WILLIAM FAULKNER

WILLIAM FAULKNER

NOVELS 1936–1940

Absalom, Absalom!

The Unvanquished

If I Forget Thee, Jerusalem
[The Wild Palms]

The Hamlet

THE LIBRARY OF AMERICA

Absalom, Absalom! copyright 1936 by William Faulkner. Copyright
renewed 1964 by Estelle Faulkner and Jill Faulkner Summers.
The Unvanquished copyright 1934, 1935, 1936, 1938 by William Faulkner.
Copyright renewed 1961, 1962 by William Faulkner. Copyright
renewed 1964, 1965 by Estelle Faulkner and Jill Faulkner Summers.
The Wild Palms copyright 1939 by Random House, Inc. Copyright renewed
1966 by Mrs. William Faulkner and Mrs. Paul D. Summers.
The Hamlet copyright 1931, 1932, 1936, 1940 by William Faulkner.
Copyright renewed 1958, 1960 by William Faulkner. Copyright renewed
1964, 1967 by Estelle Faulkner and Jill Faulkner Summers.
Published by arrangement with Random House, Inc.

The paper used in this publication meets the
minimum requirements of the American National Standard for
Information Sciences—Permanence of Paper for Printed
Library Materials, ANSI Z39.48—1984.

Distributed to the trade in the United States
by Penguin Books USA Inc
and in Canada by Penguin Books Canada Ltd.

Library of Congress Catalog Number: 89-62931
For cataloging information, see end of Notes.
ISBN 0–940450–55–0

Fifth Printing
The Library of America—48

JOSEPH BLOTNER AND NOEL POLK
WROTE THE NOTES AND SELECTED AND EDITED
THE TEXTS FOR THIS VOLUME

The texts of Absalom, Absalom!, The Unvanquished,
If I Forget Thee, Jerusalem [The Wild Palms],
and The Hamlet have been established by Noel Polk
for publication by Faulkner's publisher.

The publishers wish to thank Mrs. Paul D. Summers, Jr., the University
of Southern Mississippi, the Harry Ransom Humanities Research Center
of the University of Texas at Austin, the Alderman Library of the University of Virginia, and the John Davis Williams Library of the University of Mississippi for use of archival materials. They also wish to thank
Lieutenant Colonel John D. Hart of the Faulkner Concordance Project
at the United States Military Academy for technical assistance.

Contents

ABSALOM, ABSALOM!

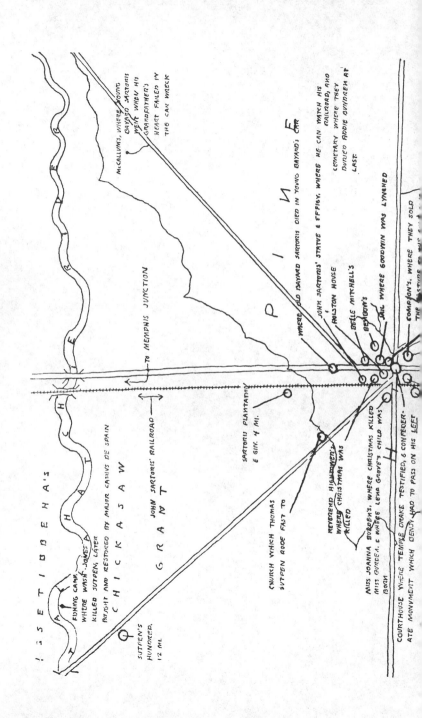

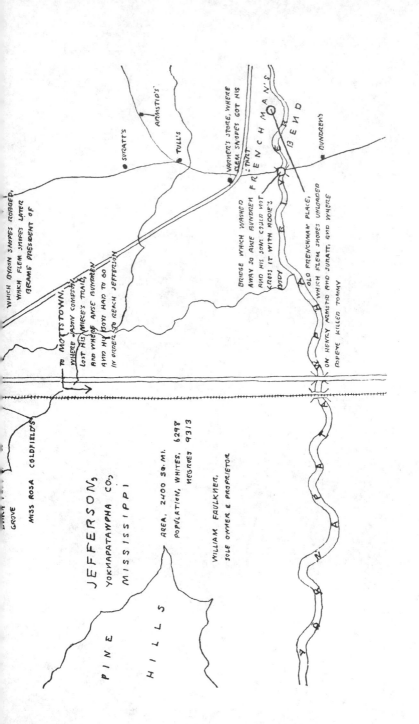

I.

FROM A LITTLE after two oclock until almost sundown of
the long still hot weary dead September afternoon they
sat in what Miss Coldfield still called the office because her
father had called it that—a dim hot airless room with the
blinds all closed and fastened for forty-three summers because
when she was a girl someone had believed that light and
moving air carried heat and that dark was always cooler, and
which (as the sun shone fuller and fuller on that side of the
house) became latticed with yellow slashes full of dust motes
which Quentin thought of as being flecks of the dead old
dried paint itself blown inward from the scaling blinds as
wind might have blown them. There was a wistaria vine
blooming for the second time that summer on a wooden trel-
lis before one window, into which sparrows came now and
then in random gusts, making a dry vivid dusty sound before
going away: and opposite Quentin, Miss Coldfield in the
eternal black which she had worn for forty-three years now,
whether for sister, father, or nothusband none knew, sitting
so bolt upright in the straight hard chair that was so tall for
her that her legs hung straight and rigid as if she had iron
shinbones and ankles, clear of the floor with that air of impotent and static rage like children's feet, and talking in that
grim haggard amazed voice until at last listening would renege
and hearing-sense self-confound and the long-dead object of
her impotent yet indomitable frustration would appear, as
though by outraged recapitulation evoked, quiet inattentive
and harmless, out of the biding and dreamy and victorious
dust.

Her voice would not cease, it would just vanish. There
would be the dim coffin-smelling gloom sweet and oversweet
with the twice-bloomed wistaria against the outer wall by the
savage quiet September sun impacted distilled and hyper-
distilled, into which came now and then the loud cloudy flutter of the sparrows like a flat limber stick whipped by an idle
boy, and the rank smell of female old flesh long embattled
in virginity while the wan haggard face watched him above
the faint triangle of lace at wrists and throat from the too tall

chair in which she resembled a crucified child; and the voice
not ceasing but vanishing into and then out of the long intervals like a stream, a trickle running from patch to patch of
dried sand, and the ghost mused with shadowy docility as if it
were the voice which he haunted where a more fortunate one
would have had a house. Out of quiet thunderclap he would
abrupt (man-horse-demon) upon a scene peaceful and decorous as a schoolprize water color, faint sulphur-reek still in
hair clothes and beard, with grouped behind him his band of
wild niggers like beasts half tamed to walk upright like men,
in attitudes wild and reposed, and manacled among them the
French architect with his air grim, haggard, and tatter-ran.
Immobile, bearded and hand palm-lifted the horseman sat;
behind him the wild blacks and the captive architect huddled
quietly, carrying in bloodless paradox the shovels and picks
and axes of peaceful conquest. Then in the long unamaze
Quentin seemed to watch them overrun suddenly the hundred square miles of tranquil and astonished earth and drag
house and formal gardens violently out of the soundless
Nothing and clap them down like cards upon a table beneath
the up-palm immobile and pontific, creating the Sutpen's
Hundred, the *Be Sutpen's Hundred* like the oldentime *Be
Light*. Then hearing would reconcile and he would seem to
listen to two separate Quentins now—the Quentin Compson
preparing for Harvard in the South, the deep South dead
since 1865 and peopled with garrulous outraged baffled
ghosts, listening, having to listen, to one of the ghosts which
had refused to lie still even longer than most had, telling him
about old ghost-times; and the Quentin Compson who was
still too young to deserve yet to be a ghost but nevertheless
having to be one for all that, since he was born and bred in
the deep South the same as she was—the two separate
Quentins now talking to one another in the long silence of
notpeople in notlanguage, like this: *It seems that this demon—
his name was Sutpen—(Colonel Sutpen)—Colonel Sutpen. Who
came out of nowhere and without warning upon the land with a
band of strange niggers and built a plantation—(Tore violently a
plantation, Miss Rosa Coldfield says)—tore violently. And married her sister Ellen and begot a son and a daughter which—
(Without gentleness begot, Miss Rosa Coldfield says)—without*

gentleness. Which should have been the jewels of his pride and the shield and comfort of his old age, only—(Only they destroyed him or something or he destroyed them or something. And died)—and died. Without regret, Miss Rosa Coldfield says—(Save by her) Yes, save by her. (And by Quentin Compson) Yes. And by Quentin Compson.

"Because you are going away to attend the college at Harvard they tell me," she said. "So I dont imagine you will ever come back here and settle down as a country lawyer in a little town like Jefferson since Northern people have already seen to it that there is little left in the South for a young man. So maybe you will enter the literary profession as so many Southern gentlemen and gentlewomen too are doing now and maybe some day you will remember this and write about it. You will be married then I expect and perhaps your wife will want a new gown or a new chair for the house and you can write this and submit it to the magazines. Perhaps you will even remember kindly then the old woman who made you spend a whole afternoon sitting indoors and listening while she talked about people and events you were fortunate enough to escape yourself when you wanted to be out among young friends of your own age."

"Yessum," Quentin said. *Only she dont mean that* he thought. *It's because she wants it told.* It was still early then. He had yet in his pocket the note which he had received by the hand of a small negro boy just before noon, asking him to call and see her—the quaint, stiffly formal request which was actually a summons, out of another world almost—the queer archaic sheet of ancient good notepaper written over with the neat faded cramped script which, due to his astonishment at the request from a woman three times his age and whom he had known all his life without having exchanged a hundred words with her or perhaps to the fact that he was only twenty years old, he did not recognise as revealing a character cold, implacable, and even ruthless. He obeyed it immediately after the noon meal, walking the half mile between his home and hers through the dry dusty heat of early September and so into the house (it too somehow smaller than its actual size— it was of two storeys—unpainted and a little shabby, yet with an air, a quality of grim endurance as though like her it had

been created to fit into and complement a world in all ways a
little smaller than the one in which it found itself) where in
the gloom of the shuttered hallway whose air was even hotter
than outside, as if there were prisoned in it like in a tomb all
the suspiration of slow heat-laden time which had recurred
during the forty-three years, the small figure in black which
did not even rustle, the wan triangle of lace at wrists and
throat, the dim face looking at him with an expression speculative, urgent, and intent, waited to invite him in.

It's because she wants it told he thought *so that people whom
she will never see and whose names she will never hear and who
have never heard her name nor seen her face will read it and know
at last why God let us lose the War: that only through the blood of
our men and the tears of our women could He stay this demon and
efface his name and lineage from the earth.* Then almost immediately he decided that neither was this the reason why she
had sent the note, and sending it, why to him, since if she had
merely wanted it told, written and even printed, she would
not have needed to call in anybody—a woman who even in
his (Quentin's) father's youth had already established (even if
not affirmed) herself as the town's and the county's poetess
laureate by issuing to the stern and meagre subscription list of
the county newspaper poems, ode eulogy and epitaph, out of
some bitter and implacable reserve of undefeat; and these
from a woman whose family's martial background as both
town and county knew consisted of the father who, a conscientious objector on religious grounds, had starved to death in
the attic of his own house, hidden (some said, walled up)
there from Confederate provost marshals' men and fed secretly at night by this same daughter who at the very time was
accumulating her first folio in which the lost cause's unregenerate vanquished were name by name embalmed; and the
nephew who served for four years in the same company with
his sister's fiance and then shot the fiance to death before the
gates to the house where the sister waited in her wedding
gown on the eve of the wedding and then fled, vanished,
none knew where.

It would be three hours yet before he would learn why she
had sent for him because this part of it, this first part of it,
Quentin already knew. It was a part of his twenty years' heri-

tage of breathing the same air and hearing his father talk about the man; a part of the town's—Jefferson's—eighty years' heritage of the same air which the man himself had breathed between this September afternoon in 1909 and that Sunday morning in June in 1833 when he first rode into town out of no discernible past and acquired his land no one knew how and built his house, his mansion, apparently out of nothing and married Ellen Coldfield and begot his two children— the son who widowed the daughter who had not yet been a bride—and so accomplished his allotted course to its violent (Miss Coldfield at least would have said, just) end. Quentin had grown up with that; the mere names were interchangeable and almost myriad. His childhood was full of them; his very body was an empty hall echoing with sonorous defeated names; he was not a being, an entity, he was a commonwealth. He was a barracks filled with stubborn back-looking ghosts still recovering, even forty-three years afterward, from the fever which had cured the disease, waking from the fever without even knowing that it had been the fever itself which they had fought against and not the sickness, looking with stubborn recalcitrance backward beyond the fever and into the disease with actual regret, weak from the fever yet free of the disease and not even aware that the freedom was that of impotence.

("But why tell me about it?" he said to his father that evening, when he returned home, after she had dismissed him at last with his promise to return for her in the buggy; "why tell me about it? What is it to me that the land or the earth or whatever it was got tired of him at last and turned and destroyed him? What if it did destroy her family too? It's going to turn and destroy us all someday, whether our name happens to be Sutpen or Coldfield or not."

"Ah," Mr Compson said. "Years ago we in the South made our women into ladies. Then the War came and made the ladies into ghosts. So what else can we do, being gentlemen, but listen to them being ghosts?" Then he said, "Do you want to know the real reason why she chose you?" They were sitting on the gallery after supper, waiting for the time Miss Coldfield had set for Quentin to call for her. "It's because she will need someone to go with her—a man, a gentleman, yet

one still young enough to do what she wants, do it the way
she wants it done. And she chose you because your grandfather was the nearest thing to a friend which Sutpen ever had
in this county, and she probably believes that Sutpen may
have told your grandfather something about himself and her,
about that engagement which did not engage, that troth
which failed to plight. Might even have told your grandfather
the reason why at the last she refused to marry him. And that
your grandfather might have told me and I might have told
you. And so, in a sense, the affair, no matter what happens
out there tonight, will still be in the family; the skeleton (if it
be a skeleton) still in the closet. She may believe that if it
hadn't been for your grandfather's friendship, Sutpen could
never have got a foothold here, and that if he had not got that
foothold, he could not have married Ellen. So maybe she considers you partly responsible through heredity for what happened to her and her family through him.")

Whatever her reason for choosing him, whether it was that
or not, the getting to it, Quentin thought, was taking a long
time. Meanwhile, as though in inverse ratio to the vanishing
voice, the invoked ghost of the man whom she could neither
forgive nor revenge herself upon began to assume a quality
almost of solidity, permanence. Itself circumambient and enclosed by its effluvium of hell, its aura of unregeneration, it
mused (mused, thought, seemed to possess sentience, as if,
though dispossessed of the peace—who was impervious anyhow to fatigue—which she declined to give it, it was still
irrevocably outside the scope of her hurt or harm) with that
quality peaceful and now harmless and not even very attentive—the ogre-shape which, as Miss Coldfield's voice went
on, resolved out of itself before Quentin's eyes the two half-
ogre children, the three of them forming a shadowy background for the fourth one. This was the mother, the dead
sister Ellen: this Niobe without tears who had conceived to
the demon in a kind of nightmare, who even while alive had
moved but without life and grieved but without weeping,
who now had an air of tranquil and unwitting desolation, not
as if she had either outlived the others or had died first, but as
if she had never lived at all. Quentin seemed to see them, the
four of them arranged into the conventional family group of

the period, with formal and lifeless decorum, and seen now as the fading and ancient photograph itself would have been seen enlarged and hung on the wall behind and above the voice and of whose presence there the voice's owner was not even aware, as if she (Miss Coldfield) had never seen this room before—a picture, a group which even to Quentin had a quality strange, contradictory and bizarre; not quite comprehensible, not (even to twenty) quite right—a group the last member of which had been dead twenty-five years and the first, fifty, evoked now out of the airless gloom of a dead house between an old woman's grim and implacable unforgiving and the passive chafing of a youth of twenty telling himself even amid the voice *Maybe you have to know anybody awful well to love them but when you have hated somebody for forty-three years you will know them awful well so maybe it's better then maybe it's fine then because after forty-three years they cant any longer surprise you or make you either very contented or very mad.* And maybe it (the voice, the talking, the incredulous and unbearable amazement) had even been a cry aloud once, Quentin thought, long ago when she was a girl—of young and indomitable unregret, of indictment of blind circumstance and savage event; but not now: now only the lonely thwarted old female flesh embattled for forty-three years in the old insult, the old unforgiving outraged and betrayed by the final and complete affront which was Sutpen's death:

"He wasn't a gentleman. He wasn't even a gentleman. He came here with a horse and two pistols and a name which nobody ever heard before, knew for certain was his own anymore than the horse was his own or even the pistols, seeking some place to hide himself, and Yoknapatawpha County supplied him with it. He sought the guarantee of reputable men to barricade him from the other and later strangers who might come seeking him in turn, and Jefferson gave him that. Then he needed respectability, the shield of a virtuous woman, to make his position impregnable even against the men who had given him protection on that inevitable day and hour when even they must rise against him in scorn and horror and outrage; and it was mine and Ellen's father who gave him that. Oh, I hold no brief for Ellen: blind romantic fool who had only youth and inexperience to excuse her even if that; blind romantic fool, then later blind woman mother fool when she no longer had either youth or inexperience to excuse her, when she lay dying in that house for which she had exchanged pride and peace both and nobody there but the daughter who was already the same as a widow without ever having been a bride and was, three years later, to be a widow sure enough without having been anything at all, and the son who had repudiated the very roof under which he had been born and to which he would return but once more before disappearing for good, and that as a murderer and almost a fratricide; and he, fiend blackguard and devil, in Virginia fighting, where the chances of the earth's being rid of him were the best anywhere under the sun, yet Ellen and I both knowing that he would return, that every man in our armies would have to fall before bullet or ball found him; and only I, a child, a child, mind you, four years younger than the very niece I was asked to save, for Ellen to turn to and say, 'Protect her. Protect Judith at least.' Yes, blind romantic fool, who did not even have that hundred miles of plantation which apparently moved our father nor that big house and the notion of slaves underfoot day and night which reconciled, I wont say moved, her aunt. No: just the face of a man who contrived somehow to swagger even on a horse—a man who so far as anyone (including the father who was to give him a daughter in marriage) knew either had no past at all or did not dare reveal it—a man who rode into town out of nowhere with a horse and two pistols and a herd of wild beasts that he had hunted down singlehanded because he was stronger in fear than even they were in whatever heathen place he had fled from, and that French architect who looked like he had been hunted down and caught in turn by the negroes—a man who fled here and hid, concealed himself behind respectability, behind that hundred miles of land which he took from a tribe of ignorant Indians, nobody knows how, and a house the size of a courthouse where he lived for three years without a window or door or bedstead in it and still called it Sutpen's Hundred as if it had been a King's grant in unbroken perpetuity from his great grandfather—a home, position: a wife and family which, being necessary to concealment, he accepted along with the rest of respectability as he would have accepted the necessary discomfort and even pain of the briers and thorns in a thicket if the thicket could have given him the protection he sought.

"No: not even a gentleman. Marrying Ellen or marrying ten thousand Ellens could not have made him one. Not that he wanted to be one, or even be taken for one. No. That was not necessary since all he would need would be Ellen's and our father's names on a wedding license (or on any other patent of respectability) that people could look at and read just as he would have wanted our father's (or any other reputable man's) signature on a note of hand because our father knew who his father was in Tennessee and who his grandfather had been in Virginia and our neighbors and the people we lived among knew that we knew and we knew they knew we knew and we knew that they would have believed us about who and where we came from even if we had lied, just as anyone could have looked at him once and known that he would be lying about who and where and why he came from by the very fact that apparently he had to refuse to say at all. And the very fact that he had had to choose respectability to hide behind was proof enough (if anyone needed further proof) that what he fled from must have been some opposite of respectability too dark to talk about. Because he was too young. He was just twenty-five and a man of twenty-five does not voluntarily undertake the hardship and privation of clearing virgin land and establishing a plantation in a new country just for money; not a young man without any past that he apparently cared to discuss, in Mississippi in 1833, with a river full of steamboats loaded with drunken fools covered with diamonds and bent on throwing away their cotton and slaves before the boat reached New Orleans;—not with this just one night's hard ride away and the only handicap or obstacle being the other blackguards or the risk of being put ashore on a sandbar and at the remotest, a hemp rope. And he was no younger son sent out from some old quiet country like Virginia or Carolina with the surplus negroes to take up new land, because anyone could look at those negroes of his and tell that they may have come (and probably did) from a much older country than Virginia or Carolina but it wasn't a quiet one. And anyone could have looked once at his face and known that he would have chosen the River and even the certainty of the hemp rope, to undertaking what he undertook even if he had known that he would find gold buried and waiting for him in the very land which he had bought.

"No. I hold no more brief for Ellen than I do for myself. I hold even less for myself, because I had had twenty years in which to watch him, where Ellen had had but five. And not even those five to see him but only to hear at second hand what he was doing, and not even to hear more than half of that since apparently half of what he actually did during those five years nobody at all knew about, and half of the remainder no man would have repeated to a wife, let alone a young girl; he came here and set up a raree show which lasted five years and Jefferson paid him for the entertainment by at least shielding him to the extent of not telling their womenfolks what he was doing. But I had had all my life to watch him in, since apparently and for what reason Heaven has not seen fit to divulge, my life was destined to end on an afternoon in April forty-three years ago, since anyone who even had as little to call living as I had had up to that time would not call what I have had since, living. I saw what had happened to Ellen, my sister. I saw her almost a recluse, watching those two doomed children growing up whom she was helpless to save. I saw the price which she had paid for that house and that pride; I saw the notes of hand on pride and contentment and peace and all to which she had put her signature when she walked into the church that night, begin to fall due in succession. I saw Judith's marriage forbidden without rhyme or reason or shadow of excuse; I saw Ellen die with only me, a child, to turn to and ask to protect her remaining child; I saw Henry repudiate his home and birthright and then return and practically fling the bloody corpse of his sister's sweetheart at the hem of her wedding gown; I saw that man return—the evil's source and head which had outlasted all its victims—who had created two children not only to destroy one another and his own line, but my line as well, yet I agreed to marry him.

"No. I hold no brief for myself. I dont plead youth, since what creature in the South since 1861, man woman nigger or mule, had had time or opportunity not only to have been

young but to have heard what being young was like from
those who had. I dont plead propinquity: the fact that I, a
woman young and at the age for marrying and in a time when
most of the young men whom I would have known ordinarily
were dead on lost battlefields, that I lived for two years under
the same roof with him. I dont plead material necessity: the
fact that, an orphan a woman and a pauper, I turned naturally
not for protection but for actual food to my only kin: my
dead sister's family: though I defy anyone to blame me, an
orphan of twenty, a young woman without resources, who
should desire not only to justify her situation but to vindicate
the honor of a family the good name of whose women has
never been impugned, by accepting the honorable proffer of
marriage from the man whose food she was forced to subsist
on. And most of all, I do not plead myself: a young woman
emerging from a holocaust which had taken parents security
and all from her, who had seen all that living meant to her fall
into ruins about the feet of a few figures with the shapes of
men but with the names and statures of heroes;—a young
woman I say thrown into daily and hourly contact with one
of these men who, despite what he might have been at one
time and despite what she might have believed or even known
about him, had fought for four honorable years for the soil
and traditions of the land where she had been born (and the
man who had done that, villain dyed though he be, would
have possessed in her eyes, even if only from association with
them, the stature and shape of a hero too) and now he also
emerging from the same holocaust in which she had suffered,
with nothing to face what the future held for the South but
his bare hands and the sword which he at least had never
surrendered and the citation for valor from his defeated
Commander-in-Chief. Oh he was brave. I have never gainsaid
that. But that our cause, our very life and future hopes and
past pride, should have been thrown into the balance with
men like that to buttress it—men with valor and strength but
without pity or honor. Is it any wonder that Heaven saw fit
to let us lose?"

"Nome," Quentin said.

"But that it should have been our father, mine and Ellen's
father of all of them that he knew, out of all the ones who

used to go out there and drink and gamble with him and watch him fight those wild negroes, whose daughters he might even have won at cards. That it should have been our father. How he could have approached papa, on what grounds; what there could have been beside the common civility of two men meeting on the street, between a man who came from nowhere or dared not tell where and our father; what there could have been between a man like that and papa—a Methodist steward, a merchant who was not rich and who not only could have done nothing under the sun to advance his fortunes or prospects but could by no stretch of the imagination even have owned anything that he would have wanted, even picked up in the road—a man who owned neither land nor slaves except two house servants whom he had freed as soon as he got them, bought them, who neither drank nor hunted nor gambled;—what there could have been between papa and a man who to my certain knowledge was never in a Jefferson church but three times in his life—the once when he first saw Ellen, the once when they rehearsed the wedding, the once when they performed it;—a man that anyone could look at and see that, even if he apparently had none now, he was accustomed to having money and intended to have it again and would have no scruples about how he got it—that man to discover Ellen inside a church. In church, mind you, as though there were a fatality and curse on our family and God Himself were seeing to it that it was performed and discharged to the last drop and dreg. Yes, fatality and curse on the South and on our family as though because some ancestor of ours had elected to establish his descent in a land primed for fatality and already cursed with it, even if it had not rather been our family, our father's progenitors, who had incurred the curse long years before and had been coerced by Heaven into establishing itself in the land and the time already cursed. So that even I, a child still too young to know more than that, though Ellen was my own sister and Henry and Judith my own nephew and niece, I was not even to go out there save when papa or my aunt was with me and that I was not to play with Henry and Judith at all except in the house (and not because I was four years younger than Judith and six years younger than Henry: wasn't it to me that Ellen turned before she died and said 'Protect them'?)—even I used to wonder what our father or his father could have done before he married our mother that Ellen and I would have to expiate and neither of us alone be sufficient; what crime committed that would leave our family cursed to be instruments not only for that man's destruction but for our own."

"Yessum," Quentin said.

"Yes," the grim quiet voice said from beyond the unmoving triangle of dim lace; and now, among the musing and decorous wraiths Quentin seemed to watch resolving the figure of a little girl, in the prim skirts and pantalettes, the smooth prim decorous braids, of the dead time. She seemed to stand, to lurk, behind the neat picket fence of a small, grimly middleclass yard or lawn, looking out upon the whatever ogreworld of that quiet village street with that air of children born too late into their parents' lives and doomed to contemplate all human behavior through the complex and needless follies of adults—an air Cassandralike and humorless and profoundly and sternly prophetic out of all proportion to the actual years even of a child who had never been young. "Because I was born too late. I was born twenty-two years too late—a child to whom out of the overheard talk of adults my own sister's and my sister's children's faces had come to be like the faces in an ogre-tale between supper and bed long before I was old enough or big enough to be permitted to play with them, yet to whom that sister must have to turn at the last when she lay dying, with one of the children vanished and doomed to be a murderer and the other doomed to be a widow before she had even been a bride, and say, 'Protect her, at least. At least save Judith.' A child, yet whose child's vouchsafed instinct could make that reply which the mature wisdom of her elders apparently could not make: 'Protect her? From whom and from what? He has already given them life: he does not need to harm them further. It is from themselves that they need protection.'"

It should have been later than it was; it should have been late, yet the yellow slashes of mote-palpitant sunlight were latticed no higher up the impalpable wall of gloom which separated them; the sun seemed hardly to have moved. It (the talking, the telling) seemed (to him, to Quentin) to partake of that logic- and reason-flouting quality of a dream which the sleeper knows must have occurred, stillborn and complete, in a second, yet the very quality upon which it must depend to move the dreamer (verisimilitude) to credulity—horror or pleasure or amazement—depends as completely upon a formal recognition of and acceptance of elapsed and yet-elapsing time as music or a printed tale. "Yes. I was born too late. I was a child who was to remember those three faces (and his, too) as seen for the first time in the carriage on that first Sunday morning when this town finally realised that he had turned that road from Sutpen's Hundred in to the church into a race track. I was three then, and doubtless I had seen them before; I must have. But I do not remember it. I do not even remember ever having seen Ellen before that Sunday. It was as though the sister whom I had never laid eyes on, who before I was born had vanished into the stronghold of an ogre or a djinn, was now to return through a dispensation of one day only, to the world which she had quitted, and I a child of three, waked early for the occasion, dressed and curled as if for Christmas, for an occasion more serious than Christmas even, since now and at last this ogre or djinn had agreed for the sake of the wife and the children to come to church, to permit them at least to approach the vicinity of salvation, to at least give Ellen one chance to struggle with him for those children's souls on a battleground where she could be supported not only by Heaven but by her own family and people of her own kind; yes, even for the moment submitting himself to redemption, or lacking that, at least chivalrous for the instant even though still unregenerate. That is what I expected. This is what I saw as I stood there before the church between papa and our aunt and waited for the carriage to arrive from the twelve mile drive. And though I must have seen Ellen and the children before this, this is the vision of my first sight of them which I shall carry to my grave: a glimpse like the forefront of a tornado, of the carriage and Ellen's high white face within it and the two replicas of his face in miniature flanking her, and on the front seat the face and teeth of the wild negro who was driving, and he, his face exactly like the negro's save for the teeth (this because of his beard, doubtless)—all in a thunder and a fury of wildeyed horses and of galloping and of dust.

"Oh, there were plenty of them to abet him, assist him, make a race of it; ten oclock on Sunday morning, the carriage racing on two wheels up to the very door to the church with that wild negro in his christian clothes looking exactly like a performing tiger in a linen duster and a top hat, and Ellen with no drop of blood in her face, holding those two children who were not crying and who did not need to be held, who sat on either side of her perfectly still too, with in their faces that infantile enormity which we did not then quite comprehend. Oh yes, there were plenty to aid and abet him; even he could not have held a horse race without someone to race against. Because it was not even public opinion that stopped him, not even the men who might have had wives and children in carriages to be ridden down and into ditches: it was the minister himself, speaking in the name of the women of Jefferson and Yoknapatawpha County. So he quit coming to church himself; now it would be just Ellen and the children in the carriage on Sunday morning, so we knew now that at least there would be no betting now, since no one could say if it was an actual race or not, since now, with his face absent, it was only the wild negro's perfectly inscrutable one with the teeth glinting a little, so that now we could never know if it were a race or a runaway, and if there was triumph, it was on the face twelve miles back there at Sutpen's Hundred, which did not even require to see or be present. It was the negro now, who in the act of passing another carriage spoke to that team too as well as to his own—something without words, not needing words probably, in that tongue in which they slept in the mud of that swamp and brought here out of whatever dark swamp he had found them in and brought them here:—the dust, the thunder, the carriage whirling up to the church door while women and children scattered and screamed before it and men caught at the bridles of the other team. And the negro would let Ellen and the children out at the door and take the carriage on around to the hitching grove and beat the horses for running away; there was even a fool who tried to interfere once, whereupon the negro turned

upon him with the stick lifted and his teeth showing a little
and said, 'Marster say; I do. You tell Marster.'

"Yes. From them; from themselves. And this time it was
not even the minister. It was Ellen. Our aunt and papa were
talking and I came in and my aunt said 'Go out and play'
though even if I could not have heard through the door at
all, I could have repeated the conversation for them: 'Your
daughter, your own daughter' my aunt said; and papa: 'Yes.
She is my daughter. When she wants me to interfere she will
tell me so herself'. Because this Sunday when Ellen and the
children came out of the front door, it was not the carriage
waiting, it was Ellen's phaeton with the old gentle mare
which she drove and the stableboy that he had bought instead
of the wild negro. And Judith looked once at the phaeton and
realised what it meant and began to scream, screaming and
kicking while they carried her back into the house and put her
to bed. No, he was not present. Nor do I claim a lurking
triumphant face behind a window curtain. Probably he would
have been as amazed as we were since we would all realise
now that we were faced by more than a child's tantrum or
even hysteria: that his face had been in that carriage all the
time; that it had been Judith, a girl of six, who had instigated
and authorised that negro to make the team run away. Not
Henry, mind; not the boy, which would have been outrageous enough; but Judith, the girl. As soon as papa and I
entered those gates that afternoon and began to go up the
drive toward the house, I could feel it. It was as though somewhere in that Sunday afternoon's quiet and peace the screams
of that child still existed, lingered, not as sound now but as
something for the skin to hear, the hair on the head to hear.
But I did not ask at once. I was just four then; I sat in the
buggy beside papa as I had stood between him and our aunt
before the church on that first Sunday when I had been
dressed to come and see my sister and my nephew and niece
for the first time, looking at the house (I had been inside it
before too, of course, but even when I saw it for the first time
that I could remember I seemed already to know how it was
going to look just as I seemed to know how Ellen and Judith
and Henry would look before I saw them for the time which
I always remember as being the first). No, not asking even

then, but just looking at that huge quiet house, saying 'What room is Judith sick in, papa?' with that quiet aptitude of a child for accepting the inexplicable, though I now know that even then I was wondering what Judith saw when she came out the door and found the phaeton instead of the carriage, the tame stableboy instead of the wild man; what she had seen in that phaeton which looked so innocent to the rest of us—or worse, what she had missed when she saw the phaeton and began to scream. Yes, a still hot quiet Sunday afternoon like this afternoon; I remember yet the utter quiet of that house when we went in and from which I knew at once that he was absent without knowing that he would now be in the scuppernong arbor drinking with Wash Jones. I only knew, as soon as papa and I crossed the threshold, that he was not there: as though with some almost omniscient conviction (that same instinctive knowledge which enabled me to tell Ellen that it was not from him that Judith would need protection) knowing that he did not need to stay and observe his triumph—and that, in comparison with what was to be, this one was a mere trivial business even beneath our notice too. Yes, that quiet darkened room with the blinds closed and a negro woman sitting beside the bed with a fan and Judith's white face on the pillow beneath a camphor cloth, asleep as I supposed then: possibly it was sleep, or would be called sleep: and Ellen's face white and calm and papa said 'Go out and find Henry and ask him to play with you, Rosa' and so I stood just outside that quiet door in that quiet upper hall because I was afraid to go away even from it because I could hear the sabbath afternoon quiet of that house louder than thunder, louder than laughing even with triumph.

" 'Think of the children,' papa said.

" 'Think?' Ellen said. 'What else do I do? What else do I lie awake at night and do but think of them?' Neither papa nor Ellen said Come back home. No: This occurred before it became fashionable to repair your mistakes by turning your back on them and running. It was just the two quiet voices beyond that blank door which might have been discussing something printed in a magazine; and I, a child standing close beside that door because I was afraid to be there but more afraid to leave it, standing motionless beside that door as though trying to make myself blend with the dark wood and become invisible, like a chameleon, listening to the living spirit, presence, of that house, since some of Ellen's life and breath had now gone into it as well as his, breathing away in a long neutral sound of victory and despair, of triumph and terror too.

" 'Do you love this——' papa said.

" 'Papa,' Ellen said. That was all. But I could see her face then as clearly as papa could have, with that same expression which it had worn in the carriage on that first Sunday and the others. Then a servant came and said our buggy was ready.

"Yes. From themselves. Not from him, not from anybody, just as nobody could have saved them, even himself. Because he now showed us why that triumph had been beneath his notice. He showed Ellen, that is: not I. I was not there; it was six years now, during which I had scarcely seen him. Our aunt was gone now and I was keeping house for papa. Perhaps once a year papa and I would go out there and have dinner, and maybe four times a year Ellen and the children would come in and spend the day with us. Not he; that I know of, he never entered this house again after he and Ellen married. I was young then; I was even young enough to believe that this was due to some stubborn coal of conscience, if not remorse, even in him. But I know better now. I know now that it was simply because since papa had given him respectability through a wife there was nothing else he could want from papa and so not even sheer gratitude, let alone appearances, could force him to forego his own pleasure to the extent of taking a family meal with his wife's people. So I saw little of them. I did not have time now to play, even if I had ever had any inclination. I had never learned how and I saw no reason to try to learn now even if I had had the time.

"So it was six years now, though it was actually no secret to Ellen since it had apparently been going on ever since he drove the last nail in the house, the only difference between now and the time of his bachelorhood being that now they would hitch the teams and saddle horses and mules in the grove beyond the stable and so come up across the pasture unseen from the house. Because there were plenty of them still; it was as if God or the devil had taken advantage of his

very vices in order to supply witnesses to the discharge of our
curse not only from among gentlefolks, our own kind, but
from the very scum and riffraff who could not have approached the house itself under any other circumstances, not
even from the rear. Yes, Ellen and those two children alone in
that house twelve miles from town, and down there in the
stable a hollow square of faces in the lantern light, the white
faces on three sides, the black ones on the fourth, and in the
center two of his wild negroes fighting, naked, fighting not
like white men fight, with rules and weapons, but like negroes
fight to hurt one another quick and bad. Ellen knew that, or
thought she did; that was not it. She accepted that—not reconciled: accepted—as though there is a breathing-point in
outrage where you can accept it almost with gratitude since
you can say to yourself, *Thank God this is all; at least I now
know all of it*—thinking that, clinging still to that when she
ran into the stable that night while the very men who had
stolen into it from the rear fell back away from her with at
least some grain of decency, and Ellen seeing not the two
black beasts she had expected to see but instead a white one
and a black one, both naked to the waist and gouging at one
another's eyes as if their skins should not only have been the
same color but should have been covered with fur too. Yes. It
seems that on certain occasions, perhaps at the end of the
evening, the spectacle, as a grand finale or perhaps as a matter
of sheer deadly forethought toward the retention of suprem-
acy, domination, he would enter the ring with one of the
negroes himself. Yes. That is what Ellen saw: her husband and
the father of her children standing there naked and panting
and bloody to the waist and the negro just fallen evidently,
lying at his feet and bloody too save that on the negro it
merely looked like grease or sweat—Ellen running down the
hill from the house, bareheaded, in time to hear the sound,
the screaming, hearing it while she still ran in the darkness
and before the spectators knew that she was there, hearing it
even before it occurred to one spectator to say, 'It's a horse'
then 'It's a woman' then 'My God, it's a child'—ran in, and
the spectators falling back to permit her to see Henry plunge
out from among the negroes who had been holding him,
screaming and vomiting—not pausing, not even looking at

the faces which shrank back away from her as she knelt in the
stable filth to raise Henry and not looking at Henry either but
up at *him* as he stood there with even his teeth showing beneath his beard now and another negro wiping the blood
from his body with a towsack. 'I know you will excuse us,
gentlemen,' Ellen said. But they were already departing, nigger and white, slinking out again as they had slunk in, and
Ellen not watching them now either but kneeling in the dirt
while Henry clung to her, crying, and *he* standing there yet
while a third nigger prodded his shirt or coat at him as
though the coat were a stick and he a caged snake. 'Where is
Judith, Thomas?' Ellen said.

" 'Judith?' he said. Oh, he was not lying; his own triumph
had outrun him; he had builded even better in evil than even
he could have hoped. 'Judith? Isn't she in bed?'

" 'Dont lie to me, Thomas,' Ellen said. 'I can understand
your bringing Henry here to see this, wanting Henry to see
this; I will try to understand it; yes, I will make myself try to
understand it. But not Judith, Thomas. Not my baby girl,
Thomas.'

" 'I dont expect you to understand it,' he said. 'Because you
are a woman. But I didn't bring Judith down here. I would
not bring her down here. I dont expect you to believe that.
But I swear to it.'

" 'I wish I could believe you,' Ellen said. 'I want to believe
you.' Then she began to call. 'Judith!' she called in a voice
calm and sweet and filled with despair: 'Judith honey! Time to
come to bed.'

"But I was not there. I was not there to see the two Sutpen
faces this time—once on Judith and once on the negro girl
beside her—looking down through the square entrance to
the loft."

II.

IT WAS a summer of wistaria. The twilight was full of it and of the smell of his father's cigar as they sat on the front gallery after supper until it would be time for Quentin to start, while in the deep shaggy lawn below the veranda the fireflies blew and drifted in soft random—the odor, the scent, which five months later Mr Compson's letter would carry up from Mississippi and over the long iron New England snow and into Quentin's sitting-room at Harvard. It was a day of listening too—the listening, the hearing in 1909 even yet mostly that which he already knew since he had been born in and still breathed the same air in which the church bells had rung on that Sunday morning in 1833 (and, on Sundays, heard even one of the original three bells in the same steeple where descendants of the same pigeons strutted and crooned or wheeled in short courses resembling soft fluid paint-smears on the soft summer sky);—a Sunday morning in June with the bells ringing peaceful and peremptory and a little cacophonous—the denominations in concord though not in tune—and the ladies and children, and house negroes to carry the parasols and flywhisks, and even a few men (the ladies moving in hoops among the miniature broadcloth of little boys and the pantalettes of little girls, in the skirts of the time when ladies did not walk but floated) when the other men sitting with their feet on the railing of the Holston House gallery looked up, and there the stranger was. He was already halfway across the square when they saw him, on a big hard-ridden roan horse, man and beast looking as though they had been created out of thin air and set down in the bright summer sabbath sunshine in the middle of a tired foxtrot—face and horse that none of them had ever seen before, name that none of them had ever heard, and origin and purpose which some of them were never to learn. So that in the next four weeks (Jefferson was a village then: the Holston House, the courthouse, six stores, a blacksmith and livery stable, a saloon frequented by drovers and peddlers, three churches and perhaps thirty residences) the stranger's name went back and forth among the places of business and of idleness and among the residences in steady strophe and antistrophe: *Sutpen. Sutpen. Sutpen. Sutpen.*

That was all that the town was to know about him for almost a month. He had apparently come into town from the south—a man of about twenty-five as the town learned later, because at the time his age could not have been guessed because at that time he looked like a man who had been sick. Not like a man who had been peacefully ill in bed and had recovered to move with a sort of diffident and tentative amazement in a world which he had believed himself on the point of surrendering, but like a man who had been through some solitary furnace experience which was more than just fever, like an explorer say, who not only had to face the normal hardship of the pursuit which he chose but was overtaken by the added and unforeseen handicap of the fever also and fought through it at enormous cost not so much physical as mental, alone and unaided and not through blind instinctive will to endure and survive but to gain and keep to enjoy it the material prize for which he accepted the original gambit. A man with a big frame but gaunt now almost to emaciation, with a short reddish beard which resembled a disguise and above which his pale eyes had a quality at once visionary and alert, ruthless and reposed in a face whose flesh had the appearance of pottery, of having been colored by that oven's fever either of soul or environment, deeper than sun alone beneath a dead impervious surface as of glazed clay. That was what they saw, though it was years before the town learned that that was all which he possessed at the time—the strong spent horse and the clothes on his back and a small saddlebag scarcely large enough to contain the spare linen and the razors, and the two pistols of which Miss Coldfield told Quentin, with the butts worn smooth as pickhandles and which he used with the precision of knitting needles; later Quentin's grandfather saw him ride at a canter around a sapling at twenty feet and put both bullets into a playing card fastened to the tree. He had a room in the Holston House but he carried the key with him and each morning he fed and saddled the horse and rode away before daylight, where to the town likewise failed to learn, probably due to the fact that he gave the pistol demonstration on the third day after his arrival. So they had to depend on inquiry to find out what they could about him, which would of necessity be at night, at the supper table in the Holston House dining room or in the lounge which he would have to cross to gain his room and lock the door again, which he would do as soon as he finished eating. The bar opened into the lounge too, and that would or should have been the place to accost him and even inquire, except for the fact that he did not use the bar. He did not drink at all, he told them. He did not say that he used to drink and had quit, nor that he had never used alcohol. He just said that he would not care for a drink; it was years later before even Quentin's grandfather (he was a young man too then; it would be years yet before he would become General Compson) learned that the reason Sutpen did not drink was that he did not have the money with which to pay his share or return the courtesy; it was General Compson who first re-alised that at this time Sutpen lacked not only the money to spend for drink and conviviality, but the time and inclination as well: that he was at this time completely the slave of his secret and furious impatience, his conviction gained from whatever that recent experience had been—that fever mental or physical—of a need for haste, of time fleeing beneath him, which was to drive him for the next five years—as General Compson computed it, roughly until about nine months before his son was born.

So they would catch him, run him to earth, in the lounge between the supper table and his locked door to give him the opportunity to tell them who he was and where he came from and what he was up to, whereupon he would move gradually and steadily until his back came in contact with something— a post or a wall—and then stand there and tell them nothing whatever as pleasantly and courteously as a hotel clerk. It was the Chickasaw Indian agent with or through whom he dealt and so it was not until he waked the County Recorder that Saturday night with the deed, patent, to the land and the gold Spanish coin, that the town learned that he now owned a hundred square miles of some of the best virgin bottom land in the country, though even that knowledge came too late because Sutpen himself was gone, where to again they did not know. But he owned land among them now and some of

them began to suspect what General Compson apparently
knew: that the Spanish coin with which he had paid to have
his patent recorded was the last one of any kind which he
possessed. So they were certain now that he had departed to
get more; there were several who even anticipated in believing (and even in saying aloud, now that he was not present)
what Sutpen's future and then unborn sister-in-law was to tell
Quentin almost eighty years later: that he had found some
unique and practical way of hiding loot and that he had returned to the cache to replenish his pockets, even if he had
not actually ridden with the two pistols back to the River and
the steamboats full of gamblers and cotton- and slavedealers
to replenish the cache. At least some of them were telling one
another that when two months later he returned, again without warning and accompanied this time by the covered
wagon with a negro driving it and on the seat with the negro
a small, alertly resigned man with a grim, harried Latin face,
in a frock coat and a flowered waistcoat and a hat which
would have created no furore on a Paris boulevard, all of
which he was to wear constantly for the next two years—the
sombrely theatric clothing and the expression of fatalistic and
amazed determination—while his white client and the negro
crew which he was to advise though not direct went stark
naked save for a coating of dried mud. This was the French
architect. Years later the town learned that he had come all the
way from Martinique on Sutpen's bare promise and lived for
two years on venison cooked over a camp fire, in an unfloored
tent made of the wagon hood, before he so much as saw any
color or shape of pay. And until he passed through town on
his way back to New Orleans two years later, he was not even
to see Jefferson again; he would not come, or Sutpen would
not bring him, to town even on the few occasions when Sutpen would be seen there, and he did not have much chance to
look at Jefferson on that first day because the wagon did not
stop. Apparently it was only by sheer geographical hap that
Sutpen passed through town at all, pausing only long enough
for someone (not General Compson) to look beneath the
wagon hood and into a black tunnel filled with still eyeballs
and smelling like a wolfden.

But the legend of Sutpen's wild negroes was not to begin at

once, because the wagon went on as though even the wood
and iron which composed it, as well as the mules which drew
it, had become imbued by sheer association with him with
that quality of gaunt and tireless driving, that conviction for
haste and of fleeing time; later Sutpen told Quentin's grandfather that on that afternoon when the wagon passed through
Jefferson they had been without food since the previous night
and that he was trying to reach Sutpen's Hundred and the
river bottom to try to kill a deer before dark, so he and the
architect and the negroes would not have to spend another
night without food. So the legend of the wild men came
gradually back to town, brought by the men who would ride
out to watch what was going on, who began to tell how Sutpen would take stand beside a game trail with the pistols and
send the negroes in to drive the swamp like a pack of hounds;
it was they who told how during that first summer and fall
the negroes did not even have (or did not use) blankets to
sleep in, even before the coon-hunter Akers claimed to have
walked one of them out of the absolute mud like a sleeping
alligator and screamed just in time. The negroes could speak
no English yet and doubtless there were more than Akers
who did not know that the language in which they and Sutpen communicated was a sort of French and not some dark
and fatal tongue of their own.

There were many more than Akers, though the others were
responsible citizens and landowners and so did not have to
lurk about the camp at night. In fact, as Miss Coldfield told
Quentin, they would make up parties to meet at the Holston
House and go out horseback, often carrying lunch. Sutpen
had built a brick kiln and he had set up the saw and planer
which he had brought in the wagon—a capstan with a long
sapling walking-beam, with the wagon team and the negroes
in shifts and himself too when necessary, when the machinery
slowed, hitched to it—as if the negroes actually were wild
men; as General Compson told his son, Quentin's father,
while the negroes were working Sutpen never raised his voice
at them, that instead he led them, caught them at the psycho-
logical instant by example, by some ascendancy of forbearance
rather than by brute fear. Without dismounting (usually
Sutpen did not even greet them with as much as a nod, ap-

parently as unaware of their presence as if they had been idle shades) they would sit in a curious quiet clump as though for mutual protection and watch his mansion rise, carried plank by plank and brick by brick out of the swamp where the clay and timber waited—the bearded white man and the twenty black ones and all stark naked beneath the croaching and pervading mud. Being men, these spectators did not realise that the garments which Sutpen had worn when he first rode into Jefferson were the only ones in which they had ever seen him, and few of the women in the county had seen him at all yet. Otherwise, some of them would have anticipated Miss Coldfield in this too: in divining that he was saving his clothes, since decorum even if not elegance of appearance would be the only weapon (or rather, ladder) with which he could conduct the last assault upon what Miss Coldfield and perhaps others believed to be respectability—that respectability which, according to General Compson, consisted in Sutpen's secret mind of a great deal more than the mere acquisition of a chatelaine for his house. So he and the twenty negroes worked together, plastered over with mud against the mosquitoes and, as Miss Coldfield told Quentin, distinguishable one from another by his beard and eyes alone and only the architect resembling a human creature because of the French clothes which he wore constantly with a sort of invincible fatality until the day after the house was completed save for the windowglass and the ironware which they could not make by hand and the architect departed—working in the sun and heat of summer and the mud and ice of winter, with quiet and unflagging fury.

It took him two years, he and his crew of imported slaves which his adopted fellow citizens still looked on as being a good deal more deadly than any beast he could have started and slain in that country. They worked from sunup to sundown while parties of horsemen rode up and sat their horses quietly and watched, and the architect in his formal coat and his Paris hat and his expression of grim and embittered amazement lurked about the environs of the scene with his air something between a casual and bitterly disinterested spectator and a condemned and conscientious ghost—amazement, General Compson said, not at the others and what they were doing so much as at himself, at the inexplicable and incredible fact of his own presence. But he was a good architect; Quentin knew the house, twelve miles from Jefferson, in its grove of cedar and oak, seventy-five years after it was finished. And not only an architect, as General Compson said, but an artist since only an artist could have borne those two years in order to build a house which he doubtless not only expected but firmly intended never to see again. Not, General Compson said, the hardship to sense and the outrage to sensibility of the two years' sojourn, but Sutpen: that only an artist could have borne Sutpen's ruthlessness and hurry and still manage to curb the dream of grim and castlelike magnificence at which Sutpen obviously aimed, since the place as Sutpen planned it would have been almost as large as Jefferson itself at the time; that the little grim harried foreigner had single-handed given battle to and vanquished Sutpen's fierce and overweening vanity or desire for magnificence or for vindication or whatever it was (even General Compson did not know yet) and so created of Sutpen's very defeat the victory which, in conquering, Sutpen himself would have failed to gain.

So it was finished then, down to the last plank and brick and wooden pin which they could make themselves. Unpainted and unfurnished, without a pane of glass or a doorknob or hinge in it, twelve miles from town and almost that far from any neighbor, it stood for three years more surrounded by its formal gardens and promenades, its slave quarters and stables and smokehouses; wild turkey ranged within a mile of the house and deer came light and colored like smoke and left delicate prints in the formal beds where there would be no flowers for four years yet. Now there began a period, a phase, during which the town and the county watched him with more puzzlement yet. Perhaps it was because the next step toward that secret end which General Compson claimed to have known but which the town and the county comprehended but dimly or not at all, now required patience or passive time instead of that driving fury to which he had accustomed them; now it was the women who first suspected what he wanted, what the next step would be. None of the men, certainly not those who knew him well enough to call him by name, suspected that he wanted a wife.

Doubtless there were some of them, husbands and bachelors both, who not only would have refused to entertain the idea but would even have protested against it, because for the next three years he led what must have been to them a perfect existence. He lived out there, eight miles from any neighbor, in masculine solitude in what might be called the halfacre gunroom of a baronial splendor. He lived in the spartan shell of the largest edifice in the county, not excepting the court-house itself, whose threshold no woman had so much as seen, without any feminised softness of window pane or door or mattress; where there was not only no woman to object if he should elect to have his dogs in to sleep on the pallet bed with him, he did not even need dogs to kill the game which left footprints within sight of the kitchen door but hunted it instead with human beings who belonged to him body and soul and of whom it was believed (or said) that they could creep up to a bedded buck and cut its throat before it could move.

It was at this time that he began to invite the parties of men of which Miss Coldfield told Quentin, out to Sutpen's Hun-dred to camp in blankets in the naked rooms of his embry-onic formal opulence; they hunted, and at night played cards and drank, and on occasion he doubtless pitted his negroes against one another and perhaps even at this time participated now and then himself—that spectacle which, according to Miss Coldfield, his son was unable to bear the sight of while his daughter looked on unmoved. Sutpen drank himself now, though there were probably others beside Quentin's grand-father who remarked that he drank very sparingly save when he himself had managed to supply some of the liquor. His guests would bring whiskey out with them but he drank of this with a sort of sparing calculation as though keeping men-tally, General Compson said, a sort of balance of spiritual solvency between the amount of whiskey he accepted and the amount of running meat which he supplied to the guns.

He lived like that for three years. He now had a plantation; inside of two years he had dragged house and gardens out of virgin swamp, and plowed and planted his land with seed cot-ton which General Compson loaned him. Then he seemed to quit. He seemed to just sit down in the middle of what he had almost finished, and to remain so for three years during which he did not even appear to intend or want anything more. Perhaps it is not to be wondered at that the men in the county came to believe that the life he now led had been his aim all the time; it was General Compson, who seemed to have known him well enough to offer to lend him seed cotton for his start, who knew any better, to whom Sutpen ever told anything about his past. It was General Compson who knew first about the Spanish coin being his last one, as it was Compson (so the town learned later) who offered to lend Sutpen the money to finish and furnish his house, and was refused. So doubtless General Compson was the first man in the county to tell himself that Sutpen did not need to borrow money with which to complete the house, supply what it yet lacked, because he intended to marry it. Not the first person: the first man, since, according to what Miss Coldfield told Quentin seventy-five years later, the women in the county had been telling one another and their husbands as well that Sutpen did not intend to quit there, that he had already gone to too much trouble, gone through too much privation and hardship, to settle down and live exactly as he had lived while the house was being built save that now he had a roof to sleep under in place of an unfloored wagon hood. Probably the women had already cast about among the families of the men who might now be called his friends, for that prospective bride whose dowry might complete the shape and substance of that respectability Miss Coldfield anyway believed to be his aim. So when, at the expiration of this second phase, three years after the house was finished and the architect departed, and again on Sunday morning and again without warning, the town saw him cross the square, on foot now but in the same garments in which he had ridden into town five years ago and which no one had seen since (he or one of the negroes had ironed the coat with heated bricks, General Compson told Quentin's father) and enter the Methodist church, only some of the men were surprised. The women merely said that he had exhausted the possibilities of the families of the men with whom he had hunted and gambled and that he had now come to town to find a wife exactly as he would have gone to the Memphis market to buy livestock or slaves. But when they comprehended whom it was that he had apparently come to town and into church to invest with his choice, the assurance of the women became one with the men's surprise, and then even more than that: amazement.

Because the town now believed that it knew him. For two years it had watched him as with that grim and unflagging fury he had erected that shell of a house and laid out his fields, then for three years he had remained completely static, as if he were run by electricity and someone had come along and removed, dismantled the wiring or the dynamo, while the women of the county gradually convinced it that he was merely waiting to find a wife with a dowry to finish it with. So that when he entered the Methodist church that Sunday morning in his ironed coat, there were men as well as women who believed that they had only to look around the congregation in order to anticipate the direction his feet would take him, until they became aware that he had apparently marked down Miss Coldfield's father with the same cold and ruthless deliberation with which he had probably marked down the French architect. They watched in shocked amazement while he laid deliberate siege to the one man in the town with whom he could have had nothing in common, least of all, money—a man who obviously could do nothing under the sun for him save give him credit at a little cross-roads store or cast a vote in his favor if he should ever seek ordination as a Methodist minister—a Methodist steward, a merchant not only of modest position and circumstances but who already had a wife and family of his own, let alone a dependent mother and sister, to support out of the proceeds of a business which he had brought to Jefferson ten years ago in a single wagon—a man with a name for absolute and undeviating and even puritan uprightness in a country and time of lawless opportunity, who neither drank nor gambled nor even hunted. In their surprise they forgot that Mr Coldfield had a marriageable daughter. They did not consider the daughter at all. They did not think of love in connection with Sutpen. They thought of ruthlessness rather than justice and of fear rather than respect, but not of pity or love: besides being too lost in amazed speculation as to just how Sutpen intended or could contrive to use Mr Coldfield to further whatever secret

ends he still had. They were never to know: even Miss Rosa
Coldfield did not. Because from that day there were no more
hunting parties out at Sutpen's Hundred, and when they saw
him now it would be in town. But not loafing, idling. The
men who had slept and matched glasses with him under his
roof (some of them had even come to call him Sutpen without the formal Mister) watched him pass along the street before the Holston House with a single formal gesture to his
hat and go on and enter Mr Coldfield's store, and that was all.

"Then one day he quitted Jefferson for the second time,"
Mr Compson told Quentin. "The town should have been
accustomed to that by now. Nevertheless, his position had
subtly changed, as you will see by the town's reaction to this
second return. Because when he came back this time, he was
in a sense a public enemy. Perhaps this was because of what
he brought back with him this time: the material he brought
back this time, as compared to the simple wagon load of wild
niggers which he had brought back before. But I dont think
so. That is, I think it was a little more involved than the sheer
value of his chandeliers and mahogany and rugs. I think that
the affront was born of the town's realization that he was
getting it involved with himself; that whatever the felony
which produced the mahogany and crystal, he was forcing the
town to compound it. Heretofore, until that Sunday when he
came to church, if he had misused or injured anybody, it was
only old Ikkemotubbe, from whom he got his land—a matter
between his conscience and Uncle Sam and God. But now
his position had changed, because when, about three months
after he departed, four wagons left Jefferson to go to the
River and meet him, it was known that Mr Coldfield was
the man who hired and dispatched them. They were big wagons, drawn by oxen, and when they returned the town looked
at them and knew, no matter what they might have contained, that Mr Coldfield could not have mortgaged everything that he owned for enough to fill them; doubtless this
time there were more men than women even who pictured
him during this absence with a handkerchief over his face and
the two pistol barrels glinting beneath the candelabra of a
steamboat's saloon, even if no worse: if not something performed in the lurking dark of a muddy landing and with a

knife from behind. They saw him pass, on the roan horse beside his four wagons; it seems that even the ones who had eaten his food and shot his game and even called him 'Sutpen' without the 'Mister', didn't accost him now. They just waited while reports and rumors came back to town of how he and his now somewhat tamed negroes had installed the windows and doors and the spits and pots in the kitchen and the crystal chandeliers in the parlors and the furniture and the curtains and the rugs; it was that same Akers who had blundered onto the mudcouched negro five years ago who came, a little wild-eyed and considerably slack-mouthed, into the Holston House bar one evening and said, 'Boys, this time he stole the whole durn steamboat!'

"So at last civic virtue came to a boil. One day and with the sheriff of the county among them, a party of eight or ten took the road out to Sutpen's Hundred. They did not go all the way because about six miles from town they met Sutpen himself. He was riding the roan horse, in the frock coat and the beaver hat which they knew and with his legs wrapped in a piece of tarpaulin; he had a portmanteau on his pommel and he was carrying a small woven basket on his arm. He stopped the roan (it was April then, and the road was still a quagmire) and sat there in his splashed tarpaulin and looked from one face to the next; your grandfather said that his eyes looked like pieces of a broken plate and that his beard was strong as a curry-comb. That was how he put it: strong as a curry-comb. 'Good morning, gentlemen,' he said. 'Were you look-ing for me?'

"Doubtless something more than this transpired at the time, though none of the vigilance committee ever told it that I know of. All I ever heard is how the town, the men on the gallery of the Holston House saw Sutpen and the committee ride onto the square together, Sutpen a little in front and the others bunched behind him—Sutpen with his legs and feet wrapped neatly in his tarpaulin and his shoulders squared in-side the worn broadcloth coat and that worn brushed beaver cocked a little, talking to them over his shoulder and those eyes hard and pale and reckless and probably quizzical and maybe contemptuous even then. He pulled up at the door and the negro hostler ducked out and took the roan's head

and Sutpen got down, with his portmanteau and the basket
and mounted the steps, and I heard how he turned there and
looked at them again where they huddled on their horses, not
knowing what to do exactly. And it might have been a good
thing that he had that beard and they could not see his
mouth. Then he turned, and he looked at the other men sitting with their feet on the railing and watching him too, men
who used to come out to his place and sleep on the floor and
hunt with him, and he saluted them with that florid, swaggering gesture to the hat (yes, he was underbred. It showed like
this always, your grandfather said, in all his formal contacts
with people. He was like John L. Sullivan having taught himself painfully and tediously to do the schottische, having
drilled himself and drilled himself in secret until he now believed it no longer necessary to count the music's beat, say.
He may have believed that your grandfather or Judge Benbow
might have done it a little more effortlessly than he, but he
would not have believed that anyone could have beat him in
knowing when to do it and how. And besides, it was in his
face; that was where his power lay, your grandfather said:
that anyone could look at him and say, *Given the occasion and
the need, this man can and will do anything*) and went on into
the house and commanded a chamber.

"So they sat on their horses and waited for him. I suppose
they knew that he would have to come out sometime: I suppose they sat there and thought about those two pistols. Because there was still no warrant for him, you see: it was just
public opinion in an acute state of indigestion; and now other
horsemen rode into the square and became aware of the situation, so that there was quite a posse waiting when he walked
out onto the gallery. He wore a new hat now, and a new
broadcloth coat, so they knew what the portmanteau had
contained. They even knew now what the basket had contained because he did not have that with him now either,
though doubtless at the time it merely puzzled them more
than ever. Because, you see, they had been too busy speculat-
ing on just how he was planning to use Mr Coldfield and,
since his return, too completely outraged by the belief that
they now saw the results even if the means were still an
enigma, to remember about Miss Ellen at all.

"So he stopped again doubtless and looked from face to face again, doubtless memorising the new faces, without any haste, with still the beard to hide whatever his mouth might have shown. But he seems to have said nothing at all this time. He just descended the steps and walked on across the square, the committee (your grandfather said it had grown to almost fifty by now) moving too, following him across the square. They say he did not even look back. He just walked on, erect, with the new hat cocked and carrying in his hand now that which must have seemed to them the final gratuitous bafflement and even insult, with the committee riding along in the street beside him and not quite parallel, and others who did not happen to have horses at the moment joining in and following the committee in the road, and ladies and children and women slaves coming to the doors and windows of the homes as they passed to watch as they went on in grim tableau, and Sutpen, still without once looking back, entered Mr Coldfield's gate and strode on up the brick walk to the door, carrying his newspaper cornucopia of flowers.

"They waited for him again. The crowd was growing fast now—other men and a few boys and even some negroes from the adjacent houses, clotting behind the eight original members of the committee who sat watching Mr Coldfield's door until he emerged. It was a good while and he no longer carried the flowers, and when he returned to the gate, he was engaged to be married. But they did not know this, because as soon as he reached the gate, they arrested him. They took him back to town, with the ladies and children and house niggers watching from behind curtains and behind the shrubbery in the yards and the corners of the houses, the kitchens where doubtless food was already beginning to scorch, and so back to the square where the rest of the able-bodied men left their offices and stores to follow, so that when he reached the courthouse, Sutpen had a larger following than if he actually had been the runaway slave. They arraigned him before a justice, but by that time your grandfather and Mr Coldfield had got there. They signed his bond and late that afternoon he returned home with Mr Coldfield, walking along the same street as of the forenoon, with doubtless the same faces watching him from behind the window curtains, to the betrothal supper with no wine at table and no whiskey before or after. I have heard how during none of his three passages that day through that street did his bearing alter—the same unhurried stride to which that new frock coat swung, the same angle to the new hat above the eyes and the beard. Your grandfather said that some of the faience appearance which the flesh of his face had had when he came to town five years ago was gone now and that his face had an honest sunburn. And he was not fleshier either; your grandfather said that was not it: it was just that the flesh on his bones had become quieter, as though passive after some actual breasting of atmosphere like in running, so that he actually filled his clothes now, with that quality still swaggering but without braggadocio or belligerence, though according to your grandfather the quality had never been belligerence, only watchfulness. And now that was gone, as though after the three years he could trust his eyes alone to do the watching, without the flesh on his bones standing sentry also. Two months later, he and Miss Ellen were married.

"It was in June of 1838, almost five years to the day from that Sunday morning when he rode into town on the roan horse. It (the wedding) was in the same Methodist church where he saw Ellen for the first time, according to Miss Rosa. The aunt had even forced or nagged (not cajoled: that would not have done it) Mr Coldfield into allowing Ellen to wear powder on her face for the occasion. The powder was to hide the marks of tears. But before the wedding was over the powder was streaked again, caked and channelled. Ellen seems to have entered the church that night out of weeping as though out of rain, gone through the ceremony and then walked back out of the church and into the weeping again, the tears again, the same tears even, the same rain. She got into the carriage and departed in it (the rain) for Sutpen's Hundred.

"It was the wedding which caused the tears: not marrying Sutpen. Whatever tears there were for that, granted there were tears, came later. It was not intended to be a big wedding. That is, Mr Coldfield seems not to have intended it to be. Of the two men (I dont speak of Ellen, of course: in fact, you will notice that most divorces occur with women who were married by tobacco-chewing j.p.'s in country court-

houses or by ministers waked after midnight, with their suspenders showing beneath their coattails and no collar on and
a wife or spinster sister in curl papers for witness. So is it too
much to believe that these women come to long for divorce
from a sense not of incompleteness but of actual frustration
and betrayal? that regardless of the breathing evidence of children and all else, they still have in their minds even yet the
image of themselves walking to music and turning heads, in
all the symbolical trappings and circumstances of ceremonial
surrender of that which they no longer possess? and why not,
since to them the actual and authentic surrender can only be
(and have been) a ceremony like the breaking of a banknote
to buy a ticket for the train)—of the two men, it was Sutpen
who desired (or hoped: I have this from something your
grandfather let drop one day and which he doubtless had
from Sutpen himself in the same accidental fashion, since Sutpen never even told Ellen that he wanted it, which—the fact
that at the last minute he refused to support her in her desire
and insistence upon it—accounts partly for the tears) the big
wedding, the full church and all the ritual. Mr Coldfield apparently intended merely to employ, use, the church, apart
from its spiritual significance, exactly as he might or would
have used any other object, concrete or abstract, to which he
had given a certain amount of his time. He seems to have
intended to use the church into which he had invested a certain amount of sacrifice and doubtless self-denial and certainly
actual labor and money for the sake of what might be called a
demand balance of spiritual solvency, exactly as he would
have used a cotton gin in which he considered himself to have
incurred either interest or responsibility, for the ginning of
any cotton which he or any member of his family, by blood
or by marriage, had raised—that, and no more. Perhaps this
was due to the same tedious and unremitting husbandry
which had enabled him to support mother and sister and
marry and raise a family on the proceeds of that store which
ten years ago had fitted into a single wagon; or perhaps it was
some innate sense of delicacy and fitness (which his sister and
daughter did not seem to possess, by the way) regarding the
prospective son-in-law whom just two months ago he had
been instrumental in getting out of jail. But not from any lack

of courage regarding the son-in-law's still anomalous position
in the town. Regardless of what their relations before that
had been and of what their future relations might be, if Mr
Coldfield had believed Sutpen guilty at the time of any crime,
he would not have raised a finger to take Sutpen out. He
might not have gone out of his way to keep Sutpen in jail,
but doubtless the best possible moral fumigation which Sutpen could have received at the time in the eyes of his fellow
citizens was the fact that Mr Coldfield signed his bond—
something he would not have done to save his own good
name even though the arrest had been a direct result of the
business between himself and Sutpen—that affair which,
when it reached a point where his conscience refused to sanction it, he had withdrawn from and let Sutpen take all the
profit, refusing even to allow Sutpen to reimburse him for the
loss which, in withdrawing, he had suffered, though he did
permit his daughter to marry this man of whose actions his
conscience did not approve. This was the second time he did
something like that.

"When they were married, there were just ten people in the
church, including the wedding party, of the hundred who had
been invited; though when they emerged from the church (it
was at night: Sutpen had brought in a half dozen of his wild
negroes to wait at the door with burning pine knots) the rest
of the hundred were there in the persons of boys and youths
and men from the drovers' tavern on the edge of town—
stock traders and hostlers and such who had not been invited.
That was the other half of the reason for Ellen's tears. It was
the aunt who persuaded or cajoled Mr Coldfield into the big
wedding. Sutpen had not expressed himself. But he wanted it.
In fact, Miss Rosa was righter than she knew: he did want,
not the anonymous wife and the anonymous children, but the
two names, the stainless wife and the unimpeachable father-
in-law, on the license, the patent. Yes, patent, with a gold seal
and red ribbons too if that had been practicable. But not for
himself. She (Miss Rosa) would have called the gold seal and
the ribbons vanity. But then, so had vanity conceived that
house and, in a strange place and with little else but his bare
hands and further handicapped by the chance and probability
of meddling interference arising out of the disapprobation of

all communities of men toward any situation which they
do not understand, built it. And pride: she admitted to you
that he was brave; perhaps she will even allow him pride: the
same pride which wanted such a house, which would accept
nothing less, and drove through to get it at whatever cost
and then lived in it, alone, on a pallet on the floor for three
years until he could furnish it as it should be furnished—not
the least of which furniture was that wedding license. She
was quite right. It was not just shelter, just anonymous wife
and children that he wanted, just as he did not want just
wedding. But he never told Ellen, nor anyone; in fact, when
the female crisis came, when Ellen and the aunt tried to enlist
him on their side to persuade Mr Coldfield to the big wedding, he refused to support them. He doubtless remembered
even better than Mr Coldfield that two months ago he had
been in jail; that public opinion which at some moment during the five preceding years had swallowed him even though
he never had quite ever lain quiet on its stomach, had performed one of mankind's natural and violent and inexplicable
volte faces and regurgitated him. And it did not help him any
that at least two of the citizens who should have made two
of the teeth in the outraged jaw served instead as props to
hold the jaw open and impotent while he walked out of it
unharmed.

"Ellen and the aunt remembered this too. The aunt did.
Being a woman, she was doubtless one of that league of Jefferson women who on the second day after the town saw him
five years ago, had agreed never to forgive him for not having
any past, and who had remained consistent. Since the marriage was now a closed incident, she probably looked upon it
as the one chance to thrust him back into the gullet of public
opinion which had tried at last to refuse him, not only to
secure her niece's future as his wife but to justify the action of
her brother in getting him out of jail and her own position as
having apparently sanctioned and permitted the wedding
which in reality she could not have prevented—this, as Miss
Rosa told you, for the sake of that big house and the position
and state which the women realised long before the men did
that he not only aimed at but was going to attain. Or maybe
women are even less complex than that and to them any

wedding is better than no wedding and a big wedding with a villain preferable to a small one with a saint.

"So the aunt even used Ellen's tears; and Sutpen, who probably knew about what was going to happen, becoming as the time drew near graver and graver. Not concerned: just watchful, like he must have been from the day when he turned his back upon all that he knew—the faces and the customs—and (he was just fourteen then, he told your grandfather. Just the same age that Henry was that night in the stable which Miss Rosa told you about, which Henry could not quite stand up to) set out into a world which even in theory, the average geographical schooling of the normal boy of fourteen, he knew nothing about, and with a fixed goal in his mind which most men do not set up until the blood begins to slow at thirty or more and then only because the image represents peace and indolence or at least a crowning of vanity, not the vindication of a past affront in the person of a son whose seed is not yet, and would not be for years yet, planted. That same alertness which he had to wear day and night without changing or laying aside, like the clothing which without doubt and for a time at least he had to sleep in as well as live in, and in a country and among a people whose very language he had to learn and where because of this he was to make that mistake which if he had acquiesced to it would not even have been an error and which, since he refused to accept it or be stopped by it, became his doom;— that unsleeping care which must have known that it could permit itself but one mistake; that alertness for measuring and weighing event against eventuality, circumstance against human nature, his own fallible judgment and mortal clay against not only human but natural forces, choosing and discarding, compromising with his dream and his ambition like you must with the horse which you take across country, over timber, which you control only through your ability to keep the animal from realising that actually you cannot, that actually it is the stronger.

"His was the curious position now. He was the solitary one. Not Ellen. She not only had the aunt to support her, but the fact that women never plead nor claim loneliness until impenetrable and insurmountable circumstance forces them to give up all hope of attaining the particular bauble which at the moment they happen to want. And not Mr Coldfield. He had not only public opinion but his own disinclination for the big wedding to support it without incongruity or paradox, as Ellen had her aunt as well as her own desire for the big wedding to support it without incongruity or paradox. While Sutpen wanted the big wedding more than Ellen did, or for a deeper reason than she did, yet his judgment forewarned him how the town would take it even more than Mr Coldfield's did. So while Ellen was using her tears not only to coerce her father but to persuade Sutpen to put his weight into the balance on her side, he had but one enemy—Mr Coldfield. But when he refused her, when he remained neutral, he had three, counting the aunt. Then (the tears won; Ellen and the aunt wrote out a hundred invitations—Sutpen brought in one of the wild negroes who carried them from door to door by hand—and even sent out a dozen more personal ones for the dress rehearsal) when they reached the church for the rehearsal on the night before the wedding and found the church itself empty and a handful of men from the town's purlieus (including two of old Ikkemotubbe's Chickasaws) standing in the shadows outside the door, the tears came down again. Ellen went through the rehearsal, but afterward the aunt took her home in a state very near hysteria, though by the next day it had become just quiet intermittent weeping again. There was some talk even of putting the wedding off. I dont know who it came from, perhaps from Sutpen. But I know who vetoed it. It was as though the aunt were now bent, no longer on merely thrusting Sutpen down the town's throat, but thrusting the wedding itself. She spent all the next day going from house to house, the invitation list in her hand, in a house dress and a shawl and one of the Coldfield negroes (they were both women) following her, perhaps for protection, perhaps just sucked along like a leaf in the wake of that grim virago fury of female affront; yes, she came to our house, though your grandfather had never intended anything else but to attend the wedding: the aunt must have had no doubts about Father since Father had helped take Sutpen out of jail, though she was probably past all ratiocination by then; she came to our house too. Father and your grandmother were just married then and Mother was a stranger in Jefferson and I dont know what she thought except that she would never talk about what happened: about the mad woman whom she had never seen before, who came bursting into the house, not to invite her to a wedding but to dare her not to come, and then rushed out again. Mother could not even tell what wedding she meant at first, and when Father came home he found Mother in hysterics too, and even twenty years later Mother could not tell what actually happened. There was nothing comic in it to her. Father used to tease her about it, but even twenty years after that day, when he would tease her I have seen her begin to raise her hand (perhaps with the thimble on one finger) as though to protect herself and the same look come into her face that must have been there when Ellen's aunt departed.

"She covered the town that morning. It did not take her long and it was complete; by nightfall the circumstances of the situation had spread not only beyond the town but beneath it, penetrating the livery stable and the drovers' tavern which was to supply the guests who did attend it, not only as notice but as a blanket threat and dare. Ellen of course was not aware of this, anymore than the aunt herself was, or would have believed what was going to happen even if she had been clairvoyant, could actually have seen the rehearsal of events before time produced them. Not that the aunt would have considered herself insulated against being thus affronted, she simply could not have believed that her intentions and actions of the day could have any result other than the one for which she had surrendered for the time not only all Coldfield dignity but all female modesty as well. Sutpen I suppose could have told her, but doubtless he knew that the aunt would not have believed him. Probably he did not even try: he just did the only thing he could do, which was to send out to Sutpen's Hundred and bring in six or seven more of his negroes, men on whom he could depend, the only men on whom he could depend, and arm them with the lighted pine knots which they were holding at the door when the carriage came up and the wedding party got out. And this is where the tears stopped, because now the street before the church was lined with carriages and buggies, though only Sutpen and

possibly Mr Coldfield remarked that instead of being drawn
up before the door and empty, they were halted across the
street and still occupied, and that now the banquette before
the church door was a sort of arena lighted by the smoking
torches which the negroes held above their heads, the light
of which wavered and gleamed upon the two lines of faces
between which the party would have to pass to enter the
church. There were no catcalls yet, no jeering; evidently neither Ellen nor the aunt suspected that anything was wrong.

"Because for the time Ellen even walked out of the weeping, the tears, and so into the church. It was empty yet save
for your grandfather and grandmother and perhaps a half
dozen more who might have come out of loyalty to the Coldfields or perhaps to be close and so miss nothing of that
which the town, as represented by the waiting carriages,
seemed to have anticipated as well as Sutpen did. It was still
empty even after the ceremony started and concluded. Because Ellen had something of pride too, or at least that vanity
which at times can assume the office of pride and fortitude;
besides, nothing had happened yet. The crowd outside was
quiet yet, perhaps out of respect for the church, out of that
aptitude and eagerness of the Anglo-Saxon for complete mystical acceptance of immolated sticks and stones. She seems to
have walked out of the church and so into it without any
warning whatever. Perhaps she was still moving beneath that
pride which would not allow the people inside the church to
see her weep. She just walked into it, probably hurrying toward the seclusion of the carriage where she could weep; perhaps her first intimation was the voice shouting, 'Look out!
Dont hit her now!' and then the object—dirt, filth, whatever
it was—passing her, or perhaps the changing light itself as
she turned and saw one of the negroes, his torch raised and in
the act of springing toward the crowd, the faces, when Sutpen spoke to him in that tongue which even now a good part
of the county did not know was a civilised language. That was
what she saw, what the others saw from the halted carriages
across the street—the bride shrinking into the shelter of his
arm as he drew her behind him and he standing there, not
moving even after another object (they threw nothing which
could actually injure: it was only clods of dirt and vegetable

refuse) struck the hat from his head, and a third struck him
full in the chest—standing there motionless, with an expression almost of smiling where his teeth showed through the
beard, holding his wild negroes with that one word (there
were doubtless pistols in the crowd; certainly knives: the negro would not have lived ten seconds if he had sprung) while
about the wedding party the circle of faces with open mouths
and torch-reflecting eyes seemed to advance and waver and
shift and vanish in the smoky glare of the burning pine. He
retreated to the carriage, shielding the two women with his
body, ordering the negroes to follow with another word. But
they threw nothing else. Apparently it was that first spontaneous outburst, though they had come armed and prepared
with the ones they did throw. In fact, that seemed to have
been the entire business which had come to a head when the
vigilance committee followed him to Mr Coldfield's gate that
day two months before. Because the men who had composed
the mob, the traders and drovers and teamsters, returned,
vanished back into the region from which they had emerged
for this one occasion like rats; scattered, departed about the
country—faces which even Ellen was not to remember, seen
for the night or the meal or just the drink at other taverns
twenty and fifty and a hundred miles further on along nameless roads and then gone from there too; and those who had
come in the carriages and buggies to see a Roman holiday,
driving out to Sutpen's Hundred to call and (the men) to
hunt his game and eat his food again and on occasion gathering at night in his stable while he matched two of his wild
negroes against one another as men match game cocks or perhaps even entered the ring himself. It blew away, though not
out of memory. He did not forget that night, even though
Ellen, I think, did, since she washed it out of her remembering with tears. Yes, she was weeping again now; it did, indeed, rain on that marriage."

III.

I F HE THREW her over, I wouldn't think she would want to tell anybody about it *Quentin said*.

Ah *Mr Compson said again* After Mr Coldfield died in '64, Miss Rosa moved out to Sutpen's Hundred to live with Judith. She was twenty then, four years younger than the niece whom, in obedience to her sister's dying request, she set out to save from the family's doom which Sutpen seemed bent on accomplishing, apparently by the process of marrying him. She (Miss Rosa) was born in 1845, with her sister already seven years married and the mother of two children and Miss Rosa born into her parents' middleage (her mother must have been at least forty and she died in that childbed and Miss Rosa never forgave her father for it) and at a time when— granted that Miss Rosa merely mirrored her parents' attitude toward the son-in-law—the family wanted only peace and quiet and probably did not expect and maybe did not even want another child. But she was born, at the price of her mother's life and never to be permitted to forget it, and raised by the same spinster aunt who tried to force not only the elder sister's bridegroom but the wedding too down the throat of a town which did not want it, growing up in that closed masonry of females to see in the fact of her own breathing not only the lone justification for the sacrifice of her mother's life, not only a living and walking reproach to her father, but a breathing indictment ubiquitous and even transferable of the entire male principle (that principle which had left the aunt a virgin at thirty-five) above dust. So for the first sixteen years of her life she lived in that grim tight little house with the father whom she hated without knowing it—that queer silent man whose only companion and friend seems to have been his conscience and the only thing he cared about his reputation for probity among his fellow men—that man who was later to nail himself in his attic and starve to death rather than look upon his native land in the throes of repelling an invading army—and the aunt who even ten years later was still taking revenge for the fiasco of Ellen's wedding by striking at the town, the human race, through any and all of

its creatures—brother nieces nephew-in-law herself and all—
with the blind irrational fury of a shedding snake; who had
taught Miss Rosa to look upon her sister as a woman who
had vanished not only out of the family and the house but out
of life too, into an edifice like Bluebeard's and there transmogrified into a mask looking back with passive and hopeless
grief upon the irrevocable world, held there not in durance
but in a kind of jeering suspension by a man (his face the
same which Mr Coldfield now saw and had seen since that
day when, with his future son-in-law for ostensible yokemate
but actually whip, Mr Coldfield's conscience had set the
brakes and, surrendering even his share of the cargo, he and
the son-in-law had parted) who had entered hers and her
family's life before she was born with the abruptness of a
tornado, done irrevocable and incalculable damage, and gone
on—a grim mausoleum air of puritan righteousness and outraged female vindictiveness in which Miss Rosa's childhood
(that aged and ancient and timeless absence of youth which
consisted of a Cassandra-like listening beyond closed doors,
of lurking in dim halls filled with that presbyterian effluvium
of lugubrious and vindictive anticipation while she waited for
the infancy and childhood with which nature had confounded
and betrayed her to overtake the precocity of convinced disapprobation regarding any and every thing which could penetrate the walls of that house through the agency of any man,
particularly her father, which the aunt seems to have invested
her with at birth along with the swaddling clothes) was
passed.

Perhaps she saw in her father's death, in the resulting
necessity upon her as not only an orphan but a pauper, to
turn to her next of kin for food and shelter and protection—
and this kin the niece whom she had been asked to save—;
perhaps she saw in this fate itself supplying her with the
opportunity to observe her sister's dying request. Perhaps she
even saw herself as an instrument of retribution: if not in herself an active instrument strong enough to cope with him, at
least as a kind of passive symbol of inescapable reminding to
rise bloodless and without dimension from the sacrificial
stone of the marriage-bed. Because until he came back from
Virginia in '66 and found her living there with Judith and

Clytie——(Yes, Clytie was his daughter too: Clytemnestra.
He named her himself. He named them all himself: all his
own get and all the get of his wild niggers after the country
began to assimilate them. Miss Rosa didn't tell you that two
of the niggers in the wagon that day were women?

No, sir *Quentin said.*

Yes. Two of them. And brought here neither by chance nor
oversight. He saw to that, who had doubtless seen even further ahead than the two years it actually took him to build his
house and show his good intentions to his neighbors until
they allowed him to mix his wild stock with their tame, since
the difference in tongue between his niggers and theirs could
have been a barrier only for a matter of weeks or perhaps even
days. He brought the two women deliberately; he probably
chose them with the same care and shrewdness with which he
chose the other livestock—the horses and mules and cattle—
which he bought later on. And he lived out there for almost
five years before he had speaking acquaintance with any white
woman in the county, just as he had no furniture in his house
and for the same reason: he had at the time nothing to exchange for it them or her. Yes. He named Clytie as he named
them all, the one before Clytie and Henry and Judith even,
with that same robust and sardonic temerity, naming with his
own mouth his own ironic fecundity of dragon's teeth which
with the two exceptions were girls. Only I have always liked
to believe that he intended to name her Cassandra, prompted
by some pure dramatic economy not only to beget but to
designate the presiding augur of his own disaster, and that he
just got the name wrong through a mistake natural in a man
who must have almost taught himself to read)——When he
returned home in '66, she had not seen him a hundred times
in her whole life. And what she saw then was just that ogre-
face of her childhood seen once and then repeated at intervals
and on occasions which she could neither count nor recall,
like the mask in Greek tragedy interchangeable not only from
scene to scene but from actor to actor and behind which the
events and occasions took place without chronology or sequence and leaving her actually incapable of saying how many
separate times she had seen him for the reason that, waking or
sleeping, the aunt had taught her to see nothing else. On

those guarded and lugubrious and even formal occasions
when she and the aunt went out to Sutpen's Hundred to
spend the day and the aunt would order her to go and play
with her nephew and niece exactly as the aunt might have
ordered her to play a piece for company on the piano, she
would not see him even at the dinner table because the aunt
would have arranged the visit to coincide with his absence;
and probably Miss Rosa would have tried to avoid meeting
him even if he had been there. And on the four or five occasions during the year when Ellen would bring the children in
to spend the day at her father's, the aunt (that strong vindictive consistent woman who seems to have been twice the man
that Mr Coldfield was and who in very truth was not only
Miss Rosa's mother but her father too) cast over these visits
also that same atmosphere of grim embattled conspiracy and
alliance against the two adversaries, one of whom—Mr Coldfield—whether he could have held his own or not, had long
since drawn in his picquets and dismantled his artillery and
retired into the impregnable citadel of his passive rectitude:
and the other—Sutpen—who probably could have engaged
and even routed them but who did not even know that he
was an embattled foe. Because he would not even come to the
house to the noon meal. His reason may have been because of
some delicacy for his father-in-law, the true reason for and
beginning of the relationship between whom and himself
neither the aunt nor Ellen nor Miss Rosa ever knew, which
Sutpen was to divulge to but one man—and that under the
pledge of confidence as long as Mr Coldfield lived—out of
regard for Mr Coldfield's carefully nurtured name for immaculate morality—and which, your grandfather said, Mr Coldfield himself never divulged for the same reason. Or perhaps
the reason was the one which Miss Rosa told you and which
the aunt gave her: that now since he had got out of his father-
in-law all which Mr Coldfield possessed that Sutpen could
have used or wanted, he (Sutpen) had neither the courage to
face his father-in-law nor the grace and decency to complete
the ceremonial family group even four times a year. Or perhaps it was the reason which Sutpen gave himself and which
the aunt refused to believe because of that very fact: that he
did not get to town every day and when he did he preferred

to spend it (he used the bar now) with the men who gathered
each noon at the Holston House.

That was the face which, when she saw it at all, was across
his own dining table—the face of a foe who did not even
know that it was embattled. She was ten now and following
the aunt's dereliction (Miss Rosa now kept her father's house
as the aunt had done until the night the aunt climbed out the
window and vanished) there was not only no one to make her
try to play with her nephew and niece on those days formal
and funereal, she did not even have to go out there and
breathe the same air which he breathed and where, even
though absent, he still remained, lurked, in what she called
sardonic and watchful triumph. She went out to Sutpen's
Hundred just once a year now when, in their Sunday clothes,
she and her father drove the twelve miles in a stout battered
buggy behind the stout scrubby team, to spend the day. It
was now Mr Coldfield who insisted on the visits, who had
never gone out with them while the aunt was there, perhaps
from a sense of duty, which was the reason he gave and which
in this case even the aunt would have believed, perhaps because it was not the true one, since doubtless even Miss Rosa
would not have believed the true one: which was that Mr
Coldfield wanted to see his grandchildren regarding whom he
was in a steadily increasing unease of that day when their father would tell the son at least of that old business between
father and grandfather which Mr Coldfield was not sure yet
that his son-in-law had never told. Though the aunt was
gone, she still managed to bequeath and invoke upon each of
these expeditions something of the old flavor of grim sortie,
more than ever now against a foe who did not know that he
was at war. Because now that the aunt was gone, Ellen had
reneged from that triumvirate of which Miss Rosa tried without realising it to make two. Now she was completely alone
and facing across the dinner table and without support now
even from Ellen (at this time Ellen went through a complete
metamorphosis, emerging into her next lustrum with the
complete finality of actual re-birth);—facing across the table
the foe who was not even aware that he sat there not as host
and brother-in-law but as the second party to an armistice.
He probably did not even look at her twice as compared with,

weighed against, his own family and children—the small slight child whose feet, even when she would be grown, would never quite reach the floor even from her own chairs, the ones which she would inherit nor the ones—the objects—which she would accumulate as complement to and expression of individual character, as people do, as against Ellen who, though small-boned also, was what is known as fullbodied (and who would have been, if her life had not declined into a time when even men found little enough to eat and the end of her days had been without trouble, fullbodied indeed. Not fat: just rounded and complete, the hair white, the eyes still even young, even a faint bloom yet on what would be dewlaps and not cheeks any longer, the small plump ringed unscarified hands folded in tranquil anticipation of the food, on the damask before the Haviland beneath the candelabra which he had fetched to town years and years ago in wagons, to the astonished and affronted outrage of his fellow citizens), and against Judith already taller than Ellen, and Henry though not as tall for sixteen as Judith was for fourteen, yet giving promise of someday standing eye to eye with his father;—this creature, this face which hardly ever spoke during the meal, with eyes like (as you put it) pieces of coal pressed into soft dough and prim hair of that peculiar mouselike shade of hair on which the sun does not often shine, against Judith's and Henry's out-of-doors faces: Judith with her mother's hair and her father's eyes and Henry with his hair halfway between his father's red and Ellen's black and eyes of a bright dark hazel;—this small body with its air of curious and paradoxical awkwardness like a costume borrowed at the last moment and of necessity for a masquerade which she did not want to attend: that aura of a creature cloistered now by deliberate choice and still in the throes of enforced apprenticeship to, rather than voluntary or even acquiescent participation in, breathing—this bound maidservant to flesh and blood waiting even now to escape it by writing a schoolgirl's poetry about the also-dead—the face, the smallest face in company, watching him across the table with still and curious and profound intensity as though she actually had some intimation gained from that rapport with the fluid cradle of events (time) which she had acquired or cultivated by listening beyond closed doors not to what she heard there but by becoming supine and receptive, incapable of either discrimination or opinion or incredulity, to the prefever's temperature of disaster which makes soothsayers and sometimes makes them right, of the future catastrophe in which the ogre-face of her childhood would apparently vanish so completely that she would agree to marry the late owner of it.

That may have been the last time she saw him. Because they quit going out there. Mr Coldfield quit. There had never been any day set for the visit. One morning he would merely appear at breakfast in the decent and heavy black coat in which he had been married and had worn fifty-two times each year since until Ellen married and then fifty-three times a year after the aunt deserted them until he put it on for good the day he climbed to the attic and nailed the door behind him and threw the hammer out the window and so died in it. Then Miss Rosa would retire and reappear in the formidable black or brown silk which the aunt had chosen for her years ago and which she continued to wear on Sundays and occasions even after it was worn out, until the day when her father decided that the aunt would not return and permitted Miss Rosa to use the clothing which the aunt had left in the house the night of her elopement. Then they would get into the buggy and depart, Mr Coldfield first docking the two negroes for the noon meal which they would not have to prepare and (so the town believed) charging them for the crude one of left-overs which they would have to eat. Then one year they did not go. Doubtless Mr Coldfield failed to come to breakfast in the black coat, and more days passed and still he did not, and that was all. Perhaps he felt, now that the grandchildren were grown, that the draft on his conscience had been discharged what with Henry away at the State University at Oxford and Judith gone even further than that:—into that transition stage between childhood and womanhood where she was even more inaccessible to the grandfather of whom she had seen but little during her life and probably cared less anyway—that state where, though still visible, young girls appear as though seen through glass and where even the voice cannot reach them; where they exist (this the hoyden who could—and did—outrun and outclimb, and ride and fight both with and beside her brother) in a pearly lambence without shadows and themselves partaking of it; in nebulous suspension held, strange and unpredictable, even their very shapes fluid and delicate and without substance; not in themselves floating and seeking but merely waiting, parasitic and potent and serene, drawing to themselves without effort the post-genitive upon and about which to shape, flow into back, breast; bosom, flank, thigh.

Now the period began which ended in the catastrophe which caused a reversal so complete in Miss Rosa as to permit her to agree to marry the man whom she had grown up to look upon as an ogre. It was not a volte face of character: that did not change. Even her behavior did not change to any extent. Even if Charles Bon had not died, she would in all probability have gone out to Sutpen's Hundred to live after her father's death sooner or later, and once she had done so she would have probably passed the remainder of her life there, as she doubtless expected to do when she did go out. But if Bon had lived and he and Judith married and Henry had remained in the known world, she would have moved (if she had moved) out there only when she was ready to, and she would have lived (if she had lived) in her dead sister's family only as the aunt which she actually was. It was not her character: despite the probably six years since she had actually seen him and certainly the four years which she had spent feeding her father secretly at night while he hid from Confederate provost marshals in the attic and at the same time writing heroic poetry about the very men from whom her father was hiding and who would have shot him or hung him without trial if they had found him—and incidentally of whom the ogre of her childhood made one and (he brought home with him a citation for valor in Lee's own hand) a good one—the face which she carried out there to live for the rest of her life was the same face which had watched him across the dinner table and which he likewise could not have said how many times he had seen it nor when and where, not for the reason that he was unable to forget it but because he could probably not have remembered it enough to have described it ten minutes after looking away, and from behind

which the same woman who had been that child now
watched him with that same grim and cold intensity.

Although she was not to see Sutpen again for years, she
now saw her sister and niece more often than ever. Ellen was
now at the full peak of what the aunt would have called her
renegadery. She seemed not only to acquiesce, to be reconciled to her life and marriage, but to be actually proud of it.
She had bloomed, as if Fate were crowding the normal Indian
summer which should have bloomed gradually and faded
gracefully through six or eight years, into three or four, either
for compensation for what was to come or to clear the books,
pay the check to which his wife, Nature, had signed his name.
She was in her late thirties, plump, her face unblemished still.
It was as though whatever marks being in the world had left
upon it up to the time the aunt vanished had been removed,
eradicated at least, from between the skeleton and the skin,
between the sum of experience and the envelope in which it
resides, by the intervening years of annealing and untroubled
flesh. Her carriage, air, now was a little regal—she and Judith
made frequent trips to town now, calling upon the same ladies, some of whom were now grandmothers, whom the aunt
had tried to force to attend the wedding twenty years ago,
and, to the meagre possibilities which the town offered, shopping—as though she had succeeded at last in evacuating not
only the puritan heritage but reality itself; had immolated
outrageous husband and incomprehensible children into
shades; escaped at last into a world of pure illusion in which,
safe from any harm, she moved, lived, from attitude to attitude against her background of chatelaine to the largest, wife
to the wealthiest, mother of the most fortunate. When she
shopped (there were twenty stores in Jefferson now) she un-
bent without even getting out of the carriage, gracious and
assured and talking the most complete nonsense, voluble,
speaking her bright set meaningless phrases out of the part
which she had written for herself, of the duchess peripatetic
with property soups and medicines among a soilless and un-
compelled peasantry—a woman who, if she had had the fortitude to bear sorrow and trouble, might have risen to actual
stardom in the role of the matriarch arbitrating from the fire-
side corner of a crone the pride and destiny of her family,

instead of turning at the last to the youngest member of it and asking her to protect the others.

Often twice and sometimes three times a week the two of them came to town and into the house—the foolish unreal voluble preserved woman now six years absent from the world—the woman who had quitted home and kin on a flood of tears and in a shadowy miasmic region something like the bitter purlieus of Styx had produced two children and then rose like the swamp-hatched butterfly, unimpeded by weight of stomach and all the heavy organs of suffering and experience, into a perennial bright vacuum of arrested sun— and the young girl dreaming, not living, in her complete detachment and imperviousness to actuality almost like physical deafness. To them, Miss Rosa must not have been anything at all now: not the child who had been the object and victim of the vanished aunt's vindictive unflagging care and attention, and not even the woman which her office as housekeeper would indicate, and certainly not the factual aunt herself. And it would be hard to say which of the two, sister or niece, was the most unreal to Miss Rosa in turn—the adult who had escaped reality into a bland region peopled by dolls, or the young girl who slept waking in some suspension so completely physical as to resemble the state before birth and as far removed from reality's other extreme as Ellen was from hers, driving up to the house twice and three times a week, and one time, in the summer when Judith was seventeen, stopping in on their way overland to Memphis to buy Judith clothes; yes: trousseau. That was the summer following Henry's first year at the University, after he had brought Charles Bon home with him for Christmas and then again to spend a week or so of the summer vacation before Bon rode on to the River to take the steamboat home to New Orleans; the summer in which Sutpen himself went away, on business, Ellen said, told, doubtless unaware, such was her existence then, that she did not know where her husband had gone and not even conscious that she was not curious, and no one but your grandfather and perhaps Clytie ever to know that Sutpen had gone to New Orleans too. They would enter that dim grim tight little house where even yet, after four years, the aunt still seemed to be just beyond any door with her hand already on

the knob and which Ellen would fill with ten or fifteen minutes of shrill uproar and then depart, taking with her the
dreamy and volitionless daughter who had not spoken one
word; and Miss Rosa who in actual fact was the girl's aunt
and who by actual years should have been her sister and who
in actual experience and hope and opportunity should have
been the niece, ignoring the mother to follow the departing
and inaccessible daughter with myopic and inarticulate yearning and not one whit of jealousy, projecting upon Judith all
the abortive dreams and delusions of her own doomed and
frustrated youth, offering Judith the only gift (it of necessity
offered to the bride's equipment and not the bride; it was
Ellen who told this, with shrieks of amusement, more than
once) in her power: she offered to teach Judith how to keep
house and plan meals and count laundry, receiving for the
offer the blank fathomless stare, the unhearing "What? What
did you say?" while even now Ellen was shrieking with astonished appreciation. Then they were gone—carriage, bundles,
Ellen's peacock amusement, the niece's impenetrable dreaming. When they came to town next and the carriage stopped
before Mr Coldfield's house, one of the negresses came out
and said that Miss Rosa was not at home.

That summer she saw Henry again too. She had not seen
him since the summer before although he had been home
Christmas with his friend from the University, and she had
heard about the balls and parties at Sutpen's Hundred during
the holidays but she and her father had not gone out. And
when Henry stopped with Bon on the way back to school the
day after New Year's to speak to his aunt, she actually was not
at home. So she did not see him until the following summer,
after a full year. She was downtown, shopping; she was standing on the street talking to your grandmother when he rode
past. He didn't see her; he passed on a new mare which his
father had given him, in the coat and hat of a man now; your
grandmother said he was as tall as his father now and that he
sat the mare with the same swagger although lighter in the
bone than Sutpen, as if his bones were capable of bearing
the swagger but were still too light and quick to support the
pomposity. Because Sutpen was acting his role too. He had
corrupted Ellen in more ways than one. He was the biggest

single landowner and cotton-planter in the county now,
which state he had attained by the same tactics with which he
had built his house—the same singleminded unflagging effort
and utter disregard of how his actions which the town could
see might look and how the indicated ones which the town
could not see must appear to it. That is, there were some
among his fellow citizens who believed even yet that there
was a nigger in the woodpile somewhere, ranging from the
ones who believed that the plantation was just a blind to his
actual dark avocation, through the ones who believed that he
had found some way to juggle the cotton market itself and so
get more per bale for his cotton than honest men could, to
the ones who believed apparently that the wild niggers which
he had brought there had the power to actually conjure more
cotton per acre from the soil than any tame ones had ever
done. He was not liked (which he evidently did not want,
anyway) but feared, which seemed to amuse, if not actually
please, him. But he was accepted; he obviously had too much
money now to be rejected or even seriously annoyed any
more. He accomplished this—got his plantation to running
smoothly (he had an overseer now; it was the son of that
same sheriff who had arrested him at his bride-to-be's gate on
the day of the betrothal) within ten years of the wedding, and
now he acted his role too—a role of arrogant ease and leisure
which, as the leisure and ease put flesh on him, became a little
pompous. Yes, he had corrupted Ellen to more than renegadery, though, like her, unaware that his flowering was a forced
blooming too and that while he was still playing the scene to
the audience, behind him fate, destiny, retribution, irony—
the stage manager, call him what you will—was already striking the set and dragging on the synthetic and spurious
shadows and shapes of the next one.—"There goes——"
your grandmother said. But Miss Rosa had already seen him,
standing there beside your grandmother, her head hardly
reaching your grandmother's shoulder, thin, in one of the
dresses which the aunt had left in the house and which Miss
Rosa had cut down to fit herself who had never been taught
to sew either, just as she had assumed the housekeeping and
offered to teach Judith to do the same, who had never been
taught to cook nor taught to do anything save listen through

closed doors, standing there with a shawl over her head like she might have been fifty instead of fifteen, looking after her nephew and saying, "Why . . . he's shaved."

Then she stopped seeing Ellen even. That is, Ellen also stopped coming to the house, stopped breaking the carriage's weekly ritual of store to store where, without getting out, Ellen bade merchant and clerk fetch out to her the cloth and the meagre fripperies and baubles which they carried and which they knew even better than she that she would not buy but instead would merely finger and handle and disarrange and then reject, all in that flow of bright pettish volubility. Not contemptuous, not even patronising exactly, but with a bland and even childlike imposition upon the sufferance or good manners or sheer helplessness of the men, the merchants and clerks; then to come to the house and fill it too with that meaningless uproar of vanity, of impossible and foundation-less advice about Miss Rosa and her father and the house, about Miss Rosa's clothes and the arrangement of the furni-ture and the food and how prepared and even the hours at which eaten. Because the time now approached (it was 1860, even Mr Coldfield probably admitted that war was unavoid-able) when the destiny of Sutpen's family which for twenty years now had been like a lake welling from quiet springs into a quiet valley and spreading, rising almost imperceptibly and in which the four members of it floated in sunny sus-pension, felt the first subterranean movement toward the out-let, the gorge which would be the land's catastrophe too, and the four peaceful swimmers turning suddenly to face one an-other, not yet with alarm or distrust but just alert, feeling the dark set, none of them yet at that point where man looks about at his companions in disaster and thinks *When will I stop trying to save them and save only myself?* and not even aware that that point was approaching. So Miss Rosa did not see any of them, who had never seen (and was never to see alive) Charles Bon at all; Charles Bon of New Orleans, Henry's friend who was not only some few years older than Henry but actually a little old to be still in college and certainly a little out of place in that one where he was—a small new college in the Mississippi hinterland and even wilderness, three hundred miles from that worldly and even foreign city which was his

home—a young man of a worldly elegance and assurance beyond his years, handsome, apparently wealthy and with for
background the shadowy figure of a legal guardian rather
than any parents—a personage who in the remote Mississippi
of that time must have appeared almost phoenix-like, full-
sprung from no childhood, born of no woman and impervious
to time and, vanished, leaving no bones nor dust anywhere—
a man with an ease of manner and a swaggering gallant air
in comparison with which Sutpen's pompous arrogance was
clumsy bluff and Henry actually a hobble-de-hoy. Miss Rosa
never saw him; this was a picture, an image. It was not what
Ellen told her: Ellen at the absolute halcyon of her butterfly's
summer and now with the added charm of gracious and
graceful voluntary surrendering of youth to her blood's and
sex's successor, that concurrent attitude and behavior with
the engagement's span with which mothers who want to can
almost make themselves the brides of their daughters' weddings. Listening to Ellen, a stranger would have almost believed that the marriage, which subsequent events would
indicate had not even been mentioned between the young
people and the parents, had been actually performed. Ellen
did not once mention love between Judith and Bon. She did
not hint around it. Love, with reference to them, was just a
finished and perfectly dead subject like the matter of virginity
would be after the birth of the first grandchild. She spoke of
Bon as if he were three inanimate objects in one or perhaps
one inanimate object for which she and her family would find
three concordant uses: a garment which Judith might wear as
she would a riding habit or a ball gown, a piece of furniture
which would complement and complete the furnishing of her
house and position, and a mentor and example to correct
Henry's provincial manners and speech and clothing. She
seemed to have encompassed time. She postulated the elapsed
years during which no honeymoon nor any change had taken
place, out of which the (now) five faces looked with a sort of
lifeless and perennial bloom like painted portraits hung in a
vacuum, each taken at its forewarned peak and smoothed of
all thought and experience, the originals of which had lived
and died so long ago that their joys and griefs must now be
forgotten even by the very boards on which they had strutted

and postured and laughed and wept. This, while Miss Rosa, not listening, who had got the picture from the first word, perhaps from the name, Charles Bon; the spinster doomed for life at sixteen, sitting beneath this bright glitter of delusion like it was one of those colored electric beams in cabarets and she there for the first time in her life and the beam filled with a substanceless glitter of tinsel motes darting suddenly upon her, halting for a moment then going on. She wasn't jealous of Judith. It was not selfpity either, sitting there in one of those botched-over house dresses (the clothes, castoff sometimes but usually new, which Ellen gave her from time to time were always silk, of course) which the aunt had abandoned when she eloped with the horse- and mule-trader, perhaps in the hope or even the firm intention of never wearing such again, blinking steadily at her sister while Ellen talked. It was probably just peaceful despair and relief at final and complete abnegation, now that Judith was about to immolate the frustration's vicarious recompense into the living fairy tale. It sounded like a fairy tale when Ellen told it later to your grandmother, only it was a fairy tale written for and acted by a fashionable ladies' club. But to Miss Rosa it must have been authentic, not only plausible but justified: hence the remark which sent Ellen again (she told this too, for the childish joke it was) into shrieks of amused and fretted astonishment. "We deserve him," Miss Rosa said. "Deserve? Him?" Ellen said, probably shrieked too. "Of course we deserve him—if you want to put it that way. I certainly hope and expect you to feel that the Coldfields are qualified to reciprocate whatever particularly signal honor marriage with anyone might confer upon them."

Naturally there is no known rejoinder to this. At least, as far as Ellen ever told, Miss Rosa did not try to make one. She just saw Ellen depart and then set about to make Judith the second only gift in her power. She possessed two now, this one likewise bequeathed to her by the aunt who taught her both to keep house and how to fit clothes by climbing out a window one night, though this second gift developed late (you might say, repercussed) due to the fact that when the aunt left, Miss Rosa was not yet large enough to be able to use the discarded clothing even by cutting the garments down. She set about secretly making garments for Judith's trousseau. She got the cloth from her father's store. She could not have got it anywhere else. Your grandmother told me that at that time Miss Rosa actually could not count money, change, that she knew the progression of the coins in theory but that apparently she had never had the actual cash to see, touch, experiment and prove with; that on certain days of the week she would go down town with a basket and shop at certain stores which Mr Coldfield had already designated, with no coin nor sum of money changing lip or hand, and that later in the day Mr Coldfield would trace her course by the debits scratched on paper or on walls and counters, and pay them. So she would have to get the material from him. And as he had brought his entire business to Jefferson in one wagon, and this at a time when he had mother sister wife and children to support out of it as against now when he had but one child to support out of it, and weighed along with this that profound disinterest in material accumulation which had permitted conscience to cause him to withdraw from that old affair in which his son-in-law had involved him not only at the cost of his just profits but at the sacrifice of his original investment, his stock which had begun as a collection of the crudest necessities and which apparently could not even feed himself and his daughter from its own shelves, had not increased, let alone diversified. Yet this was where she had to go to get the material to make those intimate young girl garments which were to be for her own vicarious bridal—and you can imagine too what Miss Rosa's notion of such garments would be, let alone what her notion of them would look like when she had finished them unassisted. Nobody knows how she managed to get the material from her father's store. He didn't give it to her. He would have felt it incumbent on him to supply his granddaughter with clothes if she were indecently clad or if she were ragged or cold, but not to marry in. So I believe she stole it. She must have. She must have taken it almost from under her father's nose (it was a small store and he was his own clerk and from any point in it he could see any other point) with that amoral boldness, that affinity for brigandage of women, but more likely, or so I would like to think, by some subterfuge of such bald and desperate transparence concocted by innocence that its very simplicity fooled him.

So she didn't even see Ellen anymore. Apparently Ellen had now served her purpose, completed the bright pointless noon and afternoon of the butterfly's summer and vanished, perhaps not out of Jefferson, but out of her sister's life anyway, to be seen but the one time more dying in bed in a darkened room in the house on which fateful mischance had already laid its hand to the extent of scattering the black foundation on which it had been erected and removing its two male mainstays, husband and son—the one into the risk and danger of battle, the other apparently into oblivion. Henry had just vanished. She heard of that too while she was spending her days (and nights; she would have to wait until her father was asleep) sewing tediously and without skill on the garments which she was making for her niece's trousseau and which she had to keep hidden not only from her father but from the two negresses, who might have told Mr Coldfield—whipping lace out of ravelled and hoarded string and thread and sewing it onto garments while news came of Lincoln's election and of the fall of Sumpter and she scarce listening, hearing and losing the knell and doom of her native land between two tedious and clumsy stitches on a garment which she would never wear and never remove for a man whom she was not even to see alive. Henry just vanished: she heard just what the town heard—that on this next Christmas Henry and Bon came home again to spend the holidays, the handsome and wealthy New Orleansian whose engagement to the daughter the mother had been filling the town's ears with for six months now. They came again and now the town listened for the announcement of the actual day. And then something happened. Nobody knew what: whether something between Henry and Bon on one hand and Judith on the other, or between the three young people on one hand and the parents on the other. But anyway, when Christmas day came, Henry and Bon were gone. And Ellen was not visible (she seemed to have retired to the darkened room which she was not to quit until she died two years later) and nobody could have told from either Sutpen's or Judith's faces or actions or behavior, and so the tale came through the negroes: of how on the

night before Christmas there had been a quarrel between, not
Bon and Henry or Bon and Sutpen, but between the son and
the father and that Henry had formally abjured his father and
renounced his birthright and the roof under which he had
been born and that he and Bon had ridden away in the night
and that the mother was prostrate—though, the town believed, not at the upset of the marriage but at the shock of
reality entering her life: this the merciful blow of the axe before the beast's throat is cut. Though Ellen of course did not
know this either.

That's what Miss Rosa heard. Nobody knows what she
thought. The town believed that Henry's action was just the
fiery nature of youth, let alone a Sutpen, and that time would
cure it. Doubtless Sutpen's and Judith's behavior toward one
another and toward the town had something to do with this.
They would be seen together in the carriage in town now and
then as though nothing had occurred between them at least,
which certainly would not have been the case if the quarrel
had been between Bon and the father, and probably not the
case if the trouble had been between Henry and his father
because the town knew that between Henry and Judith there
had been a relationship closer than the traditional loyalty of
brother and sister even; a curious relationship: something of
that fierce impersonal rivalry between two cadets in a crack
regiment who eat from the same dish and sleep under the
same blanket and chance the same destruction and who would
risk death for one another not for the other's sake but for the
sake of the unbroken front of the regiment itself. That's all
Miss Rosa knew. She could have known no more about it
than the town knew because the ones who did know (Sutpen
or Judith: not Ellen, who would have been told nothing in
the first place and would have forgot, failed to assimilate, it if
she had been—Ellen the butterfly, from beneath whom without warning the very sunbuoyed air had been withdrawn,
leaving her now with the plump hands folded on the coverlet
in the darkened room and the eyes above them probably not
even suffering but merely filled with baffled incomprehension) would not have told her anymore than they would have
told anyone in Jefferson or anywhere else. She probably went
out there, probably once and then no more, and doubtless she

did not ask, not even Judith, perhaps knowing she would not
be told or perhaps because she was waiting. And she must
have told Mr Coldfield that there was nothing wrong and
evidently she believed that herself since she continued to sew
on the garments for Judith's wedding. She was still doing that
when Mississippi seceded and when the first Confederate uniforms began to appear in Jefferson where Colonel Sartoris
and Sutpen were raising the regiment which departed in '61,
with Sutpen, second in command, riding at Colonel Sartoris'
left hand, on the black stallion named out of Scott, beneath
the regimental colors which he and Sartoris had designed and
which Sartoris' womenfolks had sewed together out of silk
dresses. He had filled out physically from what he had been
not only when he first rode into Jefferson that Sunday in '33,
but from what he had been when he and Ellen married. He
was not portly yet, though he was now getting on toward
fifty-five. The fat, the stomach, came later. It came upon him
suddenly, all at once, in the year after whatever it was happened to his engagement to Miss Rosa and she quitted his
roof and returned to town to live alone in her father's house
and did not ever speak to him again except when she addressed him that one time when they told her that he was
dead. The flesh came upon him suddenly, as though what the
negroes and Wash Jones too called the fine figure of a man
had reached and held its peak after the foundation had given
away and something between the shape of him that people
knew and the uncompromising skeleton of what he actually
was had gone fluid and, earthbound, had been snubbed up
and restrained, balloonlike unstable and lifeless, by the envelope which it had betrayed.

   She did not see the regiment depart because her father forbade her to leave the house until it was gone, refusing to
allow her to take part in or be present with the other women
and girls in the ceremony of its departure, though not because
his son-in-law happened to be in it. He had never been an
irascible man and before war was actually declared and Mississippi seceded, his acts and speeches of protest had been not
only calm but logical and quite sensible. But after the die was
cast he seemed to change overnight, just as his daughter Ellen
changed her nature a few years before. As soon as troops

began to appear in Jefferson he closed his store and kept it
closed all during the period that soldiers were being mobilised
and drilled, not only then but later, after the regiment was
gone, whenever casual troops would bivouac for the night in
passing, refusing to sell any goods for any price not only to
the military but, so it was told, to the families not only of
soldiers but of men or women who had supported secession
and war only in talk, opinion. Not only did he refuse to permit his sister to come back home to live while her horse-
trader husband was in the army, he would not even allow
Miss Rosa to look out the window at passing soldiers. He
had closed his store permanently and was at home all day
now. He and Miss Rosa lived in the back of the house, with
the front door locked and the front shutters closed and fastened, and where, so the neighbors said, he spent the day
behind one of the slightly opened blinds like a picquet on
post, armed not with a musket but with the big family bible
in which his and his sister's birth and his marriage and Ellen's
birth and marriage and the birth of his two grandchildren and
of Miss Rosa, and his wife's death (but not the marriage of
the aunt; it was Miss Rosa who entered that, along with
Ellen's death, on the day when she entered Mr Coldfield's own
and Charles Bon's and even Sutpen's) had been duly entered
in his neat clerk's hand, until a detachment of troops would
pass: whereupon he would open the bible and declaim in a
harsh loud voice even above the sound of the tramping feet,
the passages of the old violent vindictive mysticism which he
had already marked as the actual picquet would have ranged
his row of cartridges along the window sill. Then one morning he learned that his store had been broken into and looted,
doubtless by a company of strange troops bivouacked on the
edge of town and doubtless abetted, if only vocally, by his
own fellow citizens. That night he mounted to the attic with
his hammer and his handful of nails and nailed the door behind him and threw the hammer out the window. He was not
a coward. He was a man of uncompromising moral strength,
coming into a new country with a small stock of goods and
supporting five people out of it in comfort and security at
least. He did it by close trading, to be sure: he could not have
done it save by close trading or dishonesty; and as your

grandfather said, a man who, in a country such as Mississippi was then, would restrict dishonesty to the selling of straw hats and hame strings and salt meat would have been already locked up by his own family as a kleptomaniac. But he was not a coward, even though his conscience may have objected, as your grandfather said, not so much to the idea of pouring out human blood and life, but at the idea of waste: of wearing out and eating up and shooting away material in any cause whatever.

Now Miss Rosa's life consisted of keeping it in herself and her father. Up to the night of the looting of the store, they had lived out of it. She would go to the store after dark with a basket and fetch back enough food to last for a day or two. So the stock, not renewed for some time before that, was considerably reduced even before the looting; and soon she, who had never been taught to do anything practical because the aunt had raised her to believe that she was not only delicate but actually precious, was cooking the food which as time passed became harder and harder to come by and poorer and poorer in quality, and hauling it up to her father at night by means of a well pulley and rope attached to the attic window. She did this for three years, feeding in secret and at night and with food which in quantity was scarcely sufficient for one, the man whom she hated. And she may not have known before that she hated him and she may not have known it now even, nevertheless the first of the odes to Southern soldiers in that portfolio which when your grandfather saw it in 1885 contained a thousand or more, was dated in the first year of her father's voluntary incarceration and dated at two oclock in the morning.

Then he died. One morning the hand did not come out to draw up the basket. The old nails were still in the door and neighbors helped her break it in with axes and they found him, who had seen his sole means of support looted by the defenders of his cause, even if he had repudiated it and them, with three days' uneaten food beside his pallet bed as if he had spent the three days in a mental balancing of his terrestrial accounts, found the result and proved it and then turned upon his contemporary scene of folly and outrage and injustice the dead and consistent impassivity of a cold and inflexible disapproval. Now Miss Rosa was not only an orphan, but a pauper too. The store was now just a shell, the deserted building vacated even by rats and containing nothing, not even goodwill since he had irrevocably estranged himself from neighbors town and embattled land all three by his behavior. Even the two negresses which he had freed as soon as he came into possession of them (through a debt, by the way, not purchase), writing out their papers of freedom which they could not read and putting them on a weekly wage which he held back in full against the discharge of the current market value at which he had assumed them on the debt—and in return for which they had been among the first Jefferson negroes to desert and follow the Yankee troops— were gone now. So when he died, he had nothing, not only saved but kept. Doubtless the only pleasure which he had ever had was not in the meagre spartan hoard which he had accumulated before his path crossed that of his future son-in-law;—not in the money but in its representation of a balance in whatever spiritual counting-house he believed would some day pay his sight drafts on self-denial and fortitude. And doubtless what hurt him most in the whole business with Sutpen was not the loss of the money but the fact that he had had to sacrifice the hoarding, the symbol of the fortitude and abnegation, to keep intact the spiritual solvency which he believed that he had already established and secured. It was as if he had had to pay the same note twice because of some trifling oversight of date or signature.

So Miss Rosa was both pauper and orphan, with no kin above dust but Judith and the aunt who had been last heard of two years ago while trying to pass the Yankee lines to reach Illinois and so be near the Rock Island prison where her husband, who had offered his talents for horse- and mule-getting to the Confederate cavalry remount corps and had been caught at it, now was. Ellen was dead two years now—the butterfly, the moth caught in a gale and blown against a wall and clinging there beating feebly, not with any particular stubborn clinging to life, not in particular pain since it was too light to have struck hard, nor even with very much rememberance of the bright vacuum before the gale, but just in bewildered and uncomprehending amazement—the bright

trivial shell not even to any great extent changed despite the
year of bad food, since all of Sutpen's negroes had deserted
also to follow the Yankee troops away; the wild blood which
he had brought into the country and tried to mix, blend, with
the tame which was already there, with the same care and for
the same purpose with which he blended that of the stallion
and that of his own. And with the same success: as though his
presence alone compelled that house to accept and retain human life; as though houses actually possess a sentience, a personality and character acquired not from the people who
breathe or have breathed in them so much as rather inherent
in the wood and brick or begotten upon the wood and brick
by the man or men who conceived and built them—in this
one an incontrovertible affirmation for emptiness, desertion;
an insurmountable resistance to occupancy save when sanctioned and protected by the ruthless and the strong. She had
lost some flesh of course, but it was as the butterfly itself
enters dissolution by actually dissolving: the area of wing and
body decreasing a little, the pattern of the spots drawing a
little closer together, but with no wrinkle to show—the same
smooth, almost girlish face on the pillow (though Miss Rosa
now discovered that Ellen had been dyeing her hair evidently
for years), the same almost plump soft (though now un-
ringed) hands on the coverlet, and only the bafflement in the
dark uncomprehending eyes to indicate anything of present
life by which to postulate approaching death as she asked
the seventeen-year-old sister (Henry up to now was just vanished, his birthright voluntarily repudiated; he had not yet
returned to play his final part in his family's doom—and this,
your grandfather said, spared Ellen too, not that it would
have been the crushing and crowning blow but that it would
have been wasted on her since the clinging moth, even alive,
would have been incapable now of feeling anymore of wind
or violence) to protect the remaining child. So the natural
thing would have been for her to go out and live with Judith,
the natural thing for her or any Southern woman, gentlewoman. She would not have needed to be asked; no one
would expect her to wait to be. Because that's what a Southern lady is. Not the fact that, penniless and with no prospect
of ever being otherwise and knowing that all who know her

know this, yet moving with a parasol and a private chamber pot and three trunks into your home and into the room where your wife uses the hand-embroidered linen and not only takes command of all the servants who likewise know that she will never tip them because they know as well as the white folks that she will never have anything to tip them with but goes into the kitchen and dispossesses the cook and seasons the very food you are going to eat to suit her own palate;—it's not this, not this that she is depending on to keep body and soul together: it is as though she were living on the actual blood itself like a vampire, not with insatiability, certainly not with voracity, but with that serene and idle splendor of flowers arrogating to herself, because it fills her veins also, nourishment from the old blood that crossed uncharted seas and continents and battled wilderness hardships and lurking circumstances and fatalities, with tranquil disregard of whatever onerous carks to leisure and even peace which the preservation of it incurs upon what might be called the contemporary transmutable fountainhead who contrives to keep the crass foodbearing corpuscles sufficiently numerous and healthy in the stream.

That's what she would have been expected to do. But she didn't. Though Judith was an orphan too, yet Judith still had those abandoned acres to draw from, let alone Clytie to help her, keep her company, and Wash Jones to feed her as Wash had fed Ellen before she died. But Miss Rosa didn't go out there at once. Perhaps she never would have gone. Although Ellen had asked her to protect Judith, possibly she felt that Judith did not need protection yet, since if even deferred love could have supplied her with the will to exist, endure for this long, then that same love, even though deferred, must and would preserve Bon until the folly of men would stalemate from sheer exhaustion and he would return from wherever he was and bring Henry with him—Henry, victim too of the same folly and mischance. She must have seen Judith now and then and Judith probably urged her to come out to Sutpen's Hundred to live, but I believe that this is the reason she did not go, even though she did not know where Bon and Henry were and Judith apparently never thought to tell her. Because Judith knew. She may have known for some time; even Ellen may have known, only probably to Ellen at that time absence was not a qualitative state, absence into ignominy or into oblivion being identical, and so it may not have occurred to Ellen either to tell her sister, that to another the uncertainty of battle and the certainty of oblivion might be two things. Or perhaps Judith never told her mother either. Perhaps Ellen did not know before she died that Henry and Bon were now privates in the company which their classmates at the University had organised. Miss Rosa did not know it at all. The first intimation she had had in four years that her nephew was still alive was the afternoon when Wash Jones, riding Sutpen's remaining mule, stopped in front of the house and began to shout her name. She had seen him before but she did not recognise him—a gaunt gangling man malaria-ridden with pale eyes and a face that might have been any age between twenty-five and sixty, sitting on the saddleless mule in the street before the gate, shouting "Hello. Hello." at intervals until she came to the door; whereupon he lowered his voice somewhat, though not much. "Air you Rosie Coldfield?" he said.

IV.

IT WAS STILL not dark enough for Quentin to start, not yet dark enough to suit Miss Coldfield at least, even discounting the twelve miles out there and the twelve miles back. Quentin knew that. He could almost see her, waiting in one of the dark airless rooms in the little grim house's impregnable solitude. She would have no light burning because she would be out of the house soon, and probably some mental descendant or kinsman of him or her who had told her once that light and moving air carried heat had also told her that the cost of electricity was not in the actual time the light burned but in the retroactive overcoming of primary inertia when the switch was snapped: that that was what showed on the meter. She would be wearing already the black bonnet with jet sequins; he knew that: and a shawl, sitting there in the augmenting and defunctive twilight; she would have even now in her hand or on her lap the reticule with all the keys, entrance closet and cupboard, that the house possessed which she was about to desert for perhaps six hours; and a parasol, an umbrella too, he thought, thinking how she would be impervious to weather and season since although he had not spoken a hundred words to her in his life before this afternoon, he did know that she had never before tonight quitted that house after sundown save on Sundays and Wednesdays for prayer meeting, in the entire forty-three years probably. Yes, she would have the umbrella. She would emerge with it when he called for her and carry it invincibly into the spent suspiration of an evening without even dew, where even now the only alteration toward darkness was in the soft and fuller random of the fireflies—a fuller and more profound random in the twilight following sixty days without rain and forty-two without even dew—below the gallery where he rose from his chair as Mr Compson, carrying the letter, emerged from the house, snapping on the porch light as he passed. "You will probably have to go inside to read it," Mr Compson said.

"Maybe I can read it here all right," Quentin said.

"Perhaps you are right," Mr Compson said. "Maybe even

the light of day, let alone this—" he indicated the single globe stained and bug-fouled from the long summer and which even when clean gave off but little light—"which man had to invent to his need since, relieved of the onus of sweating to live, he is apparently reverting (or evolving) back into a nocturnal animal, would be too much for it, for them. Yes, for them: of that day and time, of a dead time; people too as we are and victims too as we are, but victims of a different circumstance, simpler and therefore, integer for integer, larger, more heroic and the figures therefore more heroic too, not dwarfed and involved but distinct, uncomplex who had the gift of loving once or dying once instead of being diffused and scattered creatures drawn blindly limb from limb from a grab bag and assembled, author and victim too of a thousand homicides and a thousand copulations and divorcements. Perhaps you are right. Perhaps any more light than this would be too much for it." But he did not give Quentin the letter at once. He sat again, Quentin sitting again too, and took up the cigar from the veranda rail, the coal glowing again, the wistaria colored smoke drifting again unwinded across Quentin's face as Mr Compson raised his feet once more to the railing, the letter in his hand and the hand looking almost as dark as a negro's against his linen leg. "Because Henry loved Bon. He repudiated blood birthright and material security for his sake, for the sake of this man who was at least an intending bigamist even if not an out and out blackguard, and on whose dead body four years later Judith was to find the photograph of the other woman and the child. So much so that he (Henry) could give his father the lie about a statement which he must have realised that his father could not and would not have made without foundation and proof. Yet he did it, Henry himself striking the blow with his own hand, even though he must have known that what his father told him about the woman and the child was true. He must have said to himself, must have said when he closed the library door for the last time behind himself that Christmas eve and must have repeated while he and Bon rode side by side through the iron dark of that Christmas morning, away from the house where he had been born and which he would see but one time more and that with the fresh blood of the man who now rode beside him, on his hands: *I will believe; I will. I will. Even if it is so, even if what my father told me is true and which, in spite of myself, I cannot keep from knowing is true, I will still believe.* Because what else could he have hoped to find in New Orleans, if not the truth, if not what his father had told him, what he had denied and refused to accept even though, despite himself, he must have already believed? But who knows why a man, though suffering, clings, above all the other well members, to the arm or leg which he knows must come off? Because he loved Bon. I can imagine him and Sutpen in the library that Christmas eve, the father and the brother, percussion and repercussion like a thunderclap and its echo and as close; the statement and the giving of the lie, the decision instantaneous and irrevocable between father and friend, between (so Henry must have believed) that where honor and love lay and this where blood and profit ran, even though at the instant of giving the lie he knew that it was the truth. That was why the four years, the probation. He must have known that it would be vain, even then, on that Christmas eve, not to speak of what he learned, saw with his own eyes in New Orleans. He may even have known Bon that well by then, who had not changed until then and so would in all probability not change later; and he (Henry) who could not say to his friend, *I did that for love of you; do this for love of me.* He couldn't say that, you see—this man, this youth scarcely twenty, who had turned his back upon all that he knew, to cast his lot with the single friend whom, even as they rode away that night, he must have known, as he knew that what his father had told him was true, that he was doomed and destined to kill. He must have known that just as he knew that his hope was vain, what hope and what for he could not have said; what hope and dream of change in Bon or in the situation, what dream that he could someday wake from and find it had been a dream, as in the injured man's fever dream the dear suffering arm or leg is strong and sound and only the well ones sick.

"It was Henry's probation; Henry holding all three of them in that durance to which even Judith acquiesced up to a certain point. She did not know what happened in the library that night. I dont think she ever did, suspected, until that afternoon four years later when she saw them again, when they brought Bon's body into the house and she found in his coat the photograph which was not her face, not her child; she just waked the next morning and they were gone and only the letter, the note, remaining, the note written by Henry since doubtless he refused to allow Bon to write—this announcement of the armistice, the probation, and Judith acquiescing up to that point, who would have refused as quickly to obey any injunction of her father as Henry had been to defy him yet who did obey Henry in this matter—not the male relative, the brother, but because of that relationship between them—that single personality with two bodies both of which had been seduced almost simultaneously by a man whom at the time Judith had never even seen—she and Henry both knowing that she would observe the probation, give him (Henry) the benefit of that interval, only up to that mutually recognised though unstated and undefined point and both doubtless aware that when that point was reached she would, and with the same calm, the same refusal to accept or give because of any traditional weakness of sex, recall the armistice and face him as a foe, not requiring or even wishing that Bon be present to support her, doubtless even refusing to allow him to intervene if he were, fighting the matter out with Henry like a man first before consenting to revert to the woman, the loved, the bride. And Bon: Henry would have no more told Bon what his father had told him than he would have returned to his father and told him that Bon denied it, since to do one he would have to do the other and he knew that Bon's denial would be a lie and though he could have borne Bon's lie himself, he could not have borne for either Judith or his father to hear it. Besides, Henry would not need to tell Bon what had happened. Bon must have learned of Sutpen's visit to New Orleans as soon as he (Bon) reached home that first summer. He must have known that Sutpen now knew his secret—if Bon, until he saw Sutpen's reaction to it, ever looked upon it as a cause for secrecy, certainly not as a valid objection to marriage with a white woman—a situation in which probably all his contemporaries who could afford it were likewise involved and which it would no more have occurred to him to mention to his bride or wife or to

her family than he would have told them the secrets of a fra-
ternal organization which he had joined before he married. In
fact, the manner in which his intended bride's family reacted
to the discovery of it was doubtless the first and last time
when the Sutpen family ever surprised him. He is the curious
one to me. He came into that isolated puritan country household almost like Sutpen himself came into Jefferson: apparently complete, without background or past or childhood—a
man a little older than his actual years and enclosed and surrounded by a sort of Scythian glitter, who seems to have seduced the country brother and sister without any effort or
particular desire to do so, who caused all the pother and uproar yet from the moment when he realised that Sutpen was
going to prevent the marriage if he could, he (Bon) seems to
have withdrawn into a mere spectator, passive, a little sardonic, and completely enigmatic. He seems to hover, shadowy, almost substanceless, a little behind and above all the
other straightforward and logical even though (to him) incomprehensible ultimatums and affirmations and defiances
and challenges and repudiations, with an air of sardonic and
indolent detachment like that of a youthful Roman consul
making the Grand Tour of his day among the barbarian
hordes which his grandfather conquered, benighted in a
brawling and childish and quite deadly mud-castle household
in a miasmic and spirit-ridden forest. It was as if he found the
whole business, not inexplicable of course, just unnecessary;
that he knew at once that Sutpen had found out about the
mistress and child and he now found Sutpen's action and
Henry's reaction a fetich-ridden moral blundering which did
not deserve to be called thinking, which he contemplated
with the detached attentiveness of a scientist watching the
muscles in an anesthetised frog;—watching, contemplating
them from behind that barrier of sophistication in comparison with which Henry and Sutpen were troglodytes. Not just
the outside, the way he walked and talked and wore his
clothes and handed Ellen into the dining room or into the
carriage and (perhaps, probably) kissed her hand and which
Ellen envied for Henry, but the man himself—that fatalistic
and impenetrable imperturbability with which he watched
them while he waited for them to do whatever it would be

that they would do, as if he had known all the while that the
occasion would arise when he would have to wait and that all
he would need to do would be to wait; that he had seduced
Henry and Judith both too thoroughly to have any fear that
he might not marry Judith when he wished to. Not that stupid shrewdness half instinct and half belief in luck, and half
muscular habit of the senses and nerves of the gambler waiting to take what he can from what he sees, but a certain
reserved and inflexible pessimism stripped long generations
ago of all the rubbish and claptrap of people (yes, Sutpen
and Henry and the Coldfields too) who have not quite yet
emerged from barbarism, who two thousand years hence will
still be throwing triumphantly off the yoke of Latin culture
and intelligence of which they were never in any great permanent danger to begin with.

"Because he loved Judith. He would have added doubtless
'after his fashion' since, as his intended father-in-law soon
learned, this was not the first time he had played this part,
pledged what he had pledged to Judith, let alone the first time
he would have gone through a ceremony to commemorate it,
make what distinction (he was a Catholic of sorts) he might
between this one with a white woman and that other. Because
you will see the letter, not the first one he ever wrote to her
but at least the first, the only one she ever showed, as your
grandmother knew then: and, so we believe, now that she is
dead, the only one which she kept unless of course Miss Rosa
or Clytie destroyed the others after she herself died: and this
one here preserved not because Judith put it away to keep but
because she brought it herself and gave it to your grandmother after Bon's death, possibly on the same day when she
destroyed the others which he had written her (provided of
course it was she herself who destroyed them) which would
have been when she found in Bon's coat the picture of the
octoroon mistress and the little boy. Because he was her first
and last sweetheart. She must have seen him in fact with exactly the same eyes that Henry saw him with. And it would
be hard to say to which of them he appeared the more splendid—to the one with hope, even though unconscious, of
making the image hers through possession; to the other with
the knowledge, even though subconscious to the desire, of

the insurmountable barrier which the similarity of gender
hopelessly intervened;—this man whom Henry first saw
riding perhaps through the grove at the University on one of
the two horses which he kept there or perhaps crossing the
campus on foot in the slightly Frenchified cloak and hat
which he wore, or perhaps (I like to think this) presented
formally to the man reclining in a flowered, almost feminised
gown, in a sunny window in his chambers—this man handsome elegant and even catlike and too old to be where he was,
too old not in years but in experience, with some tangible
effluvium of knowledge, surfeit: of actions done and satia-
tions plumbed and pleasures exhausted and even forgotten.
So that he must have appeared, not only to Henry but to the
entire undergraduate body of that small new provincial college, as a source not of envy because you only envy whom
you believe to be, but for accident, in no way superior to
yourself: and what you believe, granted a little better luck
than you have had heretofore, you will someday possess;—
not of envy but of despair: that sharp shocking terrible hopeless despair of the young which sometimes takes the form of
insult toward and even physical assault upon the human subject of it or, in extreme cases like Henry's, insult toward and
assault upon any and all detractors of the subject, as witness
Henry's violent repudiation of his father and his birthright
when Sutpen forbade the marriage. Yes, he loved Bon, who
seduced him as surely as he seduced Judith—the country boy
born and bred who, with the five or six others of that small
undergraduate body composed of other planters' sons whom
Bon permitted to become intimate with him, who aped his
clothing and manner and (to the extent which they were able)
his very manner of living, looked upon Bon as though he
were a hero out of some adolescent Arabian Nights who had
stumbled upon (or rather, had thrust upon him) a talisman or
touchstone not to invest him with wisdom or power or
wealth, but with the ability and opportunity to pass from the
scene of one scarce imaginable delight to the next one without interval or pause or satiety; and the very fact that, lounging before them in the outlandish and almost feminine
garments of his sybaritic privacy, he professed satiety but increased not only the amazement but the bitter and hopeless

outrage;—Henry, the provincial, the clown almost, given to
instinctive and violent action rather than to thinking, ratiocination, who may have been conscious that his fierce provincial's pride in his sister's virginity was a false quantity which
must incorporate in itself an inability to endure in order to be
precious, to exist, and so must depend upon its loss, absence,
to have existed at all. In fact, perhaps this is the pure and
perfect incest: the brother realising that the sister's virginity
must be destroyed in order to have existed at all, taking that
virginity in the person of the brother-in-law, the man whom
he would be if he could become, metamorphose into, the
lover, the husband; by whom he would be despoiled, choose
for despoiler, if he could become, metamorphose into the sister, the mistress, the bride. Perhaps that is what went on, not
in Henry's mind but in his soul. Because he never thought.
He felt, and acted immediately. He knew loyalty and acted it,
he knew pride and jealousy; he loved grieved and killed, still
grieving and, I believe, still loving Bon, the man to whom he
gave four years of probation, four years in which to renounce
and dissolve the other marriage, knowing that the four years
of hoping and waiting would be in vain.

"Yes, Henry: not Bon, as witness the entire queerly placid
course of Bon's and Judith's courtship—an engagement, if
engagement it ever was, lasting for a whole year yet com-
prising two holiday visits as her brother's guest and which
periods Bon seems to have spent either in riding and hunting
with Henry or as acting as an elegant and indolent esoteric
hothouse bloom possessing merely the name of a city for origin history and past, about which Ellen preened and fluttered
out her unwitting butterfly's Indian summer; he, the living
man, was usurped, you see. There was no time, no interval,
no niche in the crowded days when he could have courted
Judith. You can not even imagine him and Judith alone together. Try to do it and the nearest you can come is a projection of them while the two actual people were doubtless
separate and elsewhere—two shades pacing, serene and untroubled by flesh, in a summer garden—the same two serene
phantoms who seem to watch, hover, impartial attentive and
quiet, above and behind the inexplicable thunderhead of in-
terdictions and defiances and repudiations out of which the

rocklike Sutpen and the volatile and violent Henry flashed and glared and ceased;—Henry who up to that time had never even been to Memphis, who had never been away from home before that September when he went to the University with his countrified clothes and his saddle horse and negro groom; the six or seven of them, of an age and background, only in the surface matter of food and clothing and daily occupation any different from the negro slaves who supported them—the same sweat, the only difference being that on the one hand it went for labor in fields where on the other it went as the price of the spartan and meagre pleasures which were available to them because they did not have to sweat in the fields: the hard violent hunting and riding; the same pleasures: the one, gambling for worn knives and brass jewelry and twists of tobacco and buttons and garments because they happened to be easiest and quickest to hand; on the other for the money and horses, the guns and watches, and for the same reason; the same parties: the identical music from identical instruments, crude fiddles and guitars, now in the big house with candles and silk dresses and champagne, now in dirt-floored cabins with smoking pine knots and calico and water sweetened with molasses;—it was Henry, because at that time Bon had not even seen Judith. He had probably not paid enough attention to Henry's inarticulate recounting of his brief and conventional background and history to have remembered that Henry had a sister—this indolent man too old to find even companionship among the youths, the children, with whom he now lived; this man miscast for the time and knowing it, accepting it for a reason obviously good enough to cause him to endure it and apparently too serious or at least too private to be divulged to what acquaintances he now possessed:—this man who later showed the same indolence, almost uninterest, the same detachment when the uproar about that engagement which, so far as Jefferson knew, never formally existed, which Bon himself never affirmed or denied, arose and he in the background, impartial and passive as though it were not himself involved or he acting on behalf of some absent friend, but as though the person involved and interdict were someone whom he had never heard of and cared nothing about. There does not even seem to have been any courtship. Apparently he paid Judith the dubious compliment of not even trying to ruin her, let alone insisting on the marriage either before or after Sutpen forbade it—this, mind you, in a man who had already acquired a name for prowess among women while at the University, long before Sutpen was to find actual proof. No engagement, no courtship even: he and Judith saw one another three times in two years, for a total period of twelve days, counting the time which Ellen consumed; they parted without even saying goodbye. And yet, four years later, Henry had to kill Bon to keep them from marrying. So it must have been Henry who seduced Judith, not Bon: seduced her along with himself from that distance between Oxford and Sutpen's Hundred, between herself and the man whom she had not even seen yet, as though by means of that telepathy with which as children they seemed at times to anticipate one another's actions as two birds leave a limb at the same instant; that rapport not like the conventional delusion of that between twins but rather such as might exist between two people who, regardless of sex or age or heritage of race or tongue, had been marooned at birth on a desert island: the island here Sutpen's Hundred; the solitude, the shadow of that father with whom not only the town but their mother's family as well had merely assumed armistice rather than accepting and assimilating.

"You see? there they are: this girl, this young countrybred girl who sees a man for an average of one hour a day for twelve days during his life and that over a period of a year and a half, yet is bent on marrying him to the extent of forcing her brother to the last resort of homicide, even if not murder, to prevent it and that after a period of four years during which she could not have been always certain that he was still alive; this father who should see that man one time, yet have reason to make a six hundred mile journey to investigate him and either discover what he already and apparently by clairvoyance suspected, or at least something which served just as well as reason for forbidding the marriage; this brother in whose eyes that sister's and daughter's honor and happiness, granted that curious and unusual relationship which existed between them, should have been more jealous and precious than to the father even, yet who must

champion the marriage to the extent of repudiating father
and blood and home to become a follower and dependent of
the rejected suitor for four years before killing him apparently
for the very identical reason which four years ago he quitted
home to champion; and this lover who apparently without
volition or desire became involved in an engagement which
he seems neither to have sought nor avoided, who took his
dismissal in the same passive and sardonic spirit, yet four
years later was apparently so bent upon the marriage to which
up to that time he had been completely indifferent as to force
the brother who had championed it to kill him to prevent it.
Yes, granted that, even to the unworldly Henry, let alone the
more travelled father, the existence of the eighth part negro
mistress and the sixteenth part negro son, granted even the
morganatic ceremony—a situation which was as much a part
of a wealthy young New Orleanian's social and fashionable
equipment as his dancing slippers—was reason enough,
which is drawing honor a little fine even for the shadowy
paragons which are our ancestors born in the South and come
to man- and womanhood about eighteen sixty or sixty one.
It's just incredible. It just does not explain. Or perhaps that's
it: they dont explain and we are not supposed to know. We
have a few old mouth-to-mouth tales; we exhume from old
trunks and boxes and drawers letters without salutation or
signature, in which men and women who once lived and
breathed are now merely initials or nicknames out of some
now incomprehensible affection which sound to us like
Sanskrit or Chocktaw; we see dimly people, the people in
whose living blood and seed we ourselves lay dormant and
waiting, in this shadowy attenuation of time possessing now
heroic proportions, performing their acts of simple passion
and simple violence, impervious to time and inexplicable—
Yes, Judith, Bon, Henry, Sutpen: all of them. They are there,
yet something is missing; they are like a chemical formula
exhumed along with the letters from that forgotten chest,
carefully, the paper old and faded and falling to pieces, the
writing faded, almost indecipherable, yet meaningful, familiar
in shape and sense, the name and presence of volatile and
sentient forces; you bring them together in the proportions
called for, but nothing happens; you re-read, tedious and

intent, poring, making sure that you have forgotten nothing, made no miscalculation; you bring them together again and again nothing happens: just the words, the symbols, the shapes themselves, shadowy inscrutable and serene, against that turgid background of a horrible and bloody mischancing of human affairs.

"They came from the University to spend that first Christmas. Judith and Ellen and Sutpen saw him for the first time— Judith, the man whom she was to see for an elapsed time of twelve days, yet to remember so that four years later (he never wrote her during that time. Henry would not let him; it was the probation, you see) when she received a letter from him saying *We have waited long enough*, she and Clytie should begin at once to fashion a wedding dress and veil out of rags and scraps; Ellen, the esoteric, the almost baroque, the almost epicene objet d'art which with childlike voracity she essayed to include in the furnishing and decoration of her house; Sutpen, the man whom, after seeing once and before any engagement existed anywhere save in his wife's mind, he saw as a potential threat to the (now and at last) triumphant coronation of his old hardships and ambition, of which threat he was apparently sure enough to warrant a six hundred mile journey to prove it—this in a man who might have challenged and shot someone whom he disliked or feared but who would not have made even a ten mile journey to investigate him. You see? You would almost believe that Sutpen's trip to New Orleans was just sheer chance, just a little more of the illogical machinations of a fatality which had chosen that family in preference to any other in the county or the land exactly as a small boy chooses one ant-hill to pour boiling water into in preference to any other, not even himself knowing why. They stayed two weeks and rode back to school, stopping to see Miss Rosa but she was not at home; they passed the long term before the summer vacation talking together and riding and reading (Bon was reading law. He would be, would almost have to, since only that could have made his residence bearable, regardless of what reason he may have brought with him for remaining;—this, the perfect setting for his dilatory indolence: this digging into musty Blackstone and Coke where, of an undergraduate body

still numbered in two figures, the law school probably consisted of six others beside Henry—yes, he corrupted Henry
to the law also; Henry changed in midterm—and himself)
while Henry aped his clothing and speech, caricatured rather,
perhaps, and Bon, though he had now seen Judith, very likely
the same lazy and catlike man and it Henry who foisted upon
him now the role of his sister's intended as during the fall
term Henry and his companions had foisted upon Bon the
role of Lothario; and Ellen and Judith now shopping two and
three times a week in town and stopping once to see Miss
Rosa while on their way by carriage to Memphis, with a
wagon preceding them to fetch back the plunder and an extra
nigger on the box with the coachman to stop every few miles
and build a fire and re-heat the bricks on which Ellen's and
Judith's feet rested, shopping, buying the trousseau for that
wedding whose formal engagement existed no where yet save
in Ellen's mind; and Sutpen, who had seen Bon once and was
in New Orleans investigating him when Bon next entered the
house: who knows what he was thinking, what waiting for,
what moment, day, to go to New Orleans and find what he
seems to have known all the while that he would find? There
was no one for him to tell, talk to about it, about his fear and
suspicion. He trusted no man nor woman, who had no man's
nor woman's love, since Ellen was incapable of love and Judith was too much like him and he must have seen at a glance
that Bon, even though the daughter might still be saved from
him, had already corrupted the son. He had been too successful, you see; his was that solitude of contempt and distrust
which success brings to him who gained it because he was
strong instead of merely lucky.

  "Then June came and the end of the school year and Henry
and Bon returned to Sutpen's Hundred, Bon to spend a day
or two before riding on to the River to take the steamboat
home, to New Orleans where Sutpen had already gone
though none knew it, least of all Ellen. He stayed but two
days, yet now if ever was his chance to come to an understanding with Judith, perhaps even to fall in love with her. It
was his only chance, his last chance, though of course neither
he nor Judith could have known it, since Sutpen, though but
two weeks absent from home, had doubtless already found

out about the octoroon mistress and the child. So for the first
and last time Bon and Judith might have been said to have a
free field—might have been, since it was really Ellen who had
the free field. I can imagine her engineering that courtship,
supplying Judith and Bon with opportunities for trysts and
pledges with a coy and unflagging ubiquity which they must
have tried in vain to evade and escape, Judith with annoyed
yet still serene concern, Bon with that sardonic and surprised
distaste which seems to have been the ordinary manifestation
of the impenetrable and shadowy character. Yes, shadowy: a
myth, a phantom: something which they engendered and created whole themselves; some effluvium of Sutpen blood and
character, as though as a man he did not exist at all. Yet there
was the body which Miss Rosa saw, which Judith buried in
the family plot beside her mother. And this: the fact that even
an undefined and never-spoken engagement survived, speaking well for the postulation that they did love one another,
since during that two days mere romance would have perished, died of sheer saccharinity and opportunity. Then Bon
rode on to the River and took the boat. And now this: who
knows, perhaps if Henry had gone with him that summer
instead of waiting until the next, Bon would not have had to
die as he did; if Henry had only gone then to New Orleans
and found out then about the mistress and the child; Henry
who, before it was too late, might have reacted to the discovery exactly as Sutpen did, as a jealous brother might have
been expected to react, since who knows but what it was not
the fact of the mistress and child, the possible bigamy, to
which Henry gave the lie, but to the fact that it was his father
who told him, his father who anticipated him, the father who
is the natural enemy of any son and son-in-law of whom the
mother is the ally, just as after the wedding the father will be
the ally of the actual son-in-law who has for mortal foe the
mother of his wife. But Henry did not go this time. He rode
to the River with Bon and then returned; after a time Sutpen
returned home too, from where and for what purpose none
were to know until the next Christmas, and that summer
passed, the last summer, the last summer of peace and content, with Henry, doubtless without deliberate intent, plead-
ing Bon's suit far better than Bon, than that indolent fatalist

had ever bothered to plead it himself, and Judith listening with that serenity, that impenetrable tranquillity which a year or so before had been the young girl's vague and pointless and dreamy unvolition but was now already a mature woman's—a mature woman in love—repose. That's when the letters came, and Henry reading them all, without jealousy, with that complete abnegant transference, metamorphosis into the body which was to become his sister's lover. And Sutpen saying nothing yet about what he had learned in New Orleans but just waiting, unsuspected even by Henry and Judith, waiting for what nobody knows, perhaps in the hope that when Bon learned, as he would be obliged to, that Sutpen had discovered his secret, he (Bon) would realise that the game was up and not even return to school the next year. But Bon did return. He and Henry met again at the University; the letters—from Henry and Bon both now—making weekly journeys by the hand of Henry's groom; and Sutpen still waiting, certainly no one could say for what now, incredible that he should wait for Christmas, for the crisis to come to him—this man of whom it was said that he not only went out to meet his troubles, he sometimes went out and manufactured them. But this time he waited and it came to him: Christmas, and Henry and Bon rode again to Sutpen's Hundred and even the town convinced now by Ellen that the engagement existed; that twenty-fourth of December, 1860, and the nigger children, with branches of mistletoe and holly for excuses, already lurking about the rear of the big house to shout 'Christmas gift' at the white people, the rich city man come to court Judith, and Sutpen saying nothing even yet, not suspected yet unless possibly by Henry, possibly Henry who brought the matter to its crisis that same night, and Ellen at the absolute flood's peak of her unreal and weightless life which with the next dawn was to break beneath her and wash her, spent amazed and uncomprehending, into the shuttered room where she died two years later;—the Christmas eve, the explosion, and none to ever know just why or just what happened between Henry and his father and only the cabin-to-cabin whispering of negroes to spread the news that Henry and Bon had ridden away in the dark and that Henry had formally abjured his home and birthright.

"They went to New Orleans. They rode through the bright cold of that Christmas day, to the River and took the steamboat, it still Henry doing the leading, the bringing, as he always did until the very last, when for the first time during their entire relationship Bon led and Henry followed. He didn't have to go. He had voluntarily made himself a pauper but he could have gone to his grandfather since although he was probably better mounted than any other at the University, not excepting Bon himself, he probably had very little money beyond what he could raise hurriedly on his horse and what valuables he happened to have on his body when he and Bon rode away. No, he didn't have to go, and he doing the leading this time too, and Bon riding beside him trying to find out from him what had happened. Bon knew of course what Sutpen had discovered in New Orleans, but he would need to know just what, just how much, Sutpen had told Henry, and Henry not telling him, doubtless with the new mare which he probably knew he would have to surrender, sacrifice too, along with all the rest of his life, inheritance, going fast now and his back rigid and irrevocably turned upon the house, his birthplace and all the familiar scenes of his childhood and youth which he had repudiated for the sake of that friend with whom, despite the sacrifice which he had just made out of love and loyalty, he still could not be perfectly frank. Because he knew that what Sutpen had told him was true. He must have known that at the very instant when he gave his father the lie. So he dared not ask Bon to deny it; he dared not, you see. He could face poverty, disinheritance, but he could not have borne that lie from Bon. Yet he went to New Orleans. He went straight there, to the only place, the very place, where he could not help but prove conclusively the very statement which, coming from his father, he had called a lie. He went there for that purpose; he went there to prove it. And Bon, riding beside him, trying to find out what Sutpen had told him,—Bon who for a year and a half now had been watching Henry ape his clothing and speech, who for a year and a half now had seen himself as the object of that complete and abnegant devotion which only a youth, never a woman, gives to another youth or a man; who for exactly a year now had seen the sister succumb to that same

spell which the brother had already succumbed to, and this
with no volition on the seducer's part, without so much as
the lifting of a finger, as though it actually were the brother
who had put the spell on the sister, seduced her to his own
vicarious image which walked and breathed with Bon's body.
Yet here is the letter, sent four years afterward, written on a
sheet of paper salvaged from a gutted house in Carolina, with
stove polish found in some captured Yankee stores; four years
after she had had any message from him save the messages
from Henry that he (Bon) was still alive. So whether Henry
now knew about the other woman or not, he would now
have to know. Bon realised that. I can imagine them as they
rode, Henry still in the fierce repercussive flush of vindicated
loyalty, and Bon, the wiser, the shrewder even if only from
wider experience and a few more years of age, learning from
Henry without Henry's being aware of it, what Sutpen had
told him. Because Henry would have to know now. And I
dont believe it was just to preserve Henry as an ally, for the
crisis of some future need. It was because Bon not only loved
Judith after his fashion but he loved Henry too and I believe
in a deeper sense than merely after his fashion. Perhaps in his
fatalism he loved Henry the better of the two, seeing perhaps
in the sister merely the shadow, the woman vessel with which
to consummate the love whose actual object was the youth: —
this cerebral Don Juan who, reversing the order, had learned
to love what he had injured; perhaps it was even more than
Judith or Henry either: perhaps the life, the existence, which
they represented. Because who knows what picture of peace
he might have seen in that monotonous provincial backwater;
what alleviation and escape for a parched traveller who had
travelled too far at too young an age, in this granite-bound
and simple country spring.

   "And I can imagine how Bon told Henry, broke it to him.
I can imagine Henry in New Orleans, who had not yet even
been to Memphis, whose entire worldly experience consisted
of sojourns at other houses, plantations, almost interchangeable with his own, where he followed the same routine which
he did at home—the same hunting and cockfighting, the
same amateur racing of horses on crude homemade tracks,
horses sound enough in blood and lineage yet not bred to

race and perhaps not even thirty minutes out of the shafts of a trap or perhaps even a carriage; the same square dancing with identical and also interchangeable provincial virgins, to music exactly like that at home, the same champagne, the best doubtless yet crudely dispensed out of the burlesqued panto-mime elegance of negro butlers who (and likewise the drink-ers who gulped it down like neat whiskey between flowery and unsubtle toasts) would have treated lemonade the same way. I can imagine him, with his puritan heritage—that her-itage peculiarly Anglo-Saxon—of fierce proud mysticism and that ability to be ashamed of ignorance and inexperience, in that city foreign and paradoxical, with its atmosphere at once fatal and languorous, at once feminine and steel-hard—this grim humorless yokel out of a granite heritage where even the houses, let alone clothing and conduct, are built in the image of a jealous and sadistic Jehovah, put suddenly down in a place whose denizens had created their All-Powerful and His supporting hierarchy-chorus of beautiful saints and handsome angels in the image of their houses and personal ornaments and voluptuous lives. Yes, I can imagine how Bon led up to it, to the shock: the skill, the calculation, preparing Henry's pu-ritan mind as he would have prepared a cramped and rocky field and planted it and raised the crop which he wanted. It would be the fact of the ceremony, regardless of what kind, that Henry would balk at: Bon knew this. It would not be the mistress or even the child, not even the negro mistress and even less the child because of that fact, since Henry and Judith had grown up with a negro half sister of their own; not the mistress to Henry, certainly not the nigger mistress to a youth with Henry's background, a young man grown up and living in a milieu where the other sex is separated into three sharp divisions, separated (two of them) by a chasm which could be crossed but one time and in but one direction—ladies, women, females—the virgins whom gentlemen someday married, the courtesans to whom they went while on sabbat-icals to the cities, the slave girls and women upon whom that first caste rested and to whom in certain cases it doubtless owed the very fact of its virginity;—not this to Henry, young, strong-blooded, victim of the hard celibacy of riding and hunting to heat and make importunate the blood of a

young man, to which he and his kind were forced to pass
time away, with girls of his own class interdict and inaccessible and women of the second class just as inaccessible because
of money and distance, and hence only the slave girls, the
housemaids neated and cleaned by white mistresses or perhaps girls with sweating bodies out of the fields themselves
and the young man rides up and beckons the watching overseer and says Send me Juno or Missylena or Chlory and then
rides on into the trees and dismounts and waits. No: it would
be the ceremony, a ceremony entered into, to be sure, with a
negro, yet still a ceremony; this is what Bon doubtless
thought. So I can imagine him, the way he did it: the way in
which he took the innocent and negative plate of Henry's
provincial soul and intellect and exposed it by slow degrees to
this esoteric milieu, building gradually toward the picture
which he desired it to retain, accept. I can see him corrupting
Henry gradually into the purlieus of elegance, with no fore-
word, no warning, the postulation to come after the fact, exposing Henry slowly to the surface aspect—the architecture a
little curious, a little femininely flamboyant and therefore to
Henry opulent, sensuous, sinful; the inference of great and
easy wealth measured by steamboat loads in place of a tedious
inching of sweating human figures across cotton fields; the
flash and glitter of a myriad carriage wheels, in which women,
enthroned and immobile and passing rapidly across the
vision, appeared like painted portraits beside men in linen a
little finer and diamonds a little brighter and in broadcloth
a little trimmer and with hats raked a little more above faces a
little more darkly swaggering than any Henry had ever seen
before: and the mentor, the man for whose sake he had repudiated not only blood and kin but food and shelter and clothing too, whose clothing and walk and speech he had tried to
ape, along with his attitude toward women and his ideas of
honor and pride too, watching him with that cold and catlike
inscrutable calculation, watching the picture resolve and become fixed and then telling Henry, 'But that's not it. That's
just the base, the foundation. It can belong to anyone': and
Henry, 'You mean, this is not it? That it is above this, higher
than this, more select than this?': and Bon, 'Yes. This is only
the foundation. This belongs to anybody.': a dialogue with-

out words, speech, which would fix and then remove without
obliterating one line the picture, this background, leaving the
background, the plate prepared and innocent again: the plate
docile, with that puritan's humility toward anything which is
a matter of sense rather than logic, fact, the man, the struggling and suffocating heart behind it saying *I will believe! I
will! I will! Whether it is true or not, I will believe!* waiting for
the next picture which the mentor, the corruptor, intended
for it: that next picture, following the fixation and acceptance
of which the mentor would say again, perhaps with words
now, still watching the sober and thoughtful face but still secure in his knowledge and trust in that puritan heritage which
must show disapproval instead of surprise or even despair and
nothing at all rather than have the disapprobation construed
as surprise or despair: 'But even this is not it': and Henry,
'You mean, it is still higher than this, still above this?' Because
he (Bon) would be talking now, lazily, almost cryptically,
stroking onto the plate himself now the picture which he
wanted there; I can imagine how he did it—the calculation,
the surgeon's alertness and cold detachment, the exposures
brief, so brief as to be cryptic, almost staccato, the plate unaware of what the complete picture would show, scarce-seen
yet ineradicable:—a trap, a riding horse standing before a
closed and curiously monastic doorway in a neighborhood a
little decadent, even a little sinister, and Bon mentioning the
owner's name casually—this, corruption subtly anew by putting into Henry's mind the notion of one man of the world
speaking to another, that Henry knew that Bon believed that
Henry would know even from a disjointed word what Bon
was talking about, and Henry the puritan who must show
nothing at all rather than surprise or incomprehension;—a
façade shuttered and blank, drowsing in steamy morning sunlight, invested by the bland and cryptic voice with something
of secret and curious and unimaginable delights. Without his
knowing what he saw it was as though to Henry the blank
and scaling barrier in dissolving produced and revealed not
comprehension to the mind, the intellect which weighs and
discards, but striking instead straight and true to some primary blind and mindless foundation of all young male living
dream and hope—a row of faces like a bazaar of flowers,

the supreme apotheosis of chattelry, of human flesh bred of
the two races for that sale—a corridor of doomed and tragic
flower faces walled between the grim duenna row of old
women and the elegant shapes of young men trim predatory
and (at the moment) goatlike: this seen by Henry quickly,
exposed quickly and then removed, the mentor's voice still
bland, pleasant, cryptic, postulating still the fact of one man
of the world talking to another about something they both
understand, depending upon, counting upon still, the puritan's provincial horror of revealing surprise or ignorance, who
knew Henry so much better than Henry knew him, and
Henry not showing either, suppressing still that first cry of
terror and grief, *I will believe! I will! I will!* Yes, that brief,
before Henry had had time to know what he had seen, but
now slowing: now would come the instant for which Bon
had builded:—a wall, unscalable, a gate ponderously locked,
the sober and thoughtful country youth just waiting, looking,
not yet asking why? or what? the gate of solid beams in place
of the lacelike iron grilling and they passing on, Bon knocking at a small adjacent doorway from which a swarthy man
resembling a creature out of an old woodcut of the French
Revolution erupts, concerned, even a little aghast, looking
first at the daylight and then at Henry and speaking to Bon in
French which Henry does not understand and Bon's teeth
glinting for an instant before he answers in French: 'With
him? An American? He is a guest; I would have to let him
choose weapons and I decline to fight with axes. No, no; not
that. Just the key.' Just the key; and now, the solid gates
closed behind them instead of before, no sight or evidence
above the high thick walls of the low city and scarce any
sound of it, the labyrinthine mass of oleander and jasmine,
lantana and mimosa walling yet again the strip of bare earth
combed and curried with powdered shell, raked and immaculate and only the most recent of the brown stains showing
now, and the voice—the mentor, the guide standing aside
now to watch the grave provincial face—casually and pleasantly anecdotal: 'The customary way is to stand back to back,
the pistol in your right hand and the corner of the other cloak
in your left. Then at the signal you begin to walk and when
you feel the cloak tauten you turn and fire. Though there are

some now and then, when the blood is especially hot or when
it is still peasant blood, who prefer knives and one cloak.
They face one another inside the same cloak, you see, each
holding the other's wrist with the left hand. But that was
never my way';—casual, chatty, you see, waiting for the
countryman's slow question, who knew already now before
he asked it: 'What would you—they be fighting for?'

"Yes, Henry would know now, or believe that he knew
now; anymore he would probably consider anti-climax
though it would not be, it would be anything but that, the
final blow, stroke, touch, the keen surgeonlike compounding
which the now shocked nerves of the patient would not even
feel, not know that the first hard shocks were the random and
crude. Because there was that ceremony. Bon knew that that
would be what Henry would resist, find hard to stomach and
retain. Oh he was shrewd, this man whom for weeks now
Henry was realising that he knew less and less, this stranger
immersed and oblivious now in the formal, almost ritual,
preparations for the visit, finicking almost like a woman over
the fit of the new coat which he would have ordered for
Henry, forced Henry to accept for this occasion, by means of
which the entire impression which Henry was to receive from
the visit would be established before they even left the house,
before Henry ever saw the woman: and Henry, the countryman, the bewildered, with the subtle tide already setting beneath him toward the point where he must either betray
himself and his entire upbringing and thinking, or deny the
friend for whom he had already repudiated home and kin and
all; the bewildered, the (for that time) helpless, who wanted
to believe yet did not see how he could, being carried by the
friend, the mentor, through one of those inscrutable and
curiously lifeless doorways like that before which he had seen
the horse or the trap, and so into a place which to his puritan's provincial mind all of morality was upside down and all
of honor perished—a place created for and by voluptuous-
ness, the abashless and unabashed senses, and the country boy
with his simple and erstwhile untroubled code in which females were ladies or whores or slaves looked at the apotheosis
of two doomed races presided over by its own victim—a
woman with a face like a tragic magnolia, the eternal female,

the eternal Who-suffers; the child, the boy, sleeping in silk
and lace to be sure yet complete chattel of him who, begetting him, owned him body and soul to sell (if he chose) like
a calf or puppy or sheep; and the mentor watching again,
perhaps even the gambler now thinking *Have I won or lost?*
as they emerged and returned to Bon's rooms, for that while
impotent even with talk, shrewdness, no longer counting
upon that puritan character which must show neither surprise
nor despair, having to count now (if on anything) on the
corruption itself, the love; he could not even say, 'Well? What
do you say about it?' He could only wait, and that upon
the absolutely unpredictable actions of a man who lived by
instinct and not reason, until Henry should speak, 'But a
bought woman. A whore': and Bon, even gently now, 'Not
whore. Dont say that. In fact, never refer to one of them by
that name in New Orleans: otherwise you may be forced to
purchase that privilege with some of your blood from probably a thousand men', and perhaps still gently, perhaps now
even with something of pity: that pessimistic and sardonic
cerebral pity of the intelligent for any human injustice or folly
or suffering: 'Not whores. And not whores because of us, the
thousand. We—the thousand, the white men—made them,
created and produced them; we even made the laws which
declare that one eighth of a specified kind of blood shall out-
weigh seven eighths of another kind. I admit that. But that
same white race would have made them slaves too, laborers,
cooks, maybe even field hands, if it were not for this thousand, these few men like myself without principles or honor
either, perhaps you will say. We cannot, perhaps we do not
even want to, save all of them; perhaps the thousand we save
are not one in a thousand. But we save that one. God may
mark every sparrow, but we do not pretend to be God, you
see. Perhaps we do not even want to be God, since no man
would want but one of these sparrows. And perhaps when
God looks into one of these establishments like you saw tonight, He would not choose one of us to be God either, now
that He is old. Though He must have been young once,
surely He was young once, and surely someone who has existed as long as He has, who has looked at as much crude and
promiscuous sinning without grace or restraint or decorum as

He has had to, to contemplate at last, even though the instances are not one in a thousand thousand, the principles of honor, decorum and gentleness applied to perfectly normal human instinct which you Anglo-Saxons insist upon calling lust and in whose service you revert in sabbaticals to the primordial caverns, the fall from what you call grace fogged and clouded by Heaven-defying words of extenuation and explanation, the return to grace heralded by Heaven-placating cries of satiated abasement and flagellation, in neither of which—the defiance or the placation—can Heaven find interest or even, after the first two or three times, diversion. So perhaps, now that God is an old man, He is not interested in the way we serve what you call lust either. Perhaps He does not even require of us that we save this one sparrow, anymore than we save the one sparrow which we do save for any commendation from Him. But we do save that one, who but for us would have been sold to any brute who had the price, not sold to him for the night like a white prostitute, but body and soul for life to him who could have used her with more impunity than he would dare to use an animal, heifer or mare, and then discarded or sold or even murdered when worn out or when her keep and her price no longer balanced. Yes: a sparrow which God Himself neglected to mark. Because though men, white men, created her, God did not stop it. He planted the seed which brought her to flower—the white blood to give the shape and pigment of what the white man calls female beauty, to a female principle which existed, queenly and complete, in the hot equatorial groin of the world long before that white one of ours came down from trees and lost its hair and bleached out—a principle apt docile and instinct with strange and ancient curious pleasures of the flesh (which is all: there is nothing else) which her white sisters of a mushroom yesterday flee from in moral and outraged horror—a principle which, where her white sister must needs try to make an economic matter of it like someone who insists upon installing a counter or a scales or a safe in a store or business for a certain percentage of the profits, reigns, wise supine and all-powerful, from the sunless and silken bed which is her throne. No: not whores. Not even courtesans:— creatures taken at childhood, culled and chosen and raised more carefully than any white girl, any nun, than any blooded mare even, by a person who gives them the unsleeping care and attention which no mother ever gives. For a price, of course, but a price offered and accepted or declined through a system more formal than any that white girls are sold under since they are more valuable as commodities than white girls, raised and trained to fulfill a woman's sole end and purpose: to love, to be beautiful, to divert; never to see a man's face hardly until brought to the ball and offered to and chosen by some man who in return, not can and not will but *must*, supply her with the surroundings proper in which to love and be beautiful and divert, and who must usually risk his life or at least his blood for that privilege. No, not whores. Sometimes I believe that they are the only true chaste women, not to say virgins, in America, and they remain true and faithful to that man not merely until he dies or frees them, but until they die. And where will you find whore or lady either whom you can count on to do that?' and Henry, 'But you married her. You married her.': and Bon—it would be a little quicker now, sharper now, though still gentle, still patient, though still the iron, the steel—the gambler not quite yet reduced to his final trump: 'Ah. That ceremony. I see. That's it, then. A formula, a shibboleth meaningless as a child's game, performed by someone created by the situation whose need it answered: a crone mumbling in a dungeon lighted by a handful of burning hair, something in a tongue which not even the girls themselves understand anymore, maybe not even the crone herself, rooted in nothing of economics for her or for any possible progeny since the very fact that we acquiesced, suffered the farce, was her proof and assurance of that which the ceremony itself could never enforce; vesting no new rights in anyone, denying to none the old—a ritual as meaningless as that of college boys in secret rooms at night, even to the same archaic and forgotten symbols?—you call that a marriage, when the night of a honeymoon and the casual business with a hired prostitute consists of the same suzerainty over a (temporarily) private room, the same order of removing the same clothes, the same conjunction in a single bed? Why not call that a marriage too?' and Henry: 'Oh I know. I know. You give me two and two and you tell me it makes five and it does

make five. But there is still the marriage. Suppose I assume
an obligation to a man who cannot speak my language, the
obligation stated to him in his own and I agree to it: am I
any the less obligated because I did not happen to know the
tongue in which he accepted me in good faith? No: the more,
the more.' and Bon—the trump now, the voice gentle now:
'Have you forgot that this woman, this child, are niggers?
You, Henry Sutpen of Sutpen's Hundred in Mississippi? You,
talking of marriage, a wedding, here?' and Henry—the despair now, the last bitter cry of irrevocable undefeat: 'Yes. I
know. I know that. But it's still there. It's not right. Not
even you doing it makes it right. Not even you.'

    "So that was all. It should have been all; that afternoon
four years later should have happened the next day, the four
years, the interval, mere anti-climax: an attenuation and prolongation of a conclusion already ripe to happen, by the War,
by a stupid and bloody aberration in the high (and impossible) destiny of the United States, maybe instigated by that
family fatality which possessed, along with all circumstance,
that curious lack of economy between cause and effect which
is always a characteristic of fate when reduced to using human
beings for tools, material. Anyway, Henry waited four years,
holding the three of them in that abeyance, that durance,
waiting, hoping, for Bon to renounce the woman and dissolve the marriage which he (Henry) admitted was no marriage, and which he must have known as soon as he saw the
woman and the child that Bon would not renounce. In fact,
as time passed and Henry became accustomed to the idea of
that ceremony which was still no marriage, that may have
been the trouble with Henry—not the two ceremonies but
the two women; not the fact that Bon's intention was to commit bigamy but that it was apparently to make his (Henry's)
sister a sort of junior partner in a harem. Anyway, he waited,
hoped, for four years. That spring they returned north, into
Mississippi. Bull Run had been fought and there was a company organising at the University, among the student body.
Henry and Bon joined it. Probably Henry wrote Judith where
they were and what they intended to do. They enlisted together, you see, Henry watching Bon and Bon permitting
himself to be watched, the probation, the durance: the one

who dared not let the other out of his sight, not from fear
that Bon would marry Judith with Henry not there to stop it,
but that Bon would marry Judith and then he (Henry) would
have to live for the rest of his life with the knowledge that he
was glad that he had been so betrayed, with the coward's joy
of surrendering without having been vanquished; the other
for that same reason too, who could not have wanted Judith
without Henry since he must never have doubted but what he
could marry Judith when he wished, in spite of brother and
father both, because as I said before, it was not Judith who
was the object of Bon's love or of Henry's solicitude. She was
just the blank shape, the empty vessel in which each of them
strove to preserve, not the illusion of himself nor his illusion
of the other but what each conceived the other to believe him
to be—the man and the youth, seducer and seduced, who
had known one another, seduced and been seduced, victimised in turn each by the other, conquerer vanquished by his
own strength, vanquished conquering by his own weakness,
before Judith came into their joint lives even by so much as
girlname. And who knows? there was the War now; who
knows but what the fatality and the fatality's victims did not
both think, hope, that the War would settle the matter, leave
free one of the two irreconciliables, since it would not be the
first time that youth has taken catastrophe as a direct act of
Providence for the sole purpose of solving a personal problem
which youth itself could not solve.

"And Judith: how else to explain her but this way? Surely
Bon could not have corrupted her to fatalism in twelve days,
who not only had not tried to corrupt her to unchastity but
not even to defy her father. No: anything but a fatalist, who
was the Sutpen with the ruthless Sutpen code of taking what
it wanted provided it were strong enough, of the two children
as Henry was the Coldfield with the Coldfield cluttering of
morality and rules of right and wrong; who while Henry
screamed and vomited, looked down from the loft that night
on the spectacle of Sutpen fighting halfnaked with one of his
halfnaked niggers with the same cold and attentive interest
with which Sutpen would have watched Henry fighting with
a negro boy of his own age and weight. Because she could
not have known the reason for her father's objection to the

marriage. Henry would not have told her, and she would not have asked her father. Because, even if she had known it, it would have made no difference to her. She would have acted as Sutpen would have acted with anyone who tried to cross him: she would have taken Bon anyway. I can imagine her if necessary even murdering the other woman. But she certainly would have made no investigation and then held a moral debate between what she wanted and what she thought was right. Yet she waited. She waited four years, with no word from him save through Henry that he (Bon) was alive, because Henry would not let Bon write her. He would not have. And Bon would not have tried to. It was the probation, the durance; they all three accepted it; I dont believe there was ever any promise between Henry and Bon demanded or offered. But Judith, who could not have known what happened nor why. — Have you noticed how so often when we try to reconstruct the causes which lead up to the actions of men and women, how with a sort of astonishment we find ourselves now and then reduced to the belief, the only possible belief, that they stemmed from some of the old virtues? the thief who steals not for greed but for love, the murderer who kills not out of lust but pity? Judith, giving implicit trust where she had given love, giving implicit love where she had derived breath and pride: that true pride, not that false kind which transforms what it does not at the moment understand into scorn and outrage and so vents itself in pique and lacerations, but true pride which can say to itself without abasement *I love, I will accept no substitute; something has happened between him and my father; if my father was right, I will never see him again, if wrong he will come or send for me; if happy I can be I will, if suffer I must I can.* Because she waited; she made no effort to do anything else; her relations with her father had not altered one jot; to see them together, Bon might never have even existed—the same two calm impenetrable faces seen together in the carriage in town during the next few months after Ellen took to her bed, between that Christmas day and the day when Sutpen rode away with his and Sartoris' regiment. They didn't talk, tell one another anything, you see—Sutpen, what he had learned about Bon; Judith, that she knew where Bon and Henry now were. They did not need to talk. They were too much alike. They were as two people become now and then, who seem to know one another so well or are so much alike that the power, the need, to communicate by speech atrophies from disuse and, comprehending without need of the medium of ear or intellect, they no longer understand one another's actual words. So she did not tell him where Henry and Bon were and he did not discover it until after the University company departed, because Bon and Henry enrolled and then hid themselves somewhere. They must have; they must have paused in Oxford only long enough to enroll before riding on, because no one who knew them either in Oxford or in Jefferson knew that they were members of the company at the time, which would have been almost impossible to conceal otherwise. Because now people—fathers and mothers and sisters and kin and sweethearts of those young men—were coming to Oxford from further away than Jefferson—families with food and bedding and servants, to bivouac among the families, the houses, of Oxford itself, to watch the gallant mimic marching and countermarching of the sons and the brothers, drawn all of them, rich and poor, aristocrat and redneck, by what is probably the most moving mass-sight of all human mass-experience, far more so than the spectacle of so many virgins going to be sacrificed to some heathen Principle, some Priapus—the sight of young men, the light quick bones, the bright gallant deluded blood and flesh dressed in a martial glitter of brass and plumes, marching away to a battle. And there would be music at night—fiddle and triangle among the blazing candles, the blowing of curtains in tall windows on the April darkness, the swing of crinoline indiscriminate within the circle of plain gray cuff of the soldier or the banded gold of rank, of an army even if not a war of gentlemen, where private and colonel called each other by their given names not as one farmer to another across a halted plow in a field or across a counter in a store laden with calico and cheese and strap oil, but as one man to another above the suave powdered shoulders of women, above the two raised glasses of scuppernong claret or bought champagne;—music, the nightly repetitive last waltz as the days passed and the company waited to move, the brave trivial glitter against a black night not catastrophic but merely background, the perennial last scented spring of youth; and Judith not there and Henry the romantic not there and Bon the fatalist, hidden somewhere, the watcher and the watched: and the recurrent flower-laden dawns of that April and May and June filled with bugles, entering a hundred windows where a hundred still unbrided widows dreamed virgin unmeditant upon the locks of black or brown or yellow hair and Judith not one of these: and five of the company, mounted, with grooms and body servants in a forage wagon, in their new and unstained gray made a tour of the State with the flag, the company's colors, the segments of silk cut and fitted but not sewn, from house to house until the sweetheart of each man in the company had taken a few stitches in it, and Henry and Bon not of these either, since they did not join the company until after it departed, who must have emerged from whatever place it was that they lurked in, emerging as though unnoticed from the roadside brake or thicket, to fall in as the marching company passed; the two of them—the youth and the man, the youth deprived twice now of his birthright, who should have made one among the candles and fiddles, the kisses and the desperate tears, who should have made one of the color guard itself which toured the State with the unsewn flag; and the man who should not have been there at all, who was too old to be there at all, both in years and experience: that mental and spiritual orphan whose fate it apparently was to exist in some limbo halfway between where his corporeality was and his mentality and moral equipment desired to be—an undergraduate at the University, yet by the sheer accumulation of too full years behind him forced into the extra-academnic of a law class containing six members; in the War, by that same force removed into the isolation of commissioned rank. He received a lieutenancy before the company entered its first engagement even. I dont think he wanted it; I can even imagine him trying to avoid it, refuse it. But there it was, he was, orphaned once more by the very situation to which and by which he was doomed—the two of them officer and man now but still watcher and watched, waiting for something but not knowing what, what act of fate, destiny, what irrevocable sentence of what Judge or Arbiter between them since nothing less would do, nothing

halfway or reversible would seem to suffice—the officer, the
lieutenant who possessed the slight and authorised advantage
of being able to say *You* go there, of at least sometimes remaining behind the platoon which he directed; the private
who carried that officer, shot through the shoulder, on his
back while the regiment fell back under the Yankee guns at
Pittsburg Landing, carried him to safety apparently for the
sole purpose of watching him for two years more, writing
Judith meanwhile that they were both alive, and that was all.

"And Judith. She lived alone now. Perhaps she had lived
alone ever since that Christmas day last year and then year
before last and then three years and then four years ago, since
though Sutpen was gone now with his and Sartoris' regiment
and the negroes—the wild stock with which he had created
Sutpen's Hundred—had followed the first Yankee troops to
pass through Jefferson, she lived in anything but solitude,
what with Ellen in bed in the shuttered room, requiring the
unremitting attention of a child while she waited with that
amazed and passive uncomprehension to die; and she (Judith)
and Clytie making and keeping a kitchen garden of sorts to
keep them alive; and Wash Jones, living in the abandoned and
rotting fishing camp in the river bottom which Sutpen had
built after the first woman—Ellen—entered his house and
the last deer and bear hunter went out of it, where he now
permitted Wash and his daughter and infant granddaughter to
live, performing the heavy garden work and supplying Ellen
and Judith and then Judith with fish and game now and then,
even entering the house now who until Sutpen went away
had never approached nearer than the scuppernong arbor behind the kitchen where on Sunday afternoons he and Sutpen
would drink from the demijohn and the bucket of spring
water which Wash fetched from almost a mile away, Sutpen in
the barrel stave hammock talking and Wash squatting against
a post, chortling and guffawing;—not solitude and certainly
not idleness: the same impenetrable and serene face, only a
little older now, a little thinner now, which had appeared in
town in the carriage beside her father's within a week after it
was learned that her fiance and her brother had quitted the
house in the night and vanished, none knew why or where
and none asked, just as now none asked when she came to

town now, in the made-over dress which all Southern women
now wore, in the carriage still but drawn now by a mule, a
plow mule, soon the plow mule, and no coachman to drive
it either, to put the mule in the harness and take it out, to
join the other women where—there were wounded in Jefferson then—in the improvised hospital where (the nurtured
virgin, the supremely and traditionally idle) they cleaned
and dressed the self-fouled bodies of strange injured and dead
and made lint of the window curtains and sheets and linen
of the houses in which they had been born;—none to ask
her about brother and sweetheart while they talked among
themselves of sons and brothers and husbands with tears
and grief perhaps but at least with certainty, knowledge;
she waiting too, like Henry and Bon, not knowing for what,
but unlike Henry and Bon, she not even knowing for why.
Then Ellen died, the butterfly of a forgotten summer two
years defunctive now—the substanceless shell, the shade impervious to any alteration or dissolution because of its very
weightlessness: no body to be buried: just the shape, the rec-
ollection, translated on some peaceful afternoon without bell
or catafalque into that cedar grove, to lie in powder-light
paradox beneath the thousand pounds of marble monument which Sutpen (Colonel Sutpen now, since Sartoris had
been deposed at the annual election of regimental officers the
year before) brought in the regimental forage wagon from
Charleston, South Carolina and set above the faint grassy
depression which Judith told him was Ellen's grave. And then
her grandfather died, starved to death nailed up in his own
attic, and Judith doubtless inviting Miss Rosa to come out to
Sutpen's Hundred to live and Miss Rosa declining, waiting
too apparently upon this letter, this first direct word from
Bon in four years and which, a week after she buried him too
beside her mother's tombstone, she brought to town herself,
in the surrey drawn by the mule which both she and Clytie
had learned to catch and harness, and gave to your grandmother, bringing the letter voluntarily to your grandmother,
who (Judith) never called on anyone now, had no friends
now, doubtless knowing no more why she chose your grandmother to give the letter to than your grandmother knew; not
thin now but gaunt, the Sutpen skull showing indeed now

through the worn, the Coldfield, flesh, the face which had long since forgotten how to be young and yet absolutely impenetrable, absolutely serene: no mourning, not even grief, and your grandmother saying, 'Me? You want me to keep it?'

" 'Yes,' Judith said. 'Or destroy it. As you like. Read it if you like or dont read it if you like. Because you make so little impression, you see. You get born and you try this and you dont know why only you keep on trying it and you are born at the same time with a lot of other people, all mixed up with them, like trying to, having to, move your arms and legs with strings only the same strings are hitched to all the other arms and legs and the others all trying and they dont know why either except that the strings are all in one another's way like five or six people all trying to make a rug on the same loom only each one wants to weave his own pattern into the rug; and it cant matter, you know that, or the Ones that set up the loom would have arranged things a little better, and yet it must matter because you keep on trying or having to keep on trying and then all of a sudden it's all over and all you have left is a block of stone with scratches on it provided there was someone to remember to have the marble scratched and set up or had time to, and it rains on it and the sun shines on it and after a while they dont even remember the name and what the scratches were trying to tell, and it doesn't matter. And so maybe if you could go to someone, the stranger the better, and give them something—a scrap of paper— something, anything, it not to mean anything in itself and them not even to read it or keep it, not even bother to throw it away or destroy it, at least it would be something just because it would have happened, be remembered even if only from passing from one hand to another, one mind to another, and it would be at least a scratch, something, something that might make a mark on something that *was* once for the reason that it can die someday, while the block of stone cant be *is* because it never can become *was* because it cant ever die or perish. . . . . . .' and your grandmother watching her, the impenetrable, the calm, the absolutely serene face, and crying:

" 'No! No! Not that! Think of your——' and the face watching her, comprehending, still serene, not even bitter:

" 'Oh. I? No, not that. Because somebody will have to take

care of Clytie, and Father too soon, who will want something
to eat after he comes home because it wont last much longer
since they have begun to shoot one another now. No. Not
that. Women dont do that for love. I dont even believe that
men do. And not now, anyway. Because there wouldn't be
any room now, for them to go to, wherever it is, if it is. It
would be full already. Glutted. Like a theatre, an opera house,
if what you expect to find is forgetting, diversion, entertainment; like a bed already too full if what you want to find is a
chance to lie still and sleep and sleep and sleep'——" Mr
Compson moved. Half rising, Quentin took the letter from
him and beneath the dim bug-fouled globe opened it, carefully, as though the sheet, the desiccated square, were not the
paper but the intact ash of its former shape and substance:
and meanwhile Mr Compson's voice speaking on while
Quentin heard it without listening: "Now you can see why I
said that he loved her. Because there were other letters, many
of them, gallant flowery indolent frequent and insincere, sent
by hand over that forty miles between Oxford and Jefferson
after that first Christmas—the metropolitan gallant's idle and
delicately flattering (and doubtless to him, meaningless) gesture to the bucolic maiden—and that bucolic maiden, with
that profound and absolutely inexplicable tranquil patient
clairvoyance of women against which that metropolitan gallant's foppish posturing was just the jackanape antics of a
small boy, receiving the letters without understanding them,
not even keeping them, for all their elegant and gallant and
tediously contrived turns of form and metaphor, until the
next one arrived. But keeping this one which must have
reached her out of a clear sky after an interval of four years,
considering this one worthy to give to a stranger to keep or
not to keep, even to read or not to read as the stranger saw
fit, to make that scratch, that undying mark on the blank face
of the oblivion to which we are all doomed, of which she
spoke——"; Quentin hearing without having to listen as he
read the faint spidery script not like something impressed
upon the paper by a once-living hand but like a shadow cast
upon it which had resolved on the paper the instant before he
looked at it and which might fade, vanish, at any instant while
he still did: the dead tongue speaking after the four years and

then after almost fifty more, gentle sardonic whimsical and
incurably pessimistic, without date or salutation or signature:

*You will notice how I insult neither of us by claiming this to be a
voice from the defeated even, let alone from the dead. In fact, if
I were a philosopher I should deduce and derive a curious and
apt commentary on the times and augur of the future from this
letter which you now hold in your hands—a sheet of notepaper
with, as you can see, the best of French watermarks dated seventy years ago, salvaged (stolen if you will) from the gutted
mansion of a ruined aristocrat; and written upon in the best of
stove polish manufactured not twelve months ago in a New England factory. Yes. Stove polish. We captured it: a story in itself.
Imagine us, an assortment of homogeneous scarecrows, I wont
say hungry because to a woman, lady or female either, below
Mason's and Dixon's in this year of grace 1865, that word
would be sheer redundancy, like saying that we were breathing.
And I wont say ragged or even shoeless, since we have been both
long enough to have grown accustomed to it, only, thank God
(and this restores my faith not in human nature perhaps but at
least in man) that he really does not become inured to hardship
and privation: it is only the mind, the gross omnivorous carrion-
heavy soul which becomes inured; the body itself, thank God,
never reconciled from the old soft feel of soap and clean linen and
something between the sole of the foot and the earth to distinguish it from the foot of a beast. So say we merely needed ammunition. And imagine us, the scarecrows with one of those
concocted plans of scarecrow desperation which not only must but
do work, for the reason that there is absolutely no room for alternative before man or heaven, no niche on earth or under it for
failure to find space either to pause or breathe or be graved and
sepulchred; and we (the scarecrows) bringing it off with a great
deal of elan, not to say noise; imagine, I say, the prey and prize,
the ten plump defenceless sutlers' wagons, the scarecrows tumbling out box after beautiful box after beautiful box stencilled
each with that U. and that S. which for four years now has been
to us the symbol of the spoils which belong to the vanquished, of
the loaves and the fishes as was once the incandescent Brow, the
shining nimbus of the Thorny Crown; and the scarecrows clawing at the boxes with stones and bayonets and even with bare*

hands and opening them at last and finding—What? Stove polish. Gallons and gallons and gallons of the best stove polish, not a box of it a year old yet and doubtless still trying to overtake General Sherman with some belated amended field order requiring him to polish the stove before firing the house. How we laughed. Yes, we laughed, because I have learned this at least during these four years: that it really requires an empty stomach to laugh with, that only when you are hungry or frightened do you extract some ultimate essence out of laughing just as the empty stomach extracts the ultimate essence out of alcohol. But at least we have stove polish. We have plenty of it. We have too much, because it does not take much to say what I have to say, as you can see. And so the conclusion and augury which I draw, even though no philosopher, is this.

We have waited long enough. You will notice how I do not insult you either by saying I have waited long enough. And therefore, since I do not insult you by saying that only I have waited, I do not add, expect me. Because I cannot say when to expect me. Because what WAS is one thing, and now it is not because it is dead, it died in 1861, and therefore what IS—— (There. They have started firing again. Which—to mention it—is redundancy too, like the breathing or the need of ammunition. Because sometimes I think it has never stopped. It hasn't stopped of course; I dont mean that. I mean, there has never been any more of it, that there was that one fusillade four years ago which sounded once and then was arrested, mesmerised raised muzzle by raised muzzle, in the frozen attitude of its own aghast amazement and never repeated and it now only the loud aghast echo jarred by the dropped musket of a weary sentry or by the fall of the spent body itself, out of the air which lies over the land where that fusillade first sounded and where it must remain yet because no other space under heaven will receive it. So that means that it is dawn again and that I must stop. Stop what? you will say. Why, thinking, remembering—remark that I do not say, hoping—; to become once more for a period without boundaries or location in time, mindless and irrational companion and inmate of a body which, even after four years, with a sort of dismal and incorruptible fidelity which is incredibly admirable to me, is still immersed and obliviously bemused in

recollections of old peace and contentment the very names of
whose scents and sounds I do not know that I remember, which
ignores even the presence and threat of a torn arm or leg as
though through some secretly incurred and infallible promise
and conviction of immortality. ——*But to finish.) I cannot say*
when to expect me. Because what IS is something else again
because it was not even alive then. And since because within this
sheet of paper you now hold the best of the old South which is
dead, and the words you read were written upon it with the best
(each box said, the very best) of the new North which has con-
quered and which therefore, whether it likes it or not, will have
to survive, I now believe that you and I are, strangely enough,
included among those who are doomed to live.

"And that's all," Mr Compson said. "She received it and
she and Clytie made the wedding gown and the veil from
scraps—perhaps scraps intended for, which should have gone
for, lint and did not. She didn't know when he would come
because he didn't know himself: and maybe he told Henry,
showed Henry the letter before he sent it, and maybe he did
not; maybe still just the watching and the waiting, the one
saying to Henry *I have waited long enough* and Henry saying
to the other *Do you renounce then? Do you renounce?* and the
other saying *I do not renounce. For four years now I have given
chance the opportunity to renounce for me, but it seems that I am
doomed to live, that she and I both are doomed to live;*—the defiance and the ultimatum delivered beside a bivouac fire, the
ultimatum discharged before the gate to which the two of
them must have ridden side by side almost: the one calm and
undeviating, perhaps unresisting even, the fatalist to the last;
the other remorseless with implacable and unalterable grief
and despair——" (It seemed to Quentin that he could actually see them, facing one another at the gate. Inside the gate
what was once a park now spread, unkempt, in shaggy desolation, with an air dreamy remote and aghast like the unshaven face of a man just waking from ether, up to a huge
house where a young girl waited in a wedding dress made
from stolen scraps, the house partaking too of that air of scaling desolation, not having suffered from invasion but a shell
marooned and forgotten in a backwater of catastrophe—a

skeleton giving of itself in slow driblets of furniture and carpet, linen and silver, to help to die torn and anguished men who knew, even while dying, that for months now the sacrifice and the anguish were in vain. They faced one another on the two gaunt horses, two men, young, not yet in the world, not yet breathed over long enough, to be old but with old eyes, with unkempt hair and faces gaunt and weathered as if cast by some spartan and even niggard hand from bronze, in worn and patched gray weathered now to the color of dead leaves, the one with the tarnished braid of an officer, the other plain of cuff, the pistol lying yet across the saddle bow unaimed, the two faces calm, the voices not even raised: *Dont you pass the shadow of this post, this branch, Charles;* and *I am going to pass it, Henry*) "——and then Wash Jones sitting that saddleless mule before Miss Rosa's gate, shouting her name into the sunny and peaceful quiet of the street, saying, 'Air you Rosie Coldfield? Then you better come on out yon. Henry has done shot that durn French feller. Kilt him dead as a beef.' "

V.

So they will have told you doubtless already how I told that Jones to take that mule which was not his around to the barn and harness it to our buggy while I put on my hat and shawl and locked the house. That was all I needed to do since they will have told you doubtless that I would have had no need for either trunk or bag since what clothing I possessed, now that the garments which I had been fortunate enough to inherit from my aunt's kindness or haste or oversight were long since worn out, consisted of the ones which Ellen had remembered from time to time to give me and now Ellen these two years dead; that I had only to lock the house and take my place in the buggy and traverse those twelve miles which I had not done since Ellen died, beside that brute who until Ellen died was not even permitted to approach the house from the front —that brute progenitor of brutes whose granddaughter was to supplant me, if not in my sister's house at least in my sister's bed to which (so they will tell you) I aspired —that brute who (brute instrument of that justice which presides over human events which, incept in the individual, runs smooth, less claw than velvet: but which, by man or woman flouted, drives on like fiery steel and overrides both weakly just and unjust strong, both vanquisher and innocent victimised, ruthless for appointed right and truth) brute who was not only to preside upon the various shapes and avatars of Thomas Sutpen's devil's fate but was to provide at the last the female flesh in which his name and lineage should be sepulchred — that brute who appeared to believe that he had served and performed his appointed end by yelling of blood and pistols in the street before my house, who seemed to believe that what further information he might have given me was too scant or too bland and free of moment to warrant the discarding of his tobacco cud, because during the entire subsequent twelve miles he could not even tell me what had happened.

And how I traversed those same twelve miles once more after the two years since Ellen died (or was it the four years since Henry vanished or was it the nineteen years since I saw light and breathed?) knowing nothing, able to learn nothing save this: a shot heard, faint and far away and even direction and source indeterminate, by two women, two young women alone in a rotting house where no man's footstep had sounded in two years—a shot, then an interval of aghast surmise above the cloth and needles which engaged them, then feet, in the hall and then on the stairs, running, hurrying, the feet of a man: and Judith with just time to snatch up the unfinished dress and hold it before her as the door burst open upon her brother, the wild murderer whom she had not seen in four years and whom she believed to be (if he was, still lived and breathed at all) a thousand miles away: and then the two of them, the two accursed children on whom the first blow of their devil's heritage had but that moment fallen, looking at one an-other across the up-raised and unfinished wedding dress. Twelve miles toward that I rode, beside an animal who could stand in the street before my house and bellow placidly to the populous and listening solitude that my nephew had just murdered his sister's fiance, yet who could not permit himself to force the mule which drew us beyond a walk because 'hit warn't none of mine nor hisn neither and besides hit aint had a decent bait of vittles since the corn give out in February'; who, turning into the actual gate at last, must stop the mule and, pointing with the whip and spitting first, say 'Hit was right yonder.'—'What was right there, fool?' I cried, and he: 'Hit was' until I took the whip from him into my own hand and struck the mule.

But they cannot tell you how I went on up the drive, past Ellen's ruined and weed-choked flower beds and reached the house, the shell, the (so I thought) cocoon-casket marriage-bed of youth and grief and found that I had come, not too late as I had thought, but come too soon. Rotting portico and scaling walls, it stood, not ravaged, not invaded, marked by no bullet nor soldier's iron heel but rather as though reserved for something more: some desolation more profound than ruin, as if it had stood in iron juxtaposition to iron flame, to a holocaust which had found itself less fierce and less implacable, not hurled but rather fallen back before the impervious and indomitable skeleton which the flames durst not, at the in-stant's final crisis, assail; there was even one step, one plank rotted free and tilting beneath the foot (or would have if I had not touched it light and fast) as I ran up and into the hallway whose carpet had long since gone with the bed- and table-linen for lint, and saw the Sutpen face and even as I cried 'Henry! Henry! What have you done? What has that fool been trying to tell me?' realised that I had come, not too late as I had thought, but come too soon.

Because it was not Henry's face. It was Sutpen face enough, but not his; Sutpen coffee-colored face enough there in the dim light, barring the stairs: and I running out of the bright afternoon, into the thunderous silence of that brooding house where I could see nothing at first: then gradually the face, the Sutpen face not approaching, not swimming up out of the gloom, but already there, rocklike and firm and antedating time and house and doom and all, waiting there (oh yes, he chose well; he bettered choosing, who created in his own image the cold Cerberus of his private hell) — the face without sex or age because it had never possessed either: the same sphinx face which she had been born with, which had looked down from the loft that night beside Judith's and which she still wears now at seventy-four, looking at me with no change, no alteration in it at all, as though it had known to the second when I was to enter, had waited there during that entire twelve miles behind that walking mule and watched me draw nearer and nearer and enter the door at last as it had known (ay, perhaps decreed, since there is that justice whose Moloch's palate-paunch makes no distinction between gristle bone and tender flesh) that I should — the face stopping me dead (not my body: it still advanced, ran on: but I, myself, that deep existence which we lead, to which the movement of limbs is but a clumsy and belated accompanyment like so many unnecessary instruments played crudely and amateurishly out of time to the tune itself) in that barren hall with its naked stair (that carpet gone too) rising into the dim upper hallway where an echo spoke which was not mine but rather that of the lost irrevocable might-have-been which haunts all houses, all enclosed walls erected by human hands, not for shelter, not for warmth, but to hide from the world's curious looking and seeing the dark turnings which the ancient young delusions of pride and hope and ambition (ay, and love too) take. 'Judith!' I said. 'Judith!'

There was no answer. I had expected none; possibly even then I did not expect Judith to answer, just as a child, before the full instant of comprehended terror, calls on the parent whom it actually knows (this before the terror destroys all judgment whatever) is not even there to hear it. I was crying not to someone, something, but (trying to cry) through something, through that force, that furious yet absolutely rocklike and immobile antagonism which had stopped me — that presence, that familiar coffee-colored face, that body (the bare coffee-colored feet motionless on the bare floor, the curve of the stair rising just beyond her) no larger than my own which, without moving, with no alteration of visual displacement whatever (she did not even remove her gaze from mine for the reason that she was not looking at me but through me, apparently still musing upon the open door's serene rectangle which I had broken) seemed to elongate and project upward something—not soul, not spirit, but something rather of a profoundly attentive and distracted listening to or for something which I myself could not hear and was not intended to hear—a brooding awareness and acceptance of the inexplicable unseen inherited from an older and a purer race than mine, which created postulated and shaped in the empty air between us that which I believed I had come to find (nay, which I must find, else breathing and standing there, I would have denied that I was ever born):—that bedroom long-closed and musty, that sheetless bed (that nuptial couch of love and grief) with the pale and bloody corpse in its patched and weath-ered gray crimsoning the bare mattress, the bowed and unwived widow kneeling beside it—and I (my body) not stopping yet (yes, it needed the hand, the touch, for that);—I, self-mesmered fool who still believed that what must be would be, could not but be, else I must deny sanity as well as breath, running, hurling myself into that inscrutable coffee-colored face, that cold implacable mind-less (no, not mindless: anything but mindless: his own clairvoyant will tempered to amoral evil's undeviating absolute by the black willing blood with which he had crossed it) replica of his own which he had created and decreed to preside upon his absence, as you might watch a wild distracted nightbound bird flutter into the brazen and fatal lamp. 'Wait,' she said. 'Dont you go up there.' Still I did not stop; it would require the hand; and I still running on, accomplishing those last few feet across which we seemed to glare at one another not as two faces but as the two abstract contradic-tions which we actually were, neither of our voices raised, as though we spoke to one another free of the limitations and restrictions of speech and hearing. 'What?' I said.

'Dont you go up there, Rosa.' That was how she said it: that quiet, that still, and again it was as though it had not been she who spoke but the house itself that said the words—the house which he had built, which some suppuration of himself had created about him as the sweat of his body might have created, produced some (even if invisible) cocoon-like and complementary shell in which

Ellen had had to live and die a stranger, in which Henry and Judith would have to be victims and prisoners, or die. Because it was not the name, the word, the fact that she had called me Rosa. As children she had called me that, just as she had called them Henry and Judith; I knew that even now she still called Judith (and Henry too when she spoke of him) by her given name. And she might very naturally have called me Rosa still, since to every- one else whom I knew I was still a child. But it was not that. That was not what she meant at all; in fact, during that instant while we stood face to face (that instant before my still advancing body should brush past her and reach the stair) she did me more grace and respect than anyone else I knew; I knew that from the instant I had entered that door, to her of all who knew me I was no child. 'Rosa?' I cried. 'To me? To my face?' Then she touched me, and then I did stop dead. Possibly even then my body did not stop, since I seemed to be aware of it thrusting blindly still against the solid yet imponderable weight (she not owner: instrument; I still say that) of that will to bar me from the stairs; possibly the sound of the other voice, the single word spoken from the stair-head above us, had already broken and parted us before it (my body) had even paused. I do not know. I know only that my entire being seemed to run at blind full tilt into something monstrous and immobile, with a shocking impact too soon and too quick to be mere amazement and outrage at that black arresting and untimorous hand on my white woman's flesh. Because there is something in the touch of flesh with flesh which abrogates, cuts sharp and straight across the devious intricate channels of decorous ordering, which enemies as well as lovers know because it makes them both: —touch and touch of that which is the citadel of the central I-Am's private own: not spirit, soul; the liquorish and ungirdled mind is anyone's to take in any darkened hallway of this earthly tenement. But let flesh touch with flesh, and watch the fall of all the eggshell shibboleth of caste and color too. Yes, I stopped dead —no woman's hand, no negro's hand, but bitted bridle-curb to check and guide the furious and unbending will—I crying not to her, to it; speaking to it through the negro, the woman, only because of the shock which was not yet outrage because it would be terror soon, expecting and receiving no answer because we both knew it was not to her I spoke: 'Take your hand off me, nigger!'

I got none. We just stood there—I motionless in the attitude and action of running, she rigid in that furious immobility, the two of us joined by that hand and arm which held us, like a fierce rigid umbilical cord, twin sistered to the fell darkness which had produced her. As a child I had more than once watched her and Judith and even Henry scuffling in the rough games which they (possibly all children; I do not know) played, and (so I have heard) she and Judith even slept together, in the same room but with Judith in the bed and she on a pallet on the floor ostensibly. But I have heard how on more than one occasion Ellen has found them both on the pallet, and once in the bed together. But not I. Even as a child, I would not even play with the same objects which she and Judith played with, as though that warped and spartan solitude which I called my childhood, which had taught me (and little else) to listen before I could comprehend and to understand before I even heard, had also taught me not only to instinctively fear her and what she was, but to shun the very objects which she had touched. We stood there so. And then suddenly it was not outrage that I waited for, out of which I had instinctively cried; it was not terror: it was some cumulative over-reach of despair itself. I remember how as we stood there joined by that volitionless (yes: it too sentient victim just as she and I were) hand, I cried—perhaps not aloud, not with words (and not to Judith, mind: perhaps I knew already, on the instant I entered the house and saw that face which was at once both more and less than Sutpen, perhaps I knew even then what I could not, would not, must not believe) —I cried 'And you too? And you too, sister, sister?' What did I expect? I, self-mesmered fool, come twelve miles expecting—what? Henry perhaps, to emerge from some door which knew his touch, his hand on the knob, the weight of his foot on a sill which knew that weight: and so to find standing in the hall a small plain frightened creature whom neither man nor woman had ever looked at twice, whom he had not seen himself in four years and seldom enough before that but whom he would recognise if only because of the worn brown silk which had once become his mother and because the creature stood there calling him by his given name? Henry to emerge and say 'Why, it's Rosa, Aunt Rosa. Wake up, Aunt Rosa; wake up'?—I, the dreamer clinging yet to the dream as the patient clings to the last thin unbearable ecstatic instant of agony in order to sharpen the savor of the pain's surcease, waking into the reality, the more than reality, not to the unchanged and unaltered

*old time but into a time altered to fit the dream which, conjunctive
with the dreamer, becomes immolated and apotheosized: 'Mother
and Judith are in the nursery with the children, and Father and
Charles are walking in the garden. Wake up, Aunt Rosa; wake
up'? Or not expect perhaps, not even hope; not even dream since
dreams dont come in pairs, and had I not come twelve miles drawn
not by mortal mule but by some chimaera-foal of nightmare's very
self? (Ay, wake up, Rosa; wake up—not from what was, what
used to be, but from what had not, could not have ever, been;
wake, Rosa—not to what should, what might have been, but to
what cannot, what must not, be; wake, Rosa, from the hoping,
who did believe there is a seemliness to bereavement even though
grief be absent; believed there would be need for you to save not
love perhaps, not happiness nor peace, but what was left behind by
widowing—and found that there was nothing there to save; who
hoped to save her as you promised Ellen (not Charles Bon, not
Henry: not either one of these from him or even from one another)
and now too late, who would have been too late if you had come
there from the womb or had been there already at the full strong
capable mortal peak when she was born; who came twelve miles
and nineteen years to save what did not need the saving, and lost
instead yourself) I do not know, except that I did not find it. I
found only that dream-state in which you run without moving
from a terror in which you can not believe, toward a safety in
which you have no faith, held so not by the shifting and foundationless quicksand of nightmare but by a face which was its soul's
own inquisitor, a hand which was the agent of its own crucifixion,
until the voice parted us, broke the spell. It said one word: 'Clytie.'
like that, that cold, that still: not Judith, but the house itself speaking again, though it was Judith's voice. Oh, I knew it well, who
had believed in grieving's seemliness; I knew it as well as she—
Clytie—knew it. She did not move; it was only the hand, the
hand gone before I realised that it had been removed. I do not
know if she removed it or if I ran out from beneath its touch. But
it was gone; and this too they cannot tell you: How I ran, fled, up
the stairs and found no grieving widowed bride but Judith standing before the closed door to that chamber, in the gingham dress
which she had worn each time I had seen her since Ellen died,
holding something in one hanging hand; and if there had been
grief or anguish she had put them too away, complete or not*

*complete I do not know, along with that unfinished wedding dress.
'Yes, Rosa?' she said, like that again, and I stopped in running's
midstride again though my body, blind unsentient barrow of deluded clay and breath, still advanced: And how I saw that what
she held in that lax and negligent hand was the photograph, the
picture of herself in its metal case which she had given him, held
casual and forgotten against her flank as any interrupted pastime
book.*

*That's what I found. Perhaps it's what I expected, knew (even
at nineteen knew, I would say if it were not for my nineteen, my
own particular kind of nineteen years) that I should find. Perhaps
I couldn't even have wanted more than that, couldn't have accepted less, who even at nineteen must have known that living is
one constant and perpetual instant when the arras-veil before
what-is-to-be hangs docile and even glad to the lightest naked
thrust if we had dared, were brave enough (not wise enough: no
wisdom needed here) to make the rending gash. Or perhaps it is no
lack of courage either: not cowardice which will not face that sickness somewhere at the prime foundation of this factual scheme from
which the prisoner soul, miasmal-distillant, wroils ever upward
sunward, tugs its tenuous prisoner arteries and veins and prison-
ing in its turn that spark, that dream which, as the globy and
complete instant of its freedom mirrors and repeats (repeats? creates, reduces to a fragile evanescent iridescent sphere) all of space
and time and massy earth, relicts the seething and anonymous
miasmal mass which in all the years of time has taught itself no
boon of death but only how to recreate, renew; and dies, is gone,
vanished: nothing—but is that true wisdom which can comprehend that there is a might-have-been which is more true than
truth, from which the dreamer, waking, says not 'Did I but
dream?' but rather says, indicts high heaven's very self with: 'Why
did I wake since waking I shall never sleep again?'*

*Once there was—Do you mark how the wistaria, sun-impacted
on this wall here, distills and penetrates this room as though (light-
unimpeded) by secret and attritive progress from mote to mote of
obscurity's myriad components? That is the substance of remembering—sense, sight, smell: the muscles with which we see and hear
and feel—not mind, not thought: there is no such thing as memory: the brain recalls just what the muscles grope for: no more, no
less: and its resultant sum is usually incorrect and false and worthy*

only of the name of dream. —See how the sleeping outflung hand, touching the bedside candle, remembers pain, springs back and free while mind and brain sleep on and only make of this adjacent heat some trashy myth of reality's escape: or that same sleeping hand, in sensuous marriage with some dulcet surface, is transformed by that same sleeping brain and mind into that same figment-stuff warped out of all experience. Ay, grief goes, fades; we know that— but ask the tear ducts if they have forgotten how to weep. —Once there was (they cannot have told you this either) a summer of wistaria. It was a pervading everywhere of wistaria (I was fourteen then) as though of all springs yet to capitulate condensed into one spring, one summer: the spring and summertime which is every female's who breathed above dust, beholden of all betrayed springs held over from all irrevocable time, repercussed, bloomed again. It was a vintage year of wistaria: vintage year being that sweet conjunction of root bloom and urge and hour and weather; and I (I was fourteen)—I will not insist on bloom, at whom no man had yet to look—nor would ever—twice, as not as child but less than even child; as not more child than woman but even as less than any female flesh. Nor do I say leaf—warped bitter pale and crimped half-fledging intimidate of any claim to green which might have drawn to it the tender mayfly childhood sweetheart games or given pause to the male predacious wasps and bees of later lust. But root and urge I do insist and claim, for had I not heired too from all the unsistered Eves since the Snake? Yes, urge I do: warped chrysalis of what blind perfect seed: for who shall say what gnarled forgotten root might not bloom yet with some globed concentrate more globed and concentrate and heady-perfect because the neglected root was planted warped and lay not dead but merely slept forgot?

That was the miscast summer of my barren youth which (for that short time, that short brief unreturning springtime of the female heart) I lived out not as a woman, a girl, but rather as the man which I perhaps should have been. I was fourteen then, fourteen in years if they could have been called years while in that unpaced corridor which I called childhood, which was not living but rather some projection of the lightless womb itself; I gestate and complete, not aged, just overdue because of some caesarean lack, some cold head-nuzzling forceps of the savage time which should have torn me free, I waited not for light but for that doom which we call female victory which is: endure and then endure, without rhyme or reason or hope of reward—and then endure; I like that blind subterranean fish, that insulated spark whose origin the fish no longer remembers, which pulses and beats at its crepuscular and lethargic tenement with the old unsleeping itch which has no words to speak with other than 'This was called light', that 'smell', that 'touch', that other something which has bequeathed not even name for sound of bee or bird or flower's scent or light or sun or love;—yes, not even growing and developing, beloved by and loving light, but equipped only with that cunning, that inverted canker-growth of solitude which substitutes the omnivorous and unrational hearing-sense for all the others: so that instead of accomplishing the processional and measured milestones of the normal childhood's time I lurked, unapprehended as though, shod with the very damp and velvet silence of the womb, I displaced no air, gave off no betraying sound, from one closed forbidden door to the next and so acquired all I knew of that light and space in which people moved and breathed as I (that same child) might have gained conception of the sun from seeing it through a piece of smoky glass;—fourteen, four years younger than Judith, four years later than Judith's moment which only virgins know: when the entire delicate spirit's bent is one anonymous climaxless epicene and unravished nuptial—not that widowed and nightly violation by the inescapable and scornful dead which is the meed of twenty and thirty and forty, but a world filled with living marriage like the light and air which she breathes. But it was no summer of a virgin's itching discontent; no summer's caesarean lack which should have torn me, dead flesh or even embryo, from the living: or else, by friction's ravishing of the male-furrowed meat, also weaponed and panoplied as a man instead of hollow woman.

It was the summer after that first Christmas that Henry brought him home, the summer following the two days of that June vacation which he spent at Sutpen's Hundred before he rode on to the River to take the steamboat home, that summer after my aunt left and papa had to go away on business and I was sent out to Ellen (possibly my father chose Ellen as a refuge for me because at that time Thomas Sutpen was also absent) to stay so that she could take care of me, who had been born too late, born into some curious disjoint of my father's life and left on his (now twice) widowed hands, I competent enough to reach a kitchen shelf, count spoons

and hem a sheet and measure milk into a churn yet good for noth-
ing else, yet still too valuable to be left alone. I had never seen him
(I never saw him. I never even saw him dead. I heard a name, I
saw a photograph, I helped to make a grave: and that was all)
though he had been in my house once, that first New Year's Day
when Henry brought him from nephew duty to speak to me on
their way back to school and I was not at home. Until then I had
not even heard his name, did not know that he existed. Yet on the
day when I went out there to stay that summer, it was as though
that casual pause at my door had left some seed, some minute
virulence in this cellar earth of mine quick not for love perhaps (I
did not love him; how could I? I had never even heard his voice,
had only Ellen's word for it that there was such a person) and
quick not for the spying which you will doubtless call it, which
during the past six months between that New Year's and that
June gave substance to that shadow with a name emerging from
Ellen's vain and garrulous folly, that shape without even a face yet
because I had not even seen the photograph then, reflected in the
secret and bemused gaze of a young girl: because I who had
learned nothing of love, not even parents' love —that fond dear
constant violation of privacy, that stultification of the burgeoning
and incorrigible I which is the meed and due of all mammalian
meat, became not mistress, not beloved, but more than even love; I
became all polymath love's androgynous advocate.

There must have been some seed he left, to cause a child's vacant
fairy-tale to come alive in that garden. Because I was not spying
when I would follow her. I was not spying, though you will say I
was. And even if it was spying, it was not jealousy, because I did
not love him. (How could I have, when I had never seen him?)
And even if I did, not as women love, as Judith loved him, or as we
thought she did. If it was love (and I still say, How could it be?) it
was the way that mothers love when, punishing the child she strikes
not it but through it strikes the neighbor boy whom it has just
whipped or been whipped by; caresses not the rewarded child but
rather the nameless man or woman who gave the palm-sweated
penny. But not as women love. Because I asked nothing of him, you
see. And more than that: I gave him nothing, which is the sum of
loving. Why, I didn't even miss him. I dont know even now if I
was ever aware that I had seen nothing of his face but that photo-
graph, that shadow, that picture in a young girl's bedroom: a

*picture casual and framed upon a littered dressing table yet bow-
ered and dressed (or so I thought) with all the maiden and invisible lily-roses, because even before I saw the photograph I could have
recognised, nay, described, the very face. But I never saw it. I do
not even know of my own knowledge that Ellen ever saw it, that
Judith ever loved it, that Henry slew it: so who will dispute me
when I say, Why did I not invent, create it?—And I know this: if
I were God I would invent out of this seething turmoil we call
progress something (a machine perhaps) which would adorn the
barren mirror altars of every plain girl who breathes with such as
this—which is so little since we want so little—this pictured face.
It would not even need a skull behind it; almost anonymous, it
would only need vague inference of some walking flesh and blood
desired by someone else even if only in some shadow-realm of make-
believe.—A picture seen by stealth, by creeping (my childhood
taught me that instead of love and it stood me in good stead; in
fact, if it had taught me love, love could not have stood me so) into
the deserted midday room to look at it. Not to dream, since I dwelt
in the dream, but to renew, rehearse, the part as the faulty though
eager amateur might steal wingward in some interim of the visible
scene to hear the prompter's momentary voice. And if jealousy, not
man's jealousy, the jealousy of the lover; not even the lover's self
who spies from love, who spies to watch, taste, touch that maiden
revery of solitude which is the first thinning of that veil we call
virginity; not to spring out, force that shame which is such a part
of love's declaring, but to gloat upon the rich instantaneous bosom
already rosy with the flushy sleep though shame itself does not yet
need to wake. No, it was not that; I was not spying, who would
walk those raked and sanded garden paths and think 'This print
was his save for this obliterating rake, that even despite the rake it
is still there and hers beside it in that slow and mutual rhythm
wherein the heart, the mind, does not need to watch the docile (ay,
the willing) feet'; would think 'What suspiration of the twinning
souls have the murmurous myriad ears of this secluded vine or
shrub listened to? what vow, what promise, what rapt biding fire
has the lilac rain of this wistaria, this heavy rose's dissolution,
crowned?' But best of all, better far than this, the actual living
and the dreamy flesh itself. Oh no, I was not spying while I
dreamed in the lurking harborage of my own shrub or vine as I
believed she dreamed upon the nooky seat which held invisible im-*

*print of his absent thighs just as the obliterating sand, the million
finger-nerves of frond and leaf, the very sun and moony constellations which had looked down at him, the circumambient air, held
somewhere yet his foot, his passing shape, his face, his speaking
voice, his name: Charles Bon, Charles Good, Charles Husband-
soon-to-be. No, not spying, not even hiding, who was child enough
not to need to hide, whose presence would have been no violation
even though he sat with her, yet woman enough to have gone to
her entitled to be received (perhaps with pleasure, gratitude) into
that maiden shameless confidence where young girls talk of love —
Yes, child enough to go to her and say 'Let me sleep with you';
woman enough to say 'Let us lie in bed together while you tell me
what love is', yet who did not do it because I should have had to say
'Dont talk to me of love but let me tell you, who know already
more of love than you will ever know or need.' Then my father
returned and came for me and took me home and I became again
that nondescript too long a child yet too short a woman, in the
fitless garments which my aunt had left behind, keeping a fitless
house, who was not spying, hiding, but waiting, watching, for no
reward, no thanks, who did not love him in the sense we mean it
because there is no love of that sort without hope; who (if it were
love) loved with that sort beyond the compass of glib books: that love
which gives up what it never had — that penny's modicum which is
the donor's all yet whose infinitesimal weight adds nothing to the
substance of the loved — and yet I gave it. And not to him, to her;
it was as though I said to her, 'Here, take this too. You cannot love
him as he should be loved, and though he will no more feel this
giving's weight than he would ever know its lack, yet there may
come some moment in your married lives when he will find this
atom's particle as you might find a cramped small pallid hidden
shoot in a familiar flower bed and pause and say, "Where did this
come from?"; you need only answer, "I dont know." ' And then I
went back home and stayed five years, heard an echoed shot, ran
up a nightmare flight of stairs, and found —*

*Why, a woman standing calmly in a gingham dress before a
closed door which she would not allow me to enter — a woman more
strange to me than to any grief for being so less its partner — a
woman saying 'Yes, Rosa?' calmly into the midstride of my running which (I know it now) had begun five years ago, since he had
been in my house too and had left no more trace than he had left*

*in Ellen's, where he had been but a shape, a shadow: not of a man,
a being, but of some esoteric piece of furniture—vase or chair or
desk—which Ellen wanted, as though his very impression (or lack
of it) on Coldfield or Sutpen walls held portentous prophecy of what
was to be;—Yes, running out of that first year (that year before
the War) during which Ellen talked to me of trousseau (and it my
trousseau), of all the dreamy panoply of surrender which was my
surrender, who had so little to surrender that it was all I had
because there is that might-have-been which is the single rock we
cling to above the maelstrom of unbearable reality;—the four
years while I believed she waited as I waited, while the stable world
we had been taught to know dissolved in fire and smoke until peace
and security were gone, and pride and hope, and there was left
only maimed honor's veterans, and love. Yes, there should, there
must, be love and faith: these left with us by fathers, husbands,
sweethearts, brothers, who carried the pride and the hope of peace
in honor's vanguard as they did the flags; there must be these, else
what do men fight for? what else worth dying for? Yes, dying not
for honor's empty sake, nor pride nor even peace, but for that love
and faith they left behind. Because he was to die; I know that,
knew that, as both pride and peace were: else how to prove love's
immortality? But not love, not faith itself, themselves. Love without
hope perhaps, faith with little to be proud with: but love and faith
at least above the murdering and the folly, to salvage at least from
the humbled indicted dust something anyway of the old lost en-
chantment of the heart.—Yes, found her standing before that
closed door which I was not to enter (and which she herself did not
enter again to my knowledge until Jones and the other man carried the coffin up the stairs) with the photograph hanging at her
side and her face absolutely calm, looking at me for a moment and
just raising her voice enough to be heard in the hall below: 'Clytie.
Miss Rosa will be here for dinner; you had better get out some
more meal': then 'Shall we go down stairs? I will have to speak to
Mr Jones about some planks and nails.'*

*That was all. Or rather, not all, since there is no all, no finish;
it not the blow we suffer from but the tedious repercussive anti-
climax of it, the rubbishy aftermath to clear away from off the very
threshold of despair. You see, I never saw him. I never even saw
him dead. I heard an echo, but not the shot; I saw a closed door
but did not enter it: I remember how that afternoon when we*

carried the coffin from the house (Jones and another white man which he produced, exhumed, from somewhere made it of boards torn from the carriage house; I remember how while we ate the food which Judith —yes, Judith: the same face calm cold and tranquil above the stove —had cooked, ate it in the very room which he lay over, we could hear them hammering and sawing in the back yard, and how I saw Judith once, in a faded gingham sunbonnet to match the dress, giving them directions about making it; I remember how during all that slow and sunny afternoon they hammered and sawed right under the back parlor window —the slow, maddening rasp. rasp. rasp. of the saw, the flat deliberate hammer blows that seemed as though each would be the last but was not, repeated and resumed just when the dulled attenuation of the wearied nerves, stretched beyond all resiliency, relaxed to silence and then had to scream again: until at last I went out there (and saw Judith in the barnlot in a cloud of chickens, her apron cradled about the gathered eggs) and asked them why? why there? why must it be just there? and they both stopped long and more than long enough for Jones to turn and spit again and say, 'Because hit wouldn't be so fur to tote the box': and how before my very back was turned he —one of them —added further, out of some amazed and fumbling ratiocination of inertia, how 'Hit would be simpler yit to fetch him down and nail the planks around him, only maybe Missus Judy wouldn't like hit.') —I remember how as we carried him down the stairs and out to the waiting wagon I tried to take the full weight of the coffin to prove to myself that he was really in it. And I could not tell. I was one of his pall bearers, yet I could not, would not believe something which I knew could not but be so. Because I never saw him. You see? There are some things which happen to us which the intelligence and the senses refuse just as the stomach sometimes refuses what the palate has accepted but which digestion cannot compass —occurrences which stop us dead as though by some impalpable intervention, like a sheet of glass through which we watch all subsequent events transpire as though in a soundless vacuum, and fade, vanish; are gone, leaving us immobile, impotent, helpless; fixed, until we can die. That was I. I was there; something of me walked in measured cadence with the measured tread of Jones and his companion, and Theophilus Mc-Caslin who had heard the news somehow back in town, and Clytie as we bore the awkward and unmanageable box past the stair's close turning while Judith, following, steadied it from behind, and so down and out to the wagon; something of me helped to raise that which it could not have raised alone yet which it still could not believe, into the waiting wagon; something of me stood beside the gashy earth in the cedars' somber gloom and heard the clumsy knell of clods upon the wood and answered No when Judith at the grave's mounded end said, 'He was a Catholic. Do any of you all know how Catholics——' and Theophilus McCaslin said, 'Catholic be damned; he was a soldier. And I can pray for any Confedrit soldier' and then cried in his old man's shrill harsh loud cacophonous voice: 'Yaaaay, Forrest! Yaaaay, John Sartoris! Yaaaaaay!' And something walked with Judith and Clytie back across that sunset field and answered in some curious serene suspension to the serene quiet voice which talked of plowing corn and cutting winter wood, and in the lamplit kitchen helped this time to cook the meal and helped to eat it too within the room beyond whose ceiling he no longer lay, and went to bed (yes, took a candle from that firm untrembling hand and thought 'She did not even weep' and then in a lamp-gloomed mirror saw my own face and thought 'Nor did you either') within that house where he had sojourned for another brief (and this time final) space and left no trace of him, not even tears. Yes. One day he was not. Then he was. Then he was not. It was too short, too fast, too quick; six hours of a summer afternoon saw it all—a space too short to leave even the imprint of a body on a mattress, and blood can come from anywhere—if there was blood, since I never saw him. For all I was allowed to know, we had no corpse; we even had no murderer (we did not even speak of Henry that day, not one of us; I did not say—the aunt, the spinster—'Did he look well or ill?' I did not say one of the thousand trivial things with which the indomitable woman-blood ignores the man's world in which the blood kinsman shows the courage or cowardice, the folly or lust or fear, for which his fellows praise or crucify him) who came and crashed a door and cried his crime and vanished, who for the fact that he was still alive was just that much more shadowy than the abstraction which we had nailed into a box—a shot heard only by its echo, a strange gaunt half-wild horse, bridled and with empty saddle, the saddle bags containing a pistol, a worn clean shirt, a lump of iron-like bread, captured by a man four miles away and two days later while trying to force the crib door in his stable. Yes, more than that: he was absent, and he was; he returned, and he was not; three women put something into the earth and covered it, and he had never been.

Now you will ask me why I stayed there. I could say, I do not know, could give ten thousand paltry reasons, all untrue, and be believed:—that I stayed for food, who could have combed ditch-banks and weed-beds, made and worked a garden as well at my own home in town as here, not to speak of neighbors, friends whose alms I might have accepted, since necessity has a way of obliterating from our conduct various delicate scruples regarding honor and pride; that I stayed for shelter, who had a roof of my own in fee simple now indeed; or that I stayed for company, who at home could have had the company of neighbors who were at least of my own kind, who had known me all my life and even longer in the sense that they thought not only as I thought but as my forbears thought, while here I had for company one woman whom, for all she was blood kin to me, I did not understand and, if what my observation warranted me to believe was true, I did not wish to understand, and another who was so foreign to me and to all that I was that we might have been not only of different races (which we were), not only of different sexes (which we were not), but of different species, speaking no language which the other understood, the very simple words with which we were forced to adjust our days to one another being even less inferential of thought or intention than the sounds which a beast and a bird might make to each other. But I dont say any of these. I stayed there and waited for Thomas Sutpen to come home. Yes. You will say (or believe) that I waited even then to become engaged to him; if I said I did not, you would believe I lied. But I do say I did not. I waited for him exactly as Judith and Clytie waited for him: because now he was all we had, all that gave us any reason for continuing to exist, to eat food and sleep and wake and rise again: knowing that he would need us, knowing as we did (who knew him) that he would begin at once to salvage what was left of Sutpen's Hundred and restore it. Not that we would or did need him. (I had never for one instant thought of marriage, never for one instant imagined that he would look at me, see me, since he never had. You may believe me, because I shall make no bones to say so when the moment comes to tell you when I did think of it.) No. It did not even require the first day of the life we were to lead together to show us that we did not need him, had not the need for any man so long as Wash Jones

*lived or stayed there—I who had kept my father's house and he
alive for almost four years, Judith who had done the same out here,
and Clytie who could cut a cord of wood or run a furrow better (or
at least quicker) than Jones himself.—And this the sad fact, one of
the saddest: that weary tedium which the heart and spirit feel
when they no longer need that to whose need they (the spirit and
the heart) are necessary. No. We did not need him, not even vicar-
iously, who could not even join him in his furious (that almost mad
intention which he brought home with him, seemed to project, ra-
diate ahead of him before he even dismounted) desire to restore the
place to what it had been that he had sacrificed pity and gentleness
and love and all the soft virtues for—if he had ever had them to
sacrifice, felt their lack, desired them of others. Not even that. Neither Judith nor I wanted that. Perhaps it was because we did not
believe it could be done, but I think it was more than that: that we
now existed in an apathy which was almost peace, like that of the
blind unsentient earth itself which dreams after no flower's stalk
nor bud, envies not the airy musical solitude of the springing leaves
it nourishes.*

*So we waited for him. We led the busy eventless lives of three
nuns in a barren and poverty-stricken convent: the walls we had
were safe, impervious enough, even if it did not matter to the walls
whether we ate or not. And amicably, not as two white women and
a negress, not as three negroes or three whites, not even as three
women, but merely as three creatures who still possessed the need to
eat but took no pleasure in it, the need to sleep but from no joy in
weariness or regeneration, and in whom sex was some forgotten
atrophy like the rudimentary gills we call the tonsils or the still-
opposable thumbs for old climbing. We kept the house, what part of
it we lived in, used; we kept the room which Thomas Sutpen would
return to—not that one which he left, a husband, but the one to
which he should return a sonless widower, barren of that posterity
which he doubtless must have wanted who had gone to the trouble
and expense of getting children and housing them among imported
furniture beneath crystal chandeliers—just as we kept Henry's
room, as Judith and Clytie kept it that is, as if he had not run up
the stairs that summer afternoon and then run down again; we
grew and tended and harvested with our own hands the food we
ate, made and worked that garden just as we cooked and ate the
food which came out of it: with no distinction among the three of*

*us of age or color but just as to who could build this fire or stir this
pot or weed this bed or carry this apron full of corn to the mill for
meal with least cost to the general good in time or expense of other
duties. It was as though we were one being, interchangeable and
indiscriminate, which kept that garden growing, spun thread and
wove the cloth we wore, hunted and found and rendered the meagre ditch-side herbs to protect and guarantee what spartan compro-
mise we dared or had the time to make with illness, harried and
nagged that Jones into working the corn and cutting the wood
which was to be our winter's warmth and sustenance; —the three
of us, three women: I drafted by circumstance at too soon an age
into a pinch-penny housewifery which might have existed just as
well upon a lighthouse rock, which had not even taught me how to
cultivate a bed of flowers, let alone a kitchen garden, which had
taught me to look upon fuel and meat as something appearing by
its own volition in a woodbox or on a pantry shelf; Judith created
by circumstance (circumstance? a hundred years of careful nurtur-
ing, perhaps not by blood, not even Coldfield blood, but certainly by
the tradition in which Thomas Sutpen's ruthless will had carved a
niche) to pass through the soft insulated and unscathed cocoon
stages: bud, served prolific queen, then potent and soft-handed matriarch of old age's serene and well-lived content—Judith handicapped by what in me was a few years' ignorance but which in her
was ten generations of iron prohibition, who had not learned that
first principle of penury which is to scrimp and save for the sake of
scrimping and saving, who (and abetted by Clytie) would cook
twice what we could eat and three times what we could afford and
give it to anyone, any stranger in a land already beginning to fill
with straggling soldiers who stopped and asked for it; and (but
not least) Clytie. Clytie, not inept, anything but inept: perverse
inscrutable and paradox: free, yet incapable of freedom who had
never once called herself a slave, holding fidelity to none like the
indolent and solitary wolf or bear (yes, wild: half untamed black,
half Sutpen blood: and if 'untamed' be synonymous with 'wild',
then 'Sutpen' is the silent unsleeping viciousness of the tamer's lash)
whose false seeming holds it docile to fear's hand but which is not,
which if this be fidelity, fidelity only to the prime fixed principle of
its own savageness; —Clytie who in the very pigmentation of her
flesh represented that debacle which had brought Judith and me to
what we were and which had made of her (Clytie) that which she*

declined to be just as she had declined to be that from which its purpose had been to emancipate her, as though presiding aloof upon the new, she deliberately remained to represent to us the threatful portent of the old.

We were three strangers. I do not know what Clytie thought, what life she led which the food we raised and cooked in unison, the cloth we spun and wove together, nourished and sheltered. But I expected that because she and I were open, ay honorable, enemies. But I did not even know what Judith thought and felt. We slept in the same room, the three of us (this for more than to conserve the firewood which we had to carry in ourselves. We did it for safety. It was winter soon and already soldiers were beginning to come back—the stragglers, not all of them tramps, ruffians, but men who had risked and lost everything, suffered beyond endurance and had returned now to a ruined land, not the same men who had marched away but transformed—and this the worst, the ultimate degradation to which war brings the spirit, the soul—into the likeness of that man who abuses from very despair and pity the beloved wife or mistress who in his absence has been raped. We were afraid. We fed them; we gave them what and all we had and we would have assumed their wounds and left them whole again if we could. But we were afraid of them.), we waked and fulfilled the endless tedious obligations which the sheer holding to life and breath entailed; we would sit before the fire after supper, the three of us in that state where the very bones and muscles are too tired to rest, when the attenuated and invincible spirit has changed and shaped even hopelessness into the easy obliviousness of a worn garment, and talk, talk of a hundred things—the weary recurrent triviata of our daily lives, of a thousand things but not of one. We talked of him, Thomas Sutpen, of the end of the War (we could all see it now) and when he would return, of what he would do: how begin the Herculean task which we knew he would set himself, into which (oh yes, we knew this too) he would undoubtedly sweep us with the old ruthlessness whether we would or no; we talked of Henry, quietly—that normal useless impotent woman-worrying about the absent male—as to how he fared, if he were cold or hungry or not, just as we talked of his father, as if both they and we still lived in that time which that shot, those running mad feet, had put a period to and then obliterated, as though that afternoon had never been. But not once did we mention Charles Bon. There

*were two afternoons in the late fall when Judith was absent, re-
turning at supper time serene and calm. I did not ask and I did
not follow her, yet I knew and I knew that Clytie knew that she
had gone to clear that grave of dead leaves and the sere brown
refuse of the cedars—that mound vanishing slowly back into the
earth, beneath which we had buried nothing. No, there had been
no shot. That sound was merely the sharp and final clap-to of a
door between us and all that was, all that might have been—a
retroactive severance of the stream of event: a forever crystallised
instant in imponderable time accomplished by three weak yet indomitable women which, preceding the accomplished fact which we
declined, refused, robbed the brother of the prey, reft the murderer
of a victim for his very bullet. That was how we lived for seven
months. And then one afternoon in January Thomas Sutpen came
home; someone looked up from where we were preparing the garden
for another year's food and saw him riding up the drive. And then
one evening I became engaged to marry him.*

*It took me just three months. (Do you mind how I dont say he,
but I?) Yes, I, just three months, who for twenty years had looked
on him (when I did—had to—look) as an ogre, some beast out of
a tale to frighten children with; who had seen his own get upon my
dead sister's body already begin to destroy one another, yet who
must come to him like a whistled dog at that first opportunity, that
noon when he who had been seeing me for twenty years should first
raise his head and pause and look at me. Oh, I hold no brief for
myself who could (and would; ay, doubtless have already) give you
a thousand specious reasons good enough for women, ranging from
woman's natural inconsistency to the desire (or even hope) for possible wealth, position, or even the fear of dying manless which (so
they will doubtless tell you) old maids always have, or for revenge.
No. I hold no brief for me. I could have gone home and I did not.
Perhaps I should have gone home. But I did not. As Judith and
Clytie did, I stood there before the rotting portico and watched him
ride up on that gaunt and jaded horse on which he did not seem to
sit but rather seemed to project himself ahead like a mirage, in
some fierce dynamic rigidity of impatience which the gaunt horse,
the saddle, the boots, the leaf-colored and threadbare coat with its
tarnished and flapping braid containing the sentient though
nerveless shell, could not keep up with, which seemed to precede him
as he dismounted and out of which he said 'Well, daughter' and*

stooped and touched his beard to Judith's forehead, who had not, did not, move, who stood rigid and still and immobile of face, and within which they spoke four sentences, four sentences of simple direct words behind beneath above which I felt that same rapport of communal blood which I had sensed that day while Clytie held me from the stairs: 'Henry's not——?' 'No. He's not here.' —'Ah. And——?' 'Yes. Henry killed him.' and then burst into tears. Yes, burst, who had not wept yet, who had brought down the stairs that afternoon and worn ever since that cold calm face which had stopped me in midrunning at that closed door; yes, burst, as if that entire accumulation of seven months were erupting spontaneously from every pore in one incredible evacuation (she not moving, not moving a muscle) and then vanishing, disappearing as instantaneously as if the very fierce and arid aura which he had enclosed her in were drying the tears faster than they emerged: and still standing with his hands on her shoulders and looked at Clytie and said, 'Ah, Clytie' and then at me—the same face which I had last seen, only a little thinner, the same ruthless eyes, the hair grizzled a little now, and no recognition in the face at all until Judith said, 'It's Rosa. Aunt Rosa. She lives here now.'

That was all. He rode up the drive and into our lives again and left no ripple save those instantaneous and incredible tears. Because he himself was not there, not in the house where we spent our days, had not stopped there. The shell of him was there, using the room which we had kept for him and eating the food which we produced and prepared as if it could neither feel the softness of the bed nor make distinction between the viands either as to quality or taste. Yes. He wasn't there. Something ate with us; we talked to it and it answered questions; it sat with us before the fire at night and, rousing without any warning from some profound and bemused complete inertia, talked, not to us, the six ears, the three minds capable of listening, but to the air, the waiting grim decaying presence, spirit, of the house itself, talking that which sounded like the bombast of a madman who creates within his very coffin walls his fabulous immeasurable Camelots and Carcassonnes. Not absent from the place, the arbitrary square of earth which he had named Sutpen's Hundred: not that at all. He was absent only from the room, and that because he had to be elsewhere, a part of him encompassing each ruined field and fallen fence and crumbling wall of cabin or cotton house or crib; himself diffused and in solution held by that electric furious immobile urgency and awareness of short time and the need for haste as if he had just drawn breath and looked about and realised that he was old (he was fifty-nine) and was concerned (not afraid: concerned) not that old age might have left him impotent to do what he intended to do, but that he might not have time to do it in before he would have to die. We were right about what he would intend to do: that he would not even pause for breath before undertaking to restore his house and plantation as near as possible to what it had been. We did not know how he would go about it, nor I believe did he. He could not have known, who came home with nothing, to nothing, to four years less than nothing. But it did not stop him, intimidate him. His was that cold alert fury of the gambler who knows that he may lose anyway but that with a second's flagging of the fierce constant will he is sure to: and who keeps suspense from ever quite crystallising by sheer fierce manipulation of the cards or dice until the ducts and glands of luck begin to flow again. He did not pause, did not take that day or two to let the bones and flesh of fifty-nine recuperate—the day or two in which he might have talked, not about us and what we had been doing, but about himself, the past four years (for all he ever told us, there might not have been any war at all, or it on another planet and no stake of his risked on it, no flesh and blood of his to suffer by it)—that natural period during which bitter though unmaimed defeat might have exhausted itself to something like peace, like quiet in the raging and incredulous recounting (which enables man to bear with living) of that feather's balance between victory and disaster which makes that defeat unbearable which, turning against him, yet declined to slay him who, still alive, yet cannot bear to live with it.

We hardly ever saw him. He would be gone from dawn until dark, he and Jones and another man or two that he had got from somewhere and paid with something, perhaps the same coin in which he had paid that foreign architect—cajolery, promise, threat, and at last force. That was the winter when we began to learn what carpet-bagger meant and people—women—locked doors and windows at night and began to frighten each other with tales of negro uprisings, when the ruined, the four years' fallow and neglected land lay more idle yet while men with pistols in their pockets gathered daily at secret meeting places in the towns. He did not make one of these; I remember how one night a deputation

*called, rode out through the mud of early March and put him to
the point of definite yes or no, with them or against them, friend or
enemy: and he refused, declined, offered them (with no change of
gaunt ruthless face nor level voice) defiance if it was defiance they
wanted, telling them that if every man in the South would do as
he himself was doing, would see to the restoration of his own land,
the general land and South would save itself: and ushered them
from the room and from the house and stood plain in the doorway
holding the lamp above his head while their spokesman delivered
his ultimatum: 'This may be war, Sutpen', and answered, 'I am
used to it.' Oh yes, I watched him, watched his old man's solitary
fury fighting now not with the stubborn yet slowly tractable earth
as it had done before, but now against the ponderable weight of the
changed new time itself as though he were trying to dam a river
with his bare hands and a shingle: and this for the same spurious
delusion of reward which had failed (failed? betrayed: and would
this time destroy) him once; I see the analogy myself now: the accelerating circle's fatal curving course of his ruthless pride, his lust
for vain magnificence, though I did not then. And how could I?
turned twenty true enough yet still a child, still living in that
womb-like corridor where the world came not even as living echo
but as dead incomprehensible shadow, where with the quiet and
unalarmed amazement of a child I watched the miragy antics of
men and women—my father, my sister, Thomas Sutpen, Judith,
Henry, Charles Bon—called honor, principle, marriage, love, bereavement, death; the child who watching him was not a child but
one of that triumvirate mother-woman which we three, Judith
Clytie and I, made, which fed and clothed and warmed the static
shell and so gave vent and scope to the fierce vain illusion and so
said, 'At last my life is worth something, even though it only shields
and guards the antic fury of an insane child.' And then one afternoon (I was in the garden with a hoe, where the path came up
from the stable lot) I looked up and saw him looking at me. He
had seen me for twenty years, but now he was looking at me; he
stood there in the path looking at me, in the middle of the afternoon. That was it: that it should have been in the middle of the
afternoon, when he should not have been anywhere near the house
at all but miles away and invisible somewhere among his hundred
square miles which they had not troubled to begin to take away
from him yet, perhaps not even at this point or at that point but*

diffused (not attenuated to thinness but enlarged, magnified, en-
compassing as though in a prolonged and unbroken instant of tre-
mendous effort embracing and holding intact that ten-mile square
while he faced from the brink of disaster, invincible and unafraid,
what he must have known would be the final defeat) but instead of
that standing there in the path looking at me with something
curious and strange in his face as if the barnlot, the path at the
instant when he came in sight of me had been a swamp out of
which he had emerged without having been forewarned that he
was about to enter light, and then went on —the face, the same
face: it was not love; I do not say that, not gentleness or pity: just a
sudden over-burst of light, illumination, who had been told that
his son had done murder and vanished and said 'Ah.—Well,
Clytie.' He went on to the house. But it was not love: I do not
claim that; I hold no brief for myself, I do not excuse it. I could
have said that he had needed, used me; why should I rebel now,
because he would use me more? but I did not say it; I could say this
time, I do not know, and I would tell the truth. Because I do not
know. He was gone; I did not even know that either since there is a
metabolism of the spirit as well as of the entrails, in which the
stored accumulations of long time burn, generate, create and
break some maidenhead of the ravening meat; ay, in a second's
time;—yes, lost all the shibboleth erupting of cannot, will not,
never will in one red instant's fierce obliteration. This was my
instant, who could have fled then and did not, who found that he
had gone on and did not remember when he had walked away,
who found my okra bed finished without remembering the complet-
ing of it, who sat at the supper table that night with the familiar
dream-cloudy shell which we had grown used to (he did not look at
me again during the meal; I might have said then, To what de-
luded sewer-gush of dreaming does the incorrigible flesh betray us:
but I did not) and then before the fire in Judith's bedroom sat as
we always did until he came in the door and looked at us and said,
'Judith, you and Clytie——' and ceased, still entering, then said,
'No, never mind. Rosa will not mind if you both hear it too, since
we are short for time and busy with what we have of it' and came
and stopped and put his hand on my head and (I do not know
what he looked at while he spoke, save that by the sound of his voice
it was not at us nor at anything in that room) said, 'You may
think I made your sister Ellen no very good husband. You probably

*do think so. But even if you will not discount the fact that I am
older now, I believe I can promise that I shall do no worse at least
for you.'*

*That was my courtship. That minute's exchanged look in a
kitchen garden, that hand upon my head in his daughter's bedroom; a ukase, a decree, a serene and florid boast like a sentence
(ay, and delivered in the same attitude) not to be spoken and
heard but to be read carved in the bland stone which pediments a
forgotten and nameless effigy. I do not excuse it. I claim no brief,
no pity, who did not answer 'I will' not because I was not asked,
because there was no place, no niche, no interval for reply. Because
I could have made one. I could have forced that niche myself if I
had willed to—a niche not shaped to fit mild 'Yes' but some blind
desperate female weapon's frenzied slash whose very gaping wound
had cried 'No! No!' and 'Help!' and 'Save me!' No, no brief, no
pity, who did not even move, who sat beneath that hard oblivious
childhood ogre's hand and heard him speak to Judith now, heard
Judith's feet, saw Judith's hand, not Judith—that palm in which I
read as from a printed chronicle the orphaning, the hardship, the
bereave of love; the four hard barren years of scoriating loom, of
axe and hoe and all the other tools decreed for men to use: and
upon it lying the ring which he gave Ellen in the church almost
thirty years ago. Yes, analogy and paradox and madness too. I sat
there and felt not watched him slip the ring onto my finger in my
turn (he was sitting now also, in the chair which we called Clytie's
while she stood just beyond the firelight's range beside the chimney)
and listened to his voice as Ellen must have listened in her own
spirit's April thirty years ago: he talking not about me or love or
marriage, not even about himself and to no sane mortal listening
nor out of any sanity, but to the very dark forces of fate which he
had evoked and dared, out of that wild braggart dream where an
intact Sutpen's Hundred which no more had actual being now
(and would never have again) than it had when Ellen first heard
it, as though in the restoration of that ring to a living finger he
had turned all time back twenty years and stopped it, froze it. Yes.
I sat there and listened to his voice and told myself, 'Why, he is
mad. He will decree this marriage for tonight and perform his own
ceremony, himself both groom and minister; pronounce his own
wild benediction on it with the very bedward candle in his hand:
and I mad too, for I will acquiesce, succumb; abet him and plunge*

down.' No, I hold no brief, ask no pity. If I was saved that night (and I was saved; mine was to be some later, colder sacrifice when we —I —should be free of all excuse of the surprised importunate traitorous flesh) it was no fault, no doing of my own but rather because, once he had restored the ring, he ceased to look at me save as he had looked for the twenty years before that afternoon, as if he had reached for the moment some interval of sanity such as the mad know, just as the sane have intervals of madness to keep them aware that they are sane. It was more than that even. For three months now he had seen me daily though he had not looked at me since I merely made one of that triumvirate who received his gruff unspoken man's gratitude for the spartan ease we supplied, not to his comfort perhaps but at least to the mad dream he lived in. But for the next two months he did not even see me. Perhaps the reason was the obvious one: he was too busy; that having accomplished his engagement (granted that was what he wanted) he did not need to see me. Certainly he did not: there was not even any date set for the wedding. It was almost as though that very afternoon did not exist, had never happened. I might not have even been there in the house. Worse: I could have gone, returned home, and he would not have missed me. I was (whatever it was he wanted of me —not my being, my presence: just my existence, whatever it was that Rosa Coldfield or any young female no blood kin to him represented in whatever it was he wanted —because I will do him this credit: he had never once thought about what he asked me to do until the moment he asked it because I know that he would not have waited two months or even two days to ask it) —my presence was to him only the absence of black morass and snarled vine and creeper to that man who had struggled through a swamp with nothing to guide or drive him —no hope, no light: only some incorrigibility of undefeat —and blundered at last and without warning onto dry solid ground and sun and air —if there could have been such thing as sun to him, if anyone or any thing could have competed with the white glare of his madness. Yes, mad, yet not so mad. Because there is a practicality to viciousness: the thief, the liar, the murderer even, has faster rules than virtue ever has; why not madness too? If he was mad, it was only his compelling dream which was insane and not his methods: it was no madman who bargained and cajoled hard manual labor out of men like Jones; it was no madman who kept clear of the sheets and hoods and night-

galloping horses with which men who were once his acquaintances
even if not his friends discharged the canker suppuration of defeat;
it was no madman's plan or tactics which gained him at the lowest
possible price the sole woman available to wive him, and by the one
device which could have gained his point;—not madman, no:
since surely there is something in madness, even the demoniac,
which Satan flees, aghast at his own handiwork, and which God
looks on in pity—some spark, some crumb to leaven and redeem
that articulated flesh, that speech sight hearing taste and being
which we call human man. But no matter. I will tell you what he
did and let you be the judge. (Or try to tell you, because there are
some things for which three words are three too many, and three
thousand words that many words too less, and this is one of them.
It can be told; I could take that many sentences, repeat the bold
blank naked and outrageous words just as he spoke them, and
bequeath you only that same aghast and outraged unbelief I knew
when I comprehended what he meant; or take three thousand sentences and leave you only that Why? Why? and Why? that I have
asked and listened to for almost fifty years.) But I will let you be
the judge and let you tell me if I was not right.

You see, I was that sun, or thought I was who did believe there
was that spark, that crumb in madness which is divine, though
madness know no word itself for terror or for pity. There was an
ogre of my childhood which before my birth removed my only sister
to its grim ogre-bourne and produced two half phantom children
whom I was not encouraged, and did not desire, to associate with
as if my late-born solitude had taught me presentiment of that
fateful intertwining, warned me of that fatal snarly climax before
I knew the name for murder—and I forgave it; there was a shape
which rode away beneath a flag and (demon or no) courageously
suffered—and I did more than just forgive: I slew it, because the
body, the blood, the memory which that ogre had dwelt in returned
five years later and held out its hand and said 'Come' as you
might say it to a dog, and I came. Yes, the body, the face, with the
right name and memory, even the correct remembering of what
and whom (except myself: and was that not but further proof?) it
had left behind and returned to: but not the ogre; villain true
enough, but a mortal fallible one less to invoke fear than pity: but
no ogre; mad true enough, but I told myself, Why should not
madness be its own victim also? or, Why may it be not even

madness but solitary despair in titan conflict with the lonely and foredoomed and indomitable iron spirit: but no ogre, because it was dead, vanished, consumed somewhere in flame and sulphur-reek perhaps among the lonely craggy peaks of my childhood's solitary remembering—or forgetting; I was that sun, who believed that he (after that evening in Judith's room) was not oblivious of me but only unconscious and receptive like the swamp-freed pilgrim feeling earth and tasting sun and light again and aware of neither but only of darkness' and morass's lack—who did believe there was that magic in unkin blood which we call by the pallid name of love that could be, might be sun for him (though I the youngest, weakest) where Judith and Clytie both would cast no shadow; yes, I the youngest there yet potently without measured and measurable age since I alone of them could say, 'O furious mad old man, I hold no substance that will fit your dream but I can give you airy space and scope for your delirium.' And then one afternoon—oh there was a fate in it: afternoon and afternoon and afternoon: do you see? the death of hope and love, the death of pride and principle, and then the death of everything save the old outraged and aghast unbelieving which has lasted for forty-three years—he returned to the house and called me, shouting from the back gallery until I came down; oh I told you he had not thought of it until that moment, that prolonged moment which contained the distance between the house and wherever it was he had been standing when he thought of it: and this too coincident: it was the very day on which he knew definitely and at last exactly how much of his hundred square miles he would be able to save and keep and call his own on the day when he would have to die, that no matter what happened to him now, he would at least retain the shell of Sutpen's Hundred even though a better name for it would now be Sutpen's One—called, shouted for me until I came down. He had not even waited to tether his horse; he stood with the reins over his arm (and no hand on my head now) and spoke the bald outrageous words exactly as if he were consulting with Jones or with some other man about a bitch dog or a cow or mare.

They will have told you how I came back home. Oh yes, I know: 'Rosie Coldfield, lose him, weep him; caught a man but couldn't keep him'—Oh yes, I know (and kind too; they would be kind): Rosa Coldfield, warped bitter orphaned country stick called Rosa Coldfield, safely engaged at last and so off the town, the county;

they will have told you: How I went out there to live for the rest of my life, seeing in my nephew's murdering an act of God enabling me ostensibly to obey my dying sister's request that I save at least one of the two children which she had doomed by conceiving them but actually to be in the house when he returned who, being a demon, would therefore be impervious to shot and shell and so would return; I waiting for him because I was young still (who had buried no hopes to bugles, beneath a flag) and ripe for marrying in this time and place where most of the young men were dead and all the living ones either old or already married or tired, too tired for love; he my best my only chance in this: an environment where at best and even lacking war my chances would have been slender enough since I was not only a Southern gentlewoman but the very modest character of whose background and circumstances must needs be their own affirmation since had I been the daughter of a wealthy planter I could have married almost anyone but being the daughter merely of a small store-keeper I could even afford to accept flowers from almost no one and so would have been doomed to marry at last some casual apprentice-clerk in my father's business; — Yes, they will have told you: who was young and had buried hopes only during that night which was four years long when beside a shuttered and unsleeping candle she embalmed the War and its heritage of suffering and injustice and sorrow on the backsides of the pages within an old account book, embalming blotting from the breathable air the poisonous secret effluvium of lusting and hating and killing; — they will have told you: daughter of an embusque who had to turn to a demon, a villain: and therefore she had been right in hating her father since if he had not died in that attic she would not have had to go out there to find food and protection and shelter and if she had not had to depend on his food and clothing (even if she did help to grow and weave it) to keep her alive and warm until simple justice demanded that she make what return for it he might require of her commensurate with honor she would not have become engaged to him and if she had not become engaged to him she would not have had to lie at night asking herself Why and Why and Why as she has done for forty-three years: as if she had been instinctively right even as a child in hating her father and so these forty-three years of impotent and unbearable outrage were the revenge of some sophisticated and ironic sterile nature on her for having hated that which gave her life. —

Yes, Rosa Coldfield engaged at last who, lacking the fact that her sister had bequeathed her at least something of shelter and kin, might have become a charge upon the town: and now Rosie Coldfield, lose him, weep him; found a man but failed to keep him; Rosa Coldfield who would be right only right, being right, is not enough for women who had rather be wrong than just that who want the man who was wrong to admit it. And that's what she cant forgive him for: not for the insult, not even for having jilted her: but for being dead. Oh yes, I know, I know: How two months later they learned that she had packed up her belongings (that is, put on the shawl and hat again) and come back to town, to live alone in the house where her parents were dead and gone and where Judith would come now and then and bring her some of what food they had out at Sutpen's Hundred and which only dire necessity, the brute inexplicable flesh's stubborn will to live, brought her (Miss Coldfield) to accept. And it dire indeed: because now the town —farmers passing, negro servants going to work in white kitchens—would see her before sunup gathering greens along garden fences, pulling them through the fence since she had no garden of her own, no seed to plant one with, no tools to work it with herself even if she had known completely how who had had only the freshman year at gardening and doubtless would not have worked it if she had known who had never surrendered; reaching through the garden fence and gathering vegetables who would have been welcome to enter the garden and get them and they would have even done the gathering and sent them to her since there were more people than Judge Benbow who would leave baskets of provisions on her front porch at night but she would not permit them who would not even use a stick to reach through the fence and draw the vegetables to where she could grasp them, the reach of her unaided arm being the limit of brigandage which she never passed, and it not to keep from being seen stealing which sent her forth before the town was awake because if she had had a nigger she would have sent him forth in broad daylight to forage, where, she would not have cared, exactly as the cavalry heroes whom she wrote verse about would have sent their men. —Yes, Rosie Coldfield, lose him, weep him; caught a beau but couldn't keep him; (oh yes, they will tell you) found a beau and was insulted, something heard and not forgiven, not so much for the saying of it but for having thought it about her so that when she heard it she realised like thunderclap that it must have been in his mind for a day, a week, even a month maybe, he looking at her daily with that in his mind and she not even knowing it. But I forgave him. They will tell you different, but I did. Why shouldn't I? I had nothing to forgive; I had not lost him because I never owned him: a certain segment of rotten mud walked into my life, spoke that to me which I had never heard before and never shall again, and then walked out; that was all. I never owned him; certainly not in that sewer sense which you would mean by that and maybe think (but you are wrong) I mean. That did not matter. That was not even the nub of the insult. I mean that he was not owned by anyone or anything in this world, had never been, would never be, not even by Ellen, not even by Jones' granddaughter. Because he was not articulated in this world. He was a walking shadow. He was the light-blinded bat-like image of his own torment cast by the fierce demoniac lantern up from beneath the earth's crust and hence in retrograde, reverse; from abysmal and chaotic dark to eternal and abysmal dark completing his descending (do you mark the gradation?) ellipsis, clinging, trying to cling with vain unsubstantial hands to what he hoped would hold him, save him, arrest him—Ellen (do you mark them?), myself, then last of all that fatherless daughter of Wash Jones' only child who, so I heard once, died in a Memphis brothel—to find severance (even if not rest and peace) at last in the stroke of a rusty scythe. I was told, informed of that too, though not by Jones this time but by someone else kind enough to turn aside and tell me he was dead. 'Dead?' I cried. 'Dead? You? You lie; you're not dead; heaven cannot, and hell dare not, have you!'

But Quentin was not listening, because there was also something which he too could not pass—that door, the running feet on the stairs beyond it almost a continuation of the faint shot, the two women, the negress and the white girl in her underthings (made of flour sacking when there had been flour, of window curtains when not) pausing, looking at the door, the yellowed creamy mass of old intricate satin and lace spread carefully on the bed and then caught swiftly up by the white girl and held before her as the door crashed in and the brother stood there, hatless, with his shaggy bayonet-trimmed hair, his gaunt worn unshaven face, his patched and faded gray tunic, the pistol still hanging against his flank: the two of them, brother and sister, curiously alike as if the difference in sex had merely sharpened the common blood to a terrific, an almost unbearable, similarity, speaking to one another in short brief staccato sentences like slaps, as if they stood breast to breast striking one another in turn, neither making any attempt to guard against the blows:

Now you cant marry him.

Why cant I marry him?

Because he's dead.

Dead?

Yes. I killed him.

He (Quentin) couldn't pass that. He was not even listening to her; he said, "Ma'am? What's that? What did you say?"

"There's something in that house."

"In that house? It's Clytie. Dont she——"

"No. Something living in it. Hidden in it. It has been out there for four years, living hidden in that house."

VI.

T HERE WAS snow on Shreve's overcoat sleeve, his un-
gloved blond square hand red and raw with cold, vanishing. Then on the table before Quentin, lying on the open text
book beneath the lamp, the white oblong of envelope, the
familiar blurred mechanical *Jefferson Jan 10 1910 Miss* and then,
opened, the *My dear son* in his father's sloped fine hand out of
that dead dusty summer where he had prepared for Harvard
so that his father's hand could lie on a strange lamplit table in
Cambridge; that dead summer twilight—the wistaria, the
cigar-smell, the fireflies—attenuated up from Mississippi and
into this strange room, across this strange iron New England
snow:

> *My dear son,*
> *Miss Rosa Coldfield was buried yesterday. She remained in the*
> *coma for almost two weeks and two days ago she died without*
> *regaining consciousness and without pain they say and whatever*
> *they mean by that since it has always seemed to me that the only*
> *painless death must be that which takes the intelligence by*
> *violent surprise and from the rear so to speak since if death be*
> *anything at all beyond a brief and peculiar emotional state of*
> *the bereaved it must be a brief and likewise peculiar state of the*
> *subject as well and if aught can be more painful to any intelli-*
> *gence above that of a child or an idiot than a slow and gradual*
> *confronting with that which over a long period of bewilderment*
> *and dread it has been taught to regard as an irrevocable and*
> *unplumbable finality, I do not know it. And if there can be*
> *either access of comfort or cessation of pain in the ultimate escape*
> *from a stubborn and amazed outrage which over a period of*
> *forty-three years has been companionship and bread and fire*
> *and all, I do not know that either—*

—bringing with it that very September evening itself (and he
soon needing, required, to say "No, neither aunt cousin nor
uncle Rosa. Miss Rosa. Miss Rosa Coldfield, an old lady that
died young of outrage in 1866 one summer" and then Shreve,
"You mean she was no kin to you, no kin to you at all, that
there was actually one Southern Bayard or Guinevere who

was no kin to you? then what did she die for?" and that not Shreve's first time, nobody's first time in Cambridge since September: *Tell about the South. What's it like there. What do they do there. Why do they live there. Why do they live at all*) —that very September evening when Mr Compson stopped talking at last, he (Quentin) walked out of his father's talking at last because it was now time to go, not because he had heard it all because he had not been listening since he had something which he still was unable to pass: that door, that gaunt tragic dramatic self-hypnotised youthful face like the tragedian in a college play, an academic Hamlet waked from some trancement of the curtain's falling and blundering across the dusty stage from which the rest of the cast had departed last commencement, the sister facing him across the wedding dress which she was not to use, not even to finish, the two of them slashing at one another with twelve or fourteen words and most of these the same words repeated two or three times so that when you boiled it down they did it with eight or ten. And she (Miss Coldfield) had on the shawl, as he had known she would, and the bonnet (black once but faded now to that fierce muted metallic green of old peacock feathers) and the black reticule almost as large as a carpet bag containing all the keys which the house possessed: cupboard closet and door, some of which would not even turn in locks which, shot home, could be solved by any child with a hairpin or a wad of chewing gum, some of which no longer even fit the locks they had been made for like old married people who no longer have anything in common, to do or to talk about, save the same general weight of air to displace and breathe and general oblivious biding earth to bear their weight;—that evening, the twelve miles behind the fat mare in the moonless September dust, the trees along the road not rising soaring as trees should but squatting like huge fowl, their leaves ruffled and heavily separate like the feathers of panting fowls, heavy with sixty days of dust, the roadside undergrowth coated with heat-vulcanised dust and, seen through the dustcloud in which the horse and buggy moved, appeared like masses stranding delicate and rigid and immobly upward at perpendicular's absolute in some old dead volcanic water refined to the oxygenless first principle of liquid, the dustcloud in which the buggy moved not blowing away because it had been raised by no wind and was supported by no air but evoked, materialised about them, instantaneous and eternal, cubic foot for cubic foot of dust to cubic foot for cubic foot of horse and buggy, peripatetic beneath the branch-shredded vistas of flat black fiercely and heavily starred sky, the dustcloud moving on, enclosing them with not threat exactly but maybe warning, bland, almost friendly, warning, as if to say, *Come on if you like. But I will get there first; accumulating ahead of you I will arrive first, lifting, sloping gently upward under hooves and wheels so that you will find no destination but will merely abrupt gently onto a plateau and a panorama of harmless and inscrutable night and there will be nothing for you to do but return and so I would advise you not to go, to turn back now and let what is, be;* he (Quentin) agreeing to this, sitting in the buggy beside the implacable doll-sized old woman clutching her cotton umbrella, smelling the heat-distilled old woman-flesh, the heat-distilled camphor in the old fold-creases of the shawl, feeling exactly like an electric bulb blood and skin since the buggy disturbed not enough air to cool him with motion, created not enough motion within him to make his skin sweat, thinking *Good Lord yes, let's dont find him or it, try to find him or it, risk disturbing him or it:* (then Shreve again, "Wait. Wait. You mean that this old gal, this Aunt Rosa——"

"Miss Rosa," Quentin said.

"All right all right.——that this old dame, this Aunt Rosa——"

"Miss Rosa, I tell you."

"All right all right all right.——that this old——this Aunt R—— All right all right all right all right.——that hadn't been out there, hadn't set foot in the house even in forty-three years, yet who not only said there was somebody hidden in it but found somebody that would believe her, would drive that twelve miles out there in a buggy at midnight to see if she was right or not?"

"Yes," Quentin said.

"That this old dame that grew up in a household like an overpopulated mausoleum, with no call or claim on her time but the hating of her father and aunt and her sister's husband in peace and comfort and waiting for the day when they

would prove not only to themselves but to everybody else
that she had been right: so one night the aunt slid down the
rainpipe with a horse trader and she was right about the aunt
so that fixed that: then her father nailed himself up in the attic
to keep from being drafted into the Rebel army and starved
to death so that fixed that except for the unavoidable possibility that when the moment came for him to admit to himself
that she had been right he may not have been able to speak or
may not have had anyone to tell it to: so she was right about
the father too since if he hadn't made General Lee and Jeff
Davis mad he wouldn't have had to nail himself up and die
and if he hadn't died he wouldn't have left her an orphan and
a pauper and so situated, left susceptible to a situation where
she could receive this mortal affront: and right about the
brother-in-law because if he hadn't been a demon his children
wouldn't have needed protection from him and she wouldn't
have had to go out there and be betrayed by the old meat and
find instead of a widowed Agamemnon to her Cassandra an
ancient stiff-jointed Pyramus to her eager though untried
Thisbe who could approach her in this unbidden April's compounded demonry and suggest that they breed together for
test and sample and if it was a boy they would marry; would
not have had to be blown back to town on the initial blast of
that horror and outrage to eat of gall and wormwood stolen
through paling fences at dawn: so this was not fixed at all and
forever because she couldn't even tell it because of who her
successor was, not because he found a successor by just turning around and no day's loss of time even but because of who
the successor was, that she might conceivably have ever suffered a situation where she could or would have to decline
any office which her successor could have been deemed
worthy, even by a demon, to fill; this not fixed at all since
when the moment came for him to admit he had been wrong
she would have the same trouble with him she had with her
father, he would be dead too since she doubtless foresaw the
scythe if for no other reason than that it would be the final
outrage and affront like the hammer and nails in her father's
business—that scythe, symbolic laurel of a caesar's triumph
—that rusty scythe loaned by the demon himself to Jones more
than two years ago to cut the weeds away from the shanty

doorway to smooth the path for rutting—that rusty blade garlanded with each successive day's gaudy ribbon or cheap bead for the (how did she put it? slut wasn't all, was it?) to walk in—that scythe beyond whose symbolic shape he, even though dead, even when earth itself declined any longer to bear his weight, jeered at her?"

"Yes," Quentin said.

"That this Faustus, this demon, this Beelzebub fled hiding from some momentary flashy glare of his Creditor's outraged face exasperated beyond all endurance, hiding, scuttling into respectability like a jackal into a rockpile so she thought at first until she realised that he was not hiding, did not want to hide, was merely engaged in one final frenzy of evil and harm-doing before the Creditor overtook him this next time for good and all;—this Faustus who appeared suddenly one Sunday with two pistols and twenty subsidiary demons and skul-dugged a hundred miles of land out of a poor ignorant Indian and built the biggest house on it you ever saw and went away with six wagons and came back with the crystal tapestries and the Wedgwood chairs to furnish it and nobody knew if he had robbed another steamboat or had just dug up a little more of the old loot, who hid horns and tail beneath human raiment and a beaver hat and chose (bought her, outswapped his father-in-law, wasn't it?) a wife after three years to scruti-nise weigh and compare, not from one of the local ducal houses but from the lesser baronage whose principality was so far decayed that there would be no risk of his wife bringing him for dowry delusions of grandeur before he should be equipped for it yet not so far decayed but that she might keep them both from getting lost among the new knives and forks and spoons that he had bought—a wife who not only would consolidate the hiding but could would and did breed him two children to fend and shield both in themselves and in their progeny the brittle bones and tired flesh of an old man against the day when the Creditor would run him to earth for the last time and he couldn't get away: and so sure enough the daughter fell in love, the son the agent for the providing of that living bulwark between him (the demon) and the Creditor's bailiff hand until the son should marry and thus insure him doubled and compounded—and then the demon must turn square around and run not only the fiance out of the house and not only the son out of the house but so corrupt seduce and mesmerise the son that he (the son) should do the office of the outraged father's pistol-hand when fornication threatened: so that the demon should return from the war five years later and find accomplished and complete the situation he had been working for: son fled for good now with a noose behind him, daughter doomed to spinsterhood—and then almost before his foot was out of the stirrup he (the demon) set out and got himself engaged again in order to replace that progeny the hopes of which he had himself destroyed?"

"Yes," Quentin said.

"Came back home and found his chances of descendants gone where his children had attended to that, and his plantation ruined, fields fallow except for a fine stand of weeds, and taxes and levies and penalties sowed by United States marshals and such and all his niggers gone where the Yankees had attended to that, and you would have thought he would have been satisfied: yet before his foot was out of the stirrup he not only set out to try to restore his plantation to what it used to be, like maybe he was hoping to fool the Creditor by illusion and obfuscation by concealing behind the illusion that time and change had not elapsed and occurred the fact that he was now almost sixty years old until he could get himself a new batch of children to bulwark him, but chose for this purpose the last woman on earth he might have hoped to prevail on, this Aunt R——all right all right all right.—that hated him, that had always hated him, yet choosing her with a kind of outrageous bravado as if a kind of despairing conviction of his irresistibility or invulnerability were a part of the price he had got for whatever it was he had sold the Creditor since according to the old dame he never had had a soul; proposed to her and was accepted—then three months later, with no date ever set for the wedding and marriage itself not mentioned one time since, and on the very day when he established definitely that he would be able to keep at least some of his land and how much, he approached her and suggested they breed like a couple of dogs together, inventing with fiendish cunning the thing which husbands and fiances have

been trying to invent for ten million years: the thing that
without harming her or giving her grounds for civil or tribal
action would not only blast the little dream-woman out of
the dovecote but leave her irrevocably husbanded (and himself, husband or fiance, already safely cuckolded before she
can draw breath) with the abstract carcass of outrage and revenge; who said it and was free now, forever more now of
threat or meddling from anyone since he had at last eliminated the last member of his late wife's family, free now: son
fled to Texas or California or maybe even South America,
daughter doomed to spinsterhood to live until he died, since
after that it wouldn't matter, in that rotting house, caring for
him and feeding him, raising chickens and peddling the eggs
for the clothes she and Clytie couldn't make: so that he didn't
even need to be a demon now but just mad impotent old man
who had realised at last that his dream of restoring his Sutpen's Hundred was not only vain but that what he had left of
it would never support him and his family and so running his
little crossroads store with a stock of plowshares and hame
strings and calico and kerosene and cheap beads and ribbons
and a clientele of freed niggers and (what is it? the word?
white what?—Yes, trash) with Jones for clerk and who knows
maybe what delusions of making money out of the store to
rebuild the plantation; who had escaped twice now, got himself into it and been freed by the Creditor who set his children
to destroying one another before he had posterity, and he
decided that maybe he was wrong in being free and so got
into it again and then decided that he was wrong in being
unfree and so got out of it again—and then turned right
around and bought his way back into it with beads and calico
and striped candy out of his own showcase and off his
shelves?"

"Yes," Quentin said. *He sounds just like Father* he thought,
glancing (his face quiet, reposed, curiously almost sullen) for
a moment at Shreve leaning forward into the lamp, his naked
torso pink-gleaming and baby-smooth, cherubic, almost hairless, the twin moons of his spectacles glinting against his
moonlike rubicund face, smelling (Quentin) the cigar and the
wistaria, seeing the fireflies blowing and winking in the September dusk. *Just exactly like Father if Father had known as*

*much about it the night before I went out there as he did the day
after I came back* thinking *Mad impotent old man who realised at
last that there must be some limit even to the capabilities of a
demon for doing harm, who must have seen his situation as that of
the show girl, the pony, who realises that the principal tune she
prances to comes not from horn and fiddle and drum but from a
clock and calendar, must have seen himself as the old wornout
cannon which realises that it can deliver just one more fierce shot
and crumble to dust in its own furious blast and recoil, who looked
about upon the scene which was still within his scope and compass
and saw son gone, vanished, more insuperable to him now than if
the son were dead since now (if the son still lived) his name would
be different and those to call him by it strangers and whatever
dragon's outcropping of Sutpen blood the son might sow on the body
of whatever strange woman would therefore carry on the tradition,
accomplish the hereditary evil and harm under another name and
upon and among people who will never have heard the right one;
daughter doomed to spinsterhood who had chosen spinsterhood already before there was anyone named Charles Bon since the aunt
who came to succor her in bereavement and sorrow found neither
but instead that calm absolutely impenetrable face between a
homespun dress and sunbonnet seen before a closed door and again
in a cloudy swirl of chickens while Jones was building the coffin and
which she wore during the next year while the aunt lived there
and the three women wove their own garments and raised their
own food and cut the wood they cooked it with (excusing what help
they had from Jones who lived with his granddaughter in the
abandoned fishing camp with its collapsing roof and rotting porch
against which the rusty scythe which Sutpen was to lend him, make
him borrow to cut away the weeds from the door—and at last
forced him to use though not to cut weeds, at least not vegetable
weeds—would lean for two years) and wore still after the aunt's
indignation had swept her back to town to live on stolen garden
truck and out of anonymous baskets left on her front steps at night,
the three of them, the two daughters negro and white and the
aunt twelve miles away watching from her distance as the two
daughters watched from theirs the old demon, the ancient varicose
and despairing Faustus fling his final main now with the Creditor's hand already on his shoulder, running his little country store
now for his bread and meat, haggling tediously over nickels and*

*dimes with rapacious and poverty-stricken whites and negroes, who
at one time could have galloped for ten miles in any direction
without crossing his own boundary, using out of his meagre stock
the cheap ribbons and beads and the stale violently-colored candy
with which even an old man can seduce a fifteen-year-old country
girl, to ruin the granddaughter of his partner, this Jones—this
gangling malaria-ridden white man whom he had given permission fourteen years ago to squat in the abandoned fishing camp
with the year-old grandchild—Jones, partner porter and clerk who
at the demon's command removed with his own hand (and maybe
delivered too) from the showcase the candy beads and ribbons, measured the very cloth from which Judith (who had not been bereaved
and did not mourn) helped the granddaughter to fashion a dress
to walk past the lounging men in, the side-looking and the
tongues, until her increasing belly taught her embarrassment—or
perhaps fear;—Jones who before '61 had not even been allowed to
approach the front of the house and who during the next four years
got no nearer than the kitchen door and that only when he
brought the game and fish and vegetables on which the seducer-
to-be's wife and daughter (and Clytie too, the one remaining servant, negro, the one who would forbid him to pass the kitchen door
with what he brought) depended on to keep life in them, but who
now entered the house itself on the (quite frequent now) afternoons
when the demon would suddenly curse the store empty of customers
and lock the door and repair to the rear and in the same tone in
which he used to address his orderly or even his house servants when
he had them (and in which he doubtless ordered Jones to fetch from
the showcase the ribbons and beads and candy) direct Jones to fetch
the jug, the two of them (and Jones even sitting now who in the old
days, the old dead Sunday afternoons of monotonous peace which
they spent beneath the scuppernong arbor in the back yard, the
demon lying in the hammock while Jones squatted against a post,
rising from time to time to pour for the demon from the demijohn
and the bucket of spring water which he had fetched from the
spring more than a mile away then squatting again, chortling
and chuckling and saying 'Sho, Mister Tawm' each time the demon paused)—the two of them drinking turn and turn about
from the jug and the demon not lying down now nor even sitting
but reaching after the third or second drink that old man's state of
impotent and furious undefeat in which he would rise, swaying*

and plunging and shouting for his horse and pistols to ride single-handed into Washington and shoot Lincoln (a year or so too late here) and Sherman both, shouting, 'Kill them! Shoot them down like the dogs they are!' and Jones: 'Sho, Kernel; sho now' and catching him as he fell and commandeering the first passing wagon to take him to the house and carry him up the front steps and through the paintless formal door beneath its fanlight imported pane by pane from Europe which Judith held open for him to enter with no change, no alteration in that calm frozen face which she had worn for four years now, and on up the stairs and into the bedroom and put him to bed like a baby and then lie down himself on the floor beside the bed though not to sleep since before dawn the man on the bed would stir and groan and Jones would say, 'Hyer I am, Kernel. Hit's all right. They aint whupped us yit, air they?'—this Jones who after the demon rode away with the regiment when the granddaughter was only eight years old would tell people that he 'was lookin after Major's place and niggers' even before they had time to ask him why he was not with the troops and perhaps in time came to believe the lie himself, who was among the first to greet the demon when he returned, to meet him at the gate and say, 'Well, Kernel, they kilt us but they aint whupped us yit, air they?' who even worked, labored, sweat at the demon's behest during that first furious period while the demon believed he could restore by sheer indomitable willing the Sutpen's Hundred which he remembered and had lost, labored with no hope of pay or reward who must have seen long before the demon did (or would admit it) that the task was hopeless—blind Jones who apparently saw still in that furious lecherous wreck the old fine figure of the man who once galloped on the black thoroughbred about that domain two boundaries of which the eye could not see from any point

"Yes," Quentin said.

So that Sunday morning came and the demon up and away before dawn, Judith thinking she knew why since that morning the black stallion which he rode to Virginia and led back had a son born on his wife Penelope, only it was not that foal which the demon had got up early to look at and it was almost a week before they caught, found, the old negress, the midwife who was squatting beside the quilt pallet that dawn while Jones sat on the porch where the rusty scythe had leaned for two years, so that she could tell how she heard the horse and then the demon entered and stood over the pallet with the riding whip in his hand and looked down at the mother and the child and said, 'Well, Milly, too bad you're not a mare like Penelope. Then I could give you a decent stall in the stable' and turned and went out and the old negress squatted there and heard them, the voices, he and Jones: 'Stand back. Dont you touch me, Wash.'—'I'm going to tech you, Kernel' and she heard the whip too though not the scythe, no whistling air, no blow, nothing since always that which merely consummates punishment evokes a cry while that which evokes the last silence occurs in silence. And that night they finally found him and fetched him home in a wagon and carried him, quiet and bloody and with his teeth still showing in his parted beard (which was hardly grizzled although his hair was almost white now) in the light of the lanterns and the pine torches, up the steps where the tearless and stonefaced daughter held the door open for him too who used to like to drive fast to church and who rode fast there this time, only when it was all over he had never reached the church since the daughter (the woman of thirty now and looking older, not as the weak grow old, either enclosed in a static ballooning of already lifeless flesh or through a series of stages of gradual collapsing whose particles adhere not to some iron and still impervious framework but to one another as though in some communal and oblivious and mindless life of their own like a colony of maggots, but as the demon himself had grown old: with a kind of condensation, an anguished emergence of the primary indomitable ossification which the soft color and texture, the light electric aura of youth, had merely temporarily assuaged but never concealed—the spinster in homemade and shapeless clothing, with hands which could either transfer eggs or hold a plow straight in furrow) decided that he should be driven in to that same Methodist church in town where he had married her mother before returning to the grave in the cedar grove, who borrowed two half-wild young mules to pull the wagon: so he rode fast toward church as far as he went, in his homemade coffin, in his regimentals and sabre and embroidered gauntlets, until the young mules bolted and turned the wagon over and tumbled him, sabre plumes and all, into a ditch from which the daughter extricated him and fetched him back to the cedar grove and read the service herself. And no tears, no bereavement this time too, whether or not it was because she had no time to mourn since she ran the store herself now until she found a buyer for it, not keeping it open but carrying the keys to it in her apron pocket, hailed from the kitchen or the garden or even from the field since she and Clytie now did all the plowing which was done, now that Jones was gone too, having followed the demon within twelve hours on that same Sunday (and maybe to the same place; maybe They would even have a scuppernong vine for them and no compulsions now of bread or ambition or fornication or vengeance and maybe they wouldn't even have to drink only they would miss this now and then without knowing what it was that they missed but not often; serene, pleasant, unmarked by time or change of weather, only just now and then something, a wind, a shadow, and the demon would stop talking and Jones would stop guffawing and they would look at one another, groping, grave, intent, and the demon would say, 'What was it, Wash? Something happened. What was it?' and Jones looking at the demon, groping too, sober too, saying, 'I dont know, Kernel. Whut?' each watching the other. Then the shadow would fade, the wind die away until at last Jones would say, serene, not even triumphant: 'They mought have kilt us, but they aint whupped us yit, air they?') —hailed by women and children with pails and baskets, whereupon she or Clytie would go to the store, unlock it, serve the customer, lock the store and return: until she sold the store at last and spent the money for a tombstone.— ("How was it?" Shreve said. "You told me; how was it? you and your father shooting quail, the gray day after it had rained all night and the ditch the horses couldn't cross so you and your father got down and gave the reins to—what was his name? the nigger on the mule? Luster.—Luster to lead them around the ditch" and he and his father crossed just as the rain began to come down again gray and solid and slow, making no sound, Quentin not aware yet of just where they were because he had been riding with his head lowered against the drizzle, until he looked up the slope before them where the wet yellow sedge died upward into the rain like melting gold and saw the grove, the clump of cedars on the crest of the hill dissolving into the rain as if the trees had been drawn in ink on a wet blotter—the cedars beyond which, beyond the ruined fields beyond which, would be the oak grove and the gray huge rotting deserted house half a mile away. Mr Compson had stopped to look back at Luster on the mule, the towsack he had been using for saddle now wrapped

around his head, his knees drawn up under it, leading the
horses on down the ditch to find a place to cross. "Better get
on out of the rain," Mr Compson said. "He's not going to
come within a hundred yards of those cedars anyway."

They went on up the slope. They could not see the two
dogs at all, only the steady furrowing of the sedge where,
invisible, the dogs quartered the slope until one of them flung
up his head to look back. Mr Compson gestured with his
hand toward the trees, he and Quentin following. It was dark
among the cedars, the light more dark than gray even, the
quiet rain, the faint pearly globules, materialising on the
gun barrels and the five headstones like drops of not-
quite-congealed meltings from cold candles on the marble:
the two flat heavy vaulted slabs, the other three headstones
leaning a little awry, with here and there a carved letter or
even an entire word momentary and legible in the faint light
which the raindrops brought particle by particle into the
gloom and released; now the two dogs came in, drifted in like
smoke, their hair close-plastered with damp, and curled down
in one indistinguishable and apparently inextricable ball for
warmth. Both the flat slabs were cracked across the middle by
their own weight (and vanishing into the hole where the
brick coping of one vault had fallen in was a smooth faint
path worn by some small animal—possum probably—by
generations of some small animal since there could have been
nothing to eat in the grave for a long time) though the lettering was quite legible: *Ellen Coldfield Sutpen. Born October 9,
1817. Died January 23, 1863* and the other: *Thomas Sutpen, Colonel, 23rd Mississippi Infantry, C.S.A. Died August 12, 1869*: this
last, the date, added later, crudely with a chisel, who even
dead did not divulge where and when he had been born.
Quentin looked at the stones quietly, thinking *Not beloved wife
of. No. Ellen Coldfield Sutpen* "I wouldn't have thought they
would have had any money to buy marble with in 1869," he
said.

"He bought them himself," Mr Compson said. "He bought
the two of them while the regiment was in Virginia, after
Judith got word to him that her mother was dead. He ordered them from Italy, the best, the finest to be had—his
wife's complete and his with the date left blank: and this

while on active service with an army which had not only the
highest mortality rate of any before or since but which had a
custom of electing a new set of regimental officers each year
(and by which system he was at the moment entitled to call
himself colonel, since he had been voted in and Colonel Sartoris voted out only last summer) so that for all he could
know, before his order could be filled or even received he
might be already under ground and his grave marked (if at
all) by a shattered musket thrust into the earth, or lacking that
he might be a second lieutenant or even a private—provided
of course that his men would have the courage to demote
him—yet he not only ordered the stones and managed to pay
for them, but stranger still he managed to get them past a
seacoast so closely blockaded that the incoming runners
refused any cargo except ammunition——" It seemed to
Quentin that he could actually see them: the ragged and starving troops without shoes, the gaunt powder-blackened faces
looking backward over tattered shoulders, the glaring eyes
in which burned some indomitable desperation of undefeat
watching that dark interdict ocean across which a grim lightless solitary ship fled with in its hold two thousand precious
pounds-space containing not bullets, not even something to
eat, but that much bombastic and inert carven rock which for
the next year was to be a part of the regiment, to follow it
into Pennsylvania and be present at Gettysburg, moving behind the regiment in a wagon driven by the demon's body
servant through swamp and plain and mountain pass, the regiment moving no faster than the wagon could, with starved
gaunt men and gaunt spent horses knee deep in icy mud or
snow, sweating and cursing it through bog and morass like a
piece of artillery, speaking of the two stones as 'Colonel' and
'Mrs Colonel'; then through the Cumberland Gap and down
through the Tennessee mountains, travelling at night to
dodge Yankee patrols, and into Mississippi in the late fall of
'64, where the daughter waited whose marriage he had interdict and who was to be a widow the next summer though
apparently not bereaved, where his wife was dead and his son
self-excommunicated and -banished, and put one of the stones
over his wife's grave and set the other upright in the hall of
the house, where Miss Coldfield possibly (maybe doubtless)

looked at it every day as though it were his portrait, possibly
(maybe doubtless here too) reading among the lettering more
of maiden hope and virgin expectation than she ever told
Quentin about, since she never mentioned the stone to him at
all, and (the demon) drank the parched corn coffee and ate
the hoe cake which Judith and Clytie prepared for him and
kissed Judith on the forehead and said, 'Well, Clytie' and returned to the war, all in twenty-four hours; he could see it; he
might even have been there. Then he thought *No. If I had
been there I could not have seen it this plain*

"But that dont explain the other three," he said. "They
must have cost something too."

"Who would have paid for them?" Mr Compson said.
Quentin could feel him looking at him. "Think." Quentin
looked at the three identical headstones with their faint identical lettering, slanted a little in the soft loamy decay of accumulated cedar needles, these decipherable too when he looked
close, the first one: *Charles Bon. Born in New Orleans, Louisiana. Died at Sutpen's Hundred, Mississippi, May 3, 1865. Aged 33
years and 5 months.* He could feel his father watching him.

"She did it," he said. "With that money she got when she
sold the store."

"Yes," Mr Compson said. Quentin had to stoop and brush
away some of the cedar needles to read the next one. As he
did so one of the dogs rose and approached him, thrusting its
head in to see what he was looking at like a human being
would, as if from association with human beings it had acquired the quality of curiosity which is an attribute only of
men and apes.

"Get away," he said, thrusting the dog back with one hand
while with the other he brushed the cedar needles away,
smoothing with his hand into legibility the faint lettering, the
graved words: *Charles Etienne Saint-Valery Bon. 1859–1884* feeling his father watching him, remarking before he rose that the
third stone bore that same date, 1884. "It couldn't have been
the store this time," he said. "Because she sold the store in
'70, and besides 1884 is the same date that's on hers" thinking
how it would have been terrible for her sure enough if she
had wanted to put *Beloved Husband of* on that first one.

"Ah," Mr Compson said. "That was the one your grandfather attended to. Judith came into town one day and brought him the money, some of it, where she got it from he never knew, unless it was what she had left out of the price of the store which he sold for her; brought the money in with the inscription (except the date of death of course) all written out as you see it, during that three weeks while Clytie was in New Orleans finding the boy to fetch him back though your grandfather of course did not know this, money and inscription not for herself but for him."

"Oh," Quentin said.

"Yes. They lead beautiful lives—women. Lives not only divorced from, but irrevocably excommunicated from, all reality. That's why although their deaths, the instant of dissolution, are of no importance to them since they have a courage and fortitude in the face of pain and annihilation which would make the most spartan man resemble a puling boy, yet to them their funerals and graves, the little puny affirmations of spurious immortality set above their slumber, are of incalculable importance. You had an aunt once (you do not remember her because I never saw her myself but only heard the tale) who was faced with a serious operation which she became convinced she would not survive, at a time when her nearest female kin was a woman between whom and herself there had existed for years one of those bitter inexplicable (to the man mind) amicable enmities which occur between women of the same blood, whose sole worry about departing this world was to get rid of a certain brown dress which she owned and knew that the kinswoman knew she had never liked, which must be burned, not given away but burned in the back yard beneath the window where, by being held up to the window (and suffering excruciating pain) she could see it burned with her own eyes, because she was convinced that after she died the kinswoman, the logical one to take charge, would bury her in it."

"And did she die?" Quentin said.

"No. As soon as the dress was consumed she began to mend. She stood the operation and recovered and outlived the kinswoman by several years. Then one afternoon she died peacefully of no particular ailment and was buried in her wedding gown."

"Oh," Quentin said.

"Yes. But there was one afternoon in the summer of '70 when one of these graves (there were only three here then) was actually watered by tears. Your grandfather saw it; that was the year Judith sold the store and your grandfather attended to it for her and he had ridden out to see her about the matter and he witnessed it: the interlude, the ceremonial widowhood's bright dramatic pageantry. He didn't know at the time how the octoroon came to be here, how Judith could even have known about her to write her where Bon was dead. But there she was, with the eleven-year-old boy who looked more like eight. It must have resembled a garden scene by the Irish poet, Wilde: the late afternoon, the dark cedars with the level sun in them, even the light exactly right and the graves, the three pieces of marble (your grandfather had advanced Judith the money to buy the third stone with against the price of the store) looking as though they had been cleaned and polished and arranged by scene shifters who with the passing of twilight would return and strike them and carry them, hollow fragile and without weight, back to the warehouse until they should be needed again; the pageant, the scene, the act, entering upon the stage—the magnolia-faced woman a little plumper now, a woman created of by and for darkness whom the artist Beardsley might have dressed, in a soft flowing gown designed not to infer bereavement or widowhood but to dress some interlude of slumbrous and fatal insatiation, of passionate and inexorable hunger of the flesh, walking beneath a lace parasol and followed by a bright gigantic negress carrying a silk cushion and leading by the hand the little boy whom Beardsley might not only have dressed but drawn—a thin delicate child with a smooth ivory sexless face who, after his mother handed the negress the parasol and took the cushion and knelt beside the grave and arranged her skirts and wept, never released the negress' apron but stood blinking quietly who, having been born and lived all his life in a kind of silken prison lighted by perpetual shaded candles, breathing for air the milklike and absolutely physical lambence which his mother's days and hours emanated, had seen little enough of sunlight before, let alone out-of-doors, trees and grass and earth; and last of all, the other woman, Judith *(who, not bereaved, did not need to mourn* Quentin thought, thinking *Yes, I have had to listen too long)* who stood just inside the cedars, in the calico dress and the sunbonnet to match it, both faded and shapeless—the calm face, the hands which could plow or cut wood and cook or weave cloth folded before her, standing in the attitude of an indifferent guide in a museum, waiting, probably not even watching. Then the negress came and handed the octoroon a crystal bottle to smell and helped her to rise and took up the silk cushion and gave the octoroon the parasol and they returned to the house, the little boy still holding to the negress' apron, the negress supporting the woman with one arm and Judith following with that face like a mask or like marble, back to the house, across the tall scaling portico and into the house where Clytie was cooking the eggs and the cornbread on which she and Judith lived.

"She stayed a week. She passed the rest of that week in the one remaining room in the house whose bed had linen sheets, passed it in bed, in the new lace and silk and satin negligees subdued to the mauve and lilac of mourning—that room airless and shuttered, impregnated behind the sagging closed blinds with the heavy fainting odor of her flesh, her days, her hours, her garments, of eau-de-cologne from the cloth upon her temples, of the crystal phial which the negress alternated with the fan as she sat beside the bed between trips to the door to receive the trays which Clytie carried up the stairs—Clytie, who did that fetching and carrying as Judith made her, who must have perceived whether Judith told her or not that it was another negro whom she served, yet who served the negress just as she would quit the kitchen from time to time and search the rooms downstairs until she found that little strange lonely boy sitting quietly on a straight hard chair in the dim and shadowy library or parlor, with his four names and his sixteenth-part black blood and his expensive esoteric Fauntleroy clothing who regarded with an aghast fatalistic terror the grim coffee-colored woman who would come on bare feet to the door and look in at him, who gave him not teacakes but the coarsest cornbread spread with as coarse molasses (this surreptitiously, not that the mother or the duenna might object, but because the household did not have food for eating between meals), gave it to him, thrust it at him with restrained savageness, and who found him one afternoon playing with a negro boy about his own size in the road outside the gates and cursed the negro child out of sight with level and deadly violence and sent him, the other, back to the house in a voice the very absence from which of vituperation or rage made it seem just that much more deadly and cold.

"Yes, Clytie, who stood impassive beside the wagon on that last day, following the second ceremonial to the grave with the silk cushion and the parasol and the smelling-bottle, when mother and child and duenna departed for New Orleans. And your grandfather never knew if it was Clytie who watched, kept in touch by some means, waited for the day, the moment, to come, the hour when the little boy would be an orphan, and so went herself to fetch him; or if it was Judith who did the waiting and the watching and sent Clytie for him that winter, that December of 1871;—Clytie who had never been further from Sutpen's Hundred than Jefferson in her life, yet who made that journey alone to New Orleans and returned with the child, the boy of twelve now and looking ten, in one of the outgrown Fauntleroy suits but with a new oversize overall jumper coat which Clytie had bought for him (and made him wear, whether against the cold or whether not your grandfather could not say either) over it and what else he owned tied up in a bandana handkerchief—this child who could speak no English as the woman could speak no French who had found him, hunted him down, in a French city and brought him away, this child with a face not old but without age, as if he had had no childhood, not in the sense that Miss Rosa Coldfield says she had no childhood, but as if he had not been human born but instead created without agency of man or agony of woman and orphaned by no human being (your grandfather said you did not wonder what had become of the mother, you did not even care: death or elopement or marriage: who would not grow from one metamorphosis— dissolution or adultery—to the next carrying along with her all the old accumulated rubbish-years which we call memory, the recognisable *I*, but changing from phase to phase as the butterfly changes once the cocoon is cleared, carrying nothing of what was into what is, leaving nothing of what is behind but eliding complete and intact and unresisting into the next

avatar as the overblown rose or magnolia elides from one rich
June to the next, leaving no bones, no substance, no dust of
whatever dead pristine soulless rich surrender anywhere between sun and earth) but produced complete and subject to
no microbe in that cloyed and scented maze of shuttered silk
as if he were the delicate and perverse spirit-symbol, immortal
page of the ancient immortal Lilith, entering the actual world
not at the age of one second but of twelve years, the delicate
garments of his pagehood already half concealed beneath that
harsh and shapeless denim cut to an iron pattern and sold by
the millions—that burlesque uniform and regalia of the tragic
burlesque of the sons of Ham;—a slight silent child who
could not even speak English, picked suddenly up out of
whatever debacle the only life he knew had disintegrated into,
by a creature whom he had seen once and learned to dread
and fear yet could not flee, held helpless and passive in a state
which must have been some incredible compound of horror
and trust, since although he could not even talk to her (they
made, they must have made, that week's journey by steamboat among the cotton bales on the freight deck, eating and
sleeping with negroes, where he could not even tell his companion when he was hungry or when he had to relieve himself) and so could have only suspected, surmised, where she
was taking him, could have known nothing certainly except
that all he had ever been familiar with was vanishing about
him like smoke, yet he made no resistance, returning quietly
and docilely to that decaying house which he had seen one
time, where the fierce brooding woman who had come and
got him lived with the calm white one who was not even
fierce, who was not anything except calm, who to him did not
even have a name yet who was somehow so closely related to
him as to be the owner of the one spot on earth where he had
ever seen his mother weep;—returned, crossed that strange
threshold, that irrevocable demarcation, not led, not dragged,
but driven and herded by that stern implacable presence, into
that gaunt and barren household where his very silken remaining clothes, his delicate shirt and stockings and shoes
which still remained to remind him of what he had once
been, vanished, fled from arms and body and legs as if they
had been woven of chimaeras or of smoke.—Yes, sleeping in

the trundle bed beside Judith's, beside that of the woman who
looked upon him and treated him with a cold unbending detached gentleness more discouraging than the fierce ruthless
constant guardianship of the negress who, with a sort of invincible spurious humility slept on a pallet on the floor, the
child lying there between them unasleep in some hiatus of
passive and hopeless despair aware of this, aware of the
woman on the bed whose every look and action toward him,
whose every touch of the capable hands seemed at the moment of touching his body to lose all warmth and become
imbued with cold implacable antipathy, and the woman on
the pallet upon whom he had already come to look as might
some delicate talonless and fangless wild beast crouched in its
cage in some hopeless and desperate similitude of ferocity
(and your grandfather said, 'Suffer little children to come
unto Me': and what did He mean by that? how, if He meant
that little children should need to *be* suffered to approach
Him, what sort of earth had He created; that if they had to
suffer in order to approach Him, what sort of heaven did He
have?) look upon the human creature who feeds it, who fed
him, thrust food which he himself could discern to be the
choicest of what they had, food which he realised had been
prepared for him by deliberate sacrifice, with that curious
blend of savageness and pity, of yearning and hatred; who
dressed him and washed him, thrust him into tubs of water
too hot or too cold yet against which he dared make no outcry, and scrubbed him with harsh rags and soap, sometimes
scrubbing at him with repressed fury as if she were trying to
wash the smooth faint olive tinge from his skin as you might
watch a child scrubbing at a wall long after the epithet, the
chalked insult, has been obliterated;—lying there unsleeping
in the dark between them, feeling them unasleep too, feeling
them thinking about him, projecting about him and filling the
thunderous solitude of his despair louder than speech could:
*You are not up here in this bed with me, where through no fault
nor willing of your own you should be, and you are not down here
on this pallet floor with me, where through no fault nor willing of
your own you must and will be, not through any fault or willing of
our own who would not what we cannot just as we will and wait
for what must be.*

"And your grandfather did not know either just which of them it was who told him that he was, must be, a negro, who could neither have heard yet nor recognised the term 'nigger', who even had no word for it in the tongue he knew who had been born and grown up in a padded silken vacuum cell which might have been suspended on a cable a thousand fathoms in the sea, where pigmentation had no more moral value than the silk walls and the scent and the rose-colored candle shades, where the very abstractions which he might have observed—monogamy and fidelity and decorum and gentleness and affection—were as purely rooted in the flesh's offices as the digestive processes. Your grandfather did not know if he was sent from the trundle bed at last or if he quitted it by his own wish and will; if when the time came when his loneliness and grief became calloused, he retired himself from Judith's bedroom or was sent from it, to sleep in the hall (where Clytie had likewise moved her pallet) though not on a pallet like her but on a cot, elevated still and perhaps not by Judith's decree either but by the negress' fierce inexorable spurious humility; and then in the attic, the cot moved there, the few garments (the rags of the silk and broadcloth in which he had arrived, the harsh jeans and homespun which the two women bought and made for him, he accepting them with no thanks, no comment, accepting his garret room with no thanks, no comment, asking for and making no alteration in its spartan arrangements that they knew of until that second year when he was fourteen and one of them, Clytie or Judith, found hidden beneath his mattress the shard of broken mirror: and who to know what hours of amazed and tearless grief he might have spent before it, examining himself in the delicate and outgrown tatters in which he perhaps could not even remember himself, with quiet and incredulous incomprehension) hanging behind a curtain contrived of a piece of old carpet nailed across a corner. And Clytie sleeping in the hall below, barring the foot of the attic stairs, guarding his escape or exit as inexorably as a Spanish duenna, teaching him to chop wood and to work the garden and then to plow as his strength (his resiliency rather, since he would never be other than light in the bone and almost delicate) increased—the boy with his light bones and womanish hands struggling with

what anonymous avatar of intractable Mule, whatever tragic
and barren clown was his bound fellow and complement beneath his first father's curse, getting the hang of it gradually
and the two of them, linked by the savage steel-and-wood
male symbol, ripping from the prone rich female earth corn
to feed them both while Clytie watched, never out of sight of
him, with that brooding fierce unflagging jealous care, hurrying out whenever anyone white or black stopped in the road
as if to wait for the boy to complete the furrow and pause
long enough to be spoken to, sending the boy on with a single quiet word or even gesture a hundred times more fierce
than the level murmur of vituperation with which she drove
the passerby on. So he (your grandfather) believed that it was
neither of them. Not Clytie, who guarded him as if he were a
Spanish virgin, who even before she could have even suspected that he would ever come there to live, had interrupted
his first contact with a nigger and sent him back to the house;
not Judith, who could have refused at any time to let him
sleep in that white child's bed in her room, who even if she
could not have reconciled herself to his sleeping on the floor
could have forced Clytie to take him into another bed with
her, who would have made a monk, a celibate, of him perhaps
yet not a eunuch, who may not have permitted him to pass
himself for a foreigner, yet who certainly would not have
driven him to consort with negroes. Your grandfather didn't
know, even though he did know more than the town, the
countryside, knew, which was that there was a strange little
boy living out there who had apparently emerged from the
house for the first time at the age of about twelve years,
whose presence was not even unaccountable to the town and
county since they now believed they knew why Henry had
shot Bon and they wondered only where and how Clytie and
Judith had managed to keep him concealed all the time, believing now that it had been a widow who had buried Bon
even though she had no paper to show for it, and only the
incredulous (and shocked) speculation of your grandfather
who, though he had that hundred dollars and the written directions in Judith's hand for this fourth tombstone in his safe
at the time, had not yet associated the boy with the child he
had seen two years ago when the octoroon came there to

weep at the grave, to believe that the child might be Clytie's, got by its father on the body of his own daughter—a boy seen always near the house with Clytie always nearby, then a youth learning to plow and Clytie somewhere nearby too and it soon well known with what grim and unflagging alertness she discovered and interrupted any attempt to speak to him, and only your grandfather to couple at last the boy, the youth, with the child who had been there three or four years ago to visit that grave;—your grandfather to whose office Judith came that afternoon five years later and he could not remember when he had seen her in Jefferson before—the woman of forty now, in the same shapeless calico and faded sunbonnet, who would not even sit down, who despite the impenetrable mask which she used for face emanated a terrible urgency, who insisted that they walk on toward the courthouse while she talked, told him, toward the crowded room where the justice's court sat, the crowded room which they entered and your grandfather saw him, the boy (only a man now) handcuffed to an officer, his other arm in a sling and his head bandaged since they had taken him to the doctor first, your grandfather gradually learning what had happened or as much of it as he could since the Court itself couldn't get very much out of the witnesses, the ones who had fled and sent for the sheriff, the ones (excepting that one whom he had injured too badly to be present) with whom he had fought—a negro ball held in a cabin a few miles from Sutpen's Hundred and he there, present and your grandfather never to know how often he had done this before, whether he had gone there to engage in the dancing or for the dice game in progress in the kitchen where the trouble started, trouble which he and not the negroes started according to the witnesses and for no reason, no accusation of cheating, nothing; and he making no denial, saying nothing, refusing to speak at all, sitting there sullen pale and silent: so that at this point all truth, evidence vanished into a moiling clump of negro backs and heads and black arms and hands clutching sticks of stove wood and cooking implements and razors, the white man the focal point of it and using a knife which he had produced from somewhere, clumsily, with obvious lack of skill and practice, yet with deadly earnestness and a strength which his slight build

denied, a strength composed of sheer desperate will and imperviousness to the punishment, the blows and slashes which
he took in return and did not even seem to feel;—no cause,
no reason for it; none to ever know exactly what happened,
what curses and ejaculations which might have indicated what
it was that drove him and only your grandfather to fumble,
grope, grasp the presence of that furious protest, that indictment of heaven's ordering, that gage flung into the face of
what is with a furious and indomitable desperation which the
demon himself might have shown, as if the child and then the
youth had acquired it from the walls in which the demon had
lived, the air which he had once walked in and breathed until
that moment when his own fate which he had dared in his
turn struck back at him; only your grandfather to sense that
because the justice and the others present did not recognise
him, did not recognise this slight man with his bandaged
head and arm, his sullen impassive (and now bloodless) olive
face, who refused to answer any questions, make any statement: so that the justice (Jim Hamblett it was) was already
making his speech of indictment when your grandfather entered, utilising opportunity and audience to orate, his eyes
already glazed with that cessation of vision of people who like
to hear themselves talk in public: 'At this time, while our
country is struggling to rise from beneath the iron heel of a
tyrant oppressor, when the very future of the South as a place
bearable for our women and children to live in depends on
the labor of our own hands, when the tools which we have to
use, to depend on, are the pride and integrity and forbearance
of black men and the pride and integrity and forbearance of
white; that you, I say, a white man, a white——' and your
grandfather trying to reach him, stop him, trying to push
through the crowd, saying, 'Jim. Jim. *Jim!*' and it already too
late, as if Hamblett's own voice had waked him at last or as if
someone had snapped his fingers under his nose and waked
him, he looking at the prisoner now but saying 'white' again
even while his voice died away as if the order to stop the
voice had been shocked into short circuit, and every face in
the room turned toward the prisoner as Hamblett cried,
'*What are you? Who and where did you come from?*'

"Your grandfather got him out, quashed the indictment

and paid the fine and brought him back to his office and talked to him while Judith waited in the anteroom. 'You are Charles Bon's son,' he said. 'I dont know,' the other answered, harsh and sullen. 'You dont remember?' your grandfather said. The other did not answer. Then your grandfather told him he must go away, disappear, giving him money to go on: 'Whatever you are, once you are among strangers, people who dont know you, you can be whatever you will. I will make it all right; I will talk to—to——What do you call her?' And he had gone too far now, but it was too late to stop; he sat there and looked at that still face which had no more expression than Judith's, nothing of hope nor pain: just sullen and inscrutable and looking down at the calloused womanish hands with their cracked nails which held the money while your grandfather thought how he could not say 'Miss Judith', since that would postulate the blood more than ever. Then he thought *I dont even know whether he wants to hide it or not.* So he said Miss Sutpen. 'I will tell Miss Sutpen, not where you are going of course, because I wont know that myself. But just that you are gone and that I knew you were going and that you will be all right.'

"So he departed, and your grandfather rode out to tell Judith, and Clytie came to the door and looked full and steadily at his face and said nothing and went to call Judith, and your grandfather waited in that dim shrouded parlor and knew that he would not have to tell either of them. He did not have to. Judith came presently and stood and looked at him and said, 'I suppose you wont tell me.'—'Not wont, cant,' your grandfather said. 'But not now because of any promise I made him. But he has money; he will be——' and stopped, with that forlorn little boy invisible between them who had come there eight years ago with the overall jumper over what remained of his silk and broadcloth, who had become the youth in the uniform—the tattered hat and the overalls—of his ancient curse, who had become the young man with a young man's potence yet was still that lonely child in his parchment-and-denim hairshirt, and your grandfather speaking the lame vain words, the specious and empty fallacies which we call comfort, thinking *Better that he were dead, better that he had never lived:* then thinking what vain and empty recapitulation that would be to her if he were to say it, who doubtless had already said it, thought it, changing only the person and the number. He returned to town. And now, next time, he was not sent for; he learned it as the town learned it: by that country grapevine whose source is among negroes, and he, Charles Etienne Saint-Valery Bon, already returned (not home again; returned) before your grandfather learned how he had come back, appeared, with a coal black and ape-like woman and an authentic wedding license, brought back by the woman since he had been so severely beaten and mauled recently that he could not even hold himself on the spavined and saddleless mule on which he rode while his wife walked beside it to keep him from falling off; rode up to the house and apparently flung the wedding license in Judith's face with something of that invincible despair with which he had attacked the negroes in the dice game. And none ever to know what incredible tale lay behind that year's absence which he never referred to and which the woman who, even a year later and after their son was born, still existed in that aghast and automaton-like state in which she had arrived, did not, possibly could not, recount but which she seemed to exude gradually and by a process of terrific and incredulous excretion like the sweat of fear or anguish: how he had found her, dragged her out of whatever two dimensional backwater (the very name of which, town or village, she either had never known or the shock of her exodus from it had driven the name forever from her mind and memory) her mentality had been capable of coercing food and shelter from, and married her, held her very hand doubtless while she made the laborious cross on the register before she even knew his name or knew that he was not a white man (and this last none knew even now if she knew for certain, even after the son was born in one of the dilapidated slave cabins which he rebuilt after renting his parcel of land from Judith); how there followed something like a year composed of a succession of periods of utter immobility like a broken cinema film, which the white-colored man who had married her spent on his back recovering from the last mauling he had received, in frowsy stinking rooms in places—towns and cities—which likewise had no names to her, broken by other periods, intervals, of furious and incomprehensible and apparently reasonless moving, progression—a maelstrom of faces and bodies through which the man thrust, dragging her behind him, toward or from what, driven by what fury which would not let him rest, she did not know, each one to end, finish, as the one before it had so that it was almost a ritual—the man apparently hunting out situations in order to flaunt and fling the ape-like body of his charcoal companion in the faces of all and any who would retaliate: the negro stevedores and deckhands on steamboats or in city honky-tonks who thought he was a white man and believed it only the more strongly when he denied it; the white men who, when he said he was a negro, believed that he lied in order to save his skin, or worse: from sheer besotment of sexual perversion; in either case the result the same: the man with body and limbs almost as light and delicate as a girl's giving the first blow, usually unarmed and heedless of the numbers opposed to him, with that same fury and implacability and physical imperviousness to pain and punishment, neither cursing nor panting, but laughing.

"So he showed Judith the license and took his wife, already far gone with the child, to the ruined cabin which he had chosen to repair and installed her, kenneled her with a gesture perhaps, and returned to the house. And nobody to know what transpired that evening between him and Judith, in whatever carpetless room furnished with whatever chairs and such which they had not had to chop up and burn to cook food or for warmth or maybe to heat water for illness from time to time—the woman who had been widowed before she had been a bride, the son of the man who had bereaved her and a hereditary negro concubine, who had not resented his black blood so much as he had denied the white, and this with a curious and outrageous exaggeration in which was inherent its own irrevocability, almost exactly as the demon himself might have done it. (*Because there was love* Mr Compson said *There was that letter she brought and gave to your grandmother to keep* He (Quentin) could see it, as plainly as he saw the one open upon the open text book on the table before him, white in his father's dark hand against his linen leg in the September twilight where the cigar-smell, the wistaria-smell, the fireflies drifted, thinking *Yes. I have heard too much,*

I have been told too much; I have had to listen to too much, too long thinking Yes, almost exactly like Father: that letter, and who to know what moral restoration she might have contemplated in the privacy of that house, that room, that night, what hurdling of iron old traditions since she had seen almost everything else she had learned to call stable vanish like straws in a gale;—she sitting there beside the lamp in a straight chair, erect, in the same calico save that the sunbonnet would be missing now, the head bare now, the once coal-black hair streaked with gray now while he faced her, standing. He would not have sat; perhaps she would not even have asked him to, and the cold level voice would not be much louder than the sound of the lamp's flame: 'I was wrong. I admit it. I believed that there were things which still mattered just because they had mattered once. But I was wrong. Nothing matters but breath, breathing, to know and to be alive. And the child, the license, the paper. What about it? That paper is between you and one who is inescapably negro; it can be put aside, no one will anymore dare bring it up than any other prank of a young man in his wild youth. And as for the child, all right. Didn't my own father beget one? and he none the worse for it? We will even keep the woman and the child if you wish; they can stay here and Clytie will . . . ' watching him, staring at him yet not moving, immobile, erect, her hands folded motionless on her lap, hardly breathing as if he were some wild bird or beast which might take flight at the expansion and contraction of her nostrils or the movement of her breast: 'No: I. I will. I will raise it, see that it. . . . It does not need to have any name; you will neither have to see it again nor to worry. We will have General Compson sell some of the land; he will do it, and you can go. Into the North, the cities, where it will not matter even if——But they will not. They will not dare. I will tell them that you are Henry's son and who could or would dare to dispute——' and he standing there, looking at her or not looking at her she cannot tell since his face would be lowered—the still expressionless thin face, she watching him, not daring to move, her voice murmuring, clear enough and full enough yet hardly reaching him: 'Charles': and he: 'No, Miss Sutpen': and she again, still without moving, not stirring so much as a muscle, as if she stood on the outside of the thicket into which she had cajoled the animal which she knew was watching her though she could not see it, not quite cringing, not in any terror or even alarm but in that restive

light incorrigibility of the free which would leave not even a print
on the earth which lightly bore it and she not daring to put out the
hand with which she could have actually touched it but instead
just speaking to it, her voice soft and swooning, filled with that
seduction, that celestial promise which is the female's weapon: 'Call
me Aunt Judith, Charles') Yes, who to know if he said anything or nothing, turning, going out, she still sitting there,
not moving, not stirring, watching him, still seeing him, penetrating walls and darkness too to watch him walk back down
the weedy lane between the deserted collapsed cabins toward
that one where his wife waited, treading the thorny and flint-
paved path toward the Gethsemane which he had decreed and
created for himself, where he had crucified himself and come
down from his cross for a moment and now returned to it.

    "Not your grandfather. He knew only what the town, the
county, knew: that the strange little boy whom Clytie had
used to watch and had taught to farm, who had sat, a grown
man, in the justice's court that day with his head bandaged
and one arm in a sling and the other in a handcuff, who had
vanished and then returned with an authentic wife resembling
something in a zoo, now farmed on shares a portion of the
Sutpen plantation, farmed it pretty well, with solitary and
steady husbandry within his physical limitations, the body
and limbs which still looked too light for the task which he
had set himself, who lived like a hermit in the cabin which he
rebuilt and where his son was presently born, who consorted
with neither white nor black (Clytie did not watch him now;
she did not need to) and who was not seen in Jefferson but
three times during the next four years and then to appear, be
reported by the negroes who seemed to fear either him or
Clytie or Judith, as being either blind or violently drunk in
the negro store district on Depot Street, where your grandfather would come and take him away (or if he were too
drunk, had become violent, the town officers) and keep him
until his wife, the black gargoyle, could hitch the team back
into the wagon and come, with nothing alive about her but
her eyes and hands, and load him into it and take him home.
So they did not even miss him from town at first; it was the
County Medical Officer who told your grandfather that he
had yellow fever and that Judith had had him moved into the

big house and was nursing him and now Judith had the disease too, and your grandfather told him to notify Miss Coldfield and he (your grandfather) rode out there one day. He did not dismount; he sat his horse and called until Clytie looked down at him from one of the upper windows and told him 'they didn't need nothing'. Within the week your grandfather learned that Clytie had been right, or was right now anyway, though it was Judith who died first."

"Oh," Quentin said. —*Yes* he thought *Too much, too long* remembering how he had looked at the fifth grave and thought how whoever had buried Judith must have been afraid that the other dead would contract the disease from her, since her grave was at the opposite side of the enclosure, as far from the other four as the enclosure would permit, thinking *Father wont have to say 'think' this time* because he knew who had ordered and bought that headstone before he read the inscription on it, thinking about, imagining what careful printed directions Judith must have roused herself (from delirium possibly) to write down for Clytie when she knew that she was going to die; and how Clytie must have lived during the next twelve years while she raised the child which had been born in the old slave cabin and scrimped and saved the money to finish paying out the stone on which Judith had paid his grandfather the hundred dollars twenty-four years ago and which, when his grandfather tried to refuse it, she (Clytie) set the rusty can full of nickels and dimes and frayed paper money on the desk and walked out of the office without a word. He had to brush the clinging cedar needles from this one also to read it, watching these letters also emerge beneath his hand, wondering quietly how they could have clung there, not have been blistered to ashes at the instant of contact with the harsh and unforgiving threat: *Judith Coldfield Sutpen. Daughter of Ellen Coldfield. Born October 3, 1841. Suffered the Indignities and Travails of this World for 42 Years, 4 Months, 9 Days, and went to Rest at Last February 12, 1884. Pause, Mortal; Remember Vanity and Folly and Beware* thinking (Quentin) *Yes. I didn't need to ask who invented that, put that one up* thinking *Yes, to too much, too long. I didn't need to listen then but I had to hear it and now I am having to hear it all over again because he sounds just like Father: Beautiful lives—women do. In*

*very breathing they draw meat and drink from some beautiful
attenuation of unreality in which the shades and shapes of facts—
of birth and bereavement, of suffering and bewilderment and
despair—move with the substanceless decorum of lawn party
charades, perfect in gesture and without significance or any ability
to hurt. Miss Rosa ordered that one. She decreed that headstone of
Judge Benbow. He had been the executor of her father's estate,
appointed by no will since Mr Coldfield left neither will nor estate
except the house and the rifled shell of the store. So he appointed
himself, elected himself probably out of some conclave of neighbors
and citizens who came together to discuss her affairs and what to
do with her after they realised that nothing under the sun, certainly no man nor committee of men, would ever persuade her to
go back to her niece and brother-in-law—the same citizens and
neighbors who left baskets of food on her doorstep at night, the
dishes (the plates containing the food, the napkins which covered it)
from which she never washed but returned soiled to the empty basket and set the basket back on the same step where she had found it
as if to carry completely out the illusion that it had never existed or
at least that she had never touched, emptied, it, had not come out
and taken the basket up with that air which had nothing whatever
of furtiveness in it nor even defiance, who doubtless tasted the food,
criticised its quality or cooking, chewed and swallowed it and felt it
digest yet still clung to that delusion, that calm incorrigible insistence that that which all incontrovertible evidence tells her is so
does not exist, as women can; —that same self deluding which declined to admit that the liquidation of the store had left her something, that she had been left anything but a complete pauper, who
would not accept the actual money from the sale of the store from
Judge Benbow yet would accept the money's value (and after a few
years, over-value) in a dozen ways: would use casual negro boys
who happened to pass the house, stopping them and commanding
them to rake her yard and they doubtless as aware as the town was
that there would be no mention of pay from her, that they would
not even see her again though they knew she was watching them
from behind the curtains of a window, but that Judge Benbow
would pay them—would enter the stores and command objects
from the shelves and showcases exactly as she commanded that two
hundred dollar headstone from Judge Benbow, and walk out of the
store with them—who with the same aberrant cunning which*

would not wash the dishes and napkins from the baskets declined to have any discussion of her affairs with Benbow since she must have known that the sums which she had received from him must have years ago over-balanced (he, Benbow, had in his office a portfolio, a fat one, with Estate of Goodhue Coldfield. Private *written across it in indelible ink. After the Judge died his son Percy opened it. It was filled with racing forms and cancelled betting tickets on horses whose very bones were no man knew where now, which had won and lost races on the Memphis track forty years ago, and a ledger, a careful tabulation in the Judge's hand, each entry indicating the date and the horse's name and his wager and whether he won or lost; and another one showing how for forty years he had put each winning and an amount equal to each loss, to that mythical account) whatever the store had brought*

But you were not listening, because you knew it all already, had learned, absorbed it already without the medium of speech somehow from having been born and living beside it, with it, as children will and do: so that what your father was saying did not tell you anything so much as it struck, word by word, the resonant strings of remembering, who had been here before, seen these graves more than once in the rambling expeditions of boyhood whose aim was more than the mere hunting of game, just as you had seen the old house too, been familiar with how it would look before you even saw it, became large enough to go out there one day with four or five other boys of your size and age and dare one another to evoke the ghost, since it would have to be haunted, could not but be haunted although it had stood there empty and unthreatening for twenty-six years and nobody to meet or report any ghost until the wagon full of strangers moving from Arkansas tried to stop and spend the night in it and something happened before they could begin to unload the wagon even, what they did not or could not or would not tell but which had them back in the wagon and the mules going back down the drive at a gallop, all in about ten minutes, not to stop until they reached Jefferson—the rotting shell with its sagging portico and scaling walls, its sagging blinds and blank-shuttered windows, set in the middle of the domain which had reverted to the state and had been bought and sold and bought and sold again and again and again. No, you were not listening; you didn't have to: then the dogs stirred, rose; you looked up and sure enough, just as your father had said he would, Luster had *halted the mule and the two horses in the rain about fifty yards from the cedars, sitting there with his knees drawn up under the towsack and enclosed by the cloudy vapor of the steaming animals as though he were looking at you and your father out of some lugubrious and painless purgatory. 'Come on in out of the rain, Luster,' your father said. 'I wont let the old Colonel hurt you.' — 'Yawl come on and less go home,' Luster said. 'Aint no more hunting today.' — 'We'll get wet,' your father said. 'I'll tell you what: we'll ride on over to that old house. We can keep good and dry there.' But Luster didn't budge, sitting there in the rain and inventing reasons not to go to the house — that the roof would leak or that you would all three catch cold with no fire or that you would all get so wet before you reached it that the best thing to do would be to go straight home: and your father laughing at Luster but you not laughing so much because even though you were not black like Luster was, you were not any older, and you and Luster had both been there that day when the five of you, the five boys all of an age, began daring one another to enter the house long before you reached it, coming up from the rear, into the old street of the slave quarters — a jungle of sumach and persimmon and briers and honeysuckle, and the rotting piles of what had once been log walls and stone chimneys and shingle roofs among the undergrowth except one, that one; you coming up to it; you didn't see the old woman at all at first because you were watching the boy, the Jim Bond, the hulking slack-mouthed saddle-colored boy a few years older and bigger than you were, in patched and faded yet quite clean shirt and overalls too small for him, working in the garden patch beside the cabin: so you didn't even know she was there until all of you started and whirled as one and found her watching you from a chair tilted back against the cabin wall — a little dried-up woman not much bigger than a monkey and who might have been any age up to ten thousand years, in faded voluminous skirts and an immaculate headrag, her bare coffee-colored feet wrapped around the chair rung like monkeys do, smoking a clay pipe and watching you with eyes like two shoe buttons buried in the myriad wrinkles of her coffee-colored face, who just looked at you and said without even removing the pipe and in a voice almost like a white woman's: 'What do you want?' and after a moment one of you said 'Nothing' and then you were all running without knowing which of you began to run first nor why since you were not scared,*

back across the fallow and rain-gutted and brier-choked old fields
until you came to the old rotting snake fence and crossed it, hurled
yourselves over it, and then the earth, the land, the sky and trees
and woods, looked different again, all right again

"Yes," Quentin said.

"And that was the one Luster was talking about now,"
Shreve said. "And your father watching you again because
you hadn't heard the name before, hadn't even thought that
he must have a name that day when you saw him in the vegetable patch, and you said, 'Who? Jim what?' and Luster said,
'Das him. Bright-colored boy whut stay wid dat ole woman'
and your father still watching you and you said, 'Spell it' and
Luster said, 'Dat's a lawyer word. Whut dey puts you under
when de Law ketches you. I des spells readin words.' And
that was him, the name Bond now and he wouldn't care
about that, who had inherited what he was from his mother
and only what he could never have been from his father, and
if your father had asked him if he was Charles Bon's son he
not only would not have known either, he wouldn't have
cared: and if you had told him he was, it would have touched
and then vanished from what you (not he) would have had to
call his mind long before it could have set up any reaction at
all, either of pride or pleasure, anger or grief?"

"Yes," Quentin said.

"And that he lived in that cabin behind the haunted house
for twenty-six years, he and the old woman who must be
more than seventy now yet who had no white hair under that
headrag, whose flesh had not sagged but looked instead like
she had grown old up to a certain point just like normal people do, then had stopped, and instead of turning gray and soft
she had begun to shrink so that the skin of her face and hands
broke into a million tiny cross-hair wrinkles and her body just
grew smaller and smaller like something being shrunk in a
furnace, like the Bornese do their captured heads—who
might well have been the ghost if one was ever needed, if
anybody ever had so little else to do as to prowl around the
house, which there was not; if there could have been anything
in it to protect from prowlers, which there was not; if there
had been anyone of them left to hide or need concealment in
it, which there was not. And yet this old gal, this Aunt Rosa,

told you that someone was hiding out there and you said it was Clytie or Jim Bond and she said No and you said it would have to be because the demon was dead and Judith was dead and Bon was dead and Henry gone so far he hadn't even left a grave: and she said No and so you went out there, drove the twelve miles at night in a buggy and you found Clytie and Jim Bond both in it and you said You see? and she (the Aunt Rosa) still said No and so you went on: and there was?"

"Yes."

"Wait then," Shreve said. "For God's sake wait.")

VII.

THERE WAS no snow on Shreve's arm now, no sleeve on his arm at all now: only the smooth cupid-fleshed forearm and hand coming back into the lamp and taking a pipe from the empty coffee can where he kept them, filling it and lighting it. *So it is zero outside,* Quentin thought; *soon he will raise the window and do deep-breathing in it, clench-fisted and naked to the waist, in the warm and rosy orifice above the iron quad.* But he had not done so yet, and now the moment, the thought, was an hour past and the pipe lay smoked out and overturned and cold, with a light sprinkling of ashes about it, on the table before Shreve's crossed pink bright-haired arms while he watched Quentin from behind the two opaque and lamp-glared moons of his spectacles. "So he just wanted a grandson," he said. "That was all he was after. Jesus, the South is fine, isn't it. It's better than the theatre, isn't it. It's better than Ben Hur, isn't it. No wonder you have to come away now and then, isn't it."

Quentin did not answer. He sat quite still, facing the table, his hands lying on either side of the open text book on which the letter rested: the rectangle of paper folded across the middle and now open, three quarters open, whose bulk had raised half itself by the leverage of the old crease in weightless and paradoxical levitation, lying at such an angle that he could not possibly have read it, deciphered it, even without this added distortion. Yet he seemed to be looking at it, or as near as Shreve could tell, he was, his face lowered a little, brooding, almost sullen. "He told Grandfather about it," he said. "That time when the architect escaped, tried to, tried to escape into the river bottom and go back to New Orleans or wherever it was, and he—" ("The demon, hey?" Shreve said. Quentin did not answer him, did not pause, his voice level, curious, a little dreamy yet still with that overtone of sullen bemusement, of smoldering outrage: so that Shreve, still too, resembling in his spectacles and nothing else (from the waist down the table concealed him; anyone entering the room would have taken him to be stark naked) a baroque effigy created out of colored cake dough by someone with a faintly night-

marish affinity for the perverse, watched him with thoughtful and intent curiosity.) "—sent word in to Grandfather
and some others and got his dogs and his wild niggers out
and hunted the architect down and made him take earth in a
cave under the river bank two days later. That was in the
second summer, when they had finished all the brick and had
the foundations laid and most of the big timbers cut and
trimmed, and one day the architect couldn't stand it anymore
or he was afraid he would starve or that the wild niggers
(and maybe Colonel Sutpen too) would run out of grub and
eat him or maybe he got homesick or maybe he just had to
go—" ("Maybe he had a girl," Shreve said. "Or maybe he
just wanted a girl. You said the demon and the niggers didn't
have but two." Quentin did not answer this either; again he
might not have heard, talking in that curious repressed calm
voice as though to the table before him or the book upon it
or the letter upon the book or his hands lying on either side
of the book.) "—and so he went. He seemed to vanish in
broad daylight, right out from the middle of twenty-one people. Or maybe it was just Sutpen's back that was turned, and
that the niggers saw him go and didn't think it needed mentioning; that being wild men they probably didn't know what
Sutpen himself was up to and him naked in the mud with
them all day. So I reckon they never did know what the architect was there for, supposed to do or had done or could do or
was, so maybe they thought Sutpen had sent him, told him to
go away and drown himself, go away and die, or maybe just
go away. So he did, jumped up in broad daylight, in his embroidered vest and Fauntleroy tie and a hat like a Baptist con-
gressman and probably carrying the hat in his hand, and ran
into the swamp and the niggers watched him out of sight and
then went back to work and Sutpen didn't see it, didn't even
miss him until night, suppertime probably, and the niggers
told him and he declared a holiday tomorrow because he
would have to get out and borrow some dogs. Not that he
would have needed dogs, with his niggers to trail, but maybe
he thought that the guests, the others, would not be used to
trailing with niggers and would expect dogs. And Grandfather (he was young then too) brought some champagne and
some of the others brought whiskey and they began to gather

out there a little after sundown, at his house that didn't even
have walls yet, that wasn't anything yet but some lines of
bricks sunk into the ground but that was all right because
they didn't go to bed anyhow, Grandfather said, they just sat
around the fire with the champagne and the whiskey and a
quarter of the last venison he had killed, and about midnight
the man with the dogs came. Then it was daylight and the
dogs had a little trouble at first because some of the wild niggers had run out about a mile of the trail just for fun. But
they got the trail straightened out at last, the dogs and the
niggers in the bottom and most of the men riding along the
edge of it where the going was good. But Grandfather and
Colonel Sutpen went with the dogs and the niggers because
Sutpen was afraid the niggers might catch the architect before
he could reach them. He and Grandfather had to walk a good
deal, sending one of the niggers to lead the horses on around
the bad places until they could ride again. Grandfather said it
was fine weather and the trail lay pretty good but he said it
would have been fine if the architect had just waited until
October or November. And so he told Grandfather something about it.

"His trouble was innocence. All of a sudden he discovered,
not what he wanted to do but what he just had to do, had to
do it whether he wanted to or not, because if he did not do it
he knew that he could never live with himself for the rest of
his life, never live with what all the men and women that had
died to make him had left inside of him for him to pass on,
with all the dead ones waiting and watching to see if he was
going to do it right, fix things right so that he would be able
to look in the face not only the old dead ones but all the
living ones that would come after him when he would be one
of the dead. And that at the very moment when he discovered
what it was, he found out that this was the last thing in the
world he was equipped to do because he not only had not
known that he would have to do this, he did not even know
that it existed to be wanted, to need to be done, until he was
almost fourteen years old. Because he was born in West Virginia, in the mountains where—" ("Not in West Virginia,"
Shreve said. "—What?" Quentin said. "Not in West Virginia," Shreve said. "Because if he was twenty-five years old

in Mississippi in 1833, he was born in 1808. And there wasn't any West Virginia in 1808 because—" "All right," Quentin said. "—West Virginia wasn't admitted—" "All right all right," Quentin said. "—into the United States until—" "All right all right all right," Quentin said.) "—where what few other people he knew lived in log cabins boiling with children like the one he was born in—men and grown boys who hunted or lay before the fire on the floor while the women and older girls stepped back and forth across them to reach the fire to cook, where the only colored people were Indians and you only looked down at them over your rifle sights, where he had never even heard of, never imagined, a place, a land divided neatly up and actually owned by men who did nothing but ride over it on fine horses or sit in fine clothes on the galleries of big houses while other people worked for them; he did not even imagine then that there was any such way to live or to want to live, or that there existed all the objects to be wanted which there were, or that the ones who owned the objects not only could look down on the ones that didn't, but could be supported in the down-looking not only by the others who owned objects too but by the very ones that were looked down on that didn't own objects and knew they never would. Because where he lived the land belonged to anybody and everybody and so the man who would go to the trouble and work to fence off a piece of it and say 'This is mine' was crazy; and as for objects, nobody had any more of them than you did because everybody had just what he was strong enough or energetic enough to take and keep, and only that crazy man would go to the trouble to take or even want more than he could eat or swap for powder and whiskey. So he didn't even know there was a country all divided and fixed and neat with a people living on it all divided and fixed and neat because of what color their skins happened to be and what they happened to own, and where a certain few men not only had the power of life and death and barter and sale over others, they had living human men to perform the endless repetitive personal offices such as pouring the very whiskey from the jug and putting the glass into his hand or pulling off his boots for him to go to bed that all men have had to do for themselves since time began and would have to do until they died and which no man ever has or ever will like to do but which no man that he knew had ever anymore thought of evading than he had thought of evading the effort of chewing and swallowing and breathing. When he was a child he didn't listen to the vague and cloudy tales of Tidewater splendor that penetrated even his mountains because then he could not understand what the people meant, and when he became a boy he didn't listen to them because there was nothing in sight to compare and gauge the tales by and so give the words life and meaning, and no chance that he ever would (certainly no belief or thought that someday he might), and because he was too busy doing the things that boys do; and when he got to be a youth and curiosity itself exhumed the tales which he did not know he had heard and speculated about them, he was interested and would have liked to see the places once, but without envy or regret, because he just thought that some people were spawned in one place and some in another, some spawned rich (lucky, he may have called it: or maybe he called lucky, rich) and some not, and that (so he told Grandfather) the men themselves had little to do with the choosing and less of the regret because (he told Grandfather this too) it had never once occurred to him that any man should take any such blind accident as that as authority or warrant to look down at others, any others. So he had hardly heard of such a world until he fell into it.

"That's how it was. They fell into it, the whole family, returned to the coast from which the first Sutpen had come (when the ship from the Old Bailey reached Jamestown probably), tumbled head over heels back to Tidewater by sheer altitude, elevation and gravity, as if whatever slight hold the family had had (he said something to Grandfather about his mother dying about that time and how his pap said she was a fine wearying woman and that he would miss her; and something about how it was the wife that had got his father even that far West) on the mountain had broken and now the whole passel of them from the father through the grown daughters down to one that couldn't even walk yet, sliding back down out of the mountains and skating in a kind of accelerating and sloven and inert coherence like a useless collection of flotsam on a flooded river moving by some perverse automotivation such as inanimate objects sometimes show, backward against the very current of the stream, across the Virginia plateau and into the slack lowlands about the mouth of the James River. He didn't know why they moved, or didn't remember the reason if he ever knew it—whether it was optimism, hope in his father's breast or nostalgia, since he didn't know just where his father had come from, whether the country to which they returned was it or not, or even if his father knew, remembered, wanted to remember and find it again;—whether somebody, some traveler, had told him of some easy place or time, some escape from the hardship of getting food and keeping warm in the mountain way, or if perhaps somebody his father knew once or who knew his father once and remembered him, happened to think about him, or someone kin to him who had tried to forget him and couldn't quite do it, had sent for him and he obeying, going not for the promised job but for the ease, having faith perhaps in the blood kinship to evade the labor if it was kinship, in his own inertia and in whatever gods had watched over him this far if it were not. But he—" ("The demon," Shreve said) "—didn't know, or remember, whether he had ever heard, been told, the reason or not. All he remembered was that one morning the father rose and told the older girls to pack what food they had, and somebody wrapped up the baby and somebody else threw water on the fire and they walked down the mountain to where roads existed. They had a lopsided two-wheeled cart and two spavined oxen now. He told Grandfather he did not remember just where nor when nor how his father had got it, and he (he was ten then; the two older boys had left home some time before and had not been heard of since) driving the oxen since almost as soon as they got the cart his father began the practice of accomplishing that part of the translation devoted to motion flat on his back in the cart, oblivious among the quilts and lanterns and well buckets and bundles of clothing and children, snoring with alcohol. That was how he told it. He didn't remember if it was weeks or months or a year they traveled (except that one of the older girls who had left the cabin unmarried was still unmarried when they finally stopped, though she had become a mother before they lost the last blue mountain range),

whether it was that winter and then spring and then summer
overtook and passed them on the road or whether they overtook and passed in slow succession the seasons as they descended or whether it was the descent itself that did it and
they not progressing parallel in time but descending perpen-
dicularly through temperature and climate—a (you couldn't
call it a period because as he remembered it or as he told
Grandfather he did, it didn't have either a definite beginning
or a definite ending. Maybe attenuation is better)—an attenuation from a kind of furious inertness and patient immobility
while they sat in the cart outside the doors of doggeries and
taverns and waited for the father to drink himself insensible,
to a sort of dreamy and destinationless locomotion after they
had got the old man out of whatever shed or outhouse or
barn or ditch and loaded him into the cart again and during
which they did not seem to progress at all but just to hang
suspended while the earth itself altered, flattened and broad-
ened out of the mountain cove where they had all been born,
mounting, rising about them like a tide in which the strange
harsh rough faces about the doggery doors into which the old
man was just entering or was just being carried or thrown out
(and this one time by a huge bull of a nigger, the first black
man, slave, they had ever seen, who emerged with the old
man over his shoulder like a sack of meal and his—the nigger's—mouth loud with laughing and full of teeth like tombstones) swam up and vanished and were replaced; the earth,
the world, rising about them and flowing past as if the cart
moved on a treadmill (and it now spring and now summer
and they still moving on toward a place they had never seen
and had no conception of, let alone wanted to go to; and
from a place, a little lost spot on the side of a hill back to
which probably not one of them—excepting possibly the
usually insensible father who made one stage of the journey
accompanied by the raspberry-colored elephants and snakes
which he seems to have been hunting for—could have led the
way) bringing into and then removing from their sober static
country astonishment the strange faces and places, both faces
and places—doggeries and taverns now become hamlets,
hamlets now become villages, villages now towns and the
country flattened out now with good roads and fields and

niggers working in the fields while white men sat fine horses and watched them, and more fine horses and men in fine clothes, with a different look in the face from mountain men about the taverns where the old man was not even allowed to come in by the front door and from which his mountain drinking manners got him ejected before he would have time to get drunk good (so that now they began to make really pretty good time) and no laughter and jeers to the ejecting now, even if the laughter and jeers had been harsh and without much gentleness in them.

"That's the way he got it. He had learned the difference not only between white men and black ones, but he was learning that there was a difference between white men and white men not to be measured by lifting anvils or gouging eyes or how much whiskey you could drink then get up and walk out of the room. That is, he had begun to discern that without being aware of it yet. He still thought that that was just a matter of where you were spawned and how; lucky or not lucky; and that the lucky ones would be even slower and lother than the unlucky to take any advantage of it or credit for it, feel that it gave them anything more than the luck; that they would feel if anything more tender toward the unlucky than the unlucky would ever need to feel toward them. He was to find all that out later. He remembered when he did it, because that was the same second when he discovered the innocence. It was not the second, the moment, that he was long about: it was the getting to it: the moment when they must have realised, believed at last that they were no longer traveling, moving, going somewhere—not the being still at last and in a fashion settled, because they had done that before on the road; he remembered how one time the gradual difference in comfort between the presence and absence of shoes and warm clothing occurred in one place: a cowshed where the sister's baby was born and, as he told Grandfather, for all he could remember, locate in elapsed time, conceived too. Because they were stopped now at last. He didn't know where they were. For a time, during the first days or weeks or months, the woodsman's instinct which he had acquired from the environment where he grew up or maybe had been bequeathed him by the two brothers who had vanished, one of

which had been as far West as the Mississippi River one
time—bequeathed him along with the wornout buckskin garments and such which they left in the cabin when they departed the last time for good—and which he had sharpened
by boy's practice at small game and such, kept him oriented
so that he could have (so he said) found his way back to the
mountain cabin in time. But that was past now, the moment
when he last could have said exactly where he had been born
now weeks and months (maybe a year, the year, since that
was when he became confused about his age and was never
able to straighten it out again, so that he told Grandfather
that he did not know within a year on either side just how old
he was) behind him. So he knew neither where he had come
from nor where he was nor why. He was just there, surrounded by the faces, almost all the faces which he had ever
known, always known (though the number of them, despite
the efforts of the unmarried sister who pretty soon, so he told
Grandfather, and still without any wedding had another baby,
decreasing, thinning out, because of the climate, the warmth,
the dampness) living in a cabin that was almost a replica of
the mountain one except that it didn't sit up in the bright
wind but sat instead beside a big flat river that sometimes
showed no current at all and even sometimes ran backward,
where his sisters and brothers seemed to take sick after supper
and die before the next meal, where regiments of niggers with
white men watching them planted and raised things that he
had never heard of (the old man did something too, something besides drink now. At least, he would leave the cabin
after breakfast and return sober to supper, and he fed them
somehow) and the man who owned all the land and the niggers and apparently the white men who superintended the
work, lived in the biggest house he had ever seen and spent
most of the afternoon (he told how he would creep up among
the tangled shrubbery of the lawn and lie hidden and watch
the man) in a barrel stave hammock between two trees, with
his shoes off and a nigger who wore every day better clothes
than he or his father and sisters had ever owned and ever
expected to, who did nothing else but fan him and bring him
drinks; and he (he was eleven or twelve or thirteen now because this was where he realised that he had irrevocably lost

count of his age) lying there all afternoon while the sisters would come from time to time to the door of the cabin two miles away and scream at him for wood or water, watching that man who not only had shoes in the summertime too, but didn't even have to wear them.

"But he still didn't envy the man he was watching. He coveted the shoes, and probably he would have liked for his father to have a broadcloth monkey to hand him the jug and to carry the wood and water into the cabin for his sisters to wash and cook with and keep the house warm so that he himself would not have to do it. Maybe he even realised, understood the pleasure it would have given his sisters for their neighbors (other whites like them, who lived in other cabins not quite as well built and not at all as well kept and preserved as the ones the nigger slaves lived in but still nimbused with freedom's bright aura, which the slave quarters were not for all their sound roofs and white wash) to see them being waited on. Because he had not only not lost the innocence yet, he had not yet discovered that he possessed it. He no more envied the man than he would have envied a mountain man who happened to own a fine rifle. He would have coveted the rifle, but he would himself have supported and confirmed the owner's pride and pleasure in its ownership because he could not have conceived of the owner taking such crass advantage of the luck which gave the rifle to him rather than to another as to say to other men: *Because I own this rifle, my arms and legs and blood and bones are superior to yours* except as the victorious outcome of a fight with rifles: and how in the world could a man fight another man with dressed-up niggers and the fact that he could lie in a hammock all afternoon with his shoes off? and what in the world would he be fighting for if he did? He didn't even know he was innocent that day when his father sent him to the big house with the message. He didn't remember (or did not say) what the message was, apparently he still didn't know exactly just what his father did, what work (or maybe supposed to do) the old man had in relation to the plantation—a boy either thirteen or fourteen, he didn't know which, in garments his father had got from the plantation commissary and had worn out and which one of the sisters had patched and cut down to fit him and he no more

conscious of his appearance in them or of the possibility that
anyone else would be than he was of his skin, following the
road and turning into the gate and following the drive up
past where still more niggers with nothing to do all day but
plant flowers and trim grass were working, and so to the
house, the portico, the front door, thinking how at last he
was going to see the inside of it, see what else a man was
bound to own who could have a special nigger to hand him
his liquor and pull off his shoes that he didn't even need to
wear, never for one moment thinking but what the man
would be as pleased to show him the balance of his things as
the mountain man would have been to show the powder horn
and bullet mold that went with the rifle. Because he was still
innocent. He knew it without being aware that he did; he
told Grandfather how, before the monkey nigger who came
to the door had finished saying what he did, he seemed to
kind of dissolve and a part of him turn and rush back through
the two years they had lived there like when you pass through
a room fast and look at all the objects in it and you turn and
go back through the room again and look at all the objects
from the other side and you find out you had never seen them
before, rushing back through those two years and seeing a
dozen things that had happened and he hadn't even seen
them before: a certain flat level silent way his older sisters and
the other white women of their kind had of looking at niggers, not with fear or dread but with a kind of speculative
antagonism not because of any known fact or reason but inherited by both white and black, the sense, effluvium of it
passing between the white women in the doors of the sagging
cabins and the niggers in the road and which was not quite
explainable by the fact that the niggers had better clothes, and
which the niggers did not return as antagonism or in any
sense of dare or taunt but through the very fact that they were
apparently oblivious of it, too oblivious of it (you knew that
you could hit them, he told Grandfather, and they would not
hit back or even resist. But you did not want to, because they
(the niggers) were not it, not what you wanted to hit; that
when you hit them you would just be hitting a child's toy
balloon with a face painted on it, a face slick and smooth and
distended and about to burst into laughing and so you did

not dare strike it because it would merely burst and you would rather let it walk on out of your sight than to have stood there in the loud laughing)—of talk at night before the fire when they had company or had themselves gone visiting after supper to another cabin, the voices of the women sober enough, even calm, yet filled with a quality dark and sullen and only some man, usually his father in drink, to break out into harsh recapitulation of his own worth, the respect which his own physical prowess commanded from his fellows, and the boy of either thirteen or fourteen or maybe twelve know-ing that the men and the women were talking about the same thing though it had never once been mentioned by name, like when people talk about privation without mentioning the siege, about sickness without ever naming the epidemic;—of one afternoon when he and his sister were walking along the road and he heard the carriage coming up behind them and stepped off the road and then realised that his sister was not going to give way to it, that she still walked in the middle of the road with a sort of sullen implacability in the very angle of her head and he shouted at her: and then it was all dust and rearing horses and glinting harness buckles and wheel spokes; he saw two parasols in the carriage and the nigger coachman in a plug hat shouting: 'Hoo dar, gal! Git outen de way dar!' and then it was over, gone: the carriage and the dust, the two faces beneath the parasols glaring down at his sister: then he was throwing vain clods of dirt after the dust as it spun on, knowing now, while the monkey-dressed nigger butler kept the door barred with his body while he spoke, that it had not been the nigger coachman that he threw at at all, that it was the actual dust raised by the proud delicate wheels, and just that vain;—of one night late when his father came home, blundered into the cabin; he could smell the whiskey even while still dulled with broken sleep, hearing that same fierce exultation, vindication, in his father's voice: 'We whupped one of Pettibone's niggers tonight' and he roused at that, waked at that, asking which one of Pettibone's niggers and his father said he did not know, had never seen the nigger before: and he asked what the nigger had done and his father said, 'Hell fire, that goddamn son of a bitch Pettibone's nigger.'— how, without knowing it then since he had not yet discovered innocence, he must have meant the question the same way his father meant the answer: no actual nigger, living creature, living flesh to feel pain and writhe and cry out. He could even seem to see them: the torch-disturbed darkness among trees, the fierce hysterical faces of the white men, the balloon face of the nigger. Maybe the nigger's hands would be tied or held but that would be all right because they were not the hands with which the balloon face would struggle and writhe for freedom, not the balloon face: it was just poised among them, levitative and slick with paper-thin distension. Then someone would strike the balloon one single desperate and despairing blow and then he would seem to see them fleeing, running, with all about them, overtaking them and passing and going on and then returning to overwhelm them again, the roaring waves of mellow laughter meaningless and terrifying and loud. And now he stood there before that white door with the monkey nigger barring it and looking down at him in his patched made-over jeans clothes and no shoes and I dont reckon he had even ever experimented with a comb because that would be one of the things that his sisters would keep hidden good—who had never thought about his own hair or clothes or anybody else's hair or clothes until he saw that monkey nigger, who through no doing of his own happened to have had the felicity of being housebred in Richmond maybe, looking—" ("Or maybe even in Charleston," Shreve breathed.) "—at them and he never even remembered what the nigger said, how it was the nigger told him, even before he had had time to say what he came for, never to come to that front door again but to go around to the back.

"He didn't even remember leaving. All of a sudden he found himself running and already some distance from the house, and not toward home. He was not crying, he said. He wasn't even mad. He just had to think, so he was going to where he could be quiet and think, and he knew where that place was. He went into the woods. He says he did not tell himself where to go: that his body, his feet, just went there— a place where a game trail entered a cane brake and an oak tree had fallen across it and made a kind of cave where he kept an iron griddle that he would cook small game on some- times. He said he crawled back into the cave and sat with his back against the uptorn roots, and thought. Because he couldn't get it straight yet. He couldn't even realise yet that his trouble, his impediment, was innocence because he would not be able to realise that until he got it straight. So he was seeking among what little he had to call experience for something to measure it by, and he couldn't find anything. He had been told to go around to the back door even before he could state his errand, who had sprung from a people whose houses didn't have back doors but only windows and anyone entering or leaving by a window would be either hiding or escaping, neither of which he was doing. In fact, he had actually come on business, in the good faith of business which he had believed that all men accepted. Of course he had not expected to be invited in to eat a meal since time, the distance from one cooking pot to the next, did not need to be measured in hours or days; perhaps he had not expected to be asked into the house at all. But he did expect to be listened to because he had come, been sent, on some business which, even though he didn't remember what it was and maybe at the time (he said) he might not even have comprehended, was certainly connected somehow with the plantation that supported and endured that smooth white house and that smooth white brass-decorated door and the very broadcloth and linen and silk stockings the monkey nigger stood in to tell him to go around to the back before he could even state the business. It was like he might have been sent with a lump of lead or even a few molded bullets so that the man who owned the fine rifle could shoot it, and the man came to the door and told him to leave the bullets on a stump at the edge of the woods, not even letting him come close enough to look at the rifle.

"Because he was not mad. He insisted on that to Grandfather. He was just thinking, because he knew that something would have to be done about it; he would have to do something about it in order to live with himself for the rest of his life and he could not decide what it was because of that innocence which he had just discovered he had, which (the innocence, not the man, the tradition) he would have to compete with. He had nothing to compare and gauge it by but the rifle analogy, and it would not make sense by that. He was quite calm about it, he said, sitting there with his arms

around his knees in his little den beside the game trail where
more than once when the wind was right he had seen deer
pass within ten feet of him, arguing with himself quietly and
calmly while both debaters agreed that if there were only
someone else, some older and smarter person to ask. But
there was not, there was only himself, the two of them inside
that one body which was maybe thirteen or maybe fourteen
or maybe was already fifteen but would never know it for
certain forever more, arguing quiet and calm: *But I can shoot
him.* (Not the monkey nigger. It was not the nigger anymore
than it had been the nigger that his father had helped to whip
that night. The nigger was just another balloon face slick and
distended with that mellow loud and terrible laughing so that
he did not dare to burst it, looking down at him from within
the half closed door during that instant in which, before he
knew it, something in him had escaped and—he unable to
close the eyes of it—was looking out from within the balloon
face just as the man who did not even have to wear the shoes
he owned, whom the laughter which the balloon held barricaded and protected from such as he, looked out from whatever invisible place he (the man) happened to be at the
moment, at the boy outside the barred door in his patched
garments and splayed bare feet, looking through and beyond
the boy, he himself seeing his own father and sisters and
brothers as the owner, the rich man (not the nigger) must
have been seeing them all the time—as cattle, creatures heavy
and without grace, brutely evacuated into a world without
hope or purpose for them, who would in turn spawn with
brutish and vicious prolixity, populate, double treble and
compound, fill space and earth with a race whose future
would be a succession of cut-down and patched and made-
over garments bought on exorbitant credit because they were
white people, from stores where niggers were given the garments free, with for sole heritage that expression on a balloon
face bursting with laughter which had looked out at some
unremembered and nameless progenitor who had knocked at
a door when he was a little boy and had been told by a nigger
to go around to the back.): *But I can shoot him:* and the other:
No. That wouldn't do no good: and the first: *What shall we do
then?* and the other: *I dont know:* and the first: *But I can shoot*

him. I could slip right up there through them bushes and lay there until he come out to lay in the hammock and shoot him: and the other: *No. That wouldn't do no good:* and the first: *Then what shall we do?* and the other: *I dont know.*

"Now he was hungry. It was before dinner when he went to the big house, and now there was no sun at all where he crouched though he could still see sun in the tops of the trees around him. But his stomach had already told him it was late and that it would be later still when he reached home. And then he said he began to think *Home. Home* and that he thought at first that he was trying to laugh and that he kept on telling himself it was laughing even after he knew better; home, as he came out of the woods and approached it, still hidden yet, and looked at it—the rough partly rotten log walls, the sagging roof whose missing shingles they did not replace but just set pans and buckets under the leaks, the leanto room which they used for kitchen and which was all right because in good weather it didn't even matter that it had no chimney since they did not attempt to use it at all when it rained, and his sister pumping rhythmic up and down above a washtub in the yard, her back toward him, shapeless in a calico dress and a pair of the old man's shoes unlaced and flapping about her bare ankles and broad in the beam as a cow, the very labor she was doing brutish and stupidly out of all proportion to its reward: the very primary essence of labor, toil, reduced to its crude absolute which only a beast could and would endure; and now (he said) the thought striking him for the first time as to what he would tell his father when the old man asked him if he had delivered the message, whether he would lie or not, since if he did lie he would be found out maybe at once, since probably the man had already sent a nigger down to see why whatever it was his father had failed to do and had sent the excuse for was not done— granted that that was what his errand to the house had been, which (granted his old man) it probably was. But it didn't happen at once because his father was not at home yet. So it was only the sister, as if she had been waiting not for the wood but just for him to return, for the opportunity to use her vocal cords, nagging at him to fetch the wood and he not refusing, not objecting, just not hearing her, paying any at-

tention to her because he was still thinking. Then the old man
came and the sister told on him and the old man made him
fetch the wood: and still nothing said about the errand while
they ate supper nor when he went and lay down on the pallet
where he slept and where he went to bed by just lying down,
only not to sleep now, just lying there with his hands under
his head and still nothing said about it and he still not knowing if he was going to lie or not. Because he said how the
terrible part of it had not occurred to him yet, he just lay
there while the two of them argued inside of him, speaking in
orderly turn, both calm, even leaning backward to be calm
and reasonable and unrancorous: *But I can kill him. —No.
That wouldn't do no good —Then what shall we do about it? —I
dont know:* and he just listening, not especially interested he
said, hearing the two of them without listening. Because what
he was thinking about now he hadn't asked for. It was just
there, natural in a boy, a child, and he not paying any attention to it either because it was what a boy would have
thought, and he knew that to do what he had to do in order
to live with himself he would have to think it out straight as a
man would, thinking *The nigger never give me a chance to tell
him what it was and so he* (not the nigger now either) *wont
know it and whatever it is wont get done and he wont know it aint
done until too late so he will get paid back that much for what he
set that nigger to do and if it only was to tell him that the stable,
the house, was on fire and the nigger wouldn't even let me tell
him, warn him* and then he said that all of a sudden it was not
thinking, it was something shouting it almost loud enough
for his sisters on the other pallet and his father in the bed
with the two youngest and filling the room with alcohol snoring, to hear too: *He never even give me a chance to say it. Not
even to tell it, say it:* it too fast, too mixed up to be thinking, it
all kind of shouting at him at once, boiling out and over him
like the nigger laughing: *He never gave me a chance to say it
and Pap never asked me if I told him or not and so he cant even
know that Pap sent him any message and so whether he got it or
not cant even matter, not even to Pap; I went up to that door for
that nigger to tell me never to come to that front door again and I
not only wasn't doing any good to him by telling it or any harm to
him by not telling it, there aint any good or harm either in the*

living world that I can do to him. It was like that, he said, like an explosion—a bright glare that vanished and left nothing, no ashes nor refuse: just a limitless flat plain with the severe shape of his intact innocence rising from it like a monument; that innocence instructing him as calm as the others had ever spoken, using his own rifle analogy to do it with, and when it said *them* in place of *he* or *him*, it meant more than all the human puny mortals under the sun that might lie in hammocks all afternoon with their shoes off: 'If you were fixing to combat them that had the fine rifles, the first thing you would do would be to get yourself the nearest thing to a fine rifle you could borrow or steal or make, wouldn't it?' and he said Yes. 'But this aint a question of rifles. So to combat them you have got to have what they have that made them do what he did. You got to have land and niggers and a fine house to combat them with. You see?' and he said Yes again. He left that night. He waked before day and departed just like he went to bed: by rising from the pallet and tiptoeing out of the house. He never saw any of his family again.

"He went to the West Indies." Quentin had not moved, not even to raise his head from its attitude of brooding bemusement upon the open letter which lay on the open textbook, his hands lying on the table before him on either side of the book and the letter, one half of which slanted upward from the transverse crease without support, as if it had learned half the secret of levitation. "That was how he said it. He and Grandfather were sitting on a log now because the dogs had faulted. That is, they had treed—a tree from which he (the architect) could not have escaped yet which he had undoubtedly mounted because they found the sapling pole with his suspenders still knotted about one end of it that he had used to climb the tree though at first they could not understand why the suspenders and it was three hours before they comprehended that the architect had used architecture, physics, to elude them as a man always falls back upon what he knows best in a crisis—the murderer upon murder, the thief thieving, the liar lying. He (the architect) knew about the wild negroes even if he couldn't have known that Sutpen would get dogs; he had chosen that tree and hauled that pole up after him and calculated stress and distance and trajectory and had crossed a gap to the next nearest tree that a flying squirrel could not have crossed and traveled from there on from tree to tree for almost half a mile before he put foot on the ground again. It was three hours before one of the wild niggers (the dogs wouldn't leave the tree; they said he was in it) found where he had come down. So he and Grandfather sat on the log and talked, and one of the wild niggers went back to camp for grub and the rest of the whiskey and they blew the other men in with horns and they ate, and he told Grandfather some more of it while they waited.

"He went to the West Indies. That's how he said it: not how he managed to find where the West Indies were nor where ships departed from to go there, nor how he got to where the ships were and got in one nor how he liked the sea nor about the hardships of a sailor's life and it must have been hardship indeed for him, a boy of fourteen or fifteen who had never seen the ocean before, going to sea in 1823. He just said, 'So I went to the West Indies,' sitting there on the log with Grandfather while the dogs still bayed the tree where they believed the architect was because he would have to be there—saying it just like that day thirty years later when he sat in Grandfather's office (in his fine clothes now, even though they were a little soiled and worn with three years of war, with money to rattle in his pocket and his beard at its prime too: beard body and intellect at that peak which all the different parts that make a man reach, where he can say *I did all that I set out to do and I could stop here if I wanted to and no man to chide me with sloth, not even myself*—and maybe this the instant which Fate always picks out to blackjack you, only the peak feels so sound and stable that the beginning of the falling is hidden for a little while—with his head flung up a little in that attitude that nobody ever knew exactly who he had aped it from or if he did not perhaps learn it too from the same book out of which he taught himself the words, the bombastic phrases with which Grandfather said he even asked you for a match for his cigar or offered you the cigar—and nothing of vanity, nothing comic in it either Grandfather said, because of that innocence which he had never lost because after it finally told him what to do that night he forgot about it and didn't know that he still had it) and told Grand-

father—told him, mind; not excusing, asking for no pity; not
explaining, asking for no exculpation: just told Grandfather
how he had put his first wife aside like eleventh and twelfth
century kings did: 'I found that she was not and could never
be, through no fault of her own, adjunctive or incremental to
the design which I had in mind, so I provided for her and put
her aside.'—telling Grandfather in that same tone while they
sat on the log waiting for the niggers to come back with the
other guests and the whiskey: 'So I went to the West Indies. I
had had some schooling during a part of one winter, enough
to have learned something about them, to realise that they
would be most suitable to the expediency of my requirements.' He didn't remember how he came to go to the
school. That is, why his father decided all of a sudden to send
him, what nebulous vision or shape might have evolved out
of the fog of alcohol and nigger-beating and scheming to
avoid work which his old man called his mind—the image
not of ambition nor glory, not to see his son better himself
for his own sake, probably not even some blind instant of
revolt against that same house whose roof had leaked on
probably a hundred families like his which had come and
lived beneath it and vanished and left no trace, nothing, not
even rags and broken crockery, but was probably mere vindictive envy toward one or two men, planters, whom he had to
see every now and then. Anyway, he was sent to school for
about three months one winter—an adolescent boy of thirteen or fourteen in a room full of children three or four years
younger than he and three or four years further advanced, and
he not only probably bigger than the teacher (the kind of
teacher that would be teaching a one-room country school in
a nest of Tidewater plantations) but a good deal more of a
man, who probably brought into the school with him along
with his sober watchful mountain reserve a good deal of latent insubordination that he would not be aware of any more
than he would be aware at first that the teacher was afraid of
him. It would not be intractability and maybe you couldn't
call it pride either, but maybe just the self reliance of mountains and solitude, since some of his blood at least (his mother
was a mountain woman, a Scottish woman who, so he told
Grandfather, never did quite learn to speak English) had been

bred in mountains, but which, whatever it was, was that which forbade him to condescend to memorise dry sums and such but which did permit him to listen when the teacher read aloud.—Sent to school, 'where,' he told Grandfather, 'I learned little save that most of the deeds, good and bad both, incurring opprobrium or plaudits or reward either, within the scope of man's abilities, had already been performed and were to be learned about only from books. So I listened when he would read to us. I realise now that on most of these occasions he resorted to reading aloud only when he saw that the moment had come when his entire school was on the point of rising and leaving the room. But whatever the reason, he read to us and I anyway listened, though I did not know that in that listening I was equipping myself better for what I should later design to do than if I had learned all the addition and subtraction in the book. That was how I learned of the West Indies. Not where they were, though if I had known at the time that that knowledge would someday serve me, I would have learned that too. What I learned was that there was a place called the West Indies to which poor men went in ships and became rich, it didn't matter how, so long as that man was clever and courageous: the latter of which I believed that I possessed, the former of which I believed that, if it were to be learned by energy and will in the school of endeavor and experience, I should learn. I remember how I remained one afternoon when school was out and waited for the teacher, waylaid him (he was a smallish man who always looked dusty, as if he had been born and lived all his life in attics and store rooms) and stepped out. I recall how he started back when he saw me and how I thought at the time that if I were to strike him there would be no resulting outcry but merely the sound of the blow and a puff of dust in the air as when you strike a rug hanging from a line. I asked him if it were true, if what he had read us about the men who got rich in the West Indies were true. "Why not?" he answered, starting back. "Didn't you hear me read it from the book?"—"How do I know that what you read was in the book?" I said. I was that green, that countrified, you see. I had not then learned to read my own name; although I had been attending the school for almost three months, I daresay I knew no more than I did when I entered the schoolroom for the first time. But I had to know, you see. Perhaps a man builds for his future in more ways than one, builds not only toward the body which will be his tomorrow or next year, but toward actions and the subsequent irrevocable courses of resultant action which his weak senses and intellect cannot foresee but which ten or twenty or thirty years from now he will take, will have to take in order to survive the act. Perhaps it was that instinct and not I who grasped one of his arms as he drew back (I did not actually doubt him. I think that even then, even at my age, I realised that he could not have invented it, that he lacked that something which is necessary in a man to enable him to fool even a child by lying. But you see, I had to be sure, had to take whatever method that came to my hand to make sure. And there was nothing else to hand except him) glaring at me and beginning to struggle, and I holding him and saying—I was quite calm, quite calm; I just had to know—saying, "Suppose I went there and found out that it was not so?" and he shrieking now, shouting "Help! Help!" so that I let him go. So when the time came when I realised that to accomplish my design I should need first of all and above all things money in considerable quantities and in the quite immediate future, I remembered what he had read to us and I went to the West Indies.'

"Then the other guests began to ride up, and after a while the niggers came back with the coffee pot and a deer haunch and the whiskey (and one bottle of champagne which they had overlooked, Grandfather said) and he stopped talking for a while. He didn't tell anymore of it until they had eaten and were sitting around smoking while the niggers and the dogs (they had to drag the dogs away from the tree, but especially away from the sapling pole with the architect's suspenders tied to it, as if it was not only that the pole was the last thing the architect had touched but it was the thing his exultation had touched when he saw another chance to elude them, and so it was not only the man but the exultation too which the dogs smelled that made them wild) made casts in all directions, getting further and further away until just before sundown one of the niggers whooped and he (he hadn't spoken for some time, Grandfather said, lying there on one elbow, in the fine boots and the only pants he had and the shirt he had put on when he came out of the mud and washed himself off after he realised that he would have to hunt the architect down himself if he wanted him back alive probably, not talking himself and maybe not even listening while the men talked about cotton and politics, just smoking the cigar Grandfather had given him and looking at the fire embers and maybe making that West Indian voyage again that he had made when he was fourteen and didn't even know where he was going or if he would ever get there or not, no more way of knowing whether the men who said the ship was going there were lying or not than he had of knowing whether or not the school teacher was telling the truth about what was in the book. And he never told whether the voyage was hard or not, how much he must have had to endure to make it. Which of course he did have to endure, but then he believed that all necessary was courage and shrewdness and the one he knew he had and the other he believed he could learn if it were to be taught, and it probably the hardship of the voyage which comforted him that the men who said the ship was going to the West Indies had not lied to him because at that time, Grandfather said, he probably could not have believed in anything that was easy.)—he said, 'There it is' and got up and they all went on and found where the architect had come back to the ground again, with a gain of almost three hours. So they had to go fast now and there wasn't much time to talk, or at least, Grandfather said, he did not appear to intend to resume. Then the sun went down and the other men had to start back to town; they all went except Grandfather, be- cause he wanted to listen some more. So he sent word in by one of the others (he was not married then either) that he would not be home, and he and Sutpen went on until the light failed. Two of the niggers (they were thirteen miles from Sutpen's camp then) had already gone back to get blankets and more grub. Then it was dark and the niggers began to light pine knots and they went on for a little while yet, gain- ing what they could now since they knew that the architect would have had to den soon after dark to keep from traveling in a circle. That was how Grandfather remembered it: he and Sutpen leading their horses (he would look back now and

then and see the horses' eyes shining in the torch light and the
horses' heads tossing and the shadows slipping along their
shoulders and flanks) and the dogs and the niggers (the niggers mostly still naked except for a pair of pants here and
there) with the pine torches smoking and flaring above them
and the red light on their round heads and arms and the mud
they wore in the swamp to keep the mosquitoes off dried
hard and shiny, glinting like glass or china and the shadows
they cast taller than they were at one moment then gone the
next and even the trees and brakes and thickets there one
moment and gone the next though you knew all the time that
they were still there because you could feel them with your
breathing, as though, invisible, they pressed down and condensed the invisible air you breathed. And he said how Sutpen was talking about it again, telling him again before he
realised that this was some more of it, and he said how he
thought how there was something about a man's destiny (or
about the man) that caused the destiny to shape itself to him
like his clothes did, like the same coat that new might have
fitted a thousand men, yet after one man has worn it for a
while it fits no one else and you can tell it anywhere you see it
even if all you see is a sleeve or a lapel: so that his—" ("the
demon's," Shreve said) "—destiny had fitted itself to him, to
his innocence, his pristine aptitude for platform drama and
childlike heroic simplicity just as the fine broadcloth uniform
which you could have seen on ten thousand men during those
four years, which he wore when he came in the office on that
afternoon thirty years later had fitted itself to the swaggering
of all his gestures and to the forensic verbiage in which he
stated calmly, with that frank innocence which we call 'of a
child' except that a human child is the only living creature
that is never either frank or innocent, the most simple and the
most outrageous things. He was telling some more of it, already into what he was telling yet still without telling how he
got to where he was nor even how what he was now involved
in (obviously at least twenty years old now, crouching behind
a window in the dark and firing the muskets through it which
someone else loaded and handed to him) came to occur, getting himself and Grandfather both into that besieged Haitian
room as simply as he got himself to the West Indies by saying

that he decided to go to the West Indies and so he went there;
this anecdote no deliberate continuation of the other one but
merely called to his mind by the picture of the niggers and
torches in front of them; he not telling how he got there,
what had happened during the six years between that day
when he, a boy of fourteen who knew no tongue but English
and not much of that, had decided to go to the West Indies
and become rich, and this night when, overseer or foreman or
something to a French sugar planter, he was barricade in the
house with the planter's family (and now Grandfather said
there was the first mention—a shadow that almost emerged
for a moment and then faded again but not completely
away—of the——" ("It's a girl," Shreve said. "Dont tell me.
Just go on.") "——whom he was to tell Grandfather thirty
years afterward he had found unsuitable to his purpose and so
put aside, though providing for her) and a few frightened
half-breed servants which he would have to turn from the
window from time to time and kick and curse into helping
the girl load the muskets which he and the planter fired
through the windows, and I reckon Grandfather was saying
'Wait wait for God's sake wait' about like you are until he
finally did stop and back up and start over again with at least
some regard for cause and effect even if none for logical sequence and continuity. Or maybe it was the fact that they
were sitting again now, having decided that they had gone far
enough for that night, and the niggers had made camp and
cooked supper and they (he and Grandfather) drank some of
the whiskey and ate and then sat before the fire drinking some
more of the whiskey and he telling it all over and still it was
not absolutely clear—the how and the why he was there and
what he was—since he was not talking about himself. He was
telling a story. He was not bragging about something he had
done; he was just telling a story about something a man
named Thomas Sutpen had experienced, which would still
have been the same story if the man had had no name at all, if
it had been told about any man or no man over whiskey at
night.

"That may have been what slowed him down. But it was
not enough to clarify the story much. He still was not
recounting to Grandfather the career of somebody named

Thomas Sutpen. Grandfather said the only mention he ever
made to those six or seven years which must have existed
somewhere, must have actually occurred, was about the patois
he had to learn in order to oversee the plantation, and the
French he had to learn, maybe not to get engaged to be
married, but which he would certainly need to be able to repudiate the wife after he had already got her—how, so he told
Grandfather, he had believed that courage and shrewdness
would be enough but found that he was wrong and how
sorry he was that he had not taken the schooling along with
the West Indian lore when he discovered that all people did
not speak the same tongue and realised that he would not
only need courage and skill, he would have to learn to speak a
new language, else that design to which he had dedicated
himself would die still-born. So he learned the language just
like he learned to be a sailor I reckon, because Grandfather
asked him why he didn't get himself a girl to live with and
learn it the easy way and Grandfather said how he sat there
with the firelight on his face and the beard and his eyes quiet
and sort of bright, and said—and Grandfather said it was the
only time he ever knew him to say anything quiet and simple:
'On this night I am speaking of (and until my first marriage, I
might add) I was still a virgin. You will probably not believe
that, and if I were to try to explain it you would disbelieve me
more than ever. So I will only say that that too was a part of
the design which I had in my mind' and Grandfather said,
'Why shouldn't I believe it?' and he looking at Grandfather
still with that quiet bright expression about the eyes, saying,
'But do you? Surely you dont hold me in such small contempt
as to believe that at twenty I could neither have suffered
temptation nor offered it?' and Grandfather said, 'You're
right. I shouldn't believe it. But I do.' So it was no tale about
women, and certainly not about love: the woman, the girl,
just that shadow which could load a musket but could not
have been trusted to fire one out the window that night (or
the seven or eight nights while they huddled in the dark and
watched from the windows the barns or granaries or whatever
it is you harvest sugar into, and the fields too, blazing and
smoking: he said how you could smell it, you could smell
nothing else, the rank sweet rich smell as if the hatred and the

implacability, the thousand secret dark years which had created the hatred and implacability, had intensified the smell of
the sugar: and Grandfather said how he remembered then
that he had seen Sutpen each time decline sugar for his coffee
and so he (Grandfather) knew why now but he asked anyway
to be sure and Sutpen told him it was true; that he had not
been afraid until after the fields and barns were all burned and
they had even forgot about the smell of the burning sugar,
but that he had never been able to bear sugar since)—the girl
just emerging for a second of the telling, in a single word
almost, so that Grandfather said it was like he had just seen
her too for a second by the flash of one of the muskets—a
bent face, a single cheek, a chin for an instant beyond a curtain of fallen hair, a white slender arm raised, a delicate hand
clutching a ramrod, and that was all. No more detail and information about that than about how he got from the field,
his overseeing, into the besieged house when the niggers
rushed at him with their machetes, than how he got from the
rotting cabin in Virginia to the fields he oversaw: and this,
Grandfather said, more incredible to him than the getting
there from Virginia because that did infer time, a space the
getting across which did indicate something of leisureliness
since time is longer than any distance, while the other, the
getting from the fields into the barricaded house, seemed to
have occurred with a sort of violent abrogation which must
have been almost as short as his telling about it—a very condensation of time which was the gauge of its own violence,
and he telling it in that pleasant faintly forensic anecdotal
manner apparently just as he remembered it, was impressed
by it through detached and impersonal interest and curiosity
which even fear (that once when he mentioned fear by that
same inverse process of speaking of a time when he was not
afraid, before he became afraid, he put it) failed to leaven very
much. Because he was not afraid until after it was all over,
Grandfather said, because that was all it was to him—a spectacle, something to be watched because he might not have a
chance to see such again, since his innocence still functioned
and he not only did not know what fear was until afterward,
he did not even know that at first he was not terrified; did not
even know that he had found the place where money was to

be had quick if you were courageous and shrewd (he did not
mean shrewdness, Grandfather said. What he meant was un-
scrupulousness only he didn't know that word because it
would not have been in the book from which the school
teacher read. Or maybe that was what he meant by courage,
Grandfather said) but where high mortality was concomitant
with the money and the sheen on the dollars was not from
gold but from blood—a spot of earth which might have been
created and set aside by Heaven itself, Grandfather said, as a
theatre for violence and injustice and bloodshed and all the
satanic lusts of human greed and cruelty, for the last despairing fury of all the pariah-interdict and all the doomed—a
little island set in a smiling and fury-lurked and incredible
indigo sea, which was the halfway point between what we call
the jungle and what we call civilization, halfway between the
dark inscrutable continent from which the black blood, the
black bones and flesh and thinking and remembering and
hopes and desires, was ravished by violence, and the cold
known land to which it was doomed, the civilised land and
people which had expelled some of its own blood and thinking and desires that had become too crass to be faced and
borne longer, and set it homeless and desperate on the lonely
ocean—a little lost island in a latitude which would require
ten thousand years of equatorial heritage to bear its climate, a
soil manured with black blood from two hundred years of
oppression and exploitation until it sprang with an incredible
paradox of peaceful greenery and crimson flowers and sugar
cane sapling size and three times the height of a man and a
little bulkier of course but valuable pound for pound almost
with silver ore, as if nature held a balance and kept a book
and offered a recompense for the torn limbs and outraged
hearts even if man did not, the planting of nature and man
too watered not only by the wasted blood but breathed over
by the winds in which the doomed ships had fled in vain, out
of which the last tatter of sail had sunk into the blue sea,
along which the last vain despairing cry of woman or child
had blown away;—the planting of men too: the yet intact
bones and brains in which the old unsleeping blood that had
vanished into the earth they trod still cried out for vengeance.
And he overseeing it, riding peacefully about on his horse

while he learned the language (that meagre and fragile thread, Grandfather said, by which the little surface corners and edges of men's secret and solitary lives may be joined for an instant now and then before sinking back into the darkness where the spirit cried for the first time and was not heard and will cry for the last time and will not be heard then either), not knowing that what he rode upon was a volcano, hearing the air tremble and throb at night with the drums and the chanting and not knowing that it was the heart of the earth itself he heard, who believed (Grandfather said) that earth was kind and gentle and that darkness was merely something you saw, or could not see in; overseeing what he oversaw and not knowing that he was overseeing it, making his daily expeditions from an armed citadel until the day itself came. And he not telling that either, how that day happened, the steps leading up to it because Grandfather said he apparently did not know, comprehend, what he must have been seeing every day because of that innocence—a pig's bone with a little rotten flesh still clinging to it, a few chicken feathers, a stained dirty rag with a few pebbles tied up in it found on the old man's pillow one morning and none knew (least of all, the planter himself who had been asleep on the pillow) how it had come there because they learned at the same time that all the servants, the half breeds, were missing, and he did not know until the planter told him that the stains on the rag were neither dirt nor grease but blood, nor that what he took to be the planter's gallic rage was actually fear, terror, and he just curious and quite interested because he still looked upon the planter and the daughter both (he told Grandfather how until that first night of the siege he had not once thought that he did not know the girl's christian name, whether he had ever heard it or not. He also told Grandfather, dropped this into the telling as you might flick the joker out of a pack of fresh cards without being able to remember later whether you had removed the joker or not, that the old man's wife had been a Spaniard, and so it was Grandfather and not Sutpen who realised that until that first night of the attack he had possibly not seen the girl as much as a dozen times) as foreigners;— the body of one of the half breeds found at last (he found it, hunted for it for two days without even knowing that what

he was meeting was a blank wall of black secret faces, a wall
behind which almost anything could be preparing to happen
and, as he learned later, almost anything was, and on the third
day found the body where he could not possibly have missed
it during the first hour of the first day if it had been there)
and he sitting on the log, Grandfather said, telling it, making
the gestures to tell it with, whom Grandfather himself had
seen fight naked chest to chest with one of his wild niggers by
the light of the camp fire while his house was building and
who still fought with them by lantern light in the stable after
he had got at last that wife who would be adjunctive to the
forwarding of that design he had in mind, and no bones
about the fighting either, no handshaking and gratulations
while he washed the blood off and donned his shirt because at
the end of it the nigger would be flat on his back with his
chest heaving and another nigger throwing water on him;—
sitting there and telling Grandfather how at last he found the
half breed, or what used to be the half breed, and that he
(Sutpen) had seen as much as most men and had done as
much as most, including some things which he did not boast
about: but that there were some things which a man who
pretended to be civilised saw when he had to but which he
did not talk about, so he would only say that he found the
half breed at last and so began to comprehend that the situation might become serious; then the house, the barricade, the
five of them—the planter, the daughter, two women servants
and himself—shut up in it and the air filled with the smoke
and smell of burning cane and the glare and smoke of it on
the sky and the air throbbing and trembling with the drums
and the chanting—the little lost island beneath its down-
cupped bowl of alternating day and night like a vacuum into
which no help could come, where not even winds from the
outer world came but only the trades, the same weary winds
blowing back and forth across it and burdened still with the
weary voices of murdered women and children homeless and
graveless about the isolating and solitary sea—while the two
servants and the girl whose christian name he did not yet
know loaded the muskets which he and the father fired at no
enemy but at the Haitian night itself, lancing their little vain
and puny flashes into the brooding and blood-weary and

throbbing darkness: and it the very time of year, the season
between hurricanes and any hope of rain: and how on the
eighth night the water gave out and something had to be
done so he put the musket down and went out and subdued
them. That was how he told it: he went out and subdued
them, and when he returned he and the girl became engaged
to marry and Grandfather saying 'Wait wait' sure enough
now, saying, 'But you didn't even know her; you told me that
when the siege began you didn't even know her name' and he
looked at Grandfather and said, 'Yes. But you see, it took me
some time to recover.' Not how he did it. He didn't tell that
either, that of no moment to the story either; he just put the
musket down and had someone unbar the door and then bar
it behind him, and walked out into the darkness and subdued
them, maybe by yelling louder, maybe by standing, bearing
more than they believed any bones and flesh could or should
(should, yes: that would be the terrible thing: to find flesh to
stand more than flesh should be asked to stand); maybe at last
they themselves turning in horror and fleeing from the white
arms and legs shaped like theirs and from which blood could
be made to spurt and flow as it could from theirs and containing an indomitable spirit which should have come from the
same primary fire which theirs came from but which could
not have, could not possibly have (he showed Grandfather
the scars, one of which, Grandfather said, came pretty near
leaving him that virgin for the rest of his life too) and then
daylight came with no drums in it for the first time in eight
days, and they emerged (probably the man and the daughter)
and walked across the burned land with the bright sun shining down on it as if nothing had happened, walking now in
what must have been an incredible desolate solitude and
peaceful quiet, and found him and brought him to the house:
and when he recovered he and the girl were engaged. Then he
stopped."

"All right," Shreve said. "Go on."

"I said he stopped," Quentin said.

"I heard you. Stopped what? How got engaged and then
stopped yet still had a wife to repudiate later? You said he
didn't remember how he got to Haiti, and then he didn't
remember how he got into the house with the niggers sur-

rounding it. Now are you going to tell me he didn't even remember getting married? That he got engaged and then he decided he would stop, only one day he found out he hadn't stopped but on the contrary he was married? And all you called him was just a virgin?"

"He stopped talking, telling it," Quentin said. He had not moved, talking apparently (if to anything) to the letter lying on the open book on the table between his hands. Opposite him Shreve had filled the pipe and smoked it out again. It lay again overturned, a scattering of white ashes fanning out from the bowl, onto the table before his crossed naked arms with which he appeared at the same time both to support and hug himself, since although it was only eleven oclock the room was beginning to cool toward that point where about midnight there would be only enough heat in the radiators to keep the pipes from freezing, though (he would not perform his deep-breathing in the open window tonight at all) he had yet to go to the bedroom and return first with his bathrobe on and next with his overcoat on top of the bathrobe and Quentin's overcoat on his arm. "He just said that he was now engaged to be married and then he stopped telling it. He just stopped, Grandfather said, flat and final like that, like that was all there was, all there could be to it, all of it that made good listening from one man to another over whiskey at night. Maybe it was." His (Quentin's) face was lowered. He spoke still in that curious, that almost sullen flat tone which had caused Shreve to watch him from the beginning with intent detached speculation and curiosity, to watch him still from behind his (Shreve's) expression of cherubic and erudite amazement which the spectacles intensified or perhaps actually created. "He just got up and looked at the whiskey bottle and said, 'No more tonight. We'll get to sleep; we want to get an early start tomorrow. Maybe we can catch him before he limbers up.'

"But they didn't. It was late afternoon before they caught him—the architect I mean—and then only because he had hurt his leg trying to architect himself across the river. But he made a mistake in the calculation this time so the dogs and the niggers bayed him and the niggers making the racket now (Grandfather said how maybe the niggers believed that by fleeing the architect had voluntarily surrendered his status as interdict meat, had voluntarily offered the gambit by fleeing, which the niggers had accepted by chasing him and won by catching him, and that now they would be allowed to cook and eat him, both victors and vanquished accepting this in the same spirit of sport and sportsmanship and no rancor or hard feelings on either side) as they hauled him out (all the men who had started the race yesterday had come back except three, and the ones that returned had brought others, so there were more of them now than when the race started, Grandfather said)—hauled him out of his cave under the river bank: a little man with one sleeve missing from his frock coat and his flowered vest ruined by water and mud where he had fallen in the river and one pants leg ripped down so they could see where he had tied up his leg with a piece of his shirt tail and the rag bloody and the leg swollen, and his hat was completely gone. They never did find it so Grandfather gave him a new hat the day he left when the house was finished. It was in Grandfather's office and Grandfather said the architect took the new hat and looked at it and burst into tears.—a little harried wild-faced man with a two-days' stubble of beard, who came out of the cave fighting like a wildcat, hurt leg and all, with the dogs barking and the niggers whooping and hollering with deadly and merry anticipation, like they were under the impression that since the race had lasted more than twenty-four hours the rules would be automatically abrogated and they would not have to wait to cook him until Sutpen waded in with a short stick and beat niggers and dogs all away, leaving the architect standing there, not scared worth a damn either, just panting a little and Grandfather said a little sick in the face where the niggers had mishandled his leg in the heat of the capture, and making them a speech in French, a long one and so fast that Grandfather said probably another Frenchman could not have understood all of it. But it sounded fine; Grandfather said even he—all of them—could tell that the architect was not apologising; it was fine, Grandfather said, and he said how Sutpen turned toward him but he (Grandfather) was already approaching the architect, holding out the bottle of whiskey already uncorked. And Grandfather saw the eyes in the gaunt face, the eyes desperate and hopeless but indomitable too, invincible too, not beaten yet by a damn sight Grandfather said, and all that fifty-odd hours of dark and swamp and sleeplessness and fatigue and no grub and nowhere to go and no hope of getting there: just a will to endure and a foreknowing of defeat but not beat yet by a damn sight: and he took the bottle in one of his little dirty coon-like hands and raised the other hand and even fumbled about his head for a second before he remembered that the hat was gone, then flung the hand up in a gesture that Grandfather said you simply could not describe, that seemed to gather all misfortune and defeat that the human race ever suffered into a little pinch in his fingers like dust and fling it backward over his head, and raised the bottle and bowed first to Grandfather then to all the other men sitting their horses in a circle and looking at him, and then he took not only the first drink of neat whiskey he ever took in his life but the drink of it that he could no more have conceived himself taking than the Brahmin can believe that that situation can conceivably arise in which he will eat dog."

Quentin ceased. At once Shreve said, "All right. Dont bother to say he stopped now; just go on." But Quentin did not continue at once—the flat, curiously dead voice, the downcast face, the relaxed body not stirring except to breathe; the two of them not moving except to breathe, both young, both born within the same year: the one in Alberta, the other in Mississippi; born half a continent apart yet joined, connected after a fashion in a sort of geographical transubstantiation by that Continental Trough, that River which runs not only through the physical land of which it is the geologic umbilical, not only runs through the spiritual lives of the beings within its scope, but is very Environment itself which laughs at degrees of latitude and temperature, though some of these beings, like Shreve, have never seen it—the two of them who four months ago had never laid eyes on one another yet who since had slept in the same room and eaten side by side of the same food and used the same books from which to prepare to recite in the same freshman courses, facing one another across the lamplit table on which lay the fragile pandora's box of scrawled paper which had filled with violent and unratiocinative djinns and demons this snug monastic coign, this dreamy and heatless alcove of what we call the best of thought. "Just dont bother," Shreve said. "Just get on with it."

"That would take thirty years," Quentin said. "It was thirty years before he told Grandfather any more of it. Maybe he was too busy. All his time for spare talking taken up with furthering that design which he had in mind, and his only relaxation fighting his wild niggers in the stable where the men could hitch their horses and come up from the back and not be seen from the house because he was already married now, his house finished and he already arrested for stealing it and freed again so that was all settled, with a wife and two children—no, three—in it and his land cleared and planted with the seed Grandfather loaned him and him getting rich good and steady now——"

"Yes," Shreve said; "Mr Coldfield: what was that?"

"I dont know," Quentin said. "Nobody ever did know for certain. It was something about a bill of lading, some way he persuaded Mr Coldfield to use his credit: one of those things that when they work you were smart and when they dont you change your name and move to Texas: and Father said how Mr Coldfield must have sat back there in his little store and watched his wagonload of stock double maybe every ten years or at least not lose any ground and seen the chance to do that very same thing all the time, only his conscience (not his courage: Father said he had plenty of that) wouldn't let him. Then Sutpen came along and offered to do it, he and Mr Coldfield to divide the loot if it worked, and he (Sutpen) to take all the blame if it didn't. And Mr Coldfield let him. Father said it was because Mr Coldfield did not believe it would work, that they would get away with it, only he couldn't quit thinking about it, and so when they tried it and it failed he (Mr Coldfield) would be able to get it out of his mind then; and that when it did fail and they were caught, Mr Coldfield would insist on taking his share of the blame as penance and expiation for having sinned in his mind all those years. Because Mr Coldfield never did believe it would work, so when he saw that it was going to work, had worked, the least thing he could do was to refuse to take his share of the profits; that when he saw that it had worked it was his conscience he hated, not Sutpen;—his conscience and the land, the country which had created his conscience and then offered the opportunity to have made all that money to the conscience which it had created, which could do nothing but decline; hated that country so much that he was even glad when he saw it drifting closer and closer to a doomed and fatal war; that he would have joined the Yankee army, Father said, only he was not a soldier and knew that he would either be killed or die of hardship and so not be present on that day when the South would realise that it was now paying the price for having erected its economic edifice not on the rock of stern morality but on the shifting sands of opportunism and moral brigandage. So he chose the only gesture he could think of to impress his disapproval on those who should outlive the fighting and so participate in the remorse—"

"Sure," Shreve said. "That's fine. But Sutpen. The design. Get on, now."

"Yes," Quentin said. "The design.—Getting richer and richer. It must have looked fine and clear ahead for him now: house finished, and even bigger and whiter than the one he had gone to the door of that day and the nigger came in his monkey clothes and told him to go to the back, and he with his own brand of niggers even, which the man who lay in the hammock with his shoes off didn't have, to cull one from and train him to go to the door when his turn came for a little boy without any shoes on and with his pap's cutdown pants for clothes to come and knock on it. Only Father said that that wasn't it now, that when he came to Grandfather's office that day after the thirty years, and not trying to excuse now anymore than he had tried in the bottom that night when they ran the architect, but just to explain now, trying hard to explain now because now he was old and knew it, knew it was being old that he had to talk against: time shortening ahead of him that could and would do things to his chances and possibilities even if he had no more doubt of his bones and flesh than he did of his will and courage, telling Grandfather that the boy-symbol at the door wasn't it because the boy-symbol was just the figment of the amazed and desperate child; that now he would take that boy in where he would never again need to stand on the outside of a white door and knock at it: and not at all for mere shelter but so that that boy, that whatever nameless stranger, could shut that door himself forever behind him on all that he had ever known, and look ahead along the still undivulged light rays in which his descendants who might not even ever hear his (the boy's) name, waited to be born without even having to know that they had once been riven forever free from brutehood just as his own (Sutpen's) children were——"

"Dont say it's just me that sounds like your old man," Shreve said. "But go on. Sutpen's children. Go on."

"Yes," Quentin said. "The two children" thinking *Yes. Maybe we are both Father. Maybe nothing ever happens once and is finished. Maybe happen is never once but like ripples maybe on water after the pebble sinks, the ripples moving on, spreading, the pool attached by a narrow umbilical water-cord to the next pool which the first pool feeds, has fed, did feed, let this second pool contain a different temperature of water, a different molecularity of having seen, felt, remembered, reflect in a different tone the infinite unchanging sky, it doesn't matter: that pebble's watery echo whose fall it did not even see moves across its surface too at the original ripple-space, to the old ineradicable rhythm* thinking *Yes, we are both Father. Or maybe Father and I are both Shreve, maybe it took Father and me both to make Shreve or Shreve and me both to make Father or maybe Thomas Sutpen to make all of us.* "Yes, the two children, the son and the daughter by sex and age so glib to the design that he might have planned that too, by character mental and physical so glib to it that he might have culled them out of the celestial herd of seraphs and cherubim like he chose his twenty niggers out of whatever swapping there must have been when he repudiated that first wife and that child when he discovered that they would not be adjunctive to the forwarding of the design. And Grandfather said there was no conscience about that, that Sutpen sat in the office that afternoon after thirty years and told him how his conscience had bothered him somewhat at first but that he had argued calmly and logically with his conscience until it was settled, just as he must have argued with his conscience about his and Mr Coldfield's bill of lading (only prob-

ably not as long here, since time here would be pressing) until
that was settled;—how he granted that by certain lights there
was injustice in what he did but that he had obviated that as
much as lay in his power by being above-board in the matter;
that he could have simply deserted her, could have taken his
hat and walked out, but he did not: and that he had what
Grandfather would have to admit was a good and valid claim,
if not to the whole place which he alone had saved, as well as
the lives of all the white people on it, at least to that portion
of it which had been specifically described and deeded to him
in the marriage settlement which he had entered in good
faith, with no reservations as to his obscure origin and material equipment, while there had been not only reservation but
actual misrepresentation on their part and misrepresentation
of such a crass nature as to have not only voided and frustrated without his knowing it the central motivation of his
entire design, but would have made an ironic delusion of all
that he had suffered and endured in the past and all that he
could ever accomplish in the future toward that design—
which claim he had voluntarily relinquished, taking only the
twenty niggers out of all he might have claimed and which
many another man in his place would have insisted upon
keeping and (in which contention) would have been supported by both legal and moral sanction even if not the
delicate one of conscience: and Grandfather not saying 'Wait
wait' now because it was that innocence again, that innocence
which believed that the ingredients of morality were like the
ingredients of pie or cake and once you had measured them
and balanced them and mixed them and put them into the
oven it was all finished and nothing but pie or cake could
come out.—Yes, sitting there in Grandfather's office trying to
explain with that patient amazed recapitulation, not to Grandfather and not to himself because Grandfather said that his
very calmness was indication that he had long since given up
any hope of ever understanding it, but trying to explain to
circumstance, to fate itself, the logical steps by which he had
arrived at a result absolutely and forever incredible, repeating
the clear and simple synopsis of his history (which he and
Grandfather both now knew) as if he were trying to explain it
to an intractable and unpredictable child: 'You see, I had a

design in my mind. Whether it was a good or a bad design is
beside the point; the question is, Where did I make the mistake in it, what did I do or misdo in it, whom or what injure
by it to the extent which this would indicate. I had a design.
To accomplish it I should require money, a house, a plantation, slaves, a family—incidentally of course, a wife. I set out
to acquire these, asking no favor of any man. I even risked my
life at one time, as I told you, though as I also told you I did
not undertake this risk purely and simply to gain a wife,
though it did have that result. But that is beside the point
also: suffice that I had the wife, accepted her in good faith,
with no reservations about myself, and I expected as much
from them. I did not even demand, mind, as one of my obscure origin might have been expected to do (or at least be
condoned in the doing) out of ignorance of gentility in dealing with gentleborn people. I did not demand; I accepted
them at their own valuation while insisting on my own part
upon explaining fully about myself and my progenitors: yet
they deliberately withheld from me the one fact which I have
reason to know they were aware would have caused me to
decline the entire matter, otherwise they would not have
withheld it from me—a fact which I did not learn until after
my son was born. And even then I did not act hastily. I could
have reminded them of these wasted years, these years which
would now leave me behind with my schedule not only the
amount of elapsed time which their number represented, but
that compensatory amount of time represented by their number which I should now have to spend to advance myself once
more to the point I had reached and lost. But I did not. I
merely explained how this new fact rendered it impossible
that this woman and child be incorporated in my design, and
following which, as I told you, I made no attempt to keep not
only that which I might consider myself to have earned at the
risk of my life but which had been given to me by signed
testimonials, but on the contrary I declined and resigned all
right and claim to this in order that I might repair whatever
injustice I might be considered to have done by so providing
for the two persons whom I might be considered to have
deprived of anything I might later possess: and this was
agreed to, mind; agreed to between the two parties. And yet,

and after more than thirty years, more than thirty years after
my conscience had finally assured me that if I had done an
injustice, I had done what I could to rectify it——' and
Grandfather not saying Wait now but saying, hollering maybe
even: 'Conscience? Conscience? Good God, man, what else
did you expect? Didn't the very affinity and instinct for misfortune of a man who had spent that much time in a monastery even, let alone one who had lived that many years as
you lived them, tell you better than that? didn't the dread and
fear of females which you must have drawn in with the
primary mammalian milk teach you better? What kind of
abysmal and purblind innocence could that have been which
someone told you to call virginity? what conscience to trade
with which would have warranted you in the belief that you
could have bought immunity from her for no other coin but
justice?'——"

It was at this point that Shreve went to the bedroom and
put on the bathrobe. He did not say Wait, he just rose and left
Quentin sitting before the table, the open book and the letter,
and went out and returned in the robe and sat again and took
up the cold pipe, though without filling it anew or lighting
it as it was. "All right," he said. "So that Christmas Henry
brought him home, into the house, and the demon looked up
and saw the face he believed he had paid off and discharged
twenty-eight years ago. Go on."

"Yes," Quentin said. "Father said he probably named him
himself. Charles Bon. Charles Good. He didn't tell Grandfather that he did, but Grandfather believed he did, would
have. That would have been a part of the cleaning up, just as
he would have done his share toward cleaning up the exploded caps and musket cartridges after the siege if he hadn't
been sick (or maybe engaged); he would have insisted on it
maybe, the conscience again which could not allow her and
the child any place in the design even though he could have
closed his eyes and, if not fooled the rest of the world as they
had fooled him, at least have frightened any man out of
speaking the secret aloud—the same conscience which would
not permit the child, since it was a boy, to bear either his
name or that of its maternal grandfather, yet which would
also forbid him to do the customary and provide a quick

husband for the discarded woman and so give his son an authentic name. He chose the name himself, Grandfather believed, just as he named them all—the Charles Goods and
the Clytemnestras and Henry and Judith and all of them—
that entire fecundity of dragons' teeth as Father called it. And
Father said——"

"Your father," Shreve said. "He seems to have got an awful
lot of delayed information awful quick, after having waited
forty-five years. If he knew all this, what was his reason for
telling you that the trouble between Henry and Bon was the
octoroon woman?"

"He didn't know it then. Grandfather didn't tell him all of
it either, like Sutpen never told Grandfather quite all of it."

"Then who did tell him?"

"I did." Quentin did not move, did not look up while
Shreve watched him. "The day after we——after that night
when we——"

"Oh," Shreve said. "After you and the old aunt. I see. Go
on. And Father said——"

"——said how he must have stood there on the front
gallery that afternoon and waited for Henry and the friend
Henry had been writing home about all fall to come up the
drive, and that maybe after Henry wrote the name in the first
letter Sutpen probably told himself it couldn't be, that there
was a limit even to irony beyond which it became either just
vicious but not fatal horseplay or harmless coincidence, since
Father said that even Sutpen probably knew that nobody
yet ever invented a name that somebody didn't own now or
hadn't owned once: and they rode up at last and Henry said,
'Father, this is Charles' and he——" ("the demon," Shreve
said) "——saw the face and knew that there are situations
where coincidence is no more than the little child that rushes
out onto a football field to take part in the game and the
players run over and around the unscathed head and go on
and shock together and in the fury of the struggle for the
facts called gain or loss nobody even remembers the child nor
saw who came and snatched it back from dissolution;—that
he stood there at his own door, just as he had imagined,
planned, designed, and sure enough and after fifty years the
forlorn nameless and homeless lost child came to knock at it

and no monkey-dressed nigger anywhere under the sun to come to the door and order the child away; and Father said that even then, even though he knew that Bon and Judith had never laid eyes on one another, he must have felt and heard the design—house, position, posterity and all—come down like it had been built out of smoke, making no sound, creating no rush of displaced air and not even leaving any debris. And he not calling it retribution, no sins of the father come home to roost; not even calling it bad luck, but just a mistake: that mistake which he could not discover himself and which he came to Grandfather, not to excuse but just to review the facts for an impartial (and Grandfather said he believed, a legally trained) mind to examine and find and point out to him. Not moral retribution you see: just an old mistake in fact which a man of courage and shrewdness (the one of which he now knew he possessed, the other of which he believed that he had now learned, acquired) could still combat if he could only find out what the mistake had been. Because he did not give up. He never did give up; Grandfather said that his subsequent actions (the fact that for a time he did nothing and so perhaps helped to bring about the very situation which he dreaded) were not the result of any failing of courage or shrewdness or ruthlessness, but were the result of his conviction that it had all come from a mistake and until he discovered what that mistake had been he did not intend to risk making another one.

"So he invited Bon into the house, and for the two weeks of the vacation (only it didn't take that long; Father said that probably Mrs Sutpen had Judith and Bon already engaged from the moment she saw Bon's name in Henry's first letter) he watched Bon and Henry and Judith, or watched Bon and Judith rather because he would have already known about Henry and Bon from Henry's letters about him from the school; watched them for two weeks, and did nothing. Then Henry and Bon went back to school and now the nigger groom that fetched the mail back and forth each week between Oxford and Sutpen's Hundred brought letters to Judith now that were not in Henry's hand (and that not necessary either, Father said, because Mrs Sutpen was already covering the town and county both with news of that engagement that

Father said didn't exist yet) and still he did nothing. He
didn't do anything at all until spring was almost over and
Henry wrote that he was bringing Bon home with him to
stay a day or two before Bon went home. Then Sutpen went
to New Orleans. Whether he chose that time to go in order
to get Bon and his mother together and thrash the business
out for good and all or not, nobody knows, just as nobody
knows whether he ever saw the mother or not while he was
there, if she received him or refused to receive him; or if she
did and he tried once more to come to terms with her, buy
her off maybe with money now, since Father said that a man
who could believe that a scorned and outraged and angry
woman could be bought off with formal logic would believe
that she could be placated with money too, and it didn't
work; or if Bon was there and it was Bon himself who refused
the offer, though nobody ever did know if Bon ever knew
Sutpen was his father or not, whether he was trying to revenge his mother or not at first and only later fell in love, only
later succumbed to the current of retribution and fatality
which Miss Rosa said Sutpen had started and had doomed all
his blood to, black and white both. But it didn't work evidently, and the next Christmas came and Henry and Bon
came to Sutpen's Hundred again and now Sutpen saw that
there was no help for it, that Judith was in love with Bon and
whether Bon wanted revenge or was just caught and sunk and
doomed too, it was all the same. So it seems that he sent for
Henry that Christmas eve just before supper time (Father said
that maybe by now, after his New Orleans trip, he had
learned at last enough about women to know it wouldn't do
any good to go to Judith first) and told Henry. And he knew
what Henry would say and Henry said it and he took the lie
from his son and Henry knew by his father taking the lie that
what his father had told him was true; and Father said that
he (Sutpen) probably knew what Henry would do too and
counted on Henry doing it because he still believed that it
had been only a minor tactical mistake, and so he was like a
skirmisher who is outnumbered yet cannot retreat who believes that if he is just patient enough and clever enough and
calm enough and alert enough he can get the enemy scattered
and pick them off one by one. And Henry did it. And he

(Sutpen) probably knew what Henry would do next too, that Henry too would go to New Orleans to find out for himself. Then it was '61 and Sutpen knew what they would do now, not only what Henry would do but what he would force Bon to do; maybe (being a demon—though it would not require a demon to foresee war now) he even foresaw that Henry and Bon would join that student company at the University; he may have had some way of watching, knowing the day their names appeared on the roster, some way of knowing where the company was even before Grandfather became colonel of the regiment the company was in until he got hurt at Pittsburg Landing (where Bon was wounded) and came home to get used to not having any right arm and Sutpen came home in '64 with the two tombstones and talked to Grandfather in the office that day before both of them went back to the war;—knew all the time where Henry and Bon were, that they had been all the time in Grandfather's regiment where Grandfather could look after them in a fashion even if Grandfather didn't know that he was doing it—even if they needed watching, because Sutpen must have known about the probation too, what Henry was doing now: holding all three of them—himself and Judith and Bon—in that suspension while he wrestled with his conscience to make it come to terms with what he wanted to do just like his father had that time more than thirty years ago, maybe even turned fatalist like Bon now and giving the war a chance to settle the whole business by killing him or Bon or both of them (but with no help, no fudging, on his part because it was him that carried Bon to the rear after Pittsburg Landing) or maybe he knew that the South would be whipped and then there wouldn't be anything left that mattered that much, worth getting that heated over, worth protesting against or suffering for or dying for or even living for. That was the day he came to the office, his——" ("the demon's," Shreve said) "——one day of leave at home, came home with his tombstones and Judith was there and I reckon he looked at her and she looked at him and he said, 'You know where he is' and Judith didn't lie to him, and (he knew Henry) he said, 'But you have not heard from him yet' and Judith didn't lie about that either and she didn't cry either because both of them knew what would be in the letter when it came so he didn't have to ask, 'When he writes you that he is coming, you and Clytie will start making the wedding dress' even if Judith would have lied to him about that, which she would not have: so he put one of the stones on Ellen's grave and set the other one up in the hall and came in to see Grandfather, trying to explain it, seeing if Grandfather could discover that mistake which he believed was the sole cause of his problem, sitting there in his worn and shabby uniform, with his worn gauntlets and faded sash and (he would have had the plume by all means. He might have had to discard his sabre, but he would have had the plume) the plume in his hat broken and frayed and soiled, with his horse saddled and waiting in the street below and a thousand miles to ride to find his regiment, yet he sitting there on the one afternoon of his leave as though he had a thousand of them, as if there were no haste nor urgency anywhere under the sun and that when he departed he had no further to go than the twelve miles out to Sutpen's Hundred and a thousand days or maybe even years of monotony and rich peace, and he, even after he would become dead, still there, still watching the fine grandsons and great-grandsons springing as far as eye could reach; he still, even though dead in the earth, that same fine figure of a man that Wash Jones called him, but not now. Now fogbound by his own private embattlement of personal morality: that picayune splitting of abstract hairs while (Grandfather said) Rome vanished and Jericho crumbled, that *this would be right if* or *that would be wrong but* of slowing blood and stiffening bones and arteries that Father says men resort to in senility who while young and supple and strong reacted to a single simple Yes and a single simple No as instantaneous and complete and unthinking as the snapping on and off of electricity, sitting there and talking and now Grandfather not knowing what he was talking about because now Grandfather said he did not believe that Sutpen himself knew because even yet Sutpen had not quite told him all of it. And this that morality again, Grandfather said: that morality which would not permit him to malign or traduce the memory of his first wife, or at least the memory of the marriage even though he felt that he had been tricked by it, not even to an acquaintance in whose confidence

and discretion he trusted enough to wish to justify himself,
not even to his son by another marriage in order to preserve
the status of his life's attainment and desire, except as a last
resort. Not that he would hesitate then, Grandfather said: but
not until then. He had been tricked by it himself, but he had
extricated himself without asking or receiving help from any
man; let anyone else who might be so imposed upon do the
same.—Sitting there and moralising on the fact that, no
matter which course he chose, the result would be that that
design and plan to which he had given fifty years of his life
had just as well never have existed at all by almost exactly fifty
years, and Grandfather not knowing what choice he was talking about even, what second choice he was faced with until
the very last word he spoke before he got up and put on his
hat and shook Grandfather's left hand and rode away; this
second choice, need to choose, as obscure to Grandfather as
the reason for the first, the repudiation, had been: so that
Grandfather did not even say 'I dont know which you should
choose' not because that was all he could have said and so to
say that would be less than no answer at all, but that anything
he might have said would have been less than no answer at all
since Sutpen was not listening, did not expect an answer, who
had not come for pity and there was no advice that he could
have taken, and justification he had already coerced from his
conscience thirty years ago. And he still knew that he had
courage, and though he may have come to doubt lately that
he had acquired that shrewdness which at one time he believed he had, he still believed that it existed somewhere in
the world to be learned and that if it could be learned he
would yet learn it—and maybe even this, Grandfather said: if
shrewdness could not extricate him this second time as it had
before, he could at least depend on the courage to find him
will and strength to make a third start toward that design as it
had found him to make the second with—who came into the
office not for pity and not for help because Grandfather said
he had never learned how to ask anybody for help or anything
else and so he would not have known what to do with the
help if Grandfather could have given it to him, but came just
with that sober and quiet bemusement, hoping maybe (if he
hoped at all, if he were doing anything but just thinking out

loud at all) that the legal mind might perceive and clarify that initial mistake which he still insisted on, which he himself had not been able to find: 'I was faced with condoning a fact which had been foisted upon me without my knowledge during the process of building toward my design, which meant the absolute and irrevocable negation of the design; or in holding to my original plan for the design in pursuit of which I had incurred this negation. I chose, and I made to the fullest what atonement lay in my power for whatever injury I might have done in choosing, paying even more for the privilege of choosing as I chose than I might have been expected to, or even (by law) required. Yet I am now faced with a second necessity to choose, the curious factor of which is not, as you pointed out and as first appeared to me, that the necessity for a new choice should have arisen, but that either choice which I might make, either course which I might choose, leads to the same result: either I destroy my design with my own hand, which will happen if I am forced to play my last trump card, or do nothing, let matters take the course which I know they will take and see my design complete itself quite normally and naturally and successfully to the public eye, yet to my own in such fashion as to be a mockery and a betrayal of that little boy who approached that door fifty years ago and was turned away, for whose vindication the whole plan was conceived and carried forward to the moment of this choice, this second choice devolving out of that first one which in its turn was forced on me as the result of an agreement, an arrangement which I had entered in good faith, concealing nothing, while the other party or parties to it concealed from me the one very factor which would destroy the entire plan and design which I had been working toward, concealed it so well that it was not until after the child was born that I discovered that this factor existed'——"

"Your old man," Shreve said. "When your grandfather was telling this to him, he didn't know any more what your grandfather was talking about than your grandfather knew what the demon was talking about when the demon told it to him, did he? And when your old man told it to you, you wouldn't have known what anybody was talking about if you hadn't been out there and seen Clytie. Is that right?"

"Yes," Quentin said. "Grandfather was the only friend he had."

"The demon had?" Quentin didn't answer, didn't move. It was cold in the room now. The heat was almost gone out of the radiators: the cold iron fluting stern signal and admonition for sleeping, the little death, the renewal. It had been some time now since the chimes had rung eleven. "All right," Shreve said. He was hugging himself into the bathrobe now as he had formerly hugged himself inside his pink naked almost hairless skin. "He chose. He chose lechery. So do I. But go on." His remark was not intended for flippancy nor even derogation. It was born (if from any source) of that incorrigible unsentimental sentimentality of the young which takes the form of hard and often crass levity—to which, by the way, Quentin paid no attention whatever, resuming as if he had never been interrupted, his face still lowered, still brooding apparently on the open letter upon the open book between his hands.

"He left for Virginia that night. Grandfather said how he went to the window and watched him ride across the square on the gaunt black stallion, erect in his faded gray, the hat with its broken plume cocked a little yet not quite so much as the beaver of the old days, as if (Grandfather said) even with his martial rank and prerogatives he did not quite swagger like he used to do, not because he was chastened by misfortune or spent or even war-wearied but as though even while riding he was still bemused in that state in which he struggled to hold clear and free above a maelstrom of unpredictable and unreasoning human beings, not his head for breath and not so much his fifty years of effort and striving to establish a posterity, but his code of logic and morality, his formula and recipe of fact and deduction whose balanced sum and product declined, refused to swim or even float;—saw him approach the Holston House and saw old Mr McCaslin and two other old men hobble out and stop him, he sitting the stallion and talking to them and his voice not raised, Grandfather said, yet the very sober quality of his gestures and the set of his shoulders forensic, oratorical. Then he went on. He could still reach Sutpen's Hundred before dark, so it was probably after supper that he headed the stallion toward the Atlantic Ocean, he and Judith facing one another again for maybe a full minute, he not needing to say 'I will stop it if I can', she not needing to say 'Stop it then—if you can' but just goodbye, the kiss on the brow and no tears; a word to Clytie and to Wash: master to slave, baron to retainer: 'Well, Clytie, take care of Miss Judith.—Wash, I'll send you a piece of Abe Lincoln's coat tail from Washington' and I reckon Wash answering like it used to be under the scuppernongs with the demijohn and the well bucket: 'Sho, Kernel; kill ever one of the varmints!' So he ate the hoecake and drank the parched acorn coffee and rode away. Then it was '65 and the army (Grandfather had gone back to it too; he was a brigadier now though I reckon this was for more reason than because he just had one arm) had retreated across Georgia and into Carolina and they all knew it wouldn't be very much longer now. Then one day Lee sent Johnston some reinforcements from one of his corps and Grandfather found out that the Twenty-third Mississippi was one of the regiments. And he (Grandfather) didn't know what had happened: whether Sutpen had found out in some way that Henry had at last coerced his conscience into agreeing with him as his (Henry's) father had done thirty years ago, whether Judith perhaps had written her father that she had heard from Bon at last and what she and Bon intended to do, or if the four of them had just reached as one person that point where something had to be done, had to happen, he (Grandfather) didn't know. He just learned one morning that Sutpen had ridden up to Grandfather's old regiment's headquarters and asked and received permission to speak to Henry and did speak to him and then rode away again before midnight."

"So he got his choice made, after all," Shreve said. "He played that trump after all. And so he came home and found——"

"Wait," Quentin said.

"——what he must have wanted to find or anyway what he was going to find——"

"Wait, I tell you!" Quentin said, though still he did not move nor even raise his voice—that voice with its tense suffused restrained quality: "I am telling" *Am I going to have to hear it all again* he thought *I am going to have to hear it all over again I am already hearing it all over again I am listening to it all over again I shall have to never listen to anything else but this again forever so apparently not only a man never outlives his father but not even his friends and acquaintances do:*—(that at least regarding which he should have needed no word nor warning even if Judith would have sent him one, sent him acknowledgement that she was beaten, who according to Mr Compson would no more have sent him acknowledgement that he had beat her than she waited (who Miss Coldfield said was not bereaved) and met him on his return, not with the fury and despair perhaps which he might have expected even though knowing as little, having learned as little, about women as Mr Compson said he had, yet certainly with something other than the icy calm with which, according to Miss Coldfield, she met him—the kiss again after almost two years, on the brow; the voices, the speeches, quiet, contained, almost impersonal: "And—?" "Yes. Henry killed him" followed by the brief tears which ceased on the instant when they began, as if the moisture consisted of a single sheet or layer thin as a cigarette paper and in the shape of a human face; the "Ah, Clytie. Ah, Rosa.—Well, Wash. I was unable to penetrate far enough behind the Yankee lines to cut a piece from that coat tail as I promised you"; the (from Jones) guffaw, the chortle, the old imbecile stability of the articulated mud which, Mr Compson said, outlasts the victories and the defeats both: "Well, Kernel, they kilt us but they aint whupped us yit, air they?": and that was all. He had returned. He was home again where his problem now was haste, passing time, the need to hurry. *He was not concerned,* Mr Compson said, *about the courage and the will, nor even about the shrewdness now. He was not for one moment concerned about his ability to start the third time. All that he was concerned about was the possibility that he might not have time sufficient to do it in, regain his lost ground in. He did not waste any of what time he had either. The will and the shrewdness too he did not waste, though he doubtless did not consider it to have been either his will or his shrewdness which supplied waiting to his hand the opportunity, and it was probably less of shrewdness and more of courage than even will which got him engaged to Miss Rosa within a period of three months and almost before she was*

*aware of the fact—Miss Rosa, the chief disciple and advocate
of that cult of demon-harrying of which he was the chief object
(even though not victim), engaged to him before she had got accustomed to having him in the house;—yes, more of courage than
even will, yet something of shrewdness too: the shrewdness acquired
in excruciating driblets through the fifty years suddenly capitulant
and retroactive or suddenly sprouting and flowering like a seed
lain fallow in a vacuum or in a single iron clod. Because he seemed
to perceive without stopping, in that passage through the house
which was an unbroken continuation of the long journey from
Virginia, the pause not to greet his family but merely to pick up
Jones and drag him on out to the brier-choked fields and fallen
fences and clap axe or mattock into his hands, the one weak spot,
the one spot vulnerable to assault in Miss Rosa's embattled
spinsterhood, and to assault and carry this in one stride, with
something of the ruthless tactical skill of his old master (the
Twenty-third Mississippi was in Jackson's corps at one time). And
then the shrewdness failed him again. It broke down, it vanished
into that old impotent logic and morality which had betrayed him
before: and what day might it have been, what furrow might he
have stopped dead in, one foot advanced, the unsentient plow handles in his instantaneous unsentient hands, what fence panel held
in midair as though it had no weight by muscles which could not
feel it, when he realised that there was more in his problem than
just lack of time, that the problem contained some super-distillation
of this lack: that he was now past sixty and that possibly he could
get but one more son, had at best but one more son in his loins, as
the old cannon might know when it has just one more shot in its
corporeality. So he suggested what he suggested to her, and she did
what he should have known she would do and would have known
probably if he had not bogged himself again in his morality which
had all the parts but which refused to run, to move. Hence the
proposal, the outrage and unbelief; the tide, the blast of indignation and anger upon which Miss Rosa vanished from Sutpen's
Hundred, her air-ballooned skirts spread upon the flood, chip-light,
her bonnet (possibly one of Ellen's which she had prowled out of
the attic) clapped fast onto her head rigid and precarious with
rage. And he standing there with the reins over his arm, with perhaps something like smiling inside his beard and about the eyes
which was not smiling but the crinkled concentration of furious*

*thinking:—the haste, the need for it; the urgency but not fear,
not concern: just the fact that he had missed that time, though
luckily it was just a spotting shot with a light charge, and the old
gun, the old barrel and carriage none the worse; only next time
there might not be enough powder for both a spotting shot and
then a full-sized load;—the fact that the thread of shrewdness and
courage and will ran onto the same spool which the thread of his
remaining days ran onto and that spool almost near enough for
him to reach out his hand and touch it. But this was no grave
concern yet, since it (the old logic, the old morality which had never
yet failed to fail him) was already falling into pattern, already
showing him conclusively that he had been right, just as he knew
he had been, and therefore what had happened was just a delusion
and did not actually exist)*

"No," Shreve said; "you wait. Let me play a while now.
Now, Wash. Him (the demon) standing there with the horse,
the saddled charger, the sheathed sabre, the gray waiting to
be laid peaceful away among the moths and all lost save dishonor: then the voice of the faithful grave-digger who opened
the play and would close it, coming out of the wings like
Shakespeare's very self: 'Well, Kernel, they mought have
whupped us but they aint kilt us yit, air they?'——" This was
not flippancy either. It too was just that protective coloring
of levity behind which the youthful shame of being moved
hid itself, out of which Quentin also spoke, the reason for
Quentin's sullen bemusement, the (on both their parts) flip-
ness, the strained clowning: the two of them, whether they
knew it or not, in the cold room (it was quite cold now)
dedicated to that best of ratiocination which after all was a
good deal like Sutpen's morality and Miss Coldfield's demon-
ising—this room not only dedicated to it but set aside for it
and suitably so since it would be here above any other place
that it (the logic and the morality) could do the least amount
of harm;—the two of them back to back as though at the last
ditch, saying No to Quentin's Mississippi shade who in life
had acted and reacted to the minimum of logic and morality,
who dying had escaped it completely, who dead remained not
only indifferent but impervious to it, somehow a thousand
times more potent and alive. There was no harm intended by
Shreve and no harm taken, since Quentin did not even stop.

He did not even falter, taking Shreve up in stride without comma or colon or paragraph:

"——no reserve to risk a spotting shot with now so he started this one like you start a rabbit out of a brier patch, with a little chunk of dried mud thrown by hand. Maybe it was the first string of beads out of his and Wash's little store where he would get mad at his customers, the niggers and the trash and the haggling, and turn them out and lock the door and drink himself blind. And maybe Wash delivered the beads himself, Father said, that was down at the gate when he rode back from the war that day, that after he went away with the regiment would tell folks that he (Wash) was looking after Kernel's place and niggers until after a while maybe he even believed it. Father's mother said how when the Sutpen niggers first heard about what he was saying, they would stop him in the road that came up out of the bottom where the old fishing camp was that Sutpen let him and the granddaughter (she was about eight then) live in. There would be too many of them for him to whip them all, to even try to, risk trying to: and they would ask him why he wasn't at the war and he would say, 'Git outen my road, niggers!' and then it would be the outright laughing, asking one another (except it was not one another but him): 'Who him, calling us niggers?' and he would rush at them with a stick and them avoiding him just enough, not mad at all, just laughing. And he was still carrying fish and animals he killed (or maybe stole) and vegetables up to the house when that was about all Mrs Sutpen and Judith (and Clytie too) had to live on, and Clytie would not let him come into the kitchen with the basket even, saying, 'Stop right there, white man. Stop right where you is. You aint never crossed this door while Colonel was here and you aint going to cross it now.' Which was true, only Father said there was a kind of pride in it: that he had never tried to enter the house, even though he believed that if he had tried, Sutpen would not have let them repulse him; like (Father said) he might have said to himself *The reason I wont try it aint that I refuse to give any black nigger the chance to tell me I cant but because I aint going to force Mister Tom to have to cuss a nigger or take a cussing from his wife on my account* But they would drink together under the scuppernong arbor on the Sunday after-

noons, and on the week days he would see Sutpen (the fine
figure of the man as he called it) on the black stallion, galloping about the plantation, and Father said how for that moment Wash's heart would be quiet and proud both and that
maybe it would seem to him that this world where niggers,
that the Bible said had been created and cursed by God to be
brute and vassal to all men of white skin, were better found
and housed and even clothed than he and his granddaughter—that this world where he walked always in mocking and
jeering echoes of nigger laughter, was just a dream and an
illusion and that the actual world was the one where his own
lonely apotheosis (Father said) galloped on the black thoroughbred, thinking maybe, Father said, how the Book said
that all men were created in the image of God and so all men
were the same in God's eyes anyway, looked the same to God
at least, and so he would look at Sutpen and think *A fine
proud man. If God Himself was to come down and ride the natural earth, that's what He would aim to look like.* Maybe he even
delivered the first string of beads himself, and Father said
maybe each of the ribbons afterward during the next three
years while the girl matured fast like girls of that kind do; or
anyway he would know and recognise each and every ribbon
when he saw it on her even when she lied to him about where
and how she got it, which she probably did not, since she
would be bound to know that he had been seeing the ribbons
in the showcase every day for three years and would have
known them as well as he knew his own shoes. And not only
he knew them, but all the other men, the customers and the
loungers, the white and the black that would be sitting and
squatting about the store's gallery to watch her pass, not quite
defiant and not quite cringing and not quite flaunting the ribbons and the beads, but almost; not quite any of them but a
little of all: bold sullen and fearful. But Father said how
Wash's heart was probably still quiet even after he saw the
dress and spoke about it, probably only a little grave now and
watching her secret defiant frightened face while she told him
(before he had asked, maybe too insistent, too quick to volun-
teer it) that Miss Judith had given it to her, helped her to
make it: and Father said maybe he realised all of a sudden and
without warning that when he passed the men on the gallery

they would look after him too and that they already knew that
which he had just thought they were probably thinking. But
Father said his heart was still quiet, even now, and that he
answered, if he answered at all, stopped the protestations and
disclaimers at all: 'Sho, now. Ef Kernel and Miss Judith
wanted to give hit to you, I hope you minded to thank
them.'—Not alarmed, Father said: just thoughtful, just
grave; and Father said how that afternoon Grandfather rode
out to see Sutpen about something and there was nobody in
the front of the store and he was about to go out and go up
to the house when he heard the voices from the back and he
walked on toward them and so he overheard them before he
could begin to not listen and before he could make them hear
him calling Sutpen's name. Grandfather couldn't see them yet,
he hadn't even got to where they could hear him yet, but he
said he knew exactly how they would be: Sutpen having already told Wash to get the jug out and then Wash spoke and
Sutpen beginning to turn, realising that Wash wasn't getting
the jug before he comprehended the import of what Wash
was saying, then comprehending that and still half turned and
then all of a sudden kind of reared back and flinging his head
up, looking at Wash and Wash standing there, not cringing
either, in that attitude dogged and quiet and not cringing,
and Sutpen said, 'What about the dress?' and Grandfather
said it was Sutpen's voice that was short and sharp: not
Wash's; that Wash's voice was just flat and quiet, not abject:
just patient and slow: 'I have knowed you for going on
twenty years now. I aint never denied yit to do what you told
me to do. And I'm a man past sixty. And she aint nothing but
a fifteen-year-old gal.' and Sutpen said, 'Meaning that I'd
harm the girl? I, a man as old as you are?' and Wash: 'If you
was arra other man, I'd say you was as old as me. And old or
no old, I wouldn't let her keep that dress nor nothing else
that come from your hand. But you are different.' and Sutpen: 'How different?' and Grandfather said how Wash did not
answer and that he called again now and neither of them
heard him; and then Sutpen said: 'So that's why you are
afraid of me?' and Wash said, 'I aint afraid. Because you are
brave. It aint that you were a brave man at one second or
minute or hour of your life and got a paper to show hit from

General Lee. But you are brave, the same as you are alive and breathing. That's where it's different. Hit dont need no ticket from nobody to tell me that. And I know that whatever your hands tech, whether hit's a regiment of men or a ignorant gal or just a hound dog, that you will make hit right.' Then Grandfather heard Sutpen move, sudden and sharp, and Grandfather said he reckoned, thought just about what he imagined Wash was thinking. But all Sutpen said was, 'Get the jug.'—'Sho, Kernel,' Wash said.

"So that Sunday came, a year after that day and three years after he had suggested to Miss Rosa that they try it first and if it was a boy and lived, they would be married. It was before daylight and he was expecting his mare to foal to the black stallion, so when he left the house before day that morning Judith thought he was going to the stable, who knew what and how much about her father and Wash's granddaughter nobody knew, how much she could not have helped but know from what Clytie must have known (may have or may not have told her, whether or no) since everybody else white or black in the neighborhood knew who had ever seen the girl pass in the ribbons and beads which they all recognised, how much she may have refused to discover during the fitting and sewing of that dress (Father said Judith actually did this; this was no lie that the girl told Wash: the two of them alone all day long for about a week in the house: and what they must have talked about, what Judith must have talked about while the girl stood around in what she possessed to call under clothes, with her sullen defiant secret watchful face, answering what, telling what that Judith may or may not have tried to shut her eyes to, nobody knew). So it was not until he failed to return at dinner time that she went or sent Clytie to the stable and found that the mare had foaled in the night but that her father was not there. And it was not until mid-afternoon that she found a halfgrown boy and paid him a nickel to go down to the old fish camp and ask Wash where Sutpen was, and the boy walked whistling around the corner of the rotting cabin and saw maybe the scythe first, maybe the body first lying in the weeds which Wash had not yet cut, and as he screamed he looked up and saw Wash in the window, watching him. Then about a week later they caught the nigger, the midwife, and she told how she didn't know that Wash was there at all that dawn when she heard the horse and then Sutpen's feet and he came in and stood over the pallet where the girl and the baby were and said, 'Penelope—("that was the mare")—foaled this morning. A damned fine colt. Going to be the spit and image of his daddy when I rode him North in '61. Do you remember?' and the old nigger said she said, 'Yes, Marster' and that he jerked the riding whip toward the pallet and said, 'Well? Damn your black hide: horse or mare?' and that she told him and that he stood there for a minute and he didn't move at all, with the riding whip against his leg and the lattices of sunlight from the unchinked wall falling upon him, across his white hair and his beard that hadn't turned at all yet, and she said she saw his eyes and then his teeth inside his beard and that she would have run then only she couldn't, couldn't seem to make her legs bear to get up and run: and then he looked at the girl on the pallet again and said, 'Well, Milly; too bad you're not a mare too. Then I could give you a decent stall in the stable' and turned and went out. Only she could not move even yet, and she didn't even know that Wash was outside there; she just heard Sutpen say, 'Stand back, Wash. Dont you touch me': and then Wash, his voice soft and hardly loud enough to reach her: 'I'm going to tech you, Kernel': and Sutpen again: 'Stand back, Wash!' sharp now, and then she heard the whip on Wash's face but she didn't know if she heard the scythe or not because now she found out that she could move, get up, run out of the cabin and into the weeds, running——"

"Wait," Shreve said; "wait. You mean that he had got the son at last that he wanted, yet still he——"

"——walked the three miles and back before midnight to fetch the old nigger, then sat on the sagging gallery until daylight came and the granddaughter stopped screaming inside the cabin and he even heard the baby once, waiting for Sutpen. And Father said his heart was quiet then too, even though he knew what they would be saying in every cabin about the land by nightfall, just as he had known what they were saying during the last four or five months while his granddaughter's condition (which he had never tried to conceal) could no longer be mistaken: *Wash Jones has fixed old*

Sutpen at last. It taken him twenty years to do it, but he has got a holt of old Sutpen at last where Sutpen will either have to tear meat or squeal That's what Father said he was thinking while he waited outside on the gallery where the old nigger had sent him, ordered him out, standing there maybe by the very post where the scythe had leaned rusting for two years, while the granddaughter's screams came steady as a clock now but his own heart quiet, not at all concerned nor alarmed; and Father said that maybe while he stood befogged in his fumbling and groping (that morality of his that was a good deal like Sutpen's, that told him he was right in the face of all fact and usage and everything else) which had always been somehow mixed up and involved with galloping hooves even during the old peace that nobody remembered, and in which during the four years of the war which he had not attended the galloping had been only the more gallant and proud and thunderous;—Father said that maybe he got his answer; that maybe there broke free and plain in midgallop against the yellow sky of dawn the fine proud image of the man on the fine proud image of the stallion and that the fumbling and the groping broke clear and free too, not in justification or explanation or extenuation or excuse, Father said, but as the apotheosis lonely, explicable, beyond all human fouling: *He is bigger than all them Yankees that killed us and ourn, that killed his wife and widowed his daughter and druv his son from home, that stole his niggers and ruined his land; bigger than this whole county that he fit for and in payment for which has brung him to keeping a little country store for his bread and meat; bigger than the scorn and denial which hit helt to his lips like the bitter cup in the Book. And how could I have lived nigh to him for twenty years without being touched and changed by him? Maybe I am not as big as he is and maybe I did not do any of the galloping. But at least I was drug along where he went. And me and him can still do hit and will ever so, if so be he will show me what he aims for me to do;* and maybe still standing there and holding the stallion's reins after Sutpen had entered the cabin, still hearing the galloping, watching the proud galloping image merge and pass, galloping through avatars which marked the accumulation of years, time, to the fine climax where it galloped without weariness or progress, forever and forever immortal beneath the brandished sabre and the shot-torn flags rushing down a sky in color like thunder; stood there and heard Sutpen inside the house speak his single sentence of salutation inquiry and farewell to the granddaughter, and Father said that for a second Wash must not have felt the very earth under his feet while he watched Sutpen emerge from the house, the riding whip in his hand, thinking quietly, like in a dream: *I kaint have heard what I know I heard. I just know I kaint* thinking *That was what got him up. It was that colt. It aint me or mine either. It wasn't even his own that got him out of bed* maybe feeling no earth, no stability, even yet, maybe not even hearing his own voice when Sutpen saw his face (the face of the man who in twenty years he had no more known to make any move save at command than he had the stallion which he rode) and stopped: 'You said if she was a mare you could give her a decent stall in the stable', maybe not even hearing Sutpen when he said, sudden and sharp: 'Stand back. Dont you touch me' only he must have heard that because he answered it: 'I'm going to tech you, Kernel' and Sutpen said 'Stand back, Wash' again before the old woman heard the whip. Only there were two blows with the whip; they found the two welts on Wash's face that night. Maybe the two blows even knocked him down; maybe it was while he was getting up that he put his hand on the scythe——"

"Wait," Shreve said; "for Christ's sake wait. You mean that he——"

"——sat there all that day in the little window where he could watch the road; probably laid the scythe down and went straight into the house where maybe the granddaughter on the pallet asked querulously what it was and he answered, 'Whut? Whut racket, honey?' and maybe he tried to persuade her to eat too—the side meat he had probably brought home from the store Saturday night or maybe the candy, trying to tempt her with it maybe—the nickel's worth of stale jellified glue out of a striped sack, and maybe ate himself and then sat at the window where he could look out above the body and the scythe in the weeds below, and watch the road. Because he was sitting there when the half grown boy came around the corner of the house whistling and saw him. And Father said he must have realised then that it would not be much

after dark when it would happen; that he must have sat there
and sensed, felt them gathering with the horses and dogs and
guns—the curious and the vengeful—men of Sutpen's own
kind, who used to eat at his table with him back when he
(Wash) had yet to approach nearer the house than the scuppernong arbor—men who had led the way, shown the other
and lesser ones how to fight in battles, who might also possess signed papers from the generals saying that they were
among the first and foremost of the brave—who had galloped also in the old days arrogant and proud on the fine
horses about the fine plantations—symbol also of admiration
and hope, instruments too of despair and grief; these it was
whom he was expected to run from and it seeming to him
probably that he had no less to run from than he had to run
to; that if he ran he would be fleeing merely one set of bragging and evil shadows for another, since they (men) were all
of a kind throughout all of earth which he knew, and he old,
too old to run far even if he were to run who could never
escape them, no matter how much or how far he ran; a man
past sixty could not expect to run that far, far enough to escape beyond the boundaries of earth where such men lived,
set the order and the rule of living: and Father said that
maybe for the first time in his life he began to comprehend
how it had been possible for Yankees or any other army to
have whipped them—the gallant, the proud, the brave; the
acknowledged and chosen best among them all to bear the
courage and honor and pride. It would probably be about
sunset now and probably he could feel them quite near now;
Father said it probably seemed to him that he could even hear
them: all the voices, the murmuring of tomorrow and tomorrow and tomorrow beyond the immediate fury: *Old Wash
Jones come a tumble at last. He thought he had Sutpen, but Sutpen fooled him. He thought he had him, but old Wash Jones got
fooled* and then maybe even saying it aloud, shouting it Father
said: 'But I never expected that, Kernel! You know I never!'
until maybe the granddaughter stirred and spoke querulously
again and he went and quieted her and returned to talk to
himself again but careful now, quiet now since Sutpen was
close enough to hear him easy, without shouting: 'You know
I never. You know I never expected or asked or wanted

nothing from arra living man but what I expected from you. And I never asked that. I didn't think hit would need: I just said to myself *I dont need to. What need has a fellow like Wash Jones to question or doubt the man that General Lee himself said in a hand-wrote ticket that he was brave?* Brave' (and maybe it would be loud again, forgetting again) 'Brave! Better if narra one of them had ever rid back in '65' thinking *Better if his kind and mine too had never drawn the breath of life on this earth. Better that all who remain of us be blasted from the face of it than that another Wash Jones should see his whole life shredded from him and shrivel away like a dried shuck thrown onto the fire* Then they rode up. He must have been listening to them as they came down the road, the dogs and the horses, and seen the lanterns since it was dark now. And Major de Spain who was sheriff then got down and saw the body, though he said he did not see Wash nor know that he was there until Wash spoke his name quietly from the window almost in his face: 'That you, Major?' De Spain told him to come on out and he said how Wash's voice was quite quiet when he said he would be out in just a minute; it was too quiet, too calm; so much too quiet and calm that de Spain said he did not realise for a moment that it was too calm and quiet: 'In just a minute. Soon as I see about my granddaughter.' 'We'll see to her,' de Spain said. 'You come on out.' 'Sho, Major,' Wash said. 'In just a minute.' So they waited in front of the dark house, and the next day Father said there were a hundred that remembered about the butcher knife that he kept hidden and razor-sharp—the one thing in his sloven life that he was ever known to take pride in or care of—only by the time they remembered all this it was too late. So they didn't know what he was about. They just heard him moving inside the dark house, then they heard the granddaughter's voice, fretful and querulous: 'Who is it? Light the lamp, Grandpaw' then his voice: 'Hit wont need no light, honey. Hit wont take but a minute' then de Spain drew his pistol and said, 'You, Wash! Come out of there!' and still Wash didn't answer, murmuring still to the granddaughter: 'Where air you?' and the fretful voice answering, 'Right here. Where else would I be? What is——' then de Spain said, 'Jones!' and he was already fumbling at the broken steps when the granddaughter screamed;

and now all the men there claimed that they heard the knife on both the neckbones, though de Spain didn't. He just said he knew that Wash had come out onto the gallery and that he sprang back before he found out that it was not toward him Wash was running but toward the end of the gallery, where the body lay, but that he did not think about the scythe: he just ran backward a few feet when he saw Wash stoop and rise again and now Wash was running toward him. Only he was running toward them all, de Spain said, running into the lanterns so that now they could see the scythe raised above his head; they could see his face, his eyes too, as he ran with the scythe above his head, straight into the lanterns and the gun barrels, making no sound, no outcry while de Spain ran backward before him, saying, 'Jones! Stop! Stop, or I'll kill you. Jones! Jones! JONES!' "

"Wait," Shreve said. "You mean that he got the son he wanted, after all that trouble, and then turned right around and——"

"Yes. Sitting in Grandfather's office that afternoon, with his head kind of flung back a little, explaining to Grandfather like he might have been explaining arithmetic to Henry back in the fourth grade: 'You see, all I wanted was just a son. Which seems to me, when I look about at my contemporary scene, no exorbitant gift from nature or circumstance to demand——' "

"*Will you wait?*" Shreve said. "——that with the son he went to all that trouble to get lying right there behind him in the cabin, he would have to taunt the grandfather into killing first him and then the child too?"

"—What?" Quentin said. "It wasn't a son. It was a girl."

"Oh," Shreve said. "——Come on. Let's get out of this damn icebox and go to bed."

VIII.

THERE WOULD be no deep breathing tonight. The window would remain closed above the frozen and empty quad beyond which the windows in the opposite wall were, with two or three exceptions, already dark; soon the chimes would ring for midnight, the notes melodious and tranquil, faint and clear as glass in the fierce (it had quit snowing) still air. "So the old man sent the nigger for Henry," Shreve said. "And Henry came in and the old man said 'They cannot marry because he is your brother' and Henry said 'You lie' like that, that quick: no space, no interval, no nothing between like when you press the button and get light in the room. And the old man just sat there, didn't even move and strike him and so Henry didn't say 'You lie' again because he knew now it was so; he just said 'It's not true', not 'I dont believe it' but 'It's not true' because he could maybe see the old man's face again now and demon or no it was a kind of grief and pity, not for himself but for Henry, because Henry was just young while he (the old man) knew that he still had the courage and even all the shrewdness too——"

Shreve stood beside the table, facing Quentin again though not seated now. In the overcoat buttoned awry over the bathrobe he looked huge and shapeless like a disheveled bear as he stared at Quentin (the Southerner, whose blood ran quick to cool, more supple to compensate for violent changes of temperature perhaps, perhaps merely nearer the surface) who sat hunched in his chair, his hands thrust into his pockets as if he were trying to hug himself warm between his arms, looking somehow fragile and even wan in the lamplight, the rosy glow which now had nothing of warmth, coziness, in it, while both their breathing vaporised faintly in the cold room where there was now not two of them but four, the two who breathed not individuals now yet something both more and less than twins, the heart and blood of youth (Shreve was nineteen, a few months younger than Quentin. He looked exactly nineteen; he was one of those people whose correct age you never know because they look exactly that and so you tell yourself that he or she cannot possibly be that because he or she looks too exactly that not to take advantage of the appearance: so you never believe implicitly that he or she is either that age which they claim or that which in sheer desperation they agree to or which someone else reports them to be) strong enough and willing enough for two, for two thousand, for all. Not two of them in a New England college sitting-room but one in a Mississippi library sixty years ago, with holly and mistletoe in vases on the mantel or thrust behind, crowning and garlanding with the season and time the pictures on the walls, and a sprig or so decorating the photograph, the group—mother and two children—on the desk behind which the father sat when the son entered; and they—Quentin and Shreve—thinking how after the father spoke and before what he said stopped being shock and began to make sense, the son would recall later how he had seen through the window beyond his father's head the sister and the lover in the garden, pacing slowly, the sister's head bent with listening, the lover's head leaned above it while they paced slowly on in that rhythm which not the eyes but the heart marks and calls the beat and measure for, to disappear slowly beyond some bush or shrub starred with white bloom—jasmine, spiraea, honeysuckle, perhaps myriad scentless unpickable Cherokee roses—names, blooms which Shreve possibly had never heard and never seen although the air had blown over him first which became tempered to nourish them—and it would not matter here that the time had been winter in that garden too and hence no bloom nor leaf even if there had been someone to walk there and be seen there since, judged by subsequent events, it had been night in the garden also. But that did not matter because it had been so long ago. It did not matter to them (Quentin and Shreve) anyway, who could without moving, as free now of flesh as the father who decreed and forbade, the son who denied and repudiated, the lover who acquiesced, the beloved who was not bereaved, and with no tedious transition from hearth and garden (granted the garden) to saddle, be already clattering over the frozen ruts of that December night and that Christmas dawn, that day of peace and cheer, of holly and goodwill and logs on the hearth; not two of them there and then either but four of them riding the two horses through the iron darkness and that not mattering either: what faces and what names they called themselves and were called by so long as the blood coursed—the blood, the immortal brief recent intransient blood which could hold honor above slothy unregret and love above fat and easy shame.

"And Bon didn't know it," Shreve said. "The old man didn't move and this time Henry didn't say 'You lie', he said 'It's not true' and the old man said, 'Ask him. Ask Charles then' and then Henry knew that that was what his father had meant all the time and that that was what he meant himself when he told his father he lied, because what the old man said wasn't just 'He is your brother' but 'He has known all the time that he is yours and your sister's brother'. But Bon didn't. Listen, dont you remember how your father said it, about how not one time did he—the old guy, the demon—ever seem to wonder either how the other wife managed to find him, track him down, had never once seemed to wonder what she might have been doing all that time, how she might have passed that time, the thirty years since that day when he paid his bill with her and got it receipted, so he thought, and saw with his own eyes that it was (so he thought) destroyed, torn up and thrown to the wind; never once wondered about this but only that she had done it, had tracked him down, could have and would have wanted to? So it wasn't her that told Bon. She wouldn't have, maybe for the reason that she knew he—the demon—would believe she had. Or maybe she didn't get around to telling him. Maybe she just never thought that there could be anyone as close to her as a lone child out of her own body who would have to be told how she had been scorned and suffered. Or maybe she was already telling it before he was big enough to know words and so by the time he was big enough to understand what was being told him she had told it so much and so hard that the words didn't make sense to her anymore either because they didn't have to make sense to her, and so she had got to the point where when she thought she was saying it she was quiet, and when she thought she was quiet it was just the hate and the fury and the unsleeping and the unforgetting. Or maybe she didn't intend for him to know it then. Maybe she was grooming him for that hour and moment which she couldn't foresee

but that she knew would arrive some day because it would
have to arrive or else she would have to do like the Aunt Rosa
and deny that she had ever breathed—the moment when he
would stand side by side (not face to face) with his father
where fate or luck or justice or whatever she called it could do
the rest (and it did, better than she could have invented or
hoped or even dreamed, and your father said how being a
woman she probably wasn't even surprised)—grooming him
herself, bringing him on by hand herself, washing and feeding
and putting him to bed and giving him the candy and the
toys and the other child's fun and diversion and needs in measured doses like medicine with her own hand: not because she
had to, who could have hired a dozen or bought a hundred to
do it for her with the money, the jack that he (the demon)
had voluntarily surrendered, repudiated to balance his moral
ledger: but like the millionaire who could have a hundred
hostlers and handlers but who has just the one horse, the one
maiden, the one moment, the one matching of heart and muscle and will with the one instant: and himself (the millionaire)
patient in the overalls and the sweat and the stable muck,
bringing him along to the moment when she would say 'He is
your father. He cast you and me aside and denied you his
name. Now go' and then sit down and let God finish it: pistol
or knife or rack; destruction or grief or anguish: God to call
the shot or turn the wheel. Jesus, you can almost see him: a
little boy already come to learn, to expect, before he could
remember having learned his own name or the name of the
town where he lived or how to say either of them, that every
so often he would be snatched up from playing and held,
gripped between the two hands fierce with (what passed at
least with him for it) love, against the two fierce rigid knees,
the face that he remembered since before remembering began
as supervising all the animal joys of palate and stomach and
entrails, of warmth and pleasure and security, swooping down
at him in a kind of blazing immobility: he taking the inter-
ruption as a matter of course, as just another natural phenomenon of existence; the face filled with furious and almost
unbearable unforgiving almost like fever (not bitterness and
despair: just implacable will for revenge) as just another manifestation of mammalian love—and he not knowing what in

hell it was all about, who would be too young to curry any
connected fact out of the fury and hate and the tumbling
speed; not comprehending or caring: just curious, creating
for himself (without help since who to help him) his own
notion of that Porto Rico or Haiti or wherever it was he understood vaguely that he had come from like orthodox children do of heaven or the cabbage patch or wherever it was
that they came from, except that his was different in that you
were not supposed (your mother didn't intend to, anyway) to
ever go back there (and maybe when you got as old as she
was you would be horrified too every time you found hidden
in your thoughts anything that just smelled or tasted like it
might be a wish to go back there); which you were not supposed to know when and why you left but only that you had
escaped, that whatever power had created the place for you to
hate it had likewise got you away from the place so you could
hate it good and never forgive it in quiet and monotony
(though not exactly in what you would call peace); that you
were to thank God you didn't remember anything about it yet
at the same time you were not to, maybe dared not to, ever
forget it—he not even knowing maybe that he took it for
granted that all kids didn't have fathers too and that getting
snatched every day or so from whatever harmless pursuit in
which you were not bothering anybody or even thinking
about them, by someone because that someone was bigger
than you, stronger than you, and being held for a minute or
five minutes under a kind of busted water pipe of incomprehensible fury and fierce yearning and vindictiveness and
jealous rage was a part of childhood which all mothers of
children had received in turn from their mothers and from
their mothers in turn from that Porto Rico or Haiti or wherever it was we all came from but none of us ever lived in: so
that when he grew up and had children he would have to pass
it on too (and maybe deciding then and there that it was too
much trouble and bother and that he would not have any
children or at least hoped he would not) and hence no man
had a father, no one personal Porto Rico or Haiti, but all
mother faces which ever bred swooping down at those almost calculable moments out of some obscure ancient general
affronting and outraging which the actual living articulate

meat had not even suffered but merely inherited; all boy flesh that walked and breathed stemming from that one ambiguous eluded dark fatherhead and so brothered perennial and ubiquitous everywhere under the sun——"

They stared at one another—glared rather—their quiet regular breathing vaporising faintly and steadily in the now tomblike air. There was something curious in the way they looked at one another, curious and quiet and profoundly intent, not at all as two young men might look at each other but almost as a youth and a very young girl might out of virginity itself—a sort of hushed and naked searching, each look burdened with youth's immemorial obsession not with time's dragging weight which the old live with but with its fluidity: the bright heels of all the lost moments of fifteen and sixteen. "Then he got older and got out from under the apron despite her (him too maybe; maybe the both of them) and he didn't even care. He found out that she was up to something and he not only didn't care, he didn't even care that he didn't know what it was; got older and found out that she had been shaping and tempering him to be the instrument for whatever it was her hand was implacable for, maybe came to believe (or saw) that she had tricked him into receiving that shape and temper, and didn't care about that too because probably by that time he had learned that there were three things and no more: breathing, pleasure, darkness; and without money there could be no pleasure, and without pleasure it would not even be breathing but mere protoplasmic inhale and collapse of blind unorganism in a darkness where light never began. And he had the money because he knew that she knew that the money was the only thing she could coerce and smoothe him into the barrier with when Derby Day came so she didn't dare pinch him there and she knew he knew it: so that maybe he even blackmailed her, bought her off that way: 'You give me the jack as I want it and I wont ask why or what for yet.' Or maybe she was so busy grooming him that she never thought of the money now, who probably never had had much time to remember it or count it or wonder how much there was in the intervals of the hating and the being mad, and so all to check him up about the money would be the lawyer and he (Bon) probably learned that the first thing: that

he could go to his mother and hold the lawyer's feet to the
fire anytime, like the millionaire horse has only to come in
one time with a little extra sweat on him, and tomorrow he
will have a new jock. Sure, that's who it would be: the lawyer, that lawyer with his private mad female millionaire to
farm, who probably wasn't interested enough in the money to
see whether the checks had any other writing on them when
she signed them—that lawyer who, with Bon's mother already plotting and planning him since before he could remember (and even if she didn't know it or whether she knew
it or not or would have cared or not) for that day when he
should be translated quick into so much rich and rotting dirt,
had already been plowing and planting and harvesting him
and the mother both as if he already was—that lawyer who
maybe had the secret drawer in the secret safe and the secret
paper in it, maybe a chart with colored pins stuck into it like
generals have in campaigns, and all the notations in code: *Today he finished robbing a drunken Indian of a hundred miles of
virgin land, val. 25,000. At 2:31 today came up out of swamp with
final plank for house. val in conj. with land 40,000. 7:52 p.m. today
married. Bigamy threat val. minus nil. unless quick buyer. Not
probable. Doubtless conjoined with wife same day. Say 1 year* and
then with maybe the date and the hour too: *Son. Intrinsic val.
possible though not probable forced sale of house & land plus val.
crop minus child's one quarter. Emotional val. plus 100% times nil.
plus val. crop. Say 10 years, one or more children. Intrinsic val.
forced sale house & improved land plus liquid assets minus children's share. Emotional val. 100% times increase yearly for each
child plus intrinsic val. plus liquid assets plus working acquired
credit* and maybe here with the date too: *Daughter* and you
could maybe even have seen the question mark after it and the
other words even: *daughter? daughter? daughter?* trailing off
not because thinking trailed off, but on the contrary thinking
stopping right still then, backing up a little and spreading like
when you lay a stick across a trickle of water, spreading and
rising slow all around him in whatever place it was that he
could lock the door to and sit quiet and subtract the money
that Bon was spending on his whores and his champagne
from what his mother had, and figure up how much would be
left of it tomorrow and next month and next year or until

Sutpen would be good and ripe—thinking about the good hard cash that Bon was throwing away on his horses and clothes and the champagne and gambling and women (he would have known about the octoroon and the left handed marriage long before the mother did even if it had been any secret; maybe he even had a spy in the bedroom like he seems to have had in Sutpen's; maybe he even planted her, said to himself like you do about a dog: *He is beginning to ramble. He needs a block. Not a tether: just a light block of some sort, so he cant get inside of anything that might have a fence around it*) and only him to try to check it, or as much as he dared, and not getting far because he knew too that all Bon had to do was to go to his mother and the racehorse would have a gold eating trough if he wanted it and, if the jock wasn't careful, a new jockey too—counting up the money, figuring what he would net at this normal rate over the next few years, against what it looked like would be left of it to net from by that time, and meanwhile crucified between his two problems: whether maybe what he ought to do was to wash his hands of the Sutpen angle and clean up what was left and light out for Texas: except whenever he thought about doing that he would have to think about all the money that Bon had already spent, and that if he had only gone to Texas ten years ago or five years ago or even last year: so that maybe at night while he would be waiting for the window to begin to turn gray he would be like the Aunt Rosa said she was and he would have to deny that he breathed (or maybe wished he didn't) except for that two hundred percent. times the intrinsic value every New Year's;—the water backing up from the stick and rising and spreading about him steady and quiet as light and him sitting there in the actual white glare of clairvoyance (or second sight or faith in human misfortune and folly or whatever you want to call it) that was showing him not only what might happen but what was actually going to happen and him declining to believe it was going to happen, not because it had come to him as a vision, but because it would have to have love and honor and courage and pride in it; and believing it might happen, not because it was logical and possible, but because it would be the most unfortunate thing for all concerned that could occur; and though you could no more

have proved vice or virtue or courage or cowardice to him
without showing him the moving people than you could have
proved death to him without showing him a corpse, he did
believe in misfortune because of that rigorous and arduous
dusty eunuch's training which taught to leave man's good
luck and joys to God, who would in return surrender all his
miseries and follies and misfortunes to the lice and fleas of
Coke and Littleton. And the old Sabine——"

They stared—glared—at one another, their voices (it was
Shreve speaking, though save for the slight difference which
the intervening degrees of latitude had inculcated in them
(differences not in tone or pitch but of turns of phrase and
usage of words), it might have been either of them and was in
a sense both: both thinking as one, the voice which happened
to be speaking the thought only the thinking become audible,
vocal; the two of them creating between them, out of the
rag-tag and bob-ends of old tales and talking, people who
perhaps had never existed at all anywhere, who, shadows,
were shadows not of flesh and blood which had lived and
died but shadows in turn of what were (to one of them at
least, to Shreve) shades too) quiet as the visible murmur of
their vaporising breath. The chimes now began to ring for
midnight, melodious slow and faint beyond the closed, the
snow-sealed, window. "——the old Sabine, who couldn't to
save her life have told you or the lawyer or Bon or anybody
else probably what she wanted, expected, hoped for because
she was a woman and didn't need to want or hope or expect
anything, but just to want and expect and hope (and besides,
your father said that when you have plenty of good strong
hating you dont need hope because the hating will be enough
to nourish you);—the old Sabine (not so old yet, but she
would have just let herself go in the sense that you keep the
engines clean and oiled and the best of coal in the bunkers but
you dont bother to shine the brightwork or holystone the
decks anymore; just let herself go on the outside. Not fat; she
would burn it up too fast for that, shrivel it away in the gullet
between swallowing and stomach; no pleasure in the chewing; having to chew just another nuisance like no pleasure in
the clothing; having the old wear out and having to choose
the new just another nuisance: and no pleasure in the fine

figure he—" neither of them said 'Bon' "—cut in the fine
pants that fit his leg and the fine coats that fit his shoulders
nor in the fact that he had more watches and cuff buttons and
finer linen and horses and yellow-wheeled buggies (not to
mention the gals) than most others did, but all that too just
an unavoidable nuisance that he would have to get shut of
before he could do her any good just like he had to get shut
of the teething and the chicken pox and the light boy's bones
in order to be able to do her any good)—the old Sabine
getting the faked reports from the lawyer like reports sent
back to headquarters from a battle front, with maybe a special
nigger in the lawyer's anteroom to do nothing else but carry
them and that maybe once in two years or five times in two
days, depending on when she would begin to itch for news
and began to worry him—the report, the communique about
how we are not far behind him in Texas or Missouri or maybe
California (California would be fine, that far away; conve-
nient, proof inherent in the sheer distance, the necessity to
accept and believe) and we are going to catch up with him
any day now and so do not worry. So she wouldn't, she
wouldn't worry at all: she would just have out the carriage
and go to the lawyer, busting in in the black dress that looked
like a section of limp stove pipe and maybe not even a hat but
just a shawl over her head, so that the only things missing
would be the mop and the pail—busting in and saying 'He's
dead. I know he is dead and how can he, how can he be', not
meaning what the Aunt Rosa meant: *where did they find or
invent a bullet that could kill him* but *How can he be allowed to
die without having to admit that he was wrong and suffer and
regret it* and so in the next two seconds they would almost
catch him (he—the lawyer—would show her the actual letter, the writing in the English she couldn't read, that had just
come in, that he had just sent for the nigger to carry to her
when she came in, and the lawyer done practised putting the
necessary date on the letter until he could do it now while his
back would be toward her, in the two seconds it would take
him to get the letter out of the file)—catch him, get so close
to him as to have ample satisfaction that he was alive; so close
indeed that he would be able to get her out of the office before she had sat down and into the carriage again and on the

way home again where, among the Florentine mirrors and
Paris drapes and tufted camisoles, she would still look like the
one that had come in to scrub the floors, in the black dress
that the cook wouldn't have looked at even when it was new
five or six years ago, holding, clutching the letter she couldn't
read (maybe the only word in it she could even recognise
would be the word 'Sutpen') in one hand and brushing back a
rope of lank iron-colored hair with the other and not looking
at the letter like she was reading it even if she could have, but
swooping at it, blazing down at it as if she knew she would
have only a second to read it in, only a second for it to remain
intact in after her eyes would touch it, before it took fire and
so would not be perused but consumed, leaving her sitting
there with a black crumbling blank carbon ash in her hand.
And him—" (Neither of them said 'Bon') "—there watching
her, who had got old enough to have learned that what he
thought was childhood wasn't childhood, that other children
had been made by fathers and mothers where he had been
created new when he began to remember, new again when he
came to the point where his carcass quit being a baby and
became a boy, new again when he quit being a boy and became a man, between a woman whom he had thought was
feeding and washing and putting him to bed and finding him
in the extra ticklings for his palate and his pleasure because he
was himself, until he got big enough to find out that it wasn't
him at all she was washing and feeding the candy and the fun
to but it was a man that hadn't even arrived yet, whom even
she had never seen yet, who would be something else beside
that boy when he did arrive like the dynamite which destroys
the house and the family and maybe even the whole community aint the old peaceful paper that maybe would rather be
blowing aimless and light along the wind or the old merry
sawdust or the old quiet chemicals that had rather be still and
dark in the quiet earth like they had been before the meddling
guy with ten-power spectacles came and dug them up and
strained warped and kneaded them;—created between this
woman and a hired lawyer (the woman who since before he
could remember he now realised had been planning and
grooming him for some moment that would come and pass
and following which he saw that to her he would be little

more than so much rich rotting dirt; the lawyer who since
before he could remember he now realised had been plowing
and planting and watering and manuring and harvesting him
as if he already was):—him watching her, lounging there
against the mantel maybe in the fine clothes, in the harem
incense odor of what you might call easy sanctity, watching
her looking at the letter, not even thinking *I am looking upon
my mother naked* since if the hating was nakedness, she had
worn it long enough now for it to do the office of clothing
like they say that modesty can do, does——

"So he went away. He went away to school at the age of
twenty-eight. And he wouldn't know nor care about that
either: which of them—mother or lawyer—it was who decided he should go to school nor why, because he had known
all the time that his mother was up to something and that the
lawyer was up to something, and he didn't care enough about
what either of them was to try to find out, who knew that the
lawyer knew that his mother was up to something but that his
mother didn't know that the lawyer was up to something, and
that it would be all right with the lawyer if his mother got
whatever it was she wanted, provided he (the lawyer) got
what he wanted one second before or at least at the same
time. He went away to school; he said 'All right' and told the
octoroon goodbye and went to school, who not in all the
twenty-eight years had ever been told by anyone, 'Do as these
others do; have this task done at nine a.m. tomorrow or Friday or Monday'; maybe it was even the octoroon whom they
(or the lawyer) used—the light block (not tether) which the
lawyer had put on him to keep him from getting inside of
something which might be found to have a fence around it
later. Maybe the mother found out about the octoroon and
the child and the ceremony and discovered more than the
lawyer had (or would believe, who considered Bon only dull,
not a fool) and sent for him and he came and lounged against
the mantel again and maybe knowing what was up, what had
happened before she told him, lounging there with an expression on his face you might call smiling except it was not that
but just something you couldn't see through or past, and she
watching him with maybe the lank iron-colored strand of hair
down again and not even bothering to brush it back now

because she was not looking at any letter now but her eyes
blazing at him, her voice trying to blaze at him out of the
urgency of alarm and fear, but she managing to keep it down
since she could not talk about betrayal because she had not
told him yet, and now, at this moment, she would not dare
risk it;—he looking at her from behind the smiling that
wasn't smiling but was just something you were not supposed
to see beyond, saying, admitting it: 'Why not? All young men
do it. The ceremony too. I didn't set out to get the child,
but now that I have. . . . . . . It's not a bad child, either'
and she watching him, glaring at him and not being able to
say what she would because she had put off too long now
saying what she could: 'But you. This is different' and he (she
would not need to say it. He would know because he already
knew why she had sent for him, even if he did not know and
did not care what she had been up to since before he could
remember, since before he could take a woman whether in
love or not): 'Why not? Men seem to have to marry some
day, sooner or later. And this is one whom I know, who
makes me no trouble. And with the ceremony, that bother,
already done. And as for a little matter like a spot of negro
blood——' not needing to talk much, say much either, not
needing to say *I seem to have been born into this world with so
few fathers that I have too many brothers to outrage and shame
while alive and hence too many descendants to bequeath my little
portion of hurt and harm to, dead;* not that, just 'a little spot of
negro blood——' and then to watch the face, the desperate
urgency and fear, then to depart, kissing her maybe, her hand
maybe which would lie in his and even touch his lips like a
dead hand because of the desperate casting for this straw or
that; maybe as he went out he said *she will go to him* (the
lawyer); *if I were to wait five minutes I could see her in the shawl.
So probably by tonight I will be able to know—if I cared to know.*
Maybe by night he did, maybe before that if they managed to
find him, get word to him, because she went to the lawyer.
And it was right in the lawyer's alley. Maybe before she even
got started telling it good that gentle white glow began like
when you turn up a wick; maybe he could even almost see his
hand writing on into the space where the *daughter? daughter?
daughter?* never had quite showed. Because maybe that had

been the lawyer's trouble and worry and concern all the time; that ever since she had made him promise he would never tell Bon who his father was, he had been waiting and wondering how to do it, since maybe he knew that if he were to tell Bon, Bon might believe it or he might not, but certainly he would go and tell his mother that the lawyer had told him and then he (the lawyer) would be sunk, not for any harm done because there would be no harm, since this could not alter the situation, but for having crossed his paranoiac client. Maybe while he would sit in his office adding and subtracting the money and adding what they would get out of Sutpen (he was never worried about what Bon would do when he found out; he had probably a long time ago paid Bon that compliment of thinking that even if he was too dull or too indolent to suspect or find out about his father himself, he wasn't fool enough not to be able to take advantage of it once somebody showed him the proper move; maybe if the thought had ever occurred to him that because of love or honor or anything else under heaven or jurisprudence either, Bon would not, would refuse to, he (the lawyer) would even have furnished proof that he no longer breathed)—maybe all the time it was this that racked him: how to get Bon where he would either have to find it out himself, or where somebody—the father or the mother—would have to tell him. So maybe she wasn't out of the office good—or at least as soon as he had had time to open the safe and look in the secret drawer and make sure that it was the University of Mississippi that Henry attended—before his hand was writing steady and even into the space where the *daughter? daughter? daughter?* never had showed—and with the date here too: *1859. Two children. Say 1860, 20 years. Increase 200% times intrinsic val. yearly plus liquid assets plus credit earned. Approx'te val. 1860, 100,000. Query: bigamy threat, Yes or No. Possible No. Incest threat: Credible Yes* and the hand going back before it put down the period, lining out the *Credible*, writing in *Certain*, underlining it.

"And he didn't care about that too; he just said, 'All right.' Because maybe he knew now that his mother didn't know and never would know what she wanted, and so he couldn't beat her (maybe he had learned from the octoroon that you cant beat women anyhow and that if you are wise or dislike trouble

and uproar you dont even try to), and he knew that all the
lawyer wanted was just the money; and so if he just didn't
make the mistake of believing that he could beat all of it, if he
just remembered to be quiet and be alert he could beat some
of it.— So he said, 'All right' and let his mother pack the fine
clothes and the fine linen into the bags and trunks, and maybe
he lounged into the lawyer's office and watched from behind
that something which could have been called smiling while
the lawyer made the elbow motion about getting his horses
onto the steamboat and maybe buying him an extra special
body servant and arranging about the money and all; watching from behind the smiling while the lawyer did the heavy
father even, talking about the scholarship, the culture, the
Latin and the Greek that would equip and polish him for the
position which he would hold in life and how a man to be
sure could get that anywhere, in his own library even, who
had the will; but how there was something, some quality to
culture which only the monastic, the cloistral monotony of
a—say obscure and small (though high class, high class) college;—and he——" (neither of them said 'Bon'. Never at any
time did there seem to be any confusion between them as to
whom Shreve meant by 'he') "——listening courteous and
quiet behind that expression which you were not supposed to
see past, asking at last, interrupting maybe, courteous and affable—nothing of irony, nothing of sarcasm—'What did you
say this college was?': and now a good deal of elbow motion
here while the lawyer would shuffle through the papers to
find the one from which he could read that name which he
had been memorising ever since he first talked to the mother:
'The University of Mississippi, at'—— Where did you say?"

"Oxford," Quentin said. "It's about forty miles from——"

"——'Oxford.' And then the papers could be still again
because he would be talking: about a small college only ten
years old, about how there wouldn't be anything to distract
him from his studies there (where, in a sense, wisdom herself
would be a virgin or at least not very second hand) and how
he would have a chance to observe another and a provincial
section of the country in which his high destiny (granted the
outcome of this war which was without doubt imminent,
the successful conclusion of which we all hoped for, had no

doubt of) as the man he would be and the economic power
he would represent when his mother passed on, was rooted;
and he listening behind that expression, saying, 'Then you
dont recommend the law as a vocation?' and now for just a
moment the lawyer would stop, but not long; maybe not
long enough or perceptible enough for you to call it pause:
and he would be looking at Bon too: 'It hadn't occurred to
me that the law might appeal to you' and Bon: 'Neither did
practising with a rapier appeal to me while I was doing it. But
I can recall at least one occasion in my life when I was glad I
had' and then the lawyer, smooth and easy: 'Then by all
means let it be the law. Your mother will ag—be pleased.' 'All
right,' he said, not 'goodbye'; he didn't care; maybe not even
goodbye to the octoroon, to those tears and lamentations and
maybe even the clinging, the soft despairing magnolia-colored
arms about his knees, and (say) three and a half feet above
that boneless steel gyves that expression which was not smiling but just something not to be seen through. Because you
cant beat them: you just flee (and thank God you can flee, can
escape from that massy five-foot-thick maggot-cheesy solidarity which overlays the earth, in which men and women in
couples are ranked and racked like ninepins; thanks to whatever Gods for that masculine hipless tapering peg which fits
light and glib to move where the cartridge-chambered hips of
women hold them fast);—not goodbye: all right: and one
night he walked up the gangplank between the torches and
probably only the lawyer there to see him off and this not for
godspeed but to make sure that he actually took the boat.
And the new extra nigger opening the bags in the stateroom,
spreading the fine clothes, and the ladies already gathered in
the saloon for supper and the men in the bar, preparing for it
but not he; he alone, at the rail, with a cigar maybe, watching
the city drift and wink and glitter and sink away and then all
motion cease, the boat suspended immobile and without
progress from the stars themselves by the two ropes of spark-
filled smoke streaming upward from the stacks. And who
knows what thinking, what sober weighing and discarding,
who had known for years that his mother was up to something even though he did not (probably believed he never
would) know what; that the lawyer was up to something and

though he knew that was just money, yet he knew that within
his (the lawyer's) known masculine limitations he (the lawyer) could be almost as dangerous as the unknown quantity
which was his mother; and now this—school, college—and
he twenty-eight years old. And not only that, but this particular college, which he had never heard of, which ten years ago
did not even exist; and knowing too that it was the lawyer
who had chosen it for him—what sober, what intent, what
almost frowning *Why? Why? Why this college, this particular
one above all others?*—maybe leaning there in that solitude between panting smoke and engines and almost touching the
answer, aware of the jigsaw puzzle picture integers of it
waiting, almost lurking, just beyond his reach, inextricable,
jumbled, and unrecognisable yet on the point of falling into
pattern which would reveal to him at once, like a flash of
light, the meaning of his whole life, past—the Haiti, the
childhood, the lawyer, the woman who was his mother. And
maybe the letter itself right there under his feet, somewhere in
the darkness beneath the deck on which he stood—the letter
addressed not to Thomas Sutpen at Sutpen's Hundred but to
Henry Sutpen, Esquire, in Residence at the University of Mississippi, near Oxford, Mississippi: and one day Henry showed
it to him and there was no gentle spreading glow but a flash,
a glare (who not only had no visible father but had found
himself to be, even in infancy, enclosed by an unsleeping
cabal bent apparently on teaching him that he had never had,
that his mother had emerged from a sojourn in limbo, from
that state of blessed amnesia in which the weak senses can
take refuge from the godless dark forces and powers which
weak human flesh cannot stand, to wake pregnant, shrieking
and screaming and thrashing, not against the ruthless agony
of labor but in protest against the outrage of her swelling
loins; that he had been fathered on her not through that natural process but had been blotted onto and out of her body
by the old infernal immortal male principle of all unbridled
terror and darkness) in which he stood looking at the innocent face of the youth almost ten years his junior, while one
part of him said *My brow my skull my jaw my hands* and the
other said *Wait. Wait. You cant know yet. You cannot know
yet whether what you see is what you are looking at or what*

you are believing. Wait. Wait. —The letter which he——" it was
not Bon he meant now, yet again Quentin seemed to comprehend without difficulty or effort whom he meant "——wrote
maybe as soon as he finished that last entry in the record, into
the *daughter? daughter? daughter?* while he thought *By all
means he must not know now, must not be told before he can get
there and he and the daughter*—not remembering anything
about young love from his own youth and would not have
believed it if he had, yet willing to use that too as he would
have used courage and pride, thinking not of any hushed wild
importunate blood and light hands hungry for touching, but
of the fact that this Oxford and this Sutpen's Hundred were
only a day's ride apart and Henry already established in the
University and so maybe for once in his life the lawyer even
believed in God: *My Dear Mr Sutpen: The undersigned name
will not be known to you, nor are the writer's position and circumstances, for all their reflected worth and (I hope) value, so unob-
scure as to warrant the hope that he will ever see you in person or
you he*—*worth reflected from and value rendered to two persons of
birth and position, one of whom, a lady and widowed mother, resides in that seclusion befitting her condition in the city from which
this letter is inscribed, the other of whom, a young gentleman her
son, will either be as you read this, or will shortly thereafter be a
petitioner before the same Bar of knowledge and wisdom as yourself. It is in his behalf that I write. No: I will not say behalf;
certainly I shall not let his lady mother nor the young gentleman
himself suspect that I used that term, even to one, Sir, scion of the
principal family of that county as it is your fortunate lot to be.
Indeed, it were better for me if I had not written at all. But I do;
I have; it is irrevocable now; if you discern aught in this letter
which smacks of humility, take it as coming not from the mother
and certainly not from the son, but from the pen of one whose
humble position as legal adviser and man of business to the above
described lady and young gentleman, whose loyalty and gratitude
toward one whose generosity has found him (I do not confess this; I
proclaim it) in bread and meat and fire and shelter over a period
long enough to have taught him gratitude and loyalty even if he
had not known them, has led him into an action whose means fall
behind its intention for the reason that he is only what he is and
professes himself to be, not what he would. So take this, Sir, neither*

as the unwarranted insolence which an unsolicited communication
from myself to you would be, not as a plea for sufferance on behalf
of an unknown, but as an introduction (clumsy though it be) to
one young gentleman whose position needs neither detailing nor
recapitulation in the place where this letter is read, of another
young gentleman whose position requires neither detailing nor re-
capitulation in the place where it was written. —Not goodbye;
all right, who had had so many fathers as to have neither love
nor pride to receive or inflict, neither honor nor shame to
share or bequeath; to whom one place was the same as another, like to a cat—cosmopolitan New Orleans or bucolic
Mississippi: his own inherited and heritable Florentine lamps
and gilded toilet seats and tufted mirrors, or a little jerkwater
college not ten years old; champagne in the octoroon's boudoir or whiskey on a harsh new table in a monk's cell and a
country youth, a bucolic heir apparent who had probably
never spent a dozen nights outside of his paternal house (unless perhaps to lie fully dressed beside a fire in the woods
listening to dogs running) until he came to school, whom he
watched aping his clothing carriage speech and all and (the
youth) completely unaware that he was doing it, who (the
youth) over the bottle one night said, blurted—no, not
blurted: it would be fumbling, groping: and he (the cosmop-
olite ten years the youth's senior almost, lounging in one of
the silk robes the like of which the youth had never seen before and believed that only women wore) watching the youth
blush fiery red yet still face him, still look him straight in the
eye while he fumbled, groped, blurted with abrupt complete
irrelevance: 'If I had a brother, I wouldn't want him to be a
younger brother' and he: 'Ah?' and the youth: 'No. I would
want him to be older than me' and he: 'No son of a landed
father wants an older brother' and the youth: 'Yes. I do',
looking straight at the other, the esoteric, the sybarite, standing (the youth) now, erect, thin (because he was young), his
face scarlet but his head high and his eyes steady: 'Yes. And I
would want him to be just like you' and he: 'Is that so? The
whiskey's your side. Drink or pass.'

"And now," Shreve said, "we're going to talk about love."
But he didn't need to say that either, any more than he had
needed to specify which *he* he meant by *he*, since neither of

them had been thinking about anything else; all that had gone
before just so much that had to be overpassed and none else
present to overpass it but them, as someone always has to
rake the leaves up before you can have the bonfire. That was
why it did not matter to either of them which one did the
talking, since it was not the talking alone which did it, performed and accomplished the overpassing, but some happy
marriage of speaking and hearing wherein each before the
demand, the requirement, forgave condoned and forgot the
faulting of the other—faultings both in the creating of this
shade whom they discussed (rather, existed in) and in the
hearing and sifting and discarding the false and conserving
what seemed true, or fit the preconceived—in order to overpass to love, where there might be paradox and inconsistency
but nothing fault nor false. "And now, love. He must have
known all about her before he ever saw her—what she
looked like, her private hours in that provincial women's
world that even men of the family were not supposed to
know a great deal about; he must have learned it without
even having to ask a single question. Jesus, it must have kind
of boiled out all over him. There must have been nights and
nights while Henry was learning from him how to lounge
about a bedroom in a gown and slippers such as women
wore, in a faint though unmistakable effluvium of scent such
as women used, smoking a cigar almost as a woman might
smoke it, yet withal such an air of indolent and lethal assurance that only the most reckless man would have gratuitously
drawn the comparison (and with no attempt to teach, train,
play the mentor on his part—and then maybe yes; maybe
who could know what times he looked at Henry's face and
thought, not *there but for the intervening leaven of that blood
which we do not have in common is my skull, my brow, sockets,
shape and angle of jaw and chin and some of my thinking behind
it, and which he could see in my face in his turn if he but knew to
look as I know*   but   *there, just behind a little, obscured a little
by that alien blood whose admixing was necessary in order that he
exist is the face of the man who shaped us both out of that blind
chancy darkness which we call the future; there —there —at any
moment, second, I shall penetrate by something of will and intensity and dreadful need, and strip that alien leavening from it and*

*look not on my brother's face whom I did not know I possessed and
hence never missed, but my father's, out of the shadow of whose
absence my spirit's posthumeity has never escaped;* —at what moment thinking, watching the eagerness which was without ab-
jectness, the humility which surrendered no pride—the entire
proffering of the spirit of which the unconscious aping of
clothes and speech and mannerisms was but the shell—thinking *what cannot I do with this willing flesh and bone if I wish;
this flesh and bone and spirit which stemmed from the same source
that mine did, but which sprang in quiet peace and contentment
and ran in steady even though monotonous sunlight, where that
which he bequeathed me sprang in hatred and outrage and unforgiving and ran in shadow—what could I not mold of this mallea-
ble and eager clay which that father himself could not—to what
shape of what good there might, must, be in that blood and none
handy to take and mold that portion of it in me until too late:* or
what moments when he might have told himself that it was
nonsense, it could not be true; that such coincidences only
happened in books, thinking—the weariness, the fatalism, the
incorrigible cat for solitude—*That young clodhopper bastard.
How shall I get rid of him:* and then the voice, the other voice:
You dont mean that: and he: *No. But I do mean the clodhopper
bastard*) and the days, the afternoons, while they rode together (and Henry aping him here too, who was the better
horseman, who maybe had nothing of what Bon would have
called style but who had done more of it, to whom a horse
was as natural as walking, who would ride anything anywhere
and at anything) while he must have watched himself being
swamped and submerged in the bright unreal flood of Henry's speech, translated (the three of them: himself and Henry
and the sister whom he had never seen and perhaps did not
even have any curiosity to see) into a world like a fairy tale in
which nothing else save them existed, riding beside Henry,
listening, needing to ask no questions, to prompt to further
speech in any manner that youth who did not even suspect
that he and the man beside him might be brothers, who each
time his breath crossed his vocal cords was saying *From now
on mine and my sister's house will be your house and mine and my
sister's lives your life,* wondering (Bon)—or maybe not wondering at all—how if conditions were reversed and Henry

was the stranger and he (Bon) the scion and still knew what
he suspected, if he would say the same; then (Bon) agreeing
at last, saying at last, 'All right. I'll come home with you for
Christmas', not to see the third inhabitant of Henry's fairy
tale, not to see the sister because he had not once thought of
her: he had merely listened about her: but thinking *So at last I
shall see him, whom it seems I was bred up never to expect to see,
whom I had even learned to live without,* thinking maybe how
he would walk into the house and see the man who made him
and then he would know; there would be that flash, that instant of indisputable recognition between them and he would
know for sure and forever—thinking maybe *That's all I want.
He need not even acknowledge me; I will let him understand just
as quickly that he need not do that, that I do not expect that, will
not be hurt by that, just as he will let me know that quickly that I
am his son,* thinking maybe, maybe again with that expression
you might call smiling but which was not, which was just
something that even just a clodhopper bastard was not intended to see beyond: *I am my mother's son, at least: I do not
seem to know what I want either.* Because he knew exactly what
he wanted; it was just the saying of it—the physical touch
even though in secret, hidden—the living touch of that flesh
warmed before he was born by the same blood which it
had bequeathed him to warm his own flesh with, to be bequeathed by him in turn to run hot and loud in veins and
limbs after that first flesh and then his own were dead. So the
Christmas came and he and Henry rode the forty miles to
Sutpen's Hundred, with Henry still talking, still keeping distended and light and iridescent with steady breathing that
fairy balloon-vacuum in which the three of them existed,
lived, moved even maybe, in attitudes without flesh—himself
and the friend and the sister whom the friend had never seen
and (though Henry did not know it) had not even thought
about yet but only listened about from behind the more urgent thinking, and Henry probably not even noticing that the
nearer they came to home the less Bon talked, had to say on
any subject, and maybe even (and certainly Henry would not
know this) listening less. And went into the house: and
maybe somebody looking at him would have seen on his face
an expression a good deal like the one—that proffering with

humility yet with pride too, of complete surrender—which
he had used to see on Henry's face, and maybe he telling
himself *I not only dont know what it is I want but apparently I
am a good deal younger than I thought also:* and saw face to face
the man who might be his father, and nothing happened—no
shock, no hot communicated flesh that speech would have
been too slow even to impede—nothing. And he spent ten
days there, not only the esoteric, the sybarite, the steel blade
in the silken tesselated sheath which Henry had begun to ape
at the University, but the object of art, the mold and mirror
of form and fashion which Mrs Sutpen (so your father said)
accepted him as and insisted (didn't your father say?) that he
be (and would have purchased him as and paid for him with
Judith even, if there had been no other bidder among the four
of them—or didn't your father say?) and which he did remain to her until he disappeared, taking Henry with him, and
she never saw him again and war and trouble and grief and
bad food filled her days until maybe she didn't even remember after a while that she had ever forgot him. (And the girl,
the sister, the virgin—Jesus, who to know what she saw that
afternoon when they rode up the drive, what prayer, what
maiden meditative dream ridden up out of whatever fabulous
land, not in harsh stove iron but the silken and tragic Launcelot nearing thirty, ten years older than she was and wearied,
sated with what experiences and pleasures, which Henry's letters must have created for her.) And the day came to depart
and no sign yet; he and Henry rode away and still no sign, no
more sign at parting than when he had seen it first, in that
face where he might (he would believe) have seen for himself
the truth and so would have needed no sign, if it hadn't been
for the beard; no sign in the eyes which could see his face
because there was no beard to hide it, could have seen the
truth if it were there: yet no flicker in them: and so he knew it
was in his face because he knew that the other had seen it
there just exactly as Henry was to know the next Christmas
eve in the library that his father was not lying by the fact that
the father said nothing, did nothing. Maybe he even thought,
wondered if perhaps that was not why the beard, if maybe the
other had not hidden behind that beard against this very
day, and if so, why? why? thinking *But why? Why?* since he

wanted so little, could have understood if the other had wanted the signal to be in secret, would have been quick and glad to let it be in secret even if he could not have understood why, thinking in the middle of this *My God, I am young, young, and I didn't even know it; they didn't even tell me, that I was young,* feeling that same despair and shame like when you have to watch your father fail in physical courage, thinking *It should have been me that failed; me, I, not he who stemmed from that blood which we both bear before it could have become corrupt and tainted by whatever it was in Mother's that he could not brook.* —Wait," Shreve cried, though Quentin had not spoken: it had been merely some quality, some gathering of Quentin's still laxed and hunched figure which presaged speech, because Shreve said Wait. Wait. before Quentin could have begun to speak. "Because he hadn't even looked at her. Oh, he had seen her all right, he had had plenty of opportunity for that; he could not have helped but that because Mrs Sutpen would have seen to it—ten days of that kind of planned and ar-ranged and executed privacies like the campaigns of dead gen-erals in the text books, in libraries and parlors and drives in the buggy in the afternoons—all planned three months ago when Mrs Sutpen read Henry's first letter with Bon's name in it, until maybe even Judith too began to feel like the other one to a pair of goldfish: and him even talking to her too, or what talking he could have found to do to a country girl who prob-ably never saw a man young or old before who sooner or later didn't smell like manure; talking to her about like he would talk to the old dame on the gold chairs in the parlor, except that in the one case he would have to make all the conversa-tion and in the other he would not even be able to make his own escape but would have to wait for Henry to come and get him. And maybe he had even thought about her by that time; maybe at the times when he would be telling himself *it cant be so; he could not look at me like this every day and make no sign if it were so* he would even tell himself *She would be easy* like when you have left the champagne on the supper table and are walking toward the whiskey on the sideboard and you happen to pass a cup of lemon sherbet on a tray and you look at the sherbet and tell yourself, That would be easy too only who wants it.——Does that suit you?"

"But it's not love," Quentin said.

"Because why not? Because listen. What was it the old dame, the Aunt Rosa, told you about how there are some things that just have to be whether they are or not, have to be a damn sight more than some other things that maybe are and it dont matter a damn whether they are or not? That was it. He just didn't have time yet. Jesus, he must have known it would be. Like that lawyer thought, he wasn't a fool; the trouble was, he wasn't the kind of not-fool the lawyer thought he would be. He must have known it was going to happen. It would be like you passed that sherbet and maybe you knew you would even reach the sideboard and the whiskey, yet you knew that tomorrow morning you would want that sherbet, then you reached the whiskey and you knew you wanted that sherbet now; maybe you didn't even go to the sideboard, maybe you even looked back at that champagne on the supper table among the dirty haviland and the crumpled damask, and all of a sudden you knew you didn't want to go back there even. It would be no question of choosing, having to choose between the champagne or whiskey and the sherbet, but all of a sudden (it would be spring then, in that country where he had never spent a spring before and you said North Mississippi is a little harder country than Louisiana, with dogwood and violets and the early scentless flowers but the earth and the nights still a little cold and the hard tight sticky buds like young girls' nipples on alder and Judas trees and beech and maple and even something young in the cedars like he never saw before) you find that you dont want anything but that sherbet and that you haven't been wanting anything else but that and you have been wanting that pretty hard for some time—besides knowing that that sherbet is there for you to take. Not just for anybody to take but for you to take, knowing just from looking at that cup that it would be like a flower that, if any other hand reached for it, it would have thorns on it but not for your hand; and him not used to that since all the other cups that had been willing and easy for him to take up hadn't contained sherbet but champagne or at least kitchen wine. And more than that. There was the knowing what he suspected might be so, or not knowing if it was so or not. And who to say if it wasn't maybe the possibility of incest, because who (without a sister: I dont know about the others) has been in love and not discovered the vain evanescence of the fleshly encounter; who has not had to realise that when the brief all is done you must retreat from both love and pleasure, gather up your own rubbish and refuse—the hats and pants and shoes which you drag through the world—and retreat since the gods condone and practise these and the dreamy immeasurable coupling which floats oblivious above the trammelling and harried instant, the: *was-not: is: was:* is a perquisite only of balloony and weightless elephants and whales: but maybe if there were sin too maybe you would not be permitted to escape, uncouple, return.—Aint that right?" He ceased; he could have been interrupted easily now. Quentin could have spoken now, but Quentin did not. He just sat as before, his hands in his trousers pockets, his shoulders hugged inward and hunched, his face lowered and he looking somehow curiously smaller than he actually was because of his actual height and spareness— that quality of delicacy about the bones, articulation, which even at twenty still had something about it, some last echo about it, of adolescence—that is, as compared with the cherubic burliness of the other who faced him, who looked younger, whose very superiority in bulk and displacement made him look even younger, as a plump boy of twelve who outweighs the other by twenty or thirty pounds still looks younger than the boy of fourteen who had that plumpness once and lost it, sold it (whether with his consent or not) for that state of virginity which is neither boy's nor girl's.

"I dont know," Quentin said.

"All right," Shreve said. "Maybe I dont either. Only, Jesus, some day you are bound to fall in love. They just wouldn't beat you that way. It would be like if God had got Jesus born and saw that He had the carpenter tools and then never gave Him anything to build with them. Dont you believe that?"

"I dont know," Quentin said. He did not move. Shreve looked at him. Even while they were not talking their breaths in the tomblike air vaporised gently and quietly. The chimes for midnight would have rung some time ago now.

"You mean, it dont matter to you?" Quentin did not answer. "That's right. Dont say it. Because I would know you

are lying.—All right then. Listen. Because he never had to
worry about the love because that would take care of itself.
Maybe he knew there was a fate, a doom on him, like what
the old Aunt Rosa told you about some things that just have
to be whether they are or not, just to balance the books, write
Paid on the old sheet so that whoever keeps them can take it
out of the ledger and burn it, get rid of it. Maybe he knew
then that whatever the old man had done, whether he meant
well or ill by it, it wasn't going to be the old man who would
have to pay the check; and now that the old man was bankrupt with the incompetence of age, who should do the paying
if not his sons, his get, because wasn't it done that way in the
old days? the old Abraham full of years and weak and incapable now of further harm, caught at last and the captains and
the collectors saying, 'Old man, we dont want you' and Abraham would say, 'Praise the Lord, I have raised about me sons
to bear the burden of mine iniquities and persecutions; yea,
perhaps even to restore my flocks and herds from the hand of
the ravisher: that I might rest mine eyes upon my goods and
chattels, upon the generations of them and of my descendants
increased an hundred fold as my soul goeth out from me.' He
knew all the time that the love would take care of itself.
Maybe that was why he didn't have to think about her during
those three months between that September and that Christmas while Henry talked about her to him, saying every time
he breathed: *Hers and my lives are to exist within and upon
yours;* did not need to waste any time over the love after it
happened, backfired on him, why he never bothered to write
her any letters (except that last one) which she would want to
save, why he never actually proposed to her and gave her a
ring for Mrs Sutpen to show around. Because the fate was on
her too: the same old Abraham who was so old and weak
now nobody would want him in the flesh on any debt; maybe
he didn't even have to wait for that Christmas to see her to
know this; maybe that's what it was that came out of the
three months of Henry's talking that he heard without listening to: *I am not hearing about a young girl, a virgin; I am
hearing about a narrow delicate fenced virgin field already fur-
rowed and bedded so that all I shall need to do is drop the seeds in,
caress it smooth again,* saw her that Christmas and knew it for

certain and then forgot it, went back to school and did not even remember that he had forgotten it, because he did not have time then; maybe it was just one day in that spring you told about when he stopped and said, right quiet: *All right. I want to go to bed with who might be my sister. All right* and then forgot that too. Because he didn't have time. That is, he didn't have anything else but time, because he had to wait. But not for her. That was all fixed. It was the other. Maybe he thought it would be in the mail bag each time the nigger rode over from Sutpen's Hundred and Henry believing it was the letter from her that he was waiting for when what he was thinking was *Maybe he will write it then. He would just have to write 'I am your father. Burn this' and I would do it. Or if not that, a sheet a scrap of paper with the one word 'Charles' in his hand, and I would know what he meant and he would not even have to ask me to burn it. Or a lock of his hair or a paring from his finger nail and I would know them because I believe now that I have known what his hair and his finger nails would look like all my life, could choose that lock and that paring out of a thousand.* And it did not come, and his letter went to her every two weeks and hers came back to him, and maybe he thought *If one of mine to her should come back to me unopened then. That would be a sign.* And that didn't happen: and then Henry began to talk about his stopping at Sutpen's Hundred for a day or so on his way home and he said all right to it, said *It will be Henry who will get the letter, the letter saying it is inconvenient for me to come at that time; so apparently he does not intend to acknowledge me as his son, but at least I shall have forced him to admit that I am.* And that one did not come either and the date was set and the family at Sutpen's Hundred notified of it and that letter did not come either and he thought *It will be then; I wronged him; maybe this is what he has been waiting for* and maybe his heart sprang then, maybe he said *Yes. Yes. I will renounce her; I will renounce love and all; that will be cheap, cheap, even though he say to me 'never look upon my face again; take my love and my acknowledgement in secret, and go' I will do that; I will not even demand to know of him what it was my mother did that justified his action toward her and me.* So the day came and he and Henry rode the forty miles again, into the gates and up the drive to the house. He knew what would

be there—the woman whom he had seen once and seen
through, the girl whom he had seen through without even
having to see once, the man whom he had seen daily, watched
out of his fearful intensity of need and had never penetrated;—the mother who had taken Henry aside before they
had been six hours in the house on that Christmas visit and
informed him of the engagement almost before the fiance had
had time to associate the daughter's name with the daughter's face: so that probably before they even reached school
again, and without his being aware that he had done so,
Henry had already told Bon what was in his mother's mind
(who had already told Bon what was in his); so that maybe
before they even started on Bon's second visit—(It would be
June now and what would it be in North Mississippi? what
was it you said? the magnolias in bloom and the mockingbirds, and in fifty years more, after they had gone and fought
it and lost it and come back home, the Decoration Day and
the veterans in the neat brushed hand-ironed gray and the
spurious bronze medals that never meant anything to begin
with, and the chosen young girls in white dresses bound at
the waist with crimson sashes and the band would play Dixie
and all the old doddering men would yell that you would not
have thought would have had wind enough to get there, walk
down town to sit on the rostrum even)—it would be June
now, with the magnolias and mockingbirds in the moonlight
and the curtains blowing in the June air of commencement
and the music, fiddles and triangles, inside among the swirling and dipping hoops: and Henry would be a little tight,
that should have been saying 'I demand to know your intentions toward my sister' but wasn't saying it, instead maybe
blushing again even in the moonlight, but standing straight
and blushing because when you are proud enough to be humble you dont have to cringe (who every time he breathed over
his vocal cords he was saying *We belong to you; do as you will
with us*), saying 'I used to think that I would hate the man
that I would have to look at every day and whose every move
and action and speech would say to me, I have seen and
touched parts of your sister's body that you will never see and
touch: and now I know that I shall hate him and that's why I
want that man to be you', knowing that Bon would know

what he meant, was trying to say, tell him, thinking, telling
himself (Henry): *Not just because he is older than I am and has
known more than I shall ever know and has remembered more of
it; but because of my own free will, and whether I knew it at the
time or not does not matter, I gave my life and Judith's both to
him*——"

"That's still not love," Quentin said.

"All right," Shreve said. "Just listen.—— Rode the forty
miles and into the gates and up to the house. And this time
Sutpen wasn't even there. And Ellen didn't even know where
he had gone, believing blandly and volubly that he had gone
to Memphis or maybe even to Saint Louis on business, and
Henry and Judith not even caring that much, and only he,
Bon, to know where Sutpen had gone, saying to himself *Of
course; he wasn't sure; he had to go there to make sure,* telling
himself that loud now, loud and fast too so he would not,
could not, hear the thinking, the *But if he suspected, why not
have told me? I would have done that, gone to him first, who have
the blood after it was tainted and corrupt by whatever it was in
Mother;* loud and fast now, telling himself *That's what it is;
maybe he has gone on ahead to wait for me; he left no message for
me here because the others are not to suspect yet and he knows that
I will know at once where he is when I find him gone,* thinking of
the two of them, the sombre vengeful woman who was his
mother and the grim rocklike man who had looked at him
every day for ten days with absolutely no alteration of expression at all, facing one another in grim armistice after almost
thirty years in that rich baroque drawing room in that house
which he called home since apparently everybody seemed to
have to have a home, the man who he was now sure was his
father not humble now either (and he, Bon, proud of that),
not saying even now *I was wrong* but *I admit that it is so*—
Jesus, think of his heart then, during those two days, with the
old gal throwing Judith at him every minute now because she
had been spreading the news of the engagement confidentially
through the county ever since Christmas—didn't your father
say how she had even taken Judith to Memphis in the spring
to buy the trousseau?—and Judith neither having to accede to
the throwing nor to resist it but just being, just existing and
breathing like Henry did who maybe one morning during

that spring waked up and lay right still in the bed and took
stock, added the figures and drew the balance and told himself, *All right. I am trying to make myself into what I think he
wants me to be; he can do anything he wants to with me; he has
only to tell me what to do and I will do it; even though what he
asked me to do looked to me like dishonor, I would still do it,* only
Judith, being a female and so wiser than that, would not even
consider dishonor: she would just say, *All right. I will do anything he might ask me to do and that is why he will never ask me
to do anything that I consider dishonorable:* so that (maybe he
even kissed her that time, the first time she had ever been
kissed maybe and she too innocent to be coy or modest or
even to know that she had been temporised with, maybe afterward just looking at him with a kind of peaceful and blank
surprise at the fact that your sweetheart apparently kissed you
the first time like your brother would—provided of course
that your brother ever thought of, could be brought to, kissing you on the mouth)—so that when the two days were up
and he was gone again and Ellen shrieking at her, 'What? No
engagement, no troth, no ring?' she would be too astonished
even to lie about it because that would be the first time it
would have occurred to her that there had been no proposal.—Think of his heart then, while he rode to the River,
and then on the steamboat itself where he walked up and
down the deck, feeling through the deck the engines driving
him nearer and nearer day and night to the moment which he
must have realised now he had been waiting for ever since he
had got big enough to comprehend. Of course every now and
then he would have to say it pretty fast and loud, *That's all it
is. He just wants to make sure first* to drown out the old *But
why do it this way? Why not back there? He knows that I shall
never make any claim upon any part of what he now possesses,
gained at the price of what sacrifice and endurance and scorn (so
they told me; not he: they) only he knows; knows that so well that
it would never have occurred to him just as he knows it would
never occur to me that this might be his reason, who is not only
generous but ruthless, who must have surrendered everything he
and Mother owned to her and to me as the price of repudiating
her,* not because the doing it this way hurt him, flouted him
and kept him in suspense that much unnecessary longer, be-

cause he didn't matter; whether he was irked or even crucified didn't matter: it was the fact that he had to be kept constantly reminded that he would not have done it this way himself, yet he had stemmed from the blood after whatever it was his mother had been or done had tainted and corrupted it.— Nearer and nearer, until suspense and puzzlement and haste and all seemed blended into one sublimation of passive surrender in which he thought only *All right. All right. Even this way. Even if he wants to do it this way. I will promise never to see her again. Never to see him again.* Then he reached home. And he never learned if Sutpen had been there or not. He never knew. He believed it, but he never knew—his mother the same sombre unchanged fierce paranoiac whom he had left in September, from whom he could learn nothing by indirection and whom he dared not ask outright—the very fact that he saw through the skillful questions of the lawyer (as to how he had liked the school and the people of that country and how perhaps—or had he not perhaps?—he had made friends up there among the country families) only that much more proof to him at that time that Sutpen had not been there, or at least the lawyer was not aware that he had, since now that he believed he had fathomed the lawyer's design in sending him to that particular school to begin with, he saw nothing in the questions to indicate that the lawyer had learned anything new since. (Or what he could have learned in that interview with the lawyer, because it would be a short one; it would be next to the shortest one ever to transpire between them, the shortest one of all next to the last one of course, the one which would occur in the next summer, when Henry would be with him.) Because the lawyer would not dare risk asking him outright, just as he (Bon) did not dare to ask his mother outright. Because, though the lawyer believed him to be rather a fool than dull or dense, yet even he (the lawyer) never for one moment believed that even Bon was going to be the kind of a fool he was going to be. So he told the lawyer nothing and the lawyer told him nothing, and the summer passed and September came and still the lawyer (his mother too) had not once asked him if he wanted to return to the school. So that at last he had to say it himself, that he intended to return; and maybe he knew that he had lost that

move since there was nothing whatever in the lawyer's face
save an agent's acquiescence. So he returned to school, where
Henry was waiting (oh yes; waiting) for him, who did not
even say 'You didn't answer my letters. You didn't even write
to Judith' who had already said *What my sister and I have and
are belongs to you* but maybe he did write to Judith now, by
the first nigger post which rode to Sutpen's Hundred, about
how it had been an uneventful summer and hence nothing to
write about, with maybe *Charles Bon* plain and inelidible on
the outside of the envelope and he thinking *He will have to see
that. Maybe he will send it back* thinking *Maybe if it comes back
nothing will stop me then and so maybe at last I will know what I
am going to do.* But it didn't come back. And the others didn't
come back. And the fall passed and Christmas came and they
rode again to Sutpen's Hundred and this time he was not
there again, he was in the field, he had gone to town, he was
hunting—something; Sutpen not there when they rode up
and Bon knew he had not expected him to be there, saying
*Now. Now. Now. It will come now. It will come this time, and I
am young, young, because I still dont know what I am going to do.*
So maybe what he was doing that twilight (because he knew
that Sutpen had returned, was now in the house; it would be
like a wind, something, dark and chill, breathing upon him
and he stopping, grave, quiet, alert, thinking *What? What is
it?* Then he would know; he could feel the other entering the
house, and he would let his held breath go quiet and easy, a
profound exhalation, his heart quiet too) in the garden while
he walked with Judith and talked to her, gallant and elegant
and automatic (and Judith thinking about that like she
thought about that first kiss back in the summer: *So that's it.
That's what love is,* bludgeoned once more by disappointment
but still unbowed);—maybe what he was doing there now
was waiting, telling himself *Maybe even yet he will send for me.
At least say it to me* even though he knew better: *He is in the
library now, he has sent the nigger for Henry, now Henry is entering the room:* so that maybe he stopped and faced her, with
something in his face that was smiling now, and took her by
the elbows and turned her, easy and gentle, until she faced the
house, and said 'Go. I wish to be alone to think about love'
and she went just as she took the kiss that day, with maybe

the feel of the flat of his hand light and momentary upon her behind. And he stood there facing the house until Henry came out, and they looked at one another for a while with no word said and then turned and walked together through the garden, across the lot and into the stable, where maybe there was a nigger there and maybe they saddled the two horses themselves and waited until the house nigger came with the two repacked saddlebags. And maybe he didn't even say then, 'But he sent no word to me?' "

Shreve ceased. That is, for all the two of them, Shreve and Quentin, knew he had stopped, since for all the two of them knew he had never begun, since it did not matter (and possibly neither of them conscious of the distinction) which one had been doing the talking. So that now it was not two but four of them riding the two horses through the dark over the frozen December ruts of that Christmas eve: four of them and then just two—Charles-Shreve and Quentin-Henry, the two of them both believing that Henry was thinking *He* (meaning his father) *has destroyed us all,* not for one moment thinking *He* (meaning Bon) *must have known or at least suspected this all the time; that's why he has acted as he has, why he did not answer my letters last summer nor write to Judith, why he has never asked her to marry him;* believing that that must have occurred to Henry, certainly during that moment after Henry emerged from the house and he and Bon looked at one another for a while without a word then walked down to the stable and saddled the horses, but that Henry had just taken that in stride because he did not yet believe it even though he knew that it was true, because he must have now understood with complete despair the secret of his whole attitude toward Bon from that first instinctive moment when he had seen him a year and a quarter ago; he knew, yet he did not, had to refuse to, believe. So it was four of them who rode the two horses through that night and then across the bright frosty North Mississippi Christmas day, in something very like pariah-hood passing the plantation houses with sprigs of holly thrust beneath the knockers on the doors and mistletoe hanging from the chandeliers and bowls of eggnog and toddy on tables in the halls and the blue unwinded wood smoke standing above the plastered chimneys of the slave quarters, to the River and the steamboat. There would be Christmas on the boat too: the same holly and mistletoe, the same eggnog and toddy; perhaps, doubtless, a Christmas supper and a ball, but not for them: the two of them in the dark and the cold standing at the guard rail above the dark water and still not talking since there was nothing to say, the two of them (the four of them) held in that probation, that suspension, by Henry who knew but still did not believe, who was going deliberately to look upon and prove to himself that which, so Shreve and Quentin believed, would be like death for him to learn. So it was four of them still who got off the boat in New Orleans, which Henry had never seen before (whose entire cosmopolitan experience, apart from his sojourn at the school, consisted probably of one or two trips to Memphis with his father to buy live stock or slaves) and had no time to look at now—Henry who knew yet did not believe, and Bon whom Mr Compson had called a fatalist but who, according to Shreve and Quentin, did not resist Henry's dictum and design for the reason that he neither knew nor cared what Henry intended to do because he had long since realised that he did not know yet what he himself was going to do;—four of them who sat in that drawing room of baroque and fusty magnificence which Shreve had invented and which was probably true enough, while the Haiti-born daughter of the French sugar planter and the woman who Sutpen's first father-in-law had told him was a Spaniard (the slight dowdy woman with untidy gray-streaked raven hair coarse as a horse's tail, with parchment-colored skin and implacable pouched black eyes which alone showed no age because they showed no forgetting, whom Shreve and Quentin had likewise invented and which was likewise probably true enough) told them nothing because she did not need to because she had already told it, who did not say, 'My son is in love with your sister?' but 'So she has fallen in love with him' and then sat laughing harshly and steadily at Henry who could not have lied to her even if he would have, who did not even have to answer at all either Yes or No.—Four of them there, in that room in New Orleans in 1860, just as in a sense there were four of them here in this tomblike room in Massachusetts in 1910. And Bon may have, probably did, take Henry to call on the octoroon mistress and the child, as Mr Compson said, though neither Shreve nor Quentin believed that the visit affected Henry as Mr Compson seemed to think. In fact, Quentin did not even tell Shreve what his father had said about the visit. Perhaps Quentin himself had not been listening when Mr Compson related (recreated?) it that evening at home; perhaps at that moment on the gallery in the hot September twilight Quentin took that in stride without even hearing it just as Shreve would have, since both he and Shreve believed—and were probably right in this too—that the octoroon and the child would have been to Henry only something else about Bon to be, not envied but aped if that had been possible, if there had been time and peace to ape it in—peace not between men of the same race and nation but peace between two young embattled spirits and the incontrovertible fact which embattled them, since neither Henry and Bon, anymore than Quentin and Shreve, were the first young men to believe (or at least apparently act on the assumption) that wars were sometimes created for the sole aim of settling youth's private difficulties and discontents.

"So the old dame asked Henry that one question and then sat there laughing at him, so he knew then, they both knew then. And so now it would be short, this time with the lawyer, the shortest one of all. Because the lawyer would have been watching him; maybe there had even been a letter during that second fall while the lawyer was waiting and still nothing seemed to be happening up there (and maybe the lawyer was the reason why Bon never answered Henry's and Judith's letters during that summer: because he never got them)—a letter, two or maybe three pages of your humble and obedient e and t and c that boiled down to eighteen words *I know you are a fool, but just what kind of a fool are you going to be?* and Bon was at least enough of a not-fool to do the boiling down.—Yes, watching him, not concerned yet, just considerably annoyed, giving Bon plenty of time to come to him, giving him all of a week maybe (after he—the lawyer—would have contrived to get hold of Henry and find out a good deal of what Henry was thinking without Henry ever knowing it) before he would contrive Bon too, and maybe so good at the contriving that even Bon would not know at once what was coming. It would be a short one. It would be no

secret between them now; it would just be unsaid: the lawyer
behind the desk (and maybe in the secret drawer the ledger
where he had just finished adding in the last past year's interest compounded between the intrinsic and the love and pride
at two hundred percent.)—the lawyer fretted, annoyed, but
not at all concerned since he not only knew he had the screws,
but he still did not really believe that Bon was that kind of a
fool, though he was about to alter his opinion somewhat
about the dullness, or at least the backwardness;—the lawyer
watching him and saying, smooth and oily, since it would be
no secret now, who would know now that Bon knew all he
would ever know or would need to know to make the coup:
'Do you know that you are a very fortunate young man? With
most of us, even when we are lucky enough to get our revenge, we must pay for it, sometimes in actual dollars. While
you are not only in a position to get your revenge, clear your
mother's name, but the balm with which you will assuage her
injury will have a collateral value which can be translated into
the things which a young man needs, which are his due and
which, whether we like it or not, may be had only in exchange for hard dollars——' and Bon not saying *What do
you mean?* and not moving yet; that is, the lawyer would not
be aware that he was beginning to move, continuing (the lawyer) smooth and easy: 'And more than this, than the revenge,
as lagniappe to the revenge as it were, this nosegay of an
afternoon, this scentless prairie flower which will not be
missed and which might as well bloom in your lapel as in
another's; this—How do you young men put it?—a nice little piece——' and then he would see Bon, maybe the eyes,
maybe he would just hear the feet moving. And then, pistol
(derringer, horse pistol, revolver, whatever it was) and all, he
would be crouched back against the wall behind the overturned chair, snarling, 'Stand back! Stop!' then screaming
'Help! Help! He——!' then just screaming, because he would
hear and feel his own wrenching bones before he could free
his fingers of the pistol, and his neck bone too as Bon would
strike him with the palm on one cheek and then with the back
of the hand on the other; maybe he could even hear Bon too
saying, 'Stop it. Hush. I'm not going to hurt you' or maybe it
was the lawyer in him that said the Hush which he obeyed,

who got him back into the righted chair again, half lying upon the desk; the lawyer in him that warned him not to say *You will pay for this* but instead to half lie there, nursing his wrenched hand in his handkerchief while Bon stood looking down at him, holding the pistol by the barrel against his leg, saying, 'If you feel that you require satisfaction, of course you know——' and the lawyer, sitting back now, dabbing the handkerchief at his cheek now: 'I was wrong. I misunderstood your feeling about the matter. I ask your pardon' and Bon: 'Granted. As you wish. I will accept either an apology or a bullet, as you prefer' and the lawyer (there would be a faint fading red in his cheek, but that would be all: nothing in the voice or in the eyes): 'I see you are going to collect full measure for my unfortunate misconception—even ridicule. Even if I felt that right was on my side (which I do not) I would still have to decline your offer. I would not be your equal with pistols' and Bon: 'Nor with knives or rapiers too?' and the lawyer, smooth and easy: 'Nor knives or rapiers too.' So that now the lawyer wouldn't even need to say *You will pay for this* because Bon would be saying that for him, who would stand there with the lax pistol, thinking *But only with knives or pistols or rapiers. So I cant beat him. I could shoot him. I would shoot him with no more compunction than I would a snake or a man who cuckolded me. But he would still beat me.* thinking *Yes. He did beat me* while he—he—("Listen," Shreve said, cried. "It would be while he would be lying in a bedroom of that private house in Corinth after Pittsburg Landing while his shoulder got well two years later and the letter from the octoroon (maybe even the one that contained the photograph of her and the child) finally overtaking him, wailing for money and telling him that the lawyer had departed for Texas or Mexico or somewhere at last and that she (the octoroon) could not find his mother either and so without doubt the lawyer had murdered her before he stole the money, since it would be just like both of them to flee or get themselves killed without providing for her at all.")—Yes, they knew now. And Jesus, think of him, Bon, who had wanted to know, who had had the most reason to want to know, who as far as he knew had never had any father but had been created somehow between that woman who wouldn't let him play

with other children, and that lawyer who even told the
woman whether or not each time she bought a piece of meat
or a loaf of bread—two people neither of whom had taken
pleasure or found passion in getting him or suffered pain and
travail in borning him—who perhaps if one of the two had
only told him the truth, none of what happened would ever
have come to pass; while there was Henry who had father and
security and contentment and all, yet was told the truth by
both of them while he (Bon) was told by neither. And think
of Henry, who had said at first it was a lie and then when he
knew it was not a lie had still said 'I dont believe it', who had
found even in that 'I dont believe it' enough of strength to
repudiate home and blood in order to champion his defiance,
and in which championing he proved his contention to be the
false one and was more than ever interdict against returning
home; Jesus, think of the load he had to carry, born of two
Methodists (or of one long invincible line of Methodists) and
raised in provincial North Mississippi, faced with incest, incest of all things that might have been reserved for him, that
all his heredity and training had to rebel against on principle,
and in a situation where he knew that neither incest nor training was going to help him solve it. So that maybe when they
left and walked the streets that night and at last Bon said,
'Well? Now what?' Henry said, 'Wait. Wait. Let me get used
to it.' And maybe it was two days or three days, and Henry
said, 'You shall not. Shall not' and then it was Bon that said,
'Wait. I am your older brother: do you say *shall not* to me?'
And maybe it was a week, maybe Bon took Henry to see the
octoroon and Henry looked at her and said, 'Aint that
enough for you?' and Bon said, 'Do you want it to be
enough?' and Henry said, 'Wait. Wait. I must have time to get
used to it. You will have to give me time.' Jesus, think how
Henry must have talked during that winter and then that
spring with Lincoln elected and the Alabama convention and
the South began to draw out of the Union, and then there
were two presidents in the United States and the telegraph
brought the news about Charleston and Lincoln called out his
army and it was done, irrevocable now, and Henry and Bon
already decided to go without having to consult one another,
who would have gone anyway even if they had never seen one

another but certainly now, because after all you dont waste a war;—think how they must have talked, how Henry would say, 'But must you marry her? Do you have to do it?' and Bon would say, 'He should have told me. He should have told me, myself, himself. I was fair and honorable with him. I waited. You know now why I waited. I gave him every chance to tell me himself. But he didn't do it. If he had, I would have agreed and promised never to see her or you or him again. But he didn't tell me. I thought at first it was because he didn't know. Then I knew that he did know, and still I waited. But he didn't tell me. He just told you, sent me a message like you send a command by a nigger servant to a beggar or a tramp to clear out. Dont you see that?' and Henry would say, 'But Judith. Our sister. Think of her' and Bon: 'All right. Think of her. Then what?' because they both knew what Judith would do when she found it out because they both knew that women will show pride and honor about almost anything except love, and Henry said, 'Yes. I see. I understand. But you will have to give me time to get used to it. You are my older brother; you can do that little for me.' Think of the two of them: Bon who didn't know what he was going to do and had to say, pretend, he did; and Henry who knew what he was going to do and had to say he didn't. Then it was Christmas again, then 1861, and they hadn't heard from Judith because Judith didn't know for sure where they were because Henry wouldn't let Bon write to her yet; then they heard about the company, the University Grays, organising up at Oxford and maybe they had been waiting for that. So they took the steamboat North again, and more gayety and excitement on the boat now than Christmas even, like it always is when a war starts, before the scene gets cluttered up with bad food and wounded soldiers and widows and orphans, and them taking no part in it now either but standing at the rail again above the churning water, and maybe it would be two or three days, then Henry said suddenly, cried suddenly: 'But kings have done it! Even dukes! There was that Lorraine duke named John something that married his sister. The Pope excommunicated him but it didn't hurt! It didn't hurt! They were still husband and wife. They were still alive. They still loved!' then again, loud, fast: 'But you will

have to wait! You will have to give me time! Maybe the war
will settle it and we wont need to!' And maybe this was one
place where your old man was right: and they rode into
Oxford without touching Sutpen's Hundred and signed the
company roster and then hid somewhere to wait, and Henry
let Bon write Judith one letter; they would send it by hand,
by a nigger that would steal into the quarters by night and
give it to Judith's maid, and Judith sent the picture in the
metal case and they rode on ahead to wait until the company
got through making flags and riding about the state telling
girls farewell and started for the front.

"Jesus, think of them. Because Bon would know what
Henry was doing, just as he had always known what Henry
was thinking since that first day when they had looked at one
another. Maybe he would know all the better what Henry
was doing because he did not know what he himself was going to do, that he would not know until all of a sudden some
day it would burst clear and he would know then that he had
known all the time what it would be, so he didn't have to
bother about himself and so all he had to do was just to
watch Henry trying to reconcile what he (Henry) knew he
was going to do with all the voices of his heredity and training which said *No. No. You cannot. You must not. You shall not*.
Maybe they would even be under fire now, with the shells
rushing and rumbling past overhead and bursting and them
lying there waiting to charge and Henry would cry again,
'But that Lorraine duke did it! There must have been lots in
the world who have done it that people dont know about,
that maybe they suffered for it and died for it and are in hell
now for it. But they did it and it dont matter now; even the
ones we do know about are just names now and it dont matter now' and Bon watching him and listening to him and
thinking *It's because I dont know myself what I am going to do
and so he is aware that I am undecided without knowing that he
is aware. Perhaps if I told him now that I am going to do it, he
would know his own mind and tell me, You shall not*. And maybe
your old man was right this time and they did think maybe
the war would settle it and they would not have to themselves, or at least maybe Henry hoped it would because
maybe your old man was right here too and Bon didn't care;

that since both of the two people who could have given him a father had declined to do it, nothing mattered to him now, revenge or love or all, since he knew now that revenge could not compensate him nor love assuage. Maybe it wasn't even Henry who wouldn't let him write to Judith but Bon himself who did not write her because he didn't care about anything, not even that he didn't know yet what he was going to do. Then it was the next year and Bon was an officer now and they were moving toward Shiloh without knowing that either, talking again as they moved along in column, the officer dropping back alongside the file in which the private marched and Henry crying again, holding his desperate and urgent voice down to undertone: 'Dont you know yet what you are going to do?' while Bon would look at him for a moment with that expression which could have been smiling: 'Suppose I told you I did not intend to go back to her?' and Henry would walk there beside him, with his pack and his eight feet of musket, and he would begin to pant, panting and panting while Bon watched him: 'I am out in front of you a lot now; going into battle, charging, I will be out in front of you——' and Henry panting, 'Stop! Stop!' and Bon watching him with that faint thin expression about the mouth and eyes: '——and who would ever know? You would not even have to know for certain yourself, because who could say but what a Yankee ball might have struck me at the exact second you pulled your trigger, or even before——' and Henry panting and looking, glaring at the sky, with his teeth showing and the sweat on his face and the knuckles of the hand on his musket butt white, saying, panting, 'Stop! Stop! Stop! Stop!' Then it was Shiloh, the second day and the lost battle and the brigade falling back from Pittsburg Landing——And listen," Shreve cried; "wait, now; wait!" (glaring at Quentin, panting himself, as if he had had to supply his shade not only with a cue but with breath to obey it in): "Because your old man was wrong here, too! He said it was Bon who was wounded, but it wasn't. Because who told him? Who told Sutpen, or your grandfather either, which of them it was who was hit? Sutpen didn't know because he wasn't there, and your grandfather wasn't there either because that was where he was hit too, where he lost his arm. So who told them? Not Henry, because his father never saw Henry but that one time and maybe they never had time to talk about wounds and besides to talk about wounds in the Confederate army in 1865 would be like coal miners talking about soot; and not Bon, because Sutpen never saw him at all because he was dead;—it was not Bon, it was Henry; Bon that found Henry at last and stooped to pick him up and Henry fought back, struggled, saying, 'Let be! Let me die! I wont have to know it then' and Bon said, 'So you do want me to go back to her' and Henry lay there struggling and panting, with the sweat on his face and his teeth bloody inside his chewed lip, and Bon said, 'Say you do want me to go back to her. Maybe then I wont do it. Say it' and Henry lay there struggling, with the fresh red staining through his shirt and his teeth showing and the sweat on his face until Bon held his arms and lifted him onto his back——"

First, two of them, then four; now two again. The room was indeed tomblike: a quality stale and static and moribund beyond any mere vivid and living cold. Yet they remained in it, though not thirty feet away was bed and warmth. Quentin had not even put on his overcoat, which lay on the floor where it had fallen from the arm of the chair where Shreve had put it down. They did not retreat from the cold. They both bore it as though in deliberate flagellant exaltation of physical misery transmogrified into the spirits' travail of the two young men during that time fifty years ago, or forty-eight rather, then forty-seven and then forty-six, since it was '64 and then '65 and the starved and ragged remnant of an army having retreated across Alabama and Georgia and into Carolina, swept onward not by a victorious army behind it but rather by a mounting tide of the names of lost battles from either side—Chickamauga and Franklin, Vicksburg and Corinth and Atlanta—battles lost not alone because of superior numbers and failing ammunition and stores, but because of generals who should not have been generals, who were generals not through training in contemporary methods or aptitude for learning them, but by the divine right to say 'Go there' conferred upon them by an absolute caste system; or because the generals of it never lived long enough to learn how to fight massed cautious accretionary battles, since they were already as obsolete as Richard or Roland or du Guesclin, who wore plumes and cloaks lined with scarlet at twenty-eight and thirty and thirty-two and captured warships with cavalry charges but no grain nor meat nor bullets, who would whip three separate armies in as many days and then tear down their own fences to cook meat robbed from their own smokehouses, who on one night and with a handful of men would gallantly set fire to and destroy a million dollar garrison of enemy supplies and on the next night be discovered by a neighbor in bed with his wife and be shot to death;—two, four, now two again, according to Quentin and Shreve, the two the four the two still talking—the one who did not yet know what he was going to do, the other who knew what he would have to do yet could not reconcile himself—Henry citing himself authority for incest, talking about his Duke John of Lorraine as if he hoped possibly to evoke that condemned and excommunicated shade to tell him in person that it was all right, as people both before and since have tried to evoke God or devil to justify them in what their glands insisted upon;—the two the four the two facing one another in the tomblike room: Shreve, the Canadian, the child of blizzards and of cold in a bathrobe with an overcoat above it, the collar turned up about his ears; Quentin, the Southerner, the morose and delicate offspring of rain and steamy heat in the thin suitable clothing which he had brought from Mississippi, his overcoat (as thin and vain for what it was as the suit) lying on the floor where he had not even bothered to raise it:

(——*the winter of '64 now, the army retreated across Alabama, into Georgia; now Carolina was just at their backs and Bon, the officer, thinking 'We will either be caught and annihilated or Old Joe will extricate us and we will make contact with Lee in front of Richmond and then we will at least have the privilege of surrender': and then one day all of a sudden he thought of it, remembered, how that Jefferson regiment of which his father was now colonel was in Longstreet's corps, and maybe from that moment the whole purpose of the retreat seemed to him to be that of bringing him within reach of his father, to give his father one more chance. So that it must have seemed to him now that he knew at last why he had not been able to decide what he wanted to do.*

Maybe he thought for just a second, 'My God, I am still young;
even after these four years I am still young' but just for a second,
because maybe in the same breath he said, 'All right. Then I am
young. But I still believe, even though what I believe probably is
that war, suffering, these four years of keeping his men alive and
able in order to swap them blood and flesh for the largest amount
of ground at its bargain price, will have changed him (which I
know that it does not do) to where he will say to me not: Forgive
me: but: You are my oldest son. Protect your sister; never see either
of us again:' Then it was '65 and what was left of the Army of the
West with nothing remaining now but the ability to walk back-
ward slow and stubborn and to endure musketry and shelling;
maybe they didn't even miss the shoes and overcoats and food any
more now and that was why he could write about the captured
stove polish like he did in the letter to Judith when he finally knew
what he was going to do at last and told Henry and Henry said
'Thank God. Thank God', not for the incest of course but because
at last they were going to do something, at last he could be some-
thing even though that something was the irrevocable repudiation
of the old heredity and training and the acceptance of eternal
damnation. Maybe he could even quit talking about his Lorraine
duke then, because he could say now, 'It isn't yours nor his nor the
Pope's hell that we are all going to: it's my mother's and her moth-
er's and father's and their mothers' and fathers' hell, and it isn't
you who are going there, but we, the three —no: four of us. And so
at least we will all be together where we belong, since even if only
he went there we would still have to be there too since the three of
us are just illusions that he begot, and your illusions are a part of
you like your bones and flesh and memory. And we will all be
together in torment and so we will not need to remember love and
fornication, and maybe in torment you cannot even remember why
you are there. And if we cannot remember all this, it cant be much
torment'. Then they were in Carolina, that January and Febru-
ary of '65 and what was left of them had been walking backward
for almost a year now and the distance between them and Rich-
mond was less far than the distance they had come; the distance
between them and the end a good deal less far. But to Bon it was
not the space between them and defeat but the space between him
and the other regiment, between him and the hour, the moment:
'He will not even have to ask me; I will just touch flesh with him

and I will say it myself: You will not need to worry; she shall never see me again'. Then March in Carolina and still the walking backward slow and stubborn and listening to the Northward now because there was nothing to hear from any other direction because in all the other directions it was finished now, and all they expected to hear from the North was defeat. Then one day (he was an officer; he would have known, heard, that Lee had detached some troops and sent them down to reinforce them; perhaps he even knew the names and numbers of the regiments before they arrived) he saw Sutpen. Maybe that first time Sutpen actually did not see him, maybe that first time he could tell himself, 'That was why; he didn't see me', so that he had to put himself in Sutpen's way, make his chance and situation. Then for the second time he looked at the expressionless and rocklike face, at the pale boring eyes in which there was no flicker, nothing, the face in which he saw his own features, in which he saw recognition, and that was all. That was all, there was nothing further now; perhaps he just breathed once quietly, with on his own face that expression which might at a glance have been called smiling while he thought, 'I could force him. I could go to him and force him', knowing that he would not because it was all finished now, that was all of it now and at last. And maybe it was that same night or maybe a night a week later while they were stopped (because even Sherman would have to stop sometimes at night) with the fires burning for warmth at least because at least warmth is cheap and doesn't remain consumed, that Bon said, 'Henry' and said, 'It wont be much longer now and then there wont be anything left; we wont even have anything to do left, not even the privilege of walking backward slowly for a reason, for the sake of honor and what's left of pride. Not God; evidently we have done without Him for four years, only He just didn't think to notify us; and not only not shoes and clothing but not even any need for them, and not only no land nor any way to make food, but no need for the food since we have learned to live without that too; and so if you dont have God and you dont need food and clothes and shelter, there isn't anything for honor and pride to climb on and hold to and flourish. And if you haven't got honor and pride, then nothing matters. Only there is something in you that doesn't care about honor and pride yet that lives, that even walks backward for a whole year just to live; that probably even when this is over and there is not even defeat left, will still

decline to sit still in the sun and die, but will be out in the woods,
moving and seeking where just will and endurance could not move
it, grubbing for roots and such—the old mindless sentient un-
dreaming meat that doesn't even know any difference between de-
spair and victory, Henry'. And then Henry would begin to say
'Thank God. Thank God' panting and saying 'Thank God', say-
ing, 'Dont try to explain it. Just do it' and Bon: 'You authorise
me? As her brother you give me permission?' and Henry: 'Brother?
Brother? You are the oldest: why do you ask me?' and Bon: 'No.
He has never acknowledged me. He just warned me. You are the
brother and the son. Do I have your permission, Henry?' and
Henry: 'Write. Write. Write'. So Bon wrote the letter, after the
four years, and Henry read it and sent it off. But they didn't quit
then and follow the letter. They still walked backward, slow and
stubborn, listening toward the North for the end of it because it
takes an awful lot of character to quit anything when you are
losing, and they had been walking backward slow for a year now so
all they had left was not the will but just the ability, the grooved
habit to endure. Then one night they had stopped again since
Sherman had stopped again, and an orderly came along the biv-
ouac line and found Henry at last and said, 'Sutpen, the colonel
wants you in his tent.')

"And so you and the old dame, the Aunt Rosa, went out
there that night and the old nigger Clytie tried to stop you,
stop her; she held your arm and said, 'Dont let her go up
there, young marster' but you couldn't stop her either because she was strong with forty-three years of hate like forty-
three years of raw meat and all Clytie had was just forty-five
or fifty years of despair and waiting; and you, you didn't even
want to be there at all to begin with. And you couldn't stop
her either and then you saw that Clytie's trouble wasn't anger
nor even distrust; it was terror, fear. And she didn't tell you
in so many words because she was still keeping that secret for
the sake of the man who had been her father too as well as for
the sake of the family which no longer existed, whose here-
to-fore inviolate and rotten mausoleum she still guarded;—
didn't tell you in so many words anymore than she told you
in so many words how she had been in the room that day
when they brought Bon's body in and Judith took from his
pocket the metal case she had given him with her picture in it;

she didn't tell you, it just came out of the terror and the fear
after she turned you loose and caught the Aunt Rosa's arm
and the Aunt Rosa turned and struck her hand away and
went on to the stairs and Clytie ran at her again and this time
the Aunt Rosa stopped and turned on the second step and
knocked Clytie down with her fist like a man would and
turned and went on up the stairs: and Clytie lay there on the
floor, more than eighty years old and not much more than
five feet tall and looking like a little bundle of clean rags so
that you went and took her arm and helped her up and her
arm felt like a stick, as light and dry and brittle as a stick: and
she looked at you and you saw it was not rage but terror, and
not nigger terror because it was not about herself but was
about whatever it was that was up stairs, that she had kept
hidden up there for almost four years; and she didn't tell you
in the actual words because even in the terror she kept the
secret; nevertheless she told you, or at least all of a sudden
you knew——"

He ceased again. It was just as well, since he had no
listener. Perhaps he was aware of it. Then suddenly he had
no talker either, though possibly he was not aware of this.
Because now neither of them was there. They were both in
Carolina and the time was forty-six years ago, and it was not
even four now but compounded still further, since now both
of them were Henry Sutpen and both of them were Bon,
compounded each of both yet either neither, smelling the
very smoke which had blown and faded away forty-six years
ago from the *bivouac fires burning in a pine grove, the gaunt
and ragged men sitting or lying about them, talking not about the
war yet all curiously enough (or perhaps not curiously at all) facing the South where further on in the darkness the pickets stood —
the pickets who, watching to the South, could see the flicker and
gleam of the Federal bivouac fires myriad and faint and encircling
half the horizon and counting ten fires for each Confederate one,
and between whom and which (Rebel picket and Yankee fire) the
Yankee outposts watched the darkness also, the two picket lines so
close that each could hear the challenge of the other's officers passing from post to post and dying away: and when gone, the voice,
invisible, cautious, not loud yet carrying:*
—*Hey, Reb.*

—*Yah.*
—*Where you fellers going?*
—*Richmond.*
—*So are we. Why not wait for us?*
—*We air.*

The men about the fires would not hear this exchange, though they would presently hear the orderly plainly enough as he passes from fire to fire, asking for Sutpen and being directed on and so reaches the fire at last, the smoldering log, with his monotonous speech: 'Sutpen? I'm looking for Sutpen' until Henry sits up and says, 'Here.' He is gaunt and ragged and unshaven; because of the last four years and because he had not quite got his height when the four years began, he is not as tall by two inches as he gave promise of being, and not as heavy by thirty pounds as he probably will be a few years after he has outlived the four years, if he do outlive them.

—*Here, he says.* —*What is it?*
—*The colonel wants you.*

The orderly does not return with him. Instead, he walks alone through the darkness along a rutted road, a road rutted and cut and churned where the guns have passed over it that afternoon, and reaches the tent at last, one of the few tents, the canvas wall gleaming faintly from a candle within, the silhouette of a sentry before it, who challenges him.

—*Sutpen, Henry says.* —*The colonel sent for me.*

The sentry gestures him into the tent. He stoops through the entrance, the canvas falls behind him as someone, the only occupant of the tent, rises from a camp chair behind the table on which the candle sits, his shadow swooping high and huge up the canvas wall. He (Henry) comes to salute facing a gray sleeve with colonel's braid on it, one bearded cheek, a jutting nose, a shaggy droop of iron-riddled hair—a face which Henry does not recognise, not because he has not seen it in four years and does not expect to see it here and now, but rather because he is not looking at it. He just salutes the braided cuff and stands so until the other says,

—*Henry.*

Even now Henry does not start. He just stands so, the two of them stand so, looking at one another. It is the older man who moves first, though they meet in the center of the tent, where they embrace and kiss before Henry is aware that he has moved, was going

*to move, moved by what of close blood which in the reflex instant
arrogates and reconciles even though it does not yet (perhaps never
will) forgive, who stands now while his father holds his face between
both hands, looking at it.*

    —Henry, Sutpen says.—My son.

*Then they sit, one on either side of the table, in the chairs reserved
for officers, the table (an open map lies on it) and the candle between them.*

    —You were hit at Shiloh, Colonel Willow tells me, Sutpen says.

    —Yes, sir, Henry says.

*He is about to say Charles carried me back but he does not, because
already he knows what is coming. He does not even think Surely
Judith didn't write him about that letter or It was Clytie who sent
him word somehow that Charles has written her. He thinks neither
of these. To him it is logical and natural that their father should
know of his and Bon's decision: that rapport of blood which should
bring Bon to decide to write, himself to agree to it and their father
to know of it at the same identical instant, after a period of four
years, out of all time. Now it does come, almost exactly as he has
known that it will:*

    —I have seen Charles Bon, Henry.

*Henry says nothing. It is coming now. He says nothing, he merely
stares at his father—the two of them in leaf-faded gray, a single
candle, a crude tent walling them away from a darkness where
alert pickets face one another and where weary men sleep without
shelter, waiting for dawn and the firing, the weary backward
walking to commence again: yet in a second tent candle gray and
all are gone and it is the holly-decked Christmas library at
Sutpen's Hundred four years ago and the table not a camp table
suitable for the spreading of maps but the heavy carved rosewood
one at home with the group photograph of his mother and sister
and himself sitting upon it, his father behind the table and behind
his father the window above the garden where Judith and Bon
strolled in that slow rhythm where the heart matches the footsteps
and the eyes need only look at one another.*

    —You are going to let him marry Judith, Henry.

*Still Henry does not answer. It has all been said before, and now
he has had four years of bitter struggle following which, whether it
be victory or defeat which he has gained, at least he has gained it
and has peace now, even if the peace be mostly despair.*

—*He cannot marry her, Henry.*
Now Henry speaks.
—*You said that before. I told you then. And now, and now it wont be much longer now and then we wont have anything left: honor nor pride nor God since God quit us four years ago only He never thought it necessary to tell us; no shoes nor clothes and no need for them; not only no land to make food out of but no need for the food and when you dont have God and honor and pride, nothing matters except that there is the old mindless meat that dont even care if it was defeat or victory, that wont even die, that will be out in the woods and fields, grubbing up roots and weeds.*—*Yes. I have decided. Brother or not, I have decided. I will. I will.*
—*He must not marry her, Henry.*
—*Yes. I said Yes at first, but I was not decided then. I didn't let him. But now I have had four years to decide in. I will. I am going to.*
—*He must not marry her, Henry. His mother's father told me that her mother had been a Spanish woman. I believed him; it was not until after he was born that I found out that his mother was part negro.*
Nor did Henry ever say that he did not remember leaving the tent. He remembers all of it. He remembers stooping through the entrance again and passing the sentry again; he remembers walking back down the cut and rutted road, stumbling in the dark among the ruts on either side of which the fires have now died to embers, so that he can barely distinguish the men sleeping on the earth about them. It must be better than eleven oclock, he thinks. And another eight miles tomorrow. If it were only not for those damned guns. Why doesn't Old Joe give the guns to Sherman. Then we could make twenty miles a day. We could join Lee then. At least Lee stops and fights some of the time. He remembers it. He remembers how he did not return to his fire but stopped presently in a lonely place and leaned against a pine, leaning quietly and easily, with his head back so he could look up at the shabby shaggy branches like something in wrought iron spreading motionless against the chill vivid stars of early spring, thinking I hope he remembers to thank Colonel Willow for letting us use his tent, thinking not what he would do but what he would have to do. Because he knew what he would do; it now depended on what Bon would do, would force him

to do, since he knew that he would do it. So I must go to him, he thought, thinking, Now it is better than two oclock and it will be dawn soon.

Then it was dawn, or almost, and it was cold: a chill which struck through the worn patched thin clothing, through the something of weariness and undernourishment; the passive ability, not the volitional will, to endure; there was light somewhere, enough of it for him to distinguish Bon's sleeping face from among the others where he lay wrapped in his blankets, beneath his spread cloak; enough light for him to wake Bon by and for Bon to distinguish his face (or perhaps something communicated by Henry's hand) because Bon does not speak, demand to know who it is: he merely rises and puts the cloak about his shoulders and approaches the smoldering fire and is kicking it into a blaze when Henry speaks:

—Wait.

Bon pauses and looks at Henry; now he can see Henry's face. He says,

—You will be cold. You are cold now. You haven't been asleep, have you? Here.

He swings the cloak from his shoulders and holds it out.

—No, Henry says.

—Yes. Take it. I'll get my blanket.

Bon puts the cloak about Henry and goes and takes up his tumbled blanket and swings it about his shoulders, and they move aside and sit on a log. Now it is dawn. The east is gray; it will be primrose soon and then red with firing and once more the weary backward marching will begin, retreating from annihilation, falling back upon defeat, though not quite yet. There will be a little time yet for them to sit side by side upon the log in the making light of dawn, the one in the cloak, the other in the blanket; their voices are not much louder than the silent dawn itself:

—So it's the miscegenation, not the incest, which you cant bear. Henry doesn't answer.

—And he sent me no word? He did not ask you to send me to him? No word to me, no word at all? That was all he had to do, now, today; four years ago or at any time during the four years. That was all. He would not have needed to ask it, require it, of me. I would have offered it. I would have said, I will never see her

*again before he could have asked it of me. He did not have to do
this, Henry. He didn't need to tell you I am a nigger to stop me.
He could have stopped me without that, Henry.*

—*No! Henry cries.* —*No! No! I will* —*I'll* ——

*He springs up; his face is working; Bon can see his teeth within the
soft beard which covers his sunken cheeks, and the whites of Henry's
eyes as though the eyeballs struggled in their sockets as the panting
breath struggled in his lungs* —*the panting which ceased, the
breath held, the eyes too looking down at him where he sat on the
log, the voice now not much louder than an expelled breath:*

—*You said, could have stopped you. What do you mean by that?*
*Now it is Bon who does not answer, who sits on the log looking at
the face stooped above him. Henry says, still in that voice no louder
than breathing:*

—*But now? You mean you* ——

—*Yes. What else can I do now? I gave him the choice. I have
been giving him the choice for four years.*

—*Think of her. Not of me: of her.*

—*I have. For four years. Of you and her. Now I am thinking
of myself.*

—*No, Henry says.* —*No. No.*

—*I cannot?*

—*You shall not.*

—*Who will stop me, Henry?*

—*No, Henry says.* —*No. No. No.*

*Now it is Bon who watches Henry; he can see the whites of Henry's
eyes again as he sits looking at Henry with that expression which
might be called smiling. His hand vanishes beneath the blanket
and reappears, holding his pistol by the barrel, the butt extended
toward Henry.*

—*Then do it now, he says.*

*Henry looks at the pistol; now he is not only panting, he is trem-
bling; when he speaks now his voice is not even the exhalation, it is
the suffused and suffocating inbreath itself:*

—*You are my brother.*

—*No I'm not. I'm the nigger that's going to sleep with your
sister. Unless you stop me, Henry.*

*Suddenly Henry grasps the pistol, jerks it free of Bon's hand and
stands so, the pistol in his hand, panting and panting; again Bon
can see the whites of his inrolled eyes while he sits on the log and*

*watches Henry with that faint expression about the eyes and
mouth which might be smiling.*

—Do it now, Henry, he says.

*Henry whirls; in the same motion he hurls the pistol from him and
stoops again, gripping Bon by both shoulders, panting.*

—You shall not! he says. —You shall not! Do you hear me?

*Bon does not move beneath the gripping hands; he sits motionless,
with his faint fixed grimace; his voice is gentler than that first
breath in which the pine branches begin to move a little:*

—You will have to stop me, Henry. "And he never slipped
away," Shreve said. "He could have, but he never even tried.
Jesus, maybe he even went to Henry and said, 'I'm going,
Henry' and maybe they left together and rode side by side
dodging Yankee patrols all the way back to Mississippi and
right up to that gate; side by side and it only then that one of
them ever rode ahead or dropped behind and that when
Henry spurred ahead and turned his horse to face Bon and
took out the pistol; and Judith and Clytie heard the shot, and
maybe Wash Jones was hanging around somewhere in the
back yard and so he was there to help Clytie and Judith carry
him into the house and lay him on the bed, and Wash went to
town to tell the Aunt Rosa and the Aunt Rosa comes boiling
out that afternoon and finds Judith standing without a tear
before the closed door, holding the metal case she had given
him with her picture in it but that didn't have her picture in it
now but that of the octoroon and the kid. And your old man
wouldn't know about that too: why the black son of a bitch
should have taken her picture out and put the octoroon's picture in, so he invented a reason for it. But I know. And you
know too. Dont you? Dont you, huh?" He glared at Quentin,
leaning forward over the table now, looking huge and shapeless as a bear in his swaddling of garments. "Dont you know?
It was because he said to himself, 'If Henry dont mean what
he said, it will be all right; I can take it out and destroy it. But
if he does mean what he said, it will be the only way I will
have to say to her, *I was no good; do not grieve for me.*' Aint that
right? Aint it? By God, aint it?"

"Yes," Quentin said.

"Come on," Shreve said. "Let's get out of this refrigerator
and go to bed."

IX.

AT FIRST, in bed in the dark, it seemed colder than ever, as if there had been some puny quality of faint heat in the single light bulb before Shreve turned it off and that now the iron and impregnable dark had become one with the iron and icelike bedclothing lying upon the flesh slacked and thin-clad for sleeping. Then the darkness seemed to breathe, to flow back; the window which Shreve had opened became visible against the faintly unearthly glow of the outer snow as, forced by the weight of the darkness, the blood surged and ran warmer, warmer. "University of Mississippi," Shreve's voice said in the darkness to Quentin's right. "Bayard attenuated forty miles (it was forty miles, wasn't it?); out of the wilderness proud honor semestrial regurgitant."

"Yes," Quentin said. "They were in the tenth graduating class since it was founded."

"I didn't know there were ten in Mississippi that went to school at one time," Shreve said. Quentin didn't answer. He lay watching the rectangle of window, feeling the warming blood driving through his veins, his arms and legs. And now, although he was warm and though while he had sat in the cold room he merely shook faintly and steadily, now he began to jerk all over, violently and uncontrollably until he could even hear the bed, until even Shreve felt it and turned, raising himself (by the sound) onto his elbow to look at Quentin, though Quentin himself felt perfectly all right. He felt fine even, lying there and waiting in peaceful curiosity for the next violent unharbingered jerk to come. "Jesus, are you that cold?" Shreve said. "Do you want me to spread the overcoats on you?"

"No," Quentin said. "I'm not cold. I'm all right. I feel fine."

"Then what are you doing that for?"

"I dont know. I cant help it. I feel fine."

"All right. But let me know if you want the coats. Jesus, if I was going to have to spend nine months in this climate, I would sure hate to have come from the South. Maybe I wouldn't come from the South anyway, even if I could stay there. Wait. Listen. I'm not trying to be funny, smart. I just

296

want to understand it if I can and I dont know how to say it better. Because it's something my people haven't got. Or if we have got it, it all happened long ago across the water and so now there aint anything to look at every day to remind us of it. We dont live among defeated grandfathers and freed slaves (or have I got it backward and was it your folks that are free and the niggers that lost?) and bullets in the dining room table and such, to be always reminding us to never forget. What is it? something you live and breathe in like air? a kind of vacuum filled with wraithlike and indomitable anger and pride and glory at and in happenings that occurred and ceased fifty years ago? a kind of entailed birthright father and son and father and son of never forgiving General Sherman, so that forever more as long as your children's children produce children you wont be anything but a descendant of a long line of colonels killed in Pickett's charge at Manassas?"

"Gettysburg," Quentin said. "You cant understand it. You would have to be born there."

"Would I then?" Quentin did not answer. "Do you understand it?"

"I dont know," Quentin said. "Yes, of course I understand it." They breathed in the darkness. After a moment Quentin said: "I dont know."

"Yes. You dont know. You dont even know about the old dame, the Aunt Rosa."

"Miss Rosa," Quentin said.

"All right. You dont even know about her. Except that she refused at the last to be a ghost. That after almost fifty years she couldn't reconcile herself to letting him lie dead in peace. That even after fifty years she not only could get up and go out there to finish up what she found she hadn't quite completed, but she could find someone to go with her and bust into that locked house because instinct or something told her it was not finished yet. Do you?"

"No," Quentin said peacefully. He could taste the dust. Even now, with the chill pure weight of the snow-breathed New England air on his face, he could taste and feel the dust of that breathless (rather, furnace-breathed) Mississippi September night. He could even smell the old woman in the buggy beside him, smell the fusty camphor-reeking shawl and even the airless black cotton umbrella in which (he would not discover until they had reached the house) she had concealed a hatchet and a flashlight. He could smell the horse; he could hear the dry plaint of the light wheels in the weightless permeant dust and he seemed to feel the dust itself move sluggish and dry across his sweating flesh just as he seemed to hear the single profound suspiration of the parched earth's agony rising toward the imponderable and aloof stars. Now she spoke, for the first time since they had left Jefferson, since she had climbed into the buggy with a kind of clumsy and fumbling and trembling eagerness (which he thought derived from terror, alarm, until he found that he was quite wrong) before he could help her, to sit on the extreme edge of the seat, small, in the fusty shawl and clutching the umbrella, leaning forward as if by leaning forward she would arrive the sooner, arrive immediately after the horse and before he, Quentin, would, before the prescience of her desire and need could warn its consummation. "Now," she said. "We are on the Domain. On his land, his and Ellen's and Ellen's descendants. They have taken it away from them since, I understand. But it still belongs to him, to Ellen and her descendants." But Quentin was already aware of that. Before she spoke he had said to himself, 'Now. Now' and (as during the long hot afternoon in the dim hot little house) it seemed to him that if he stopped the buggy and listened, he might even hear the galloping hooves; might even see at any moment now the black stallion and the rider rush across the road before them and gallop on—the rider who at one time owned, lock stock and barrel, everything he could see from a given point, with every stick and blade and hoof and heel on it to remind him (if he ever forgot it) that he was the biggest thing in their sight and in his own too; who went to war to protect it and lost the war and returned home to find that he had lost more than the war even, though not absolutely all; who said *At least I have life left* but did not have life but only old age and breathing and horror and scorn and fear and indignation: and all remaining to look at him with unchanged regard was the girl who had been a child when he saw her last, who doubtless used to watch him from window or door as he passed unaware of her as she would have looked at God probably, since everything else within her view belonged to him too. Maybe he would even stop at the cabin and ask for water and she would take the bucket and walk the mile and back to the spring to fetch it fresh and cool for him, no more thinking of saying "The bucket is empty" to him than she would have said it to God;—this the not-all, since at least there was breathing left.

Now Quentin began to breathe hard again, who had been peaceful for a time in the warm bed, breathing hard the heady pure snowborn darkness. She (Miss Coldfield) did not let him enter the gate. She said "Stop" suddenly; he felt her hand flutter on his arm and he thought, 'Why, she is afraid'. He could hear her panting now, her voice almost a wail of diffident yet iron determination: "I dont know what to do. I dont know what to do." ('I do,' he thought. 'Go back to town and go to bed.') But he did not say it. He looked at the two huge rotting gate posts in the starlight, between which no gates swung now, wondering from what direction Bon and Henry had ridden up that day, wondering what had cast the shadow which Bon was not to pass alive; if some living tree which still lived and bore leaves and shed or if some tree gone, vanished, burned for warmth and food years ago now or perhaps just gone; or if it had been one of the two posts themselves, thinking, wishing that Henry were there now to stop Miss Coldfield and turn them back, telling himself that if Henry were there now, there would be no shot to be heard by anyone. "She's going to try to stop me," Miss Coldfield whimpered. "I know she is. Maybe this far from town, out here alone at midnight, she will even let that negro man——And you didn't even bring a pistol. Did you?"

"Nome," Quentin said. "What is it she's got hidden there? What could it be? And what difference does it make? Let's go back to town, Miss Rosa."

She didn't answer this at all. She just said, "That's what I have got to find out", sitting forward on the seat, trembling now and peering up the tree-arched drive toward where the rotting shell of the house would be. "And now I will have to find it out," she whimpered, in a kind of amazed self-pity. She moved suddenly. "Come," she whispered, beginning to get out of the buggy.

"Wait," Quentin said. "Let's drive up to the house. It's a half a mile."

"No, no," she whispered, a tense fierce hissing of words filled with that same curious terrified yet implacable determination, as though it were not she who had to go and find out but she only the helpless agent of someone or something else who must know. "Hitch the horse here. Hurry." She got out, scrambled awkwardly down, before he could help her, clutching the umbrella. It seemed to him that he could still hear her whimpering panting where she waited close beside one of the posts while he led the mare from the road and tied one rein about a sapling in the weed-choked ditch. He could not see her at all, so close she stood against the post: she just stepped out and fell in beside him when he passed and turned into the gate, still breathing in those whimpering pants as they walked on up the rutted tree-arched drive. The darkness was intense; she stumbled; he caught her. She took his arm, clutching it in a dead rigid hard grip as if her fingers, her hand, were a small mass of wire. "I will have to take your arm," she whispered, whimpered. "And you haven't even got a pistol—Wait," she said. She stopped. He turned; he could not see her but he could hear her hurried breathing and then a rustling of cloth. Then she was prodding something at him. "Here," she whispered. "Take it." It was a hatchet; not sight but touch told him—a hatchet with a heavy worn handle and a heavy gapped rust-dulled blade.

"What?" he said.

"Take it!" she whispered, hissed. "You didn't bring a pistol. It's something."

"Here," he said; "wait."

"Come," she whispered. "You will have to let me take your arm, I am trembling so bad." They went on again, she clinging to one of his arms, the hatchet in his other hand. "We will probably need it to get into the house, anyway," she said, stumbling along beside him, almost dragging him. "I just know she is somewhere watching us," she whimpered. "I can feel her. But if we can just get to the house, get into the house——" The drive seemed interminable. He knew the place. He had walked from the gate to the house as a child, a boy, when distances seem really long (so that to the man

grown the long crowded mile of his boyhood becomes less
than the throw of a stone) yet now it seemed to him that
the house would never come in sight: so that presently he
found himself repeating her words: 'If we can just get to the
house, get inside the house', telling himself, recovering himself in that same breath: 'I am not afraid. I just dont want to
be here. I just dont want to know about whatever it is she
keeps hidden in it'. But they reached it at last. It loomed,
bulked, square and enormous, with jagged half-toppled chimneys, its roofline sagging a little; for an instant as they moved,
hurried, toward it Quentin saw completely through it a ragged segment of sky with three hot stars in it as if the house
were of one dimension, painted on a canvas curtain in which
there was a tear; now, almost beneath it, the dead furnace-
breath of air in which they moved seemed to reek in slow and
protracted violence with a smell of desolation and decay as if
the wood of which it was built were flesh. She was trotting
beside him now, her hand trembling on his arm yet gripping
it still with that lifeless and rigid strength; not talking, not
saying words, yet producing a steady whimpering, almost a
moaning, sound. Apparently she could not see at all now, so
that he had to guide her toward where he knew the steps
would be and then restrain her, whispering, hissing, aping
without knowing it her own tense fainting haste: "Wait. This
way. Be careful, now. They're rotten." He almost lifted, carried, her up the steps, supporting her from behind by both
elbows as you lift a child; he could feel something fierce and
implacable and dynamic driving down the thin rigid arms and
into his palms and up his own arms; lying in the Massachusetts bed he remembered how he thought, knew, said suddenly to himself, 'Why, she's not afraid at all. It's something.
But she's not afraid', feeling her flee out of his hands, hearing
her feet cross the gallery, overtaking her where she now stood
beside the invisible front door, panting. "Now what?" he
whispered.

"Break it," she whispered. "It will be locked, nailed. You
have the hatchet. Break it."

"But——" he began.

"Break it!" she hissed. "It belonged to Ellen. I am her sister, her only living heir. Break it. Hurry." He pushed against

the door. It did not move. She panted beside him. "Hurry," she said. "Break it."

"Listen, Miss Rosa," he said. "Listen."

"Give me the hatchet."

"Wait," he said. "Do you really want to go inside?"

"I'm going inside," she whimpered. "Give me the hatchet."

"Wait," he said. He moved along the gallery, guiding himself by the wall, moving carefully since he did not know just where the floor planks might be rotten or even missing, until he came to a window. The shutters were closed and apparently locked, yet they gave almost at once to the blade of the hatchet, making not very much sound—a flimsy and sloven barricading done either by an old feeble person—woman— or by a shiftless man; he had already inserted the hatchet blade beneath the sash before he discovered that there was no glass in it, that all he had to do now was to step through the vacant frame. Then he stood there for a moment, telling himself to go on in, telling himself that he was not afraid, he just didn't want to know what might be inside. "Well?" Miss Coldfield whispered from the door. "Have you opened it?"

"Yes," he said. He did not whisper, though he did not speak overloud; the dark room which he faced repeated his voice with hollow profundity, as an unfurnished room will. "You wait there. I'll see if I can open the door."—'So now I shall have to go in,' he thought, climbing over the sill. He knew that the room was empty; the echo of his voice had told him that, yet he moved as slowly and carefully here as he had along the gallery, feeling along the wall with his hand, following the wall when it turned, and found the door and passed through it. He would be in the hall now; he almost believed that he could hear Miss Coldfield breathing just beyond the wall beside him. It was pitch dark; he could not see, he knew that he could not see, yet he found that his eyelids and muscles were aching with strain while merging and dissolving red spots wheeled and vanished across the retinae. He went on; he felt the door under his hand at last and now he could hear Miss Coldfield's whimpering breathing beyond it as he fumbled for the lock. Then behind him the sound of the scraped match was like an explosion, a pistol; even before the puny following light appeared all his organs lifted sickeningly; he

could not even move for a moment even though something of
sanity roared silently inside his skull: 'It's all right! If it were
danger, he would not have struck the match!' Then he could
move, and turned to see the tiny gnomelike creature in headrag and voluminous skirts, the worn coffee-colored face staring at him, the match held in one coffee-colored and doll-like
hand above her head. Then he was not watching her but
watching the match as it burned down toward her fingers; he
watched quietly as she moved at last and lit a second match
from the first and turned; he saw then the square-ended saw
chunk beside the wall and the lamp sitting upon it as she
lifted the chimney and held the match to the wick. He remembered it, lying here in the Massachusetts bed and breathing fast now, now that peace and quiet had fled again. He
remembered how she did not say one word to him, not Who
are you? or What do you want here? but merely came with a
bunch of enormous old fashioned iron keys, as if she had
known all the time that this hour must come and that it could
not be resisted, and opened the door and stepped back a little
as Miss Coldfield entered. And how she (Clytie) and Miss
Coldfield said no word to one another, as if Clytie had looked
once at the other woman and knew that that would do no
good; that it was to him, Quentin, that she turned, putting
her hand on his arm and saying, "Dont let her go up there,
young marster." And how maybe she looked at him and knew
that would do no good either, because she turned and overtook Miss Coldfield and caught her arm and said, "Dont you
go up there, Rosie" and Miss Coldfield struck the hand away
and went on toward the stairs (and now he saw that she had a
flashlight; he remembered how he thought, 'It must have
been in the umbrella too along with the axe') and Clytie said,
"Rosie" and ran after the other again, whereupon Miss Coldfield turned on the step and struck Clytie to the floor with a
full-armed blow like a man would have, and turned and went
on up the stairs. She (Clytie) lay on the bare floor of the
scaling and empty hall like a small shapeless bundle of quiet
clean rags. When he reached her he saw that she was quite
conscious, her eyes wide open and calm; he stood above her,
thinking, 'Yes. She is the one who owns the terror'. When he
raised her it was like picking up a handful of sticks concealed

in a rag bundle, so light she was. She could not stand; he had
to hold her up, aware of some feeble movement or intention
in her limbs until he realised that she was trying to sit on the
bottom step. He lowered her to it. "Who are you?" she said.

"I'm Quentin Compson," he answered.

"Yes. I remember your grandpaw. You go up there and
make her come down. Make her go away from here. Whatever he done, me and Judith and him have paid it out. You go
and get her. Take her away from here." So he mounted the
stairs, the worn bare treads, the cracked and scaling wall on
one side, the balustrade with its intermittent missing spindles
on the other. He remembered how he looked back and she
was still sitting as he had left her, and that now (and he had
not heard him enter) there stood in the hall below a hulking
young light-colored negro man in clean faded overalls and
shirt, his arms dangling, no surprise, no nothing in the
saddle-colored and slack-mouthed idiot face. He remembered
how he thought, 'The scion, the heir, the apparent (though
not obvious)' and how he heard Miss Coldfield's feet and saw
the light of the torch approaching along the upper hall and
how she came and passed him, how she stumbled a little and
caught herself and looked full at him as if she had never seen
him before—the eyes wide and unseeing like a sleepwalker's,
the face which had always been tallow-hued now possessing
some still profounder, some almost unbearable, quality of
bloodlessness—and he thought, 'What? What is it now? It's
not shock. And it never has been fear. Can it be triumph?' and
how she passed him and went on. He heard Clytie say to the
man, "Take her to the gate, the buggy" and he stood there
thinking, 'I should go with her' and then, 'But I must see too
now. I will have to. Maybe I shall be sorry tomorrow, but I
must see'. So when he came back down the stairs (and he
remembered how he thought, 'Maybe my face looks like hers
did, but it's not triumph') there was only Clytie in the hall,
sitting still on the bottom step, sitting still in the attitude in
which he had left her. She did not even look at him when he
passed her. Nor did he overtake Miss Coldfield and the negro.
It was too dark to go fast, though he could presently hear
them ahead of him. She was not using the flashlight now; he
remembered how he thought, 'Surely she cant be afraid to

show a light now'. But she was not using it and he wondered
if she were holding to the negro's arm now; he wondered that
until he heard the negro's voice, flat, without emphasis or
interest: "Wawkin better over here" and no answer from her,
though he was close enough now to hear (or believe he did)
her whimpering panting breath. Then he heard the other
sound and he knew that she had stumbled and fallen; he
could almost see the hulking slack-faced negro stopped in his
tracks, looking toward the sound of the fall, waiting, without
interest or curiosity, as he (Quentin) hurried forward, hurried
toward the voices:

"You, nigger! What's your name?"

"Calls me Jim Bond."

"Help me up! You aint any Sutpen! You dont have to leave
me lying in the dirt!"

When he stopped the buggy at her gate she did not offer to
get out alone this time. She sat there until he got down and
came around to her side; she still sat there, clutching the umbrella in one hand and the hatchet in the other, until he spoke
her name. Then she stirred; he helped, lifted her down; she
was almost as light as Clytie had been; when she moved it
was like a mechanical doll, so that he supported and led her
through the gate and up the short walk and into the doll-
sized house and turned on the light for her and looked at the
fixed sleep-walking face, the wide dark eyes as she stood there,
still clutching the umbrella and the hatchet, the shawl and the
black dress both stained with dirt where she had fallen, the
black bonnet jerked forward and awry by the shock of the fall.
"Are you all right now?" he said.

"Yes," she said. "Yes. I'm all right. Goodnight."—'Not
thank you,' he thought: 'Just goodnight', outside the house
now, breathing deep and fast now as he returned to the
buggy, finding that he was about to begin to run, thinking
quietly, 'Jesus. Jesus. Jesus', breathing fast and hard of the dark
dead furnace-breath of air, of night where the fierce aloof
stars hung. His own home was dark; he was still using the
whip when he turned into the lane and then into the stable
lot. He sprang out and took the mare from the buggy, stripping the harness from her and tumbling it into the harness
room without stopping to hang it up, sweating, breathing

fast and hard; when he turned at last toward the house he did
begin to run. He could not help it. He was twenty years old;
he was not afraid, because what he had seen out there could
not harm him, yet he ran; even inside the dark familiar house,
his shoes in his hand, he still ran, up the stairs and into his
room and began to undress, fast, sweating, breathing fast. 'I
ought to bathe,' he thought: then he was lying on the bed,
naked, swabbing his body steadily with the discarded shirt,
sweating still, panting: so that when, his eye-muscles aching
and straining into the darkness and the almost dried shirt still
clutched in his hand, he said 'I have been asleep' it was all the
same, there was no difference: waking or sleeping he walked
down that upper hall between the scaling walls and beneath
the cracked ceiling, toward the faint light which fell outward
from the last door and paused there, saying 'No. No' and
then 'Only I must. I have to' and went in, entered the bare
stale room whose shutters were closed too, where a second
lamp burned dimly on a crude table; waking or sleeping it
was the same: the bed, the yellow sheets and pillow, the
wasted yellow face with closed, almost transparent eyelids on
the pillow, the wasted hands crossed on the breast as if he
were already a corpse; waking or sleeping it was the same and
would be the same forever as long as he lived:

    And you are ——?
    Henry Sutpen.
    And you have been here ——?
    Four years.
    And you came home ——?
    To die. Yes.
    To die?
    Yes. To die.
    And you have been here ——?
    Four years.
    And you are ——?
    Henry Sutpen.

It was quite cold in the room now; the chimes would ring
for one any time now; the chill had a compounded, a gathered quality, as though preparing for the dead moment before
dawn. "And she waited three months before she went back to
get him," Shreve said. "Why did she do that?" Quentin didn't

answer. He lay still and rigid on his back with the cold New England night on his face and the blood running warm in his rigid body and limbs, breathing hard but slow, his eyes wide open upon the window, thinking 'Nevermore of peace. Nevermore of peace. Nevermore. Nevermore. Nevermore'. "Do you suppose it was because she knew what was going to happen when she told it, took any steps, that it would be over then, finished, and that hating is like drink or drugs and she had used it so long that she did not dare risk cutting off the supply, destroying the source, the very poppy's root and seed?" Still Quentin didn't answer. "But at last she did reconcile herself to it, for his sake, to save him, to bring him into town where the doctors could save him, and so she told it then, got the ambulance and the men and went out there. And old Clytie maybe watching for just that out of the upstairs window for three months now: and maybe even your old man was right this time and when she saw the ambulance turn into the gate she believed it was that same black wagon for which she probably had had that nigger boy watching for three months now, coming to carry Henry into town for the white folks to hang him for shooting Charles Bon. And I guess it had been him who had kept that closet under the stairs full of tinder and trash all that time too, like she told him to, maybe he not getting it then either but keeping it full just like she told him, the kerosene and all, for three months now, until the hour when he could begin to howl—" Now the chimes began, ringing for one oclock. Shreve ceased, as if he were waiting for them to cease or perhaps were even listening to them. Quentin lay still too, as if he were listening too, though he was not; he just heard them without listening as he heard Shreve without listening or answering, until they ceased, died away into the icy air delicate and faint and musical as struck glass. And he, Quentin, could see that too, though he had not been there—the ambulance with Miss Coldfield between the driver and the second man, perhaps a deputy sheriff, in the shawl surely and perhaps even with the umbrella too, though probably no hatchet nor flashlight in it now, entering the gate and picking its way gingerly up the rutted and frozen (and now partially thawed) drive; and it may have been the howling or it may have been the deputy or

the driver or it may have been she who cried first: "It's
on fire!" though she would not have cried that; she would
have said, "Faster. Faster." leaning forward on this seat too
—the small furious grim implacable woman not much
larger than a child. But the ambulance could not go fast in
that drive; doubtless Clytie knew, counted upon, that; it
would be a good three minutes before it could reach the
house, the monstrous tinder-dry rotten shell seeping smoke
through the warped cracks in the weather-boarding as if it
were made of gauze wire and filled with roaring and beyond
which somewhere something lurked which bellowed, something human since the bellowing was in human speech, even
though the reason for it would not have seemed to be. And
the deputy and the driver would spring out and Miss Coldfield would stumble out and follow them, running too, onto
the gallery too, where the creature which bellowed followed
them, wraith-like and insubstantial, looking at them out of
the smoke, whereupon the deputy even turned and ran at
him, whereupon he retreated, fled, though the howling did
not diminish nor even seem to get any further away. They ran
onto the gallery too, into the seeping smoke, Miss Coldfield
screaming harshly, "The window! The window!" to the
second man at the door. But the door was not locked; it
swung inward; the blast of heat struck them. The entire stair-
case was on fire. Yet they had to hold her; Quentin could
see it: the light thin furious creature making no sound at all
now, struggling with silent and bitter fury, clawing and
scratching and biting at the two men who held her, who
dragged her back and down the steps as the draft created by
the open door seemed to explode like powder among the
flames as the whole lower hall vanished. He, Quentin, could
see it, could see the deputy holding her while the driver
backed the ambulance to safety and returned, the three faces
all a little wild now since they must have believed her;—the
three of them staring, glaring at the doomed house: and then
for a moment maybe Clytie appeared in that window from
which she must have been watching the gates constantly day
and night for three months—the tragic gnome's face beneath
the clean headrag, against a red background of fire, seen for
a moment between two swirls of smoke, looking down at

them, perhaps not even now with triumph and no more of despair than it had ever worn, possibly even serene above the melting clapboards before the smoke swirled across it again. —and he, Jim Bond, the scion, the last of his race, seeing it too now and howling with human reason now since now even he could have known what he was howling about. But they couldn't catch him. They could hear him; he didn't seem to ever get any further away but they couldn't get any nearer and maybe in time they could not even locate the direction of the howling anymore. They—the driver and the deputy—held Miss Coldfield as she struggled: he (Quentin) could see her, them; he had not been there but he could see her, struggling and fighting like a doll in a nightmare, making no sound, foaming a little at the mouth, her face even in the sunlight lit by one last wild crimson reflection as the house collapsed and roared away, and there was only the sound of the idiot negro left.

"And so it was the Aunt Rosa that came back to town inside the ambulance," Shreve said. Quentin did not answer; he did not even say, *Miss Rosa*. He just lay there staring at the window without even blinking, breathing the chill heady pure snowgleamed darkness. "And she went to bed because it was all finished now, there was nothing left now, nothing out there now but that idiot boy to lurk around those ashes and those four gutted chimneys and howl until someone came and drove him away. They couldn't catch him and nobody ever seemed to make him go very far away, he just stopped howling for a little while. Then after a while they would begin to hear him again. And so she died." Quentin did not answer, staring at the window; then he could not tell if it was the actual window or the window's pale rectangle upon his eyelids, though after a moment it began to emerge. It began to take shape in its same curious, light, gravity-defying attitude—the once-folded sheet out of the wistaria Mississippi summer, the cigar smell, the random blowing of the fireflies. "The South," Shreve said. "The South. Jesus. No wonder you folks all outlive yourselves by years and years and years." It was becoming quite distinct; he would be able to decipher the words soon, in a moment; even almost now, now, now.

"I am older at twenty than a lot of people who have died," Quentin said.

"And more people have died than have been twenty-one," Shreve said. Now he (Quentin) could read it, could finish it—the sloped whimsical ironic hand out of Mississippi attenuated, into the iron snow:

—or perhaps there is. Surely it can harm no one to believe that perhaps she has escaped not at all the privilege of being outraged and amazed and of not forgiving but on the contrary has herself gained that place or bourne where the objects of the outrage and of the commiseration also are no longer ghosts but are actual people to be actual recipients of the hatred and the pity. It will do no harm to hope—You see I have written hope, not think. So let it be hope.—that the one cannot escape the censure which no doubt he deserves, that the other no longer lack the commiseration which let us hope (while we are hoping) that they have longed for, if only for the reason that they are about to receive it whether they will or no. The weather was beautiful though cold and they had to use picks to break the earth for the grave yet in one of the deeper clods I saw a redworm doubtless alive when the clod was thrown up though by afternoon it was frozen again.

"So it took Charles Bon and his mother to get rid of old Tom, and Charles Bon and the octoroon to get rid of Judith, and Charles Bon and Clytie to get rid of Henry; and Charles Bon's mother and Charles Bon's grandmother got rid of Charles Bon. So it takes two niggers to get rid of one Sutpen, dont it?" Quentin did not answer; evidently Shreve did not want an answer now; he continued almost without a pause: "Which is all right, it's fine; it clears the whole ledger, you can tear all the pages out and burn them, except for one thing. And do you know what that is?" Perhaps he hoped for an answer this time, or perhaps he merely paused for emphasis, since he got no answer. "You've got one nigger left. One nigger Sutpen left. Of course you cant catch him and you dont even always see him and you never will be able to use him. But you've got him there still. You still hear him at night sometimes. Dont you?"

"Yes," Quentin said.

"And so do you know what I think?" Now he did expect an answer, and now he got one:

"No," Quentin said.

"Do you want to know what I think?"

"No," Quentin said.

"Then I'll tell you. I think that in time the Jim Bonds are going to conquer the western hemisphere. Of course it wont quite be in our time and of course as they spread toward the poles they will bleach out again like the rabbits and the birds do, so they wont show up so sharp against the snow. But it will still be Jim Bond; and so in a few thousand years, I who regard you will also have sprung from the loins of African kings. Now I want you to tell me just one thing more. Why do you hate the South?"

"I dont hate it," Quentin said, quickly, at once, immediately; "I dont hate it," he said. *I dont hate it* he thought, panting in the cold air, the iron New England dark: *I dont. I dont! I dont hate it! I dont hate it!*

Chronology

1807   Thomas Sutpen born in West Virginia mountains. Poor whites of Scottish-English stock. Large family.

1817   Sutpen family moved down into Tidewater Virginia, Sutpen ten years old. Ellen Coldfield born in Tennessee.

1820   Sutpen ran away from home. Fourteen years old.

1827   Sutpen married first wife in Haiti.

1828   Goodhue Coldfield moved to Yoknapatawpha County (Jefferson) Mississippi: mother, sister, wife and daughter Ellen.

1831   Charles Bon born, Haiti. Sutpen learns his wife has negro blood, repudiates her and child.

1833   Sutpen appears in Yoknapatawpha County, Mississippi, takes up land, builds his house.

1834   Clytemnestra (Clytie) born to slave woman.

1838   Sutpen married Ellen Coldfield.

1839   Henry Sutpen born, Sutpen's Hundred.

1841   Judith Sutpen born.

1845   Rosa Coldfield born.

1850   Wash Jones moves into abandoned fishing camp on Sutpen's plantation, with his daughter.

1853   Milly Jones born to Wash Jones' daughter.

1859   Henry Sutpen and Charles Bon meet at University of Mississippi. Judith and Charles meet that Xmas. Charles Etienne St. Valery Bon born, New Orleans.

1860   Xmas, Sutpen forbids marriage between Judith and Bon. Henry repudiates his birthright, departs with Bon.

1861   Sutpen, Henry, and Bon depart for war.

1863   Ellen Coldfield dies.

1864   Goodhue Coldfield dies.

1865   Henry kills Bon at gates. Rosa Coldfield moves out to Sutpen's Hundred.

1866 Sutpen becomes engaged to Rosa Coldfield, insults her. She returns to Jefferson.

1867 Sutpen takes up with Milly Jones.

1869 Milly's child is born. Wash Jones kills Sutpen.

1870 Charles E. St. V. Bon appears at Sutpen's Hundred.

1871 Clytie fetches Charles E. St. V. Bon to Sutpen's Hundred to live.

1881 Charles E. St. V. Bon returns with negro wife.

1882 Jim Bond born.

1884 Judith and Charles E. St. V. Bon die of yellow fever.

1909

September Rosa Coldfield and Quentin find Henry Sutpen hidden in the house.

December Rosa Coldfield goes out to fetch Henry to town, Clytie sets fire to the house.

Genealogy

THOMAS SUTPEN. Born in West Virginia mountains, 1807. One of several children of poor whites, Scotch-English stock. Established plantation of Sutpen's Hundred in Yoknapatawpha County, Mississippi, 1833. Married (1) Eulalia Bon, Haiti, 1827. (2) Ellen Coldfield, Jefferson, Mississippi, 1838. Major, later Colonel, —th Mississippi Infantry, C.S.A. Died, Sutpen's Hundred, 1869.

EULALIA BON. Born in Haiti. Only child of Haitian sugar planter of French descent. Married Thomas Sutpen, 1827, divorced from him, 1831. Died in New Orleans, date unknown.

CHARLES BON. Son of Thomas and Eulalia Bon Sutpen. Only child. Attended University of Mississippi, where he met Henry Sutpen and became engaged to Judith. Private, later lieutenant, —th Company, (University Grays) —th Mississippi Infantry, C.S.A. Died, Sutpen's Hundred, 1865.

GOODHUE COLDFIELD. Born in Tennessee. Moved to Jefferson, Miss., 1828, established small mercantile business. Died, Jefferson, 1864.

ELLEN COLDFIELD. Daughter of Goodhue Coldfield. Born in Tennessee, 1817. Married Thomas Sutpen, Jefferson, Miss., 1838. Died, Sutpen's Hundred, 1863.

ROSA COLDFIELD. Daughter of Goodhue Coldfield. Born, Jefferson, 1845. Died, Jefferson, 1910.

HENRY SUTPEN. Born, Sutpen's Hundred, 1839, son of Thomas and Ellen Coldfield Sutpen. Attended University of Mississippi. Private, —th Company, (University Grays) —th Mississippi Infantry, C.S.A. Died, Sutpen's Hundred, 1909.

JUDITH SUTPEN. Daughter of Thomas and Ellen Coldfield Sutpen. Born, Sutpen's Hundred, 1841. Became engaged to Charles Bon, 1860. Died, Sutpen's Hundred, 1884.

CLYTEMNESTRA SUTPEN. Daughter of Thomas Sutpen and a negro slave. Born, Sutpen's Hundred, 1834. Died, Sutpen's Hundred, 1909.

WASH JONES. Date and location of birth unknown. Squatter, residing in an abandoned fishing camp belonging to Thomas Sutpen, hanger-on of Sutpen, handy man about Sutpen's place while Sutpen was away between '61–'65. Died, Sutpen's Hundred, 1869.

MELICENT JONES. Daughter of Wash Jones. Date of birth unknown. Rumored to have died in a Memphis brothel.

MILLY JONES. Daughter of Melicent Jones. Born 1853. Died, Sutpen's Hundred, 1869.

UNNAMED INFANT. Daughter of Thomas Sutpen and Milly Jones. Born, died, Sutpen's Hundred, same day, 1869.

CHARLES ETIENNE DE SAINT VALERY BON. Only child of Charles Bon and an octoroon mistress whose name is not recorded. Born, New Orleans, 1859. Married a full-blood negress, name unknown, 1879. Died, Sutpen's Hundred, 1884.

JIM BOND (BON). Son of Charles Etienne de Saint Valery Bon. Born, Sutpen's Hundred, 1882. Disappeared from Sutpen's Hundred, 1910. Whereabouts unknown.

QUENTIN COMPSON. Grandson of Thomas Sutpen's first Yoknapatawpha County friend. Born, Jefferson, 1891. Attended Harvard, 1909–1910. Died, Cambridge, Mass., 1910.

SHREVLIN MCCANNON. Born, Edmonton, Alberta, Canada, 1890. Attended Harvard, 1909–1914. Captain, Royal Army Medical Corps, Canadian Expeditionary Forces, France, 1914–1918. Now a practising surgeon, Edmonton, Alta.

THE UNVANQUISHED

Drawings by

EDWARD SHENTON

Contents

AMBUSCADE

I.

BEHIND THE SMOKEHOUSE that summer, Ringo and I had a living map. Although Vicksburg was just a handful of chips from the woodpile and the River a trench scraped into the packed earth with the point of a hoe, it (river, city, and terrain) lived, possessing even in miniature that ponderable though passive recalcitrance of topography which outweighs artillery, against which the most brilliant of victories and the most tragic of defeats are but the loud noises of a moment. To Ringo and me it lived, if only because of the fact that the sunimpacted ground drank water faster than we could fetch it from the well, the very setting of the stage for conflict a prolonged and wellnigh hopeless ordeal in which we ran, panting and interminable, with the leaking bucket between wellhouse and battlefield, the two of us needing first to join forces and spend ourselves against a common enemy, time, before we could engender between us and hold intact the pattern of recapitulant mimic furious victory like a cloth, a shield between ourselves and reality, between us and fact and doom. This afternoon it seemed as if we would never get it filled, wet enough, since there had not even been dew in three weeks. But at last it was damp enough, damp-colored enough at least, and we could begin. We were just about to begin. Then suddenly Loosh was standing there, watching us. He was Joby's son and Ringo's uncle; he stood there (we did not know where he had come from; we had not seen him appear, emerge) in the fierce dull early afternoon sunlight, bareheaded, his head slanted a little, tilted a little yet firm and not askew, like a cannonball (which it resembled) bedded hurriedly and carelessly in concrete, his eyes a little red at the inner corners as negroes' eyes get when they have been drinking, looking down at what Ringo and I called Vicksburg. Then I saw Philadelphy, his wife, over at the woodpile, stooped, with an armful of wood already gathered into the crook of her elbow, watching Loosh's back.

"What's that?" Loosh said.

"Vicksburg," I said.

Loosh laughed. He stood there laughing, not loud, looking at the chips.

"Come on here, Loosh," Philadelphy said from the woodpile. There was something curious in her voice too—urgent, perhaps frightened. "If you wants any supper, you better tote me some wood." But I didn't know which, urgency or fright; I didn't have time to wonder or speculate, because suddenly Loosh stooped before Ringo or I could have moved, and with his hand he swept the chips flat.

"There's your Vicksburg," he said.

"Loosh!" Philadelphy said. But Loosh squatted, looking at me with that expression on his face. I was just twelve then; I didn't know triumph; I didn't even know the word.

"And I tell you nother un you aint know," he said. "Corinth."

"Corinth?" I said. Philadelphy had dropped the wood and she was coming fast toward us. "That's in Mississippi too. That's not far. I've been there."

"Far dont matter," Loosh said. Now he sounded as if he were about to chant, to sing; squatting there with the fierce dull sun on his iron skull and the flattening slant of his nose, he was not looking at me or Ringo either; it was as if his redcornered eyes had reversed in his skull and it was the blank flat obverses of the balls which we saw. "Far dont matter. Case hit's on the way!"

"On the way? On the way to what?"

"Ask your paw. Ask Marse John."

"He's at Tennessee, fighting. I cant ask him."

"You think he at Tennessee? Aint no need for him at Tennessee now." Then Philadelphy grabbed him by the arm.

"Hush your mouth, nigger!" she cried, in that tense desperate voice. "Come on here and get me some wood!"

Then they were gone. Ringo and I didn't watch them go. We stood there above our ruined Vicksburg, our tedious hoe-scratch not even damp-colored now, looking at one another quietly. "What?" Ringo said. "What he mean?"

"Nothing," I said. I stooped and set Vicksburg up again. "There it is."

But Ringo didn't move, he just looked at me. "Loosh laughed. He say Corinth too. He laughed at Corinth too. What you reckon he know that we aint?"

"Nothing!" I said. "Do you reckon Loosh knows anything that Father dont know?"

"Marse John at Tennessee. Maybe he aint know either."

"Do you reckon he'd be away off at Tennessee if there were Yankees at Corinth? Do you reckon that if there were Yankees at Corinth, Father and General Van Dorn and General Pemberton all three wouldn't be there too?" But I was just talking too, I knew that, because niggers know, they know things; it would have to be something louder, much louder, than words to do any good. So I stooped and caught both hands full of dust and rose: and Ringo still standing there, not moving, just looking at me even as I flung the dust. "I'm General Pemberton!" I cried. "Yaaay! Yaay!" stooping and catching up more dust and flinging that too. Still Ringo didn't move. "All right!" I cried. "I'll be Grant this time, then. You can be General Pemberton." Because it was that urgent, since negroes knew. The arrangement was that I would be General Pemberton twice in succession and Ringo would be Grant, then I would have to be Grant once so Ringo could be General Pemberton or he wouldn't play anymore. But now it was that urgent even though Ringo was a nigger too, because Ringo and I had been born in the same month and had both fed at the same breast and had slept together and eaten together for so long that Ringo called Granny 'Granny' just like I did, until maybe he wasn't a nigger anymore or maybe I wasn't a white boy anymore, the two of us neither, not even people any longer: the two supreme undefeated like two moths, two feathers riding above a hurricane. So we were both at it; we didn't see Louvinia, Joby's wife and Ringo's grandmother, at all. We were facing one another at scarcely arms' length, to the other each invisible in the furious slow jerking of the flung dust, yelling "Kill the bastuds! Kill them! Kill them!" when her voice seemed to descend upon us like an enormous hand, flattening the very dust which we had raised, leaving us now visible to one another, dust-colored ourselves to the eyes and still in the act of throwing:

"You, Bayard! You, Ringo!" She stood about ten feet away, her mouth still open with shouting. I noticed that she did not now have on the old hat of Father's which she wore on top of her head rag even when she just stepped out of the kitchen for wood. "What was that word?" she said. "What did I hear you say?" Only she didn't wait to be answered, and then I saw that she had been running too. "Look who coming up the big road!" she said.

We—Ringo and I—ran as one, in midstride out of frozen immobility, across the back yard and around the house, where Granny was standing at the top of the front steps and where Loosh had just come around the house from the other side and stopped, looking down the drive toward the gate. In the spring, when Father came home that time, Ringo and I ran down the drive to meet him and return, I standing in one stirrup with Father's arm around me, and Ringo holding to the other stirrup and running beside the horse. But this time we didn't. I mounted the steps and stood beside Granny, and with Ringo and Loosh on the ground below the gallery we watched the claybank stallion enter the gate which was never closed now, and come up the drive. We watched them—the big gaunt horse almost the color of smoke, lighter in color than the dust which had gathered and caked on his wet hide where they had crossed at the ford three miles away, coming up the drive at a steady gait which was not a walk and not a run, as if he had held it all the way from Tennessee because there was a need to encompass earth which abrogated sleep or rest and relegated to some insulated bourne of perennial and pointless holiday so trivial a thing as galloping; and Father damp too from the ford, his boots dark and dustcaked too, the skirts of his weathered gray coat shades darker than the breast and back and sleeves where the tarnished buttons and the frayed braid of his field officer's rank glinted dully, the sabre hanging loose yet rigid at his side as if it were too heavy to jounce or perhaps were attached to the living thigh itself and took no more motion from the horse than he did. He stopped; he looked at Granny and me on the porch and at Ringo and Loosh on the ground.

"Well, Miss Rosa," he said. "Well, boys."

"Well, John," Granny said. Loosh came and took Jupiter's head; Father dismounted stiffly, the sabre clashing dully and heavily against his wet boot and leg.

"Curry him," Father said. "Give him a good feed, but dont turn him into the pasture. Let him stay in the lot. . . . Go with Loosh," he said, as if Jupiter were a child, slapping him on the flank as Loosh led him on. Then we could see him good. I mean, Father. He was not big; it was just the things he did, that we knew he was doing, had been doing in Virginia and Tennessee, that made him seem big to us. There were others besides him that were doing the things, the same things, but maybe it was because he was the only one we knew, had ever heard snoring at night in a quiet house, had watched eating, had heard when he talked, knew how he liked to sleep and what he liked to eat and how he liked to talk. He was not big, yet somehow he looked even smaller on the horse than off of him, because Jupiter was big and when you thought of Father you thought of him as being big too and so when you thought of Father being on Jupiter it was as if you said, 'Together they will be too big; you wont believe it.' So you didn't believe it and so it wasn't. He came toward the steps and began to mount, the sabre heavy and flat at his side. Then I began to smell it again, like each time he returned, like the day back in the spring when I rode up the drive standing in one of his stirrups — that odor in his clothes and beard and flesh too which I believed was the smell of powder and glory, the elected victorious but know better now: know now to have been only the will to endure, a sardonic and even humorous declining of self-delusion which is not even kin to that optimism which believes that that which is about to happen to us can possibly be the worst which we can suffer. He mounted four of the steps, the sabre (that's how tall he actually was) striking against each one of the steps as he mounted, then he stopped and removed his hat. And that's what I mean: about his doing bigger things than he was. He could have stood on the same level with Granny and he would have only needed to bend his head a little for her to kiss him. But he didn't. He stopped two steps below her, with his head bared and his forehead held for her to touch her lips to, and the fact that Granny had to stoop a little now took nothing from the illusion of height and size which he wore for us at least.

"I've been expecting you," Granny said.

"Ah," Father said. Then he looked at me, who was still looking at him, as Ringo at the foot of the steps beneath still was.

"You rode hard from Tennessee," I said.

"Ah," Father said again.

"Tennessee sho gaunted you," Ringo said. "What does they eat up there, Marse John? Does they eat the same things that folks eat?"

Then I said it, looking him in the face while he looked at me: "Loosh says you haven't been at Tennessee."

"Loosh?" Father said. "Loosh?"

"Come in," Granny said. "Louvinia is putting your dinner on the table. You will just have time to wash."

2.

That afternoon we built the stock pen. We built it deep in the creek bottom, where you could not have found it unless you had known where to look, and you could not have seen it until you came to the new sap-sweating, axe-ended rails woven through and into the jungle growth itself. We were all there—Father and Joby and Ringo and Loosh and me— Father in the boots still but with his coat off now, so that we saw for the first time that his trousers were not Confederate ones but were Yankee ones, of new strong blue cloth, which they (he and his troop) had captured, and without the sabre now too. We worked fast, felling the saplings—the willow and pin oak, the swamp maple and chinkapin—and, without even waiting hardly to trim them, dragging them behind the mules and by hand too, through the mud and the briers to where Father waited. And that was it too; Father was everywhere, with a sapling under each arm going through the brush and briers almost faster than the mules; racking the rails into place while Joby and Loosh were still arguing about which end of the rail went where. That was it: not that Father worked faster and harder than anyone else, even though you do look bigger (to twelve, at least, to me and Ringo at twelve, at least) standing still and saying, 'Do this or that' to the ones who are doing; it was the way he did it. When he sat at his old place at the table in the dining room and finished the side meat and greens and the cornbread and milk which Louvinia brought him (and we watching and waiting, Ringo and I at least, waiting for night and the talking, the telling) and wiped his beard and said, "Now we're going to build a new pen. We'll have to cut the rails, too"; when he said that, Ringo and I probably had exactly the same vision. There would be all of us there—Joby and Loosh and Ringo and me on the edge of the bottom and drawn up into a kind of order—an order partaking not of any lusting and sweating for assault or even victory, but rather of that passive yet dynamic affirmation which Napoleon's troops must have felt—and facing us, between us and the bottom, between us and the waiting sap-running boles which were about to be transposed into dead rails, Father. He was on Jupiter now; he wore the frogged gray field-officer's tunic; and while we watched he drew the sabre. Giving us a last embracing and comprehensive glance he drew it, already pivoting Jupiter on the tight snaffle; his hair tossed beneath the cocked hat, the sabre flashed and glinted; he cried, not loud yet stentorian: "Trot! Canter! *Charge!*" Then, without even having to move, we could both watch and follow him—the little man (who in conjunction with the horse looked exactly the right size because that was as big as he needed to look and—to twelve years old—bigger than most folks could hope to look) standing in the stirrups above the smoke-colored diminishing thunderbolt, beneath the arcy and myriad glitter of the sabre from which the chosen saplings, sheared trimmed and lopped, sprang into neat and waiting windrows, requiring only the carrying and the placing to become a fence.

The sun had gone out of the bottom when we finished the fence, that is, left Joby and Loosh with the last three panels to put up, but it was still shining up the slope of the pasture when we rode across it, I behind Father on one of the mules and Ringo on the other one. But it was gone even from the pasture by the time I had left Father at the house and returned to the stable, where Ringo already had a lead rope on the cow. So we went back to the new pen, with the calf following nuzzling and prodding at the cow every time she stopped to snatch a mouthful of grass, and the sow trotting on ahead. She (the sow) was the one who moved slow. She seemed to be moving slower than the cow even while the cow was stopped with Ringo leaned to the taut jerk of the rope and hollering at the cow, so it was dark sure enough when we reached the new pen. But there was still plenty of gap left to drive the stock through. But then, we never had worried about that.

We drove them in—the two mules, the cow and calf, the sow; we put up the last panel by feel, and went back to the house. It was full dark now, even in the pasture; we could see the lamp in the kitchen and the shadow of someone moving across the window. When Ringo and I came in, Louvinia was just closing one of the big trunks from the attic, which hadn't been down stairs since the Christmas four years ago which we spent at Hawkhurst, when there wasn't any war and Uncle Dennison was still alive. It was a big trunk and heavy even when empty; it had not been in the kitchen when we left to build the pen so it had been fetched down some time during the afternoon, while Joby and Loosh were in the bottom and nobody there to carry it down but Granny and Louvinia, and then Father later, after we came back to the house on the mule, so that was a part of the need and urgency too; maybe it was Father who carried the trunk down from the attic too. And when I went in to supper, the table was set with the kitchen knives and forks in place of the silver ones, and the sideboard (on which the silver service had been sitting when I began to remember and where it had been sitting ever since except on each Tuesday afternoon, when Granny and Louvinia and Philadelphy would polish it, why, nobody except Granny maybe knew, since it was never used) was bare.

It didn't take us long to eat. Father had already eaten once early in the afternoon, and besides that was what Ringo and I were waiting for: for after supper, the hour of laxed muscles and full entrails, the talking. In the spring when he came home that time, we waited as we did now, until he was sitting in his old chair with the hickory logs popping and snapping on the hearth and Ringo and I squatting on either side of the hearth, beneath the mantel above which the captured musket which he had brought home from Virginia two years ago rested on two pegs, loaded and oiled for service. Then we listened. We heard: the names—Forrest and Morgan and Barksdale and Van Dorn; the words like Gap and Run which we didn't have in Mississippi even though we did own Barksdale, and Van Dorn until somebody's husband killed him, and one day General Forrest rode down South Street in Oxford where there watched him through a window pane a young girl who scratched her name on it with a diamond ring: Celia Cook.

But we were just twelve; we didn't listen to that. What Ringo and I heard was the cannon and the flags and the anonymous yelling. That's what we intended to hear tonight. Ringo was waiting for me in the hall; we waited until Father was settled in his chair in the room which he and the negroes called the Office—Father because his desk was here in which he kept the seed cotton and corn and in this room he would remove his muddy boots and sit in his stocking feet while the boots dried on the hearth and where the dogs could come and go with impunity, to lie on the rug before the fire or even to sleep there on the cold nights—these whether Mother, who died when I was born, gave him this dispensation before she died or whether Granny carried it on afterward or whether Granny gave him the dispensation herself because Mother died I dont know: and the negroes called the Office because into this room they would be fetched to face the Patroller (sitting in one of the straight hard chairs and smoking one of Father's cigars too but with his hat off) and swear that they could not possibly have been either who or where he (the Patroller) said they were—and which Granny called the library because there was one bookcase in it containing a Coke upon Littleton, a Josephus, a Koran, a volume of

Mississippi Reports dated 1848, a Jeremy Taylor, a Napoleon's Maxims, a thousand and ninety-eight page treatise on astrology, a History of Werewolf Men in England, Ireland and Scotland and Including Wales by the Reverend Ptolemy Thorndyke, M.A. (Edinburgh), F.R.S.S., a complete Walter Scott, a complete Fenimore Cooper, a paper-bound Dumas complete, too, save for the volume which Father lost from his pocket at Manassas (retreating, he said).

So Ringo and I squatted again and waited quietly while Granny sewed beside the lamp on the table and Father sat in his old chair in its old place, his muddy boots crossed and lifted into the old heel-marks beside the cold and empty fireplace, chewing the tobacco which Joby had loaned him. Joby was a good deal older than Father. He was too old to have been caught short of tobacco just by a war. He had come to Mississippi from Carolina with Father and he had been Father's body servant all the time that he was raising and training Simon, Ringo's father, to take over when he (Joby) got too old, which was to have been some years yet except for the War. So Simon went with Father; he was still in Tennessee with the army. We waited for Father to begin; we waited so long that we could tell from the sounds that Louvinia was almost through in the kitchen: so that I decided Father was waiting for Louvinia to finish and come in to hear too, so I said, "How can you fight in mountains, Father?"

And that's what he was waiting for, though not in the way Ringo and I thought, because he said, "You cant. You just have to. Now you boys run on to bed."

We went up the stairs. But not all the way; we stopped and sat on the top step, just out of the light from the hall lamp, watching the door to the Office, listening; after a while Louvinia crossed the hall without looking up and entered the Office; we could hear Father and her:

"Is the trunk ready?"

"Yes sir. Hit's ready."

"Then tell Loosh to get the lantern and the shovels and wait in the kitchen for me."

"Yes sir," Louvinia said. She came out; she crossed the hall again without even looking up the stairs, who used to follow us up and stand in the bedroom door and scold at us until we were in bed—I in the bed itself, Ringo on the pallet beside it. But this time she not only didn't wonder where we were, she didn't even think about where we might not be.

"I knows what's in that trunk," Ringo whispered. "Hit's the silver. What you reckon—"

"Shhhh," I said. We could hear Father's voice, talking to Granny. After a while Louvinia came back and crossed the hall again. We sat on the top step, listening to Father's voice telling Granny and Louvinia both.

"Vicksburg?" Ringo whispered. We were in the shadow; I couldn't see anything but his eyeballs. "Vicksburg *fell*? Do he mean hit fell off in the River? With Ginrul Pemberton in hit too?"

"Shhhhh!" I said. We sat close together in the shadow, listening to Father. Perhaps it was the dark or perhaps we were the two moths, the two feathers again or perhaps there is a point at which credulity firmly and calmly and irrevocably declines, because suddenly Louvinia was standing over us, shaking us awake. She didn't even scold us. She followed us up stairs and stood in the door to the bedroom and she didn't even light the lamp; she couldn't have told whether or not we had undressed even if she had been paying enough attention to suspect that we had not. She may have been listening as Ringo and I were, to what we thought we heard, though I knew better, just as I knew that we had slept on the stairs for some time; I was telling myself, 'They have already carried it out, they are in the orchard now, digging.' Because there is that point at which credulity declines; somewhere between waking and sleeping I believed I saw or I dreamed that I did see the lantern in the orchard, under the apple trees. But I dont know whether I saw it or not, because then it was morning and it was raining and Father was gone.

3.

He must have ridden off in the rain, which was still falling at breakfast and then at dinnertime too, so that it looked as if we wouldn't have to leave the house at all, until at last Granny put the sewing away and said, "Very well. Get the cook book, Marengo." Ringo got the cook book from the kitchen and he and I lay on our stomachs on the floor while Granny opened the book. "What shall we read about today?" she said.

"Read about cake," I said.

"Very well. What kind of cake?" Only she didn't need to say that because Ringo was already answering that before she spoke:

"Cokynut cake, Granny." He said coconut cake every time because we never had been able to decide whether Ringo had ever tasted coconut cake or not. We had had some that Christmas before it started and Ringo had tried to remember whether they had had any of it in the kitchen or not, but he couldn't remember. Now and then I used to try to help him decide, get him to tell me how it tasted and what it looked like and sometimes he would almost decide to risk it before he would change his mind. Because he said that he would rather just maybe have tasted coconut cake without remembering it than to know for certain he had not; that if he were to describe the wrong kind of cake, he would never taste coconut cake as long as he lived.

"I reckon a little more wont hurt us," Granny said.

The rain stopped in the middle of the afternoon; the sun was shining when I stepped out onto the back gallery, with Ringo already saying, "Where we going?" behind me and still saying it after we passed the smokehouse where I could see the stable and the cabins: "Where we going now?" Before we reached the stable Joby and Loosh came into sight beyond the pasture fence, bringing the mules up from the new pen. "What we ghy do now?" Ringo said.

"Watch him," I said.

"Watch him? Watch who?" I looked at Ringo. He was staring at me, his eyeballs white and quiet like last night. "You talking about Loosh. Who tole us to watch him?"

"Nobody. I just know."

"Bayard, did you dream hit?"

"Yes. Last night. It was Father and Louvinia. Father said to watch Loosh, because he knows."

"Knows?" Ringo said. "Knows what?" But he didn't need to ask that either; in the next breath he answered it himself, staring at me with his round quiet eyes, blinking a little: "Yes-tiddy. Vicksburg. When he knocked hit over. He knowed it then, already. Like when he said Marse John wasn't at no Tennessee and sho enough Marse John wasn't. Go on; what else did the dream tole you?"

"That's all. To watch him. That he would know before we did. Father said that Louvinia would have to watch him too, that even if he was her son, she would have to be white a little while longer. Because if we watched him, we could tell by what he did when it was getting ready to happen."

"When what was getting ready to happen?"

"I dont know." Ringo breathed deep, once.

"Then hit's so," he said. "If somebody tole you, hit could be a lie. But if you dremp hit, hit cant be a lie case aint nobody there to tole hit to you. So we got to watch him."

We followed them when they put the mules to the wagon and went down beyond the pasture to where they had been cutting wood. We watched them for two days, hidden. We realised then what a close watch Louvinia had kept on us all the time. Sometimes while we were hidden watching Loosh and Joby load the wagon we would hear her yelling at us and we would have to sneak away and then run to let Louvinia find us coming from the other direction. Sometimes she would even meet us before we had time to circle, and Ringo hiding behind me then while she scolded at us: "What devilment yawl into now? Yawl up to something. What is it?" But we didn't tell her and we would follow her back to the kitchen while she scolded at us over her shoulder and when she was inside the house we would move quietly until we were out of sight again and then run back to hide and watch Loosh.

So we were outside of his and Philadelphy's cabin that night when he came out. We followed him down to the new pen and heard him catch the mule and ride away. We ran, but when we reached the road too we could only hear the mule loping, dying away. But we had come a good piece, because even Louvinia calling us sounded faint and small. We looked up the road in the starlight, after the mule. "That's where Corinth is," I said.

He didn't get back until after dark the next day. We stayed close to the house and watched the road by turns, to get Louvinia calmed down in case it would be late before he got back.

It was late; she had followed us up to bed and we had slipped out again; we were just passing Joby's cabin when the door opened and Loosh kind of surged up out of the darkness right beside us. He was almost close enough for me to have touched him and he did not see us at all; all of a sudden he was just kind of hanging there against the lighted doorway like he had been cut out of tin in the act of running and was inside the cabin and the door shut black again almost before we knew what we had seen. And when we looked in the window he was standing in front of the fire, with his clothes torn and muddy where he had been hiding in swamps and bottoms from the Patrollers and with that look on his face again which resembled drunkenness but was not, as if he had not slept in a long time and did not want to sleep now, and Joby and Philadelphy leaning into the firelight and looking at him and Philadelphy's mouth open too and the same look on her face. Then I saw Louvinia standing in the door. We had not heard her behind us yet there she was, with one hand on the door jamb, looking at Loosh, and again she didn't have on Father's old hat.

"You mean they gwinter free us all?" Philadelphy said. "We gonter all be free?"

"Yes," Loosh said, loud, with his head flung back; he didn't even look at Joby when Joby said, "Hush up, Loosh!"— "Yes!" Loosh said. "Ginral Sherman gonter sweep the earth and the Race gonter all be free!"

Then Louvinia crossed the floor in two steps and hit Loosh across the head hard with her flat hand. "You black fool!" she said. "Do you think there's enough Yankees in the whole world to whip the white folks?"

We ran to the house, we didn't wait for Louvinia; again we didn't know that she was behind us. We ran into the room where Granny was sitting beside the lamp with the bible open on her lap and her neck arched to look at us across her spectacles. "They're coming here!" I said. "They're coming to set us free!"

"What?" she said.

"Loosh saw them! They're just down the road. It's General Sherman and he's going to make us all free!" And we watching her, waiting to see who she would send for to take down the musket: whether it would be Joby because he was the oldest, or Loosh because he had seen them and would know what to shoot at. Then she shouted too, and her voice was strong and loud as Louvinia's:

"You, Bayard Sartoris! Aint you in bed yet? Louvinia!" she shouted. Louvinia came in. "Take these children up to bed and if you hear another sound out of them tonight you have my permission and my insistence too to whip them both."

It didn't take us long to get to bed. But we couldn't talk even then, because Louvinia was going to bed on the cot in the hall. And Ringo was afraid to come up in the bed with me, so I got down on the pallet with him. "We'll have to watch the road," I said. Ringo whimpered.

"Look like hit haf to be us," he said.

"Are you scared?"

"I aint very," he said. "I just wish Marse John was here."

"Well he's not," I said. "It'll have to be us."

We watched the road for two days, lying in the cedar copse. Now and then Louvinia hollered at us but we told her where we were and that we were making another map, and besides she could see the cedar copse from the kitchen. It was cool and shady there, and quiet, and Ringo slept most of the time and I slept some too. I was dreaming, it was like I was looking at our place and suddenly the house and stable and cabins and trees and all were gone and I was looking at a place flat and empty as the sideboard and it was growing darker and darker and then all of a sudden I wasn't looking at it, I was there: a sort of frightened drove of little tiny figures moving on it, they were Father and Granny and Joby and Louvinia and Loosh and Philadelphy and Ringo and me and we were wandering around on it lost and it getting darker and darker and we forever more without any home to go to because we were forever free; that's what it was and then Ringo made a choked sound and I was looking at the road and there in the middle of it, sitting on a bright bay horse and looking at the house through a field glass, was a Yankee. For a long time we just lay there looking at him. I dont know what we had expected to see but we knew what he was at once; I remember thinking *He looks just like a man* and then Ringo and I were glaring at one another and then we were crawling backward down the hill without remembering when we started to crawl and then we were running across the pasture toward the house without remembering when we got to our feet. We seemed to run forever, with our heads back and our fists clenched before we reached the fence and fell over it and ran on into the house. Granny's chair was empty beside the table where her sewing lay. "Quick!" I said. "Shove it up here!" But Ringo didn't move; his eyes looked like door knobs while I dragged the chair up and climbed onto it and began to lift down the musket. It weighed about fifteen pounds, though it was not the weight so much as the length; when it came free it and the chair and all went down with a tremendous clatter; we heard Granny sit up in her bed upstairs and then we heard her voice:

"Who is it?"

"Quick!" I said. "Hurry!"

"I'm scared," Ringo said.

"You, Bayard!" Granny said. "Louvinia!"

We held the musket between us like a log of wood. "Do you want to be free?" I said. "Do you want to be free?"

We carried it that way, like a log, one at each end, running. We ran through the grove toward the road and ducked down behind the honeysuckle just as the horse came around the curve. We didn't hear anything else, maybe because of our own breathing or maybe because we were not expecting to hear anything else. We didn't look again either; we were too busy cocking the musket. We had practiced before, once or twice when Granny was not there and Joby would come in to examine it and change the cap on the nipple. Ringo held it up and I took the barrel in both hands, high, and drew myself up and shut my legs about it and slid down over the hammer until it clicked. That's what we were doing, we were too busy to look, the musket was already riding up across Ringo's back as he stooped, his hands on his knees and panting "Shoot the bastud! Shoot him!" and then the sights came level and as I shut my eyes I saw the man and the bright horse vanish in smoke. It sounded like thunder and it made as much smoke as a brushfire and I heard the horse scream but I didn't see anything else; it was Ringo wailing, "Great God, Bayard! Hit's the whole army!"

4.

The house didn't seem to get any nearer, it just hung there in front of us floating and increasing slowly in size like something in a dream, and I could hear Ringo moaning behind me and further back still the shouts and the hooves. But we reached the house at last; Louvinia was just inside the door, with Father's old hat on her headrag and her mouth open, but we didn't stop. We ran on into the room where Granny was standing beside the righted chair, her hand at her chest. "We shot him, Granny!" I cried. "We shot the bastud!"

"What?" She looked at me, her face the same color as her hair almost, her spectacles shining against her hair above her forehead. "Bayard Sartoris, what did you say?"

"We killed him, Granny! At the gate. Only there was the whole army too and we never saw them and now they are coming——" She sat down, she dropped into the chair, hard, her hand at her breast. But her voice was strong as ever:

"What's this? You, Marengo! What have you done?"

"We shot the bastud, Granny!" Ringo said. "We kilt him!" Then Louvinia was there too, with her mouth still open too and her face like somebody had thrown ashes at her. Only it didn't need her face; we heard the hooves jerking and sliding in the dirt and one of them hollering, "Get around to the back there, some of you!" and we looked up and saw them ride past the window—the blue coats and the guns. Then we heard the boots and spurs on the porch.

"Granny!" I said. "Granny!" But it seemed like none of us could move at all, we just had to stand there looking at Granny with her hand at her breast and her face looking like she had died and her voice like she had died too:

"Louvinia! What is this? What are they trying to tell me?" That's how it happened, like when once the musket decided to go off, all that was to occur afterward tried to rush into the sound of it all at once. I could still hear it, my ears were still ringing, so that Granny and Ringo and I all seemed to be talking far away. Then she said, "Quick! Here!" and then

Ringo and I were squatting with our chins under our knees, on either side of her against her legs, with the hard points of the chair rockers jammed into our backs and her skirts spread over us like a tent, and the heavy feet coming in and (Louvinia told us afterward) the Yankee sergeant shaking the musket at Granny and saying,

"Come on, grandma. Where are they? We saw them run in here."

We couldn't see, we just squatted in a kind of faint gray light and that smell of Granny that her clothes and bed and room all had and Ringo's eyes looking like two plates of chocolate pudding and maybe both of us thinking how Granny had never whipped us for anything in our lives except lying, and that even when it wasn't even a told lie but just keeping quiet, how she would whip us first and then make us kneel down and kneel down with us herself to ask the Lord to forgive us.

"You are mistaken," she said. "There are no children in this house nor on this place. There is no one here at all except my servant and myself and the people in the quarters."

"You mean you deny ever having seen this gun before?"

"I do." It was that quiet; she didn't move at all, sitting bolt upright and right on the edge of the chair to keep her skirts spread over us. "If you doubt me, you may search the house."

"Dont you worry about that, I'm going to. Send some of the boys upstairs," he said. "If you find any locked doors, you know what to do. And tell them fellows out back to comb and curry the barn and the cabins too."

"You wont find any locked doors," Granny said. "At least let me ask you——"

"Dont you ask anything, grandma. You set still. Better for you if you had done a little asking before you sent them little devils out with this gun."

"Was there. . . . . . ." We could hear her voice die away and then speak again, like she was behind it with a switch, making it talk. "Is he. . . . . . .it. . . . . . .the one who——"

"Dead? Hell, yes. Broke his back and we had to shoot him."

"Had to——you had——shoot. . . . . . ." I didn't know

horrified astonishment either, but Ringo and Granny and I were all three it.

"Yes, by God. Had to shoot him. The best damn horse in the whole army. The whole damn regiment betting on him for next Sunday——" He said some more, but we were not listening. We were not breathing either, glaring at one another in the gray gloom and I was almost shouting too, until Granny said it:

"Didn't——they didn't——Oh, thank God! Thank God!"

"We didn't——" Ringo said.

"Hsh!" I said. Because we didn't have to say it, it was like we had had to hold our breaths for a long time without knowing it, and that now we could let go and breathe again. Maybe that was why we never heard the other man when he came in at all, it was Louvinia that saw that too—a colonel, with a bright short beard and hard bright gray eyes, who looked at Granny sitting in the chair with her hand at her breast and took off his hat. Only he was talking to the sergeant.

"What's this?" he said. "What's going on here, Harrison?"

"This is where they run to," the sergeant said. "I'm searching the house."

"Ah," the colonel said. He didn't sound mad at all. He just sounded cold and short and pleasant. "By whose authority?"

"Well, somebody here fired on United States troops. I guess this is authority enough." We could just hear the sound; it was Louvinia that told us how he shook the musket and banged the butt on the floor.

"And killed one horse," the colonel said.

"It was a United States horse. I heard the general say myself that if he had enough horses, he wouldn't always care whether there was anybody to ride them or not. And so here we are, riding peaceful along the road, not bothering nobody yet, and these two little devils. . . . . . The best horse in the army, the whole damn regiment betting——"

"Ah," the colonel said. "I see. Well? Have you found them?"

"We aint yet. But these rebels are like rats when it comes to hiding. She says that there aint even any children here."

"Ah," said the colonel. And Louvinia said how he looked at

Granny now for the first time. She said how she could see his eyes going from Granny's face down to where her skirt was spread and looking at her skirt for a whole minute and then going back to her face. And that Granny gave him look for look while she lied. "Do I understand, madam, that there are no children in or about this house?"

"There are none, sir," Granny said.

Louvinia said he looked back at the sergeant. "There are no children here, sergeant. Evidently the shot came from some-where else. You may call the men in and mount them."

"But, Colonel, we saw them two kids run in here. All of us saw them——"

"Didn't you just hear this lady say there are no children here? Where are your ears, sergeant? Or do you really want the artillery to overtake us, with a creek bottom not five miles away to be got over?"

"Well, sir, you're colonel. But if it was me was colonel——"

"Then doubtless I should be Sergeant Harrison. In which case I think I should be more concerned about getting an-other horse to protect my wager next Sunday than over a grandchildless old lady—" Louvinia said his eyes just kind of touched Granny now and flicked away "—alone in a house which in all probability (and for her pleasure and satisfaction I am ashamed to say I hope) I shall never see again. Mount your men and get along with you."

We squatted there, not breathing, and heard them leave the house; we heard the sergeant calling the men up from the barn and we heard them ride away. But we did not move yet, because Granny's body had not relaxed at all and so we knew that the colonel was still there even before he spoke:—the voice short, brisk, hard, with that something of laughing be-hind it: "So you have no grandchildren. What a pity, in a place like this which two boys would enjoy—sports, fishing, game to shoot at, perhaps the most exciting game of all and none the less so for being possibly a little rare this near the house. And with a gun, a very dependable weapon, I see. . . . . . ." Louvinia said how the sergeant had set the musket in the corner and how the colonel looked at it now, and now we didn't breathe. "——though I understand that this weapon does not belong to you? Which is just as well.

Because if it were your weapon (which it is not) and you had two grandsons, or say a grandson and a negro playfellow (which you have not), and if this were the first time, which it is not, someone next time might be seriously hurt. But what am I doing? trying your patience by keeping you in that uncomfortable chair while I waste my time delivering a homily suitable only for a lady with grandchildren—or one grandchild and a negro companion." Now he was about to go too, we could tell it even beneath the skirt; this time it was Granny herself:

"There is little of refreshment I can offer you, sir. But if a glass of cool milk after your ride—"

Only for a long time he didn't answer at all; Louvinia said how he just looked at Granny with his hard bright eyes and that hard bright silence full of laughing. "No, no," he said. "I thank you. You are taxing yourself beyond mere politeness and into sheer bravado."

"Louvinia," Granny said, "conduct the gentleman to the diningroom and serve him with what we have."

He was out of the room now because Granny began to tremble now, trembling and trembling but not relaxing yet; we could hear her panting now. And we breathed too now, looking at one another. "We never killed him!" I whispered. "We never killed him! We haven't killed anybody at all!" So it was Granny's body that told us again, only this time I could almost feel him looking at Granny's spread skirt where we crouched while he thanked her for the milk and told her his name and regiment.

"Perhaps it is just as well that you have no grandchildren," he said. "Since doubtless you wish to live in peace. I have three boys myself, you see. And I have not even had time to become a grandparent." And now there wasn't any laughing behind his voice and Louvinia said he was standing there in the door, with the brass bright on his dark blue and his hat in his hand and his bright beard and hair, looking at Granny without the laughing now: "I wont apologise; fools cry out at wind or fire. But permit me to say and hope that you will never have anything worse than this to remember us by." Then he was gone. We heard his spurs in the hall and on the porch, then the horse, dying away, ceasing, and then Granny let go. She went back into the chair with her hand at her breast and her eyes closed and the sweat on her face in big drops; all of a sudden I began to holler, "Louvinia! Louvinia!" But she opened her eyes then and looked at me; they were looking at me when they opened. Then she looked at Ringo for a moment, but she looked back at me, panting.

"Bayard," she said. "What was that word you used?"

"Word?" I said. "When, Granny?" Then I remembered; I didn't look at her and she lying back in the chair, looking at me and panting.

"Dont repeat it. You cursed. You used obscene language, Bayard."

I didn't look at her. I could see Ringo's feet too. "Ringo did too," I said. She didn't answer, but I could feel her looking at me; I said suddenly: "And you told a lie. You said we were not here."

"I know it," she said. She moved. "Help me up." She got out of the chair, holding to us. We didn't know what she was trying to do. We just stood there while she held to us and to the chair and let herself down to her knees beside it. It was Ringo that knelt first. Then I knelt too while she asked the Lord to forgive her for telling the lie. Then she rose; we didn't have time to help her. "Go to the kitchen and get a pan of water and the soap," she said. "Get the new soap."

5.

It was late, as if time had slipped up on us while we were still caught, enmeshed by the sound of the musket and were too busy to notice it; the sun shone almost level into our faces while we stood at the edge of the back gallery, spitting, rinsing the soap from our mouths turn and turn about from the gourd dipper, spitting straight into the sun. For a while, just by breathing we could blow soap bubbles, but soon it was just the taste of the spitting. Then even that began to go away although the impulse to spit did not, while away to the north we could see the cloudbank, faint and blue and faraway at the base and touched with copper sun along the crest. When Father came home in the spring, we tried to understand about mountains. At last he pointed out the cloudbank to tell us

what mountains looked like. So ever since then Ringo believed that the cloudbank was Tennessee.

"Yonder they," he said, spitting. "Yonder hit. Tennessee,
where Marse John use to fight um at. Looking mighty far,
too."

"Too far to go just to fight Yankees," I said, spitting too.
But it was gone now—the suds, the glassy weightless iridescent bubbles; even the taste of it.

RETREAT

I.

IN THE AFTERNOON Loosh drove the wagon up beside the
back gallery and took the mules out; by suppertime we
had everything loaded into the wagon but the bedclothes we
would sleep under that night. Then Granny went up stairs
and when she came back down she had on her Sunday black
silk and her hat, and there was color in her face now and her
eyes were bright.

"Is we gonter leave tonight?" Ringo said. "I thought we
wasn't going to start until in the morning."

"We're not," Granny said. "But it's been three years now
since I have started anywhere; I reckon the Lord will forgive
me for getting ready one day ahead of time." She turned (we
were in the diningroom then, the table set with supper) to
Louvinia. "Tell Joby and Loosh to be ready with the lantern
and the shovels as soon as they have finished eating."

Louvinia had set the cornbread on the table and was going
out when she stopped and looked at Granny. "You mean you
gonter take that heavy trunk all the way to Memphis with
you? You gonter dig hit up from where hit been hid safe since
last summer, and take hit all the way to Memphis?"

"Yes," Granny said. "I am following Colonel Sartoris' instructions as I believe he meant them." She was eating; she
didn't even look at Louvinia. Louvinia stood there in the
pantry door, looking at the back of Granny's head.

"Whyn't you leave hit here where hit hid good and I can take care of hit? Who gonter find hit even if They was to come here again? Hit's Marse John They done called the reward on, hit aint no trunk full of——"

"I have my reasons," Granny said. "You do what I told you."

"All right. But how come you wanter dig hit up tonight when you aint leaving until tomor——"

"You do what I said," Granny said.

"Yessum," Louvinia said. She went out. I looked at Granny eating, with her hat sitting on the exact top of her head and Ringo looking at me across the back of Granny's chair with his eyes rolling a little.

"Why not leave it hid?" I said. "It'll be just that much more load on the wagon. Joby says that trunk will weigh a thousand pounds."

"A thousand fiddlesticks," Granny said. "I dont care if it weighed ten thousand——" Louvinia came in.

"They be ready," she said. "I wish you'd tell me why you got to dig hit up tonight."

Granny looked at her. "I had a dream about it last night."

"Oh," Louvinia said. She and Ringo looked exactly alike except Louvinia's eyes were not rolling as much as his.

"I dreamed I was looking out my window and a man walked into the orchard and went to where it is and stood there pointing at it," Granny said. She looked at Louvinia. "A black man."

"A nigger?" Louvinia said.

"Yes."

For a while Louvinia didn't say anything. Then she said, "Did you know him?"

"Yes," Granny said.

"Is you going to tell who hit was?"

"No," Granny said.

Louvinia turned to Ringo. "Gawn tell your pappy and Loosh to get the lantern and the shovels and come on up here."

Joby and Loosh were in the kitchen. Joby was sitting behind the stove with a plate on his knees, eating. Loosh was sitting on the woodbox, still, with the two shovels between his knees but I didn't see him at first because of Ringo's shadow. The lamp was on the table and I could see the shadow of Ringo's head bent over and his arm working back and forth and Louvinia standing between us and the lamp, her hands on her hips and her elbows spread and her shadow filling the room. "Clean that chimney good," she said.

Joby carried the lantern with Granny behind him and then Loosh; I could see her bonnet and Loosh's head and the two shovel blades over his shoulder. Ringo was breathing behind me. "Which un you reckon she drempt about?" he said.

"Why dont you ask her?" I said. We were in the orchard now.

"Hoo," Ringo said. "Me ask her? I bet if she stayed here wouldn't no Yankee nor nothing else bother that trunk nor Marse John neither if he knowed hit."

Then they stopped—Joby and Granny, and while Granny held the lantern at arm's length, Joby and Loosh dug the trunk up from where they had buried it that night last summer while Father was at home, while Louvinia stood in the door of the bedroom without even lighting the lamp while Ringo and I went to bed and later I either looked out or dreamed I looked out the window and saw (or dreamed I saw) the lantern. Then, with Granny in front and still carrying the lantern and with Ringo and me both helping to carry it, we returned toward the house. Before we reached the house Joby began to bear away toward where the loaded wagon stood.

"Take it into the house," Granny said.

"We'll just load hit now and save having to handle hit again in the morning," Joby said. "Come on here, nigger," he said to Loosh.

"Take it into the house," Granny said. So after a while Joby moved on toward the house. We could hear him breathing now, saying "Hah!" every few steps. Inside the kitchen he let his end down, hard.

"Hah!" he said. "That's done, thank God."

"Take it upstairs," Granny said.

Joby turned and looked at her. He hadn't straightened up yet, he turned half stooping and looked at her. "Which?" he said.

"Take it upstairs," Granny said. "I want it in my room."

"You mean you gonter tote this thing all the way upstairs and then tote it back down tomorrow?"

"Somebody is," Granny said. "Are you going to help or are me and Bayard going to do it alone?"

Then Louvinia came in. She had already undressed. She looked tall as a ghost, in one dimension like a bolster case, taller than a bolster case in her nightgown; silent as a ghost on her bare feet which were the same color as the shadow in which she stood so that she seemed to have no feet, the twin rows of her toenails lying weightless and faint and still as two rows of faintly soiled feathers on the floor about a foot below the hem of her nightgown as if they were not connected with her. She came and shoved Joby aside and stooped to lift the trunk. "Git away, nigger," she said. Joby groaned, then he shoved Louvinia aside.

"Git away, woman," he said. He lifted his end of the trunk, then he looked back at Loosh who had never let his end down. "If you gonter ride on hit, pick up your feet," he said. We carried the trunk up to Granny's room and Joby was setting it down again until Granny made him and Loosh pull the bed out from the wall and slide the trunk in behind it; Ringo and I helped again. I dont believe it lacked much of weighing a thousand pounds.

"Now I want everybody to go right to bed so we can get an early start tomorrow," Granny said.

"That's you," Joby said. "Git everybody up at crack of day and it be noon fore we get started."

"Nummine about that," Louvinia said. "You do like Miss Rosa tell you." We went out; we left Granny there beside her bed now well away from the wall and in such an ungainly position that anyone would have known at once that something was concealed, even if the trunk which Ringo and I as well as Joby believed now to weigh at least a thousand pounds, could have been hidden. As it was, the bed merely underlined it. Then Granny shut the door behind us and then Ringo and I stopped dead in the hall and looked at one another. Since I could remember, there had never been a key to any door, inside or outside, about the house. Yet we had heard a key turn in the lock.

"I didn't know there was ere a key would fit hit," Ringo said, "let alone turn."

"And that's some more of yawl's and Joby's business," Louvinia said. She had not stopped; she was already reclining on her cot and as we looked toward her she was already in the act of drawing the quilt up over her face and head. "Yawl get on to bed."

We went on to our room and began to undress. The lamp was lighted and there was already laid out across two chairs our Sunday clothes which we too would put on tomorrow to go to Memphis in. "Which un you reckin she dremp about?" Ringo said. But I didn't answer that; I knew that Ringo knew I didn't need to.

2.

We put on our Sunday clothes by lamplight, we ate breakfast by it and listened to Louvinia above stairs as she removed from Granny's and my beds the linen we had slept under last night and rolled up Ringo's pallet and carried them downstairs; in the first beginning of day we went out to where Loosh and Joby had already put the mules into the wagon and where Joby stood in what he called his Sunday clothes too—the old frock coat, the napless beaver hat, of Father's. Then Granny came out (still in the black silk and the bonnet as if she had slept in them, passed the night standing rigidly erect with her hand on the key which she had produced from we knew not where and locked her door for the first time Ringo and I knew of) with her shawl over her shoulders and carrying her parasol and the musket from the pegs over the mantel. She held out the musket to Joby. "Here," she said. Joby looked at it.

"We wont need hit," he said.

"Put it in the wagon," Granny said.

"Nome. We wont need nothing like that. We be in Memphis so quick wont nobody even have time to hear we on the road. I speck Marse John got the Yankees pretty well cleant out between here and Memphis anyway."

This time Granny didn't say anything at all. She just stood there holding out the musket until after a while Joby took it and put it into the wagon. "Now go get the trunk," Granny said. Joby was still putting the musket into the wagon; he stopped, his head turned a little.

"Which?" he said. He turned a little more, still not looking at Granny standing on the steps and looking at him; he was not looking at any of us, not speaking to any of us in particular. "Aint I tole you?" he said.

"If anything ever came into your mind that you didn't tell to somebody inside of ten minutes, I dont remember it," Granny said. "But just what do you refer to now?"

"Nummine that," Joby said. "Come on here, Loosh. Bring that boy with you." They passed Granny and went on. She didn't look at them; it was as if they had walked not only out of her sight but out of her mind. Evidently Joby thought they had. He and Granny were like that; they were like a man and a mare, a blooded mare, which takes just exactly so much from the man and the man knows the mare will take just so much and the man knows that when that point is reached, just what is going to happen. Then it does happen: the mare kicks him, not viciously but just enough, and the man knows it was going to happen and so he is glad then, it is over then, or he thinks it is over, so he lies or sits on the ground and cusses the mare a little because he thinks it is over, finished, and then the mare turns her head and nips him. That's how Joby and Granny were and Granny always beat him, not bad: just exactly enough, like now; he and Loosh were just about to go in the door and Granny still not even looking after them, when Joby said, "I done tole um. And I reckin even you cant dispute hit." Then Granny, without moving anything but her lips, still looking out beyond the waiting wagon as if we were not going anywhere and Joby didn't even exist, said,

"And put the bed back against the wall." This time Joby didn't answer. He just stopped perfectly still, not even looking back at Granny, until Loosh said quietly,

"Gawn, pappy. Get on." They went on; Granny and I stood at the end of the gallery and heard them drag the trunk out, then shove the bed back where it had been yesterday; we heard them on the stairs with the trunk—the slow, clumsy, coffinsounding thumps. Then they came out onto the gallery.

"Go and help them," Granny said without looking back.

"Remember, Joby is getting old." We put the trunk into the wagon, along with the musket and the basket of food and the bedclothing, and got in ourselves—Granny on the seat beside Joby, the bonnet on the exact top of her head and the parasol raised even before the dew had begun to fall—and we drove away. Loosh had already disappeared, but Louvinia still stood at the end of the gallery with Father's old hat on top of her headrag. Then I stopped looking back, though I could feel Ringo beside me on the trunk turning every few yards, even after we were outside the gate and in the road to town. Then we came to the curve where we had seen the Yankee sergeant on the bright horse last summer.

"Hit gone now," Ringo said. "Goodbye, Sartoris; Memphis, how-dy-do!"

The sun was just rising when we came in sight of Jefferson; we passed a company of troops bivouacked in a pasture beside the road, eating breakfast. Their uniforms were not gray anymore now; they were almost the color of dead leaves and some of them didn't even have uniforms and one man waved a skillet at us and he had on a pair of blue Yankee pants with a yellow cavalry stripe like Father wore home last summer. "Hey, Missippi!" he shouted. "Hooraw for Arkansaw!"

We left Granny at Mrs Compson's, to tell Mrs Compson goodbye and to ask her to drive out home now and then and look after the flowers. Then Ringo and I drove the wagon on to the store and we were just coming out with the sack of salt when Uncle Buck McCaslin came hobbling across the square, waving his stick and hollering, and behind him the captain of the company we had passed eating breakfast in the pasture. There were two of them; I mean, there were two McCaslins, Amodeus and Theophilus, twins, only everybody called them Buck and Buddy except themselves. They were bachelors, they had a big bottom-land plantation about fifteen miles from town. It had a big colonial house on it which their father had built and which people said was still one of the finest houses in the country when they inherited it. But it wasn't now, because Uncle Buck and Buddy didn't live in it. They never had lived in it since their father died. They lived in a two-room log house with about a dozen dogs, and they kept their niggers in the manor house. It didn't have any windows

now and a child with a hairpin could unlock any lock in it,
but every night when the niggers came up from the fields
Uncle Buck or Uncle Buddy would drive them into the house
and lock the door with a key almost as big as a horse pistol;
probably they would still be locking the front door long after
the last nigger had escaped out the back. And folks said that
Uncle Buck and Uncle Buddy knew this and that the niggers
knew they knew it, only it was like a game with rules—neither one of Uncle Buck or Uncle Buddy to peep around the
corner of the house while the other was locking the door,
none of the niggers to escape in such a way as to be seen even
by unavoidable accident, nor to escape at any other time; they
even said that the ones who couldn't get out while the door
was being locked voluntarily considered themselves interdict
until the next evening. Then they would hang the key on a
nail beside the door and go back to their own little house full
of dogs and eat supper and play head-and-head poker; and
they said how no man in the state or on the River either
would have dared to play with them even if they did not
cheat, but that in the game as they played it between themselves, betting niggers and wagon-loads of cotton with one
another on the turn of a single card, the Lord Himself might
have held His own with one of them at a time, but that with
both of them even He would have lost His shirt.

There was more to Uncle Buck and Buddy than just that.
Father said they were ahead of their time; he said they not
only possessed, but put into practice, ideas about social relationship that maybe fifty years after they were both dead people would have a name for. These ideas were about land.
They believed that land did not belong to people but that
people belonged to land and that the earth would permit
them to live on and out of it and use it only so long as they
behaved and that if they did not behave right, it would shake
them off just like a dog getting rid of fleas. They had some
kind of a system of book-keeping which must have been even
more involved than their betting score against one another,
by which all their niggers were to be freed, not given freedom, but earning it, buying it not in money from Uncle Buck
and Buddy, but in work from the plantation. Only there were
others besides niggers, and this was the reason why Uncle

Buck came hobbling across the square, shaking his stick at me and hollering, or at least why it was Uncle Buck who was hobbling and hollering and shaking the stick. One day Father said how they suddenly realised that if the county ever split up into private feuds either with votes or weapons, no family could contend with the McCaslins because all the other families would have only their cousins and kin to recruit from, while Uncle Buck and Buddy would already have an army. These were the dirt farmers, the people whom the niggers called 'white trash'—men who had owned no slaves and some of whom even lived worse than the slaves on big plantations. It was another side of Uncle Buck's and Buddy's ideas about men and land, which Father said people didn't have a name for yet, by which Uncle Buck and Buddy had persuaded the white men to pool their little patches of poor hill land along with the niggers and the McCaslin plantation, promising them in return nobody knew exactly what, except that their women and children did have shoes, which not all of them had had before, and a lot of them even went to school. Anyway, they (the white men, the trash) looked on Uncle Buck and Buddy like Deity Himself, so that when Father began to raise his first regiment to take to Virginia and Uncle Buck and Buddy came to town to enlist and the others decided they were too old (they were past seventy), it looked for a while as if Father's regiment would have to fight its first engagement right there in our pasture. At first Uncle Buck and Buddy said they would form a company of their own men in opposition to Father's. Then they realised that this wouldn't stop Father, since he didn't care whom the men fought under just so they fought, so then Uncle Buck and Buddy put the thumbscrews on Father sure enough. They told Father that if he did not let them go, the solid bloc of private soldier white trash votes which they controlled would not only force Father to call a special election of officers before the regiment left the pasture, it would also demote Father from colonel to major or maybe only a company commander. Father didn't mind what they called him; colonel or corporal, it would have been all the same to him, as long as they let him tell them what to do, and he probably wouldn't have minded being demoted even to private by God Himself;

it was the idea that there could be latent within the men he led the power, let alone the desire, to so affront him. So they compromised; they agreed at last that one of the McCaslins should be allowed to go. Father and Uncle Buck and Buddy shook hands on it and they stuck to it; the following summer after Second Manassas when the men did demote Father, it was the McCaslin votes who stuck with and resigned from the regiment along with Father and returned to Mississippi with him and formed his irregular cavalry. So one of them was to go, and they decided themselves which one it would be; they decided in the one possible manner in which the victor could know that he had earned his right, the loser that he had been conquered by a better man; Uncle Buddy looked at Uncle Buck and said, "All right, 'Philus, you old butter-fingered son of a bitch. Get out the cards."

Father said it was fine, that there were people there who had never seen anything like it for cold and ruthless artistry. They played three hands of draw poker, the first two hands dealt in turn, the winner of the second hand to deal the third; they sat there (somebody had spread a blanket and the whole regiment watched) facing each other with the two old faces that did not look exactly alike so much as they looked exactly like something which after a while you remembered—the portrait of someone who had been dead a long time and that you knew just by looking at him he had been a preacher in some place like Massachusetts a hundred years ago; they sat there and called those face-down cards correctly without even looking at the backs of them apparently, so that it took some-times eight and ten deals before the referees could be certain that neither of them knew exactly what was in the other's hand. And Uncle Buck lost: so that now Uncle Buddy was a sergeant in Tennant's brigade in Virginia and Uncle Buck was hobbling across the square, shaking his stick at me and hollering:

"By Godfrey, there he is! There's John Sartoris' boy!"

The captain came up and looked at me. "I've heard of your father," he said.

"Heard of him?" Uncle Buck shouted. By now people had begun to stop along the walk and listen to him, like they always did, not smiling so he could see it. "Who aint heard about him in this country? Get the Yankees to tell you about him sometime. By Godfrey, he raised the first damn regiment in Mississippi out of his own pocket, and took em to Ferginny and whipped Yankees right and left with em before he found out that what he had bought and paid for wasn't a regiment of soldiers but a congress of politicians and fools. Fools I say!" he shouted, shaking the stick at me and glaring with his watery fierce eyes like the eyes of an old hawk, with the people along the street listening to him and smiling where he couldn't see it and the strange captain looking at him a little funny because he hadn't heard Uncle Buck before; and I kept on thinking about Louvinia standing there on the porch with Father's old hat on, and wishing that Uncle Buck would get through or hush so we could go on.

"Fools, I say!" he shouted. "I dont care if some of you folks here do still claim kin with men that elected him colonel and followed him and Stonewall Jackson right up to spitting distance of Washington without hardly losing a man, and then next year turned around and voted him down to major and elected in his stead a damn feller that never even knowed which end of a gun done the shooting until John Sartoris showed him." He quit shouting just as easy as he started but the shouting was right there, waiting to start again as soon as he found something else to shout about. "I wont say God take care of you and your grandma on the road, boy, because by Godfrey you dont need God's nor nobody else's help; all you got to say is 'I'm John Sartoris' boy; rabbits, hunt the canebrake' and then watch the blue bellied sons of bitches fly."

"Are they leaving, going away?" the captain said.

Then Uncle Buck begun to shout again, going into the shouting easy, without even having to draw a breath: "Leaving? Hell's skillet, who's going to take care of them around here? John Sartoris is a damn fool; they voted him out of his own private regiment in kindness, so he could come home and take care of his family, knowing that if he didn't wouldn't nobody around here be likely to. But that dont suit John Sartoris because John Sartoris is a damned confounded selfish coward, askeered to stay at home where the Yankees might get him. Yes sir. So skeered that he has to raise him up another batch of men to protect him every time he gets within a hundred foot of a Yankee brigade. Scouring all up and down the country, finding Yankees to dodge; only if it had been me I would have took back to Ferginny and I'd have showed that new colonel what fighting looked like. But not John Sartoris. He's a coward and a fool. The best he can do is dodge and run away from Yankees until they have to put a price on his head, and now he's got to send his family out of the country; to Memphis where maybe the Union Army will take care of them, since it dont look like his own government and fellow citizens are going to." He ran out of breath then, or out of words anyway, standing there with his tobacco-stained beard trembling and more tobacco running onto it out of his mouth, and shaking his stick at me. So I lifted the reins; only the captain spoke; he was still watching me.

"How many men has your father got in his regiment?" he said.

"It's not a regiment, sir," I said. "He's got about fifty, I reckon."

"Fifty?" the captain said. "Fifty? We had a prisoner last week who said he had more than a thousand. He said that Colonel Sartoris didn't fight, he just stole horses."

Uncle Buck had enough wind to laugh though. He sounded just like a hen, slapping his leg and holding to the wagon wheel like he was about to fall. "That's it! That's John Sartoris! He gets the horses; any fool can step out and get a Yankee. These two damn boys here did that last summer: stepped down to the gate and brought back a whole regiment and them just——How old are you, boy?"

"Fourteen," I said.

"We aint fourteen yit," Ringo said. "But we will be in September if we live and nothing happens. I reckon Granny waiting on us, Bayard."

Uncle Buck quit laughing. He stepped back. "Git on," he said. "You got a long road." I turned the wagon. "You take care of your grandma, boy, or John Sartoris will skin you alive. And if he dont, I will!" When the wagon straightened out he began to hobble along beside it. "And when you see him, tell him I said to leave the horses go for a while and kill the bluebellied sons of bitches. Kill them!"

"Yes, sir," I said. We went on.

"Good thing for his mouth Granny aint here," Ringo said. She and Joby were waiting for us at the Compsons' gate. Joby had another basket with a napkin over it and a bottleneck sticking out and some rose cuttings. Then Ringo and I sat behind again and Ringo turning to look back every few feet and saying, "Goodbye, Jefferson. Memphis, how-dy-do!" And then we came to the top of the first hill and he looked back quiet this time and said, "Suppose they dont never get done fighting."

"All right," I said. "Suppose it." I didn't look back. At noon we stopped by a spring and Granny opened the basket and she took out the rose cuttings and handed them to Ringo.

"Dip the roots into the spring after you drink," she said. They had earth still on the roots, in a cloth; when Ringo stooped down to the water I watched him pinch off a little of the dirt and start to put it into his pocket. Then he looked up and saw me watching him and he made like he was going to throw it away. But he didn't.

"I reckon I can save dirt if I want to," he said.

"It's not Sartoris dirt, though," I said.

"I know hit," he said. "Hit's closer than Memphis dirt though. Closer than what you got."

"What'll you bet?" I said. He looked at me. "What'll you swap?" I said. He looked at me.

"What you swap?" he said.

"You know," I said. He reached into his pocket and brought out the buckle we had shot off the Yankee saddle when we shot the horse last summer. "Gimmit here," he said. So I took the snuff box from my pocket and emptied half the soil (it was more than Sartoris earth; it was Vicksburg too: the yelling was in it, the embattled, the iron-worn, the supremely invincible) into his hand. "I know hit," he said. "Hit come from hind the smokehouse. You brung a lot of hit."

"Yes," I said. "I brought enough to last."

We soaked the cuttings every time we stopped and opened the basket, and there was some of the food left on the fourth day because at least once a day we stopped at houses on the road and ate with them, and on the second night we had supper and breakfast at the same house. But even then Granny would not come inside to sleep. She made her bed down in the wagon by the chest and Joby slept under the wagon with the gun beside him like when we camped on the road. Only it would not be exactly on the road but back in the woods a way; on the third night Granny was in the wagon and Joby and Ringo and I were under the wagon and some cavalry rode up and Granny said, "Joby! the gun!" and somebody got down and took the gun away from Joby and they lit a pine knot and we saw the gray.

"Memphis?" the officer said. "You cant get to Memphis. There was a fight at Cockrum yesterday and the roads ahead are full of Yankee patrols. How in hell—Excuse me, ma'am" (behind me Ringo said, "Git the soap") "—you ever got this far I dont see. If I were you, I wouldn't even try to go back, I'd stop at the first house I came to and stay there."

"I reckon we'll go on," Granny said, "like John—Colonel Sartoris told us to. My sister lives in Memphis; we are going there."

"Colonel Sartoris?" the officer said. "Colonel Sartoris told you?"

"I'm his mother-in-law," Granny said. "This is his son."

"Good Lord, ma'am! You cant go a step further. Dont you know that if They captured you and this boy, They could almost force him to come in and surrender?"

Granny looked at him, she was sitting up in the wagon and her hat was on. "My experience with Yankees has evidently been different from yours. I have no reason to believe that their officers—I suppose they still have officers among them—will bother a woman and two children. I thank you, but my son has directed us to go to Memphis. If there is any information about the roads which my driver should know, I will be obliged if you will instruct him."

"Then let me give you an escort.—Or better still, there is a house about a mile back; return there and wait. Colonel Sartoris was at Cockrum yesterday, by tomorrow night I believe I can find him and bring him to you."

"Thank you," Granny said. "Wherever Colonel Sartoris is, he is doubtless busy with his own affairs. I think we will continue to Memphis as he instructed us."

So they rode away and Joby came back under the wagon and put the musket between us only every time I turned over I rolled on it so I made him move it and he tried to put it in the wagon with Granny and she wouldn't let him so he leaned it against a tree and we slept and ate breakfast and went on, with Ringo and Joby looking behind every tree we passed. "You aint going to find them behind a tree we have already passed," I said. We didn't. We had passed where a house had burned and then we were passing another house with an old white horse looking at us out of the stable door behind it and then I saw six men running in the next field and then we saw a dustcloud coming fast out of a lane that crossed the road; Joby said, "Them folks look like they trying to make the Yankees take they stock, running hit up and down the big road in broad daylight like that." They rode right out of the dustcloud without seeing us at all, crossing the road and the first ten or twelve had already jumped the ditch with pistols in their hands like when you run with a stick of stove wood balanced on your palm, and the last ones came out of the dust with five men running and holding to stirrups and us sitting there in the wagon with Joby holding the mules like they were sitting down on the whiffletrees and his mouth hanging open and his eyes like two eggs, and I had forgotten what the blue coats looked like. It was fast, like that: all sweating horses with wild eyes and men with wild faces full of yelling and then Granny standing up in the wagon and beating the five men about their heads and shoulders with the umbrella while they unfastened the traces and cut the harness off the mules with pocket knives. They didn't say a word, they didn't even look at Granny while she was hitting them, they just took the mules out of the wagon and then the two mules and the five men disappeared together in another cloud of dust and the mules came out of the dust soaring like hawks with two men on them and two more just falling backward over the mules' tails and the fifth man already running too and the two that were on their backs in the road getting up with little scraps of cut leather sticking to them like a kind of black shavings in a sawmill; the three of them went off across the field after the mules and then we heard the pistols away off like striking a handful of matches at one time and Joby still sitting on the seat with his mouth still open and the ends of the cut reins in his hands and Granny still standing in the wagon with the bent umbrella lifted and hollering at Ringo and me while we jumped out of the wagon and ran across the road.

"The stable," I said. "The stable!" While we were running up the hill toward the house we could see our mules still galloping in the field and we could see the three men running too. When we ran around the house we could see the wagon too in the road, with Joby on the seat above the wagon tongue sticking straight out ahead and Granny standing up and shaking the umbrella toward us and even though I couldn't hear her I knew she was still shouting. Our mules had run into the woods but the three men were still in the field and the old white horse was watching them too in the barn door; he never saw us until he snorted and jerked back and kicked over something behind him. It was a homemade shoeing box and he was tied by a rope halter to the ladder to the loft and there was even a pipe still burning on the ground.

We climbed onto the ladder and got on him and when we came out of the barn we could still see the three men but we had to stop while Ringo got down and opened the lot gate and got back on again and so they were gone too by then. When we reached the woods there was no sign of them and we couldn't hear anything either but the old horse's insides. We went on slower then because the old horse wouldn't go fast again anyway and so we tried to listen and so it was almost sunset when we came out into a road. "Here where they went," Ringo said. They were mule tracks. "Tinney and Old Hundred's tracks bofe," Ringo said. "I know um anywhere. They done throwed them Yankees and heading back home."

"Are you sure?" I said.

"Is I sure? You reckon I aint followed them mules all my life and cant tell they tracks when I see um? Git up there, horse!"

We went on, but the old horse could not go very fast. After a while the moon came up, but Ringo still said he could see the tracks of our mules. So we went on, only now the old horse went even slower than ever because presently I caught Ringo and held him as he slipped off and then a little later

Ringo caught and held me from slipping before I even knew that I had been asleep. We didn't know what time it was, we didn't care; we only heard after a time the slow hollow repercussion of wood beneath the horse's feet and we turned from the road and hitched the bridle to a sapling; we probably both crawled beneath the bridge already asleep; still sleeping, we doubtless continued to crawl. Because if we had not moved, they would not have found us. I waked, still believing I dreamed of thunder. It was light; even beneath the close weed-choked bridge Ringo and I could sense the sun though not at once; for the time we just sat there beneath the loud drumming, while the loose planks of the bridge floor clattered and danced to the hooves; we sat there for a moment staring at one another in the pale jonquil-colored light almost before we were awake. Perhaps that was it, perhaps we were still asleep, were taken so suddenly in slumber that we had not time to think of Yankees or anything else; we were out from beneath the bridge and already running before we remembered having begun to move; I looked back one time and (the road, the bridge, was five or six feet higher than the earth beside it) it looked as if the whole rim of the world was full of horses running along the sky. Then everything ran together again as it had yesterday; even while our legs still continued to run Ringo and I had dived like two rabbits into a brier patch, feeling no thorn, and lay on our faces in it while men shouted and horses crashed around us, then hard hands dragged us, clawing and kicking and quite blind, out of the thicket and onto our feet. Then sight returned—a vacuum, an interval, of amazing and dewy-breathed peace and quiet while Ringo and I stood in a circle of mounted and dismounted men and horses. Then I recognised Jupiter standing big and motionless and pale in the dawn as a mesmerised flame, then Father was shaking me and shouting, "Where's your grandmother? Where's Miss Rosa?" and then Ringo, in a tone of complete amazement: "We done fergot Granny!"

"Forgot her?" Father shouted. "You mean you ran away and left her sitting there in that wagon in the middle of the road?"

"Lord, Marse John," Ringo said. "You know hit aint no Yankee gonter bother her if he know hit."

Father swore. "How far back did you leave her?"

"It was about three oclock yesterday," I said. "We rode some last night."

Father turned to the others. "Two of you boys take them up behind you; we'll lead that horse." Then he stopped and turned back to us. "Have you all had anything to eat?"

"Eat?" Ringo said. "My stomach think my throat been cut."

Father took a pone of bread from his saddle bags and broke it and gave it to us. "Where did you get that horse?" he said.

After a while I said, "We borrowed it."

"Who from?" Father said.

After a while Ringo said, "We aint know. The man wasn't there." One of the men laughed. Father looked at him quick and he hushed. But just for a minute, because all of a sudden they all began to whoop and holler, and Father looking around at them and his face getting redder and redder.

"Dont you say a word, Colonel," one of them said. "Hooraw for Sartoris!"

We galloped back; it was not far; we came to the field where the men had run, and the house with the barn, and in the road we could still see the scraps of harness where they had cut it. But the wagon was gone. Father led the old horse up to the house himself and knocked on the porch floor with his pistol and the door of the house was still open but nobody came. We put the old horse back into the barn, the pipe was still on the ground by the overturned shoeing box. We came back to the road and Father sat Jupiter in the middle of the litter of harness scraps. "You damn boys," he said. "You damn boys."

When we went on now we went slower, there were three men riding on ahead out of sight. In the afternoon one of them came galloping back and Father left Ringo and me three others and he and the rest rode on; it was almost sunset when they came back with their horses sweated a little and leading two new horses with blue blankets under the saddles and U.S. burned on the horses' hips.

"I tole you they wasn't no Yankees gonter stop Granny," Ringo said. "I bet she in Memphis right now."

"I hope for your sake she is," Father said. He jerked his hand at the new horses. "You and Bayard get on them."

Ringo went to one of the new horses. "Wait," Father said, "the other one is yours."

"You mean hit belong to me?" Ringo said.

"No," Father said. "You borrowed it." Then we all stopped and watched Ringo trying to get on his horse. The horse would stand perfectly still until he would feel Ringo's weight on the stirrup, then he would whirl completely around until his off side faced Ringo; the first time Ringo wound up lying on his back in the road. "Get on him from that side," Father said laughing.

Ringo looked at the horse and then at Father. "Git up from the wrong side?" Ringo said. "I knowed Yankees wasn't folks but I never knowed before they horses aint horses."

"Get on up," Father said. "He's blind in his near eye."

It got dark while we were still riding and after a while I waked up with somebody holding me in the saddle and we were stopped in some trees and there was a fire but Ringo and I didn't even stay awake to eat, and then it was morning again and all of them were gone but Father and eleven more, but we didn't start off even then, we stayed there in the trees all day. "What are we going to do now?" I said.

"I'm going to take you damn boys home and then I've got to go to Memphis and find your grandmother," Father said.

Just before dark we started, we watched Ringo trying to get on his horse from the nigh side for a while and then we went on. We rode until dawn and stopped again. This time we didn't build a fire, we didn't even unsaddle right away; we lay hidden in the woods and then Father was waking me with his hand, it was after sunup and we lay there and listened to a column of Yankee infantry pass in the road and then I slept again. It was noon when I waked. There was a fire now and a shoat cooking over it and we ate. "We'll be home by midnight," Father said.

Jupiter was rested. He didn't want the bridle for a while and then he didn't want Father to get on him and even after we were started he still wanted to go; Father had to hold him back between Ringo and me. Ringo was on his right. "You and Bayard better swap sides," Father told Ringo. "So your horse can see what's beside him."

"He going all right," Ringo said. "He like hit this way. Maybe because he can smell Jupiter another horse and know Jupiter aint fixing to git on him and ride."

"All right," Father said. "Watch him, though." We went on. Mine and Ringo's horses could go pretty well too; when I looked back the others were a good piece behind, out of our dust. It wasn't far to sundown.

"I wish I knew your grandmother was all right," Father said.

"Lord, Marse John," Ringo said, "is you still worrying about Granny? I been knowed her all my life; I aint worried about her."

Jupiter was fine to watch, with his head up and watching my horse and Ringo's and boring a little and just beginning to drive a little. "I'm going to let him go a little," Father said. "You and Ringo watch yourselves." I thought Jupiter was gone then. He went out like a rocket, flattening a little. But I should have known that Father still held him because I should have seen that he was still boring, but there was a snake fence along the road and all of a sudden it began to blur and then I realised that Father and Jupiter had not moved up at all, that it was all three of us flattening out up toward the crest of the hill where the road dipped like three swallows and I was thinking *We're holding Jupiter. We're holding Jupiter* when Father looked back and I saw his eyes and his teeth in his beard and I knew he still had Jupiter on the bit; he said, "Watch out, now," and then Jupiter shot out from between us; he went out exactly like I have seen a hawk come out of a sage field and rise over a fence; when they reached the crest of the hill I could see sky under them and the tops of the trees beyond the hill like they were flying, sailing out into the air to drop down beyond the hill like the hawk; only they didn't. It was like Father stopped Jupiter in midair on top of the hill; I could see him standing in the stirrups and his arm up with his hat in it and then Ringo and I were on them before we could even begin to think to pull, and Jupiter reined back onto his haunches and then Father hit Ringo's horse across his blind eye with the hat and I saw Ringo's horse swerve and jump clean over the snake fence and I heard Ringo hollering as I went on over the crest of the hill with Father just behind me shooting his pistol and shouting, "Surround them, boys! Dont let a man escape!"

There is a limit to what a child can accept, assimilate; not to what it can believe because a child can believe anything, given time, but to what it can accept, a limit in time, in the very time which nourishes the believing of the incredible. And I was still a child at that moment when Father's and my horses came over the hill and seemed to cease galloping and to float, hang suspended rather in a dimension without time in it while Father held my horse reined back with one hand and I heard Ringo's half blind beast crashing and blundering among the trees to our right and Ringo yelling, and looked quietly down at the scene beneath rather than before us—the dusk, the fire, the creek running quiet and peaceful beneath a bridge, the muskets all stacked carefully and neatly and no-body within fifty feet of them; and the men, the faces, the blue Yankee coats and pants and boots, squatting about the fire with cups in their hands and looking toward the crest of the hill with the same peaceful expression on all their faces like so many dolls. Father's hat was flung onto his head now, his teeth were showing and his eyes were bright as a cat's.

"Lieutenant," he said, loud, jerking my horse around, "ride back up the hill and close in with your troop on their right. Git!" he whispered, slapping my horse across the rump with his hand. "Make a fuss! Holler! See if you can keep up with Ringo.—Boys," he said, while they still looked up at him; they hadn't even put the cups down: "Boys, I'm John Sartoris, and I reckon I've got you."

Ringo was the only difficult one to capture. The rest of Father's men came piling over the hill, reining back, and I reckon that for a minute their faces looked about like the Yan-kees' faces did, and now and then I would quit thrashing the bushes and I could hear Ringo on his side hollering and moaning and hollering again, "Marse John! You Marse John! You come here quick!" and hollering for me, calling Bayard and Colonel and Marse John and Granny until it did sound like a company at least, and then hollering at his horse again and it running back and forth; I reckon he had forgotten again and was trying to get up on the nigh side again, until at last Father said, "All right, boys. You can come on in."

It was almost dark then. They had built up the fire and the Yankees still sitting around it and Father and the others standing over them with their pistols while two of them were taking the Yankees' pants and boots off. Ringo was still hollering off in the trees. "I reckon you better go and extricate Lieutenant Marengo," Father said. Only about that time Ringo's horse came bursting out with his blind eye looking big as a plate and still trotting in a circle with his knees up to his chin and then Ringo came out; he looked wilder than the horse, he was already talking, he was saying, "I'm gonter tell Granny on you, making my horse run—" when he saw the Yankees. His mouth was already open and he kind of squatted for a second, looking at them. Then he hollered, "Look *out!* Ketch um! Ketch um, Marse John! They stole Old Hundred and Tinney!"

We all ate supper together: Father and us and the Yankees in their underclothes. The officer talked to Father. He said, "Colonel, by God I believe you have fooled us. I dont believe there's another man of you but what I see."

"You might try to depart, and prove your point," Father said.

"Depart? Like this? And have every darky and old woman between here and Memphis shooting at us for ghosts? . . . . I suppose we can have our blankets to sleep in, cant we?"

"Certainly, Captain," Father said. "And with your permission I shall now retire and leave you to set about that business."

We went back into the darkness. We could see them about the fire, spreading their blankets on the ground. "What in the tarnation do you want with sixty prisoners, John?" one of Father's men said.

"I dont," Father said. He looked at me and Ringo. "You boys captured them; what do you want to do with them?"

"Shoot em," Ringo said. "This aint the first time me and Bayard ever shot Yankees."

"No," Father said. "I have a better plan than that. One that Joe Johnston will thank us for." He turned to the others behind him. "Have you got the muskets and ammunition?"

"Yes, Colonel," somebody said.

"Grub, boots, clothes?"

"Everything but the blankets, Colonel."

"We'll pick them up in the morning," Father said. "Now wait."

We sat there in the dark. The Yankees were going to bed. One of them went to the fire and picked up a stick. Then he stopped. He didn't turn his head and we didn't hear anything or see anybody move. Then he put the stick down again and came back to his blanket. "Wait," Father whispered. After a while the fire had died down. "Now listen," Father whispered. So we sat there in the dark and listened to the Yankees sneaking off into the bushes in their underclothes. Once we heard a splash and somebody cursing and then a sound like somebody had shut his hand over his mouth. Father didn't laugh out loud; he just sat there shaking. "Look out for moccasins," one of the others whispered behind us.

It must have taken them two hours to get done sneaking off into the bushes. Then Father said, "Everybody get a blanket and let's go to bed."

3.

The sun was high when he waked us. "Home for dinner," he said. And so after a while we came to the creek; we passed the hole where Ringo and I learned to swim and we began to pass the fields too and we came to where Ringo and I hid last summer and saw the first Yankee we ever saw and then we could see the house too and Ringo said, "Sartoris, here we is; let them that want Memphis take hit and keep hit bofe." Because we were looking at the house, it was like that day when we ran across the pasture and the house would not seem to get any nearer at all, we never saw the wagon at all, it was Father that saw it; it was coming up the road from Jefferson with Granny sitting thin and straight on the seat with Mrs Compson's rose cuttings wrapped in a new piece of paper in her hand, and Joby yelling and lashing the strange horses and Father stopping us at the gate with his hat raised while the wagon went in first. Granny didn't say a word. She just looked at Ringo and me and went on with us coming behind and she didn't stop at the house. The wagon went on into the orchard and stopped by the hole where we had dug the trunk up and still Granny didn't say a word, it was Father that got down and got into the wagon and took up one end of the trunk and said over his shoulder, "Jump up here, boys."

We buried the trunk again and we walked behind the wagon to the house. We went into the back parlor and Father put the musket back onto the pegs over the mantel and Granny put down Mrs Compson's rose cuttings and took off her hat and looked at Ringo and me. "Get the soap," she said.

"We haven't cussed any," I said. "Ask Father."

"They behaved all right, Miss Rosa," Father said.

Granny looked at us. Then she came and put her hand on me and then on Ringo. "Go up stairs——" she said.

"How did you and Joby manage to get those horses?" Father said.

Granny was looking at us. "I borrowed them," she said. "——upstairs and take off your——"

"Who from?" Father said.

Granny looked at Father for a second, then back at us. "I dont know. There was nobody there.—take off your Sunday clothes," she said.

It was hot the next day, so we only worked on the new pen until dinner and quit. It was even too hot for Ringo and me to ride our horses. Even at six oclock it was still hot, the resin was still cooking out of the front steps at six oclock. Father was sitting in his shirt sleeves and his stockings, with his feet on the porch railing and Ringo and I were sitting on the steps waiting for it to get cool enough to ride, when we saw them coming into the gate, about fifty of them, coming fast, and I remember how hot the blue coats looked. "Father," I said; "Father!"

"Dont run," Father said. "Ringo, you go around the house and catch Jupiter; Bayard you go through the house and tell Louvinia to have my boots and pistols at the back door, then you go and help Ringo. Dont run, now: walk."

Louvinia was shelling peas in the kitchen. When she stood up the bowl broke on the floor. "Oh Lord," she said. "Oh Lord. Again?"

I ran then. Ringo was just coming around the corner of the house; we both ran. Jupiter was in his stall, eating; he slashed out at us, his feet banged against the wall right by my head twice like pistols before Ringo jumped down from the hayrack onto his head. We got the bridle on him but he wouldn't take the saddle. "Get your horse and shove his blind side up——" I was hollering at Ringo when Father came in running, with his boots in his hand and we looked up the hill toward the house and saw one of them riding around the corner with a short carbine, carrying it in one hand like a lamp. "Get away," Father said. He went up onto Jupiter's bare back like a bird, holding him for a moment and looking down at us. He didn't speak loud at all; he didn't even sound in a hurry. "Take care of Granny," he said. "All right, Jupe. Let's go." Jupiter's head was pointing down the hallway toward the lattice half doors at the back; he went out again, out from between me and Ringo like he did yesterday, with Father already lifting him and I thinking, He cant jump through that little hole. Jupiter took the doors on his chest only they seemed to burst before he even touched them and I saw him and Father again like they were flying in the air, with broken planks whirling and spinning around them when they went out of sight. And then the Yankee rode into the barn and saw us and threw down with the carbine and shot at us point blank with one hand, like it was a pistol, and said, "Where'd he go, the rebel goddamn son of a bitch!"

Louvinia kept on trying to tell us about it while we were running and looking back at the smoke beginning to come out of the downstairs windows: "Marse John setting on the porch and them Yankees riding through the flowerbeds and say, 'Brother, we wanter know where the rebel John Sartoris live' and Marse John say 'Hey?' with his hand to his ear and his face look like he born loony like Unc Few Mitchell and Yankee say 'Sartoris. John Sartoris' and Marse John say 'Which? Say which?' until he know Yankee stood about all he going to and Marse John say 'Oh, John Sartoris; whyn't you say so in the first place' and Yankee cussing him for idiot fool and Marse John say 'Hey? How's that?' and Yankee say 'Nothing! Nothing! Show me where John Sartoris is fore I put rope round your neck too' and Marse John say 'Lemme git my shoes and I show you' and come into house limping and then run down the hall at me and say 'Boots and pistols, Louvinia.

Take care of Miss Rosa and the chillen' and I go to the door
but I just a nigger; Yankee say 'That woman's lying. I believe
that man was Sartoris himself. Go look in the barn quick and
see if that claybank stallion there'——" until Granny stopped
and began to shake her.

"Hush!" Granny said. "Hush! Cant you understand that
Loosh has shown them where the silver is buried? Call Joby.
Hurry!" She turned Louvinia toward the cabins and hit her
exactly like Father turned my horse and hit him when we rode
down the hill and into the Yankees, and then Granny turned
to run back toward the house, only now it was Louvinia
holding her and Granny trying to get away.

"Dont you go back there, Miss Rosa!" Louvinia said.
"Bayard, hold her; help me, Bayard! They'll kill her!"

"Let me go!" Granny said. "Call Joby! Loosh has shown
them where the silver is buried!" But we held her; she was
strong and thin and light as a cat, but we held her. The smoke
was boiling up now and we could hear it or them, something:
maybe all of them making one sound, the Yankees and the
fire. And then I saw Loosh. He was coming up from his
cabin, with a bundle on his shoulder tied up in a bandanna
and Philadelphy behind him, and his face looked like it had
that night last summer when Ringo and I looked into the
window and saw him after he came back from seeing the
Yankees. Granny stopped fighting. She said, "Loosh."

He stopped and looked at her; he looked like he was asleep,
like he didn't even see us or was seeing something we
couldn't. But Philadelphy saw us; she cringed back behind
him, looking at Granny. "I tried to stop him, Miss Rosa," she
said. "Fore God I tried."

"Loosh," Granny said. "Are you going too?"

"Yes," Loosh said. "I going. I done been freed; God's own
angel proclamated me free and gonter general me to Jordan. I
dont belong to John Sartoris now; I belongs to me and God."

"But the silver belongs to John Sartoris," Granny said.
"Who are you to give it away?"

"You ax me that?" Loosh said. "Where John Sartoris?
Whyn't he come and ax me that? Let God ax John Sartoris
who the man name that give me to him. Let the man that
buried me in the black dark ax that of the man what dug me

free." He wasn't looking at us; I dont think he could even see us. He went on.

"Fore God, Miss Rosa," Philadelphy said. "I tried to stop him. I done tried."

"Dont you go, Philadelphy," Granny said. "Dont you know he's leading you into misery and starvation?"

Philadelphy began to cry. "I knows hit. I knows whut they tole him cant be true. But he my husband. I reckon I got to go with him."

They went on. Louvinia had come back; she and Ringo were behind us. The smoke boiled up, yellow and slow and turning coppercolored in the sunset like dust; it was like dust from a road above the feet that made it and then went on, boiling up slow and hanging and waiting to die away. "The bastuds, Granny!" I said. "The bastuds!" Then we were all three saying it, Granny and me and Ringo, saying it together: "The bastuds!" we cried. "The bastuds! The bastuds!"

RAID

I.

Granny wrote the note with pokeberry juice. "Take it straight to Mrs Compson and come straight back," she said. "Dont you all stop anywhere."

"You mean we got to *walk*?" Ringo said. "You gonter make us walk all them four miles to Jefferson and back, with them two horses standing in the lot doing nothing?"

"They are borrowed horses," Granny said. "I'm going to take care of them until I can return them."

"I reckon you calls starting out to be gone you dont know where and you dont know how long taking care of——" Ringo said.

"Do you want me to whup you?" Louvinia said.

"Nome," Ringo said.

We walked to Jefferson and gave Mrs Compson the note and got the hat and the parasol and the hand mirror and walked back home. That afternoon we greased the wagon and that night after supper Granny got the pokeberry juice again and wrote on a scrap of paper *Colonel Nathaniel G. Dick. —th Ohio Cavalry* and folded it and pinned it inside her dress. "Now I wont forget it," she said.

"If you was to, I reckon these hellion boys can remind you," Louvinia said. "I reckon they aint forgot him. Walking in that door just in time to keep them others from snatching them out from under your dress and nailing them to the barn door like two coon hides."

"Yes," Granny said. "Now we'll go to bed."

We lived in Joby's cabin then, with a red quilt nailed by one edge to a rafter and hanging down to make two rooms. Joby was waiting with the wagon when Granny came out with Mrs Compson's hat on and got into the wagon and told Ringo to open the parasol and took up the reins. Then we all stopped and watched Joby stick something into the wagon, beneath the quilts; it was the barrel and the iron parts of the musket after Ringo and I found it in the ashes of the house. "What's that?" Granny said. Joby didn't look at her.

"Maybe if They just seed the end of hit They mought think hit was the whole gun," he said.

"Then what?" Granny said. Joby didn't look at anybody now.

"I was just doing what I could to help git the silver and the mules back," he said. Louvinia didn't say anything either. She and Granny just looked at Joby. After a while he took the musket barrel out of the wagon. Granny gathered up the reins.

"Take him with you," Louvinia said. "Leastways he can tend the horses."

"No," Granny said. "Dont you see I have got about all I can look after now?"

"Then you stay here and lemme go," Louvinia said. "I'll git um back."

"No," Granny said. "I'll be all right. I shall inquire until I find Colonel Dick and then we will load the chest in the wagon and Loosh can lead the mules and we will come back home."

Then Louvinia began to act just like Uncle Buck McCaslin did the morning we started to Memphis. She stood there holding to the wagon wheel and looked at Granny from under Father's old hat and began to holler. "Dont you waste no time on colonels or nothing!" she hollered. "You tell them niggers to send Loosh to you and you tell him to get that chest and them mules and then you whup him!" The wagon was moving now, she had turned loose the wheel and she walked along beside it, hollering at Granny. "Take that pair-sawl and wear hit out on him!"

"All right," Granny said. The wagon went on; we passed the ash pile and the chimneys standing up out of it: Ringo and I found the insides of the big clock too. The sun was just coming up, shining back on the chimneys; I could still see Louvinia between them, standing in front of the cabin, shading her eyes with her hand to watch us. Joby was still standing behind her, holding the musket barrel. They had broken the gates clean off and then we were in the road.

"Dont you want me to drive?" I said.

"I'll drive," Granny said. "These are borrowed horses."

"Case even Yankee could look at um and tell they couldn't keep up with even a walking army," Ringo said. "And I like to know how anybody can hurt this team lessen he aint got strength enough to keep um from laying down in the road and getting run over with they own wagon."

We drove until dark, and camped. By sunup we were on the road again. "You better let me drive a while," I said.

"I'll drive," Granny said. "I was the one who borrowed them."

"You can tote this pairsawl a while, if you want something to do," Ringo said. "And give my arm a rest." I took the parasol and he laid down in the wagon and put his hat over his eyes. "Call me when we gitting nigh to Hawkhurst," he said, "so I can commence to look out for that railroad you tells about."

That was how he travelled for the next six days—lying on his back in the wagon bed with his hat over his eyes, sleeping, or taking his turn holding the parasol over Granny and keeping me awake by talking of the railroad which he had never seen though which I had seen that Christmas we spent at Hawkhurst. That's how Ringo and I were. We were almost the same age, and Father always said that Ringo was a little smarter than I was, but that didn't count with us, any-more than the difference in the color of our skins counted. What counted was, what one of us had done or seen that the other had not, and ever since that Christmas I had been ahead of Ringo because I had seen a railroad, a locomotive. Only I know now it was more than that with Ringo, though neither of us was to see the proof of my belief for some time yet and we were not to recognise it as such even then. It was as if Ringo felt it too and that the railroad, the rushing locomotive which he hoped to see symbolised it—the motion, the impulse to move which had already seethed to a head among his people, darker than themselves, reasonless, following and seeking a delusion, a dream, a bright shape which they could not know since there was nothing in their heritage, nothing in the memory even of the old men to tell the others, 'This is what we will find'; he nor they could not have known what it was yet it was there—one of those impulses inexplicable yet invincible which appear among races of people at intervals and drive them to pick up and leave all security and familiarity of earth and home and start out, they dont know where, empty handed, blind to everything but a hope and a doom.

We went on; we didn't go fast. Or maybe it seemed slow because we had got into a country where nobody seemed to live at all; all that day we didn't even see a house. I didn't ask and Granny didn't say; she just sat there under the parasol with Mrs Compson's hat on and the horses walking and even our own dust moving ahead of us; after a while even Ringo sat up and looked around. "We on the wrong road," he said. "Aint even nobody live here, let alone pass here."

But after a while the hills stopped, the road ran out flat and straight and all of a sudden Ringo hollered, "Look out! Here they come again to git these uns!" We saw it too then, a cloud of dust away to the west, moving slow, too slow for men riding, and then the road we were on ran square into a big broad one running straight on into the east as the railroad at Hawkhurst did when Granny and I were there that Christmas before the War; all of a sudden I remembered it.

"This is the road to Hawkhurst," I said. But Ringo was not listening; he was looking at the dust, and the wagon stopped now in the road with the horses' heads hanging and our dust overtaking us again and the big dustcloud coming slow up in the west.

"Cant you see um coming?" Ringo hollered. "Git on away from here!"

"They aint Yankees," Granny said. "The Yankees have

already been here." Then we saw it too: a burned house like ours; three chimneys standing above a mound of ashes and then we saw a white woman and a child looking at us from a cabin behind them. Granny looked at the dustcloud, then she looked at the empty broad road going on into the east. "This is the way," she said.

We went on. It seemed like we went slower than ever now, with the dustcloud behind us and the burned houses and gins and thrown down fences on either side and the white women and children—we never saw a nigger at all—watching us from the nigger cabins where they lived now like we lived at home; we didn't stop. "Poor folks," Granny said. "I wish we had enough to share with them."

At sunset we drew off the road and camped; Ringo was looking back. "Whatever hit is, we done went off and left hit," he said. "I dont see no dust." We slept in the wagon this time, all three of us; I dont know what time it was, only that all of a sudden I was awake. Granny was already sitting up in the wagon, I could see her head against the branches and the stars; all of a sudden all three of us were sitting up in the wagon, listening. They were coming up the road. It sounded like about fifty of them; we could hear the feet hurrying, and a kind of panting murmur. It was not singing exactly, it was not that loud; it was just a sound, a breathing, a kind of gasping murmuring chant and the feet whispering fast in the deep dust. I could hear women too and then all of a sudden I began to smell them. "Niggers," I whispered.

"Shhhhhh," I whispered. We couldn't see them and they did not see us; maybe they didn't even look, just walking fast in the dark with that panting hurrying murmuring, going on. And then the sun rose and we went on too, along that big broad empty road between the burned houses and gins and fences. Before it had been like passing through a country where nobody had ever lived; now it was like passing through one where everybody had died at the same moment. That night we waked up three times and sat up in the wagon in the dark and heard niggers pass in the road. The last time it was after dawn and we had already fed the horses. It was a big crowd of them this time and they sounded like they were running, like they had to run to keep ahead of daylight. Then they were gone. Ringo and I had taken up the harness again when Granny said, "Wait. Hush." It was just one; we could hear her panting and sobbing, and then we heard another sound. Granny began to get down from the wagon. "She fell," she said. "You all hitch up and come on."

When we turned into the road the woman was kind of crouched beside it, holding something in her arms and Granny standing beside her. It was a baby, a few months old; she held it like she thought maybe Granny was going to take it away from her. "I been sick and I couldn't keep up," she said. "They went off and left me."

"Is your husband with them?" Granny said.

"Yessum," the woman said. "They's all there."

"Who do you belong to?" Granny said. Then she didn't answer. She squatted there in the dust, crouched over the baby. "If I give you something to eat, will you turn around and go back home?" Granny said. Still she didn't answer. She just squatted there. "You see you cant keep up with them and that they aint going to wait for you," Granny said. "Do you want to die here in the road for buzzards to eat?" But she didn't even look at Granny, she just squatted there.

"Hit's Jordan we coming to," she said. "Jesus gonter see me that far."

"Get in the wagon," Granny said. She got in, she squatted again just like she had in the road, holding the baby and not looking at anything, just hunkered down and swaying on her hams as the wagon rocked and jolted. The sun was up, we went down a long hill and began to cross a creek bottom.

"I'll get out here," she said. Granny stopped the wagon and she got out. There was nothing at all but the thick gum and cypress and thick underbrush still full of shadow.

"You go back home, girl," Granny said. She just stood there. "Hand me the basket," Granny said. I handed it to her and she opened it and gave the woman a piece of bread and meat. We went on; we began to mount the hill. When I looked back she was still standing there, holding the baby and the bread and meat Granny had given her. She was not looking at us. "Were the others there in that bottom?" Granny asked Ringo.

"Yessum," Ringo said. "She done found um. Reckon she gonter lose um again tonight though."

We went on; we mounted the hill and crossed the crest of it. When I looked back this time the road was empty. That was the morning of the sixth day.

2.

Late that afternoon we were descending again; we came around a curve in the late level shadows and our own quiet dust and I saw the graveyard on the knoll and the marble shaft at Uncle Dennison's grave; there was a dove somewhere in the cedars. Ringo was asleep again under his hat in the wagon bed but he waked as soon as I spoke, even though I didn't speak loud and didn't speak to him. "There's Hawkhurst," I said.

"Hawkhurst?" he said, sitting up. "Where's that railroad?" on his knees now and looking for something which he would have to find in order to catch up with me and which he would have to recognise only through hearsay when he saw it: "Where is it? Where?"

"You'll have to wait for it," I said.

"Seem like I been waiting on hit all my life," he said. "I reckon you'll tell me next the Yankees done moved hit too."

The sun was going down. Because suddenly I saw it shining level across the place where the house should have been and there was no house there. And I was not surprised; I remember that; I was just feeling sorry for Ringo, since (I was just fourteen then) if the house was gone, they would have taken the railroad too, since anybody would rather have a railroad than a house. We didn't stop; we just looked quietly at the same mound of ashes, the same four chimneys standing gaunt and blackened in the sun like the chimneys at home. When we reached the gate Cousin Denny was running down the drive toward us. He was ten; he ran up to the wagon with his eyes round and his mouth already open for hollering. "Denny," Granny said. "Do you know us?"

"Yessum," Cousin Denny said. He looked at me, hollering. "Great God, come——"

"Where's your mother?" Granny said.

"In Jingus' cabin," Cousin Denny said; he didn't even look at Granny. "They burnt the house.—Great God," he hollered, "come see what They done to the railroad!"

We ran, all three of us. Granny hollered something and I turned and put the parasol back into the wagon and hollered Yessum back at her and ran on and caught up with Cousin Denny and Ringo in the road and we ran on over the hill and then it came in sight. When Granny and I were here before Cousin Denny showed me the railroad but he was so little then that Jingus had to carry him. It was the straightest thing I ever saw, running straight and empty and quiet through a long empty gash cut through the trees and the ground too and full of sunlight like water in a river only straighter than any river, with the crossties cut off even and smooth and neat and the light shining on the rails like on two spider threads running straight on to where you couldn't even see that far. It looked clean and neat, like the yard behind Louvinia's cabin after she had swept it on Saturday morning, with those two little threads that didn't look strong enough for anything to run on, running straight and fast and light like they were getting up speed to jump clean off the world. Jingus knew when the train would come, he held my hand and carried Cousin Denny and we stood between the rails and he showed us where it would come from, and then he showed us where the shadow of a dead pine would come to a stob he had driven in the ground and then you would hear the whistle. And we got back and watched the shadow and then we heard it; it whistled and then it got louder and louder fast and Jingus went to the track and took his hat off and held it out with his face turned back toward us and his mouth hollering "Watch now! Watch!" even after we couldn't hear him for the train; and then it passed. It came roaring up and went past; the river they had cut through the trees was all full of smoke and noise and sparks and jumping brass and then empty again and just Jingus' old hat bouncing and jumping along the empty track behind it like the hat was alive. But this time what I saw was something that looked like piles of black straws heaped up every few yards and we ran into the cut and we could see where they had dug the ties up and piled them and set them on fire. But Cousin Denny was still hollering.

"Come see what They done to the rails," he said. They were back in the trees; it looked like four or five men had taken each rail and tied it around a tree like you knot a green cornstalk around a wagon stake, and Ringo was hollering too now.

"What's them?" he hollered. "What's them?"

"That's what it runs on!" Cousin Denny hollered.

"You mean hit have to come in here and run up and down around these here trees like a squirrel?" Ringo hollered. Then we all heard the horse at once; we just had time to look when Bobolink came up the road out of the trees and went across the railroad and into the trees again like a bird, with Cousin Drusilla riding astride like a man and sitting straight and light as a willow branch in the wind. They said she was the best woman rider in the country.

"There's Dru!" Cousin Denny hollered. "Come on. She's been up to the river to see them niggers! Come on!" He and Ringo ran again. When I passed the chimneys they were just running into the stable. Cousin Drusilla had already unsaddled Bobolink and she was rubbing him down with a croker sack when I came in. Cousin Denny was still hollering, "What did you see? What are they doing?"

"I'll tell about it at the house," Cousin Drusilla said. Then she saw me. She was not tall, it was the way she stood and walked. She had on pants, like a man. She was the best woman rider in the country; when Granny and I were here that Christmas before the War and Gavin Breckbridge had just given Bobolink to her, they looked fine together; it didn't need Jingus to say that they were the finest looking couple in Alabama or Mississippi either. But Gavin was killed at Shiloh and so they didn't marry. She came and put her hand on my shoulder. "Hello," she said. "Hello, John Sartoris." She looked at Ringo. "Is this Ringo?" she said.

"That's what they tells me," Ringo said. "What about that railroad?"

"How are you?" Cousin Drusilla said.

"I manages to stand hit," Ringo said. "What about that railroad?"

"I'll tell you about that tonight too," Drusilla said.

"I'll finish Bobolink for you," I said.

"Will you?" she said. She went to Bobolink's head. "Will you stand for Cousin Bayard, lad?" she said. "I'll see you all at the house, then," she said. She went out.

"Yawl sho must a had this horse hid good when the Yankees come," Ringo said.

"This horse?" Cousin Denny said. "Aint no damn Yankee going to fool with Dru's horse no more." He didn't holler now, but pretty soon he began again. "When They come to burn the house Dru grabbed the pistol and run out here, she had on her Sunday dress and Them right behind her, she run in here and she jumped on Bobolink bareback without even waiting for the bridle and one of Them right there in the door hollering Stop and Dru said Get away or I'll ride you down and Him hollering Stop Stop with his pistol out too——" Cousin Denny was hollering good now: "——and Dru leaned down to Bobolink's ear and said Kill him Bob and the Yankee jumped back just in time; the lot was full of Them too and Dru stopped Bobolink and jumped down in her Sunday dress and put the pistol to Bobolink's ear and said I cant shoot you all because I haven't enough bullets and it wouldn't do any good anyway but I wont need but one shot for the horse and which shall it be? So They burned the house and went away——" He was hollering good now, with Ringo staring at him so you could have raked Ringo's eyes off his face with a stick. "Come on," Cousin Denny hollered. "Les go hear about them niggers at the river!"

"I been having to hear about niggers all my life," Ringo said. "I got to hear about that railroad."

When we reached the house Cousin Drusilla was already talking, telling Granny mostly, though it was not about the railroad. Her hair was cut short; it looked like Father's would when he would tell Granny about him and the men cutting each other's hair with a bayonet. She was sunburned and her hands were hard and scratched like a man's that works. She was telling Granny mostly: "They began to pass in the road yonder while the house was still burning. We couldn't count them: men and women carrying children who couldn't walk and carrying old men and women who should have been at home waiting to die. They were singing, walking along the road singing, not even looking to either side; the dust didn't even settle for two days because all that night they still passed; we sat up listening to them, and the next morning every few yards along the road would be the old ones who couldn't keep up anymore, sitting or lying down and even crawling along, calling to the others to help them, and the others, the young strong ones, not stopping, not even looking at them; I dont think they even heard or saw them. Going to Jordan, they told me. Going to cross Jordan——"

"That was what Loosh said," Granny said. "That General Sherman was leading them all to Jordan."

"Yes," Cousin Drusilla said. "The river. They have stopped there; it's like a river itself dammed up. The Yankees have thrown out a brigade of cavalry to hold them back while they build the bridge to cross the infantry and artillery; they are all right until they get up there and see or smell the water. That's when they go mad. Not fighting; it's like they cant even see the horses shoving them back and the scabbards beating them, it's like they cant see anything but the water and the other bank. They aren't angry, aren't fighting: just men women and children singing and chanting and trying to get to that unfinished bridge or even down into the water itself and the cavalry beating them back with sword scabbards. I dont know when they have eaten, nobody knows just how far some of them have come, they just pass here without food or anything, exactly as they rose up from whatever they were doing when the spirit or the voice or whatever it was told them to go. They stop during the day and rest in the woods, then at night they move again; we will hear them later: I'll wake you, marching on up the road until the cavalry stops them; there was an officer, a major, who finally took time to see I wasn't one of his men; he said, 'Cant you do anything with them? Promise them anything to go back home?' But it was like they couldn't see me or hear me speaking; it was only that water and that bank on the other side. But you will see for yourself tomorrow when we go back."

"Drusilla," Aunt Louisa said, "you're not going back tomorrow or any other time."

"They are going to mine the bridge and blow it up when the army has crossed," Cousin Drusilla said. "Nobody knows what they will do then."

"But we cannot be responsible," Aunt Louisa said. "The Yankees brought it on themselves; let them pay the price."

"Those negroes are not Yankees, Mother," Cousin Drusilla said. "At least there will be one person there who is not a Yankee either." She looked at Granny. "Four, counting Bayard and Ringo."

Aunt Louisa looked at Granny. "Rosa, you shant go. I forbid it. Brother John will thank me to do so."

"I reckon I will," Granny said. "I've got to get the silver anyway."

"And the mules," Ringo said; "dont forget them. And dont yawl worry about Granny. She cide what she want and then she kneel down about ten seconds and tell God what she aim to do and then she git up and do hit. And them that dont like hit can git outen the way or git tromped. But that railroad—"

"And now I reckon we better go to bed," Granny said. But we didn't go to bed then. I had to hear about the railroad too; possibly it was more the need to keep even with Ringo (or even ahead of him, since I had seen the railroad when it was a railroad, which he had not) than a boy's affinity for smoke and fury and thunder and speed. We sat there in that slave cabin partitioned, like Louvinia's cabin at home, into two rooms by that suspended quilt beyond which Aunt Louisa and Granny were already in bed and where Cousin Denny should have been too except for the evening's dispensation he had received, listening too who did not need to hear it again since he had been there to see it when it happened;— we sat there, Ringo and I, listening to Cousin Drusilla and staring at each other with the same amazed and incredulous question: *Where could we have been at that moment? What could we have been doing, even a hundred miles away, not to have sensed, felt this, paused to look at one another, aghast and uplifted, while it was happening?* Because this, to us, was it. Ringo and I had seen Yankees; we had shot at one; we had crouched like two rats and heard Granny, unarmed and not even rising from her chair, rout a whole regiment of them from the library. And we had heard about battles and fighting and seen those who had taken part in them, not only in the person of Father when once or twice each year and without warning he

would appear on the strong gaunt horse, arrived from beyond
that cloudbank region which Ringo believed was Tennessee,
but in the persons of other men who returned home with
actual arms and legs missing. But that was it: men had lost
arms and legs in sawmills; old men had been telling young
men and boys about wars and fighting before they discovered
how to write it down: and what petty precisian to quibble
about locations in space or in chronology, who to care or
insist *Now come, old man, tell the truth: did you see this? were you
really there?* Because wars are wars: the same exploding powder when there was powder, the same thrust and parry of iron
when there was not—one tale, one telling, the same as the
next or the one before. So we knew a war existed; we had to
believe that, just as we had to believe that the name for the
sort of life we had led for the last three years was hardship
and suffering. Yet we had no proof of it. In fact, we had even
less than no proof; we had had thrust into our faces the very
shabby and unavoidable obverse of proof, who had seen
Father (and the other men too) return home, afoot like
tramps or on crowbait horses, in faded and patched (and at
times obviously stolen) clothing, preceded by no flags nor
drums and followed not even by two men to keep step with
one another, in coats bearing no glitter of golden braid and
with scabbards in which no sword reposed, actually almost
sneaking home to spend two or three or seven days performing actions not only without glory (plowing land, repairing
fences, killing meat for the smoke house) and in which they
had no skill but the very necessity for which was the fruit of
the absent occupations from which, returning, they bore no
proof—actions in the very clumsy performance of which
Father's whole presence seemed (to us, Ringo and me) to
emanate a kind of humility and apology, as if he were saying,
"Believe me, boys; take my word for it: there's more to it
than this, no matter what it looks like. I cant prove it, so
you'll just have to believe me." And then to have it happen,
where we could have been there to see it, and were not: and
this no poste and riposte of sweat-reeking cavalry which all
war-telling is full of, no galloping thunder of guns to wheel
up and unlimber and crash and crash into the lurid grime-
glare of their own demon-served inferno which even children

would recognise, no ragged lines of gaunt and shrill-yelling infantry beneath a tattered flag which is a very part of that child's make-believe. Because this was it: an interval, a space, in which the toad-squatting guns, the panting men and the trembling horses paused, amphitheatric about the embattled land, beneath the fading fury of the smoke and the puny yelling, and permitted the sorry business which had dragged on for three years now to be congealed into an irrevocable instant and put to an irrevocable gambit, not by two regiments or two batteries or even two generals, but by two locomotives.

Cousin Drusilla told it while we sat there in the cabin which smelled of new white wash and even (still faintly) of negroes. She probably told us the reason for it (she must have known)—what point of strategy, what desperate gamble not for preservation, since hope of that was gone, but at least for prolongation, which it served. But that meant nothing to us. We didn't hear, we didn't even listen; we sat there in that cabin and waited and watched that railroad which no longer existed, which was now a few piles of charred ties among which green grass was already growing, a few threads of steel knotted and twisted about the trunks of trees and already annealing into the living bark, becoming one and indistinguishable with the jungle growth which had now accepted it, but which for us ran still pristine and intact and straight and narrow as the path to glory itself, as it ran for all of them who were there and saw when Ringo and I were not. Drusilla told about that too; 'Atlanta' and 'Chattanooga' were in it—the names, the beginning and the end—but they meant no more to us than they did to the other watchers—the black and the white, the old men, the children, the women who would not know for months yet if they were widows or childless or not—gathered, warned by grapevine, to see the momentary flash and glare of indomitable spirit starved by three years free of the impeding flesh. She told it (and now Ringo and I began to see it; we were there too)—the roundhouse in Atlanta where the engine waited; we were there, we were of them who (they must have) would slip into the roundhouse in the dark, to caress the wheels and pistons and iron flanks, to whisper to it in the darkness like lover to mistress or rider to

horse, cajoling ruthlessly of her or it one supreme effort in
return for making which she or it would receive annihilation
(and who would not pay that price), cajoling, whispering, ca-
ressing her or it toward the one moment; we were of them—
the old men, the children, the women—gathered to watch,
drawn and warned by that grapevine of the oppressed,
deprived of everything now save the will and the ability to
deceive, turning inscrutable and impassive secret faces to the
blue enemies who lived among them. Because they knew it
was going to happen; Drusilla told that too: how they
seemed to know somehow the very moment when the engine
left Atlanta; it was as if the gray generals themselves had sent
the word, had told them, "You have suffered for three years;
now we will give to you and your children a glimpse of that
for which you have suffered and been denied." Because that's
all it was. I know that now. Even the successful passage of a
hundred engines with trains of cars could not have changed
the situation or its outcome; certainly not two free engines
shrieking along a hundred yards apart up that drowsing solitude of track which had seen no smoke and heard no bell in
more than a year. I dont think it was intended to do that. It
was like a meeting between two iron knights of the old time,
not for material gain but for principle—honor denied with
honor, courage denied with courage—the deed done not for
the end but for the sake of the doing, put to the ultimate test
and proving nothing save the finality of death and the vanity
of all endeavor. We saw it, we were there, as if Drusilla's voice
had transported us to the wandering light-ray in space in
which was still held the furious shadow—the brief section of
track which existed inside the scope of a single pair of eyes
and nowhere else, coming from nowhere and having, needing, no destination, the engine not coming into view but arrested in human sight in thunderous yet dreamy fury, lonely,
inviolate and forlorn, wailing through its whistle precious
steam which could have meant seconds at the instant of passing and miles at the end of its journey (and cheap at ten times
this price)—the flaring and streaming smoke stack, the tossing bell, the starred Saint Andrew's cross nailed to the cab
roof, the wheels and the flashing driving rods on which the
brass fittings glinted like the golden spurs themselves—then

gone, vanished. Only not gone or vanished either, so long as there should be defeated or the descendants of defeated to tell it or listen to the telling.

"The other one, the Yankee one, was right behind it," Drusilla said. "But they never caught it. Then the next day they came and tore the track up. They tore the track up so we couldn't do it again; they could tear the track up but they couldn't take back the fact that we had done it. They couldn't take that from us."

We—Ringo and I—knew what she meant; we stood together just outside the door before Ringo went on to Missy Lena's cabin, where he was to sleep. "I know what you thinking," Ringo said. Father was right; he was smarter than me. "But I heard good as you did. I heard every word you heard."

"Only I saw the track before they tore it up. I saw where it was going to happen."

"But you didn't know hit was fixing to happen when you seed the track. So nemmine that. I heard. And I reckon they aint gonter git that away from me, neither."

He went on, then I went back into the house and behind the quilt where Denny was already asleep on the pallet. Drusilla was not there only I didn't have time to wonder where she was because I was thinking how I probably wouldn't be able to go to sleep at all now though it was late. Then it was later still and Denny was shaking me and I remember how I thought then that he did not seem to need sleep either, that just by having been exposed for three or four seconds to war he had even at just ten acquired that quality which Father and the other men brought back from the front—the power to do without sleep and food both, needing only the opportunity to endure. "Dru says to come on out doors if you want to hear them passing," he whispered.

She was outside the cabin; she hadn't undressed even. I could see her in the starlight: her short jagged hair and the man's shirt and pants. "Hear them?" she said. We could hear it again, like we had in the wagon—the hurrying feet, the sound like they were singing in panting whispers, hurrying on past the gate and dying away up the road. "That's the third tonight," Cousin Drusilla said. "Two passed while I was down at the gate. You were tired and so I didn't wake you before."

"I thought it was late," I said. "You haven't been to bed even. Have you?"

"No," she said. "I've quit sleeping."

"Quit sleeping?" I said. "Why?"

She looked at me. I was as tall as she was; we couldn't see one another's face: it was just her head with the short jagged hair like she had cut it herself without bothering about a mirror, and her neck that had got thin and hard like her hands since Granny and I were here before. "I'm keeping a dog quiet," she said.

"A dog?" I said. "I haven't seen any dog."

"No. It's quiet now," she said. "It doesn't bother anybody anymore now. I just have to show it the stick now and then." She was looking at me. "Why not stay awake now? Who wants to sleep now, with so much happening, so much to see? Living used to be dull, you see. Stupid. You lived in the same house your father was born in and your father's sons and daughters had the sons and daughters of the same negro slaves to nurse and coddle, and then you grew up and you fell in love with your acceptable young man and in time you would marry him, in your mother's wedding gown perhaps and with the same silver for presents she had received, and then you settled down forever more while your husband got children on your body for you to feed and bathe and dress until they grew up too; and then you and your husband died quietly and were buried together maybe on a summer afternoon just before suppertime. Stupid, you see. But now you can see for yourself how it is, it's fine now; you dont have to worry now about the house and the silver because they get burned up and carried away, and you dont have to worry about the negroes because they tramp the roads all night waiting for a chance to drown in homemade Jordan, and you dont have to worry about getting children on your body to bathe and feed and change because the young men can ride away and get killed in the fine battles and you dont even have to sleep alone, you dont even have to sleep at all and so all you have to do is show the stick to the dog now and then and say Thank God for nothing. You see? . . . . There.

They've gone now. And you'd better get back to bed so we can get an early start in the morning. It will take a long time to get through them."

"You're not coming in now?" I said.

"Not yet," she said. But we didn't move. And then she put her hand on my shoulder. "Listen," she said. "When you go back home and see Uncle John, ask him to let me come there and ride with his troop. Tell him I can ride, and maybe I can learn to shoot. Will you?"

"Yes," I said. "I'll tell him you are not afraid too."

"Aren't I?" she said. "I hadn't thought about it. It doesn't matter, anyway. Just tell him I can ride and that I dont get tired." Her hand was on my shoulder; it felt thin and hard. "Will you do that for me? Ask him to let me come, Bayard."

"All right," I said. Then I said, "I hope he will let you."

"So do I," she said. "Now you go back to bed. Good-night."

I went back to the pallet and then to sleep; again it was Denny shaking me awake; by sunup we were on the road again, Drusilla on Bobolink riding beside the wagon. But not for long.

We began to see the dust almost at once and I even believed that I could already smell them though the distance between us did not appreciably decrease, since they were travelling almost as fast as we were. We never did overtake them, just as you do not overtake a tide. You just keep moving, then suddenly you know that the set is about you, beneath you, overtaking you, as if the slow and ruthless power, become aware of your presence at last, had dropped back a tentacle, a feeler, to gather you in and sweep you remorselessly on. Singly, in couples, in groups and families they began to appear from the woods, ahead of us, alongside of us and behind; they covered and hid from sight the road exactly as an infiltration of flood water would have, hiding the road from sight and then the very wheels of the wagon in which we rode, our two horses as well as Bobolink breasting slowly on, enclosed by a mass of heads and shoulders—men and women carrying babies and dragging older children by the hand, old men and women on improvised sticks and crutches, and very old ones sitting beside the road and even calling to us when we passed; there was one old woman who even walked along beside the wagon, holding to the bed and begging Granny to at least let her see the river before she died.

But mostly they did not look at us. We might not have even been there. We did not even ask them to let us through because we could look at their faces and know they couldn't have heard us. They were not singing yet, they were just hurrying, while our horses pushed slow through them, among the blank eyes not looking at anything out of faces caked with dust and sweat, breasting slowly and terrifically through them as if we were driving in midstream up a creek full of floating logs and the dust and the smell of them everywhere and Granny in Mrs Compson's hat sitting bolt upright under the parasol which Ringo held and looking sicker and sicker, and it already afternoon though we didn't know it anymore than we knew how many miles we had come. Then all of a sudden we reached the river, where the cavalry was holding them back from the bridge. It was just a sound at first, like wind, like it might be in the dust itself. We didn't even know what it was until we saw Drusilla holding Bobolink reined back, her face turned toward us wan and small above the dust and her mouth open and crying thinly: "Look out, Aunt Rosa! Oh, look out!"

It was like we all heard it at the same time—we in the wagon and on the horse, they all around us in the sweat-caking dust. They made a kind of long wailing sound, and then I felt the whole wagon lift clear of the ground and begin to rush forward. I saw our old rib-gaunted horses standing on their hind feet one minute and then turned sideways in the traces the next, and Drusilla leaning forward a little and taut as a pistol hammer holding Bobolink, and I saw men and women and children going down under the horses and we could feel the wagon going over them and we could hear them screaming. And we couldn't stop anymore than if the earth had tilted up and was sliding us all down toward the river.

It went fast, like that, like it did every time anybody named Sartoris or Millard came within sight hearing or smell of Yankees, as if Yankees were not a people nor a belief nor even a form of behavior, but instead were a kind of gully, precipice, into which Granny and Ringo and I were sucked pell-mell every time we got close to them. It was sunset; now there was a high bright rosy glow quiet beyond the trees and shining on the river, and now we could see it plain—the tide of niggers dammed back from the entrance to the bridge by a detachment of cavalry, the river like a sheet of rosy glass beneath the delicate arch of the bridge which the tail of the Yankee column was just crossing. They were in silhouette, running tiny and high above the placid water; I remember the horses' and mules' heads all mixed up among the bayonets, and the barrels of cannon tilted up and kind of rushing slow across the high peaceful rosy air like split-cane clothespins being jerked along a clothesline, and the singing everywhere up and down the river bank, with the voices of the women coming out of it thin and high: "Glory! Glory! Hallelujah!"

They were fighting now, the horses rearing and shoving against them, the troopers beating at them with their scabbards, holding them clear of the bridge while the last of the infantry began to cross; all of a sudden there was an officer beside the wagon, holding his scabbarded sword by the little end like a stick and hanging onto the wagon and screaming at us. I dont know where he came from, how he ever got to us, but there he was with his little white face with a stubble of beard and a long streak of blood on it, bareheaded and with his mouth open. "Get back!" he shrieked. "Get back! We're going to blow the bridge!" screaming right into Granny's face while she shouted back at him with Mrs Compson's hat knocked to one side of her head and hers and the Yankee's faces not a yard apart:

"I want my silver! I'm John Sartoris' mother-in-law! Send Colonel Dick to me!" Then the Yankee officer was gone, right in the middle of shouting and beating at the nigger heads with his sabre, with his little bloody shrieking face and all. I dont know where he went anymore than I know where he came from; he just vanished still holding onto the wagon and flailing about him with the sabre, and then Cousin Drusilla was there on Bobolink; she had our nigh horse by the headstall and was trying to turn the wagon sideways. I started to jump down to help. "Stay in the wagon," she said. She didn't shout; she just said it. "Take the lines and turn them."

When we got the wagon turned sideways we stopped. And then for a minute I thought we were going backward, until I saw it was the niggers. Then I saw that the cavalry had broken; I saw the whole mob of it—horses and men and sabres and niggers—rolling on toward the end of the bridge like when a dam breaks, for about ten clear seconds behind the last of the infantry. And then the bridge vanished. I was looking right at it; I could see the clear gap between the infantry and the wave of niggers and cavalry, with a little empty thread of bridge joining them together in the air above the water, and then there was a bright glare and I felt my insides suck and a clap of wind hit me on the back of the head. I didn't hear anything at all. I just sat there in the wagon with a funny buzzing in my ears and a funny taste in my mouth, and watched little toy men and horses and pieces of plank floating along in the air above the water. But I didn't hear anything at all; I couldn't even hear Cousin Drusilla. She was right beside the wagon now, leaning toward us, her mouth urgent and wide and no sound coming out of it at all.

"What?" I said.

"Stay in the wagon!"

"I cant hear you!" I said. That's what I said, that's what I was thinking; I didn't realise even then that the wagon was moving again. But then I did; it was like the whole long bank of the river had turned and risen under us and was rushing us down toward the water, we sitting in the wagon and rushing down toward the water on another river of faces that couldn't see or hear either. Cousin Drusilla had the nigh horse by the bridle again and I dragged at them too and Granny was standing up in the wagon and beating at the faces with Mrs Compson's parasol, and then the whole rotten bridle came off in Cousin Drusilla's hand. "Get away!" I said. "The wagon will float!"

"Yes," she said, "it will float. Just stay in it. Watch Aunt Rosa and Ringo."

"Yes," I said. Then she was gone, we passed her, turned and holding Bobolink like a rock again and leaning down talking to him and patting his cheek; she was gone. Then maybe the bank did cave, I dont know. I didn't even know

we were in the river, it was just like the earth had fallen
out from under the wagon and the faces and all and we all
rushed down slow, with the faces looking up and their eyes
blind and their mouths open and their arms held up; high
up in the air across the river I saw a cliff and a big fire on it
running fast sideways and then all of a sudden the wagon
was moving fast sideways and then a dead horse came
shining up from out of the yelling faces and went down slow
again exactly like a fish feeding, with hanging over his rump
by one stirrup a man in a black uniform and then I realised
that the uniform was blue, only it was wet. They were
screaming then and now I could feel the wagon bed tilt and
slide as they caught at it. Granny was kneeling beside me
now, hitting at the screaming faces with Mrs Compson's parasol. Behind us they were still marching down the bank and
into the river, singing.

3.

A Yankee patrol helped Ringo and me cut the drowned
horses out of the harness and drag the wagon ashore. We
sprinkled water on Granny until she came to and they
rigged harness with ropes and hitched up two of their
horses. There was a road on top of the bluff and then we
could see the fires along the bank. They were still singing on
the other side of the river but it was quieter now. But there
were patrols still riding up and down the cliff on this side,
and squads of infantry down at the water where the fires
were. Then we began to pass between rows of tents, with
Granny lying against me and I could see her face then, it was
white and still and her eyes were shut. She looked old and
tired, I hadn't realised how old and little she was. Then we
began to pass big fires, with niggers in wet clothes crouching
around them and soldiers going among them passing out
food, then we came to a broad street and stopped before a
tent with a sentry at the door and a light inside. The soldiers
looked at Granny. "We better take her to the hospital," one
of them said.

Granny opened her eyes, she tried to sit up. "No," she said.
"Just take me to Colonel Dick. I will be all right then."

They carried her into the tent and put her in a chair. She hadn't moved, she was sitting there with her eyes closed and a strand of wet hair sticking to her face when Colonel Dick came in. I had never seen him before, only his voice while Ringo and I were squatting under Granny's skirt and holding our breath, but I knew him at once with his bright beard and his hard bright eyes stooping over Granny and saying, "Damn this war. Damn it. Damn it."

"They took the silver and the darkies and the mules," Granny said. "I have come to get them."

"Have them you shall," he said. "If they are anywhere in this corps. I'll see the General myself." He was looking at Ringo and me now. "Ha," he said. "I believe we have met before also." Then he was gone again.

It was hot in the tent, and quiet, with three bugs swirling around the lantern and outside the sound of the army like wind far away. Ringo was already asleep, sitting on the ground with his head on his knees, and I wasn't much better because all of a sudden Colonel Dick was back and there was an orderly writing at the table, and Granny sitting again with her eyes closed in her white face.

"Maybe you can describe them," Colonel Dick said to me.

"I will do it," Granny said. She didn't open her eyes. "The chest of silver tied with hemp rope. The rope was new. Two darkies, Loosh and Philadelphy. The mules, Old Hundred and Tinney."

Colonel Dick turned and watched the orderly writing. "Have you got that?" he said.

The orderly looked at what he had written. "I guess the General will be glad to give them twice the silver and mules just for taking that many niggers," he said.

"Now I'll go see the General," Colonel Dick said.

Then we were moving again; I dont know how long it had been because they had to wake me and Ringo both; we were in the wagon again, with two army horses pulling it on down the long broad street, and there was another officer with us and Colonel Dick was gone. We came to a pile of chests and boxes that looked higher than a mountain. There was a rope pen behind it full of mules and then standing to one side and waiting was what looked like a thousand niggers, men women and children, with their wet clothes dried on them. And now it began to go fast again: there was Granny in the wagon with her eyes wide open now and the lieutenant reading from the paper and the soldiers jerking chests and trunks out of the pile. "Ten chests tied with hemp rope," the lieutenant read. "Got them? A hundred and ten mules. It says from Philadelphia; that's in Mississippi. Get these Mississippi mules. They are to have rope and halters."

"We aint got a hundred and ten Mississippi mules," the sergeant said.

"Get what we have got. Hurry." He turned to Granny. "And there are your niggers, madam."

Granny was looking at him with her eyes wide as Ringo's. She was drawn back a little, with her hand at her chest. "But they're not——They aint——" she said.

"They aint all yours?" the lieutenant said. "I know it. The General said to give you another hundred with his compliments."

"But that aint——We didn't——" Granny said.

"She wants the house back too," the sergeant said. "We aint got any houses, Grandma," he said. "You'll just have to make out with trunks and niggers and mules. You wouldn't have room for it on the wagon, anyway."

We sat there while they loaded the ten trunks into the wagon. It just did hold them all. They got another set of trees and harness and hitched four mules to it. "One of you darkies that can handle two span come here," the lieutenant said. One of the niggers came and got on the seat with Granny; none of us had ever seen him before. Behind us they were leading the mules out of the pen. "You want to let some of the women ride?" the lieutenant said.

"Yes," Granny whispered.

"Come on," the lieutenant said. "Just one to a mule, now." Then he handed me the paper. "Here you are. There's a ford about twenty miles up the river; you can cross there. You better get on away from here before any more of these niggers decide to go with you."

We rode until daylight, with the ten chests in the wagon and the mules and our army of niggers behind. Granny had not moved, sitting there beside the strange nigger with Mrs

Compson's hat on and the parasol in her hand. But she was not asleep because when it got light enough to see she said, "Stop the wagon." The wagon stopped. She turned and looked at me. "Let me see that paper," she said.

We opened the paper and looked at it, at the neat writing:

> Field Headquarters,
> —th Army Corps,
> Department of Tennessee
> August 14, 1863.

To all Brigade Regimental and Other Commanders:

You will see that bearer is repossessed in full of the following property, to wit: Ten (10) chests tied with hemp rope and containing silver. One hundred ten (110) mules captured loose near Philadelphia in Mississippi. One hundred ten (110) negroes of both sexes belonging to and having strayed from the same locality.

You will further see that bearer is supplied with necessary food and forage to expedite his passage to his destination.

By order of the General Commanding.

We looked at each other in the gray light. "I reckon you gonter take um back now," Ringo said.

Granny looked at me. "We can get food and fodder too," I said.

"Yes," Granny said. "I tried to tell them better. You and Ringo heard me. It's the hand of God."

We stopped and slept until noon. That afternoon we came to the ford. We had already started down the bluff when we saw the troop of cavalry camped there. It was too late to stop. "They done found hit out and headed us off," Ringo said. It was too late; already an officer and two men were riding toward us.

"I will tell them the truth," Granny said. "We have done nothing." She sat there, drawn back a little again, with her hand already raised and holding the paper out in the other when they rode up. The officer was a heavy built man with a red face, he looked at us and took the paper and read it and began to swear. He sat there on his horse swearing while we watched him.

"How many do you lack?" he said.

"How many do I what?" Granny said.

"Mules!" the officer shouted. "Mules! Mules! Do I look like I had any chests of silver or niggers tied with hemp rope?"

"Do we——" Granny said with her hand to her chest, looking at him; I reckon it was Ringo that knew first what he meant.

"We like fifty," Ringo said.

"Fifty, hey?" the officer said. He cursed again; he turned to one of the men behind him and cursed him now. "Count em!" he said. "Do you think I'm going to take their word for it?"

The man counted the mules; we didn't move, I dont think we even breathed hardly. "Sixty-three," the man said.

The officer looked at us. "Sixty-three from a hundred and ten leaves forty-seven," he said. He cursed. "Get forty-seven mules," he hollered. "Hurry." He looked at us again. "Think you can beat me out of three mules, hey?" he hollered.

"Forty-seven will do," Ringo said. "Only I reckon maybe we better eat something, like the paper mention."

We crossed the ford; we didn't stop, we went on as soon as they brought up the other mules and some more of the women got on them. We went on, it was after sundown then but we didn't stop. "Hah," Ringo said. "Whose hand was that?"

We went on until midnight before we stopped. This time it was Ringo that Granny was looking at. "Ringo," she said.

"I never nothing the paper never said," Ringo said. "Hit was the one that said it, hit wasn't me. All I done was to told him how much the hundred and ten liked; I never said we liked that many. Sides, hit aint no use in praying about hit now; aint no telling what we gonter run into fore we gits home. The main thing now is, whut we gonter do with all these niggers."

"Yes," Granny said. We cooked and ate the food the cavalry officer gave us, then Granny told all the niggers that lived in Alabama to come forward. It was about half of them. "I sup-

pose you all want to cross some more rivers and run after the
Yankee Army, dont you?" Granny said. They stood there,
moving their feet in the dust. "What? Dont any of you want
to?" They just stood there. "Then who are you going to mind
from now on?"

After a while, one of them said, "You, missy."

"All right," Granny said. "Now listen to me. Go home.
And if I ever hear of any of you straggling off like this again,
I'll see to it. Now line up and come up here one at a time
while we divide the food."

It took a long time until the last one was gone; when we
started again, we had almost enough mules for everybody to
ride, but not quite, and Ringo drove now. He didn't ask; he
just got in and took the reins, with Granny on the seat by
him; it was just once that she told him not to go so fast. So I
rode in the back then, on one of the chests, and that afternoon I was asleep; it was the wagon stopping that woke me.
We had just come down a hill onto a flat, and then I saw them
beyond a field, about a dozen of them, cavalry in blue coats.
They hadn't seen us yet, trotting along, while Granny and
Ringo watched them.

"They aint hardly worth fooling with," Ringo said. "Still,
they's horses."

"We've already got a hundred and ten," Granny said.
"That's all the paper calls for."

"All right," Ringo said. "You wanter go on?" Granny
didn't answer, sitting there drawn back a little, with her hand
at her breast again. "Well, what you wanter do?" Ringo said.
"You got to cide quick, or they be gone." He looked at her;
she didn't move. Ringo leaned out of the wagon. "Hey!" he
hollered. They looked back quick and saw us and whirled
about. "Granny say come here!" Ringo hollered.

"You, Ringo," Granny whispered.

"All right," Ringo said. "You want me to tell um to never
mind?" She didn't answer; she was looking past Ringo at the
two Yankees who were riding toward us across the field, with
that kind of drawn-back look on her face and her hand holding the front of her dress. It was a lieutenant and a sergeant;
the lieutenant didn't look much older than Ringo and me. He
saw Granny and took off his hat. And then all of a sudden she

took her hand away from her chest; it had the paper in it; she held it out to the lieutenant without saying a word. The lieutenant opened it, the sergeant looking over his shoulder. Then the sergeant looked at us.

"This says mules, not horses," he said.

"Just the first hundred was mules," Ringo said. "The extra twelve is horses."

"Damn it!" the lieutenant said. He sounded like a girl swearing. "I told Captain Bowen not to mount us with captured stock!"

"You mean you're going to give them the horses?" the sergeant said.

"What else can I do?" the lieutenant said. He looked like he was fixing to cry. "It's the General's own signature!"

So then we had enough stock for all of them to ride except about fifteen or twenty. We went on. The soldiers stood under a tree by the road, with their saddles and bridles on the ground beside them—all but the lieutenant. When we started again, he ran along by the wagon; he looked like he was going to cry, trotting along by the wagon with his hat in his hand, looking at Granny.

"You'll meet some troops somewhere," he said. "I know you will. Will you tell them where we are and to send for us? something—mounts or wagons—anything we can ride in? You wont forget?"

"They's some of yawl about twenty or thirty miles back that claim to have three extry mules," Ringo said. "But when we sees any more of um, we'll tell um about yawl."

We went on. We came in sight of a town, but we went around it; Ringo didn't even want to stop and send the lieutenant's message in, but Granny made him stop and we sent the message in by one of the niggers.

"That's one more mouth to feed we got shed of," Ringo said.

We went on. We went fast now, changing the mules every few miles; a woman told us we were in Mississippi again, and then, in the afternoon, we came over the hill, and there our chimneys were, standing up into the sunlight, and the cabin behind them and Louvinia bending over a washtub and the clothes on the line, flapping bright and peaceful.

"Stop the wagon," Granny said.

We stopped—the wagon, the hundred and twenty-two mules and horses, and the niggers we never had had time to count.

Granny got out slow and turned to Ringo. "Get out," she said; then she looked at me. "You too," she said. "Because you said nothing at all." We got out of the wagon. She looked at us. "We have lied," she said.

"Hit was the paper that lied; hit wasn't us," Ringo said.

"The paper said a hundred and ten. We have a hundred and twenty-two," Granny said. "Kneel down."

"But they stole them fore we did," Ringo said.

"But we lied," Granny said. "Kneel down." She knelt first. Then we all three knelt by the road while she prayed. The washing blew soft and peaceful and bright on the clothesline. And then Louvinia saw us; she was already running across the pasture while Granny was praying.

RIPOSTE IN TERTIO

I.

WHEN AB SNOPES left for Memphis with the nine mules, Ringo and Joby and I worked on a new fence. Then Ringo went off on his mule and there was just Joby and me. Once Granny came down and looked at the new section of rails; the pen would be almost two acres larger now. That was the second day after Ringo left. That night while Granny and I were sitting before the fire, Ab Snopes came back. He said that he had got only four hundred and fifty dollars for the nine mules. That is, he took some money out of his pocket and gave it to Granny, and she counted it and said:

"That's only fifty dollars apiece."

"All right," Ab said. "If you can do any better, you are welcome to take the next batch in yourself. I done already admitted I cant hold a candle to you when it comes to getting mules; maybe I cant even compete with you when it comes to selling them." He chewed something—tobacco when he could get it; willow bark when he couldn't—all the time and he never wore a collar and nobody ever admitted they ever saw him in a uniform, though when Father was away he would talk a lot now and then about when he was in Father's troop and about what he and Father used to do. But when I asked Father about it once Father said, "Who? Ab Snopes?" and then laughed. But it was Father that told Ab to kind of look out for Granny while he was away; only he

told me and Ringo to look out for Ab too, that Ab was all
right in his way, but he was like a mule; while you had him in
the traces, you better watch him. But Ab and Granny got
along all right, though each time Ab took a batch of mules to
Memphis and came back with the money, it would be like
this. "Yes, sir," Ab said, "it's easy to talk about hit, setting
here without no risk. But I'm the one that has to dodge them
durn critters nigh a hundred miles into Memphis, with Forrest and Smith fighting on ever side of me and me never
knowing when I wull run into a Confederit or Yankee patrol
and have ever last one of them confiscated off of me right
down to the durn halters. And then I got to take them into
the very heart of the Yankee army in Memphis and try to sell
them to a e-quipment officer that's liable at any minute to
recognise them as the same mules he bought from me not
two weeks ago. Yes. Hit's easy enough for them to talk that
sets here getting rich and takes no risk."

"I suppose you consider getting them back for you to sell
taking no risk," Granny said.

"The risk of running out of them printed letterheads, sho,"
Ab said. "If you aint satisfied with making just five or six
hundred dollars at a time, why dont you requisition for more
mules at a time? Why dont you write out a letter and have
General Smith turn over his commissary train to you, with
about four wagonloads of new shoes in hit? Or better than
that: pick out the day when the pay officer is coming around
and draw for the whole pay wagon: then we wouldn't even
have to bother about finding somebody to buy hit——"

The money was in new bills. Granny folded them carefully
and put them into the can, but she didn't put the can back
inside her dress right away (and she never put it back under
the loose board beneath her bed while Ab was about the
place). She sat there looking at the fire, with the can in her
hands and the string which suspended it looping down from
around her neck. She didn't look any thinner or any older.
She didn't look sick either. She just looked like somebody
that has quit sleeping at night. "We have more mules," she
said, "if you would just sell them. There are more than a hundred of them that you refuse——"

"Refuse is right," Ab said; he began to holler now. "Yes,

sir! I reckon I aint got much sense or I wouldn't be doing this a-tall. But I got better sense than to take them mules to a Yankee officer and tell him that them hip patches where you and that durn nigger burned out the U.S. brand are trace galls. By Godfrey, I——"

"That will do," Granny said. "Have you had some supper?"

"I——" Ab said. Then he quit hollering: he chewed again. "Yessum," he said. "I done et."

"Then you had better go home and get some rest," Granny said. "There is a new relief regiment at Mottstown. Ringo went down two days ago to see about it. So we may need that new fence soon."

Ab stopped chewing. "Is, huh?" he said. "Out of Memphis, likely. Likely got them nine mules in it we just got shet of."

Granny looked at him. "So you sold them further back than three days ago, then," Granny said. Ab started to say something but Granny didn't give him time. "You go on home and rest up," she said. "Ringo will probably be back tomorrow; and then you'll have a chance to see if they are the same mules. I may even have a chance to find out what they say they paid you for them."

Ab stood in the door and looked at Granny. "You're a good un," he said. "Yessum, you got my respect. John Sartoris himself cant tech you. He hells all over the country day and night with a hundred armed men, and it's all he can do to keep them in crowbait to ride on. And you set here in this cabin, without nothing but a handful of durn printed letterheads, and you got to build a bigger pen to hold the stock you aint got no market yet to sell. . . . . . . How many head of mules have you sold back to the Yankees?"

"A hundred and five," Granny said.

"A hundred and five," Ab said. "For how much active cash money, in round numbers?" Only he didn't wait for her to answer; he told her himself: "For six thou-sand and seven hun-dred and twen-ty-two dollars and six-ty-five cents, lessen the dollar and thirty-five cents I spent for whisky that time the snake bit one of the mules." It sounded round when he said it, like big sawn oak wheels running in wet sand. "You started out a year ago with two. You got forty-odd in the pen and twice that many out on receipt. And I reckon you have sold about fifty-odd more back to the Yankees a hundred and five times, for a grand total of six thousand, seven hundred and twenty-two dollars and sixty-five cents, and in a day or so you are aiming to requisition a few of them back again, I understand." He looked at me. "Boy," he said, "when you grow up and start out for yourself, dont you waste your time learning to be a lawyer or nothing; you just save your money and buy you a handful of printed letterheads, it dont matter much what's on them, I reckon, and you hand them to your grandmaw here and just ask her to give you the job of counting the money when hit comes in." He looked at Granny again. "When Kernel Sartoris left here, he told me to look out for you against General Grant and them. What I wonder is, if somebody hadn't better tell Abe Lincoln to look out for General Grant against Miz Rosa Millard. I bid you one and all good night."

He went out. Granny looked at the fire, the tin can in her hand. But it didn't have any six thousand dollars in it. It didn't have a thousand dollars in it. Ab Snopes knew that, only I dont suppose that it was possible for him to believe it. Then she got up; she looked at me, quiet. She didn't look sick; that wasn't it. "I reckon it's bedtime," she said. She went beyond the quilt; it came back and hung straight down from the rafter and I heard the loose board when she put the can away under the floor, and then I heard the sound the bed made when she would hold to the post to kneel down. It would make another sound when she got up, but when it made that sound I was already undressed and on my pallet. The quilts were cold, but when the sound came I had been there long enough for them to begin to get warm.

Ab Snopes came and helped me and Joby with the new fence the next day, so we finished it early in the afternoon and I went back to the cabin; I was almost there when I saw Ringo and the mule turning in the gate. Granny had seen him too, because when I went inside the quilt she was kneeling in the corner, taking the window shade from under the loose floor board. While she was unrolling the shade on the bed we heard Ringo getting off the mule, hollering at it while he hitched it to Louvinia's clothesline. Then Granny stood up and looked at the quilt until Ringo pushed it aside and came in. And then they sounded like two people playing a guessing game in code.

"——th Illinois Infantry," Ringo said. He came on toward the map on the bed. "Col. G. W. Newberry. Eight days out of Memphis."

Granny watched him while he came toward the bed. "How many?" she said.

"Nineteen head," Ringo said. "Four with; fifteen without." Granny just watched him; she didn't have to speak at all for the next one. "Twelve," Ringo said. "Out of that Oxford batch."

Granny looked at the map; they both looked at it. "July the twenty-second," Granny said.

"Yessum," Ringo said. Granny sat down on the saw chunk before the map. It was the only window shade Louvinia had; Ringo had drawn it (Father was right; he was smarter than me; he had even learned to draw, who had declined even to try to learn to print his name when Loosh was teaching me; who had learned to draw immediately by merely taking up the pen, who had no affinity for it and never denied he had not but who learned to draw simply because somebody had to.) with Granny showing him where to draw in the towns. But it was Granny who had done the writing, in her neat spidery hand like she wrote in the cookbook with, written on the map by each town: *Colonel* or *Major* or *Captain So-and-So, Such-and-Such Regiment* or *Troop* Then, under that: *12* or *9* or *21 mules* And around four of them, town and writing and all, in purple pokeberry juice instead of ink, a circle with a date in it, and in big neat letters *Complete*.

They looked at the map, Granny's head white and still where the light came through the window on it, and Ringo leaning over her. He had got taller during the summer; he was taller than me now, maybe from the exercise of riding around the country, listening out for fresh regiments with mules, and he had got to treating me like Granny did—like he and Granny were the same age instead of him and me.

"We just sold that twelve in July," Granny said. "That leaves only seven. And you say that four of them are branded."

"That was back in July," Ringo said. "It's October now. They done forgot about hit. Sides, look here"—he put his finger on the map.—"We captived these here fourteen at Madison on the twelf of April, sont um to Memphis and sold um, and had all fourteen back and three more besides, here at Caledonia on the third of May."

"But that was four counties apart," Granny said. "Oxford and Mottstown are only a few miles apart."

"Phut," Ringo said, "these folks is too busy keeping us conquered to recognise no little ten or twelve head of stock. Sides, if they does recognise um in Memphis, that's Ab Snopes' trouble, not ourn."

"Mister Snopes," Granny said.

"All right," Ringo said. He looked at the map. "Nineteen head, and not two days away. Jest forty-eight hours to have um in the pen."

Granny looked at the map. "I dont think we ought to risk it. We have been successful so far. Too successful perhaps."

"Nineteen head," Ringo said. "Four to keep, and fifteen to sell back to um. That will make a even two hundred and forty-eight head of Confedrit mules we done recovered and collected interest on, let alone the money."

"I dont know what to do," Granny said. "I want to think about it."

"All right," Ringo said. Granny sat still beside the map. Ringo didn't seem patient or impatient either; he just stood there, thin and taller than me against the light from the window, scratching himself; then he began to dig with his right hand little fingernail between his front teeth; he looked at his fingernail and spat something and then he said, "Must been five minutes now." He turned his head a little toward me without moving. "Get the pen and ink," he said.

They kept the paper under the same floor board with the map and the tin can. I dont know how or where Ringo got it; he just came back one night with about a hundred sheets of it, stamped with the official letterhead: *United States Forces. Department of Tennessee*. He had got the pen and the ink at the same time, too; he took them from me and now it was Ringo sitting on the saw chunk and Granny leaning over him. Granny still had the first letter, the order that Colonel Dick had given us in Alabama last year; she kept it in the can, too, and by now Ringo had learned to copy it so that I dont believe that Colonel Dick himself could have told the difference; all they had to do was to put in the right regiment and whatever number of mules Ringo had examined and approved, and sign the right general's name to it. At first Ringo had wanted to sign Grant's name every time, and when Granny said that would not do anymore, Lincoln's. At last Granny found out that Ringo objected to having the Yankees think that Father's folks would have any dealings with anybody under the General-in-Chief. But at last he realised that Granny was right, that they would have to be careful about what general's name was on the letter, as well as what mules they requisitioned. They were using General Smith now; he and Forrest were fighting every day up and down the road to Memphis, and Ringo always remembered to put in rope.

He wrote the date and the town, the headquarters; he wrote in Colonel Newberry's name and the first line. Then he stopped; he didn't lift the pen. "What name you want this time?" he said.

"I'm worried about this," Granny said. "We ought not to risk it."

"We was on 'F' last time," Ringo said. "It's 'H' now. Think of a name in 'H.' "

"Mrs Mary Harris," Granny said.

"We done used Mary before," Ringo said. "How about Plurella Harris?"

"I'm worried about this time," Granny said.

"Miz Plurella Harris," Ringo said, writing. "Now we done used up 'P' too. Member that, now. I reckon when we run out of letters, maybe we can start in on numbers. We will have nine hundred and ninety-nine before we have to worry, then." He finished the order and signed General Smith to it; it looked exactly like the man who had signed the one Colonel Dick gave us was named General Smith, except for the number of mules. Then Granny turned and looked at me. "Tell Mr Snopes to be ready at sunup," she said.

We went in the wagon, with Ab Snopes and his two men following on two of the mules. We went just fast enough so that we would reach the bivouac at supper time, because

Granny and Ringo had found out that that was the best time; that the stock would all be handy, and the men would be too hungry or sleepy or something to think very quick in case they happened to think, and we would just have time to get the mules and get out of sight before dark came. Then, if they should decide to chase us, by the time they found us in the dark, there wouldn't be anything but the wagon with me and Granny in it to capture. So we did; only this time it was a good thing we did. We left Ab Snopes and his men in the woods beyond the bivouac, and Granny and Ringo and I drove up to Colonel Newberry's tent at exactly the right time and Granny passed the sentry and went into the tent, walking thin and straight, with the shawl over her shoulders and Mrs Compson's hat on her head and the parasol in one hand and hers and Ringo's General Smith order in the other, and Ringo and I sat in the wagon and looked at the cook fires about the grove and smelled the coffee and the meat. It was always the same. Granny would disappear into the tent or the house and then in about a minute somebody would holler inside the tent or the house and then the sentry at the door would holler and then a sergeant or even sometimes an officer, only it would be a lieutenant, would hurry into the tent or the house and then Ringo and I would hear somebody cursing and then they would all come out, Granny walking straight and stiff and not looking much bigger than Cousin Denny at Hawkhurst and three or four mad Yankee officers behind her and getting madder all the time. Then they would bring up the mules, tied together; Granny and Ringo could guess to the second now; it would be just enough light left to tell that they were mules, and Granny would get into the wagon and Ringo would hang his legs over the tail gate, holding the lead rope, and we would go on, not fast, so that when we came back to where Ab Snopes and his men waited in the woods you could not even tell that they were mules. Then Ringo would get onto the lead mule, and they would turn off into the woods, and Granny and I would go on home.

That's what we did this time, only this time it happened. We couldn't even see our own team, when we heard them coming, the galloping hooves. They came up fast and mad;

Granny jerked up quick and straight, holding Mrs Compson's parasol. "Damn that Ringo!" she said. "I had my doubts about this time all the while." Then they were all around us, like the dark itself had fallen down on us full of horses and mad men shouting "Halt! Halt! If they try to escape, shoot the damn horses." with me and Granny sitting in the wagon and men jerking the team back and the team jerking and clashing in the traces and some of them hollering, "Where are the mules? The mules are gone!" and the officer cursing and shouting of course they are gone and cursing Granny and the darkness and the men and the mules. Then somebody struck a light and we saw the officer sitting his horse beside the wagon while one of the soldiers lit one lightwood splinter from another.

"Where are the mules?" the officer shouted.

"What mules?" Granny said.

"Dont lie to me!" the officer shouted. "The mules you just left camp with on that forged order. By God, we've got you this time. We knew you'd turn up again. Orders went out to the whole department to watch for you a month ago! That damn Newberry had his copy in his pocket while you were talking to him." He cursed Colonel Newberry now. "By God, they ought to let you go free and courtmartial him. Where's the nigger boy and the mules, Mrs Plurella Harris?"

"I dont know what you are talking about," Granny said. "I have no mules except this team I am driving. And my name is Rosa Millard; I am on my way home, beyond Jefferson."

The officer began to laugh; he sat on the horse, laughing. "So that's your real name, hey? Well, well, well. So you have begun to tell the truth at last. Come now, tell me where those mules are, and tell me where the others you have stolen from us are hid——"

Then Ringo hollered. He and Ab Snopes and the mules had turned off into the woods on the right side of the road, but when he hollered now he was on the left side. "Heyo the road!" he hollered. "One busted loose! head um off the road!"

And that was all of that. The soldier dropped the lightwood splinter and the officer whirled his horse, already spurring him, hollering, "Two men stay here." Maybe they all thought he meant two others, because there was just a big noise of bushes and trees like a cyclone was going through them, and then Granny and I were sitting in the wagon like before we had even heard the hooves. "Come on," Granny said. She was already getting out of the wagon.

"Are we going to leave the team and wagon," I said.

"Yes," Granny said. "I misdoubted this all the time."

We could not see at all in the woods; we felt our way, and me helping Granny along and her arm didn't feel any bigger than a pencil almost, but it wasn't trembling. "This is far enough," she said. I found a log and we sat down. Beyond the road we could hear them thrashing around, shouting and cursing. It sounded far away now. "And the team too," Granny said.

"But we have nineteen new ones," I said. "That makes two hundred and forty-eight."

It seemed like a long time, sitting there on the log in the dark. After a while they came back; we could hear the officer cursing and the horses crashing and thumping back into the road. And then he found the wagon empty and he cursed sure enough—Granny and me and the two men he had told to stay there. He was still cursing while they turned the wagon around. Then they went away. After a while we couldn't hear them. Granny got up and we felt our way back to the road and we went on too, toward home. After a while I persuaded her to stop and rest and while we were sitting beside the road we heard the buggy coming. We stood up and Ringo saw us and stopped the buggy.

"Did I holler loud enough?" he said.

"Yes," Granny said. Then she said, "Well?"

"All right," Ringo said. "I told Ab Snopes to hide out with them in Hickahala bottom until tomorrow night. All cep these two."

"Mister Snopes," Granny said.

"All right," Ringo said. "Git in and les go home."

Granny didn't move; I knew why even before she spoke: "Where did you get this buggy?"

"I borrowed hit," Ringo said. "Twarn't no Yankees handy, so I never needed no paper."

We got in. The buggy went on. It seemed to me like it had

already been all night, but it wasn't midnight yet: I could tell by the stars; we would be home by midnight almost. We went on. "I reckon you went and told um who we is now," Ringo said.

"Yes," Granny said.

"Well I reckon that completes that," Ringo said. "Anyway, we handled two hundred and forty-eight head while the business lasted."

"Two hundred and forty-six," Granny said. "We have lost the team."

2.

It was after midnight when we reached home; it was already Sunday and when we reached the church that morning there was the biggest crowd waiting there had ever been, though Ab Snopes would not get back with the new mules until tomorrow. So I believed that somehow they had heard about last night and they knew too, like Ringo, that this was the end and that now the books would have to be balanced and closed. We were late, because Granny made Ringo get up at sunup and take the buggy back where he had got it. So when we reached the church they were already inside, waiting. Brother Fortinbride met us at the door, and they all turned in the pews and watched Granny—the old men and the women and the children and the maybe a dozen niggers that didn't have any white people now; they looked at her exactly like Father's fox hounds would look at him when he would go into the dogrun while we went up the aisle to our pew. Ringo had the book; he went up to the gallery; I looked back and saw him leaning his arms on the book on the balustrade. We sat down in our pew, like before there was a war only for Father: Granny still and straight in her Sunday calico dress and the shawl and the hat Mrs Compson had loaned her a year ago, straight and quiet with her hands holding her prayer book in her lap like always, though there hadn't been an Episcopal service in the church in almost three years now. Brother Fortinbride was a Methodist, and I dont know what the people were. Last summer when we got back with the first batch of mules from Alabama, Granny sent for them, sent out word back into the hills where they lived in dirt-floored cabins, on the little poor farms without slaves. It took three or four times to get them to come in, but at last they all came—men and women and children and the dozen niggers that had got free by accident and didn't know what to do about it—I reckon this was the first church with a slave gallery some of them had ever seen, with Ringo and the other twelve sitting up there in the high shadows where there was room enough for two hundred; and I could remember back when Father would be in the pew with us and the grove outside would be full of carriages from the other plantations, and Doctor Worsham in his stole beneath the altar and for each white person in the auditorium there would be ten niggers in the gallery. And I reckon that on that first Sunday when Granny knelt down in public, it was the first time they had ever seen anyone kneel in a church.

Brother Fortinbride wasn't a minister either. He was a private in Father's regiment and he got hurt bad in the first battle the regiment was in; they thought that he was dead but he said that Jesus came to him and told him to rise up and live and Father sent him back home to die only he didn't die; but they said that he didn't have any stomach left at all and everybody thought that the food we had to eat in 1862 and 63 would finish killing him, even if he had eaten it with women to cook it instead of gathering weeds from ditch banks and cooking them himself. But it didn't kill him and so maybe it was Jesus after all like he said. And so when we came back with the first batch of mules and the silver and the food, and Granny sent word out for all that needed, it was like Brother Fortinbride sprang right up out of the ground with the names and histories of all the hill folks at his tongue's end, like maybe what he claimed was true, that the Lord had both him and Granny in mind when He created the other. So he would stand there where Doctor Worsham used to stand, and talk quiet for a little while about God, with his hair showing where he cut it himself and the bones looking like they were coming right out through his face, in a frock coat that had turned green a long time ago and with patches on it that he had sewed on himself, one of them was green horsehide and the other was a piece of tent canvas with the U.S.A. stencil still showing a little on it. He never talked long. There wasn't much anybody could say about Confederate armies now; I reckon there is a time when even preachers quit believing that God is going to change His plan and give victory where there is nothing left to hang victory on; he just said how victory without God is mockery and delusion, but that defeat with God is not defeat. Then he quit talking, and he stood there with the old men, and the women and children and the eleven or twelve niggers lost in freedom, in clothes made out of cotton bagging and flour sacks, still watching Granny. Only now it was not like the hounds used to look at Father; but like they would watch the food in Loosh's hands when he would go in to feed them, and then he said, "Brethren and sisters, Sister Millard wishes to bear public witness."

Granny stood up. She would not go to the altar. She just stood there, in our pew with her face straight ahead, in the shawl and Mrs Compson's hat and the dress that Louvinia washed and ironed every Saturday, holding the prayer book. It used to have her name on it in gold letters, but now the only way you could read them was to run your finger over them; she said quiet too, quiet as Brother Fortinbride: "I have sinned. I want you all to pray for me."

She knelt down in the pew; she looked littler than Cousin Denny; it was only Mrs Compson's hat above the pew back they had to look at now. I dont know if she prayed herself or not. And Brother Fortinbride didn't pray either, not aloud anyway. Ringo and I were just past fifteen then, but I could imagine what Doctor Worsham would have thought up to say, about all soldiers did not carry arms, and about they also serve and how one child saved from hunger and cold is better in heaven's sight than a thousand slain enemies. But Brother Fortinbride didn't say it. I reckon he thought of that; he always had plenty of words when he wanted to. It was like he said to himself, "Words are fine in peacetime, when everybody is comfortable and easy. But now I think that we can be excused." He just stood there where Doctor Worsham used to stand and where the bishop would stand, too, with his ring looking big as a pistol target. Then Granny rose up; I didn't have time to help her; she stood up and then the long sound

went through the church, a sound kind of like a sigh that
Ringo said was the sound of the cotton bagging and the flour
sacking when they breathed again, and Granny turned and
looked back toward the gallery; only Ringo was already moving. "Bring the book," she said.

It was a big blank account book; it weighed almost fifteen
pounds; they opened it on the reading desk, Granny and
Ringo side by side, while Granny drew the tin can out of her
dress and spread the money on the book. But nobody moved
until she began to call out the names. Then they came up one
at a time, while Ringo read the names off the book, and the
date, and the amount they had received before. Each time
Granny would make them tell what they intended to do with
the money; and now she would make them tell her how they
had spent it, and she would look at the book to see whether
they had lied or not. And the ones that she had loaned the
brand blotted mules that Ab Snopes was afraid to try to sell
would have to tell her how the mule was getting along and
how much work it had done; and now and then she would
take the mule away from one man or woman and give it to
another, tearing up the old receipt and making the man or the
woman sign the new one, telling them on what day to go and
get the mule.

So it was afternoon when Ringo closed the book and got
the new receipts together, and Granny stopped putting the
rest of the money back into the can and she and Brother Fortinbride did what they did each time. "I'm making out fine
with the mule," he said. "I dont need any money."

"Fiddlesticks," Granny said. "You'll never grow enough
food out of the ground to feed a bird the longest day you live.
You take this money."

"No," Brother Fortinbride said. "I'm making out fine."

We walked back home, Ringo carrying the book. "You
done receipted out four mules you aint hardly laid eyes on
yet," he said. "What you gonter do about that?"

"They will be here tomorrow morning, I reckon," Granny
said. They were; Ab Snopes came in while we were eating
breakfast; he leaned in the door with his eyes a little red from
lack of sleep and looked at Granny.

"Yes, ma'am," he said. "I dont never want to be rich; I just

want to be lucky. Do you know what you done?" Only nobody asked him what, so he told us anyway: "Hit was taking
place all day yestiddy; I reckon by now there aint a Yankee
regiment left in Mississippi. You might say that this here war
has turned around at last and went back North. Yes, sir. That
regiment you requisitioned on Sattidy never even stayed long
enough to warm the ground. You managed to requisition the
last batch of Yankee live stock, at the last possible moment hit
could have been done by living man. You made just one mistake: you drawed them last nineteen mules just too late to
have anybody to sell them back to."

3.

It was a bright warm day; we saw the guns and the bits
shining a long way down the road, but this time Ringo didn't
even move. He just quit drawing and looked up from the
paper and said, "So Ab Snopes was lying. Gret God, aint we
gonter never get shet of them?"

It was just a lieutenant; by this time Ringo and I could tell
the different officers' ranks better than we could tell Confederate ranks because one day we counted up and the only Confederate officers we had ever seen were Father and the captain
that talked to us with Uncle Buck McCaslin that day in Jefferson before Grant burned it. And this was to be the last
time we would see any uniforms at all except as the walking
symbols of defeated men's pride and indomitable unregret,
but we didn't know that now. So it was just a lieutenant. He
looked about forty and kind of mad and gleeful both at the
same time; Ringo didn't recognise him because he had not
been in the wagon with us, but I did: from the way he sat the
horse, or maybe from the way he looked mad and happy
both, like he had been mad for several days, thinking about
how much he was going to enjoy being mad when the right
time came. And he recognised me too; he looked at me once
and said, "Hah!" with his teeth showing and pushed his horse
up and looked at Ringo's picture. There were maybe a dozen
cavalry behind him; we never noticed especially. "Hah," he
said again, then he said, "What's that?"

"A house," Ringo said. Ringo had never even looked at

him good yet. He had seen even more of them than I had. "Look at it."

The lieutenant looked at me and said "Hah" again behind his teeth; every now and then while he was talking to Ringo he would do that. He looked at Ringo's picture. Then he looked up the grove to where the chimneys rose out of the pile of rubble and ashes. Grass and weeds had come up out of the ashes now and unless you knew better, all you saw was the four chimneys. Some of the golden rod was still in bloom. "Oh," the officer said. "I see. You're drawing it like it used to be."

"Co-rect," Ringo said. "What I wanter draw hit like hit is now for? I can walk down here ten times a day and look at hit like hit is now. I can even ride in that gate on a horse and do that."

The lieutenant didn't say "Hah!" this time. He didn't do anything yet; I reckon he was still enjoying waiting a little longer to get good and mad. He just kind of grunted. "When you get done here, you can move into town and keep busy all winter, cant you?" he said. Then he sat back in the saddle. He didn't say "Hah" now either; it was his eyes that said it, looking at me; they were a kind of thin milk color, like the chine knuckle bone in a ham. "All right," he said. "Who lives up there now? What's her name today, hey?"

Ringo was watching him now, though I dont think he suspected yet who he was. "Dont nobody," he said. "The roof leaks." One of the men made a kind of sound; maybe it was laughing. The lieutenant started to whirl around and then he started not to; then he sat there glaring down at Ringo with his mouth beginning to open. "Oh," Ringo said. "You mean way back yonder in the quarters. I thought you was still worrying about them chimneys."

This time the soldier did laugh, and this time the lieutenant did whirl around, cursing at the soldier; I would have known him now even if I hadn't before; he cursed at them all now, sitting there with his face swelling up. "Blank blank blank," he shouted. "Get to hell on out of here. He said that pen is down there in the creek bottom beyond the pasture. If you meet man woman or child and they so much as smile at you, shoot them. Get!" The soldiers went on, galloping up the drive; we watched them scatter out across the pasture. The lieutenant looked at me and Ringo; he said "Hah" again, glaring at us. "You boys come with me. Jump!"

He didn't wait for us; he galloped, too, up the drive. We ran; Ringo looked at me. "*He* said the pen was in the creek bottom," Ringo said. "Who you reckon *he* is?"

"I dont know," I said.

"Well, I reckon I know," Ringo said. But we didn't talk anymore. We ran on up the drive. The lieutenant had reached the cabin now, and Granny came out the door; I reckon she had seen him too because she already had her sunbonnet on. They looked at us once, then Granny went on, too, walking straight, not fast, down the path toward the lot, with the lieutenant behind her on the horse. We could see his shoulders and his head, and now and then his hand and arm, but we couldn't hear what he was saying. "I reckon this does complete hit," Ringo said.

But we could hear him before we reached the new fence. Then we could see them standing at the fence that Joby and I had just finished: Granny straight and still, with her sunbonnet on and the shawl drawn tight over her shoulders where she had her arms folded in it so that she looked littler than anybody I could remember, like during the four years she hadn't got any older or weaker, but just littler and littler and straighter and straighter and more and more indomitable, and the lieutenant beside her with one hand on his hip and waving a whole handful of letters at Granny's face with the other. "Look like he got all we ever wrote there," Ringo said. The soldiers' horses were all tied along the fence; they were inside the pen now, and they and Joby and Ab Snopes had the forty-odd old mules and the nineteen new ones hemmed into the corner. The mules were still trying to break out, only it didn't look like that: it looked like every one of them was trying to keep the big burned smear where Granny and Ringo had blotted the U.S. brand turned so that the lieutenant would have to look at it.

"And I guess you will call those scars left handed trace galls!" the lieutenant said. "You have been using castoff band-saw bands for traces, hey? By God, I'd rather engage Forrest's whole brigade every morning for six months than spend that same length of time trying to protect United States property from defenseless Southern women and niggers and children. Defenseless!" he shouted: "Defenseless! God help the North if Davis and Lee had ever thought of the idea of forming a brigade of grandmothers and nigger orphans and invading us with it." He hollered, shaking the letters at Granny. In the pen the mules huddled and surged, with Ab Snopes waving his arms at them now and then. Then the lieutenant quit shouting: he even quit shaking the letters at Granny.

"Listen," he said. "We are on evacuation orders now. Likely I am the last Federal soldier you will have to look at. And I'm not going to harm you; orders to that effect too. All I'm going to do is take back this stolen property. And now I want you to tell me, as enemy to enemy, or even man to man, if you like. I know from these forged orders how many head of stock you have taken from us, and I know from the records how many times you have sold a few of them back to us. I even know what we paid you. But how many of them did you actually sell back to us more than one time?"

"I dont know," Granny said.

"You dont know," the lieutenant said. He didn't start to shout now, he just stood there, breathing slow and hard, looking at Granny; he talked now with a kind of furious patience, as if she were an idiot or an Indian: "Listen. I know you dont have to tell me, and you know I cant make you. I ask it only out of pure respect. Respect? Envy. Wont you tell me?"

"I dont know," Granny said.

"You dont know," the lieutenant said. "You mean, you——" He talked quiet now. "I see. You really dont know. You were too busy running the reaper to count the——" We didn't move: Granny wasn't even looking at him; it was Ringo and me that watched him fold the letters that Granny and Ringo had written and put them carefully into his pocket. He still talked quiet, like he was tired: "All right, boys. Rope them together and haze them out of there."

"The gate is a quarter of a mile from here," a soldier said.

"Throw down some fence," the lieutenant said. They began to throw down the fence that Joby and I had worked two months on. The lieutenant took a pad from his pocket and he went to the fence and laid the pad on the rail and took out a pencil. Then he looked back at Granny; he still talked quiet: "I believe you said the name now is Rosa Millard?"

"Yes," Granny said.

The lieutenant wrote on the pad and tore the sheet out and came back to Granny. He still talked quiet, like when somebody is sick in a room: "We are under orders to pay for all property damaged in the process of evacuation," he said. "This is a voucher on the quartermaster at Memphis for ten dollars. For the fence." He didn't give the paper to her at once; he just stood there, looking at her. "Confound it, I dont mean promise. If I just knew what you believed in, held——" He cursed again, not loud and not at anybody or anything. "Listen. I dont say promise; I never mentioned the word. But I have a family; I am a poor man; I have no grandmother. And if in about four months the auditor should find a warrant in the records for a thousand dollars to Mrs Rosa Millard, I would have to make it good. Do you see?"

"Yes," Granny said. "You need not worry."

Then they were gone. Granny and Ringo and Joby and I stood there and watched them drive the mules up across the pasture and out of sight. We had forgot about Ab Snopes until he said, "Well, hit looks like that's all they are to hit. But you still got that ere hundred-odd that are out on receipt, provided them hill folks dont take a example from them Yankees. I reckon you can still be grateful for that much anyway. So I'll bid you one and all good day and get on home and rest a spell. If I can help you again, just send for me." He went on too. After a while Granny said, "Joby, put those rails back up." I reckon Ringo and I were both waiting for her to tell us to help Joby, but she didn't. She just said, "Come" and turned and went on, not toward the cabin, but across the pasture toward the road. We didn't know where we were going until we reached the church. She went straight up the aisle to the chancel and stood there until we came up. "Kneel down," she said.

We knelt in the empty church. She was small between us, little; she talked quiet, not loud, not fast and not slow; her voice sounded quiet and still, but strong and clear: "I have sinned. I have stolen and I have borne false witness against my neighbor, though that neighbor was an enemy of my country. And more than that, I have caused these children to sin. I hereby take their sin upon my conscience." It was one of those bright, soft days. It was cool in the church, the floor was cold to my knees. There was a hickory branch just outside the window, turning yellow; when the sun touched it, the leaves looked like gold. "But I did not sin for gain or for greed," Granny said. "I did not sin for revenge; I defy You or anyone to say I did. I sinned first for justice. And after that first time, I sinned for more than justice: I sinned for the sake of food and clothes for Your own creatures who could not help themselves; for children who had given their fathers, for wives who had given their husbands, for old people who had given their sons, to a holy cause, even though You have seen fit to make it a lost cause. What I gained, I shared with them. It is true that I kept some of it back, but I am the best judge of that because I, too, have dependents who may be orphans, too, at this moment for all I know. And if this be sin in Your sight, I take this on my conscience too. Amen."

She rose up. She got up easy, like she had no weight to herself. It was warm outside; it was the finest October that I could remember. Or maybe it was because you are not conscious of weather until you are fifteen. We walked slow back home, though Granny said she wasn't tired. "I just wish I knew how they found out about that pen," she said.

"Dont you know?" Ringo said. Granny looked at him. "Ab Snopes told them."

This time she didn't even say, "Mister Snopes." She just stopped dead still and looked at Ringo. "Ab Snopes?"

"Do you reckon he was going to be satisfied until he had sold them last nineteen mules to somebody?" Ringo said.

"Ab Snopes," Granny said. "Well." Then she walked on; we walked on. "Ab Snopes," she said. "I reckon he beat me, after all. But it cant be helped now. And anyway, we did pretty well, taken by and large."

"We done damn well——" Ringo said. He caught himself, but it was already too late. Granny didn't even stop.

"Go on home and get the soap," she said.

He went on. We could watch him cross the pasture and go into the cabin, and then come out and go down the hill toward the spring. We were close now; when I left Granny and went down to the spring, he was just rinsing his mouth, the can of soap in one hand and the gourd dipper in the other. He spit and rinsed his mouth and spit again; there was a long smear of suds up his cheek; a light froth of colored bubbles flicking away while I watched them, without any sound at all. "I still says we done damn well," he said.

4.

We tried to keep her from doing it, we both tried: Ringo had told her about Ab Snopes and after that we both knew it: it was like all three of us should have known it all the time, only I dont believe now that he meant to happen what did happen. But I believe that if he had known what was going to happen, he would still have egged her on to do it. And Ringo and I tried, we tried, but Granny just sat there before the fire (it was cold in the cabin now) with her arms folded in the shawl and with that look on her face when she had quit either arguing or listening to you at all, saying just this one time more and that even a rogue will be honest for enough pay. It was Christmas: we had just heard from Aunt Louisa at Hawkhurst and found out where Drusilla was: she had been missing from home for almost a year now and at last Aunt Louisa found out that she was with Father away in Carolina like she had told me, riding with the troop like she was a man; Ringo and I had just got back from Jefferson with the letter, and Ab Snopes was in the cabin, telling Granny about it, and Granny listening and believing him because she still believed that what side of a war a man fought on made him what he is. And she knew better with her own ears, she must have known; everybody knew about them and were either mad if they were men or terrified if they were women. There was one negro in the county that everybody knew that they had murdered and burned him up in his cabin. They called themselves Grumby's Independents—about fifty or sixty of them that wore no uniform and came from nobody knew where as soon as the last Yankee regiment was out of the country, raiding smoke houses and stables, and houses where they were sure there were no men,

tearing up beds and floors and walls, frightening white
women and torturing negroes to find where money or silver
was hidden; they were caught once and the one that said he
was Grumby produced a tattered raiding commission actually
signed by General Forrest, though you couldn't tell if the
original name was Grumby or not. But it got them off, because it was just some old men that captured them, and now
women who had lived alone for three years surrounded by
invading armies were afraid to stay in the houses at night, and
the negroes who had lost their white people lived hidden in
caves back in the hills like animals. That's who Ab Snopes was
talking about, with his hat on the floor and his hands flapping
and his hair bent up across the back of his head where he had
slept on it. The band had a thoroughbred stallion and three
mares, how Ab Snopes knew it he didn't say, that they had
stolen; and how he knew they were stolen he didn't say. But
all Granny had to do was to write out one of the orders and
sign Forrest's name to it; he, Ab, would guarantee to get two
thousand dollars for the horses. He swore to that, and
Granny sitting there with her arms rolled into the shawl and
that expression on her face, and Ab Snopes' shadow leaping
and jerking up the wall while he waved his arms and talked
about that was all she had to do: to look at what she had
made out of the Yankees, enemies, and that these were Southern men and, therefore, there would not even be any risk to
this, because Southern men would not harm a woman, even if
the letter failed to work. Oh, he did it well: I can see now that
Ringo and I had no chance against him: about how the business with the Yankees had stopped without warning, before
she had made what she had counted on, and how she had
given most of that away under the belief that she would be
able to replace that and more, but as it was now, she had
made independent and secure almost everyone in the county
save herself and her own blood; that soon Father would return home to his ruined plantation and most of his slaves
vanished; and how it would be if, when he came home and
looked about at his desolate future, she could take fifteen hundred dollars in cash out of her pocket and say, "Here. Start
over with this"—fifteen hundred dollars more than she had
hoped to have. He would take one of the mares for his com-

mission and he would guarantee her fifteen hundred dollars for the other three. Oh, we had no chance against him. We begged her to let us ask advice from Uncle Buck McCaslin, anyone, any man. But she just sat there with that expression on her face, saying that the horses did not belong to him, that they had been stolen, and that all she had to do was to frighten them with the order, and even Ringo and I knowing at fifteen that Grumby, or whoever he was, was a coward and that you might frighten a brave man, but that nobody dared frighten a coward; and Granny, sitting there without moving at all and saying, "But the horses do not belong to them because they are stolen property," and we said, "Then no more will they belong to us," and Granny said, "But they do not belong to them."

But we didn't quit trying; all that day (Ab Snopes had located them; it was an abandoned cotton compress on Tallahatchie River, sixty miles away) while we rode in the rain in the wagon Ab Snopes got for us to use, we tried. But Granny just sat there on the seat between us, with the order signed by Ringo for General Forrest in the tin can under her dress and her feet on some hot bricks in a croker sack that we would stop every ten miles and build a fire in the rain and heat again, until we came to the crossroads, where Ab Snopes told us to leave the wagon and walk. And then she would not let me and Ringo go with her. "You and Ringo look like men," she said. "They wont hurt a woman." It had rained all day; it had fallen gray and steady and slow and cold on us all day long, and now it was like twilight had thickened it without being able to make it any grayer or colder. The crossroad was not a road anymore; it was no more than a faint gash turning off at right angles into the bottom, so that it looked like a cave. We could see the hoof marks in it.

"Then you shant go," I said. "I'm stronger than you are; I'll hold you." I held her; her arm felt little and light and dry as a stick. But it wasn't that: her size and appearance had no more to do with it than it had in her dealings with the Yankees; she just turned and looked at me and then I began to cry. I would be sixteen years old before another year was out, yet I sat there in the wagon, crying. I didn't even know when she freed her arm. And then she was out of the wagon, standing there looking at me in the gray rain and the gray darkening light.

"It's for all of us," she said—"for John, and you, and Ringo and Joby and Louvinia. So we will have something when John comes back home. You never cried when you knew he was going into a battle, did you? And now I am taking no risk: I am a woman. Even Yankees do not harm old women. You and Ringo stay here until I call you."

We tried. I keep on saying that because I know now that I didn't. I could have held her, turned the wagon, driven away, holding her in it. I was just fifteen, and for most of my life her face had been the first thing I saw in the morning and the last thing I saw at night, but I could have stopped her and I didn't. I sat there in the wagon in the cold rain and let her walk on into the wet twilight and never come out of it again. How many of them there were in the old compress, I dont know and when and why they took fright and left, I dont know. We just sat there in the wagon in that cold dissolving December twilight until at last I couldn't bear it any longer. Then Ringo and I were both running, trying to run, in the ankle deep mud of that old road pocked with the prints of ingoing hooves but of no wheel, knowing that we had waited too long either to help her or to share in her defeat. Because there was no sound nor sign of life at all; just the huge rotting building with the gray afternoon dying wetly upon it, and then at the end of the hall a faint crack of light beneath a door.

I dont remember touching the door at all, because the room was a floor raised about two feet from the earth, so that I ran into the step and fell forward into and then through the door, onto my hands and knees in the room, looking at Granny. There was a tallow dip still burning on a wooden box, but it was the powder I smelled, stronger even than the tallow. I couldn't seem to breathe for the smell of the powder, looking at Granny. She had looked little alive, but now she looked like she had collapsed, like she had been made out of a lot of little thin dry light sticks notched together and braced with cord, and now the cord had broken and all the little sticks had collapsed in a quiet heap on the floor, and somebody had spread a clean and faded calico dress over them.

VENDÉE

I.

Tʜᴇʏ ᴀʟʟ ᴄᴀᴍᴇ in again when we buried Granny, Brother Fortinbride and all of them—the old men and the women and the children, and the niggers—the twelve who used to come in when word would spread that Ab Snopes was back from Memphis, and the hundred more who had returned to the county since, who had followed the Yankees away and then returned, to find their families and owners gone, to scatter into the hills and live in caves and hollow trees like animals I suppose, not only with no one to depend on but with no one depending on them, caring whether they returned or not or lived or died or not: and that I suppose is the sum, the sharp serpent's fang, of bereavement and loss— all coming in from the hills in the rain. Only there were no Yankees in Jefferson now so they didn't have to walk in; I could look across the grave and beyond the other headstones and monuments and see the dripping cedar grove full of mules with long black smears on their hips where Granny and Ringo had burned out the U.S. brand.

Most of the Jefferson people were there too, and there was another preacher—a big preacher refugeeing from Memphis or somewhere—and I found out how Mrs Compson and some of them had arranged for him to preach the funeral. But Brother Fortinbride didn't let him. He didn't tell him not to; he just didn't say anything to him at all, he just acted like a grown person coming in where the children are getting ready to play a game and telling the children that the game is all right but that the grown folks need the room and the furniture for a while. He came walking fast up from the grove where he had hitched his mule with the others, with his gaunted face and his frock coat with the horse-hide and the Yankee-tent patches, into where the town people were standing around under umbrellas with Granny in the middle and the big refugeeing preacher with his book already open and one of the Compson niggers holding an umbrella over him and the rain splashing slow and cold and gray on the umbrella and splashing slow on the yellow boards where Granny was and into the dark red dirt beside the red grave without splashing at all. Brother Fortinbride just walked in and looked at the umbrellas and then at the hill people in cotton bagging and split flour-sack clothes that didn't have umbrellas, and went to Granny and said, "Come, you men."

The town men would have moved. Some of them did. Uncle Buck McCaslin was the first man of them all, town and hill, to come forward. By Christmas his rheumatism would be so bad that he couldn't hardly lift his hand, but he was there now, with his peeled hickory stick, shoving up through the hill men with croker sacks tied over their heads and the town men with umbrellas getting out of his way; then Ringo and I stood there and watched Granny going down into the earth with the quiet rain splashing on the yellow boards until they quit looking like boards and began to look like water with thin sunlight reflected in it, sinking away into the ground. Then the wet red dirt began to flow into the grave, with the shovels darting and flicking slow and steady and the hill men waiting to take turns with the shovels because Uncle Buck would not let anyone spell him with his.

It didn't take long, and I reckon the refugeeing preacher would have tried again even then, but Brother Fortinbride didn't give him a chance. Brother Fortinbride didn't even put down his shovel; he stood there leaning on it like he was in the field and he sounded just like he used to in the church when Ab Snopes would be home from Memphis again: strong and quiet and not loud: "I dont reckon that Rosa Millard or anybody that ever knew her has to be told where she has gone. And I dont reckon that anybody that ever knew her would want to insult her by telling her to rest anywhere in peace. And I reckon that God has already seen to it that there are men women and children, black white yellow or red, waiting for her to tend and worry over. And so you folks go home. Some of you aint come far and you came that distance in carriages with tops. But most of you didn't, and it's by the grace of Rosa Millard that you didn't come on foot. I'm talking to you. You have wood to cut and split, at least. And what do you reckon Rosa Millard would say about you all standing around here, keeping old folks and children out here in the rain?"

Mrs Compson asked me and Ringo to come home and live with her until Father came back, and some others did: I dont remember who; and then when I thought they had all gone I looked around and there was Uncle Buck. He came up to us, with one elbow jammed into his side and his beard drawn over to one side like it was another arm, and his eyes red and mad like he hadn't slept much, and holding his stick like he was fixing to hit somebody with it and he didn't much care who. "What you boys going to do now?" he said.

The earth was loose and soft now, dark and red with rain, so that the rain didn't splash on Granny at all: it just dissolved slow and gray into the dark red mound, so that after a while the mound began to dissolve too without changing shape, like the soft yellow color of the boards had dissolved and stained up through the earth and mound and boards and rain were all melting into one vague quiet reddish gray. "I want to borrow a pistol," I said.

He begun to holler then, but quiet. Because he was older than us; it was like it had been at the old compress that night with Granny. "Need me or not," he hollered, "by Godfrey, I'm going. You cant stop me. You mean to tell me you dont *want* me to go with you?"

"I dont care," I said. "I just want a pistol. Or a gun. Ours got burned up with the house."

"All right," he hollered. "Me and the pistol, or you and this damn nigger horse thief and a fence rail; you aint even got a poker at home. Have you?"

"We got the barl of the musket yet," Ringo said. "I reckon that's all we'll need for Ab Snopes."

"Ab Snopes?" Uncle Buck hollered. "Do you think it's Ab Snopes this boy is thinking about? Hey?" he hollered, hollering at me now. "Hey, boy?" It was changing all the time, with the slow gray rain lancing slow and gray and cold into the red earth, yet it did not change. It would be some time yet, it would be days and weeks and then months before it would be smooth and quiet and level with the other earth. Now Uncle Buck was talking at Ringo, and not hollering now. "Catch my mule," he said. "I got the pistol in my britches."

Ab Snopes lived back in the hills too. Uncle Buck knew where; it was midafternoon by then and we were riding up a long red hill between pines when Uncle Buck stopped. He and Ringo had croker sacks tied over their heads. Uncle Buck's handworn stick stuck out from under his sack, with the rain shining on it like a long wax candle. "Wait," he said. "I got a idea." We turned from the road and came to a creek bottom; there was a faint path. It was dark under the trees and the rain didn't fall on us now: it was like the bare trees themselves were dissolving slow and steady and cold into the end of the December day. We rode in single file, in our wet clothes and in the wet ammonia steam of the mules.

The pen was just like the one he and Ringo and Joby and I had built at home, only smaller and better hidden; I reckon he had got the idea from ours. We stopped at the wet rails; they were still new enough for the split sides to be still yellow with sap, and on the far side of the pen there was something that looked like a yellow cloud in the twilight until it moved. And then we saw that it was a claybank stallion and three mares. "I thought so," Uncle Buck said.

Because I was mixed up. Maybe it was because Ringo and I were tired and we hadn't slept much lately. Because the days were mixed up with the nights: all the while we had been riding I would keep on thinking how Ringo and I would catch it from Granny when we got back home for going off in the rain without telling her. Because for a minute I sat there and looked at the horses and I believed that Ab Snopes was Grumby. But Uncle Buck begun to holler again.

"Him, Grumby?" he hollered. "Ab Snopes? Ab Snopes? By Godfrey, if he was Grumby, if it was Ab Snopes that shot your grandmaw, I'd be ashamed to have it known. I'd be ashamed to be caught catching him. No, sir. He aint Grumby: he's better than that." He sat sideways on his mule with the sack over his head and his beard jerking and wagging out of it while he talked. "He's the one that's going to show us where Grumby is. They just hid them horses here because they thought this would be the last place you boys would think to look for them. And now Ab Snopes has went off with Grumby to get some more, since your grandmaw has gone out of business as far as he is concerned. And thank Godfrey for that: it wont be a house or a cabin they will ever pass as long as Ab Snopes is with them that he wont leave a indelible signature, even if it aint nothing to capture but a chicken or a kitchen clock. By Godfrey, the one thing we dont want is to catch Ab Snopes."

And we didn't catch him that night. We went back to the road and went on and then we came in sight of the house. I rode up to Uncle Buck. "Give me the pistol," I said.

"We aint going to need a pistol," Uncle Buck said. "He aint even here, I tell you. You and that nigger stay back and let me do this. I'm going to find out which a way to start hunting. Get back, now."

"No," I said, "I want——"

He looked at me from under the croker sack. "You want what? You want to lay your two hands on the man that shot Rosa Millard. Dont you?" He looked at me. I sat there on the mule, in the slow gray cold rain, in the dying daylight. Maybe it was the cold. I didn't feel cold, but I could feel my bones jerking and shaking. "And then what you going to do with him?" Uncle Buck said. He was almost whispering now. "Hey? Hey?"

"Yes," I said. "Yes."

"Yes. That's what. Now you and Ringo stay back. I'll do this."

It was just a cabin. I reckon there were a thousand of them just like it about our hills, with the same canted plow lying under a tree and the same bedraggled chickens roosting on the plow and the same gray twilight dissolving onto the gray shingles of the roof. Then we saw a faint crack of fire and a woman's face looking at us around the crack of the door. "Mister Snopes aint here, if that's what you want," she said. "He's done gone to Alabama. On a visit."

"Sho, now," Uncle Buck said. "To Alabama. Did he leave any word when to expect him home?"

"No," the woman said.

"Sho, now," Uncle Buck said. "Then I reckon we better get on back home and out of the rain."

"I reckon you had," the woman said. Then the door closed. We rode away. We rode back toward home. It was like it had been while we waited at the old compress: it hadn't got darker exactly, the twilight had just thickened.

"Well well well," Uncle Buck said. "They aint in Alabama, because she told us so. And they aint toward Memphis, because there are still Yankees there yet. So I reckon we better try down toward Grenada first. By Godfrey, I'll bet this mule against that nigger's pocket knife that we wont ride two days before we come on a mad woman hollering down the road with a handful of chicken feathers in her hand. You come on here and listen to me. By Godfrey, we're going to do this thing but by Godfrey we're going to do it right."

2.

So we didn't get Ab Snopes that day. We didn't get him for a lot of days, and nights too—days in which we rode, the three of us, on relays of Granny's and Ringo's Yankee mules along the known roads and the unknown (and sometimes unmarked) trails and paths, in the wet and the iron frost, and nights when we slept in the same wet and the same freeze and (once) in the snow, beneath whatever shelter we found when night found us. They had neither name nor number. They lasted from that December afternoon until late February, until one night we realised that we had been hearing geese and ducks going north for some time. At first Ringo kept a pine stick and each night he would cut a notch in it, with a big one for Sunday and two long ones which meant Christmas and New Year's. But one night when the stick had almost forty notches in it, we stopped in the rain to make camp without any roof to get under and we had to use the stick to start a fire, because of Uncle Buck's arm. And so, when we came to where we could get another pine stick, we couldn't remember whether it had been five or six or ten days, and so Ringo didn't start another. Because he said he would fix the stick up the day we got Grumby and that it wouldn't need but two notches on it—one for the day we got him and one for the day Granny died.

We had two mules apiece, to swap onto at noon each day. We got the mules back from the hill people; we could have got a cavalry regiment if we had wanted it—of old men and women and children, too—with cotton bagging and flour sacking for uniforms and hoes and axes for arms, on the Yankee mules that Granny had loaned to them. But Uncle Buck told them that we didn't need any help; that three was enough to catch Grumby.

They were not hard to follow. One day we had about twenty notches on the stick and we came onto a house where the ashes were still smoking and a boy almost as big as Ringo and me still unconscious in the stable with even his shirt cut to pieces like they had had a wire snapper on the whip, and a woman with a little thread of blood still running out of her mouth and her voice sounding light and far away like a locust from across the pasture, telling us how many there were and which way they would likely go, saying, "Kill them. Kill them."

It was a long way, but it wasn't far. You could have put a silver dollar down on the geography page with the center of it at Jefferson and we would have never ridden out from under it. And we were closer behind them than we knew, because one night we had ridden late without coming to a house or a shed to camp in, and so we stopped and Ringo said he would scout around a little, because all we had left to eat was the bone of a ham; only it was more likely Ringo was trying to dodge helping to get in the firewood. So Uncle Buck and I were spreading down pine branches to sleep on when we heard a shot and then a sound like a brick chimney falling onto a rotten shingle roof, and then the horses, starting fast and dying away, and then I could hear Ringo yelling. He had come onto a house; he thought it was deserted, and then he said it looked too dark, too quiet. So he climbed onto a shed against the back wall, and he said he saw the crack of light and he was trying to pull the shutter open careful, but it came loose with a sound like a shot, and he was looking into a room with a candle stuck into a bottle and either three or thirteen men looking right at him; and how somebody hollered, "There they are!" and another man jerked out a pistol and one of the others grabbed his arm as it went off, and then the whole shed gave way under him, and he said how he lay there hollering and trying to get untangled from the broken planks and heard them ride away.

"So he didn't shoot at you," Uncle Buck said.

"Hit warn't none of his fault if he never," Ringo said.

"But he didn't," Uncle Buck said. But he wouldn't let us go on that night. "We wont lose any distance," he said. "They are flesh and blood, the same as we are. And we aint scared."

So we went on at daylight, following the hoofprints now. Then we had three more notches in the stick; that night Ringo put the last notch in it that he was going to but we didn't know it; we were sitting in front of the cotton pen where we were going to sleep, eating a shote that Ringo had found, when we heard the horse. Then the man begun to holler "Hello! Hello!" and then we watched him ride up on a good short coupled sorrel mare, with his neat little fine made boots and his linen shirt without any collar and a coat that had been good too once, and a broad hat pulled down so that all we could see was his eyes and nose between the hat and his black beard. "Howdy, men," he said.

"Howdy," Uncle Buck said. He was eating a spare rib; he sat now with the rib in his left hand and his right hand lying on his lap, just inside his coat; he wore the pistol on a loop of lace leather around his neck and stuck into his pants like a lady's watch. But the stranger wasn't looking at him; he just looked at each of us once and then sat there on the mare, with both his hands on the pommel in front of him.

"Mind if I light and warm?" he said.

"Light," Uncle Buck said.

He got off. But he didn't hitch the mare. He led her up and he sat down opposite us, with the reins in his hand. "Give the stranger some meat, Ringo," Uncle Buck said. But he didn't

take it. He didn't move. He just said that he had eaten, sitting
there on the log with his little feet side by side and his elbows
out a little and his two hands on his knees as small as a
woman's hands and covered with a light mat of fine black hair
right down to the fingernails, and not looking at any of us
now. I dont know what he was looking at now.

"I have just ridden out from Memphis," he said. "How far
do you call it to Alabama?"

Uncle Buck told him, not moving either, with the spare rib
still raised in his left hand and the other hand lying just inside
his coat. "You going to Alabama, hey?"

"Yes," the stranger said. "I'm looking for a man." And now
I saw that he was looking at me from under his hat. "A man
named Grumby. You people in these parts may have heard of
him too."

"Yes," Uncle Buck said. "We have heard of him."

"Ah," the stranger said. He smiled; for a second his teeth
looked white as rice inside his inkcolored beard. "Then what
I am doing does not have to be secret." He looked at Uncle
Buck now. "I live up in Tennessee. Grumby and his gang
killed one of my niggers and ran my horses off. I'm going to
get the horses back. If I have to take Grumby in the bargain,
that will suit me too."

"Sho, now," Uncle Buck said. "So you look to find him in
Alabama?"

"Yes. I happen to know that he is now headed there. I
almost caught him yesterday; I did get one of his men,
though the others escaped me. They passed you all sometime
last night, if you were in this neighborhood then. You would
have heard them, because when I last saw them, they were
not wasting any time. I managed to persuade the man I
caught to tell me where they are to rondyvoo."

"Alabama?" Ringo said. "You mean, they headed back toward Alabama?"

"Correct," the stranger said. He looked at Ringo now.
"Did Grumby steal your hog too, boy?"

"Hawg," Ringo said. "Hawg?"

"Put some wood on the fire," Uncle Buck told Ringo.
"Save your breath to snore with tonight."

Ringo hushed but he didn't move; he sat there staring back

at the stranger, with his eyes looking a little red in the firelight. "So you folks are out to catch a man too, are you?" the
stranger said.

"Two is correct," Ringo said. "I reckon Ab Snopes can pass
for a man."

So then it was too late; we just sat there with the stranger
facing us across the fire, with the mare's reins in his little
still hand, looking at the three of us from between his hat
and his beard. "Ab Snopes," he said. "I dont believe I am
acquainted with Ab Snopes. But I know Grumby. And you
want Grumby too." He was looking at all of us now. "You
want to catch Grumby. Dont you think that's dangerous?"

"Not exactly," Uncle Buck said. "You see, we done got a
little Alabama Grumby evidence ourselves. That something or
somebody has give Grumby a change of heart about killing
women and children." He and the stranger looked at one another. "Maybe it's the wrong season for women and children.
Or maybe it's public opinion, now that Grumby is what you
might call a public character. Folks hereabouts is got used to
having ther menfolks killed and even shot from behind. But
even the Yankees never got them used to the other. And evidently somebody has done reminded Grumby of this. Aint
that correct?"

They looked at one another; they didn't move. "But you
are neither a woman nor a child, old man," the stranger said.
He stood up, easy; his eyes glinted in the firelight as he
turned and put the reins over the mare's head. "I reckon I'll
get along," he said. We watched him get into the saddle and
sit there again, with his little black haired hands lying on the
pommel, looking down at us, at me and Ringo now. "So you
want Ab Snopes," he said. "Take a stranger's advice and stick
to him."

He turned the mare. I was watching him, then I was thinking *I wonder if he knows that her off back shoe is gone* when
Ringo hollered, "Look *out!*" and then it seemed to me that I
saw the spurred mare jump before I saw the pistol flash; and
then the mare was galloping and Uncle Buck was lying on the
ground cussing and yelling and dragging at his pistol, and
then all three of us were dragging and fighting over it but the
front sight was caught in his suspenders and the three of us

fighting over it and Uncle Buck panting and cussing and the sound of the galloping mare dying away.

The bullet went through the flesh of the inner side of the arm that had the rheumatism; that was why Uncle Buck cussed so bad: he said the rheumatism was bad enough, and the bullet was bad enough, but to have them both at once was too much for any man. And then when Ringo told him he ought to be thankful, that to suppose the bullet had hit his good arm and then he wouldn't even be able to feed himself, he reached back and, still lying down, he caught up a stick of firewood and tried to hit Ringo with it. We cut his sleeve away and stopped the blood and he made me cut a strip off his shirt tail and Ringo handed him his stick and he sat there cussing us while we soaked the strip in hot salt water, and he held the arm himself with his good hand, cussing a steady streak and made us run the strip back and forth through the hole the bullet had made; he cussed then sure enough, looking a little like Granny looked, like all old people look when they have been hurt, with his beard jerking and his eyes snapping and his heels and the stick jabbing into the ground like the stick had been with him so long that it felt the rag and the salt too.

And at first I thought that the black man was Grumby, like I had thought that maybe Ab Snopes was. But Uncle Buck said not. It was the next morning; we hadn't slept much because Uncle Buck wouldn't go to sleep; only we didn't know then that it was his arm, because he wouldn't even let us talk about taking him back home. And now we tried again, after we had finished breakfast, but he wouldn't listen, already on his mule with his left arm tied across his chest and the pistol stuck between the arm and his chest, where he could get to it quick, saying Wait. Wait and his eyes hard and snapping with thinking. "It's something I aint quite got yet," he said. "Something he was telling us last night without aiming to have us know yet that he had told us. Something that we are going to find out today."

"Likely a bullet that's fixing to hit you halfway betwixt both arms stid of halfway betwixt one," Ringo said.

Uncle Buck rode fast; we could watch his stick rising and falling against the mule's flank, not hard, just steady and fast,

like a crippled man in a hurry that has used the stick so long
he dont even know it anymore. Because we didn't know that
his arm was making him sick yet; he hadn't given us time to
realise it. So we hurried on, riding along beside a slough, and
then Ringo saw the snake. It had been warm for a week until
last night. But last night it made ice and now we saw the
moccasin where it had crawled out and was trying to get back
into the water when the cold got it, so that it lay with its
body on the land and its head fixed in the skim ice like it was
set into a mirror, and Uncle Buck turned sideways on his
mule, hollering at us: "There it is, by Godfrey! There's the
sign! Didn't I tell you we would——"

We all heard it at once: the three or maybe four shots and
then the sound of horses galloping, except that some of the
galloping came from Uncle Buck's mule and he had his pistol
out now before he turned from the road and into the trees,
with the stick jammed under his hurt arm and his beard flying
back over his shoulder. But we didn't find anything. We saw
the marks in the mud where the five horses had stood while
the men that rode them had watched the road, and we saw the
sliding tracks where the horses had begun to gallop and I
thinking quietly, *He still dont know that that shoe is gone.* But
that was all, and Uncle Buck sitting on his mule with the
pistol raised in his hand and his beard blown back over his
shoulder and the leather thong of the pistol hanging down his
back like a girl's pigtail, and his mouth open and his eyes
blinking at me and Ringo. "What in the tarnation hell," he
said. "Well. Let's go back to the road. Whatever it was has
done gone that way too." So we had turned; Uncle Buck had
put the pistol up and his stick had begun to beat the mule
again when we saw what it was, what it meant.

It was Ab Snopes. He was lying on his side, tied hand and
foot and hitched to a sapling; we could see the marks in the
mud where he had tried to roll back into the underbrush until
the rope stopped him. He had been watching us all the time,
lying there with his face in the shape of snarling and not making a sound after he found out he could not roll out of sight.
He was watching our mules' legs and feet under the bushes;
he hadn't thought to look any higher yet and so he did not
know that we could see him; he must have thought that we

had just spied him because all of a sudden he began to jerk
and thrash on the ground, hollering, "Help! Help! Help!"

We untied him and got him onto his feet and he was still
hollering, loud, with his face and his arms jerking, about how
they had caught and robbed him and they would have killed
him if they hadn't heard us coming and run away: only his
eyes were not hollering. They were watching us, going fast
and quick from Ringo to me to Uncle Buck and then at
Ringo and me again and they were not hollering, like his eyes
belonged to one man and his gaped and yelling mouth belonged to another. "So they caught you, hey?" Uncle Buck
said. "A innocent and unsuspecting traveler. I reckon the
name of them would never be Grumby now, would it?"

It was like we might have stopped and built a fire and
thawed out that moccasin, just enough for it to find out
where it was but not enough for it to know what to do about
it. Only I reckon it was a high compliment to set Ab Snopes
up with a moccasin, even a little one. I reckon it was bad for
him. I reckon he realised that they had thrown him back to us
without mercy, and that if he tried to save himself from us at
their expense, they would come back and kill him. I reckon he
decided that the worst thing that could happen to him would
be for us not to do anything to him at all. Because he quit
jerking his arms; he even quit lying: for a minute his eyes and
his mouth were telling the same thing.

"I made a mistake," he said. "I admit hit. I reckon everbody
does. The question is, what are you fellows going to do about
hit?"

"Yes," Uncle Buck said. "Everybody makes mistakes. Your
trouble is, you make too many. Because mistakes are bad.
Look at Rosa Millard. She just made one, and look at her.
And you have made two."

Ab Snopes watched Uncle Buck. "What's them?"

"Being born too soon and dying too late," Uncle Buck said.

He looked at all of us, fast; he didn't move, still talking to
Uncle Buck. "You aint going to kill me. You dont dast."

"I dont even need to," Uncle Buck said. "It wasn't my
grandmaw you sicced onto that snake den."

He looked at me now, but his eyes were going again, back
and forth across me at Ringo and Uncle Buck; it was the two

of them again now, the eyes and the voice. "Why, then I'm all right. Bayard aint got no hard feelings against me. He knows hit was a pure accident; that we was doing hit for his sake and his paw and them niggers at home; why, here hit's a whole year and it was me that holp and tended Miss Rosa when she never had ara living soul but them chil——" Now the voice began to tell the truth again; it was the eyes and the voice that I was walking toward. He fell back, crouching, his hands flung up; behind me Uncle Buck said,

"You, Ringo! Stay back."

He was walking backward now, with his hands flung up, hollering, "Three on one! Three on one!"

"Stand still," Uncle Buck said. "Aint no three on you. I dont see nobody on you but one of them children you was just mentioning." Then we were both down in the mud: and then I couldn't see him and I couldn't seem to find him anymore, not even with the hollering: and then I was fighting three or four for a long time before Uncle Buck and Ringo held me and then I could see him again, lying on the ground with his arms over his face. "Get up," Uncle Buck said.

"No," he said. "Three of you can jump on me and knock me down again, but you got to pick me up first to do hit. I aint got no rights and justice here, but you cant keep me from protesting hit."

"Lift him up," Uncle Buck said. "I'll hold Bayard."

Ringo lifted him; it was like lifting a half filled cotton sack. "Stand up, *Mister* Ab Snopes," Ringo said. But he would not stand, not even after Ringo and Uncle Buck tied him to the sapling and Ringo had taken off his and Uncle Buck's and Ab Snopes' galluses and knotted them together with the bridle reins from the mules. He just hung there in the rope, not even flinching when the lash fell, saying,

"That's hit. Whup me. Lay hit on me; you got me three to one."

"Wait," Uncle Buck said. Ringo stopped. "You want another chance with one to one? You can take your choice of the three of us."

"I got my rights," he said. "I'm helpless, but I can still protest hit. Whup me."

I reckon he was right. I reckon if we had let him go clean,

they would have circled back and killed him themselves before dark. Because (that was the night it began to rain and we had to burn Ringo's stick because Uncle Buck admitted now that his arm was getting bad) we all ate supper together and it was Ab Snopes that was the most anxious about Uncle Buck, saying how it wasn't any hard feelings and that he could see himself that he had made a mistake in trusting the folks he did and that all he wanted to do now was to go back home because it was only the folks you had known all your life that you could trust and when you put faith in a stranger you deserved what you got when you found that what you had been eating and sleeping with was no better than a passel of rattlesnakes. But as soon as Uncle Buck tried to find out if it actually was Grumby, he shut up and denied that he had ever even seen him.

They left us early the next morning. Uncle Buck was sick by then; we offered to ride back home with him, or to let Ringo ride back with him and I would keep Ab Snopes with me, but Uncle Buck wouldn't have it. "Grumby might capture him again and tie him to another sapling in the road and you would lose time burying him," Uncle Buck said. "You boys go on. It aint going to be long now. And catch them!" He begun to holler, with his face flushed and his eyes bright, taking the pistol from around his neck and giving it to me. "Catch them! Catch them!"

3.

So Ringo and I went on. It rained all that day; now it began to rain all the time. We had the two mules apiece; we went fast. It rained; sometimes we had no fire at all; that was when we lost count of time because one morning we came to a fire still burning and a hog they had not even had time to butcher and sometimes we would ride all night, swapping mules when we had guessed that it had been two hours, and so sometimes it would be night when we slept and sometimes it would be daylight and we knew that they must have watched us from somewhere every day and that now that Uncle Buck was not with us, they didn't even dare to stop and try to hide.

Then one afternoon—the rain had stopped but the clouds
had not broken and it was turning cold again—it was about
dusk and we were galloping along an old road in the river
bottom; it was dim and narrow under the trees and we were
galloping when my mule shied and swerved and stopped and
I just did catch myself before I went over his head; and then
we saw the thing hanging over the middle of the road from a
limb. It was an old negro man, with a rim of white hair and
with his bare toes pointing down and his head on one side
like he was thinking about something quiet. The note was
pinned to him, but we couldn't read it until we rode on into a
clearing. It was a scrap of dirty paper, with big crude printed
letters like a child might have made them:

> Last woning not thret. Turn back. The barer of this my
> promise and garntee. I have stood all I aim to stand chil-
> dren no children.
>
> G.

And something else, written beneath it in a hand neat and
small and prettier than Granny's, only you knew that a man
had written it and while I looked at the dirty paper I could
see him again, with his neat little feet and his little black
haired hands and his fine soiled shirt and his fine muddy coat,
across the fire from us that night:

> This is signed by others beside G., one of wh$^{\underline{m}}$ in particular
> hav$^{\underline{ng}}$ less scruples re children than he has. Nethless under-
> s$^{\underline{gnd}}$ desires to give both you and G. one more chance. Take
> it, and someday become a man. Refuse it, and cease even to
> be a child.

Ringo and I looked at one another. There had been a house
here once, but it was gone now. Beyond the clearing the road
went on again into the thick trees, in the gray twilight.
"Maybe it will be tomorrow," Ringo said.

It was tomorrow; we slept that night in a haystack but
we were riding again by daylight, following the dim road
along the river bottom. This time it was Ringo's mule that
shied: the man had stepped out of the bushes that quick,
with his fine muddy boots and coat and the pistol in his
little black haired hand and only his eyes and his nose

showing between his hat and his beard. "Stay where you are,"
he said. "I will still be watching you." We didn't move. We
watched him step back in to the bushes, then the three of
them came out: the bearded man and another man walking
abreast and leading two saddled horses, and the third man
walking just in front of them with his hands behind him—a
thick built man with a reddish stubble and pale eyes, in a
faded Confederate uniform coat and Yankee boots, bareheaded, with a long smear of dried blood on his cheek and
one side of his coat caked with dried mud and that sleeve
ripped away at the shoulder, but we didn't realise at once
that what made his shoulders look so thick was that his
arms were tied tight behind him. And then all of a sudden we
knew that at last we were looking at Grumby. We knew it
long before the bearded man said, "You want Grumby. Here
he is."

We just sat there. Because from then on, the other two men
did not even look at us again. "I'll take him now," the
bearded man said. "Get on your horse." The other man got
on one of the horses. We could see the pistol in his hand then,
pointed at Grumby's back. "Hand me your knife," the
bearded man said.

Without moving the pistol, the other man passed his knife
to the bearded man. Then Grumby spoke; he had not moved
until now; he just stood there with his shoulders hunched and
his little pale eyes blinking at me and Ringo.

"Boys," he said, "boys—"

"Shut your mouth," the bearded man said, in a cold, quiet,
almost pleasant voice. "You've already talked too much. If
you had done what I wanted done that night in December,
you wouldn't be where you are now." We saw his hand with
the knife; I reckon maybe for a minute Ringo and I and
Grumby, too, all thought the same thing. But he just cut
Grumby's hands loose and stepped back quick. But when
Grumby turned, he turned right into the pistol in the bearded
man's hand.

"Steady," the bearded man said. "Have you got him,
Bridger?"

"Yes," the other man said. The bearded man backed to
the other horse and got on it without lowering his pistol or

ceasing to watch Grumby. Then he sat there, too, looking down at Grumby, with his little hooked nose and his eyes alone showing between the hat and the inkcolored beard. Grumby began to move his head from side to side.

"Boys," he said, "boys, you aint going to do this to me."

"We're not going to do anything to you," the bearded man said. "I cant speak for these boys there. But since you are so delicate about children, maybe they will be delicate with you. But we'll give you a chance though." His other hand went inside his coat too fast to watch; it had hardly disappeared before the other pistol flicked out and turned once and fell at Grumby's feet; again Grumby moved, but the pistols stopped him. The bearded man sat easy on the horse, looking down at Grumby, talking in that cold, still, vicious voice that wasn't even mad:

"We had a good thing in this country. We would have it yet, if it hadn't been for you. And now we've got to pull out. Got to leave it because you lost your nerve and killed an old woman and then lost your nerve again and refused to cover the first mistake. Scruples," he said. "Scruples. So afraid of raising the country that there aint a man woman or child black or white in it that aint on the watch for us. And all because you got scared and killed an old woman you never saw before. Not to get anything: not for one single Confed. banknote. But because you got scared of a piece of paper on which someone had signed Bedford Forrest's name. And you with one exactly like it in your pocket now." He didn't look at the other man, Bridger, he just said, "All right. Ease off. But watch him. He's too tender hearted to turn your back on." They backed the horses away, side by side, the two pistols trained on Grumby's belly, until they reached the underbrush. "We're going to Texas. If you should leave this place, I would advise you to go at least that far, also. But just remember that Texas is a wide place, and use that knowledge. Ride!" he shouted.

He whirled the mare. Bridger whirled too. As they did so, Grumby leaped and caught the pistol from the ground and ran forward, crouching and shouting into the bushes, cursing. He shot three times toward the fading sound of the horses, then he whirled back to face us. Ringo and I were on the ground, too; I dont remember when we got down nor why, but we were down, and I remember how I looked once at Ringo's face and then how I stood there with Uncle Buck's pistol feeling heavy as a firedog in my hand. Then I saw that he had quit whirling; that he was standing there with the pistol hanging against his right leg and that he was looking at me; and then all of a sudden he was smiling.

"Well, boys," he said, "it looks like you have got me. Durn my hide for letting Matt Bowden fool me into emptying my pistol at him."

And I could hear my voice; it sounded faint and far away, like the woman's in Alabama that day, so that I wondered if he could hear me: "You shot three times. You have got two more shots in it."

His face didn't change, or I couldn't see it change. It just lowered, looking down, but the smile was gone from it. "In this pistol?" he said. It was like he was examining a pistol for the first time, so slow and careful it was that he passed it from his right to his left hand and let it hang again, pointing down again. "Well, well, well. Sholy I aint forgot how to count as well as how to shoot." There was a bird somewhere—a yellowhammer—I had been hearing it all the time; even the three shots hadn't frightened it. And I could hear Ringo, too, making a kind of whimpering sound when he breathed, and it was like I wasn't trying to watch Grumby so much as to keep from looking at Ringo. "Well, she's safe enough now, since it dont look like I can even shoot with my right hand."

Then it happened. I know what did happen, but even now I dont know how, in what order. Because he was big and squat, like a bear. But when we had first seen him he was a captive, and so, even now he seemed more like a stump than even an animal, even though we had watched him leap and catch up the pistol and run firing after the other two. All I know is, one second he was standing there in his muddy Confederate coat, smiling at us, with his ragged teeth showing a little in his red stubble, with the thin sunlight on the stubble and on his shoulders and cuffs, on the dark marks where the braid had been ripped away; and the next second there were two bright orange splashes, one after the other, against the middle of the gray coat and the coat itself swelling slow down

on me like when Granny told us about the balloon she saw in
St Louis and we would dream about it.

I reckon I heard the sound, and I reckon I must have heard
the bullets, and I reckon I felt him when he hit me, but I dont
remember it. I just remember the two bright flashes and the
gray coat rushing down, and then the ground hitting me. But
I could smell him—the smell of man sweat, and the gray coat
grinding into my face and smelling of horse sweat and wood
smoke and grease—and I could hear him, and then I could
hear my arm socket, and I thought *In a minute I will hear my
fingers breaking, but I have got to hold onto it* and then—I dont
know whether it was under or over his arm or his leg—I saw
Ringo, in the air, looking exactly like a frog, even to the eyes,
with his mouth open too and his open pocket knife in his
hand.

Then I was free. I saw Ringo straddle of Grumby's back
and Grumby getting up from his hands and knees and I tried
to raise the pistol only my arm wouldn't move. Then Grumby
bucked Ringo off just like a steer would and whirled again,
looking at us, crouched, with his mouth open too; and then
my arm began to come up with the pistol and he turned and
ran. He shouldn't have tried to run from us in boots. Or
maybe that made no difference either, because now my arm
had come up and now I could see Grumby's back (he didn't
scream, he never made a sound) and the pistol both at the
same time and the pistol was level and steady as a rock.

4.

It took us the rest of that day and part of the night to reach
the old compress. But it didn't take very long to ride home
because we went fast with the two mounts apiece to change
to, and what we had to carry now, wrapped in a piece of the
skirt of Grumby's coat, didn't weigh anything.

It was almost dark when we rode through Jefferson; it was
raining again when we rode past the brick piles and the sooty
walls that hadn't fallen down yet, and went on through what
used to be the square. We hitched the mules in the cedars
and Ringo was just starting off to find a board when we
saw that somebody had already put one up—Mrs Compson,

I reckon, or maybe Uncle Buck when he got back home. We already had the piece of wire.

The earth had sunk too now, after two months; it was almost level now, like at first Granny had not wanted to be dead either but now she had begun to be reconciled. We unwrapped it from the jagged square of stained faded gray cloth and fastened it to the board. "Now she can lay good and quiet," Ringo said.

"Yes," I said. And then we both began to cry. We stood there in the slow rain, crying. We had ridden a lot, and during the last week we hadn't slept much and we hadn't always had anything to eat.

"It wasn't him or Ab Snopes either that kilt her," Ringo said. "It was them mules. That first batch of mules we got for nothing."

"Yes," I said. "Let's go home. I reckon Louvinia is worried about us."

So it was good and dark when we came to the cabin. And then we saw that it was lighted like for Christmas; we could see the big fire and the lamp clean and bright when Louvinia opened the door long before we had got to it and ran out into the rain and began to paw at me, crying and hollering.

"What?" I said. "Father? Father's home? *Father?*"

"And Miss Drusilla!" Louvinia hollered, crying and praying and pawing at me and hollering and scolding at Ringo all at once. "Home! Hit done finished! All but the surrendering. And now Marse John done home." She finally told us, how Father and Drusilla had come home about a week ago and Uncle Buck told Father where Ringo and I were, and how Father had tried to make Drusilla wait at home but she refused, and how they were looking for us with Uncle Buck to show the way.

So we went to bed. We couldn't even stay awake to eat the supper Louvinia cooked for us; Ringo and I went to bed in our clothes on the pallet and went to sleep all in one motion, with Louvinia's face hanging over us and still scolding and Joby in the chimney corner where Louvinia had made him get up out of Granny's chair. And then somebody was pulling at me and I thought I was fighting Ab Snopes again and then it was the rain in Father's beard and clothes that I smelled. But Uncle Buck was still hollering, and Father holding me and Ringo and I held to him and then it was Drusilla kneeling and holding me and Ringo and we could smell the rain in her hair too while she was hollering at Uncle Buck to hush. Father's hand was hard; I could see his face beyond Drusilla and I was trying to say "Father. Father" while she was holding me and Ringo with the rain smell of her hair all around us and Uncle Buck hollering and Joby looking at Uncle Buck with his mouth open and his eyes round:

"Yes, by Godfrey! Not only tracked him down and caught him, but brought back the actual proof of it to where Rosa Millard could rest quiet."

"The which?" Joby hollered. "Fotch back the which?"

"Hush! Hush!" Drusilla said. "That's all done, all finished. You, Uncle Buck!"

"The proof and the expiation!" Uncle Buck hollered. "When me and John Sartoris and Drusilla rode up to that old compress, the first thing we see was that murdering scoundrel pegged out on the door to it like a coon hide, all except the right hand. 'And if anybody wants to see that too,' I told John Sartoris, 'just let them ride into Jefferson and look on Rosa Millard's grave!' Aint I told you he is John Sartoris' boy? Hey? Aint I told you?"

SKIRMISH AT SARTORIS

I.

WHEN I THINK of that day, of Father's old troop on their horses drawn up facing the house, and Father and Drusilla on the ground with that carpet bagger voting box in front of them, and opposite them the women—Aunt Louisa, Mrs Habersham and all the others—on the porch and the two sets of them, the men and the women, facing one another like they were both waiting for a bugle to sound the charge, I think I know the reason. I think it was because Father's troop (like all the other Southern soldiers too), even though they had surrendered and said that they were whipped, were still soldiers. Maybe from the old habit of doing everything as one man; maybe when you have lived for four years in a world ordered completely by men's doings, even when it is danger and fighting, you dont want to quit that world: maybe the danger and the fighting are the reasons, because men have been pacifists for every reason under the sun except to avoid danger and fighting. And so now Father's troop and all the other men in Jefferson, and Aunt Louisa and Mrs Habersham and all the women in Jefferson were actually enemies for the reason that the men had given in and admitted that they belonged to the United States but the women had never surrendered.

I remember the night we got the letter and found out at last where Drusilla was. It was just before Christmas in 1864,

446

after the Yankees had burned Jefferson and gone away, and we didn't even know for sure if the War was still going on or not. All we knew was that for three years the country had been full of Yankees, and then all of a sudden they were gone and there were no men there at all anymore. We hadn't even heard from Father since July, from Carolina, so that now we lived in a world of burned towns and houses and ruined plantations and fields inhabited only by women. Ringo and I were fifteen then; we felt almost exactly like we had to eat and sleep and change our clothes in a hotel built only for ladies and children.

The envelope was worn and dirty and it had been opened once and then glued back, but we could still make out *Hawkhurst, Gihon County, Alabama* on it even though we did not recognise Aunt Louisa's hand at first. It was addressed to Granny; it was six pages cut with scissors from wallpaper and written on both sides with pokeberry juice and I thought of that night eighteen months ago when Drusilla and I stood outside the cabin at Hawkhurst and listened to the niggers passing in the road, the night when she told me about the dog, about keeping the dog quiet, and then asked me to ask Father to let her join his troop and ride with him. But I didn't tell Father. Maybe I forgot it. Then the Yankees went away, and Father and his troop went away too. Then, six months later, we had a letter from him about how they were fighting in Carolina, and a month after that we had one from Aunt Louisa that Drusilla was gone too, a short letter on the wallpaper that you could see where Aunt Louisa had cried in the pokeberry juice about how she did not know where Drusilla was but that she had expected the worst ever since Drusilla had deliberately tried to unsex herself by refusing to feel any natural grief at the death in battle not only of her affianced husband but of her own father and that she took it for granted that Drusilla was with us and though she did not expect Drusilla to take any steps herself to relieve a mother's anxiety, she hoped that Granny would. But we didn't know where Drusilla was either. She had just vanished. It was like the Yankees in just passing through the South had not only taken along with them all living men blue and gray and white and black, but even one young girl who had happened to try to look and act like a man after her sweet-heart was killed.

So then the next letter came. Only Granny wasn't there to read it because she was dead then (it was the time when Grumby doubled back past Jefferson and so Ringo and I spent one night at home and found the letter when Mrs Compson had sent it out) and so for a while Ringo and I couldn't make out what Aunt Louisa was trying to tell us. This one was on the same wallpaper too, six pages this time, only Aunt Louisa hadn't cried in the pokeberry juice this time: Ringo said because she must have been writing too fast:

Dear sister:

I think this will be news to you as it was to me though I both hope and pray it will not be the heart-rending shock to you it was to me as naturally it cannot since you are only an aunt while I am the mother. But it is not myself I am thinking of since I am a woman, a mother, a Southern woman, and it has been our lot during the last four years to learn to bear anything. But when I think of my husband who laid down his life to protect a heritage of courageous men and spotless women looking down from heaven upon a daughter who had deliberately cast away that for which he died, and when I think of my half orphan son who will one day ask of me why his martyred father's sacrifice was not enough to preserve his sister's good name——

That's how it sounded. Ringo was holding a pineknot for me to read by, but after a while he had to light another pine-knot and all the farther we had got was how when Gavin Breckbridge was killed at Shiloh before he and Drusilla had had time to marry, there had been reserved for Drusilla the highest destiny of a Southern woman—to be the bride-widow of a lost cause—and how Drusilla had not only thrown that away, she had not only become a lost woman and a shame to her father's memory but she was now living in a word that Aunt Louisa would not even repeat but that Granny knew what it was, though at least thank God that Father and Drusilla were not actually any blood kin, it being

Father's wife who was Drusilla's cousin by blood and not
Father himself. So then Ringo lit the other pineknot and
then we put the sheets of wallpaper down on the floor and
then we found out what it was: how Drusilla had been gone
for six months and no word from her except she was alive,
and then one night she walked into the cabin where Aunt
Louisa and Denny were (and now it had a line drawn under
it, like this:) <u>in the garments not alone of a man but of a
common private soldier</u> and told them how she had been
a member of Father's troop for six months, bivouacking
at night surrounded by sleeping men and not even bothering
to put up the tent for her and Father except when the weather
was bad, and how Drusilla not only showed neither shame
nor remorse but actually pretended she did not even know
what Aunt Louisa was talking about; how when Aunt Louisa
told her that she and Father must marry at once Drusilla said
Cant you understand that I am tired of burying husbands in
this war? that I am riding in Cousin John's troop not to find a
man but to hurt Yankees? and how Aunt Louisa said At least
dont call him *Cousin* John where strangers can hear you.

2.

The third letter did not come to us at all. It came to Mrs
Compson. Drusilla and Father were home then. It was in
the spring and the War was over now, and we were busy
getting the cypress and oak out of the bottom to build the
house and Drusilla working with Joby and Ringo and Father
and me like another man, with her hair shorter than it had
been at Hawkhurst and her face sunburned from riding in
the weather and her body thin from living like soldiers lived.
After Granny died Ringo and Louvinia and I all slept in the
cabin, but after Father came Ringo and Louvinia moved back
to the other cabin with Joby and now Father and I slept on
Ringo's and my pallet and Drusilla slept in the bed behind the
quilt curtain where Granny used to sleep. And so one night I
remembered Aunt Louisa's letter and I showed it to Drusilla
and Father, and Father found out that Drusilla had not written to tell Aunt Louisa where she was and Father said she
must, and so one day Mrs Compson came out with the third

letter. Drusilla and Ringo and Louvinia too were down in the bottom at the sawmill and I saw that one too, on the wall-paper with the pokeberry juice and the juice not cried on this time either, and this the first time Mrs Compson had come out since Granny died and not even getting out of her surrey but sitting there holding to her parasol with one hand and her shawl with the other and looking around like when Drusilla would come out of the house or from around the corner it would not be just a thin sunburned girl in a man's shirt and pants but maybe something like a tame panther or bear. This one sounded just like the others: about how Aunt Louisa was addressing a stranger to herself but not a stranger to Granny and that there were times when the good name of one family was the good name of all and that she naturally did not expect Mrs Compson to move out and live with Father and Drusilla because even that would be too late now to preserve the appearance of that which had never existed anyway. But that Mrs Compson was a woman too, Aunt Louisa believed, a Southern woman too, and had suffered too, Aunt Louisa didn't doubt, only she did hope and pray that Mrs Compson had been spared the sight of her own daughter if Mrs Compson had one flouting and outraging all Southern principles of purity and womanhood that our husbands had died for, though Aunt Louisa hoped again that Mrs Compson's husband (Mrs Compson was a good deal older than Granny and the only husband she had ever had had been locked up for crazy a long time ago because in the slack part of the afternoons he would gather up eight or ten little niggers from the quarters and line them up across the creek from him with sweet potatoes on their heads and he would shoot the potatoes off with a rifle; he would tell them he might miss a potato but he wasn't going to miss a nig-ger, and so they would stand mighty still) had not made one of the number. So I couldn't make any sense out of that one too and I still didn't know what Aunt Louisa was talk-ing about and I didn't believe that Mrs Compson knew either.

Because it was not her: it was Mrs Habersham, that never had been out here before and that Granny never had been to see that I knew of. Because Mrs Compson didn't stay, she didn't even get out of the surrey, sitting there kind of drawn up under the shawl and looking at me and then at the cabin like she didn't know just what might come out of it or out from behind it. Then she began to tap the nigger driver on his head with the parasol and they went away, the two old horses going pretty fast back down the drive and back down the road to town. And the next afternoon when I came out of the bottom to go to the spring with the water bucket there were five surreys and buggies in front of the cabin and inside the cabin there were fourteen of them that had come the four miles out from Jefferson, in the Sunday clothes that the Yankees and the War had left them, that had husbands dead in the War or alive back in Jefferson helping Father with what he was doing, because they were strange times then. Only like I said, maybe times are never strange to women: that it is just one continuous monotonous thing full of the repeated follies of their menfolks. Mrs Compson was sitting in Granny's chair, still holding the parasol and drawn up under her shawl and looking like she had finally seen whatever it was she had expected to see, and it had been the panther. It was Mrs Habersham who was holding back the quilt for the others to go in and look at the bed where Drusilla slept and then showing them the pallet where Father and I slept. Then she saw me and said, "And who is this?"

"That's Bayard," Mrs Compson said.

"You poor child," Mrs Habersham said. So I didn't stop. But I couldn't help but hear them. It sounded like a ladies' club meeting with Mrs Habersham running it, because every now and then Mrs Habersham would forget to whisper: "——mother should come, be sent for at once. But lacking her presence. . . . . . .we, the ladies of the community, mothers ourselves. . . . . . .child probably taken advantage of by gallant romantic. . . . . . .before realising the price she must——" and Mrs Compson said, "Hush! Hush!" and then somebody else said, "Do you really suppose——" and then Mrs Habersham forgot to whisper good: "What else? What other reason can you name why she should choose to conceal herself down there in the woods all day long, lifting heavy weights like logs and——"

Then I went away. I filled the bucket at the spring and

went back to the log-yard where Drusilla and Ringo and Joby were feeding the bandsaw and the blindfolded mule going round and round in the sawdust. And then Joby kind of made a sound and we all stopped and looked and there was Mrs Habersham, with three of the others kind of peeping out from behind her with their eyes round and bright, looking at Drusilla standing there in the sawdust and shavings, in her dirty sweated overalls and shirt and brogans, with her face sweat-streaked with sawdust and her short hair yellow with it. "I am Martha Habersham," Mrs Habersham said. "I am a neighbor and I hope to be a friend." And then she said, "You poor child."

We just looked at her; when Drusilla finally spoke, she sounded like Ringo and I would when Father would say something to us in Latin for a joke. "Ma'am?" Drusilla said. Because I was just fifteen; I still didn't know what it was all about; I just stood there and listened without even thinking much, like when they had been talking in the cabin. "My condition?" Drusilla said. "My——"

"Yes," Mrs Habersham said. "No mother, no woman to . . . . . . .forced to these straits——" kind of waving her hand at the mules that hadn't stopped and at Joby and Ringo goggling at her and the three others still peeping around her at Drusilla. ". . . to offer you not only our help, but our sympathy."

"My condition," Drusilla said. "My con—— Help and sym——" Then she began to say, "Oh. Oh. Oh." standing there, and then she was running. She began to run like a deer, that starts to run and then decides where it wants to go: she turned right in the air and came toward me, running light over the logs and planks, with her mouth open, saying "John. John." not loud; for a minute it was like she thought I was Father until she waked up and found I was not; she stopped without even ceasing to run, like a bird stops in the air, motionless yet still furious with movement. "Is that what you think too?" she said. Then she was gone. Every now and then I could see her footprints, spaced and fast, just inside the woods, but when I came out of the bottom, I couldn't see her. But the surreys and buggies were still in front of the cabin and I could see Mrs Compson and the other ladies on the porch, looking out across the pasture toward the bottom, so I did not go there. But before I came to the other cabin, where Louvinia and Joby and Ringo lived, I saw Louvinia come up the hill from the spring, carrying her cedar water bucket and singing. Then she went into the cabin and the singing stopped short off and so I knew where Drusilla was. But I didn't hide. I went to the window and looked in and saw Drusilla just turning from where she had been leaning her head in her arms on the mantel when Louvinia came in with the water bucket and a gum twig in her mouth and Father's old hat on top of her headrag. Drusilla was crying. "That's what it is, then," she said. "Coming down there to the mill and telling me that in my condition— sympathy and help—— Strangers; I never saw any of them before and I dont care a damn what they—— But you and Bayard. Is that what you believe? that John and I—that we——" Then Louvinia moved. Her hand came out quicker than Drusilla could jerk back and lay flat on the belly of Drusilla's overalls, then Louvinia was holding Drusilla in her arms like she used to hold me and Drusilla was crying hard. "That John and I—that we— And Gavin dead at Shiloh and John's home burned and his plantation ruined, that he and I—— We went to the War to hurt Yankees, not hunting women!"

"I knows you aint," Louvinia said. "Hush now. Hush."

And that's about all. It didn't take them long. I dont know whether Mrs Habersham made Mrs Compson send for Aunt Louisa or whether Aunt Louisa just gave them a deadline and then came herself. Because we were busy, Drusilla and Joby and Ringo and me at the mill, and Father in town; we wouldn't see him from the time he would ride away in the morning until when he would get back, sometimes late, at night. Because they were strange times then. For four years we had lived for just one thing, even the women and children who could not fight: to get Yankee troops out of the country; we thought that when that happened, it would be all over. And now that had happened, and then before the summer began I heard Father say to Drusilla, "We were promised Federal troops; Lincoln himself promised to send us troops. Then things will be all right." That, from a man who had commanded a regiment for four years with the avowed purpose of driving Federal troops from the country. Now it was as though we had not surrendered at all, we had joined forces with the men who had been our enemies against a new foe whose means we could not always fathom but whose aim we could always dread. So he was busy in town all day long. They were building Jefferson back, the courthouse and the stores, but it was more than that which Father and the other men were doing; it was something which he would not let Drusilla or me or Ringo go into town to see. Then one day Ringo slipped off and went to town and came back and he looked at me with his eyes rolling a little.

"Do you know what I aint?" he said.

"What?" I said.

"I aint a nigger anymore. I done been abolished." Then I asked him what he was, if he wasn't a nigger anymore and he showed me what he had in his hand. It was a new scrip dollar; it was drawn on the United States Resident Treasurer, Yoknapatawpha County, Mississippi, and signed "Cassius Q. Benbow, Acting Marshal" in a neat clerk's hand, with a big sprawling X under it.

"Cassius Q. Benbow?" I said.

"Co-rect," Ringo said. "Uncle Cash that druv the Benbow carriage twell he run off with the Yankees two years ago. He back now and he gonter be elected Marshal of Jefferson. That's what Marse John and the other white folks is so busy about."

"A nigger?" I said. "A nigger?"

"No," Ringo said. "They aint no more niggers, in Jefferson nor nowhere else." Then he told me about the two Burdens from Missouri, with a patent from Washington to organise the niggers into Republicans, and how Father and the other men were trying to prevent it. "Naw, suh," he said. "This War aint over. Hit just started good. Used to be when you seed a Yankee you knowed him because he never had nothing but a gun or a mule halter or a handful of hen feathers. Now you dont even know him and stid of the gun he got a clutch of this stuff in one hand and a clutch of nigger voting tickets in the yuther." So we were busy; we just saw Father at night and sometimes then Ringo and I and even Drusilla would take one look at him and we wouldn't ask him any questions. So it didn't take them long, because Drusilla was already beaten; she was just marking time without knowing it from that afternoon when the fourteen ladies got into the surreys and buggies and went back to town until one afternoon about two months later when we heard Denny hollering even before the wagon came in the gates, and Aunt Louisa sitting on one of the trunks (that's what beat Drusilla: the trunks. They had her dresses in them that she hadn't worn in three years; Ringo never had seen her in a dress until Aunt Louisa came) in mourning even to the crepe bow on her umbrella handle, that hadn't worn mourning when we were at Hawkhurst two years ago though Uncle Dennison was just as dead then as he was now. She came to the cabin and got out of the wagon, already crying and talking just like the letters sounded, like even when you listened to her you had to skip around fast to make any sense:

"I have come to appeal to them once more with a mother's tears though I dont think it will do any good though I had prayed until the very last that this boy's innocence might be spared and preserved but what must be must be and at least we can all three bear our burden together"; sitting in Granny's chair in the middle of the room, without even laying down the umbrella or taking her bonnet off, looking at the pallet where Father and I slept and then at the quilt nailed to the rafter to make a room for Drusilla, dabbing at her mouth with a handkerchief that made the whole cabin smell like dead roses. And then Drusilla came in from the mill, in the muddy brogans and the sweaty shirt and overalls and her hair sunburned and full of sawdust, and Aunt Louisa looked at her once and began to cry again, saying, "Lost, lost. Thank God in His mercy that Dennison Hawk was taken before he lived to see what I see."

She was already beaten. Aunt Louisa made her put on a dress that night; we watched her run out of the cabin in it and run down the hill toward the spring while we were waiting for Father. And he came and walked into the cabin where Aunt Louisa was still sitting in Granny's chair with the handkerchief before her mouth. "This is a pleasant surprise, Miss Louisa," Father said.

"It is not pleasant to me, Colonel Sartoris," Aunt Louisa said. "And after a year, I suppose I cannot call it surprise. But it is still a shock." So Father came out too and we went down to the spring and found Drusilla hiding behind the big beech, crouched down like she was trying to hide the skirt from Father even while he raised her up. "What's a dress?" he said. "It dont matter. Come. Get up, soldier."

But she was beaten, like as soon as she let them put the dress on her she was whipped; like in the dress she could neither fight back nor run away. And so she didn't come down to the log-yard anymore, and now that Father and I slept in the cabin with Joby and Ringo, I didn't even see Drusilla except at mealtime. And we were busy getting the timber out, and now everybody was talking about the election and how Father had told the two Burdens before all the men in town that the election would never be held with Cash Benbow or any other nigger in it and how the Burdens had dared him to stop it. And besides, the other cabin would be full of Jefferson ladies all day; you would have thought that Drusilla was Mrs Habersham's daughter and not Aunt Louisa's. They would begin to arrive right after breakfast and stay all day, so that at supper Aunt Louisa would sit in her black mourning except for the bonnet and umbrella, with a wad of some kind of black knitting she carried around with her and that never got finished and the folded handkerchief handy in her belt (only she ate fine; she ate more than Father even because the election was just a week off and I reckon he was thinking about the Burdens) and refusing to speak to anybody except Denny; and Drusilla trying to eat, with her face strained and thin and her eyes like somebody's that had been whipped a long time now and is going just on nerve.

Then Drusilla broke; they beat her. Because she was strong; she wasn't much older than I was, but she had let Aunt Louisa and Mrs Habersham choose the game and she had beat them both until that night when Aunt Louisa went behind her back and chose a game she couldn't beat. I was coming up to supper; I heard them inside the cabin before I could stop: "Cant you believe me?" Drusilla said. "Cant you understand that in the troop I was just another man and not much of one at that, and since we came home here I am just another mouth for John to feed, just a cousin of John's wife and not much older than his own son?" And I could almost see Aunt Louisa sitting there with that knitting that never progressed:

"You wish to tell me that you, a young woman, associated with him, a still young man, day and night for a year, running about the country with no guard nor check of any sort upon—— Do you take me for a complete fool?" So that night Aunt Louisa beat her; we had just sat down to supper when Aunt Louisa looked at me like she had been waiting for the noise of the bench to stop: "Bayard, I do not ask your forgiveness for this because it is your burden too; you are an innocent victim as well as Dennison and I——" Then she looked at Father, thrust back in Granny's chair (the only chair we had) in her black dress, the black wad of knitting beside her plate. "Colonel Sartoris," she said, "I am a woman; I must request what the husband whom I have lost and the man son which I have not would demand, perhaps at the point of a pistol— Will you marry my daughter?"

I got out. I moved fast; I heard the light sharp sound when Drusilla's head went down between her flungout arms on the table, and the sound the bench made when Father got up too; I passed him standing beside Drusilla with his hand on her head. "They have beat you, Drusilla," he said.

3.

Mrs Habersham got there before we had finished breakfast the next morning. I dont know how Aunt Louisa got word in to her so quick. But there she was, and she and Aunt Louisa set the wedding for the day after tomorrow. I dont reckon they even knew that that was the day Father had told the Burdens Cash Benbow would never be elected Marshal in Jefferson. I dont reckon they paid any more attention to it than if all the men had decided that day after tomorrow all the clocks in Jefferson were to be set back or up an hour. Maybe they didn't even know there was to be an election, that all the men in the county would be riding toward Jefferson tomorrow with pistols in their pockets, and that the Burdens already had their nigger voters camped in a cotton gin on the edge of town under guard. I dont reckon they even cared. Because like Father said, women cannot believe that anything can be right or wrong or even be very important that can be decided by a lot of little scraps of scribbled paper dropped into a box.

It was to be a big wedding; all Jefferson was to be invited and Mrs Habersham planning to bring the three bottles of Madeira she had been saving for five years now when Aunt Louisa began to cry again. But they caught on quick now; now all of them were patting Aunt Louisa's hands and giving her vinegar to smell and Mrs Habersham saying, "Of course. You poor thing. A public wedding now, after a year, would be a public notice of the . . . ." So they decided it would be a reception, because Mrs Habersham said how a reception could be held for a bridal couple at any time, even ten years later. So Drusilla was to ride into town, meet Father and be married as quick and quiet as possible, with just me and one other for witnesses to make it legal; none of the ladies themselves would even be present. Then they would come back home and we would have the reception.

So they began to arrive early the next morning, with baskets of food and tablecloths and silver like for a church supper. Mrs Habersham brought a veil and a wreath and they all helped Drusilla to dress, only Aunt Louisa made Drusilla put on Father's big riding cloak over the veil and wreath too, and Ringo brought the horses up, all curried and brushed, and I helped Drusilla on with Aunt Louisa and the others all watching from the porch. But I didn't know that Ringo was missing when we started, not even when I heard Aunt Louisa hollering for Denny while we rode down the drive. It was Louvinia that told about it, about how after we left the ladies set and decorated the table and spread the wedding breakfast and how they were all watching the gate and Aunt Louisa still hollering for Denny now and then when they saw Ringo and Denny come up the drive riding double on one of the mules at a gallop, with Denny's eyes round as doorknobs and already hollering, "They kilt um! They kilt um!"

"Who?" Aunt Louisa hollered. "Where have you been?"

"To town!" Denny hollered. "Them two Burdens! They kilt um!"

"Who killed them?" Aunt Louisa hollered.

"Drusilla and Cousin John!" Denny hollered. Then Louvinia said how Aunt Louisa hollered sure enough.

"Do you mean to tell me that Drusilla and that man are not married yet?"

Because we didn't have time. Maybe Drusilla and Father would have, but when we came into the square we saw the crowd of niggers kind of huddled beyond the hotel door with six or eight strange white men herding them, and then all of a sudden I saw the Jefferson men, the men that I knew, that Father knew, running across the square toward the hotel with each one holding his hip like a man runs with a pistol in his pocket. And then I saw the men who were Father's troop lined up before the hotel door, blocking it off. And then I was sliding off my horse too and watching Drusilla struggling with George Wyatt. But he didn't have hold of her, he just had hold of the cloak, and then she was through the line of them and running toward the hotel with her wreath on one side of her head and the veil streaming behind. But George held me. He threw the cloak down and held me. "Let go," I said. "Father."

"Steady, now," George said, holding me. "John's just gone in to vote."

"But there are two of them!" I said. "Let me go!"

"John's got two shots in the derringer," George said. "Steady, now."

But they held me. And then we heard the three shots and we all turned and looked at the door. I dont know how long it was. "The last two was that derringer," George said. I dont know how long it was. The old nigger that was Mrs Holston's porter, that was too old even to be free, stuck his head out once and said "Gret Gawd" and ducked back. Then Drusilla came out, carrying the ballot box, the wreath on one side of her head and the veil twisted about her arm, and then Father came out behind her, brushing his new beaver hat on his sleeve. And then it was loud; I could hear them when they drew in their breath like when the Yankees used to hear it begin:

"Yaaaaa—" But Father raised his hand and they stopped. Then you couldn't hear anything.

"We heard a pistol too," George said. "Did they touch you?"

"No," Father said. "I let them fire first. You all heard. You boys can swear to my derringer."

"Yes," George said. "We all heard." Now Father looked at all of them, at all the faces in sight, slow.

"Does any man here want a word with me about this?" he said. But you could not hear anything, not even moving. The herd of niggers stood like they had when I first saw them, with the Northern white men herding them together. Father put his hat on and took the ballot box from Drusilla and helped her back onto her horse and handed the ballot box up to her. Then he looked around again, at all of them. "This election will be held out at my home," he said. "I hereby appoint Drusilla Hawk voting commissioner until the votes are cast and counted. Does any man here object?" But he stopped them again with his hand before it had begun good. "Not now, boys," he said. He turned to Drusilla. "Go home. I will go to the sheriff, and then I will follow you."

"Like hell you will," George Wyatt said. "Some of the boys will ride out with Drusilla. The rest of us will come with you."

But Father would not let them. "Dont you see we are working for peace through law and order?" he said. "I will make bond and then follow you. You do as I say." So we went on; we turned in the gates with Drusilla in front, the ballot box on her pommel—us and Father's men and about a hundred more, and rode on up to the cabin where the buggies and surreys were standing, and Drusilla passed the ballot box to me and got down and took the box again and was walking toward the cabin when she stopped dead still. I reckon she and I both remembered at the same time and I reckon that even the others, the men, knew all of a sudden that something was wrong. Because like Father said, I reckon women dont ever surrender: not only victory, but not even defeat. Because that's how we were stopped when Aunt Louisa and the other ladies came out on the porch, and then

Father shoved past me and jumped down beside Drusilla. But Aunt Louisa never even looked at him.

"So you are not married," she said.

"I forgot," Drusilla said.

"You forgot? You *forgot*?"

"I. . . . . . ." Drusilla said. "We. . . . . . ."

Now Aunt Louisa looked at us; she looked along the line of us sitting there in our saddles; she looked at me too just like she did at the others, like she had never seen me before. "And who are these, pray? Your wedding train of forgetters? Your bridesmaids of murder and robbery?"

"They came to vote," Drusilla said.

"To vote," Aunt Louisa said. "Ah. To vote. Since you have forced your mother and brother to live under a roof of license and adultery you think you can also force them to live in a polling booth refuge from violence and bloodshed, do you? Bring me that box." But Drusilla didn't move, standing there in her torn dress and the ruined veil and the twisted wreath hanging from her hair by a few pins. Aunt Louisa came down the steps; we didn't know what she was going to do: we just sat there and watched her snatch the polling box from Drusilla and fling it across the yard. "Come into the house," she said.

"No," Drusilla said.

"Come into the house. I will send for a minister myself."

"No," Drusilla said. "This is an election. Dont you understand? I am voting commissioner."

"So you refuse?"

"I have to. I must." She sounded like a little girl that has been caught playing in the mud. "John said that I——"

Then Aunt Louisa began to cry. She stood there in the black dress, without the knitting and for the first time that I ever saw it, without even the handkerchief, crying, until Mrs Habersham came and led her back into the cabin. Then they voted. That didn't take long either. They set the box on the sawchunk where Louvinia washed, and Ringo got the pokeberry juice and an old piece of window shade, and they cut it into ballots. "Let all who want the Honorable Cassius Q. Benbow to be Marshal of Jefferson write Yes on his ballot; opposed, No," Father said.

"And I'll do the writing and save some more time," George Wyatt said. So he made a pack of the ballots and wrote them against his saddle and fast as he would write them the men would take them and drop them into the box and Drusilla would call their names out. We could hear Aunt Louisa still crying inside the cabin and we could see the other ladies watching us through the window. It didn't take long. "You needn't bother to count them," George said. "They all voted No."

And that's all. They rode back to town then, carrying the box, with Father and Drusilla in the torn wedding dress and the crooked wreath and veil standing beside the sawchunk, watching them. Only this time even Father could not have stopped them. It came back high and thin and ragged and fierce, like when the Yankees used to hear it out of the smoke and the galloping:

"Yaaaaay, Drusilla!" they hollered. "Yaaaaaay, John Sartoris! Yaaaaaaay!"

AN ODOR OF VERBENA

I.

IT WAS JUST after supper. I had just opened my *Coke* on the table beneath the lamp; I heard Professor Wilkins' feet in the hall and then the instant of silence as he put his hand to the door knob, and I should have known. People talk glibly of presentiment, but I had none. I heard his feet on the stairs and then in the hall approaching and there was nothing in the feet because although I had lived in his house for three college years now and although both he and Mrs Wilkins called me Bayard in the house, he would no more have entered my room without knocking than I would have entered his—or hers. Then he flung the door violently inward against the doorstop with one of those gestures with or by which an almost painfully unflagging preceptory of youth ultimately aberrates, and stood there saying, "Bayard. Bayard, my son, my dear son."

I should have known; I should have been prepared. Or maybe I was prepared because I remember how I closed the book carefully, even marking the place, before I rose. He (Professor Wilkins) was doing something, bustling at something; it was my hat and cloak which he handed me and which I took although I would not need the cloak, unless even then I was thinking (although it was October, the equinox had not occurred) that the rains and the cool weather would arrive before I should see this room again and so I would need the cloak anyway to return to it if I returned, thinking 'God, if he had only done this last night, flung that door crashing and bouncing against the stop last night without knocking so I could have gotten there before it happened, been there when it did, beside him on whatever spot, wherever it was that he would have to fall and lie in the dust and dirt.'

"Your boy is downstairs in the kitchen," he said. It was not until years later that he told me (someone did; it must have been Judge Wilkins) how Ringo had apparently flung the cook aside and come on into the house and into the library where he and Mrs Wilkins were sitting and said without preamble and already turning to withdraw: "They shot Colonel Sartoris this morning. Tell him I be waiting in the kitchen" and was gone before either of them could move. "He has ridden forty miles yet he refuses to eat anything." We were moving toward the door now—the door on my side of which I had lived for three years now with what I knew, what I knew now I must have believed and expected, yet beyond which I had heard the approaching feet yet heard nothing in the feet. "If there was just anything I could do."

"Yes, sir," I said. "A fresh horse for my boy. He will want to go back with me."

"By all means take mine—Mrs Wilkins'," he cried. His tone was no different yet he did cry it and I suppose that at the same moment we both realised that was funny—a short-legged deep-barrelled mare who looked exactly like a spinster music teacher, which Mrs Wilkins drove to a basket phaeton—which was good for me, like being doused with a pail of cold water would have been good for me.

"Thank you, sir," I said. "We wont need it. I will get a fresh horse for him at the livery stable when I get my mare." Good for me, because even before I finished speaking I knew that would not be necessary either, that Ringo would have stopped at the livery stable before he came out to the college and attended to that and that the fresh horse for him and my mare both would be saddled and waiting now at the side fence and we would not have to go through Oxford at all. Loosh would not have thought of that if he had come for me, he would have come straight to the college, to Professor

Wilkins', and told his news and then sat down and let me take charge from then on. But not Ringo.

He followed me from the room. From now until Ringo and I rode away into the hot thick dusty darkness quick and strained for the overdue equinox like a laboring delayed woman, he would be somewhere either just beside me or just behind me and I never to know exactly nor care which. He was trying to find the words with which to offer me his pistol too. I could almost hear him: "Ah, this unhappy land, not ten years recovered from the fever yet still men must kill one another, still we must pay Cain's price in his own coin." But he did not actually say it. He just followed me, somewhere beside or behind me as we descended the stairs toward where Mrs Wilkins waited in the hall beneath the chandelier—a thin gray woman who reminded me of Granny, not that she looked like Granny probably but because she had known Granny—a lifted anxious still face which was thinking *Who lives by the sword shall die by it* just as Granny would have thought, toward which I walked, had to walk not because I was Granny's grandson and had lived in her house for three college years and was about the age of her son when he was killed in almost the last battle nine years ago, but because I was now The Sartoris. (The Sartoris: that had been one of the concomitant flashes, along with the *at last it has happened* when Professor Wilkins opened my door.) She didn't offer me a horse and pistol, not because she liked me any less than Professor Wilkins but because she was a woman and so wiser than any man, else the men would not have gone on with the War for two years after they knew they were whipped. She just put her hands (a small woman, no bigger than Granny had been) on my shoulders and said, "Give my love to Drusilla and your Aunt Jenny. And come back when you can."

"Only I dont know when that will be," I said. "I dont know how many things I will have to attend to." Yes, I lied even to her; it had not been but a minute yet since he had flung that door bouncing into the stop yet already I was beginning to realise, to become aware of that which I still had no yardstick to measure save that one consisting of what, despite myself, despite my raising and background (or maybe because of them) I had for some time known I was becoming and had feared the test of it; I remember how I thought while her hands still rested on my shoulders: *At least this will be my chance to find out if I am what I think I am or if I just hope; if I am going to do what I have taught myself is right or if I am just going to wish I were.*

We went on to the kitchen, Professor Wilkins still somewhere beside or behind me and still offering me the pistol and horse in a dozen different ways. Ringo was waiting; I remember how I thought then that no matter what might happen to either of us, I would never be The Sartoris to him. He was twenty-four too, but in a way he had changed even less than I had since that day when we had nailed Grumby's body to the door of the old compress. Maybe it was because he had outgrown me, had changed so much that summer while he and Granny traded mules with the Yankees that since then I had had to do most of the changing just to catch up with him. He was sitting quietly in a chair beside the cold stove, spent-looking too who had ridden forty miles (at one time, either in Jefferson or when he was alone at last on the road somewhere, he had cried; dust was now caked and dried in the tear-channels on his face) and would ride forty more yet would not eat, looking up at me a little red-eyed with weariness (or maybe it was more than just weariness and so I would never catch up with him) then rising without a word and going on toward the door and I following and Professor Wilkins still offering the horse and the pistol without speaking the words and still thinking (I could feel that too) *Dies by the sword. Dies by the sword.*

Ringo had the two horses saddled at the side gate, as I had known he would—the fresh one for himself and my mare Father had given me three years ago, that could do a mile under two minutes any day and a mile every eight minutes all day long. He was already mounted when I realised that what Professor Wilkins wanted was to shake my hand. We shook hands; I knew he believed he was touching flesh which might not be alive tomorrow night and I thought for a second how if I told him what I was going to do, since we had talked about it, about how if there was anything at all in the Book, anything of hope and peace for His blind and bewildered spawn which He had chosen above all others to offer immortality, *Thou shalt not kill* must be it, since maybe he even believed that he had taught it to me except that he had not, nobody had, not even myself since it went further than just having been learned. But I did not tell him. He was too old to be forced so, to condone even in principle such a decision; he was too old to have to stick to principle in the face of blood and raising and background, to be faced without warning and made to deliver like by a highwayman out of the dark: only the young could do that—one still young enough to have his youth supplied him gratis as a reason (not an excuse) for cowardice.

So I said nothing. I just shook his hand and mounted too, and Ringo and I rode on. We would not have to pass through Oxford now and so soon (there was a thin sickle of moon like the heel print of a boot in wet sand) the road to Jefferson lay before us, the road which I had travelled for the first time three years ago with Father and travelled twice at Christmas time and then in June and September and twice at Christmas time again and then June and September again each college term since alone on the mare, not even knowing that this was peace; and now this time and maybe last time who would not die (I knew that) but who maybe forever after could never again hold up his head. The horses took the gait which they would hold for forty miles. My mare knew the long road ahead and Ringo had a good beast too, had talked Hilliard at the livery stable out of a good horse too. Maybe it was the tears, the channels of dried mud across which his strain-reddened eyes had looked at me, but I rather think it was that same quality which used to enable him to replenish his and Granny's supply of United States Army letterheads during that time—some outrageous assurance gained from too long and too close association with white people: the one whom he called Granny, the other with whom he had slept from the time we were born until Father rebuilt the house. We spoke one time, then no more:

"We could bushwhack him," he said. "Like we done Grumby that day. But I reckon that wouldn't suit that white skin you walks around in."

"No," I said. We rode on; it was October; there was plenty

of time still for verbena although I would have to reach home before I would realise there was a need for it; plenty of time for verbena yet from the garden where Aunt Jenny puttered beside old Joby, in a pair of Father's old cavalry gauntlets, among the coaxed and ordered beds, the quaint and odorous old names, for though it was October no rain had come yet and hence no frost to bring (or leave behind) the first half-warm half-chill nights of Indian Summer—the drowsing air cool and empty for geese yet languid still with the old hot dusty smell of fox grape and sassafras—the nights when before I became a man and went to college to learn law Ringo and I, with lantern and axe and croker sack and six dogs (one to follow the trail and five more just for the tonguing, the music) would hunt possum in the pasture where, hidden, we had seen our first Yankee that afternoon on the bright horse, where for the last year now you could hear the whistling of the trains which had no longer belonged to Mr Redmond for a long while now and which at some instant, some second during the morning Father too had relinquished along with the pipe which Ringo said he was smoking, which slipped from his hand as he fell. We rode on, toward the house where he would be lying in the parlor now, in his regimentals (sabre too) and where Drusilla would be waiting for me beneath all the festive glitter of the chandeliers, in the yellow ball gown and the sprig of verbena in her hair, holding the two loaded pistols (I could see that too, who had had no presentiment; I could see her, in the formal brilliant room arranged formally for obsequy, not tall, not slender as a woman is but as a youth, a boy, is, motionless, in yellow, the face calm, almost bemused, the head simple and severe, the balancing sprig of verbena above each ear, the two arms bent at the elbows, the two hands shoulder high, the two identical duelling pistols lying upon, not clutched in, one to each: the Greek amphora priestess of a succinct and formal violence).

2.

Drusilla said that he had a dream. I was twenty then and she and I would walk in the garden in the summer twilight while we waited for Father to ride in from the railroad. I was

just twenty then: that summer before I entered the University
to take the law degree which Father decided I should have
and four years after the one, the day, the evening when Father
and Drusilla had kept old Cash Benbow from becoming
United States Marshal and returned home still unmarried and
Mrs Habersham herded them into her carriage and drove
them back to town and dug her husband out of his little
dim hole in the new bank and made him sign Father's peace
bond for killing the two carpet baggers, and took Father
and Drusilla to the minister herself and saw that they were
married. And Father had rebuilt the house too, on the same
blackened spot, over the same cellar, where the other had
burned, only larger, much larger: Drusilla said that the house
was the aura of Father's dream just as a bride's trousseau and
veil is the aura of hers. And Aunt Jenny had come to live with
us now so we had the garden (Drusilla would no more have
bothered with flowers than Father himself would have, who
even now, even four years after it was over, still seemed to
exist, breathe, in that last year of it while she had ridden in
man's clothes and with her hair cut short like any other member of Father's troop, across Georgia and both Carolinas in
front of Sherman's army) for her to gather sprigs of verbena
from to wear in her hair because she said verbena was the
only scent you could smell above the smell of horses and
courage and so it was the only one that was worth the wearing. The railroad was hardly begun then and Father and Mr
Redmond were not only still partners, they were still friends,
which as George Wyatt said was easily a record for Father,
and he would leave the house at daybreak on Jupiter, riding
up and down the unfinished line with two saddlebags of
gold coins borrowed on Friday to pay the men on Saturday,
keeping just two cross-ties ahead of the sheriff as Aunt Jenny
said. So we walked in the dusk, slowly between Aunt Jenny's
flower beds while Drusilla (in a dress now, who still would
have worn pants all the time if Father had let her) leaned
lightly on my arm and I smelled the verbena in her hair as I
had smelled the rain in it and in Father's beard that night four
years ago when he and Drusilla and Uncle Buck McCaslin
found Grumby and then came home and found Ringo and
me more than just asleep: escaped into that oblivion which

God or Nature or whoever it was had supplied us with for the time being, who had had to perform more than should be required of children because there should be some limit to the age, the youth at least below which one should not have to kill. This was just after the Saturday night when he returned and I watched him clean the derringer and reload it and we learned that the dead man was almost a neighbor, a hill man who had been in the first infantry regiment when it voted Father out of command: and we never to know if the man actually intended to rob Father or not because Father had shot too quick, but only that he had a wife and several children in a dirt-floored cabin in the hills, to whom Father the next day sent some money and she (the wife) walked into the house two days later while we were sitting at the dinner table and flung the money at Father's face.

"But nobody could have more of a dream than Colonel Sutpen," I said. He had been Father's second-in-command in the first regiment and had been elected colonel when the regiment deposed Father after Second Manassas, and it was Sutpen and not the regiment whom Father never forgave. He was underbred, a cold ruthless man who had come into the country about thirty years before the War, nobody knew from where except Father said you could look at him and know he would not dare to tell. He had got some land and nobody knew how he did that either, and he got money from somewhere—Father said they all believed he robbed steamboats, either as a card sharper or as an out-and-out highwayman—and built a big house and married and set up as a gentleman. Then he lost everything in the War like everybody else, all hope of descendants too (his son killed his daughter's fiancé on the eve of the wedding and vanished) yet he came back home and set out singlehanded to rebuild his plantation. He had no friends to borrow from and he had nobody to leave it to and he was past sixty years old, yet he set out to rebuild his place like it used to be; they told how he was too busy to bother with politics or anything; how when Father and the other men organised the night riders to keep the carpet baggers from organising the negroes into an insurrection, he refused to have anything to do with it. Father stopped hating him long enough to ride out to see Sutpen himself and he (Sutpen) came to the door with a lamp and did not even invite them to come in and discuss it; Father said, "Are you with us or against us?" and he said, "I'm for my land. If every man of you would rehabilitate his own land, the country will take care of itself" and Father challenged him to bring the lamp out and set it on a stump where they could both see to shoot and Sutpen would not. "Nobody could have more of a dream than that."

"Yes. But his dream is just Sutpen. John's is not. He is thinking of this whole country which he is trying to raise by its bootstraps, so that all the people in it, not just his kind nor his old regiment, but all the people, black and white, the women and children back in the hills who dont even own shoes— Dont you see?"

"But how can they get any good from what he wants to do for them if they are—after he has——"

"Killed some of them? I suppose you include those two carpet baggers he had to kill to hold that first election, dont you?"

"They were men. Human beings."

"They were northerners, foreigners who had no business here. They were pirates." We walked on, her weight hardly discernible on my arm, her head just reaching my shoulder. I had always been a little taller than she, even on that night at Hawkhurst while we listened to the niggers passing in the road, and she had changed but little since—the same boy-hard body, the close implacable head with its savagely cropped hair which I had watched from the wagon above the tide of crazed singing niggers as we went down into the river—the body not slender as women are but as boys are slender. "A dream is not a very safe thing to be near, Bayard. I know; I had one once. It's like a loaded pistol with a hair trigger: if it stays alive long enough, somebody is going to be hurt. But if it's a good dream, it's worth it. There are not many dreams in the world, but there are a lot of human lives. And one human life or two dozen——"

"Are not worth anything?"

"No. Not anything.—Listen. I hear Jupiter. I'll beat you to the house." She was already running, the skirts she did not like to wear lifted almost to her knees, her legs beneath it running as boys run just as she rode like men ride.

I was twenty then. But the next time I was twenty-four; I had been three years at the University and in another two weeks I would ride back to Oxford for the final year and my degree. It was just last summer, last August, and Father had just beat Redmond for the State legislature. The railroad was finished now and the partnership between Father and Redmond had been dissolved so long ago that most people would have forgotten they were ever partners if it hadn't been for the enmity between them. There had been a third partner but nobody hardly remembered his name now; he and his name both had vanished in the fury of the conflict which set up between Father and Redmond almost before they began to lay the rails, between Father's violent and ruthless dictatorialness and will to dominate (the idea was his; he did think of the railroad first and then took Redmond in) and that quality in Redmond (as George Wyatt said, he was not a coward or Father would never have teamed with him) which permitted him to stand as much as he did from Father, to bear and bear and bear until something (not his will nor his courage) broke in him. During the War Redmond had not been a soldier, he had had something to do with cotton for the Government; he could have made money himself out of it but he had not and everybody knew he had not, Father knew it, yet Father would even taunt him with not having smelled powder. He was wrong; he knew he was when it was too late for him to stop just as a drunkard reaches a point where it is too late for him to stop, where he promises himself that he will and maybe believes he will or can but it is too late. Finally they reached the point (they had both put everything they could mortgage or borrow into it for Father to ride up and down the line, paying the workmen and the waybills on the rails at the last possible instant) where even Father realised that one of them would have to get out. So (they were not speaking then; it was arranged by Judge Benbow) they met and agreed to buy or sell, naming a price which, in reference to what they had put into it, was ridiculously low but which each believed the other could not raise—at least Father claimed that Redmond did not believe he could raise it. So Redmond accepted the price, and found out that Father had the money. And according to Father, that's what started it, although Uncle Buck McCaslin said Father could not have owned a half interest in even one hog, let alone a railroad, and not dissolve the business either sworn enemy or death-pledged friend to his recent partner. So they parted and Father finished the road. By that time, seeing that he was going to finish it, some northern people sold him a locomotive on credit which he named for Aunt Jenny, with a silver oil can in the cab with her name engraved on it; and last summer the first train ran into Jefferson, the engine decorated with flowers and Father in the cab blowing blast after blast on the whistle when he passed Redmond's house; and there were speeches at the station, with more flowers and a Confederate flag and girls in white dresses and red sashes and a band, and Father stood on the pilot of the engine and made a direct and absolutely needless allusion to Mr Redmond. That was it. He wouldn't let him alone. George Wyatt came to me right afterward and told me. "Right or wrong," he said, "us boys and most of the other folks in this county know John's right. But he ought to let Redmond alone. I know what's wrong: he's had to kill too many folks, and that's bad for a man. We all know Colonel's brave as a lion, but Redmond aint no coward either and there aint any use in making a brave man that made one mistake eat crow all the time. Cant you talk to him?"

"I dont know," I said. "I'll try." But I had no chance. That is, I could have talked to him and he would have listened, but he could not have heard me because he had stepped straight from the pilot of that engine into the race for the Legislature. Maybe he knew that Redmond would have to oppose him to save his face even though he (Redmond) must have known that, after that train ran into Jefferson, he had no chance against Father, or maybe Redmond had already announced his candidacy and Father entered the race just because of that, I dont remember. Anyway they ran, a bitter contest in which Father continued to badger Redmond without reason or need, since they both knew it would be a landslide for Father. And it was, and we thought he was satisfied. Maybe he thought so himself, as the drunkard believes that he is done with drink; and it was that afternoon and Drusilla and I walked in the garden in the twilight and I said something about what George Wyatt had told me and she released my arm and turned me to face her and said, "This from you? You? Have you forgotten Grumby?"

"No," I said. "I never will forget him."

"You never will. I wouldn't let you. There are worse things than killing men, Bayard. There are worse things than being killed. Sometimes I think the finest thing that can happen to a man is to love something, a woman preferably, well, hard hard hard, then to die young because he believed what he could not help but believe and was what he could not (could not? would not) help but be." Now she was looking at me in a way she never had before. I did not know what it meant then and was not to know until tonight since neither of us knew then that two months later Father would be dead. I just knew that she was looking at me as she never had before and that the scent of the verbena in her hair seemed to have increased a hundred times, to have got a hundred times stronger, to be everywhere in the dusk in which something was about to happen which I had never dreamed of. Then she spoke. "Kiss me, Bayard."

"No. You are Father's wife."

"And eight years older than you are. And your fourth cousin too. And I have black hair. Kiss me, Bayard."

"No."

"Kiss me, Bayard." So I leaned my face down to her. But she didn't move, standing so, bent lightly back from me from the waist, looking at me; now it was she who said, "No." So I put my arms around her. Then she came to me, melted as women will and can, the arms with the wrist- and elbow-power to control horses about my shoulders, using the wrists to hold my face to hers until there was no longer need for the wrists; I thought then of the woman of thirty, the symbol of the ancient and eternal Snake and of the men who have written of her, and I realised then the immitigable chasm between all life and all print—that those who can, do, those who cannot and suffer enough because they cant, write about it. Then I was free, I could see her again, I saw her still watching me with that dark inscrutable look, looking up at me now across her down-slanted face; I watched her arms rise with almost

the exact gesture with which she had put them around me as
if she were repeating the empty and formal gesture of all
promise so that I should never forget it, the elbows angling
outward as she put her hands to the sprig of verbena in her
hair, I standing straight and rigid facing the slightly bent
head, the short jagged hair, the rigid curiously formal angle of
the bare arms gleaming faintly in the last of light as she removed the verbena sprig and put it into my lapel, and I
thought how the War had tried to stamp all the women of her
generation and class in the South into a type and how it had
failed—the suffering, the identical experience (hers and Aunt
Jenny's had been almost the same except that Aunt Jenny had
spent a few nights with her husband before they brought him
back home in an ammunition wagon while Gavin Breckbridge was just Drusilla's fiancé) was there in the eyes, yet
beyond that was the incorrigibly individual woman: not like
so many men who return from wars to live on Government
reservations like so many steers, emasculate and empty of all
save an identical experience which they cannot forget and
dare not, else they would cease to live at that moment, almost
interchangeable save for the old habit of answering to a given
name.

"Now I must tell Father," I said.

"Yes," she said. "You must tell him. Kiss me." So again it
was like it had been before. No. Twice, a thousand times and
never like—the eternal and symbolical thirty to a young man,
a youth, each time both cumulative and retroactive, immiti-
gably unrepetitive, each wherein remembering excludes experience, each wherein experience antedates remembering; the
skill without weariness, the knowledge virginal to surfeit, the
cunning secret muscles to guide and control just as within
the wrists and elbows lay slumbering the mastery of horses:
she stood back, already turning, not looking at me when she
spoke, never having looked at me, already moving swiftly on
in the dusk: "Tell John. Tell him tonight."

I intended to. I went to the house and into the office at
once; I went to the center of the rug before the cold hearth, I
dont know why, and stood there rigid like soldiers stand,
looking at eye level straight across the room and above his
head and said, "Father" and then stopped. Because he did

not even hear me. He said, "Yes, Bayard?" but he did not hear me although he was sitting behind the desk doing nothing, immobile, as still as I was rigid, one hand on the desk with a dead cigar in it, a bottle of brandy and a filled and untasted glass beside his hand, clothed quiet and bemused in whatever triumph it was he felt since the last overwhelming return of votes had come in late in the afternoon. So I waited until after supper. We went to the diningroom and stood side by side until Aunt Jenny entered and then Drusilla, in the yellow ball gown, who walked straight to me and gave me one fierce inscrutable look then went to her place and waited for me to draw her chair while Father drew Aunt Jenny's. He had roused by then, not to talk himself but rather to sit at the head of the table and reply to Drusilla as she talked with a sort of feverish and glittering volubility—to reply now and then to her with that courteous intolerant pride which had lately become a little forensic, as if merely being in a political contest filled with fierce and empty oratory had retroactively made a lawyer of him who was anything and everything except a lawyer. Then Drusilla and Aunt Jenny rose and left us and he said, "Wait" to me who had made no move to follow and directed Joby to bring one of the bottles of wine which he had fetched back from New Orleans when he went there last to borrow money to liquidate his first private railroad bonds. Then I stood again like soldiers stand, gazing at eye level above his head while he sat half-turned from the table, a little paunchy now though not much, a little grizzled too in the hair though his beard was as strong as ever, with that spurious forensic air of lawyers and the intolerant eyes which in the last two years had acquired that transparent film which the eyes of carnivorous animals have and from behind which they look at a world which no ruminant ever sees, perhaps dares to see, which I have seen before on the eyes of men who have killed too much, who have killed so much that never again as long as they live will they ever be alone. I said again, "Father," then I told him.

"Hah?" he said. "Sit down." I sat down, I looked at him, watched him fill both glasses and this time I knew it was worse with him than not hearing: it didn't even matter. "You are doing well in the law, Judge Wilkins tells me. I am pleased to hear that. I have not needed you in my affairs so far, but from now on I shall. I have now accomplished the active portion of my aims in which you could not have helped me; I acted as the land and the time demanded and you were too young for that, I wished to shield you. But now the land and the time too are changing; what will follow will be a matter of consolidation, of pettifogging and doubtless chicanery in which I would be a babe in arms but in which you, trained in the law, can hold your own—our own. Yes. I have accomplished my aim, and now I shall do a little moral house-cleaning. I am tired of killing men, no matter what the necessity nor the end. Tomorrow, when I go to town and meet Ben Redmond, I shall be unarmed."

3.

We reached home just before midnight; we didn't have to pass through Jefferson either. Before we turned in the gates I could see the lights, the chandeliers—hall, parlor, and what Aunt Jenny (without any effort or perhaps even design on her part) had taught even Ringo to call the drawing room, the light falling outward across the portico, past the columns. Then I saw the horses, the faint shine of leather and buckle-glints on the black silhouettes and then the men too—Wyatt and others of Father's old troop—and I had forgot that they would be there. I had forgot that they would be there; I remember how I thought, since I was tired and spent with strain, *Now it will have to begin tonight. I wont even have until tomorrow in which to begin to resist.* They had a watchman, a picquet out, I suppose, because they seemed to know at once that we were in the drive. Wyatt met me, I halted the mare, I could look down at him and at the others gathered a few yards behind him with that curious vulture-like formality which Southern men assume in such situations.

"Well, boy," George said.

"Was it—" I said. "Was he—"

"It was all right. It was in front. Redmond aint no coward. John had the derringer inside his cuff like always, but he never touched it, never made a move toward it." I have seen him do it, he showed me once: the pistol (it was not four inches

long) held flat inside his left wrist by a clip he made himself of
wire and an old clock spring; he would raise both hands at
the same time, cross them, fire the pistol from beneath his left
hand almost as if he were hiding from his own vision what he
was doing; when he killed one of the men he shot a hole
through his own coat sleeve. "But you want to get on to the
house," Wyatt said. He began to stand aside, then he spoke
again: "We'll take this off your hands, any of us. Me." I
hadn't moved the mare yet and I had made no move to speak,
yet he continued quickly, as if he had already rehearsed all
this, his speech and mine, and knew what I would say and
only spoke himself as he would have removed his hat on entering a house or used 'sir' in conversing with a stranger:
"You're young, just a boy, you aint had any experience in this
kind of thing. Besides, you got them two ladies in the house
to think about. He would understand, all right."

"I reckon I can attend to it," I said.

"Sure," he said; there was no surprise, nothing at all, in his
voice because he had already rehearsed this: "I reckon we all
knew that's what you would say." He stepped back then; almost it was as though he and not I bade the mare to move
on. But they all followed, still with that unctuous and voracious formality. Then I saw Drusilla standing at the top of the
front steps, in the light from the open door and the windows
like a theatre scene, in the yellow ball gown and even from
here I believed that I could smell the verbena in her hair,
standing there motionless yet emanating something louder
than the two shots must have been—something voracious
too and passionate. Then, although I had dismounted and
someone had taken the mare, I seemed to be still in the saddle
and to watch myself enter that scene which she had postulated
like another actor while in the background for chorus Wyatt
and the others stood with the unctuous formality which
the Southern man shows in the presence of death—that
Roman holiday engendered by mist-born Protestantism
grafted onto this land of violent sun, of violent alteration
from snow to heat-stroke which has produced a race impervious to both. I mounted the steps toward the figure straight
and yellow and immobile as a candle which moved only to
extend one hand; we stood together and looked down at

them where they stood clumped, the horses too gathered in a tight group beyond them at the rim of light from the brilliant door and windows. One of them stamped and blew his breath and jangled his gear.

"Thank you, gentlemen," I said. "My aunt and my— Drusilla thank you. There's no need for you to stay. Good-night." They murmured, turning. George Wyatt paused, looking back at me.

"Tomorrow?" he said.

"Tomorrow." Then they went on, carrying their hats and tiptoeing, even on the ground, the quiet and resilient earth, as though anyone in that house awake would try to sleep, any-one already asleep in it whom they could have wakened. Then they were gone and Drusilla and I turned and crossed the portico, her hand lying light on my wrist yet discharging into me with a shock like electricity that dark and passionate voracity, the face at my shoulder—the jagged hair with a verbena sprig above each ear, the eyes staring at me with that fierce exaltation. We entered the hall and crossed it, her hand guiding me without pressure, and entered the parlor. Then for the first time I realised it—the alteration which is death— not that he was now just clay but that he was lying down. But I didn't look at him yet because I knew that when I did I would begin to pant; I went to Aunt Jenny who had just risen from a chair behind which Louvinia stood. She was Father's sister, taller than Drusilla but no older, whose husband had been killed at the very beginning of the War, by a shell from a Federal frigate at Fort Moultrie, come to us from Carolina six years ago. Ringo and I went to Tennessee Junction in the wagon to meet her. It was January, cold and clear and with ice in the ruts; we returned just before dark with Aunt Jenny on the seat beside me holding a lace parasol and Ringo in the wagon bed nursing a hamper basket containing two bottles of old sherry and the two jasmine cuttings which were bushes in the garden now, and the panes of colored glass which she had salvaged from the Carolina house where she and Father and Uncle Bayard were born and which Father had set in a fan-light about one of the drawing room windows for her—who came up the drive and Father (home now from the railroad) went down the steps and lifted her from the wagon and said,

"Well, Jenny," and she said, "Well, Johnny," and began to cry. She stood too, looking at me as I approached—the same hair, the same high nose, the same eyes as Father's except that they were intent and very wise instead of intolerant. She said nothing at all, she just kissed me, her hands light on my shoulders. Then Drusilla spoke, as if she had been waiting with a sort of dreadful patience for the empty ceremony to be done, in a voice like a bell: clear, unsentient, on a single pitch, silvery and triumphant: "Come, Bayard."

"Hadn't you better go to bed now?" Aunt Jenny said.

"Yes," Drusilla said in that silvery ecstatic voice, "oh yes. There will be plenty of time for sleep." I followed her, her hand again guiding me without pressure; now I looked at him. It was just as I had imagined it—sabre, plumes, and all—but with that alteration, that irrevocable difference which I had known to expect yet had not realised, as you can put food into your stomach which for a while the stomach declines to assimilate—the illimitable grief and regret as I looked down at the face which I knew—the nose, the hair, the eyelids closed over the intolerance—the face which I realised I now saw in repose for the first time in my life; the empty hands still now beneath the invisible stain of what had been (once, surely) needless blood, the hands now appearing clumsy in their very inertness, too clumsy to have performed the fatal actions which forever afterward he must have waked and slept with and maybe was glad to lay down at last—those curious appendages clumsily conceived to begin with yet with which man has taught himself to do so much, so much more than they were intended to do or could be forgiven for doing, which had now surrendered that life to which his intolerant heart had fiercely held; and then I knew that in a minute I would begin to pant. So Drusilla must have spoken twice before I heard her and turned and saw in the instant Aunt Jenny and Louvinia watching us, hearing Drusilla now, the unsentient bell quality gone now, her voice whispering into that quiet death-filled room with a passionate and dying fall: "Bayard." She faced me, she was quite near; again the scent of the verbena in her hair seemed to have increased a hundred times as she stood holding out to me, one in either hand, the two duelling pistols. "Take them, Bayard," she said, in the same tone in which she had said "Kiss me" last summer, already pressing them into my hands, watching me with that passionate and voracious exaltation, speaking in a voice fainting and passionate with promise: "Take them. I have kept them for you. I give them to you. Oh you will thank me, you will remember me who put into your hands what they say is an attribute only of God's, who took what belongs to heaven and gave it to you. Do you feel them? the long true barrels true as justice, the triggers (you have fired them) quick as retribution, the two of them slender and invincible and fatal as the physical shape of love?" Again I watched her arms angle out and upward as she removed the two verbena sprigs from her hair in two motions faster than the eye could follow, already putting one of them into my lapel and crushing the other in her other hand while she still spoke in that rapid passionate voice not much louder than a whisper: "There. One I give to you to wear tomorrow (it will not fade), the other I cast away, like this—" dropping the crushed bloom at her feet. "I abjure it. I abjure verbena forever more; I have smelled it above the odor of courage; that was all I wanted. Now let me look at you." She stood back, staring at me—the face tearless and exalted, the feverish eyes brilliant and voracious. "How beautiful you are: do you know it? How beautiful: young, to be permitted to kill, to be permitted vengeance, to take into your bare hands the fire of heaven that cast down Lucifer. No; I. I gave it to you; I put it into your hands; oh you will thank me, you will remember me when I am dead and you are an old man saying to himself, 'I have tasted all things'.—It will be the right hand, wont it?" She moved; she had taken my right hand which still held one of the pistols before I knew what she was about to do; she had bent and kissed it before I comprehended why she took it. Then she stopped dead still, still stooping in that attitude of fierce exultant humility, her hot lips and her hot hands still touching my flesh, light on my flesh as dead leaves yet communicating to it that battery charge dark, passionate and damned forever of all peace. Because they are wise, women are—a touch, lips or fingers, and the knowledge, even clairvoyance, goes straight to the heart without bothering the laggard brain at all. She stood erect now, staring at me with intolerable and

amazed incredulity which occupied her face alone for a whole
minute while her eyes were completely empty; it seemed to
me that I stood there for a full minute while Aunt Jenny and
Louvinia watched us, waiting for her eyes to fill. There was
no blood in her face at all, her mouth open a little and pale as
one of those rubber rings women seal fruit jars with. Then
her eyes filled with an expression of bitter and passionate betrayal. "Why, he's not—" she said. "He's not— And I kissed
his hand," she said in an aghast whisper; *"I kissed his hand!"*
beginning to laugh, the laughter rising, becoming a scream
yet still remaining laughter, screaming with laughter, trying
herself to deaden the sound by putting her hand over her
mouth, the laughter spilling between her fingers like vomit,
the incredulous betrayed eyes still watching me across the
hand.

"Louvinia!" Aunt Jenny said. They both came to her.
Louvinia touched and held her and Drusilla turned her face
to Louvinia.

"I kissed his hand, Louvinia!" she cried. "Did you see it?
I kissed his hand!" the laughter rising again, becoming the
scream again yet still remaining laughter, she still trying to
hold it back with her hand like a small child who has filled its
mouth too full.

"Take her upstairs," Aunt Jenny said. But they were already
moving toward the door, Louvinia half carrying Drusilla, the
laughter diminishing as they neared the door as though it
waited for the larger space of the empty and brilliant hall to
rise again. Then it was gone; Aunt Jenny and I stood there
and I knew soon that I would begin to pant. I could feel it
beginning like you feel regurgitation beginning, as though
there were not enough air in the room, the house, not
enough air anywhere under the heavy hot low sky where the
equinox couldn't seem to accomplish, nothing in the air for
breathing, for the lungs. Now it was Aunt Jenny who said
"Bayard" twice before I heard her. "You are not going to try
to kill him. All right."

"All right?" I said.

"Yes. All right. Dont let it be Drusilla, a poor hysterical
young woman. And dont let it be him, Bayard, because he's
dead now. And dont let it be George Wyatt and those others

who will be waiting for you tomorrow morning. I know you are not afraid."

"But what good will that do?" I said. "What good will that do?" It almost began then; I stopped it just in time. "I must live with myself, you see."

"Then it's not just Drusilla? Not just him? Not just George Wyatt and Jefferson?"

"No," I said.

"Will you promise to let me see you before you go to town tomorrow?" I looked at her; we looked at one another for a moment. Then she put her hands on my shoulders and kissed me and released me, all in one motion. "Goodnight, son," she said. Then she was gone too and now it could begin. I knew that in a minute I would look at him and it would begin and I did look at him, feeling the long held breath, the hiatus before it started, thinking how maybe I should have said, "Goodbye, Father" but did not. Instead I crossed to the piano and laid the pistols carefully on it, still keeping the panting from getting too loud too soon. Then I was outside on the porch and (I dont know how long it had been) I looked in the window and saw Simon squatting on a stool beside him. Simon had been his body servant during the War and when they came home Simon had a uniform too—a Confederate private's coat with a Yankee brigadier's star on it and he had put it on now too, like they had dressed Father, squatting on the stool beside him, not crying, not weeping the facile tears which are the white man's futile trait and which negroes know nothing about but just sitting there, motionless, his lower lip slacked down a little; he raised his hand and touched the coffin, the black hand rigid and fragile-looking as a clutch of dead twigs, then dropped the hand; once he turned his head and I saw his eyes roll red and unwinking in his skull like those of a cornered fox. It had begun by that time; I panted, standing there, and this was it—the regret and grief, the despair out of which the tragic mute insensitive bones stand up that can bear anything, anything.

4.

After a while the whip-poor-wills stopped and I heard the

first day bird, a mockingbird. It had sung all night too but
now it was the day song, no longer the drowsy moony fluting. Then they all began—the sparrows from the stable, the
thrush that lived in Aunt Jenny's garden, and I heard a quail
too from the pasture and now there was light in the room.
But I didn't move at once. I still lay on the bed (I hadn't
undressed) with my hands under my head and the scent of
Drusilla's verbena faint from where my coat lay on a chair,
watching the light grow, watching it turn rosy with the sun.
After a while I heard Louvinia come up across the back yard
and go into the kitchen; I heard the door and then the long
crash of her armful of stovewood into the box. Soon they
would begin to arrive—the carriages and buggies in the
drive—but not for a while yet because they too would wait
first to see what I was going to do. So the house was quiet
when I went down to the diningroom, no sound in it except
Simon snoring in the parlor, probably still sitting on the stool
though I didn't look in to see. Instead I stood at the diningroom window and drank the coffee which Louvinia brought
me, then I went to the stable; I saw Joby watching me from
the kitchen door as I crossed the yard and in the stable Loosh
looked up at me across Betsy's head, a curry comb in his
hand, though Ringo didn't look at me at all. We curried Jupiter then. I didn't know if we would be able to without trouble or not, since always Father would come in first and touch
him and tell him to stand and he would stand like a marble
horse (or pale bronze rather) while Loosh curried him. But
he stood for me too, a little restive but he stood, then that
was done and now it was almost nine oclock and soon they
would begin to arrive and I told Ringo to bring Betsy on to
the house.

I went on to the house and into the hall. I had not had to
pant in some time now but it was there, waiting, a part of the
alteration, as though by being dead and no longer needing air
he had taken all of it, all that he had compassed and claimed
and postulated between the walls which he had built, along
with him. Aunt Jenny must have been waiting; she came out
of the diningroom at once, without a sound, dressed, the hair
that was like Father's combed and smooth above the eyes that
were different from Father's eyes because they were not in-

tolerant but just intent and grave and (she was wise too) without pity. "Are you going now?" she said.

"Yes." I looked at her. Yes, thank God, without pity. "You see, I want to be thought well of."

"I do," she said. "Even if you spend the day hidden in the stable loft, I still do."

"Maybe if she knew that I was going. Was going to town anyway."

"No," she said. "No, Bayard." We looked at one another. Then she said quietly, "All right. She's awake." So I mounted the stairs. I mounted steadily, not fast because if I had gone fast the panting would have started again or I might have had to slow for a second at the turn or at the top and I would not have gone on. So I went slowly and steadily, across the hall to her door and knocked and opened it. She was sitting at the window, in something soft and loose for morning in her bedroom only she never did look like morning in a bedroom because there was no hair to fall about her shoulders. She looked up, she sat there looking at me with her feverish brilliant eyes and I remembered I still had the verbena sprig in my lapel and suddenly she began to laugh again. It seemed to come not from her mouth but to burst out all over her face like sweat does and with a dreadful and painful convulsion as when you have vomited until it hurts you yet still you must vomit again—burst out all over her face except her eyes, the brilliant incredulous eyes looking at me out of the laughter as if they belonged to somebody else, as if they were two inert fragments of tar or coal lying on the bottom of a receptacle filled with turmoil: "I kissed his hand! *I kissed his hand!*" Louvinia entered, Aunt Jenny must have sent her directly after me; again I walked slowly and steadily so it would not start yet, down the stairs where Aunt Jenny stood beneath the chandelier in the hall as Mrs Wilkins had stood yesterday at the University. She had my hat in her hand. "Even if you hid all day in the stable, Bayard," she said. I took the hat; she said quietly, pleasantly, as if she were talking to a stranger, a guest: "I used to see a lot of blockade runners in Charleston. They were heroes in a way, you see—not heroes because they were helping to prolong the Confederacy but heroes in the sense that David

Crockett or John Sevier would have been to small boys or fool young women. There was one of them, an Englishman. He had no business there; it was the money of course, as with all of them. But he was the Davy Crockett to us because by that time we had all forgot what money was, what you could do with it. He must have been a gentleman once or associated with gentlemen before he changed his name, and he had a vocabulary of seven words, though I must admit he got along quite well with them. The first four were, 'I'll have rum, thanks', and then, when he had the rum, he would use the other three—across the champagne, to whatever ruffled bosom or low gown: 'No bloody moon'. No bloody moon, Bayard."

Ringo was waiting with Betsy at the front steps. Again he did not look at me, his face sullen, downcast even while he handed me the reins. But he said nothing, nor did I look back. And sure enough I was just in time; I passed the Compson carriage at the gates, General Compson lifted his hat as I did mine as we passed. It was four miles to town but I had not gone two of them when I heard the horse coming up behind me and I did not look back because I knew it was Ringo. I did not look back; he came up on one of the carriage horses, he rode up beside me and looked me full in the face for one moment, the sullen determined face, the eyes rolling at me defiant and momentary and red; we rode on. Now we were in town—the long shady street leading to the square, the new courthouse at the end of it; it was eleven oclock now: long past breakfast and not yet noon so there were only women on the street, not to recognise me perhaps or at least not the walking stopped sudden and dead in midwalking as if the legs contained the sudden eyes, the caught breath, that not to begin until we reached the square and I thinking *If I could only be invisible until I reach the stairs to his office and begin to mount*. But I could not, I was not; we rode up to the Holston House and I saw the row of feet along the gallery rail come suddenly and quietly down and I did not look at them, I stopped Betsy and waited until Ringo was down then I dismounted and gave him the reins. "Wait for me here," I said.

"I'm going with you," he said, not loud; we stood there

under the still circumspect eyes and spoke quietly to one another like two conspirators. Then I saw the pistol, the outline of it inside his shirt, probably the one we had taken from Grumby that day we killed him.

"No you aint," I said.

"Yes I am."

"No you aint." So I walked on, along the street in the hot sun. It was almost noon now and I could smell nothing except the verbena in my coat, as if it had gathered all the sun, all the suspended fierce heat in which the equinox could not seem to occur and were distilling it so that I moved in a cloud of verbena as I might have moved in a cloud of smoke from a cigar. Then George Wyatt was beside me (I dont know where he came from) and five or six others of Father's old troop a few yards behind, George's hand on my arm, drawing me into a doorway out of the avid eyes like caught breaths.

"Have you got that derringer?" George said.

"No," I said.

"Good," George said. "They are tricky things to fool with. Couldn't nobody but Colonel ever handle one right; I never could. So you take this. I tried it this morning and I know it's right. Here." He was already fumbling the pistol into my pocket, then the same thing seemed to happen to him that happened to Drusilla last night when she kissed my hand—something communicated by touch straight to the simple code by which he lived, without going through the brain at all: so that he too stood suddenly back, the pistol in his hand, staring at me with his pale outraged eyes and speaking in a whisper thin with fury: "Who are you? Is your name Sartoris? By God, if you dont kill him, I'm going to." Now it was not panting, it was a terrible desire to laugh, to laugh as Drusilla had, and say, "That's what Drusilla said." But I didn't. I said, "I'm tending to this. You stay out of it. I dont need any help." Then his fierce eyes faded gradually, exactly as you turn a lamp down.

"Well," he said, putting the pistol back into his pocket. "You'll have to excuse me, son. I should have knowed you wouldn't do anything that would keep John from laying quiet. We'll follow you and wait at the foot of the steps. And remember: he's a brave man, but he's been sitting in that office by himself since yesterday morning waiting for you and his nerves are on edge."

"I'll remember," I said. "I dont need any help." I had started on when suddenly I said it without having any warning that I was going to: "No bloody moon."

"What?" he said. I didn't answer. I went on across the square itself now, in the hot sun, they following though not close so that I never saw them again until afterward, surrounded by the remote still eyes not following me yet either, just stopped where they were before the stores and about the door to the courthouse, waiting. I walked steadily on enclosed in the now fierce odor of the verbena sprig. Then shadow fell upon me; I did not pause, I looked once at the small faded sign nailed to the brick *B.J. Redmond. Atty at Law* and began to mount the stairs, the wooden steps scuffed by the heavy bewildered boots of countrymen approaching litigation and stained by tobacco spit, on down the dim corridor to the door which bore the name again, *B.J. Redmond* and knocked once and opened it. He sat behind the desk, not much taller than Father but thicker as a man gets who spends most of his time sitting and listening to people, freshly shaven and with fresh linen; a lawyer yet it was not a lawyer's face— a face much thinner than the body would indicate, strained (and yes, tragic; I know that now) and exhausted beneath the neat recent steady strokes of the razor, holding a pistol flat on the desk before him, loose beneath his hand and aimed at nothing. There was no smell of drink, not even of tobacco in the neat clean dingy room although I knew he smoked. I didn't pause. I walked steadily toward him. It was not twenty feet from door to desk yet I seemed to walk in a dreamlike state in which there was neither time nor distance, as though the mere act of walking was no more intended to encompass space than was his sitting. We didn't speak. It was as if we both knew what the passage of words would be and the futility of it; how he might have said, "Go out, Bayard. Go away, boy" and then, "Draw then. I will allow you to draw" and it would have been the same as if he had never said it. So we did not speak; I just walked steadily toward him as the pistol rose from the desk. I watched it, I could see the foreshortened slant of the barrel and I knew it would miss me though his hand did not tremble. I walked toward him, toward the pistol in the rocklike hand, I heard no bullet. Maybe I didn't even hear the explosion though I remember the sudden orange bloom and smoke as they appeared against his white shirt as they had appeared against Grumby's greasy Confederate coat; I still watched that foreshortened slant of barrel which I knew was not aimed at me and saw the second orange flash and smoke and heard no bullet that time either. Then I stopped; it was done then. I watched the pistol descend to the desk in short jerks; I saw him release it and sit back, both hands on the desk, I looked at his face and I knew too what it was to want air when there was nothing in the circumambience for the lungs. He rose, shoved the chair back with a convulsive motion and rose, with a queer ducking motion of his head; with his head still ducked aside and one arm extended as though he couldn't see and the other hand resting on the desk as if he couldn't stand alone, he turned and crossed to the wall and took his hat from the rack and with his head still ducked aside and one hand extended he blundered along the wall and passed me and reached the door and went through it. He was brave; no one denied that. He walked down those stairs and out onto the street where George Wyatt and the other six of Father's old troop waited and where the other men had begun to run now; he walked through the middle of them with his hat on and his head up (they told me how someone shouted at him: "Have you killed that boy too?"), saying no word, staring straight ahead and with his back to them, on to the station where the south-bound train was just in and got on it with no baggage, nothing, and went away from Jefferson and from Mississippi and never came back.

I heard their feet on the stairs then in the corridor then in the room, but for a while yet (it wasn't that long, of course) I still sat behind the desk as he had sat, the flat of the pistol still warm under my hand, my hand growing slowly numb between the pistol and my forehead. Then I raised my head; the little room was full of men. "My God!" George Wyatt cried. "You took the pistol away from him and then missed him, missed him *twice*?" Then he answered himself— that same rapport for violence which Drusilla had and which in George's case was actual character judgment: "No; wait.

You walked in here without even a pocket knife and let him miss you twice. My God in heaven." He turned, shouting: "Get to hell out of here! You, White, ride out to Sartoris and tell his folks it's all over and he's all right. Ride!" So they departed, went away; presently only George was left, watching me with that pale bleak stare which was speculative yet not at all ratiocinative. "Well by God," he said. "—Do you want a drink?"

"No," I said. "I'm hungry. I didn't eat any breakfast."

"I reckon not, if you got up this morning aiming to do what you did. Come on. We'll go to the Holston House."

"No," I said. "No. Not there."

"Why not? You aint done anything to be ashamed of. I wouldn't have done it that way, myself. I'd a shot at him once, anyway. But that's your way or you wouldn't have done it."

"Yes," I said. "I would do it again."

"Be damned if I would.—You want to come home with me? We'll have time to eat and then ride out there in time for the—" But I couldn't do that either.

"No," I said. "I'm not hungry after all. I think I'll go home."

"Dont you want to wait and ride out with me?"

"No. I'll go on."

"You dont want to stay here, anyway." He looked around the room again, where the smell of powder smoke still lingered a little, still lay somewhere on the hot dead air though invisible now, blinking a little with his fierce pale unintroverted eyes. "Well by God," he said again. "Maybe you're right, maybe there has been enough killing in your family without— Come on." We left the office. I waited at the foot of the stairs and soon Ringo came up with the horses. We crossed the square again. There were no feet on the Holston House railing now (it was twelve oclock) but a group of men stood before the door who raised their hats and I raised mine and Ringo and I rode on.

We did not go fast. Soon it was one, maybe after; the carriages and buggies would begin to leave the square soon, so I turned from the road at the end of the pasture and I sat the mare, trying to open the gate without dismounting, until

Ringo dismounted and opened it. We crossed the pasture in the hard fierce sun; I could have seen the house now but I didn't look. Then we were in the shade, the close thick airless shade of the creek bottom; the old rails still lay in the undergrowth where we had built the pen to hide the Yankee mules. Presently I heard the water, then I could see the sunny glints. We dismounted. I lay on my back, I thought *Now it can begin again if it wants to.* But it did not. I went to sleep. I went to sleep almost before I had stopped thinking. I slept for almost five hours and I didn't dream anything at all yet I waked myself up crying, crying too hard to stop it. Ringo was squatting beside me and the sun was gone though there was a bird of some sort still singing somewhere and the whistle of the north-bound evening train sounded and the short broken puffs of starting where it had evidently stopped at our flag station. After a while I began to stop and Ringo brought his hat full of water from the creek but instead I went down to the water myself and bathed my face.

There was still a good deal of light in the pasture, though the whip-poor-wills had begun, and when we reached the house there was a mockingbird singing in the magnolia, the night song now, the drowsy moony one, and again the moon like the rim print of a heel in wet sand. There was just one light in the hall now and so it was all over though I could still smell the flowers even above the verbena in my coat. I had not looked at him again. I had started to before I left the house but I did not, I did not see him again and all the pictures we had of him were bad ones because a picture could no more have held him dead than the house could have kept his body. But I didn't need to see him again because he was there, he would always be there; maybe what Drusilla meant by his dream was not something which he possessed but something which he had bequeathed us which we could never forget, which would even assume the corporeal shape of him whenever any of us, black or white, closed our eyes. I went into the house. There was no light in the drawing room except the last of the afterglow which came through the western window where Aunt Jenny's colored glass was; I was about to go on up stairs when I saw her sitting there beside the window. She didn't call me and I didn't speak Drusilla's name, I just went to the door and stood there. "She's gone," Aunt Jenny said. "She took the evening train. She has gone to Montgomery, to Dennison." Denny had been married about a year now; he was living in Montgomery, reading law.

"I see," I said. "Then she didn't—" But there wasn't any use in that either; Jed White must have got there before one oclock and told them. And besides, Aunt Jenny didn't answer. She could have lied to me but she didn't, she said,

"Come here." I went to her chair. "Kneel down. I cant see you."

"Dont you want the lamp?"

"No. Kneel down." So I knelt beside the chair. "So you had a perfectly splendid Saturday afternoon, didn't you? Tell me about it." Then she put her hands on my shoulders. I watched them come up as though she were trying to stop them; I felt them on my shoulders as if they had a separate life of their own and were trying to do something which for my sake she was trying to restrain, prevent. Then she gave up or she was not strong enough because they came up and took my face between them, hard, and suddenly the tears sprang and streamed down her face like Drusilla's laughing had. "Oh, damn you Sartorises!" she said. "Damn you! Damn you!"

As I passed down the hall the light came up in the dining-room and I could hear Louvinia laying the table for supper. So the stairs were lighted quite well. But the upper hall was dark. I saw her open door (that unmistakable way in which an open door stands open when nobody lives in the room any more) and I realised I had not believed that she was really gone. So I didn't look into the room. I went on to mine and entered. And then for a long moment I thought it was the verbena in my lapel which I still smelled. I thought that until I had crossed the room and looked down at the pillow on which it lay—the single sprig of it (without looking she would pinch off a half dozen of them and they would be all of a size, almost all of a shape, as if a machine had stamped them out) filling the room, the dusk, the evening with that odor which she said you could smell alone above the smell of horses.

IF I FORGET THEE,
JERUSALEM
[THE WILD PALMS]

The Wild Palms

THE KNOCKING sounded again, at once discreet and peremptory, while the doctor was descending the stairs, the flashlight's beam lancing on before him down the brown-stained stairwell and into the brown-stained tongue-and-groove box of the lower hall. It was a beach cottage, even though of two stories, and lighted by oil lamps—or an oil lamp, which his wife had carried up stairs with them after supper. And the doctor wore a night shirt too, not pajamas, for the same reason that he smoked the pipe which he had never learned and knew that he would never learn to like, between the occasional cigar which clients gave him in the intervals of Sundays on which he smoked the three cigars which he felt he could buy for himself even though he owned the beach cottage as well as the one next door to it and the one, the residence with electricity and plastered walls, in the village four miles away. Because he was now forty-eight years old and he had been sixteen and eighteen and twenty at the time when his father could tell him (and he believe it) that cigarettes and pajamas were for dudes and women.

It was after midnight, though not much. He could tell that, even apart from the wind, the taste and smell and feel of wind even here behind the closed and locked doors and shutters. Because he had been born here, on this coast though not in this house but in the other, the residence in town, and had lived here all his life, including the four years at the State University's medical school and the two years as an intern in New Orleans where (a thick man even when young, with thick soft woman's hands, who should never have been a doctor at all, who even after the six more or less metropolitan years looked out from a provincial and insulated amazement at his classmates and fellows: the lean young men swaggering their drill jackets on which—to him—they wore the myriad anonymous faces of the probationer nurses with a ruthless and assured braggadocio like decorations, like flower trophies) he had sickened for it. So he graduated, nearer the foot of the class than the head though not at either, and came home and within the year married the wife his father had picked out for him and within four years owned the house which his father had built and assumed the practice which his father had created, losing nothing from it and adding nothing to it, and within ten years owned not only the beach house where he and his wife spent their childless summers but the adjoining property as well, which he rented to summer visitors or even parties—picnickers or fishermen. On the evening of the wedding he and his wife went to New Orleans and spent two days in a hotel room, though they never had a honeymoon. And though they had slept in the same bed for twenty-three years now they still had no children.

But even apart from the wind he could still tell the approximate time by the staling smell of gumbo now cold in the big earthen pot on the cold stove beyond the flimsy kitchen wall—the big pot of it which his wife had made that morning in order to send some over to their neighbors and renters in the next house: the man and the woman who four days ago had rented the cottage and who probably did not even know that the donors of the gumbo were not only neighbors but landlords too—the dark-haired woman with queer hard yellow eyes in a face whose skin was drawn thin over prominent cheekbones and a heavy jaw (the doctor called it sullen at first, then he called it afraid), young, who sat all day long in a new cheap beach chair facing the water, in a worn sweater and a pair of faded jeans pants and canvas shoes, not reading, not doing anything, just sitting there in that complete immobility which the doctor (or the doctor in the Doctor) did not need the corroboration of the drawn quality of the skin and the blank inverted fixity of the apparently unseeing eyes to recognise at once—that complete immobile abstraction from which even pain and terror are absent, in which a living creature seems to listen to and even watch some one of its own flagging organs, the heart say, the secret irreparable seeping of blood; and the man young too, in a pair of disreputable khaki slacks and a sleeveless jersey undershirt and no hat in a region where even young people believed the summer sun to be fatal, seen usually walking barefoot along the beach at tide-edge, returning with a faggot of driftwood strapped into a belt, passing the immobile woman in the beach chair with no sign from her, no movement of the head or perhaps even of the eyes.

But it was not the heart, the doctor told himself. He decided that on the first day from where, without intending to eavesdrop, he watched the woman through the screen of oleander bushes which separated the two lots. Yet this very postulation of what it was not seemed to him to contain the secret, the answer. It seemed to him that he saw the truth already, the shadowy indefinite shape of truth, as though he were separated from the truth only by a veil just as he was separated from the living woman by the screen of oleander leaves. He was not eavesdropping, not spying; perhaps he thought, *I will have plenty of time in which to learn just which organ it is she is listening to; they have paid their rent for two weeks* (perhaps at that time also the doctor in the Doctor knowing that it would not require weeks but just days), thinking how if she should need assistance it would be fortunate that he, the landlord, was also a doctor until it occurred to him that since they probably did not even know he was the landlord, they would probably not know either that he was a doctor.

The real estate agent told him over the telephone of the renting of the house. "She's got on pants," the agent said. "I mean, not these ladies' slacks but pants, man's pants. I mean, they are too little for her in just exactly the right places any man would want to see them too little but no woman would unless she had them on herself. I reckon Miss Martha aint going to like that much."

"That will be all right with her if they pay their rent on time," the doctor said.

"No damn fear," the agent said. "I saw to that. I aint been in this business this long for nothing. I said, 'It will have to be in advance' and he said 'All right. All right. How much?' like he was Vanderbilt or somebody, in them dirty fishing pants and nothing but an undershirt under his coat, hauling the wad of money out and one of the bills wasn't but a ten and I just gave him ten change back out of the other one and there wasn't but two of them to begin with and I says 'Of course if you want to take the house like it is, with just what furniture is in it now, you can get out pretty cheap' and he says 'All right. All right. How much?' I believe I could have got more than I did because if you ask me he dont want any furniture, all he wants is four walls to get inside of and a door to close afterward. She never even got out of the taxi. She just sat there, waiting, in them pants that was just exactly too little for her in just exactly the right places." The voice ceased; the doctor's head filled now with suspended wirehum, the rising inflection of a risible silence, so that he said almost sharply:

"Well? Do they want more furniture or not? There's nothing in the house but one bed, and the mattress on it aint—"

"No, no, they dont want anymore. I told him the house had a bed and a stove in it, and they had a chair with them— one of these canvas ones that fold up in the taxi along with the grip. So they are all fixed." Now that suspension of silent laughing filled the doctor's head again.

"Well?" the doctor said. "What is it? What's the matter with you?" though he seemed to know already, before the other spoke, what the voice would say:

"I reckon Miss Martha is going to have something that will set heavier on her stomach than them pants even. I dont think they are married. Oh, he says they are and I dont think he is lying about her and maybe he aint even lying about himself. The trouble is, they aint married to each other, she aint married to him. Because I can smell a husband. Show me a woman I never saw before on the streets of Mobile or New Orleans either and I can smell whether——"

They took possession that afternoon of the cottage, the shack, which contained the one bed whose springs and mattress were not very good, and the stove with its one frying pan incrusted by generations of cooking fish, and the coffee pot and the meagre collection of mismatched iron spoons and forks and knives and cracked cups and saucers and drinking vessels which had once been containers of bought jams and jellies, and the new beach chair in which the woman lay all day long apparently watching the palm fronds clashing with their wild dry bitter sound against the bright glitter of the water while the man carried driftwood into the kitchen. Two mornings ago the milk wagon which made the beach route stopped there and the doctor's wife saw the man once returning up the beach from a small grocery store owned by a

Portuguese ex-fisherman, carrying a loaf of bread and a bulky paper sack. And she told the doctor about watching him cleaning (or trying to clean) a mess of fish at the kitchen steps, told the doctor about it with bitter and outraged conviction—a shapeless woman yet not fat, not anywhere near as plump as the doctor himself, who had begun to turn gray all over about ten years ago, as if hair and complection both were being subtly altered, along with the shade of her eyes, by the color of the house dresses which she apparently chose to match them. "And a mess of it he was making!" she cried. "A mess outside the kitchen and a mess on the stove too probably!"

"Maybe she can cook," the doctor said mildly.

"Where? how? sitting out there in the yard? When he carries stove and all out to her?" But even that was not the real outrage, though she did not say so. She did not say 'They are not married' though it was in both their minds. They both knew that, once it was said aloud between them, he would turn the renters out. Yet they both refused to say it and for more reason than because when he turned them out he would feel conscience-bound to return the rent money; more than this on his part anyway, who was thinking *They had only twenty dollars. And that was three days ago. And there is something wrong with her,* the doctor now speaking louder than the provincial protestant, the Baptist born. And something (perhaps the doctor here too) talking louder than the provincial Baptist in her too because this morning she waked the doctor, calling him from the window where she stood shapeless in the cotton nightgown shaped like a shroud and with her gray hair screwed into papers, to show him the man coming up the beach at sunrise with his belted faggot of driftwood. And when he (the doctor) came home at noon she had the gumbo made, an enormous quantity of it, enough for a dozen people, made with that grim Samaritan husbandry of good women, as if she took a grim and vindictive and masochistic pleasure in the fact that the Samaritan deed would be performed at the price of its remainder which would sit invincible and inexhaustible on the stove while days accumulated and passed, to be warmed and rewarmed and then rewarmed until consumed by two people who did not even like it, who born and bred in sight of the sea had for taste in fish a predilection for the tuna, the salmon, the sardines bought in cans, immolated and embalmed three thousand miles away in the oil of machinery and commerce.

He delivered the bowl himself—a shortish fattish untidy man with linen not quite fresh, sidling a little clumsily through the oleander hedge with the bowl covered by a yet-creased (and not yet even laundered, it was that new) linen napkin, lending an air of awkward kindliness even to the symbol which he carried of the uncompromising Christian deed performed not with sincerity or pity but through duty —and lowered it (she had not risen from the chair nor moved save the hard cat's eyes) as if the bowl contained nitro glycerin, the fattish unshaven mask beaming foolishly but behind the mask the eyes of the doctor within the Doctor shrewd, missing nothing, examining without smiling and without diffidence the face of the woman who was not thin but actually gaunt, thinking *Yes. A degree or two. Perhaps three. But not the heart* then waking, rousing, to find the blank feral eyes staring at him, whom to his certain knowledge they could scarcely have seen before, with profound and illimitable hatred. It was quite impersonal, as when the person in whom joy already exists looks out at any post or tree with pleasure and happiness. He (the doctor) was without vanity; it was not at him the hatred was directed. *It's at the whole human race* he thought. *Or no, no. Wait. Wait*— the veil about to break, the cogs of deduction about to mesh—*Not at the race of mankind but at the race of man, the masculine. But why? Why?* His wife would have noticed the faint mark of the absent wedding ring, but he, the doctor, saw more than that: *She has borne children* he thought. *One, anyway; I would stake my degree on that. And if Cofer* (he was the agent) *is right about his not being her husband—and he should be, should be able to tell, smell, as he says, since he is apparently in the business of renting beach cottages for the same reason or under the same compulsion, vicarious need, which drives certain people in the cities to equip and supply rooms to clandestine and fictitious names. . . . Say she had come to hate the race of men enough to desert husband and children; good. Yet, to have gone not only to another man, but to live apparently in penury, and herself sick, really sick. Or to have deserted husband and chil-dren for another man and poverty, and then to have — to have — to.* . . . . . . He could feel, hear them: the cogs, clicking, going fast; he felt a need for terrific haste in order to keep up, a premonition that the final cog would click and the bell of comprehension ring and he would not be quite near enough to see and hear: *Yes. Yes. What is it that man as a race can have done to her that she would look upon such a manifestation of it as I, whom she has never seen before and would not look at twice if she had, with that same hatred through which he must walk each time he comes up from the beach with an armful of firewood to cook the very food which she eats.*

She did not even offer to take the dish from him. "It's not soup, it's gumbo," he said. "My wife made it. She— we. . . . . . ." She did not move, looking at him as he stooped fatly in his crumpled seersucker, with the careful tray; he did not even hear the man until she spoke to him.

"Thanks," she said. "Take it into the house, Harry." Now she was not even looking at the doctor anymore. "Thank your wife," she said.

He was thinking about his two tenants as he descended the stairs behind the jerking pencil of light, into the staling odor of gumbo in the lower hall, toward the door, the knocking. It was from no presentiment, premonition that the knocker was the man named Harry. It was because he had thought of nothing else for four days—this snuffy middleaging man in the archaic sleeping garment now become one of the national props of comedy, roused from slumber in the stale bed of his childless wife and already thinking of (perhaps having been dreaming of) the profound and distracted blaze of objectless hatred in the strange woman's eyes; and he again with that sense of imminence, of being just beyond a veil from some-thing, of groping just without the veil and even touching but not quite, almost seeing but not quite, the shape of truth, so that without being aware of it he stopped dead on the stairs in his old fashioned list slippers, thinking swiftly: *Yes. Yes. Something which the entire race of men, males, has done to her or she believes has done to her.*

The knocking came again now, as if the knocker had be-come aware that he had stopped through some alteration of

the torch's beam seen beneath the door itself and now began
to knock again with that diffident insistence of a stranger
seeking aid late at night, and the doctor moved again, not in
response to the renewed knocking who had had no presentiment, but as though the renewal of the knocking had merely
coincided with the recurrent old stale impasse of the four
days' bafflement and groping, capitulant and recapitulant; as
though instinct perhaps moved him again, the body capable
of motion, not the intellect, believing that physical advance-
ment might bring him nearer the veil at the instant when it
would part and reveal in inviolable isolation that truth which
he almost touched. So it was without premonition that he
opened the door and peered out, bringing the torch's beam
on the knocker. It was the man called Harry. He stood there
in the darkness, in the strong steady seawind filled with the
dry clashing of invisible palm fronds, as the doctor had always
seen him, in the soiled ducks and the sleeveless undershirt,
murmuring the conventional amenities about the hour and
the need, asking to use the telephone while the doctor, his
nightshirt streaming about his flabby calves, peered at the
caller and thought in a fierce surge of triumph *Now I am going
to find out what it is*. "Yes," he said, "you wont need the telephone. I am a doctor myself."

"Oh," the other said. "Can you come at once?"

"Yes. Just let me slip on my pants. What's the trouble? So I
shall know what to bring."

For an instant the other hesitated; this familiar to the doctor too who had seen it before and believed he knew its
source: that innate and ineradicable instinct of mankind to
attempt to conceal some of the truth even from the doctor or
lawyer for whose skill and knowledge they are paying. "She's
bleeding," he said. "What will your fee—"

But the doctor did not notice this. He was talking to himself: *Ah. Yes. Why didn't I. . . . Lungs, of course. Why didn't I
think of that?* "Yes," he said. "Will you wait here? Or perhaps
inside? I wont be but a minute."

"I'll wait here," the other said. But the doctor did not hear
that either. He was already running back up the stairs; he
trotted into the bedroom where his wife rose on one elbow
in the bed and watched him struggle into his trousers, his

shadow, cast by the lamp on the low table by the bed, antic
on the wall, her shadow also monstrous, gorgonlike from the
rigid paper-wrapped twists of gray hair above the gray face
above the high-necked night-dress which also looked gray, as
if every garment she owned had partaken of that grim iron-
color of her implacable and invincible morality which, the
doctor was to realise later, was almost omniscient. "Yes," he
said, "bleeding. Probably hemorrhage. Lungs. And why in
the world I didn't—"

"More likely he has cut or shot her," she said in a cold quiet
bitter voice. "Though from the look in her eyes the one time
I saw her close I would have said she would be the one to do
the cutting and shooting."

"Nonsense," he said, hunching into his suspenders.
"Nonsense." Because he was not talking to her now either.
"Yes. The fool. To bring her here, of all places. To sealevel.
To the Mississippi coast.—Do you want me to put out the
lamp?"

"Yes. You'll probably be there a long time if you are going
to wait until you are paid." He blew out the lamp and descended the stairs again behind the torch. His black bag sat
on the hall table beside his hat. The man Harry still stood just
without the front door.

"Maybe you better take this now," he said.

"What?" the doctor said. He paused, looking down, bringing the torch to bear on the single banknote in the other's
extended hand. *Even if he has spent nothing, now he will have
only fifteen dollars* he thought. "No, later," he said. "Maybe we
had better hurry." He bustled on ahead, following the torch's
dancing beam, trotting while the other walked, across his
own somewhat sheltered yard and through the dividing oleander hedge and so into the full sweep of the unimpeded sea-
wind which thrashed among the unseen palms and hissed in
the harsh salt grass of the unkempt other lot; now he could
see a dim light in the other house. "Bleeding, hey?" he said. It
was overcast; the invisible wind blew strong and steady
among the invisible palms, from the invisible sea—a harsh
steady sound full of the murmur of surf on the outside barrier
islands, the spits and scars of sand bastioned with tossing and
shabby pines. "Hemorrhage?"

"What?" the other said. "Hemorrhage?"

"No?" the doctor said. "She's just coughing a little blood then? Just spitting a little blood when she coughs, eh?"

"Spitting?" the other said. It was the tone, not the words. It was not addressed to the doctor and it was beyond laughter, as if that which it addressed were impervious to laughter; it was not the doctor who stopped; the doctor still trotted onward on his short sedentary legs, behind the jolting torch-beam, toward the dim waiting light, it was the Baptist, the provincial, who seemed to pause while the man, not the doctor now, thought not in shock but in a sort of despairing amazement: *Am I to live forever behind a barricade of perennial innocence like a chicken in a pen?* He spoke aloud quite carefully; the veil was going now, dissolving now, it was about to part now and now he did not want to see what was behind it; he knew that for the sake of his peace of mind forever afterward he did not dare and he knew that it was too late now and that he could not help himself; he heard his voice ask the question he did not want to ask and get the answer he did not want to hear:

"You say she is bleeding. Where is she bleeding?"

"Where do women bleed?" the other said, cried, in a harsh exasperated voice, not stopping. "I'm no doctor. If I were, do you think I would waste five dollars on you?"

Nor did the doctor hear this either. "Ah," he said. "Yes. I see. Yes." Now he stopped. He was aware of no cessation of motion since the steady dark wind still blew past him. *Because I am at the wrong age for this* he thought. *If I were twenty-five I could say, Thank God I am not him because I would know it was only my luck today and that maybe tomorrow or next year it will be me and so I will not need to envy him. And if I were sixty-five I could say, Thank God I am not him because then I would know I was too old for it to be possible and so it would not do me any good to envy him because he has proof on the body of love and of passion and of life that he is not dead. But now I am forty-eight and I did not think that I deserved this.* "Wait," he said; "wait." The other paused; they stood facing one another, leaning a little into the dark wind filled with the wild dry sound of the palms.

"I offered to pay you," the other said. "Isn't five enough?

And if it isn't, will you give me the name of someone who will come for that and let me use your telephone?"

"Wait," the doctor said. *So Cofer was right* he thought. *You are not married. Only why did you have to tell me so?* He didn't say that, of course, he said, "You haven't. . . . You are not. . . . . . What are you?"

The other, taller, leaned in the hard wind, looking down at the doctor with that impatience, that seething restraint. In the black wind the house, the shack, stood, itself invisible, the dim light shaped not by any door or window but rather like a strip of dim and forlorn bunting dingy and rigidly immobile in the wind. "What am I what?" he said. "I'm trying to be a painter. Is that what you mean?"

"A painter? But there is no building, no boom, no development here anymore. That died nine years ago. You mean, you came here without any offer of work, any sort of contract at all?"

"I paint pictures," the other said. "At least, I think I do.—Well? Am I to use your phone or not?"

"You paint pictures," the doctor said; he spoke in that tone of quiet amazement which thirty minutes later and then to-morrow and tomorrow would vacillate among outrage and anger and despair: "Well. She's probably still bleeding. Come along." They went on. He entered the house first; even at the moment he realised that he had preceded the other not as a guest, not even as owner, but because he believed now that he alone of the two of them had any right to enter it at all so long as the woman was in it. They were out of the wind now. It merely leaned, black, imponderable and firm, against the door which the man called Harry had closed behind them: and now and at once the doctor smelled again the odor of stale and cooling gumbo. He even knew where it would be, he could almost see it sitting uneaten (*They have not even tasted it* he thought. *But why should they? Why in God's name should they?*) on the cold stove since he knew the kitchen well—the broken stove, the spare cooking vessels, the meagre collection of broken knives and forks and spoons, the drink-ing receptacles which had once contained gaudily labelled and machine-made pickle and jam. He knew the entire house well, he owned it, he had built it—the flimsy walls (they were not even tongue-and-groove like the one in which he lived but were of ship-lap, the synthetic joints of which, weathered and warped by the damp salt air, leaked all privacy just as broken socks and trousers do) murmurous with the ghosts of a thousand rented days and nights to which he (though not his wife) had closed his eyes, insisting only that there be always an odd number in any mixed party which stayed there overnight unless the couple were strangers formally professing to be man and wife, as now, even though he knew better and knew that his wife knew better. Because this was it, this the anger and outrage which would alternate with the despair tomorrow and tomorrow: *Why did you have to tell me?* he thought. *The others didn't tell me, upset me, didn't bring here what you brought, though I dont know what they might have taken away.*

At once he could see the dim lamplight beyond the open door. But he would have known which door without the light to guide him, the one beyond which the bed would be, the bed in which his wife said she would not ask a nigger servant to sleep; he could hear the other behind him and he realised for the first time that the man called Harry was still barefoot and that he was about to pass and enter the room first, thinking (the doctor) how he who actually had the only small portion of right to enter of either of them must hold back, feeling a dreadful desire to laugh, thinking *You see, I dont know the etiquette in these cases because when I was young and lived in the cities where apparently such as this occurs, I suppose I was afraid, too afraid,* pausing because the other paused: so that it seemed to the doctor, in a steady silent glare of what he was never to know was actual clairvoyance, that they had both paused as if to allow the shade, the shadow, of the absent outraged rightful husband to precede them. It was a sound from within the room itself which moved them—the sound of a bottle against a glass.

"Just a minute," the man named Harry said. He entered the room quickly; the doctor saw, flung across the beach chair, the faded jeans that were too small for her in exactly the right places. But he did not move. He just heard the swift passage of the man's bare feet on the floor and then his voice, tense, not loud, quiet, quite gentle: so that suddenly the doctor believed he knew why there had been neither pain nor terror in the woman's face: that the man was carrying that too just as he carried the firewood and (doubtless) cooked with it the food she ate. "No, Charlotte," he said. "You mustn't. You cant. Come back to bed now."

"Why cant I?" the woman's voice said. "Why bloody cant I?" and now the doctor could hear them struggling. "Let me go, you bloody bungling bastard" (it was 'rat', the noun, which the doctor believed he heard.). "You promised, rat. That was all I asked and you promised. Because listen, rat—" the doctor could hear it, the voice cunning, secret now: "It wasn't him, you see. Not that bastard Wilbourne. I ratted off on him like I did you. It was the other one. You cant, anyway. I'll plead my ass like they used to plead their bellies and nobody ever knows just where the truth is about a whore to convict anybody—" The doctor could hear them, the two pairs of bare feet; it sounded as if they were dancing, furiously and infinitesimally and without shoes. Then this stopped and the voice was not cunning, not secret. *But where's the despair?* the doctor thought. *Where's the terror?* "Jesus, there I went again. Harry! Harry! You promised."

"I've got you. It's all right. Come back to bed."

"Give me a drink."

"No. I told you no more. I told you why not. Do you hurt bad now?"

"Jesus, I dont know. I cant tell. Give me the drink, Harry. Maybe that will start it again."

"No. It cant now. It's too late for that too. Besides, the doctor's here now. He'll start it again. I'm going to put your gown on you so he can come in."

"And risk bloodying up the only nightgown I ever owned?"

"That's why. That's why we got the gown. Maybe that's all it will take to start it again. Come on now."

"Then why the doctor? Why the five dollars? Oh you damned bloody bungling—No no no no. Quick. There I go again. Stop me quick. I am hurting. I cant help it. Oh damn bloody bloody—" she began to laugh; it was hard laughing and not loud, like retching or coughing. "There. That's it. It's like dice. Come seven come eleven. Maybe if I can just keep on saying it—" He (the doctor) could hear them, the two pair of bare feet on the floor, then the rusty plaint of the bed springs, the woman still laughing, not loud, just with that abstract and furious despair which he had seen in her eyes over the bowl of gumbo at noon. He stood there, holding his little scuffed worn serviceable black bag, looking at the faded jeans among the wadded mass of other garments on the beach chair; he saw the man called Harry reappear and select from among them a night gown and vanish again; the doctor looked at the chair. *Yes* he thought. *Just like the firewood.* Then the man called Harry was standing in the door.

"You can come in now," he said.

Old Man

ONCE (it was in Mississippi, in May, in the flood year 1927) there were two convicts. One of them was about twenty-five, tall, lean, flat-stomached, with a sunburned face and Indian-black hair and pale, china-colored outraged eyes—an outrage directed not at the men who had foiled his crime, not even at the lawyers and judges who had sent him here, but at the writers, the uncorporeal names attached to the stories, the paper novels—the Diamond Dicks and Jesse Jameses and such—whom he believed had led him into his present predicament through their own ignorance and gullibility regarding the medium in which they dealt and took money for, in accepting information on which they placed the stamp of verisimilitude and authenticity (this so much the more criminal since there was no sworn notarised statement attached and hence so much the quicker would the information be accepted by one who expected the same unspoken good faith, demanding, asking, expecting no certification, which he extended along with the dime or fifteen cents to pay for it) and retailed for money and which on actual application proved to be impractical and (to the convict) criminally false; there would be times when he would halt his mule and plow in midfurrow (there is no walled penitentiary in Mississippi; it is a cotton plantation which the convicts work under the rifles and shotguns of guards and trusties) and muse with a kind of enraged impotence, fumbling among the rubbish left him by his one and only experience with courts and law, fumbling until the meaningless and verbose shibboleth took form at last (himself seeking justice at the same blind fount where he had met justice and been hurled back and down): using the mails to defraud: who felt that he had been defrauded by the third class mail system not of crass and stupid money which he did not particularly want anyway, but of liberty and honor and pride.

He was in for fifteen years (he had arrived shortly after his nineteenth birthday) for attempted train robbery. He had laid his plans in advance, he had followed his printed (and false) authority to the letter; he had saved the paper-backs for two years, reading and rereading them, memorising them, comparing and weighing story and method against story and method, taking the good from each and discarding the dross as his workable plan emerged, keeping his mind open to make the subtle last-minute changes, without haste and without impatience, as the newer pamphlets appeared on their appointed days as a conscientious dressmaker makes the subtle alterations in a court presentation costume as the newer bulletins appear. And then when the day came, he did not even have a chance to go through the coaches and collect the watches and the rings, the brooches and the hidden money-belts, because he had been captured as soon as he entered the express car where the safe and the gold would be. He had shot no one because the pistol which they took away from him was not that kind of a pistol although it was loaded; later he admitted to the District Attorney that he had got it, as well as the dark lantern in which a candle burned and the black handkerchief to wear over the face, by peddling among his pine-hill neighbors subscriptions to the *Detectives' Gazette*. So now from time to time (he had ample leisure for it) he mused with that raging impotence because there was something else he could not tell them at the trial, did not know how to tell them. It was not the money he had wanted. It was not riches, not the crass loot; that would have been merely a bangle to wear upon the breast of his pride like the Olympic runner's amateur medal—a symbol, a badge to show that he too was the best at his chosen gambit in the living and fluid world of his time. So that at times as he trod the richly shearing black earth behind his plow or with a hoe thinned the sprouting cotton and corn or lay on his sullen back in his bunk after supper, he cursed in a harsh steady unrepetitive stream, not at the living men who had put him where he was but at what he did not even know were pen-names, did not even know were not actual men but merely the designations of shades who had written about shades.

The second convict was short and plump. Almost hairless, he was quite white. He looked like something exposed to light by turning over rotting logs or planks and he too carried (though not in his eyes like the first convict) a sense of burning and impotent outrage. So it did not show on him and hence none knew it was there. But then nobody knew very

much about him, including the people who had sent him
here. His outrage was directed at no printed word but at the
paradoxical fact that he had been forced to come here of his
own free choice and will. He had been forced to choose between the Mississippi State penal farm and the Federal Penitentiary at Atlanta, and the fact that he, who resembled a
hairless and pallid slug, had chosen the out-of-doors and
the sunlight was merely another manifestation of the close-
guarded and solitary enigma of his character, as something
recognisable roils momentarily into view from beneath stagnant and opaque water, then sinks again. None of his fellow
prisoners knew what his crime had been, save that he was in
for a hundred and ninety-nine years—this incredible and impossible period of punishment or restraint itself carrying a
vicious and fabulous quality which indicated that his reason
for being here was such that the very men, the paladins and
pillars of justice and equity who had sent him here had during
that moment become blind apostles not of mere justice but of
all human decency, blind instruments not of equity but of all
human outrage and vengeance, acting in a savage personal
concert, judge lawyer and jury, which certainly abrogated
justice and possibly even law. Possibly only the Federal and
State's attorneys knew what the crime actually was. There had
been a woman in it and a stolen automobile transported
across a state line, a filling station robbed and the attendant
shot to death. There had been a second man in the car at the
time and anyone could have looked once at the convict (as the
two attorneys did) and known he would not even have had
the synthetic courage of alcohol to pull trigger on anyone.
But he and the woman and the stolen car had been captured
while the second man, doubtless the actual murderer, had escaped, so that, brought to bay at last in the State's Attorney's
office, harried, dishevelled and snarling, the two grimly implacable and viciously gleeful attorneys in his front and the now
raging woman held by two policemen in the anteroom in his
rear, he was given his choice. He could be tried in Federal
Court under the Mann Act and for the automobile, that is, by
electing to pass through the anteroom where the woman
raged he could take his chances on the lesser crime in Federal
Court, or by accepting a sentence for manslaughter in the

State Court he would be permitted to quit the room by a back entrance, without having to pass the woman. He had chosen; he stood at the Bar and heard a judge (who looked down at him as if the District Attorney actually had turned over a rotten plank with his toe and exposed him) sentence him to a hundred and ninety-nine years at the State Farm. Thus (he had ample leisure too; they had tried to teach him to plow and had failed, they had put him in the blacksmith shop and the foreman trusty himself had asked to have him removed: so that now, in a long apron like a woman, he cooked and swept and dusted in the deputy wardens' barracks) he too mused at times with that sense of impotence and outrage though it did not show on him as on the first convict since he leaned on no halted broom to do it and so none knew it was there.

It was this second convict who, toward the end of April, began to read aloud to the others from the daily newspapers when, chained ankle to ankle and herded by armed guards, they had come up from the fields and had eaten supper and were gathered in the bunkhouse. It was the Memphis newspaper which the deputy wardens had read at breakfast; the convict read aloud from it to his companions who could have had but little active interest in the outside world, some of whom could not have read it for themselves at all and did not even know where the Ohio and Missouri river basins were, some of whom had never even seen the Mississippi river although for past periods ranging from a few days to ten and twenty and thirty years (and for future periods ranging from a few months to life) they had plowed and planted and eaten and slept beneath the shadow of the levee itself, knowing only that there was water beyond it from hearsay and because now and then they heard the whistles of steamboats from beyond it, and during the last week or so had seen the stacks and pilot houses moving along the sky sixty feet above their heads.

But they listened, and soon even those who like the taller convict had probably never before seen more water than a horse pond would hold knew what thirty feet on a river gauge at Cairo or Memphis meant and could (and did) talk glibly of sandboils. Perhaps what actually moved them were the accounts of the conscripted levee gangs, mixed blacks and whites working in double shifts against the steadily rising water; stories of men, even though they were negroes, being forced like themselves to do work for which they received no other pay than coarse food and a place in a mudfloored tent to sleep on—stories, pictures, which emerged from the shorter convict's reading voice: the mudsplashed white men with the inevitable shotguns, the antlike lines of negroes carrying sandbags, slipping and crawling up the steep face of the revetment to hurl their futile ammuntion into the face of a flood and return for more. Or perhaps it was more than this. Perhaps they watched the approach of the disaster with that same amazed and incredulous hope of the slaves—the lions and bears and elephants, the grooms and bathmen and pastrycooks—who watched the mounting flames of Rome from Ahenobarbus' gardens. But listen they did and presently it was May and the warden's newspaper began to talk in headlines two inches tall—those black staccato slashes of ink which, it would almost seem, even the illiterate should be able to read: *Crest Passes Memphis at Midnight. 4000 Homeless in White River Basin. Governor Calls out National Guard Martial Law Declared in Following Counties. Red Cross Train with Secretary Hoover Leaves Washington Tonight;* then, three evenings later (It had been raining all day—not the vivid brief thunderous downpours of April and May, but the slow steady gray rain of November and December before a cold north wind. The men had not gone to the fields at all during the day, and the very second-hand optimism of the almost twenty-four hour old news seemed to contain its own refutation.): *Crest Now Below Memphis. 22,000 Refugees Safe at Vicksburg. Army Engineers Say Levees Will Hold.*

"I reckon that means it will bust tonight," one convict said.

"Well, maybe this rain will hold on until the water gets here," a second said. They all agreed to this because what they meant, the living unspoken thought among them, was that if the weather cleared, even though the levees broke and the flood moved in upon the Farm itself, they would have to return to the fields and work, which they would have had to do. There was nothing paradoxical in this, although they could not have expressed the reason for it which they instinctively perceived: that the land they farmed and the substance they produced from it belonged neither to them who worked it nor to those who forced them at guns' point to do so, that as far as either—convicts or guards—were concerned, it could have been pebbles they put into the ground and papier-mache cotton- and corn-sprouts which they thinned. So it was that, what between the sudden wild hoping and the idle day and the evening's headlines, they were sleeping restlessly beneath the sound of the rain on the tin roof when at midnight the sudden glare of the electric bulbs and the guards' voices waked them and they heard the throbbing of the waiting trucks.

"Turn out of there!" the deputy shouted. He was fully dressed—rubber boots, slicker, and shotgun. "The levee went out at Mound's Landing an hour ago. Get up out of it!"

The Wild Palms

WHEN THE MAN called Harry met Charlotte Rittenmeyer, he was an intern in a New Orleans hospital. He
was the youngest of three children, born to his father's second
wife in his father's old age; there was a difference of sixteen
years between him and the younger of his two half sisters. He
was left an orphan at the age of two and his older half sister
had raised him. His father had been a doctor before him. He
(the father) had begun and completed his medical training
at a time when the designation Doctor of Medicine covered
everything from pharmacology through diagnostics to surgery and when an education could be paid for in kind or in
labor; the elder Wilbourne had been janitor of his dormitory
and had also waited on table in commons and had completed
his four year course at a cash outlay of two hundred dollars.
Thus when his will was opened, the last paragraph read:

> To my son, Henry Wilbourne, and realising that conditions
> as well as the intrinsic value of money have changed and
> therefore he cannot be expected to obtain his degree in Sur-
> gery and Medicine for the same outlay of money which ob-
> tained in my day, I hereby bequeath and set aside the sum
> of two thousand dollars, to be used for the futhering and
> completing of his college course and the acquiring of his
> degree and license to practise in Surgery and Medicine, be-
> lieving that the aforesaid sum will be amply sufficient for
> that purpose.

The will was dated two days after Harry's birth in 1910, and
his father died two years later of toxemia gotten from sucking
a snake bite on the hand of a child in a country cabin and his
half sister took him. She had children of her own and was
married to a man who died still a clerk in a grocery store in a
small Oklahoma town, so by the time Harry was ready to
enter medical school that two thousand dollars to be stretched
over four years, even in the modest though well-rated school
which he chose, was not much more than his father's two
hundred had been. It was less, because there was steam heat
in the dormitories now and the college was served by a cafe-
teria requiring no waiters and the only way a young man

could earn money in school now was by carrying a football or stopping the man who did carry it. His sister helped him—an occasional money order for one or two dollars or even a few stamps folded carefully into a letter. This bought his cigarettes and by stopping tobacco for a year he saved enough to pay his fee into his medical fraternity. There was nothing left over for squiring girls (the school was coeducational) but then he had no time for that; beneath the apparent serenity of his monastic life he waged a constant battle as ruthless as any in a Wall Street skyscraper as he balanced his dwindling bank account against the turned pages of his text books.

But he did it, he came in under the wire with enough of the two thousand dollars left either to return to the Oklahoma town and present his sheepskin to his sister, or to go straight to New Orleans and assume his internship, but not enough to do both. He chose New Orleans. Or rather, there was no choice; he wrote his sister and her husband a letter of gratitude and thanks, inclosing a signed note for the full amount of the postage stamps and the money orders, with interest (he also sent the diploma with its Latin and its spidery embossed salutation and its cramped faculty signatures, of which his sister and brother-in-law could decipher only his name) and mailed it to them and bought his ticket and rode fourteen hours in a day coach. He reached New Orleans with one bag and a dollar and thirty-six cents.

He had been in the hospital almost two years now. He lived in the intern's quarters with the others who, like him, had no private means; he smoked once a week now: a package of cigarettes over the week-end and he was paying the note which he had executed to his half sister, the one- and two-dollar money orders in reverse now, returning to source; the one bag would still hold all he owned, including his hospital whites—the twenty-six years, the two thousand dollars, the railroad ticket to New Orleans, the one dollar and thirty-six cents, the one bag in a corner of a barracks-like room furnished with steel army cots; on the morning of his twenty-seventh birthday he waked and looked down his body toward his foreshortened feet and it seemed to him that he saw the twenty-seven irrevocable years diminished and foreshortened beyond them in turn, as if his life were to lie passively on his back as though he floated effortless and without volition upon an unreturning stream. He seemed to see them: the empty years in which his youth had vanished—the years for wild oats and for daring, for the passionate tragic ephemeral loves of adolescence, the girl- and boy-white, the wild importunate fumbling flesh, which had not been for him; lying so he thought, not exactly with pride and certainly not with the resignation which he believed, but rather with that peace with which a middleaged eunuch might look back upon the dead time before his alteration, at the fading and (at last) edgeless shapes which now inhabited only the memory and not the flesh: *I have repudiated money and hence love. Not abjured it, repudiated. I do not need it; by next year or two years or five years I will know to be true what I now believe to be true: I will not even need to want it.*

That evening he was a little late in going off duty; when he passed the dining room he heard already the clash of cutlery and the voices, and the interns' quarters were empty save for a man named Flint who in evening trousers and shirt was tying a black tie before the mirror and who turned as Wilbourne entered and pointed to a telegram on Wilbourne's pillow. It had been opened. "It was lying on my cot," Flint said. "I was in a hurry to dress so I didn't take time to look at the name good. I just picked it up and opened it. I'm sorry."

"That's all right," Wilbourne said. "Too many people have already seen a telegram for it to be very private." He removed the folded yellow sheet from the envelope. It was decorated with symbols—garlands and scrolls; it was from his sister: one of those stereotyped birthday greetings which the telegraph company sends to any distance within the boundaries of the United States for twenty-five cents. He found that Flint was still watching him.

"So this is your birthday," Flint said. "Celebrating?"

"No," Wilbourne said. "I guess not."

"What? Listen. I'm going to a party down in French Town. Why not come along?"

"No," Wilbourne said. "Thanks, though." He did not yet begin to think *Why not?* "I'm not invited."

"That dont matter. It's not that kind of a party. It's at a studio. Painting guy. Just a mob sitting around on the floor in each others' laps, drinking. Come on. You dont want to stick here on your birthday." Now he did begin to think *Why not? Why really not?* and now he could almost see the guardian of the old trained peace and resignation rise to arms, the grim Moses, not alarmed, impervious to alarm, just gauntly and fanatically interdicting: *No. You will not go. Let well enough alone. You have peace now; you want no more.*

"Besides, I haven't any dress clothes."

"You wont need them. Your host will probably be wearing a bathrobe. You've got a dark suit, haven't you?"

"But I dont—"

"All right," Flint said. "De Montigny has a tux. He's about your size. I'll get it." He went to the closet which they used in common.

"But I dont—" Wilbourne said.

"All right," Flint said. He laid the second dinner suit on the cot and slipped his braces and began to remove his own trousers. "I'll wear de Montigny's and you can wear mine. We're all three about standard."

An hour later, in a borrowed costume such as he had never worn before, he and Flint halted in one of the narrow, dim, balcony-hung one-way streets between Jackson Square and Royal Street in the Vieux Carré—a wall of soft muted brick above which the crest of a cabbage palm exploded raggedly and from beyond which came a heavy smell of jasmine which seemed to lie visible upon the rich stagnant air already impregnated with the smell of sugar and bananas and hemp from the docks, like inert wisps of fog or even paint. A wooden gate hung slightly awry, beside it a wire bell pull which under Flint's hand produced a remote mellow jangling. They could hear a piano, it was something of Gershwin's. "There," Flint said. "You dont need to worry about this party. You can already hear the home-made gin. Gershwin might have painted his pictures for him too. Only I bet Gershwin could paint what Crowe calls his pictures better than Crowe plays what Gershwin calls his music."

Flint jerked the bell again, again nothing came of it. "It's not locked, anyway," Wilbourne said. It was not, they entered: a court paved with the same soft, quietly rotting brick. There was a stagnant pool with a terra-cotta figure, a mass of lantana, the single palm, the thick rich leaves and the heavy white stars of the jasmine bush where light fell upon it through open french doors, the court balcony-overhung too on three sides, the walls of that same annealing brick lifting a rampart broken and nowhere level against the glare of the city on the low eternally overcast sky, and over all, brittle, dissonant and ephemeral, the spurious sophistication of the piano like symbols scrawled by adolescent boys upon an ancient decayed rodent-scavengered tomb.

They crossed the court and entered the french windows and the noise—the piano, the voices—a longish room, uneven of floor, the walls completely covered with unframed paintings which at the moment impacted upon Wilbourne with that inextricable and detailless effect of an enormous circus poster seen suddenly at close range, from which vision, the very eyeballs, seem to start violently back in consternation. It contained no furniture except a piano at which a man sat in a basque cap and a bathrobe. Perhaps a dozen other people sat or stood about on the floor with glasses; a woman in a sleeveless linen frock shrieked, "My God, where was the funeral?" and came and kissed Flint, still carrying her glass.

"This is Doctor Wilbourne, boys and girls," Flint said. "Watch him. He's got a pad of blank checks in his pocket and a scalpel in his sleeve." His host did not even turn his head, though a woman brought him a drink presently. It was his hostess, though no one had told him that; she stood and talked to him for a moment, or at him because he was not listening, he was looking at the pictures on the wall; presently he stood alone, still holding his glass, before the wall itself. He had seen photographs and reproductions of such in magazines before, at which he had looked completely without curiosity because it was completely without belief, as a yokel might look at a drawing of a dinosaur. But now the yokel was looking at the monster itself and Wilbourne stood before the paintings in complete absorption. It was not at what they portrayed, the method or the coloring; they meant nothing to him. It was in a bemusement without heat or envy at a condition which could supply a man with the obvious leisure and means to spend his days painting such as this and his evenings playing the piano and feeding liquor to people whom he ignored and (in one case, at least) whose names he did not even bother to catch. He was still standing there when someone behind said, "Here's Rat and Charley"; he was still standing there when Charlotte spoke at his shoulder:

"What do you think about it, mister?" He turned and saw a young woman a good deal shorter than he and for a moment he thought she was fat until he saw it was not fat at all but merely that broad, simple, profoundly delicate and feminine articulation of Arabian mares—a woman of under twenty-five, in a print cotton dress, a face which laid no claim even to prettiness and wore no makeup save the painted broad mouth, with a faint inch-long scar on one cheek which he recognised as an old burn, doubtless from childhood. "You haven't decided yet, have you?"

"No," he said. "I dont know."

"Dont know what you think, or whether you are trying to decide or not?"

"Yes. Probably that. What do you think about it?"

"Marshmallows with horseradish," she said, too promptly. "I paint too," she added. "I can afford to say. I can afford to say I can beat that, too. What's your name? and what have you got all this on for, just to come slumming? So we can all know you are slumming?"

He told her and now she looked at him and he saw that her eyes were not hazel but yellow, like a cat's, staring at him with a speculative sobriety like a man might, intent beyond mere boldness, speculative beyond any staring. "I borrowed this suit. It's the first time in my life I ever had one on." Then he said, he did not intend to, he didn't even know he was going to say it, he seemed to be drowning, volition and will, in the yellow stare: "This is my birthday. I'm twenty-seven years old."

"Oh," she said. She turned, she took him by the wrist, a grasp simple, ruthless and firm, drawing him after her. "Come on." He followed, awkwardly, not to trod on her heels, then she released him and went on before him, across the room to where three men and two women stood about the table on which the bottles and glasses sat. She stopped, she grasped his wrist again and drew him toward a man of his own age about, in a dark double-breasted suit, with blond wavy hair going a little thin, a face not quite handsome and reasonably insensitive and shrewder than intelligent yet on the whole gentler than not, assured courteous and successful. "This is Rat," she said. "He is the senior living ex-freshman of the University of Alabama. That's why we still call him Rat. You can call him Rat too. Sometimes he is."

Later—it was after midnight and Flint and the woman who had kissed him were gone—they stood in the court beside the jasmine bush. "I've got two children, both girls," she said. "That's funny, because all my family were brothers except me. I liked my oldest brother the best but you cant sleep with your brother and he and Rat roomed together in school so I married Rat and now I've got two girls, and when I was seven years old I fell in the fireplace, my brother and I were fighting, and that's the scar. It's on my shoulder and side and hip too and I got in the habit of telling people about it before they would have time not to ask and I still do it even when it doesn't matter anymore."

"Do you tell everybody like this? At first?"

"About the brothers or about the scar?"

"Both. Maybe the scar."

"No. That's funny too. I had forgotten. I haven't told anybody in years. Five years."

"But you told me."

"Yes. And that's funny twice. No, three times now. Listen. I lied to you. I dont paint. I work with clay, and some in brass, and once with a piece of stone, with a chisel and maul. Feel." She took his hand and drew his finger-tips along the base of her other palm—the broad, blunt, strong, supple-fingered hand with nails as closely trimmed as if she had bitten them down, the skin at the base and lower joints of the fingers not calloused exactly but smoothly hardened and toughened like the heel of a foot. "That's what I make: something you can touch, pick up, something with weight in your hand that you can look at the behind side of, that displaces air and displaces water and when you drop it, it's your foot that breaks and not the shape. Not poking at a piece of cloth with a knife or a brush like you were trying to put together a jig saw puzzle with a rotten switch through the bars of a cage. That's why I said I could beat that," she said. She didn't move, she didn't even indicate by a motion of her head the room behind them. "Not just something to tickle your taste buds for a second and then swallowed and maybe not even sticking to your entrails but just evacuated whole and flushed away into the damned old sewer, the Might-just-as-well-not-have-been. Will you come to supper tomorrow night?"

"I cant. I'm on duty tomorrow night."

"The next night then? Or when?"

"Dont you have engagements yourself?"

"There are some people coming the night after tomorrow. But they wont bother you." She looked at him. "All right, if you dont want a lot of people, I'll put them off. The night after tomorrow? At seven? Do you want me to come to the hospital for you in the car?"

"No. Dont do that."

"I can, you know."

"I know it," he said. "I know it. Listen—"

"Let's go in," she said. "I'm going home. And dont wear that. Wear your own clothes. I want to see."

Two evenings later he went to dinner. He found a modest though comfortable apartment in an irreproachable neighborhood near Audubon Park, a negro maid, two not particularly remarkable children of two and four, with her hair but otherwise looking like the father (who in another dark obviously expensive double-breasted suit made a cocktail not particularly remarkable either and insisted that Wilbourne call him Rat) and she in something he knew had been purchased as a semi-formal garment and which she wore with the same ruthless indifference as she had the garment in which he had first seen her, as if both of them were overalls. After the meal, which was considerably better than the cocktails, she went out with the older child, who had dined with them, but she returned presently to lie on the sofa smoking while Rittenmeyer continued to ask Wilbourne questions about his profession such as the president of a college fraternity might ask of a pledge from the medical school. At ten oclock Wilbourne said he must go. "No," she said, "not yet." So he remained; at half past ten Rittenmeyer said he must work tomorrow and was going to bed and left them. Then she crushed out the cigarette and rose and came to where he stood before the cold hearth and stopped, facing him. "What to—Do they call you Harry? What to do about it, Harry?"

"I dont know. I never was in love before."

"I have been. But I dont know either.—Do you want me to call a cab for you?"

"No." He turned, she moved beside him across the room. "I'll walk."

"Are you that poor? Let me pay for the cab. You cant walk to the hospital. It's three miles."

"That's not far."

"It wont be his money, if that's what you mean. I have some of my own. I have been saving it for something, I dont know what." She handed him his hat and stood with her hand on the door knob.

"Three miles is not far. I would walk—"

"Yes," she said. She opened the door, they looked at one another. Then the door closed between them. It was painted white. They did not shake hands.

During the next six weeks they met five times more. This would be down town for lunch, because he would not again enter her husband's house and his destiny or luck (or ill-luck, since otherwise he might have discovered that love no more exists just at one spot and in one moment and in one body out of all the earth and all time and all the teeming breathed than sunlight does) brought him no more second hand invitations to parties. It would be in Vieux Carre places where they could lunch on the weekly two dollars which he had been sending to his sister to apply on the note. At the third of these she said abruptly, out of nothing: "I have told Rat."

"Told him?"

"About lunches. That I have been meeting you." After that she never mentioned her husband again. The fifth time they did not lunch. They went to a hotel, they planned it the day before. He discovered that he knew next to nothing about the proper procedure other than supposition and imagination; because of his ignorance he believed that there was a secret to the successful performance of the business, not a secret formula to be followed but rather a kind of white magic: a word or some infinitesimal and trivial movement of the hand such as that which opens a hidden drawer or panel. He thought once of asking her how to go about it because he was certain that she would know, just as he was certain that she would never be at a loss about anything she wished to do, not only because of her absolute co-ordination but because even in this short time he had come to realise that intuitive and infallible skill of all women in the practical affairs of love. But he did not ask her because he told himself that, when she told him how to do, which she would, and it would be correct, he might at some later time believe that she had done this before and that even if she had, he did not want to know it. So he asked Flint.

"Jesus," Flint said. "You have come out, haven't you? I didn't even know you knew a girl." Wilbourne could almost watch Flint thinking swiftly, casting backward. "Was it that brawl at Crowe's that night? But hell, that's your business, aint it? It's easy. Just take a bag with a couple of bricks wrapped up in a towel so they wont rattle, and walk in. I wouldn't pick the Saint Charles or the Roosevelt, of course. Take one of the smaller ones, not too small of course. Maybe that one down toward the station. Wrap the bricks separately, see, then roll them up together. And be sure to carry a coat with you. Raincoat."

"Yes. Do you reckon I'd better tell her to bring a coat too?"

Flint laughed, one short syllable, not loud. "I guess not. I dont guess she'll need any coaching from you or me either. — Here," he said quickly, "hold your horses. I dont know her. I aint talking about her. I'm talking about women. She could turn up with a bag of her own and a coat and a veil and the stub of a Pullman ticket sticking out of her handbag and that wouldn't mean she had done this before. That's just women. There aint any advice that Don Juan or Solomon either could give the youngest fourteen-year-old gal ever foaled about this kind of phenagling."

"It doesn't matter," he said. "She probably wont come anyway." He found that he really believed that. He still believed it even when the cab drew up to the curb where he waited with the bag. She had a coat, but no bag nor veil. She came swiftly out of the cab when he opened the door, her face was hard, sober, her eyes extraordinarily yellow, her voice harsh:

"Well? Where?"

He told her. "It's not far. We can—" She turned, already getting back into the cab. "We can walk—"

"You damned pauper," she said. "Get in. Hurry." He got in. The cab moved on. The hotel was not far. A negro porter took the bag. Then it seemed to Wilbourne that he had never been in his life, and would never be again, so aware of her as he was while she stood in the center of the dingy lobby raddled with the Saturday nights of drummers and of minor race-track hangers-on while he signed the two fictitious names on the pad and gave to the clerk the sixth two dollars which were to have gone to his sister but did not, waiting for him, making no effort for effacement, quiet, contained, and with a quality profoundly tragic which he knew (he was learning fast) was not peculiar to her but was an attribute of all women at this instant in their lives, which would invest them with a dignity, almost a modesty, to be carried over and clothe even the last prone and slightly comic attitude of ultimate surrender. He followed her down the corridor and into the door which the porter opened, he dismissed the porter and closed the rented door behind him and watched her cross the room to the single dingy window and, still in the hat and coat, turn without pausing and exactly like a child playing prisoner's base and return to him, the yellow eyes, the whole face which he had already come to call beautiful, hard and fixed. "Oh God, Harry," she said. She beat her clenched fists on his chest. "Not like this. Jesus, not like this."

"All right," he said. "Steady, now." He caught her wrists and held them, still doubled into fists against his chest while she still wrenched at them to free them to strike his chest again. *Yes* he thought. *Not like this and never.* "Steady now."

"Not like this, Harry. Not back alleys. I've always said that: that no matter what happened to me, whatever I did, anything anything but not back alleys. If it had just been hot pants, somebody with a physique I just leched for all of a sudden so that I never looked nor thought higher than his collar. But not us, Harry. Not you. Not you."

"Steady now," he said. "It's all right." He led her to the edge of the bed and stood over her, still holding her wrists.

"I told you how I wanted to make things, take the fine hard

clean brass or stone and cut it, no matter how hard, how long
it took, cut it into something fine, that you could be proud to
show, that you could touch, hold, see the behind side of it
and feel the fine solid weight so when you dropped it it
wouldn't be the thing that broke it would be the foot it
dropped on except it's the heart that breaks and not foot, if I
have a heart. But Jesus, Harry, how I have bitched it for you."
She extended her hand, then he realised what she was about
and twisted his hips away before she touched him.

"I'm all right," he said. "You mustn't worry about me. Do
you want a cigarette?"

"Please." He gave her a cigarette and a light, looking down
at the foreshortened slant of her nose and jaw as she drew at
it. He threw the match away. "Well," she said. "So that's that.
And no divorce."

"No divorce?"

"Rat's a Catholic. He wont give me one."

"You mean that he—"

"I told him. Not that I was to meet you at a hotel. I just
said, suppose I did. And he still said no soap."

"Cant you get the divorce?"

"On what grounds? He would fight it. And it would have
to be here—a Catholic judge. So there's just one other thing.
And it seems I cant do that."

"Yes," he said. "Your children."

For a moment she looked at him, smoking. "I wasn't thinking of them. I mean, I have already thought of them. So now
I dont need to think of them anymore because I know the
answer to that and I know I cant change that answer and I
dont think I can change me because the second time I ever
saw you I learned what I had read in books but I never had
actually believed: that love and suffering are the same thing
and that the value of love is the sum of what you have to pay
for it and anytime you get it cheap you have cheated yourself.
So I dont need to think about the children. I settled that a
long time ago. I was thinking about money. My brother
sends me twenty-five dollars every Christmas and for the last
five years I have saved it. I told you the other night I dont
know why I have saved it. Maybe it was for this and maybe
this is the best joke of all: that I have saved for five years and

it's only a hundred and twenty-five dollars, hardly enough to get two people to Chicago. And you have nothing." She leaned toward the table at the head of the bed and crushed the cigarette out with slow and infinite care, and rose. "So that's that. That's all of it."

"No," he said. "No! I'll be damned if it is."

"Do you want to go on like this? hanging around and staying green for me like an apple on a limb?" She took his raincoat from the chair and slung it across her arm and stood waiting.

"Dont you want to go first?" he said. "I'll wait about thirty minutes, then I——"

"And let you walk alone through that lobby carrying the bag for that clerk and that nigger to snigger at because they saw me leave before I would have even had time to take my clothes off, let alone put them back on?" She went to the door and put her hand on the key. He picked up the bag and followed. But she did not unlock the door at once. "Listen. Tell me again you haven't got any money. Say it. So I can have something my ears can listen to as making sense even if I cant understand it. Some reason why I—that I can accept as the strong reason we cant beat even if I cant believe or understand that it could be just that, just money, not anything but just money. Come on. Say it."

"I have no money."

"All right. It makes sense. It must make sense. It will have to make sense." She began to shake, not tremble, shake, like one with a violent ague, the bones themselves seeming to chatter rigid and silent inside the flesh. "It will have—"

"Charlotte," he said. He set the bag down and moved toward her. "Charlotte—"

"Dont you touch me!" she whispered in a kind of tense fury. "Dont you touch me!" Yet for an instant he believed she was coming to him; she seemed to sway forward, she turned her head and looked toward the bed with an expression of distraction and despair. Then the key clicked, the door opened, and she was out of the room.

They parted as soon as he found a cab for her. He was about to follow her into it, to ride down town to the parking lot where she had left her car. Then for the first of the two times in their lives he saw her cry. She sat there, her face harsh and wrung and savage beneath the springing tears like sweat. "Oh, you pauper, you damned pauper, you transparent fool. It's money again. After you paid the hotel the two dollars you should have sent your sister and got nothing for it, now you want to pay this cab with what you intended to take your other shirt out of the laundry with and get nothing for that either but the privilege of transporting my damned ass that at the last refused, will always refuse——" She leaned toward the driver. "Go on!" she said savagely. "Drive on! Down town!"

The cab went on fast; it disappeared almost at once, though he was not looking after it. After a while he said quietly, aloud, to nobody: "At least, there's no use in carrying the bricks too." So he walked on to where a trash bin sat at the curb-edge and, while the people passing glanced at him with curiosity or briefly or not at all, he opened the bag and removed the bricks from the towel and dropped them into the bin. It contained a mass of discarded newspapers and fruit skins, the casual anonymous droppings of the anonymous who passed it during the twelve hours like the refuse of birds in flight. The bricks struck the mass without a sound; there was no premonitory buzz or whirr at all, the edges of the papers merely tilted and produced from among them, with the magical abruptness with which the little metal torpedo containing change from a sale emerges from its tube in a store, a leather wallet. It contained the stubs of five parimutuel tickets from Washington Park, a customer's identification from a national gasoline trust and another from a B.P.O.E. lodge at Longview, Texas, and twelve hundred and seventy-eight dollars in bills.

He discovered the exact amount only after he reached the hospital however, his first thought was merely, *I ought to keep out a dollar for the reward* as he walked on toward the branch post office, then (the post office was not only six blocks away, it was in the opposite direction from the hospital) *I could even keep out taxi-fare and he should not mind. Not that I want to ride but that I've got to make it last, make everything last so there wont be any gaps between now and six oclock when I can hide behind my white jacket again, draw the old routine up over my head and face like niggers do the quilt when they go to bed.* Then he stood before the locked Saturday afternoon doors of the branch station and he had forgotten that too, thinking, as he buttoned the wallet into his hip pocket, how when he waked the name of today had been in fire letters and no word out of a nursery jingle or off a calendar, walking on, carrying the light bag, walking the now twelve useless blocks out of his way, thinking, *Only I have beat that too; I have saved myself at least forty-five minutes of time that otherwise would have been filled with leisure.*

The dormitory was empty. He put the bag away and hunted for and found a flat cardboard box stippled with holly-sprigs in which his sister had sent him one hand-embroidered handkerchief last Christmas; he found scissors and a bottle of paste and made a neat surgeon's packet of the wallet, copying the address neatly and clearly from one of the identification cards and putting it carefully away beneath the garments in his drawer; and now that was done too. *Maybe I can read* he thought. Then he cursed, thinking, *That's it. It's all exactly backward. It should be the books, the people in the books inventing and reading about us—the Does and Roes and Wilbournes and Smiths—males and females but without the pricks or cunts.*

He went on duty at six. At seven he was relieved long enough to go to supper. While he was eating one of the probationer nurses looked in and told him he was wanted on the telephone. It would be long distance, he thought. It would be his sister, he had not written her since he had sent the last two-dollar money order five weeks ago, and now she had called him, would spend two dollars herself, not to reproach him (*She's right* he thought, not meaning his sister. *It's comic. It's more than comic. It rolls you in the aisles. I fail to make the one I love and I make myself a failure toward the one who loves me.*) but to see that he was well. So when the voice on the wire said "Wilbourne?" he thought it was his brother-in-law until Rittenmeyer spoke again: "Charlotte wants to speak to you."

"Harry?" she said. Her voice was rapid but calm: "I told Rat about today, and that it was a bust. So he's right. It's his turn now. He gave me a free shot, and I didn't make it. So now it's no more than fair to give him a free shot. And it's no more than decent to tell you what the score is only decent is such a bastard word to have to use between you and me—"

"Charlotte," he said. "Listen, Charlotte—"

"So it's goodbye, Harry. And good luck. And good God damn—"

"Listen, Charlotte. Can you hear me?"

"Yes? What? What is it?"

"Listen. This is funny. I have been waiting all afternoon for you to call me, only I didn't know it until just now. I even know now that I knew then it was Saturday all the time I was walking toward that post office— Can you hear me? Charlotte?"

"Yes? Yes?"

"I've got twelve hundred and seventy-eight dollars, Charlotte."

At four oclock the next morning, in the empty laboratory, he cut up the wallet and the identification cards with a razor blade and burned the shreds of paper and leather and flushed the ashes away in a bathroom. The next day at noon, the two tickets to Chicago and the remainder of the twelve hundred and seventy-eight dollars buttoned into his pocket and the single bag on the seat facing him, he peered out the window as the train slowed into the Carrollton Avenue station. They were both there, the husband and the wife, he in the conservative, spuriously unassertive dark suit, the face of a college senior revealing nothing, lending an air of impeccable and formal rightness to the paradoxical act of handing the wife to the lover almost identical with the conventional mumbo-jumbo of father and bride at a wedding in church, she beside him in a dark dress beneath the open coat, watching the slowing car windows intently yet without doubt or nervousness, so that Wilbourne mused again upon that instinctive proficiency in and rapport for the mechanics of cohabitation even of innocent and unpractised women—that serene confidence in their amorous destinies like that of birds in their wings—that tranquil ruthless belief in an imminent deserved personal happiness which fledges them instantaneous and full-winged from the haven of respectability, into untried and un-supportive space where no shore is visible (*not sin* he thought.

I dont believe in sin. It's getting out of timing. You are born submerged in anonymous lockstep with the teeming anonymous myriads of your time and generation; you get out of step once, falter once, and you are trampled to death.) and this without terror or alarm and hence inferring neither of courage nor hardihood: just an utter and complete faith in airy and fragile and untried wings—wings, the airy and fragile symbols of love which have failed them once since by universal consent and acceptance they brooded over the very ceremony which, in taking flight, they repudiate. They slid past and vanished, Wilbourne saw the husband stoop and raise the bag as they vanished; the air hissed into the brakes and he sat thinking, *He will come in with her, he will have to do that, he will not want to anymore than I (she?) will want him to but he will have to do it just as he has to wear those dark suits which I dont believe he wants to wear either, just as he had to stay at that party that first night and drink as much as any other man there yet not once sit on the floor with a wife (his own or someone else's) sprawled across his knees.*

So he looked up presently and they were both standing beside his seat; he rose too and now the three of them stood, blocking the aisle while other passengers crowded past them or waited for them to move, Rittenmeyer carrying the bag— this man who ordinarily would no more have carried a bag into a train in the presence of a red cap or Pullman porter than he would have got up and fetched himself a glass of water in a restaurant; looking at the frozen impeccable face above the impeccable shirt and tie Wilbourne thought with a kind of amazement, *Why, he's suffering, he's actually suffering,* thinking how perhaps it is not the heart at all, not even the sensibilities, with which we suffer, but our capacity for grief or vanity or self-delusion or perhaps even merely masochism. "Go on," Rittenmeyer said. "Get out of the aisle." His voice was harsh, his hand almost rough as he pushed her into the seat and set the bag beside the other one. "Remember now. If I dont hear by the tenth of each month, I'm going to give the detective the word. And no lies, see? No lies." He turned, he did not even look at Wilbourne, he merely jerked his head toward the end of the car. "I want to talk to you," he said in that seething repressed voice. "Come on." When they were half way down the car the train began to move, Wilbourne expected the other to run for the exit, he thought again, *He is suffering; even circumstance, a trivial railroad time table, is making comedy of that tragedy which he must play to the bitter end or cease to breathe.* But the other did not even hurry. He went steadily on and swung aside the curtain to the smoking room and waited for Wilbourne to enter. He seemed to read the temporary surprise in Wilbourne's face. "I've got a ticket as far as Hammond," he said harshly. "Dont you worry about me." The unspoken question seemed to set him off; Wilbourne could almost see him struggling physically to keep his voice down. "Worry about yourself, see? Yourself. Or by God—" Now he did check the voice again, holding it on some sort of curb like a horse, yet forcing it on; he took a wallet from his pocket. "If you ever—" he said. "If you dare—"

He cant say it, Wilbourne thought. *He cant even bear to say it.* "If I'm not good to her, gentle with her. Is that what you mean?"

"I'll know it," Rittenmeyer said. "If I dont hear from her by the tenth of every month, I am going to give the detective the word to go ahead. And I'll know lies too, see? See?" He was trembling, the impeccable face suffused beneath the impeccable hair which resembled a wig. "She's got a hundred and twenty-five dollars of her own, she wouldn't take more. But damn that, she wouldn't use that, anyway. She wont have it by the time she came to need it enough to use it. So here." He removed from the wallet a check and gave it to Wilbourne. It was a cashier's check for three hundred dollars, payable to the Pullman Company of America and indorsed in the corner in red ink: *For one railroad ticket to New Orleans, Louisiana.*

"I was going to do that with some of my money," Wilbourne said.

"Damn that too," the other said. "And it's for the ticket. If it is ever cashed and returned to the bank and no ticket bought with it, I'll have you arrested for fraud. See? I'll know."

"You mean, you want her to come back? You will take her back?" But he did not need to look at the other's face; he said quickly, "I'm sorry. I retract that. That's more than any man can bear to answer."

"God," the other said; "God. I ought to sock you." He added, in a tone of incredulous amazement, "Why dont I? Can you tell me? Aint a doctor, any doctor, supposed to be an authority on human glands?"

Then suddenly Wilbourne heard his own voice speaking out of an amazed and quiet incredulity; it seemed to him that they both stood now, aligned, embattled and doomed and lost, before the entire female principle: "I dont know. Maybe it would make you feel better." But the moment passed. Rittenmeyer turned and produced a cigarette from his coat and fumbled a match from the box attached to the wall. Wilbourne watched him—the trim back; he caught himself on the point of asking if the other wished him to stay and keep him company until the train reached Hammond. But again Rittenmeyer seemed to read his mind.

"Go on," he said. "Get to hell out of here and let me alone." Wilbourne left him standing facing the window and returned to his seat. Charlotte did not look up, she sat motionless, looking out the window, an unlighted cigarette in her fingers. Now they were running beside the larger lake, soon they would begin to cross the trestle between Maurepas and Pontchartrain. Now the whistle of the engine drifted back, the train slowed as beneath the sound of it came the hollow reverberation of the trestle. Water spread on either hand now, swamp-bound and horizonless, lined with rotting wooden jetties to which small dingy boats were tied. "I love water," she said. "That's where to die. Not in the hot air, above the hot ground, to wait hours for your blood to get cool enough to let you sleep and even weeks for your hair to stop growing. The water, the cool, to cool you quick so you can sleep, to wash out of your brain and out of your eyes and out of your blood all you ever saw and thought and felt and wanted and denied. He's in the smoking room, isn't he? Can I go back and speak to him a minute?"

"Can you go?—"

"Hammond is the next station."

Why, he is your husband, he was about to say but caught himself. "It's the men's room," he said. "Maybe I had better—" But she had already risen and passed him; he thought *If she stops and looks back at me it will mean she is thinking 'Later I can always know that at least I told him good-bye'* and she did stop and they looked at each other, then she went on. Now the water slid away, the sound of the trestle ceased, the engine whistled again and the train regained speed, and almost at once they were running through an out-skirt of shabby houses which would be Hammond, and he ceased to look out the window while the train stopped and stood and then moved again; he did not even have time to rise as she slipped past him and into the seat. "So you came back," he said.

"You didn't think I was. Neither did I."

"But you did."

"Only it's not finished. If he were to get back on the train, with a ticket to Slidell—" She turned, staring at him though she did not touch him. "It's not finished. It will have to be cut."

"Cut?"

" 'If thine eye offend thee, pluck it out, lad, and be whole'. That's it. Whole. Wholly lost—something. I've got to cut it. That drawing room back there was empty. Find the conduc-tor and engage it to Jackson."

"Drawing room? But that will cost—"

"You fool!" she said. *She doesn't love me now* he thought. *She doesn't love anything now*. She spoke in a tense whisper, beat-ing on his knee with her fist. "You fool!" She rose.

"Wait," he said, catching her wrist. "I'll do it." He found the conductor in the vestibule at the end of the car; he was not gone long. "All right," he said. She rose at once, taking up her bag and coat. "The porter will be here—" he said. She didn't pause. "Let me have it," he said, taking the bag from her and then his own and followed her down the aisle. Later he was to recall that interminable walk between the filled seats where people sat with nothing else to do but watch them pass, and it seemed to him that everyone in the car must have known their history, that they must have disseminated an aura of unsanctity and disaster like a smell. They entered the draw-ing room.

"Lock the door," she said. He set the bags down and

locked the door. He had never been in a drawing room before and he fumbled at the lock for an appreciable time. When he turned she had removed her dress; it lay in a wadded circle about her feet and she stood in the scant feminine underwear of 1937, her hands over her face. Then she removed her hands and he knew it was neither shame nor modesty, he had not expected that, and he saw it was not tears. Then she stepped out of the dress and came and began to unknot his tie, pushing aside his own suddenly clumsy fingers.

Old Man

WHEN THE BELATED and streaming dawn broke the two convicts, along with twenty others, were in a truck. A trusty drove, two armed guards sat in the cab with him. Inside the high, stall-like topless body the convicts stood, packed like matches in an upright box or like the pencil-shaped ranks of cordite in a shell, shackled by the ankles to a single chain which wove among the motionless feet and swaying legs and a clutter of picks and shovels among which they stood, and was rivetted by both ends to the steel body of the truck.

Then and without warning they saw the flood about which the plump convict had been reading and they listening for two weeks or more. The road ran south. It was built on a raised levee, known locally as a dump, about eight feet above the flat surrounding land, bordered on both sides by the barrow pits from which the earth of the levee had been excavated. These barrow pits had held water all winter from the fall rains, not to speak of the rain of yesterday, but now they saw that the pit on either side of the road had vanished and instead there lay a flat still sheet of brown water which extended into the fields beyond the pits, ravelled out into long motionless shreds in the bottom of the plow furrows and gleaming faintly in the gray light like the bars of a prone and enormous grating. And then (the truck was moving at good speed) as they watched quietly (they had not been talking much anyway but now they were all silent and quite grave, shifting and craning as one to look soberly off to the west side of the road) the crests of the furrows vanished too and they now looked at a single perfectly flat and motionless steel-colored sheet in which the telephone poles and the straight hedgerows which marked section lines seemed to be fixed and rigid as though set in concrete.

It was perfectly motionless, perfectly flat. It looked, not innocent, but bland. It looked almost demure. It looked as if you could walk on it. It looked so still that they did not realise it possessed motion until they came to the first bridge. There was a ditch under the bridge, a small stream, but ditch and stream were both invisible now, indicated only by the rows of cypress and bramble which marked its course. Here they both saw and heard movement—the slow profound eastward and upstream ("It's running backward," one convict said quietly.) set of the still rigid surface, from beneath which came a deep faint subaquean rumble which (though none in the truck could have made the comparison) sounded like a subway train passing far beneath the street and which inferred a terrific and secret speed. It was as if the water itself were in three strata, separate and distinct, the bland and unhurried surface bearing a frothy scum and a miniature flotsam of twigs and screening as though by vicious calculation the rush and fury of the flood itself, and beneath this in turn the original stream, trickle, murmuring along in the opposite direction, following undisturbed and unaware its appointed course and serving its Lilliputian end, like a thread of ants between the rails on which an express train passes, they (the ants) as unaware of the power and fury as if it were a cyclone crossing Saturn.

Now there was water on both sides of the road and now, as if once they had become aware of movement in the water the water seemed to have given over deception and concealment, they seemed to be able to watch it rising up the flanks of the dump; trees which a few miles back had stood on tall trunks above the water now seemed to burst from the surface at the level of the lower branches like decorative shrubs on barbered lawns. The truck passed a negro cabin. The water was up to the window ledges. A woman clutching two children squatted on the ridgepole, a man and a halfgrown youth, standing waist-deep, were hoisting a squealing pig onto the slanting roof of a barn, on the ridgepole of which sat a row of chickens and a turkey. Near the barn was a haystack on which a cow stood tied by a rope to the center pole and bawling steadily; a yelling negro boy on a saddleless mule which he flogged steadily, his legs clutching the mule's barrel and his body leaned to the drag of a rope attached to a second mule, approached the haystack, splashing and floundering. The woman on the housetop began to shriek at the passing truck, her voice carrying faint and melodious across the brown water, becoming fainter and fainter as the truck passed and went on, ceasing at last, whether because of distance or because she had stopped screaming those in the truck did not know.

Then the road vanished. There was no perceptible slant to it yet it had slipped abruptly beneath the brown surface with no ripple, no ridgy demarcation, like a flat thin blade slipped obliquely into flesh by a delicate hand, annealed into the water without disturbance, as if it had existed so for years, had been built that way. The truck stopped. The trusty descended from the cab and came back and dragged two shovels from among their feet, the blades clashing against the serpentining of the chain about their ankles. "What is it?" one said. "What are you fixing to do?" The trusty didn't answer. He returned to the cab, from which one of the guards had descended, without his shotgun. He and the trusty, both in hip boots and each carrying a shovel, advanced into the water, gingerly, probing and feeling ahead with the shovel handles. The same convict spoke again. He was a middle-aged man with a wild thatch of iron-gray hair and a slightly mad face. "What the hell are they doing?" he said. Again nobody answered him. The truck moved, on into the water, behind the guard and the trusty, beginning to push ahead of itself a thick slow viscid ridge of chocolate water. Then the gray-haired convict began to scream. "God damn it, unlock the chain!" He began to struggle, thrashing violently about him, striking at the men nearest him until he reached the cab, the roof of which he now hammered on with his fists, screaming. "God damn it, unlock us! Unlock us! Son of a bitch!" he screamed, addressing no one. "They're going to drown us! Unlock the chain!" But for all the answer he got the men within radius of his voice might have been dead. The truck crawled on, the guard and the trusty feeling out the road ahead with the reversed shovels, the second guard at the wheel, the twenty-two convicts packed like sardines into the truck bed and padlocked by the ankles to the body of the truck itself. They crossed another bridge—two delicate and paradoxical iron railings slanting out of the water, travelling parallel to it for a distance, then slanting down into it again with an outrageous quality almost significant yet apparently meaningless like something in a dream not quite nightmare. The truck crawled on.

Along toward noon they came to a town, their destination. The streets were paved; now the wheels of the truck made a sound like tearing silk. Moving faster now, the guard and the trusty in the cab again, the truck even had a slight bone in its teeth, its bow-wave spreading beyond the submerged sidewalks and across the adjacent lawns, lapping against the stoops and porches of houses where people stood among piles of furniture. They passed through the business district; a man in hip boots emerged knee-deep in water from a store, dragging a flat-bottomed skiff containing a steel safe.

At last they reached the railroad. It crossed the street at right angles, cutting the town in two. It was on a dump, a levee, also, eight or ten feet above the town itself; the street ran blankly into it and turned at right angles beside a cotton compress and a loading platform on stilts at the level of a freight car door. On this platform was a khaki army tent and a uniformed National Guard sentry with a rifle and bandolier.

The truck turned and crawled out of the water and up the ramp which cotton wagons used and where trucks and private cars filled with household goods came and unloaded onto the platform. They were unlocked from the chain in the truck and shackled ankle to ankle in pairs they mounted the platform and into an apparently inextricable jumble of beds and trunks, gas and electric stoves, radios and tables and chairs and framed pictures which a chain of negroes under the eye of an unshaven white man in muddy corduroy and hip boots carried piece by piece into the compress, at the door of which another guardsman stood with his rifle, they (the convicts) not stopping here but herded on by the two guards with their shotguns, into the dim and cavernous building where among the piled heterogeneous furniture the ends of cotton bales and the mirrors on dressers and sideboards gleamed with an identical mute and unreflecting concentration of pallid light.

They passed on through, onto the loading platform where the army tent and the first sentry were. They waited here. Nobody told them for what nor why. While the two guards talked with the sentry before the tent the convicts sat in a line along the edge of the platform like buzzards on a fence, their shackled feet dangling above the brown motionless flood out of which the railroad embankment rose, pristine and intact, in a kind of paradoxical denial and repudiation of change and portent, not talking, just looking quietly across the track to where the other half of the amputated town seemed to float, house shrub and tree, ordered and pageant-like and without motion, upon the limitless liquid plain beneath the thick gray sky.

After a while the other four trucks from the Farm arrived. They came up, bunched closely, radiator to tail light, with their four separate sounds of tearing silk and vanished beyond the compress. Presently the ones on the platform heard the feet, the mute clashing of the shackles, the first truckload emerged from the compress, the second, the third; there were more than a hundred of them now in their bed-ticking over-alls and jumpers and fifteen or twenty guards with rifles and shotguns. The first lot rose and they mingled, paired, twinned by their clanking and clashing umbilicals; then it began to rain, a slow steady gray drizzle like November instead of May. Yet not one of them made any move toward the open door of the compress. They did not even look toward it, with longing or hope or without it. If they thought at all, they doubtless knew that the available space in it would be needed for furniture, even if it were not already filled. Or perhaps they knew that, even if there were room in it, it would not be for them, not that the guards would wish them to get wet but that the guards would not think about getting them out of the rain. So they just stopped talking and with their jumper collars turned up and shackled in braces like dogs at a field trial they stood, immobile, patient, almost ruminant, their backs turned to the rain as sheep and cattle do.

After another while they became aware that the number of soldiers had increased to a dozen or more, warm and dry be-neath rubberised ponchos, there was an officer with a pistol at his belt, then and without making any move toward it, they began to smell food and, turning to look, saw an army field kitchen set up just inside the compress door. But they made no move, they waited until they were herded into line, they inched forward, their heads lowered and patient in the rain, and received each a bowl of stew, a mug of coffee, two slices of bread. They ate this in the rain. They did not sit down because the platform was wet, they squatted on their heels as

country men do, hunching forward trying to shield the bowls
and mugs into which nevertheless the rain splashed steadily as
into miniature ponds and soaked, invisible and soundless,
into the bread.

After they had stood on the platform for three hours, a
train came for them. Those nearest the edge saw it, watched
it—a passenger coach apparently running under its own
power and trailing a cloud of smoke from no visible stack, a
cloud which did not rise but instead shifted slowly and
heavily aside and lay upon the surface of the aqueous earth
with a quality at once weightless and completely spent. It
came up and stopped, a single old fashioned open-ended
wooden car coupled to the nose of a pushing switch engine
considerably smaller. They were herded into it, crowding forward to the other end where there was a small cast iron stove.
There was no fire in it, nevertheless they crowded about it—
the cold and voiceless lump of iron stained with fading tobacco and hovered about by the ghosts of a thousand Sunday
excursions to Memphis or Moorhead and return—the peanuts, the bananas, the soiled garments of infants—huddling,
shoving for places near it. "Come on, come on," one of the
guards shouted. "Sit down, now." At last three of the guards,
laying aside their guns, came among them and broke up the
huddle, driving them back and into seats.

There were not enough seats for all. The others stood in
the aisle, they stood braced, they heard the air hiss out of the
released brakes, the engine whistled four blasts, the car came
into motion with a snapping jerk; the platform, the compress
fled violently as the train seemed to transpose from immobility to full speed with that same quality of unreality with
which it had appeared, running backward now though with
the engine in front where before it had moved forward but
with the engine behind.

When the railroad in its turn ran beneath the surface of the
water, the convicts did not even know it. They felt the train
stop, they heard the engine blow a long blast which wailed
away unechoed across the waste, wild and forlorn, and they
were not even curious; they sat or stood behind the rain-
streaming windows as the train crawled on again, feeling its
way as the truck had while the brown water swirled between

the trucks and among the spokes of the driving wheels and lapped in cloudy steam against the dragging fire-filled belly of the engine; again it blew four short harsh blasts filled with the wild triumph and defiance yet also with repudiation and even farewell, as if the articulated steel itself knew it did not dare stop and would not be able to return. Two hours later in the twilight they saw through the streaming windows a burning plantation house. Juxtaposed to nowhere and neighbored by nothing it stood, a clear steady pyre-like flame rigidly fleeing its own reflection, burning in the dusk above the watery desolation with a quality paradoxical, outrageous and bizarre.

Sometime after dark the train stopped. The convicts did not know where they were. They did not ask. They would no more have thought of asking where they were than they would have asked why and what for. They couldn't even see, since the car was unlighted and the windows fogged on the outside by rain and on the inside by the engendered heat of the packed bodies. All they could see was a milky and sourceless flick and glare of flashlights. They could hear shouts and commands, then the guards inside the car began to shout; they were herded to their feet and toward the exit, the ankle chains clashing and clanking. They descended into a fierce hissing of steam, through ragged wisps of it blowing past the car. Laid-to alongside the train and resembling a train itself was a thick blunt motor launch to which was attached a string of skiffs and flat boats. There were more soldiers; the flashlights played on the rifle barrels and bandolier buckles and flicked and glinted on the ankle chains of the convicts as they stepped gingerly down into knee-deep water and entered the boats; now car and engine both vanished completely in steam as the crew began dumping the fire from the firebox.

After another hour they began to see lights ahead—a faint wavering row of red pin-pricks extending along the horizon and apparently hanging low in the sky. But it took almost another hour to reach them while the convicts squatted in the skiffs, huddled into the soaked garments (they no longer felt the rain anymore at all as separate drops) and watched the lights draw nearer and nearer until at last the crest of the levee defined itself; now they could discern a row of army tents stretching along it and people squatting about the fires, the wavering reflections from which, stretching across the water, revealed an involved mass of other skiffs tied against the flank of the levee which now stood high and dark overhead. Flashlights glared and winked along the base, among the tethered skiffs; the launch, silent now, drifted in.

When they reached the top of the levee they could see the long line of khaki tents, interspersed with fires about which people—men, women and children, negroes and white—crouched or stood among shapeless bales of clothing, their heads turning, their eyeballs glinting in the firelight as they looked quietly at the striped garments and the chains; further down the levee, huddled together too though untethered, was a drove of mules and two or three cows. Then the taller convict became conscious of another sound. He did not begin to hear it all at once, he suddenly became aware that he had been hearing it all the time, a sound so much beyond all his experience and his powers of assimilation that up to this point he had been as oblivious of it as an ant or a flea might be of the sound of the avalanche on which it rides; he had been travelling upon water since early afternoon and for seven years now he had run his plow and harrow and planter within the very shadow of the levee on which he now stood, but this profound deep whisper which came from the further side of it he did not at once recognise. He stopped. The line of convicts behind jolted into him like a line of freight cars stopping, with an iron clashing like cars. "Get on!" a guard shouted.

"What's that?" the convict said. A negro man squatting before the nearest fire answered him:

"Dat's him. Dat's de Ole Man."

"The old man?" the convict said.

"Get on! Get on up there!" the guard shouted. They went on; they passed another huddle of mules, the eyeballs rolling too, the long morose faces turning into and out of the firelight; they passed them and reached a section of empty tents, the light pup tents of a military campaign, made to hold two men. The guards herded the convicts into them, three brace of shackled men to each tent.

They crawled in on all fours, like dogs into cramped kennels, and settled down. Presently the tent became warm from their bodies. Then they became quiet and then all of them could hear it, they lay listening to the bass whisper deep, strong and powerful. "The old man?" the train-robber convict said.

"Yah," another said. "He dont have to brag."

At dawn the guards waked them by kicking the soles of the projecting feet. Opposite the muddy landing and the huddle of skiffs an army field kitchen was set up, already they could smell the coffee. But the taller convict at least, even though he had had but one meal yesterday and that at noon in the rain, did not move at once toward the food. Instead and for the first time he looked at the River within whose shadow he had spent the last seven years of his life but had never seen before; he stood in quiet and amazed surmise and looked at the rigid steel-colored surface not broken into waves but merely slightly undulant. It stretched from the levee on which he stood, further than he could see—a slowly and heavily roiling chocolate-frothy expanse broken only by a thin line a mile away as fragile in appearance as a single hair, which after a moment he recognised. *It's another levee* he thought quietly. *That's what we look like from there. That's what I am standing on looks like from there.* He was prodded from the rear; a guard's voice carried forward: "Go on! Go on! You'll have plenty of time to look at that!"

They received the same stew and coffee and bread as the day before, they squatted again with their bowls and mugs as yesterday, though it was not raining yet. During the night an intact wooden barn had floated up. It now lay jammed by the current against the levee while a crowd of negroes swarmed over it, ripping off the shingles and planks and carrying them up the bank; eating steadily and without haste, the taller convict watched the barn dissolve rapidly down to the very water-line exactly as a dead fly vanished beneath the moiling industry of a swarm of ants.

They finished eating. Then it began to rain again, as upon a signal, while they stood or squatted in their harsh garments which had not dried out during the night but had merely become slightly warmer than the air. Presently they were haled to their feet and told off into two groups, one of which was armed from a stack of mud-clogged picks and shovels nearby, and marched away up the levee. A little later the motor launch with its train of skiffs came up across what was, fifteen feet beneath its keel, probably a cotton field, the skiffs loaded to the gunwales with negroes and a scattering of white people nursing bundles on their laps. When the engine shut off the faint plinking of a guitar came across the water. The skiffs warped in and unloaded; the convicts watched the men and women and children struggle up the muddy slope, carrying heavy towsacks and bundles wrapped in quilts. The sound of the guitar had not ceased and now the convicts saw him— a young, black, lean-hipped man, the guitar slung by a piece of cotton plow line about his neck. He mounted the levee, still picking it. He carried nothing else, no food, no change of clothes, not even a coat.

The taller convict was so busy watching this that he did not hear the guard until the guard stood directly beside him shouting his name. "Wake up!" the guard shouted. "Can you fellows paddle a boat?"

"Paddle a boat where?" the taller convict said.

"In the water," the guard said. "Where in hell do you think?"

"I aint going to paddle no boat nowhere out yonder," the tall convict said, jerking his head toward the invisible river beyond the levee behind him.

"No, it's on this side," the guard said. He stooped swiftly and unlocked the chain which joined the tall convict and the plump hairless one. "It's just down the road a piece." He rose. The two convicts followed him down to the boats. "Follow them telephone poles until you come to a filling station. You can tell it, the roof is still above water. It's on a bayou and you can tell the bayou because the tops of the trees are sticking up. Follow the bayou until you come to a cypress snag with a woman in it. Pick her up and then cut straight back west until you come to a cotton house with a fellow sitting on the ridgepole—" He turned, looking at the two convicts, who stood perfectly still, looking first at the skiff and then at the water with intense sobriety. "Well? What are you waiting for?"

"I cant row a boat," the plump convict said.

"Then it's high time you learned," the guard said. "Get in."

The tall convict shoved the other forward. "Get in," he said. "That water aint going to hurt you. Aint nobody going to make you take a bath."

As, the plump one in the bow and the other in the stern, they shoved away from the levee, they saw other pairs being unshackled and manning the other skiffs. "I wonder how many more of them fellows are seeing this much water for the first time in their lives too," the tall convict said. The other did not answer. He knelt in the bottom of the skiff, pecking gingerly at the water now and then with his paddle. The very shape of his thick soft back seemed to wear that expression of wary and tense concern.

Sometime after midnight a rescue boat filled to the guard rail with homeless men and women and children docked at Vicksburg. It was a steamer, shallow of draft; all day long it had poked up and down cypress- and gum-choked bayous and across cotton fields (where at times instead of swimming it waded) gathering its sorry cargo from the tops of houses and barns and even out of trees, and now it warped into that mushroom city of the forlorn and despairing where kerosene flares smoked in the drizzle and hurriedly-strung electrics glared upon the bayonets of martial policemen and the red cross brassards of doctors and nurses and canteen-workers. The bluff overhead was almost solid with tents, yet still there were more people than shelter for them; they sat or lay, single and by whole families, under what shelter they could find or sometimes under the rain itself, in the little death of profound exhaustion while the doctors and the nurses and the soldiers stepped over and around and among them.

Among the first to disembark was one of the penitentiary deputy wardens, followed closely by the plump convict and another white man—a small man with a gaunt unshaven wan face still wearing an expression of incredulous outrage. The deputy warden seemed to know exactly where he wished to go. Followed closely by his two companions he threaded his way swiftly among the piled furniture and the sleeping bodies and stood presently in a fiercely lighted and hastily established temporary office, almost a military post of command in fact, where the Warden of the Penitentiary sat with two army officers wearing majors' leaves. The deputy warden spoke without preamble. "We lost a man," he said. He called the tall convict's name.

"Lost him?" the Warden said.

"Yah. Drowned." Without turning his head he spoke to the plump convict. "Tell him," he said.

"He was the one that said he could row a boat," the plump convict said. "I never. I told him myself—" he indicated the deputy warden with a jerk of his head "—I couldn't. So when we got to the bayou—"

"What's this?" the Warden said.

"The launch brought word in," the deputy warden said. "Woman in a cypress snag on the bayou, then this fellow—" he indicated the third man; the Warden and the two officers looked at the third man "—on a cotton house. Never had room in the launch to pick them up. Go on."

"So we come to where the bayou was," the plump convict continued in a voice perfectly flat, without any inflection whatever. "Then the boat got away from him. I dont know what happened. I was just sitting there because he was so positive he could row a boat. I never saw any current. Just all of a sudden the boat whirled clean around and begun to run fast backward like it was hitched to a train and it whirled around again and I happened to look up and there was a limb right over my head and I grabbed it just in time and that boat was snatched out from under me like you'd snatch off a sock and I saw it one time more upside down and that fellow that said he knew all about rowing holding to it with one hand and still holding the paddle in the other—" He ceased. There was no dying fall to his voice, it just ceased and the convict stood looking quietly at a half-full quart of whiskey sitting on the table.

"How do you know he's drowned?" the Warden said to the deputy. "How do you know he didn't just see his chance to escape, and took it?"

"Escape where?" the other said. "The whole Delta's flooded. There's fifteen foot of water for fifty miles, clean back to the hills. And that boat was upside down."

"That fellow's drowned," the plump convict said. "You dont need to worry about him. He's got his pardon; it wont cramp nobody's hand signing it, neither."

"And nobody else saw him?" the Warden said. "What about the woman in the tree?"

"I dont know," the deputy said. "I aint found her yet. I reckon some other boat picked her up. But this is the fellow on the cotton house."

Again the Warden and the two officers looked at the third man, at the gaunt, unshaven wild face in which an old terror, an old blending of fear and impotence and rage still lingered. "He never came for you?" the Warden said. "You never saw him?"

"Never nobody came for me," the refugee said. He began to tremble though at first he spoke quietly enough. "I set there on that sonabitching cotton house, expecting hit to go any minute, I saw that launch and them boats come up and they never had no room for me. Full of bastard niggers and one of them setting there playing a guitar but there wasn't no room for me. A guitar!" he cried; now he began to scream, trembling, slavering, his face twitching and jerking. "Room for a bastard nigger guitar but not for me—"

"Steady now," the Warden said. "Steady now."

"Give him a drink," one of the officers said. The Warden poured the drink. The deputy handed it to the refugee, who took the glass in both jerking hands and tried to raise it to his mouth. They watched him for perhaps twenty seconds, then the deputy took the glass from him and held it to his lips while he gulped, though even then a thin trickle ran from each corner of his mouth, into the stubble on his chin.

"So we picked him and—" the deputy called the plump convict's name now "—both up just before dark and come on in. But that other fellow is gone."

"Yes," the Warden said. "Well. Here I haven't lost a prisoner in ten years, and now, like this—I'm sending you back to the Farm tomorrow. Have his family notified, and his discharge papers filled out at once."

"All right," the deputy said. "And listen, chief. He wasn't a bad fellow and maybe he never had no business in that boat. Only he did say he could paddle one. Listen. Suppose I write on his discharge, Drowned while trying to save lives in the great flood of nineteen twenty-seven, and send it down for the Governor to sign it. It will be something nice for his folks to have, to hang on the wall when neighbors come in or something. Maybe they will even give his folks a cash bonus because after all they sent him to the Farm to raise cotton, not to fool around in a boat in a flood."

"All right," the Warden said. "I'll see about it. The main thing is to get his name off the books as dead before some politician tries to collect his food allowance."

"All right," the deputy said. He turned and herded his companions out. In the drizzling darkness again he said to the plump convict: "Well, your partner beat you. He's free. He's done served his time out but you've got a right far piece to go yet."

"Yah," the plump convict said. "Free. He can have it."

The Wild Palms

ON THE SECOND MORNING in the Chicago hotel Wilbourne waked and found that Charlotte was dressed and gone, hat coat and handbag, leaving a note for him in a big sprawling untrained hand such as you associate at first glance with a man until you realise an instant later it is profoundly feminine: *Back at noon. C.* then, beneath the initial: *Or maybe later.* She returned before noon, he was asleep again; she sat on the side of the bed, her hand in his hair, rolling his head on the pillow to shake him awake, still in the open coat and the hat shoved back from her forehead, looking down at him with that sober yellow profundity, and now he mused indeed on that efficiency of women in the mechanics, the domiciling, of cohabitation. Not thrift, not husbandry, something far beyond that, who (the entire race of them) employed with infallible instinct, a completely uncerebrated rapport for the type and nature of male partner and situation, either the cold penuriousness of the fabled Vermont farmwife or the fantastic extravagance of the Broadway revue mistress as required, absolutely without regard for the intrinsic value of the medium which they saved or squandered and with little more regard or grief for the bauble which they bought or lacked, using both the presence and absence of jewel or checking account as pawns in a chess game whose prize was not security at all but respectability within the milieu in which they lived, even the love-nest under the rose to follow a rule and a pattern; he thought *It's not the romance of illicit love which draws them, not the passionate idea of two damned and doomed and isolated forever against the world and God and the irrevocable which draws men, it's because the idea of illicit love is a challenge to them, because they have an irresistible desire to (and an unshakable belief that they can, as they all believe they can successfully conduct a boarding house) take the illicit love and make it respectable, take Lothario himself and trim the very incorrigible bachelor's ringlets which snared them into the seemly decorum of Monday's hash and suburban trains.* "I've found it," she said.

"Found what?"

"An apartment. A studio. Where I can work too."

"Too?" She shook his head again with that savage oblivi-ousness, she actually hurt him a little; he thought again, *There's a part of her that doesn't love anybody, anything;* and then, a profound and silent lightning-clap—a white glare—ratiocination, instinct, he did not know which: *Why, she's alone. Not lonely, alone. She had a father and then four brothers exactly like him and then she married a man exactly like the four brothers and so she probably never even had a room of her own in all her life and so she has lived all her life in complete solitude and she doesn't even know it as a child who has never tasted cake doesn't know what cake is.*

"Yes, too. Do you think that twelve hundred dollars will last forever? You live *in* sin; you cant live on it."

"I know it. I thought of that before I told you over the phone that night I had twelve hundred dollars. But this is honeymoon; later will be—"

"I know that too." She grasped his hair again, hurting him again though now he knew she knew she was hurting him. "Listen: it's got to be all honeymoon, always. Forever and ever, until one of us dies. It cant be anything else. Either heaven, or hell: no comfortable safe peaceful purgatory be-tween for you and me to wait in until good behavior or for-bearance or shame or repentance overtakes us."

"So it's not me you believe in, put trust in; it's love." She looked at him. "Not just me; any man."

"Yes. It's love. They say love dies between two people. That's wrong. It doesn't die. It just leaves you, goes away, if you are not good enough, worthy enough. It doesn't die; you're the one that dies. It's like the ocean: if you're no good, if you begin to make a bad smell in it, it just spews you up somewhere to die. You die anyway, but I had rather drown in the ocean than be urped up onto a strip of dead beach and be dried away by the sun into a little foul smear with no name to it, just *This Was* for an epitaph. Get up. I told the man we would move in today."

They left the hotel with their bags within the hour, by cab; they mounted three flights of stairs. She even had the key, she opened the door for him to enter; he knew she was looking not at the room but at him. "Well?" she said. "Do you like it?"

It was a big oblong room with a skylight in the north wall, possibly the handiwork of a dead or bankrupt photographer or maybe a former sculptor or painter tenant, with two cubbyholes for kitchen and bath. *She rented that skylight* he told himself quietly, thinking how as a rule women rent bathrooms primarily. *It's only incidental that there is a place to sleep and cook food. She chose a place not to hold us but to hold love; she did not just run from one man to another; she did not merely mean to swap one piece of clay she made a bust with for another—* He moved now, and then he thought *Maybe I'm not embracing her but clinging to her because there is something in me that wont admit it cant swim or cant believe it can.* "It's all right," he said. "It's fine. Nothing can beat us now."

During the next six days he made the rounds of the hospitals, interviewing (or being interviewed by) Residents and Staff Heads. They were brief interviews. He was not particular what he did and he had something to offer—his degree from a good medical school, his twenty months' internship in a hospital which was known, yet always after the first three or four minutes, something began to happen. He knew what it was, though he told himself differently (this sitting after the fifth interview, on a sunny bench in a park among the bums and W.P.A. gardeners and nursemaids and children): *It's because I really dont try hard enough, dont really realise the need for trying because I have accepted completely her ideas about love; I look upon love with the same boundless faith that it will clothe and feed me as the Mississippi or Louisiana countryman, converted last week at a camp meeting revival, looks upon religion,* knowing that that was not the reason, that it was the twenty months of internship instead of twenty-four, thinking *I have been confounded by numbers,* thinking how it is apparently more seemly to die in the dulcet smell than to be saved by an apostate from convention.

At last he found a job. It was not much, it was laboratory work in a charity hospital in the negro tenement district, where victims of alcohol or pistol- and knife-wounds were brought, usually by police, and his job was making routine tests for syphilis. "You dont need a microscope or Wassermann paper," he told her that night. "All you need is enough light to tell what race they belong to." She had set two planks on trestles beneath the skylight which she called her work bench and at which for some time now she had been puttering with a package of plaster of paris from the ten cent store, though he had paid little attention to what she was doing. She now bent over this table with a scrap of paper and a pencil while he watched the blunt supple hand make the big sprawling rapid figures.

"You will make this much a month," she said. "And it costs this much for us to live a month. And we have this much to draw from to make up the difference." The figures were cold, incontrovertible, the very pencil marks had a scornful and impregnable look; incidentally she now saw to it that he made not only the current weekly remittances to his sister but that he had also sent to her the equivalent sum of the lunches and the abortive hotel during the six weeks in New Orleans. Then she wrote down a date beside the last figure; it would be in early September. "On that day we wont have any money left."

Then he repeated something he had thought while sitting on the park bench that day: "It will be all right. I've just got to get used to love. I never tried it before; you see, I'm at least ten years behind myself. I'm still free wheeling. But I'll get back into gear soon."

"Yes," she said. Then she crumpled the paper and flipped it aside, turning. "But that's not important. That's just whether it's steak or hamburger. And hunger's not here—" She struck his belly with the flat of her hand. "That's just your old guts growling. Hunger's here." She touched his breast. "Dont you ever forget that."

"I wont. Not now."

"But you may. You've been hungry down here in your guts so you are afraid of it. Because you are always a little afraid of what you have stood. If you had ever been in love before, you wouldn't have been on that train that afternoon. Would you?"

"Yes," he said. "Yes. Yes."

"So it's more than just training your brain to remember hunger's not in the belly. Your belly, your guts themselves, have got to believe it. Can yours believe it?"

"Yes," he said. *Only she's not so sure of that* he told himself, because three days later when he returned from the hospital he found the work bench littered with twisted bits of wire and bottles of shellac and glue and wood fiber, a few tubes of paint and a pan in which a mass of tissue paper soaked in water, which two afternoons later had become a collection of little figures—deer and wolfhounds and horses and men and women, lean epicene sophisticated and bizarre, with a quality fantastic and perverse; the afternoon after that when he returned she and the figures were gone. She came in an hour later, her yellow eyes like a cat's in the dark, not triumph or exultation but rather fierce affirmation, and with a new ten dollar bill.

"He took them all," she said, she named a leading department store. "Then he let me dress one of the windows. I have an order for a hundred dollars more—historical figures about Chicago, this part of the West. You know—Mrs O'Leary with Nero's face and the cow with a ukelele, Kit Carson with legs like Nijinsky and no face, just two eyes and a shelf of forehead to shade them with, buffalo cows with the heads and flanks of Arabian mares. And all the other stores on Michigan Avenue. Here. Take it."

He refused. "It's yours. You earned it." She looked at him—the unwinking yellow stare in which he seemed to blunder and fumble like a moth, a rabbit caught in the glare of a torch; an envelopment almost like a liquid, a chemical precipitant, in which all the dross of small lying and sentimentality dissolved away. "I dont—"

"You dont like the idea of your woman helping to support you, is that it? Listen. Dont you like what we've got?"

"You know I do."

"Then what does it matter what it cost us, what we pay for it? or how? You stole the money we've got now; wouldn't you do it again? Isn't it worth it, even if it all busts tomorrow and we have to spend the rest of our lives paying interest?"

"Yes. Only it's not going to bust tomorrow. Nor next month. Nor next year—"

"No. Not as long as we are worthy of keeping it. Good enough. Strong enough. Worthy to be allowed to keep it. To get what you want as decently as you can, then keep it. Keep it." She came and put her arms around him, hard, striking her body against him hard, not in caress but exactly as she would grasp him by the hair to wake him up from sleep. "That's what I'm going to do. Try to do. I like bitching, and making things with my hands. I dont think that's too much to be permitted to like, to want to have and keep."

She earned that hundred dollars, working at night now, after he was in bed and sometimes asleep; during the next five weeks she earned twenty-eight dollars more, then she filled an order amounting to fifty. Then the orders stopped; she could get no more. Nevertheless she continued to work, at night altogether now, since she was out with her samples, her completed figures all day, and she worked usually with an audience now, for now their apartment had become a sort of evening club. It began with a newspaper man named McCord who had worked on a New Orleans paper during the brief time when Charlotte's youngest brother (in a dilettanti and undergraduate heeler manner, Wilbourne gathered) had cubbed there. She met him on the street, he came to dinner one evening and took them out to dinner one evening; three nights later he appeared with three men and two women and four bottles of whiskey at their apartment, and after that Wilbourne never knew just whom he would find when he reached home, except that it would not be Charlotte alone and, regardless of who was there, idle, who even after the dearth season of sales had extended into weeks and then a month and summer was almost upon them, still worked in a cheap coverall already filthy as that of any house painter and a glass of whiskey-and-water among the twists of wire and pots of glue and paint and plaster which transformed steadily and endlessly beneath the deft untiring hands into the effigies elegant, bizarre, fantastic and perverse.

Then she made a final sale, a small one, and it was done, finished. It stopped as abruptly and inexplicably as it had begun. The summer season was on now they told her at the stores, and the tourists and natives too were leaving town to escape the heat. "Except that that's a lie," she said. "It's the saturation point," she told him, told them all: it was at night, she had returned late with the cardboard box containing the figures which had been refused, so the evening's collection of callers had already arrived. "But I expected it. Because these are just fun." She had taken the effigies from the box and set them up on the work bench again. "Like something created to live only in the pitch airless dark, like in a bank vault or maybe a poison swamp, not in the rich normal nourishing air breathed off of guts full of vegetable from Oak Park and Evanston. And so that's it and that's all. And now I'm not an artist anymore and I'm tired and I'm hungry and I'm going to curl up with one of our good books and one of our crusts. So let each and all of you step up to the bench and choose himself or herself one souvenir and memento of this occasion, and beat it."

"We can still beat a crust," he told her. *And besides, she's not done yet* he thought. *She hasn't quit yet. She never will,* thinking as he had thought before that there was a part of her which he nor Rittenmeyer either had never touched, which did not even love love. In less than a month he believed that he had proof of this; he returned and found her at the bench again, in a profound excitement which he had never seen before—an excitement without exultation but with a grim and deadly quality of irresistible driving as she told him about it. It was one of the men whom McCord had brought, a photographer. She was to make puppets, marionettes, and he to photograph them for magazine covers and advertisements; perhaps later they would use the actual puppets in charades, tableaux—a hired hall, a rented stable, something, anything. "It's my money," she told him. "The hundred and twenty-five dollars I never could get you to take."

She worked with dense and concentrated fury. She would be at the bench when he went to sleep, he would wake at two and three oclock and find the fierce working light above it still burning. Now he would return (from the hospital at first, then from the park bench where he spent his days after he lost his job, leaving and returning home at the usual hours so she would not suspect) and see the actual figures almost as large as small children—a Quixote with a gaunt mad dreamy uncoordinated face, a Falstaff with the worn face of a syphilitic barber and gross with meat (a single figure, yet when he looked at it he seemed to see two: the man and the gross flesh like a huge bear and its fragile consumptive keeper; it seemed to him that he could actually watch the man struggling with the mountain of entrails as the keeper might wrestle with the bear, not to overcome it but to pass it, escape it, as you do with the atavistic beasts in nightmare), Roxane with spit curls and a wad of gum like the sheet music demonstrator in a ten cent store, Cyrano with the face of a low-comedy Jew in vaudeville, the monstrous flare of whose nostrils ceased exactly on the instant of becoming molluscs, a piece of cheese in one hand and a check book in the other—accumulating about the apartment, filling all available spaces of floor and walls, fragile perverse and disturbing, with incredible rapidity; begun continued and completed in one sustained rush of furious industry—a space of time broken not into successive days and nights but a single interval interrupted only by eating and sleeping.

Then she finished the last one and now she would be gone all day and half the night; he would return in the afternoon and find a scrawled note on a scrap of paper or a margin torn from a newspaper or even the telephone book: *Dont wait for me. Go out and eat,* which he would do and return and go to bed and sometimes to sleep until she slid naked (she never wore a sleeping garment, she told him she had never owned one) into bed to wake him, rouse him to listen with a hard wrestling movement, holding him in her hard arms while she talked in a grim quiet rapid voice not about money or its lack, not about the details of the day's progress with the photographing, but of their present life and situation as though it were a complete whole without past or future in which themselves as individuals, the need for money, the figures she had made, were component parts like the parts of a tableau or a puzzle, none more important than another; lying still and relaxed in the darkness while she held him, not even bothering to be aware whether his eyes were open or not, he seemed to see their joint life as a fragile globe, a bubble, which she kept balanced and intact above disaster like a trained seal does its ball. *She's worse off than I am* he thought. *She doesn't even know what it is to hope.*

Then the puppet business ended, as abruptly and completely as the window dressing had. He returned one evening and she was at home, reading. The filthy overall in which she had lived for weeks (it was August now) was gone and then he saw that the work bench was not only clean of its former litter of wire and paint, it had been drawn into the center of the room and had become a table covered with a strip of chintz and stacked with the magazines and books which formerly had rested upon the floor and in the unused chairs and such, and, most surprising of all, a bowl of flowers. "I've got some things here," she said. "We'll eat at home for a change."

She had chops and such, she prepared the meal in a curiously frivolous apron new too like the chintz on the table; he thought how failure, reacting upon her like on a man by investing her with a sort of dignified humility, had yet brought out in her a quality which he had never seen before, a quality not only female but profoundly feminine. They ate, then she cleared the table. He offered to help but she refused. So he sat with a book beside the lamp, he heard her in the kitchen for a time, then she emerged and entered the bedroom. He did not hear her when she came out of the bedroom at all since her bare feet made no sound on the floor; he just looked up to see her standing beside him—the compactly simple rightness of the body lines, the sober intent yellow stare. She took the book from him and put it on the converted table. "Get your clothes off," she said. "The hell with it. I can still bitch."

But he did not tell her about the job for another two weeks. His reason was no longer concern that the news might destroy her accord with what she was concentrating on, since that was no longer valid now, if it had ever been, and it was no longer the possibility that he might find something else before she would need to know, for that was not valid either now, since he had tried that and failed, nor was it the Micawber-like faith of the inert in tomorrow; it was partly perhaps the knowledge that late enough would be soon enough, but mostly (he did not try to fool himself) it was a profound faith in her. Not in them, in her. *God wont let her starve* he thought. *She's too valuable. He did too well with her. Even the one who made everything must fancy some of it enough to want to keep it.* So each day he would leave the apartment at the usual hour and sit on his bench in the park until time to go home. And once each day he would take out the wallet and produce the slip of paper on which he kept a record of the dwindling money, as if he expected each time to find that the amount had changed or that he had misread it the day before, finding each time that it had not and he had not—the neat figures, the $182.00 less $5.00 or $10.00, with the date of each subtraction; by the day it would be due there would not be enough to pay the quarter's rent on the first day of September. And then sometimes he would take out the other paper, the pink cashier's check with its perforated legend *Only Three Hundred Dollars*. There would be something almost ceremonial about it, like the formal preparation by the addict of his opium pipe, and then for the time he would as completely renounce reality as the opium smoker himself while he invented a hundred ways to spend it, shifting the various components of the sum and their bought equivalents here and there like a jigsaw puzzle, knowing that this was a form of masturbation (thinking, *because I am still, and probably will always be, in the puberty of money*), that if it were really possible to cash the check and use the money, he would not even dare to toy with the idea.

Then he returned home one afternoon and found her at the work bench again. It was still the table, still in the center of the room; she had merely turned back the chintz and shoved the books and magazines to one end, and she wore the apron and not the coverall and she was working now with a kind of idle bemusement like someone passing time with a deck of cards. The figure was not three inches tall—a little ancient shapeless man with a foolish disorganised face, the face of a harmless imbecile clown. "It's a Bad Smell," she said. Then he understood. "That's all it is, just a bad smell. Not a wolf at the door. Wolves are Things. Keen and ruthless. Strong, even if they are cowards. But this is just a bad smell because hunger is not here—" again she struck his belly with the back of her hand. "Hunger's up there. It doesn't look like this. It looks like a skyrocket or a roman candle or at least one of those sparkler sticks for little children that sparkle away into a live red coal that's not afraid to die. But this." She looked up at him. Then he knew it was coming. "How much money have we got?"

"A hundred and forty-eight dollars. But it's all right. I—"

"Oh, then you have paid next quarter's rent already." Then it came, it was too late now. *My trouble is, everytime I tell either*

the truth or a lie I seem to have to sell myself on the idea first.
"Look at me. You mean you haven't been to the hospital in
two months?"

"It was the detective. You were busy then, that was the
month you forgot to write to New Orleans. He wasn't trying
to hur—get me fired. He just hadn't heard from you and he
was worried. He was trying to find out if you were all right.
It wasn't him, it was the detective who spilled the works. So
they let me go. It was funny. I was fired from a job which
existed because of moral turpitude, on the grounds of moral
turpitude. Only it wasn't actually that, of course. The job just
played out, as I knew in time it would—"

"Well," she said. "And we haven't got a drink in the house.
You go down to the store and get a bottle while I—No, wait.
We'll go out and eat and drink both. Besides, we'll have to
find a dog."

"A dog?" From where he stood he could see her in the
kitchen take from the ice box the two chops for supper and
wrap them again.

"But certainly, friend," she said. "Get your hat."

It was evening, the hot August, the neon flashed and
glared, alternately corpse- and hell-glowing the faces in the
street and their own too as they walked, she still carrying the
two chops in the thick slick clammy butcher's paper. Within
the block they met McCord. "We've lost our job," she told
him. "So we're looking for a dog."

Presently it began to seem to Wilbourne that the invisible
dog was actually among them. They were in a bar now, one
which they frequented, meeting perhaps twice a week by
chance or prearrangement the group which McCord had
brought into their lives. There were four of these ("We've lost
our job," McCord told them. "And now we're waiting for a
dog.") present now, the seven of them sitting about a table
set for eight, an empty chair, an empty gap, the two chops
unwrapped now and on a plate beside a glass of neat whiskey
among the highballs. They had not eaten yet; twice Wilbourne leaned to her: "Hadn't we better eat something? It's
all right; I can—"

"Yes, it's all right. It's fine." She was not speaking to him.
"We've got forty-eight dollars too much; just think of that.

Even the Armours haven't got forty-eight dollars too much. Drink up, ye armourous sons. Keep up with the dog."

"Yah," McCord said. "Set, ye armourous sons, in a sea of hemingwaves."

The neon flashed and glared, the traffic lights blinked from green to red and back to green again above the squawking cabs and hearse-like limousines. They had not eaten yet though they had lost two members of the party, they were six in the cab, sitting on each others' knees while Charlotte carried the chops (they had lost the paper now) and McCord held the invisible dog; it was named Moreover now, from the bible, the poor man's table. "But listen," McCord said. "Just listen a minute. Doc and Gillespie and I own it. Gillespie's up there now, but he will have to be back in town by the first and it will be empty. You could take your hundred bucks—"

"You're impractical," Charlotte said. "You're talking about security. Have you no soul?—How much money have we got now, Harry?"

He looked at the meter. "A hundred and twenty-two dollars."

"But listen," McCord said.

"All right," she said. "But now is no time to talk. You've made your bed; lie in it. And pull the covers over your head." They were in Evanston now; they had stopped at a drug store and they had a flashlight now, the cab crawling along a suburban and opulent curb while Charlotte, leaning across McCord, played the flashlight upon the passing midnight lawns. "There's one," she said.

"I dont see it," McCord said.

"Look at that fence. Did you ever hear of an iron fence with a wreath of pansies in each panel that didn't have an iron dog inside of it? The house has got a mansard roof too."

"I dont see any house," McCord said.

"I dont either. But look at that fence."

The cab stopped, they got out. The torch beam played on the iron fence with scrolled spear-tipped panels set in concrete; there was even a hitching-post in the effigy of a negro boy beside the small scrolled gate. "You're right," McCord said. "There'll be one here." They did not use the light now, but even in the faint starlight they could see it plainly—the cast iron Saint Bernard with its composite face of the emperor Franz Josef and a Maine banker in the year 1859. Charlotte placed the chops upon the iron pediment, between the iron feet; they returned to the cab. "Listen," McCord said. "It's completely equipped—three rooms and kitchen, bedding, cooking things, plenty of wood for the chopping; you can even bathe if you want to. And all the other cottages will be empty after the first of September and nobody to bother you and right on the lake, you can have fish for a while yet, and with your hundred dollars in grub and the cold wont come until in October, maybe not until November; you could stay up there until Christmas or even longer than that if you dont mind the cold—"

McCord drove them up to the lake on the Saturday night before Labor Day, the hundred dollars worth of food—the tins, the beans and rice and coffee and salt and sugar and flour—in the rumble. Wilbourne contemplated the equivalent of their last dollar with a certain sobriety. "You dont realise how flexible money is until you exchange it for something," he said. "Maybe this is what the economists mean by a normal diminishing return."

"You dont mean flexible," McCord said. "You mean volatile. That's what Congress means by a fluid currency. If it rains on us before we get this stuff under a roof, you'll see. Those beans and rice and truck will boil us clean out of the car like three matches in a pail of home brew." They had a bottle of whiskey and McCord and Wilbourne took turns driving while Charlotte slept. They reached the cottage just after dawn—a hundred odd acres of water surrounded by second growth spruce, four clearings with a cabin in each (from the chimney of one of them smoke stood. "That's Bradley," McCord said. "I thought he'd be out by now.") and a short pier into the water. There was a narrow finger of beach with a buck standing on it, pink in the Sunday dawn, its head up, watching them for an instant before it whirled, its white scut arcing in long bounds while Charlotte, springing from the car, her face swollen with sleep, ran to the water's edge, squealing. "That's what I was trying to make!" she cried. "Not the animals, the dogs and deer and horses: the motion, the speed."

"Sure," McCord said. "Let's eat." They unloaded the car and carried the things in and started a fire in the stove, then while Charlotte cooked breakfast Wilbourne and McCord carried the bottle down to the water and squatted. They drank from the bottle, saluting one another. Then there was one drink left. "Charlotte's," McCord said. "She can drink to the Wagon, the long drouth."

"I'm happy now," Wilbourne said. "I know exactly where I am going. It's perfectly straight, between two rows of cans and sacks, fifty dollars' worth to a side. Not street, that's houses and people. This is a solitude. Then the water, the solitude wavering slow while you lie and look up at it." Squatting and still holding the almost empty bottle he put his other hand into the water, the still, dawn-breathing liquid with the temperature of the synthetic ice water in hotel rooms, the ripples fanning slowly from his wrist. McCord stared at him. "And then fall will come, the first cold, the first red and yellow leaves drifting down, the double leaves, the reflection rising to meet the falling one until they touch and rock a little, not quite closing. And then you could open your eyes for a minute if you wanted to, remembered to, and watch the shadow of the rocking leaves on the breast beside you."

"For sweet Jesus Schopenhauer," McCord said. "What the bloody hell kind of ninth-rate Teasdale is this? You haven't near done your share of starving yet. You haven't near served your apprenticeship to destitution. If you're not careful, you'll talk that stuff to some guy who will believe it and'll hand you the pistol and see you use it. Stop thinking about yourself and think about Charlotte for a while."

"That's who I'm talking about. But I wouldn't use the pistol, anyway. Because I started this too late. I still believe in love." Then he told McCord about the cashier's check. "If I didn't believe in it, I'd give you the check and send her back with you tonight."

"And if you believed in it as much as you say you do, you would have torn that check up a long time ago."

"If I tore it up, nobody would ever get the money. He couldn't even get it back from the bank."

"Damn him. You dont owe him anything. Didn't you take

his wife off his hands for him? Yah, you're a hell of a guy. You haven't even got the courage of your fornications, have you?" McCord rose. "Come on. I smell coffee."

Wilbourne didn't move, his hand still in the water. "I haven't hurt her." Then he said, "Yes I have. If I hadn't marked her by now, I would. . . . . . ."

"What?"

"Refuse to believe it."

For a full minute McCord stood looking down at the other as he squatted, the bottle in one hand and the other wrist-deep in the water. "Shit!" he said. Then Charlotte called them from the door. Wilbourne rose.

"I wouldn't use the pistol," he said. "I'll still take this."

Charlotte did not take the drink. Instead she set the bottle on the mantel. "To remind us of our lost civilization when our hair begins to spread," she said. They ate. There were two iron cots in each of the two bedrooms, two more on the screened porch. While Wilbourne washed the dishes Charlotte and McCord made up the cots on the porch with bedding from the locker; when Wilbourne came out McCord already lay on one cot, his shoes off, smoking. "Go on," he said. "Take it. Charlotte says she dont want to sleep anymore." She came out at that moment, carrying a pad of paper, a tin cup, a new japanned color box.

"We had a dollar and a half left over, even after we bought the whiskey," she said. "Maybe that deer will come back."

"Take some salt to put on his tail," McCord said. "Maybe he will stand still and pose for you."

"I dont want him to pose. That's just what I dont want. I dont want to copy a deer. Anybody can do that." She went on, the screen door slapped behind her. Wilbourne did not look after her. He lay smoking too, his hands beneath his head.

"Listen," McCord said. "You've got a lot of food, there's plenty of wood here and cover when it turns cold, and when things begin to open up in town maybe I can sell some of that junk she made, get orders—"

"I'm not worrying. I told you I am happy. Nothing can take what I have already had away from me."

"Now, aint that just sweet. Listen. Why dont you give me

that damn check and send her back with me and you can eat
through your hundred bucks and then move into the woods
and eat ants and play Saint Anthony in a tree and on Christmas you can take a mussel shell and make yourself a present of
your own oysters. I'm going to sleep." He turned over and
seemed to go to sleep at once, and soon Wilbourne slept too.
He waked once and knew by the sun that it was past noon
and that she was not in the house. But he was not concerned;
lying awake for a moment it was not the twenty-seven barren
years he looked at, and she would not be far, the path straight
and empty and quiet between the two fifty-dollar rows of
cans and sacks, she would wait for him. *If that is to be, she will
wait* he thought. *If we are to lie so, it will be together in the
wavering solitude in spite of Mac and his ninth-rate Teasdale who
seems to remember a hell of a lot of what people read, beneath the
red and yellow drift of the waning year, the myriad kissing of
the repeated leaves.*

The sun was just above the trees when she returned. The
top sheet of the pad was still blank, though the paints had
been used. "Were they that bad?" McCord said. He was busy
at the stove with beans and rice and dried apricots—one of
those secret cooking or eating specialties such as every bachelor seems to have and which some can actually produce
though, you would have said at first glance, not McCord.

"Maybe a little bird told her what you were doing with fifty
cents' worth of our grub so she had to run," Wilbourne said.
The concoction was ready at last. It was not so bad, Wilbourne admitted. "Only I dont know whether it actually is
not foul, or if it's something protective—that what I taste is
not this at all but the forty or fifty cents it represents, if maybe
I dont have a gland for cowardice in my palate or stomach
too." He and Charlotte washed the dishes, McCord went out
and returned with an armful of wood and laid a fire. "We
wont need that tonight," Wilbourne said.

"It wont cost you anything but the wood," McCord said.
"And you've got from here to the Canadian line to get more
from. You can run all northern Wisconsin up this chimney if
you want to." Then they sat before the fire, smoking and not
talking a great deal, until time for McCord to leave. He
would not stay, holiday tomorrow or not. Wilbourne went

out to the car with him and he got into it, looking back at
Charlotte in silhouette against the fire, in the door. "Yah," he
said. "You dont need to worry, no more than an old lady
being led across the street by a policeman or an eagle scout.
Because when the damned bloody wild drunken car comes
along it wont be the old lady, it will be the cop or the scout it
busts the hell out of. Watch yourself."

"Watch myself?"

"Yah. You cant be even afraid all the time without taking
some pains."

Wilbourne returned to the house. It was late, yet she had
not begun to undress; again he mused, not on the adaptability
of women to circumstance but on the ability of women to
adapt the illicit, even the criminal, to a bourgeois standard of
respectability as he watched her, barefoot, moving about the
room, making those subtle alterations in the fixtures of this
temporary abode as they even do in hotel rooms rented for
but one night, producing from one of the boxes which he had
believed to contain only food objects from their apartment in
Chicago which he not only did not know she still had but had
forgotten they ever owned—the books they had acquired, a
copper bowl, even the chintz cover from the ex-work bench,
then from a cigarette carton which she had converted into a
small receptacle resembling a coffin, the tiny figure of the old
man, the Bad Smell; he watched her set it on the mantel and
stand looking at it for a time, musing too, then take up the
bottle with the drink they had saved her and, with the ritualistic sobriety of a child playing, pour the whiskey onto the
hearth. "The lares and penates," she said. "I dont know Latin,
but They will know what I mean."

They slept in the two cots on the porch, then, it turning
cold just before dawn, in one cot, her bare feet fast on the
boards, the hard plunge of elbow and hip waking him as she
came into the blankets smelling of bacon and balsam. There
was a gray light on the lake and when he heard the loon he
knew exactly what it was, he even knew what it would look
like, listening to the raucous idiot voice, thinking how man
alone of all creatures deliberately atrophies his natural senses
and that only at the expense of others; how the four-legged
animal gains all its information through smelling and seeing

and hearing and distrusts all else while the two-legged one believes only what it reads.

The fire felt good the next morning. While she washed the breakfast dishes he cut more wood for it behind the cabin, removing his sweater now, the sun definitely impacting now though he was not fooled, thinking how in these latitudes Labor Day and not equinox marked the suspiration of summer, the long sigh toward autumn and the cold, when she called him from the house. He entered; in the middle of the room stood a stranger carrying balanced on his shoulder a large cardboard box, a man no older than himself, barefoot, in faded khaki slacks and a sleeveless singlet, sunbrowned, with blue eyes and pale sunburned lashes and symmetrical ridges of straw-colored hair—the perfect reflexive *coiffer*—who was looking quietly at the effigy on the mantel. Through the open door behind him Wilbourne saw a beached canoe. "This is—" Charlotte said. "What did you say your name was?"

"Bradley," the stranger said. He looked at Wilbourne, his eyes almost white against his skin like a kodak negative, balancing the box on his shoulder while he extended the other hand.

"Wilbourne," Charlotte said. "Bradley's the neighbor. He's leaving today. He brought us what grub they had left."

"No use lugging it out again," Bradley said. "Your wife tells me you folks are going to stay on a while, so I thought—" he gave Wilbourne a brief hard violent bone-crushing meaningless grip—the broker's front man two years out of an eastern college.

"That's decent of you. We'll be glad to have it. Here, let me—" But the other had already swung the box to the floor; it was well filled. Charlotte and Wilbourne carefully did not look at it. "Thanks a lot. The more we have in the house, the harder it will be for the wolf to get in."

"Or to crowd us out when he does," Charlotte said. Bradley looked at her. He laughed, that is with his teeth. His eyes did not laugh, the assured, predatory eyes of the still successful prom leader.

"Not bad," he said. "Do you—"

"Thanks," Charlotte said. "Will you have some coffee?"

"Thanks, I've had breakfast. We were up at dawn. Must be back in town tonight." Now he looked at the effigy on the mantel again. "May I?" he said. He approached the mantel. "Do I know him? I seem—"

"I hope not," Charlotte said. Bradley looked at her.

"We hope not yet, she means," Wilbourne said. But Bradley continued to watch Charlotte, the pale brows courteously interrogatory above the predatory eyes which did not smile when the mouth did.

"It's the Bad Smell," Charlotte said.

"Oh. I see." He looked at the effigy. "You made it. I saw you sketching yesterday. Across the lake."

"I know you did."

"Touch," he said. "Can I apologise? I wasn't spying."

"I wasn't hiding." Bradley looked at her and now Wilbourne for the first time saw the eyes brows and mouth in accord, quizzical, sardonic, ruthless, the whole man emanating a sort of crass and insolent confidence.

"Sure?" he said.

"Sufficiently," Charlotte said. She moved to the mantel and took the effigy from it. "It's too bad you are leaving before we can return your call upon your wife. But perhaps you will accept this as a memento of your perspicuity."

"No; really, I——"

"Take it," Charlotte said pleasantly. "You must need it much worse than we do."

"Well, thanks." He took the effigy. "Thanks. We've got to get back to town tonight. But maybe we could look in on the way out. Mrs Bradley would—"

"Do," Charlotte said.

"Thanks," he said. He turned toward the door. "Thanks again."

"Thanks again too," Charlotte said. He went out, Wilbourne watched him shove the canoe off and step into it. Then Wilbourne went and stooped over the box.

"What are you going to do?" Charlotte said.

"I'm going to carry it back and throw it in his front door."

"Oh you bloody ass," she said. She came to him. "Stand up. We're going to eat it. Stand up like a man." He rose, she put her hard arms around him, wrestling him against her with restrained savage impatience. "Why dont you grow up, you damned home-wrecking boy scout? Dont you know yet that we just dont look married thank God, even to brutes?" She held him hard against her, leaning back, her hips against him and moving faintly while she stared at him, the yellow stare inscrutable and derisive and with that quality which he had come to recognise—that ruthless and almost unbearable honesty. "Like a man, I said," holding him hard and derisive against her moving hips though that was not necessary. *She dont need to touch me* he thought. *Nor the sound of her voice even nor the smell, a slipper will do it, one of those fragile instigations to venery discarded in the floor.* "Come on. That's right. That's better. That's fine now." She freed one hand and began to unfasten his shirt. "Only this is supposed to be bad luck or something in the forenoon, isn't it? Or isn't it?"

"Yes," he said. "Yes." She began to unfasten his belt.

"Or is this just the way you assuage insults to me? Or are you going to bed with me just because somebody happened to remind you I divide at the belly?"

"Yes," he said. "Yes."

Later in the forenoon they heard Bradley's car depart. Face down and half lying across him (she had been asleep, her weight heavy and relaxed, her head beneath his chin, her breath slow and full) she raised up, one elbow in his stomach and the blanket slipping away from her shoulders, while the sound of the car died away. "Well, Adam," she said. But they had always been alone, he told her.

"Ever since that first night. That picture. We couldn't be any more alone, no matter who went away."

"I know it. I mean, I can go swimming now." She slid out from beneath the blanket. He watched her, the grave simple body a little broader, a little solider than the Hollywood-magazine cod liver oil advertisements, the bare feet padding across the rough boards, toward the screen door.

"There are bathing suits in the locker," he said. She didn't answer. The screen door slapped. Then he could not see her anymore, or he would have had to raise his head.

She swam each morning, the three bathing suits still undisturbed in the locker. He would rise from breakfast and return to the porch and lie on the cot and hear presently her bare feet cross the room and then the porch; perhaps he would watch the steadily and smoothly browning body cross the porch. Then he would sleep again (this scarcely an hour after he had waked from slumber, a habit which he formed within the first six days) to wake later and look out and see her lying on the pier on stomach or back, her arms folded across or beneath her face; sometimes he would still be there, not sleeping now and not even thinking but merely existing in a drowsy and foetuslike state, passive and almost unsentient in the womb of solitude and peace, when she returned, moving then only enough to touch his lips to the sun-impacted flank as she stopped beside the cot, tasting the impacted sun. Then one day something happened to him.

September had gone, the nights and mornings were definitely chilly; she had changed her swim from after breakfast to after lunch and they were talking about when they would have to move the bedding in from the porch to the room with the fireplace. But the days themselves were unchanged—the same stationary recapitulation of golden interval between dawn and sunset, the long quiet identical days, the immaculate monotonous hierarchy of noons filled with the sun's hot honey, through which the waning year drifted in red-and-yellow retrograde of hardwood leaves sourceless and going nowhere. Each day she departed directly after her swim and sunbath, with the pad and color box, leaving him to move about the house empty yet at the same time thunderous with the hard impact of her presence—the few garments she owned, the whisper of her bare feet on the boards—while he believed that he was worrying, not about the inevitable day on which their food would run out, but at the fact that he did not seem to worry about it: a curious state which he had experienced once before when his sister's husband had taken him to task one summer because he refused to exercise his vote. He remembered the exasperation just about to become rage in which he had tried to present his reasons to his brother-in-law, realising at last that he was talking faster and faster not to convince the brother-in-law but to justify his own rage as in a mild nightmare he might be grasping for his falling trousers; that it was not even to the brother-in-law he was talking but to himself.

It became an obsession with him; he realised quite calmly that he had become secretly quietly and decently a little mad; he now thought constantly of the diminishing row of cans and sacks against which he was matching in inverse ratio the accumulating days, yet he would not go to the closet and look at them, count them. He would tell himself how it used to be he would have to steal away to a park bench and take out the wallet and produce the scrap of paper and subtract numbers from one another, while now all he would have to do would be to glance at the row of cans on a shelf; he could count the cans and know exactly how many days more they would have left, he could take a pencil and mark the shelf itself off into days and he would not even have to count cans, he could glance at the shelf and read the position at once, like on a thermometer. But he would not even look into the closet.

He knew that during these hours he was mad and he fought against it sometimes, believing that he had conquered the madness, for in the next succeeding instant the cans, save for a tragic conviction that they did not even matter, were as completely out of his mind as if they had never existed, and he would look about at his familiar surroundings with a sense of profound despair, not even knowing that he was worrying now, worrying so terribly that he did not even know it; he looked about with a kind of aghast amazement at the sunfilled solitude out of which she had walked temporarily yet still remained in and to which she would presently return and re-enter her aura which had remained behind exactly as she might re-enter a garment and find him stretched on the cot, not sleeping now and not even reading, who had lost that habit along with the habit of sleep, and said quietly to himself, *I am bored. I am bored to extinction. There is nothing here that I am needed for. Not even by her. I have already cut enough wood to last until Christmas and there is nothing else for me to do.*

One day he asked her to divide the colors and pad with him. She did so and found that he was color blind and didn't even know it. Then each day he would lie on his back in a small sunny clearing he had found, surrounded by the fierce astringent smell of balsam, smoking the cheap pipe (the one provision he had made before leaving Chicago against the day they would exhaust food and money both), his half of the sketch pad and his converted sardine can color-box intact and pristine beside him. Then one day he decided to make a calendar, a notion innocently conceived not by mind, out of a desire for a calendar, but from the sheer boredom of muscles, and put into effect with the pure quiet sensory pleasure of a man carving a basket from a peach stone or the Lord's Prayer on a pin head; he drew it neatly off on the sketch pad, numbering in the days, planning to use various appropriate colors for Sundays and the holidays. He discovered at once that he had lost count of the days, but this only added to the anticipation, prolonging the work, making more involved the pleasure, the peach basket to be a double one, the prayer to be in code. So he went back to that first morning when he and McCord squatted beside the water, whose name and number he knew, then he counted forward by reconstructing from memory the drowsing demarcations between one dawn and the next, unravelling one by one out of the wine-sharp and honey-still warp of tideless solitude the lost Tuesdays and Fridays and Sundays; when it suddenly occurred to him that he could prove his figures, establish mathematical truth out of the sunny and timeless void into which the individual days had vanished by the dates of and intervals between Charlotte's menstrual periods, he felt as some old crook-propped contemplator on the ancient sheep-drifted Syrian hills must have felt after stumbling by accident on some Alexandrian formula which proved the starry truths which he had watched nightly all his life and knew to be true but not how nor why.

That was when the thing happened to him. He sat looking at what he had made in a gleeful and amazed amusement at his own cunning in contriving for God, for Nature the unmathematical, the overfecund, the prime disorderly and illogical and patternless spendthrift, to prove his mathematical problem for him, when he discovered that he had given six weeks to the month of October and that the day in which he now stood was November twelfth. It seemed to him that he could see the actual numeral, incontrovertible and solitary, in the anonymous identical hierarchy of the lost days; he seemed to see the row of cans on the shelf a half mile away, the dynamic torpedolike solid shapes which up to now had merely dropped one by one, silently and without weight, into that

stagnant time which did not advance and which would somehow find for its two victims food as it found them breath,
now in reverse to time, time now the mover, advancing slow
and irresistible, blotting the cans one by one in steady progression as a moving cloud shadow blots. *Yes* he thought. *It's
the Indian summer that did it. I have been seduced to an imbecile's paradise by an old whore; I have been throttled and sapped of
strength and volition by the old weary Lilith of the year.*

He burned the calendar and went back to the cabin. She
had not returned yet. He went to the closet and counted the
cans. It was two hours to sunset yet; when he looked out
toward the lake he saw that there was no sun and that a mass
of cloud like dirty cotton had crossed from east to north and
west and that the feel and taste of the air too had changed. *Yes*
he thought. *The old bitch. She betrayed me and now she doesn't
need to pretend.* At last he saw her approaching, circling the
lake, in a pair of his trousers and an old sweater they had
found in the locker with the blankets. He went to meet her.
"Good Lord," she said. "I never saw you look so happy. Have
you painted a picture or have you discovered at last that the
human race really doesn't have to even try to produce art—"
He was moving faster than he knew; when he put his arms
around her he jolted her to a stop by physical contact; thrust
back, she looked at him with actual and not simulated astonishment now.

"Yes," he said. "How's for a spot of necking?"

"Why, certainly, friend," she said immediately. Then she
thrust herself back again to look at him. "What's this? What's
going on here?"

"Will you be afraid to stay here alone tonight?" Now she
began to free herself.

"Let me go. I cant see you good." He released her, though
he did manage to meet the unwinking yellow stare which he
had never yet been able to lie to. "Tonight?"

"This is the twelfth of November."

"All right. Then what?" She looked at him. "Come on.
Let's go to the house and get to the bottom of this." They
returned to the house; again she paused and faced him. "Now
let's have it."

"I just counted the cans. Measured the. . . . . . ." She

stared at him with that hard, almost grim impersonality. "We can eat for about six days more."

"All right. Then what?"

"It was the mild weather. Like time had stopped and us with it, like two chips on a pond. So I didn't think to worry, to watch. So I'm going to walk to the village. It's only twelve miles. I could be back by noon tomorrow." She stared at him. "A letter. From Mac. It will be there."

"Did you dream it would be there, or did you find it out in the coffee pot when you were measuring the grub?"

"It will be there."

"All right. But wait till tomorrow to go. You cant walk twelve miles before dark." They ate and went to bed. This time she came straight and got into the cot with him, as heedless of the hard and painful elbow which jabbed him as she would have been on her own account if the positions had been reversed, as she was of the painful hand which grasped his hair and shook his head with savage impatience. "My God, I never in my life saw anybody try as hard to be a husband as you do. Listen to me, you lug. If it was just a successful husband and food and a bed I wanted, why the hell do you think I am here instead of back there where I had them?"

"You've got to sleep and eat."

"Certainly we have. So why worry about it? That's like worrying about having to bathe just because the water in the bathroom is about to be cut off." Then she rose, got out of the cot with the same abrupt violence; he watched her cross to the door and open it and look out. He could smell the snow before she spoke. "It's snowing."

"I know it. I knew this afternoon she realised the game was up."

"She?" She closed the door. This time she went to the other cot and got into it. "Try to get to sleep. It'll be a hard walk tomorrow, if it snows much."

"It will be there though."

"Yes," she said. She yawned, her back to him. "It's probably been there a week or two."

He left the cabin shortly after daylight. The snow had ceased and it was quite cold. He reached the village in four

hours and found the letter from McCord. It contained a check
for twenty-five dollars; he had sold one of the puppets, and he
had the promise of a job for Charlotte in a department store
during the holiday season. It was well after dark when he
reached home. "You can put it all in the pot," he said. "We've
got twenty-five dollars. And Mac's got a job for you. He's
driving up Saturday night."

"Saturday night?"

"I wired him. I waited for an answer. That's why I'm late."
They ate and this time she got quietly into the narrow cot
with him and this time she even crept close to him who had
never before known her to do such at any time, to anything.

"I'll be sorry to leave here."

"Will you?" he said quietly, peacefully, lying on his back,
his arms crossed on his chest like a stone effigy on a tenth
century sepulchre. "You'll probably be glad to get back, once
you are there though. People to see again, McCord and the
others you liked, Christmas and all that. You can get your hair
clean again and your nails manicured——" This time she did
not move, whose habit it was to assault him with that cold
and disregardful savageness, shaking and jerking at him not
only for conversion but even for mere emphasis. This time
she lay perfectly still, not even breathing, her voice filled not
with a suspiration but sheer amazed incredulity:

"*You'll* probably. *You* are. *You* can. Harry, what do you
mean?"

"That I wired Mac to come and get you. You'll have your
job; that will keep you until after Christmas all right. I
thought I'd just keep half the twenty-five dollars and stay on
here. Maybe Mac can find something for me too; if nothing
else, maybe a W.P.A. job of some sort. Then I'd come on back
to town and then we could——"

"No!" she cried. "No! No! Jesus God, no! Hold me! Hold
me hard, Harry! This is what it's for, what it all was for, what
we were paying for: so we could be together, sleep together
every night: not just to eat and evacuate and sleep warm so
we can get up and eat and evacuate in order to sleep warm
again! Hold me! Hold me hard! Hard!" He held her, his arms
rigid, his face still turned upward, his lips lifted away from his
rigid teeth.

God he thought. *God help her. God help her.*

They left snow at the lake, though before they reached Chicago they had overtaken the end of the south-moving Indian summer for a little while. But it did not last and now it was winter in Chicago too, the Canadian wind made ice in the Lake and blew in the stone canyons holly-burgeoned with the imminent Christmas, crisping and frosting the faces of policemen and clerks and panhandlers and Red Cross and Salvation Army people costumed as Santa Claus, the defunctive days dying in neon upon the fur-framed petal faces of the wives and daughters of cattle and timber millionaires and the paramours of politicians returned from Europe and the dude ranches to spend the holidays in the air-carved and opulent tenements above the iron lake and the rich sprawling city before departing for Florida, and of the sons of London brokers and Midland shoe-peg knights and South African senators come to look at Chicago because they had read Whitman and Masters and Sandburg in Oxford or Cambridge—members of that race which without tact for exploration and armed with note books and cameras and sponge bags elects to pass the season of Christian holiday in the dark and bitten jungles of savages.

Charlotte's job was in a store which had been one of her first customers for the first figurines she had made. It included window- and showcase-dressing, so that her day sometimes began when the store closed in the afternoon and that of the other employees ceased. So Wilbourne and sometimes McCord would wait for her in a bar just around the corner, where they would eat an early dinner. Then McCord would depart to begin his upside down day at the newspaper and Charlotte and Wilbourne would return to the store, which would now take on a sort of bizarre and infernal inverted life—the chromium glass and synthetic marble cavern which for eight hours had been filled with the ruthless voracious murmur of furred shoppers and the fixed regimented grimaces of satin-clad robot-like saleswomen now empty of uproar, glittering and quiet and echoed with cavernous silence, dwarfing, filled now with a grim tense fury like an empty midnight clinic in which a handful of pygmy-like surgeons and nurses battle in low-toned decorum for some obscure and anonymous life, into which Charlotte would vanish too (not disappear: he would see her from time to time, consulting in pantomime with someone over some object which one of them held, or entering or leaving a window) as soon as they entered. He would have an evening paper and now for the next two or three hours he would sit on fragile chairs surrounded by jointless figures with suave organless bodies and serene almost incredible faces, by draped brocade and sequins or the glitter of rhinestones, while charwomen appeared on their knees and pushing pails before them as though they were another species just crawled molelike from some tunnel or orifice leading from the foundations of the earth itself and serving some obscure principle of sanitation not to the hushed glitter which they did not even look at but to the subterranean region which they would crawl back to before light. Then at eleven and midnight and, as Christmas approached, even later they would go home, to the apartment which had no work bench and no skylight now but which was new and neat and in a new neat district near a park (toward which, around ten oclock in the morning while lying in bed between his first and second sleep of the day, he could hear the voices of nursemaid-harried children moving) where Charlotte would go to bed and he would sit again at the typewriter at which he had already spent most of the day, the machine borrowed first from McCord then rented from an agency then purchased outright from among the firing-pinless pistols and guitars and gold-filled teeth in a pawnshop on which he wrote and sold to the confession magazines the stories beginning 'I had the body and desires of a woman yet in knowledge and experience of the world I was but a child' or 'If I had only had a mother's love to guard me on that fatal day'—stories which he wrote complete from the first capital to the last period in one sustained frenzied agonising rush like the halfback working his way through school who grasps the ball (his Albatross, his Old Man of the Sea, which, not the opposing team, not the blank incontrovertible chalk marks profoundly terrifying and meaningless as an idiot's nightmare, is his sworn and mortal enemy) and runs until the play is completed—downed or across the goal line, it doesn't matter which—then to go to bed himself, with dawn sometimes beyond the open window of the chill sleeping cubicle, to get into bed beside Charlotte who without waking would sometimes turn to him, murmuring something damp and indistinguishable out of sleep, and to lie again holding her as on that last night at the lake, himself wide awake, carefully rigid and still, knowing no desire to sleep, waiting for the smell and echo of his last batch of moron's pap to breathe out of him.

Thus he was awake mostly while she slept, and vice versa. She would get up and close the window and dress and make coffee (the breakfast which while they were poor, when they did not know for certain where the next measure of coffee to put into the pot was coming from, they would prepare and eat together, the dishes of which they would wash and dry together side by side at the sink) and be gone and he would not know it. Then he in his turn would wake and listen to the passing children while the stale coffee heated, and drink it and sit down to the typewriter, entering without effort and without especial regret the anesthesia of his monotonous inventing. At first he made a kind of ritual of his solitary lunch, fetching in the cans and slices of meat and such the night before, like a little boy with a new Daniel Boone suit hoarding crackers in the improvised forest of a broom closet. But lately, since he had actually bought the typewriter (he had voluntarily relinquished his amateur standing, he told himself then; he no longer had even to pretend to himself it was a lark) he began to dispense with lunch altogether, with the bother of eating, instead writing steadily on, pausing only to sit while his fingers rested, a cigarette scarring slowly into the edge of the rented table, staring at but not seeing the two or three current visible lines of his latest primer-bald moronic fable, his sexual gumdrop, then remembering the cigarette and raising it to rub uselessly at the new scorch before writing again. Then the hour would arrive and with the ink sometimes scarcely dry on the stamped sealed and self-addressed envelope containing the latest story beginning 'At sixteen I was an unwed mother' he would leave the apartment and walk through the crowded streets, the steadily shortening afternoons of the dying year, to the bar where he and Charlotte and McCord met.

There was Christmas in the bar too, holly sprigs and

mistletoe among the gleaming pyramids of glasses, mirror-repeated, the mirror aping the antic jackets of the barmen, the steaming seasonal bowls of hot rum and whiskey for the patrons to look at and recommend to one another while holding in their hands the same iced cocktails and highballs they had been drinking all summer. Then McCord at their usual table, with what he called breakfast—a quart stein of beer and about another quart of pretzels or salted peanuts or whatever was available, and Wilbourne would have the one drink which he allowed himself before Charlotte came ("I can afford abstemiousness now, sobriety," he told McCord. "I can pay shot for shot and no holds barred with any and all for the privilege of refusing.") and they would wait for the hour when the stores would empty, the glass doors flashing outward to erupt into the tender icy glare of neon the holly-pinned fur-framed faces, the wind-carved canyons merry and crisp with the bright voices speaking the good wishes and good will into intransigeant vapor, the employees' chute too discharging presently the regimented black satin, the feet swollen with the long standing, the faces aching with the sustained long rigid grimacing. Then Charlotte would enter; they would stop talking and watch her approach, shifting and sidling past the throng at the bar and among the waiters and the crowded tables, her coat open above the neat uniform, her hat of the current off-the-face mode thrust further back still as if she had pushed it there herself with a sweep of the forearm in the immemorial female gesture out of the immemorial female weariness, approaching the table, her face pale and tired-looking too though she moved as strongly and surely as ever, the eyes as humorlessly and incorrigibly honest as ever above the blunt strong nose, the broad pale unsubtle mouth. "Rum, men," she would say, then, sinking into the chair which one of them drew for her: "Well, papa." Then they would eat, at the wrong hour, the hour when the rest of the world was just beginning to prime itself for food ("I feel like three bears in a cage on Sunday afternoon," she said.), eating the meal which none of them wanted and then disperse, McCord to the paper, Charlotte and Wilbourne back to the store.

Two days before Christmas when she entered the bar she carried a parcel. It contained Christmas gifts for her children, the two girls. They had no work bench now and no skylight. She unwrapped and rewrapped them on the bed, the immemorial—the work bench of the child's unwitting begetting become the altar for the Child's service, she sitting on the edge of it surrounded by holly-stippled paper and the fatuous fragile red-and-green cord and gummed labels, the two gifts she had chosen reasonably costly but unremarkable, she looking at them with a sort of grim bemusement above the hands otherwise and at nearly every other human action unhesitating and swift. "They haven't even taught me how to wrap up packages," she said. "Children," she said. "It's not a child's function, really. It's for adults: a week's dispensation to return to childishness, to give something you dont want yourself to someone who doesn't want it either, and demand thanks for it. And the children swap with you. They vacate puerility and accept the role you abandoned not because they ever had any particular desire to be grown but just out of that ruthless piracy of children that will use anything—deception or secrecy or acting—to get anything. Anything, any bauble will do. Presents dont mean anything to them until they get big enough to calculate what it probably cost. That's why little girls are more interested in presents than little boys. So they take what you give them not because they will accept even that in preference to nothing but because that's about all they expected anyway from the stupid oxen among whom for some reason they have to live.—They have offered to keep me on at the store."

"What?" he said. He had not been listening to her. He had been hearing but not listening, looking down at the blunt hands among the tinsel litter, thinking *Now is the time for me to say, Go home. Be with them tomorrow night.* "What?"

"They are going to keep me on until summer at the store."

He heard this time; he went through the same experience as when he had recognised the number on the calendar he had made, now he knew what the trouble had been all the time, why he would lie rigidly and carefully beside her in the dawn, believing the reason he could not sleep was that he was waiting for the smell of his moron pandering to fade, why he would sit before an unfinished page in the typewriter, believing he was thinking of nothing, believing he was thinking only of the money, how each time they always had the wrong amount of it and that they were about money like some unlucky people were about alcohol: either none or too much. *It was the city I was thinking of* he thought. *The city and winter together, a combination too strong for us yet, for a time yet — the winter that herds people inside walls wherever they are, but winter and city together, a dungeon; the routine even of sinning, an absolution even for adultery.* "No," he said. "Because we are going to leave Chicago."

"Leave Chicago?"

"Yes. For good. You're not going to work any more just for money. Wait," he said quickly. "I know we have come to live like we had been married five years, but I am not coming the heavy husband on you. I know I catch myself thinking, 'I want my wife to have the best' but I'm not yet saying 'I dont approve of my women working'. It's not that. It's what we have come to work for, got into the habit of working for before we knew it, almost waited too late before we found it out. Do you remember how you said up at the lake when I suggested that you clear out while the clearing was good and you said 'That's what we bought, what we are paying for: to be together and eat together and sleep together'? And now look at us. When we are together, it's in a saloon or a street car or walking along a crowded street and when we eat together it's in a crowded restaurant inside a vacant hour they allow you from the store so you can eat and stay strong so they can get the value of the money they pay you every Saturday and we dont sleep together at all anymore, we take turns watching each other sleep; when I touch you I know you are too tired to wake up and you are probably too tired to touch me at all."

Three weeks later, with a scribbled address on a torn newspaper margin folded in his vest pocket, he entered a downtown office building and ascended twenty floors to an opaque glass door lettered *Callaghan Mines* and entered and passed with some difficulty a chromium-finished office girl and faced at last across a desk flat and perfectly bare save for a telephone and a deck of cards laid out for Canfield, a red-faced cold-eyed man of about fifty, with a highwayman's head and the body of a two hundred and twenty pound college fullback gone to fat, in a suit of expensive tweed which nevertheless looked on him as if he had taken it from a fire sale at the point of a pistol, to whom Wilbourne essayed to give a summary of his medical qualifications and experience.

"Never mind that," the other interrupted. "Can you take care of the ordinary injuries that men working in a mine shaft might meet?"

"I was just trying to tell you—"

"I heard you. I asked you something else. I said, Take care of them." Wilbourne looked at him.

"I dont think I—" he began.

"Take care of the mine. Of the people who own it. Have put money into it. Who will be paying your salary as long as you earn it. I dont care two damns in hell how much or how little surgery and pharmacology you know or dont know or how many degrees you might have from where to show it. Nobody else out there will; there'll be no state inspectors out there to ask to see your license. I want to know if you can be depended on to protect the mine, the company. Against backfires. Suits from wop pick-and-shovel men and bohunk powder-monkeys and chink ore-trammers to whom the notion might occur to swap the company a hand or a foot for a pension or a trip back to Canton or Hong Kong."

"Oh," Wilbourne said. "I see. Yes. I can do that."

"All right. You will be given transportation out to the mine at once. Your pay will be—" he named a sum.

"That's not much," Wilbourne said. The other looked at him with the cold flesh-bedded eyes. Wilbourne stared back at him. "I have a degree from a good university, a recognised medical school. I lacked only a few weeks of finishing my internship at a hospital which has a—"

"Then you dont want this job. This job is nowhere near up to your qualifications and, I daresay, your deserts. Good day." The cold eyes stared at him; he did not move. "I said, Good morning."

"I will have to have transportation for my wife," Wilbourne said.

Their train left at three oclock two mornings later. They waited for McCord at the apartment where they had lived for two months and left no mark other than the cigarette scars on the table. "Not even of loving," he said. "Not the wild sweet attunement, bare feet hurrying bedward in the half light, covers that wont turn back fast enough. Just the seminal groaning of box springs, the preprandial prostate relieving of the ten years' married. We were too busy; we had to rent and support a room for two robots to live in." McCord came and they carried down the luggage, the two bags with which they had left New Orleans, and the typewriter. The manager shook hands with all three of them and expressed regret at the dissolution of mutually pleasant domestic bonds. "Just two of us," Wilbourne said. "None of us are androgynous." The manager blinked, though just once.

"Ah," he said. "A pleasant journey. You have a cab?" They had McCord's car; they went out to it in a mild glitter of minor silver, the final neon and clash and clang of changing lights; the redcap turned the two bags and the typewriter over to the porter at the pullman vestibule.

"We've got time for a drink," McCord said.

"You and Harry have one," Charlotte said. "I'm going to bed." She came and put her arms around McCord, her face raised. "Goodnight, Mac." Then McCord moved and kissed her. She stepped back, turning; they watched her enter the vestibule and vanish. Then Wilbourne also knew that McCord knew he would never see her again.

"How about that drink?" McCord said. They went to the station bar and found a table and then they were sitting again as they had on so many of the afternoons while they waited for Charlotte—the same drinking faces, the same white jackets of waiters and barmen, the same racked gleaming glasses, only the steaming bowls and the holly (Christmas, McCord had said, the apotheosis of the bourgeoisie, the season when with shining fable Heaven and Nature, in accord for once, edict and postulate us all husbands and fathers under our skins, when before an altar in the shape of a gold-plated cattle-trough man may with impunity prostrate himself in an orgy of unbridled sentimental obeisance to the fairy tale which conquered the Western world, when for seven days the rich get richer and the poor get poorer in amnesty: the whitewashing of a stipulated week leaving the page blank and pristine again for the chronicling of the fresh—and for the moment, horselike ("there's the horse," McCord said), breathed—revenge and hatred.) missing now, the waiter coming up as he had used to come—the same white sleeve, the anonymous featureless waiter-face you never actually see. "Beer," McCord said. "What's yours?"

"Ginger ale," Wilbourne said.

"What?"

"I'm on the wagon."

"Since when?"

"Since last night. I cant afford to drink anymore." McCord looked at him.

"Hell," McCord said. "Bring me a double rye then." The waiter departed. McCord still stared at Wilbourne. "It seems to agree with you," he said savagely. "Listen," he said. "I know this is none of my business. But I wish I knew what it's all about. Here you were making fair money, and Charlotte with a good job, you had a nice place to live in. And then all of a sudden you quit it, make Charlotte throw up her job to start out in February to live in a mine shaft in Utah, without a railroad or a telephone or even a decent can, on a salary of—"

"That was just it. That was why. I had become—" He ceased. The waiter set the drinks on the table and went away. Wilbourne raised his ginger ale. "To freedom."

"I would," McCord snarled. "You'll probably be able to drink to a lot of it before you see any of it again. And in water too, not even in soda pop. And maybe in a tighter place than this too. Because that guy is poison. I know about him. He's wildcat. If the truth was written about him on a tombstone it wouldn't be an epitaph, it would be a police record."

"All right," Wilbourne said. "To love, then." There was a clock above the entrance—the ubiquitous and synchronised face, oracular admonitory and unsentient; he had twenty-two minutes yet. *While it will only take two minutes to tell Mac what it took me two months to discover* he thought. "I had turned into a husband," he said. "That was all. I didn't even know it until she told me the store had offered to keep her on. At first I used to have to watch myself, rehearse myself each time so I would be sure to say 'my wife' or 'Mrs Wilbourne', then I discovered I had been watching myself for months to keep from saying it; I have even caught myself twice since we came back from the lake thinking 'I want my wife to have the best' exactly like any husband with his Saturday pay envelope and his suburban bungalow full of electric wife-saving gadgets and his table cloth of lawn to sprinkle on Sunday morning that will become his actual own provided he is not fired or run down by a car in the next ten years—the doomed worm blind to all passion and dead to all hope and not even knowing it, oblivious and unaware in the face of all darkness, all unknown, the underlying All-Derisive biding to blast him. I had even stopped being ashamed of the way I earned the money, apologising even to myself for the stories I wrote; I was no more ashamed of them than the city employee buying his own bungalow on the installment plan in which his wife can have the best is ashamed of his badge of office, the rubber plunger for unstopping toilets, which he carries about with him. In fact, I had come to really like to write them, even apart from the money, like the boy who never saw ice before goes bugs about skating right after he learns how. Besides, after I started writing them I learned that I had no idea of the depths of depravity of which the human invention is capable, which is always interesting—"

"You mean, enjoys," McCord said.

"Yes. All right.— Respectability. That was what did it. I found out some time back that it's idleness breeds all our virtues, our most bearable qualities—contemplation, equableness, laziness, letting other people alone; good digestion mental and physical: the wisdom to concentrate on fleshly pleasures—eating and evacuating and fornication and sitting in the sun—than which there is nothing better, nothing to match, nothing else in all this world but to live for the short time you are loaned breath, to be alive and know it—oh yes, she taught me that; she has marked me too forever—nothing, nothing. But it was only recently I have clearly seen, followed out the logical conclusion, that it is one of what we call the prime virtues—thrift, industry, independence—that breeds all the vices—fanaticism, smugness, meddling, fear, and worst of all, respectability. Us, for instance. Because of the fact that for the first time we were solvent, knew for certain where tomorrow's food was coming from (the damned money, too much of it; at night we would lie awake and plan how to get it spent; by spring we would have been carrying steamer folders in our pockets) I had become as completely thrall and slave to respectability as any—"

"But not her," McCord said.

"No. But she's a better man than I am. You said that yourself.—as any man by drink or opium. I had become the Complete Householder. All I lacked was official sanction in the form of a registered Social Security number as head of a family. We lived in an apartment that wasn't bohemian, it wasn't even a tabloid love-nest, it wasn't even in that part of town but in a neighborhood dedicated by both city ordinance and architecture to the second year of wedlock among the five thousand a year bracket. I would be waked in the mornings by the noise of children passing in the street; by the time spring came and the windows would have to stay open I would have been hearing the fretful cries of Swede nursemaids from the park all day long and, when the wind was right, smell the smell of infant urine and animal crackers. I referred to it as home, there was a corner in it we both called my study; I had even bought the damn typewriter at last— something I had got along without for twenty-eight years and so well I didn't even know it, which is too heavy and unwieldy to carry yet which I would no more have dared desert than—"

"You've still got it, I noticed," McCord said.

"—than—Yes. A good portion of any courage is a sincere disbelief in good luck. It's not courage otherwise.—than I would my eyelashes. I had tied myself hand and foot in a little strip of inked ribbon, daily I watched myself getting more and more tangled in it like a roach in a spider web; each morning, so that my wife could leave on time for her job, I would wash the coffee pot and the sink and twice a week (for the same reason) I would buy from the same butcher the groceries we needed and the chops we would cook ourselves on Sunday; give us a little more time and we would have been dressing and undressing inside our kimonos in one another's presence and turning off the light before we made love. That's it. It's not avocation that elects our vocations, it's respectability that makes chiropractors and clerks and bill posters and motormen and pulp writers of us." There was a loudspeaker in the bar too, synchronised too; at this moment a voice cavernous and sourceless roared deliberately, a sentence in which could be distinguished a word now and then—'train', then others which the mind two or three seconds afterward recognised to be the names of cities far flung about the continent, cities seen rather than names heard, as if the listener (so enormous was the voice) were suspended in space watching the globy earth spin slowly out of its cradling cloud-wisps in fragmentary glimpses the evocative strange divisions of the sphere, spinning them on into fog and cloud again before vision and comprehension could quite grasp them. He looked at the clock again; he still had fourteen minutes. *Fourteen minutes to try to tell what I have already said in five words* he thought.

"And mind, I liked it. I never denied that. I liked it. I liked the money I made. I even liked the way I made it, the thing I did, as I told you. It wasn't because of that that one day I caught myself back from thinking 'My wife must have the best'. It was because I found out one day that I was afraid. And I found out at the same time that I will still be afraid, no matter what I do, that I will still be afraid as long as she lives or I live."

"You are still afraid now?"

"Yes. And not about money. Damn money. I can make all the money we will need; certainly there seems to be no limit to what I can invent on the theme of female sex troubles. I dont mean that, nor Utah either. I mean us. Love, if you will. Because it cant last. There is no place for it in the world today, not even in Utah. We have eliminated it. It took us a long time, but man is resourceful and limitless in inventing too, and so we have got rid of love at last just as we have got rid of Christ. We have radio in the place of God's voice and instead of having to save emotional currency for months and years to deserve one chance to spend it all for love we can now spread it thin into coppers and titillate ourselves at any newsstand, two to the block like sticks of chewing gum or chocolate from the automatic machines. If Jesus returned today we would have to crucify him quick in our own defense, to justify and preserve the civilization we have worked and suffered and died shrieking and cursing in rage and impotence and terror for two thousand years to create and perfect in man's own image; if Venus returned she would be a soiled man in a subway lavatory with a palm full of French post-cards—" McCord turned in his chair and beckoned, a single repressed violent gesture. The waiter appeared, McCord pointed to his glass. Presently the waiter's hand set the refilled glass on the table and withdrew.

"All right," McCord said. "So what?"

"I was in eclipse. It began that night in New Orleans when I told her I had twelve hundred dollars and it lasted until that night she told me the store would keep her on. I was outside of time. I was still attached to it, supported by it in space as you have been ever since there was a not-you to become you, and will be until there is an end to the not-you by means of which alone you could once have been—that's the immortal-ity—supported by it but that's all, just on it, non-conductive, like the sparrow insulated by its own hard non-conductive dead feet from the high tension line, the current of time that runs through remembering, that exists only in relation to what little of reality (I have learned that too) we know, else there is no such thing as time. You know: *I was not*. Then *I am,* and time begins, retroactive, is was and will be. Then *I was* and so I am not and so time never existed. It was like the instant of virginity, it was the instant of virginity: that condi-tion, fact, that does not actually exist except during the in-stant you know you are losing it; it lasted as long as it did because I was too old, I waited too long; twenty-seven is too long to wait to get out of your system what you should have rid yourself of at fourteen or fifteen or maybe even younger—the messy wild hurried fumbling of two panting amateurs beneath the front steps or in an afternoon hayloft. You re-member: the precipice, the dark precipice; all mankind before you went over it and lived and all after you will but that means nothing to you because they cant tell you, forewarn you, what to do in order to survive. It's the solitude, you see. You must do it in solitude and you can bear just so much solitude and still live, like electricity. And for this one or two seconds you will be absolutely alone: not before you were and not after you are not, because you are never alone then; in either case you are secure and companioned in a myriad and inextricable anonymity: in the one, dust from dust; in the other, seething worms to seething worms. But now you are going to be alone, you must, you know it, it must be, so be it; you herd the beast you have ridden all your life, the old familiar well-broken nag, up to the precipice—"

"There's the damned horse," McCord said. "I've been waiting for it. After ten minutes we sound like *Bit and Spur*. We dont talk, we moralise at each other like two circuit-riding parsons travelling the same country lane."

"—maybe you thought all the time that when the moment came you could rein back, save something, maybe not, the instant comes and you know you cannot, know you knew all the time you could not, and you cannot; you are one single abnegant affirmation, one single fluxive Yes out of the terror in which you surrender volition, hope, all—the darkness, the falling, the thunder of solitude, the shock, the death, the moment when, stopped physically by the ponderable clay, you yet feel all your life rush out of you into the pervading immemorial blind receptive matrix, the hot fluid blind foundation—grave-womb or womb-grave, it's all one. But you return; maybe you knew that all the time, but you return, maybe you even live out your three score and ten or whatever it is but forever afterward you will know that forever more you have lost some of it, that for that one second or two seconds you were present in space but not in time, that you are not the three score and ten they have credited you with and that you will have to discharge someday to make the books balance, but three score and nine and three hundred and sixty-four and twenty-three and fifty-eight—"

"Sweet Jesus," McCord said. "Holy choriated cherubim. If I am ever unlucky enough to have a son, I'm going to take him to a nice clean whore-house myself on his tenth birthday."

"So that's what happened to me," Wilbourne said. "I waited too long. What would have been two seconds at fourteen or fifteen was eight months at twenty-seven. I was in eclipse, and we almost scraped bottom on that snow-bound Wisconsin lake with nine dollars and twenty cents' worth of food between us and starving. I beat that, I thought I did. I believed I waked up in time and beat that; we came back here and I thought we were going great guns, until that night before Christmas when she told me about the store and I realised what we had got into, that the starving was nothing, it could have done nothing but kill us, while this was worse than death or division even: it was the mausoleum of love, it was the stinking catafalque of the dead corpse borne between the olfactoryless walking shapes of the immortal unsentient demanding ancient meat." The loudspeaker spoke again; they made to rise at the same time; at the same moment the waiter materialised and McCord paid him. "So I am afraid," Wilbourne said. "I wasn't afraid then because I was in eclipse but I am awake now and I can be afraid now, thank God. Because this Anno Domini 1938 has no place in it for love. They used money against me while I was asleep because I was vulnerable in money. Then I waked up and rectified the money and I thought I had beat Them until that night when I found out They had used respectability on me and that it was harder to beat than money. So I am vulnerable in neither money nor respectability now and so They will have to find something else to force us to conform to the pattern of human life which has now evolved to do without love—to conform, or die." They entered the train shed—the cavernous gloom in which the constant electricity which knew no day from night burned wanly on toward the iron winter dawn among wisps of steam, in which the long motionless line of darkened pullmans seemed to stand knee-deep, bedded and fixed forever in concrete. They passed the soot-dulled steel walls, the serried cubicles filled with snoring, to the open vestibule. "So I am afraid. Because They are smart, shrewd, They will have to be; if They were to let us beat Them, it would be like unchecked murder and robbery. Of course we cant beat Them; we are doomed of course; that's why I am afraid. And not for me: do you remember that night at the lake when you said I was an old woman being led across the street by a policeman or a boy scout, and that when the drunken car came it would not be the old lady, it would—"

"But why go to Utah in February to beat it? And if you cant beat it, why in hell go to Utah?"

"Because I—" Steam, air, hissed behind them in a long

sigh; the porter appeared suddenly from nowhere like the waiter had done.

"All right, gentlemen," he said. "We're going."

Wilbourne and McCord shook hands. "Maybe I'll write you," Wilbourne said. "Charlotte probably will, anyway. She's a better gentleman than I am, too." He stepped into the vestibule and turned, the porter behind him, his hand on the door knob, waiting; he and McCord looked at one another, the two speeches unspoken between them, each knowing they would not be spoken: *I wont see you again* and *No. You wont see us again.* "Because crows and sparrows get shot out of trees or drowned by floods or killed by hurricanes and fires, but not hawks. And maybe I can be the consort of a falcon, even if I am a sparrow." The train gathered itself, the first, the beginning of motion, departure came back car by car and passed under his feet. "And something I told myself up there at the lake," he said. "That there is something in me she is not mistress to but mother. Well, I have gone a step further." The train moved, he leaned out, McCord moving too to keep pace with him. "That there is something in me you and she parented between you, that you are father of. Give me your blessing."

"Take my curse," McCord said.

Old Man

As the short convict had testified, the tall one, when he returned to the surface, still retained what the short one called the oar. He clung to it, not instinctively against the time when he would be back inside the boat and would need it, because for a time he did not believe he would ever regain the skiff or anything else that would support him, but because he did not have time to think about turning it loose. Things had moved too fast for him. He had not been warned, he had felt the first snatching tug of the current, he had seen the skiff begin to spin and his companion vanish violently upward like in a translation out of Isaiah, then he himself was in the water, struggling against the drag of the paddle which he did not know he still held each time he fought back to the surface and grasped at the spinning skiff which at one instant was ten feet away and the next poised above his head as though about to brain him, until at last he grasped the stern, the drag of his body becoming a rudder to the skiff, the two of them, man and boat and with the paddle perpendicular above them like a jackstaff, vanishing from the view of the short convict (who had vanished from that of the tall one with the same celerity though in a vertical direction) like a tableau snatched offstage intact with violent and incredible speed.

He was now in the channel of a slough, a bayou, in which until today no current had run probably since the old subterranean outrage which had created the country. There was plenty of current in it now though; from his trough behind the stern he seemed to see the trees and sky rushing past with vertiginous speed, looking down at him between the gouts of cold yellow in lugubrious and mournful amazement. But they were fixed and secure in something; he thought of that, he remembered in an instant of despairing rage the firm earth fixed and founded strong and cemented fast and stable forever by the generations of laborious sweat, somewhere beneath him, beyond the reach of his feet, when, and again without warning, the stern of the skiff struck him a stunning blow across the bridge of his nose. The instinct which had caused him to cling to it now caused him to fling the paddle into the

boat in order to grasp the gunwale with both hands just
as the skiff pivoted and spun away again. With both hands
free he now dragged himself over the stern and lay prone on
his face, streaming with blood and water and panting, not
with exhaustion but with that furious rage which is terror's
aftermath.

But he had to get up at once because he believed he had
come much faster (and so further) than he had. So he rose,
out of the watery scarlet puddle in which he had lain, streaming, the soaked denim heavy as iron on his limbs, the black
hair plastered to his skull, the blood-infused water streaking
his jumper, and dragged his forearm gingerly and hurriedly
across his lower face and glanced at it then grasped the paddle
and began to try to swing the skiff back upstream. It did not
even occur to him that he did not know where his companion
was, in which tree among all which he had passed or might
pass. He did not even speculate on that for the reason that he
knew so incontestably that the other was upstream from him,
and after his recent experience the mere connotation of the
term upstream carried a sense of such violence and force and
speed that the conception of it as other than a straight line
was something which the intelligence, reason, simply refused
to harbor, like the notion of a rifle bullet the width of a
cotton field.

The bow began to swing back upstream. It turned readily,
it outpaced the aghast and outraged instant in which he realised it was swinging far too easily, it had swung on over the
arc and lay broadside to the current and began again that vicious spinning while he sat, his teeth bared in his bloody
streaming face while his spent arms flailed the impotent paddle at the water, that innocent-appearing medium which at
one time had held him in iron-like and shifting convolutions
like an anaconda yet which now seemed to offer no more
resistance to the thrust of his urge and need than so much air,
like air: the boat which had threatened him and at last actually
struck him in the face with the shocking violence of a mule's
hoof now seemed to poise weightless upon it like a thistle
bloom, spinning like a wind vane while he flailed at the water
and thought of, envisioned, his companion safe inactive and
at ease in the tree with nothing to do but wait, musing with

impotent and terrified fury upon that arbitrariness of human affairs which had abrogated to the one the secure tree and to the other the hysterical and unmanageable boat for the very reason that it knew that he alone of the two of them would make any attempt to return and rescue his companion.

The skiff had paid off and now ran with the current again. It seemed again to spring from immobility into incredible speed, and he thought he must already be miles away from where his companion had quitted him, though actually he had merely described a big circle since getting back into the skiff and the object (a clump of cypress trees choked by floating logs and debris) which the skiff was now about to strike was the same one it had careened into before when the stern had struck him. He didn't know this because he had not yet ever looked higher than the bow of the boat. He didn't look higher now, he just saw that he was going to strike; he seemed to feel run through the very insentient fabric of the skiff a current of eager gleeful vicious incorrigible wilfulness; and he who had never ceased to flail at the bland treacherous water with what he had believed to be the limit of his strength now from somewhere, some ultimate absolute reserve, produced a final measure of endurance, will to endure which adumbrated mere muscle and nerves, continuing to flail the paddle right up to the instant of striking, completing one last reach thrust and recover out of pure desperate reflex, as a man slipping on ice reaches for his hat and money-pocket, as the skiff struck and hurled him once more flat on his face in the bottom of it.

This time he did not get up at once. He lay flat on his face, slightly spread-eagled and in an attitude almost peaceful, a kind of abject meditation. He would have to get up sometime, he knew that, just as all life consists of having to get up sooner or later and then having to lie down again sooner or later after a while. And he was not exactly exhausted and he was not particularly without hope and he did not especially dread getting up. It merely seemed to him that he had accidentally been caught in a situation in which time and environment, not himself, was mesmerised; he was being toyed with by a current of water going nowhere, beneath a day which would wane toward no evening; when it was done with him it would spew him back into the comparatively safe world he had been snatched violently out of and in the meantime it did not much matter just what he did or did not do. So he lay on his face, now not only feeling but hearing the strong quiet rustling of the current on the underside of the planks, for a while longer. Then he raised his head and this time touched his palm gingerly to his face and looked at the blood again, then he sat up onto his heels and leaning over the gunwale he pinched his nostrils between thumb and finger and expelled a gout of blood and was in the act of wiping his fingers on his thigh when a voice slightly above his line of sight said quietly, "It taken you a while," and he who up to this moment had had neither reason nor time to raise his eyes higher than the bows looked up and saw, sitting in a tree and looking at him, a woman. She was not ten feet away. She sat on the lowest limb of one of the trees holding the jam he had grounded on, in a calico wrapper and an army private's tunic and a sunbonnet, a woman whom he did not even bother to examine since that first startled glance had been ample to reveal to him all the generations of her life and background, who could have been his sister if he had a sister, his wife if he had not entered the penitentiary at an age scarcely out of adolescence and some years younger than that at which even his prolific and monogamous kind married—a woman who sat clutching the trunk of the tree, her stockingless feet in a pair of man's unlaced brogans less than a yard from the water, who was very probably somebody's sister and quite certainly (or certainly should have been) somebody's wife, though this too he had entered the penitentiary too young to have had more than mere theoretical female experience to discover yet. "I thought for a minute you wasn't aiming to come back."

"Come back?"

"After the first time. After you run into this brush pile the first time and got into the boat and went on." He looked about, touching his face tenderly again; it could very well be the same place where the boat had hit him in the face.

"Yah," he said. "I'm here now though."

"Could you maybe get the boat a little closer? I taken a right sharp strain getting up here; maybe I better. . . ." He was not listening; he had just discovered that the paddle was gone; this time when the skiff hurled him forward he had flung the paddle not into it but beyond it. "It's right there in them brush tops," the woman said. "You can get it. Here. Catch a holt of this." It was a grapevine. It had grown up into the tree and the flood had torn the roots loose. She had taken a turn with it about her upper body; she now loosed it and swung it out until he could grasp it. Holding to the end of the vine he warped the skiff around the end of the jam, picking up the paddle, and warped the skiff on beneath the limb and held it and now he watched her move, gather herself heavily and carefully to descend—that heaviness which was not painful but just excruciatingly careful, that profound and almost lethargic awkwardness which added nothing to the sum of that first aghast amazement which had served already for the catafalque of invincible dream since even in durance he had continued (and even with the old avidity, even though they had caused his downfall) to consume the impossible pulp-printed fables carefully censored and as carefully smuggled into the penitentiary; and who to say what Helen, what living Garbo, he had not dreamed of rescuing from what craggy pinnacle or dragoned keep when he and his companion embarked in the skiff. He watched her, he made no further effort to help her beyond holding the skiff savagely steady while she lowered herself from the limb—the entire body, the deformed swell of belly bulging the calico, suspended by its arms, thinking *And this is what I get. This, out of all the female meat that walks, is what I have to be caught in a runaway boat with.*

"Where's that cottonhouse?" he said.

"Cottonhouse?"

"With that fellow on it. The other one."

"I dont know. It's a right smart of cottonhouses around here. With folks on them too, I reckon." She was examining him. "You're bloody as a hog," she said. "You look like a convict."

"Yah," he said, snarled. "I feel like I done already been hung. Well, I got to pick up my pardner and then find that cottonhouse." He cast off. That is, he released his hold on the vine. That was all he had to do, for even while the bow of the skiff hung high on the log jam and even while he held it by the vine in the comparatively dead water behind the jam, he felt steadily and constantly the whisper, the strong purring power of the water just one inch beyond the frail planks on which he squatted and which, as soon as he released the vine, took charge of the skiff not with one powerful clutch but in a series of touches light, tentative, and catlike; he realised now that he had entertained a sort of foundationless hope that the added weight might make the skiff more controllable. During the first moment or two he had a wild (and still foundation-less) belief that it had; he had got the head upstream and managed to hold it so by terrific exertion continued even after he discovered that they were travelling straight enough but stern-first and continued somehow even after the bow began to wear away and swing: the old irresistible movement which he knew well by now, too well to fight against it, so that he let the bow swing on downstream with the hope of utilising the skiff's own momentum to bring it through the full circle and so upstream again, the skiff travelling broadside then bow-first then broadside again, diagonally across the channel, toward the other wall of submerged trees; it began to flee beneath him with terrific speed, they were in an eddy but did not know it, he had no time to draw conclusions or even wonder; he crouched, his teeth bared in his blood-caked and swollen face, his lungs bursting, flailing at the water while the trees stooped hugely down at him. The skiff struck, spun, struck again; the woman half lay in the bow, clutching the gunwales, as if she were trying to crouch behind her own pregnancy; he banged now not at the water but at the living sapblooded wood with the paddle, his desire now not to go anywhere, reach any destination, but just to keep the skiff from beating itself to fragments against the tree trunks. Then something exploded, this time against the back of his head, and stooping trees and dizzy water, the woman's face and all, fled together and vanished in bright soundless flash and glare.

An hour later the skiff came slowly up an old logging road and so out of the bottom, the forest, and into (or onto) a cottonfield—a gray and limitless desolation now free of tur-moil, broken only by a thin line of telephone poles like a wading millipede. The woman was now paddling, steadily and deliberately, with that curious lethargic care, while the convict squatted, his head between his knees, trying to stanch the fresh and apparently inexhaustible flow of blood from his nose with handsfull of water. The woman ceased paddling, the skiff drifted on, slowing, while she looked about. "We're done out," she said.

The convict raised his head and also looked about. "Out where?"

"I thought maybe you might know."

"I dont even know where I used to be. Even if I knowed which way was north, I wouldn't know if that was where I wanted to go." He cupped another handfull of water to his face and lowered his hand and regarded the resulting crimson marbling on his palm, not with dejection, not with concern, but with a kind of sardonic and vicious bemusement. The woman watched the back of his head.

"We got to get somewhere."

"Dont I know it? A fellow on a cottonhouse. Another in a tree. And now that thing in your lap."

"It wasn't due yet. Maybe it was having to climb that tree quick yesterday, and having to set in it all night. I'm doing the best I can. But we better get somewhere soon."

"Yah," the convict said. "I thought I wanted to get somewhere too and I aint had no luck at it. You pick out a place to get to now and we'll try yours. Gimme that oar." The woman passed him the paddle. The boat was a double-ender; he had only to turn around.

"Which way you fixing to go?" the woman said.

"Never you mind that. You just keep on holding on." He began to paddle, on across the cottonfield. It began to rain again, though not hard at first. "Yah," he said. "Ask the boat. I been in it since breakfast and I aint never knowed, where I aimed to go or where I was going either."

That was about one oclock. Toward the end of the afternoon the skiff (they were in a channel of some sort again, they had been in it for some time; they had got into it before they knew it and too late to get out again, granted there had been any reason to get out, as, to the convict anyway, there was certainly none and the fact that their speed had increased again was reason enough to stay in it) shot out upon a broad expanse of debris-filled water which the convict recognised as a river and, from its size, the Yazoo River though it was little enough he had seen of this country which he had not quitted for so much as one single day in the last seven years of his life. What he did not know was that it was now running backward. So as soon as the drift of the skiff indicated the set of the current, he began to paddle in that direction which he believed to be downstream, where he knew there were towns—Yazoo City, and as a last resort, Vicksburg, if his luck was that bad; if not, smaller towns whose names he did not know but where there would be people, houses, something, anything he might reach and surrender his charge to and turn his back on her forever, on all pregnant and female life forever and return to that monastic existence of shotguns and shackles where he would be secure from it. Now, with the imminence of habitations, release from her, he did not even hate her. When he looked upon the swelling and unmanageable body before him it seemed to him that it was not the woman at all but rather a separate demanding threatening inert yet living mass of which both he and she were equally victims; thinking, as he had been for the last three or four hours, of that minute's—nay, second's—aberration of eye or hand which would suffice to precipitate her into the water to be dragged down to death by that senseless millstone which in its turn would not even have to feel agony, he no longer felt any glow of revenge toward her as its custodian, he felt sorry for her as he would for the living timber in a barn which had to be burned to rid itself of vermin.

He paddled on, helping the current, steadily and strongly, with a calculated husbandry of effort, toward what he believed was downstream, towns, people, something to stand upon, while from time to time the woman raised herself to bail the accumulated rain from the skiff. It was raining steadily now though still not hard, still without passion, the sky, the day itself dissolving without grief; the skiff moved in a nimbus, an aura of gray gauze which merged almost without demarcation with the roiling spittle-frothed debris-choked water. Now the day, the light, definitely began to end and the convict permitted himself an extra notch or two of effort because it suddenly seemed to him that the speed of the skiff had lessened. This was actually the case though the convict did not know it. He merely took it as a phenomenon of the increasing obfuscation, or at most as a result of the long day's continuous effort with no food complicated by the ebbing and fluxing phases of anxiety and impotent rage at his absolutely gratuitous predicament. So he stepped up his stroke a beat or so, not from alarm but on the contrary, since he too had received that lift from the mere presence of a known stream, a river known by its ineradicable name to generations of men who had been drawn to live beside it as man always has been drawn to dwell beside water, even before he had a name for water and fire, drawn to the living water, the course of his destiny and his actual physical appearance rigidly coerced and postulated by it. So he was not alarmed. He paddled on, upstream without knowing it, unaware that all the water which for forty hours now had been pouring through the levee break to the north was somewhere ahead of him, on its way back to the River.

It was full dark now. That is, night had completely come, the gray dissolving sky had vanished, yet as though in perverse ratio surface visibility had sharpened, as though the light which the rain of the afternoon had washed out of the air had gathered upon the water as the rain itself had done, so that the yellow flood spread on before him now with a quality almost phosphorescent, right up to the instant where vision ceased. The darkness in fact had its advantages; he could now stop seeing the rain. He and his garments had been wet for more than twenty-four hours now so he had long since stopped feeling it, and now that he could no longer see it either it had in a certain sense ceased for him. Also, he now had to make no effort even not to see the swell of his passenger's belly. So he was paddling on, strongly and steadily, not alarmed and not concerned but just exasperated because he had not yet begun to see any reflection on the clouds which would indicate the city or cities which he believed he was approaching but which were actually now miles behind him, when he heard a sound. He did not know what it was because he had never heard it before and he would never be expected to hear such again since it is not given to every man to hear such at all and to none to hear it more than once in his life. And he was not alarmed now either because there was not time, for although the visibility ahead, for all its clarity, did not extend very far, yet in the next instant to the hearing he was also seeing something such as he had never seen before. This was that the sharp line where the phosphorescent water met the darkness was now about ten feet higher than it had been an instant before and that it was curled forward upon itself like a sheet of dough being rolled out for a pudding. It reared, stooping; the crest of it swirled like the mane of a galloping horse and, phosphorescent too, fretted and flickered like fire. And while the woman huddled in the bow, aware or not aware the convict did not know which, he (the convict), his swollen and blood-streaked face gaped in an expression of aghast and incredulous amazement, continued to paddle directly into it. Again he simply had not had time to order his rhythm-hypnotised muscles to cease. He continued to paddle though the skiff had ceased to move forward at all but seemed to be hanging in space while the paddle still reached thrust recovered and reached again; now instead of space the skiff became abruptly surrounded by a welter of fleeing debris— planks, small buildings, the bodies of drowned yet antic animals, entire trees leaping and diving like porpoises above which the skiff seemed to hover in weightless and airy indecision like a bird above a fleeing countryside, undecided where to light or whether to light at all, while the convict squatted in it still going through the motions of paddling, waiting for an opportunity to scream. He never found it. For an instant the skiff seemed to stand erect on its stern and then shoot scrabbling and scrambling up the curling wall of water like a cat, and soared on above the licking crest itself and hung cradled into the high actual air in the limbs of a tree, from which bower of new-leafed boughs and branches the convict, like a bird in its nest and still waiting his chance to scream and still going through the motions of paddling though he no longer even had the paddle now, looked down upon a world turned to furious motion and in incredible retrograde.

Sometime about midnight, accompanied by a rolling cannonade of thunder and lightning like a battery going into action, as though some forty hours' constipation of the elements, the firmament itself, were discharging in clapping and glaring salute to the ultimate acquiescence to desperate and furious motion, and still leading its charging welter of dead cows and mules and outhouses and cabins and hencoops, the skiff passed Vicksburg. The convict didn't know it. He wasn't looking high enough above the water, who still squatted, clutching the gunwales and glaring at the yellow turmoil about him out of which entire trees, the sharp gables of houses, the long mournful heads of mules which he fended off with a splintered length of plank snatched from he knew not where in passing (and which seemed to glare reproachfully back at him with sightless eyes, in limber-lipped and incredulous amazement) rolled up and then down again, the skiff now travelling forward now sideways now sternward, sometimes in the water, sometimes riding for yards upon the roofs of houses and trees and even upon the backs of the mules as though even in death they were not to escape that burden-bearing doom with which their eunuch race was cursed. But he didn't see Vicksburg; the skiff, travelling at express speed, was in a seething gut between soaring and dizzy banks with a glare of light above them but he did not see it, he saw the flotsam ahead of him divide violently and begin to climb upon itself, mounting, and he was sucked through the resulting gap too fast to recognise it as the trestling of a railroad bridge; for a horrible moment the skiff seemed to hang in static indecision before the looming flank of a steamboat as though undecided whether to climb over it or dive under it, then a hard icy wind filled with the smell and taste and sense of wet and boundless desolation blew upon him; the skiff made one long bounding lunge as the convict's native state, in a final paroxysm, regurgitated him onto the wild bosom of the Father of Waters.

This is how he told about it seven weeks later, sitting in new bedticking garments, shaved and with his hair cut again, on his bunk in the barracks:

During the next three or four hours after the thunder and lightning had spent itself the skiff ran in pitch streaming darkness upon a roiling expanse which, even if he could have seen, apparently had no boundaries. Wild and invisible, it tossed and heaved about and beneath the boat, ridged with dirty phosphorescent foam and filled with a debris of destruction— objects nameless and enormous and invisible which struck and slashed at the skiff and whirled on. He did not know he was now upon the River. At that time he would have refused to believe it, even if he had known. Yesterday he had known he was in a channel by the regularity of the spacing between the bordering trees. Now, since even by daylight he could have seen no boundaries, the last place under the sun (or the streaming sky rather) he would have suspected himself to be would have been a river; if he had pondered at all about his present whereabouts, about the geography beneath him, he would merely have taken himself to be travelling at dizzy and inexplicable speed above the largest cottonfield in the world; if he who yesterday had known he was in a river, had accepted that fact in good faith and earnest, then had seen that river turn without warning and rush back upon him with furious and deadly intent like a frenzied stallion in a lane,—if he had suspected for one second that the wild and limitless expanse on which he now found himself was a river, consciousness would simply have refused; he would have fainted.

When daylight—a gray and ragged dawn filled with driving scud between icy rain-squalls—came and he could see again, he knew he was in no cottonfield. He knew that the wild water on which the skiff tossed and fled flowed above no soil tamely trod by man, behind the straining and surging buttocks of a mule. That was when it occurred to him that its present condition was no phenomenon of a decade, but that the intervening years during which it consented to bear upon its placid and sleepy bosom the frail mechanicals of man's clumsy contriving was the phenomenon and this the norm and the river was now doing what it liked to do, had waited patiently the ten years in order to do, as a mule will work for you ten years for the privilege of kicking you once. And he also learned something else about fear too, something he had even failed to discover on that other occasion when he was really afraid—that three or four seconds of that night in his youth while he looked down the twice-flashing pistol barrel of the terrified mail clerk before the clerk could be persuaded that his (the convict's) pistol would not shoot: that if you just held on long enough a time would come in fear after which it would no longer be agony at all but merely a kind of horrible outrageous itching, as after you have been burned bad.

He did not have to paddle now, he just steered (who had been without food for twenty-four hours now and without any sleep to speak of for fifty) while the skiff sped on across that boiling desolation where he had long since begun to not dare believe he could possibly be where he could not doubt he was, trying with his fragment of splintered plank merely to keep the skiff intact and afloat among the houses and trees and dead animals (the entire towns, stores residences parks and farmyards, which leaped and played about him like fish), not trying to reach any destination, just trying to keep the skiff afloat until he did. He wanted so little. He wanted nothing for himself. He just wanted to get rid of the woman, the belly, and he was trying to do that in the right way, not for himself, but for her. He could have put her back into another tree at any time——

"Or you could have jumped out of the boat and let her and it drown," the plump convict said. "Then they could have give you the ten years for escaping and then hung you for the murder and charged the boat to your folks."

"Yah," the tall convict said.—But he had not done that. He wanted to do it the right way, find somebody, anybody he could surrender her to, something solid he could set her down on and then jump back into the river, if that would please anyone. That was all he wanted—just to come to something, anything. That didn't seem like a great deal to ask. And he couldn't do it. He told how the skiff fled on——

"Didn't you pass nobody?" the plump convict said. "No steamboat, nothing?"

"I dont know," the tall one said.—while he tried merely to keep it afloat, until the darkness thinned and lifted and revealed—

"Darkness?" the plump convict said. "I thought you said it was already daylight."

"Yah," the tall one said. He was rolling a cigarette, pouring the tobacco carefully from a new sack, into the creased paper. "This was another one. They had several while I was gone."
—the skiff to be moving still rapidly up a winding corridor bordered by drowned trees which the convict recognised again to be a river running again in the direction that, until two days ago, had been upstream. He was not exactly warned

through instinct that this one, like that of two days ago, was in reverse. He would not say that he now believed himself to be in the same river, though he would not have been surprised to find that he did believe this, existing now, as he did and had and apparently was to continue for an unnamed period, in a state in which he was toy and pawn on a vicious and inflammable geography. He merely realised that he was in a river again, with all the subsequent inferences of a comprehensible, even if not familiar, portion of the earth's surface. Now he believed that all he had to do would be to paddle far enough and he would come to something horizontal and above water even if not dry and perhaps even populated; and, if fast enough, in time, and that his only other crying urgency was to refrain from looking at the woman who, as vision, the incontrovertible and apparently inescapable presence of his passenger, returned with dawn, had ceased to be a human being and (you could add twenty-four more hours to the first twenty-four and the first fifty now, even counting the hen. It was dead, drowned, caught by one wing under a shingle on a roof which had rolled momentarily up beside the skiff yesterday and he had eaten some of it raw though the woman would not) had become instead one single inert monstrous sentient womb from which, he now believed, if he could only turn his gaze away and keep it away, would disappear, and if he could only keep his gaze from pausing again at the spot it had occupied, would not return. That's what he was doing this time when he discovered the wave was coming.

He didn't know how he discovered it was coming back. He heard no sound, it was nothing felt nor seen. He did not even believe that finding the skiff to be now in slack water—that is, that the motion of the current which, whether right or wrong, had at least been horizontal, had now stopped that and assumed a vertical direction—was sufficient to warn him. Perhaps it was just an invincible and almost fanatic faith in the inventiveness and innate viciousness of that medium on which his destiny was now cast, apparently forever; a sudden conviction far beyond either horror or surprise that now was none too soon for it to prepare to do whatever it was it intended doing. So he whirled the skiff, spun it on its heel like a running horse, whereupon, reversed, he could not even distinguish the very channel he had come up. He did not know whether he simply could not see it or if it had vanished some time ago and he not aware at the time; whether the river had become lost in a drowned world or if the world had become drowned in one limitless river. So now he could not tell if he were running directly before the wave or quartering across its line of charge; all he could do was keep that sense of swiftly accumulating ferocity behind him and paddle as fast as his spent and now numb muscles could be driven, and try not to look at the woman, to wrench his gaze from her and keep it away until he reached something flat and above water. So, gaunt, hollow-eyed, striving and wrenching almost physically at his eyes as if they were two of those suction-tipped rubber arrows shot from the toy gun of a child, his spent muscles obeying not will now but that attenuation beyond mere exhaustion which, mesmeric, can continue easier than cease, he once more drove the skiff full tilt into something it could not pass and, once more hurled violently forward onto his hands and knees, crouching, he glared with his wild swollen face up at the man with the shotgun and said in a harsh, croaking voice: "Vicksburg? Where's Vicksburg?"

Even when he tried to tell it, even after the seven weeks and he safe, secure, rivetted warranted and doubly guaranteed by the ten years they had added to his sentence for attempted escape, something of the old hysteric incredulous outrage came back into his face, his voice, his speech. He never did even get on the other boat. He told how he clung to a strake (it was a dirty unpainted shanty boat with a drunken rake of tin stove pipe, it had been moving when he struck it and apparently it had not even changed course even though the three people on it must have been watching him all the while—a second man, barefoot and with matted hair and beard also at the steering sweep, and then—he did not know how long—a woman leaning in the door, in a filthy assortment of men's garments, watching him too with the same cold speculation) being dragged violently along, trying to state and explain his simple (and to him at least) reasonable desire and need; telling it, trying to tell it, he could feel again the old unforgettable affronting like an ague fit as he watched the abortive tobacco rain steadily and faintly from between his shaking hands and then the paper itself part with a thin dry snapping report:

"Burn my clothes?" the convict cried. "Burn them?"

"How in hell do you expect to escape in them billboards?" the man with the shotgun said. He (the convict) tried to tell it, tried to explain as he had tried to explain not to the three people on the boat alone but to the entire circumambience— desolate water and forlorn trees and sky—not for justification because he needed none and knew that his hearers, the other convicts, required none from him, but rather as, on the point of exhaustion, he might have picked dreamily and incredulously at a suffocation. He told the man with the gun how he and his partner had been given the boat and told to pick up a man and a woman, how he had lost his partner and failed to find the man, and now all in the world he wanted was something flat to leave the woman on until he could find an officer, a sheriff. He thought of home, the place where he had lived almost since childhood, his friends of years whose ways he knew and who knew his ways, the familiar fields where he did work he had learned to do well and to like, the mules with characters he knew and respected as he knew and respected the characters of certain men; he thought of the barracks at night, with screens against the bugs in summer and good stoves in winter and someone to supply the fuel and the food too; the Sunday ball games and the picture shows—things which, with the exception of the ball games, he had never known before. But most of all, his own character (Two years ago they had offered to make a trusty of him. He would no longer need to plow or feed stock, he would only follow those who did with a loaded gun, but he declined. "I reckon I'll stick to plowing," he said, absolutely without humor. "I done already tried to use a gun one time too many.") his good name, his responsibility not only toward those who were responsible toward him but to himself, his own honor in the doing of what was asked of him, his pride in being able to do it, no matter what it was. He thought of this and listened to the man with the gun talking about escape and it seemed to him that, hanging there, being dragged violently along (it was here he said that he first noticed the goats' beards of moss in the trees, though it could have been there for several days so far as he knew. It just happened that he first noticed it here.) that he would simply burst.

"Cant you get it into your head that the last thing I want to do is run away?" he cried. "You can set there with that gun and watch me; I give you fair lief. All I want is to put this woman—"

"And I told you she could come aboard," the man with the gun said in his level voice. "But there aint no room on no boat of mine for nobody hunting a sheriff in no kind of clothes, let alone a penitentiary suit."

"When he steps aboard, knock him in the head with the gun barrel," the man at the sweep said. "He's drunk."

"He aint coming aboard," the man with the gun said. "He's crazy."

Then the woman spoke. She didn't move, leaning in the door, in a pair of faded and patched and filthy overalls like the two men: "Give them some grub and tell them to get out of here." She moved, she crossed the deck and looked down at the convict's companion with her cold sullen face. "How much more time have you got?"

"It wasn't due till next month," the woman in the boat said. "But I—" The woman in overalls turned to the man with the gun.

"Give them some grub," she said. But the man with the gun was still looking down at the woman in the boat.

"Come on," he said to the convict. "Put her aboard, and beat it."

"And what'll happen to you," the woman in overalls said, "when you try to turn her over to an officer. When you lay alongside a sheriff and the sheriff asks you who you are?" Still the man with the gun didn't even look at her. He hardly even shifted the gun across his arm as he struck the woman across the face with the back of his other hand, hard. "You son of a bitch," she said. Still the man with the gun did not even look at her.

"Well?" he said to the convict.

"Dont you see I cant?" the convict cried. "Cant you see that?"

Now, he said, he gave up. He was doomed. That is, he knew now that he had been doomed from the very start never to get rid of her, just as the ones who sent him out with the skiff knew that he never would actually give up; when he recognised one of the objects which the woman in overalls was hurling into the skiff to be a can of condensed milk, he believed it to be a presage, gratuitous and irrevocable as a death-notice over the telegraph, that he was not even to find a flat stationary surface in time for the child to be born on it. So he told how he held the skiff alongside the shanty boat while the first tentative toying of the second wave made up beneath him, while the woman in overalls passed back and forth between house and rail, flinging the food—the hunk of salt meat, the ragged and filthy quilt, the scorched lumps of cold bread which she poured into the skiff from a heaped dishpan like so much garbage—while he clung to the strake against the mounting pull of the current, the new wave which for the moment he had forgotten because he was still trying to state the incredible simplicity of his desire and need until the man with the gun (the only one of the three who wore shoes) began to stamp at his hands, he snatching his hands away one at a time to avoid the heavy shoes then grasping the rail again until the man with the gun kicked at his face, he flinging himself sideways to avoid the shoe and so breaking his hold on the rail, his weight canting the skiff off at a tangent on the increasing current so that it began to leave the shanty boat behind and he paddling again now, violently, as a man hurries toward the precipice for which he knows at last he is doomed, looking back at the other boat, the three faces sullen derisive and grim and rapidly diminishing across the wideing water and at last, apoplectic, suffocating with the intolerable fact not that he had been refused but that he had been refused so little, had wanted so little, asked for so little, yet there had been demanded of him in return the one price out of all breath which (they must have known) if he could have paid it, he would not have been where he was, asking what he asked, raising the paddle and shaking it and screaming curses back at them even after the shotgun flashed and the charge went scuttering past along the water to one side.

So he hung there, he said, shaking the paddle and howling, when suddenly he remembered that other wave, the second wall of water full of houses and dead mules building up behind him back in the swamp. So he quit yelling then and went back to paddling. He was not trying to outrun it. He just knew from experience that when it overtook him, he would have to travel in the same direction it was moving in anyway, whether he wanted to or not, and when it did overtake him, he would begin to move too fast to stop, no matter what places he might come to where he could leave the woman, land her in time. Time: that was his itch now, so his only chance was to stay ahead of it as long as he could and hope to reach something before it struck. So he went on, driving the skiff with muscles which had been too tired so long they had quit feeling it, as when a man has had bad luck for so long that he ceases to believe it is even bad, let alone luck. Even when he ate—the scorched lumps the size of baseballs and the weight and durability of cannel coal even after having lain in the skiff's bilge where the shanty boat woman had thrown them—the iron-like lead-heavy objects which no man would have called bread outside of the crusted and scorched pan in which they had cooked—it was with one hand, begrudging even that from the paddle.

He tried to tell that too—that day while the skiff fled on among the bearded trees while every now and then small quiet tentative exploratory feelers would come up from the wave behind and toy for a moment at the skiff, light and curious, then go on with a faint hissing sighing, almost a chuckling, sound, the skiff going on, driving on with nothing to see but trees and water and solitude: until after a while it no longer seemed to him that he was trying to put space and distance behind him or shorten space and distance ahead but that both he and the wave were now hanging suspended simultaneous and unprogressing in pure time, upon a dreamy desolation in which he paddled on not from any hope even to reach anything at all but merely to keep intact what little of distance the length of the skiff provided between himself and the inert and inescapable mass of female meat before him; then night and the skiff rushing on, fast since any speed over anything unknown and invisible is too fast, with nothing before him and behind him the outrageous idea of a volume of moving water toppling forward, its crest frothed and shredded like fangs, and then dawn again (another of those dreamlike alterations day to dark then back to day again with that quality truncated anachronic and unreal as the waxing and waning of lights in a theatre scene) and the skiff emerging now with the woman no longer supine beneath the shrunken soaked private's coat but sitting bolt upright, gripping the gunwales with both hands, her eyes closed and her lower lip caught between her teeth and he driving the splintered board furiously now, glaring at her out of his wild swollen sleepless face and crying, croaking, "Hold on! For God's sake hold on!"

"I'm trying to," she said. "But hurry! Hurry!" He told it, the unbelievable: hurry, hasten: the man falling from a cliff being told to catch onto something and save himself; the very telling of it emerging shadowy and burlesque, ludicrous comic and mad, from the ague of unbearable forgetting with a quality more dreamily furious than any fable behind proscenium lights:

He was in a basin now— "A basin?" the plump convict said. "That's what you wash in."

"All right," the tall one said, harshly, above his hands. "I did." With a supreme effort he stilled them long enough to release the two bits of cigarette paper and watched them waft in light fluttering indecision to the floor between his feet, holding his hands motionless even for a moment longer.—a basin, a broad peaceful yellow sea which had an abruptly and curiously ordered air, giving him, even at that moment, the impression that it was accustomed to water even if not total submersion; he even remembered the name of it, told to him two or three weeks later by someone: Atchafalaya—

"Louisiana?" the plump convict said. "You mean you were clean out of Mississippi? Hell fire." He stared at the tall one. "Shucks," he said. "That aint but just across from Vicksburg."

"They never named any Vicksburg across from where I was," the tall one said. "It was Baton Rouge they named." And now he began to talk about a town, a little neat white portrait town nestling among enormous very green trees, appearing suddenly in the telling as it probably appeared in actuality, abrupt and airy and miragelike and incredibly serene before him behind a scattering of boats moored to a line of freight cars standing flush to the doors in water. And now he tried to tell that too: how he stood waist-deep in water for a moment looking back and down at the skiff in which the woman half lay, her eyes still closed, her knuckles white on the gunwales and a tiny thread of blood creeping down her chin from her chewed lip, and he looking down at her in a kind of furious desperation.

"How far will I have to walk?" she said.

"I dont know, I tell you!" he cried. "But it's land somewhere yonder! It's land, houses."

"If I try to move, it wont even be born inside a boat," she said. "You'll have to get closer."

"Yes," he cried, wild, desperate, incredulous. "Wait. I'll go and surrender, then they will have—" He didn't finish, wait to finish; he told that too: himself splashing, stumbling, trying to run, sobbing and gasping; now he saw it—another loading platform standing above the yellow flood, the khaki figures on it as before, identical, the same; he said how the intervening days since that first innocent morning telescoped, vanished as if they had never been, the two contiguous succeeding instants (succeeding? simultaneous) and he transported across no intervening space but merely turned in his own footsteps, plunging, splashing, his arms raised, croaking harshly. He heard the startled shout, "There's one of them!", the command, the clash of equipment, the alarmed cry: "There he goes! There he goes!"

"Yes!" he cried, running, plunging, "here I am! Here! Here!" running on, into the first scattered volley, stopping among the bullets, waving his arms, shrieking, "I want to surrender! I want to surrender!" watching not in terror but in amazed and absolutely unbearable outrage as a squatting clump of the khaki figures parted and he saw the machine gun, the blunt thick muzzle slant and drop and probe toward him and he still screaming in his hoarse crow's voice, "I want to surrender! Cant you hear me?", continuing to scream even as he whirled and plunged splashing, ducking, went completely under and heard the bullets going thuck-thuck-thuck on the water above him and he scrabbling still on the bottom, still trying to scream even before he regained his feet and still all submerged save his plunging unmistakable buttocks, the outraged screaming bubbling from his mouth and about his face since he merely wanted to surrender. Then he was comparatively screened, out of range, though not for long. That is (he didn't tell how nor where) there was a moment in which he paused, breathed for a second before running again, the course back to the skiff open for the time being though he could still hear the shouts behind him and now and then a shot, and he panting, sobbing, a long savage tear in the flesh of one hand, got when and how he did not know, and he wasting precious breath, speaking to no one now anymore than the scream of the dying rabbit is addressed to any mortal ear but rather an indictment of all breath and its folly and suffering, its infinite capacity for folly and pain, which seems to be its only immortality: "All in the world I want is just to surrender."

He returned to the skiff and got in and took up his splintered plank. And now when he told this, despite the fury of element which climaxed it, it (the telling) became quite simple; he now even creased another cigarette paper between fingers which did not tremble at all and filled the paper from the tobacco sack without spilling a flake, as though he had passed from the machine gun's barrage into a bourne beyond any more amazement: so that the subsequent part of his narrative seemed to reach his listeners as though from beyond a sheet of slightly milky though still transparent glass, as something not heard but seen—a series of shadows, edgeless yet distinct, and smoothly flowing, logical and unfrantic and making no sound: They were in the skiff, in the center of the broad placid trough which had no boundaries and down which the tiny forlorn skiff flew to the irresistible coercion of a current going once more he knew not where, the neat small liveoak-bowered towns unattainable and miragelike and apparently attached to nothing upon the airy and unchanging horizon. He did not believe them, they did not matter, he was doomed; they were less than the figments of smoke or of delirium, and he driving his unceasing paddle without destination or even hope now, looking now and then at the woman sitting with her knees drawn up and locked and her entire body one terrific clench while the threads of bloody saliva crept from her teeth-clenched lower lip. He was going nowhere and fleeing from nothing, he merely continued to paddle because he had paddled so long now that he believed if he stopped his muscles would scream in agony. So when it happened he was not surprised. He heard the sound which he knew well (he had heard it but once before, true enough, but no man needed hear it but once) and he had been expecting it; he looked back, still driving the paddle, and saw it, curled, crested with its strawlike flotsam of trees and debris and dead beasts and he glared over his shoulder at it for a full minute out of that attenuation far beyond the point of outragement where even suffering, the capability of being further affronted, had ceased, from which he now contemplated with savage and invulnerable curiosity the further extent to which his now anesthetised nerves could bear, what next could be invented for them to bear, until the wave actually began to rear above his head into its thunderous climax. Then only did he turn his head. His stroke did not falter, it neither slowed nor increased; still paddling with that spent hypnotic steadiness, he saw the swimming deer. He did not know what it was nor that he had altered the skiff's course to follow it, he just watched the swimming head before him as the wave boiled down and the skiff rose bodily in the old familiar fashion on a welter of tossing trees and houses and bridges and fences, he still paddling even while the paddle found no purchase save air and still paddled even as he and the deer shot forward side by side at arm's length, he watching the deer now, watching the deer begin to rise out of the water bodily until it was actually running along upon the surface, rising still, soaring clear of the water altogether, vanishing upward in a dying crescendo of splashings and snapping branches, its damp scut flashing upward, the entire animal vanishing upward as smoke vanishes. And now the skiff struck and canted and he was out of it too, standing knee-deep, springing out and falling to his knees, scrambling up, glaring after the vanished deer. "Land!" he croaked. "Land! Hold on! Just hold on!" He caught the woman beneath the arms, dragging her out of the boat, plunging and panting after the vanished deer. Now earth actually appeared—an acclivity smooth and swift and steep, bizarre solid and unbelievable; an Indian mound, and he plunging at the muddy slope, slipping back, the woman struggling in his muddy hands.

"Let me down!" she cried. "Let me down!" But he held her, panting, sobbing, and rushed again at the muddy slope; he had almost reached the flat crest with his now violently unmanageable burden when a stick under his foot gathered itself with thick convulsive speed. *It was a snake* he thought as his feet fled beneath him and with the indubitable last of his strength he half pushed and half flung the woman up the bank as he shot feet first and face down back into that medium upon which he had lived for more days and nights than he could remember and from which he himself had never completely emerged, as if his own failed and spent flesh were attempting to carry out his furious unflagging will for severance at any price, even that of drowning, from the burden with which, unwitting and without choice, he had been doomed. Later it seemed to him that he had carried back beneath the surface with him the sound of the infant's first mewling cry.

The Wild Palms

NEITHER THE MANAGER of the mine nor his wife met them—a couple even less old though considerably harder, in the face at least, than Charlotte and Wilbourne. Their name was Buckner, they called each other Buck and Bill. "Only the name is Billie, i,e," Mrs Buckner said in a harsh Western voice. "I'm from Colorado" (she pronounced the a like in radish). "Buck's from Wyoming."

"It's a perfect whore's name, isn't it?" Charlotte said pleasantly.

"Just what do you mean by that?"

"That's all. I didn't mean to offend. It would be a good whore. That's what I would try to be."

Mrs Buckner looked at her. (This was while Buckner and Wilbourne were up at the commissary, getting the blankets and the sheep coats and woollen underwear and socks.) "You and him aint married, are you?"

"What made you think that?"

"I dont know. You can just tell somehow."

"No we're not. I hope you dont mind, since we're going to live in the same house together."

"Why should I? Me and Buck wasn't married for a while either. But we are now all right." Her voice was not triumphant, it was smug. "And I've got it put away good too. Even Buck dont know where. Not that that would make any difference. Buck's all right. But it dont do a girl any harm to be safe."

"What put away?"

"The paper. The license." Later (she was cooking the evening meal now and Wilbourne and Buckner were still across the canyon at the mine) she said, "Make him marry you."

"Maybe I will," Charlotte said.

"You make him. It's better that way. Especially when you get jammed."

"Are you jammed?"

"Yes. About a month."

In fact, when the ore train—a dummy engine with neither

616

head nor rear and three cars and a cubicle of caboose containing mostly stove—reached the snow-choked railhead there was no one in sight at all save a grimed giant upon whom they had apparently come by complete surprise, in a grimed sheep-lined coat, with pale eyes which looked as if he had not slept much lately in a grimed face which obviously had not been shaved and doubtless not been washed in some time—a Pole, with an air fierce proud and wild and a little hysterical, who spoke no English, jabbering, gesturing violently toward the opposite wall of the canyon where a half dozen houses made mostly of sheet iron and window-deep in drifts, clung. The canyon was not wide, it was a ditch, a gutter, it soared, swooping, the pristine snow scarred and blemished by and dwarfing the shaft entrance, the refuse dump, the few buildings; beyond the canyon rims the actual unassailable peaks rose, cloud-ravelled in some incredible wind, on the dirty sky. "It will be beautiful in the spring," Charlotte said.

"It had better be," Wilbourne said.

"It will be. It is now. But let's go somewhere. I'm going to freeze in a minute."

Again Wilbourne tried the Pole. "Manager," he said. "Which house?"

"Yah; boss," the Pole said. He flung his hand again toward the opposite canyon wall, he moved with incredible speed for all his size and, Charlotte starting momentarily back before she caught herself, he pointed at her thin slippers in the trodden ankle-deep snow then took both lapels of her coat in his grimed hands and drew them about her throat and face with almost a woman's gentleness, the pale eyes stooping at her with an expression at once fierce wild and tender; he shoved her forward, patting her back, he actually gave her a definite hard slap on the bottom. "Ron," he said. "Ron."

Then they saw and entered the path crossing the narrow valley. That is, it was not exactly a path free of snow or snow-packed by feet, it was merely that here the snow level was lower, the width of a single man between the two snow banks and so protected somewhat from the wind. "Maybe he lives in the mine and only comes home over the week-end," Charlotte said.

"But he's got a wife, they told me. What would she do?"

"Maybe the ore train just comes once a week too."

"You must not have seen the engineer."

"We haven't seen his wife, either," she said. She made a sound of disgust. "That wasn't even funny. Excuse me, Wilbourne."

"I do."

"Excuse me, mountains. Excuse me, snow. I think I'm going to freeze."

"She wasn't there this morning, anyway," Wilbourne said. Nor was the manager at the mine. They chose a house, not at random and not because it was the largest, which it was not, and not even because there was a thermometer (it registered fourteen degrees above zero) beside the door, but simply because it was the first house they came to and now they had both become profoundly and ineradicably intimate with cold for the first time in their lives, a cold which left an ineffaceable and unforgettable mark somewhere on the spirit and memory like first sex experience or the experience of taking human life. Wilbourne knocked once at this door with a hand which could not even feel the wood and did not wait for an answer, opening it and thrusting Charlotte ahead of him into a single room where a man and a woman, sitting identical in woollen shirts and jeans pants and shoeless woollen socks on either side of a dog-eared pack of cards laid out for a game of some sort on a plank across a nail keg, looked up at them in amazement.

"You mean *he* sent you out here? Callaghan himself?" Buckner said.

"Yes," Wilbourne said. He could hear Charlotte and Mrs Buckner where Charlotte stood over the heater about ten feet away (it burned gasoline; when a match was struck to it, which happened only when they had to turn it off to refill the tank, since it burned otherwise all the time, night and day, it took fire with a bang and glare which after a while even Wilbourne got used to and no longer clapped his mouth shut just before his heart jumped out) talking: "Is them all the clothes you brought out here? You'll freeze. Buck'll have to go to the commissary." — "Yes," Wilbourne said. "Why? Who else would send me?"

"You — ah — you didn't bring anything? Letter or nothing?"

"No. He said I wouldn't—"

"Oh, I see. You paid your own way. Railroad fare."

"No. He paid it."

"Well I'll be damned," Buckner said. He turned his head toward his wife. "You hear that, Bill?"

"What?" Wilbourne said. "What's wrong?"

"Never mind now," Buckner said. "We'll go up to the commissary and get you fixed up for sleeping, and some warmer clothes than them you've got. He didn't even tell you to buy yourself a couple of Roebuck sheep coats, did he?"

"No," Wilbourne said. "But let me get warm first."

"You wont never get warm out here," Buckner said. "If you sit over a stove trying to, waiting to, you wont ever move. You'll starve, you wont even get up to fill the stove tank when it burns out. The thing is, to make up your mind you will always be a little cold even in bed and just go on about your business and after a while you will get used to it and forget it and then you wont even notice you are cold because you will have forgotten what being warm was ever like. So come on now. You can take my coat."

"What will you do?"

"It aint far. I have a sweater. Carrying the stuff will warm us up some."

The commissary was another iron single room filled with the iron cold and lighted by the hushed iron glare of the snow beyond a single window. The cold in it was a dead cold. It was like aspic, almost solid to move through, the body reluctant as though, and with justice, more than to breathe, live, was too much to ask of it. On either side rose wooden shelves, gloomy and barren save for the lower ones, as if this room too were a thermometer not to measure cold but moribundity, an incontrovertible centigrade (*We should have brought the Bad Smell* Wilbourne was already thinking), a contracting mercury of sham which was not even grandiose. They hauled down the blankets, the sheep coats and woollens and galoshes; they felt like ice, like iron, stiff; carrying them back to the cabin Wilbourne's lungs (he had forgot the altitude) labored at the rigid air which felt like fire in them.

"So you're a doctor," Buckner said.

"I'm the doctor," Wilbourne said. They were outside

now. Buckner locked the door again. Wilbourne looked out across the canyon, toward the opposite wall with its tiny life-less scar of mine entrance and refuse dump. "Just what's wrong here?"

"I'll show you after a while. Are you a doctor?"

Now Wilbourne looked at him. "I just told you I was. What do you mean?"

"Then I guess you've got something to show it. Degree: what do they call them?"

Wilbourne looked at him. "Just what are you getting at? Am I to be responsible to you for my capabilities, or to the man who is paying my salary?"

"Salary?" Buckner laughed harshly. Then he stopped. "I guess I am going about this wrong. I never aimed to rub your fur crossways. When a man comes into my country and you offer him a job and he claims he can ride, we want proof that he can and he wouldn't get mad when we asked him for it. We would even furnish him a horse to prove it on only it wouldn't be the best horse we had and if we never had but one horse and it would be a good horse, it wouldn't be that one. So we wouldn't have a horse for him to prove it on and we would have to ask him. That's what I'm doing now." He looked at Wilbourne, sober and intent, out of hazel eyes in a gaunt face like raw beef muscle.

"Oh," Wilbourne said. "I see. I have a degree from a pretty fair medical school. I had almost finished my course in a well-known hospital. Then I would have been—known, anyway; that is, they would have admitted publicly that I knew—about what any doctor knows, and more than some probably. Or at least I hope so. Does that satisfy you?"

"Yes," Buckner said. "That's all right." He turned and went on. "You wanted to know what's wrong here. We'll leave these things at the cabin and go over to the shaft and I'll show you." They left the blankets and woollens at the cabin and crossed the canyon, the path which was no path just as the commissary had not been a commissary but a sort of in-scrutable signpost like a code word set beside a road.

"That ore train we came up on," Wilbourne said. "What was in it when it went down to the valley?"

"Oh, it was loaded," Buckner said. "It has to get there

loaded. Leave here loaded, anyway. I see to that. I dont want my throat cut until I know it."

"Loaded with what?"

"Ah," Buckner said. The mine was not a shaft, it was a gallery pitching at once straight back into the bowels of the rock—a round tube like the muzzle of a howitzer, shored with timbers and filled with the dying snow-glare as they advanced, and the same dead aspic-like cold that was in the commissary and lined by two light gauge rails along which as they entered (they stepped quickly aside for it or they would have been run down) came a filled ore tram pushed by a running man whom Wilbourne recognised also to be a Pole though shorter, thicker, squatter (he was to realise later that none of them were the giants they seemed, that the illusion of size was an aura, an emanation of that wild childlike innocence and credulity which they possessed in common)—the same pale eyes, the same grimed unshaven face above the same filthy sheep-lined coat.

"I thought—" Wilbourne began. But he did not say it. They went on; the last glare of the snow faded and now they entered a scene like something out of an Eisenstein Dante. The gallery became a small amphitheatre, branching off in smaller galleries like the spread fingers from a palm, lighted by an incredible extravagance of electricity as though for a festival—an extravagance of dirty bulbs which had, though in inverse ratio, that same air of sham and moribundity which the big, almost barren building labeled *Commissary* in tremendous new letters had—in the light from which still more of the grimed, giant-seeming men in sheep coats and with eyes which had not slept much lately worked with picks and shovels with that same frenzy of the man running behind the loaded tram, with shouts and ejaculations in that tongue which Wilbourne could not understand almost exactly like a college baseball team cheering one another on, while from the smaller galleries which they had not penetrated yet and where still more electric bulbs glared in the dust-laden and icy air came either echoes or the cries of still other men, meaningless and weird, filling the heavy air like blind erratic birds. "He told me you had Chinese and Italians too," Wilbourne said.

"Yah," Buckner said. "They left. The chinks left in October.

I waked up one morning and they were gone. All of them.
They walked down, I guess. With their shirt tails hanging out
and in them straw slippers. But then there wasn't much snow
in October. Not all the way down, anyhow. They smelled it.
The wops—"

"Smelled it?"

"There hasn't been a payroll in here since September."

"Oh," Wilbourne said. "I see now. Yes. So they smelled it.
Like niggers do."

"I dont know. I never had any smokes here. The wops
made a little more noise. They struck, all proper. Threw down
their picks and shovels and walked out. There was a—what
do you call it? deputation?—waited on me. Considerable talk,
all pretty loud, and a lot of hands, the women standing outside in the snow, holding up the babies for me to look at. So
I opened the commissary and gave them all a woollen shirt
apiece, men women and children (you should have seen them,
the kids in a man's shirt, the ones that were just big enough
to walk I mean. They wore them outside, like overcoats.) and
a can of beans apiece and sent them out on the ore train.
There was still a considerable hands, fists now, and I could
hear them for a good while after the train was out of sight.
Going down Hogben (he runs the ore train; the railroad pays
him) just uses the engine to brake with, so it dont make much
fuss. Not as much as they did, anyway. But the hunkies
stayed."

"Why? Didn't they—"

"Find out that everything had blew? They dont understand
good. Oh, they could hear all right; the wops could talk to
them: one of the wops was the interpreter for them. But they
are queer people; they dont understand dishonesty. I guess
when the wops tried to tell them, it just didn't make sense,
that a man could let folks keep on working without intending
to pay them. So now they think they are making overtime.
Doing all the work. They are not trammers or miners either,
they are blasters. There's something about a hunky that likes
dynamite. Maybe it's the noise. But now they are doing it all.
They wanted to put their women in here too. I understood
that after a while and stopped it. That's why they dont sleep
much. They think that when the money comes tomorrow,

they'll get all of it. They probably think now you brought it
and that Saturday night they'll all get thousands of dollars
apiece. They're like kids. They will believe anything. That's
why when they find out you have kidded them, they kill you.
Oh, not with a knife in the back and not even with a knife,
they walk right up to you and stick the stick of dynamite into
your pocket and hold you with one hand while they strike the
match to the fuse with the other."

"And you haven't told them?"

"Told them how? I cant talk to them; the interpreter was
one of the wops. Besides, he's got to keep his mine looking
like it's running and that's what I am supposed to do. So he
can keep on selling the stock. That's why you are here—a
doctor. When he told you there wouldn't be any medical inspectors out here to worry you about a license, he told you
the truth. But there are mining inspectors out here, laws and
regulations for running mines that say there must be a doctor.
That's why he paid you and your wife's fare out here. Besides,
the money might come in. When I saw you this morning I
thought you had brought it too. Well? Seen enough?"

"Yes," Wilbourne said. They returned toward the entrance;
once more they stepped quickly aside to let a filled ore tram
pass, pushed at a run by another grimed and frantic Pole.
They emerged into the living cold of the immaculate snow,
the fading day. "I dont believe it," Wilbourne said.

"You saw, didn't you?"

"I mean the reason you are still here. You were not expecting any money."

"Maybe I'm waiting for a chance to slip away. And these
bastards wont even go to sleep at night and give me one.—
Hell," he said. "That's a lie too. I waited here because it's
winter and I might as well be here as any where else, long as
there is enough grub in the commissary and we can keep
warm. And because I knew he would have to send another
doctor soon or come here himself and tell me and them wild
bastards in there the mine is closed."

"Well, here I am," Wilbourne said. "He sent another doctor. What is it you want of a doctor?"

For a long moment Buckner looked at him—the hard little
eyes which would have had to be good at measuring and

commanding men of a sort, a class, a type, or he would not be where he now was; the hard eyes which perhaps never before, Wilbourne told himself, had been faced with the need of measuring a man who merely claimed to be a doctor. "Listen," he said. "I've got a good job, only I haven't had any pay since September. We've saved about three hundred bucks, to get out of here with when this does blow, and to live on until I can find something else. And now Bill turns up a month gone with a kid and we cant afford a kid. And you claim to be a doctor and I believe you are. How about it?"

"No," Wilbourne said.

"It's my risk. I'll see you are clear."

"No," Wilbourne said.

"You mean you dont know how?"

"I know how. It's simple enough. One of the men in the hospital did it once—emergency patient—maybe to show us what never to do. He didn't need to show me."

"I'll give you a hundred bucks."

"I've got a hundred bucks," Wilbourne said.

"A hundred and fifty bucks. That's half of it. You see I cant do more."

"I've got a hundred and fifty bucks too. I've got a hundred and eighty-five bucks. And even if I didn't have but ten bucks—"

Buckner turned away. "You're lucky. Let's go eat."

He told Charlotte about it. Not in bed, as they had used to talk, because they all slept in the same room—the cabin had but one, with a lean-to for what privacy was absolutely required—but outside the cabin where, knee-deep in snow, in the galoshes now, they could see the opposite canyon wall and the serrated cloud-ravelled peaks beyond, where Charlotte said again, indomitable: "It will be beautiful in the spring."

"And you said no," she said. "Why? Was it the hundred dollars?"

"You know better than that. It was a hundred and fifty, incidentally."

"Low I may be, but not that low?"

"No. It was because I——"

"You are afraid?"

"No. It's nothing. Simple enough. A touch with the blade to let the air in. It's because I—"

"Women do die of it though."

"Because the operator was no good. Maybe one in ten thousand. Of course there are no records. It's because I—"

"It's all right. It's not because the price was too low, nor because you are afraid. That's all I wanted to know. You dont have to. Nobody can make you. Kiss me. We cant even kiss inside, let alone——"

The four of them (Charlotte now slept in the woollen underwear like the others) slept in the one room, not in beds but on mattresses on the floor ("It's warmer that way," Buckner explained. "Cold comes from underneath.") and the gasoline stove burned constantly. They had opposite corners but even at that the two mattresses were not fifteen feet apart, so Wilbourne and Charlotte could not even talk, whisper. It meant less to the Buckners though, even though they seemed to have little enough of preliminary talking and whispering to do; at times and with the lamp not five minutes dark Wilbourne and Charlotte would hear the abrupt stallion-like surge from the other bed, the violent blanket-muffled motion ceasing into the woman's panting moans and at times a series of pure screams tumbling over one another, though such was not for them. Then one day the thermometer reversed itself from fourteen below to forty-one below and they moved the two mattresses together and slept as a unit, the two women in the middle, and still sometimes before the light was scarcely out (or perhaps they would be wakened by it) there would come the ruthless stallion crash with no word spoken, as if they had been drawn violently and savagely to one another out of pure slumber like steel and magnet, the fierce breathing, the panting and shuddering woman-moans, and Charlotte saying, "Cant you all do that without pulling the covers loose?" and still it was not for them.

They had been there a month, it was almost March now and the spring for which Charlotte waited that much nearer, when one afternoon Wilbourne returned from the mine where the dirty and unsleeping Poles still labored in that fierce deluded frenzy and the blind birdlike incomprehensible voices still flew back and forth among the dusty extravagant electric bulbs, and found Charlotte and Mrs Buckner watching the cabin door as he entered. And he knew what was coming and perhaps even that he was already done for. "Listen, Harry," she said. "They are going to leave. They've got to. It's all up here and they have only three hundred dollars, to get where they are going and to live on until he can find work. So they've got to do something before it's too late."

"So have we," he said. "And we haven't got three hundred dollars."

"We haven't got a baby either. We haven't had bad luck. You said it's simple, that only one in ten thousand die, that you know how to do it, that you are not afraid. And they want to take the risk."

"Do you want a hundred dollars that bad?"

"Have I ever? ever talked about money, except the hundred and twenty-five of mine you wouldn't take? You know that. Just as I know you wouldn't take their money."

"I'm sorry. I didn't mean that. It's because I—"

"It's because they are in trouble. Suppose it was us. I know you will have to throw away something. But we have thrown away a lot, threw it away for love and we're not sorry."

"No," he said. "Not sorry. Never."

"This is for love too. Not ours maybe. But love." She went to the shelf on which they kept their personal effects and took down the meagre case of instruments with which he had been equipped before he left Chicago, along with the two railroad tickets. "This would be good for him to know, if he could know it: that the only time you ever used them was to amputate his manager from the mine. What else do you need?"

Buckner came up beside Wilbourne. "All right?" he said. "I'm not afraid and she aint. Because you're all right. I aint watched you for a month for nothing. Maybe if you had agreed quick, right off, that first day, I wouldn't let you, I'd be afraid. But not now. I'll take all the risk and I'll remember my promise: I'll see you are clear. And it aint a hundred, it's still a hundred and fifty."

He tried to say No, he tried hard. *Yes* he thought quietly *I have thrown away lots, but apparently not this. Honesty about money, security, degree* and then for a terrible moment he thought *Maybe I would have thrown away love first too* but he stopped this in time; he said, "You haven't got enough money, even if your name were Callaghan. I'll just take all the risk instead."

Three days later they who had not been met walked with the Buckners across the canyon to the waiting ore train. Wilbourne had steadily refused even the hundred dollars, accepting at last and instead of it a hundred dollar assignment on Buckner's back pay which they both knew would never be paid, this to be expended against its equivalent in food from the commissary, whose key Buckner had surrendered to him. "It sounds damn foolish to me," Buckner said. "The commissary is yours anyway."

"It will keep the books balanced," Wilbourne said. They followed the path which was no path, to the train, the engine with neither head nor tail, the three ore cars, the toy caboose. Buckner looked up at the mine, the gaping orifice, the refuse dump scarring the pristine snow. It was clear now, the sun low and thin above the serrated rosy peaks in a sky of incredible blue. "What will they think when they find you are gone?"

"Maybe they will think I have gone after the money myself. I hope they do, for your sake." Then he said, "They are better off here. No worries about rent and such and getting drunk and then getting sober again, enough food to keep you all until spring. And they have something to do, keep the days filled, and nights to lie in bed and count up that overtime. A man can go a long way on what he thinks he's going to get. And he may send some money yet."

"Do you believe that?"

"No," Buckner said. "Dont you believe it either."

"I dont think I ever have," Wilbourne said. "Not even that day in his office. Maybe even less then than at any time." They were standing a little aside from the two women. "Look, when you get out and find a chance, have her see a doctor. A good one. Tell him the truth."

"What for?" Buckner said.

"I'd rather you would. I'd feel easier."

"Nah," the other said. "She's all right. Because you're all right. If I hadn't known that, do you think I'd a let you do it?" Now it was time, the locomotive blew a shrill peanut-whistle blast, the Buckners got into the caboose and it began to move. Charlotte and Wilbourne looked after it for only a moment, then Charlotte turned, already running. The sun was almost down, the peaks ineffable and tender, the sky amber and azure; for an instant Wilbourne heard the voices from the mine, wild faint and incomprehensible.

"Oh God," Charlotte said. "Let's dont even eat tonight. Hurry. Run." She ran on, then she stopped and turned, the broad blunt face rosy in the reflected pink, the eyes now green with it above the shapeless sheep collar of the shapeless coat. "No," she said. "You run in front, so I can be undressing us both in the snow. But run." But he did not go ahead, he did not even run, he walked so he could watch her diminishing ahead of him along the path which was no path, then mounting the other wall toward the cabin, who, save for the fact that she wore them with the same abrupt obliviousness with which she wore dresses, should never have worn pants at all, and entered the cabin and found her now stripping off even the woollen underwear. "Hurry," she said. "Hurry. Six weeks. I have almost forgotten how. No," she said, "I'll never forget that. You never forget that, thank you sweet God." Then she said, holding him, the hard arms and thighs: "I guess I am a sissy about love. I never could, even with just one other people in the bed with us."

They didn't get up to prepare or eat supper. After a time they slept; Wilbourne waked somewhere in the rigid night to find the stove had gone out and the room freezing cold. He thought of Charlotte's undergarment where she had flung it away onto the floor; she would need it, she should have it on now. But it too would be like iron ice and he thought for a while about getting up and fetching it into the bed and thawing it, warming it beneath his body until she could put it on and at last he found will power to begin to move but at once she clutched him. "Where you going?" He told her. She clutched him, hard. "When I get cold, you can always cover me."

Each day he would visit the mine, where the frenzied and unabated work continued. On the first visit the men looked at him not with curiosity or surprise but merely with interrogation, obviously looking for Buckner too. But nothing else happened and he realised that they did not even know probably that he was merely the mine's official doctor, that they recognised in him only another American (he almost said white man), another representative of that remote golden unchallengeable Power in which they held blind faith and trust. He and Charlotte began to discuss the question of telling them, trying to. "Only what good would it do?" he said. "Buckner was right. Where would they go, and what would they do when they got there? There's plenty of food for them here to last out the winter, and they probably haven't saved any money (granted they ever got square with the commissary even when they were being paid enough wages to save) and like Buckner said, you can live pretty happy a long time on illusion. Maybe you aren't happy any other time. I mean, if you are a hunky that never learned anything else but how to time a dynamite fuse five hundred feet underground. And another thing. We've still got three quarters of the hundred dollars in grub ourselves, and if everybody left here, somebody would hear about it and he might even send a man in here to pick up the other three cans of beans."

"And something else too," Charlotte said. "They cant go now. They cant walk out in this snow. Hadn't you noticed?"

"Noticed what?"

"That little toy train hasn't been back since it took the Buckners out. That's two weeks ago."

He hadn't noticed this, he did not know if it would come back again, so they agreed that the next time it appeared they would wait no longer, they would tell (or try to tell) the men in the mine. Then two weeks later the train did return. They crossed the canyon to where the wild filthy jabbering men were already beginning to load the cars. "Now what?" Wilbourne said. "I cant talk to them."

"Yes you can. Someway. They believe you are the boss now and nobody yet ever failed to understand the man he believes is his boss. Try to get them over to the commissary."

Wilbourne moved forward, over to the loading chute in which the first tram of ore was already rattling, and raised his hand. "Wait," he said loudly. The men paused, looking at him out of the gaunt pale-eyed faces. "Commissary," he shouted. "Store!" jerking his arm toward the opposite canyon wall;

now he recalled the word which the first one, the one who drew up Charlotte's coat for her that first day, had used. "Ron," he said. "Ron." They looked at him a moment longer, silently, the eyes round beneath the brute-like and terrific arching of pale brows, the expressions eager, puzzled, and wild. Then they looked at one another, they huddled, jabbering in that harsh incomprehensible tongue. Then they moved toward him in a body. "No, no," he said. "All." He gestured toward the mine shaft. "All of you." Someone comprehended quickly this time, almost at once the short one whom Wilbourne had seen behind the galloping ore tram on his first visit to the mine dashed out of the group and up the snowy slope on his short strong thick piston-like legs and vanished into the orifice and reappeared, followed by the rest of the endless shift. These mingled with the first group, jabbering and gesticulating. Then they all ceased and looked at Wilbourne, obedient and subdued. "Look at their faces," he said. "God, I hate to be the one to have to do this. Damn Buckner anyway."

"Come on," Charlotte said. "Let's get it over." They crossed the valley, the miners following, incredibly dirty against the snow—the faces of a poorly made-up and starving black-face minstrel troupe—to the commissary. Wilbourne unlocked the door. Then he saw at the rear of the group five women. He and Charlotte had never seen them before; they seemed to have sprung from the snow itself, shawled; two of them carried infants, one of which could not have been a month old.

"My God," Wilbourne said. "They dont even know I'm a doctor. They dont even know they are supposed to have a doctor, that the law requires that they have one." He and Charlotte entered. In the gloom after the snow-glare the faces vanished and only the eyes watched him out of nothing, subdued, patient, obedient, trusting and wild. "Now what?" he said again. Then he began to watch Charlotte and now they all watched her, the five women pushing forward also to see, as she fastened with four tacks produced from somewhere a sheet of wrapping paper to the end of a section of shelves where the light from the single window fell on it and began to draw swiftly with one of the scraps of charcoal she had brought from Chicago—the elevation of a wall in cross section with a grilled window in it unmistakably a pay window and as unmistakably shut, on one side of the window a number of people unmistakably miners (she had even included the woman with the baby); on the other side of the window an enormous man (she had never seen Callaghan, he had merely described him to her, yet the man was Callaghan) sitting behind a table heaped with glittering coins which the man was shovelling into a sack with a huge hand on which glittered a diamond the size of a ping pong ball. Then she stepped aside. For a moment longer there was no sound. Then an indescribable cry rose, fierce but not loud, only the shrill voices of the women much more than a whisper, wailing, and they turned as one upon Wilbourne, the wild pale frenzied eyes glaring at him with at once incredulous ferocity and profound reproach.

"Wait!" Charlotte cried. "Wait!" They paused; they watched her once more as the crayon moved, and now, at the rear of the throng waiting outside the closed window Wilbourne saw his own face emerge from beneath the flying chalk; anyone would have recognised him: they did at once. The sound ceased, they looked at Wilbourne then at one another in bewilderment. Then they looked at Charlotte again as she ripped the paper from the wall and began to attach a fresh sheet; this time one of them stepped forward and helped her, Wilbourne too watching the flying crayon again. This time it was himself, indubitably himself and indubitably a doctor, anyone would have known it—the horn glasses, the hospital tunic every charity patient, every hunky gutted by flying rock or steel or premature dynamite and coming to in company emergency stations, has seen, a bottle which was indubitably medicine in one hand, a spoonful of which he was offering to a man who was compositely all of them, every man who ever labored in the bowels of earth—the same wild unshaven look, even the sheepskin collar, and behind the doctor the same huge hand with its huge diamond in the act of extracting from the doctor's pocket a wallet thin as paper. Again the eyes turned toward Wilbourne, the reproach gone now and only the ferocity remaining and that not at him. He gestured toward the remaining laden shelves. Presently he was able to reach Charlotte in the pandemonium and take her arm.

"Come on," he said. "Let's get out of here." Later (he had returned to the ore train, where Hogben, its entire crew, sat over the red hot stove in the caboose not much larger than a broom closet. "You'll be back in thirty days then," Wilbourne said. "I have to make a trip every thirty days for us to hold the franchise," Hogben said. "You better bring your wife on out now."—"We'll wait," Wilbourne said. Then he returned to the cabin and he and Charlotte stood in the door and watched the crowd emerge from the commissary with its piti-ful loot and later cross the canyon and board the ore train, filling the three open cars. The temperature was not forty-one now, neither was it back up to fourteen. The train moved; they could see the tiny faces looking back at the mine en-trance, the refuse dump, with incredulous bewilderment, a kind of shocked and unbelieving sorrow; as the train moved a burst of voices reached across the canyon to them, faint with distance, forlorn, grieving, and wild) he said to Charlotte, "Thank God we got our grub out first."

"Maybe it wasn't ours," she said soberly.

"Buckner's then. They hadn't paid him either."

"But he ran away. They didn't."

It was still nearer spring then; by the time the ore train made its next ritualistic and empty visitation perhaps they would see the beginning of the mountain spring which nei-ther of them had seen and did not know would not appear until that time which in their experience was the beginning of summer. They talked of this at night now, with the thermom-eter again sometimes at forty-one. But they could at least talk in bed now, in the dark where beneath the blankets Charlotte would, after an amount of savage heaving and twisting (this too ritualistic) emerge from the woollen undergarment to sleep in the old fashion. She would not fling it out from be-neath the blankets but would keep it inside, a massy wad upon and beneath and around which they slept, so it would be warm for the morning. One night she said, "You haven't heard from Buckner yet. But of course you haven't; how could you have."

"No," he said, suddenly sober. "And I wish I would. I told

him to take her to a doctor soon as they got out. But he probably— He promised to write me."

"I wish you would too."

"We may have a letter when the ore train comes back for us."

"If it comes back." But he suspected nothing, though later it seemed incredible to him that he had not, even though at the time he could not have said why he should have suspected, on what evidence. But he did not. Then one day about a week before the ore train was due there was a knock and he opened the door upon a man with a mountain face and a pack and a pair of slung snow shoes on his back.

"You Wilbourne?" he said. "Got a letter for you." He produced it—a pencilled envelope smudged with handling and three weeks old.

"Thanks," Wilbourne said. "Come in and eat."

But the other declined. "One of them big airplanes fell somewhere back in yonder just before Christmas. You hear or see anything about that time?"

"I wasn't here then," Wilbourne said. "You better eat first."

"There's a reward for it. I guess I wont stop."

The letter was from Buckner. It said *Everything O K Buck*. Charlotte took it from him and stood looking at it. "That's what you said. You said it was simple, didn't you. Now you feel all right about it."

"Yes," Wilbourne said. "I am relieved."

Charlotte looked at the letter, the four words, counting O and K as two. "Just one in ten thousand. All you have to do is be reasonably careful, isn't it. Boil the tools and so forth. Does it matter who you do it on?"

"They have to be fe—" Then he stopped. He looked at her, he thought swiftly *Something is about to happen to me. Wait. Wait.* "Do it on?"

She looked at the letter. "That was foolish, wasn't it. Maybe I was mixed up with incest." Now it did happen to him. He began to tremble, he was trembling even before he grasped her shoulder and jerked her about to face him.

"Do it on?"

She looked at him, still holding the cheap ruled sheet with its heavy pencilling—the sober intent gaze with that greenish cast which the snow gave her eyes. She spoke in short brutal sentences like out of a primer. "That night. That first night alone. When we couldn't wait to cook supper. When the stove went out my douche bag was hanging behind it. It froze and when we lit the stove again I forgot it and it burst."

"And every time since then you didn't—"

"I should have known better. I always did take easy. Too easy. I remember somebody telling me once, I was young then, that when people loved, hard, really loved each other, they didn't have children, the seed got burned up in the love, the passion. Maybe I believed it. Wanted to believe it because I didn't have a douche bag anymore. Or maybe I just hoped. Anyway it's done."

"When?" he said, shaking her, trembling. "How long since you missed? Are you sure?"

"Sure that I missed? Yes. Sixteen days."

"But you're not sure," he said, rapidly, knowing he was talking only to himself: "You cant be sure yet. Sometimes they miss, any woman. You can never be sure until two—"

"Do you believe that?" she said quietly. "That's just when you want a child. And I dont and you dont because we cant. I can starve and you can starve but not it. So we must, Harry."

"No!" he cried. "No!"

"You said it was simple. We have proof it is, that it's nothing, no more than clipping an ingrowing toenail. I'm strong and healthy as she is. Dont you believe that?"

"Ah," he cried. "So you tried it on her first. That was it. You wanted to see if she would die or not. That's why you were so bent on selling me the idea when I had already said no—"

"The stove went out the night after they left, Harry. But yes, I did wait to hear from her first. She would have done the same if it had been me first. I would have wanted her to. I would have wanted her to live whether I did or not just as she would want me to live whether she did or not, just as I want to live."

"Yes," he said. "I know. I didn't mean that. But you— you—"

"So it's all right. It's simple. You know that now by your own hand."

"No! No!"

"All right," she said quietly. "Maybe we can find a doctor to do it when we go out next week."

"No!" he cried, shouted, gripping her shoulder, shaking her. "Do you hear me?"

"You mean no one else shall do it, and you wont?"

"Yes! That's what I mean! That's exactly what I mean!"

"Are you that afraid?"

"Yes!" he said. "Yes!"

The next week passed. He took to walking, slogging and plunging in the waist-deep drifts, *not to not see her; it's because I cant breathe in there* he told himself; once he went up to the mine even, the deserted gallery dark now of the extravagant and unneeded bulbs though it still seemed to him that he could hear the voices, the blind birds, the echoes of that frenzied and incomprehensible human speech which still remained, hanging batlike and perhaps head-down about the dead corridors until his presence startled them into flight. But sooner or later the cold—something—would drive him back to the cabin and they did not quarrel simply because she refused to be drawn into one and again he would think *She is not only a better man and a better gentleman than I am, she is a better everything than I will ever be* They ate together, went through the day's routine, they slept together to keep from freezing; now and then he took her (and she accepted him) in a kind of frenzy of immolation, saying, crying, "At least it doesn't matter now; at least you wont have to get up in the cold." Then it would be day again; he would refill the tank when the stove burned out; he would carry out and throw into the snow the cans which they had opened for the last meal, and there would be nothing else for him to do, nothing else under the sun for him to do. So he would walk (there was a pair of snow shoes in the cabin but he never tried to use them) among but mostly into the drifts which he had not yet learned to distinguish in time to avoid, wallowing and plunging, thinking, talking to himself aloud, weighing a thousand expedients: *A kind of pill* he thought—this, a trained doctor: *whores use them, they are supposed to work, they must work, something must; it cant be this difficult, this much of a price* and not believing it, knowing that he would never be able to make himself believe it, thinking *And this is the price of the twenty-six years, the two thousand dollars I stretched over four of them by not smoking, by keeping my virginity until it damn near spoiled on me, the dollar and two dollars a week or a month my sister could not afford to send: that I should have deprived myself of all hope forever of anesthesia from either pills or pamphlets. And now anything else is completely out* "So there's just one thing left," he said, aloud, in a kind of calm like that which follows the deliberate ridding of the stomach of a source of nausea. "Just one thing left. We'll go where it is warm, where it wont cost so much to live, where I can find work and we can afford a baby and if no work, charity wards, orphanages, doorsteps anyway. No, no, not orphanage; not doorstep. We can do it, we must do it; I will find something, anything.—Yes!" he thought, cried aloud into the immaculate desolation, with harsh and terrible sardonicism, "I will set up as a professional abortionist." Then he would return to the cabin and still they did not quarrel simply because she would not, this not through any forbearance feigned or real nor because she herself was subdued and afraid but simply because (and he knew this too and he cursed himself for this too in the snow) she knew that one of them must keep some sort of head and she knew beforehand it would not be him.

Then the ore train came. He had packed the remaining provisions out of Buckner's theoretical hundred dollars into a box. They loaded this and the two bags with which they had left New Orleans almost exactly a year ago and themselves into the toy caboose. At the mainline junction he sold the cans of beans and salmon and lard, the sacks of sugar and coffee and flour, to a small store-keeper for twenty-one dollars. They rode two nights and a day in day coaches and left the snow behind and found buses now, cheaper now, her head tilted back against the machine-made doily, her face in profile against the dark fleeing snow-free countryside and the little lost towns, the neon, the lunch rooms with broad strong Western girls got up out of Hollywood magazines (Hollywood which is no longer in Hollywood but is stippled by a billion feet of burning colored gas across the face of the American earth) to resemble Joan Crawford, asleep or not he could not tell.

They reached San Antonio, Texas, with a hundred and fifty-two dollars and a few cents. It was warm here, it was almost like New Orleans; the pepper trees had been green all winter and the oleander and mimosa and lantana were already in bloom and cabbage palms exploded shabbily in the mild air as in Louisiana. They had a single room with a decrepit gas plate, reached by an outside gallery in a shabby wooden house. And now they did quarrel. "Cant you see?" she said. "My period would come now, tomorrow. Now is the time, the simple time to do it. Like you did with her—what's her name? the whore's name? Bill. Billie, i,e. You shouldn't have let me learn so much about it. I wouldn't know how to pick my time to worry you then."

"Apparently you learned about it without any help from me," he said, trying to restrain himself, cursing himself: *You bastard, she's the one that's in trouble; it's not you.* "I had settled it. I had said no. You were the one who—" Now he did stop himself, rein himself in. "Listen. There's a pill of some sort. You take it when your time is due. I'll try to get some of them."

"Try where?'

"Where would I try? Who would ever need such? At a brothel. Oh God, Charlotte! Charlotte!"

"I know," she said. "We cant help it. It's not us now. That's why: dont you see? I want it to be us again, quick, quick. We have so little time. In twenty years I cant anymore and in fifty years we'll both be dead. So hurry. Hurry."

He had never been in a brothel in his life and had never even sought one before. So now he discovered what a lot of people have: how difficult it is to find one; how you lived in the duplex for ten years before you discovered that the late-sleeping ladies next door were not night-shift telephone girls. At last that occurred to him which the veriest yokel seems to inherit with breath: he asked a taxi-driver and was presently set down before a house a good deal like the one he lived in and pressed a button which made no audible response though presently a curtain over the narrow window beside the door fell a second before he could have sworn someone had looked out at him. Then the door opened, a negro maid conducted him down a dim hallway and into a room containing a bare veneered dining-table bearing an imitation cut-glass punch bowl and scarred by the white rings from damp glass-bottoms, a pianola slotted for coins, and twelve chairs ranged along the four walls in orderly sequence like tombstones in a military graveyard, where the maid left him to sit and look at a lithograph of the Saint Bernard dog saving the child from the snow and another of President Roosevelt, until there entered a double-chinned woman of no especial age more than forty, with blondined hair and a lilac satin gown not quite clean. "Good evening," she said. "Stranger in town?"

"Yes," he told her. "I asked a taxi-driver. He—"

"Dont apologise," she said. "The drivers is all my friends here."

He remembered the driver's parting advice: "The first white person you see, buy them some beer. You'll be jake then."—"Wont you have some beer?" he said.

"Why, I dont mind if I do," the woman said. "It might refresh us." Immediately (she had rung no bell that Wilbourne could see) the maid entered. "Two beers, Louisa," the woman said. The maid went out. The woman sat down too. "So you're a stranger in San Tone. Well, some of the sweetest friendships I ever seen was made in one night or even after one session between two folks that never even seen one another an hour ago. I got American girls here or Spanish (strangers like Spanish girls, once, anyway. It's the influence of the moving pictures, I always say) and one little Eyetalian that just—" The maid entered with two tankards of beer. It could not have been much further away than wherever it was she had been standing when the woman in purple had rung no bell that Wilbourne could see. The maid went out.

"No," he said. "I dont want—I came here—I—" The woman was watching him; she had started to raise her mug. Instead she set it back on the table, watching him. "I'm in trouble," he said quietly. "I hoped you could help me."

Now the woman even withdrew her hand from the tankard and he saw now that her eyes, even if they were no less muddy, were also no less cold than the big diamond at her breast. "And just what made you think I could or would help you out of whatever your trouble is? the driver tell you that too? What'd he look like? You take his number?"

"No," Wilbourne said. "I—"

"Never mind that now. What kind of trouble are you in?" He told her, simply and quietly, while she watched him. "H'm," she said. "And so you, a stranger here, found right off a taxi-driver that brought you straight to me to find a doctor to do your business. Well, well." Now she did ring the bell, not violently, just hard.

"No, no, I dont—" *She even keeps a doctor in the house* he thought. "I dont—"

"Undoubtless," the woman said. "It's all a mistake. You'll get back to the hotel or wherever it is and find you just drempt your wife was knocked up or even that you had a wife."

"I wish I would," Wilbourne said. "But I—" The door opened and a man entered, a biggish man, fairly young, bulging his clothes a little, who gave Wilbourne a hot, embracing, almost loverlike glare out of hot brown flesh-bedded eyes beneath the straight innocently parted hair of a little boy and continued to look at him from then on. His neck was shaved.

"Thatim?" he said over his shoulder to the woman in purple, in a voice husky with prolonged whiskey begun at too early an age yet withal the voice of a disposition cheerful, happy, even joyous. He did not even wait for an answer, he came straight to Wilbourne and before the other could move plucked him from the chair with one hamlike hand. "Whadya mean, you sonafabitch, coming into a respectable house and acting like a sonafabitch? hah?" He glared at Wilbourne happily. "Out?" he said.

"Yah," the woman in purple said. "Then I want to find that taxi-driver." Wilbourne began to struggle. At once the young man turned upon him with loverlike joy, beaming. "Not in here," the woman said sharply. "Out, like I told you, you ape."

"I'll go," Wilbourne said. "You can turn me loose."

"Yah; sure, you sonafabitch," the young man said. "I'll just help you. You got helped in, see. This way." They were in the hall again, now there was a small slight black-haired dark-faced man also, in dingy trousers and a tieless blue shirt: a Mexican servant of some sort. They went on to the door, the back of Wilbourne's coat bunched in the young man's huge hand. The young man opened it. *The brute will have to hit me once* Wilbourne thought. *Or he will burst, suffocate. But all right. All right.*

"Maybe you could tell me," he said. "All I want is—"

"Yah; sure," the young man said. "Maybe I awda sockm, Pete. Whadya think?"

"Sockm," the Mexican said.

He did not even feel the fist. He felt the low stoop strike him across the back, then the grass already damp with dew, before he began to feel his face at all. "Maybe you could tell me—" he said.

"Yah; sure," the young man said in his hoarse happy voice, "ask me another." The door slammed. After a while Wilbourne got up. Now he could feel his eye, the whole side of his face, his whole head, the slow painful pounding of the blood, though in the drugstore mirror presently (it was on the first corner he came to, he entered it; he was indeed learning fast the things he should have known before he was nineteen years old) he could see no discoloration yet. But the mark was apparent, something was, because the clerk said,

"What happened to your face, mister?"

"Fight," he said. "I knocked up my girl. I want something for it."

For a moment the clerk looked at him, hard. Then he said, "Cost you five bucks."

"Do you guarantee it?"

"Nah."

"All right. I'll take it."

It was a small tin box, unlettered. It contained five objects which might have been coffee beans. "He said whiskey would help, and moving around. He said to take two of them tonight and go somewhere and dance." She took all five of them, they went out and got two pints of whiskey and found at last a dance hall full of cheap colored bulbs and khaki uniforms and rentable partners or hostesses.

"Drink some of it too," she said. "Does your face hurt very bad now?"

"No," he said. "Drink it. Drink all you can."

"God," she said. "You cant dance, can you?"

"No," he said. "Yes. Yes, I can dance." They moved about the floor, bumped and shoved and bumping and shoving, somnambulistic and sometimes in step, during each short phase of hysterical music. By eleven oclock she had drunk almost half of one of the bottles but it only made her sick. He waited until she emerged from the washroom, her face the color of putty, the eyes indomitable and yellow. "You lost the pills too," he said.

"Two of them. I was afraid of that so I used the basin and washed them off and took them again. Where's the bottle?"

They had to go out for her to drink, then they returned. At twelve she had almost finished the first bottle and the lights were turned off save for a spot light which played on a revolving globe of colored glass, so that the dancers moved with the faces of corpses in a wheeling of colored mote-beams resembling a marine nightmare. There was a man with a megaphone; it was a dancing contest and they did not even know it; the music crashed and ceased, the lights flared on, the air was filled by the bellowing megaphone and the winning couple moved forward. "I'm sick again," she said. Once more he waited for her—the putty face, the indomitable eyes. "I washed them off again," she said. "But I cant drink anymore. Come on. They close at one oclock."

Perhaps they were coffee beans because after three days nothing had happened and after five days even he admitted that the time had passed. Now they did quarrel, he cursing himself for it as he sat on his park benches reading the help wanted columns in newspapers grubbed out of trash bins while he waited for his black eye, his shiner, to disappear so he could apply decently for work, cursing himself because she had borne up for so long and would and could continue to bear up save that he had worn her out at last, knowing he had done this, swearing he would change, stop it. But when he returned to the room (she was thinner now and there was something in her eyes; all the pills and whiskey had done was to put something in her eyes that had not been there before) it would be as if his promises had never been made, she cursing him now and striking at him with her hard fists then catching herself, clinging to him, crying, "Oh, God, Harry, make me stop! Make me hush! Bust the hell out of me!" Then they would lie holding one another, fully dressed now, in a sort of peace for a time.

"It'll be all right," he said. "A lot of people have to do it these days. Charity wards are not bad. Then we can find someone to take the baby until I can—"

"No. It wont do, Harry. It wont do."

"I know it sounds bad at first. Charity. But charity isn't—"

"Damn charity. Have I ever cared where money comes from, where or how we lived, had to live? It's not that. They hurt too much."

"I know that too. But women have been bearing children—You have borne two yourself—"

"Damn pain too. I take easy and breed hard but damn that, I'm used to that, I dont mind that. I said they hurt too much. Too damned much." Then he understood, knew what she meant; he thought quietly, as he had thought before, that she had already and scarcely knowing him given up more than he would ever possess to relinquish, remembering the old tried true incontrovertible words: *Bone of my bone, blood and flesh and even memory of my blood and flesh and memory*. You dont beat it, he told himself. You dont beat it that easy. He was about to say, "But this will be ours," when he realised that this was it, this was exactly it.

But still he could not say yes, could not say "All right." He could say it to himself on the park benches, he could hold his hand out and it would not shake. But he could not say the word to her; he would lie beside her, holding her while she slept, and he would watch the ultimate last of his courage and manhood leave him. "That's right," he would whisper to himself, "stall. Stall. She will be in the fourth month soon, then I can tell myself I know it is too late to risk it; even she will believe then." Then she would wake and it would start all over—the reasoning which got nowhere becoming the quarreling and then the cursing until she would catch herself and cling to him, crying in frantic despair: "Harry! Harry! What are we doing? We, we, *us!* Make me hush! Bust me! Knock me cold!" This last time he held her until she was quiet. "Harry, will you make a compact with me?"

"Yes," he said wearily. "Anything."

"A compact. And then until it's up, we will never mention

pregnancy again." She named the date when her next period would have come; it was thirteen days away. "That's the best time, and after that it will be four months and it will be too late to risk it. So from now until then we wont even talk about it; I will try to make things as easy as possible while you look for a job, a good job that will support three of us—"

"No," he said. "No! No!"

"Wait," she said. "You promised. —then if you haven't found a job by that time, you will do it, take it away from me."

"No!" he cried. "I wont! Never!"

"But you promised," she said, quietly, gently, slowly, as if he were a child just learning English. "Dont you see there is nothing else?"

"I promised; yes. But I didn't mean—"

"I told you once how I believe it isn't love that dies, it's the man and the woman, something in the man and the woman that dies, doesn't deserve the chance anymore to love. And look at us now. We have the child, only we both know we cant have it, cant afford to have it. And they hurt too bad, Harry. Too damned bad. I'm going to hold you to the promise, Harry. And so from now until that day comes, we wont even have to mention it, think about it again. Kiss me." After a moment he leaned to her. Not touching otherwise, they kissed, as brother and sister might.

Now it was like Chicago again, the first weeks there while he went from hospital to hospital, the interviews which seemed to die, to begin to wilt and fade tranquilly at a given identical instant, he already foreknowing this and expecting it and so meeting the obsequy decently. But not now, not this time. In Chicago he would think *I imagine I am going to fail* and he would fail; now he knew he was going to fail and he refused to believe it, refused to accept no for an answer until threatened almost with physical violence. He was not trying hospitals alone, he was trying anyone, anything. He told lies, any lie; he approached appointments with a frantic cold maniacal determination which was inherent with its own negation; he promised anyone that he could and would do anything; walking along the street one afternoon he glanced up by sheer chance and saw a doctor's sign and entered and actually offered to perform any abortions thrown his way for half the fee, stated his experience and (he realised later when comparatively sane again) only his ejection by force forestalled his showing Buckner's letter as a testimonial to his ability.

Then one day he returned home in the middle of the afternoon. He stood outside his own door for a long time before he opened it. And even then he did not enter but stood instead in the opening with on his head a cheap white bellows-topped peaked cap with a yellow band—the solitary insigne of a rankless W.P.A. school crossing guard—and his heart cold and still with a grief and despair that was almost peaceful. "I get ten dollars a week," he said.

"Oh you monkey!" she said, then for the last time in his life he saw her cry. "You bastard! You damned bastard! So you can rape little girls in parks on Saturday afternoons!" She came and snatched the cap from his head and hurled it into the fireplace (a broken grate hanging by one side and stuffed with faded frilled paper which had once been either red or purple) and then clung to him, crying hard, the hard tears springing and streaming. "You bastard, you damned bastard, you damned damned damned—"

She boiled the water herself and fetched out the meagre instruments they had supplied him with in Chicago and which he had used but once, then lying on the bed she looked up at him. "It's all right. It's simple. You know that; you did it before."

"Yes," he said. "Simple. You just have to let the air in. All you have to do is let the air—" Then he began to tremble again. "Charlotte. Charlotte."

"That's all. Just a touch. Then the air gets in and tomorrow it will be all over and I will be all right and it will be us again forever and ever."

"Yes. Ever and ever. But I'll have to wait a minute, until my hand—Look. It wont stop. I cant make it stop."

"All right. We'll wait a minute. It's simple. It's funny. New, I mean. We've done this lots of ways but not with knives, have we? There. Now your hand has stopped."

"Charlotte," he said. "Charlotte."

"It's all right. We know how. What was it you told me nigger women say? Ride me down, Harry."

And now, sitting on his bench in Audubon Park lush green and bright with the Louisiana summer already fully accomplished although it was not yet June, and filled with the cries of children and the sound of pram wheels like the Chicago apartment had been, he watched against his eyelids the cab (it had been told to wait) stopping before the neat and unremarkable though absolutely unimpugnable door and she getting out of the cab in the dark dress carried a full year and better, for three thousand miles and better, in the bag from last spring and mounting the steps. Now the bell, perhaps the same negro maid: "Why, Miss—" then nothing, remembering who paid the wages, though probably not since by ordinary negroes quit an employment following death or division. And now the room, as he had first seen it, the room in which she said, "Harry—do they call you Harry?—what are we going to do?" (*Well, I did it* he thought. *She will have to admit that*) He could see them, the two of them, Rittenmeyer in the double-breasted suit (it might be flannel now but it would be dark flannel, obtruding smoothly its unobtrusive cut and cost); the four of them, Charlotte here and the three others yonder, the two children which were unremarkable, the daughters, the one with the mother's hair but nothing else, the other, the younger one, with nothing, the younger sitting perhaps on the father's knee, the other, the older, leaning against him; the three faces, the one impeccable, the two of them invincible and irrevocable, the second cold and unwinking, the third merely unwinking; he could see them, he could hear them:

'*Go speak to your mother, Charlotte. Take Ann with you.*'

'*I dont want to.*'

'*Go. Take Ann's hand.*' He could hear, see them: Rittenmeyer setting the little one onto the floor, the older one takes her hand and they approach. *And now she will take the little one onto her lap, it staring at her still with that intent absolutely blank detachment of infants, the older one leans to her, obedient, cold, suffering the caress, already withdrawing before the kiss is completed, and returns to her father; an instant later Charlotte sees her beckoning, gesturing in violent surreptitious pantomime to the little one. So Charlotte sets the little one onto the floor again and it returns to the father, turning against his knee and already hunching one buttock toward its father's lap as children do, still staring at Charlotte with that detachment empty even of curiosity.*

'Let them go,' Charlotte says.

'You want them sent away?'

'Yes. They want to go.' The children depart. And now he hears her; it is not Charlotte; he knows that as Rittenmeyer never will: *'So that's what you have taught them.'*

'I? I taught them? I taught them nothing!' he cries. *'Nothing! It wasn't me who—'*

'I know. I'm sorry. I didn't mean that. I have not—Have they been well?'

'Yes. As I wrote you. If you will recall, for several months I had no address. The letters were returned. You may have them when and if you like. You dont look well yourself. Is that why you came back home? or have you come back home?'

'To see the children. And to give you this.' She produces the check, double-signed and perforated against any tampering, the slip of paper more than a year old, creased and intact and only a little worn.

'You came home on his money then. Then it belongs to him.'

'No. It's yours.'

'I refuse to accept it.'

'So would he.'

'Then burn it. Destroy it.'

'Why? Why do you wish to hurt yourself? Why do you like suffering, when there is so much of it that has to be done, so damned much. Give it to the children. A bequest. If not from me, from Ralph then. He is still their uncle. He has not harmed you.'

'A bequest?' he says. Then she tells him. Oh yes, Wilbourne told himself, she will tell him; he could see it, hear it—the two people between whom something like love must have existed once, or who at least had known together the physical striving with which alone the flesh can try to capture what little it is ever to know of love. Oh, she will tell him; he could see and hear her as she lays the check upon the table at her hand and tells him:

'It was a month ago. It was all right, only I kept on losing blood

and it got to be pretty bad. Then all of a sudden two days ago the blood stopped and so there is something wrong, which might be something badder still—what do they call it? toxemia, septicemia? It doesn't matter—that we are watching for. Waiting for.'

The men who passed the bench he sat on walked in linen suits, and now he began to notice a general exodus from the park—the negro nursemaids who managed to lend a quality bizarre and dazzling even to their starched white-crossed blue, the children moving with thin cries in bright random like blown petals, across the green. It was near noon; Charlotte would have been in the house more than half an hour. *Because it will take that long* he thought, seeing and hearing them: *He is trying to persuade her to go to a hospital at once, the best, the best doctors; he will assume all blame, tell all the lies; he insists, calm, not at all importunate and not to be denied.*

'No. H— he knows a place. On the Mississippi coast. We are going there. We will get a doctor there if necessary.'

'The Mississippi coast? Why in God's name the Mississippi coast? A country doctor in a little lost Mississippi shrimping village when in New Orleans there are the best, the very best—'

'We may not need a doctor after all. And we can live cheaper there until we find out.'

'You have money for coast vacations then.'

'We have money.' It was dead noon now; the air fell still, the stippled shadows unmoving upon his lap, upon the six bills in his hand, the two twenties, the five, the three ones, hearing them, seeing them:

'Take up the check again. It is not mine.'

'Nor mine. Let me go my way, Francis. A year ago you let me choose and I chose. I will stick to it. I wont have you retract, break your oath to yourself. But I want to ask one thing of you.'

'Of me? A favor?'

'If you like. I dont ask a promise. Maybe what I am trying to express is just a wish. Not hope; wish. If anything happens to me.'

'If anything happens to you. What am I to do?'

'Nothing.'

'Nothing?'

'Yes. Against him. I dont ask it for his sake nor even for mine. I ask it for the sake of—of—I dont even know what I am trying to

say. For the sake of all the men and women who ever lived and blundered but meant the best and all that ever will live and blunder but mean the best. For your sake maybe, since yours is suffering too—if there is any such thing as suffering, if any of us ever did, if any of us were ever born strong enough and good enough to be worthy to love or suffer either. Maybe what I am trying to say is justice.'

'*Justice?*' And now he could hear Rittenmeyer laughing, who had never laughed since laughter is the yesterday's slight beard, the negligee among emotions. '*Justice? This, to me? Justice?*' *Now she rises; he too: they face one another.*

'*I didn't ask a promise,*' *she says.* '*That would have been too much to ask.*'

'*Of me.*'

'*Of anyone. Any man or woman. Not only you.*'

'*But it is I who give none. Remember. Remember. I said you could come back home when you wished, and I would take you back, into my house at least. But can you expect that again? from any man? Tell me; you spoke once of justice; tell me that.*'

'*I dont expect it. I told you before that maybe what I was trying to say was hope.*' *She will turn now,* he told himself, *approaching the door, and they will stand looking at one another and maybe it will be like McCord and me in the Chicago station that night last*—He stopped. He was about to say 'last year' and he ceased and sat perfectly still and said aloud in quiet amazement, "That night was not five months ago."—*and they will both know they will never see one another again and neither of them will say it.* '*Goodbye, Rat,*' *she says. And he will not answer* he thought *No. He will not answer, this man of ultimatums, upon whom for the rest of his life will yearly devolve the necessity for decrees which he knows before hand he cannot support, who would have denied the promise she did not ask yet would perform the act and she to know this well, too well too well;—this face impeccable and invincible upon which all existing light in the room will have seemed to gather as though in benediction, affirmation not of righteousness but rightness, having been consistently and incontrovertibly right; and withal tragic too since in the being right there was nothing of consolation nor of peace.*

Now it would be time. He rose from the bench and followed the curve of blanched oyster shells between the massy bloom of oleander and wygelia, jasmine japonica and orange, toward the exit and the street, beneath the noon. The cab came up, slowing into the curb; the driver opened the door. "Station," Wilbourne said.

"Union Station?"

"No. The one for Mobile. The coast." He got in. The door closed, the cab went on; the scaling palm trunks began to flee past. "They were both well?" he said.

"Listen," she said. "If we're going to get it."

"Get it?"

"You'll know in time, wont you?"

"We're not going to get anything. I'm going to hold you. Haven't I held you so far?"

"Dont be a fool now. There's no time now. You'll know in time. Get to hell out, do you hear?"

"Out?"

"Promise me. Dont you know what they'll do to you? You cant lie to anybody, even if you would. And you couldn't help me. But you'll know in time. Just telephone an ambulance or the police or something and wire Rat and get to hell out fast. Promise me."

"I'm going to hold you," he said. "That's what I'll promise you. They were both well?"

"Yes," she said; the scaling palm trunks fled constantly past. "They were all right."

Old Man

WHEN THE WOMAN asked him if he had a knife, standing there in the streaming bedticking garments which had got him shot at, the second time by a machine gun, on the two occasions when he had seen any human life after leaving the levee four days ago, the convict felt exactly as he had in the fleeing skiff when the woman suggested that they had better hurry. He felt the same outrageous affronting of a condition purely moral, the same raging impotence to find any answer to it; so that, standing above her, spent suffocating and inarticulate, it was a full minute before he comprehended that she was now crying, "The can! The can in the boat!" He did not anticipate what she could want with it, he did not even wonder nor stop to ask. He turned running; this time he thought *It's another moccasin* as the thick body truncated in that awkward reflex which had nothing of alarm in it but only alertness, he not even shifting his stride though he knew his running foot would fall within a yard of the flat head. The bow of the skiff was well up the slope now where the wave had set it and there was another snake just crawling over the stern into it and as he stooped for the bailing can he saw something else swimming toward the mound, he didn't know what—a head, a face at the apex of a vee of ripples. He snatched up the can; by pure juxtaposition of it and water he scooped it full, already turning. He saw the deer again, or another one. That is, he saw a deer—a side glance, the light smoke-colored phantom in a cypress vista then gone, vanished, he not pausing to look after it, galloping back to the woman and kneeling with the can to her lips until she told him better.

It had contained a pint of beans or tomatoes, something, hermetically sealed and opened by four blows of an axe heel, the metal flap turned back, the jagged edges razor-sharp. She told him how, and he used this in lieu of a knife, he removed one of his shoelaces and cut it in two with the sharp tin. Then she wanted warm water—"If I just had a little hot water," she said in a weak serene voice without particular hope, only when he thought of matches it was again a good deal like when she had asked him if he had a knife, until she fumbled in the pocket of the shrunken tunic (it had a darker double vee on one cuff and a darker blotch on one shoulder where service stripes and a divisional emblem had been ripped off but this meant nothing to him) and produced a matchbox contrived by telescoping two shotgun shells. So he drew her back a little from the water and went to hunt wood dry enough to burn, thinking this time *It's just another snake* only, he said, he should have thought *ten thousand other snakes*: and now he knew it was not the same deer because he saw three at one time, does or bucks he did not know which since they were all antlerless in May and besides he had never seen one of any kind anywhere before except on a Christmas card; and then the rabbit, drowned, dead anyway, already torn open, the bird, the hawk, standing upon it—the erected crest, the hard vicious patrician nose, the intolerant omnivorous yellow eye—and he kicking at it, kicking it lurching and broad-winged into the actual air.

When he returned with the wood and the dead rabbit the baby, wrapped in the tunic, lay wedged between two cypress-knees and the woman was not in sight, though while the convict knelt in the mud, blowing and nursing his meagre flame, she came slowly and weakly from the direction of the water. Then, the water heated at last and there produced from somewhere he was never to know, she herself perhaps never to know until the need comes, no woman perhaps ever to know, only no woman will even wonder, that square of something somewhere between sackcloth and silk;—squatting, his own wet garments steaming in the fire's heat, he watched her bathe the child with a savage curiosity and interest that became amazed unbelief, so that at last he stood above them both, looking down at the tiny terra cotta colored creature resembling nothing, and thought *And this is all. This is what severed me violently from all I ever knew and did not wish to leave and cast me upon a medium I was born to fear, to fetch up at last in a place I never saw before and where I do not even know where I am.*

Then he returned to the water and refilled the bailing can. It was drawing toward sunset now (or what would have been sunset save for the high prevailing overcast) of this day whose beginning he could not even remember; when he returned to where the fire burned in the interlaced gloom of the cypresses, even after this short absence, evening had definitely come, as though darkness too had taken refuge upon that quarter-acre mound, that earthen ark out of Genesis, that dim wet cypress-choaked life-teeming constricted desolation in what direction and how far from what and where he had no more idea than of the day of the month, and had now with the setting of the sun crept forth again to spread upon the waters. He stewed the rabbit in sections while the fire burned redder and redder in the darkness where the shy wild eyes of small animals— once the tall mild almost plate-sized stare of one of the deer— glowed and vanished and glowed again, the broth hot and rank after the four days; he seemed to hear the roar of his own saliva as he watched the woman sip the first canful. Then he drank too, they ate the other fragments which had been charring and scorching on willow twigs; it was full night now. "You and him better sleep in the boat," the convict said. "We want to get an early start tomorrow." He shoved the bow of the skiff off the land so it would lie level, he length-ened the painter with a piece of grapevine and returned to the fire and tied the grapevine about his wrist and lay down. It was mud he lay upon, but it was solid underneath, it was earth, it did not move; if you fell upon it you broke your bones against its incontrovertible passivity sometimes but it did not accept you substanceless and enveloping and suffocat-ing, down and down and down; it was hard at times to drive a plow through, it sent you spent, weary, and cursing its light-long insatiable demands back to your bunk at sunset at times but it did not snatch you violently out of all familiar knowing and sweep you thrall and impotent for days against any returning. *I dont know where I am and I dont reckon I know the way back to where I want to go* he thought. *But at least the boat has stopped long enough to give me a chance to turn it around*

He waked at dawn, the light faint, the sky jonquil-colored; the day would be fine. The fire had burned out; on the op-posite side of the cold ashes lay three snakes motionless and parallel as underscoring, and in the swiftly making light others seemed to materialise: earth which an instant before had been mere earth broke up into motionless coils and loops, branches which a moment before had been mere branches now become immobile ophidian festoons even as the convict stood thinking about food, about something hot before they started. But he decided against this, against wasting this much time, since there still remained in the skiff quite a few of the rocklike objects which the shanty woman had flung into it, besides (thinking this) no matter how fast nor successfully he hunted, he would never be able to lay up enough food to get them back to where they wanted to go. So he returned to the skiff, paying himself back to it by his vine-spliced painter, back to the water on which a low mist thick as cotton batting (though apparently not very tall, deep) lay, into which the stern of the skiff was already beginning to disappear although it lay with its prow almost touching the mound. The woman waked, stirred. "We fixing to start now?" she said.

"Yah," the convict said. "You aint aiming to have another one this morning, are you?" He got in and shoved the skiff clear of the land, which immediately began to dissolve into the mist. "Hand me the oar," he said over his shoulder, not turning yet.

"The oar?"

He turned his head. "The oar. You're laying on it." But she was not, and for an instant during which the mound, the island continued to fade slowly into the mist which seemed to enclose the skiff in weightless and impalpable wool like a precious or fragile bauble or jewel, the convict squatted not in dismay but in that frantic and astonished outrage of a man who, having just escaped a falling safe, is struck by the following two-ounce paper weight which was sitting on it: this the more unbearable because he knew that never in his life had he less time to give way to it. Because he did not hesitate. Grasping the grapevine end he sprang into the water, vanishing in the violent action of climbing and reappeared still climbing and (who had never learned to swim) plunged and threshed on toward the almost-vanished mound, moving through the water then upon it as the deer had done yesterday and scrabbled up the muddy slope and lay gasping and panting, still clutching the grapevine end.

Now the first thing he did was to choose what he believed to be the most suitable tree (for an instant in which he knew he was insane he thought of trying to saw it down with the flange of the bailing can) and build a fire against the butt of it. Then he went to seek food. He spent the next six days seeking it while the tree burned through and fell and burned through again at the proper length and he nursing little constant cunning flames along the flanks of the log to make it paddle-shaped, nursing them at night too while the woman and baby (it was eating, nursing now, he turning his back or even retiring into the woods each time she prepared to open the faded tunic) slept in the skiff. He learned to watch for stooping hawks and so found more rabbits and twice possums; they ate some drowned fish which gave them both a rash and then a violent flux and one snake which the woman thought was turtle and which did them no harm, and one night it rained and he got up and dragged brush, shaking the snakes (he no longer thought *It aint nothing but another moccasin*, he just stepped aside for them as they, when there was time, telescoped sullenly aside for him) out of it with the old former feeling of personal invulnerability and built a shelter and the rain stopped at once and did not recommence and the woman went back to the skiff.

Then one night—the slow tedious charring log was almost a paddle now—one night and he was in bed, in his bed in the bunkhouse and it was cold, he was trying to pull the covers up only his mule wouldn't let him, prodding and bumping heavily at him, trying to get into the narrow bed with him and now the bed was cold too and wet and he was trying to get out of it only the mule would not let him, holding him by his belt in its teeth, jerking and bumping him back into the cold wet bed and, leaning, gave him a long swipe across the face with its cold limber musculated tongue and he waked to no fire, no coal even beneath where the almost-finished paddle had been charring and something else prolonged and coldly limber passed swiftly across his body where he lay in four inches of water while the nose of the skiff alternately tugged at the grapevine tied about his waist and bumped and shoved him back into the water again. Then something else came up and began to nudge at his ankle (the log, the oar, it was) even as he groped frantically for the skiff, hearing the swift rustling going to and fro inside the hull as the woman began to thrash about and scream. "Rats!" she cried. "It's full of rats!"

"Lay still!" he cried. "It's just snakes. Cant you hold still long enough for me to find the boat?" Then he found it, he got into it with the unfinished paddle; again the thick muscular body convulsed under his foot; it did not strike; he would not have cared, glaring astern where he could see a little—the faint outer luminosity of the open water. He poled toward it, thrusting aside the snake-looped branches, the bottom of the skiff resounding faintly to thick solid plops, the woman shrieking steadily. Then the skiff was clear of the trees, the mound, and now he could feel the bodies whipping about his ankles and hear the rasp of them as they went over the gunwale. He drew the log in and scooped it forward along the bottom of the boat and up and out; against the pallid water he could see three more of them in lashing convolutions before they vanished. "Shut up!" he cried. "Hush! I wish I was a snake so I could get out too!"

When once more the pale and heatless wafer disc of the early sun stared down at the skiff (whether they were moving or not the convict did not know) in its nimbus of fine cotton batting, the convict was hearing again that sound which he had heard twice before and would never forget—that sound of deliberate and irresistible and monstrously disturbed water. But this time he could not tell from what direction it came. It seemed to be everywhere, waxing and fading; it was like a phantom behind the mist, at one instant miles away, the next on the point of overwhelming the skiff within the next second; suddenly in the instant he would believe (his whole weary body would spring and scream) that he was about to drive the skiff point-blank into it and with the unfinished paddle of the color and texture of sooty bricks, like something gnawed out of an old chimney by beavers and weighing twenty-five pounds, he would whirl the skiff frantically and find the sound dead ahead of him again. Then something bellowed tremendously above his head, he heard human voices, a bell jangled and the sound ceased and the mist vanished like when you draw your hand across a frosted pane, and the skiff now lay upon a sunny glitter of brown water flank to flank with, and about thirty yards away from, a steamboat. The decks were crowded and packed with men women and children sitting or standing beside and among a homely conglomeration of hurried furniture, who looked mournfully and silently down into the skiff while the convict and the man with a megaphone in the pilot house talked to each other in alternate puny shouts and roars above the chuffing of the reversed engines:

"What in hell are you trying to do? Commit suicide?"

"Which is the way to Vicksburg?"

"Vicksburg? Vicksburg? Lay alongside and come aboard."

"Will you take the boat too?"

"Boat? Boat?" Now the megaphone cursed, the roaring waves of blasphemy and biological supposition empty cavernous and bodiless in turn, as if the water, the air, the mist had spoken it, roaring the words then taking them back to itself and no harm done, no scar, no insult left anywhere. "If I took aboard every floating sardine can you sonabitchin mushrats want me to I wouldn't even have room forrard for a leadsman. Come aboard! Do you expect me to hang here on stern engines till hell freezes?"

"I aint coming without the boat," the convict said. Now another voice spoke, so calm and mild and sensible that for a moment it sounded more foreign and out of place than even the megaphone's bellowing and bodiless profanity:

"Where is it you are trying to go?"

"I aint trying," the convict said. "I'm going. Parchman." The man who had spoken last turned and appeared to converse with a third man in the pilot house. Then he looked down at the skiff again.

"Carnarvon?"

"What?" the convict said. "Parchman?"

"All right. We're going that way. We'll put you off where you can get home. Come aboard."

"The boat too?"

"Yes yes. Come along. We're burning coal just to talk to you." So the convict came alongside then and watched them help the woman and baby over the rail and he came aboard himself, though he still held to the end of the vine-spliced painter until the skiff was hoisted onto the boiler deck. "My God," the man, the gentle one, said, "is that what you have been using for a paddle?"

"Yah," the convict said. "I lost the plank."

"The plank," the mild man (the convict told how he seemed to whisper it), "the plank. Well. Come along and get something to eat. Your boat is all right now."

"I reckon I'll wait here," the convict said. Because now, he told them, he began to notice for the first time that the other people, the other refugees who crowded the deck, who had gathered in a quiet circle about the upturned skiff on which he and the woman sat, the grapevine painter wrapped several times about his wrist and clutched in his hand, staring at him and the woman with queer hot mournful intensity, were not white people—

"You mean niggers?" the plump convict said.

"No. Not Americans."

"Not Americans? You was clean out of *America* even?"

"I dont know," the tall one said. "They called it Atchafalaya."—because after a while he said "What?" to the man and the man did it again, gobble-gobble—

"Gobble-gobble?" the plump convict said.

"That's the way they talked," the tall one said. "Gobble-gobble, whang, caw-caw-to-to."—and he sat there and watched them gobbling at one another and then looking at him again, then they fell back and the mild man (he wore a Red Cross brassard) entered, followed by a waiter with a tray of food. The mild man carried two glasses of whiskey.

"Drink this," the mild man said. "This will warm you." The woman took hers and drank it but the convict told how he looked at his and thought *I aint tasted whiskey in seven years*. He had not tasted it but once before that; it was at the still itself back in a pine hollow; he was seventeen, he had gone there with four companions, two of whom were grown men, one of twenty-two or -three, the other about forty; he remembered it. That is, he remembered perhaps a third of that evening—a fierce turmoil in the hell-colored firelight, the shock and shock of blows about his head (and likewise of his own fists on other hard bone), then the waking to a splitting and blinding sun in a place, a cowshed, he had never seen before and which later turned out to be twenty miles from his home. He said he thought of this and he looked about at the faces watching him and he said,

"I reckon not."

"Come, come," the mild man said. "Drink it."

"I dont want it."

"Nonsense," the mild man said. "I'm a doctor. Here. Then you can eat." So he took the glass and even then he hesitated but again the mild man said, "Come along, down with it; you're still holding us up" in that voice still calm and sensible but a little sharp too—the voice of a man who could keep calm and affable because he wasn't used to being crossed —and he drank the whiskey and even in the second between the sweet full fire in his belly and when it began to happen he was trying to say, "I tried to tell you! I tried to!" But it was too late now in the pallid sun-glare of the tenth day of terror and hopelessness and despair and impotence and rage and outrage and it was himself and the mule, his mule (they had let him name it—John Henry) which no man save he had plowed for five years now and whose ways and habits he knew and respected and who knew his ways and habits so well that each of them could anticipate the other's very movements and intentions; it was himself and the mule, the little gobbling faces flying before them, the familiar hard skull-bones shocking against his fists, his voice shouting, "Come on, John Henry! Plow them down! Gobble them down, boy!" even as the bright hot red wave turned back, meeting it joyously, happily, lifted, poised, then hurling through space, triumphant and yelling, then again the old shocking blow at the back of his head: he lay on the deck, flat on his back and pinned arm and leg and cold sober again, his nostrils gushing again, the mild man stooping over him with behind the thin rimless glasses the coldest eyes the convict had ever seen— eyes which the convict said were not looking at him but at the gushing blood with nothing in the world in them but complete impersonal interest.

"Good man," the mild man said. "Plenty of life in the old carcass yet, eh? Plenty of good red blood too. Anyone ever suggest to you that you were hemophilic?" ("What?" the plump convict said. "Hemophilic? You know what that means?" The tall convict had his cigarette going now, his body jackknifed backward into the coffinlike space between the upper and lower bunks, lean, clean, motionless, the blue smoke wreathing across his lean dark aquiline shaven face. "That's a calf that's a bull and a cow at the same time."

"No it aint," a third convict said. "It's a calf or a colt that aint neither one."

"Hell fire," the plump one said. "He's got to be one or the other to keep from drownding." He had never ceased to look at the tall one in the bunk; now he spoke to him again: "You let him call you that?") The tall one had done so. He did not answer the doctor (this was where he stopped thinking of him as the mild man) at all. He could not move either, though he felt fine, he felt better than he had in ten days. So they helped him to his feet and steadied him over and low-ered him onto the upturned skiff beside the woman, where he sat bent forward, elbows on knees in the immemorial attitude, watching his own bright crimson staining the mud-trodden deck, until the doctor's clean clipped hand appeared under his nose with a phial.

"Smell," the doctor said. "Deep." The convict inhaled, the sharp ammoniac sensation burned up his nostrils and into his throat. "Again," the doctor said. The convict inhaled obedi-ently. This time he choked and spat a gout of blood, his nose now had no more feeling than a toenail, other than it felt about the size of a ten-inch shovel, and as cold.

"I ask you to excuse me," he said. "I never meant—"

"Why?" the doctor said. "You put up as pretty a scrap against forty or fifty men as I ever saw. You lasted a good two seconds. Now you can eat something. Or do you think that will send you haywire again?"

They both ate, sitting on the skiff, the gobbling faces no longer watching them now, the convict gnawing slowly and painfully at the thick sandwich, hunched, his face laid side-ways to the food and parallel to the earth as a dog chews; the steamboat went on. At noon there were bowls of hot soup and bread and more coffee; they ate this too, sitting side by side on the skiff, the grapevine still wrapped about the con-vict's wrist. The baby waked and nursed and slept again and they talked quietly:

"Was it Parchman he said he was going to take us?"

"That's where I told him I wanted to go."

"It never sounded exactly like Parchman to me. It sounded like he said something else." The convict had thought that too. He had been thinking about that fairly soberly ever since they boarded the steamboat and soberly indeed ever since he had remarked the nature of the other passengers, those men and women definitely a little shorter than he and with skin a little different in pigmentation from any sunburn, even though the eyes were sometimes blue or gray, who talked to one another in a tongue he had never heard before and who apparently did not understand his own, people the like of whom he had never seen about Parchman nor anywhere else and whom he did not believe were going there or beyond there either. But after his hill-billy country fashion and kind he would not ask, because to his raising asking information was asking a favor and you did not ask favors of strangers; if they offered them perhaps you accepted and you expressed gratitude almost tediously recapitulant, but you did not ask. So he would watch and wait, as he had done before, and do or try to do to the best of his ability what the best of his judgment dictated.

So he waited, and in midafternoon the steamboat chuffed and thrust through a willow-choked gorge and emerged from it, and now the convict knew it was the River. He could believe it now—the tremendous reach yellow and sleepy in the afternoon—("Because it's too big," he told them soberly. "Aint no flood in the world big enough to make it do more than stand a little higher so it can look back and see just where the flea is, just exactly where to scratch. It's the little ones, the little piddling creeks that run backward one day and forward the next and come busting down on a man full of dead mules and hen houses.")—and the steamboat moving up this now (*like a ant crossing a plate* the convict thought, sitting beside the woman on the upturned skiff, the baby nursing again, apparently looking too out across the water where, a mile away on either hand, the twin lines of levee resembled parallel unbroken floating thread) and then it was nearing sunset and he began to hear, to notice, the voices of the doctor and of the man who had first bawled at him through the megaphone now bawling again from the pilot house overhead:

"Stop? Stop? Am I running a street car?"

"Stop for the novelty then," the doctor's pleasant voice said. "I dont know how many trips back and forth you have made in yonder nor how many of what you call mushrats you have fetched out. But this is the first time you ever had two people—no, three—who not only knew the name of some place they wished to go to but were actually trying to go there." So the convict waited while the sun slanted more and more and the steamboat-ant crawled steadily on across its vacant and gigantic plate turning more and more to copper. But he did not ask, he just waited. *Maybe it was Carrollton he said* he thought. *It begun with a C.* But he did not believe that either. He did not know where he was, but he did know that this was not anywhere near the Carrollton he remembered from that day seven years ago when, shackled wrist to wrist with the deputy sheriff, he had passed through it on the train—the slow spaced repeated shattering banging of trucks where two railroads crossed, a random scattering of white houses tranquil among trees on green hills lush with summer, a pointing spire, the finger of the hand of God. But there was no river there. *And you aint never close to this river without knowing it* he thought. *I dont care who you are nor where you have been all your life.* Then the head of the steamboat began to swing across the stream, its shadow swinging too, travelling long before it across the water, toward the vacant ridge of willow-massed earth empty of all life. There was nothing there at all, the convict could not even see either earth or water beyond it; it was as though the steamboat were about to crash slowly through the thin low frail willow barrier and embark into space, or lacking this, slow and back and fill and disembark him into space, granted it was about to disembark him, granted this was that place which was not near Parchman and was not Carrollton either, even though it did begin with c. Then he turned his head and saw the doctor stooping over the woman, pushing the baby's eyelid up with his forefinger, peering at it.

"Who else was there when he came?" the doctor said.

"Nobody," the convict said.

"Did it all yourselves, eh?"

"Yes," the convict said. Now the doctor stood up and looked at the convict.

"This is Carnarvon," he said.

"Carnarvon?" the convict said. "That aint—" Then he stopped, ceased. And now he told about that—the intent eyes as dispassionate as ice behind the rimless glasses, the clipped quick-tempered face that was not accustomed to being crossed or lied to either. ("Yes," the plump convict said. "That's what I was aiming to ask. Them clothes. Anybody would know them. How if this doctor was as smart as you claim he was—"

"I had slept in them for ten nights, mostly in the mud," the tall one said. "I had been rowing since midnight with that sapling oar I had tried to burn out that I never had time to scrape the soot off. But it's being scared and worried and then scared and then worried again in clothes for days and days and days that changes the way they look. I dont mean just your pants." He did not laugh. "Your face too. That doctor knowed."

"All right," the plump one said. "Go on.")

"I know it," the doctor said. "I discovered that while you were lying on the deck yonder sobering up again. Now dont lie to me. I dont like lying. This boat is going to New Orleans."

"No," the convict said immediately, quietly, with absolute finality. He could hear them again—the thuck-thuck-thuck on the water where an instant before he had been. But he was not thinking of the bullets. He had forgotten them, forgiven them. He was thinking of himself crouching, sobbing, panting before running again—the voice, the indictment, the cry of final and irrevocable repudiation of the old primal faithless Manipulator of all the lust and folly and injustice: *All in the world I wanted was just to surrender;* thinking of it, remembering it but without heat now, without passion now and briefer than an epitaph: *No. I tried that once. They shot at me.*

"So you dont want to go to New Orleans. And you didn't exactly plan to go to Carnarvon. But you will take Carnarvon in preference to New Orleans." The convict said nothing. The doctor looked at him, the magnified pupils like the heads of two bridge nails. "What were you in for? Hit him harder than you thought, eh?"

"No. I tried to rob a train."

"Say that again." The convict said it again. "Well? Go on. You dont say that in the year 1927 and just stop, man." So the convict told it, dispassionately too—about the magazines, the pistol which would not shoot, the mask and the dark lantern in which no draft had been arranged to keep the candle burning so that it died almost with the match but even then left the metal too hot to carry, won with subscriptions. *Only it aint my eyes or my mouth either he's watching* he thought. *It's like he is watching the way my hair grows on my head.* "I see," the doctor said. "But something went wrong. But you've had plenty of time to think about it since. To decide what was wrong, what you failed to do."

"Yes," the convict said. "I've thought about it a right smart since."

"So next time you are not going to make that mistake."

"I dont know," the convict said. "There aint going to be a next time."

"Why? If you know what you did wrong, they wont catch you next time."

The convict looked at the doctor steadily. They looked at each other steadily; the two sets of eyes were not so different after all. "I reckon I see what you mean," the convict said presently. "I was eighteen then. I'm twenty-five now."

"Oh," the doctor said. Now (the convict tried to tell it) the doctor did not move, he just simply quit looking at the convict. He produced a pack of cheap cigarettes from his coat. "Smoke?" he said.

"I wouldn't care for none," the convict said.

"Quite," the doctor said in that affable clipped voice. He put the cigarettes away. "There has been conferred upon my race (the Medical race) also the power to bind and to loose, if not by Jehovah perhaps, certainly by the American Medical Association—on which incidentally, in this day of Our Lord, I would put my money, at any odds, at any amount, at any time. I dont know just how far out of bounds I am on this specific occasion but I think we'll put it to the touch." He cupped his hands to his mouth, toward the pilot house overhead. "Captain!" he shouted. "We'll put these three passengers ashore here." He turned to the convict again. "Yes," he said, "I think I shall let your native state lick its own vomit. Here." Again his hand emerged from his pocket, this time with a bill in it.

"No," the convict said.

"Come, come; I dont like to be disputed either."

"No," the convict said. "I aint got any way to pay it back."

"Did I ask you to pay it back?"

"No," the convict said. "I never asked to borrow it either."

So once more he stood on dry land, who had already been toyed with twice by that risible and concentrated power of water, once more than should have fallen to the lot of any one man, any one lifetime, yet for whom there was reserved still another unbelievable recapitulation, he and the woman standing on the empty levee, the sleeping child wrapped in the faded tunic and the grapevine painter still wrapped about the convict's wrist, watching the steamboat back away and turn and once more crawl onward up the platter-like reach of vacant water burnished more and more to copper, its trailing smoke roiling in slow copper-edged gouts, thinning out along the water, fading, stinking away across the vast serene desolation, the boat growing smaller and smaller until it did not seem to crawl at all but to hang stationary in the airy substanceless sunset, dissolving into nothing like a pellet of floating mud.

Then he turned and for the first time looked about him, behind him, recoiling, not through fear but through pure reflex and not physically but the soul, the spirit, that profound sober alert attentiveness of the hillman who will not ask anything of strangers, not even information, thinking quietly *No. This aint Carrollton neither.* Because he now looked down the almost perpendicular landward slope of the levee through sixty feet of absolute space, upon a surface, a terrain flat as a waffle and of the color of a waffle or perhaps of the summer coat of a claybank horse and possessing that same piled density of a rug or peltry, spreading away without undulation yet with that curious appearance of imponderable solidity like fluid, broken here and there by thick humps of arsenical green which nevertheless still seemed to possess no height and by

writhen veins of the color of ink which he began to suspect to
be actual water but with judgment reserved, with judgment
still reserved even when presently he was walking in it. That's
what he said, told: So they went on. He didn't tell how he
got the skiff singlehanded up the revetment and across the
crown and down the opposite sixty foot drop, he just said he
went on, in a swirling cloud of mosquitoes like hot cinders,
thrusting and plunging through the saw-edged grass which
grew taller than his head and which whipped back at his arms
and face like limber knives, dragging by the vine-spliced
painter the skiff in which the woman sat, slogging and stumbling knee-deep in something less of earth than water, along
one of those black winding channels less of water than earth:
and then (he was in the skiff too now, paddling with the
charred log, what footing there had been having given away
beneath him without warning thirty minutes ago, leaving
only the air-filled bubble of his jumper-back ballooning
lightly on the twilit water until he rose to the surface and
scrambled into the skiff) the house, the cabin a little larger
than a horse-box, of cypress boards and an iron roof, rising
on ten-foot stilts slender as spiders' legs, like a shabby and
death-stricken (and probably poisonous) wading creature
which had got that far into that flat waste and died with nothing anywhere in reach or sight to lie down upon, a pirogue
tied to the foot of a crude ladder, a man standing in the open
door holding a lantern (it was that dark now) above his head,
gobbling down at them.

He told it—of the next eight or nine or ten days, he did
not remember which, while the four of them—himself and
the woman and baby and the little wiry man with rotting
teeth and soft wild bright eyes like a rat or a chipmunk,
whose language neither of them could understand—lived in
the room and a half. He did not tell it that way, just as he
apparently did not consider it worth the breath to tell how he
had got the hundred-and-sixty-pound skiff singlehanded up
and across and down the sixty-foot levee. He just said, "After
a while we come to a house and we stayed there eight or nine
days then they blew up the levee with dynamite so we had to
leave." That was all. But he remembered it, but quietly now,
with the cigar now, the good one the Warden had given him

(though not lighted yet) in his peaceful and steadfast hand, remembering that first morning when he waked on the thin pallet beside his host (the woman and baby had the one bed) with the fierce sun already latticed through the warped rough planking of the wall, and stood on the ricketty porch looking out upon that flat fecund waste neither earth nor water, where even the senses doubted which was which, which rich and massy air and which mazy and impalpable vegetation, and thought quietly *He must do something here to eat and live. But I dont know what. And until I can go on again, until I can find where I am and how to pass that town without them seeing me I will have to help him do it so we can eat and live too, and I dont know what.* And he had a change of clothing too, almost at once on that first morning, not telling any more than he had about the skiff and the levee how he had begged borrowed or bought from the man whom he had not laid eyes on twelve hours ago and with whom on the day he saw him for the last time he still could exchange no word, the pair of dungaree pants which even the Cajan had discarded as no longer wearable, filthy, buttonless, the legs slashed and frayed into fringe like that on an 1890 hammock, in which he stood naked from the waist up and holding out to her the mud-caked and soot-stained jumper and overall when the woman waked on that first morning in the crude bunk nailed into one corner and filled with dried grass, saying, "Wash them. Good. I want all them stains out. All of them."

"But the jumper," she said. "Aint he got ere old shirt too? That sun and them mosquitoes—" But he did not even answer, and she said no more either, though when he and the Cajan returned at dark the garments were clean, stained a little still with the old mud and soot, but clean, resembling again what they were supposed to resemble as (his arms and back already a fiery red which would be blisters by tomorrow) he spread the garments out and examined them and then rolled them up carefully in a six-months-old New Orleans paper and thrust the bundle behind a rafter, where it remained while day followed day and the blisters on his back broke and suppurated and he would sit with his face expressionless as a wooden mask beneath the sweat while the Cajan doped his back with something on a filthy rag from a filthy saucer, she still saying nothing since she too doubtless knew what his reason was, not from that rapport of the wedded conferred upon her by the two weeks during which they had jointly suffered all the crises emotional social economic and even moral which do not always occur even in the ordinary fifty married years (the old married: you have seen them, the electroplate reproductions, the thousand identical coupled faces with only a collarless stud or a fichu out of Louisa Alcott to denote the sex, looking in pairs like the winning braces of dogs after a field trial out from among the packed columns of disaster and alarm and baseless assurance and hope and incredible insensitivity and insulation from tomorrow propped by a thousand morning sugar bowls or coffee urns; or singly, rocking on porches or sitting in the sun beneath the tobacco-stained porticoes of a thousand county courthouses, as though with the death of the other having inherited a sort of rejuvenescence, immortality; relict, they take a new lease on breath and seem to live forever, as though that flesh which the old ceremony or ritual had morally purified and made legally one had actually become so with long tedious habit and he or she who entered the ground first took all of it with him or her, leaving only the old permanent enduring bone, free and tramelless)—not because of this but because she too had stemmed at some point from the same dim hill-bred Abraham.

So the bundle remained behind the rafter and day followed day while he and his partner (he was in partnership now with his host, hunting alligators on shares, on the halvers he called it— "Halvers?" the plump convict said. "How could you make a business agreement with a man you claim you couldn't even talk to?"

"I never had to talk to him," the tall one said. "Money aint got but one language.") departed at dawn each day, at first together in the pirogue but later singly, the one in the pirogue and the other in the skiff, the one with the battered and pitted rifle, the other with the knife and a piece of knotted rope and a lightwood club the size and weight and shape of a Thuringian mace, stalking their pleistocene nightmares up and down the secret inky channels which writhed the flat brass-colored land. He remembered that too: that first

morning when turning in the sunrise from the ricketty platform he saw the hide nailed drying to the wall and stopped
dead, looking at it quietly, thinking quietly and soberly *So
that's it. That's what he does in order to eat and live* knowing it
was a hide, a skin, but from what animal, by association, ratiocination or even memory of any picture out of his dead
youth, he did not know but knowing that it was the reason,
the explanation, for the little lost spider-legged house (which
had already begun to die, to rot from the legs upward almost
before the roof was nailed on) set in that teeming and myriad
desolation, enclosed and lost within the furious embrace of
flowing mare earth and stallion sun, divining through pure
rapport of kind for kind, hill-billy and bayou-rat, the two one
and identical because of the same grudged dispensation and
niggard fate of hard and unceasing travail not to gain future
security, a balance in bank or even in a buried soda can for
slothful and easy old age, but just permission to endure and
endure to buy air to feel and sun to drink for each's little
while, thinking (the convict) *Well, anyway I am going to find
out what it is sooner than I expected to* and did so, re-entered the
house where the woman was just waking in the one sorry
built-in straw-filled bunk which the Cajan had surrendered to
her, and ate the breakfast (the rice, a semi-liquid mess violent
with pepper and mostly fish considerably high, the chicory-
thickened coffee) and shirtless followed the little scuttling
bobbing bright-eyed rotten-toothed man down the crude ladder and into the pirogue. He had never seen a pirogue either
and he believed that it would not remain upright—not that it
was light and precariously balanced with its open side upward
but that there was inherent in the wood, the very log, some
dynamic and unsleeping natural law, almost will, which its
present position outraged and violated—yet accepting this
too as he had the fact that that hide had belonged to something larger than any calf or hog and that anything which
looked like that on the outside would be more than likely to
have teeth and claws too, accepting this, squatting in the
pirogue, clutching both gunwales, rigidly immobile as though
he had an egg filled with nitroglycerin in his mouth and
scarcely breathing, thinking *If that's it, then I can do it too and
even if he cant tell me how I reckon I can watch him and find out.*

And he did this too, he remembered it, quietly even yet, thinking *I thought that was how to do it and I reckon I would still think that even if I had it to do again now for the first time*—the brazen day already fierce upon his naked back, the crooked channel like a voluted thread of ink, the pirogue moving steadily to the paddle which both entered and left the water without a sound; then the sudden cessation of the paddle behind him and the fierce hissing gobble of the Cajan at his back and he squatting bate-breathed and with that intense immobility of complete sobriety of a blind man listening while the frail wooden shell stole on at the dying apex of its own parted water. Afterward he remembered the rifle too—the rust-pitted single-shot weapon with a clumsily wired stock and a muzzle you could have driven a whisky cork into, which the Cajan had brought into the boat—but not now; now he just squatted, crouched, immobile, breathing with infinitesimal care, his sober unceasing gaze going here and there constantly as he thought *What? What? I not only dont know what I am looking for, I dont even know where to look for it.* Then he felt the motion of the pirogue as the Cajan moved and then the tense gobbling hissing actually, hot rapid and repressed, against his neck and ear, and glancing downward saw projecting between his own arm and body from behind the Cajan's hand holding the knife, and glaring up again saw the flat thick spit of mud which as he looked at it divided and became a thick mud-colored log which in turn seemed, still immobile, to leap suddenly against his retinae in three—no, four—dimensions: volume, solidity, shape, and another: not fear but pure and intense speculation and he looking at the scaled motionless shape, thinking not *It looks dangerous* but *It looks big* thinking *Well maybe a mule standing in a lot looks big to a man that never walked up to one with a halter before* thinking *Only if he could just tell me what to do it would save time*, the pirogue drawing nearer now, creeping now, with no ripple now even and it seemed to him that he could even hear his companion's held breath and he taking the knife from the other's hand now and not even thinking this since it was too fast, a flash; it was not a surrender, not a resignation, it was too calm, it was a part of him, he had drunk it with his mother's milk and lived with it all his life: *After all a man cant only do what he has to do, with what he has to do it with, with what he has learned, to the best of his judgment. And I reckon a hog is still a hog, no matter what it looks like. So here goes* sitting still for an instant longer until the bow of the pirogue grounded lighter than the falling of a leaf and stepped out of it and paused just for one instant while the words *It does look big* stood for just a second, unemphatic and trivial, somewhere where some fragment of his attention could see them and vanished, and stooped straddling, the knife driving even as he grasped the near foreleg, this all in the same instant when the lashing tail struck him a terrific blow upon the back. But the knife was home, he knew that even on his back in the mud, the weight of the thrashing beast longwise upon him, its ridged back clutched to his stomach, his arm about its throat, the hissing head clamped against his jaw, the furious tail lashing and flailing, the knife in his other hand probing for the life and finding it, the hot fierce gush: and now sitting beside the profound up-bellied carcass, his head again between his knees in the old attitude while his own blood freshened the other which drenched him, thinking *It's my durn nose again.*

So he sat there, his head, his streaming face, bowed between his knees in an attitude not of dejection but profoundly bemused, contemplative while the shrill voice of the Cajan seemed to buzz at him from an enormous distance; after a time he even looked up at the antic wiry figure bouncing hysterically about him, the face wild and grimacing, the voice gobbling and high; while the convict, holding his face carefully slanted so the blood would run free, looked at him with the cold intentness of a curator or custodian paused before one of his own glass cases, the Cajan threw up the rifle, cried "Boom-boom-boom!" flung it down and in pantomime re-enacted the recent scene then whirled his hands again, crying "Magnifique! Magnifique! Cent d'argent! mille d'argent! Tout l'argent sous le ciel de Dieu!" But the convict was already looking down again, cupping the coffee-colored water to his face, watching the constant bright carmine marble it, thinking *It's a little late to be telling me that now* and not even thinking this long because presently they were in the pirogue again, the convict squatting again with that unbreathing rigidity as though he were trying by holding his breath to decrease his very weight, the bloody skin in the bows before him and he looking at it, thinking *And I cant even ask him how much my half will be*.

But this not for long either, because as he was to tell the plump convict later, money has but one language. He remembered that too (they were at home now, the skin spread on the platform, where for the woman's benefit now the Cajan once more went through the pantomime—the gun which was not used, the hand-to-hand battle; for the second time the invisible alligator was slain amid cries, the victor rose and found this time that not even the woman was watching him. She was looking at the once more swollen and inflamed face of the convict. "You mean it kicked you right in the face?" she said.

"Nah," the convict said harshly, savagely. "It never had to. I done seem to got to where if that boy was to shoot me in the tail with a bean blower my nose would bleed.")—remembered that too but he did not try to tell it. Perhaps he could not have—how two people who could not even talk to one another made an agreement which both not only understood but which each knew the other would hold true and protect (perhaps for this reason) better than any written and witnessed contract. They even discussed and agreed somehow that they should hunt separately, each in his own vessel, to double the chances of finding prey. But this was easy: the convict could almost understand the words in which the Cajan said, "You do not need me and the rifle; we will only hinder you, be in your way." And more than this, they even agreed about the second rifle: that there was someone, it did not matter who—friend, neighbor, perhaps one in business in that line—from whom they could rent a second rifle; in their two patois, the one bastard English, the other bastard French—the one volatile, with his wild bright eyes and his voluble mouth full of stumps of teeth, the other sober, almost grim, swollen-faced and with his naked back blistered and scoriated like so much beef—they discussed this, squatting on either side of the pegged-out hide like two members of a corporation facing each other across a mahogany board table, and decided against it, the convict deciding: "I reckon not," he said. "I reckon if I had knowed enough to wait to start out with a gun, I still would. But since I done already started out without one, I dont reckon I'll change." Because it was a question of the money in terms of time, days. (Strange to say, that was the one thing which the Cajan could not tell him: how much the half would be. But the convict knew it was half.) He had so little of them. He would have to move on soon, thinking (the convict) *All this durn foolishness will stop soon and I can get on back* and then suddenly he found that he was thinking *Will have to get on back* and he became quite still and looked about at the rich strange desert which surrounded him, in which he was temporarily lost in peace and hope and into which the last seven years had sunk like so many trivial pebbles into a pool, leaving no ripple, and he thought quietly, with a kind of bemused amazement *Yes. I reckon I had done forgot how good making money was. Being let to make it.*

So he used no gun, his the knotted rope and the Thuringian mace, and each morning he and the Cajan took their separate ways in the two boats to comb and creep the secret channels about the lost land from (or out of) which now and then still other pint-sized dark men appeared gobbling, abruptly and as though by magic from nowhere, in other hollowed logs, to follow quietly and watch him at his single combats — men named Tine and Toto and Theodule, who were not much larger than and looked a good deal like the muskrats which the Cajan (the host did this too, supplied the kitchen too, he expressed this too like the rifle business, in his own tongue, the convict comprehending this too as though it had been English: "Do not concern yourself about food, O Hercules. Catch alligators; I will supply the pot.") took now and then from traps as you take a shoat pig at need from a pen, and varied the eternal rice and fish (the convict did tell this: how at night, in the cabin, the door and one sashless window battened against mosquitoes — a form, a ritual, as empty as crossing the fingers or knocking on wood — sitting beside the bug-swirled lantern on the plank table in a temperature close to blood heat he would look down at the swimming segment of meat on his sweating plate and think *It must be Theodule. He was the fat one.*) — day following day, unemphatic and identical, each like the one before and the one which would follow while his theoretical half of a sum to be reckoned in pennies, dollars, or tens of dollars he did not know mounted—the mornings when he set forth to find waiting for him like the *matador* his *aficionados* the small clump of constant and deferential pirogues, the hard noons when ringed half about by little motionless shells he fought his solitary combats, the evenings, the return, the pirogues departing one by one into inlets and passages which during the first few days he could not even distinguish, then the platform in the twilight where before the static woman and the usually nursing infant and the one or two bloody hides of the day's take the Cajan would perform his ritualistic victorious pantomime before the two growing rows of knifemarks in one of the boards of the wall; then the nights when, the woman and child in the single bunk and the Cajan already snoring on the pallet and the reeking lantern set close, he (the convict) would sit on his naked heels, sweating steadily, his face worn and calm, immersed and indomitable, his bowed back raw and savage as beef beneath the suppurant old blisters and the fierce welts of tails, and scrape and chip at the charred sapling which was almost a paddle now, pausing now and then to raise his head while the cloud of mosquitoes about it whined and whirled, to stare at the wall before him until after a while the crude boards themselves must have dissolved away and let his blank unseeing gaze go on and on unhampered, through the rich oblivious darkness, beyond it even perhaps, even perhaps beyond the seven wasted years during which, so he had just realised, he had been permitted to toil but not to work. Then he would retire himself, he would take a last look at the rolled bundle behind the rafter and blow out the lantern and lie down as he was beside his snoring partner, to lie sweating (on his stomach, he could not bear the touch of anything to his back) in the whining oven-like darkness filled with the forlorn bellowing of alligators, thinking not *They never gave me time to learn* but *I had forgot how good it is to work*.

Then on the tenth day it happened. It happened for the third time. At first he refused to believe it, not that he felt that now he had served out and discharged his apprenticeship to mischance, had with the birth of the child reached and crossed the crest of his Golgotha and would now be, possibly not permitted so much as ignored, to descend the opposite slope free-wheeling. That was not his feeling at all. What he declined to accept was the fact that a power, a force such as that which had been consistent enough to concentrate upon him with deadly undeviation for weeks, should with all the wealth of cosmic violence and disaster to draw from, have been so barren of invention and imagination, so lacking in pride of artistry and craftmanship, as to repeat itself twice. Once he had accepted, twice he even forgave, but three times he simply declined to believe, particularly when he was at last persuaded to realise that this third time was to be instigated not by the blind potency of volume and motion but by human direction and hands: that now the cosmic joker, foiled twice, had stooped in its vindictive concentration to the employing of dynamite.

He did not tell that. Doubtless he did not know himself how it happened, what was happening. But he doubtless remembered it (but quietly above the thick rich-colored pristine cigar in his clean steady hand) what he knew, divined of it. It would be evening, the ninth evening, he and the woman on either side of their host's empty place at the evening meal, he hearing the voices from without but not ceasing to eat, still chewing steadily, because it would be the same as though he were seeing them anyway—the two or three or four pirogues floating on the dark water beneath the platform on which the host stood, the voices gobbling and jabbering, incomprehensible and filled not with alarm and not exactly with rage or even perhaps absolute surprise but rather just cacophony like those of disturbed marsh fowl, he (the convict) not ceasing to chew but just looking up quietly and maybe without a great deal of interrogation or surprise too as the Cajan burst in and stood before them, wild-faced, glaring, his blackened teeth gaped against the inky orifice of his distended mouth, watching (the convict) while the Cajan went through his violent pantomime of violent evacuation, ejection, scooping something invisible into his arms and hurling it out and downward and in the instant of completing the gesture changing from instigator to victim of that which he had set into pantomimic motion, clasping his head and, bowed over and not otherwise moving, seeming to be swept on and away before it, crying "Boom! Boom! Boom!", the convict watching him, his jaw not chewing now, though for just that moment, thinking *What? What is it he is trying to tell me?* thinking (this a flash too, since he could not have expressed this, and hence did not even know that he had ever thought it) that though his life had been cast here, circumscribed by this environment, accepted by this environment and accepting it in turn (and he had done well here—this quietly, soberly indeed, if he had been able to phrase it, think it instead of merely knowing it—better than he had ever done, who had not even known until now how good work, making money, could be) yet it was not his life, he still and would ever be no more than the water bug upon the surface of the pond, the plumbless and lurking depths of which he would never know, his only actual contact with it being the instants when on lonely and glaring mudspits under the pitiless sun and amphitheatred by his motionless and rivetted semicircle of watching pirogues, he accepted the gambit which he had not elected, entered the lashing radius of the armed tail and beat at the thrashing and hissing head with his lightwood club, or this failing, embraced without hesitation the armored body itself with the frail web of flesh and bone in which he walked and lived and sought the raging life with an eight-inch knife-blade.

So he and the woman merely watched the Cajan as he acted out the whole charade of eviction—the little wiry man gesticulant and wild, his hysterical shadow leaping and falling upon the rough wall as he went through the pantomime of abandoning the cabin, gathering in pantomime his meagre belongings from the walls and corners—objects which no other man would want and only some power or force like blind water or earthquake or fire would ever dispossess him of, the woman watching too, her mouth slightly open upon a mass of chewed food, on her face an expression of placid astonishment, saying, "What? What's he saying?"

"I dont know," the convict said. "But I reckon if it's something we ought to know we will find it out when it's ready for us to." Because he was not alarmed, though by now he had read the other's meaning plainly enough. *He's fixing to leave* he thought *He's telling me to leave too*—this later, after they had quitted the table and the Cajan and the woman had gone to bed and the Cajan had risen from the pallet and approached the convict and once more went through the pantomime of abandoning the cabin, this time as one repeats a speech which may have been misunderstood, tediously, carefully repetitional as to a child, seeming to hold the convict with one hand while he gestured, talked, with the other, gesturing as though in single syllables, the convict (squatting, the knife open and the almost-finished paddle across his lap) watching, nodding his head, even speaking in English: "Yah; sure. You bet. I got you."—trimming again at the paddle but no faster, with no more haste than on any other night, serene in his belief that when the time came for him to know whatever it was, that would take care of itself, having already and without even knowing it, even before the possibility, the question, ever arose, declined, refused to accept even the thought of moving also, thinking about the hides, thinking *If there was just someway he could tell me where to carry my share to get the money* but thinking this only for an instant between two delicate strokes of the blade because almost at once he thought *I reckon as long as I can catch them I wont have no big trouble finding whoever it is that will buy them.*

So the next morning he helped the Cajan load his few belongings—the pitted rifle, a small bundle of clothing (again they traded, who could not even converse with one another, this time the few cooking vessels by definite allocation, and something embracing and abstractional which included the stove, the crude bunk, the house or its occupancy—something—in exchange for one alligator hide) a few rusty traps—into the pirogue, then, squatting and as two children divide sticks they divided the hides, separating them into two piles, one-for-me-and-one-for-you, two-for-me-and-two-for-you, and the Cajan loaded his share and shoved away from the platform and paused again, though this time he only put the paddle down, gathered something invisibly into his two hands and flung it violently upward, crying "Boom? Boom?" on a rising inflection, nodding violently to the half-naked and savagely scoriated man on the platform who stared with a sort of grim equability back at him and said, "Sure. Boom. Boom." Then the Cajan went on. He did not look back. They watched him, already paddling rapidly, or the woman did; the convict had already turned.

"Maybe he was trying to tell us to leave too," she said.

"Yah," the convict said. "I thought of that last night. Hand me the paddle." She fetched it to him—the sapling, the one he had been trimming at nightly, not quite finished yet though one more evening would do it (he had been using a spare one of the Cajan's. The other had offered to let him keep it, to include it perhaps with the stove and the bunk and the cabin's freehold, but the convict had declined. Perhaps he had computed it by volume against so much alligator hide, this weighed against one more evening with the tedious and careful blade.) and he departed too with his knotted rope and mace, in the opposite direction, as though not only not content with refusing to quit the place he had been warned against, he must establish and affirm the irrevocable finality of his refusal by penetrating even further and deeper into it. And then and without warning the high fierce drowsing of his solitude gathered itself and struck at him.

He could not have told this if he had tried—this not yet midmorning and he going on, alone for the first time, no pirogue emerging anywhere to fall in behind him, but he had not expected this anyway, he knew that the others would have departed too; it was not this, it was his very solitude, his desolation which was now his alone and in full since he had elected to remain; the sudden cessation of the paddle, the skiff shooting on for a moment yet while he thought *What? What?* then *No. No. No.* as the silence and solitude and emptiness roared down upon him in a jeering bellow: and now reversed, the skiff spun violently on its heel, he the betrayed driving furiously back toward the platform where he knew it was already too late, that citadel where the very crux and dear breath of his life—the being allowed to work and earn money, that right and privilege which he believed he had earned to himself unaided, asking no favor of anyone or anything save the right to be let alone to pit his will and strength against the sauric Protagonist of a land, a region, which he had not asked to be projected into—was being threatened, driving the home-made paddle in grim fury, coming in sight of the platform at last and seeing the motor launch lying alongside it with no surprise at all but actually with a kind of pleasure as though at a visible justification of his outrage and fear, the privilege of saying *I told you so* to his own affronting, driving on toward it in a dreamlike state in which there seemed to be no progress at all, in which, unimpeded and suffocating, he strove dreamily with a weightless oar, with muscles without strength or resiliency, at a medium without resistance, seeming to watch the skiff creep infinitesimally across the sunny water and up to the platform while a man in the launch (there were five of them in all) gobbled at him in that same tongue he had been hearing constantly now for ten days and still knew no word of, just as a second man, followed by the woman carrying the baby and dressed again for departure in the faded tunic and the sunbonnet, emerged from the house, carrying (the man carried several other things but the convict saw nothing else) the paper-wrapped bundle which the convict had put behind the rafter ten days ago and no other hand had touched since, he (the convict) on the platform too now, holding the skiff's painter in one hand and the bludgeon-like paddle in the other, contriving to speak to the woman at last in a voice dreamy and suffocating and incredibly calm: "Take it away from him and carry it back into the house."

"So you can talk English, can you?" the man in the launch said. "Why didn't you come out like they told you to last night?"

"Out?" the convict said. Again he even looked, glared, at the man in the launch, contriving even again to control his voice: "I aint got time to take trips. I'm busy", already turning to the woman again, his mouth already open to repeat as the dreamy buzzing voice of the man came to him and he turning once more, in a terrific and absolutely unbearable exasperation, crying, "Flood? What flood? Hell a mile, it's done passed me twice months ago! It's gone! What flood?" and then (he did not think this in actual words either but he knew it, suffered that flashing insight into his own character or destiny: how there was a peculiar quality of repetitiveness about his present fate, how not only the almost seminal crises recurred with a certain monotony, but the very physical circumstances followed a stupidly unimaginative pattern) the man in the launch said "Take him" and he was on his feet for a few minutes yet, lashing and striking in panting fury, then once more on his back on hard unyielding planks while the four men swarmed over him in a fierce wave of hard bones and panting curses and at last the thin dry vicious snapping of handcuffs.

"Damn it, are you mad?" the man in the launch said. "Cant you understand they are going to dynamite that levee at noon today?—Come on," he said to the others. "Get him aboard. Let's get out of here."

"I want my hides and boat," the convict said.

"Damn your hides," the man in the launch said. "If they dont get that levee blowed pretty soon you can hunt plenty more of them on the capitol steps at Baton Rouge. And this is all the boat you will need and you can say your prayers about it."

"I aint going without my boat," the convict said. He said it calmly and with complete finality, so calm, so final that for almost a minute nobody answered him, they just stood looking quietly down at him as he lay, half-naked, blistered and scarred, helpless and manacled hand and foot, on his back, delivering his ultimatum in a voice peaceful and quiet as that in which you talk to your bedfellow before going to sleep. Then the man in the launch moved; he spat quietly over the side and said in a voice as calm and quiet as the convict's:

"All right. Bring his boat." They helped the woman, carrying the baby and the paper-wrapped parcel, into the launch. Then they helped the convict to his feet and into the launch too, the shackles on his wrists and ankles clashing. "I'd unlock you if you'd promise to behave yourself," the man said. The convict did not answer this at all, he said,

"I want to hold the rope."

"The rope?"

"Yes," the convict said. "The rope." So they lowered him into the stern and gave him the end of the painter after it had passed the towing cleat, and they went on. The convict did not look back. But then, he did not look forward either, he lay half sprawled, his shackled legs before him, the end of the skiff's painter in one shackled hand. The launch made two other stops; when the hazy wafer of the intolerable sun began

to stand once more directly overhead there were fifteen people in the launch; and then the convict, sprawled and motionless, saw the flat brazen land begin to rise and become a
greenish-black mass of swamp, bearded and convoluted, this
in turn stopping short off and there spread before him an
expanse of water embraced by a blue dissolution of shore line
and glittering thinly under the noon, larger than he had ever
seen before, the sound of the launch's engine ceasing, the
hull sliding on behind its fading bow-wave. "What are you
doing?" the leader said.

"It's noon," the helmsman said. "I thought we might hear
the dynamite." So they all listened, the launch lost of all forward motion, rocking slightly, the glitter-broken small waves
slapping and whispering at the hull, but no sound, no tremble
even, came anywhere under the fierce hazy sky; the long moment gathered itself and turned on and noon was past. "All
right," the leader said. "Let's go." The engine started again,
the hull began to gather speed. The leader came aft and
stooped over the convict, key in hand. "I guess you'll have to
behave now, whether you want to or not," he said, unlocking
the manacles. "Wont you?"

"Yes," the convict said. They went on; after a time the
shore vanished completely and a little sea got up. The convict
was free now but he lay as before, the end of the skiff's
painter in his hand, bent now with three or four turns about
his wrist; he turned his head now and then to look back at the
towing skiff as it slewed and bounced in the launch's wake;
now and then he even looked out over the lake, the eyes alone
moving, the face grave and expressionless, thinking *This is a
greater immensity of water, of waste and desolation, than I have
ever seen before;* perhaps not; thinking three or four hours
later, the shoreline raised again and broken into a clutter of
sailing sloops and power cruisers, *These are more boats than I
believed existed, a maritime race of which I also had no cognizance*
or perhaps not thinking it but just watching as the launch
opened the shored gut of the ship canal, the low smoke of the
city beyond it, then a wharf, the launch slowing in; a quiet
crowd of people watching with that same forlorn passivity he
had seen before and whose race he did recognise even though
he had not seen Vicksburg when he passed it—the brand,

the unmistakable hallmark of the violently homeless, he more so than any, who would have permitted no man to call him one of them.

"All right," the leader said to him. "Here you are."

"The boat," the convict said.

"You've got it. What do you want me to do—give you a receipt for it?"

"No," the convict said. "I just want the boat."

"Take it. Only you ought to have a bookstrap or something to carry it in." ("Carry it in?" the plump convict said. "Carry it where? Where would you have to carry it?")

He (the tall one) told that: how he and the woman disembarked and how one of the men helped him haul the skiff up out of the water and how he stood there with the end of the painter wrapped around his wrist and the man bustled up, saying, "All right. Next load! Next load!" and how he told this man too about the boat and the man cried, "Boat? Boat?" and how he (the convict) went with them when they carried the skiff over and racked, berthed, it with the others and how he lined himself up by a coca cola sign and the arch of a draw bridge so he could find the skiff again quick when he returned, and how he and the woman (he carrying the paper-wrapped parcel) were herded into a truck and after a while the truck began to run in traffic, between close houses, then there was a big building, an armory—

"Armory?" the plump one said. "You mean a jail."

"No. It was a kind of warehouse, with people with bundles laying on the floor." And how he thought maybe his partner might be there and how he even looked about for the Cajan while waiting for a chance to get back to the door again, where the soldier was and how he got back to the door at last, the woman behind him and his chest actually against the dropped rifle.

"Gwan, gwan," the soldier said. "Get back. They'll give you some clothes in a minute. You cant walk around the streets that way. And something to eat too. Maybe your kinfolks will come for you by that time." And he told that too: how the woman said,

"Maybe if you told him you had some kinfolks here he would let us out." And how he did not; he could not have expressed this either, it too deep, too ingrained; he had never yet had to think it into words through all the long genera- tions of himself—his hill-man's sober and jealous respect not for truth but for the power, the strength, of lying—not to be niggard with lying but rather to use it with respect and even care, delicate quick and strong, like a fine and fatal blade. And how they fetched him clothes—a blue jumper and overalls, and then food too (a brisk starched young woman saying "But the baby must be bathed, cleaned. It will die if you dont" and the woman saying "Yessum. He might holler some, he aint never been bathed before. But he's a good baby") and now it was night, the unshaded bulbs harsh and savage and forlorn above the snorers and he rising, gripping the woman awake, and then the window. He told that: how there were doors in plenty, leading he did not know where, but he had a hard time finding a window they could use but he found one at last, he carrying the parcel and the baby too while he climbed through first—"You ought to tore up a sheet and slid down it," the plump convict said. But he needed no sheet, there were cobbles under his feet now, in the rich darkness. The city was there too but he had not seen it yet and would not—the low constant glare; Bienville had stood there too, it had been the figment of an emasculate also calling himself Napoleon but no more, Andrew Jackson had found it one step from Pennsylvania Avenue. But the convict found it considerably further than one step back to the ship canal and the skiff, the coca cola sign dim now, the draw bridge arching spidery against the jonquil sky at dawn: nor did he tell, anymore than about the sixty-foot levee, how he got the skiff back into the water. The lake was behind him now; there was but one direction he could go. When he saw the River again he knew it at once. He should have; it was now ineradicably a part of his past, his life; it would be a part of what he would bequeath, if that were in store for him. But four weeks later it would look different from what it did now and did: he (the old man) had recovered from his debauch, back in banks again, the Old Man, rimpling placidly toward the sea, brown and rich as chocolate between levees whose inner faces were wrinkled as though in a frozen and aghast amazement, crowned with the rich green of summer in the willows; beyond them, sixty feet below, slick mules squatted against the broad pull of middle-busters in the richened soil which would not need to be planted, which would need only to be shown a cotton seed to sprout and make; there would be the symmetric miles of strong stalks by July, purple bloom in August, in September the black fields snowed over, spilled, the middles dragged smooth by the long sacks, the long black limber hands plucking, the hot air filled with the whine of gins, the September air then but now June air heavy with locust and (the towns) the smell of new paint and the sour smell of the paste which holds wall paper—the towns, the villages, the little lost wood landings on stilts on the inner face of the levee, the lower storeys bright and rank under the new paint and paper and even the marks on spile and post and tree of May's raging water-height fading beneath each bright silver gust of summer's loud and inconstant rain; there was a store at the levee's lip, a few saddled and rope-bridled mules in the sleepy dust, a few dogs, a handful of negroes sitting on the steps beneath the chewing tobacco and malaria medicine signs, and three white men, one of them a deputy sheriff canvassing for votes to beat his superior (who had given him his job) in the August primary, all pausing to watch the skiff emerge from the glitter-glare of the afternoon water and approach and land, a woman carrying a child stepping out, then a man, a tall man who, approaching, proved to be dressed in a faded but recently-washed and quite clean suit of penitentiary clothing, stopping in the dust where the mules dozed and watching with pale cold humorless eyes while the deputy sheriff was still making toward his armpit that gesture which everyone present realised was to have produced a pistol in one flashing motion for a considerable time while still nothing came of it. It was apparently enough for the new-comer, however.

"You a officer?" he said.

"You damn right I am," the deputy said. "Just let me get this damn gun—"

"All right," the other said. "Yonder's your boat, and here's the woman. But I never did find that bastard on the cotton-house."

The Wild Palms

THIS TIME the doctor and the man called Harry walked out of the door together, onto the dark porch, into the dark wind still filled with the clashing of invisible palms. The doctor carried the whiskey—the pint bottle half full; perhaps he did not even know it was in his hand, perhaps it was only the hand and not the bottle which he shook in the invisible face of the man standing above him. His voice was cold, precise, and convinced—the puritan who some would have said was about to do what he had to do because he was a puritan, who perhaps believed himself he was about to do it to protect the ethics and sanctity of his chosen profession, but who was actually about to do it because though not old yet he believed he was too old for this, too old to be wakened at midnight and dragged, haled, unwarned and still dull with sleep, into this, this bright wild passion which had somehow passed him up when he had been young enough, worthy enough, and to whose loss he believed he had not only become reconciled but had been both fortunate and right in having been elected to lose.

"You have murdered her," he said.

"Yes," the other said, almost impatiently; this the doctor noticed now, this alone. "The hospital. Will you telephone, or—"

"Yes, murdered her! Who did this?"

"I did. Dont stand here talking. Will you tel—"

"Who did this, I say? Who performed it? I demand to know."

"I did, I tell you. Myself. In God's name, man!" He took the doctor's arm, he gripped it, the doctor felt it, felt the hand, he (the doctor) heard his own voice too:

"What?" he said. "You? *You* did it? Yourself? But I thought you were the. . . ." *I thought you were the lover* was what he meant. *I thought you were the one who* because what he was thinking was *This is too much! There are rules! Limits! To fornication, adultery, to abortion, crime* and what he meant was *To that of love and passion and tragedy which is allowed to anyone lest he become as God Who has suffered likewise all that Satan can*

684

have known. He even said some of it at last, flinging the other's hand violently off, not exactly as if it had been a spider or a reptile or even a piece of filth, but rather as if he had found clinging to his sleeve a piece of atheistic or Communist propaganda—something not violating so much as affronting that profound and now deathless desiccated spirit which had contrived to retire into pure morality. "This is too much!" he cried. "Stay here! Dont try to escape! You cannot hide where you will not be found!"

"Escape?" the other said. "Escape? Will you telephone for the ambulance, in God's dear name?"

"I'll telephone, never you fear!" the doctor cried. He was on the earth below the porch now, in the hard black wind, already moving away, beginning to run suddenly and heavily on his thick sedentary legs. "Dont you dare to try!" he cried back. "Dont you dare to try!" He still had the flashlight; Wilbourne watched the beam of it jouncing on toward the oleander hedge as though it too, the little futile moth-light beam, struggled too against the constant weight of the black pitiless wind. *He didn't forget that* Wilbourne thought, watching it. *But then he probably never forgot anything in his life except that he was alive once, must have been born alive at least*. Then at that word he became aware of his heart, as though all profound terror had merely waited until he should prompt himself. He could feel the hard black wind too as he blinked after the floundering light until it passed through the hedge and vanished; he blinked steadily in the black wind, he could not stop it. *My lachrymae are not functioning* he thought, hearing his roaring and laboring heart. *As though it were pumping sand not blood, not liquid* he thought. *Trying to pump it. It's just this wind I think I cant breathe in, it's not that I really cant breathe, find something somewhere to breathe because apparently the heart can stand anything anything anything*.

He turned and crossed the porch. This time as before he and the black steady wind were like two creatures trying to use the same single entrance. *Only it dont really want to come in* he thought. *Dont need to. Dont have to. It's just interfering for the fun, the hell of it*. He could feel it on the door when he touched the knob, then, close, he could hear it too, a sibilance, a whisper. It was risible, it was almost a chuckling, leaning its weight on the door along with his weight, making the door easy, too easy, surreptitious, making its weight really felt only when he came to close the door and this time too just easy because so steady, just risible and chuckling; it did not really want to come in. He closed the door, watching the faint light which fell into the hall from the lamp inside the bedroom suck shift and recover steadily as what of the wind might have remained in the house if it had wanted to, might have been trapped inside the house by the closing door, licked quietly out through the ultimate closing crack, risible and constant, not at all departing, and turned listening, his head slanted a little toward the bedroom door with listening. But no sound came from beyond it, no sound in the hall but the wind murmuring against the door of the barren rented hall where he stood, quiet with listening, thinking quietly, *I guessed wrong. It's incredible, not that I should have had to guess but that I should have guessed so wrong* not meaning the doctor, not thinking about the doctor now (With a part of his mind he was not using now he could see it: the other neat, tight, brown-stained wind-proof tongue-and-groove hall, the flashlight still burning on the table beside the hurried bag, the thick bulging varicose planted calves as he had first seen them beneath the nightshirt, planted outraged and convinced and unassuageable by anything else but this; he could even hear the voice not raised but risen, a little shrill, unappeasable too, into the telephone: "And a policeman. A *policeman*. Two if necessary. Do you hear?" *He'll wake her too* he thought, seeing this too: the upper room, the gorgon-headed woman in the gray high-necked gown risen onto her elbow in the stale gray bed, her head cocked to listen and without surprise, who would be hearing only what she had been expecting for four days to hear. *She will come back with him — if he himself comes back* he thought. *If he dont just sit outside with the pistol to guard the exits. And maybe she will even be there too.*). Because this didn't matter, it was just like putting a letter into the mail; it didn't matter what box, only that he should have waited so late to mail the letter, he, after the four years and then the twenty months, the almost two years more and then done, complete. *I have made a bust even of that part of my life which I threw away* he thought, motionless in the risible murmur of the waiting and unhurried wind, his head turned slightly toward the bedroom door with listening, thinking with that trivial layer of his mind which he did not need to use, *So it's not just the wind I cant breathe in so maybe forever after I have gained, earned, some little of suffocation* beginning to breathe not faster but deeper, he could not stop it, each breath shallower and shallower and harder and harder and nearer and nearer the top of his lungs until in a moment it would escape the lungs altogether and there would indeed be no breath left anywhere forever, blinking steadily and painfully at the sudden granulation of his lids as though the black sand dammed forever of any moisture at which his strong heart scooped and surged were about to burst out of him through all his ducts and pores as they say the sweat of agony does, thinking *Steady now. Careful now. When she comes back this time she will have to begin to hold on.*

He crossed the hall to the bedroom door. There was still no sound save the wind (there was a window, the sash did not fit; the black wind whispered and murmured at it but did not enter, it did not want to, did not need to). She lay on her back, her eyes closed, the nightgown (that garment which she had never owned, never worn before) twisted about her just under the arms, the body not sprawled, not abandoned, but on the contrary even a little tense. The whisper of the black wind filled the room but coming from nothing, so that presently it began to seem to him that the sound was rather the murmur of the lamp itself sitting on an up-ended packing case beside the bed, the rustle and murmur of faint dingy light itself on her flesh—the waist ever narrower than he had believed, anticipated, the thighs merely broad since they were flat too, the swell and neat nip of belly between the navel's flattened crease and the neat close cupping of female hair, and nothing else, no croaching shadow of ineradicable blackness, no shape of death cuckolding him; nothing to see, yet it was there, he not permitted to watch his own cuckolding but only to look down upon the invisible pregnancy of his horning. And then he could not breathe and he began to back away from the door but it was too late because she was lying on the bed looking at him.

He didn't move. He couldn't help his breathing but he

didn't move, one hand on the door frame and his foot already lifted for the first step back, the eyes open full upon him though still profoundly empty of sentience. Then he saw it begin: the *I*. It was like watching a fish rise in water—a dot, a minnow, and still increasing; in a second there would be no more pool but all sentience. He crossed to the bed in three strides, fast but quiet; he put his hand flat on her chest, his voice quiet, steady, insistent: "No, Charlotte. Not yet. You can hear me. Go back. Go back, now. It's all right now", quiet and urgent and contained out of his need, as though departure only followed farewell, and goodbye was not something to precede the going away—provided there was time for it. "That's right," he said. "Go back. It's not time yet. I will tell you when the time comes." And she heard him from somewhere because at once the fish became the minnow again and then the dot; in another second the eyes would be empty again and blank. Only he lost her. He watched it: the dot growing too fast this time, no serene minnow but a vortex of cognizant pupil in the yellow stare spinning to blackness while he watched, the black shadow not on the belly but in the eyes. Her teeth caught her lower lip, she rolled her head and tried to rise, struggling against the flat of his hand on her breast.

"I'm hurting. Jesus, where is he? Where's he gone? Tell him to give me something. Quick."

"No," he said. "He cant. You've got to hurt. That's what you've got to hold on to." Now it must have been laughing; it couldn't have been anything else. She lay back and began to thresh from hip to hip, still threshing as he untwisted the gown and drew it down and covered her.

"I thought you said you would do the holding."

"I am. But you've got to hold on too. You've got to do most of it for a while. Just a little while. The ambulance will be here soon, but you must stay here and hurt now. Do you hear? You cant go back now."

"Then take the knife and cut it out of me. All of it. Deep. So there wont be anything left but just a shell to hold the cold air, the cold—" Her teeth, glinting in the lamplight, caught her lower lip again; a thread of blood appeared at the corner of her mouth. He took a soiled handkerchief from his hip and leaned to her but she rolled her head away from his hand. "All right," she said. "I'm holding on. You say the ambulance is coming?"

"Yes. In a minute we will hear it. Let me—" She rolled her head again away from the handkerchief.

"All right. Now get to hell out. You promised."

"No. If I leave, you wont hold on. And you've got to hold on."

"I am holding on. I'm holding on so you can go, get out of here before they come. You promised me you would. I want to see you go. I want to watch you."

"All right. But dont you want to say goodbye first?"

"All right. But Jesus God, dont touch me. It's like fire, Harry. It doesn't hurt. It's just like fire. Just dont touch me." So he knelt beside the bed; she stopped her head now; her lips lay still under his for a moment, hot and dry to the taste, with the thin sweetish taste of the blood. Then she pushed his face away with her hand, it hot and dry too, he hearing her heart still, even now, a little too fast, a little too strong. "Jesus, we had fun, didn't we? bitching, and making things. In the cold, the snow. That's what I'm thinking about. That's what I'm holding on to now: the snow, the cold, the cold. But it doesn't hurt; it's just like fire; it's just—Now go. Get to hell out. Quick." She began to roll her head again. He rose from his knees.

"All right. I'm going. But you must hold on. You will have to hold on a long time. Can you do it?"

"Yes. But go. Go quick. We've got enough money for you to get to Mobile. You can lose yourself quick there; they cant find you there. But go. Get to hell away from here quick for God's sake." This time when the teeth caught the bright thin blood spurted all the way to her chin. He didn't move at once. He was trying to remember something out of a book, years ago, of Owen Wister's, the whore in the pink ball dress who drank the laudanum and the cowboys taking turns walking her up and down the floor, keeping her on her feet, keeping her alive, remembering and forgetting it in the same instant since it would not help him. He began to move toward the door.

"All right," he said. "I'm going now. But remember, you

will have to hold on by yourself then. Do you hear? Charlotte?" The yellow eyes were full on him, she released the
bitten lip and as he sprang back toward the bed he heard over
the chuckling murmur of the wind the two voices at the front
door, the porch—the plump-calved doctor's high, almost
shrill, almost breaking, that of the gray gorgon wife cold and
level, at a baritone pitch a good deal more masculine than the
man's voice, the two of them unorientable because of the
wind like the voices of two ghosts quarrelling about nothing,
he (Wilbourne) hearing them and losing them too in the
same instant as he bent over the wide yellow stare in the head
which had ceased to roll, above the relaxed bleeding lip.
"Charlotte!" he said. "You cant go back now. You're hurting.
You're hurting. It wont let you go back. You can hear me."
He slapped her, fast, with two motions of the same hand.
"You're hurting, Charlotte."

"Yes," she said. "You and your best doctors in New Orleans. When anybody with one mail-order stethoscope could
give me something. Come on, Rat. Where are they?"

"They're coming. But you've got to hurt now. You're hurting now."

"All right. I'm holding on. But you mustn't hold him. That
was all I asked. It wasn't him. Listen, Francis—See, I called
you Francis. If I were lying to you do you think I would call
you Francis instead of Rat?—Listen, Francis. It was the other
one. Not that Wilbourne bastard. Do you think I would let
that bloody bungling bastard that never even finished hospital
poke around in me with a knife——" The voice stopped;
there was nothing in the eyes at all now though they were still
open—no minnow, no dot even—nothing. *But the heart* he
thought. *The heart.* He laid his ear to her chest, hunting the
wrist pulse with one hand; he could hear it before his ear
touched her, slow, strong enough still but each beat making a
curious hollow reverberation as though the heart itself had
retreated, seeing at the same moment (his face was toward the
door) the doctor enter, still carrying the scuffed bag in one
hand and in the other a cheap-looking nickel-plated revolver
such as you could find in almost any pawnshop and which, as
far as serviceability was concerned, should still have been
there, and followed by the gray-faced Medusa-headed woman

in a shawl. Wilbourne rose, already moving toward the doctor, his hand already extended for the bag. "It will last this time," he said, "but the heart's—Here. Give me the bag. What do you carry? Strychnine?" He watched the bag as it fled, snatched, behind the thick leg, the other hand he did not even look at as it came up but only in the next instant, at the cheap pistol pointed at nothing and being shaken in his face as the whiskey bottle had been.

"Dont move!" the doctor cried.

"Put that thing down," the wife said, in that same cold baritone. "I told you not to bring it. Give him the bag if he wants it and can do anything with it."

"No!" the doctor cried. "I'm a doctor. He is not. He's not even a successful criminal!" Now the gray wife spoke to Wilbourne so abruptly that for a moment he did not even know he was being addressed:

"Is there anything in that bag that would cure her?"

"Cure her?"

"Yes. Get her on her feet and get both of you out of this house." The doctor turned on her now, speaking in that shrill voice on the point of breaking:

"Cant you understand that this woman is dying?"

"Let her die. Let them both die. But not in this house. Not in this town. Get them out of here and let them cut on one another and die as much as they please." Now Wilbourne watched the doctor shaking the pistol in the wife's face as the other had shaken it in his.

"I will not be interfered with!" he cried. "This woman is dying and this man must suffer for it."

"Suffer fiddlesticks," the wife said. "You're mad because he used a scalpel without having a diploma. Or did something with it the Medical Association said he mustn't. Put that thing down and give her whatever it is so she can get out of that bed. Then give them some money and call a taxi-cab, not an ambulance. Give him some of my money if you wont your own."

"Are you mad?" the doctor cried. "Are you insane?" The wife looked at him coldly with her gray face beneath the screws of gray hair.

"So you will aid and abet him to the last, wont you? I'm

not surprised. I never yet saw one man fail to back up another, provided what they wanted to do was just foolish enough." Again she turned on (not to) Wilbourne with that cold abruptness which for an instant left him unaware that he was being addressed: "You haven't eaten anything, I imagine. I'm going to heat some coffee. You'll probably need it by the time he and those others get through with you."

"Thank you," Wilbourne said. "I couldn't—" But she was already gone. He caught himself about to say, "Wait, I'll show you" then forgot this without even having to think that she would know the kitchen better than he since she owned it, moving aside as the doctor passed him and went to the bed, following the doctor, watching him set the bag down then seem to discover the pistol in his hand and look about for something to lay it upon before remembering, then remembering and turning over his shoulder his dishevelled face.

"Dont you move!" he cried. "Dont you dare to move!"

"Get your stethoscope," Wilbourne said. "I had thought about something now, but maybe we had better wait. Because she will come out of it once more, wont she? She'll rally another time. Of course she will. Go on. Get it out."

"You should have thought of that before!" The doctor still watched Wilbourne, glaring, still holding the pistol while he fumbled the bag open and extracted the stethoscope; then, still holding the pistol he ducked into the pronged tubes and leaned, seeming to forget the pistol again because he actually laid it on the bed, his hand still resting upon it but unconscious of the pistol, merely supporting his leaning weight, because there was peace in the room now, the fury gone; Wilbourne could now hear the gray wife at the stove in the kitchen and he could hear the black wind again, risible, jeering, constant, inattentive, and it even seemed to him that he could hear the wild dry clashing of the palms in it. Then he heard the ambulance, the first faint mounting wail, far away yet, on the highway from the village, and almost immediately the wife came in, carrying a cup.

"Here comes your joyride," she said. "It never had time to get hot. But it will be something in your stomach."

"I thank you," Wilbourne said. "I do thank you. It wouldn't stay down, you see."

"Nonsense. Drink it."

"I do thank you." The ambulance was wailing louder, loud, it was coming fast, it was close now, the wail sinking into a grumble as it slowed, then rising into the wail again. It seemed to be just outside the house, loud and peremptory and with an illusion of speed and haste even though Wilbourne knew it was now merely crawling up the rutted weed-choked lane which led from the highway to the house; this time when it sank to the groan it was just outside the house, the sound now possessing a baffled grunting tone almost like the voice of an animal, a large one, bewildered, maybe even injured. "I do thank you. I realise there is always a certain amount of inevitable cleaning up in vacating a house. It would be foolish to add to it this late." Now he heard the feet on the porch, hearing them above his heart, the profound strong ceaseless shallow dredging at air, breath on the point of escaping his lungs altogether; now (there was no knock) they were in the hall, the trampling; three men entered, in civilian clothes—a youth with a close cap of curly hair, in a polo shirt and no socks, a neat wiry man of no age and fully dressed even to a pair of horn glasses, pushing a wheeled stretcher, and behind them a third man with the indelible mark of ten thousand Southern deputy sheriffs, urban and suburban—the snapped hat-brim, the sadist's eyes, the slightly and unmistakably bulged coat, the air not swaggering exactly but of a formally pre-absolved brutality. The two men with the stretcher wheeled it up to the bed in a business-like manner; it was the officer whom the doctor addressed, indicating Wilbourne with his hand, and now Wilbourne knew the other had really forgot that the hand still held the pistol.

"This is your prisoner," the doctor said. "I will prefer formal charges against him as soon as we get to town. As soon as I can."

"Look out, Doc— Evening, Miss Martha," the officer said. "Put that thing down. It might go off at any time. That fellow you got it from might of pulled the trigger before he turned it over to you." The doctor looked at the pistol, then Wilbourne seemed to remember him stowing it methodically into the scuffed bag along with the stethoscope; he just seemed to remember this because he had followed the stretcher to the bed.

"Easy now," he said. "Dont rouse her up. She wont—"

"I'll take charge of this," the doctor said, in that weary voice which had become peaceful at last after a fashion, as if it had worn itself out yet which would have, could have risen again at need quick and easy, as if it had renewed itself, renewed the outragement. "This case has been turned over to me, remember that. I didn't ask for it." He approached the bed (it was now that Wilbourne seemed to remember him putting the pistol into the bag) and lifted Charlotte's wrist. "Go as easy with her as you can. But hurry. Doctor Richardson will be there and I will follow in my car." The two men lifted Charlotte onto the stretcher. It was on rubber-tired wheels; with the hatless youth pushing it seemed to cross the room and vanish into the hall with incredible rapidity, as though sucked there and not pushed (the very wheels making a sucking sound on the floor), by no human agency but by time perhaps, by some vent-pipe through which the irrevocable seconds were fleeing, crowding; even the night itself.

"All right," the officer said. "What's your name? Wilson?"

"Yes," Wilbourne said. It went through the hall too that way, sucked through, where the wiry man now had a flashlight; the risible dark wind chuckled and murmured into the open door, leaning its weight against him like a black palpy hand, he leaning into it, onto it. There would be the porch, the steps beyond. "She's light," Wilbourne said in a thin anxious voice. "She's lost a lot of weight lately. I could carry her if they would—"

"They can too," the officer said. "Besides, they are being paid for it. Take it easy."

"I know. But that short one, that small one with the light—"

"He saves his strength for this. He likes it. You dont want to hurt his feelings. Take it easy."

"Look," Wilbourne said thinly, murmuring, "why dont you put the handcuffs on me? Why dont you?"

"Do you want them?" the officer said. And now the stretcher without stopping sucked off the porch too, into space, still on the same parallel plane as though it possessed displacement perhaps but no weight; it didn't even pause, the white shirt and trousers of the youth seemed merely to walk behind it as it moved on behind the flashlight, toward the corner of the house, toward what the man from whom he had rented the house called the drive. Now he could hear the threshing of the invisible palms, the wild dry sound of them.

The hospital was a low building, vaguely Spanish (or Los Angeles), of stucco, almost hidden by a massy lushness of oleander. There were more of the shabby palms too, the ambulance turning in at speed, the siren's wail dying into the grunting animal-like fall, the tires dry and sibilant in oyster shells; when he emerged from the ambulance he could hear the palms rustling and hissing again as if they were being played upon by a sand-blower and he could smell the sea still, the same black wind, but not so strong since the sea was four miles away, the stretcher coming out fast and smooth again as though sucked out, the feet of the four of them crisp in the dry fragile shells; and now in the corridor he began to blink again at his sanded lids, painfully in the electric light, the stretcher sucking on, the wheels whispering on the linoleum, so that it was between two blinks that he saw that the stretcher was now propelled by two nurses in uniform, a big one and a little one, he thinking how apparently there was no such thing as a matched stretcher team, how apparently all the stretchers in the world must be propelled not by two physical bodies in accord but rather by two matched desires to be present and see what was going on. Then he saw an open door fierce with light, a surgeon already in operating tunic beside it, the stretcher turning in, sucked through the door, the surgeon looking at him once, not with curiosity but as you memorise a face, then turning and following the stretcher as Wilbourne was about to speak to him, the door (it sounded rubber-tired too) clapping to soundlessly in his face, almost slapping his face, the officer at his elbow saying, "Take it easy." Then there was another nurse; he had not heard her, she did not look at him at all, speaking briefly to the officer. "Okay," the officer said. He touched Wilbourne's elbow. "Straight ahead. Just take it easy."

"But let me—"

"Sure. Just take it easy." It was another door, the nurse turning and stepping aside, her skirts crisp and sibilant too like the oyster shells; she did not look at him at all. They entered, an office, a desk, another man in sterilised cap and tunic seated at the desk with a blank form and a fountain pen. He was older than the first one. He did not look at Wilbourne either.

"Name?" he said.

"Charlotte Rittenmeyer."

"Miss?"

"Mistress." The man at the desk wrote on the pad.

"Husband?"

"Yes."

"Name?"

"Francis Rittenmeyer." Then he told the address too. The pen flowed, smooth and crisp. *Now it's the fountain pen I cant breathe in* Wilbourne thought. "Can I—"

"He will be notified." Now the man at the desk looked up at him. He wore glasses, the pupils behind them distorted slightly and perfectly impersonal. "How do you account for it? Instruments not clean?"

"They were clean."

"You think so."

"I know it."

"Your first attempt?"

"No. Second."

"Other one come off? But you wouldn't know."

"Yes. I know. It did."

"Then how do you account for this failure?" He could have answered that: *I loved her.* He could have said it: *A miser would probably bungle the blowing of his own safe too. Should have called in a professional, a cracksman who didn't care, didn't love the very iron flanks that held the money.* So he said nothing at all, and after a moment the man at the desk looked down and wrote again, the pen travelling smoothly across the card. He said, still writing, without looking up: "Wait outside."

"I aint to take him in now?" the officer said.

"No." The man at the desk still did not look up.

"Couldn't I—" Wilbourne said. "Will you let. . . . . . ."
The pen stopped, but for a time longer the man at the desk

looked at the card, perhaps reading what he had written. Then he looked up.

"Why? She wouldn't know you."

"But she might come back. Rouse one more time. So I could—we could. . . ." The other looked at him. The eyes were cold. They were not impatient, not quite palpably patient. They merely waited until Wilbourne's voice ceased. Then the man at the desk spoke:

"Do you think she will—Doctor?" For a moment Wilbourne blinked painfully at the neat scrawled card beneath the day-colored desk lamp, the clean surgeon's hand holding the uncapped pen beside it.

"No," he said quietly. The man at the desk looked down again, at the card too since the hand holding the pen moved to it and wrote again.

"You will be notified." Now he spoke to the officer, not looking up, writing steadily: "That's all."

"I better get him out of here before that husband blows in with a gun or something, hadn't I, Doc?" the officer said.

"You will be notified," the man at the desk repeated without looking up.

"All right, Jack," the officer said. There was a bench, slotted and hard, like in old-time open trolley cars. From it he could see the rubber-tired door. It was blank, it looked final and impregnable as an iron portcullis; he saw with a kind of amazement that even from this angle it hung in its frame by only one side, lightly, so that for three-quarters of its circumference there was an unbroken line of Klieg light. *But she might* he thought. *She might.* "Jesus," the officer said. He held an unlighted cigarette in his hand now (Wilbourne had felt the movement against his elbow). "—Jesus, you played— What did you say your name was? Webster?"

"Yes," Wilbourne said. *I could get there. I could trip him if necessary and get there. Because I would know. I would. Surely They would not*

"You played hell, didn't you. Using a knife. I'm old fashioned; the old way still suits me. I dont want variety."

"Yes," Wilbourne said. There was no wind in here, no sound of it, though it seemed to him that he could smell, if not the sea, at least the dry and stubborn lingering of it in the oyster shells in the drive: and then suddenly the corridor became full of sound, the myriad minor voices of human fear and travail which he knew, remembered—the carbolised vacuums of linoleum and rubber soles like wombs into which human beings fled before something of suffering but mostly of terror, to surrender in little monastic cells all the burden of lust and desires and pride, even that of functional independence, to become as embryos for a time yet retaining still a little of the old incorrigible earthly corruption—the light sleeping at all hours, the boredom, the wakeful and fretful ringing of little bells between the hours of midnight and the dead slowing of dawn (finding perhaps at least this good use for the cheap money with which the world was now glutted and cluttered); this for a while, then to be born again, to emerge renewed, to bear the world's weight for another while as long as courage lasted. He could hear them up and down the corridor—the tinkle of the bells, the immediate sibilance of rubber heels and starched skirts, the querulous murmur of voices about nothing. He knew it well: and now still another nurse came down the hall, already looking full at him, slowing as she passed, looking at him, her head turning as she went on like an owl's head, her eyes quite wide and filled with something beyond just curiosity and not at all shrinking or horror, going on. The officer was running his tongue around inside his teeth as though seeking the remnants of food; possibly he had been eating somewhere when the call came. He still held the unlighted cigarette.

"These doctors and nurses," he said. "What a fellow hears about hospitals. I wonder if there's as much laying goes on in them as you hear about."

"No," Wilbourne said. "There never is any place."

"That's so. But you think of a place like a hospital. All full of beds every which way you turn. And all the other folks flat on their backs where they cant bother you. And after all doctors and nurses are men and women. And smart enough to take care of themselves or they wouldn't be doctors and nurses. You know how it is. How you think."

"Yes," Wilbourne said. "You've just told me." *Because after all* he thought *They are gentlemen. They must be. They are*

stronger than we are. Above all this. Above clowning. They dont
need to be anything else but gentlemen And now the second
doctor or surgeon—the one of the fountain pen—came out
of the office and down the corridor, the skirts of his tunic
sucking and snicking behind him too. He did not look at
Wilbourne at all, even when Wilbourne, watching his face,
rose as he passed and stepped toward him, about to speak, the
officer rising hurriedly too, surging up. Then the doctor
merely paused long enough to look back at the officer with
one cold brief irascible glance through the glasses.

"Aren't you in charge of this man?" he said.

"Sure, Doc," the officer said.

"Then what's the trouble?"

"Come on now, Watson," the officer said. "Take it easy, I tell
you." The doctor turned; he had scarcely paused even. "How
about smoking, Doc?" The doctor didn't answer at all. He
went on, his smock flicking. "Come on here," the officer said.
"Sit down before you get yourself in a jam or something."
Again the door went inward on its rubber tires and returned,
clapped silently to with that iron finality and that illusion of
iron impregnability which was so false since even from here
he could see how it swung in its frame by one side only, so
that a child, a breath, could move it. "Listen," the officer said.
"Just take it easy. They'll fix her up. That was Doc Richardson
himself. They brought a sawmill nigger in here couple three
years ago where somebody hit him across the guts with a
razor in a crap game. Well, what does Doc Richardson do,
opens him up, cuts out the bad guts, sticks the two ends together like you'd vulcanise an inner tube, and the nigger's
back at work right now. Of course he aint got but one gut
and it aint but two feet long so he has to run for the bushes
almost before he quits chewing. But he's all right. Doc'll fix
her up the same way. Aint that better than nothing? Huh?"

"Yes," Wilbourne said. "Yes. Do you suppose we could go
outside a while?" The officer rose with alacrity, the cigarette
still unlighted in his hand.

"That's an idea. We could smoke then." But then he could
not.

"You go on. I'll stay right here. I'm not going to leave. You
know that."

"Well, I dont know. Maybe I could stand at the door yonder and smoke."

"Yes. You can watch me from there." He looked up and down the corridor, at the doors. "Do you know where I could go if I get sick?"

"Sick?"

"Should have to vomit."

"I'll call a nurse and ask her."

"No. Never mind. I wont need it. I dont suppose I've got anything more to lose. Worth the trouble. I'll stay right here until they call me." So the officer went on down the corridor, on past the door hung in its three fierce slashes of light, and on toward the entrance through which they had come. Wilbourne watched the match snap under his thumb-nail and flare against his face, beneath the hat-brim, face and hat slanted to the match (not a bad face either exactly, just that of a fourteen-year-old boy who had to use a razor, who had begun too young to carry the authorised pistol too long), the entrance door apparently still open because the smoke, the first puff of it, streamed back up the corridor, fading: so that Wilbourne discovered that he really could smell the sea, the black shallow slumbering Sound without surf which the black wind blew over. Up the corridor, beyond an elbow, he could hear the voices of two nurses, two nurses not two patients, two females but not necessarily two women even, then beyond the same elbow one of the little bells tinkled, fretful, peremptory, the two voices murmuring on, then they both laughed, two nurses laughing not two women, the little querulous bell becoming irascible and frenzied, the laughter continuing for half a minute longer above the bell, then the rubber soles on the linoleum, hissing faint and fast; the bell ceased. It was the sea he smelled; there was the taste of the black beach the wind blew over in it, in his lungs, up near the top of his lungs, going through that again but then he had expected to have to, each fast strong breath growing shallower and shallower as if his heart had at last found a receptacle, a dumping-place, for the black sand it dredged and pumped at: and now he got up too, not going anywhere; he just got up without intending to, the officer at the entrance turning at once, snapping the cigarette backward. But Wilbourne made no further move and the officer slowed; he even paused at the light-slashed door and flattened his hat-brim against it, against the crack for a moment. Then he came on. He came on, because Wilbourne saw him; he saw the officer as you see a lamp post which happens to be between you and the street because the rubber-tired door had opened again, outward this time (*The Kliegs are off* he thought. *They are off. They are off now.*) and the two doctors emerged, the door clashing soundlessly to behind them and oscillating sharply once but opening again before it could have resumed, re-entered immobility, to produce two nurses though he saw them only with that part of vision which still saw the officer because he was watching the faces of the two doctors coming up the corridor and talking to one another in clipped voices through their mouth-pads, their smocks flicking neatly like the skirts of two women, passing him without a glance and he was sitting down again because the officer at his elbow said, "That's right. Take it easy" and he found that he was sitting, the two doctors going on, pinch-waisted like two ladies, the skirts of the smocks snicking behind them, and then one of the nurses passed too, in a face-pad also, not looking at him either, her starched skirts rustling on, he (Wilbourne) sitting on the hard bench, listening: so that for a moment his heart evacuated him, beating strong and slow and steady but re-mote, leaving him globed in silence, in a round vacuum where only the remembered wind murmured, to listen in, for the rubber soles to sibilate in, the nurse stopping at last beside the bench and now he looked up after a space.

"You can go in now," she said.

"All right," he said. But he didn't move at once. *It's the same one who didn't look at me* he thought. *She's not looking at me now. Only she is looking at me now* Then he got up; it was all right, the officer rising too, the nurse looking at him now.

"Do you want me to go in with you?"

"All right." It was all right. Probably a breath would do it yet when he put his hand on the door he found that his whole weight would not do it, that is, he could not seem to get any of his weight into it, the door actually like a fixed iron plate in the wall except at that moment it fled suddenly before him on its rubber tires and he saw the nurse's hand and arm and the operating table, the shape of Charlotte's body just indicated and curiously flattened beneath the sheet. The Kliegs were off, the standards shoved away into a corner and only a single dome light burned, and there was another nurse—he had not remembered four of them—drying her hands at a sink. But she dropped the towel into a bin at that moment and passed him, that is, walked into then out of his vision, and was gone. There was a blower, a ventilator, going somewhere near the ceiling too, invisible or at least concealed, camou-flaged, then he reached the table, the nurse's hand came and folded back the sheet and after a moment he looked back past her, blinking his dry painful eyelids, to where the officer stood in the door. "It's all right now," he said. "He can smoke now, cant he?"

"No," the nurse said.

"Never mind," he said. "You'll be through soon. Then you—"

"Come," the nurse said. "You only have a minute." Only this was not a cool wind blowing into the room but a hot one being forced out, so there was no smell in it of black sand it had blown over. But it was a wind, steady, he could feel it and see it, a lock of the dark savagely short hair stirring in it, heavily because the hair was still wet, still damp, between the closed eyes and the neat surgeon's knot in the tape which supported her lower jaw. Only it was more than this. It was more than just a slackening of joints and muscles, it was a collapsing of the entire body as undammed water collapses, arrested for the moment for him to look at but still seeking that profound and primal level much lower than that of the walking and upright, lower than the prone one of the little death called sleep, lower even than the paper-thin spurning sole; the flat earth itself and even this not low enough, spreading, disappearing, slow at first then increasing and at last with incredible speed: gone, vanished, no trace left above the insatiable dust. The nurse touched his arm. "Come," she said.

"Wait," he said; "wait." But he had to step back; it came fast as before, the same stretcher on its rubber tires, the wiry man hatless now too, his hair parted neatly with water, brushed forward then curved back at the brow like an old time barkeeper's, the flashlight in his hip pocket, the rim of his coat caught up behind it, the stretcher wheeling rapidly up broadside to the table as the nurse drew the sheet up again. "I wont need to help those two," he said. "Will I?"

"No," the nurse said. There was no especial shape beneath the sheet now at all and it came onto the stretcher as if it had no weight either. The stretcher whispered into motion again, wheeling sibilantly, sucking through the door again where the officer now stood with his hat in his hand. Then it was gone. He could hear it for a moment longer. Then he could not. The nurse reached her hand to the wall, a button clicked and the hum of the blower stopped. It cut short off as if it had run full-tilt into a wall, blotted out by a tremendous silence which roared down upon him like a wave, a sea, and there was nothing for him to hold to, picking him up, tossing and spinning him and roaring on, leaving him blinking steadily and painfully at his dry granulated lids. "Come," the nurse said. "Doctor Richardson says you can have a drink."

"Sure, Morrison." The officer put his hat back on. "Just take it easy."

The jail was somewhat like the hospital save that it was of two storeys, square, and there were no oleanders. But the palm was there. It was just outside his window, bigger, more shabby; when he and the officer passed beneath it to enter, with no wind to cause it it had set up a sudden frenzied clashing as though they had startled it, and twice more during the night while he stood, shifting his hands from time to time as that portion of the bars which they clasped grew warm and began to sweat on his palms, it clashed again in that brief sudden inexplicable flurry. Then the tide began to fall in the river and he could smell that too—the sour smell of salt flats where oyster shells and the heads of shrimp rotted, and hemp and old piling. Then dawn began (he had been hearing the shrimp boats putting out for some time) and he could see the draw bridge on which the railroad to New Orleans crossed standing suddenly against the paling sky and he heard the train from New Orleans and watched the approaching smoke then the train itself crawling across the bridge, high and toy-like and pink like something bizarre to decorate a cake with, in the flat sun that was already hot. Then the train was gone, the pink smoke. The palm beyond the window began to murmur, dry and steady, and he felt the cool morning breeze from the sea, steady and filled with salt, clean and iodinic in the cell above the smell of creosote and tobacco-spit and old vomit; the sour smell of the flats went away and now there would be a glitter on the tide-chopped water, the gars roiling sluggishly up and then down again among the floating garbage. Then he heard feet on the stairs and the jailor entered with a tin mug of coffee and a piece of factory-made coffee cake. "You want anything else?" he said. "Any meat?"

"Thanks," Wilbourne said. "Just the coffee. Or if you could get me some cigarettes. I haven't had any since yesterday."

"I'll leave you this until I go out." The jailor produced a cloth tobacco-sack and papers from his shirt. "Can you roll them?"

"I dont know," Wilbourne said. "Yes. Thanks. This will be fine." But he didn't make much of a job of it. The coffee was weak, oversweet and hot, too hot to drink or even hold in the hand, possessing seemingly a dynamic inherent inexhaustible quality of renewable heat impervious even to its own fierce radiation. So he set the cup on his stool and sat on the cot's edge above it; without realising it he had assumed the immemorial attitude of all misery, crouching, hovering not in grief but in complete guttish concentration above a scrap, a bone which would require protection not from anything which walked upright but from creatures which moved on the same parallel plane with the protector and the protected, pariah too, which would snap and snarl with the protector for it in the dust. He poured from the cloth sack into the creased paper as he knew, without being able to remember at all when and where he had seen the process, it should be done, watching in mild alarm as the tobacco sprayed off the paper in the light wind which blew in the window, turning his body to shelter the paper, realising that his hand was beginning to tremble though not concerned about it yet, laying the sack carefully and blindly aside, watching the tobacco as if he were holding the grains in the paper by the weight of his eyes, putting the other hand to the paper and finding they were both trembling now, the paper parting suddenly between his hands with an almost audible report. His hands were shaking

badly now; he filled the second paper with a terrific concentration of will, not of desire for tobacco but just to make
the cigarette; he deliberately raised his elbows from his knees
and held the filled paper before his calm unshaven faintly haggard face until the trembling stopped. But as soon as he relaxed them to roll the tobacco into the paper they began to
tremble again but this time he did not even pause, turning
the tobacco carefully into the paper, the tobacco raining
faintly and steadily from either end of the paper but the
paper turning on. He had to hold it in both hands to lick it
and then as soon as his tongue touched the paper his head
seemed to catch from the contact the same faint uncon-
trollable jerking and he sat for an instant, looking at what he
had accomplished—the splayed raddled tube already half
empty of tobacco and almost too damp to take fire. It took
both hands to hold the match to it too, it not smoke but a
single thin lance of heat, of actual fire, which shot into his
throat. Nevertheless, the cigarette in his right hand and his
left hand gripping his right wrist, he took two more draws
before the coal ran too far up the dry side of the paper to
draw again and dropped it, about to set his foot on it before
he remembered, noticed, that he was still barefoot, and so
letting it burn while he sat looking at the coffee mug with a
kind of despair, who had shown none before this and perhaps had not even begun to feel it yet, then taking up the
mug, holding it as he had held the cigarette, wrist in hand,
and brought it to his mouth, concentrated not on the coffee
but on the drinking of it so that he perhaps forgot to remember that the coffee was too hot to drink, making contact between the cup-rim and his steadily and faintly jerking
head, gulping at the still wellnigh scalding liquid, driven back
each time by the heat, blinking, gulping again, blinking, a
spoonful of the coffee sloshing out of the cup and onto the
floor, splashing over his feet and ankles like a handful of
dropped needles or maybe ice particles, realising that he had
begun to blink again too and setting the mug carefully—it
took both hands to make contact with the stool too—on the
stool again and sitting over it again, hunched a little and
blinking steadily at that granulation behind his lids, hearing
the two pair of feet on the stairs this time though he did not

even look toward the door until he heard it open then clash
again then looking around and up, at the double-breasted
coat (it was of gray palm beach now), the face above it freshly
shaved but which had not slept either, thinking (Wilbourne)
*He had so much more to do. I just had to wait. He had to get out
at a minute's notice and find someone to stay with the children.*
Rittenmeyer carried the suitcase—that one which had come
out from under the cot in the intern's quarters a year ago and
had travelled to Chicago and Wisconsin and Chicago and
Utah and San Antonio and New Orleans again and now to
jail—and he came and set it beside the cot. But even then the
hand at the end of the smooth gray sleeve was not done, the
hand going now inside the coat.

"There are your clothes," he said. "I have made your bond.
They will let you out this morning." The hand emerged and
dropped onto the cot a sheaf of banknotes folded neatly
twice. "It's the same three hundred dollars. You carried it long
enough to have gained adverse possession. It should get you a
long way. Far enough, anyhow. I'd say Mexico, but then you
can probably stay hidden anywhere if you're careful. But there
wont be anymore. Understand that. This is all."

"Jump it?" Wilbourne said. "Jump the bail?"

"Yes!" Rittenmeyer said violently. "Get to hell away from
here. I'll buy you a railroad ticket and send it to you—"

"I'm sorry," Wilbourne said.

"—New Orleans; you could even ship out on a boat—"

"I'm sorry," Wilbourne said. Rittenmeyer ceased. He was
not looking at Wilbourne; he was not looking at anything.
After a moment he said quietly:

"Think of her."

"I wish I could stop. I wish I could. No I dont. Maybe
that's it. Maybe that's the reason. . . ." Maybe that was; that
was the first time when he almost touched it. But not yet: and
that was all right too; it would return; he would find it, hold
it, when the time was ready.

"Then think about me," Rittenmeyer said.

"I wish I could stop that too. I feel—"

"Not me!" the other said, with that sudden violence again;
"dont you feel sorry for me. See? See?" And there was something else but he didn't say it, couldn't or wouldn't. He began

to shake too, in the neat dark sober beautiful suit, murmuring, "Jesus. Jesus. Jesus."

"Maybe I'm sorry because you cant do anything. And I know why you cant. Anybody else would know why you cant. But that doesn't help any. And I could do it and that would help some, not much maybe but some. Only I cant either. And I know why I cant too. I think I do. Only I just haven't. . . ." He ceased too. He said quietly: "I'm sorry." The other ceased to tremble; he spoke as quietly as Wilbourne:

"So you wont go."

"Maybe if you could tell me why," Wilbourne said. But the other didn't answer. He took an immaculate handkerchief from his breast pocket and wiped his face carefully with it and Wilbourne noticed too that the morning breeze from the sea had dropped, gone on, as if the bright still cumulus-stippled bowl of sky and earth were an empty globe, a vacuum, and what wind there was was not enough to fill it but merely ran back and forth inside it with no schedule, obeying no laws, unpredictable and coming from and going nowhere, like a drove of bridleless horses in an empty plain. Rittenmeyer went to the door and rattled it, not looking back. The jailor appeared and unlocked the door. He was not going to look back. "You've forgotten the money," Wilbourne said. The other turned and came back and took up the neat fold of notes. After a moment he looked at Wilbourne.

"So you wont do it," he said. "You wont."

"I'm sorry," Wilbourne said. *Only if he had just told me why* Wilbourne thought. *Maybe I would have* Only he knew he would not have. Yet he continued to think it from time to time while the last days of that June accomplished and became July—the dawns while he listened to the heavy beat of the shrimper engines standing down the river toward the Sound, the brief cool hour of morning while the sun was still at his back, the long glare of brazen afternoons while the salt-impinged sun slanted full and fierce into his window, printing his face and upper body with the bars to which he held— and he had even learned to sleep again, finding sometimes that he had slept between two shiftings of his hands upon the sweating bars. Then he stopped thinking it. He didn't know when; he did not even remember that Rittenmeyer's visit had gone completely out of his mind.

One day—it was toward sunset, how he had failed to see it before he did not know, it had been there twenty years—he saw, beyond the flat one-storey border of the river, across the river and toward the sea, the concrete hull of one of the emergency ships built in 1918 and never finished, the hull, the hulk; it had never moved, the ways rotted out from under it years ago, leaving it sitting on a mudflat beside the bright glitter of the river's mouth with a thin line of drying garments across the after well deck. The sun was setting behind it now and he could not distinguish much but the next morning he discovered the projecting slant of stove pipe with smoke coming out of it and he could distinguish the color of the garments flapping in the morning sea-wind and watched later a tiny figure which he knew to be a woman taking the garments from the line, believing he could distinguish the gesture with which she put the clothes pins one by one into her mouth, and he thought *If we had known it we could probably have lived there for the four days and saved ten dollars,* thinking *Four days. It could not possibly have been just four days. It could not;* and watching, one evening saw the dory come alongside and the man mount the ladder with a long skein of net cascading downward from his climbing shoulder, fragile and fairy-like, and watched the man mend the net under a morning's sun, sitting on the poop, the net across his knees, the sun on the mazy blond webbing tawnily silver. And a moon began and waxed nightly while he stood there, and he stood there in the dying light while night by night it waned; and one afternoon he saw the flags, set one above another, rigid and streaming from the slender mast above the Government station at the river mouth, against a flat steel-colored scudding sky and all that night a buoy outside the river moaned and bellowed and the palm beyond the window threshed and clashed and just before dawn, in a driving squall, the tail of the hurricane struck. Not the hurricane; it was galloping off somewhere in the Gulf, just the tail of it, a flick of the mane in passing, driving up the shore ten feet of roiled and yellow tide which did not fall for twenty hours and driving fiercely through the wild frenzied palm which still sounded dry and across the roof of the cell, so that all that second night he could hear the boom of seas against the breakwater in the crashing darkness and the buoy too, gurgling now between bellows; he could even seem to hear the roar of water streaming from it as it surged up again with each choking cry, the rain driving on, into the next dawn but with less fury now, on across the flat land before the east wind. It would be even quieter inland, it would become only a bright silver summer murmur among the heavy decorous trees, upon the clipped sward; it would be clipped; he could imagine it, it would be a good deal like the park where he had waited, maybe even with children and nurses at times, the best, the very best; there would even be a headstone soon, at just exactly the right time, when restored earth and decorum stipulated, telling nothing; it would be clipped and green and quiet, the body, the shape of it under the drawn sheet, flat and small and moving in the hands of two men as if without weight though it did, nevertheless bearing and quiet beneath the iron weight of earth. *Only that cant be all of it* he thought. *It cant be. The waste. Not of meat, there is always plenty of meat. They found that out twenty years ago preserving nations and justifying mottoes —granted the nations the meat preserved are worth the preserving with the meat it took gone. But memory. Surely memory exists independent of the flesh.* But this was wrong too. *Because it wouldn't know it was memory* he thought. *It wouldn't know what it was it remembered. So there's got to be the old meat, the old frail eradicable meat for memory to titillate.*

That was the second time he almost got it. But it escaped him again. But he was not trying yet; it was still all right, he was not worried; it would return when the time was ready and even stand still to his hand. Then one night he was allowed a bath and a barber (they had taken his razor blades away from him) came early the next morning and shaved him, and in a new shirt and manacled to an officer on one side and his court-designated lawyer on the other he walked through the still early sun, up the street where people—malaria-ridden men from the sawmill swamps and the wind- and sun-bitten professional shrimpers—turned to look after him, toward the courthouse from the balcony of which a bailiff was already crying. It was like the jail in its turn, of two storeys, of the same stucco, the same smell of creosote and tobacco spittle but not the vomit, set in a grassless plot with a half dozen palms and oleanders again too, blooming pink and white above a low thick mass of lantana. Then an entry filled yet, for a while yet, with shadow and a cellar-like coolness, the tobacco stronger, the air filled with a steady human sound, not exactly speech but that droning murmur which might have been the very authentic constant unsleeping murmur of functioning pores. They mounted stairs, a door; he walked up an aisle between filled benches while heads turned and the bailiff's voice still chanted from the balcony, and sat at a table between his lawyer and the officer then a moment later rose and stood again while the gownless judge in a linen suit and the high black shoes of an old man came with a short quick purposeful stride and took the Bench. It did not take long, it was businesslike, brief, twenty-two minutes to get a jury, his appointed lawyer (a young man with a round moon face and myopic eyes behind glasses, in a crumpled linen suit) challenging monotonously but it just took twenty-two minutes, the judge sitting high behind a pine counter grained and stained to resemble mahogany with his face which was not a lawyer's face at all but that of a Methodist Sunday School superintendent who on week days was a banker and probably a good banker, a shrewd banker, thin, with neat hair and a neat moustache and old fashioned gold-rimmed spectacles. "How does the indictment read?" he said. The clerk read it, his voice droning, almost drowsy among the redundant verbiage:

". . . . . .against the peace and dignity of the State of Mississippi. . . . . . .manslaughter. . . . . . ." A man rose at the far end of the table. He wore a suit of crumpled, almost disreputable, seersucker. He was quite fat and his was the lawyer's face, a handsome face, almost noble, cast for footlights, forensic shrewd and agile: the District Attorney.

"We believe we can prove murder, Your Honor."

"This man is not indicted for murder, Mr Gower. You should know that. Arraign the accused." Now the plump young lawyer rose. He had neither the older one's stomach nor the lawyer's face, not yet anyway.

"Guilty, Your Honor," he said. And now Wilbourne heard it from behind him—the long expulsion, the sigh.

"Is the accused trying to throw himself upon the mercy of this Court?" the judge said.

"I just plead guilty, Your Honor," Wilbourne said. He heard it again behind him, louder, but already the judge was hammering sharply with his child's croquet mallet.

"Dont speak from there!" he said. "Does the accused wish to throw himself on the mercy of the Court?"

"Yes, Your Honor," the young lawyer said.

"Then you dont need to make a case, Mr Gower. I will instruct the jury—" This time it was no sigh. Wilbourne heard the caught breath, then it was almost a roar, not that loud of course, not yet, the little hard wooden mallet furious against the wood and the bailiff shouting something too, and there was movement, a surging sound of feet in it too; a voice cried, "That's it! Go ahead! Kill him!" and Wilbourne saw it—the gray buttoned coat (the same one) moving steadily toward the Bench, the face, the outrageous face: the man who without any warning had had to stand the wrong sort of suffering, the one suffering for which he was not fitted, who even now must be saying to himself, *But why me? Why? What have I done? What in the world can I have done in my life?* coming steadily on then stopping and beginning to speak, the roar cutting short off as he opened his mouth:

"Your Honor—If the Court please—"

"Who is this?" the judge said.

"I am Francis Rittenmeyer," Rittenmeyer said. Now it was a roar again, the gavel going again, the judge himself shouting now, shouting the roar into silence:

"Order! Order! One more outbreak like this and I will clear the room! Disarm that man!"

"I'm not armed," Rittenmeyer said. "I just want—" But already the bailiff and two other men were upon him, the smooth gray sleeves pinioned while they slapped at his pockets and sides.

"He's not armed, Your Honor," the bailiff said. The judge turned upon the District Attorney, trembling too, a neat orderly man too old for this too.

"What is the meaning of this clowning, Mr Gower?"

"I dont know, Your Honor. I didn't—"

"You didn't summons him?"

"I didn't consider it necessary. Out of consideration for his—"

"If the Court please," Rittenmeyer said. "I just want to make a—" The judge lifted his hand; Rittenmeyer ceased. He stood motionless, his face calm as a carving, with something about it of the carved faces on gothic cathedrals, the pale eyes possessing something of the same unpupilled marble blankness. The judge stared at the District Attorney. It (the District Attorney's) was the lawyer's face now, completely, completely watchful, completely alert, the thinking going fast and secret behind it. The judge looked at the young lawyer, the plump one, hard. Then he looked at Rittenmeyer. "This case is closed," he said. "But if you still wish to make a statement, you may do so." Now there was no sound at all, not even that of breathing that Wilbourne could hear save his own and that of the young lawyer beside him, as Rittenmeyer moved toward the witness box. "This case is closed," the judge said. "The accused is waiting sentence. Make your statement from there." Rittenmeyer stopped. He was not looking at the judge, he was not looking at anything, his face calm, impeccable, outrageous.

"I wish to make a plea," he said. For a moment the judge did not move, staring at Rittenmeyer, the gavel still clutched in his fist like a sabre, then he leaned slowly forward, staring at Rittenmeyer: and Wilbourne heard it begin, the long insucking, the gathering of amazement and incredulity.

"You what?" the judge said. "A what? A plea? For this man? This man who wilfully and deliberately performed an operation on your wife which he knew might cause her death and which did?" And now it did roar, in waves, renewed; he could hear the feet in it and the separate screaming voices, the officers of the Court charging into the wave like a football team: a vortex of fury and turmoil about the calm immobile outrageous face above the smooth beautifully cut coat: "Hang them! Hang them both!" "Lock them up together! Let the son of a bitch work on him this time with the knife!" roaring on above the trampling and screaming, dying away at last but still not ceasing, just muffled beyond the closed doors for a time, then rising again from outside the building, the judge standing now, his arms propped on the bench, still clutching the gavel, his head jerking and trembling, the head of an old man indeed now. Then he sank slowly back, his head jerking as the heads of old men do. But his voice was quite calm, cold: "Give that man protection out of town. See that he leaves at once."

"I dont think he better try to leave the building right now, Judge," the bailiff said. "Listen at them." But nobody had to listen to hear it, not hysterical now, just outraged and angry. "They aint hanging mad, just tar-and-feathering mad. But anyway—"

"All right," the judge said. "Take him to my chambers. Keep him there until after dark. Then get him out of town.— Gentlemen of the jury, you will find the prisoner guilty as charged and so bring in your verdict, which carries with it a sentence at hard labor in the State Penitentiary at Parchman for a period of not less than fifty years. You may retire."

"I reckon there's no need of that, Judge," the foreman said. "I reckon we are all—" The judge turned upon him, the old man's thin and trembling fury:

"You will retire! Do you wish to be held in contempt?" They retired. They were gone less than two minutes, hardly long enough for the bailiff to close and then open the door. From outside the sound beat on, rising and falling.

That afternoon it rained again, a bright silver curtain roaring out of nowhere before the sun could be hidden, galloping on vagrom and coltlike, going nowhere, then thirty minutes later roaring back, bright and harmless in its own steaming footsteps. But when, shortly after dark, he was returned to his cell the sky was ineffable and stainless above the last green of twilight, arching the evening star, the palm merely murmuring beyond the bars, the bars still cool to his hands though the water, the rain, had long evaporated. So he had learned what Rittenmeyer meant. And now he learned why. He heard the two pairs of feet again but he did not turn from the window until the door had opened then clanged and clashed to and Rittenmeyer entered and stood for a moment, looking at him. Then Rittenmeyer took something from his pocket and crossed the cell, the hand extended. "Here," he said. It was a small box for medicine, unlabelled. It contained one white tablet. For a moment Wilbourne looked down at it stupidly, though only for a moment. Then he said quietly:

"Cyanide."

"Yes," Rittenmeyer said. He turned, he was already going: the face calm outrageous and consistent, the man who had been right always and found no peace in it.

"But I dont—" Wilbourne said. "How will my just being dead help—" Then he believed he understood. He said, "Wait." Rittenmeyer reached the door and put his hand on it. Nevertheless he paused, looking back. "It's because I have got stale. I dont think good. Quick." The other looked at him, waiting. "I thank you. I do thank you. I wish I knew I would do the same for you in my turn." Then Rittenmeyer shook the door once and looked again at Wilbourne—the face consistent and right and damned forever. The jailor appeared and opened the door.

"I'm not doing it for you," Rittenmeyer said. "Get that out of your damned head." Then he was gone, the door clashed; and it was no flash of comprehension, it was too quiet for that, it was just a simple falling of a jumbled pattern. *Of course* Wilbourne thought. *That last day in New Orleans. He promised her. She said, Not that bungling bastard Wilbourne, and he promised her.* And that was it. That was all. It fell into the quiet pattern and remained just long enough for him to see it then flowed, vanished, gone out of all remembering forever and so there was just memory, forever and inescapable, so long as there was flesh to titillate. And now he was about to get it, think it into words, so it was all right now and he turned to the window and, holding the open box carefully beneath and pinching the tablet in a folded cigarette paper between thumb and finger he rubbed the tablet carefully into powder on one of the lower bars, catching the last dust in the box and wiping the bar with the cigarette paper, and emptied the box onto the floor and with his shoe-sole ground it into the dust and old spittle and caked creosote until it had completely vanished and burned the cigarette paper and returned to the window. It was there, waiting, it was all right; it would stand to his hand when the moment came. Now he could see the light on the concrete hulk, in the poop porthole which he had called the kitchen for weeks now, as if he lived there, and now with a preliminary murmur in the palm the light off-shore breeze began, bringing with it the smell of swamps and wild jasmine, blowing on under the dying west and the bright star; it was the night. So it wasn't just memory. Memory was just half of it, it wasn't enough. *But it must be somewhere* he thought. *There's the waste. Not just me. At least I think I dont mean just me. Hope I dont mean just me. Let it be anyone* thinking of, remembering, the body, the broad thighs and the hands that liked bitching and making things. It seemed so little, so little to want, to ask. *With all the old graveward-creeping, the old wrinkled withered defeated clinging not even to the defeat but just to an old habit; accepting the defeat even to be allowed to cling to the habit —the wheezing lungs, the troublesome guts incapable of pleasure.* But after all memory could live in the old wheezing entrails: and now it did stand to his hand, incontrovertible and plain, serene, the palm clashing and murmuring dry and wild and faint and it the night but he could face it, thinking, *Not could. Will. I want to. So it is the old meat after all, no matter how old. Because if memory exists outside of the flesh it wont be memory because it wont know what it remembers so when she became not then half of memory became not and if I become not then all of remembering will cease to be. —Yes* he thought *Between grief and nothing I will take grief.*

Old Man

Oₙₑ ᴏꜰ ᴛʜᴇ Governor's young men arrived at the Penitentiary the next morning. That is, he was fairly young
(he would not see thirty again though without doubt he did
not want to, there being that about him which indicated a
character which never had and never would want anything it
did not, or was not about to, possess), a Phi Beta Kappa out
of an eastern university, a colonel on the Governor's staff who
did not buy it with a campaign contribution, who had stood
in his negligent eastern-cut clothes and his arched nose and
lazy contemptuous eyes on the galleries of any number of
little lost backwoods stores and told his stories and received
the guffaws of his overalled and spitting hearers and with
the same look in his eyes fondled infants named in memory of
the last administration and in honor (or hope) of the next,
and (it was said of him and doubtless not true) by lazy accident the behinds of some who were not infants any longer
though still not old enough to vote. He was in the Warden's
office with a briefcase, and presently the deputy warden of the
levee was there too. He would have been sent for presently
though not yet, but he came anyhow, without knocking, with
his hat on, calling the Governor's young man loudly by a
nickname and striking him with a flat hand on the back and
lifted one thigh to the Warden's desk, almost between the
Warden and the caller, the emissary. Or the vizier with the
command, the knotted cord, as began to appear immediately.

"Well," the Governor's young man said, "you've played the
devil, haven't you?" The Warden had a cigar. He had offered
the caller one. It had been refused, though presently, while
the Warden looked at the back of his neck with hard immobility even a little grim, the deputy leaned and reached
back and opened the desk drawer and took one.

"Seems straight enough to me," the Warden said. "He got
swept away against his will. He came back as soon as he could
and surrendered."

"He even brought that damn boat back," the deputy said.
"If he'd a throwed the boat away he could a walked back
in three days. But no sir. He's got to bring the boat back.

'Here's your boat and here's the woman but I never found no bastard on no cottonhouse.'" He slapped his knee, guffawing. "Them convicts. A mule's got twice as much sense."

"A mule's got twice as much sense as anything except a rat," the emissary said in his pleasant voice. "But that's not the trouble."

"What is the trouble?" the Warden said.

"This man is dead."

"Hell fire, he aint dead," the deputy said. "He's up yonder in that bunkhouse right now, lying his head off probly. I'll take you up there and you can see him." The Warden was looking at the deputy.

"Look," he said. "Bledsoe was trying to tell me something about that Kate mule's leg. You better go up to the stable and—"

"I done tended to it," the deputy said. He didn't even look at the Warden. He was watching, talking to, the emissary. "No sir. He aint—"

"But he has received an official discharge as being dead. Not a pardon nor a parole either: a discharge. He's either dead, or free. In either case he doesn't belong here." Now both the Warden and the deputy looked at the emissary, the deputy's mouth open a little, the cigar poised in his hand to have its tip bitten off. The emissary spoke pleasantly, extremely distinctly: "On a report of death forwarded to the Governor by the Warden of the Penitentiary." The deputy closed his mouth, though otherwise he didn't move. "On the official evidence of the officer delegated at the time to the charge and returning of the body of the prisoner to the Penitentiary." Now the deputy put the cigar into his mouth and got slowly off the desk, the cigar rolling across his lip as he spoke:

"So that's it. I'm to be it, am I?" He laughed shortly, a stage laugh, two notes. "When I done been right three times running through three separate administrations? That's on a book somewhere too. Somebody in Jackson can find that too. And if they cant, I can show——"

"Three administrations?" the emissary said. "Well, well. That's pretty good."

"You damn right it's good," the deputy said. "The woods

are full of folks that didn't." The Warden was again watching the back of the deputy's neck.

"Look," he said. "Why dont you step up to my house and get that bottle of whiskey out of the sideboard and bring it down here?"

"All right," the deputy said. "But I think we better settle this first. I'll tell you what we'll do——"

"We can settle it quicker with a drink or two," the Warden said. "You better step on up to your place and get a coat so the bottle—"

"That'll take too long," the deputy said. "I wont need no coat." He moved to the door, where he stopped and turned. "I'll tell you what to do. Just call twelve men in here and tell him it's a jury—he never seen but one before and he wont know no better—and try him over for robbing that train. Hamp can be the judge."

"You cant try a man twice for the same crime," the emissary said. "He might know that even if he doesn't know a jury when he sees one."

"Look," the Warden said.

"All right. Just call it a new train robbery. Tell him it happened yesterday, tell him he robbed another train while he was gone and just forgot it. He couldn't help himself. Besides, he wont care. He'd just as lief be here as out. He wouldn't have nowhere to go if he was out. None of them do. Turn one loose and be damned if he aint right back here by Christmas like it was a reunion or something, for doing the very same thing they caught him at before." He guffawed again. "Them convicts."

"Look," the Warden said. "While you're there, why dont you open the bottle and see if the liquor's any good. Take a drink or two. Give yourself time to feel it. If it's not good, no use in bringing it."

"O. K.," the deputy said. He went out this time.

"Couldn't you lock the door?" the emissary said. The Warden squirmed faintly. That is, he shifted his position in his chair.

"After all, he's right," he said. "He's guessed right three times now. And he's kin to all the folks in Pittman county except the niggers."

"Maybe we can work fast then." The emissary opened the briefcase and took out a sheaf of papers. "So there you are," he said.

"There what are?"

"He escaped."

"But he came back voluntarily and surrendered."

"But he escaped."

"All right," the Warden said. "He escaped. Then what?" Now the emissary said Look. That is, he said,

"Listen. I'm on per diem. That's tax-payers, votes. And if there's any possible chance for it to occur to anyone to hold an investigation about this, there'll be ten senators and twenty-five representatives here on a special train maybe. On per diem. And it will be mighty hard to keep some of them from going back to Jackson by way of Memphis or New Orleans—on per diem."

"All right," the Warden said. "What does he say to do?"

"This. The man left here in charge of one specific officer. But he was delivered back here by a different one."

"But he surren—" This time the Warden stopped of his own accord. He looked, stared almost, at the emissary. "All right. Go on."

"In specific charge of an appointed and delegated officer, who returned here and reported that the body of the prisoner was no longer in his possession; that, in fact, he did not know where the prisoner was. That's correct, isn't it?" The Warden said nothing. "Isn't that correct?" the emissary said, pleasantly, insistently.

"But you cant do that to him. I tell you he's kin to half the—"

"That's taken care of. The Chief has made a place for him on the highway patrol."

"Hell," the Warden said. "He cant ride a motorcycle. I dont even let him try to drive a truck."

"He wont have to. Surely an amazed and grateful state can supply the man who guessed right three times in succession in Mississippi general elections with a car to ride in and somebody to run it if necessary. He wont even have to stay in it all the time. Just so he's near enough so when an inspector sees the car and stops and blows the horn of it he can hear it and come out."

"I still dont like it," the Warden said.

"Neither do I. Your man could have saved all of this if he had just gone on and drowned himself, as he seems to have led everybody to believe he had. But he didn't. And the Chief says do. Can you think of anything better?" The Warden sighed.

"No," he said.

"All right." The emissary opened the papers and uncapped a pen and began to write. "Attempted escape from the Penitentiary, ten years' additional sentence," he said. "Deputy Warden Buckworth transferred to Highway Patrol. Call it for meritorious service even if you want to. It wont matter now. Done?"

"Done," the Warden said.

"Then suppose you send for him. Get it over with." So the Warden sent for the tall convict and he arrived presently, saturnine and grave, in his new bed-ticking, his jowls blue and close under the sunburn, his hair recently cut and neatly parted and smelling faintly of the prison barber's (the barber was in for life, for murdering his wife, still a barber) pomade. The Warden called him by name.

"You had bad luck, didn't you." The convict said nothing. "They are going to have to add ten years to your time."

"All right," the convict said.

"It's hard luck. I'm sorry."

"All right," the convict said. "If that's the rule." So they gave him the ten years more and the Warden gave him the cigar and now he sat, jackknifed backward into the space between the upper and lower bunks, the unlighted cigar in his hand while the plump convict and four others listened to him. Or questioned him, that is, since it was all done, finished, now and he was safe again so maybe it wasn't even worth talking about anymore.

"All right," the plump one said. "So you come back into the River. Then what?"

"Nothing. I rowed."

"Wasn't it pretty hard rowing coming back?"

"The water was still high. It was running pretty hard still. I never made much speed for the first week or two. After that it got better." Then, suddenly and quietly, something—the inarticulateness, the innate and inherited reluctance for speech, dissolved and he found himself, listened to himself, telling it quietly, the words coming not fast but easily to the tongue as he required them: How he paddled on (he found out by try-ing it that he could make better speed, if you could call it speed, next the bank—this after he had been carried suddenly and violently out to midstream before he could prevent it and found himself, the skiff, travelling back toward the region from which he had just escaped and he spent the better part of the morning getting back inshore and up to the canal again from which he had emerged at dawn) until night came and they tied up to the bank and ate some of the food he had secreted in his jumper before leaving the armory in New Or-leans and the woman and the infant slept in the boat as usual and when daylight came they went on and tied up again that night too and the next day the food gave out and he came to a landing, a town, he didn't notice the name of it, and he got a job. It was a cane farm—

"Cane?" one of the other convicts said. "What does any-body want to raise cane for? You cut cane. You have to fight it where I come from. You burn it just to get shut of it."

"It was sorghum," the tall convict said.

"Sorghum?" another said. "A whole farm just raising sor-ghum? *Sorghum?* What did they do with it?" The tall one didn't know. He didn't ask, he just came up the levee and there was a truck waiting full of niggers and a white man said, "You there. Can you run a shovel plow?" and the convict said Yes and the man said, "Jump in then" and the convict said, "Only I've got a—"

"Yes," the plump one said. "That's what I been aiming to ask. What did—" The tall convict's face was grave, his voice was calm, just a little short:

"They had tents for the folks to live in. They were behind." The plump one blinked at him.

"Did they think she was your wife?"

"I dont know. I reckon so." The plump one blinked at him.

"Wasn't she your wife? Just from time to time kind of, you might say?" The tall one didn't answer this at all. After a mo-ment he raised the cigar and appeared to examine a loosening of the wrapper because after another moment he licked the cigar carefully near the end. "All right," the plump one said. "Then what?" So he worked there four days. He didn't like it. Maybe that was why: that he too could not quite put credence in that much of what he believed to be sorghum. So when they told him it was Saturday and paid him and the white man told him about somebody who was going to Baton Rouge the next day in a motor boat, he went to see the man and took the six dollars he had earned and bought food with it and tied the skiff behind the motor boat and went to Baton Rouge. It didn't take long and even after they left the motor boat at Baton Rouge and he was paddling again it seemed to the convict that the River was lower and the current not so fast, so hard, so they made fair speed, tying up to the bank at night among the willows, the woman and baby sleeping in the skiff as of old. Then the food gave out again. This time it was a wood landing, the wood stacked and waiting, a wagon and team being unladen of another load. The men with the wagon told him about the sawmill and helped him drag the skiff up the levee; they wanted to leave it there but he would not so they loaded it onto the wagon too and he and the woman got on the wagon too and they went to the sawmill. They gave them one room in a house to live in here. They paid two dollars a day and furnish. The work was hard. He liked it. He stayed there eight days.

"If you liked it so well, why did you quit?" the plump one said. The tall convict examined the cigar again, holding it up where the light fell upon the rich chocolate-colored flank.

"I got in trouble," he said.

"What trouble?"

"Woman. It was a fellow's wife."

"You mean you had been toting one piece up and down the country day and night for over a month, and now the first time you have a chance to stop and catch your breath almost you got to get in trouble over another one?" The tall convict had thought of that. He remembered it: how there were times, seconds, at first when if it had not been for the baby he might have, might have tried. But they were just seconds because in the next instant his whole being would seem to flee the very idea in a kind of savage and horrified revulsion; he would find himself looking from a distance at this millstone

which the force and power of blind and risible Motion had
fastened upon him, thinking, saying aloud actually, with
harsh and savage outrage even though it had been two years
since he had had a woman and that a nameless and not young
negress, a casual, a straggler whom he had caught more or
less by chance on one of the fifth-Sunday visiting days, the
man—husband or sweetheart—whom she had come to see
having been shot by a trusty a week or so previous and she
had not heard about it: "She aint even no good to me for
that."

"But you got this one, didn't you?" the plump convict said.

"Yah," the tall one said. The plump one blinked at him.

"Was it good?"

"It's all good," one of the others said. "Well? Go on. How
many more did you have on the way back? Sometimes when
a fellow starts getting it it looks like he just cant miss even
if—" That was all, the convict told them. They left the sawmill fast, he had no time to buy food until they reached the
next landing. There he spent the whole sixteen dollars he had
earned and they went on. The River was lower now, there
was no doubt of it, and sixteen dollars' worth looked like a lot
of food and he thought maybe it would do, would be
enough. But maybe there was more current in the River still
than it looked like. But this time it was Mississippi, it was
cotton; the plow handles felt right to his palms again, the
strain and squat of the slick buttocks against the middle buster's blade was what he knew, even though they paid but a
dollar a day here. But that did it. He told it: they told him it
was Saturday again and paid him and he told about it—
night, a smoked lantern in a disc of worn and barren earth as
smooth as silver, a circle of crouching figures, the importunate murmurs and ejaculations, the meagre piles of worn bills
beneath the crouching knees, the dotted cubes clicking and
scuttering in the dust; that did it. "How much did you win?"
the second convict said.

"Enough," the tall one said.

"But how much?"

"Enough," the tall one said. It was enough exactly; he gave
it all to the man who owned the second motor boat (he
would not need food now), he and the woman in the launch

now and the skiff towing behind, the woman with the baby and the paper-wrapped parcel beneath his peaceful hand, on his lap; almost at once he recognised, not Vicksburg because he had never seen Vicksburg, but the trestle beneath which on his roaring wave of trees and houses and dead animals he had shot, accompanied by thunder and lightning, a month and three weeks ago; he looked at it once without heat, even without interest as the launch went on. But now he began to watch the bank, the levee. He didn't know how he would know but he knew he would, and then it was early afternoon and sure enough the moment came and he said to the launch owner: "I reckon this will do."

"Here?" the launch owner said. "This dont look like any-where to me."

"I reckon this is it," the convict said. So the launch put inshore, the engine ceased, it drifted up and lay against the levee and the owner cast the skiff loose.

"You better let me take you on until we come to some-thing," he said. "That was what I promised."

"I reckon this will do," the convict said. So they got out and he stood with the grapevine painter in his hand while the launch purred again and drew away, already curving; he did not watch it. He laid the bundle down and made the painter fast to a willow root and picked up the bundle and turned. He said no word, he mounted the levee, passing the mark, the tide-line of the old raging, dry now and lined, traversed by shallow and empty cracks like foolish and deprecatory senile grins, and entered a willow clump and removed the overalls and shirt they had given him in New Orleans and dropped them without even looking to see where they fell and opened the parcel and took out the other, the known, the desired, faded a little, stained and worn, but clean, recognisable, and put them on and returned to the skiff and took up the paddle. The woman was already in it.

The plump convict stood blinking at him. "So you come back," he said. "Well well." Now they all watched the tall convict as he bit the end from the cigar neatly and with com-plete deliberation and spat it out and licked the bite smooth and damp and took a match from his pocket and examined the match for a moment as though to be sure it was a good one, worthy of the cigar perhaps, and raked it up his thigh with the same deliberation—a motion almost too slow to set fire to it, it would seem—and held it until the flame burned clear and free of sulphur, then put it to the cigar. The plump one watched him, blinking rapidly and steadily. "And they give you ten years more for running. That's bad. A fellow can get used to what they give him at first, to start off with, I dont care how much it is, even a hundred and ninety-nine years. But ten more years. Ten years more, on top of that. When you never expected it. Ten more years to have to do without no society, no female companionship—" He blinked steadily at the tall convict. But he (the tall convict) had thought of that too. He had had a sweetheart. That is, he had gone to church singings and picnics with her—a girl a year or so younger than he, short-legged, with ripe breasts and a heavy mouth and dull eyes like ripe muscadines, who owned a baking powder can almost full of ear-rings and brooches and rings bought (or presented at suggestion) from ten-cent stores. Presently he had divulged his plan to her, and there were times later when, musing, the thought occurred to him that possibly if it had not been for her he would not actually have attempted it—this a mere feeling, unworded, since he could not have phrased this either: that who to know what Capone's uncandled bridehood she might not have dreamed to be her destiny and fate, what fast car filled with authentic colored glass and machine guns, running traffic lights. But that was all past and done when the notion first occurred to him, and in the third month of his incarceration she came to see him. She wore ear-rings and a bracelet or so which he had never seen before and it never became quite clear how she had got that far from home, and she cried violently for the first three minutes though presently (and without his ever knowing either exactly how they had got separated or how she had made the acquaintance) he saw her in animated conversation with one of the guards. But she kissed him before she left that evening and said she would return the first chance she got, clinging to him, sweating a little, smelling of scent and soft young female flesh, slightly pneumatic. But she didn't come back though he continued to write to her, and seven months later he got an answer. It was a postcard, a colored lithograph of a Birmingham hotel, a childish X inked heavily across one window, the heavy writing on the reverse slanted and primer-like too: *This is where were honnymonning at. Your friend (Mrs) Vernon Waldrip*

The plump convict stood blinking at the tall one, rapidly and steadily. "Yes sir," he said. "It's them ten more years that hurt. Ten more years to do without a woman, no woman a tall that a fellow wants—" He blinked steadily and rapidly, watching the tall one. The other did not move, jackknifed backward between the two bunks, grave and clean, the cigar burning smoothly and richly in his clean steady hand, the smoke wreathing upward across his face saturnine, humorless, and calm. "Ten more years—"

"Women, shit," the tall convict said.

THE HAMLET

To Phil Stone

Contents

FLEM
Chapter One

I.

F RENCHMAN'S BEND was a section of rich river-bottom
country lying twenty miles southeast of Jefferson. Hill-
cradled and remote, definite yet without boundaries, straddling into two counties and owning allegiance to neither, it
had been the original grant and site of a tremendous pre-Civil
War plantation, the ruins of which—the gutted shell of an
enormous house with its fallen stables and slave quarters and
overgrown gardens and brick terraces and promenades—
were still known as the Old Frenchman place, although the
original boundaries now existed only on old faded records
in the Chancery Clerk's office in the county court house in
Jefferson, and even some of the once-fertile fields had long
since reverted to the cane-and-cypress jungle from which their
first master had hewed them.

He had quite possibly been a foreigner, though not necessarily French, since to the people who had come after him
and had almost obliterated all trace of his sojourn, anyone
speaking the tongue with a foreign flavor or whose appearance or even occupation was strange, would have been a
Frenchman regardless of what nationality he might affirm,
just as to their more urban co-evals (if he had elected to settle
in Jefferson itself say) he would have been called a Dutchman.
But now nobody knew what he had actually been, not even
Will Varner, who was sixty years old and now owned a good
deal of his original grant, including the site of his ruined mansion. Because he was gone now, the foreigner, the Frenchman,
with his family and his slaves and his magnificence. His
dream, his broad acres were parcelled out now into small
shiftless mortgaged farms for the directors of Jefferson banks
to squabble over before selling finally to Will Varner, and all
that remained of him was the river bed which his slaves had
straightened for almost ten miles to keep his land from flood-
ing, and the skeleton of the tremendous house which his

heirs-at-large had been pulling down and chopping up—walnut newel posts and stair spindles, oak floors which fifty years later would have been almost priceless, the very clapboards themselves—for thirty years now for firewood. Even his name was forgotten, his pride but a legend about the land he had wrested from the jungle and tamed as a monument to that appellation which those who came after him in battered wagons and on mule-back and even on foot, with flint-lock rifles and dogs and children and home-made whiskey stills and Protestant psalm-books, could not even read, let alone pronounce, and which now had nothing to do with any once-living man at all—his dream and his pride now dust with the lost dust of his anonymous bones, his legend but the stubborn tale of the money he buried somewhere about the place when Grant over-ran the country on his way to Vicksburg.

The people who inherited from him came from the northeast, through the Tennessee mountains by stages marked by the bearing and raising of a generation of children. They came from the Atlantic seaboard and before that, from England and the Scottish and Welsh Marches, as some of the names would indicate—Turpin and Haley and Whittington, McCallum and Murray and Leonard and Littlejohn, and other names like Riddup and Armstid and Doshey which could have come from nowhere since certainly no man would deliberately select one of them for his own. They brought no slaves and no Phyfe and Chippendale highboys; indeed, what they did bring most of them could (and did) carry in their hands. They took up land and built one- and two-room cabins and never painted them, and married one another and produced children and added other rooms one by one to the original cabins and did not paint them either, but that was all. Their descendants still planted cotton in the bottom land and corn along the edge of the hills and in the secret coves in the hills made whiskey of the corn and sold what they did not drink. Federal officers went into the country and vanished. Some garment which the missing man had worn might be seen—a felt hat, a broadcloth coat, a pair of city shoes or even his pistol—on a child or an old man or woman. County officers did not bother them at all save in the heel of election years. They supported their own churches and schools, they married and committed infrequent adulteries and more frequent homicides among themselves and were their own courts judges and executioners. They were Protestants and Democrats and prolific; there was not one negro landowner in the entire section. Strange negroes would absolutely refuse to pass through it after dark.

Will Varner, the present owner of the Old Frenchman place, was the chief man of the country. He was the largest landholder and beat supervisor in one county and Justice of the Peace in the next and election commissioner in both, and hence the fountainhead if not of law at least of advice and suggestion to a countryside which would have repudiated the term constituency if they had ever heard it, which came to him, not in the attitude of *What must I do* but *What do you think you think you would like for me to do if you was able to make me do it*. He was a farmer, a usurer, a veterinarian; Judge Benbow of Jefferson once said of him that a milder mannered man never bled a mule or stuffed a ballot box. He owned most of the good land in the country and held mortgages on most of the rest. He owned the store and the cotton gin and the combined grist mill and blacksmith shop in the village proper and it was considered, to put it mildly, bad luck for a man of the neighborhood to do his trading or gin his cotton or grind his meal or shoe his stock anywhere else. He was thin as a fence rail and almost as long, with reddish-gray hair and moustaches and little hard bright innocently blue eyes; he looked like a Methodist Sunday School superintendent who on week days conducted a railroad passenger train or vice versa and who owned the church or perhaps the railroad or perhaps both. He was shrewd secret and merry, of a Rabelaisian turn of mind and very probably still sexually lusty (he had fathered sixteen children to his wife, though only two of them remained at home, the others scattered, married and buried, from El Paso to the Alabama line) as the spring of his hair which even at sixty was still more red than gray, would indicate. He was at once active and lazy; he did nothing at all (his son managed all the family business) and spent all his time at it, out of the house and gone before the son had come down to breakfast even, nobody knew where save that he and the old fat white horse which he rode might be seen anywhere within the surrounding ten miles at any time, and at least once every month during the spring and summer and early fall, the old white horse tethered to an adjacent fence post, he would be seen by someone sitting in a home-made chair on the jungle-choked lawn of the Old Frenchman's homesite. His blacksmith had made the chair for him by sawing an empty flour barrel half through the middle and trimming out the sides and nailing a seat into it, and Varner would sit there chewing his tobacco or smoking his cob pipe, with a brusque word for passers cheerful enough but inviting no company, against his background of fallen baronial splendor. The people (those who saw him sitting there and those who were told about it) all believed that he sat there planning his next mortgage foreclosure in private, since it was only to an itinerant sewing-machine agent named Ratliff—a man less than half his age—that he ever gave a reason: "I like to sit here. I'm trying to find out what it must have felt like to be the fool that would need all this"—he did not move, he did not so much as indicate with his head the rise of old brick and tangled walks topped by the columned ruin behind him— "just to eat and sleep in." Then he said—and he gave Ratliff no further clue to which might have been the truth—"For a while it looked like I was going to get shut of it, get it cleared up. But by God folks have got so lazy they wont even climb a ladder to pull off the rest of the boards. It looks like they will go into the woods and even chop up a tree before they will reach above eyelevel for a scantling of pine kindling. But after all, I reckon I'll just keep what there is left of it, just to remind me of my one mistake. This is the only thing I ever bought in my life I couldn't sell to nobody."

The son, Jody, was about thirty, a prime bulging man, slightly thyroidic, who was not only unmarried but who emanated a quality of invincible and inviolable bachelordom as some people are said to breathe out the odor of sanctity or spirituality. He was a big man, already promising a considerable belly in ten or twelve years, though as yet he still managed to postulate something of the trig and unattached cavalier. He wore, winter and summer (save that in the warm season he dispensed with the coat) and Sundays and week days, a glazed collarless white shirt fastened at the neck with a heavy gold collar-button beneath a suit of good black broadcloth. He put on the suit the day it arrived from the Jefferson tailor and wore it everyday and in all weathers thereafter until he sold it to one of the family's negro retainers, so that on almost any Sunday night one whole one or some part of one of his old suits could be met—and promptly recognised—walking the summer roads, and replaced it with the new succeeding one. In contrast to the unvarying overalls of the men he lived among he had an air not funereal exactly but ceremonial—this because of that quality of invincible bachelorhood which he possessed: so that, looking at him you saw, beyond the flabbiness and the obscuring bulk, the perennial and immortal Best Man, the apotheosis of the masculine Singular, just as you discern beneath the dropsical tissue of the '09 half-back the lean hard ghost which once carried a ball. He was the ninth of his parents' sixteen children. He managed the store of which his father was still titular owner and in which they dealt mostly in foreclosed mortgages, and the gin, and oversaw the scattered farm holdings which his father at first and later the two of them together had been acquiring during the last forty years.

One afternoon he was in the store, cutting lengths of plow-line from a spool of new cotton rope and looping them in neat seamanlike bights onto a row of nails in the wall, when at a sound behind him he turned and saw, silhouetted by the open door, a man smaller than common, in a wide hat and a frock coat too large for him, standing with a curious planted stiffness. "You Varner?" the man said, in a voice not harsh exactly, or not deliberately harsh so much as rusty from infrequent use.

"I'm one Varner," Jody said, in his bland hard quite pleasant voice. "What can I do for you?"

"My name is Snopes. I heard you got a farm to rent."

"That so?" Varner said, already moving so as to bring the other's face into the light. "Just where did you hear that?" Because the farm was a new one, which he and his father had acquired through a foreclosure sale not a week ago, and the man was a complete stranger. He had never even heard the name before.

The other did not answer. Now Varner could see his face—a pair of eyes of a cold opaque gray between shaggy graying irascible brows and a short scrabble of iron-gray beard as tight and knotted as a sheep's coat. "Where you been farming?" Varner said.

"West." He did not speak shortly. He merely pronounced the one word with a complete inflectionless finality, as if he had closed a door behind himself.

"You mean Texas?"

"No."

"I see. Just west of here. How much family you got?"

"Six." Now there was no perceptible pause, nor was there any hurrying on into the next word. But there was something. Varner sensed it even before the lifeless voice seemed deliberately to compound the inconsistency: "Boy and two girls. Wife and her sister."

"That's just five."

"Myself," the dead voice said.

"A man dont usually count himself among his own field hands," Varner said. "Is it five or is it seven?"

"I can put six hands into the field."

Now Varner's voice did not change either, still pleasant, still hard: "I dont know as I will take on a tenant this year. It's already almost first of May. I figure I might work it myself, with day labor. If I work it at all this year."

"I'll work that way," the other said. Varner looked at him.

"Little anxious to get settled, aint you?" The other said nothing. Varner could not tell whether the man was looking at him or not. "What rent were you aiming to pay?"

"What do you rent for?"

"Third and fourth," Varner said. "Furnish out of the store here. No cash."

"I see. Furnish in six-bit dollars."

"That's right," Varner said pleasantly. Now he could not tell if the man were looking at anything at all or not.

"I'll take it," he said.

Standing on the gallery of the store, above the half dozen overalled men sitting or squatting about it with pocket knives and slivers of wood, Varner watched his caller limp stiffly across the porch, looking neither right nor left, and descend and from among the tethered teams and saddled animals below the gallery choose a gaunt saddleless mule in a worn plow

bridle with rope reins and lead it to the steps and mount awkwardly and stiffly and ride away, still without once looking to
either side. "To hear that ere foot, you'd think he weighed
two hundred pounds," one of them said. "Who's he, Jody?"

Varner sucked his teeth and spat into the road. "Name's
Snopes," he said.

"Snopes?" a second man said. "Sho now. So that's him."
Now not only Varner but all the others looked at the
speaker—a gaunt man in absolutely clean though faded and
patched overalls and even freshly shaven, with a gentle, almost sad face until you unravelled what were actually two
separate expressions—a temporary one of static peace and
quiet overlaying a constant one of definite even though faint
harriedness, and a sensitive mouth which had a quality of adolescent freshness and bloom until you realised that this could
just as well be the result of a lifelong abstinence from tobacco—the face of the breathing archetype and protagonist
of all men who marry young and father only daughters and
are themselves but the eldest daughter of their own wives.
His name was Tull. "He's the fellow that wintered his family
in a old cottonhouse on Ike McCaslin's place. The one that
was mixed up in that burnt barn of a fellow named Harris
over in Grenier County two years ago."

"Huh?" Varner said. "What's that? Burnt barn?"

"I never said he done it," Tull said. "I just said he was kind
of involved in it after a fashion you might say."

"How much involved in it?"

"Harris had him arrested into court."

"I see," Varner said. "Just a pure case of mistaken identity.
He just hired it done."

"It wasn't proved," Tull said. "Leastways, if Harris ever
found any proof afterward, it was too late then. Because he
had done left the country. Then he turned up at McCaslin's
last September. Him and his family worked by the day, gathering for McCaslin, and McCaslin let them winter in a old
cottonhouse he wasn't using. That's all I know. I aint repeating nothing."

"I wouldn't," Varner said. "A man dont want to get the
name of a idle gossip." He stood above them with his broad
bland face, in his dingy formal black-and-white—the glazed

soiled white shirt and the bagging and uncared-for trousers—
a costume at once ceremonial and negligee. He sucked his
teeth briefly and noisily. "Well well well," he said. "A barn
burner. Well well well."

That night he told his father about it at the supper table.
With the exception of the rambling half-log half-sawn plank
edifice known as Littlejohn's hotel, Will Varner's was the only
house in the country with more than one storey. They had a
cook too, not only the only negro servant but the only servant
of any sort in the whole district. They had had her for years
yet Mrs Varner still said and apparently believed that she
could not be trusted even to boil water unsupervised. He told
it that evening while his mother, a plump cheery bustling
woman who had borne sixteen children and already outlived
five of them and who still won prizes for preserved fruits and
vegetables at the annual county fair, bustled back and forth
between dining room and kitchen, and his sister, a soft ample
girl with definite breasts even at thirteen and eyes like cloudy
hothouse grapes and a full damp mouth always slightly open,
sat at her place in a kind of sullen bemusement of rife young
female flesh, apparently not even having to make any effort
not to listen.

"You already contracted with him?" Will Varner said.

"I hadn't aimed to at all till Vernon Tull told me what he
did. Now I figure I'll take the paper up there tomorrow and
let him sign."

"Then you can point out to him which house to burn too.
Or are you going to leave that to him?"

"Sho," Jody said. "We'll discuss that too." Then he said—
and now all levity was gone from his voice, all poste and riposte of humor's light whimsy, tierce quarto and prime: "All
I got to do is find out for sho about that barn. But then it will
be the same thing, whether he actually did it or not. All he'll
need will be to find out all of a sudden at gathering time that
I think he did it. Listen. Take a case like this." He leaned
forward now, over the table, bulging, protuberant, intense.
The mother had bustled out, to the kitchen, where her brisk
voice could be heard scolding cheerfully at the negro cook.
The daughter was not listening at all. "Here's a piece of land
that the folks that own it hadn't actually figured on getting

nothing out of this late in the season. And here comes a man and rents it on shares that the last place he rented on a barn got burnt up. It dont matter whether he actually burnt that barn or not, though it will simplify matters if I can find out for sho he did. The main thing is, it burnt while he was there and the evidence was such that he felt called on to leave the country. So here he comes and rents this land we hadn't fig- ured on nothing out of this year nohow and we furnish him outen the store all regular and proper. And he makes his crop and the landlord sells it all regular and has the cash waiting and the fellow comes in to get his share and the landlord says, 'What's this I heard about you and that barn?' That's all. 'What's this I just heard about you and that barn?'" They stared at one another—the slightly protuberant opaque eyes and the little hard blue ones. "What will he say? What can he say except 'All right. What do you aim to do?'"

"You'll lose his furnish bill at the store."

"Sho. There aint no way of getting around that. But after all, a man that's making you a crop free gratis for nothing, at least you can afford to feed him while he's doing it.—Wait," he said. "Hell fire, we wont even need to do that; I'll just let him find a couple of rotten shingles with a match laid across them on his doorstep the morning after he finishes laying-by and he'll know it's all up then and aint nothing left for him but to move on. That'll cut two months off the furnish bill and all we'll be out is hiring his crop gathered." They stared at one another. To one of them it was already done, accom- plished: he could actually see it; when he spoke it was out of a time still six months in the future yet: "Hell fire, he'll have to! He cant fight it! He dont dare!"

"Hmph," Will said. From the pocket of his unbuttoned vest he took a stained cob pipe and began to fill it. "You better stay clear of them folks."

"Sho now," Jody said. He took a tooth pick from the china receptacle on the table and sat back. "Burning barns aint right. And a man that's got habits that way will just have to suffer the disadvantages of them."

He did not go the next day nor the one after that either. But early in the afternoon of the third day, his roan saddle horse hitched and waiting at one of the gallery posts, he sat at the roll-top desk in the rear of the store, hunched, the black hat on the back of his head and one broad black-haired hand motionless and heavy as a ham of meat on the paper and the pen in the other tracing the words of the contract in his heavy deliberate sprawling script. An hour after that and five miles from the village, the contract blotted and folded neatly into his hip pocket, he was sitting the horse beside a halted buckboard in the road. It was battered with rough usage and caked with last winter's dried mud, it was drawn by a pair of shaggy ponies as wild and active-looking as mountain goats and almost as small. To the rear of it was attached a sheet-iron box the size and shape of a dog-kennel and painted to resemble a house, in each painted window of which a painted woman's face simpered above a painted sewing-machine, and Varner sat his horse and glared in shocked and outraged consternation at its occupant, who had just said pleasantly, "Well, Jody, I hear you got a new tenant."

"Hell fire!" Varner cried. "Do you mean he set fire to another one? even after they caught him, he set fire to *another* one?"

"Well," the man in the buckboard said, "I dont know as I would go on record as saying he set ere a one of them afire. I would put it that they both taken fire while he was more or less associated with them. You might say that fire seems to follow him around, like dogs follows some folks." He spoke in a pleasant, lazy, equable voice which you did not discern at once to be even more shrewd than humorous. This was Ratliff, the sewing-machine agent. He lived in Jefferson and he travelled the better part of four counties with his sturdy team and the painted dog-kennel into which an actual machine neatly fitted. On successive days and two counties apart the splashed and battered buckboard and the strong mismatched team might be seen tethered in the nearest shade and Ratliff's bland affable ready face and his neat tieless blue shirt one of the squatting group at a cross-roads store, or— and still squatting and still doing the talking apparently though actually doing a good deal more listening than anybody believed until afterward—among the women surrounded by laden clothes lines and tubs and blackened wash pots beside springs and wells, or decorous in a splint chair on cabin galleries, pleasant, affable, courteous, anecdotal and impenetrable. He sold perhaps three machines a year, the rest of the time trading in land and livestock and second hand farming tools and musical instruments or anything else which the owner did not want badly enough, retailing from house to house the news of his four counties with the ubiquity of a newspaper and carrying personal messages from mouth to mouth about weddings and funerals and the preserving of vegetables and fruit with the reliability of a postal service. He never forgot a name and he knew everyone, man mule and dog, within fifty miles. "Just say it was following along behind the wagon when Snopes druv up to the house De Spain had give him, with the furniture piled into the wagon bed like he had druv up to the house they had been living in at Harris's or wherever it was and said 'Get in here' and the cookstove and beds and chairs come out and got in by their selves. Careless and yet good too, tight, like they was used to moving and not having no big help at it. And Ab and that big one, Flem they call him—there was another one too, a little one; I remember seeing him once somewhere. He wasn't with them. Leastways he aint now. Maybe they forgot to tell him when to get outen the barn.—setting on the seat and them two hulking gals in the two chairs in the wagon bed and Miz Snopes and her sister, the widow, setting on the stuff in back like nobody cared much whether they come along or not either, including the furniture. And the wagon stops in front of the house and Ab looks at it and says, 'Likely it aint fitten for hawgs.'"

Sitting the horse, Varner glared down at Ratliff in protuberant and speechless horror. "All right," Ratliff said. "Soon as the wagon stopped Miz Snopes and the widow got out and commenced to unload. Them two gals aint moved yet, just setting there in them two chairs, in their Sunday clothes, chewing sweet gum, till Ab turned round and cussed them outen the wagon to where Miz Snopes and the widow was wrastling with the stove. He druv them out like a pair of heifers just a little too valuable to hit hard with a stick, and then him and Flem set there and watched them two strapping gals take a wore-out broom and a lantern outen the wagon and stand there again till Ab lent out and snicked the nigh one across the stern with the end of the reins. 'And then you come back and help your maw with that stove,' he hollers after them. Then him and Flem got outen the wagon and went up to call on De Spain."

"To the barn?" Varner cried. "You mean they went right straight and—"

"No no. That was later. The barn come later. Likely they never knowed just where it was yet. The barn burnt all regular and in due course; you'll have to say that for him. This here was just a call, just pure friendship, because Snopes knowed where his fields was and all he had to do was to start scratching them, and it already the middle of May. Just like now," he added in a tone of absolutely creamlike innocence. "But then I hear tell he always makes his rent contracts later than most." But he was not laughing. The shrewd brown face was as bland and smooth as ever beneath the shrewd impenetrable eyes.

"Well?" Varner said violently. "If he sets his fires like you tell about it, I reckon I dont need to worry until Christmas. Get on with it. What does he have to do before he starts lighting matches? Maybe I can recognise at least some of the symptoms in time."

"All right," Ratliff said. "So they went up the road, leaving Miz Snopes and the widow wrastling at the cookstove and them two gals standing there now holding a wire rat-trap and a chamber pot, and went up to Major de Spain's and walked up the private road where that pile of fresh horse manure was and the nigger said Ab stepped in it on deliberate purpose. Maybe the nigger was watching them through the front window. Anyway Ab tracked it right across the front porch and knocked and when the nigger told him to wipe it offen his feet, Ab shoved right past the nigger and the nigger said he wiped the rest of it off right on that ere hundred-dollar rug and stood there hollering 'Hello. Hello, De Spain' until Miz de Spain come and looked at the rug and at Ab and told him to please go away. And then De Spain come home at dinner time and I reckon maybe Miz de Spain got in behind him because about middle of the afternoon he rides up to Ab's house with a nigger holding the rolled-up rug on a mule behind him and Ab setting in a

chair against the door jamb and De Spain hollers 'Why in hell
aint you in the field?' and Ab says, he dont get up or nothing,
'I figger I'll start tomorrow. I dont never move and start to
work the same day', only that aint neither here nor there; I
reckon Miz de Spain had done got in behind him good because he just set on the horse a while saying 'Confound you
Snopes, confound you Snopes' and Ab setting there saying 'If
I had thought that much of a rug I dont know as I would
keep it where folks coming in would have to tromp on it.'"
Still he was not laughing. He just sat there in the buckboard,
easy and relaxed, with his shrewd intelligent eyes in his
smooth brown face, well-shaved and clean in his perfectly
clean faded shirt, his voice pleasant and drawling and anecdotal, while Varner's suffused swollen face glared down at
him.

"So after a while Ab hollers back into the house and one of
them strapping gals comes out and Ab says, 'Take that ere rug
and wash it.' And so next morning the nigger found the
rolled-up rug throwed onto the front porch against the door
and there was some more tracks across the porch too only it
was just mud this time and it was said how when Miz de
Spain unrolled the rug this time it must have been hotter for
De Spain than before even—the nigger said it looked like
they had used brick bats instead of soap on it—because he
was at Ab's house before breakfast even, in the lot where Ab
and Flem was hitching up to go to the field sho enough, setting on the mare mad as a hornet and cussing a blue streak,
not at Ab exactly but just sort of at all rugs and all horse
manure in general and Ab not saying nothing, just buckling
hames and choke strops until at last De Spain says how the
rug cost him a hundred dollars in France and he is going to
charge Ab twenty bushels of corn for it against his crop that
Ab aint even planted yet. And so De Spain went back home.
And maybe he felt it was all neither here nor there now.
Maybe he felt that long as he had done something about it
Miz de Spain would ease up on him and maybe come gathering time he would a even forgot about that twenty bushels
of corn. Only that never suited Ab. So here, it's the next evening I reckon, and Major laying with his shoes off in the
barrel stave hammock in his yard and here comes the bailiff

hemming and hawing and finally gets it out how Ab has done sued him—"

"Hell fire," Varner murmured. "Hell fire."

"Sho," Ratliff said. "That's just about what De Spain his self said when he finally got it into his mind that it was so. So it come Sat-dy and the wagon druv up to the store and Ab got out in that preacher's hat and coat and tromps up to the table on that club foot where Uncle Buck McCaslin said Colonel John Sartoris his self shot Ab for trying to steal his clay-bank riding stallion during the War, and the Judge says, 'I done reviewed your suit, Mr Snopes, but I aint been able to find nothing nowhere in the law bearing on rugs, let alone horse manure. But I'm going to accept it because twenty bushels is too much for you to have to pay because a man as busy as you seem to stay aint going to have time to make twenty bushels of corn. So I am going to charge you ten bushels of corn for ruining that rug.' "

"And so he burnt it," Varner said. "Well well well."

"I dont know as I would put it just that way," Ratliff said, repeated. "I would just put it that that same night Major de Spain's barn taken fire and was a total loss. Only somehow or other De Spain got there on his mare about the same time, because somebody heard him passing in the road. I dont mean he got there in time to put it out but he got there in time to find something else already there that he felt entitled to consider enough of a foreign element to justify shooting at it, setting there on the mare and blasting away at it or them three or four times until it run into a ditch on him where he couldn't follow on the mare. And he couldn't say neither who it was because any animal can limp if it wants to and any man is liable to have a white shirt, with the exception that when he got to Ab's house (and that couldn't a been long, according to the gait the fellow heard him passing in the road) Ab and Flem wasn't there, wasn't nobody there but the four women and De Spain never had time to look under no beds and such because there was a cypress-roofed corn crib right next to that barn. So he rid back to where his niggers had done fetched up the water barrels and was soaking tow-sacks to lay on the crib, and the first person he see was Flem standing there in a white-colored shirt, watching it with his hands in his pockets, chewing tobacco. 'Evening,' Flem says. 'That ere hay goes fast' and De Spain setting on the horse hollering 'Where's your paw? Where's that—' and Flem says, 'If he aint here somewhere he's done went back home. Me and him left at the same time when we see the blaze.' And De Spain knowed where they had left from too and he knowed why too. Only that wasn't neither here nor there neither because, as it was just maintained, any two fellows anywhere might have a limp and a white shirt between them and it was likely the coal oil can he seen one of them fling into the fire when he shot the first time. And so here the next morning he's setting at breakfast with a right smart of his eyebrows and hair both swinged off when the nigger comes in and says it's a fellow to see him and he goes to the office and it's Ab, already in the preacher hat and coat and the wagon done already loaded again too, only Ab aint brought that into the house where it could be seen. 'It looks like me and you aint going to get along together,' Ab says, 'so I reckon we better quit trying before we have a misunderstanding over something. I'm moving this morning.' And De Spain says, 'What about your contract?' And Ab says, 'I done cancelled it.' and De Spain setting there saying 'Cancelled. Cancelled' and then he says, 'I would cancel it and a hundred more like it and throw in that barn too just to know for sho if it was you I was shooting at last night.' And Ab says, 'You might sue me and find out. Justices of the Peace in this country seems to be in the habit of finding for plaintiffs.' "

"Hell fire," Varner said quietly again. "Hell fire."

"So Ab turned and went stomping out on that stiff foot and went back—"

"And burnt the tenant house," Varner said.

"No no. I aint saying he might not a looked back at it with a certain regret, as the fellow says, when he druv off. But never nothing else taken all of a sudden on fire. Not right then, that is. I dont—"

"That's so," Varner said. "I recollect you did say he had to throw the balance of the coal oil into the fire when De Spain started shooting at him. Well well well," he said, bulging, slightly apoplectic. "And now, out of all the men in this country, I got to pick him to make a rent contract with." He began to laugh. That is, he began to say "Ha. Ha. Ha." rapidly, but just from the teeth, the lungs: no higher, nothing of it in the eyes. Then he stopped. "Well, I cant be setting here, no matter how pleasant it is. Maybe I can get there in time to get him to cancel with me for just a old cottonhouse."

"Or at least maybe for a empty barn," Ratliff called after him.

An hour later Varner was sitting the halted horse again, this time before a gate, or a gap that is in a fence of sagging and rusted wire. The gate itself or what remained of it lay unhinged to one side, the interstices of the rotted palings choked with grass and weeds like the ribs of a forgotten skeleton. He was breathing hard but not because he had been galloping. On the contrary, since he had approached near enough to his destination to believe he could have seen smoke if there had been smoke, he had ridden slower and slower. Nevertheless he now sat the horse before the gap in the fence, breathing hard through his nose and even sweating a little, looking at the sagging broken-backed cabin set in its inevitable treeless and grassless plot and weathered to the color of an old bee-hive, with that expression of tense and rapid speculation of a man approaching a dud howitzer shell. "Hell fire," he said again quietly. "Hell fire. He's been here three days now and he aint even set the gate up. And I dont even dare to mention it to him. I dont even dare to act like I knowed there was even a fence to hang it to." He twitched the reins savagely. "Come up!" he said to the horse. "You hang around here very long standing still and you'll be a-fire too."

The path (it was neither road nor lane: just two parallel barely discernible tracks where wagon wheels had run, almost obliterated by this year's grass and weeds) went up to the sagging and stepless porch of the perfectly blank house which he now watched with wire-taut wariness, as if he were approaching an ambush. He was watching it with such intensity as to be oblivious to detail. He saw suddenly in one of the sashless windows and without knowing when it had come there, a face beneath a gray cloth cap, the lower jaw moving steadily and rhythmically with a curious sidewise thrust, which even as he shouted "Hello!" vanished again. He was about to shout again when he saw beyond the house the stiff figure which he recognised even though the frock coat was missing now, doing something at the gate to the lot. He had already begun to hear the mournful measured plaint of a rusted well-pulley, and now he began to hear two flat meaningless loud female voices. When he passed beyond the house he saw it—the narrow high frame like an epicene gallows, two big absolutely static young women beside it, who even in that first glance postulated that immobile dreamy solidarity of statuary (this only emphasised by the fact that they both seemed to be talking at once and to some listener—or perhaps just circumambience—at a considerable distance and neither listening to the other at all) even though one of them had hold of the well-rope, her arms extended at full reach, her body bent for the down pull like a figure in a charade, a carved piece symbolising some terrific physical effort which had died with its inception, though a moment later the pulley began again its rusty plaint but stopped again almost immediately, as did the voices also when the second one saw him, the first one paused now in the obverse of the first attitude, her arms stretched downward on the rope and the two broad expressionless faces turning slowly in unison as he rode past.

He crossed the barren yard littered with the rubbish—the ashes, the shards of pottery and tin cans—of its last tenants. There were two women working beside the fence too and they were all three aware of his presence now because he had seen one of the women look around. But the man himself (Durn little clubfooted murderer, Varner thought with that furious helpless outrage) had not looked up nor even paused in whatever it was he was doing until Varner rode directly up behind him. The two women were watching him now. One wore a faded sunbonnet, the other a shapeless hat which at one time must have belonged to the man and holding in her hand a rusted can half full of bent and rusted nails. "Evening," Varner said, realising too late that he was almost shouting. "Evening, ladies." The man turned, deliberately, holding a hammer—a rusted head from which both claws had been broken, fitted onto an untrimmed stick of stove-wood—and once more Varner looked down into the cold impenetrable agate eyes beneath the writhen overhang of brows.

"Howdy," Snopes said.

"Just thought I'd ride up and see what your plans were," Varner said, too loud still; he could not seem to help it. I got too much to think about to have time to watch it, he thought, beginning at once to think, Hell fire. Hell fire, again, as though proving to himself what even a second's laxity of attention might bring him to.

"I figure I'll stay," the other said. "The house aint fitten for hogs. But I reckon I can make out with it."

"But look here!" Varner said. Now he was shouting; he didn't care. Then he stopped shouting. He stopped shouting because he stopped speaking because there was nothing else to say, though it was going through his mind fast enough: Hell fire. Hell fire. Hell fire. I dont dare say Leave here, and I aint got anywhere to say Go there. I dont even dare to have him arrested for barn-burning for fear he'll set my barn a-fire. The other had begun to turn back to the fence when Varner spoke. Now he stood half-turned, looking up at Varner not courteously and not exactly patiently, but just waiting. "All right," Varner said. "We can discuss the house. Because we'll get along all right. We'll get along. Anything that comes up, all you got to do is come down to the store. No, you dont even need to do that: just send me word and I'll ride right up here as quick as I can get here. You understand? Anything, just anything you dont like—"

"I can get along with anybody," the other said. "I been getting along with fifteen or twenty different landlords since I started farming. When I cant get along with them, I leave. That all you wanted?"

All, Varner thought. All. He rode back across the yard, the littered grassless desolation scarred with the ashes and charred stick-ends and blackened bricks where pots for washing clothes and scalding hogs had sat. I just wish I never had to have but just the little I do want now, he thought. He had been hearing the well-pulley again. This time it did not cease when he passed, the two broad faces, the one motionless, the other pumping up and down with metronome-like regularity to the wheel's not-quite-musical complaint, turning slowly again as though rivetted and synchronised to one another by a mechanical arm as he went on beyond the house and into the imperceptible lane which led to the broken gate which he knew would still be lying there in the weeds when he saw it next. He still had the contract in his pocket, which he had written out with that steady and deliberate satisfaction which, it now seemed to him, must have occurred in another time, or more likely, to another person altogether. It was still un-signed. *I could put a fire-clause in it,* he thought. But he did not even check the horse. *Sho,* he thought. *And then I could use it to start shingling the new barn.* So he went on. It was late, and he eased the horse into a rack which it would be able to hold nearly all the way home, with a little breathing on the hills, and he was travelling at a fair gait when he saw sud-denly, leaning against a tree beside the road, the man whose face he had seen in the window of the house. One moment the road had been empty, the next moment the man stood there beside it, at the edge of a small copse—the same cloth cap, the same rhythmically chewing jaw materialised appar-ently out of nothing and almost abreast of the horse, with an air of the complete and purely accidental which Varner was to remember and speculate about only later. He had almost passed the other before he pulled the horse up. He did not shout now and now his big face was merely bland and ex-tremely alert. "Howdy," he said. "You're Flem, aint you? I'm Varner."

"That so?" the other said. He spat. He had a broad flat face. His eyes were the color of stagnant water. He was soft in appearance like Varner himself, though a head shorter, in a soiled white shirt and cheap gray trousers.

"I was hoping to see you," Varner said. "I hear your father has had a little trouble once or twice with landlords. Trouble that might have been serious." The other chewed. "Maybe they never treated him right; I dont know about that and I dont care. What I'm talking about is a mistake, any mistake, can be straightened out so that a man can still stay friends with the fellow he aint satisfied with. Dont you agree to that?" The other chewed steadily. His face was as blank as a pan of uncooked dough. "So he wont have to feel that the only thing that can prove his rights is something that will make him have to pick up and leave the country next day," Varner said. "So that there wont come a time some day when he will look around and find out he has run out of new country to move to." Varner ceased. He waited so long this time that the other finally spoke, though Varner was never certain whether this was the reason or not:

"There's a right smart of country."

"Sho," Varner said pleasantly, bulging, bland. "But a man dont want to wear it out just moving through it. Especially because of a matter that if it had just been took in hand and straightened out to begin with, wouldn't have amounted to nothing. That could have been straightened out in five minutes if there had just been some other fellow handy to take a hold of a fellow that was maybe a little high-tempered to begin with say, and say to him, 'Hold up here, now; that fellow dont aim to put nothing on you. All you got to do is consult with him peaceable and it will be fixed up. I know that to be a fact because *I got his promise to that effect*.' " He paused again. "Especially if this here fellow we are speaking of, that could take a hold of him and tell him that, was going to get a benefit out of keeping him quiet and peaceable." Varner stopped again. After a while the other spoke again:

"What benefit?"

"Why, a good farm to work. Store credit. More land if he felt he could handle it."

"Aint no benefit in farming. I figure on getting out of it soon as I can."

"All right," Varner said. "Say he wanted to take up some other line, this fellow we're speaking of. He will need the good will of the folks he aims to make his money off of to do it. And what better way—"

"You run a store, dont you?" the other said.

"—better way—" Varner said. Then he stopped. "What?" he said.

"I hear you run a store."

Varner stared at him. Now Varner's face was not bland. It was just completely still and completely intent. He reached to his shirt pocket and produced a cigar. He neither smoked nor drank himself, being by nature so happily metabolised that, as he might have put it himself, he could not possibly have felt better than he naturally did. But he always carried two or three. "Have a cigar," he said.

"I dont use them," the other said.

"Just chew, hah?" Varner said.

"I chew up a nickel now and then until the suption is out of it. But I aint never lit a match to one yet."

"Sho now," Varner said. He looked at the cigar; he said quietly: "And I just hope to God you and nobody you know ever will." He put the cigar back into his pocket. He expelled a loud hiss of breath. "All right," he said. "Next fall. When he has made his crop." He had never been certain just when the other had been looking at him and when not, but now he watched the other raise his arm and with his other hand pick something infinitesimal from the sleeve with infinitesimal care. Once more Varner expelled his breath through his nose. This time it was a sigh. "All right," he said. "Next week then. You'll give me that long, wont you? But you got to guarantee it." The other spat.

"Guarantee what?" he said.

Two miles further on dusk overtook him, the shortening twilight of late April, in which the blanched dogwoods stood among the darker trees with spread raised palms like praying nuns; there was the evening star and already the whippor-wills. The horse, travelling supperward, was going well in the evening's cool, when Varner pulled it to a stop and held it for a full moment. "Hell fire," he said. "He was standing just exactly where couldn't nobody see him from the house."

Chapter Two

Ratliff, the sewing machine agent, again approaching the village, with a used music box and a set of brand new harrow teeth still fastened together by the factory shipping wire in the dog kennel box in place of the sewing machine, saw the old white horse dozing on three legs at a fence post and, an instant later, Will Varner himself sitting in the home-made chair against the rise of shaggy lawns and overgrown gardens of the Old Frenchman place.

"Evening, Uncle Will," he said in his pleasant, courteous, even deferent voice. "I hear you and Jody got a new clerk in the store." Varner looked at him sharply, the reddish eyebrows beetling a little above the hard little eyes.

"So that's done spread," he said. "How far you been since yesterday?"

"Seven-eight miles," Ratliff said.

"Hah," Varner said. "We been needing a clerk." That was true. All they needed was someone to come and unlock the store in the morning and lock it again at night—this just to keep stray dogs out, since even tramps, like stray negroes, did not stay in Frenchman's Bend after nightfall. In fact, at times Jody Varner himself (Will was never there anyhow) would be absent from the store all day. Customers would enter and serve themselves and each other, putting the price of the articles, which they knew to a penny as well as Jody himself did, into a cigar box inside the circular wire cage which protected the cheese, as though it—the cigar box, the worn bills and thumb-polished coins—were actually baited.

"At least you can get the store swept out every day," Ratliff said. "Aint everybody can get that included into a fire insurance policy."

"Hah," Varner said again. He rose from the chair. He was chewing tobacco. He removed from his mouth the chewed-out wad which resembled a clot of damp hay, and threw it away and wiped his palm on his flank. He approached the fence, where at his direction the blacksmith had contrived a clever passage which (neither the blacksmith nor Varner had ever seen one before or even imagined one) operated exactly like a modern turnstile, by the raising of a chained pin instead of inserting a coin. "Ride my horse on back to the store," Varner said. "I'll drive your rig. I want to sit down and ride."

"We can tie the horse behind the buckboard and both ride in it," Ratliff said.

"You ride the horse," Varner said. "That's close as I want you right now. Sometimes you are a little too smart to suit me."

"Why, sho, Uncle Will," Ratliff said. So he cramped the buckboard's wheel for Varner to get in, and himself mounted the horse. They went on, Ratliff a little behind the buck-board, so that Varner talked to him over his shoulder, not looking back:

"This here fire-fighter—"

"It wasn't proved," Ratliff said mildly. "Of course, that's the trouble. If a fellow's got to choose between a man that is a murderer and one he just thinks maybe is, he'll choose the murderer. At least then he will know exactly where he's at. His attention aint going to wander then."

"All right, all right," Varner said. "This here victim of libel and mis-statement then. What do you know about him?"

"Nothing to mention," Ratliff said. "Just what I hear about him. I aint seen him in eight years. There was another boy then, besides Flem. A little one. He would be about ten or twelve now if he was there. He must a been mislaid in one of them movings."

"Has what you have heard about him since them eight years ago caused you to think he might have changed his habits any?"

"Sho now," Ratliff said. What dust the three horses raised blew lightly aside on the faint breeze, among the dogfennel and bitterweed just beginning to bloom in the roadside ditches. "Eight years. And before that it was fifteen more pretty near I never saw him. I growed up next to where he was living. I mean, he lived for about two years on the same place where I growed up. Him and my pap was both renting from Old Man Anse Holland. Ab was a horse-trader then. In fact, I was there the same time the horse-trading give out on him and left him just a farmer. He aint naturally mean. He's just soured."

"Soured," Varner said. He spat. His voice was now sardonic, almost contemptuous: "Jody came in last night, late. I knowed it soon as I saw him. It was exactly like when he was a boy and had done something he knowed I was going to find out about tomorrow and so he would figure he better tell me first himself. 'I done hired a clerk,' he says. 'What for?' I says. 'Dont Sam shine your shoes on Sunday no more to suit you?' and he hollers, 'I had to! I had to hire him! I had to, I tell you!' And he went to bed without eating no supper. I dont know how he slept; I never listened to see. But this morning he seemed to feel a little better about it. He seemed to feel considerable better about it. 'He might even be useful,' he says. 'I dont doubt it,' I says. 'But there's a law against it. Besides, why not just tear them down instead? You could even sell the lumber then.' And he looked at me a while longer. Only he was just waiting for me to stop; he had done figured it all out last night. 'Take a man like that,' he says. 'A man that's independent about protecting his self, his own rights and interests. Say the advantages of his own rights and interests is another fellow's advantage and interest too. Say his benefits is the same benefits as the fellow that's paying some of his kinfolks a salary to protect his business; say it's a business where now and then (and you know it as well as I do,' Jody says) '—say benefits is always coming up that the fellow that's going to get the benefits just as lief not be actively mixed up in himself, why, a fellow that independent—'"

"He could have said 'dangerous' with the same amount of breath," Ratliff said.

"Yes," Varner said. "Well?"

Ratliff didn't answer. Instead, he said: "That store aint in Jody's name, is it?" Only he answered this himself, before the other could have spoken: "Sho now. Why did I need to ask that? Besides, it's just—Flem that Jody's mixed up with. Long as Jody keeps him, maybe old Ab will—"

"Out with it," Varner said. "What do you think about it?"

"You mean what I really think?"

"What in damnation do you think I am talking about?"

"I think the same as you do," Ratliff said quietly. "That there aint but two men I know can risk fooling with them folks. And just one of them is named Varner and his front name aint Jody."

"And who's the other one?" Varner said.

"That aint been proved yet neither," Ratliff said pleasantly.

2.

Besides Varner's store and cotton gin and the combined grist mill and blacksmith shop which they rented to the actual smith, and the schoolhouse and the church and the perhaps three dozen dwellings within sound of both bells, the village consisted of a livery barn and lot and a contiguous shady though grassless yard in which sat a sprawling rambling edifice partly of sawn boards and partly of logs, unpainted and of two storeys in places and known as Littlejohn's hotel, where behind a weathered plank nailed to one of the trees and lettered ROOMƧ AND BORD drummers and livestock-traders were fed and lodged. It had a long veranda lined with chairs. That night after supper, the buckboard and team in the stable, Ratliff was sitting here with five or six other men who had drifted in from the adjacent homes within walking distance. They would have been there on any other night, but this evening they were gathered even before the sun was completely gone, looking now and then toward the dark front of Varner's store as people will gather to look quietly at the cold embers of a lynching or at the propped ladder and open window of an elopement, since the presence of a hired white clerk in the store of a man still able to walk and with intellect still sound enough to make money mistakes at least in his own favor, was as unheard of as the presence of a hired white woman in one of their own kitchens. "Well," one said, "I dont know nothing about that one Varner hired. But blood's thick. And a man that's got kinfolks that stays mad enough all the time to set fire to a man's barn—"

"Sho now," Ratliff said. "Old man Ab aint naturally mean. He's just soured."

For a moment nobody spoke. They sat or squatted along the veranda, invisible to one another. It was almost full dark, the departed sun a pale greenish stain in the north-western sky. The whipporwills had begun and fireflies winked and drifted among the trees beyond the road.

"How soured?" one said after a while.

"Why, just soured," Ratliff said pleasantly, easily, readily. "There was that business during the War. When he wasn't bothering nobody, not harming or helping either side, just tending to his own business, which was profit and horses—things which never even heard of such a thing as a political conviction—when here comes somebody that never even owned the horses even and shot him in the heel. And that soured him. And then that business of Colonel Sartoris's ma-in-law, Miss Rosa Millard, that Ab had done went and formed a horse- and mule-partnership with in good faith and honor, not aiming to harm nobody blue or gray but just keeping his mind fixed on profit and horses, until Miz Millard had to go and get herself shot by that fellow that called his self Major Grumby, and then Colonel's boy Bayard and Uncle Buck McCaslin and a nigger caught Ab in the woods and something else happened, tied up to a tree or something and maybe even a doubled bridle rein or maybe even a heated ramrod in it too though that's just hearsay. Anyhow, Ab had to withdraw his allegiance to the Sartorises, and I hear tell he skulked for a considerable back in the hills until Colonel Sartoris got busy enough building his railroad for it to be safe to come out. And that soured him some more. But at least he still had horse-trading left to fall back on. Then he run into Pat Stamper. And Pat eliminated him from horse-trading. And so he just went plumb curdled."

"You mean he locked horns with Pat Stamper and even had the bridle left to take back home?" one said. Because they all knew Stamper. He was a legend, even though still alive, not only in that country but in all north Mississippi and west Tennessee—a heavy man with a stomach and a broad pale expensive Stetson hat and eyes the color of a new axe blade, who travelled about the country with a wagon carrying camping equipment and played horses against horses as a gambler plays cards against cards, for the pleasure of beating a worthy opponent as much as for gain, assisted by a negro hostler who was an artist as a sculptor is an artist, who could take any

piece of horseflesh which still had life in it and retire to whatever closed building or shed was empty and handy and then,
with a quality of actual legerdemain, reappear with something
which the beast's own dam would not recognise, let alone its
recent owner; the two of them, Stamper and the negro, working in a kind of outrageous rapport like a single intelligence
possessing the terrific advantage over common mortals of
being able to be in two places at once and directing two separate sets of hands and fingers at the same time.

"He done better than that," Ratliff said. "He come out exactly even. Because if it was anybody that Stamper beat, it was
Miz Snopes. And even she never considered it so. All she was
out was just having to make the trip to Jefferson herself to
finally get the separator and maybe she knowed all the time
that sooner or later she would have to do that. It wasn't Ab
that bought one horse and sold two to Pat Stamper. It was
Miz Snopes. Her and Pat just used Ab to trade through."

Once more for a moment no one spoke. Then the first
speaker said: "How did you find all this out? I reckon you
was there too."

"I was," Ratliff said. "I went with him that day to get the
separator. We lived about a mile from them. My pap and Ab
were both renting from Old Man Anse Holland then, and I
used to hang around Ab's barn with him. Because I was a fool
about a horse too, same as he was. And he wasn't curdled
then. He was married to his first wife then, the one he got
from Jefferson, that one day her pa druv up in a wagon and
loaded her and the furniture into it and told Ab that if he ever
crossed Whiteleaf bridge again he would shoot him. They
never had no children and I was just turning eight and I
would go down to his house almost every morning and stay
all day with him, setting on the lot fence with him while the
neighbors would come up and look through the fence at
whatever it was he had done swapped some more of Old Man
Anse's bob-wire or busted farm tools for this time, and Ab
lying to just exactly the right amount about how old it was
and how much he give for it. He was a fool about a horse; he
admitted it, but he wasn't the kind of a fool about a horse
Miz Snopes claimed he was that day when we brought Beasley Kemp's horse home and turned it into the lot and come

up to the house and Ab taken his shoes off on the gallery to
cool his feet for dinner and Miz Snopes standing in the door
shaking the skillet at him and Ab saying, 'Now Vynie, now
Vynie. I always was a fool about a good horse and you know
it and aint a bit of use in you jawing about it. You better
thank the Lord that when He give me a eye for horseflesh He
give me a little judgment and gumption with it.'

    "Because it wasn't the horse. It wasn't the trade. It was a
good trade because Ab had just give Beasley a straight stock
and a old wore-out sorghum mill of Old Man Anse's for the
horse, and even Miz Snopes had to admit that that was a
good swap for anything that could get up and walk from
Beasley's lot to theirn by itself, because like she said while
she was shaking the skillet at him, he couldn't get stung
very bad in a horse-trade because he never had nothing of
his own that anybody would want to swap even a sorry horse
for. And it wasn't because Ab had left the plow down in the
far field where she couldn't see it from the house and had
snuck the wagon out the back way with the plow stock and
the sorghum mill in it while she still thought he was in the
field. It was like she knowed already what me and Ab didn't:
that Pat Stamper had owned that horse before Beasley got it
and that now Ab had done caught the Pat Stamper sickness
just from touching it. And maybe she was right. Maybe to
himself Ab did call his self the Pat Stamper of the Holland
farm or maybe even of all Beat Four, even if maybe he was
fairly sho that Pat Stamper wasn't going to walk up to that lot
fence and challenge him for it. Sho, I reckon while he was
setting there on the gallery with his feet cooling and the sidemeat plopping and spitting in the kitchen and us waiting to
eat it so we could go back down to the lot and set on the
fence while the folks would come up and look at what he had
brung home this time, I reckon maybe Ab not only knowed
as much about horse-trading as Pat Stamper, but he owned
head for head of them with Old Man Anse himself. And I
reckon while we would be setting there, just moving enough
to keep outen the sun, with that empty plow standing in the
furrow down in the far field and Miz Snopes watching him
outen the back window and saying to herself, 'Horse-trader!
Setting there bragging and lying to a passel of shiftless men

with the weeds and morning glories climbing so thick in the cotton and corn I am afraid to tote his dinner down to him for fear of snakes'; I reckon Ab would look at whatever it was he had just traded the mail box or some more of Old Man Anse's bob-wire or some of the winter corn for this time, and he would say to his self, 'It's not only mine, but before God it's the prettiest drove of a horse I ever see.'

"It was fate. It was like the Lord Himself had decided to buy a horse with Miz Snopes's separator money. Though I will admit that when He chose Ab He picked out a good quick willing hand to do His trading for Him. The morning we started, Ab hadn't planned to use Beasley's horse a tall because he knowed it probably couldn't make that twenty-eight mile trip to Jefferson and back in one day. He aimed to go up to Old Man Anse's lot and borrow a mule to work with hisn and he would a done it except for Miz Snopes. She kept on taunting him about swapping for a yard ornament, about how if he could just git it to town somehow maybe he could swap it to the livery stable to prop up in front for a sign. So in a way it was Miz Snopes herself that put the idea in Ab's head of taking Beasley's horse to town. So when I got there that morning we hitched Beasley's horse into the wagon with the mule. We had done been feeding it for two-three days now by forced draft, getting it ready to make the trip, and it looked some better now than when we had brung it home. But even yet it didn't look so good. So Ab decided it was the mule that showed it up, that when it was the only horse or mule in sight it looked pretty good and that it was standing by something else on four legs that done the damage. 'If it was just some way to hitch the mule under the wagon, so it wouldn't show but could still pull, and just leave the horse in sight,' Ab says. Because he wasn't soured then. But we had done the best we could with it. Ab thought about mixing a right smart of salt in some corn so it would drink a lot of water so some of the ribs wouldn't show so bad at least, only we knowed it wouldn't never get to Jefferson then, let alone back home, besides having to stop at every creek and branch to blow it up again. So we done the best we could. That is, we hoped for the best. Ab went to the house and come back in his preacher's coat (it's the same one he's still got; it was

Colonel Sartoris's that Miss Rosa Millard give him, it would be thirty years ago) and that twenty-four dollars and sixty-eight cents Miz Snopes had been saving on for four years now, tied up in a rag, and we started out.

"We wasn't even thinking about horse-trading. We was thinking about horse all right, because we was wondering if maybe we wasn't fixing to come back home that night with Beasley's horse in the wagon and Ab in the traces with the mule. Yes sir, Ab eased that team outen the lot and on down the road easy and careful as ere a horse and mule ever moved in this world, with me and Ab walking up every hill that tilted enough to run water offen it, and we was aiming to do that right in to Jefferson. It was the weather, the hot day; it was the middle of July. Because here we was about a mile from Whiteleaf store, with Beasley's horse kind of half walking and half riding on the double tree and Ab's face looking worrieder and worrieder every time it failed to lift its feet high enough to step, when all of a sudden that horse popped into a sweat. It flung its head up like it had been touched with a hot poker and stepped up into the collar, touching the collar for the first time since the mule had taken the weight of it when Ab shaken out the whip in the lot, and so we come down the hill and up to Whiteleaf store with that horse of Beasley's eyes rolling white as darning eggs and its mane and tail swirling like a grass fire. And I be dog if it hadn't not only sweated itself into as pretty a dark blood bay as you ever saw, but even its ribs didn't seem to show so much. And Ab that had been talking about taking the back road so we wouldn't have to pass the store at all, setting there on the wagon seat like he would set on the lot fence back home where he knowed he was safe from Pat Stamper, telling Hugh Mitchell and the other fellows on the gallery that that horse come from Kentucky. Hugh Mitchell never even laughed. 'Sho now,' he says. 'I wondered what had become of it. I reckon that's what taken it so long; Kentucky's a long walk. Herman Short swapped Pat Stamper a mule and buggy for that horse five years ago and Beasley Kemp give Herman eight dollars for it last summer. What did you give Beasley? Fifty cents?'

"That's what did it. It wasn't what the horse had cost Ab because you might say all it had cost Ab was the straight stock, since in the first place the sorghum mill was wore out and in the second place it wasn't Ab's sorghum mill nohow. And it wasn't the mule and buggy of Herman's. It was them eight cash dollars of Beasley's, and not that Ab held them eight dollars against Herman, because Herman had done already invested a mule and buggy in it. And besides, the eight dollars was still in the country and so it didn't actually matter whether it was Herman or Beasley that had them. It was the fact that Pat Stamper, a stranger, had come in and got actual Yoknapatawpha County cash dollars to rattling around loose that way. When a man swaps horse for horse, that's one thing and let the devil protect him if the devil can. But when cash money starts changing hands, that's something else. And for a stranger to come in and start that cash money to changing and jumping from one fellow to another, it's like when a burglar breaks into your house and flings your things ever which way even if he dont take nothing. It makes you twice as mad. So it was not just to unload Beasley Kemp's horse back onto Pat Stamper. It was to get Beasley Kemp's eight dollars back outen Pat someway. And that's what I meant about it was pure fate that had Pat Stamper camped outside Jefferson right by the road we would have to pass on that day we went to get Miz Snopes's milk separator; camped right there by the road with that nigger magician on the very day when Ab was coming to town with twenty-four dollars and sixty-eight cents in his pocket and the entire honor and pride of the science and pastime of horse-trading in Yoknapatawpha County depending on him to vindicate it.

"I dont recollect just when and where we found out Pat was in Jefferson that day. It might have been at Whiteleaf store. Or it might have just been that in Ab's state it was not only right and natural that Ab would have to pass Stamper to get to Jefferson, but it was foreordained and fated that he would have to. So here we come, easing them eight dollars of Beasley Kemp's up them long hills with Ab and me walking and Beasley's horse laying into the collar the best it could but with the mule doing most of the pulling and Ab walking on his side of the wagon and cussing Pat Stamper and Herman Short and Beasley Kemp and Hugh Mitchell; and we went down the hills with Ab holding the wagon braked with a sapling pole so it wouldn't shove Beasley's horse through the collar and turn it wrong-side-out like a sock, and Ab still cussing Pat Stamper and Herman and Beasley and Mitchell, until we come to the Three Mile bridge and Ab turned the team outen the road and druv into the bushes and taken the mule out and knotted up one rein so I could ride and give me the quarter and told me to ride for town and get a dime's worth of salt-peter and a nickel's worth of tar and a number ten fish hook and hurry back.

"So we didn't get into town until after dinner time. We went straight to Pat's camp and druv in with that horse of Beasley's laying into the collar now sho enough, with its eyes looking nigh as wild as Ab's and foaming a little at the mouth where Ab had rubbed the saltpeter into its gums and a couple of as pretty tarred bob-wire cuts on its chest as you could want, and another one where Ab had worked that fish hook under its hide where he could touch it by drooping one rein a little, and Pat's nigger running up to catch the head-stall before the horse run right into the tent where Pat slept and Pat his self coming out with that ere cream colored Stetson cocked over one eye and them eyes the color of a new plow point and just about as warm and his thumbs hooked into his waist band. 'That's a pretty lively horse you got there,' he says.

" 'You damn right,' Ab says. 'That's why I got to get shut of it. Just consider you done already trimmed me and give me something in place of it I can get back home without killing me and this boy both.' Because that was the right system: to rush right up and say he had to trade instead of hanging back for Pat to persuade him. It had been five years since Pat had seen the horse, so Ab figured that the chance of his recognis-ing it would be about the same as a burglar recognising a dollar watch that happened to get caught for a minute on his vest button five years ago. And Ab wasn't trying to beat Pat bad. He just wanted to recover that eight dollars' worth of the honor and pride of Yoknapatawpha County horse-trading, doing it not for profit but for honor. And I believe it worked. I still believe that Ab fooled Pat, and that it was because of what Pat aimed to trade Ab and not because Pat recognised Beasley's horse, that Pat refused to trade any way except team for team. Or I dont know: maybe Ab was so busy fooling Pat that Pat never had to fool Ab at all. So the nigger led the span of mules out and Pat standing there with his thumbs in his pants-top, watching Ab and chewing tobacco slow and gentle, and Ab standing there with that look on his face that was desperate but not scared yet, because he was realising now he had got in deeper than he aimed to and that he would either have to shut his eyes and bust on through, or back out and quit, get back in the wagon and go on before Beasley's horse even give up to the fish hook. And then Pat Stamper showed how come he was Pat Stamper. If he had just started in to show Ab what a bargain he was getting, I reckon Ab would have backed out. But Pat didn't. He fooled Ab just exactly as one first class burglar would fool another first class burglar by purely and simply refusing to tell him where the safe was at.

" 'I already got a good mule,' Ab says. 'It's just the horse I dont want. Trade me a mule for the horse.'

" 'I dont want no wild horse neither,' Pat says. 'Not that I wont trade for anything that walks, provided I can trade my way. But I aint going to trade for that horse alone because I dont want it no more than you do. What I am trading for is that mule. And this here team of mine is matched. I aim to get about three times as much for them as a span as I would selling them single.'

" 'But you would still have a team to trade with,' Ab says.

" 'No,' Pat says. 'I aim to get more for them from you than I would if the pair was broken. If it's a single mule you want, you better try somewhere else.'

"So Ab looked at the mules again. They looked just exactly right. They didn't look extra good and they didn't look extra bad. Neither one of them looked quite as good as Ab's mule, but the two of them together looked just a little mite better than just one mule of anybody's. And so he was doomed. He was doomed from the very minute Hugh Mitchell told him about that eight dollars. I reckon Pat Stamper knowed he was doomed the very moment he looked up and seen that nigger holding Beasley's horse back from running into the tent. I reckon he knowed right then he wouldn't even have to try to trade Ab: all he would have to do would be just to say No long enough. Because that's what he done, leaning there against our wagon bed with his thumbs hooked into his pants, chewing his tobacco and watching Ab go through the motions of examining them mules again. And even I knowed that Ab had done traded, that he had done walked out into what he thought was a spring branch and then found out it was quicksand, and that now he knowed he couldn't even stop long enough to turn back. 'All right,' he says. 'I'll take them.'

"So the nigger put the new team into the harness and we went on to town. And them mules still looked all right. I be dog if I didn't begin to think that Ab had walked into that Stamper quicksand and then got out again, and when we had got back into the road and beyond sight of Stamper's tent, Ab's face begun to look like it would while he would set on the lot fence at home and tell folks how he was a fool about a horse but not a durn fool. It wasn't easy yet, it was just watchful, setting there and feeling out the new team. We was right at town now and he wouldn't have much time to feel them out in, but we would have a good chance on the road back home. 'By God,' Ab says. 'If they can walk home at all, I have got that eight dollars back, damn him.'

"But that nigger was a artist. Because I swear to God them mules looked all right. They looked exactly like two ordinary, not extra good mules you might see in a hundred wagons on the road. I had done realised how they had a kind of jerky way of starting off, first one jerking into the collar and then jerking back and then the other jerking into the collar and then jerking back, and even after we was in the road and the wagon rolling good one of them taken a spell of some sort and snatched his self crossways in the traces like he aimed to turn around and go back, maybe crawling right across the wagon to do it, but then Stamper had just told us they was a matched team; he never said they had ever worked together as a matched team, and they was a matched team in the sense that neither one of them seemed to have any idea as to just when the other one aimed to start moving. But Ab got them straightened out and we went on, and we was just starting up that big hill onto the Square when they popped into a sweat too, just like Beasley's horse had done just beyond Whiteleaf. But that was all right, it was hot enough; that was when I first noticed that that rain was coming up; I mind how I was watching a big hot-looking bright cloud over to the south-west and thinking how it was going to rain on us before we got home or to Whiteleaf either, when all of a sudden I realised that the wagon had done stopped going up the hill and was starting down it backwards and I looked around just in time to see both of them mules this time crossways in the traces and kind of glaring at one another across the tongue and Ab trying to straighten them out and glaring too, and then all of a sudden they straightened out and I mind how I was thinking what a good thing it was they was pointed away from the wagon when they straightened out. Because they moved at the same time for the first time in their lives, or for the first time since Ab owned them anyway, and here we come swurging up that hill and into the Square like a roach up a drain pipe, with the wagon on two wheels and Ab sawing at the reins and saying 'Hell fire, hell fire' and folks, ladies and children mostly, scattering and screeching and Ab just managed to swing them into the alley behind Cain's store and stopped them by locking our nigh wheel with another wagon's and the other team (they was hitched) holp to put the brakes on. So it was a good crowd by then, helping us to get untangled, and Ab led our team over to Cain's back door and tied them snubbed up close to a post, with folks still coming up and saying, 'It's that team of Stamper's,' and Ab breathing hard now and looking a right smart less easy in the face and most all-fired watchful. 'Come on,' he says. 'Let's get that damn separator and get out of here.'

"So we went in and give Cain Miz Snopes's rag and he counted the twenty-four sixty-eight and we got the separator and started back to the wagon, to where we had left it. Because it was still there; the wagon wasn't the trouble. In fact, it was too much wagon. I mind how I could see the bed and the tops of the wheels where Ab had brought it up close against the loading platform and I could see the folks from the waist up standing in the alley, twice or three times as many of them now, and I was thinking how it was too much wagon and too much folks; it was like one of these here pictures that have printed under them, *What's wrong with this picture?* and then Ab begun to say 'Hell fire, hell fire' and begun to run, still toting his end of the separator, up to the edge of the platform where we could see under it. The mules was all right too. They was laying down. Ab had snubbed them up pretty close to the same post, with the same line through both bits, and now they looked exactly like two fellows that had done hung themselves in one of these here suicide packs, with their heads snubbed up together and pointing straight up and their tongues hanging out and their eyes popping and their necks stretched about four foot and their legs doubled back under them like shot rabbits until Ab jumped down and cut them down with his pocket knife. A artist. He had give them just exactly to the inch of whatever it was to get them to town and off the Square before it played out.

"So Ab was desperate. I can see him now, backed off in a corner behind Cain's plows and cultivators, with his face white and his voice shaking and his hand shaking so he couldn't hardly hand me the six bits outen his pocket. 'Go to Doc Peabody's,' he says, 'and get me a bottle of whiskey. Hurry.' He was desperate. It wasn't even quicksand now. It was a whirlpool and him with just one jump left. He drunk that pint of whiskey in two drinks and set the empty bottle down in the corner careful as a egg and we went back to the wagon. The mules was still standing up this time and we loaded the separator in and he eased them away careful, with folks still telling each other it was that team of Stamper's. Ab's face was red instead of white now and the sun was gone but I dont think he even noticed it. And we hadn't et too, and I dont believe he knowed that either. And I be dog if it didn't seem like Pat Stamper hadn't moved either, standing there at the gate to his rope stock pen, with that Stetson cocked and his thumbs still hooked in the top of his pants and Ab sitting in the wagon trying to keep his hands from shaking and the team Stamper had swapped him stopped now with their heads down and their legs spraddled and breathing like a saw-mill. 'I come for my team,' Ab says.

" 'What's the matter?' Stamper says. 'Dont tell me these are too lively for you too. They dont look it.'

" 'All right,' Ab says. 'All right. I got to have my team. I got four dollars. Make your four-dollar profit and give me my team.'

" 'I aint got your team,' Stamper says. 'I didn't want that horse neither. I told you that. So I got shut of it.'

"Ab set there for a while. It was cooler now. A breeze had got up and you could smell the rain in it. 'But you still got my mule,' Ab says. 'All right. I'll take it.'

" 'For what?' Stamper says. 'You want to swap that team for your mule?' Because Ab wasn't trading now. He was desperate, sitting there like he couldn't even see, with Stamper leaning easy against the gate post and looking at him for a minute. 'No,' Stamper says. 'I dont want them mules. Yours is the best one. I wouldn't trade that way, even swap.' He spit, easy and careful. 'Beside I done included your mule into another team. With another horse. You want to look at it?'

" 'All right,' Ab says. 'How much?'

" 'Dont you even want to see it first?' Stamper says.

" 'All right,' Ab says. So the nigger led out Ab's mule and a horse, a little dark brown horse; I remember how even with it clouded up and no sun, how that horse shined—a horse a little bigger than the one we had traded Stamper, and hog fat. That's just exactly how it was fat: not like a horse is fat but like a hog: fat right up to its ears and looking tight as a drum; it was so fat it couldn't hardly walk, putting its feet down like they didn't have no weight nor feeling in them at all. 'It's too fat to last,' Ab says. 'It wont even get me home.'

" 'That's what I think myself,' Stamper says. 'That's why I want to get shut of it.'

" 'All right,' Ab says. 'I'll have to try it.' He begun to get outen the wagon.

" 'Try it?' Stamper says. Ab didn't answer. He got outen the wagon careful and went to the horse, putting his feet down careful and stiff too, like he never had no weight in his feet too, like the horse. It had a hackamore on and Ab taken the rope from the nigger and started to get on the horse. 'Wait,' Stamper said. 'What are you fixing to do?'

" 'Going to try it,' Ab says. 'I done swapped a horse with you once today.' Stamper looked at Ab a minute. Then he spit again and kind of stepped back.

" 'All right, Jim,' he says to the nigger. 'Help him up.' So the nigger holp Ab onto the horse, only the nigger never had time to jump back like Stamper because soon as Ab's weight come onto the horse it was like Ab had a live wire in his britches. The horse made one swirl, it looked round as a ball, without no more front or back end than a Irish potato. It throwed Ab hard and Ab got up and went back to the horse and Stamper says, 'Help him up, Jim,' and the nigger holp Ab up again and the horse slammed him off again and Ab got up with his face just the same and went back and taken the rope again when Stamper stopped him. It was just exactly like Ab wanted that horse to throw him, hard, like the ability of his bones and meat to stand that ere hard ground was all he had left to pay for something with life enough left to get us home. 'Are you trying to kill yourself?' Stamper says.

" 'All right,' Ab says. 'How much?'

" 'Come into the tent,' Stamper says.

"So I waited in the wagon. It was beginning to blow a little now, and we hadn't brought no coats with us. But we had some croker sacks in the wagon Miz Snopes had made us bring along to wrap the separator in and I was wrapping it in the sacks when the nigger come outen the tent and when he lifted up the flap I seen Ab drinking outen the bottle. Then the nigger led up a horse and buggy and Ab and Stamper come outen the tent and Ab come to the wagon, he didn't look at me, he just lifted the separator outen the sacks and went and put it into the buggy and him and Stamper went and got into it and drove away, back toward town. The nigger was watching me. 'You fixing to get wet fo you get home,' he said.

" 'I reckon so,' I said.

" 'You want to eat a snack of dinner until they get back?' he said. 'I got it on the stove.'

" 'I reckon not,' I said. So he went back into the tent and I waited in the wagon. It was most sholy going to rain, and that soon. I mind how I thought that anyway we would have the croker sacks now to try to keep dry under. Then Ab and Stamper come back and Ab never looked at me that time either. He went back into the tent and I could see him drinking outen the bottle again and this time he put it into his shirt. And then the nigger led our mule and the new horse up and put them in the wagon and Ab come out and got in. Stamper and the nigger both holp him now.

" 'Dont you reckon you better let that boy drive?' Stamper says.

" 'I'll drive,' Ab says. 'Maybe I cant swap a horse with you, but by God I can still drive it.'

" 'Sho now,' Stamper says. 'That horse will surprise you.'

"And it did," Ratliff said. He laughed, for the first time, quietly, invisible to his hearers though they knew exactly how he would look at the moment as well as if they could see him, easy and relaxed in his chair, with his lean brown pleasant shrewd face, in his faded clean blue shirt, with that same air of perpetual bachelorhood which Jody Varner had, although there was no other resemblance between them and not much here, since in Varner it was a quality of shabby and fustian gallantry where in Ratliff it was that hearty celibacy as of a lay brother in a twelfth-century monastery—a gardener, a pruner of vines, say. "That horse surprised us. The rain, the storm, come up before we had gone a mile and we rode in it for two hours, hunched under the croker sacks and watching that new shiny horse that was so fat it even put its feet down like it couldn't even feel them, that every now and then, even during the rain, would give a kind of flinching jerk like when Ab's weight had come down onto its back at Stamper's camp, until we found a old barn to shelter under. I did, that is, because Ab was laying out in the wagon bed by then, flat on his back with the rain popping him in the face and me on the seat driving now and watching that shiny black horse turning into a bay horse. Because I was just eight then, and me and Ab had done all our horse-trading up and down that lane that run past his lot. So I just drove under the first roof I come to and shaken Ab awake. The rain had cooled him off by then and he waked up sober. And he got a heap soberer fast. 'What?' he says. 'What is it?'

" 'The horse!' I hollered. 'He's changing color!'

"He was sober then. We was both outen the wagon then and Ab's eyes popping and a bay horse standing in the traces where he had went to sleep looking at a black one. He put his hand out like he couldn't believe it was even a horse and touched it at a spot where the reins most every now and then

just barely touched it and just about where his weight had
come down on it when he was trying to ride it at Stamper's,
and next I knowed that horse was plunging and swurging. I
dodged just as it slammed into the wall behind me; I could
even feel the wind in my hair. Then there was a sound like
a nail jabbed into a big bicycle tire. It went *whishhhhhhhhh*
and then the rest of that shiny fat black horse we had got
from Pat Stamper vanished. I dont mean me and Ab was
standing there with just the mule left. We had a horse too.
Only it was the same horse we had left home with that morning and that we had swapped Beasley Kemp the sorghum mill
and the straight stock for two weeks ago. We even got our
fish hook back, with the barb still bent where Ab had bent it
and the nigger had just moved it a little. But it wasn't till next
morning that Ab found the bicycle pump valve under its
hide just inside the nigh fore shoulder—the one place in the
world where a man might own a horse for twenty years and
never think to look at it.

"Because we never got home till well after sunup the next
day, and my pap was waiting at Ab's house, considerable
mad. So I didn't stay long, I just had time to see Miz Snopes
standing in the door where I reckon she had been setting all
night too, saying, 'Where's my separator?' and Ab saying
how he had always been a fool about a horse and he couldn't
help it and then Miz Snopes begun to cry. I had been hanging around them a heap by now, but I never had seen her cry
before. She looked like the kind of somebody that never had
done much crying to speak of nohow, because she cried hard,
like she didn't know just how to do it, like even the tears
never knowed just exactly what they was expected to do,
standing there in a old wrapper, not even hiding her face,
saying, 'Fool about a horse, yes! But why the horse? why the
horse?'

"So me and Pap went on. He had my arm a right smart
twisted up in his hand, but when I begun to tell him about
what happened yesterday, he changed his mind about licking
me. But it was almost noon before I got back down to Ab's.
He was setting on the lot fence and I clumb up and set by
him. Only the lot was empty. I couldn't see his mule nor
Beasley's horse neither. But he never said nothing and I never

said nothing, only after a while he said, 'You done had breakfast?' and I said I had and he said, 'I aint et yet.' So we went to the house then, and sho enough, she was gone. And I could imagine it—Ab setting there on that fence and her coming down the hill in her sunbonnet and shawl and gloves too and going into the stable and saddling the mule and putting the halter on Beasley's horse and Ab setting there trying to decide whether to go and offer to help her or not.

"So I started the fire in the stove. Ab wasn't much of a hand at cooking, so by the time he got his breakfast started it was so late we just decided to cook enough for breakfast and dinner too and we et it and I washed the dishes and we went back to the lot. The middle buster was still setting down yonder in the far field, but there wasn't nothing to pull it with nohow now lessen he walked up to Old Man Anse's and borrowed a span of mules, which would be just like going up to a rattlesnake and borrowing a rattle: but then, I reckon he felt he had stood all the excitement he could for the rest of that day at least. So we just set on the fence and looked at that empty lot. It never had been a big lot and it would look kind of crowded even with just one horse in it. But now it looked like all Texas; and sho enough, I hadn't hardly begun to think about how empty it was when he clumb down offen the fence and went across and looked at a shed that was built against the side of the barn and that would be all right if it was just propped up and had a new roof on it. 'I think next time I will trade for a mare and build me up a brood herd and raise mules,' he says. 'This here will do all right for colts with a little fixing up.' Then he come back and we set on the fence again, and about middle of the afternoon a wagon druv up. It was Cliff Odum, it had the side-boards on it and Miz Snopes was on the seat with Cliff, coming on past the house, toward the lot. 'She aint got it,' Ab says. 'He wouldn't dicker with her.' We was behind the barn now and we watched Cliff back his wagon up against a cut bank by the gate and we watched Miz Snopes get out and take off her shawl and gloves and come across the lot and into the cow shed and lead the cow back and up onto the cut bank behind the wagon and Cliff said, 'You come hold the team. I'll get her in the wagon.' But she never even stopped. She faced the cow into the tail gate and got behind it and laid her shoulder against its hams and hove that cow into the wagon before Cliff could have got out. And Cliff put up the tail gate and Miz Snopes put her shawl and gloves back on and they got into the wagon and they went on.

"So I built him another fire to cook his supper and then I had to go home; it was almost sundown then. When I come back the next morning I brung a pail of milk. Ab was in the kitchen, still cooking breakfast. 'I am glad you thought about that,' he says when he seen the milk. 'I was aiming to tell you yesterday to see if you could borrow some.' He kept on cooking breakfast because he hadn't expected her that soon, because that would make two twenty-eight mile trips in not much more than twenty-four hours. But we heard the wagon again and this time when she got out she had the separator. When we got to the barn we could see her toting it into the house. 'You left that milk where she will see it, didn't you?' Ab says.

" 'Yes sir,' I says.

" 'Likely she will wait to put on her old wrapper first,' Ab says. 'I wish I had started breakfast sooner.' Only I dont think she even waited that long, because it seemed like we begun to hear it right away. It made a fine high sound, good and strong, like it would separate a gallon of milk in no time. Then it stopped. 'It's too bad she aint got but the one gallon,' Ab says.

" 'I can bring her another one in the morning,' I said. But he wasn't listening, watching the house.

" 'I reckon you can go now and look in the door,' he says. So I went and did. She was taking Ab's breakfast offen the stove, onto two plates. I didn't know she had even seen me till she turned and handed the two plates to me. Her face was all right now, quiet. It was just busy.

" 'I reckon you can eat something more too,' she said. 'But eat it out yonder. I am going to be busy in here and I dont want you and him in my way.' So I taken the plates back and we set against the fence and et. And then we heard the separator again. I didn't know it would go through but one time. I reckon he didn't neither.

" 'I reckon Cain showed her,' he says, eating. 'I reckon if

she wants it to run through more than once, it will run through more than once.' Then it stopped and she come to the door and hollered to us to bring the dishes up so she could wash them and I taken the plates back and set them on the step and me and Ab went back and set on the fence. It looked like it would have held all Texas and Kansas too. 'I reckon she just rode up to that damn tent and said, Here's your team. You get my separator and get it quick because I got to catch a ride back home.', he said. And then we heard it again, and that evening we walked up to Old Man Anse's to borrow a mule to finish the far piece with, but he never had none to spare now. So as soon as Old Man Anse had finished cussing, we come on back and set on the fence. And sho enough, we could hear the separator start up again. It sounded strong as ever, like it could make the milk fly, like it didn't give a whoop whether that milk had been separated once or a hundred times. 'There it goes again,' Ab says. 'Dont forget that other gallon tomorrow.'

" 'No sir,' I says. We listened to it. Because he wasn't curdled then.

" 'It looks like she is fixing to get a heap of pleasure and satisfaction outen it,' he says."

3.

He halted the buckboard and sat for a moment looking down at the same broken gate which Jody Varner had sat the roan horse and looked at nine days ago—the weed-choked and grass-grown yard, the weathered and sagging house—a cluttered desolation filled already, even before he reached the gate and stopped, with the loud flat sound of two female voices. They were young voices, talking not in shouts or screams but with an unhurried profundity of volume the very apparent absence from which of any discernible human speech or language seemed but natural, as if the sound had been emitted by two enormous birds; as if the aghast and amazed solitude of some inaccessible and empty marsh or desert were being invaded and steadily violated by the constant bickering of the two last survivors of a lost species which had established residence in it—a sound which stopped short off when Ratliff shouted. A moment later the two girls came to the door and stood, big, identical, like two young tremendous cows, looking at him.

"Morning, ladies," he said. "Where's your paw?"

They continued to contemplate him. They did not seem to breathe even, though he knew they did, must; bodies of that displacement and that apparently monstrous, that almost oppressive, wellness, would need air and lots of it. He had a fleeting vision of them as the two cows, heifers, standing knee-deep in air as in a stream, a pond, nuzzling into it, the level of the pond fleeing violently and silently to one inhalation, exposing in astounded momentary amaze the teeming lesser subaerial life about the planted feet. Then they spoke exactly together, like a trained chorus: "Down to the field."

Sho now, he thought, moving on. Doing what? Because he did not believe that the Ab Snopes he had known would have more than two mules. And one of these he had already seen standing idle in the lot beyond the house; and the other he knew to be tied at this moment to a tree behind Varner's store eight miles away, because only three hours ago he had left it there, tied where for six days now he had watched Varner's new clerk ride up each morning and tie it. For an instant he actually halted the buckboard again. By God, he thought quietly, This would be exactly the chance he must have been waiting on for twenty-three years now to get his-self that new un-Stampered start. So when he came in sight of the field and recognised the stiff, harsh, undersized figure behind a plow drawn by two mules, he was not even surprised. He did not wait until he had actually recognised the mules to be a pair which until a week ago at least had belonged to Will Varner: he merely changed the tense of the possessing verb: Not *had* belonged, he thought. They still do. By God, he has done even better than that. He aint even trading horses now. He has done swapped a man for a span of them.

He halted the buckboard at the fence. The plow had reached the far end of the field. The man turned the team, their heads tossing and yawing, their stride breaking as he sawed them about with absolutely needless violence. Ratliff watched soberly. Just like always, he thought. He still handles a horse or a mule like it had done already threatened him with its fist before he even spoke to it. He knew that Snopes had seen and even recognised him too, though there was no sign of it, the team straightened out now and returning, the delicate mule-legs and narrow deer-like feet picking up swiftly and nervously, the earth shearing dark and rich from the polished blade of the plow. Now Ratliff could even see Snopes looking directly at him—the cold glints beneath the shaggy ill-tempered brows as he remembered them even after eight years, the brows only a little grayer now—though once more the other merely swung the team about with that senseless savageness, canting the plow onto its side as he stopped it. "What you doing here?" he said.

"Just heard you were here and stopped by," Ratliff said. "It's been a while, aint it? Eight years."

The other grunted. "It dont show on you, though. You still look like butter wouldn't melt in your mouth."

"Sho now," Ratliff said. "Speaking of mouths." He reached beneath the seat cushion and produced a pint bottle filled apparently with water. "Some of McCallum's best," he said. "Just run off last week. Here." He extended the bottle. The other came to the fence. Although they were now not five feet apart, still all that Ratliff could see were the two glints beneath the fierce overhang of brow.

"You brought it to me?"

"Sholy," Ratliff said. "Take it."

The other did not move. "What for?"

"Nothing," Ratliff said. "I just brought it. Try a sup of it. It's good."

The other took the bottle. Then Ratliff knew that something had gone out of the eyes. Or maybe they were just not looking at him now. "I'll wait till tonight," Snopes said. "I dont drink in the sun any more."

"How about in the rain?" Ratliff said. And then he knew that Snopes was not looking at him, although the other had not moved, no change in the harsh knotted violent face as he stood holding the bottle. "You ought to settle down pretty good here," Ratliff said. "You got a good farm now, and Flem seems to taken hold in the store like he was raised storekeeping." Now the other did not seem to be listening either.

He shook the bottle and raised it to the light as though test-ing the bead. "I hope you will," Ratliff said.

Then he saw the eyes again, fierce and intractable and cold. "What's it to you if I do or dont?"

"Nothing," Ratliff said, pleasantly, quietly. Snopes stooped and hid the bottle in the weeds beside the fence and returned to the plow and raised it.

"Go on to the house and tell them to give you some din-ner," he said.

"I reckon not," Ratliff said. "I got to get on to town."

"Suit yourself," the other said. He looped the single rein about his neck and gave another savage yank on the inside line; again the team swung with yawing heads, already break-ing stride even before they had come into motion. "Much obliged for the bottle," he said.

"Sho now," Ratliff said. The plow went on. Ratliff watched it. He never said, Come back again, he thought. He lifted his own reins. "Come up, rabbits," he said. "Let's hit for town."

Chapter Three

O N THE Monday morning when Flem Snopes came to clerk in Varner's store, he wore a brand new white shirt. It had not even been laundered yet, the creases where the cloth had lain bolted on a shelf, and the sun-browned streaks repeated zebra-like on each successive fold, were still apparent. And not only the women who came to look at him, but Ratliff himself (he did not sell sewing machines for nothing. He had even learned to operate one quite well from demonstrating them, and it was even told of him that he made himself the blue shirts which he wore) knew that the shirt had been cut and stitched by hand and by a stiff and unaccustomed hand too. He wore it all that week. By Saturday night it was soiled, but on the following Monday he appeared in a second one exactly like it, even to the zebra-stripes. By the second Saturday night that one was soiled too, in exactly the same places as the other. It was as though its wearer, entering though he had into a new life and milieu already channelled to compulsions and customs fixed long before his advent, had nevertheless established in it even on that first day his own particular soiling groove.

He rode up on a gaunt mule, on a saddle which was recognised at once as belonging to the Varners, with a tin pail tied to it. He hitched the mule to a tree behind the store and untied the pail and came and mounted to the gallery, where already a dozen men, Ratliff among them, lounged. He did not speak. If he ever looked at them individually, that one did not discern it—a thick squat soft man of no establishable age between twenty and thirty, with a broad still face containing a tight seam of mouth stained slightly at the corners with tobacco, and eyes the color of stagnant water, and projecting from among the other features in startling and sudden paradox, a tiny predatory nose like the beak of a small hawk. It was as though the original nose had been left off by the original designer or craftsman and the unfinished job taken over by someone of a radically different school or perhaps by some viciously maniacal humorist or perhaps by one who had had only time to clap into the center of the face a frantic and desperate warning.

He entered the store, carrying the pail, and Ratliff and his companions sat and squatted about the gallery all that day and watched not only the village proper but all the countryside within walking distance come up singly and in pairs and in groups, men women and children, to make trivial purchases and look at the new clerk and go away. They came not belligerently but completely wary, almost decorous, like half-wild cattle following word of the advent of a strange beast upon their range, to buy flour and patent medicine and plow lines and tobacco and look at the man whose name a week ago they had never heard, yet with whom in the future they would have to deal for the necessities of living, and then depart as quietly as they had come. About nine oclock Jody Varner rode up on his roan saddle horse and entered the store. They could hear the bass murmur of his voice inside, though for all the answer he got he might have been talking to himself. He came out at noon and mounted and rode away, though the clerk did not follow him. But they had known anyway what the tin pail would contain, and they began to disperse noonward too, looking into the store as they passed the door, seeing nothing. If the clerk was eating his lunch, he had hidden to do it. Ratliff was back on the gallery before one oclock, since he had had to walk only a hundred yards for his dinner. But the others were not long after him, and for the rest of that day they sat and squatted, talking quietly now and then about nothing at all, while the rest of the people within walking distance came and bought in nickels and dimes and went away.

By the end of that first week they had all come in and seen him, not only all those who in the future would have to deal through him for food and supplies but some who had never traded with the Varners and never would—the men, the women, the children—the infants who had never before crossed the doorsteps beyond which they had been born, the sick and the aged who otherwise might never have crossed them but once more—coming on horses and mules and by wagonsful. Ratliff was still there, the buckboard still containing the music box and the set of virgin harrow teeth standing, a plank propping its tongue and the sturdy mismatched team growing vicious with idleness, in Mrs Littlejohn's lot, watching each morning as the clerk would ride up on the mule, on the borrowed saddle, in the new white shirt growing gradually and steadily a little more and more soiled with each sunset, with the tin pail of lunch which no man had ever yet seen him eating, and hitch the mule and unlock the store with the key which they had not quite expected him to have in his possession for a few days yet at least. After the first day or so he would even have the store open when Ratliff and the others arrived. Jody Varner would appear on the horse about nine oclock and mount the steps and jerk his head bluffly at them and enter the store, though after the first morning he remained only about fifteen minutes. If Ratliff and his companions had hoped to divine any hidden undercurrent or secret spark between the younger Varner and the clerk, they were disappointed. There would be the heavy bass matter-of-fact murmur, still talking apparently to itself for all the audible answer it ever got, then he and the clerk would come to the door and stand in it while Varner finished his instructions and sucked his teeth and departed; when they looked toward the door, it would be empty.

Then at last, on Friday afternoon, Will Varner himself appeared. Perhaps it was for this Ratliff and his companions had been waiting. But if it was, it was doubtless not Ratliff but the others who even hoped that anything would divulge here. So it was very likely Ratliff alone who was not surprised, since what did divulge was the obverse of what they might have hoped for; it was not the clerk who now discovered at last whom he was working for, but Will Varner who discovered who was working for him. He came up on the old fat white horse. A young man squatting on the top step rose and descended and took the reins and tied the horse and Varner got down and mounted the steps, speaking cheerily to their deferential murmur, to Ratliff by name: "Hell fire, aint you gone back to work yet?" Two more of them vacated the knife-gnawed wooden bench, but Varner did not approach it at once. Instead, he paused in front of the open door in almost exactly the same attitude of the people themselves, lean, his neck craned a little like a turkey as he looked into the store, though only for an instant because almost at once he shouted, "You there. What's your name? Flem. Bring me a plug of my tobacco. Jody showed you where he keeps it." He came and approached the group, two of whom vacated the knife-gnawed wooden bench for him, and he sat down and took out his knife and had already begun his smoking car story in his cheerful drawling bishop's voice when the clerk (Ratliff had not heard his feet at all) appeared at his elbow with the tobacco. Still talking, Varner took the plug and cut off a chew and shut the knife with his thumb and straightened his leg to put the knife back into his pocket, when he stopped talking and looked sharply upward. The clerk was still standing at his elbow. "Hey?" Varner said. "What?"

"You aint paid for it," the clerk said. For an instant Varner did not move at all, his leg still extended, the plug and the severed chew in one hand and the knife in the other just about to enter his pocket. None of them moved in fact, looking quietly and attentively at their hands or at wherever their eyes had been when Varner interrupted himself. "The tobacco," the clerk said.

"Oh," Varner said. He put the knife into his pocket and drew from his hip a leather purse about the size and shape and color of an egg-plant and took a nickel from it and gave it to the clerk. Ratliff had not heard the clerk come out and he did not hear him return. Now he saw why. The clerk wore also a new pair of rubber-soled tennis shoes. "Where was I?" Varner said.

"The fellow had just begun to unbutton his over-halls," Ratliff said mildly.

The next day Ratliff departed. He was put into motion not by the compulsion of food, earning it. He could have passed from table to table in that country for six months without once putting his hand into his pocket. He was moved by his itinerary, his established and nurtured round of newsmongering, the pleasure of retailing it, not the least nor stalest of which present stock he had spent the last two weeks actually watching. It was five months before he saw the village again. His route embraced four counties. It was absolutely rigid, flexible only within itself. In ten years he had not once crossed the boundaries of these four, yet one day in this summer he found himself in Tennessee. He found himself not only on foreign soil but shut away from his native state by a golden barrier, a wall of neatly accumulating minted coins.

During the spring and summer he had done a little too well. He had oversold himself, selling and delivering the machines on notes against the coming harvest, employing what money he collected or sold the exchanged articles for which he accepted as down-payments, to make his own down-payments to the Memphis wholesaler on still other machines, which he delivered in turn on new notes, countersigning them, until one day he discovered that he had almost sold himself insolvent on his own bull market. The wholesaler made demand upon him for his (the wholesaler's) half of the outstanding twenty-dollar notes. Ratliff in his turn made a swift canvass of his own debtors. He was affable, bland, anecdotal and apparently unhurried as ever but he combed them thoroughly, not to be denied, although the cotton had just begun to bloom and it would be months yet before there would be any money in the land. He collected a few dollars, a set of used wagon harness, eight White Leghorn hens. He owed the wholesaler $120.00. He called on the twelfth customer, a distant kinsman, and found that he had departed a week ago with a string of mules to sell at the mule curbmarket at Columbia, Tennessee.

He followed at once in the buckboard, with the wagon harness and the hens. He not only saw a chance to collect his note, provided he got there before someone sold the kinsman some mules in his own turn, but he might even borrow enough to appease the wholesaler. He reached Columbia four days later, where, after the first amazed moment or so, he looked about him with something of the happy surmise of the first white hunter blundering into the idyllic solitude of a virgin African vale teeming with ivory, his for the mere shooting and fetching out. He sold a machine to the man whom he asked the whereabouts of his cousin, he went with the kinsman to pass the night at the home of the kinsman's wife's cousin ten miles from Columbia and sold a machine there. He sold three in the first four days; he remained a month and sold eight in all, collecting $80.00 in down-payments, with

the $80.00 and the wagon harness and the eight hens he
bought a mule, took the mule to Memphis and sold it at curb
auction for $135.00, gave the wholesaler $120.00 and the new
notes for a quit-claim on the old ones in Mississippi, and
reached home at gathering-time with $2.53 in cash and full
title to the twelve twenty-dollar notes which would be paid as
the cotton was ginned and sold.

When he reached Frenchman's Bend in November, it had
returned to normal. It had acquiesced to the clerk's presence
even if it had not accepted him, though the Varners seemed to
have done both. Jody had used to be in the store at some time
during the day and not far from it at any time. Ratliff now
discovered that for months he had been in the habit of sometimes not appearing at all, customers who had traded there
for years, mostly serving themselves and putting the correct
change into the cigar box inside the cheese cage, now having
to deal for each trivial item with a man whose name they had
not even heard two months ago, who answered Yes and No
to direct questions and who apparently never looked directly
or long enough at any face to remember the name which
went with it, yet who never made mistakes in any matter per-
taining to money. Jody Varner had made them constantly.
They were usually in his own favor to be sure, letting a customer get away with a spool of thread or a tin of snuff now
and then, but getting it back sooner or later. They had come
to expect mistakes of him, just as they knew he would correct
them when caught with a bluff, hearty amiability, making a
joke of it, which sometimes left the customer wondering just
a little about the rest of the bill. But they expected this too,
because he would give them credit for food and plow-gear
when they needed it, long credit, though they knew they
would pay interest for that which on its face looked like generosity and open-handedness, whether that interest showed in
the final discharge or not. But the clerk never made mistakes.

"Nonsense," Ratliff said. "Somebody's bound to catch him
sooner or later. There aint a man woman or child in twenty-
five miles that dont know what's in that store and what it cost
as well as Will or Jody Varner either."

"Hah," the other said—a sturdy short-legged black-browed
ready-faced man named Odum Bookwright. "That's it."

"You mean aint nobody ever caught him *once* even?"

"No," Bookwright said. "And folks dont like it. Otherwise, how can you tell?"

"Sho," Ratliff said. "How can you?"

"There was that credit business too," another said—a lank man with a bulging dreamy scant-haired head and pale myopic eyes named Quick, who operated a sawmill. He told about it: how they had discovered almost at once that the clerk did not want to credit anyone with anything. He finally flatly refused further credit to a man who had been into and out of the store's debt at least once a year for the last fifteen, and how that afternoon Will Varner himself came galloping up on the old fat grumble-gutted white horse and stormed into the store, shouting loud enough to be heard in the black-smith shop across the road: "Who in hell's store do you think this is, anyway?"

"Well, we know whose store it is yet, anyway," Ratliff said.

"Or whose store some folks still thinks it is yet," Book-wright said. "Anyhow, he aint moved into Varner's house yet."

Because the clerk now lived in the village. One Saturday morning someone noticed that the saddled mule was not hitched behind the store. The store remained open until ten and later on Saturdays and there was always a crowd about it and several men saw him put out the lamps and lock the door and depart, on foot. And the next morning he who had never been seen in the village between Saturday night and Monday morning appeared at the church, and those who saw him looked at him for an instant in incredulous astonishment. In addition to the gray cloth cap and the gray trousers, he wore not only a clean white shirt but a necktie—a tiny machine-made black bow which snapped together at the back with a metal fastener. It was not two inches long and with the exception of the one which Will Varner himself wore to church it was the only tie in the whole Frenchman's Bend country, and from that Sunday morning until the day he died he wore it or one just like it (it was told of him later, after he had become president of his Jefferson bank, that he had them made for him by the gross)—a tiny viciously depthless cryptically bal-anced splash like an enigmatic punctuation symbol against the

expanse of white shirt which gave him Jody Varner's look of
ceremonial heterodoxy raised to its tenth power and which
postulated to those who had been present on that day that
quality of outrageous overstatement of physical displacement
which the sound of his father's stiff foot made on the gallery
of the store that afternoon in the spring. He departed on
foot; he came to the store the next morning still walking and
still wearing the tie. By nightfall the countryside knew that
since the previous Saturday he had boarded and lodged in the
home of a family living about a mile from the store.

Will Varner had long since returned to his old idle busy
cheerful existence—if he had ever left it. The store had not
seen him since the Fourth of July. And now that Jody no
longer came in, during the dead slack days of August while
the cotton ripened and there was nothing for anyone to do, it
had actually seemed as if not only the guiding power but the
proprietorial and revenue-deriving as well was concentrated in
that squat reticent figure in the steadily-soiling white shirts
and the minute invulnerable bow, which in those abeyant
days lurked among the ultimate shadows of the deserted and
rich-odored interior with a good deal of the quality of a spider of that bulbous blond omnivorous though non-poisonous
species.

Then in September something happened. It began rather,
though at first they did not recognise it for what it was. The
cotton had opened and was being picked. One morning the
first of the men to arrive found Jody Varner already there. The
gin was unlocked and Trumbull, Varner's blacksmith, and his
apprentice and the negro fireman were overhauling the machinery, getting it ready for the season's run, and presently
Snopes came out of the store and went across to the gin and
entered it and passed from sight and so, for the moment,
from remembering too. It was not until the store closed that
afternoon that they realised that Jody Varner had been inside
it all day. But even then they attached little importance to
this. They thought that without doubt Jody himself had sent
the clerk to superintend the opening of the gin, which Jody
himself had used to do, out of laziness, assuming himself the
temporary onus of tending store so he could sit down. It took
the actual firing-up of the gin and the arrival of the first

loaded wagons to disabuse them. Then they saw that it was
Jody who was now tending store again, fetching and carrying
for the nickels and dimes, while the clerk sat all day long on
the stool behind the scale-beam as the wagons moved in turn
onto it and so beneath the suction pipe. Jody had used to do
both. That is, he was mostly behind the scales, letting the
store take care of itself, as it always had, though now and
then, just to rest himself, he would keep a wagon standing
upon the scales, blocking them for fifteen minutes or even
forty-five minutes, while he was in the store; maybe there
would not even be any customers during that time, just
loungers, listeners for him to talk to. But that was all right.
Things got along just as well. And now that there were two
of them, there was no reason why one should not remain in
the store while the other did the weighing, and there was no
reason why Jody should not have designated the weighing to
the clerk. The cold surmise which now began to dawn upon
them was that——

"Sho," Ratliff said. "I know. That Jody should have stayed
there a tall. Just who it was that told him to stay there." He
and Bookwright looked at each other. "It wasn't Uncle Will.
That store and that gin had been running themselves at the
same time for nigh forty years all right, with just one fellow
between them. And a fellow Uncle Will's age aint likely to
change his notions. Sho now. All right. Then what?"

They could watch them both from the gallery. They would
come in on their laden wagons and draw into line, mule-nose
to tail-gate, beside the road, waiting for their turn to move
onto the scales and then under the suction pipe, and dismount and wrap the reins about a stanchion and cross to the
gallery, from which they could watch the still, impenetrable,
steadily-chewing face throned behind the scale-beam, the
cloth cap, the minute tie, while from within the store they
could hear now and then the short surly grunts with which
Varner answered when his customers forced him to speak at
all. Now and then they would even go in themselves and buy
sacks or plugs of tobacco or tins of snuff which they did not
actually need yet, or maybe just to drink from the cedar water
bucket. Because there was something in Jody's eyes that had
not been there before either—a shadow, something between

annoyance and speculation and purest foreknowledge, which was not quite bafflement yet but was certainly sober. This was the time they referred to later, two and three years later, when they told one another: "That was when he passed Jody," though it was Ratliff who amended it: "You mean, that was when Jody begun to find it out."

But that was to be sometime in the future yet. Now they just watched, missing nothing. During that month the air was filled from daylight until dark with the whine of the gin; the wagons stood in line for the scales and moved up one by one beneath the suction pipe. Now and then the clerk would cross the road to the store, the cap, the trousers, even the tie wisped with cotton; the men lounging upon the gallery while they waited their turns at the suction pipe or the scales would watch him enter the store now and a moment later hear his voice this time, murmuring, matter-of-fact, succinct. But Jody Varner would not come to the door with him to stand for a moment as before, and they would watch the clerk return to the gin—the thick squat back, shapeless, portentous, without age. After the crops were in and ginned and sold, the time came when Will Varner made his yearly settlement with his tenants and debtors. He had used to do this alone, not even allowing Jody to help him. This year he sat at the desk with the iron cash box while Snopes sat on a nail keg at his knee with the open ledgers. In the tunnel-like room lined with canned food and cluttered with farming implements and now crowded with patient earth-reeking men waiting to accept almost without question whatever Varner should compute he owed them for their year's work, Varner and Snopes resembled the white trader and his native parrot-taught headman in an African outpost.

That headman was acquiring the virtues of civilization fast. It was not known what the Varners paid him, except that Will Varner had never been known to pay very much for anything. Yet this man who five months ago was riding eight miles back and forth to work on a plow mule and a cast-off saddle with a tin pail of cold turnip greens or field pease tied to it, was now not only sleeping in a rented bed and eating from a furnished table like a drummer, he had also made a considerable cash loan, security and interest not specified, to a resident of the village, and before the last of the cotton was ginned it was generally known that any sum between twenty-five cents and ten dollars could be borrowed from him at any time, if the borrower agreed to pay enough for the accommodation. In the next spring Tull, in Jefferson with a drove of cattle for shipping on the railroad, came to see Ratliff who was sick in bed in the house which he owned and which his widowed sister kept for him, with a recurrent old gall-bladder trouble. Tull told him of a considerable herd of scrub cattle which had passed the winter in pasture on the farm which Snopes' father had rented from the Varners for another year—a herd which, by the time Ratliff had been carried to a Memphis hospital and operated on and returned home and once more took an interest in what went on about him, had increased gradually and steadily and then overnight vanished, its disappearance coincident with the appearance of a herd of good Herefords in a pasture on another place which Varner owned and kept himself as his home farm, as though transmogrified, translated complete and intact save for their altered appearance and obviously greater worth, it only later becoming known that the cattle had reached the pasture via a foreclosed lien nominally held by a Jefferson bank. Bookwright and Tull both came to see him and told him of this.

"Maybe they was in the bank vault all the time," Ratliff said weakly. "Who did Will say they belonged to?"

"He said they was Snopeses'," Tull said. "He said, 'Ask that son-of-a-gun of Jody's.'"

"And did you?" Ratliff said.

"Bookwright did. And Snopes said, 'They're in Varner's pasture.' And Bookwright said, 'But Will says they are yourn.' And Snopes turned his head and spit and says, 'They're in Varner's pasture.'"

And Ratliff, ill, did not see this either. He only heard it second hand, though by that time he was mending, well enough to muse upon it, speculate, curious, shrewd, and inscrutable himself, sitting up now in a chair propped with pillows in a window where he could watch the autumn begin, feel the bright winy air of October noons: How one morning in that second spring a man named Houston, heeled by a magnificent grave blue-ticked Walker hound, led a horse up to the blacksmith shop and saw, stooping over the forge and trying to start a fire in it with liquid from a rusty can, a stranger—a young, well-made, muscle-bound man who, turning, revealed an open equable face beginning less than an inch below his hairline, who said, "Howdy. I cant seem to get this here fire started. Everytime I put this here coal oil onto it, it just goes further out. Watch." He prepared to pour from the can again.

"Hold on," Houston said. "Is that coal oil you've got?"

"It was setting on that ere ledge yonder," the other said. "It looks like the kind of a can coal oil would be in. It's a little rusty, but I never heard tell of even rusty coal oil that wouldn't burn before." Houston came and took the can from him and sniffed it. The other watched him. The splendid hound sat in the doorway and watched them both. "It dont smell exactly like coal oil, does it?"

"—t," Houston said. He set the can back on the sooty ledge above the forge. "Go on. Haul that mud out. You'll have to start over. Where's Trumbull?" Trumbull was the smith who had been in the shop for almost twenty years, until this morning.

"I dont know," the other said. "Wasn't nobody here when I come."

"What are you doing here? Did he send you?"

"I dont know," the other said. "It was my cousin hired me. He told me to be here this morning and get the fire started and tend to the business till he come. But everytime I put that ere coal oil—"

"Who is your cousin?" Houston said. At that moment a gaunt aged horse came up rapidly, drawing a battered and clattering buggy one of whose wheels was wired upright by two crossed slats, which looked as if its momentum alone held it intact and that the instant it stopped it would collapse into kindling. It contained another stranger—a frail man none of whose garments seemed to belong to him, with a talkative weasel's face—who halted the buggy, shouting at the horse as if they were a good-sized field apart, and got out of the buggy and came into the shop, already (or still) talking.

"Morning, morning," he said, his little bright eyes darting. "Want that horse shod, hey? Good, good: save the hoof and save all. Good-looking animal. Seen a considerable better one in a field a piece back. But no matter; love me, love my horse, beggars cant be choosers, if wishes was horseflesh we'd all own thoroughbreds. What's the matter?" he said to the man in the apron. He paused, though still he seemed to be in violent motion, as though the attitude and position of his garments gave no indication whatever of what the body within them might be doing—indeed, if it were still inside them at all. "Aint you got that fire started yet? Here." He darted to the ledge; he seemed to translate himself over beneath it without increasing his appearance of violent motion at all, and had taken the can down and sniffed at it and then prepared to empty it onto the coals in the forge before anyone could move. Then Houston intercepted him at the last second and took the can from him and flung it out the door.

"I just finished taking that damn hog piss away from him," Houston said. "What the hell's happened here? Where's Trumbull?"

"Oh, you mean the fellow that used to be here," the newcomer said. "His lease has done been cancelled. I'm leasing the shop now. My name's Snopes. I.O. Snopes. This here's my young cousin, Eck Snopes. But it's the old shop, the old stand; just a new broom in it."

"I dont give a damn what his name is," Houston said. "Can he shoe a horse?" Again the newcomer turned upon the man in the apron, shouting at him as he had shouted at the horse:

"All right. All right. Get that fire started." After watching a moment, Houston took charge and they got the fire going. "He'll pick it up though," the newcomer said. "Just give him time. He's handy with tools, even though he aint done no big sight of active blacksmithing. But give a dog a good name and you dont need to hang him. Give him a few days to practise up and he'll shoe a horse quick as Trumbull or any of them."

"I'll shoe this one," Houston said. "Just let him keep pumping that bellows. He looks like he ought to be able to do that without having to practise." Nevertheless, the shoe shaped and cooled in the tub, the newcomer darted in again. It was as if he took not only Houston but himself too by complete surprise—that weasel-like quality of existing independent of his clothing so that although you could grasp and hold that you could not restrain the body itself from doing what it was doing until the damage had been done—a furious already dissipating concentration of energy vanishing the instant after the intention took shape, the newcomer darting between Houston and the raised hoof and clapping the shoe onto it and touching the animal's quick with the second blow of the hammer on the nail and being hurled, hammer and all, into the shrinking-tub by the plunging horse which Houston and the man in the apron finally backed into a corner and held while Houston jerked nail and shoe free and flung them into the corner and backed the horse savagely out of the shop, the hound rising and resuming its position quietly at proper heeling distance behind the man. "And you can tell Will Varner— if he cares a damn, which evidently he dont," Houston said, "that I have gone to Whiteleaf to have my horse shod."

The shop and the store were just opposite, only the road between. There were several men already on the gallery, who watched Houston, followed by the big quiet regal dog, lead the horse away. They did not even need to cross the road to see one of the strangers, because presently the smaller and older one crossed to the store, in the clothes which would still appear not to belong to him on the day they finally fell off his body, with his talkative pinched face and his bright darting eyes. He mounted the steps, already greeting them. Still talking, he entered the store, his voice voluble and rapid and meaningless like something talking to itself about nothing in a deserted cavern. He came out again, still talking: "Well, gentlemen, off with the old and on with the new. Competition is the life of trade, and though a chain aint no stronger than its weakest link, I dont think you'll find the boy yonder no weak reed to have to lean on once he catches onto it. It's the old shop, the old stand; it's just a new broom in it and maybe you cant teach a old dog new tricks but you can teach a new young willing one anything. Just give him time; a penny on the waters pays interest when the flood turns. Well, well; all pleasure and no work, as the fellow says, might make Jack so sharp he might cut his self. I bid you good morning, gentlemen." He went on and got into the buggy, still talking, now to the man in the shop and now to the gaunt horse, all in one breath, without any break to indicate to the hearers which he addressed at any time. He drove away, the men on the gallery looking after him, completely expressionless. During the day they crossed to the shop, one by one, and looked at the second stranger—the quiet empty open face which seemed to have been a mere afterthought to the thatching of the skull, like the binding of a rug, harmless. A man brought up a wagon with a broken hound. The new smith even repaired it, though it took him most of the forenoon, working steadily but in a dreamlike state in which what actually lived inside him apparently functioned somewhere else, paying no heed to and having no interest in, not even in the money he would earn, what his hands were doing; busy, thick-moving, getting nowhere seemingly though at last the job was finished. That afternoon Trumbull, the old smith, appeared. But if they had waited about the store to see what would happen when he arrived who until last night anyway must have still believed himself the incumbent, they were disappointed. He drove through the village with his wife, in a wagon loaded with household goods. If he even looked toward his old shop nobody saw him do it—an old man though still hale, morose and efficient, who would have invited no curiosity even before yesterday. They never saw him again.

A few days later they learned that the new smith was living in the house where his cousin (or whatever the relationship was: nobody ever knew for certain) Flem lived, the two of them sleeping together in the same bed. Six months later the smith had married one of the daughters of the family where the two of them boarded. Ten months after that he was pushing a perambulator (once—or still—Will Varner's, like the cousin's saddle) about the village on Sundays, accompanied by a five or six year old boy, his son by a former wife which the village did not know either he had ever possessed—indicating that there was considerably more force and motion to his private life, his sex life anyway, than would appear on the surface of his public one. But that all appeared later. All they saw now was that they had a new blacksmith— a man who was not lazy, whose intentions were good and who was accommodating and unfailingly pleasant and even generous, yet in whom there was a definite limitation of physical co-ordination beyond which design and plan and pattern all vanished, disintegrated into dead components of pieces of wood and iron straps and vain tools.

Two months later Flem Snopes built a new blacksmith shop in the village. He hired it done, to be sure, but he was there most of the day, watching it going up. This was not only the first of his actions in the village which he was ever seen in physical juxtaposition to, but the first which he not only admitted but affirmed, stating calmly and flatly that he was doing it so that people could get decent work done again. He bought completely new equipment at cost price through the store and hired the young farmer who during the slack of planting and harvesting time had been Trumbull's apprentice. Within a month the new shop had got all the trade which Trumbull had had and three months after that Snopes had sold the new shop—smith clientele and goodwill and new equipment—to Varner, receiving in return the old equipment in the old shop, which he sold to a junk man, moved the new equipment to the old shop and sold the new building to a farmer for a cowshed, without even having to pay himself to have it moved, leaving his kinsman now apprentice to the new smith—at which point even Ratliff had lost count of what profit Snopes might have made. But I reckon I can guess the rest of it, he told himself, sitting, a little pale but otherwise well, in his sunny window. He could almost see it—in the store, at night, the door barred on the inside and the lamp burning above the desk where the clerk sat, chewing steadily, while Jody Varner stood over him, in no condition to sit down, with a good deal more in his eyes than had been in them last fall, shaking, trembling, saying in a shaking voice: "I want to make one pure and simple demand of you and I want a pure and simple Yes and No for a answer: How many more is there? How much longer is this going on? Just what is it going to cost me to protect one goddamn barn full of hay?"

2.

He had been sick and he showed it as, the buckboard once more with a new machine in the dog kennel box and the little sturdy team fat and slick with the year's idleness hitched in an

adjacent alley, he sat at the counter of a small side-street restaurant in which he owned a sleeping partner's half interest,
with a cup of coffee at his hand and in his pocket a contract
to sell fifty goats to a Northerner who had recently established a goat-ranch in the western part of the county. It was
actually a subcontract which he had purchased at the rate of
twenty-five cents a goat from the original contractor who held
his from the Northerner at seventy-five cents a goat and was
about to fail to complete. Ratliff bought the subcontract because he happened to know of a herd of some fifty-odd goats
in a little-travelled section near Frenchman's Bend village
which the original contractor had failed to find and which
Ratliff was confident he could acquire by offering to halve his
profit with the owner of them.

He was on his way to Frenchman's Bend now, though he
had not started yet and did not know just when he would
start. He had not seen the village in a year now. He was looking forward to his visit not only for the pleasure of the
shrewd dealing which far transcended mere gross profit, but
with the sheer happiness of being out of bed and moving
once more at free will, even though a little weakly, in the sun
and air which men drank and moved in and talked and dealt
with one another—a pleasure no small part of which lay in
the fact that he had not started yet and there was absolutely
nothing under heaven to make him start until he wanted to.
He did not still feel weak, he was merely luxuriating in that
supremely gutful lassitude of convalescence in which time,
hurry, doing, did not exist, the accumulating seconds and
minutes and hours to which in its well state the body is slave
both waking and sleeping, now reversed and time now the
lip-server and mendicant to the body's pleasure instead of
the body thrall to time's headlong course. So he sat, thin, the
fresh clean blue shirt quite loose upon him now, yet looking
actually quite well, the smooth brown of his face not pallid
but merely a few shades lighter, cleaner-looking; emanating
in fact a sort of delicate robustness like some hardy odorless
infrequent woodland plant blooming into the actual heel of
winter's snow, nursing his coffee cup in one thin hand and
telling three or four listeners about his operation in that
shrewd humorous voice which would require a good deal

more than just illness to other than merely weaken its volume
a little, when two men entered. They were Tull and Bookwright. Bookwright had a stock whip rolled about its handle
and thrust into the back pocket of his overalls.

"Howdy, boys," Ratliff said. "You're in early."

"You mean late," Bookwright said. He and Tull went to the
counter.

"We just got in last night with some cattle to ship today,"
Tull said. "I heard you was sick. I thought I'd missed you."

"We all missed him," Bookwright said. "My wife aint mentioned nobody's new sewing machine in almost a year. What
was it that Memphis fellow cut outen you anyway?"

"My pocket book," Ratliff said. "I reckon that's why he put
me to sleep first."

"He put you to sleep first to keep you from selling him a
sewing machine or a bushel of harrow teeth before he could
get his knife open," Bookwright said. The counterman came
and slid two plates of bread and butter before them.

"I'll have steak," Tull said.

"I wont," Bookwright said. "I been watching the dripping
sterns of steaks for two days now. Let alone running them
back out of corn fields and vegetable patches. Bring me some
ham and a half a dozen fried eggs." He began to eat the
bread, wolfing it. Ratliff turned slightly on his stool to face
them.

"So I been missed," he said. "I would a thought you folks
would a had so many new citizens in Frenchman's Bend by
now you wouldn't a missed a dozen sewing machine agents.
How many kinfolks has Flem Snopes brought in to date? Is it
two more, or just three?"

"Four," Bookwright said shortly, eating.

"Four?" Ratliff said. "That's that blacksmith—I mean, the
one that uses the blacksmith shop for his address until it's
time to go back home and eat again—what's his name? Eck.
And that other one, the contractor, the business executive—"

"He's going to be the new school professor next year," Tull
said mildly. "Or so they claim."

"No no," Ratliff said. "I'm talking about them Snopeses.
That other one. I.O. That Jack Houston throwed into the
water tub that day in the blacksmith shop."

"That's him," Tull said. "They claim he's going to teach the school next year. The teacher we had left all of a sudden just after Christmas. I reckon you never heard about that neither."

But Ratliff wasn't listening to this. He wasn't thinking about the other teacher. He stared at Tull, for the moment surprised out of his own humorous poise. "What?" he said. "Teach the school? That fellow? That Snopes? The one that came to the shop that day that Jack Houston—— Here, Odum," he said; "I been sick, but sholy it aint affected my ears that much."

Bookwright didn't answer. He had finished his bread; he leaned and took a piece from Tull's plate. "You aint eating it," he said. "I'll tell him to bring some more in a minute."

"Well," Ratliff said. "I'll be damned. By God, I knowed there was something wrong with him soon as I saw him. That was it. He was standing in front of the wrong thing—a blacksmith shop or a plowed field. But teaching the school. I just hadn't imagined that yet. But that's it, of course. He has found the one and only place in the world or Frenchman's Bend either where he not only can use them proverbs of hisn all day long but he will be paid for doing it. Well," he said. "So Will Varner has caught that bear at last. Flem has grazed up the store and he has grazed up the blacksmith shop and now he is starting in on the school. That just leaves Will's house. Of course, after that he will have to fall back on you folks, but that house will keep him occupied for a while because Will—"

"Hah!" Bookwright said shortly. He finished the slice of bread he had taken from Tull's plate and called to the counterman: "Here. Bring me a piece of pie while I'm waiting."

"What kind of pie, Mr Bookwright?" the counterman said.

"Eating pie," Bookwright said.

"—because Will might be a little hard to dislodge outen the actual house," Ratliff went on. "He might even draw the line there altogether. So maybe Flem will have to start in on you folks sooner than he had figured on—"

"Hah," Bookwright said again, harsh and sudden. The counterman slid the pie along to him. Ratliff looked at him.

"All right," Ratliff said. "Hah what?"

Bookwright sat with the wedge of pie poised in his hand

before his mouth. He turned his fierce dark face toward Ratliff. "I was sitting on the sawdust pile at Quick's mill last week. His fireman and another nigger were shovelling the chips over toward the boiler, to fire with. They were talking. The fireman wanted to borrow some money, said Quick wouldn't let him have it. 'Go to Mr Snopes at the store,' the other nigger says. 'He will lend it to you. He lent me five dollars over two years ago and all I does, every Saturday night I goes to the store and pays him a dime. He aint even mentioned that five dollars.' " Then he turned his head and bit into the pie, taking a little less than half of it. Ratliff watched him with a faint quizzical expression which was almost smiling.

"Well well well," he said. "So he's working the top and the bottom both at the same time. At that rate it will be a while yet before he has to fall back on you ordinary white folks in the middle." Bookwright took another huge bite of the pie. The counterman brought his and Tull's meal and Bookwright crammed the rest of the pie into his mouth. Tull began to cut his steak neatly into bites as though for a child to eat it. Ratliff watched them. "Aint none of you folks out there done nothing about it?" he said.

"What could we do?" Tull said. "It aint right. But it aint none of our business."

"I believe I would think of something if I lived there," Ratliff said.

"Yes," Bookwright said. He was eating his ham as he had the pie. "And wind up with one of them bow ties in place of your buckboard and team. You'd have room to wear it."

"Sho now," Ratliff said. "Maybe you're right." He stopped looking at them now and raised his spoon, but lowered it again. "This here cup seems to have a draft in it," he said to the counterman. "Maybe you better warm it up a little. It might freeze and bust, and I would have to pay for the cup too." The counterman swept the cup away and refilled it and slid it back. Ratliff spooned sugar into it carefully, his face still wearing that faint expression which would have been called smiling for lack of anything better. Bookwright had mixed his six eggs into one violent mess and was now eating them audibly with a spoon. He and Tull both ate with expedition, though Tull even contrived to do that with almost niggling primness. They did not talk, they just cleaned their plates and rose and went to the cigar case and paid their bills.

"Or maybe them tennis shoes," Bookwright said. "He aint wore them in a year now.—No," he said. "If I was you I would go out there nekkid in the first place. Then you wont notice the cold coming back."

"Sho now," Ratliff said mildly. After they left he drank his coffee again, sipping it without haste, talking again to the three or four listeners, finishing the story of his operation. Then he rose too and paid for his coffee, scrupulously, and put on his overcoat. It was now March but the doctor had told him to wear it, and in the alley now he stood for a while beside the buckboard and the sturdy little horses overfat with idleness and sleek with new hair after their winter coats, looking quietly at the dog kennel box where, beneath the cracked paint of their fading and incredible roses, the women's faces smiled at him in fixed and sightless invitation. It would need painting again this year; he must see to that. It will have to be something that will burn, he thought. And in his name. Known to be in his name. Yes, he thought, if my name was Will Varner and my partner's name was Snopes I believe I would insist that some part of our partnership at least, that part of it that will burn anyway, would be in his name. He walked on slowly, buttoned into the overcoat. It was the only one in sight. But then the sick grow well fast in the sun; perhaps when he returned to town he would no longer need it. And soon he would not need the sweater beneath it either—May and June, the summer, the long good days of heat. He walked on, looking exactly as he always had save for the thinness and the pallor, pausing twice to tell two different people that yes, he felt all right now, the Memphis doctor had evidently cut the right thing out whether by accident or design, crossing the Square now beneath the shaded marble gaze of the Confederate soldier, and so into the court house and the Chancery Clerk's office, where he found what he sought—some two hundred acres of land, with buildings, recorded to Flem Snopes.

Toward the end of the afternoon he was sitting in the halted buckboard in a narrow back road in the hills, reading the name on a mail box. The post it sat on was new, but the box was not. It was battered and scarred; at one time it had apparently been crushed flat as though by a wagon wheel and straightened again, but the crude lettering of the name might have been painted on it yesterday. It seemed to shout at him, all capitals, MINK SNOPES, sprawling, without any spacing between the two words, trailing off and uphill and over the curve of the top to include the final letters. Ratliff turned in beside it—a rutted lane now, at the end of it a broken-backed cabin of the same two rooms which were scattered without number through these remote hill sections which he travelled. It was built on a hill; below it was a foul muck-trodden lot and a barn leaning away downhill as though a human breath might flatten it. A man was emerging from it, carrying a milk pail, and then Ratliff knew that he was being watched from the house itself though he had seen no one. He pulled the team up. He did not get down. "Howdy," he said. "This Mr Snopes? I brought your machine."

"Brought my what?" the man in the lot said. He came through the gate and set the pail on the end of the sagging gallery. He was slightly less than medium height also but thin, with a single line of heavy eyebrow. But it's the same eyes, Ratliff thought.

"Your sewing machine," he said pleasantly. Then he saw from the corner of his eye a woman standing on the gallery—a big-boned hard-faced woman with incredible yellow hair, who had emerged with a good deal more lightness and quickness than the fact that she was barefoot would have presaged. Behind her were two towheaded children. But Ratliff did not look at her. He watched the man, his expression bland courteous and pleasant.

"What's that?" the woman said. "A sewing machine?"

"No," the man said. He didn't look at her either. He was approaching the buckboard. "Get on back in the house." The woman paid no attention to him. She came down from the gallery, moving again with that speed and co-ordination which her size belied. She stared at Ratliff with pale hard eyes.

"Who told you to bring it here?" she said.

Now Ratliff looked at her, still bland, still pleasant. "Have I done made a mistake?" he said. "The message come to me in Jefferson, from Frenchman's Bend. It said Snopes. I taken it to mean you, because if your. . . . . . .cousin?" Neither of them spoke, staring at him. "Flem. If Flem had wanted it, he would have waited till I got there. He knowed I was due there tomorrow. I reckon I ought to made sho." The woman laughed harshly, without mirth.

"Then take it on to him. If Flem Snopes sent you word about anything that cost more than a nickel, it wasn't to give away. Not to his kinfolks anyhow. Take it on to the Bend."

"I told you to go in the house," the man said. "Go on." The woman didn't look at him. She laughed harshly and steadily, staring at Ratliff.

"Not to give away," she said. "Not the man that owns a hundred head of cattle and a barn and pasture to feed them in his own name." The man turned and walked toward her. She turned and began to scream at him, the two children watching Ratliff quietly from behind her skirts as if they were deaf or as if they lived in another world from that in which the woman screamed, like two dogs might. "Deny it if you can!" she cried at the man. "He'd let you rot and die right here and glad of it, and you know it! Your own kin you're so proud of because he works in a store and wears a necktie all day! Ask him to give you a sack of flour even and see what you get. Ask him! Maybe he'll give you one of his old neckties someday so you can dress like a Snopes too!" The man walked steadily toward her. He did not even speak again. He was the smaller of the two of them; he walked steadily toward her with a curious sidling deadly, almost deferential, air until she broke, turned swiftly and went back toward the house, the herded children before her still watching Ratliff over their shoulders. The man approached the buckboard.

"You say the message came from Flem?" he said.

"I said it come from Frenchman's Bend," Ratliff said. "The name mentioned was Snopes."

"Who was it seems to done all this mentioning about Snopes?"

"A friend," Ratliff said pleasantly. "He seems to made a

mistake. I ask you to excuse it. Can I follow this lane over to
the Whiteleaf Bridge road?"

"If Flem sent you word to leave it here, suppose you leave
it."

"I just told you I thought I had made a mistake and ask you
to excuse it," Ratliff said. "Does this lane—"

"I see," the other said. "That means you aim to have a little
cash down. How much?"

"You mean on the machine?"

"What do you think I am talking about?"

"Ten dollars," Ratliff said. "A note for twenty more in six
months. That's gathering time."

"Ten dollars? With the message you got from—"

"We aint talking about messages now," Ratliff said. "We're
talking about a sewing machine."

"Make it five."

"No," Ratliff said pleasantly.

"All right," the other said, turning. "Fix up your note."
He went back to the house. Ratliff got out and went to the
rear of the buckboard and opened the dog kennel's door
and drew from beneath the new machine a tin dispatch
box. It contained a pen, a carefully corked ink bottle, a pad of
note forms. He was filling in the note when Snopes returned,
reappeared at his side. As soon as Ratliff's pen stopped
Snopes slid the note toward himself and took the pen from
Ratliff's hand and dipped it and signed the note, all in one
continuous motion, without even reading it, and shoved the
note back to Ratliff and took something from his pocket
which Ratliff did not look at yet because he was looking at
the signed note, his face perfectly expressionless. He said
quietly,

"This is Flem Snopes' name you have signed."

"All right," the other said. "Then what?" Ratliff looked at
him. "I see. You want my name on it too, so one of us anyway
cant deny it has been signed. All right." He took the note and
wrote again on it and passed it back. "And here's your ten
dollars. Give me a hand with the machine." But Ratliff did
not move again, because it was not money but another paper
which the other had given him, folded, dog-eared and soiled.
Opened, it was another note. It was dated a little more than

three years ago, for ten dollars with interest, payable on demand one year after date of execution, to *Isaac Snopes or bearer*, and signed *Flem Snopes*. It was indorsed on the back (and Ratliff recognised the same hand which had just signed the two names to the first note) to *Mink Snopes*, by *Isaac Snopes (X) his mark*, and beneath that and still in the same hand and blotted (or dried at least), to *V. K. Ratliff*, by *Mink Snopes*, and Ratliff looked at it quite quietly and quite soberly for almost a minute. "All right," the other said. "Me and Flem are his cousins. Our grandma left us all three ten dollars a piece. We were to get it when the least of us—that was him—come twenty-one. Flem needed some cash and he borrowed his from him on this note. Then he needed some cash a while back and I bought Flem's note from him. Now if you want to know what color his eyes are or anything else, you can see for yourself when you get to Frenchman's Bend. He's living there now with Flem."

"I see," Ratliff said. "Isaac Snopes. He's twenty-one, you say?"

"How could he have got that ten dollars to lend Flem if he hadn't been?"

"Sho," Ratliff said. "Only this here aint just exactly a cash ten dollars—"

"Listen," the other said. "I dont know what you are up to and I dont care. But you aint fooling me any more than I am fooling you. If you were not satisfied Flem is going to pay that first note, you wouldn't have taken it. And if you aint afraid of that one, why are you afraid of this one, for less money, on the same machine, when this one has been collectible by law for more than two years? You take these notes on to him down yonder. Just hand them to him. Then you give him a message from me. Say 'From one cousin that's still scratching dirt to keep alive, to another cousin that's risen from scratching dirt to owning a herd of cattle and a hay barn. To owning cattle and a hay barn.' Just say that to him. Better keep on saying it over to yourself on the way down there so you will be sure not to forget it."

"You dont need to worry," Ratliff said. "Does this road lead over to Whiteleaf bridge?"

He spent that night in the home of kin people (he had

been born and raised not far away) and reached French-man's Bend the next afternoon and turned his team into Mrs Littlejohn's lot and walked down to the store, on the gallery of which apparently the same men who had been there when he saw it last a year ago were still sitting, including Bookwright. "Well, boys," he said. "A quorum as usual, I see."

"Bookwright says it was your pocket book that Memphis fellow cut outen you," one said. "No wonder it taken you a year to get over it. I'm just surprised you didn't die when you reached back and found it gone."

"That's when I got up," Ratliff said. "Otherwise I'd a been laying there yet." He entered the store. The front of it was empty but he did not pause, not even long enough for his contracted pupils to have adjusted themselves to the obscu-rity, as he might have been expected to. He went on to the counter, saying pleasantly, "Howdy, Jody. Howdy, Flem. Dont bother; I'll get it myself." Varner, standing beside the desk at which the clerk sat, looked up.

"So you got well, hah," he said.

"I got busy," Ratliff said, going behind the counter and opening the store's single glassed-in case which contained a jumble of shoe strings and combs and tobacco and patent medicines and cheap candy. "Maybe that's the same thing." He began to choose sticks of the striped gaudy candy with care, choosing and rejecting. He did not once look toward the rear of the store, where the clerk at the desk had never looked up at all. "You know if Uncle Ben Quick is at home or not?"

"Where would he be?" Varner said. "Only I thought you sold him a sewing machine two-three years back."

"Sho," Ratliff said, rejecting a stick of candy and substitut-ing another one for it. "That's why I want him to be at home: so his folks can look after him when he faints. I'm going to buy something from him this time."

"What in thunder has he got you had to come all the way out here to buy?"

"A goat," Ratliff said. He was counting the candy sticks into a sack now.

"A what?"

"Sho," Ratliff said. "You wouldn't think it, would you? But there aint another goat in Yoknapatawpha and Grenier County both except them of Uncle Ben's."

"No I wouldn't," Varner said. "But what's curiouser than that is what you want with it."

"What does a fellow want with a goat?" Ratliff said. He moved to the cheese cage and put a coin into the cigar box. "To pull a wagon with. You and Uncle Will and Miss Maggie all well, I hope."

"Ah-h-h!" Varner said. He turned back to the desk. But Ratliff had not paused to see him do it. He returned to the gallery, offering his candy about.

"Doctor's orders," he said. "He'll probably send me another bill now for ten cents for advising me to eat a nickel's worth of candy. I dont mind that though. What I mind is the order he give me to spend so much time setting down." He looked now, pleasant and quizzical, at the men sitting on the bench. It was fastened against the wall, directly beneath one of the windows which flanked the door, a little longer than the window was wide. After a moment a man on one end of the bench rose.

"All right," he said. "Come on and set down. Even if you wasn't sick you will probably spend the next six months pretending like you was."

"I reckon I got to get something outen that seventy-five dollars it cost me," Ratliff said. "Even if it aint no more than imposing on folks for a while. Only you are fixing to leave me setting in a draft. You folks move down and let me set in the middle." They moved and made room for him in the middle of the bench. He sat now directly before the open window. He took a stick of his candy himself and began to suck it, speaking in the weak thin penetrating voice of recent illness: "Yes sir. I'd a been in that bed yet if I hadn't a found that pocket book gone. But it wasn't till I got up that I got sho enough scared. I says to myself, here I been laying on my back for a year now and I bet some enterprising fellow has done come in and flooded not only Frenchman's Bend but all Yoknapatawpha County too with new sewing machines. But the Lord was watching out for me. I be dog if I had hardly got outen bed before Him or somebody had done sent me a sheep just like He done to save Isaac in the Book. He sent me a goat-rancher."

"A what?" one said.

"A goat-rancher. You never heard of a goat-rancher. Because wouldn't nobody in this country think of it. It would take a northerner to do that. This here one thought of it away up yonder in Massachusetts or Boston or Ohio and here he come all the way down to Mississippi with his hand grip bulging with greenback money and bought him up two thousand acres of as fine a hill-gully and rabbit-grass land as ever stood on one edge about fifteen miles west of Jefferson and built him a ten foot practically water-proof fence around it and was just getting ready to start getting rich, when he run out of goats."

"Shucks," another said. "Never nobody in the world ever run out of goats."

"Besides," Bookwright said, suddenly and harshly, "if you want to tell them folks at the blacksmith shop about it too, why dont we all just move over there."

"Sho now," Ratliff said. "You fellows dont know how good a man's voice feels running betwixt his teeth until you have been on your back where folks that didn't want to listen could get up and go away and you couldn't follow them." Nevertheless he did lower his voice a little, thin, clear, anecdotal, unhurried: "This one did. You got to keep in mind he is a northerner. They does things different from us. If a fellow in this country was to set up a goat-ranch, he would do it purely and simply because he had too many goats already. He would just declare his roof or his front porch or his parlor or wherever it was he couldn't keep the goats out of a goat-ranch and let it go at that. But a northerner dont do it that way. When he does something, he does it with a organised syndicate and a book of printed rules and a gold-filled diploma from the Secretary of State at Jackson saying for all men to know by these presents, greeting, that them twenty thousand goats or whatever it is, is goats. He dont start off with goats or a piece of land either. He starts off with a piece of paper and a pencil and measures it all down setting in the library— so many goats to so many acres and so much fence to hold them. Then he writes off to Jackson and gets his diploma for

that much land and fence and goats and he buys the land first
so he can have something to build the fence on, and he builds
the fence around it so nothing cant get outen it, and then he
goes out to buy some things not to get outen the fence. So
everything was going just fine at first. He picked out land that
even the Lord hadn't never thought about starting a goat-
ranch on and bought it without hardly no trouble at all except
finding the folks it belonged to and making them understand
it was actual money he was trying to give them, and that
fence practically taken care of itself because he could set in
one place in the middle of it and pay out the money for it.
And then he found he had done run out of goats. He combed
this country up and down and backwards and forwards to
find the right number of goats to keep that gold diploma
from telling him to his face he was lying. But he couldn't do
it. In spite of all he could do, he still liked fifty goats to take
care of the rest of that fence. So now it aint a goat-ranch; it's
a insolvency. He's either got to send that diploma back, or get
them fifty goats from somewhere. So here he is, done come
all the way down here from Boston, Maine, and paid for two
thousand acres of land and built forty-four thousand feet of
fence around it, and now the whole blame pro-jeck is hung
up on that passel of goats of Uncle Ben Quick's because
they aint another goat betwixt Jackson and the Tennessee line
apparently."

"How do you know?" one said.

"Do you reckon I'd a got up outen bed and come all the
way out here if I hadn't?" Ratliff said.

"Then you better get in that buckboard right now and go
and make yourself sure," Bookwright said. He was sitting
against a gallery post, facing the window at Ratliff's back.
Ratliff looked at him for a moment, pleasant and inscrutable
behind his faint constant humorous mask.

"Sho," he said. "He's had them goats a good while now. I
reckon he'll be still telling me I cant do this and must do that
for the next six months, not to mention sending me bills for
it"—changing the subject so smoothly and completely that,
as they realised later, it was as if he had suddenly produced a
signboard with Hush in red letters on it, glancing easily and
pleasantly upward as Varner and Snopes came out. Snopes did

not speak. He went on across the gallery and descended the steps. Varner locked the door. "Aint you closing early, Jody?" Ratliff said.

"That depends on what you call late," Varner said shortly. He went on after the clerk.

"Maybe it is getting toward supper time," Ratliff said.

"Then if I was you I'd go eat it and then go and buy my goats," Bookwright said.

"Sho now," Ratliff said. "Uncle Ben might have a extra dozen or so by tomorrow. Howsomedever——" He rose and buttoned the overcoat about him.

"Go buy your goats first," Bookwright said. Again Ratliff looked at him, pleasant, impenetrable. He looked at the others. None of them were looking at him.

"I figure I can wait," he said. "Any of you fellows eating at Mrs Littlejohn's?" Then he said, "What's that?" and the others saw what he was looking at—the figure of a grown man but barefoot and in scant faded overalls which would have been about right for a fourteen-year-old boy, passing in the road below the gallery, dragging behind him on a string a wooden block with two snuff tins attached to its upper side, watching over his shoulder with complete absorption the dust it raised. As he passed the gallery he looked up and Ratliff saw the face too—the pale eyes which seemed to have no vision in them at all, the open drooling mouth encircled by a light fuzz of golden virgin beard.

"Another one of them," Bookwright said, in that harsh short voice. Ratliff watched the creature as it went on—the thick thighs about to burst from the overalls, the mowing head turned backward over its shoulder, watching the dragging block.

"And yet they tell us we was all made in His image," Ratliff said.

"From some of the things I see here and there, maybe he was," Bookwright said.

"I dont know as I would believe that, even if I knowed it was true," Ratliff said. "You mean he just showed up here one day?"

"Why not?" Bookwright said. "He aint the first."

"Sho," Ratliff said. "He would have to be somewhere."

The creature, opposite Mrs Littlejohn's now, turned in the gate.

"He sleeps in her barn," another said. "She feeds him. He does some work. She can talk to him some how."

"Maybe she's the one that was then," Ratliff said. He turned; he still held the end of the stick of candy. He put it into his mouth and wiped his fingers on the skirt of his overcoat. "Well, how about supper?"

"Go buy your goats," Bookwright said. "Wait till after that to do your eating."

"I'll go tomorrow," Ratliff said. "Maybe by then Uncle Ben will have another fifty of them even." Or maybe the day after tomorrow, he thought, walking on toward the brazen sound of Mrs Littlejohn's supper-bell in the winy chill of the March evening. So he will have plenty of time. Because I believe I done it right. I had to trade not only on what I think he knows about me, but on what he must figure I know about him, as conditioned and restricted by that year of sickness and abstinence from the science and pastime of skullduggery. But it worked with Bookwright. He done all he could to warn me. He went as far and even further than a man can let his self go in another man's trade.

So tomorrow he not only did not go to see the goat-owner, he drove six miles in the opposite direction and spent the day trying to sell a sewing machine he did not even have with him. He spent the night there and did not reach the village until midmorning of the second day, halting the buckboard before the store, to one of the gallery posts of which Varner's roan horse was tied. So he's even riding the horse now, he thought. Well well well. He did not get out of the buckboard. "One of you fellows mind handing me a nickel's worth of candy?" he said. "I might have to bribe Uncle Ben through one of his grandchillen." One of the men entered the store and fetched out the candy. "I'll be back for dinner," he said. "Then I'll be ready for another needy young doc to cut at again."

His destination was not far: a little under a mile to the river bridge, a little more than a mile beyond it. He drove up to a neat well-kept house with a big barn and pasture beyond it; he saw the goats. A hale burly old man was sitting in his stocking feet on the veranda, who roared, "Howdy, V. K. What in thunder are you fellows up to over at Varner's?"

Ratliff did not get out of the buckboard. "So he beat me," he said.

"Fifty goats," the other roared. "I've heard of a man paying a dime to get shut of two or three, but I never in my life heard of a man buying fifty."

"He's smart," Ratliff said. "If he bought fifty of anything he knowed before hand he was going to need exactly that many."

"Yes, he's smart. But fifty goats. Hell and sulphur. I still got a passel left, bout one hen-house full, say. You want them?"

"No," Ratliff said. "It was just them first fifty."

"I'll give them to you. I'll even pay you a quarter to get the balance of them outen my pasture."

"I thank you," Ratliff said. "Well, I'll just charge this to social overhead."

"Fifty goats," the other said. "Stay and eat dinner."

"I thank you," Ratliff said. "I seem to done already wasted too much time eating now. Or sitting down doing something, anyway." So he returned to the village—that long mile then the short one, the small sturdy team trotting briskly and without synchronization. The roan horse still stood before the store and the men still sat and squatted about the gallery, but Ratliff did not stop. He went on to Mrs Littlejohn's and tied his team to the fence and went and sat on the veranda, where he could see the store. He could smell food cooking in the kitchen behind him and soon the men on the store's gallery began to rise and disperse, noonward, though the saddled roan still stood there. Yes, he thought. He has passed Jody. A man takes your wife and all you got to do to ease your feelings is to shoot him. But your horse.

Mrs Littlejohn spoke behind him: "I didn't know you were back. You going to want some dinner, aint you?"

"Yessum," he said. "I want to step down to the store first. But I wont be long." She went back into the house. He took the two notes from his wallet and separated them, putting one into his inside coat pocket, the other into the breast pocket of his shirt, and walked down the road in the March noon, treading the noon-impacted dust, breathing the un-

breathing suspension of the meridian, and mounted the steps
and crossed the now deserted gallery stained with tobacco
and scarred with knives. The store, the interior, was like a
cave, dim, cool, smelling of cheese and leather; it needed a
moment for his eyes to adjust themselves. Then he saw the
gray cap, the white shirt, the minute bow tie. The face looked
up at him, chewing. "You beat me," Ratliff said. "How
much?" The other turned his head and spat into the sand-
filled box beneath the cold stove.

"Fifty cents," he said.

"I paid twenty-five for my contract," Ratliff said. "All I am
to get is seventy-five. I could tear the contract up and save
hauling them to town."

"All right," Snopes said. "What'll you give?"

"I'll trade you this for them," Ratliff said. He drew the first
note from the pocket where he had segregated it. And he saw
it—an instant, a second of a new and completer stillness and
immobility touch the blank face, the squat soft figure in the
chair behind the desk. For that instant even the jaw had
stopped chewing, though it began again almost at once.
Snopes took the paper and looked at it. Then he laid it on the
desk and turned his head and spat into the sand-box.

"You figure this note is worth fifty goats," he said. It was
not a question, it was a statement.

"Yes," Ratliff said. "Because there is a message goes with it.
Do you want to hear it?"

The other looked at him, chewing. Otherwise he didn't
move, he didn't even seem to breathe. After a moment he
said, "No." He rose, without haste. "All right," he said. He
took his wallet from his hip and extracted a folded paper and
gave it to Ratliff. It was Quick's bill-of-sale for the fifty goats.
"Got a match?" Snopes said. "I dont smoke." Ratliff gave him
the match and watched him set fire to the note and hold it,
blazing, then drop it still blazing into the sand-box and then
crush the carbon to dust with his toe. Then he looked up;
Ratliff had not moved. And now just for another instant
Ratliff believed he saw the jaw stop. "Well?" Snopes said.
"What?" Ratliff drew the second note from his pocket. And
then he knew that the jaw had stopped chewing. It did not
move at all during the full minute while the broad impene-

trable face hung suspended like a balloon above the soiled dog-eared paper, front back then front again. The face looked at Ratliff again with no sign of life in it, not even breathing, as if the body which belonged to it had learned somehow to use over and over again its own suspirations. "You want to collect this too," he said. He handed the note back to Ratliff. "Wait here," he said. He crossed the room to the rear door and went out. What, Ratliff thought. He followed. The squat reluctant figure was going on, in the sunlight now, toward the fence to the livery lot. There was a gate in it. Ratliff watched Snopes pass through the gate and go on across the lot, toward the barn. Then something black blew in him, a suffocation, a sickness, nausea. They should have told me! he cried to himself. Somebody should have told me! Then, remembering: Why, he did! Bookwright did tell me. He said Another one. It was because I have been sick, was slowed up, that I didn't— He was back beside the desk now. He believed he could hear the dragging block long before he knew it was possible, though presently he did hear it as Snopes entered and turned, moving aside, the block thumping against the wooden step and the sill, the hulking figure in the bursting overalls blotting the door, still looking back over its shoulder, entering, the block thumping and scraping across the floor until it caught and lodged behind the counter leg where a three-year-old child would have stooped and lifted it clear though the idiot himself merely stood jerking fruitlessly at the string and beginning a wet whimpering moaning at once pettish and concerned and terrified and amazed until Snopes kicked the block free with his toe. They came on to the desk where Ratliff stood—the mowing and bobbing head, the eyes which at some instant, some second once, had opened upon, been vouchsafed a glimpse of, the Gorgon-face of that primal injustice which man was not intended to look at face to face and had been blasted empty and clean forever of any thought, the slobbering mouth in its mist of soft gold hair. "Say what your name is," Snopes said. The creature looked at Ratliff, bobbing steadily, drooling. "Say it," Snopes said, quite patiently. "Your name."

"Ike H-mope," the idiot said hoarsely.

"Say it again."

"Ike H-mope." Then he began to laugh, though almost at once it stopped being laughing and Ratliff knew that it had never been laughing, cachinnant, sobbing, already beyond the creature's power to stop it, galloping headlong and dragging breath behind it like something still alive at the galloping heels of a cossack holiday, the eyes above the round mouth fixed and sightless.

"Hush," Snopes said. "Hush." At last he took the idiot by the shoulder, shaking him until the sound began to fall, bubbling and gurgling away. Snopes led him toward the door, pushing him on ahead, the other moving obediently, looking backward over his shoulder at the block with its two raked snuff tins dragging at the end of the filthy string, the block about to lodge again behind the same counter leg though this time Snopes kicked it free before it stopped. The hulking shape—the backlooking face with its hanging mouth and pointed faun's ears, the bursting overalls drawn across the incredible female thighs—blotted the door again and was gone. Snopes closed the door and returned to the desk. He spat again into the sand-box. "That was Isaac Snopes," he said. "I'm his guardian. Do you want to see the papers?"

Ratliff didn't answer. He looked down at the note where he had laid it on the desk when he returned from the door, with that same faint, quizzical, quiet expression which his face had worn when he looked at his coffee cup in the restaurant four days ago. He took up the note, though he did not look at Snopes yet. "So if I pay him his ten dollars myself, you will take charge of it as his guardian. And if I collect the ten dollars from you, you will have the note to sell again. And that will make three times it has been collected. Well well well." He took another match from his pocket and extended it and the note to Snopes. "I hear tell you said once you never set fire to a piece of money. This here's your chance to see what it feels like." He watched the second note burn too and drift, still blazing, onto the stained sand in the box, curling into carbon which vanished in its turn beneath the shoe.

He descended the steps, again into the blaze of noon upon the pocked quiet dust of the road; actually it was not ten minutes later. Only thank God men have done learned how to forget quick what they aint brave enough to try to cure,

he told himself, walking on. The empty road shimmered
with mirage, the pollen-roiled chiaroscuro of spring. Yes, he
thought, I reckon I was sicker than I knowed. Because I
missed it, missed it clean. Or maybe when I have et I will feel
better. Yet, alone in the diningroom where Mrs Littlejohn had
set a plate for him, he could not eat. He could feel what he
had thought was appetite ebbing with each mouthful becoming heavy and tasteless as dirt. So at last he pushed the plate
aside and onto the table he counted the five dollars profit he
had made—the thirty-seven-fifty he would get for the goats,
less the twelve-fifty his contract had cost him, plus the twenty
of the first note. With a chewed pencil stub he calculated the
three years' interest on the ten-dollar note, plus the principal
(that ten dollars would have been his commission on the
machine, so it was no actual loss anyway) and added to the five
dollars the other bills and coins—the frayed banknotes, the
worn coins, the ultimate pennies. Mrs Littlejohn was in the
kitchen, where she cooked what meals she sold and washed
the dishes too, as well as caring for the rooms in which they
slept who ate them. He put the money on the table beside the
sink. "That what's-his-name, Ike. Isaac. They tell me you feed
him some. He dont need money. But maybe—"

"Yes," she said. She dried her hands on her apron and took
the money and folded the bills carefully about the silver and
stood holding it. She didn't count it. "I'll keep it for him.
Dont you worry. You going on to town now?"

"Yes," he said. "I got to get busy. No telling when I will
run into another starving and eager young fellow that aint got
no way to get money but to cut meat for it." He turned, then
paused again, not quite looking back at her, with that faint
quizzical expression on his face that was smiling now, sardonic, humorous. "I got a message I would like to get to Will
Varner. But it dont matter especially."

"I'll give it to him," Mrs Littlejohn said. "If it aint too long
I will remember it."

"It dont matter," Ratliff said. "But if you happen to think
of it. Just tell him Ratliff says it aint been proved yet neither.
He'll know what it means."

"I'll try to remember it," she said.

He went out to the buckboard and got into it. He would

not need the overcoat now, and next time he would not even have to bring it along. The road began to flow beneath the flickering hooves of the small hickory-tough horses. I just never went far enough, he thought. I quit too soon. I went as far as one Snopes will set fire to another Snopes's barn and both Snopeses know it, and that was all right. But I stopped there. I never went on to where that first Snopes will turn around and stomp the fire out so he can sue that second Snopes for the reward and both Snopeses know that too.

3.

Those who watched the clerk now saw, not the petty dispossession of a blacksmith, but the usurpation of an heirship. At the next harvest the clerk not only presided at the gin scales but when the yearly settling of accounts between Varner and his tenants and debtors occurred, Will Varner himself was not even present. It was Snopes who did what Varner had never even permitted his son to do—sat alone at the desk with the cash from the sold crops and the accountbooks before him and cast up the accounts and charged them off and apportioned to each tenant his share of the remaining money, one or two of them challenging his figures as they had when he first entered the store, on principle perhaps, the clerk not even listening, just waiting in his soiled white shirt and the minute tie, with his steady thrusting tobacco and his opaque still eyes which they never knew whether or not were looking at them, until they would finish, cease; then, without speaking a word, taking pencil and paper and proving to them that they were wrong. Now it was not Jody Varner who would come leisurely to the store and give the clerk directions and instructions and leave him to carry them out; it was the ex-clerk who would enter the store, mounting the steps and jerking his head at the men on the gallery exactly as Will Varner himself would do, and enter the store, from which presently the sound of his voice would come, speaking with matter-of-fact succinctness to the bull-goaded bafflement of the man who once had been his employer and who still seemed not to know just exactly what had happened to him. Then Snopes would depart, to be seen no more that day, for Will Varner's old fat white horse had a companion now. It was the roan which Jody had used to ride, the white and the roan now tied side by side to the same fence while Varner and Snopes examined fields of cotton and corn or herds of cattle or land boundaries, Varner cheerful as a cricket and shrewd and bowel-less as a tax-collector, idle and busy and Rabelaisian; the other chewing his steady tobacco, his hands in the pockets of the disreputable bagging gray trousers, spitting now and then his contemplative bullet-like globules of chocolate saliva. One morning he came to the village carrying a brand new straw suitcase. That evening he carried it up to Varner's house. A month after that Varner bought a new runabout buggy with bright red wheels and a fringed parasol top, which, the fat white horse and the big roan in new brass-studded harness and the wheels glinting in vermilion and spokeless blurs, swept all day long along back country roads and lanes while Varner and Snopes sat side by side in outrageous paradox above a spurting cloud of light dust, in a speeding aura of constant and invincible excursion. And one afternoon in that same summer Ratliff again drove up to the store, on the gallery of which was a face which he did not recognise for a moment because he had only seen it once before and that two years ago, though only for a moment for almost at once he said, "Howdy. Machine still running good?" and sat looking with an expression quite pleasant and absolutely impenetrable at the fierce intractable face with its single eyebrow, thinking *Fox? cat? oh yes, mink.*

"Howdy," the other said. "Why not? Aint you the one that claims not to sell no other kind?"

"Sholy," Ratliff said, still quite pleasant, impenetrable. He got out of the buckboard and tied it to a gallery post and mounted the steps and stood among the four men who sat and squatted about the gallery. "Only it aint quite that, I would put it. I would say, folks named Snopes dont buy no other kind." Then he heard the horse and turned his head and saw it, coming up fast, the fine hound running easily and strongly beside it as Houston pulled up, already dismounting, and dropped the loose reins over its head as a Western rider does and mounted the steps and stopped before the post against which Mink Snopes squatted.

"I reckon you know where that yearling is," Houston said.

"I can guess," Snopes said.

"All right," Houston said. He was not shaking, trembling, anymore than a stick of dynamite does. He didn't even raise his voice. "I warned you. You know the law in this country. A man must keep his stock up after ground's planted, or take the consequences."

"I would have expected you to have fences that would keep a yearling up," Snopes said. Then they cursed each other, hard and brief and without emphasis, like blows or pistol-shots, both speaking at the same time and neither moving, the one still standing in the middle of the steps, the other still squatting against the gallery post. "Try a shotgun," Snopes said. "That might keep it up." Then Houston went on into the store and those on the gallery stood or squatted quietly, the man with his single eyebrow no less quiet than any, until Houston came out again and passed without looking at any of them and mounted and galloped off, the hound following again, strong, high-headed, indefatiguable, and after another moment or so Snopes rose too and went up the road on foot. Then one leaned and spat carefully over the gallery-edge, into the dust, and Ratliff said,

"I dont quite understand about that fence. I gathered it was Snopes's yearling in Houston's field."

"It was," the man who had spat said. "He lives on a piece of what used to be Houston's land. It belongs to Will Varner now. That is, Varner foreclosed on it about a year ago."

"That is, it was Will Varner Houston owed the money to," a second said. "It was the fences on that he was talking about."

"I see," Ratliff said. "Just conversational remarks. Unnecessary."

"It wasn't losing the land that seems to rile Houston," a third said. "Not that he dont rile easy."

"I see," Ratliff said again. "It's what seems to happened to it since. Or who it seems Uncle Will has rented it to. So Flem's got some more cousins still. Only this here seems to be a different kind of Snopes like a cotton-mouth is a different kind of snake." So that wasn't the last time this one is going to make his cousin trouble, he thought. But he did not say it, he just said, absolutely pleasant, easy, inscrutable: "I wonder where Uncle Will and his partner would be about now. I aint learned the route good yet like you folks."

"I passed them two horses and the buggy tied to the Old Frenchman fence this morning," the fourth man said. He too leaned and spat carefully over the gallery-edge. Then he added, as if in trivial afterthought: "It was Flem Snopes that was setting in the flour barrel."

BOOK TWO
EULA
Chapter One

WHEN FLEM SNOPES came to clerk in her father's store, Eula Varner was not quite thirteen. She was the last of the sixteen children, the baby, though she had overtaken and passed her mother in height in her tenth year. Now, though not yet thirteen years old, she was already bigger than most grown women and even her breasts were no longer the little, hard, fiercely-pointed cones of puberty or even maidenhood. On the contrary, her entire appearance suggested some symbology out of the old Dionysic times—honey in sunlight and bursting grapes, the writhen bleeding of the crushed fecundated vine beneath the hard rapacious trampling goat-hoof. She seemed to be not a living integer of her contemporary scene, but rather to exist in a teeming vacuum in which her days followed one another as though behind sound-proof glass, where she seemed to listen in sullen bemusement, with a weary wisdom heired of all mammalian maturity, to the enlarging of her own organs.

Like her father, she was incorrigibly lazy, though what was in him a constant bustling cheerful idleness was in her an actual force impregnable and even ruthless. She simply did not move at all of her own volition, save to and from the table and to and from bed. She was late in learning to walk. She had the first and only perambulator the countryside had ever seen, a clumsy expensive thing almost as large as a dog-cart. She remained in it long after she had grown too large to straighten her legs out. When she reached the stage where it almost took the strength of a grown man to lift her out of it, she was graduated from it by force. Then she began to sit in chairs. It was not that she insisted upon being carried when she went anywhere. It was rather as though, even in infancy, she already knew there was nowhere she wanted to go, nothing new or novel at the end of any progression, one place like another anywhere and everywhere. Until she was five and six,

817

when she did have to go anywhere because her mother declined to leave her at home while she herself was absent, she would be carried by their negro manservant. The three of them would be seen passing along the road—Mrs Varner in her Sunday dress and shawl, followed by the negro man staggering slightly beneath his long, dangling, already indisputably female burden like a bizarre and chaperoned Sabine rape.

She had the usual dolls. She would place them in chairs about the one in which she sat, and they would remain so, none with either more or less of the semblance of life than any other. Finally her father had his blacksmith make her a miniature of the perambulator in which she had spent her first three years. It was crude and heavy also, but it was the only doll perambulator anyone in that country had ever seen or even heard of. She would place all the dolls in it and sit in a chair beside it. At first they decided it was mental backwardness, that she merely had not yet reached the maternal stage of female adulthood in miniature, though they soon realised that her indifference to the toy was that she would have to move herself to keep it in motion.

She grew from infancy to the age of eight in the chairs, moving from one to another about the house as the exigencies of sweeping and cleaning house and eating meals forced her to break cover. At her mother's insistence, Varner continued to have the blacksmith make miniatures of housekeeping implements—little brooms and mops, a small actual stove—hoping to make a sport, a game, of utility, all of which, singly and collectively, was apparently no more to her than the tot of cold tea to the old drunkard. She had no playmates, no inseparable girl companion. She did not want them. She never formed one of those violent, sometimes short-lived intimacies in which two female children form embattled secret cabal against their masculine co-evals and the mature world too. She did nothing. She might as well still have been a foetus. It was as if only half of her had been born, that mentality and body had somehow become either completely separated or hopelessly involved; that either only one of them had ever emerged, or that one had emerged, itself not accompanied by, but rather pregnant with, the other. "Maybe she's fixing to be a tomboy," her father said.

"When?" Jody said—a spark, a flash, even though born of enraged exasperation. "At the rate she's going at it, there aint a acorn that will fall in the next fifty years that wont grow up and rot down and be burnt for firewood before she'll ever climb it."

When she was eight, her brother decided she should start to school. Her parents had intended that she should start someday, perhaps mainly because Will Varner was, with the nominal designation of Trustee, the principal mainstay and arbiter of the school's existence. It was, as the other parents of the countryside considered it, actually another Varner enterprise, and sooner or later Varner would have insisted that his daughter attend it, for a while at least, just as he would have insisted upon collecting the final odd cents of an interest calculation. Mrs Varner did not particularly care whether the daughter went to school or not. She was one of the best housewives in the county and was indefatiguable at it. She derived an actual physical pleasure which had nothing at all to do with mere satisfaction in husbandry and forehandedness, from the laying-away of ironed sheets and the sight of packed shelves and potato cellars and festooned smoke-house rafters. She did not read herself, though at the time of her marriage she had been able to read a little. She did not practise it much then and during the last forty years she had lost even that habit, preferring now to be face to face with the living breath of event, fiction or news either, and being able to comment and moralise upon it. So she saw no need for literacy in women. Her conviction was that the proper combining of food ingredients lay not on any printed page but in the taste of the stirring spoon, and that the housewife who had to wait until she had been to school to know how much money she had left after subtracting from it what she had spent, would never be a housewife.

It was the brother, Jody, who emerged almost violently in her eighth summer as erudition's champion, and three months later came bitterly to regret it. He did not regret that it had been himself who had insisted that she go to school. His regret was that he was still convinced, and knew that he would remain convinced, of the necessity of that for which he now paid so dear a price. Because she refused to walk to school. She did not object to attending it, to being in school, she just declined to walk to it. It was not far. It was not a half mile from the Varner home. Yet during the five years she attended it, which, if it had been computed in hours based upon what she accomplished while there, would have been measured not in years or even months but in days, she rode to and from it. While other children living three and four and five times the distance walked back and forth in all weathers, she rode. She just calmly and flatly refused to walk. She did not resort to tears and she did not even fight back emotionally, let alone physically. She just sat down, where, static, apparently not even thinking, she emanated an outrageous and immune perversity like a blooded and contrary filly too young yet to be particularly valuable, though which in another year or so would be, and for which reason its raging and harried owner does not dare whip it. Her father immediately and characteristically washed his hands of the business. "Let her stay at home then," he said. "She aint going to lift her hand here either, but at least maybe she will learn something about housekeeping from having to move from one chair to another to keep out of the way of it. All we want anyway is to keep her out of trouble until she gets old enough to sleep with a man without getting me and him both arrested. Then you can marry her off. Maybe you can even find a husband that will keep Jody out of the poorhouse too. Then we will give them the house and store and the whole shebang and me and you will go to that world's fair they are talking about having in Saint Louis, and if we like it by God we will buy a tent and settle down there."

But the brother insisted that she go to school. She still declined to walk there, sitting supine and female and soft and immovable and not even thinking and apparently not even listening either, while the battle between her mother and brother roared over her tranquil head. So at last the negro man who had used to carry her when her mother went visiting would bring up the family surrey and drive her the half mile to school and would be waiting there with the surrey at noon and at three oclock when school dismissed. This lasted about two weeks. Mrs Varner stopped it because it was too wasteful, like firing up a twenty-gallon pot to make a bowl of soup would be wasteful. She delivered an ultimatum; if Jody wanted his sister to go to school, he would have to see that she got there himself. She suggested that, since he rode his horse to and from the store every day anyhow, he might carry Eula to and from school behind him, the daughter sitting there again, neither thinking nor listening while this roared and concussed to the old stalemate, sitting on the front porch in the mornings with the cheap oilcloth booksatchel they had bought her until her brother rode the horse up to the gallery-edge and snarled at her to come and mount behind him. He would carry her to the school and go and fetch her at noon and carry her back afterward and be waiting when school was out for the day. This lasted for almost a month. Then Jody decided that she should walk the two hundred yards from the schoolhouse to the store and meet him there. To his surprise, she agreed without protest. This lasted for exactly two days. On the second afternoon the brother fetched her home at a fast single-foot, bursting into the house and standing over his mother in the hall and trembling with anger and outrage, shouting. "No wonder she agreed so easy and quick to walk to the store and meet me!" he cried. "If you could arrange to have a man standing every hundred feet along the road, she would walk all the way home! She's just like a dog! Soon as she passes anything in long pants she begins to give off something. You can smell it! You can smell it ten feet away!"

"Fiddlesticks," Mrs Varner said. "Besides, dont worry me with it. It was you insisted she had to go to school. It wasn't me. I raised eight other daughters, I thought they turned out pretty well. But I am willing to agree that maybe a twenty-seven-year-old bachelor knows more about them than I do. Anytime you want to let her quit school, I reckon your pa and me wont object. Did you bring me that cinnamon?"

"No," Jody said. "I forgot it."

"Try to remember it tonight. I'm already needing it."

So she no longer began the homeward journey at the store. Her brother would be waiting for her at the schoolhouse. It had been almost five years now since this sight had become an integral part of the village's life four times a day and five days a week—the roan horse bearing the seething and angry man and the girl of whom, even at nine and ten and eleven, there was too much—too much of leg, too much of breast, too much of buttock; too much of mammalian female meat which, in conjunction with the tawdry oilcloth receptacle that was obviously a grammar-grade booksatchel, was a travesty and paradox on the whole idea of education. Even while sitting behind her brother on the horse, the inhabitant of that meat seemed to lead two separate and distinct lives as infants in the act of nursing do. There was one Eula Varner who supplied blood and nourishment to the buttocks and legs and breasts; there was the other Eula Varner who merely inhabited them, who went where they went because it was less trouble to do so, who was comfortable there but in their doings she intended to have no part, as you are in a house which you did not design but where the furniture is all set- tled and the rent paid up. On the first morning Varner had put the horse into a fast trot, to get it over with quick, but almost at once he began to feel the entire body behind him, which even motionless in a chair seemed to postulate an in- vincible abhorrence of straight lines, jigging its component boneless curves against his back. He had a vision of himself transporting not only across the village's horizon but across the embracing proscenium of the entire inhabited world like the sun itself, a kaleidoscopic convolution of mammalian ellipses. So he would walk the horse. He would have to, his sister clutching the cross of his suspenders or the back of his coat with one hand and holding the booksatchel with the other, passing the store where the usual quota of men would be squatting and sitting, past Mrs Littlejohn's veranda where there would usually be an itinerant drummer or horse- trader—and Varner now believing, convinced, that he knew why they were there too, the real reason why they had driven twenty miles from Jefferson—and so up to the school where the other children in overalls and coarse calico and cast-off adult shoes as often as not when they wore shoes at all, were already gathered after walking three and four and five times the distance. She would slide off the horse and her brother would sit for a moment longer, seething, watching the back which already used its hips to walk with as women used them, and speculate with raging impotence whether to call the school-teacher (he was a man) outside at once and have it out with him, warn or threaten or even use his fists, or whether to wait until that happened which he, Varner, was convinced must occur. They would repeat that at one oclock and in the reverse direction at twelve and three, Varner riding on a hundred yards up the road to where, hidden by a copse, a fallen tree lay. The negro manservant had felled it one night while he sat the horse and held the lantern; he would ride up beside it, snarling fiercely to her the third time she mounted from it: "God damn it, cant you try to get on without making it look like the horse is twenty feet tall?"

He even decided one day that she should not ride astride anymore. This lasted one day, until he happened to look aside and so behind him and saw the incredible length of out-rageously curved dangling leg and the bare section of thigh between dress and stocking-top looking as gigantically and profoundly naked as the dome of an observatory. And his rage was only intensified by the knowledge that she had not deliberately exposed it. He knew that she simply did not care, doubtless did not even know it was exposed, and if she had known, would not have gone to the trouble to cover it. He knew that she was sitting even on the moving horse exactly as she would in a chair at home, and, as he knew, inside the schoolhouse itself, so that he wondered at times in his raging helplessness how buttocks as constantly subject to the impact of that much steadily increasing weight could in the mere act of walking seem actually to shout aloud that rich mind- and will-sapping fluid softness; sitting, even on the moving horse, secret and not even sullen, bemused with that whatever it was which had nothing to do with flesh, meat, at all; emanating that outrageous quality of being, existing, actually on the out-side of the garments she wore and not only being unable to help it but not even caring.

She attended the school from her eighth year until shortly after Christmas in her fourteenth. She would undoubtedly have completed that year and very probably the next one or two, learning nothing, except that in January of that year the school closed. It closed because the teacher vanished. He disappeared overnight, with no word to anyone. He neither collected his term's salary nor removed his meagre and monklike personal effects from the fireless rented lean-to room in which he had lived for six years.

His name was Labove. He came from the adjoining county, where Will Varner himself had discovered him by sheer chance. The incumbent, the Professor at that time, was an old man bibulous by nature, who had been driven still further into his cups by the insubordination of his pupils. The girls had respect neither for his ideas and information nor for his ability to convey them; the boys had no respect for his capacity, not to teach them but to make them obey and behave or even be civil to him—a condition which had long since passed the stage of mere mutiny and had become a kind of bucolic Roman holiday, like the baiting of a mangy and toothless bear.

Thus everyone, including the Professor, knew that he would not be there next term. But nobody minded especially whether the school functioned next year or not. They owned it. They had built the schoolhouse themselves and paid the teacher and sent their children to it only when there was no work for them to do at home, so it only ran between harvest-time and planting—from mid-October through March. Nothing had been done yet about replacing the Professor until one day in the summer Varner happened to make a business trip into the next county, was benighted, and was invited to pass the night in a bleak puncheon-floored cabin on a barren little hill farm. When he entered the house he saw, sitting beside the cold hearth and sucking a foul little clay pipe, an incredibly old woman wearing a pair of stout-looking man's shoes slightly unorthodox or even a little bizarre in appearance. But Varner paid no attention to them until he heard a clattering scraping noise behind him and turned and saw a girl of about ten, in a tattered though quite clean gingham dress and a pair of shoes exactly like those of the old lady—if anything, even a little larger. Before he departed the next morning Varner had seen three more pairs of the same shoes, by which time he had discovered that they resembled no other shoes he had ever seen or even heard of. His host told him what they were.

"What?" Varner said. "Football shoes?"

"It's a game," Labove said. "They play it at the University."

He explained. It was the eldest son. He was not at home now, off working at a sawmill to earn money to return to the University, where he had been for one summer normal term and then half of the following academic term. It was then that the University played the game out of which the shoes had come. The son had wanted to learn to be a school-teacher, or so he said when he left for the University the first time. That is, he wanted to go to the University. The father saw no point in it. The farm was clear and would belong to the son someday and it had always made them a living. But the son insisted. He could work at mills and such and save enough to attend the summer terms and learn to be a teacher anyway, since this was all they taught in the summer sessions. He would even be back home in the late summer in time to help finish the crop. So he earned the money—"Doing harder work than farming too," the elder Labove said. "But he was almost twenty-one. I couldn't have stood in his way even if I would have."—and enrolled for the summer session, which would last eight weeks and so would have had him back home in August but did not do so. When September arrived, he still had not returned. They did not know for certain where he was, though they were not worried so much as annoyed, concerned, even a little outraged that he should have deserted them with the remaining work on the crop— the picking and ginning of the cotton, the gathering and crib-bing of the corn—to be done. In mid-September the letter came. He was going to stay on longer at the University, through the fall. He had a job there; they must gather the crops without him. He did not say what kind of a job it was and the father took it for granted as being another sawmill, since he would never have associated any sort of revenue-producing occupation with going to school, and they did not hear from him again until in October, when the first package arrived. It contained two pair of the curious cleated shoes. A third pair came early in November. The last two came just after Thanksgiving, which made five pair, although there were seven in the family. So they all used them indis-criminately, anyone who found a pair available, like umbrel-las, four pair of them that is, Labove explained. The old lady (she was the elder Labove's grandmother) had fastened upon the first pair to emerge from the box and would let no one else wear them at all. She seemed to like the sound the cleats made on the floor when she sat in a chair and rocked. But that still left four pair. So now the children could go shod to school, removing the shoes when they reached home for whoever else needed to go out doors. In January the son came home. He told them about the game. He had been playing it all that fall. They let him stay at the University for the entire fall term for playing it. The shoes were provided them free of charge to play it in.

"How did he happen to get six pairs?" Varner asked.

Labove did not know that. "Maybe they had a heap of them on hand that year," he said. They had also given the son a sweater at the University, a fine heavy warm dark blue sweater with a big red M on the front of it. The great-grandmother had taken that too, though it was much too big for her. She would wear it on Sundays, winter and summer, sitting beside him on the seat of the churchward wagon on the bright days, the crimson accolade of the color of courage and fortitude gallant in the sun, or on the bad days, sprawled and quiet but still crimson, still brave, across her shrunken chest and stomach as she sat in her chair and rocked and sucked the dead little pipe.

"So that's where he is now," Varner said. "Playing the football."

No, Labove told him. He was at the sawmill now. He had calculated that by missing the current summer term and working instead, he could save enough money to stay on at the University even after they stopped letting him stay to play the football, thus completing a full year in the regular school instead of just the summer school in which they only taught people how to be school-teachers.

"I thought that's what he wanted to be," Varner said.

"No," Labove said. "That was all he could learn in the summer school. I reckon you'll laugh when you hear this. He says he wants to be Governor."

"Sho now," Varner said.

"You'll laugh, I reckon."

"No," Varner said. "I aint laughing. Governor. Well well well. Next time you see him, if he would consider putting off the governor business for a year or two and teach school, tell him to come over to the Bend and see me."

That was in July. Perhaps Varner did not actually expect Labove to come to see him. But he made no further effort to fill the vacancy, which he certainly could not have forgotten about. Even apart from his obligation as Trustee, he would have a child of his own ready to start to school within another year or so. One afternoon in early September he was lying with his shoes off in the barrel stave hammock slung between two trees in his yard, when he saw approaching on foot across the yard the man whom he had never seen before but knew at once—a man who was not thin so much as actually gaunt, with straight black hair coarse as a horse's tail and high Indian cheekbones and quiet pale hard eyes and the long nose of thought but with the slightly curved nostrils of pride and the thin lips of secret and ruthless ambition. It was a forensic face, the face of invincible conviction in the power of words as a principle worth dying for if necessary. A thousand years ago it would have been a monk's, a militant fanatic who would have turned his uncompromising back upon the world with actual joy and gone to a desert and passed the rest of his days and nights calmly and without an instant's self-doubt battling, not to save humanity about which he would have cared nothing, for whose sufferings he would have had nothing but contempt, but with his own fierce and unappeasable natural appetites.

"I came to tell you I cant teach for you this year," he said. "I haven't got time. I've got things fixed now so I can stay at the University the whole year."

Varner did not rise. "That's just one year. What about next year?"

"I have arranged about the sawmill too. I am going back to it next summer. Or something else."

"Sho," Varner said. "I been thinking about it some myself. Because the school here dont need to open until first of November. You can stay at Oxford until then and play your game. Then you can come and open the school and get it started. You can bring your books here from the University and keep up with the class and on the day you have to play the game again you can go back to Oxford and play it and let them find out whether you have kept up in the books or not or whether you have learned anything or whatever they would need to know. Then you could come back to the school; even a day or two wont matter. I will furnish you a horse that can make the trip in eight hours. It aint but forty miles to Oxford from here. Then when the time comes for the examination in January your pa was telling me about, you can shut up the school here and go back and stay until you are through with them. Then you can close the school here in March and go back for the rest of the year, until the last of next October if you wanted. I dont reckon a fellow that really wanted to would have much trouble keeping up with his class just forty miles away. Well?"

For some time now Varner knew that the other no longer saw him though he had not moved and his eyes were still open. Labove stood quite still, in a perfectly clean white shirt which had been washed so often that it now had about the texture of mosquito netting, in a coat and trousers absolutely clean too and which were not mates and the coat a little too small for him and which Varner knew were the only ones he owned and that he owned them only because he believed, or had been given to understand, that one could not wear overalls to a University classroom. He stood there enveloped in no waking incredulous joy and hope but in that consuming fury, the gaunt body not shaped by the impact of its environment but as though shrunken and leaned by what was within it, like a furnace. "All right," he said. "I'll be here the first of November." He was already turning away.

"Dont you want to know what your pay will be?"

"All right," Labove said, pausing. Varner told him. He (Varner) had not moved in the hammock, his home-knit socks crossed at the ankles.

"That game," he said. "Do you like to play it?"

"No," Labove said.

"I hear it aint much different from actual fighting."

"Yes," Labove said, again shortly, paused, courteous and waiting, looking at the lean shrewd shoeless old man prone and profoundly idle in the hammock, who seemed to have laid upon him already the curse of his own invincible conviction of the absolute unimportance of this or any other given

moment or succession of them, holding him there and forcing
him to spend time thinking about what he had never told anyone and did not intend to talk about since it did not matter
now. It began just before the end of the summer term a year
ago. He had intended to return home at the end of the term,
as he had told his father he would, to help finish the crop. But
just before the term ended he found a job. It was practically
dropped into his lap. There would be two or three weeks yet
before the cotton would be ready to pick and gin and he was
already settled where he could stay on until the middle of
September at little additional expense. So most of what the
work would bring him would be clear profit. He took the job.
It was grading and building a football field. He didn't know
then what a football field was and he did not care. To him it
was merely an opportunity to earn so much additional money
each day and he did not even stop his shovel when he would
speculate now and then with cold sardonicism on the sort of
game the preparation of ground for which demanded a good
deal more care and expense both than the preparing of that
same ground to raise a paying crop on; indeed, to have warranted that much time and money for a crop, a man would
have had to raise gold at least. So it was still sardonicism and
not curiosity when in September and before the field was finished, it began to be used, and he discovered that the young
men engaged upon it were not even playing the game but just
practising. He would watch them at it. He was probably
watching them more closely or at least more often than he
was aware and with something in his face, his eyes, which he
did not know was there too, because one afternoon one of
them (he had already discovered that the game had a paid
teacher) said to him, "You think you can do it better, do you?
All right. Come here." That night he sat on the front steps of
the coach's house in the dry dusty September darkness, still
saying No quietly and patiently.

"I aint going to borrow money just to play a game on," he
said.

"You wont have to, I tell you!" the coach said. "Your tu-
ition will be paid. You can sleep in my attic and you can feed
my horse and cow and milk and build the fires and I will give
you your meals. Dont you understand?" It could not have

been his face because that was in darkness, and he did not believe it had been in his voice. Yet the coach said, "I see. You dont believe it."

"No," he said. "I dont believe anybody will give me all that just for playing a game."

"Will you try it and see? Will you stay here and do it until somebody comes to you and asks you for money?"

"Will I be free to go when they do?"

"Yes," the coach said. "You have my word." So that night he wrote his father he would not be home to help finish the harvest and if they would need an extra hand in his place he would send money. And they gave him a uniform and on that afternoon, as on the one before when he had still worn the overalls in which he had been working, one of the other play-ers failed to rise at once and they explained that to him—how there were rules for violence, he trying patiently to make this distinction, understand it: "But how can I carry the ball to that line if I let them catch me and pull me down?"

He didn't tell this. He just stood beside the hammock, in the clean unmatching garments, composed and grave, answer-ing Yes or No briefly and quietly to Varner's questions while it recapitulated, ran fast and smooth and without significance now in his memory, finished and done and behind him, meaning nothing, the fall itself going fast, dreamlike and tele-scoped. He would rise in the icy attic at four oclock and build fires in the houses of five different faculty members and return to feed and milk. Then the lectures, the learning and wisdom distilled of all man had ever thought, plumbed, the ivied walls and monastic rooms impregnated with it, abundant, no limit save that of the listener's capacity and thirst; the afternoons of practice (soon he was excused from this on alternate days, which afternoons he spent raking leaves in the five yards), the preparing of coal and wood against tomorrow's fires. Then the cow again and then in the overcoat which the coach had given him he sat with his books beneath the lamp in his fire-less garret until he went to sleep over the printed page. He did this for five days, up to the Saturday's climax when he carried a trivial contemptible obloid across fleeing and mean-ingless white lines. Yet during these seconds, despite his con-tempt, his ingrained conviction, his hard and spartan heritage, he lived, fiercely free—the spurning earth, the shocks, the hard breathing and the grasping hands, the speed, the rocking roar of massed stands, his face even then still wearing the expression of sardonic not-quite-belief. And the shoes. Varner was watching him, his hands beneath his head. "Them shoes," Varner said. It was because I never did really believe it was going to last until the next Saturday, Labove could have answered. But he did not, he just stood, his hands quiet at his sides, looking at Varner. "I reckon they always had a plenty of them on hand," Varner said.

"They bought them in lots. They kept all sizes on hand."

"Sho now," Varner said. "I reckon all a fellow had to do was just to say his old pair didn't fit good or had got lost."

Labove did not look away. He stood quietly facing the man in the hammock. "I knew what the shoes cost. I tried to get the coach to say what a pair was worth. To the University. What a touchdown was worth. Winning was worth."

"I see. You never taken a pair except when you beat. And you sent five pairs home. How many times did you play?"

"Seven," Labove said. "One of them nobody won."

"I see," Varner said. "Well, I reckon you want to get on back home before dark. I'll have that horse ready by November."

Labove opened the school in the last week of October. Within that week he had subdued with his fists the state of mutiny which his predecessor had bequeathed him. On Friday night he rode the horse Varner had promised him the forty-odd miles to Oxford, attended morning lectures and played a football game in the afternoon, slept until noon Sunday and was on his pallet bed in the unheated lean-to room in Frenchman's Bend by midnight. It was in the house of a widow who lived near the school. He owned a razor, the unmatching coat and trousers he stood in, two shirts, the coach's overcoat, a Coke, a Blackstone, a volume of Mississippi Reports, an original Horace and a Thucydides which the classics professor, in whose home he had built the morning fires, had given him at Christmas, and the brightest lamp the village had ever seen. It was nickel, with valves and pistons and gauges; as it sat on his plank table it obviously cost more than everything else he owned lumped together and

people would come in from miles away at night to see the
fierce still glare it made.

By the end of that first week they all knew him—the
hungry mouth, the insufferable humorless eyes, the intense
ugly blue-shaved face like a composite photograph of Voltaire
and an Elizabethan pirate. They called him Professor too
even though he looked what he was—twenty-one—and even
though the school was a single room in which pupils ranging
in age from six to the men of nineteen whom he had had to
meet with his fists to establish his professorship, and classes
ranging from bald a b c's to the rudiments of common frac-
tions were jumbled together. He taught them all and everything. He carried the key to the building in his pocket as a
merchant carries the key to his store. He unlocked it each
morning and swept it, he divided the boys by age and size
into water-carrying and wood-cutting details and by precept,
bullying, ridicule and force saw that they did it, helping them
at times not as an example but with a kind of contemptuous
detached physical pleasure in burning up his excess energy.
He would ruthlessly keep the older boys after school, standing before the door and barring it and beating them to the
open windows when they broke for these. He forced them to
climb with him to the roof and replace shingles and such
which heretofore Varner, as Trustee, had seen to after the
teacher had nagged and complained to him enough. At night
passers would see the fierce dead glare of the patent lamp
beyond the lean-to window where he would be sitting over
the books which he did not love so much as he believed that
he must read, compass and absorb and wring dry with something of that same contemptuous intensity with which he
chopped firewood, measuring the turned pages against the
fleeing seconds of irrevocable time like the implacable inching
of a leaf worm.

Each Friday afternoon he would mount the wiry strong
hammer-headed horse in Varner's lot and ride to where the
next day's game would be played or to the railroad which
would get him there, sometimes arriving only in time to
change into his uniform before the whistle blew. But he was
always back at the school on Monday morning, even though
on some occasions it meant he had spent only one night—

Saturday—in bed between Thursday and Monday. After the Thanksgiving game between the two State colleges, his picture was in a Memphis paper. He was in the uniform and the picture (to the people in the village, and for that reason) would not have looked like him. But the name was his and that would have been recognised, except that he did not bring the paper back with him. They did not know what he did on those week-ends, except that he was taking work at the University. They did not care. They had accepted him, and although his designation of professor was a distinction, it was still a woman's distinction, functioning actually in a woman's world like the title of reverend. Although they would not have actually forbidden him the bottle, they would not have drunk with him, and though they were not quite as circumspect in what they said before him as they would have been with the true minister, if he had responded in kind he might have found himself out of a position when the next term began and he knew it. This distinction he accepted in the spirit offered and even met it more than half way, with that same grim sufficiency, not pride quite and not quite actual belligerence, grave and composed.

He was gone for a week at the time of the mid-term examinations at the University. He returned and hounded Varner into clearing a basket ball court. He did a good deal of the work himself, with the older boys, and taught them the game. At the end of the next year the team had beaten every team they could find to play against and in the third year, himself one of the players, he carried the team to Saint Louis, where, in overalls and barefoot, they won a Mississippi Valley tournament against all comers.

When he brought them back to the village, he was through. In three years he had graduated, a master of arts and a bachelor of laws. He would leave the village now for the last time —the books, the fine lamp, the razor, the cheap reproduction of an Alma Tadema picture which the classics professor had given him on the second Christmas—to return to the University to his alternating academic and law classes, one following another from breakfast time to late afternoon. He had to read in glasses now, leaving one class to walk blinking painfully against the light to the next, in the single unmatching costume he owned, through throngs of laughing youths and girls in clothes better than he had ever seen until he came here, who did not stare through him so much as they did not see him at all anymore than they did the poles which supported the electric lights which until he arrived two years ago he had never seen before either. He would move among them and look with the same expression he would wear above the cleat-spurned fleeing lines of the football field, at the girls who had apparently come there to find husbands, the young men who had come there for what reason he knew not.

Then one day he stood in a rented cap and gown among others and received the tightly-rolled parchment scroll no larger than a rolled calendar yet which, like the calendar, contained those three years—the spurned cleat-blurred white lines, the nights on the tireless horse, the other nights while he had sat in the overcoat and with only the lamp for heat, above spread turning pages of dead verbiage. Two days after that he stood with his class before the Bench in an actual courtroom in Oxford and was admitted to the Bar, and it was finished. He made one that night at a noisy table in the hotel diningroom, at which the Judge presided, flanked by the law professors and the other legal sponsors. This was the anteroom to that world he had been working to reach for three years now—four, counting that first one when he could not yet see his goal. He had only to sit with that fixed expression and wait until the final periphrase died, was blotted by the final concussion of palms, and rise and walk out of the room and on, his face steady in the direction he had chosen to set it, as it had been for three years now anyway, not faltering, not looking back. And he could not do it. Even with that already forty miles of start toward freedom and (he knew it, said it) dignity and self-respect, he could not do it. He must return, drawn back into the radius and impact of an eleven-year-old girl who, even while sitting with veiled eyes against the sun like a cat on the schoolhouse steps at recess and eating a cold potato, postulated that ungirdled quality of the very goddesses in his Homer and Thucydides: of being at once corrupt and immaculate, at once virgins and the mothers of warriors and of grown men.

On that first morning when her brother had brought her to

the school, Labove had said to himself: No. No. Not here. Dont leave her here. He had taught the school for only one year, a single term of five months broken by the weekly night ride to Oxford and return and the two-weeks' gap of the mid-term examinations in January, yet he had not only extricated it from the chaos in which his predecessor had left it, he had even coerced the curriculum itself into something resembling order. He had no assistant, there was not even a partition in the single room, yet he had segregated the pupils according to capacity into a routine which they not only observed but had finally come to believe in. He was not proud of it, he was not even satisfied. But he was satisfied that it was motion, progress, if not toward increasing knowledge to any great extent, at least toward teaching order and discipline. Then one morning he turned from the crude blackboard and saw a face eight years old and a body of fourteen with the female shape of twenty, which on the instant of crossing the threshold brought into the bleak, ill-lighted, poorly-heated room dedicated to the harsh functioning of Protestant primary education a moist blast of spring's liquorish corruption, a pagan triumphal prostration before the supreme primal uterus.

He took one look at her and saw what her brother would doubtless be the last to discern. He saw that she not only was not going to study, but there was nothing in books here or anywhere else that she would ever need to know, who had been born already completely equipped not only to face and combat but to overcome anything the future could invent to meet her with. He saw a child whom for the next two years he was to watch with what he thought at first was only rage, already grown at eight, who apparently had reached and passed puberty in the foetus, who, tranquil bemused and not even sullen, obedient to whatever outside compulsion it had been had merely transferred from one set of walls to another that quality of static waiting through and beneath the accumulating days of burgeoning and unhurryable time until whatever man it was to be whose name and face she probably had neither seen nor heard yet, would break into and disperse it. For five years he was to watch her, fetched each morning by the brother and remaining just as he had left her, in the same place and almost in the same position, her hands lying motionless for hours on her lap like two separate slumbering bodies. She would answer "I dont know" when her attention was finally attracted at last, or, pressed, "I never got that far." It was as if her muscles and flesh too were even impervious to fatigue and boredom or as if, the drowsing maidenhead symbol's self, she possessed life but not sentience and merely waited until the brother came, the jealous seething eunuch priest, and removed her.

She would arrive each morning with the oilcloth satchel in which if she carried anything else beside the baked sweet potatoes which she ate at recess, Labove did not know it. By merely walking down the aisle between them she would transform the very wooden desks and benches themselves into a grove of Venus and fetch every male in the room, from the children just entering puberty to the grown men of nineteen and twenty, one of whom was already a husband and father, who could turn ten acres of land between sunup and sundown, springing into embattled rivalry, importunate each for precedence in immolation. Sometimes on Friday nights there would be parties in the schoolhouse, where the pupils would play the teasing games of adolescence under his supervision. She would take no part in them, yet she would dominate them. Sitting beside the stove exactly as she had sat during the hours of school, inattentive and serene amid the uproar of squeals and trampling feet, she would be assaulted simultaneously beneath a dozen simultaneous gingham or calico dresses in a dozen simultaneous shadowy nooks and corners. She was neither at the head nor at the foot of her class, not because she declined to study on the one hand and not because she was Varner's daughter on the other and Varner ran the school, but because the class she was in ceased to have either head or foot twenty-four hours after she entered it. Within the year there even ceased to be any lower class for her to be promoted from, for the reason that she would never be at either end of anything in which blood ran. It would have but one point, like a swarm of bees, and she would be that point, that center, swarmed over and importuned yet serene and intact and apparently even oblivious, tranquilly abrogating the whole long sum of human thinking and suffering which is called knowledge, education, wisdom, at once supremely unchaste and inviolable: the queen, the matrix.

He watched that for two years, still with what he thought was only rage. He would graduate at the end of the second year, take his two degrees. He would be done then, finished. His one reason for having taken the school would be cancelled and discharged. His aim and purpose would be gained at the price it had cost him, not the least of which was riding that horse forty miles at night to and from the University, since after his dirt-farmer tradition and heritage, he did not ride a horse for fun. Then he could go on, quit the village and never lay eyes upon it again. For the first six months he believed he was going to do that and for the next eighteen he still told himself he was. This was especially easy not only to tell himself but to believe too while he was away from the village during the last two months of the spring term at the University and the following eight weeks of the summer term into which he was crowding by sections his fourth academic year, then the eight weeks of what the school called his vacation, which he spent at the sawmill although he did not need the money now, he could graduate without it, but it would be that much more in his pocket when he passed through the last door and faced the straight hard road with nothing between him and his goal save himself; then the six fall weeks when each Saturday afternoon the spurned white lines fled beneath him and the hysteric air screamed and roared and he for those fleet seconds and despite himself did live, fierce, concentrated, even though still not quite believing it.

Then one day he discovered that he had been lying to himself for almost two years. It was after he had returned to the University in the second spring and about a month before he would graduate. He had not formally resigned from the school, though when he left the village a month ago he believed it was for the last time, considering it understood between Varner and himself that he was teaching the school only to enable himself to finish at the University. So he believed he had quitted the village for the last time. The final examinations were only a month away, then the Bar examination and the door would be open to him. There was even the promise of a position in the profession he had chosen. Then one afternoon, he had no warning at all, he had entered the diningroom of his boarding house for the evening meal when the landlady came and said, "I have a treat for you. My sister's husband brought them to me," and set a dish before him. It was a single baked sweet potato, and while the landlady cried, "Why, Mr Labove, you are sick!" he managed to rise and leave the room. In his room at last it seemed to him that he must go at once, start now, even on foot. He could see her, even smell her, sitting there on the school steps, eating the potato, tranquil and chewing and with that terrible quality of being not only helplessly and unawares on the outside of her clothing, but of being naked and not even knowing it. He knew now that it was not on the school steps but in his mind that she had constantly been for two years now, that it had not been rage at all but terror, and that the vision of that gate which he had held up to himself as a goal was not a goal but just a point to reach, as the man fleeing a holocaust runs not for a prize but to escape destruction.

But he did not really give up then, though for the first time he said the words, I will not go back. It had not been necessary to say them before because until now he had believed he was going on. But at least he could still assure himself aloud that he would not, which was something and which got him on through the graduation and the Bar initiation and banquet too. Just before the ceremony he had been approached by one of his fellow neophytes. After the banquet they were going to Memphis, for further and informal celebrating. He knew what that meant: drinking in a hotel room and then, for some of them at least, a brothel. He declined, not because he was a virgin and not because he did not have the money to spend that way but because up to the very last he still believed, still had his hill-man's purely emotional and foundationless faith in education, the white magic of Latin degrees, which was an actual counterpart of the old monk's faith in his wooden cross. Then the last speech died into the final clapping and scraping of chairs; the door was open and the road waited and he knew he would not take it. He went to the man who had invited him to Memphis and accepted. He descended with the group from the train in the Memphis station and asked quietly how to find a brothel. "Hell, man," the other said. "Restrain yourself. At least let's go through the formality of registering at the hotel." But he would not. He went alone to the address given him. He knocked firmly at the equivocal door. This would not help him either. He did not expect it to. His was that quality lacking which no man can ever be completely brave or completely craven: the ability to see both sides of the crisis and visualise himself as already vanquished—itself inherent with its own failure and disaster. At least it wont be my virginity that she is going to scorn, he told himself. The next morning he borrowed a sheet of cheap ruled tablet paper (the envelope was pink and had been scented once) from his companion of the night, and wrote Varner that he would teach the school for another year.

He taught it for three more years. By then he was the monk indeed, the bleak schoolhouse, the little barren village, was his mountain, his Gethsemane and, he knew it, his Golgotha too. He was the virile anchorite of old time. The heatless lean-to room was his desert cell, the thin pallet bed on the puncheon floor the couch of stones on which he would lie prone and sweating in the iron winter nights, naked, rigid, his teeth clenched in his scholar's face and his legs haired-over like those of a faun. Then day would come and he could rise and dress and eat the food which he would not even taste. He had never paid much attention to what he ate anyway, but now he would not always know that he had eaten it. Then he would go and unlock the school and sit behind his desk and wait for her to walk down the aisle. He had long since thought of marrying her, waiting until she was old enough and asking for her in marriage, attempting to, and had discarded that. In the first place, he did not want a wife at all, certainly not yet and probably not ever. And he did not want her as a wife, he just wanted her one time as a man with a gangrened hand or foot thirsts after the axe-stroke which will leave him comparatively whole again. But he would have paid even this price to be free of his obsession, only he knew that this could never be, not only because her father would never agree to it, but because of her, that quality in her which absolutely abrogated the exchange value of any single life's promise or capacity for devotion, the puny asking-price of any one man's reserve of so-called love. He could almost see the husband which she would someday have. He would be a dwarf, a gnome, without glands or desire, who would be no more a physical factor in her life than the owner's name on the fly-leaf of a book. There it was again, out of the books again, the dead defacement of type which had already betrayed him: the crippled Vulcan to that Venus, who would not possess her but merely own her by the single strength which power gave, the dead power of money, wealth, gewgaws, baubles, as he might own, not a picture, statue: a field, say. He saw it: the fine land rich and fecund and foul and eternal and impervious to him who claimed title to it, oblivious, drawing to itself ten fold the quantity of living seed its owner's whole life could have secreted and compounded, producing a thousand fold the harvest he could ever hope to gather and save.

So that was out. Yet still he stayed on. He stayed for the privilege of waiting until the final class was dismissed and the room was empty so that he could rise and walk with his calm damned face to the bench and lay his hand on the wooden plank still warm from the impact of her sitting or even kneel and lay his face to the plank, wallowing his face against it, embracing the hard unsentient wood, until the heat was gone. He was mad. He knew it. There would be times now when he did not even want to make love to her but wanted to hurt her, see blood spring and run, watch that serene face warp to the indelible mark of terror and agony beneath his own; to leave some indelible mark of himself on it and then watch it even cease to be a face. Then he would exorcise that. He would drive it from him, whereupon their positions would reverse. It would now be himself importunate and prostrate before that face which, even though but fourteen years old, postulated a weary knowledge which he would never attain, a surfeit, a glut of all perverse experience. He would be as a child before that knowledge. He would be like a young girl, a maiden, wild distracted and amazed, trapped not by the seducer's maturity and experience but by blind and ruthless forces inside herself which she now realised she had lived with for years without even knowing they were there. He would grovel in the dust before it, panting: "Show me what to do. Tell me. I will do anything you tell me, anything, to learn and know what you know." He was mad. He knew it. He knew that sooner or later something was going to happen. And he knew too that, whatever it would be, he would be the vanquished, even though he did not know yet what the one crack in his armor was and that she would find it unerringly and instinctively and without ever being aware that she had been in deadly danger. Danger? he thought, cried. Danger? Not to her: to me. I am afraid of what I might do, not because of her because there is nothing I or any man could do to her that would hurt her. It's because of what it will do to me.

Then one afternoon he found his axe. He continued to hack in almost an orgasm of joy at the dangling nerves and tendons of the gangrened member long after the first bungling blow. He had heard no sound. The last footfall had ceased and the door had closed for the last time. He did not hear it open again, yet something caused him to raise his wallowing face from the bench. She was in the room again, looking at him. He knew that she not only recognised the place at which he knelt, but that she knew why. Possibly at that instant he believed she had known all the time, because he knew at once that she was neither frightened nor laughing at him, that she simply did not care. Nor did she know that she was now looking at the face of a potential homicide. She merely released the door and came down the aisle toward the front of the room where the stove sat. "Jody aint come yet," she said. "It's cold out there. What are you doing down there?"

He rose. She came steadily on, carrying the oilcloth satchel which she had carried for five years now and which he knew she had never opened outside of the schoolhouse save to put into it the cold potatoes. He moved toward her. She stopped, watching him. "Dont be afraid," he said. "Dont be afraid."

"Afraid?" she said. "Of what?" She took one step back, then no more, watching his face. She was not afraid. She aint got that far either, he thought; and then something furious and cold, of repudiation and bereavement both, blew in him though it did not show in his face which was even smiling a little, tragic and sick and damned.

"That's it," he said. "That's the trouble. You are not afraid. That's what you have got to learn. That's one thing I am going to teach you, anyway." He had taught her something else, though he was not to find it out for a minute or so yet.

She had indeed learned one thing during the five years in school and was presently to take and pass an examination on it. He moved toward her. She still stood her ground. Then he had her. He moved as quickly and ruthlessly as if she had a football or as if he had the ball and she stood between him and the final white line which he hated and must reach. He caught her, hard, the two bodies hurling together violently because she had not even moved to avoid him, let alone to begin resisting yet. She seemed to be momentarily mesmerised by a complete inert soft surprise, big, immobile, almost eye to eye with him in height, the body which seemed always to be on the outside of its garments, which without even knowing it apparently had made a priapic hullabaloo of that to which, at the price of three years of sacrifice and endurance and flagellation and unceasing combat with his own implacable blood, he had bought the privilege of dedicating his life, as fluid and muscleless as a miraculous intact milk.

Then the body gathered itself into furious and silent resistance which even then he might have discerned to be neither fright nor even outrage but merely surprise and annoyance. She was strong. He had expected that. He had wanted that, he had been waiting for it. They wrestled furiously. He was still smiling, even whispering. "That's it," he said. "Fight it. Fight it. That's what it is: a man and a woman fighting each other. The hating. To kill, only to do it in such a way that the other will have to know for ever afterward he or she is dead. Not even to lie quiet dead because forever afterward there will have to be two in that grave and those two can never again lie quiet anywhere together and neither can ever lie anywhere alone and be quiet until he or she is dead." He held her loosely, the better to feel the fierce resistance of bones and muscles, holding her just enough to keep her from actually reaching his face. She had made no sound, although her brother, who was never late in calling for her, must by now be just outside the building. Labove did not think of this. He would not have cared probably. He held her loosely, still smiling, whispering his jumble of fragmentary Greek and Latin verse and American-Mississippi obscenity, when suddenly she managed to free one of her arms, the elbow coming up hard under his chin. It caught him off-balance; before he regained it her other hand struck him a full-armed blow in the face. He stumbled backward, struck a bench and went down with it and partly beneath it. She stood over him, breathing deep but not panting and not even dishevelled.

"Stop pawing me," she said. "You old headless horseman Ichabod Crane."

After the sound of her feet and the closing door had ceased, he could hear the cheap clock which he had brought back with him from his room at the University, loud in the silence, with a tinny sound like minute shot being dropped into a can, though before he could begin to get up the door opened again and, sitting on the floor, he looked up at her as she came back down the aisle. "Where's my—" she said. Then she saw it, the booksatchel, and lifted it from the floor and turned again. He heard the door again. So she hasn't told him yet, he thought. He knew the brother too. He would not have waited to take her home first, he would have come in at once, vindicated at last after five years of violent and unsupported conviction. That would be something, anyway. It would not be penetration, true enough, but it would be the same flesh, the same warm living flesh in which the same blood ran, under impact at least—a paroxysm, an orgasm of sorts, a kathar-sis, anyway—something. So he got up and went to his desk and sat down and squared the clock-face (it sat at an oblique angle, so he could see it from the point before the recitation bench where he usually stood) toward him. He knew the dis-tance between the school and the Varner home and he had ridden that horse back and forth to the University enough to calculate time in horse-distance. He will gallop back too, he thought. So he measured the distance the minute hand would have to traverse and sat watching it as it crept toward the mark. Then he looked up at the only comparatively open space in the room, which still had the stove in it, not to speak of the recitation bench. The stove could not be moved, but the bench could. But even then. . . . Maybe he had better meet the brother out doors, or someone might get hurt. Then he thought that that was exactly what he wanted: for some-body to get hurt, and then he asked himself quietly, Who? and answered himself: I dont know. I dont care. So he looked back at the clock-face. Yet even when a full hour had passed he still could not admit to himself that the final disaster had befallen him. He is lying in ambush for me with the pistol, he thought. But where? What ambush? What ambush could he want better than here? already seeing her entering the room again tomorrow morning, tranquil, untroubled, not even remembering, carrying the cold potato which at recess she would sit on the sunny steps and eat like one of the unchaste and perhaps even anonymously pregnant immortals eating bread of Paradise on a sunwise slope of Olympus.

So he rose and gathered up the books and papers which, with the clock, he carried to his barren room each afternoon and fetched back the next morning, and put them into the desk drawer and closed it and with his handkerchief he wiped off the desk top, moving without haste yet steadily, his face calm, and wound the clock and set it back on the desk. The overcoat which the football coach had given him six years ago hung on its nail. He looked at it for a moment, though presently he went and got it and even put it on and left the room, the now deserted room in which there were still and forever would be too many people; in which, from that first day when her brother had brought her into it, there had been too many people, who would make one too many forever after in any room she ever entered and remained in long enough to expel breath.

As soon as he emerged, he saw the roan horse tied to the post before the store. Of course, he thought quietly. Naturally he would not carry a pistol around with him, and it would not do him any good hidden under a pillow at home. Of course. That's it. That's where the pistol will be; telling himself that perhaps the brother even wanted witnesses, as he himself wanted them, his face tragic and calm now, walking on down the road toward the store. That will be proof, he cried silently. Proof in the eyes and beliefs of living men that that happened which did not. Which will be better than nothing, even though I am not here to know men believe it. Which will be fixed in the beliefs of living men forever and ever ineradicable, since one of the two alone who know different will be dead.

It was a gray day, of the color and texture of iron, one of those windless days of a plastic rigidity too dead to make or release snow even, in which even light did not alter but seemed to appear complete out of nothing at dawn and would expire into darkness without gradation. The village was lifeless—the shuttered and silent gin and blacksmith shop, the weathered store; the motionless horse alone postulating life and that not because it moved but because it resembled something known to be alive. But they would be inside the store. He could see them—the heavy shoes and boots, the overalls and jumper coats bulging over the massed indiscriminate garments beneath—planted about the box of pocked sand in which the stove, squatting, radiated the strong good heat which had an actual smell, masculine, almost monastic —a winter's concentration of unwomaned and deliberate tobacco-spittle annealing into the iron flanks. The good heat: he would enter it, not out of the bleak barren cold but out of life, mounting steps and walking through a door and out of living. The horse raised its head and looked at him as he passed it. But not you, he said to it. You've got to stand outside, stand here and remain intact for the blood to contrive to run through. I dont. He mounted the steps, crossing the heelgnawed planks of the gallery. On the closed door was tacked a paper placard advertising a patent medicine, half defaced— the reproduction of a portrait, smug, bearded, successful, living far away and married, with children, in a rich house and beyond the reach of passion and blood's betrayal and not even needing to be dead to be embalmed with spaced tacks, ubiquitous and immortal in ten thousand fading and tattered effigies on ten thousand weathered and paintless doors and walls and fences in all the weathers of rain and ice and summer's harsh heat, about the land.

Then, with his hand already on the knob to turn it, he stopped. Once—it was one of the football trips of course, he had never ridden in a train otherwise save on that night visit to Memphis—he had descended onto a bleak station platform. There was a sudden commotion about a door. He heard a man cursing, shouting, a negro ran out the door, followed by a shouting white man. The negro turned, stooping, and as the onlookers scattered the white man shot the negro in the body with a blunt pistol. He remembered how the negro, clutching his middle, dropped onto his face then suddenly flopped over onto his back, actually appearing to elongate himself, to add at least a yard to his stature; the cursing white man was overpowered and disarmed, the train whistled once and began to draw away, a uniformed trainman breaking out of the crowd and running to overtake it and still looking back from the moving step. And he remembered how he shoved himself up, instinctively using his football tactics to make a place, where he looked down upon the negro lying rigid on his back, still clutching his middle, his eyes closed and his face quite peaceful. Then there was a man—a doctor or an officer, he did not know—kneeling over the negro. He was trying to draw the negro's hands away. There was no outward show of resistance; the forearms and hands at which the doctor or officer was tugging merely seemed to have become iron. The negro's eyes did not open nor his peaceful expression alter; he merely said: "Look out, white folks. I awready been shot." But they unclasped his hands at last, and he remembered the peeling away of the jumper, the overalls, a ragged civilian coat beneath which revealed itself to have been a long overcoat once, the skirts cut away at the hips as with a razor; beneath that a shirt and a pair of civilian trousers. The waist of them was unbuttoned and the bullet rolled out onto the platform, bloodless. He released the doorknob and removed the overcoat and hung it over his arm. At least I wont make a failure with one of us, he thought, opening the door, entering. At first he believed the room was empty. He saw the stove in its box of pocked sand, surrounded by the nail kegs and upended boxes; he even smelled the rank scorch of recent spitting. But no one sat there, and when a moment later he saw the brother's thick humorless surly face staring at him over the desk, for an instant he felt rage and outrage. He believed that Varner had cleared the room, sent them all away deliberately in order to deny him that last vindication, the ratification of success which he had come to buy with his life; and suddenly he knew a furious disinclination, even a raging refusal, to die at all. He stooped quickly aside, already dodging, scrabbling about him for some weapon as Varner's face rose still further above the desk-top like a bilious moon.

"What in hell are you after?" Varner said. "I told you two days ago that window sash aint come yet."

"Window sash?" Labove said.

"Nail some planks over it," Varner said. "Do you expect me to make a special trip to town to keep a little fresh air out of your collar?"

Then he remembered it. The panes had been broken out during the Christmas holidays. He had nailed boards over them at the time. He did not remember doing it. But then he did not remember being told about the promised sash two days ago, let alone asking about it. And now he stopped remembering the window at all. He rose quietly and stood, the overcoat over his arm; now he did not even see the surly suspicious face anymore. Yes, he thought quietly; Yes. I see. She never told him at all. She didn't even forget to. She doesn't even know anything happened that was worth mentioning. Varner was still talking; apparently someone had answered him:

"Well, what do you want, then?"

"I want a nail," he said.

"Get it, then." The face had already disappeared beyond the desk. "Bring the hammer back."

"I wont need the hammer," he said. "I just want a nail."

The house, the heatless room in which he had lived for six years now with his books and his bright lamp, was between the store and the school. He did not even look toward it when he passed. He returned to the schoolhouse and closed and locked the door. With a fragment of brick he drove the nail into the wall beside the door and hung the key on the nail. The schoolhouse was on the Jefferson road. He already had the overcoat with him.

Chapter Two

I.

Through that spring and through the long succeeding summer of her fourteenth year, the youths of fifteen and sixteen and seventeen who had been in school with her and others who had not, swarmed like wasps about the ripe peach which her full damp mouth resembled. There were about a dozen of them. They formed a group, close, homogeneous, and loud, of which she was the serene and usually steadily and constantly eating axis, center. There were three or four girls in the group, lesser girls, though if she were deliberately using them for foils, nobody knew it for certain. They were smaller girls, even though mostly older. It was as though that abundance which had invested her cradle, not content with merely overshadowing them with the shape of features and texture of hair and skin, must also dwarf and extinguish them ultimately with sheer bulk and mass.

They were together at least once a week and usually oftener. They would meet at the church on Sunday mornings and sit together in two adjacent pews which presently became their own by common consent of the congregation and authorities, like a class or an isolation place. They met at the community parties which would be held in the now empty schoolhouse, which was to be used for nothing else for almost two years before another teacher was installed. They arrived in a group, they chose one another monotonously in the twosing games, the boys clowning and ruthless, loud. They might have been a masonic lodge set suddenly down in Africa or China, holding a weekly meeting. They departed together, walking back down the star- or moonlit road in a tight noisy clump, to leave her at her father's gate before dispersing. If the boys had been sparring for opportunities to walk home with her singly, nobody knew that either because she was never known to walk home singly from anywhere or to walk anywhere anyhow when she could help it.

They would meet again at the singings and baptisings and picnics about the country. It was election year and after the last of the planting and the first of the laying-by of the crops, there were not only the first-Sunday all-day singings and baptisings, but the vote-rousing picnics as well. The Varner surrey would be seen now week after week among the other tethered vehicles at country churches or on the edge of groves within which the women spread a week's abundance of cold food on the long plank tables while the men stood beneath the raised platforms on which the candidates for the county offices and the legislature and Congress spoke, and the young people in groups or pairs moved about the grove or, in what-ever of seclusion the girls could be enticed into, engaged in the clumsy horseplay of adolescent courtship or seduction. She listened to no speeches and set no tables and did no sing-ing. Instead, with those two or three or four lesser girls she sat, nucleus of that loud frustrated group; the nucleus, the center, the centrice; here as at the school parties of last year, casting over them all that spell of incipient accouchement while refusing herself to be pawed at, preserving even within that aura of license and invitation in which she seemed to breathe and walk—or sit rather—a ruthless chastity impervi-ous even to the light precarious balance, the actual overlap-ping, of Protestant religious and sexual excitement. It was as if she really knew what instant, moment, she was reserved for, even if not his name and face, and was waiting for that mo-ment rather than merely for the time for the eating to start, as she seemed to be.

They would meet again at the homes of the girls. This would be by prearrangement without doubt, and doubtless contrived by the other girls, though if she were aware that they invited her so that the boys would come, nobody ever divined this from her behavior either. She would make visits of overnight or of two and three days with them. She was not allowed to attend the dances which would be held in the vil-lage schoolhouse or in other schoolhouses or country stores at night. She had never asked permission; it had rather been violently refused her by her brother before anyone knew whether she was going to ask it or not. The brother did not object to the house visits though. He even fetched her back and forth on the horse as he had used to do to and from the school and for the same reason he would not let her walk from the school to the store to meet him, still seething and grimly outraged and fanatically convinced of what he believed he was battling against, riding for miles, the oilcloth booksatchel containing the nightgown and the toothbrush which her mother compelled her to bring held in the same hand which clutched the cross of his suspenders, the soft mammalian rubbing against his back and the steady quiet sound of chewing and swallowing in his ear, stopping the horse at last before the house she had come to visit and snarling at her, "Cant you stop eating that damn potato long enough to get down and let me go back to work?"

In early September the annual County Fair was held in Jefferson. She and her parents went to town and lived for four days in a boarding-house. The youths and the three girls were already there waiting for her. While her father looked at livestock and farm tools and her mother bustled cheerful and martinettish among ranked cans and jars and decorated cakes, she moved all day long in the hem-lengthened dresses she had worn last year to school and surrounded by her loud knot of loutish and belligerent adolescents, from shooting gallery to pitch game to pop stand, usually eating something, or time after time without even dismounting and still eating, rode, her long Olympian legs revealed halfway to the thigh astride the wooden horses of merry-go-rounds.

By her fifteenth year they were men. They were the size of men and doing the work of grown men at least—eighteen and nineteen and twenty, who in that time and country should have been thinking of marriage and, for her sake anyway, looking toward other girls; for their own sakes, almost any other girl. But they were not thinking of marriage. There was about a dozen of them too, who at some moment, instant, during that second spring which her brother still could not definitely put his finger on, had erupted into her placid orbit like a stampede of wild cattle, trampling ruthlessly aside the children of last summer's yesterday. Luckily for her brother, the picnics were not as frequent this year as during the election summer, because he went with the family now in the surrey—the humorless seething raging man in his hot bagging broadcloth and collarless glazed shirt who now, as if in a kind of unbelieving amazement, did not even snarl at her anymore. He had nagged Mrs Varner into making her

wear corsets. He would grasp her each time he saw her outside the house, in public or alone, and see for himself if she
had them on.

Although the brother declined to attend the singings and
baptisings, he had badgered the parents into standing in his
stead then. So the young men had what might be called a free
field only on Sundays. They would arrive in a body at the
church, riding up on horses and mules taken last night from
the plow and which would return to the plow with tomorrow's sun, and wait for the Varner surrey to arrive. That was
all the adolescent companions of last year ever saw of her
now—that glimpse of her between the surrey and the church
door as she moved stiff and awkward in the corset and the
hem-lengthened dress of last year's childhood, seen for an
instant then hidden by the crowding surge of those who
had dispossessed them. Within another year it would be the
morning's formal squire in a glittering buggy drawn by a
horse or mare bred for harness, and the youths of this year
would be crowded aside in their turn. But that would be next
year; now it was a hodge-podge though restrained into something like decorum or at least discretion by the edifice and the
day, a leashed turmoil of lust like so many lowering dogs after
a scarce-fledged and apparently unawares bitch, filing into the
church to sit on a back bench where they could watch the
honey-colored head demure among those of her parents and
brother.

After church the brother would be gone, courting himself,
it was believed, and through the long drowsing afternoons
the trace-galled mules would doze along the Varner fence
while their riders sat on the veranda, doggedly and vainly sitting each other out, crass and loud and baffled and raging not
at one another but at the girl herself who apparently did not
care whether they stayed or not, apparently not even aware
that the sitting-out was going on. Older people, passing,
would see them—the half dozen or so bright Sunday shirts
with pink or lavender sleeve-garters, the pomaded hair above
the shaved sun-burned necks, the polished shoes, the hard
loud faces, the eyes filled with the memory of a week of hard
labor in fields behind them and knowledge of another week of
it ahead; among them the girl, the centrice here too—the

body of which there was simply too much dressed in the
clothing of childhood, like a slumberer washed out of Paradise by a night flood and discovered by chance passers and
covered hurriedly with the first garment to hand, still sleeping. They would sit leashed and savage and loud and wild at
the vain galloping seconds while the shadows lengthened and
the frogs and whipporwills began and the fireflies began to
blow and drift above the creek. Then Mrs Varner would come
bustling out, talking, and still talking herd them all in to eat
the cold remains of the heavy noon meal beneath the bug-
swirled lamp, and they would give up. They would depart in
a body, seething and decorous, to mount the patient mules
and horses and ride in furious wordless amity to the creek
ford a half mile away and dismount and hitch the horses and
mules and with bare fists fight silently and savagely and wash
the blood off in the water and mount again and ride their
separate ways, with their skinned knuckles and split lips and
black eyes and for the time being freed even of rage and frustration and desire, beneath the cold moon, across the planted
land.

By the third summer the trace-galled mules had given way
to the trotting horses and the buggies. Now it was the
youths, the outgrown and discarded of last year, who waited
about the churchyard on Sunday mornings to watch in impotent and bitter turn their own dispossession—the glittering
buggy powdered only lightly over with dust, drawn by a
bright mare or horse in brass-studded harness, driven by the
man who owned them both—a man grown in his own right
and never again to be haled from an attic bed in an iron dawn
to milk cows or break land not his own, by a father who still
held over him legally and sometimes physically too the power
to bind and loose. Beside him would be the girl who last year,
after a fashion at least, had been their own and who had outgrown them, escaped them like the dead summer itself, who
had learned at last to walk without proclaiming the corsets
beneath the dresses of silk in which she looked, not like a girl
of sixteen dressed like twenty, but a woman of thirty dressed
in the garments of her sixteen-year-old sister.

At one time in the spring, for an afternoon and evening, to
be exact, there were four buggies. The fourth one belonged to

a drummer, rented. He appeared in the village by accident
one day, having lost his way and blundered upon Frenchman's Bend to ask directions without even knowing there was
a store there, in a battered rig which a Jefferson livery stable
rented to travelling men. He saw the store and stopped and
tried to sell the clerk, Snopes, a bill of goods and got nowhere
quickly. He was a youngish city man with city ways and
assurance and insistence. He had presently wormed from the
usual loungers on the gallery who the actual owner of the
store was and where he lived, and went on to Varner's house
and doubtless knocked and was or was not admitted, since
that was all they knew then. Two weeks later he was back, in
the same rig. This time he did not even try to sell the Varners
anything; it was learned later that he had taken supper at the
Varner house. That was Tuesday. On Friday he returned. He
was now driving the best turnout which the Jefferson stable
had—a runabout and a fair horse—and he not only wore a
necktie, he had on the first white flannel trousers Frenchman's
Bend ever saw. They were the last ones too, and they were
not there long: he ate supper with the Varners and that
evening he drove the daughter to a dance in a schoolhouse
about eight miles away, and vanished. Someone else brought
the daughter home and at daylight the next morning the hostler found the rented horse and buggy tied to the stable door
in Jefferson and that afternoon the night station agent told
of a frightened and battered man in a pair of ruined ice cream
pants who had bought a ticket on the early train. The train
was going south, though it was understood that the drummer
lived in Memphis, where it was later learned he had a wife
and family, but about this nobody in Frenchman's Bend
either knew or cared.

That left three. They were constant, almost in rotation,
week and week and Sunday and Sunday about, last summer's
foreclosed bankrupts waiting at the church to watch him of
that morning lift her out of the buggy. They still waited there
to look at her exposed leg when she got back into it, or, a
lowering clot further along the road, they would stand suddenly out of the undergrowth as the buggy swept past to
shout vicious obscenity after it out of the spinning and choking dust. At some time during the afternoon one or two or

three of them would pass the Varner house, to see without looking at them the horse and buggy hitched to the fence and Will Varner napping in his wooden hammock in its small grove in the yard and the closed blinds of the parlor windows beyond, shuttered after the local fashion, against the heat. They would lurk in the darkness, usually with a jug of white hill whiskey, just beyond the light-radius of the homes or stores or school buildings within the lamplit doors and windows of which the silhouettes of dancing couples moved athwart the whine and squeal of fiddles. Once they charged yelling from a clump of shadow beside the moonlit road, upon the moving buggy, the mare rearing and plunging, the driver standing up in the buggy and slashing at them with the whip and laughing at them as they ducked and dodged. Because it was not the brother, it was this dead last summer's vain and raging jetsam, who divined or at least believed that there had never been but one buggy all the time. It was almost a year now since Jody had ceased to wait for her in the hall until she came out, dressed, the buggy waiting, to grasp her arm and exactly as he would have felt the back of a new horse for old saddle sores, grimly explore with his hard heavy hand to see if she had the corset on or not.

This buggy belonged to a man named McCarron who lived about twelve miles from the village. He was the only child of a widow, herself the only child of a well-to-do landowner. Motherless, she had eloped at nineteen with a handsome, ready-tongued, assured and pleasant man who had come into the country without specific antecedents and no definite past. He had been there about a year. His occupation seemed to be mainly playing poker in the back rooms of country stores or the tack rooms of stables, and winning, though perfectly honestly; there had never been any question of that. All the women said he would make a poor husband. The men said that only a shotgun would ever make him a husband of any sort, and most of them would have declined him as a son-in-law even on those terms, because he had that about him which loved the night—not the night's shadows, but the bright hysteric glitter-glare which made them, the perversity of unsleeping. Nevertheless, Alison Hoake climbed out a second storey window one night. There was no ladder, no drainpipe, no rope of knotted sheets. They said she jumped and McCarron caught her in his arms and they vanished for ten days and returned, McCarron walking, his fine teeth exposed though the rest of his face took no part in the smile, into the room where old Hoake had sat for ten days now with a loaded shotgun across his lap.

To everyone's surprise, he made not only a decent husband, but son-in-law too. He knew little about farming and did not pretend to like it, nevertheless he served as his father-in-law's overseer, carrying out the old man's verbatim instructions like a dictaphone record would have of course, but having himself the gift of getting along well with, and even dominating somewhat, all men not as ready of tongue as he, though it was actually his jolly though lightly-balanced temper and his reputation as a gambler which got him the obedience of the negro field hands even more than his position as the son-in-law or even his proved prowess with a pistol. He even stayed home at night and quit the poker-playing. In fact, later nobody could decide for certain if the cattle-buying scheme had not been the father-in-law's instead of his. But within a year, by which time he was a father himself, he was buying up cattle and taking them in droves overland to the railroad and Memphis every two or three months. This went on for ten years, by which time the father-in-law had died and left the property to his grandson. Then McCarron made his last trip. Two nights later one of his drovers galloped up to the house and waked his wife. McCarron was dead, and the countryside never did know much about that either, shot in a gambling house apparently. His wife left the nine-year-old boy with the negro servants and went in the farm wagon and fetched her husband's body home and buried it on the oak and cedar knoll beside her father and mother. Shortly after that a rumor, a tale of a brief day or two, went about that a woman had shot him. But that died; they only said to one another, "So that's what he was doing all the time," and there remained only the legend of the money and jewels he was supposed to have won during the ten years and fetched home at night and, with his wife's help, bricked up in one of the chimneys of the house.

The son, Hoake, at twenty-three looked older. This was his

father's assurance in his face which was bold and handsome too. It was also a little swaggering and definitely spoiled though not vain so much as intolerant, which his father's face had not been. It also lacked humor and equability and perhaps intelligence too, which his father's face had not lacked, but which that of the man who sat for ten days after his daughter's elopement with a loaded shotgun on his lap, probably did. He grew up with a negro lad for his sole companion. They slept in the same room, the negro on a pallet on the floor, until he was ten years old. The negro was a year older. When they were six and seven, he conquered the negro with his fists in fair fight. Afterward he would pay the negro out of his pocket money at a standard rate fixed between them, for the privilege of whipping the negro, not severely, with a miniature riding crop.

At fifteen his mother sent him to a military boarding school. Precocious, well-co-ordinated and quick to learn whatever he saw was to his benefit, he acquired enough credits in three years to enter college. His mother chose an agricultural college. He went there and spent a whole year in the town without even matriculating while his mother believed he was passing his freshman work. The next fall he did matriculate, remained five months and was given the privilege of withdrawing from the school following a scandalous denouement involving the wife of a minor instructor. He returned home and spent the next two years ostensibly overseeing the plantation which his mother now ran. This meant that he spent some part of the day riding about it in the dress boots of his military school days which still fitted his small feet and which were the first riding boots the countryside had ever seen. Five months ago he happened by chance to ride through Frenchman's Bend village and saw Eula Varner.

This was he against whom, following the rout of the Memphis drummer, the youths of last summer's trace-galled mules rose in embattled concert to defend that in which apparently they and the brother both had no belief, even though they themselves had failed signally to disprove it, as knights before them have probably done. A scout of two or three would lurk about the Varner fence to watch the buggy depart and find which road it would take. They would follow or precede it to whatever plank-trampling fiddle-impregnated destination, to wait there with the jug of raw whiskey and follow it back home or toward home—the long return through night-time roads across the mooned or unmooned sleeping land, the mare's feet like slow silk in the dust as a horse moves when the reins are wrapped about the upright whip in its dashboard socket, the fords into which the unguided mare would step gingerly down and stop unchidden and drink, nuzzling and blowing among the broken reflections of stars, raising its dripping muzzle and maybe drinking again or maybe just blowing into the water as a thirst-quenched horse will. There would be no voice, no touch of rein to make it move on; anyway, it would be standing there too long, too long, too long. One night they charged the moving buggy from the roadside shadows and were driven off by the whip because they had no concerted plan but were moved by a spontaneous combustion of rage and grief. A week after that, the horse and buggy tied to the Varner fence, they burst with yells and banging pans around the corner of the dark veranda, McCarron presently strolling composedly out, not from the porch but from the clump of trees where Varner's wooden hammock hung, and called upon two or three of them by name and cursed them in a pleasant, drawling, conversational voice and dared any two of them to meet him down the road. They could see the pistol hanging in his hand against his flank.

Then they gave him formal warning. They could have told the brother but they did not, not because the brother would more than likely have turned upon the informers with physical violence. Like the teacher Labove, they would have welcomed that, they would have accepted that with actual joy. As with Labove, it would at least have been the same living flesh warm under furious impact, bruising, scoriating, springing blood, which, like Labove, was what they actually desired now whether they knew it or not. It was because they were already insulated against acceptance of the idea of telling him by the fact that their rage would be wasted then upon the agent of their vengeance and not the betrayer; they would have met the profferer of a mortal affronting and injury with their hands bound up in boxing gloves. So they sent McCarron a formal warning in writing with their names signed.

One of them rode the twelve miles to his mother's house one night and fastened the notice to the door. The next afternoon McCarron's negro, a grown man too now, brought the five separate answers and escaped from them at last, bloody about the head but not seriously hurt.

Yet for almost another week he foiled them. They were trying to take him when he was in the buggy alone, either before he had reached the Varner house or after he had left it. But the mare was too fast for them to overtake, and their spiritless plow-animals would not stand ground and halt the mare, and they knew from the previous attempt that, if they tried to stop the mare on foot, he would ride them down, standing up in the buggy with the slashing whip and his hard bare jeering teeth. Besides, he had the pistol, they had learned enough about him to know that he had never been without it since he turned twenty-one. And there was still the matter to be settled between him and the two who had beaten his negro messenger.

So they were forced at last to ambush him at the ford with Eula in the buggy when the mare stopped to drink. Nobody ever knew exactly what happened. There was a house near the ford, but there were no yells and shouts this time, merely abrasions and cuts and missing teeth on four of the five faces seen by daylight tomorrow. The fifth one, the other of the two who had beaten the negro, still lay unconscious in the nearby house. Someone found the butt of the buggy whip. It was clotted with dried blood and human hair and later, years later, one of them told that it was the girl who had wielded it, springing from the buggy and with the reversed whip beating three of them back while her companion used the reversed pistol-butt against the wagon-spoke and the brass knuckles of the other two. That was all that was ever known, the buggy reaching the Varner house not especially belated. Will Varner, in his nightshirt and eating a piece of cold peach pie with a glass of buttermilk in the kitchen, heard them come up from the gate and onto the veranda, talking quietly, murmuring as she and her young men did about what her father believed was nothing, and on into the house, the hall, and on to the kitchen door. Varner looked up and saw the bold handsome face, the pleasant hard revelation of teeth which would have

been called smiling at least, though it was not particularly deferent, the swelling eye, the long welt down the jaw, the hanging arm flat against the side. "He bumped into something,"
the daughter said.

"I see he did," Varner said. "He looks like it kicked him
too."

"He wants some water and a towel," she said. "It's over
yonder," she said, turning; she did not come into the kitchen,
the light. "I'll be back in a minute." Varner heard her mount
the stairs and move about in her room overhead but he paid
no further attention. He looked at McCarron and saw that
the exposed teeth were gritted rather than smiling, and he was
sweating. After he saw that, Varner paid no more attention to
the face either.

"So you bumped into something," he said. "Can you get
that coat off?"

"Yes," the other said. "I did it catching my mare. A piece of
scantling."

"Serve you right for keeping a mare like that in a wood-
shed," Varner said. "This here arm is broke."

"All right," McCarron said. "Aint you a veterinary? I
reckon a man aint so different from a mule."

"That's correct," Varner said. "Usually he aint got quite as
much sense." The daughter entered. Varner had heard her on
the stairs again, though he did not notice that she now wore
another dress from that in which she had left the house.
"Fetch my whiskey jug," he said. It was beneath his bed,
where it stayed. She fetched it down. McCarron sat now with
his bared arm flat on the kitchen table. He fainted once, erect
in the chair, but not for long. After that it was only the fixed
teeth and the sweat until Varner had done. "Pour him another
drink and go wake Sam to drive him home," Varner said. But
McCarron would not, either be driven home or go to bed
where he was. He had a third drink from the jug and he and
the girl went back to the veranda and Varner finished his pie
and milk and carried the jug back up stairs and went to bed.

It was not the father and not even the brother, who for five
or six years now had actually been supported upright and
intact in breathing life by an idea which had not even grown
through the stage of suspicion at all but had sprung fullblown

as a conviction only the more violent for the fact that the most unremitting effort had never been able to prove it, whom divination descended upon. Varner took a drink himself from the jug and shoved it back under the bed where a circle of dust marked the place where it had sat for years, and went to sleep. He entered his accustomed state of unsnoring and childlike slumber and did not hear his daughter mount the stairs, to remove this time the dress which had her own blood on it. The mare, the buggy, was gone by then, though McCarron fainted in it again before he reached home. The next morning the doctor found that, although the break had been properly set and splinted, nevertheless it had broken free since, the two bone-ends telescoping, and so had to be set again. But Varner did not know that—the father, the lean pleasant shrewd unillusioned man asleep in the bed above the whiskey jug twelve miles away, who, regardless of what error he might have made in the reading of the female heart in general and his daughter's in particular, had been betrayed at the last by failing to anticipate that she would not only essay to, but up to a certain point actually support, with her own braced arm from underneath, the injured side.

Three months later, when the day came for the delicate buggies and the fast bright horses and mares to be seen no more along the Varner fence, Will Varner himself was the last to discover it. They and the men who drove them were gone, vanished overnight, not only from Frenchman's Bend but from the country itself. Although one of the three knew certainly one who was guilty, and the other two knew collectively two who were not, all three of them fled, secretly and by back roads probably, with saddle-bags or single hurried portmanteaus for travelling fast. One of them went because of what he believed the Varner men would do. The other two fled because they knew that the Varners would not do it. Because the Varners too would know by now from the one incontrovertible source, the girl herself, that two of them were not guilty, and so those two would thus be relegated also to the flotsam of a vain dead yesterday of passionate and eternal regret and grief, along with the impotent youths who by badgering them also, along with him who had been successful, had conferred upon them likewise blindly and unearned the accolade of success. By fleeing too, they put in a final and despairing bid for the guilt they had not compassed, the glorious shame of the ruin they did not do.

So when the word went quietly from house to house about the country that McCarron and the two others had vanished and that Eula Varner was in what everyone else but her, as it presently appeared, called trouble, the last to learn of it was the father—this man who cheerfully and robustly and undeviatingly declined to accept any such theory as female chastity other than as a myth to hoodwink young husbands with just as some men decline to believe in free tariff or the efficacy of prayer; who, as it was well known, had spent and was still spending no inconsiderable part of his time proving to himself his own contention, who at the present moment was engaged in a liaison with the middle-fortyish wife of one of his own tenants. He was too old, he told her baldly and plainly, to be tomcatting around at night, about his own house or any other man's. So she would meet him in the afternoons, on pretence of hunting hen-nests, in a thicket beside the creek near her house, in which sylvan Pan-hallowed retreat, the fourteen-year-old boy whose habit it was to spy on them told, Varner would not even remove his hat. He was the last to hear about it, waked where he slept in his sock feet in the wooden hammock, by the peremptory voice of his wife, hurrying, lean, loose-jointed and still not quite awake, in his stockings across the yard and into the hall where Mrs Varner, in a loose old wrapper and the lace boudoir cap in which she took her afternoon naps, shouted at him in an immediate irate voice above the uproar of his son's voice from the daughter's room upstairs: "Eula's got a baby. Go up there and knock that fool in the head."

"Got a what?" Varner said. But he did not pause. He hurried on, Mrs Varner following, up the stairs and into the room in which for the last day or two the daughter had remained more or less constantly, not even coming down for meals, suffering from what, if Varner had thought about it at all, he would have judged merely a stomach disorder from eating too much, possibly accumulated and suddenly and violently retroactive after sixteen years of visceral forbearance and outragement. She sat in a chair beside the window in her loosened hair and a bright near-silk negligee she had ordered recently from a Chicago mail order house. Her brother stood over her, shaking her arm and shouting: "Which one was it? Tell me which one!"

"Stop shoving me," she said. "I dont feel good." Again Varner did not pause. He came between them and thrust Jody back.

"Let her alone," he said. "Get on out of here." Jody turned on Varner his suffused face.

"Let her alone?" he said. He laughed fiercely, with no mirth, his eyes pale, popping and enraged. "That's what's the matter now! She's done been let alone too damn much already! I tried. I knowed what was coming. I told both of you five years ago. But no. You both knew better. And now see what you got! See what's happened! But I'll make her talk. By God, I'll find out who it was. And then I—"

"All right," Varner said. "What's happened?" For a moment, a minute almost, Jody appeared to be beyond speech. He glared at Varner. He looked as though only a supreme effort of will kept him from bursting where he stood.

"And he asks me what's happened," he said at last, in an amazed and incredulous whisper. "He asks me what's happened." He whirled; he jerked one hand upward in a gesture of furious repudiation and, Varner following, rushed upon Mrs Varner, who had just reached the door, her hand upon her fleshy now heaving breast and her mouth open for speech as soon as breath returned. Jody weighed two hundred pounds and Mrs Varner, although not much over five feet tall, weighed almost as much. Yet he managed somehow to run past her in the door, she grasping at him as Varner, eel-like, followed. "Stop the fool!" she shouted, following again as Varner and Jody thundered back down the stairs and into the ground floor room which Varner still called his office though for the last two years now the clerk, Snopes, had slept on a cot in it, where Varner now overtook Jody bending over the open drawer of the clumsy (and now priceless, though Varner did not know it) walnut secretary which had belonged to Varner's grandfather, scrabbling a pistol from among the jumble of dried cotton bolls and seed pods and harness buckles and cartridges and old papers which it contained. Through the window beside the desk the negress, the cook, could be seen running across the back yard toward her cabin, her apron over her head, as negroes do when trouble starts among the white people. Sam, the man, was following, though slower, looking back at the house, when both Varner and Jody saw him at the same time.

"Sam! Saddle my horse!" Jody roared.

"You, Sam!" Varner shouted. They both grasped the pistol now, the four hands now apparently hopelessly inextricable in the open drawer. "Dont touch that horse! Come back here this minute!" Mrs Varner's feet were now pounding in the hall. The pistol came free of the drawer, they stepped back, their hands locked and tangled, to see her now in the door, her hand still at her heaving breast, her ordinarily cheerful opinionated face suffused and irate.

"Hold him till I get a stick of stove wood," she gasped. "I'll fix him. I'll fix both of them. Turning up pregnant and yelling and cursing here in the house when I am trying to take a nap!"

"All right," Varner said. "Go and get it." She went out; she seemed to have been sucked violently out of the door by her own irate affrontment. Varner wrenched the pistol free and hurled Jody (he was quite strong, incredibly wiry and quick for all his sixty years, though he had cold intelligence for his ally where the son had only blind rage) back into the desk and went and threw the pistol into the hall and slammed the door and turned the key and came back, panting a little but not much. "What in hell are you trying to do?" he said.

"Nothing!" Jody cried. "Maybe you dont give a damn about your name, but I do. I got to hold my head up before folks even if you aint."

"Hah," Varner said. "I aint noticed you having any trouble holding it up. You have just about already got to where you cant get it far enough down to lace your own shoes." Jody glared at him, panting.

"By God," he said, "maybe she wont talk but I reckon I can find somebody that will. I'll find all three of them. I'll—"

"What for? Just out of curiosity to find out for certain just which of them was and wasn't diddling her?" Again for a long moment Jody could not speak at all. He stood against the desk, huge, bull-goaded, impotent and outraged, actually suffering, not from lese-Varner but from frustration. Mrs Varner's heavy stockinged feet pounded again in the hall; she began now to hammer at the door with the stick of wood.

"You, Will!" she shouted. "Open this door!"

"You mean you aint going to do *nothing*?" Jody said. "Not anything?"

"Do what?" Varner said. "To who? Dont you know them damn tomcats are half way to Texas now? Where would you be about now, if it was you? Where would I be, even at my age, if I was footloose enough to prowl any roof I wanted to and could get in when I did? I know damn well where, and so would you—right where they are and still lathering horsemeat." He went to the door and unlocked it, though the steady irate tattoo of Mrs Varner's stick was so loud that she apparently did not hear the key turn at all. "Now you go on out to the barn and set down until you cool off. Make Sam dig you some worms and go fishing. If this family needs any head-holding-up done, I'll tend to it myself." He turned the knob. "Hell and damnation, all this hullabaloo and uproar because one confounded running bitch finally foxed herself. What did you expect—that she would spend the rest of her life just running water through it?"

That was Saturday afternoon. On the next Monday morning the seven men squatting about the gallery of the store saw the clerk, Snopes, coming on foot down the road from Varner's house, followed by a second man who was carrying a suitcase. The clerk not only wore the gray cloth cap and the minute tie but a coat too, and then they saw that the suitcase which the second man carried was the straw one which Snopes had carried new to Varner's house one afternoon a year ago and left there. Then they began to look at the man who was carrying it. They saw that the clerk was heeled as by a dog by a man a little smaller than himself but shaped exactly like him. It was as though the two of them were merely graded by perspective. At first glance even the two faces were identical, until the two of them mounted the steps. Then they saw that the second face was a Snopes face right enough, differing from the other only by that unpredictable variation within the iron kinship to which they had become accustomed—in this case a face not smaller than the other exactly but closer, the features plucked together at the center of it not by some inner impulse but rather from the outside, as though by a single swift gesture of the fingers of one hand; a face quick and bright and not derisive exactly as profoundly and incorrigibly merry behind the bright, alert, amoral eyes of a squirrel or a chipmunk.

They mounted the steps and crossed the gallery, carrying the suitcase. Snopes jerked his head at them exactly as Will Varner himself did it, chewing; they entered the store. After a while three more men came out of the blacksmith shop opposite, so there was a dozen of them about within sight of the gallery when, an hour later, the Varner surrey came up. The negro, Sam, was driving. Beside him in front was the tremendous battered telescope bag which Mr and Mrs Varner had made their honeymoon to Saint Louis with and which all travelling Varners had used since, even the daughters marrying, sending it back empty, when it would seem to be both symbol and formal notice of moon-set, the mundane return, the valedictory of bright passion's generous impulsive abandon, as the printed card had been of its hopeful dawn. Varner, in the back seat with his daughter, called a general greeting, short, perfectly inflectionless, unreadable. He did not get out, and those on the gallery looked quietly once and then away from the calm beautiful mask beside him beneath the Sunday hat, the veil, above the Sunday dress, even the winter coat, seeing without looking at him as Snopes came out of the store, carrying the straw suitcase, and mounted to the front seat beside the telescope bag. The surrey moved on. Snopes turned his head once and spat over the wheel. He held the straw suitcase on his knees like the coffin of a baby's funeral.

The next morning Tull and Bookwright returned from Jefferson, where they had delivered another drove of cattle to the railroad. By that night the countryside knew the rest of it—how on that Monday afternoon Varner and his daughter and his clerk had visited his bank, where Varner had cashed a considerable check. Tull said it was for three hundred dollars. Bookwright said that meant a hundred and fifty then, since Varner would discount even his own paper to himself fifty percent. From there they had gone to the court house, to the

Chancery Clerk's office, where a deed to the Old Frenchman place was recorded to Flem and Eula Varner Snopes. A Justice of the Peace had a desk in the Circuit Clerk's office, where they bought the license.

Tull blinked rapidly, telling it. He coughed. "The bride and groom left for Texas right after the ceremony," he said.

"That makes five," a man named Armstid said. "But they say Texas is a big place."

"It's beginning to need to be," Bookwright said. "You mean six."

Tull coughed. He was still blinking rapidly. "Mr Varner paid for it too," he said.

"Paid for what too?" Armstid said.

"The wedding license," Tull said.

2.

She knew him well. She knew him so well that she never had to look at him anymore. She had known him ever since her fourteenth summer, when the people said that he had "passed" her brother. They did not say it to her. She would not have heard them. She would not have cared. She saw him almost every day, because in her fifteenth summer he began to come to the house itself, usually after supper, to sit with her father on the veranda, not talking but listening, spitting his tobacco neatly over the railing. Sometimes on Sunday afternoons he would come and squat against a tree beside the wooden hammock where her father lay in his stockings, still not talking and still chewing; she would see him there from where she sat on the veranda surrounded by her ravening crowd of that year's Sunday beaux. By then she had learned to recognise the mute hissing of his tennis shoes on the veranda planks; without rising or even turning her head she would call toward the interior of the house: "Papa, here's that man", or, presently, "the man",—"papa, here's the man again," though sometimes she said Mr Snopes, saying it exactly as she would have said Mr Dog.

In the next summer, her sixteenth, she not only did not look at him, she never saw him again because he now lived in the same house, eating at the same table, using her brother's saddle horse to attend to his and her father's interminable business. He would pass her in the hall where her brother held her, dressed to go out to the waiting buggy, while his hard raging hand explored to see if she had the corset on, and she would not see him. She faced him across the table to eat twice a day because she ate her own breakfast in the kitchen, at whatever mid-morning hour her mother finally got her up, though once she was awake it was no further trouble to get her down to the table; harried at last from the kitchen by the negress or her mother, the last half-eaten biscuit in her hand and her face unwashed and looking, in the rich deshabille of her loose hair and the sloven and not always clean garments she had groped into between bed and breakfast-table, as if she had just been surprised from a couch of illicit love by a police raid, she would meet and pass him returning to his noon meal, in the hall, and he had never been. And so one day they clapped her into her Sunday clothes and put the rest of her things—the tawdry mail-order negligees and nightgowns, the big cheap flimsy shoes and what toilet things she had—into the tremendous bag and took her to town in the surrey and married her to him.

Ratliff was in Jefferson that Monday afternoon too. He saw the three of them cross the Square from the bank to the court house and followed them. He walked past the door to the Chancery Clerk's office and saw them inside; he could have waited and seen them go from there to the Circuit Clerk's office and he could have witnessed the marriage, but he did not. He did not need to. He knew what was happening now and he had already gone on to the station, there waiting an hour before the train was due, and he was not wrong; he saw the straw suitcase and the big telescope bag go into the vestibule, in that juxtaposition no more paradoxical and bizarre; he saw the calm beautiful mask beneath the Sunday hat once more beyond a moving window, looking at nothing, and that was all. If he had lived in Frenchman's Bend itself during that spring and summer, he would have known no more—a little lost village, nameless, without grace, forsaken, yet which wombed once by chance and accident one blind seed of the spendthrift Olympian ejaculation and did not even know it, without tumescence conceived, and bore—one bright brief

summer, concentric, during which three fairly well-horsed
buggies stood in steady rotation along a picket fence or spun
along adjacent roads between the homes and the cross-
roads stores and the schoolhouses and churches where people
gathered for pleasure or at least for escape, and then overnight and simultaneously were seen no more; then eccentric:
buggies gone, vanished—a lean, loose-jointed, cotton-socked,
shrewd, ruthless old man, the splendid girl with her beautiful
masklike face, the froglike creature which barely reached her
shoulder, cashing a check, buying a license, taking a train—a
word, a single will to believe born of envy and old deathless
regret, murmured from cabin to cabin above the washing pots
and the sewing, from wagon to horseman in roads and lanes
or from rider to halted plow in field furrows; the word, the
dream and wish of all male under sun capable of harm—the
young who only dreamed yet of the ruins they were still incapable of; the sick and the maimed sweating in sleepless
beds, impotent for the harm they willed to do; the old, now-
glandless earth-creeping, the very buds and blossoms, the garlands of whose yellowed triumphs had long fallen into the
profitless dust, embalmed now and no more dead to the living
world if they were sealed in buried vaults, behind the impregnable matronly calico of others' grandchildren's grandmothers—the word, with its implications of lost triumphs and
defeats of unimaginable splendor—and which best: to have
that word, that dream and hope for future, or to have had
need to flee that word and dream, for past. Even one of the
actual buggies remained. Ratliff was to see it, discovered a
few months afterward, standing empty and with propped
shafts in a stable shed a few miles from the village, gathering
dust; chickens roosted upon it, steadily streaking and marring
the once-bright varnish with limelike droppings, until the
next harvest, the money-time, when the father of its late
driver sold it to a negro farm-hand, after which it would be
seen passing through the village a few times each year, perhaps recognised, perhaps not, while its new owner married
and began to get a family and then turn gray, spilling children, no longer glittering, its wheels wired upright in succession by crossed barrel staves until staves and delicate wheels

both vanished, translated apparently in motion at some point into stout, not new, slightly smaller wagon-wheels, giving it a list, the list too interchangeable, ranging from quarter to quarter between two of its passing appearances behind a succession of spavined and bony horses and mules in wire- and rope-patched harness, as if its owner had horsed it ten minutes ago out of a secret boneyard for this particular final swan-song's apotheosis which, woefully misinformed as to its own capacities, was each time not the last.

But when he at last turned his little tough team toward Frenchman's Bend again, Bookwright and Tull had long since returned home and told it. It was now September. The cotton was open and spilling into the fields; the very air smelled of it. In field after field as he passed along the pickers, arrested in stooping attitudes, seemed fixed amid the constant surf of bursting bolls like piles in surf, the long, partly-filled sacks streaming away behind them like rigid frozen flags. The air was hot, vivid and breathless—a final fierce concentration of the doomed and dying summer. The feet of the small horses twinkled rapidly in the dust and he sat, loose and easy to the motion, the reins loose in one hand, inscrutable of face, his eyes darkly impenetrable, quizzical and bemused, remembering, still seeing them—the bank, the court house, the station; the calm beautiful mask seen once more beyond a moving pane of glass, then gone. But that was all right, it was just meat, just galmeat he thought, and God knows there was a plenty of that, yesterday and tomorrow too. Of course there was the waste, not wasted on Snopes but on all of them, himself included—Except was it waste? he thought suddenly, seeing the face again for an instant as though he had recalled not only the afternoon but the train too—the train itself, which had served its day and schedule and so, despite the hard cars, the locomotive, no more existed. He looked at the face again. It had not been tragic, and now it was not even damned, since from behind it there looked out only another mortal natural enemy of the masculine race. And beautiful: but then, so did the highwayman's daggers and pistols make a pretty shine on him; and now as he watched, the lost calm face vanished. It went fast; it was as if the moving glass were in retrograde, it too merely a part, a figment, of the concentric flotsam and jetsam of the translation, and there remained only the straw bag, the minute tie, the constant jaw:

Until at last, baffled, they come to the Prince his-self. 'Sire,' they says. 'He just wont. We cant do nothing with him.'

'What?' the Prince hollers.

'He says a bargain is a bargain. That he swapped in good faith and honor, and now he has come to redeem it, like the law says. And we cant find it,' they says. 'We done looked everywhere. It wasn't no big one to begin with nohow, and we was specially careful in handling it. We sealed it up in a asbestos matchbox and put the box in a separate compartment to itself. But when we opened the compartment, it was gone. The matchbox was there and the seal wasn't broke. But there wasn't nothing in the matchbox but a little kind of dried-up smear under one edge. And now he has come to redeem it. But how can we redeem him into eternal torment without his soul?'

'Damn it,' the Prince hollers. 'Give him one of the extra ones. Aint there souls turning up here everyday, banging at the door and raising all kinds of hell to get in here, even bringing letters from Congressmen, that we never even heard of? Give him one of them.'

'We tried that,' they says. 'He wont do it. He says he dont want no more and no less than his legal interest according to what the banking and the civil laws states in black and white is hisn. He says he has come prepared to meet his bargain and signature, and he sholy expects you of all folks to meet yourn.'

'Tell him he can go then. Tell him he had the wrong address. That there aint nothing on the books here against him. Tell him his note was lost—if there ever was one. Tell him we had a flood, even a freeze.'

'He wont go, not without his—'

'Turn him out. Eject him.'

'How?' they says. 'He's got the law.'

'Oho,' the Prince says. 'A sawmill advocate. I see. All right,' he says. 'Fix it. Why bother me?' And he set back and raised his glass and blowed the flames offen it like he thought they was already gone. Except they wasn't gone.

'Fix what?' they says.

'His bribe!' the Prince hollers. 'His bribe! Didn't you just tell

*me he come in here with his mouth full of law? Did you expect him
to hand you a wrote-out bill for it?'*

'We tried that,' they says. 'He wont bribe.'

*Then the Prince set up there and sneered at them with his sharp
bitter tongue and no talkback, about how likely what they thought
was a bribe would be a cash discount with maybe a trip to the
Legislature throwed in, and them standing there and listening
and taking it because he was the Prince. Only there was one of
them that had been there in the time of the Prince's pa. He used to
dandle the Prince on his knee when the Prince was a boy; he even
made the Prince a little pitchfork and learned him how to use it
practising on Chinees and Dagoes and Polynesians, until his arms
would get strong enough to handle his share of white folks. He
didn't appreciate this and he drawed his-self up and he looked at
the Prince and he says,*

*'Your father made, unreproved, a greater failure. Though
maybe a greater man tempted a greater man.'*

*'Or you have been reproved by a lesser,' the Prince snaps back.
But he remembered them old days too, when the old fellow was
smiling fond and proud on his crude youthful inventions with BB
size lava and brimstone and such, and bragging to the old Prince
at night about how the boy done that day, about what he invented
to do to that little Dago or Chinee that even the grown folks
hadn't thought of yet. So he apologised and got the old fellow
smoothed down, and says, 'What did you offer him?'*

'The gratifications.'

'And —?'

*'He has them. He says that for a man that only chews, any
spittoon will do.'*

'And then?'

'The vanities.'

'And —?'

*'He has them. He brought a gross with him in the suitcase,
specially made up for him outen asbestos, with unmeltable snaps.'*

*'Then what does he want?' the Prince hollers. 'What does he
want? Paradise?' And the old one looks at him and at first the
Prince thinks it's because he aint forgot that sneer. But he finds
out different.*

'No,' the old one says. 'He wants hell.'

And now for a while there aint a sound in that magnificent kingly hall hung about with the proud battle-torn smokes of the old martyrs but the sound of frying and the faint constant screams of authentic Christians. But the Prince was the same stock and blood his pa was. In a flash the sybaritic indolence and the sneers was gone; it might have been the old Prince his-self that stood there. 'Bring him to me,' he says. 'Then leave us.'

So they brought him in and went away and closed the door. His clothes was still smoking a little, though soon he had done brushed most of it off. He come up to the Throne, chewing, toting the straw suitcase.

'Well?' the Prince says.

He turned his head and spit, the spit frying off the floor quick in a little blue ball of smoke. 'I come about that soul,' he says.

'So they tell me,' the Prince says. 'But you have no soul.'

'Is that my fault?' he says.

'Is it mine?' the Prince says. 'Do you think I created you?'

'Then who did?' he says. And he had the Prince there and the Prince knowed it. So the Prince set out to bribe him his-self. He named over all the temptations, the gratifications, the satieties; it sounded sweeter than music the way the Prince fetched them up in detail. But he didn't even stop chewing, standing there holding the straw suitcase. Then the Prince said, 'Look yonder,' pointing at the wall, and there they was, in order and rite for him to watch, watching his-self performing them all, even the ones he hadn't even thought about inventing to his-self yet, until they was done, the last unimaginable one. And he just turned his head and spit another scorch of tobacco onto the floor and the Prince flung back on the Throne in very exasperation and baffled rage.

'Then what do you want?' the Prince says. 'What do you want? Paradise?'

'I hadn't figured on it,' he says. 'Is it yours to offer?'

'Then whose is it?' the Prince says. And the Prince knowed he had him there. In fact, the Prince knowed he had him all the time, ever since they had told him how he had walked in the door with his mouth already full of law; he even leaned over and rung the fire-bell so the old one could be there to see and hear how it was done, then he leaned back on the Throne and looked down at him standing there with his straw suitcase, and says, 'You have admitted and even argued that I created you. Therefore your soul was mine all the time. And therefore when you offered it as security for

*this note, you offered that which you did not possess and so laid
yourself liable to —'*

'I have never disputed that,' he says.

*'—criminal action. So take your bag and —' the Prince says.
'Eh?' the Prince says. 'What did you say?'*

'I have never disputed that,' he says.

*'What?' the Prince says. 'Disputed what?' Except that it dont
make any noise, and now the Prince is leaning forward, and now
he feels that ere hot floor under his knees and he can feel his-self
grabbing and hauling at his throat to get the words out like he
was digging potatoes outen hard ground. 'Who are you?' he says,
choking and gasping and his eyes a-popping up at him setting
there with that straw suitcase on the Throne among the bright,
crown-shaped flames. 'Take Paradise!' the Prince screams. 'Take
it! Take it!' And the wind roars up and the dark roars down and
the Prince scrabbling across the floor, clawing and scrabbling at
that locked door, screaming. . . . . . .*

THE LONG SUMMER
Chapter One

I.

S ITTING IN THE halted buckboard, Ratliff watched the old
fat white horse emerge from Varner's lot and come down
the lane beside the picket fence, surrounded and preceded by
the rich sonorous organ-tone of its entrails. So he's back to
the horse again, he thought. He's got to straddle his legs at
least once to keep on moving. So he had to pay that too. Not
only the deed to the land and the two-dollar wedding license
and them two tickets to Texas and the cash, but the riding in
that new buggy with somebody to do the driving, to get that
patented necktie out of his store and out of his house. The
horse came up and stopped, apparently of its own accord,
beside the buckboard in which Ratliff sat neat, decorous, and
grave like a caller in a house of death.

"You must have been desperate," he said quietly. He meant
no insult. He was not even thinking of Varner's daughter's
shame or of his daughter at all. He meant the land, the Old
Frenchman place. He had never for one moment believed that
it had no value. He might have believed this if anyone else
had owned it. But the very fact that Varner had ever come
into possession of it and still kept it, apparently making no
effort to sell it or do anything else with it, was proof enough
for him. He declined to believe that Varner ever had been or
ever would be stuck with anything; that if he acquired it, he
got it cheaper than anyone else could have, and if he kept it, it
was too valuable to sell. In the case of the Old Frenchman
place he could not see why this was so, but the fact that
Varner had bought it and still had it was sufficient. So when
Varner finally did let it go, Ratliff believed it was because
Varner had at last got the price for which he had been holding
it for twenty years, or at least some sufficient price, whether it
was in money or not. And when he considered who Varner
had relinquished possession to, he believed that the price had
been necessity and not cash.

Varner knew that Ratliff was thinking it. He sat the old horse and looked down at Ratliff, the little hard eyes beneath their bushy rust-colored brows glinting at the man who was a good deal nearer his son in spirit and intellect and physical appearance too than any of his own get. "So you think pure liver aint going to choke that cat," he said.

"Maybe with that ere little piece of knotted-up string in it?" Ratliff said.

"What little piece of knotted-up string?"

"I dont know," Ratliff said.

"Hah," Varner said. "You going my way?"

"I reckon not," Ratliff said. "I'm going to mosey down to the store." Unless maybe he even feels he can set around it too again now, he thought.

"So am I," Varner said. "I got that damn trial this morning. That damn Jack Houston and that What's-his-name. Mink. About that durned confounded scrub yearling."

"You mean Houston sued him?" Ratliff said. *Houston?*"

"No no. Houston just kept the yearling up. He kept it up all last summer and Snopes let him pasture and feed it all winter, and it run in Houston's pasture all this spring and summer too. Then last week for some reason he decided to go and get it. I reckon he figured to beef it. So he went to Houston's with a rope. He was in Houston's pasture, trying to catch it, when Houston come up and stopped him. He finally had to draw his pistol, he claims. He says Snopes looked at the pistol and said, 'That's what you'll need. Because you know I aint got one.' And Houston said all right, they would lay the pistol on a fence-post and back off one post apiece on each side and count three and run for it."

"Why didn't they?" Ratliff said.

"Hah," Varner said shortly. "Come on. I want to get it over with. I got some business to tend to."

"You go on," Ratliff said. "I'll mosey on slow. I aint got no yearling calf nor trial neither today."

So the old fat clean horse (it looked always as if it had just come back from the dry-cleaner's; you could almost smell the benzine) moved on again, with a rich preliminary internal chord, going on along the gapped and weathered picket fence. Ratliff sat in the still-motionless buckboard and watched it and the lean, loose-jointed figure which, with the exception of the three-year runabout interval, had bestridden it, the same saddle between them, for twenty-five years, thinking how if, as dogs do, the white horse or his own two either had snuffed along that fence for yellow-wheeled buggies now, they would not have found them, thinking: *And all the other two-legged feice in this country between thirteen and eighty can pass here now without feeling no urge to stop and raise one of them against it.* And yet those buggies were still there. He could see them, sense them. Something was; it was too much to have vanished that quickly and completely—the air polluted and rich and fine which had flowed over and shaped that abundance and munificence, which had done the hydraulic office to that almost unbroken progression of chewed food, which had held intact the constant impact of those sixteen years of sitting down: so why should not that body at the last have been the unscalable sierra, the rosy virginal mother of barricades for no man to conquer scot-free or even to conquer at all, but on the contrary to be hurled back and down, leaving no scar, no mark of himself (*That ere child aint going to look no more like nobody this country ever saw than she did,* he thought.)—the buggy merely a part of the whole, a minor and trivial adjunct, like the buttons on her clothing, the clothes themselves, the cheap beads which one of the three of them had given her. That would never have been for him, not even at the prime summer peak of what he and Varner both would have called his tom-catting's heyday. He knew that without regret or grief, he would not have wanted it to be (*It would have been like giving me a pipe organ, that never had and never would know any more than how to wind up the second-hand music-box I had just swapped a mail-box for,* he thought.) and he even thought of the cold and froglike victor without jealousy: and this not because he knew that, regardless of whatever Snopes had expected or would have called what it was he now had, it would not be victory. What he felt was outrage at the waste, the useless squandering; at a situation intrinsically and inherently wrong by any economy, like building a log dead-fall and baiting it with a freshened heifer to catch a rat; or no, worse: as though the gods themselves had funnelled all the concentrated bright wet-slanted unparadised June onto a dung-heap, breeding pismires. Beyond the white horse, beyond the corner of the picket fence, the faint, almost overgrown lane turned off which led to the Old Frenchman place. The horse attempted to turn into it until Varner hauled it roughly back. Not to mention the poorhouse, Ratliff thought. But then, he wouldn't have been infested. He shook his own reins slightly. "Boys," he said, "advance."

The team, the buckboard, went on in the thick dust of the spent summer. Now he could see the village proper—the store, the blacksmith shop, the metal roof of the gin with a thin rapid shimmer of exhaust above the stack. It was now the third week in September; the dry, dust-laden air vibrated steadily to the rapid beat of the engine, though so close were the steam and the air in temperature that no exhaust was visible but merely a thin feverish shimmer of mirage. The very hot, vivid air, which seemed to be filled with the slow laborious plaint of laden wagons, smelled of lint; wisps of it clung among the dust-stiffened roadside weeds and small gouts of cotton lay imprinted by hoof- and wheel-marks into the trodden dust. He could see the wagons too, the long motionless line of them behind the patient, droop-headed mules, waiting to advance a wagon-length at a time, onto the scales and then beneath the suction-pipe where Jody Varner would now be again, what with a second new clerk in the store—the new clerk exactly like the old one but a little smaller, a little compacter, as if they had both been cut with the same die but in inverse order to appearance, the last first and after the edges of the die were dulled and spread a little—with his little, full, bright-pink mouth like a kitten's button and his bright, quick, amoral eyes like a chipmunk and his air of merry and incorrigible and unflagging conviction of the inherent constant active dishonesty of all men, including himself.

Jody Varner was at the scales; Ratliff craned his turkey's neck in passing and saw the heavy bagging broadcloth, the white collarless shirt with a yellow halfmoon of sweat at each armpit, the dusty, lint-wisped black hat. So I reckon maybe everybody is satisfied now, he thought. Or everybody except one, he added to himself because before he reached the store Will Varner came out of it and got onto the white horse which someone had just untied and held for him, and on the gallery beyond Ratliff now saw the eruption of men whose laden wagons stood along the road opposite, waiting for the scales, and as he drove up to the gallery in his turn, Mink Snopes and the other Snopes, the proverbist, the schoolteacher (he now wore a new frock coat which, for all its newness, looked no less like it belonged to him than the old one in which Ratliff had first seen him did) came down the steps. Ratliff saw the intractable face now cold and still with fury behind the single eyebrow; beside it the rodent's face of the teacher, the two of them seeming to pass him in a whirling of flung unco-ordinated hands and arms out of the new, black, swirling frock coat, the voice that, also like the gestures, seemed to be not servant but master of the body which supplied blood and wind to them:

"Be patient; Caesar never built Rome in one day; patience is the horse that runs steadiest; justice is the right man's bread but poison for the evil man if you give it time. I done looked the law up; Will Varner has misread it pure and simple. We'll take a appeal. We will—" until the other turned his furious face with its single violent emphasis of eyebrow upon him and said fiercely: "—t!" They went on. Ratliff moved up to the gallery. While he was tying his team, Houston came out, followed by the big hound, and mounted and rode away. Ratliff mounted to the gallery where now at least twenty men were gathered, Bookwright among them.

"The plaintiff seems to had legal talent," he said. "What was the verdict?"

"When Snopes pays Houston three dollars pasturage, he can get his bull," Quick said.

"Sho now," Ratliff said. "Wasn't his lawyer even allowed nothing by the court?"

"The lawyer was fined what looked like the considerable balance of one uncompleted speech," Bookwright said. "If that's what you want to know."

"Well well," Ratliff said. "Well well well. So Will couldn't do nothing to the next succeeding Snopes but stop him from talking. Not that anymore would have done any good. Snopes can come and Snopes can go, but Will Varner looks like he is fixing to snopes forever. Or Varner will Snopes forever—take your pick. What is it the fellow says? off with the old and on with the new; the old job at the old stand, maybe a new fellow doing the jobbing but it's the same old stern getting reamed out?" Bookwright was looking at him.

"If you would stand closer to the door, he could hear you a heap better," he said.

"Sholy," Ratliff said. "Big ears have little pitchers, the world beats a track to the rich man's hog-pen but it aint every family has a new lawyer, not to mention a prophet. Waste not want not, except that a full waist dont need no prophet to prophesy a profit and just whose." Now they were all watching him—the smooth, impenetrable face with something about the eyes and the lines beside the mouth which they could not read.

"Look here," Bookwright said. "What's the matter with you?"

"Why, nothing," Ratliff said. "What could be wrong with nothing nowhere nohow in this here best of all possible worlds? Likely the same folks that sells him the neckties will have a pair of long black stockings too. And any sign-painter can paint him a screen to set up alongside the bed to look like looking up at a wall full of store shelves of canned goods—"

"Here," Bookwright said.

"—so he can know to do what every man and woman that ever seen her between thirteen and Old Man Hundred-and-One McCallum has been thinking about for twenty-nine days now. Of course, he could fix it with a shed roof to climb up on and a window to crawl through too. But that aint necessary; that aint his way. No sir. This here man aint no trifling eave-cat. This here man—" A little boy of eight or ten came up, trotting, in overalls, and mounted the steps and gave them a quick glance out of eyes as blue and innocent as periwinkles and trotted intently into the store. "—this here man that all he needs is just to set back there in the store until after a while one comes in to get a nickel's worth of lard, not buy it: come and ax Mr Snopes for it, and he gives it to her and writes in a book about it and her not knowing no more about what he wrote in that book and why than she does how that ere lard got into that tin bucket with the picture of a hog on it that even she can tell is a hog, and he puts the bucket back and puts the book away and goes and shuts the door and puts the bar up and she has done already went around behind the counter and laid down on the floor because maybe she thinks by now that's what you have to do, not to pay for the lard because that's done already been wrote down in the book, but to get out of that door again—" The new clerk appeared suddenly among them. He bounced out of the store, his features all seeming to hasten into the center of his face in a fierce depthless glare of bright excitement, the little periwinkle-eyed boy trotting intently around him and on down the steps without waiting.

"All right, boys," the clerk said rapidly, tensely. "He's started. You better hurry. I cant go this time. I got to stay here. Kind of make a swing around from the back so old Littlejohn cant see you. She's done already begun to look cross-eyed." Five or six men had already risen, with a curious, furtive, defiant sort of alacrity. They began to leave the gallery. The little boy was now trotting indefatiguably along the fence which enclosed the end of Mrs Littlejohn's lot.

"What's this?" Ratliff said.

"Come on, if you aint seen it yet," one of the departing men said.

"Seen what?" Ratliff said. He looked about at the ones who had not risen. Bookwright was one of them. He was whittling steadily and deeply into a stick of white pine, his face lowered.

"Go on, go on," a second said behind the man who had paused on the steps. "It'll be over before we get there." The group went on then. Ratliff watched them too hurry along Mrs Littlejohn's lot fence after the little boy, still with that curiously furtive defiance.

"What's this you all have got here now?" he said.

"Go and see it," Bookwright said harshly. He did not look up from his knife. Ratliff looked at him.

"Have you seen it?"

"No."

"You going to?"

"No."

"You know what it is?"

"Go on and see it," Bookwright said again, harshly and violently.

"It looks like I'll have to, since aint nobody going to tell me," Ratliff said. He moved toward the steps. The group was now well on ahead, hurrying along the fence. Ratliff began to descend. He was still talking. He continued to talk as he went down the steps, not looking back; nobody could have told whether he was actually talking to the men behind him or not, if he was talking to anyone or not: "—goes and puts the bar up on the inside and comes back and this here black brute from the field with the field sweat still drying on her that she dont know it's sweat she smells because she aint never smelled nothing else, just like a mule dont know it's mule he smells for the same reason, and the one garment to her name and that's the one she's laying there on the floor behind the counter in and looking up past him at them rows of little tight cans with fishes and devils on them that she dont know what's on the inside either because she aint never had the dime or the fifteen cents that even if he was to give her the nickel, not to mention the lard she come after, she would have after the next two or three times she come after lard, but just heard somewhere one day the name of what folks said was inside them, laying there and looking up at them every time his head would get out of the way long enough, and says, 'Mr Snopes, whut you ax fer dem sardines?' "

2.

As winter became spring and the spring itself advanced, he had less and less of darkness to flee through and from. Soon it was dark only when he left the barn, backed carefully, with one down-groping foot, from the harness-room where his quilt-and-straw bed was, and turned his back on the long rambling loom of the house where last night's new drummer-faces snored on the pillows of the beds which he had now learned to make as well as Mrs Littlejohn could; by April it was the actual thin depthless suspension of false dawn itself, in which he could already see and know himself to be an entity solid and cohered in visibility instead of the uncohered all-sentience of fluid and nerve-springing terror alone and terribly free in the primal sightless inimicality. That was gone now. Now the terror existed only during that moment after the false dawn, that interval's second between it and the moment which birds and animals know: when the night at last succumbs to day; and then he would begin to hurry, trot, not to get there quicker but because he must get back soon, without fear and calmly now in the growing visibility, the gradation from gray through primrose to the morning's ultimate gold, to the brow of the final hill, to let himself downward into the creekside mist and lie in the drenched myriad waking life of grasses and listen for her approach.

Then he would hear her, coming down the creekside in the mist. It would not be after one hour, two hours, three; the dawn would be empty, the moment and she would not be, then he would hear her and he would lie drenched in the wet grass, serene and one and indivisible in joy, listening to her approach. He would smell her; the whole mist reeked with her; the same malleate hands of mist which drew along his prone drenched flanks palped her pearled barrel too and shaped them both somewhere in immediate time, already married. He would not move. He would lie amid the waking instant of earth's teeming minute life, the motionless fronds of water-heavy grasses stooping into the mist before his face in black, fixed curves, along each parabola of which the marching drops held in minute magnification the dawn's rosy miniatures, smelling and even tasting the rich, slow, warm barn-reek milk-reek, the flowing immemorial female, hearing the slow planting and the plopping suck of each deliberate cloven mud-spreading hoof, invisible still in the mist loud with its hymeneal choristers.

Then he would see her; the bright thin horns of morning, of sun, would blow the mist away and reveal her, planted, blond, dew-pearled, standing in the parted water of the ford, blowing into the water the thick, warm, heavy, milk-laden breath; and lying in the drenched grasses, his eyes now blind with sun, he would wallow faintly from thigh to thigh, making a faint, thick, hoarse moaning sound. Because he cannot make one with her through the day's morning and noon and evening. It is not that he must return to work. There is no work, no travail, no muscular and spiritual reluctance to over-

come, constantly war against; yesterday was not, tomorrow is
not, today is merely a placid and virginal astonishment at the
creeping ridge of dust and trash in front of the broom, at
sheets coming smooth and taut at certain remembered motions of the hands—a routine grooved, irkless; a firm gentle
compelling hand, a voice to hold and control him through joy
out of kindness as a dog is taught and held.

It is because he can go no further. He tried it. It was the
third time he lay and waited for her; the mist blew away and
he saw her and this time there was no today even—no beds
to return to, no hand, no voice: he repudiated fidelity and
even habit. He rose and approached her, speaking to her, his
hand extended. She raised her head and looked at him and
scrambled up the further bank, out of the water. He followed,
stepping gingerly down into the water, and began to cross,
lifting his feet high at each step, moaning a little, urgent and
concerned yet not to alarm her more. He fell once, at full
length into the water, making no effort to catch himself, vanishing completely with one loud cry and rising again, streaming, his breath already indrawn to cry again. But he stopped
the cry, speaking to her instead, and climbed out onto the
bank and approached her again, his hand extended. This time
she ran, rushed on a short distance and turned, her head lowered; she whirled and rushed away again before his hand
touched her, he following, speaking to her, urgent and cajoling. Finally she broke back past him and went back to the
ford. She ran faster than he could; trotting, moaning, he
watched the vain stippling of leaf-shadows as they fled across
the intact and escaping shape of love as she recrossed the
creek and galloped on up the path for a short way, where
once more she stopped to graze.

He ceased to moan. He hurried back to the creek and began to cross it, lifting his feet high out of the water at each
step as if he expected each time to find solidity there, or perhaps at each step did not know whether he would or not.
This time he did not fall. But as soon as he climbed the bank,
she moved again, on up the path, not galloping now but
purposefully, so that he once more had to run, once more
steadily losing ground, moaning again now with that urgent
and now alarmed and bewildered amazement. She was now

retracing the path by which she had appeared that morning and all the other mornings. Probably he did not even know it, was paying no attention at all to where he was going, seeing nothing but the cow; perhaps he did not even realise they were in the lot, even when she went on across it and entered the milking shed which she had left less than an hour ago, though he probably knew generally where she would come from each morning, since he knew most of the adjacent countryside and was never disoriented: objects became fluid in darkness but they did not alter in place and juxtaposition. Perhaps he did not even comprehend that she was in her stable, in any stable, but only that she had stopped at last, ceased to flee at last, because at once he stopped the alarmed and urgent moaning and followed her into the shed, speaking to her again, murmurous, drooling, and touched her with his hand. She whirled; possibly he saw, not that she could not, but only that she did not flee. He touched her again, his hand, his voice, thin and hungry with promise. Then he was lying on his back, her heels were still thudding against the plank wall beside his head and then the dog was standing over him and an instant later the man was hauling him savagely to his feet by the slack of his shirt. Then he was outside the shed while Houston still clutched him by the shirt and cursed in what he could not know was not rage but angry exasperation. The dog stood a few feet away, watching.

"Ike H-mope," he said. "Ike H-mope."

"Ike hell," Houston said, cursing, shaking him. "Go on!" he said. "Git!" He spoke to the dog. "Take him out of here. Easy, now." Now the dog shouted at him. It did not move yet, it merely shouted once; it was as if it said "Boo!" and, still moaning, trying now to talk to the man with his blasted eyes, he moved on toward the still-open gate which he had just entered. Now the dog moved too, just behind him. He looked back at the shed, the cow; he tried again to speak to the man with his eyes, moaning, drooling, when the dog shouted at him again, once, taking one pace toward him but no more, whereupon he gave the dog one terrified glance and broke, trotting toward the gate. The dog shouted again, three times in rapid succession, and he cried now, hoarse and abject, running now, the thick reluctant hips working with a sort of abject and hopeless unco-ordination. "Easy, now!" Houston shouted. He did not hear. He heard only the feet of the dog just behind him. He ran heavily, bellowing.

So now he can go no further. He can lie in the grass and wait for her and hear her and then see her when the mist parts, and that is all. So he would rise from the grass and stand, still swaying faintly from side to side and making the faint, hoarse sound. Then he would turn and mount the hill, stumbling a little because his eyes were still full of sun yet. But his bare feet would know the dust of the road, and in it again, he would begin to trot again, hurrying, still moaning, his shadow shortening on the dust ahead and the mounting sun warm on his back and already drying the dust on his damp overalls; and so back to the house, the littered rooms and the unmade beds. Soon he would be sweeping again, stopping only occasionally to make the hoarse sound of baf-flement and incredulous grieving, then watching again with peaceful and absorbed astonishment the creeping ridge of dust and trash before the moving broom. Because even while sweeping he would still see her, blond among the purpling shadows of the pasture, not fixed amid the suppurant tender green but integer of spring's concentrated climax, by it crowned, garlanded.

He was upstairs sweeping when he saw the smoke. He knew exactly where it was—the hill, the sedge-and-brier over-grown hill beyond the creek. Although it was three miles away, he can even see her backing away before the flames and hear her bellowing. He began to run where he stood, carrying the broom. He ran blundering at the wall, the high small win-dow through which he had seen the smoke, which he could not have passed through even if he could have taken the eighteen-foot drop to the earth, as a moth or a trapped bird might. Then the corridor door was facing him and without pausing he ran to it and through it, still carrying the broom, and on down the corridor toward the stairs, when Mrs Little-john emerged from a second bedroom and stopped him. "You, Isaac," she said. "You, Isaac." She did not raise her voice and she did not touch him, yet he stopped, moaning, the empty eyes striving at her, picking his feet up in turn like a cat standing on something hot. Then she put her hand out and took him by the shoulder and turned him and he went obediently back up the corridor and into the room again, moaning; he even made a stroke or two with the broom before he saw the smoke again through the window. This time he found the corridor door almost at once, though he did not approach it. Instead he stood for a moment, looking at the broom in his hands, whimpering, then at the bed, smooth and neat where he had just made it up, and he stopped whimpering and went to the bed and turned the covers back and put the broom into it, the straw end on the pillow like a face, and drew the covers up smooth again, tucking them about the broom with that paradoxical unco-ordinated skill and haste, and left the room.

He made no sound now. He did not move on tiptoe, yet he went down the corridor with astonishing silence and celerity; he had reached the stairs and begun to descend before Mrs Littlejohn could have emerged from the other room. At first, three years ago, he would not try to descend them. He had ascended them alone; nobody ever knew if he had walked or crawled up, or if perhaps he had mounted them without realising he was doing so, altering his position in altitude, depth perception not functioning in reverse. Mrs Littlejohn had gone to the store. Someone passing the house heard him and when she returned there were five or six people in the hall, looking up at where he clung to the rail at the top step, his eyes shut, bellowing. He still clung to the rail, bellowing and tugging back, when she tried to break his grip and draw him downward. He stayed upstairs three days while she carried food to him and people would come in from miles away and say, "Aint you got him down yet?" before she finally coaxed him to attempt to descend. And even then it took several minutes, while faces gathered in the lower hall to watch as the firm, gentle, unremitting hand, the cold, grim, patient voice, drew him, clinging to the rail and bellowing, step by step downward. For a while after that he would fall down them each time he tried to descend. He would know he was going to fall; he would step blindly and already moaning onto nothing and plunge, topple, sprawling and bumping, terrified not by pain but by amazement, to lie at last on the floor of the lower hall, bellowing, his blasted eyes staring aghast and incredulous at nothing.

But at last he learned to negotiate them. Now he merely slowed a little before stepping, not confidently quite but not with alarm, off onto that which at each successive step, was not quite space; was almost nothing but at each advancing instant, not quite was, and hurried on through the lower hall and into the back yard, where he paused again and began to sway from side to side and moan, his empty face now filled with baffled bewilderment. Because he could not see the smoke from here and now all he remembers is the empty dawn-hill from which he will let himself downward into the creekside mist to wait for her, and it is wrong now. Because he stands in sun, visible—himself, earth, trees, house— already cohered and fixed in visibility; no darkness to flee through and from, and this is wrong. So he stood, baffled, moaning and swaying for a time, then he moved again, across the yard to the lot gate. He had learned to open it too. He turned the catch and the gate vanished from between its two posts; he passed through and after a moment he found the gate where it had swung to against the fence and closed it and turned the latch and went on across the sun-glared lot, moaning, and entered the hallway of the stable.

Because of his sun-contracted pupils, he could not see at once. But then, it always was dark when he entered the stable on his way to bed, so at once he ceased to moan and went straight to the door to the harness-room, moving now with actual assurance, and grasped the door-jamb with both hands and raised his foot to the step, and, his down-groping foot already on the ground, he backed out of darkness and into visibility, turning, visibility roaring soundless down about him, establishing him intact and cohered in it and already trotting, running, toward the crest where he will let himself downward into the creekside mist to lie and wait for her, on across the lot and through the spread place in the wire fence. His overalls snagged on the wire but he ripped free, making no sound now, and into the road, running, his thick female thighs working, his face, his eyes, urgent and alarmed.

When he reached the hill three miles away, he was still trotting; when he turned from the road and mounted to the crest of the hill and saw the smoke beyond the creek, he made the hoarse, aghast sound again and ran on down the hill and through the now-dry grass in which at dawn he had lain, and to the creek, the ford. He did not hesitate. He ran full-tilt off the bank and onto the rimpled water, continuing to run even after he began to fall, plunging face-down into the water, completely submerged, and rose, streaming, knee-deep, bellowing. He lifted one foot above the surface and stepped forward as though onto a raised floor and took another step running before he fell. This time his outflung hands touched the further bank and this time when he rose he actually heard the cow's voice, faint and terrified, from beyond the smoke-pall on the other hill. He raised one foot above the surface and ran again. When he fell this time he lay on dry land. He scrambled up and ran in his sodden overalls, across the pasture and on up the other hill, on whose crest the smokepall lay without wind, grading from blue to delicate mauve and lilac and then copper beneath the meridional sun.

A mile back he had left the rich, broad, flat river-bottom country and entered the hills—a region which typographically was the final blue and dying echo of the Appalachian mountains. Chickasaw Indians had owned it, but after the Indians it had been cleared where possible for cultivation, and after the Civil War, forgotten save by small peripatetic sawmills which had vanished too now, their sites marked only by the mounds of rotting sawdust which were not only their gravestones but the monuments of a people's heedless greed. Now it was a region of scrubby second-growth pine and oak among which dogwood bloomed until it too was cut to make cotton spindles, and old fields where not even a trace of furrow showed any more, gutted and gullied by forty years of rain and frost and heat into plateaus choked with rank sedge and briers loved of rabbits and quail coveys, and crumbling ravines striated red and white with alternate sand and clay. It was toward one of these plateaus that he now ran, running in ashes without knowing it since the earth here had had time to cool, running among the blackened stubble of last year's sedge dotted with small islands of this year's incombustible green and the blasted heads of tiny blue-and-white daisies, and so onto the crest of the hill, the plateau.

The smoke lay like a wall before him; beyond it he could hear the steady terrified bellowing of the cow. He ran into the smoke and toward the voice. The earth was now hot to his feet. He began to snatch them quickly up; he cried once himself, hoarse and amazed, whereupon, as though in answer, the smoke, the circumambience itself, screamed back at him. The sound was everywhere, above and beneath, funnelling downward at him; he heard the hooves and as he paused, his breath indrawn, the horse appeared, materialised furiously out of the smoke, monstrous and distorted, wild-eyed and with tossing mane, bearing down upon him. He screamed too. For an instant they yelled face to face, the wild eyes, the yellow teeth, the long gullet red with ravening gleeful triumph, stooping at him and then on as the horse swerved without breaking, the wind, the fierce dragon-reek of its passage, blasting at his hair and garments; it was gone. He ran again toward the cow's voice. When he heard the horse behind him again he did not even look back. He did not even scream again. He just ran, running, as again the earth, the smoke, filled and became thunderous with the hard, rapid hoofbeats and again the intolerable voice screamed down at him and he flung both arms about his head and fell sprawling as the wind, the dragon-reek, blasted at him again as the maddened horse soared over his prone body and vanished once more.

He scrambled up and ran. The cow was quite near now and now he saw the fire—a tender, rosy, creeping thread low in the smoke between him and the location of the cow's voice. Each time his feet touched the earth now he gave a short shriek like an ejaculation, trying to snatch his foot back before it could have taken his weight, then turning immediately in aghast amazement to the other foot which he had for the moment forgotten, so that presently he was not progressing at all but merely moving in one spot, like a dance, when he heard the horse coming at him again. He screamed. His voice and that of the horse became one voice, wild, furious and without hope, and he ran into and through the fire and burst into air, sun, visibility again, shedding flames which sucked away behind him like a tattered garment. The cow stood at the edge of a ravine about ten feet away, facing the fire, her head low-ered, bellowing. He had just time to reach her and turn, his body intervened and his arms about his head, as the frantic horse burst out of the smoke and bore down upon them.

It did not even swerve. It took off almost without gather-ing, at full stride. The teeth, the wild eyes, the long red gullet, stooped at him, framed out of a swirled rigidity of forelock and mane, the entire animal floating overhead in monstrous deliberation. The air was filled with furious wings and the four crescent-glints of shod hooves as, still screaming, the horse vanished beyond the ravine's lip, sucking first the cow and then himself after it as though by the violent vacuum of its passing. Earth became perpendicular and fled upward— the yawn of void without even the meretricious reassurance of graduated steps. He made no sound as the three of them plunged down the crumbling sheer, at the bottom of which the horse rolled to its feet without stopping and galloped on down the ditch and where he, lying beneath the struggling and bellowing cow, received the violent relaxing of her fear-constricted bowels. Overhead, in the down draft of the ra-vine, the last ragged flame tongued over the lip, tip-curled, and vanished, swirled off into the windless stain of pale smoke on the sunny sky.

At first he couldn't do anything with her at all. She scram-bled to her feet, facing him, her head lowered, bellowing. When he moved toward her, she whirled and ran at the crum-bling sheer of the slope, scrambling furiously at the vain and shifting sand as though in a blind paroxysm of shame, to es-cape not him alone but the very scene of the outragement of privacy where she had been sprung suddenly upon and with-out warning from the dark and betrayed and outraged by her own treacherous biological inheritance, he following again, speaking to her, trying to tell her how this violent violation of her maiden's delicacy is no shame, since such is the very iron imperishable warp of the fabric of love. But she would not hear. She continued to scrabble at the shifting rise, until at last he set his shoulder to her hams and heaved forward. Striving together, they mounted for a yard or so up the slope, the sand shifting and fleeing beneath their feet, before mo-mentum and strength were spent and, locked together and motionless, they descended once more to the floor of the ditch, planted and fixed ankle-deep in a moving block of sand like two effigies on a float. Again, his shoulder to her hams, they rushed at the precipice and up it for a yard or more before the treacherous footing completely failed. He spoke to her, exhortative; they made a supreme effort. But again the earth fled upward; footing, sand and all plucked violently from beneath them and rushed upward into the pale sky still faintly stained with smoke, and once more they lay inextricable and struggling on the floor of the ravine, he once more underneath, until, bellowing and never ceasing her mad thrashing, the cow scrambled up and galloped on down the ditch as the horse had done, vanishing before he could get to his feet to follow.

The ravine debouched onto the creek. Almost at once he was in the pasture again, though possibly he did not realise it, seeing only the cow as she galloped on ahead. Possibly at the moment he did not even recognise the ford at once, even when the cow, slowing, walked down into the water and stopped and drank and he ran up, slowing too, moaning, urgent but not loud, not to send her once more in to flight. So he approaches the bank, stilling his voice now, picking his feet up and putting them down again in one spot, his singed and scorched face urgent and tense. But she does not move, and at last he steps down into the water, onto the water, forgetting again that it will give under his weight, crying once again not so much in surprise as in alarm lest he alarm her, and steps again forward onto the receptive solid, and touches her. She does not even stop drinking; his hand has lain on her flank for a second or two before she lifts her dripping muzzle and looks back at him, once more maiden meditant, shamefree.

Houston found them there. He came across the pasture on the horse, bareback, galloping, the hound following, and saw the thick squatting shape in the water behind the cow, clumsily washing her legs with a broken willow branch. "Is she all right?" he shouted, speaking to the horse to slow it since he did not even have a hackamore: "Whoa. Whoa. Ho now. Ho now, damn you.—Why in hell didn't you try to catch the horse?" he shouted. "He might have broke—" Then the other, squatting in the water, turned his scorched face and Houston recognised him. He began to curse, checking the horse with his hand in its mane, already flinging his leg over and sliding down before the horse stopped, cursing with that fretted exasperation which was not anger, rage. He came to the creek, the hound following, and stooped and caught up a dried limb left from last winter's flood water and slashed the cow savagely with it and flung the broken end after her as she sprang forward and scrambled up the further bank. "Git!" Houston shouted. "Git on home, you damn whore!" The cow galloped on a few steps, then stopped and began to graze. "Take her home," Houston said to the dog. Without moving, only raising its head, the hound bayed once. The cow jerked her head up and trotted again, and he in the creek made again his faint hoarse sound, rising too as the hound rose. But the dog did not even cross the creek, it did not even hurry; it merely followed the bank until it came opposite the cow and bayed again, once, contemptuous and peremptory. This time the cow went off at a gallop, back up the creek toward the lot, the hound following on its side of the creek. They went out of sight so. Twice more at intervals the hound bayed, one time, as though it merely shouted "Boo!" each time the cow prepared to stop.

He stood in the water, moaning. Now he actually bellowed himself, not loud, just amazed. When Houston and the dog came up he had looked around, at first at the dog. His mouth had opened to cry then, but instead there had come into his face an expression almost intelligent in its foolish fatuity, which, when Houston began to curse, faded and became one of incredulity, amazement, and which was still incredulous and bereft as he stood in the water, moaning, while Houston on the bank looked at the stained foul front of his overalls, cursing with that baffled exasperation, saying, "Jesus Christ. Jesus Christ.—Come here," he said. "Get out of there;" gesturing his arm savagely. But the other did not move, moaning, looking away up the creek where the cow had gone, until Houston came to the edge and leaned and caught him by the strap of his overalls and drew him roughly out of the water and, his nose wrinkled fiercely and still cursing, unfastened the straps and snatched the overalls down about his hips.

"Step out!" Houston said. But he did not move until Houston jerked him, stumbling, out of the overalls, to stand in his shirt and nothing else, moaning faintly, though when Houston picked up the overalls gingerly by the strap and flung them into the creek, he cried again, once, hoarse, abject, not loud. "Go on," Houston said. "Wash them." He made violent washing motions in pantomime. But the other only looked at Houston, moaning, until Houston found another stick and twisted it into the overalls and soused and walloped them violently in the water, cursing steadily, and drew them out and, still using the stick, scrubbed them front-down on the grass. "There," he said. "Now git! Home! Home!" he shouted. "Stay there! Let her alone!" He had stopped moaning to watch Houston. Now he began to moan again, drooling, while Houston glared at him in baffled and raging exasperation. Then Houston took a handful of coins from his pocket and chose a fifty-cent piece and came and put it into his shirt pocket and buttoned the flap and went back to the horse, speaking to it until he touched it, grasped it by the mane, and vaulted onto its back. He had stopped moaning now, he just watched as, again without seeming to gather itself, just as when it had soared above him and the cow on the edge of the ravine an hour ago, the horse made two short circles under Houston's hand and then took the creek cleanly, already galloping, and was gone.

Then he began to moan again. He stood for a while, moaning, looking down at the shirt pocket which Houston had buttoned, fumbling at it. Then he looked at his soaked and wadded overalls on the ground beside him. After a while he stooped and picked them up. One leg was turned wrong-side-outward. He tried patiently for a while to put them on so, moaning. Then presently they came straight again and he got into them and fastened the straps and went to the creek and crossed, moving gingerly, raising his foot at each step as if he were mounting onto a raised floor, and climbed out and went back to the place where he had lain at each dawn for three months now, waiting for her. It was the same spot; he would return as exactly to it each time as a piston to its cylinder-head, and he stood there for a time, fumbling at the buttoned pocket, moaning. Then he went on up the hill; his feet knew the dust of the road again though perhaps he himself was unaware of it, possibly it was pure instinct functioning in the desolation of bereavement which carried him back toward the house which he had left that morning, because twice more in the first mile he stopped and fumbled at the buttoned pocket. Apparently he was not trying to unbutton the pocket without being able to do it, because presently he had the coin in his hand, looking at it, moaning. He was standing then on a plank bridge over a narrow, shallow, weed-choked ditch. He made no false motion with the hand which held the coin, he had made no motion of any kind, he was standing perfectly still at the moment, yet suddenly his palm was empty. The coin rang dully once on the dusty planks and perhaps glinted once, then vanished, though who to know what motion, infinitesimal and convulsive, of supreme repudiation there might have been, its impulse gone, vanished with the movement, because he even ceased to moan as he stood looking at his empty palm with quiet amazement, turning the hand over to look at the back, even raising and opening the other hand to look into it. Then—it was an effort almost physical, like childbirth—he connected two ideas, he progressed backward into time and recaptured an image by logical retrogression and fumbled into the shirt pocket again, peering into it, though only for a moment, as if he actually did not expect to find the coin there, though it was doubtless pure instinct which caused him to look down at the dusty planks on which he stood. And he was not moaning. He made no sound at all. He just stood there, looking at the planks, lifting his feet in turn; when he stepped off the bridge and into the ditch, he fell. You could not have told if he did step off intentionally or if he fell off, though it was doubtless a continuation of the instinct, the inherited constant awareness of gravity, which caused him to look under the bridge for the coin—if he were looking for it as he squatted in the weeds, bobbing his head faintly yet still making no sound. From then on he made no sound at all. He squatted for a time, pulling at the weeds, and now even the paradoxical dexterity was missing from his movements, even the dexterity which caused his hands to function at other times as though in spite of him; watching him you would have said he did not want to find the coin.

And then you would have said, known, that he did not intend
to find it; when after a time a wagon came up the road and
crossed the bridge and the driver spoke to him, when he
raised his face it was not even empty, it was unfathomable
and profoundly quiet; when the man spoke his name, he did
not even reply with the one sound which he knew, or at least
was ever known to make, and that infallibly when anyone
spoke to him.

He did not move until the wagon was out of sight, though
he was not watching it. Then he rose and climbed back into
the road. He was already trotting, back in the direction from
which he had just come, treading his own tracks into the hot
dust of the road beneath the May noon, back to where he
would leave the road to mount the hill, and crossed the hill
again and trotted down the slope to the creek. He passed the
place where he would lie in the wet grass each dawn without
even looking at it and turned on up the creek, trotting. It was
then about two oclock Saturday afternoon. He could not have
known that at that hour and day Houston, a childless widower who lived alone with the hound and a negro man to
cook for them both, would already be sitting on the gallery of
Varner's store three miles away; he could not have thought
that maybe Houston would not be at home. Certainly he did
not pause to find out. He entered the lot, trotting, he went
straight to the closed door of the shed. There was a halter
hanging from a nail beside it. Perhaps he merely put his hand
on the halter by chance in fumbling at the latch. But he put it
on the cow properly, as he had seen it done.

At six oclock that afternoon they were five miles away. He
did not know it was that distance. It did not matter; there is
no distance in either space or geography, no prolongation of
time for distance to exist in, no muscular fatigue to establish
its accomplishment. They are moving not toward a destination in space but a destination in time, toward the pinnacle-
keep of evening where morning and afternoon become one;
the sleight hand of May shapes them both, not in the immediate, the soon, but in the now as, facing her, braced against
the pull of the rope, he speaks to her implacable and compelling while she tugged back, shaking her head against the rope
and bellowing. She had been doing this for the last half hour,

drawn backward and barnward by the discomfort of her bag. But he held her, slacking the rope gradually until his other hand touched her, first her head then her neck, speaking to her until the resistance went out of her and she moved on again. They were in the hills now, among pines. Although the afternoon wind had fallen, the shaggy crests still made a constant murmuring sound in the high serene air. The trunks and the massy foliage were the harps and strings of afternoon; the barred inconstant shadow of the day's retrograde flowed steadily over them as they crossed the ridge and descended into shadow, into the azure bowl of evening, the windless well of night; the portcullis of sunset fell behind them. At first she would not let him touch her bag at all. Even then she kicked him once, but only because the hands were strange and clumsy. Then the milk came down, warm among his fingers and on his hands and wrists, making a thin sharp hissing on the earth.

There was a moon at that time. It waned nightly westward; juxtaposed to it, each dawn the morning star burned in fierce white period to the night, and he would smell the waking's instant as she would rise, hindquarters first, backing upward out of invisibility, attenuating then disseminating out of the nest-form of sleep, the smell of milk. Then he would rise too and tie the rope-end to a swinging branch and seek and find the basket by the smell of the feed which it contained last night, and depart. From the edge of the woods he would look back. She would be still invisible, but he could hear her; it is as though he can see her—the warm breath visible among the tearing roots of grass, the warm reek of the urgent milk a cohered shape amid the fluid and abstract earth.

The barn is less than a half-mile away. Soon it looms, forth-right and square upon the scroll and cryptogram of heaven. The dog meets him at the fence, not barking, furrowing invisibility somewhere between sight and sound, moving completely in neither. On the first morning it rushed at him, yapping furiously. He stopped then. Perhaps he remembered that other dog five miles away, but only for a moment, since such is succeeding's success, such is that about victory which out-odors the betraying stink of all past defeats: so that now it comes up to him already fawning, invisible and fluid about his walking legs, its warm wet limber tongue shaping for him out of invisibility his own swinging hand.

In the ammoniac density of the barn, filled with the waking dawn-sounds of horses and cattle, he cannot even sense space. But he does not hesitate. He finds the crib door and enters; his sightless hand which knows and remembers finds the feed-box. He sets the basket down and begins to fill it, working steadily and fast, spilling half of what his cupped hands raise, as on the two preceding mornings establishing between feed-box and basket the agent of his own betrayal. When he rises and faces the door, he can see it now, gray, lighter in tone yet paradoxically no more luminous, as if a rectangle of opaque glass had been set into nothing's self while his back was turned, to further confound obscurity. And now he becomes aware of the birds. The cattle-sounds are louder now, constant; he can actually see the dog waiting in the stable door and he knows that he should hurry, since he knows that soon someone will come to feed and milk. So he leaves the crib, pausing for a moment in the door before descending as though he were listening, breathing in the reek, the odor of cows and mares as the successful lover does that of a room full of women, his the victor's drowsing rapport with all anonymous faceless female flesh capable of love walking the female earth.

He and the dog recross the lot together in the negative dawn-wash cacophonous and loud with birds. He can see the fence now, where the dog leaves him. He climbs through the fence, hurrying now, carrying the basket awkwardly before him in both arms, leaving in the wet grass a dark fixed wake. Now he watches the recurrence of that which he discovered for the first time three days ago: that dawn, light, is not decanted onto earth from the sky, but instead is from the earth itself suspired. Roofed by the woven canopy of blind annealing grass-roots and the roots of trees, dark in the blind dark of time's silt and rich refuse—the constant and unslumbering anonymous worm-glut and the inextricable known bones—Troy's Helen and the nymphs and the snoring mitred bishops, the saviors and the victims and the kings—it wakes, upseeping, attritive in uncountable creeping channels: first, root; then frond by frond, from whose escaping tips like gas it rises and disseminates and stains the sleep-fast earth with drowsy insect-murmur; then, still upward-seeking, creeps the knitted bark of trunk and limb where, suddenly louder leaf by leaf and dispersive in diffusive sudden speed, melodious with the winged and jeweled throats, it upward bursts and fills night's globed negation with jonquil thunder. Far below, the gauzy hemisphere treads with herald-cock, and sty and pen and byre salute the day. Vanes on steeples groove the south-west wind, and fields for plowing, since sunset married to the bedded and unhorsed plow, spring into half-furrowed sight like the slumbering half-satiate sea. Then the sun itself: within the half-mile it overtakes him. The silent copper roar fires the drenched grass and flings long before him his shadow prone for the vain eluded treading; the earth mirrors his antic and constant frustration which soars up the last hill and, motionless in the void, hovers until he himself crests over, whereupon it drops an invisible bridge across the ultimate ebb of night and, still preceding him, leaps visible once more across the swale and touches the copse itself, shortening into the nearing leafy wall, head: shoulders: hips: and then the trotting legs, until at last it stands upright upon the mazy whimple of the windy leaves for one intact inconstant instant before he runs into and through it.

She stands as he left her, tethered, chewing. Within the mild enormous moist and pupilless globes he sees himself in twin miniature mirrored by the inscrutable abstraction; one with that which Juno might have looked out with, he watches himself contemplating what those who looked at Juno saw. He sets the basket before her. She begins to eat. The shifting shimmer of incessant leaves gives to her a quality of illusion as insubstantial as the prone negative of his late hurrying, but this too is not so: one blond touch stipulates and affirms both weight and mass out of the flowing shadow-maze; a hand's breadth of contact shapes her solid and whole out of the infinity of hope. He squats beside her and begins to draw the teats.

They eat from the basket together. He has eaten feed before—hulls and meal, and oats and raw corn and silage and pig-swill, never much at one time but more or less constantly while he is awake as birds do, eating not even very much of the filled plate which Mrs Littlejohn would set for him, leaving it less than half-emptied, then an hour later eating something else, anything else, things which the weary long record of shibboleth and superstition had taught his upright kind to call filth, neither liking nor disliking the taste of any thing save that of certain kinds of soil and the lime in old plaster and the dissolved ink in chewed newspapers and the formic acid of stinging ants, making but one discrimination: he is herbivorous, even the life he eats is the life of plants. Then he removed the basket. It was not empty. It contained yet almost to the measured ounce exactly half of the original feed, but he takes it away from her, drags it from beneath the swinging muzzle which continues to chew out of the center of surprise, and hangs it over a limb, who is learning fast now, who has learned success and then precaution and secrecy and how to steal and even providence; who has only lust and greed and bloodthirst and a moral conscience to keep him awake at night, yet to acquire.

They go first to the spring. He found it on the first day—a brown creep of moisture in a clump of alder and beech, sunless, which wandered away without motion among the unsunned roots of other alders and willows. He cleaned it out and scooped a basin for it, which now at each return of light stood full and clear and leaf by leaf repeating until they lean and interrupt the green reflections and with their own drinking faces break each's mirroring, each face to its own shattered image wedded and annealed. Then he rises and takes up the rope, and they go on across the swale, toward the woods, and enter them.

Dawn is now over. It is now bald and forthright day. The sun is well up the sky. The air is still loud with birds, but the cries are no longer the mystery's choral strophe and antistrophe rising vertical among the leafed altars, but are earth-parallel, streaking the lateral air in prosaic busy accompanyment to the prosaic business of feeding. They dart in ceaseless arrowings, tinted and electric, among the pines whose shaggy crests murmur dry and incessant in the high day wind. Now he slacks the rope; from now until evening they will advance only as the day itself advances, no faster. They have the same destination: sunset. They pursue it as the sun itself does and within the compass of one single immutable horizon. They pace the ardent and unheeding sun, themselves unheeding and without ardor among the shadows of the soaring trunks which are the sun-geared ratchet-spokes which wheel the axled earth, powerful and without haste, up out of the caverns of darkness, through dawn and morning and mid-morning, and on toward and at last into the slowing neap of noon, the flood, the slack of peak and crown of light garlanding all within one single coronet the fallen and unregenerate seraphim. The sun is a yellow column, perpendicular. He bears it on his back as, stooping with that thick, reluctant unco-ordination of thigh and knee, he gathers first the armful of lush grass, then the flowers. They are the bright blatant wild daisies of flamboyant summer's spendthrift beginning. At times his awkward and disobedient hand, instead of breaking the stem, merely shuts about the escaping stalk and strips the flower-head into a scatter of ravished petals. But before he reaches the windless noon-bound shade in which she stands, he has enough of them. He has more than enough; if he had only gathered two of them, there would have been too many: he lays the plucked grass before her, then out of the clumsy fumbling of the hands there emerges, already in dissolution, the abortive diadem. In the act of garlanding, it disintegrates, rains down the slant of brow and chewing head; fodder and flowers become one inexhaustible rumination. From the sideling rhythm of the jaws depends one final blossom.

That afternoon it rained. It came without warning and it did not last long. He watched it for some time and without alarm, wanton and random and indecisive before it finally developed, concentrated, drooping in narrow unperpendicular bands in two or three different places at one time, about the horizon, like gauzy umbilical loops from the bellied cumulae, the sun-belled ewes of summer grazing up the wind from the south-west. It was as if the rain were actually seeking the two of them, hunting them out where they stood amid the shade, finding them finally in a bright intransigeant fury. The pine-snoring wind dropped, then gathered; in an anti-climax of complete vacuum the shaggy pelt of earth became overblown like that of a receptive mare for the rampant crash, the furious brief fecundation which, still rampant, seeded itself in flash and glare of noise and fury and then was gone, vanished; then the actual rain, from a sky already breaking as if of its own rich over-fertile weight, running in a wild lateral turmoil among the unrecovered leaves, not in drops but in needles of fiery ice which seemed to be not trying to fall but, immune to gravity, earthless, were merely trying to keep pace with the windy uproar which had begotten and foaled them, striking in thin brittle strokes through his hair and shirt and against his lifted face, each brief lance already filled with the glittering promise of its imminent cessation like the brief bright saltless tears of a young girl over a lost flower; then gone too, fled north and eastward beyond the chromatic arch of its own insubstantial armistice, leaving behind it the spent confetti of its carnival to gather and drip leaf by leaf and twig by twig then blade by blade of grass, to gather in murmurous runnels, releasing in mirrored repetition the sky which, glint by glint of fallen gold and blue, the falling drops had prisoned.

It was over at last. He takes up the rope again and they move out from beneath the tree and go on, moving no faster than before but for the first time since they entered the woods, with purpose. Because it is nearing sunset. Although the rain had not seemed to last long, yet now it is as if there had been something in that illogical and harmless sound and fury which abrogated even the iron schedule of grooved and immutable day as the abrupt unplumbable tantrum of a child, the very violence of which is its own invincible argument against protraction, can somehow seem to set the clock up. He is soaking wet. His overalls are heavy and dank and cold upon him—the sorry refuse, the scornful lees of glory—a lifeless chill which is no kin to the vivid wet of the living water which has carried into and still retains within the very mud, the boundless freedom of the golden air as that same air glitters in the leaves and branches which globe in countless minute repetition the intact and iridescent cosmos. They walk in splendor. Joined by the golden skein of the wet grass rope, they move in single file toward the ineffable effulgence, directly into the sun. They are still pacing it. They mount the final ridge. They will arrive together. At the same moment all three of them cross the crest and descend into the bowl of evening and are extinguished.

The rapid twilight effaces them from the day's tedious recording. Original, in the womb-dimension, the unavoidable first and the inescapable last, eyeless, they descend the hill. He finds the basket by smell and lifts it down from the limb and sets it before her. She nuzzles into it, blowing the sweet breath-reek into the sweetish reek of feed until they become indistinguishable with that of the urgent and unimpatient milk as it flows among and about his fingers, hands, wrists, warm and indivisible as the strong inexhaustible life ichor itself, inherently, of itself, renewing. Then he leaves the invisible basket where he can find it again at dawn, and goes to the spring. Now he can see again. Again his head interrupts, then replaces as once more he breaks with drinking the reversed drinking of his drowned and fading image. It is the well of days, the still and insatiable aperture of earth. It holds in tranquil paradox of suspended precipitation dawn, noon, and sunset; yesterday, today, and tomorrow—star-spawn and hieroglyph, the fierce white dying rose, then gradual and invincible speeding up to and into slack-flood's coronal of nympholept noon. Then ebb's afternoon, until at last the morning, noon, and afternoon flow back, drain the sky and creep leaf by voiceless leaf and twig and branch and trunk, descending, gathering frond by frond among the grass, still creeping downward in drowsy insect murmurs, until at last the complete all of light gathers about that still and tender mouth in one last expiring inhalation. He rises. The swale is constant with random and erratic fireflies. There is the one fierce evening star, though almost at once the marching constellations mesh and gear and wheel strongly on. Blond too in that gathered last of light, she owns no dimension against the lambent and undimensional grass. But she is there, solid amid the abstract earth. He walks lightly upon it, returning, treading lightly that frail inextricable canopy of the subterrene slumber—Helen and the bishops, the kings and the graceless seraphim. When he reaches her, she has already begun to lie down—first the forequarters, then the hinder ones, lowering herself in two distinct stages into the spent ebb of evening, nestling back into the nest-form of sleep, the mammalian attar. They lie down together.

3.

It was after sunset when Houston returned home and missed the cow. He was a widower, without family. Since the death of his wife three or four years ago, the cow was the only female creature on the place, obviously. He even had a man cook, a negro, who did the milking too, but on this Saturday the negro had asked permission to attend a picnic of his race, promising to be back in plenty of time to milk and get supper too—a statement in which Houston naturally put no credence at all. Indeed, except for a certain monotonous recapitulation about the promise which finally began to impinge on him, he might not have returned home at all that night and so would not have missed the cow until the next day.

As it was, he returned home just after sunset, not for food, the presence or lack of which meant nothing to him, but to milk the cow, the prospect and necessity of which had been facing him and drawing nearer and nearer all afternoon. Because of this, he had drunk a little more than his customary Saturday afternoon quantity, which (a man naturally of a moody, though robustly and healthily so, habit) in conjunction with the savage fixation about females which the tragic circumstances of his bereavement had created in him, and the fact that not only must he return and establish once more physical contact with the female world which three years ago he had abjured but the time this would require would be that (the hour between sunset and dark) one of the entire day's hierarchy which he could least bear—when the presence of his dead wife and sometimes even that of the son which they had never had, would be everywhere about the house and the place—left him in no very predictable frame of mind when he went to the cowshed and found the cow gone.

He thought at first that she had merely continued to bump and butt at the door until the latch turned and allowed it to open. But even then he was surprised that the discomfort of her bag had not fetched her, waiting and even lowing, at the lot gate before he arrived. But she was not there, and cursing her (and himself for having neglected to close the gate which led to the creek pasture) he called the hound and took the path back to the creek. It was not yet full dark. He could (and did) see tracks, though when he did notice the prints of the man's bare feet, the cow's prints superposed, so he merely took the two sets of tracks to be six hours apart and not six feet. But primarily he did not bother with the tracks because he was convinced he knew where the cow was, even when the hound turned from the creek at the ford and bore away up the hill. He shouted it angrily back. Even when it paused and looked back at him in grave and intelligent surprise, he still acted out of that seething conviction born of drink and exasperation and the old strong uncompromising grief, shouting at the dog until it returned and then actually kicking it toward the ford and then following it across, where it now heeled him, puzzled and gravely alert, until he kicked at it again and drove it out ahead.

She was not in the pasture. Now he knew that she was not, and therefore had been led away; it was as though his very savageness toward the dog had recalled him to something like sanity. He recrossed the creek. He had in his hip pocket the weekly county paper which he had taken from his mailbox on his way to the village early in the afternoon. He rolled it into a torch. By its light he saw the prints of the idiot's feet and those of the cow where they had turned away at the ford and mounted the hill to the road, where the torch burned out, leaving him standing there in the early starlight (the moon had not risen yet) cursing again in that furious exasperation which was not rage but savage contempt and pity for all blind flesh capable of hope and grief.

He was almost a mile from his horse. What with the vain quartering of the pasture, he had already walked twice that distance, and he was boiling with that helpless rage at abstract circumstance which feeds on its own impotence, has no object to retaliate upon; it seemed to him that once more he had been victim of a useless and elaborate practical joke at the hands of the prime maniacal Risibility, the sole purpose of which had been to leave him with a mile's walk in darkness. But even if he could not actually punish, hurt, the idiot, at least he could put the fear, if not of God, at least of cowstealing and certainly of Jack Houston, into him, so that in any event he, Houston, would not leave home each time from now on wondering whether or not the cow would be there when he returned. Yet, mounted at last and in motion again and the cool wind of motion drawing about him, he found that the grim icy rage had given way to an even more familiar sardonic humor, a little clumsy and heavy-footed perhaps, but indomitable and unconquerable above even the ruthless grief: so that long before he reached the village he knew exactly what he would do. He would cure the idiot forever more of coveting cows by the immemorial and unfailing method: he would make him feed and milk her; he would return home and ride back tomorrow morning and make him feed and milk again and then lead the cow back on foot to where he had found her. So he did not stop at Mrs Littlejohn's house at all. He turned into the lane and went on toward the lot; it was Mrs Littlejohn who spoke to him from the dense moon-shade beside the fence: "Who's that?"

He stopped the horse. She aint even saw the dog, he thought. That was when he knew he was not going to say anything else to her either. He could see her now, tall, tall like a chimney and with little more shape, standing at the fence. "Jack Houston," he said.

"What you want?" she said.

"Thought I'd water my horse at your trough."

"Aint there water at the store any more?"

"I come from home."

"Oh," she said. "Then you aint—" She spoke in a harsh rush, stopping. Then he knew he was going to say more. He was saying it:

"He's all right. I saw him."

"When?"

"Before I left home. He was there this morning and again this evening. In my pasture. He's all right. I reckon he's tak-ing a Saturday holiday too."

She grunted. "That nigger of yours go to the picnic?"

"Yessum."

"Then come on in and eat. There's some cold supper left."

"I done et." He began to turn the horse. "I wouldn't worry. If he's still there, I'll tell him to get to hell on home."

She grunted again. "I thought you was going to water your horse."

"That's a fact," he said. So he rode into the lot. He had to dismount and open the gate and close it and then open it and close it again in order to do so, and then mount again. She was still standing beside the fence but when he called good-night in passing she did not answer.

He returned home. The moon was now high and full above the trees. He stabled the horse and crossed the blanched lot, passing the moony yawn of the empty cowshed, and went on to the dark and empty and silver-roofed house and undressed and lay on the monklike iron cot where he now slept, the hound on the floor beside it, the moony square of the window falling across him as it had used to fall across both of them when his wife was alive and there was a bed there in place of the cot. He was not cursing now, and it was still not rage when at sunup he sat the horse in the road where he had lost the tracks last night. He looked down at the dust blandly inscrutable with the wheel- and hoof- and human-prints of a whole Saturday afternoon, where the very virginity of the idiot at hiding had seemed to tap at need an inexhaustible reservoir of cleverness as one who has never before needed courage can seem at need to find it, cursing, not with rage but with that savage contempt and pity for the weak, nerve-raddled, yet curiously indestructible flesh already doomed and damned before it saw light and breathed.

By that time the owner of the barn had already found in the crib the tell-tale ridge of spilled feed beginning at the feedbox and ending in a shelving crescent about the shape of the absent basket; presently he even discovered it was his own basket which was gone. He tracked the feet across the lot and lost them. But there was nothing else missing, not a great quantity of feed and the basket was an old one. He gathered up the spilled feed and put it back into the box and soon even his first burst of impotent wrath at the moral outrage, the crass violation of private property, evaporated, recurring only once or twice during the day as angry and exasperated puzzle-ment: so that on the second morning when he entered the crib and saw the mute ridge of spilled feed ending in that empty embracing crescent, he experienced a shocking bewil-derment followed by a furious and blazing wrath like that of a man who, leaping to safety from in front of a runaway, slips on a banana skin. For that moment his state of mind was homicidal. He saw in this second flagrant abrogation of the ancient biblical edict (on which he had established existence, integrity, all) that man must sweat or have not, the same embattled moral point which he had fought singly and collectively with his five children for more than twenty years and in which battle, by being victorious, he had lost. He was a man past middleage, who with nothing to start with but sound health and a certain grim and puritanical affinity for abstinence and endurance, had made a fair farm out of the barren scrap of hill land which he had bought at less than a dollar an acre and married and raised a family on it and fed and clothed them all and even educated them after a fashion, taught them at least hard work, so that as soon as they became big enough to resist him, boys and girls too, they left home (one was a professional nurse, one a ward-heeler to a minor county politician, one a city barber, one a prostitute; the oldest had simply vanished completely) so that there now remained the small neat farm which likewise had been worked to the point of mute and unflagging mutual hatred and resistance but which could not leave him and so far had not been able to eject him but which possibly knew that it could and would outlast him, and his wife who possibly had the same, perhaps not hope for resisting, but maybe staff and prop for bearing and enduring.

He ran out of the barn, shouting her name. When she appeared in the kitchen door, he shouted at her to come and milk and ran on into the house and reappeared with a shotgun, and ran past her again in the barn, cursing her for her slowness, and bridled one of the mules and took up the gun and followed the tracks once more across the lot, to where they disappeared at the fence. But this time he did not quit, and presently he found them again—the dark, dragging wake still visible in the dew-heavy grass of his hayfield, crossing the field and entering the woods. Then he did lose them. But still he did not quit. He was too old for this, too old certainly for such prolonged and panting rage and thirst for blood. He had eaten no breakfast yet, and at home there was that work waiting, the constant and unflagging round of repetitive nerve-and-flesh wearing labor by which alone that piece of earth which was his mortal enemy could fight him with, which he had performed yesterday and must perform again today and again tomorrow and tomorrow, alone and unassisted or else knock under to that very defeat which had been his barren victory over his children;—this until the day came when (he knew this too) he would stumble and plunge, his eyes still open and his empty hands stiffening into the shape of the plow-handles, into the furrow behind the plow, or topple into the weedy ditch, still clutching the brush-hook or the axe, this final victory marked by a cenotaph of coiling buz-zards on the sky until some curious stranger happened there and found and buried what was left of him. Yet he went on. After a while he even found the tracks again, three of them in a sandy ditch where a branch ran, coming upon them more or less by chance since the last one he had seen was a mile away; he could have had no reason to believe they were even the right ones, though as it happened they were. But he did not for one moment doubt that they were the right ones. About the middle of the morning he even discovered whom the cow belonged to. He met Houston's negro, also on a mule, in the woods. He told the negro violently, even swinging the gun toward him, that he had seen no stray cow, there was no stray cow about there, and that this was his land although he owned nothing within three miles of where he stood unless it might have been the temporarily hidden feed-basket, and or-dered the negro to get off it and stay off.

He returned home. He had not given up; he now knew not only what he intended to do, but how to do it. He saw before him not mere revenge and reprisal, but redress. He did not want to surprise the thief; he wanted now to capture the cow and either collect a reward from its owner for returning it, or if the owner refused, resort to his legal rights and demand a pound fee on the cow as a stray—this, this legal dollar which would be little enough compensation, not for the time he had spent recovering the cow, but for the time he had lost from the endless round of that labor which he could not have hired done in his place, not because he could not pay for it but because no man in that country, white or black, would work for him at any price, and which he durst not permit to get the ascendancy of him or he would be lost. He did not even go to the house. He went straight to the field and put the mule into the plow which he had left in the furrow last night and plowed until his wife rang the bell at noon; he returned to the field after dinner and plowed on until dark.

He was in the barn, the mule already saddled and waiting in its stall, before moonset the next morning. He saw against the pallid lift of dawn the thick, bearlike figure enter with the basket and followed by his own dog, and enter the crib and then emerge, carrying the basket in both arms as a bear does, and hurry back across the lot, the dog still following. When he saw the dog he was suffused again by that almost unbearable rage. He had heard it on the first morning, but its uproar had ceased by the time he came good awake; now he understood why he had not heard it on the second and third mornings, and he knew now that even if the man did not look back and see him, if he now appeared from the barn the dog in all likelihood would bark at him. So when he did feel it safe to come out of the barn, there was nothing in sight but the dog, which stood peering through the fence after the thief, remaining unaware of his presence until he had actually kicked it, savage and raging, toward the house.

But the thief's dark wake lay again upon the dew-pearled grass of the pasture, though when he reached the woods he discovered that he had made the same error of underestimation which Houston had made: that there is perhaps something in passion too, as well as in poverty and innocence, which cares for its own. So he spent another half morning, breakfastless, seething with incredulous outrage, riding the green and jocund solitudes of the May woods, while behind him the dark reminder of his embattled and unremitting fields stood higher and higher in despotic portent. This time he even found the trail again—the stain of wasted milk on the earth (so close he was), the bent grass where the basket had sat while the cow fed from it. He should have found the basket itself hanging on the limb, since nobody had tried to conceal it. But he did not look that high, since he now had the cow's trail. He followed it, calm and contained and rigidly boiling, losing it and finding it and losing it again, on through the morning and into the access of noon—that concentration of light and heat which he could seem to feel raising not only the temperature of his blood but that of the very abstract conduits and tubes through which the current of his wrath had to flow. That afternoon though he discovered that the sun had nothing to do with it. He also stood beneath a tree while the thunder-storm crashed and glared and the furious cold rain drove at that flesh which cringed and shivered only on the outside, then galloped on in tearful and golden laughter across the glittering and pristine earth. He was then seven miles from home. There was an hour more of daylight. He had done perhaps four of the miles and the evening star had risen, when it occurred to him that the fugitives might just possibly return to the place where he had found the milk-stain on the earth. He went back there without hope. He was not even raging anymore.

He reached home about midnight, on foot, leading the mule and the cow. At first he had been afraid that the thief himself would escape. Then he had expected him to. Then for that half mile between the barn and the place where he had found them, he tried to drive away the creature which had started up from beside the cow with a hoarse, alarmed cry which he recognised, which still followed, moaning and blundering along in the darkness behind even when he would turn—a man too old for this, spent not so much by the long foodless day as by constant and unflagging rage—and shout at it, cursing. His wife was waiting at the lot gate with a lighted lantern. He entered, he handed the two halter-reins carefully to her and went and closed the gate carefully and stooped as an old man stoops and found a stick and then sprang, ran at the idiot, striking at it, cursing in a harsh spent panting voice, the wife following, calling him by name. "You stop!" she cried. "Stop it! Do you want to kill yourself?"

"Hah!" he said, panting, shaking. "I aint going to die for a few more miles yet. Go get the lock." It was a padlock. It was the only lock of any sort on the place. It was on the front gate, where he had put it the day after his last child left home. She went and got it while he still tried to drive the idiot from the lot. But he could not overtake the creature. It moved awkwardly and thickly, moaning and bubbling, but he could neither overtake it nor frighten it. It was somewhere behind him, just outside the radius of the lantern which his wife held, even while he locked the piece of chain through the door of the stall into which he had put the cow. The next morning when he unlocked the chain, the creature was inside the stall with the cow. It had even fed the cow, climbing back out and then back into the stall to do it, and for that five miles to Houston's place it still followed, moaning and slobbering, though just before they reached the house he looked back, and it was gone. He did not know just when it disappeared. Later, returning, with Houston's dollar in his pocket, he examined the road to see just where it had vanished. But he found no trace.

The cow was in Houston's lot less than ten minutes. Houston was at the house at the time; his immediate intention was to send the cow on by his negro. But he countermanded this in the next breath and sent the man instead to saddle his horse, during which time he stood waiting, cursing again with that savage and bleak contempt which was not disgust nor rage. Mrs Littlejohn was putting her horse into the buggy when he led the cow into the lot, so he did not need to tell her himself, after all. They just looked at one another, not man and woman but two integers which had both reached the same ungendered peace even if by different roads. She drew the clean, knotted rag from her pocket. "I dont want money," he said roughly. "I just dont want to see her again."

"It's his," she said, extending the rag. "Take it."

"Where'd he get money?"

"I dont know. V. K. Ratliff gave it to me. It's his."

"I reckon it is, if Ratliff gave it up. But I still dont want it."

"What else could he do with it?" she said. "What else did he ever want?"

"All right," Houston said. He took the rag. He did not open it. If he had asked how much was in it, she could not have told him since she had never counted it either. Then he said, furious and still out of his calm rigid face: "Goddamn it, keep them both away from my place. Do you hear?"

That lot was beyond the house from the road; the rear wall of the stable was not in sight from either. It was not directly in view from anywhere in the village proper, and on this September forenoon Ratliff realised that it did not need to be. Because he was walking in a path, a path which he had not seen before, which had not been there in May. Then that rear wall came into his view, the planks nailed horizontally upon it, that plank at head-height prized off and leaning, the projecting nails faced carefully inward, against the wall and no more motionless than the row of backs, the row of heads which filled the gap. He knew not only what he was going to see but that, like Bookwright, he did not want to see it, yet, unlike Bookwright, he was going to look. He did look, leaning his face in between two other heads; and it was as though it were himself inside the stall with the cow, himself looking out of the blasted tongueless face at the row of faces watching him who had been given the wordless passions but not the specious words. When they looked around at him, he already held the loose plank, holding it as if he were on the point of striking at them with it. But his voice was merely sardonic, mild even, familiar, cursing as Houston had: not in rage and not even in outraged righteousness.

"I notice you come to have your look too," one said.

"Sholy," Ratliff said. "I aint cussing you folks. I'm cussing all of us," lifting the plank and fitting it back into the orifice. "Does he—What's his name? that new one? Lump.—does he make you pay again each time, or is it a general club ticket good for every performance?" There was a half-brick on the ground beside the wall. With it he drove the nails back while they watched him, the brick splitting and shaling, crumbling away onto his hands in fine dust—a dry, arid, pallid dust of the color of shabby sin and shame, not splendid, not magnificent like blood, and fatal. "That's all," he said. "It's over. This here engagement is completed." He did not wait to see if they were departing. He crossed the lot in the bright hazy glare of the September noon, and the back yard. Mrs Littlejohn was in the kitchen. Again like Houston, he did not need to tell her.

"What do you think I think when I look out that window and watch them sneaking up along that fence?" she said.

"Only all you done was think," he said. "That new clerk," he said. "That Snopes encore. Launcelot," he said. "Lump. I remember his ma." He remembered her in life, as well as from inquiry—a thin, eager, plain woman who had never had quite enough to eat and showed it and did not even know that she had actually never had enough to eat, who taught school. Out of a moil of sisters and brothers fathered by a congenital failure who between a constant succession of not even successful petty-mercantile bankruptcies, begot on his whining and sluttish wife still more children whom he could not quite clothe and feed. Out of this, through one summer term at the State Teacher's college and into a one-room country school, and out of the school before the first year was done and into marriage with a man under indictment then because of a drummer's sample-case of shoes, all for the right foot, which had vanished from a railway baggage-room. And who brought with her into that marriage, as sole equipment and armament, the ability to wash and feed and clothe a swarm of brothers and sisters without ever enough food or clothing or soap to do it with, and a belief that there was honor and pride and salvation and hope too to be found for man's example between the pages of books, and who bore one child and named it Launcelot, flinging this quenchless defiance into the very jaws of the closing trap, and died. "Launcelot!" Ratliff cried. He did not even curse: not that Mrs Littlejohn would have minded, or perhaps even have heard him. "Lump! Just think of his shame and horror when he got big enough to realise what his ma had done to his family's name and pride so that he even had to take Lump for folks to call him in place of it! He pulled that plank off! At just exactly the right height! Not child-height and not woman-height: man-height! He just keeps that little boy there to watch and run to the store and give the word when it's about to start. Oh, he aint charging them to watch it yet, and that's what's wrong. That's what I dont understand. What I am afraid of. Because if he, Lump Snopes, Launcelot Snopes. . . . I said encore," he cried. "What I was trying to say was echo. Only what I meant was forgery." He ceased, having talked himself wordless, mute into baffled and aghast outrage, glaring at the man-tall, man-grim woman in the faded wrapper who stared as steadily back at him.

"So that's it," she said. "It aint that it is, that itches you. It's that somebody named Snopes, or that particular Snopes, is making something out of it and you dont know what it is. Or is it because folks come and watch? It's all right for it to be, but folks mustn't know it, see it."

"Was," he said. "Because it's finished now. I aint never disputed I'm a pharisee," he said. "You dont need to tell me he
aint got nothing else. I know that. Or that I can sholy leave
him have at least this much. I know that too. Or that besides,
it aint any of my business. I know that too, just as I know
that the reason I aint going to leave him have what he does
have is simply because I am strong enough to keep him from
it. I am stronger than him. Not righter. Not any better,
maybe. But just stronger."

"How are you going to stop it?"

"I dont know. Maybe I even cant. Maybe I dont even want
to. Maybe all I want is just to have been righteouser, so I can
tell myself I done the right thing and my conscience is clear
now and at least I can go to sleep tonight." But he seemed to
be at no loss as to what to do next. He did stand for a time on
Mrs Littlejohn's front steps, but he was only canvassing the
possibilities—or rather, discarding the faces as he called them
up: the fierce intractable one barred with the single eyebrow;
the high one ruddy and open and browless as a segment of
watermelon above the leather blacksmith's apron; that third
one which did not belong to the frock coat so much as it
appeared to be attached to it like a toy balloon by its string,
the features of which seemed to be in a constant state of disorganised flight from about the long, scholarly, characterless
nose as if the painted balloon-face had just been fetched in
out of a violent and driving rain—Mink, Eck, I.O.; and then
he began to think Lump again, cursing, driving his mind back
to the immediate problem with an almost physical effort,
though actually standing quite still on the top step, his face
familiar and enigmatic, quiet, actually almost smiling, bringing the three possible faces once more into his mind's eye and
watching them elide once more—the one which would not
stay at all; the second which would never even comprehend
what he was talking about; the third which in that situation
would be like one of the machines in railway waiting-rooms,
into which you could insert the copper coin or lead slug of
impulse to action, and you would get something back in
return, you would not know what, except that it would not
be worth quite as much as the copper or the slug. He
even thought of the older one, or at least the first one: Flem,

thinking how this was probably the first time anywhere where breath inhaled and suspired and men established the foundations of their existences on the currency of coin, that anyone had ever wished Flem Snopes were here instead of anywhere else, for any reason, at any price.

It was now nearing noon, almost an hour since he had seen the man he sought emerge from the store. He made inquiries at the store; ten minutes later he turned from a lane, through a gate in a new wire fence. The house was new, one-storey, paintless. There were a few of the summer's flowers blooming on dustily into the summer's arid close, all red ones—cannas and geraniums—in a raw crude bed before the steps and in rusted cans and buckets along the edge of the porch. The same little boy was in the yard beyond the house, and a big, strong, tranquil-faced young woman opened the door to him, an infant riding her hip and another child peering from behind her skirt. "He's in his room, studying," she said. "Just walk right in."

The room also was unpainted, of tongue-and-groove planking; it looked and was as airtight as a strong-box and not much larger, though even then he remarked how the odor of it was not a bachelor-uncle smell but was curiously enough that of a closet in which a middleaged widow kept her clothes. At once he saw the frock coat lying across the bed's foot, because the man (he really was holding a book, and he wore spectacles) in the chair had given the opening door one alarmed look and sprang up and snatched up the coat and began to put it on. "Never mind," Ratliff said. "I aint going to stay long. This here cousin of yours. Isaac." The other finished getting into the coat, buttoning it hurriedly about the paper dickey he wore in place of a shirt (the cuffs were attached to the coat sleeves themselves) then removing the spectacles with that same flustered haste, as if he had hurried into the coat in order to remove the spectacles, so that for that reason Ratliff noticed that the frames had no lenses in them. The other was watching him with that intentness which he had seen before, which (the concentration and intelligence both) seemed actually to be no integral part either of the organs or the process behind them, but seemed rather to be a sort of impermanent fungus-growth on the surface of the eyeballs like the light down which children blow from the burrs of dandelion blooms. "About that cow," Ratliff said.

Now the features fled. They streamed away from the long nose which burlesqued ratiocination and firmness and even made a sort of crass roman holiday of rationalised curiosity, fluid and flowing even about the fixed grimace of glee. Then Ratliff saw that the eyes were not laughing but were watching him and that there was something intelligently alert, or at least competent, behind them, even if it were not firm. "Aint he a sight now?" Snopes cackled, chortled. "I done often thought, since Houston give him that cow and Mrs Littlejohn located them in that handy stall, what a shame it is some of his folks aint running for office. Bread and circuses, as the fellow says, makes hay at the poll-box. I dont know of no cheaper way than Lump's got to get a man—"

"Beat," Ratliff said. He did not raise his voice, and he did not speak further than that one word. The other face did not change either: the long, still nose, the fixed grimace, the eyes which partook of the life of neither. After a moment Snopes said:

"Beat?"

"Beat," Ratliff said.

"Beat," the other said. If it were not intelligence, Ratliff told himself, it was a good substitute. "Except as it happens, I aint—"

"Why?" Ratliff said. "When Caesar's wife goes up to Will Varner next month to get that ere school job again, and he aint pure as a marble monument, what do you think is going to happen?" The face did not actually alter because the features were in a constant state of flux, having no relation to one another save that the same skull bore them, the same flesh fed them.

"Much obliged," Snopes said. "What do you figure we better do?"

"We aint going to do nothing," Ratliff said. "I dont want to teach school."

"But you'll help. After all, we was getting along all right until you come into it."

"No," Ratliff said harshly. "Not me. But I aim to do this much. I am going to stay here until I see if his folks are doing something about it. About letting them folks hang around that crack and watch, anyhow."

"Sholy," Snopes said. "That ere wont do. That's it. Flesh is weak, and it wants but little here below. Because sin's in the eye of the beholder; cast the beam outen your neighbors' eyes and out of sight is out of mind. A man cant have his good name drug in the alleys. The Snopes name has done held its head up too long in this country to have no such reproaches against it like stock-diddling."

"Not to mention that school," Ratliff said.

"Sholy. We'll have a conference. Family conference. We'll meet at the shop this afternoon."

When Ratliff reached the shop that afternoon, they were both there—the smith's apprentice and the school-teacher, and a third man: the minister of the village church—a farmer and a father; a harsh, stupid, honest, superstitious and up-right man, out of no seminary, holder of no degrees, functioning neither within nor without any synod but years ago ordained minister by Will Varner as he decreed his school-teachers and commissioned his bailiffs. "It's all right," I.O. said when Ratliff entered. "Brother Whitfield has done solved it. Only—"

"I said I knowed of a case before where it worked," the minister corrected. Then he told them—or the teacher did, that is:

"You take and beef the critter the fellow has done formed the habit with, and cook a piece of it and let him eat it. It's got to be a authentic piece of the same cow or sheep or what-ever it is, and the fellow has got to know that's what he is eating; he cant be tricked nor forced to eating it, and a sub-stitute wont work. Then he'll be all right again and wont want to chase nothing but human women. Only—" and now Ratliff noticed it—something in the diffusive face at once speculative and annoyed: "—only Mrs Littlejohn wont let us have the cow. You told me Houston give it to him."

"No I didn't," Ratliff said. "You told me that."

"But didn't he?"

"Mrs Littlejohn or Houston or your cousin will be the one to tell you that."

"Well, no matter. Anyway, she wont. And now we got to

buy it from her. And what I cant understand is, she says she dont know how much, but that you do."

"Oh," Ratliff said. But now he was not looking at Snopes. He was looking at the minister. "Do you know it will work, Reverend?" he said.

"I know it worked once," Whitfield said.

"Then you have knowed it to fail."

"I never knowed it to be tried but that once," Whitfield said.

"All right," Ratliff said. He looked at the two others— cousins, nephew and uncle, whatever they were. "It will cost you sixteen dollars and eighty cents."

"Sixteen dollars and eighty cents?" I.O. said. "Hell fire." The little quick pale eyes darted from face to face between them. Then he turned to the minister. "Look here. A cow is a heap of different things besides the meat. Yet it's all that same cow. It's got to be, because it's some things that cow never even had when it was born, so what else can it be but the same thing? The horns, the hair. Why couldn't we take a little of them and make a kind of soup; we could even take a little of the actual living blood so it wouldn't be no technicality in it—"

"It was the meat, the flesh," the minister said. "I taken the whole cure to mean that not only the boy's mind but his insides too, the seat of passion and sin, can have the proof that the partner of his sin is dead."

"But sixteen dollars and eighty cents," I.O. said. He looked at Ratliff. "I dont reckon you aim to put up none of it."

"No," Ratliff said.

"And Mink aint, not to mention after that law verdict Will Varner put on him this morning," the other said fretfully. "And Lump. If anything, Lump is going to be put out considerable with what after all wasn't a whole heap of your business," he told Ratliff. "And Flem aint in town. So that leaves me and Eck here. Unless Brother Whitfield would like to help us out for moral reasons. After all, what reflects on one, reflects on all the members of a flock."

"But he dont," Ratliff said. "He cant. Come to think of it, I've heard of this before myself. It's got to be done by the fellow's own blood kin, or it wont work." The little bright quick eyes went constantly between his face and the minister's.

"You never said nothing about that," he said.

"I just told you what I know happened," Whitfield said. "I dont know how they got the cow."

"But sixteen-eighty," I.O. said. "Hell fire." Ratliff watched him—the eyes which were much shrewder than they appeared—not intelligent; he revised that: shrewd. Now he even looked at his cousin or nephew for the first time. "So it's me and you, Eck." And the cousin or nephew spoke for the first time.

"You mean we got to buy it?"

"Yes," I.O. said. "You sholy wont refuse a sacrifice for the name you bear, will you?"

"All right," Eck said. "If we got to." From beneath the leather apron he produced a tremendous leather purse and opened it and held it in one grimed fist as a child holds the paper sack which it is about to inflate with its breath. "How much?"

"I'm a single man, unfortunately," I.O. said. "But you got three children—"

"Four," Eck said. "One coming."

"Four. So I reckon the only way to figure it is to divide it according to who will get the most benefits from curing him. You got yourself and four children to consider. That will be five to one. So that will be I pay the one-eighty and Eck pays the fifteen because five goes into fifteen three times and three times five is fifteen dollars. And Eck can have the hide and the rest of the beef."

"But a beef and hide aint worth fifteen dollars," Eck said. "And even if it was, I dont want it. I dont want fifteen dollars' worth of beef."

"It aint the beef and the hide. That's just a circumstance. It's the moral value we are going to get out of it."

"How do I need fifteen dollars' worth of moral value when all you need is a dollar and eighty cents?"

"The Snopes name. Cant you understand that? That aint never been aspersed yet by no living man. That's got to be kept pure as a marble monument for your children to grow up under."

"But I still dont see why I got to pay fifteen dollars, when all you got to pay is—"

"Because you got four children. And you make five. And five times three is fifteen."

"I aint got but three yet," Eck said.

"Aint that just what I said? five times three? If that other one was already here, it would make four, and five times four is twenty dollars, and then I wouldn't have to pay anything."

"Except that somebody would owe Eck three dollars and twenty cents change," Ratliff said.

"What?" I.O. said. But he immediately turned back to his cousin or nephew. "And you got the meat and the hide," he said. "Cant you even try to keep from forgetting that?"

Chapter Two

I.

THE WOMAN Houston married was not beautiful. She had neither wit nor money. An orphan, a plain girl, almost homely and not even very young (she was twenty-four) she came to him out of the home of the remote kinswoman who had raised her, with the domestic skill of her country heritage and blood and training and a small trunk of neat, plain, dove-colored clothes and the hand-stitched sheets and towels and table-linen which she had made herself and an infinite capacity for constancy and devotion, and no more. And they were married and six months later she died and he grieved for her for four years in black, savage, indomitable fidelity, and that was all.

They had known one another all their lives. They were both only children, born of the same kind of people, on farms not three miles apart. They belonged to the same country congregation and attended the same one-room country school, where, although five years his junior, she was already one class ahead of him when he entered and, although he failed twice during the two years he attended it, she was still one class ahead of him when he quit, vanished, not only from his father's house but from the country too, fleeing even at sixteen the immemorial trap, and was gone for thirteen years and then as suddenly returned, knowing (and perhaps even cursing himself) on the instant he knew he was going to return, that she would still be there and unmarried; and she was.

He was fourteen when he entered the school. He was not wild, he was merely unbitted yet; not high-spirited so much as possessed of that strong lust, not for life, not even for movement, but for that fetterless immobility called freedom. He had nothing against learning; it was merely the confinement, the regimentation, which it entailed. He could competently run his father's farm, and his mother had taught him to write his name before she died at last and so gave up trying to compel his father to send him to the school which for four years at least he had contrived to avoid by playing his

mother's spoiling fondness against the severity of his father's
pride; he really enjoyed the increasing stint of responsibility
and even work which his father set him as a training for manhood. But at last he outgeneralled himself with his own strategy: finally even his father admitted that there was nothing
else about the farm for him to learn. So he entered school,
not a paragon but a paradox. He was competent for citizen-
ship before he could vote and capable of fatherhood before he
learned to spell. At fourteen he was already acquainted with
whiskey and was the possessor of a mistress—a negro girl
two or three years his senior, daughter of his father's renter—
and so found himself submitting to be taught his a-b-c's four
and five and six years after his coevals and hence already too
big physically for where he was; bulging in Lilliput, inevitably
sophisticated, logically contemptuous, invincibly incorrigible,
not deliberately intending to learn nothing but merely convinced that he would not, did not want and did not believe he
needed to.

Afterward, it seemed to him that the first thing he saw
when he entered the room was that bent, demure, simply-
brown and straight-haired head. Still later, after he believed
he had escaped, it seemed to him that it had been in his life
always, even during those five years between his birth and
hers; and not that she had contrived somehow to exist during those five years, but that he himself had not begun to
exist until she was born, the two of them chained irrevocably
from that hour and onward forever, not by love but by implacable constancy and invincible repudiation—on the one
hand, that steadfast and undismayable will to alter and improve and remake; on the other, that furious resistance. It was
not love—worship, prostration—as he knew it, as passion
had manifested heretofore in an experience limited to be sure,
yet not completely innocent. He would have accepted that,
taken it as his due, calling himself submitting to it as he called
himself submitting when he was really using that same quality
which he called proffered slavedom in all the other women—
his mother and his mistress—so far in his life. What he did
not comprehend was that until now he had not known what
true slavery was—that single constant despotic undeviating
will of the enslaved not only for possession, complete assimi-

lation, but to coerce and reshape the enslaver into the seemliness of his victimization. She did not even want him yet, not because she was too young yet but because apparently she had not found even in him the one suitable. It was as though she had merely elected him out of all the teeming earth, not as one competent to her requirements, but as one possessing the possibilities on which she would be content to establish the structure of her life.

She was trying to get him through school. Not out of it and apparently not even educated, any wiser; apparently just through it, grade by grade in orderly progression and at the appointed times for advancing from one to the next as people commonly do. At one time the thought occurred to him that what she perhaps wanted was to get him on and into the class of his age, where he should have been; that if she could do that, perhaps she would let him alone, to fail or not fail as his nature and character dictated. Perhaps she would have. Or perhaps she, who was fond enough to attempt it at all, was also wise enough to know that he not only would never reach the grade where he should have been but he would not even keep up with the one where he was, and more: that where he was did not even matter, that even failing did not matter so long as she had a hand too in the failing.

It was a feud, a gage, wordless, uncapitulating, between that unflagging will not for love or passion but for the married state, and that furious and as unbending one for solitariness and freedom. He was going to fail that first year. He expected to. Not only himself but the whole school knew it. She never even spoke directly to him, she would pass him on the playground without even looking at him, apparently ever seeing him, yet there would be, mute and inevitable on his desk, the apple or the piece of cake from her lunch-box, and secret in one of his books the folded sheet of problems solved or spelling corrected or sentences written out in the round, steadfast child's hand—the reward and promise which he spurned, the assistance which he repudiated, raging not because his integrity and gullibility had been attempted but because he could neither publicly express the scorn of the repudiation nor be sure that the private exposition—the wanton destruction of the food or the paper—had even registered upon that head bent, decorous, intent, in profile or three-quarters and sometimes in full rear, which he had never yet heard even pronounce his name. Then one day a boy not a third his size chanted a playground doggerel at him—not that Lucy Pate and Jack Houston were sweethearts, but that Lucy Pate was forcing Jack Houston to make the rise to the second grade. He struck the child as he would one of his own size, was immediately swarmed over by four older boys and was holding his furious own when his assailants gave back and she was beside him, flailing at his enemies with her school-satchel. He struck her as blindly and furiously as he had the little boy and flung her away. For the next two minutes he was completely berserk. Even after he was down, the four of them had to bind him up with a piece of fence wire in order to turn him loose and run.

So he won that first point. He failed. When he entered school the next fall, in the same grade and surrounded (a giant knee-deep in midgets) by a swarm of still smaller children, he believed that he had even escaped. The face was still there to be sure, and it looked no smaller, no more distant. But he now believed he saw it from beyond the additional abyss of yet another intervening grade. So he believed that he had taken the last point too, and the game; it was almost two months before he discovered that she too had failed in her last year's examinations.

Now something very like panic took possession of him. Because he also discovered that the scale and tone of the contest between them had altered. It was no more deadly; that was impossible. It had matured. Up to now, for all its deadly seriousness, it had retained something of childhood, something both illogical and consistent, both reasonable and bizarre. But now it had become a contest between adults; at some instant during that summer in which they had not even seen one another except among the congregation at church, the ancient worn glove of biological differentiation had been flung and raised. It was as if, mutually unaware yet at the same moment, they had looked upon the olden Snake, had eaten of the Tree with the will and capacity for assimilation but without the equipment, even if the lack of equipment were not true in his case. There were no more apples and cake now, there was

only the paper, correct, inescapable and implacable, in the
book or in his overcoat pocket or in the mailbox before his
gate; he would submit his own blank paper at the written
monthly tests and receive back that one bearing a perfect
grade and written in that hand, even to the signature, which
was coming more and more to look like his own. And always
there was the face which still never addressed him nor even
looked at him, bent, in profile or three-quarters, sober and
undismayable. He not only looked at it all day, he carried it
home with him at night, waking from sleep to meet it, still
serene, still steadfast. He would even try to efface and exorcise
it beyond that of the negress paramour but it still remained,
constant, serene, not reproachful nor even sad nor even angry,
but already forgiving him before forgiveness had been dared
or earned; waiting, tranquil, terrifying. Once during that year
the frantic thought occurred to him of escaping her forever by
getting beyond the reach of her assistance, of applying himself
and making up the lost years, overhauling the class where he
should have been. For a short time he even attempted it. But
there was the face. He knew he could never pass it, not that it
would hold him back, but he would have to carry it on with
him in his turn, just as it had held him somehow in abeyance
during those five years before she was even born; not only
would he never pass it, he would not even ever overtake it by
that one year, so that regardless of what stage he might reach
it would still be there, one year ahead of him, inescapable and
impervious to passing. So there was but one alternative. That
was the old one: the movement not in retrograde since he
could retrograde no further than the grade in which he already was, but of braking, clapping the invincible spike-heels
of immobility into the fleeing and dizzy scope.

He did that. His mistake was in assuming a limitation
to female ruthlessness. He watched his blank monthly test
papers vanish into the teacher's hands and then return to
him, perfectly executed even to his own name at the top,
while the months passed and the final examination for pro-
motion or not arrived. He submitted the blank sheets bearing nothing but his name and the finger-smudges where he
had folded them and closed for the last time the books which
he had not even managed to soil and walked out of the

room, free save for the minor formality of being told by the
teacher that he had failed. His conviction of freedom lasted
through the afternoon and through supper and into the
evening itself. He was undressing for bed, one leg already out
of his trousers; without pause or falter he put the leg back
into the trousers, already running, barefoot and shirtless, out
of the house where his father was already asleep. The schoolhouse was not locked, though he had to break a lock to get
into the teacher's desk. Yet all three of his papers were there,
even to the same type of foolscap which he had submitted in
blank—arithmetic, geography, the paragraph of English com-
position which, if he had not known he had submitted a
blank one and if it had not been that he could neither pronounce nor recognise some of the words and could not understand all of what the ones he did know were talking about,
he could not have sworn himself he had not written.

He returned home and got a few clothes and the pistol
which he had owned for three years now, and waked his father, the two of them meeting for the last time in life in the
summer lamplit midnight room—the determined and frightened youth and the fierce thin wiry man almost a head
shorter, unshaven, with a wild flurry of gray hair, in a calf-
length nightshirt, who gave him the contents of the worn
wallet from the trousers flung across a nearby chair and, in
iron spectacles now, wrote out the note for the amount, with
interest, and made the son sign it. "All right," he said. "Go
then, and be damned to you. You certainly ought to be
enough kin to me to take care of yourself at sixteen. I was.
But I'll bet you the same amount, by God, that you'll be hollering for help before six months." He went back past the
schoolhouse and restored the papers, including the new set of
blank ones; he would have repaired the broken lock if he
could. And he even paid the bet, although he did not lose it.
He sent the money back out of three times that sum won at
dice one Saturday night a year later in the railroad construc-
tion camp in Oklahoma where he was a time-keeper.

He fled, not from his past, but to escape his future. It took
him twelve years to learn you cannot escape either of them.
He was in El Paso then, which was one end of his run as a
locomotive fireman well up the service list toward an engine

of his own, where he lived in the neat, small, urban house
which he had rented for four years now, with the woman
known to the neighborhood and the adjacent grocers and
such as his wife, whom he had taken seven years ago out of a
Galveston brothel. He had been a Kansas wheat-hand, he had
herded sheep in New Mexico, he was again with a construc-
tion gang in Arizona and west Texas and then a longshoreman
on the Galveston docks; if he were still fleeing, he did not
know it because it had been years now since he had even
remembered that he had forgotten the face. And when he
proved that at least you cannot escape either past or future
with nothing better than geography, he did not know that.
(Geography: that paucity of invention, that fatuous faith in
distance of man, who can invent no better means than geography for escaping; himself of all, to whom, so he believed he
believed, geography had never been merely something to
walk upon but was the very medium which the fetterless to-
and fro-going required to breathe in.) And if he were merely
being consistent in escaping from one woman by violating the
skirts of another, as with his mother and the negro girl of his
adolescence, he did not know that, taking almost by force out
of the house at daybreak the woman whom he had never seen
until the previous midnight; there was a scene by gaslight
between him and the curl-papered landlady as violent as if he
were ravishing from the house an only daughter with an entailed estate.

They lived together for seven years. He went back to rail-
roading and stuck with it and even came at last into the hier-
archical current of seniority; he was mentally and spiritually,
and with only an occasional aberration, physically faithful to
her who in her turn was loyal, discreet, undemanding, and
thrifty with his money. She bore his name in the boarding
houses where they lived at first, then in the rented house in
El Paso which they called home and were furnishing as they
were able to buy furniture. Although she had never suggested
it, he even thought of marrying her, so had the impact of
the West which was still young enough then to put a pre-
mium on individuality, softened and at last abolished his
inherited southern-provincial-protestant fanaticism regarding
marriage and female purity, the biblical Magdalen. There was

his father, to be sure. He had not seen him since the night he left home and he did not expect to see him again. He did not think of his father as being dead, being any further removed than the old house in Mississippi where he had seen him last; he simply could not visualise them meeting anywhere else except in Mississippi, to which he could only imagine himself returning as an old man. But he knew what his father's reaction to his marriage with a once-public woman would be, and up to this time, with all that he had done and failed to do, he had never once done anything which he could not imagine his father also doing, or at least condoning. Then he received the message that his father was dead (He received at the same time an offer from a neighbor for the farm. He did not sell it. At the time he did not comprehend why.) and so that was removed. But it had never actually existed anyway. He had already settled that as a matter purely between him and himself, long ago one night while the dim engine rocked through the darkness over the clucking rail-joints: "Maybe she was not much once, but neither was I. And for a right smart while now she has been better than I know myself to have been." Perhaps they would have a child after a while. He thought of waiting for that, letting that be the sign. At first that eventuality had never occurred to him—here again was the old mystical fanatic protestant; the hand of God lying upon the sinner even after the regeneration: the Babylonian interdict by heaven forever against reproduction. He did not know just how much time, just what span of chastity, would constitute purgatorium and absolution, but he would imagine it—some instant, mystical still, when the blight of those nameless and faceless men, the scorched scars of merchandised lust, would be effaced and healed from the organs which she had prostituted.

But that time was past now, not the mystic moment when the absolvement would be discharged, but the hour, the day before the elapse of which he had thought she would have told him she was pregnant and they would have married. It was long past now. It would never be. And one night in that twelfth year, in the boarding house at the other end of his run where he spent the alternate nights, he took out the three-year-old offer for the farm and he knew why he had not

accepted it. I'm going home, he told himself—no more than
that, not why; not even seeing the face which up to the day
he entered school he could not even have described and
which now he could not even remember. He made his run
back to El Paso the next day and drew the seven years' accumulation out of the bank and divided it into two equal parts.
The woman who had been his wife for seven years glanced
once at the money and then stood cursing him. "You are going to get married," she said. There were no tears; she just
cursed him. "What do I want with money? Look at me. Do
you think I will lack money? Let me go with you. There will
be some town, some place close where I can live. You can
come when you want to. Have I ever bothered you?"

"No," he said. She cursed him, cursing them both. If she
would just touch me, hit me, make me mad enough to hit
her, he thought. But that did not happen either. It was not
him she cursed, anymore than she could curse the woman she
had never seen and whose face even he could not quite recall.
So he divided his half of the money again—that money
which he had been lucky with: not lucky in the winning or
earning or finding, but lucky in having the vices and desiring
the pleasures which left a fair balance of it after they had been
fed and satisfied—and returned to Mississippi. But even then,
it apparently took him still another year to admit that he did
not want to escape that past and future. The countryside
believed he had come back to sell the farm. Yet the weeks
passed, and he did not. Spring came and he had made no
preparations either to rent it or work it himself. He merely
continued to live in the old pre-Civil War house which, although no mansion, owning no columns, had been too big
for three, while month after month passed, still apparently on
that vacation from the Texas railroad his father had already
told them he worked for, alone, without companionship,
meeting (when he met them at all) the contemporaries who
remembered him from youth over casual drinks or cards and
that not often. Occasionally he would be seen at the picnics
during the summer, and each Saturday afternoon he would
make one of the group on the gallery of Varner's store, talking
a little, answering questions rather, about the West, not secret
and reserved so much as apparently thinking in another

tongue from that in which he listened and would presently
have to answer. He was bitted now, even if it did not show so
much yet. There was still the mark of space and solitude in his
face, but fading a little, rationalised and corrupted even into
something consciously alert even if it was not fearful; the
beast, prime solitary and sufficient out of the wild fields,
drawn to the trap and knowing it to be a trap, not comprehending why it was doomed but knowing it was, and not
afraid now—and not quite wild.

They were married in January. His part of the Texas money
was gone then, though the countryside still believed he was
rich, else he could not have lived for a year without working
and would not have married a penniless orphan. Since he
had arrived home solvent, the neighborhood would be unalterably convinced forever that he was wealthy, just as it had
been unalterably convinced at first that only beggary had
brought him home. He borrowed money from Will Varner,
on a portion of the land, to build the new house on a new site
nearer the road. He bought the stallion too then, as if for a
wedding present to her, though he never said so. Or if that
blood and bone and muscles represented that polygamous
and bitless masculinity which he had relinquished, he never
said that. And if there were any among his neighbors and
acquaintances—Will Varner or Ratliff perhaps—who discerned that this was the actual transference, the deliberate
filling of the vacancy of his abdication, they did not say it
either.

Three months after the marriage the house was finished and
they moved into it, with a negro woman to cook although the
only other hired cook, white or black, in the country was
Varner's. Then the countryside would call, the men to the lot
to look at the stallion, the women to the house, the new
bright rooms, the new furniture and equipment and devices
for saving steps and labor whose pictures they would dream
over in the mail-order catalogues. They would watch her
moving among the new possessions, busy, indefatiguable, in
the plain, neat garments, the plain and simple hair, the plain
face blooming now with something almost like beauty—not
amazement at luck, not particularly vindication of will and
faith, but just serene, steadfast and boldly rosy when they

would remark how the house had been completed exactly in time to catch the moon's full of April through the window where the bed was placed.

Then the stallion killed her. She was hunting a missing hennest in the stable. The negro man had warned her: "He's a horse, missy. But he's a man horse. You keep out of there." But she was not afraid. It was as if she had recognised that transubstantiation, that duality, and thought even if she did not say it: Nonsense. I've married him now. He shot the stallion, running first into the stall with the now frenzied animal with nothing but an open pocket knife, until the negro grappled with him and persuaded him to wait for the pistol to be fetched from the house, and for four years and two months he had lived in the new house with the hound and the negro man to cook for them. He sold the mare which he had bought for her, and the cow he owned then, and discharged the woman cook and gave away the chickens. The new furniture had been bought on installment. He moved it all into the barn at the old place where he was born and notified the merchant to come and get it. Then he had only the stove, the kitchen table he ate from, and the cot he had substituted for the bed beneath the window. The moon was full on that first night he slept on the cot too, so he moved the cot into another room and then against a north wall where the moon could not possibly reach him, and two nights later he even went and spent one night in the old house. But there he lost everything, not only peace but even fibred and durable grief for despair to set its teeth into.

So he returned to the new house. The moon was waning then and would return only at monthly intervals, so that left only that single hour between sunset and full dark between its fulls, and weariness was an antidote for that. And weariness was cheap: he not only had the note he had given Will Varner for the loan, but there had been some trouble with the installment people who did not want to take the furniture back. So he farmed again, finding gradually how much he had forgotten about it. Thus, at times he would have actually forgotten that hour he dreaded until he would find himself entering it, walking into it, finding it suddenly upon him, drowning him with suffocation. Then that stubborn part of her and sometimes even of the son which perhaps next year they would have would be everywhere about the house he had built to please her even though it was empty now of all the objects she had touched and used and looked at except the stove and the kitchen table and the one garment—not a nightgown or an undergarment, but the gingham dress which resembled the one in which he had first seen her that day at the school— and the window itself, so that even on the hottest evenings of summer he would sit in the sweltering kitchen while the negro man cooked supper, drinking whiskey from a stone jug and tepid water from the cedar bucket and talking louder and louder, profane, intolerant, argumentative, with no challenge to be rebutted and no challenger to be vanquished and overcome.

But sooner or later the moon would wax again. There would be nights which were almost blank ones. Yet sooner or later that silver and blanched rectangle of window would fall once more, while night waxed into night then waned from night, as it had used to fall across the two of them while they observed the old country belief that the full moon of April guaranteed the fertilising act. But now there was no body beside his own for the moon to fall upon, and nothing for another body to have lain beside his own upon. Because the cot was too narrow for that and there was only the abrupt downward sheer of inky shadow in which only the invisible hound slept, and he would lie rigid, indomitable, and panting. "I dont understand it," he would say. "I dont know why. I wont ever know why. But You cant beat me. I am strong as You are. You cant beat me."

He was still alive when he left the saddle. He had heard the shot, then an instant later he knew he must have felt the blow before he heard it. Then the orderly sequence of time as he had known it for thirty-three years became inverted. He seemed to feel the shock of the ground while he knew he was still falling and had not yet reached it, then he was on the ground, he had stopped falling, and remembering what he had seen of stomach-wounds he thought: If I dont get the hurting started quick, I am going to die. He willed to start it, and for an instant he could not understand why it did not start. Then he saw the blank gap, the chasm somewhere between vision and where his feet should have been, and he lay on his back watching the ravelled and shattered ends of sentience and will projecting into the gap, hair-light and worm-blind and groping to meet and fuse again, and he lay there trying to will the sentience to meet and fuse. Then he saw the pain blast like lightning across the gap. But it came from the other direction: not from himself outward, but inward toward himself out of all the identifiable lost earth. Wait, wait, he said. Just go slow at first, and I can take it. But it would not wait. It roared down and raised him, tossed and spun. But it would not wait for him. It would not wait to hurl him into the void, so he cried, "Quick! Hurry!" looking up out of the red roar, into the face which with his own was wedded and twinned forever now by the explosion of that ten-gauge shell—the dead who would carry the living into the ground with him; the living who must bear about the repudiating earth with him forever, the deathless slain—then, as the slanted barrels did not move: "God damn it, couldn't you even borrow two shells, you fumbling ragged—" and put the world away. His eyes, still open to the lost sun, glazed over with a sudden well and run of moisture which flowed down the alien and unremembering cheeks too, already drying, with a newness as of actual tears.

2.

That shot was too loud. It was not only too loud for any shot, it was too loud for any sound, louder than any sound needed to be. It was as though the very capacity of space and echo for reproducing noise were leagued against him too in the vindication of his rights and the liquidation of his injuries, building up and building up about the thicket where he crouched and the dim faint road which ran beside it long after the gun-butt had shocked into his shoulder and the black powder smoke had reeked away and the horse had whirled, galloping, the empty stirrups clashing against the empty saddle. He had not fired the gun in four years; he had not even been certain that either two of the five shells he owned would explode. The first one had not; it was the second one—the vain click louder than thunderbolt, the furious need to realign and find the second trigger, then the crash which after the other deafening click he did not hear at all, the reek and stink of powder pressing him backward and downward into the thicket until for an instant he was physically off-balance, so that even if he could have made a second shot it would have been too late and the hound too was gone, leaving him betrayed here too, crouching behind the log, panting and trembling.

Then he would have to finish it, not in the way he wanted to but in the way he must. It was no blind, instinctive, and furious desire for flight which he had to combat and curb. On the contrary. What he would have liked to do would be to leave a printed placard on the breast itself: *This is what happens to the men who impound Mink Snopes' cattle,* with his name signed to it. But he could not, and here again, for the third time since he had pulled the trigger, was that conspiracy to frustrate and outrage his rights as a man and his feelings as a sentient creature. He must rise and quit the thicket and do what he had next to do, not to finish it but merely to complete the first step of what he had started, put into motion, who realised now that he had known already, before he heard the horse and raised the gun, that that would happen which had happened: that he had pulled trigger on an enemy but had only slain a corpse to be hidden. So he sat up behind the log and shut his eyes and counted slowly until the shaking stopped and the sound of the galloping horse and even the outrageous and incredible shot had died out of his ears and he could rise, carrying the slanted gun still loaded with the shell which had failed to explode, and emerge from the thicket, already hurrying. But even then it would be dusk before he reached home.

It was dusk. He emerged from the bottom and looked up the slope of his meagre and sorry corn and saw it—the paint-less two-room cabin with an open hallway between and a leanto kitchen, which was not his, on which he paid rent but not taxes, paying almost as much in rent in one year as the house had cost to build; not old, yet the roof of which already leaked and the weather-stripping had already begun to rot away from the wall planks and which was just like the one he had been born in which had not belonged to his father either,

and just like the one he would die in if he died indoors—
which he probably would even if in his clothes, repudiated
without warning at some instant between bed and table or
perhaps the door itself, by his unflagging furious heart-
muscles—and it was just like the more than six others he had
lived in since his marriage and like the twice that many more
he knew he would live in before he did die and although he
paid rent on this one he was unalterably convinced that his
cousin owned it and he knew that this was as near as he
would ever come to owning the roof over his head. Then he
saw the two children in the yard before it, who even as he saw
them, stood quickly up, watching him, then turned and scut-
tled toward the house. Then it seemed to him that he could
see her also, standing in the open hallway almost exactly
where she had stood eight hours before and watched his back
where he sat over the cold hearth, oiling the gun with the
bacon-drippings which was the only thing he owned that
could be used for oil, which would not lubricate but in contact with the metal would congeal into a substance like soap,
inherent with its own salty corrosion; standing there as if in
all that time she had not moved, once more framed by an
opening, though without the lamp, as she was standing in the
savage lamplight, above the loud harsh voices of invisible
men, in the open door of the mess-hall in that south Mississippi convict camp where he first saw her nine years ago. He
stopped looking at the house; he had only glanced at it as it
was, and mounted through the yellow and stunted stand of
his corn, yellow and stunted because he had had no money
to buy fertilizer to put beneath it and owned neither the
stock nor the tools to work it properly with and had had no
one to help him with what he did own in order to gamble his
physical strength and endurance against his body's liveli-
hood not only with ordinary climate but with the incredible
spring of which the dry summer was the monstrous abortion, which had rained every day from the middle of May into
July, as if the zodiac too had stacked cards against him. He
mounted on among the bitten and fruitless stalks, carrying
the gun which looked too big for him to carry or aim or dare
to fire, which he had acquired seven years ago at the sacrifice
of actual food and had acquired at all only because no other

man would want it since it carried a shell too big to shoot at anything but a wild goose or a deer and too costly to shoot at anything but a man.

He did not look toward the house again. He went on past it and entered the rotting lattice which enclosed the well and leaned the gun against the wall and removed his shoes and drew a bucket of water and began to wash the shoes. Then he knew that she was behind him. He didn't look back, sitting on the rotted bench, small, in a faded clean shirt and patched overalls, tipping the bucket over the shoe and scrubbing at it with a corn cob. She began to laugh, harshly and steadily. "I told you this morning," she said. "I said, if you do, if you left here with that gun, I was going." He didn't look up, crouched over the wet shoe into which he had slipped his hand like a shoe-last, scrubbing at it with the cob. "Never you mind where. Dont you worry about where when they come for you." He didn't answer. He finished the first shoe and set it down and slipped his hand into the second one and tipped water from the bucket over it and began to scrub it. "Because it wont be far!" she cried suddenly, yet without raising her voice at all. "Because when they come to hang you, I'm going to be where I can see it!" Now he rose. He set the unfinished second shoe carefully down and laid the cob beside it and rose, small, almost a half head shorter than she, barefoot, moving toward her, not fast, sidling a little, his head bent and apparently not even looking at her as she stood in the gaping and broken entrance—the bleached hair darkening again at the roots since it had been a year now since there had been any money to buy more dye, the harshly and steadily laughing face watching him with a curious and expectant glitter in the eyes. He struck her across the mouth. He watched his hand, almost labored, strike across the face which did not flinch, beneath the eyes which did not even blink. "You damned little murdering bastard," she said past the bright sudden blood. He struck her again, the blood smearing between mouth and palm and then renewed, striking again with that slow gathering which was not deliberation but extreme and patiently indomitable and implacable weariness, and again. "Go," he said. "Go. Go."

He followed her, across the yard and into the hallway,

though he did not enter the room. From the door he could see her, although the room itself was almost completely dark, against the small high square of the dusk-faint window. Then the match spurted and glared and steadied above the wick, and now she was framed in an opening by shadeless light and surrounded by the loud soundless invisible shades of the nameless and numberless men—that body which, even when he was actually looking at them, at times to him had never borne children, was anterior even to the two-dollar marriage which had not sanctified but sanctioned them, which each time he approached it, it was not garments intervening but the cuckolding shades which had become a part of his past too, as if he and not she had been their prone recipient; which despite the soiled and shapeless garments concealing it he would contemplate even from the cold starless night-periphery beyond both hatred and desire and tell himself: It's like drink. It's like dope to me. Then he saw the faces of the two children also, in the same flare of match and wick as if she had touched that single match to all three of them at the same time. They were sitting on the floor in the corner, not crouched, not hiding, just sitting there in the dark as they had been sitting doubtless ever since he had watched them scuttle toward the house when he came out of the bottom, looking at him with that same quality which he himself possessed: not abject but just still, with an old tired wisdom, acceptance of the immitigable discrepancy between will and capability due to that handicap of physical size in which none of the three of them had had any choice, turning from him to look without curiosity at the blood on their mother's face and watching quietly as she took a garment from a nail in the wall and spread it on the pallet bed and wrapped the other objects— the other garments, the single pair of half-size shoes which either child wore indiscriminately in cold weather, the cracked hand-glass, the wooden comb, the handleless brush—into it. "Come," she said. He moved aside and they passed him, the children huddled against her skirt and for a moment hidden from him as they emerged from the room, then visible again, moving on up the hallway before her, he following, keeping that same distance, stopping again at the entrance while they crossed the porch and descended the warped and rotting steps. When she paused on the ground beyond the steps he moved again, again with that invincible, that weary implacability, until he saw and stopped also and watched the larger child hurry across the yard, soundless and incorporeal in the dusk which was almost night now, and snatch something from the ground and return, clasping the object—a wooden block with the tops of four snuff tins nailed to it like wheels—to its breast. They went on. He did not follow further. He did not even appear to be looking at them as they passed through the broken gate.

He returned to the house and blew out the lamp, whereupon the dark became complete, as if the puny vanishing flame had carried along with it all that remained of day, so that when he returned to the well, it was by touch alone that he found the cob and the unfinished shoe and finished cleaning it. Then he washed the gun. When he first got it, when the gun was new, or new at least to him, he had had a cleaning rod for it. He had made it himself, of cane, chosen carefully and trimmed and scraped carefully and eyed neatly at the tip to take the greasy rag, and during the first year or so, when he had had money to buy powder and shot and caps to load the shells with and could hunt a little now and then, he had been no less particular in the care of the cleaning rod than of the gun because he had only bought the gun but the rod he had made. But the rod was gone now, he did not remember when nor know where, vanished along with the other accumulations of his maturity which had been dear to him too once, which he had shed somehow and somewhere along the road between the attaining of manhood and this hour when he found himself with nothing but an empty and foodless house which did not actually belong to him, and the gun, and that irremediable instant when the barrels had come level and true and his will had told his finger to contract, which nothing but his own death would ever efface from his memory. So he tipped water from the bucket over the gun and removed his shirt and wiped it dry and picked up the shoes and returned to the house and, without lighting the lamp again, stood in the dark at the cold stove and ate with his fingers from the pot of cold peas which sat on it and went and lay down, still in his overalls, on the pallet bed in the room which was empty at last even of the loud shades, lying flat on his back in the darkness with his eyes open and his arms straight beside him, thinking of nothing. Then he heard the hound.

At first he did not move; except for his regular and unhurried breathing, he might have been the corpse his attitude resembled, lying perfectly still while the first cry died away and the myriad night-silence came down and then indrew and the second cry came, ringing, deep, resonant and filled with grief. He did not move. It was as though he had been expecting it, waiting for it; had lain down and composed and emptied himself, not for sleep but to gather strength and will as distance runners and swimmers do, before assuming the phase of harried and furious endeavor which his life was about to enter, lying there for perhaps ten minutes while the long cries rang up from the dark bottom, as if he knew that those ten minutes were to be the last of peace. Then he rose. Still in the dark, he put on the still-damp shirt and the shoes he had just washed and from a nail behind the door he took down the new plowline still looped in the coils in which his cousin, Varner's clerk, had knotted it two weeks ago, and left the house.

The night was moonless. He descended through the dry and invisible corn, keeping his bearing on a star until he reached the trees, against the black solidity of which fireflies winked and drifted and from beyond which came the booming and grunting of frogs and the howling of the dog. But once among them, he could not even see the sky anymore, though he realised then what he should have before: that the hound's voice would guide him. So he followed it, slipping and plunging in the mud and tripping and thrashing among the briers and tangled undergrowth and blundering against invisible tree trunks, his arm crooked to shield his face, sweating, while the steady cries of the dog drew nearer and nearer and broke abruptly off in mid-howl. He believed for an instant that he actually saw the phosphorescent glints of eyes although he had no light to reflect them, and suddenly and without knowing that he was going to do it, he ran toward where he had seen the eyes. He struck the next tree a shocking blow with his shoulder; he was hurled sideways but

caught balance again, still plunging forward, his hands extended. He was falling now. If there's a tree in front of me
now, he thought, it will be all. He actually touched the dog.
He felt its breath and heard the click of its teeth as it slashed
at him, springing away, leaving him on his hands and knees in
the mud while the noise of its invisible flight crashed and
ceased.

He was kneeling at the brink of the depression. He had
only to rise and, half stooping, his arm still crooked to fend
his face, step down into the ankle-deep ooze of sunless mud
and rotting vegetation and follow it for another step or so to
reach the brush-pile. He thrust the coiled plowline into the
bib of his overalls and stooped and began to drag away the
slimed and rotten branches. Something gave a choked, infant-
like cry, scrabbling among the sticks; it sprawled frantically
across his foot as he kicked at it, telling himself: It's just a
possum. It aint nothing but a possum, stooping again to the
tangle of foul and sweating wood, lifting it away until he
reached the body. He wiped his hands free of mud and slime
on his shirt and overalls and took hold of the shoulders and
began to walk backward, dragging it along the depression. It
was not a ditch, it was an old logging road, choked with undergrowth and almost indistinguishable now, about two feet
below the flat level of the bottom. He followed it for better
than a mile, dragging the body which outweighed him by
fifty pounds, pausing only to wipe his sweating hands from
time to time on his shirt and to establish his whereabouts
anew whenever he could find enough visible sky to distinguish the shapes of individual trees against.

Then he turned and dragged the body up out of the depression and went on for a hundred yards, still walking backward.
He seemed to know exactly where he was, he did not even
look over his shoulder until he released the body at last and
stood erect and laid his hand upon what he sought—the shell
of a once-tremendous pin oak, topless and about ten feet tall,
standing in the clearing which the lightning bolt or age or
decay or whatever it had been, had created. Two years ago he
had lined a wild bee into it; the sapling which he had cut and
propped against the shell to reach the honey was still in place.
He took the plowline from his breast and knotted one end

about the body and removed his shoes and with the other end of the rope between his teeth, he climbed the sapling and straddled the rim of the shell and hand over hand hauled up the body which was half again as large as he, dragging it bumping and scraping up the trunk, until it lay like a half-filled sack across the lip. The knot in the rope had slipped tight. At last he took his knife and cut the rope and tumbled the body over into the shell. But it stopped almost at once, and only when it was too late did he realise that he should have reversed it. He shoved at it, probing about the shoulders, but it was not hung, it was wedged by one twisted arm. So he tied one end of the rope about the stub of a limb just below his foot and took a turn of the rope about his wrist and stood up on the wedged shoulders and began to jump up and down, whereupon without warning the body fled suddenly beneath him, leaving him dangling on the rope. He began to climb it, hand over hand, rasping off with his knuckles the rotten fibre of the wall so that a faint, constant, dry powder of decay filled his nostrils like snuff. Then he heard the stub crack, he felt the rope slip free and he leaped upward from nothing and got the finger-tips of one hand over the lip. But when his weight came down on it, a whole shard of the rotten shell carried away and he flung the other hand up but the shell crumbled beneath that one also and he climbed interminably, furiously perpetual and without gain, his mouth open for his panting breath and his eyes glaring at the remote September sky which had long since turned past midnight, until at last the wood stopped crumbling, leaving him dangling by his hands, panting, until he could pull himself up once more and straddle the rim. After a while he climbed down and lifted the propped sapling onto his shoulder and carried it fifteen or twenty yards beyond the edge of the clearing and returned and got his shoes. When he reached home dawn had already begun. He took off the muddy shoes and lay down on the pallet bed. Then, as if it had waited for him to lie down, the hound began to howl again. It seemed to him that he had even heard the intake of breath before the first cry came up from the bottom where it was still night, measured, timbrous, and prolonged.

His days and nights were now reversed. He would emerge

from the bottom with the morning star or perhaps the actual sun and mount through the untended and abortive corn. He did not wash the shoes now. He would not always remove them, and he would make no fire but would eat standing from the pot of cold peas on the stove while they lasted and drank down to its dregs the pot of cold, stale coffee while it lasted, and when they were gone he would eat handsful of raw meal from the almost empty barrel. For during the first day or so he would be hungry, since what he was doing now was harder than any work he had ever done, besides the excitement, the novelty. But after that it was not new anymore, and by then he realised it could have but one ending and so it would last forever, and he stopped being hungry. He would merely rouse, wake, to tell himself, You got to eat, and eating the raw meal (presently there was nothing in the barrel but the dried cake on the sides which he would scrape off with a knife-blade) which he did not want and apparently did not even need, as if his body were living on the incorrigible singleness of his will like so much fatty tissue. Then he would lie down on the pallet bed in his overalls and shoes on which the freshest and most recent caking of mud had not even begun to dry, still chewing and with the lengthening stubble about his mouth still full of meal grains and, as though in a continuation of the lying down, plunge not into oblivion but into an eyeless and tongueless interval of resting and recuperation like a man stepping deliberately into a bath, to wake as though to an alarm clock at the same afternoon hour, the continuity unbroken between the lying down and the opening of eyes again, since it was only the body which bore and would bear the burden which needed the rest. He would build a fire in the stove then, although there was nothing to cook save the scrapings from the meal barrel. But it was the hot drink he wanted, though there was no more coffee either. So he would fill the pot with water and heat it and drink the hot water sweetened with sugar, then in the splint chair on the porch he would watch the night, the darkness, emerge from the bottom and herd, drive, the sun gradually up the slope of the corn-patch which even in dusk stood no less barren and yellow than in sunlight, and at last take the house itself. Then the hound would begin and he would sit there for perhaps ten or fifteen minutes longer, as the holder of the annual commuter's ticket sits on his accustomed bench and continues to read his paper after the train has already whistled for the stop.

On the second afternoon when he waked a little boy was sitting on the front steps—the round-headed periwinkle-eyed son of his kinsman who operated Varner's blacksmith shop— though at the first sound of his feet on the floor the boy moved, so that when he reached the porch the boy was already on the ground beyond it and several feet away, looking back at him. "Uncle Lump says for you to come to the store," the boy said. "He says it's important." He didn't answer. He stood there with last night's mud now dried on the shoes and overalls and (so still had been his sleep) this morning's meal grains still clinging in the stubble around his mouth, until the boy turned and began to walk away and then began to run, looking back for an instant from the edge of the woods, then running on, vanishing. Still he didn't move and still there was nothing in his face. If it had been money, he could have brought it, he thought. Because it aint money. Not from them. And on the third morning he knew suddenly that someone was standing in the door watching him. He knew, even in the midst of the unreality which was not dream but a barren place where his mind, his will, stood like an unresting invincible ungrazing horse while the puny body which rode it renewed its strengh, that it was not the boy now and that it was still morning, that he had not been asleep that long. They were hid here, watching me when I come up out of the bottom, he thought, trying to speak aloud to wake himself as he might have knelt to shake his own shoulder: Wake up. Wake up: until he waked, knowing at once that it was too late, not even needing the position of the window's shadow on the floor to tell him it was that same automatic hour of afternoon. He did not hurry. He started the fire and set the pot on to heat and scooped a handful of meal scrapings from the barrel and ate it, chewing the splinters out of it, spitting them, rubbing them from his lips with his hand. In doing so, he discovered the meal already clinging in his beard and he ate that too, wiping the grains from either side with his fingers across his chewing mouth. Then he drank the cup

of sweetened water and went out into the yard. The tracks
were there. He knew the sheriff's—the heavy, deep, deliberate prints, even in the rainless summer's parched earth, of
those two hundred and forty pounds of flesh which wore the
metal shield smaller than a playing card, on which he had
gambled not only his freedom but perhaps his obliteration
too, followed by those of its satellites. He saw the prints of
the hands and the crawling knees where one of them had
searched back and forth beneath the floor while he was sleeping on top of it; he found leaning against the wall inside the
stable his own shovel with which they had cleared away the
year's accumulation of mule-droppings to examine the earth
beneath, and he found among the trees above the cabin the
place where the surrey had stood. And still there was nothing
in his face—no alarm, no terror, no dread; not even contempt or amusement—only the cold and incorrigible, the
almost peaceful, intractability.

He returned to the house and took the shotgun from its
corner. It was covered now almost completely over with a
thin, snuff-colored frost of rust, as though the very tedious
care of that first night's wiping had overreached itself, had
transferred the water from the gun to the shirt then back from
the shirt to the gun again. And it did not breech, break, but
opened slowly to steady force, exposing the thick, chocolate-
colored soap-like mass of congealed animal fat, so that at last
he dismantled it and boiled water in the coffee pot and
scalded the grease away and laid the dismembered sections
along the edge of the back porch where the sun fell on them
as long as there was sun. Then he reassembled it and loaded it
with two of the three remaining shells and leaned it against
the wall beside the chair, and again he watched the night
emerge from the bottom and mount through the bitten corn,
taking the house itself at last and, still rising, become as two
up-opening palms releasing the westward-flying ultimate bird
of evening. Below him, beyond the corn, the fireflies winked
and drifted against the breast of darkness; beyond, within, it
the steady booming of the frogs was the steady pulse and beat
of the dark heart of night, so that at last when the unvarying
moment came—that moment as unvarying from one dusk to
the next as the afternoon's instant when he would awake—

the beat of that heart seemed to fall still too, emptying silence for the first deep cry of strong and invincible grief. He reached his hand backward and took up the gun.

This time he used the hound's voice for a bearing from the start. When he entered the bottom he thought about wind and paused to test it. But there was no wind, so he went straight on toward the howling, not fast now since he was trying for silence, yet not slow either since this would not take long and then he could return home and lie down before midnight, long before midnight, telling himself as he moved cautiously and steadily toward the howling: Now I can go back to sleeping at night again. The howling was quite near now. He slanted the gun forward, his thumb on the two hammers. Then the dog's voice stopped, again in midhowl; again for an instant he saw the two yellow points of eyes before the gun-muzzle blotted them. In the glare of the explosion he saw the whole animal sharp in relief, leaping. He saw the charge strike and hurl it backward into the loud welter of following darkness. By an actual physical effort he restrained his finger before it contracted on the second trigger and with the gun still at his shoulder he crouched, holding his breath and glaring into the sightless dark while the tremendous silence which had been broken three nights ago when the first cry of the hound reached him and which had never once been restored, annealed, even while he slept, roared down about him and, still roaring, began to stiffen and set like cement, not only in his hearing but in his lungs, his breathing, inside and without him too, solidifying from tree-trunk to tree-trunk, among which the shattered echoes of the shot died away in strangling murmurs, caught in that cooling solidity before they had had time to cease. With the gun still cocked and presented, he advanced toward the place where he had seen the dog fall, panting through his bared clenched teeth, feeling about with his feet in the undergrowth. Then he realised suddenly that he had already passed the spot and that he was still advancing. He knew that he was about to start running and then he was running, blindly in the pitch darkness, speaking, hissing to himself: Stop. Stop. You'll bust your damn brains out. He stopped, panting. He got his bearings anew on a patch of sky, yet he forced himself to remain motionless until even the panting stopped. Then he let the hammer of the gun down and went on, walking now. Now he had the booming of the frogs to guide him, blending and fading then rising again in choral climax, each separate voice not a single note but an octave, almost a chord, in bass, growing louder and louder and nearer and nearer, then ceasing abruptly too into a second of frozen immobility followed by a swift random patter of small splashes like hands striking the water, so that when he saw the water it was already shattered into fluid ceaseless gleams across which reflected stars slid and vanished and recovered. He flung the gun. For an instant he saw it, spinning slowly. Then it splashed, not sinking but disintegrating among that shattered scurrying of broken stars.

When he reached home, it was not even midnight yet. Now he removed not only the shoes but the overalls too which had not passed his knees in seventy-two hours, and lay down on the pallet. But at once he knew he was not going to sleep, not because of the seventy-two hours' habit of reversed days and nights, not because of any twitching and jerking of spent and ungovernable nerves and muscles, but because of that silence which the first gunshot had broken and the second one had made whole again. So he lay again, rigid and composed on his back, his arms at his sides and his eyes open in the darkness and his head and lungs filled with that roaring silence across which the random and velvet-shod fireflies drifted and winked and beyond which the constant frogs pulsed and beat, until the rectangle of sky beyond the oblique door of the room and the open end of the hallway began to turn gray and then primrose, and already he could see three buzzards soaring in it. Now I must get up, he told himself; I will have to start staying up all day if I aim to begin sleeping again at night. Then he began to say, Wake up. Wake up, until he waked at last, with the yellow square of window-shaped sun lying once more on the floor where each unvarying afternoon it would lie. Resting upon the quilt not an inch from his face was a folded scrap of brown paper; when he rose, he found in the dust at the doorsill the print of the little boy's naked foot. The note was in pencil, on a scrap torn from a paper sack, unsigned: *Come on in here your wifes got some money for you* He stood, unshaven, in his shirt, blinking at it. Now I can go, he thought, and something began to happen in his heart. He raised his head, blinking almost painfully, looking for the first time in three days beyond the desolate and foodless cabin which symbolised the impasse his life had reached, into the limitless freedom of the sunny sky. He spoke aloud. "Now I can—" he said. Then he saw the buzzards. At dawn he had seen three. Now he might possibly have counted them, though he did not. He just watched the black concentric spiraling as if they followed an invisible funnel, disappearing one by one below the trees. He spoke aloud again. "It's the dog," he said, knowing it was not the dog. And it didn't matter. Because I'll be gone then, he thought. It was not that something lifted from his heart; it was as though he had become aware for the first time of the weight which lay on it.

It was almost sunset when, shaved and with the shoes and overalls washed again, he mounted to the empty gallery and entered the store. His kinsman was behind the open candy case, in the act of putting something into his mouth.

"Where—" he said.

The cousin closed the case, chewing. "You durned fool, I sent word to you two days ago to get away from there before that pussel-gutted Hampton come prowling around here with that surrey full of deputies. A nigger grabbling in that slough found that durn gun before the water even quit shaking."

"It's not mine," he said. "I have no gun. Where—"

"Hell fire, everybody knows it's yours. There aint another one of them old hammer-lock ten-gauge Hadleys in this country but that one. That's why I never told no lie about it, let alone that durn Hampton sitting right out there on that bench when the nigger come up the steps with it. I says, 'Sure it's Mink's gun. He's been hunting for it ever since last fall.' Then I turns to the nigger. 'What the hell you mean, you black son of a bitch,' I says, 'borrowing Mr Snopes' gun last fall to go squirl hunting and letting it fall in that ere slough and claiming you couldn't find it?' Here." The cousin stooped beneath the counter and rose and laid the gun on the counter. It had been wiped off save for a patch of now-dried mud on the stock.

He did not even look at it. "It's not mine," he said. "Where is—"

"But that's all right now. I fixed that in time. What Hampton expected was for me to deny it was yours. Then he would a had you. But I fixed that. I throwed the suspicion right onto the nigger fore Hampton could open his mouth. I figger about tonight or maybe tomorrow night I'll take a few of the boys and go to the nigger's house with a couple of trace chains or maybe a little fire under his feet. And even if he dont confess nothing, folks will hear that he has done been visited at night and there's too many votes out here for Hampton to do nothing else but take him on in and send him to the penitentiary, even if he cant quite risk hanging him, and Hampton knows it. So that's all right. Besides, what I sent you that first message for was about your wife."

"Yes," he said. "Where—"

"She's going to get you in trouble. She's done already got you in trouble. That's how come that durn vote-sucking sheriff noseying around out here. His nigger found the horse, with him and the dog both missing, but that was all right until folks begun to remember how she turned up here that same night, with them two kids and that bundle of clothes and blood still running out of her busted mouth until folks couldn't help but know you had run her out of the house. And even that might have been all right if she hadn't started in telling everybody that would listen that you never done it. Just a horse with a empty saddle; no body and no blood neither found yet, and here she is trying to help you by telling everybody she meets that you never done something that nobody knows for sure has even been done yet. Why in hell aint you got out of here? Didn't you have sense enough to do that the first day?"

"On what?" he said.

The cousin had been blinking rapidly at him. Now the little eyes stopped blinking. "On what?" he said. The other did not answer. He had not moved since he entered, small, immobile, in the middle of the floor opposite the entrance, through which the dying sunlight stained him from head to foot with a thin wash like diluted blood. "You mean you aint got any money? You mean to stand there and tell me he never had nothing in his pocket? Because I dont believe it. By God, I know better. I saw inside his purse that same morning. He never carried a cent less than fifty. . . . . . ." The voice ceased, died. Then it spoke in a dawning incredulous amazement and no louder than a whisper: "Do you mean to tell me you never even looked? *never even looked?*" The other did not answer. He might not have even heard, motionless, looking at nothing while the last of the copper light, mounting like rising water up his body, gathered for an instant in concentrated and dying crimson upon the calm and unwavering and intractable mask of his face, and faded, and the dusk, the twilight, gathered along the ranked shelves and in the shadowy corners and the old strong smells of cheese and leather and kerosene, condensed and thickened among the rafters above his head like the pall of oblivion itself. The cousin's voice seemed to emerge from it, sourceless, unlocatable, without even the weight of breath to give it volume: "Where did you put him?" and again, the cousin outside the counter now, facing him, almost breast to breast with him, the fierce repressed breathing murmuring on his face now: "By God, he had at least fifty dollars. I know. I seen it. Right here in this store. Where did you—"

"No," he said.

"Yes."

"No." Their faces were not a foot apart, their breathing steady and audible. Then the other face moved back, larger than his, higher than his, beginning to become featureless in the fading light.

"All right," the cousin said. "I'm glad you dont need money. Because if you come to me expecting any, you'd just have to keep on expecting. You know what Will Varner pays his clerks. You know about how much any man working for Will Varner's wages could get ahead in ten years, let alone two months. So you wont even need that ten dollars your wife's got. So that'll be just fine, wont it?"

"Yes," he said. "Where—"

"Staying at Will Varner's." He turned at once and went toward the door. As he passed out of it the cousin spoke again out of the shadows behind him: "Tell her to ask Will or Jody to lend her another ten to go with that one she's already got."

Although it was not quite dark yet, there was already a light in the Varner house. He could see it even at this distance, and it was as if he were standing outside of himself, watching the distance steadily shorten between himself and the light. And then that's all, he thought. All them days and nights that looked like they wasn't going to have no end, come down to the space of a little piece of dusty road between me and a lighted door. And when he put his hand on Varner's gate, it was as if she had been waiting, watching the road for him. She came out of the front door, running, framed again for an instant by the lighted doorway as when he had first seen her that night at the lumber camp to which, even nine years afterward, he did not like to remember how, by what mischance, he had come. The feeling was no less strong now than it had ever been. He did not dread to remember it nor did he try not to, and not in remorse for the deed he had done, because he neither required nor desired absolution for that. He merely wished he did not have to remember the fiasco which had followed the act, contemptuous of the body or the intellect which had failed the will to do, not writhing with impotent regret on remembering it and not snarling, because he never snarled; but just cold, indomitable, and intractable. He had lived in a dozen different sorry and ill-made rented cabins as his father had moved from farm to farm, without himself ever having been more than fifteen or twenty miles away from any one of them. Then suddenly and at night he had had to leave the roof he called home and the only land and people and customs he knew, without even time to gather up anything to take with him, if there had been anything to take, nor to say farewell to anyone if there had been anyone to say farewell to, to find himself weeks later and still on foot, more than two hundred miles away. He was seeking the sea; he was twenty-three then, that young. He had never seen it; he did not know certainly just where it was, except that it was to the south. He had never thought of it before and he could not have said why he wanted to go to it—what of repudiation of the land, the earth, where his body or intellect had faulted somehow to the cold undeviation of his will to do—seeking what of that iodinic proffer of space and oblivion of which he had no intention of availing himself, would never avail himself, as if, by deliberately refusing to cut the wires of remembering, to punish that body and intellect which had failed him. Perhaps he was seeking only the proffer of this illimitable space and irremediable forgetting along the edge of which the contemptible teeming of his own earth-kind timidly seethed and recoiled, not to accept the proffer but merely to bury himself in this myriad anonymity beside the impregnable haven of all the drowned intact golden galleons and the unattainable deathless seamaids. Then, almost there and more than twenty-four hours without food, he saw a light and approached it and heard the loud voices and saw her framed in the open door, immobile, upright and unlistening, while those harsh loud manshouts and cries seemed to rise toward her like a roaring incense. He went no further. The next morning he was at work there, an axeman, without even knowing whom he was working for, asking only incidentally of the foreman who hired him and who told him bluntly that he was too small, too light, to swing his end of a cross-cut saw, what his wage would be. He had never seen convicts' stripes before either, so it was not with that first light but only after several succeeding ones that he learned where he was—a tract of wildcatted virgin timber in process of being logged by a roaring man of about fifty who was no taller than he was, with strong, short iron-gray hair and a hard prominent belly, who through political influence or bribery or whatever got his convict labor from the State for the price of their board and keep; a widower who had lost his wife years ago at the birth of their first child and now lived openly with a magnificent quadroon woman most of whose teeth were gold and who superintended the kitchen where other convicts did the actual work, in a separate house set among the plank-and-canvas barracks in which the convicts lived. The woman in the lighted door was that child. She lived in the same house with her father and the quadroon, in a separate wing with an entrance of its own, and her hair was black then—a splendid heavy mane of it which whatever present one out of foremen and armed guards and convict laborers, and himself in his turn, after his summons came and he had long since discovered the reason for the separate entrance, contributed to keep cut almost man-short with razors.

It was strong and short and not fine, either in the glare of that first evening's lamp or in the next day's sunlight when, the axe lifted for the stroke, he turned and she was sitting a big, rangy, well-kept horse behind and above him, in overalls, looking at him not brazenly and not speculatively, but intently and boldly, as a bold and successful man would. That was what he saw: the habit of success—that perfect marriage of will and ability with a single undiffused object—which set her not as a feminine garment but as one as masculine as the overalls and her height and size and the short hair; he saw not a nympholept but the confident lord of a harem. She did not speak that time. She rode on, and now he discovered that that separate entrance was not used only at night. Sometimes she would ride past on the horse and stop and speak briefly to the foreman and ride on; sometimes the quadroon would appear on the horse and speak a name to the foreman and return, and the foreman would call that name and the man would drop his axe or saw and follow the horse. Then he, still swinging his axe and not even looking up, would seem to follow and watch that man enter the private door and then watch him emerge later and return to work—the nameless, the identical, highwayman, murderer, thief, among whom there appeared to be no favorites and no jealousy. That was to be his alone, apparently. But even before his summons came, he was resigned to the jealousy and cognizant of his fate. He had been bred by generations to believe invincibly that to every man, whatever his past actions, whatever depths he might have reached, there was reserved one virgin, at least for him to marry; one maidenhead, if only for him to deflower and destroy. Yet he not only saw that he must compete for mere notice with men among whom he saw himself not only as a child but as a child of another race and species, but that when he did approach her at last he would have to tear aside not garments alone but the ghostly embraces of thirty or forty men; and this not only once but each time and hence (he foresaw even then his fate) forever: no room, no darkness, no desert even ever large enough to contain the two of them and the constant stallion-ramp of those inexpugnable shades. Then his turn, his summons came at last, as he had known it would. He obeyed it with foreknowledge but without regret.

He entered not the hot and quenchless bed of a barren and
lecherous woman, but the fierce simple cave of a lioness—a
tumescence which surrendered nothing and asked no quarter,
and which made a monogamist of him forever, as opium and
homicide do of those whom they once accept. That was early
one afternoon, the hot sun of July falling through the shadeless and even curtainless windows open to all outdoors, upon
a bed made by hand of six-inch unplaned timbers cross-braced
with light steel cables, yet which nevertheless would advance
in short steady skidding jerks across the floor like a light and
ill-balanced rocking chair. Five months later they were married. They did not plan it. Never at any time afterward did he
fail to affirm, even to himself, that the marriage had been no
scheme or even intention of hers. What did it was the collapse
of her father's enterprise, which even he had been able to see
was inherent with its own inevitable bankruptcy which the
crash of each falling tree brought one stick nearer. Afterward
it seemed to him that that afternoon's bedding had been the
signal for that entire furious edifice of ravished acres and shotgun houses and toiling men and mules which had been
erected overnight and founded on nothing, to collapse overnight into nothing, back into the refuse—the sawdust heaps,
the lopped dead limbs and tree-butts and all the grief of
wood—of its own murdering. He had most of his five
months' pay. They walked to the nearest county-seat and
bought a license; the Justice of the Peace who sold it to them
removed his chew of tobacco and, holding it damp in his
hand, called in two passing men and pronounced them man
and wife. They returned to his native country, where he
rented a small farm on shares. They had a second-hand stove,
a shuck mattress on the floor, the razor with which he still
kept her hair cut short, and little else. At that time they
needed little else. She said: "I've had a hundred men, but I
never had a wasp before. That stuff comes out of you is rank
poison. It's too hot. It burns itself and my seed both up. It'll
never make a kid." But three years afterward it did. Five years
later it had made two; and he would watch them as they approached across whatever sorry field or patch, fetching his
cold meagre dinner or the jug of fresh water, or as they
played with blocks of wood or rusted harness buckles or

threadless and headless plow-bolts which even he could no longer use, in the dust before whatever rented porch he sat on while the sweat cooled out of him, and in a resurgence of the old hot quick invincible fury still as strong and fierce and brief as on the first time, he would think, By God, they better be mine. Then, quieter, on the pallet bed where she would already be asleep although his own spent body had not yet ceased to jerk and twitch, he would think how, even if they were not, it was the same thing. They served to shackle her too, more irrevocably than he himself was shackled, since on her fate she had even put the seal of a formal acquiescence by letting her hair grow out again and dyeing it.

She came down the walk, running heavily but fast. She reached it before he had finished opening it, flinging both him and the gate back as she ran through it and caught him by the front of his overalls. "No!" she cried, though her voice still whispered: "No! Oh God, what do you mean? You cant come in here!"

"I can go anywhere I want to," he said. "Lump said—" Then he tried to wrench free, but she had already released him and caught his arm and was hurrying, almost dragging him along the fence, away from the light. He wrenched at her grip again, setting his feet. "Wait," he said.

"You fool!" she said, in that harsh panting whisper: "You fool! Oh, God damn you! God damn you!" He began to struggle, with a cold condensed fury which did not seem quite able or perhaps ready to emerge yet from his body. Then he lashed suddenly out, still not at her but to break her grip. But she held him, with both hands now, as they faced each other. "Why didn't you go that night? God, I thought of course you were going to get out as soon as I left!" She shook him savagely, with no more effort than if he were a child. "Why didn't you? Why in hell didn't you?"

"On what?" he said. "Where? Lump said—"

"I know you didn't have any money, like I know you haven't had anything to eat except the dust in that barrel. You could have hidden! In the woods—anywhere, until I would have time to—God damn you! God damn you! If they would just let me do the hanging!" She shook him, her face bent to his, her hard, hot, panting breath on his face. "Not for killing him, but for doing it when you had no money to get away on if you ran, and nothing to eat if you stayed. If they'd just let me do it: hang you just enough to take you down and bring you to and hang you again just enough to cut you down and bring you to—" He slashed out again, viciously. But she had already released him, standing on one foot now, the other foot angled upward from the knee to meet her reaching hand. She took something from her shoe and put it into his hand. He knew at once what it was—a banknote, folded and refolded small and square and still warm with body-heat. And it was just one note. It's one dollar, he thought, knowing it was not. It was I.O. and Eck, he told himself, knowing it was not, just as he knew there was but one man in the country who would have ten dollars in one bill—or at the most, two men; now he even heard what his cousin had said as he walked out of the store fifteen minutes ago. He didn't even look toward his hand.

"Did you sell Will something for it, or did you just take it out of his pants while he was asleep? Or was it Jody?"

"What if I did? What if I can sell enough more of it tonight to get ten more. Only for God's sake dont go back to the house. Stay in the woods. Then tomorrow morning——" He did not move; she saw only the slight jerk of his hand and wrist—no coin to ring against his thumbnail or to make any sound among the dust-stiffened roadside weeds where gouts of dusty cotton clung. When he went on, she began to run after him. "Mink!" she said. He walked steadily on. She was at his shoulder, running, though he continued to walk. "For God's sake," she said. "For God's sake." Then she caught his shoulder and swung him to face her. This time he slashed free and sprang into the weeds, stooping, and rose with a stick lifted in his hand and walked toward her again with that patient and implacable weariness, until she turned. He lowered the stick, but he continued to stand there until he could no longer distinguish her, even against the pale dust of the road. Then he tossed the stick into the weeds and turned. The cousin was standing behind him. If the other had been smaller or he larger he would have stepped on him, walked him down. The other stepped aside and turned with him, the faint rasp of the repressed breathing at his shoulder.

"So you throwed that away too," the cousin said. He didn't answer. They went on side by side in the thick, ankle-deep dust. Their feet made no sound in it. "He had at least fifty dollars. I tell you I saw it. And you expect me to believe you aint got it." He didn't answer. They walked steadily on, not fast, like two people walking without destination or haste, for pleasure or exercise. "All right. I'm going to do what wouldn't no other man living do: I'm going to give you the benefit of the doubt that you aint got it, actually never looked. Now where did you put him?" He didn't answer nor pause. The cousin caught him by the shoulder, stopping him; now there was in the fierce baffled breathing, the whispering voice, not only the old amazement but a sort of cold and desperate outrage, like one trying to reach through a fleeing crisis to the comprehension of an idiot: "Are you going to let that fifty dollars lay there for Hampton and them deputies to split up between them?"

He struck the hand off. "Let me alone," he said.

"All right. I'll do this. I'll give you twenty-five dollars now. I'll go with you, all you got to do is hand me the wallet, sight unseen. Or hand me his pants, if you dont want to take it out of them. You wont even touch or even see the money." He turned to go on again. "All right. If you are too puke-stomached to do it yourself, tell me where it is. When I come back, I'll give you ten dollars, though a fellow that just throwed away a ten-dollar-bill dont——" He walked on. Again the hand caught his shoulder and swung him about; the tense fierce voice murmured from nowhere and every-where out of the breathless dark: "Wait. Listen. Listen good. Suppose I look up Hampton; he's been around here all day; he's probably still somewhere here tonight. Suppose I tell him I done recollected a mistake, that that gun wasn't lost last fall because you come in the store and bought a nickel's worth of powder just last week. Then you can explain how you was aiming to swap Houston the powder for the pound-fee on that yearling——"

This time he did not fling the hand off. He merely began to walk toward the other with that patient and invincible weari-ness which the other did not recognise, walking steadily to-ward the cousin as the other gave ground. His voice was not loud either; it was flat, absolutely toneless: "I ask you to let me alone," he said. "I dont tell you; I ask you to let me alone. Not for my sake. Because I'm tired. I ask you to let me alone." The other backed away before him, moving slightly faster, so that the distance between them increased. When he stopped, it continued to increase until he could no longer see the other and only the whisper, furious and outraged, came back:

"All right, you durn little tight-fisted murderer. See if you get away with it."

Approaching the village again, his feet made no sound in the dust and, in the darkness, seemingly no progress either, though the light in Mrs Littlejohn's kitchen window just beyond the store's dark bulk—the only light anywhere—drew steadily nearer. Just beyond it the lane turned off which led to his cabin four miles away. That's where I would have kept straight on, to Jefferson and the railroad, he thought; and suddenly, now that it was too late, now that he had lost all hope of alternative between planned and intelligent escape and mere blind desperate harried fleeing and doubling through the swamp and jungle of the bottom like a spent and starving beast cut off from its den, he knew that for three days now he had not only hoped but had actually believed that opportunity to choose would be given him. And he had not only lost that privilege of choice, but due to the blind mischance which had permitted his cousin either to see or guess what was in the wallet, even the bitter alternative was deferred for another night. It began to seem to him now that that puny and lonely beacon not only marked no ultimate point for even desperate election but was the period to hope itself, and that all which remained to him of freedom lay in the shortening space between it and his advancing foot. I thought that when you killed a man, that finished it, he told himself. But it dont. It just starts then.

When he reached home, he did not enter it. Instead, he went around to the woodpile and got his axe and stood for a moment to examine the stars. It was not much past nine; he could allow himself until midnight. Then he circled the house and entered the corn-patch. Halfway down the slope he paused, listening, then he went on. He did not enter the bottom either; he stepped behind the first tree large enough to conceal him and leaned the axe carefully against it where he could find it again and stood there, motionless, breathing quietly, and listened to the heavy body running with hurried and cautious concern among the clashing cornstalks, the tense and hurried panting drawing rapidly nearer, then the quick indraw of breath when the other ran past the tree, checking, as he stepped out from behind it and turned back up the slope.

They went back through the corn, in single file and five feet apart. He could hear the clumsy body behind him stumbling and thrashing among the sibilant rows, and the breathing fierce, outraged, and repressed. His own passage made no noise, even in the trigger-set dryness of the corn, as if his body had no substance. "Listen," the cousin said. "Let's look at this thing like two reasonable. . . . . . ." They emerged from the corn and crossed the yard and entered the house, still five feet apart. He went on to the kitchen and lit the lamp and squatted before the stove, preparing to start the fire. The cousin stood in the door, breathing heavily and watching while the other coaxed the chips into a blaze and took the coffee pot from the stove and filled it from the water pail and set it back. "Aint you even got nothing to eat?" the cousin said. The other did not answer. "You got some feed corn, aint you? We could parch some of that." The fire was burning well now. The other laid his hand on the pot, though of course it had not even begun to be warm yet. The cousin watched the back of his head. "All right," he said. "Let's go get some of it."

The other removed his hand from the pot. He did not look back. "Get it," he said. "I'm not hungry." The cousin breathed in the door, watching the still, slanted face. His breath made a faint, steady, rasping sound.

"All right," he said. "I'll go to the barn and get some." He left the door and walked heavily down the hallway and onto the back porch and stepped down to the earth, already running. He ran frantically in the blind darkness and on tiptoe, around toward the front of the house and stopped, peering around the corner toward the front door, holding his breath, then ran again, on to the steps, where he could see into the hallway lighted faintly by the lamp in the kitchen, and paused again for an instant, crouched, glaring. The son of a bitch tricked me, he thought. He went out the back: and ran up the steps, stumbling heavily and recovering, and thundered down the hall to the kitchen door and saw, in the instant of passing it, the other standing beside the stove as he had left him, his hand again on the coffee pot. The murdering little son of a bitch, he thought. I wouldn't have believed it. I wouldn't have believed a man would have to go through all this even for five hundred dollars.

But when he stood in the door again, save for the slightly increased rasp and tempo of his breathing, he might never have left it. He watched the other fetch to the stove a cracked china cup, a thick glass tumbler, a tin can containing a little sugar, and a spoon; when he spoke, he might have been talking to his employer's wife over a tea-table: "It's done made up its mind at last to get hot, has it?" The other did not answer. He filled the cup from the pot and spooned sugar into it and stirred it and stood beside the stove, turned three quarters from the cousin, his head bent, sipping from the cup. After a moment the cousin approached and filled the tumbler and put sugar into it and sipped, wry-faced, his features all seeming to flee from the tumbler's rim, upward, gathering, eyes, nose, even mouth, toward his forehead, as if the skin in which they were embedded was attached to his skull only at one point somewhere in the back. "Listen," the cousin said. "Just try to look at this thing like two reasonable people. There's that fifty dollars laying out there, not belonging to nobody. And you cant go and get it without taking me, because I aint going to let you. And I cant go get it without taking you, because I dont know where it's at. Yet here we are, setting around this house while every minute we waste is bringing that durn sheriff and them deputies just that much closer to finding it. It's just a matter of pure and simple principle. Aint no likes and dislikes about it. If I had my way, I'd keep all of it myself, the same as you would. But you cant and I cant. Yet here we are, setting here—" The other tilted the cup and drained it.

"What time is it?" he said. From the creased bulge of his waistband the cousin wrenched a dollar watch on a thong of greasy leather and looked at it and prized it back into the fob-pocket.

"Twenty-eight past nine. And it aint going to stay that forever. And I got to open the store at six oclock in the morning. And I got to walk five miles tonight before I can go to bed. But never mind that. Dont pay no attention to that, because there aint nothing personal in this because it is a pure and simple business matter. Think about your—" The other set the empty cup on the stove.

"Checkers?" he said.

"—self. You got—What?" The cousin stopped talking. He watched the other cross the room and lift from among the shadows in the corner a short, broad piece of plank. From the shelf above it he took another tin can and brought them to the table. The board was marked off with charcoal into alternate staggered squares; the can contained a handful of small china- and glass-fragments in two colors, apparently from a broken plate and a blue glass bottle. He laid the board beside the lamp and began to oppose the men. The cousin watched him, the tumbler arrested halfway to his mouth. For an instant he ceased to breathe. Then he breathed again. "Why, sholy," he said. He set the glass on the stove and drew up a chair opposite. Sitting, he seemed to be on the point of enveloping not only the chair but the table too in a collapsing mass of flabby and badly-filled flesh, like a collapsing balloon. "We'll play a nickel a game against that fifty dollars," he said. "All right?"

"Move," the other said. They began to play—the one with a cold and deadly deliberation and economy of moves, the other with a sort of clumsy speed and dash. It was that amateurish, that almost childlike, lack of premeditation and plan or even foresight of one who, depending on manipulation and not intellect in games of chance, finds himself involved in one where dexterity cannot avail, yet nevertheless attempting to cheat even at bald and simple draughts with an incredible optimism, an incorrigible dishonesty long since become pure reflex and probably now beyond his control, making his dashing and clumsy moves then withdrawing his closed fist to sit watching with his little intent unwinking eyes the still, wasted, down-looking face opposite, talking steadily about almost everything except money and death, the fist resting on the table-edge still closed about the pawn or the king's crown which it had palmed. The trouble with checkers is, he thought, It aint nothing but checkers. At the end of an hour he was thirteen games ahead.

"Make it a quarter," he said.

"What time is it?" the other said. The cousin wrung the watch from his waistband again and returned it.

"Four minutes to eleven."

"Move," the other said. They played on. The cousin was not talking now. He was keeping score now with a chewed pencil stub on the edge of the board. Thus when, thirty minutes later, he totted up the score, the pencil presented to his vision not a symbol but a sum complete with decimal and dollar mark, which seemed in the next instant to leap upward and strike comprehension with an impact almost audible; he became dead still, for an instant he did not breathe indeed, thinking rapidly: Hell fire. Hell fire. Of course he never caught me. He didn't want to. Because when I have won all of his share, he'll figure he wont need to risk going where it's at. So now he had to completely reverse his entire tactics. And now for the first time the crawling hands on the face of the watch which he now produced without being asked and laid face-up beside the board, assumed a definite significance. Because this here just cant go on forever, he thought in a resurgence of the impotent rage. It just cant. A man just cant be expected to go through much more of this even for all of fifty dollars. So he reversed himself. Whereupon it was as if even dishonesty had foresworn him. He would make the dashing, clumsy, calculated moves; he would sit back with his own pawn or king's crown in his fist now. Only now the other's thin hard hand would be gripping that wrist while the cold, flat, dead voice demonstrated how a certain pawn could not possibly have arrived at the square on which it suddenly appeared to be, and lived, or even rapping the knuckles of that gripped hand on the table until it disgorged. Yet he would attempt it again, with that baffled and desperate optimism and hope, and be caught again and then try it again, until at the end of the next hour his movements on the board were not even childlike, they were those of an imbecile or a blind person. And he was talking again now: "Listen. There's that fifty dollars that dont belong to nobody because he never had no kin, nobody to claim it. Just laying out there for the first man that comes along to——"

"Move," the other said. He moved a pawn. "No," the other said. "Jump." He made the jump. The other moved a second pawn.

"——and here you are needing money to keep from being hung maybe and you cant go and get it because I wont leave. And me that cant get up and go on home and get to bed so I can get up, and go to work tomorrow because you wont show me where that money's at——"

"Move," the other said. The cousin moved a pawn. "No," the other said. "Jump." The cousin took the jump. Then he watched the gaunt black-haired fingers holding the scrap of blue glass clear the board in five jumps.

"And now it's after midnight. It will be light in six hours. And Hampton and them durn deputies——" The cousin ceased. The other was now standing, looking down at him; the cousin rose quickly. They stared at one another across the table. "Well?" the cousin said. His breath began to make the harsh, tense, rasping sound again, not triumphant yet. "Well?" he said. "Well?" But the other was not looking at him, he was looking down, the face still, wasted, seemingly without life.

"I ask you to go," the other said. "I ask you to leave me alone."

"Sholy," the cousin said, his voice no louder than the other's. "Quit now? after I done gone through all this?" The other turned toward the door. "Wait," the cousin said. The other did not pause. The cousin blew out the lamp and overtook the other in the hallway. He was talking again, whispering now. "If you'd just listened to me six hours ago. We'd a done had it and been back, in bed, instead of setting up here half the night. Dont you see how it was tit for tat all the time? You had me and I had you, and couldn't neither— Where we going?" The other didn't answer. He went steadily on across the yard, toward the barn, the cousin following; again he heard just behind him the tense, fierce adenoidal breathing, the whispering voice: "Hell fire, maybe you dont want me to have half of it and maybe I dont want nobody to have half of it neither. But hell fire, aint just half of it better

than to think of that durn Hampton and them deputies—"
He entered the barn and opened the door to the crib and
stepped up into it, the cousin stopping just outside the door
behind him, and reached down from its nail in the wall a
short, smooth white-oak stick eyed at the end with a loop of
hemp rope—a twister which Houston had used with his stallion, which Snopes had found when he rented the foreclosed
portion of Houston's farm from the Varners—and turned
and struck all in one motion and dropped the cudgel and
caught the heavy body as it fell so that its own weight helped
to carry it into the crib and all he needed to do was to drag it
on in until the feet cleared the door. He unbuckled a hame
string and the check rein from his plow gear and bound the
other's hands and feet and tore a strip from the tail of his shirt
and made a gag with it.

When he reached the bottom, he could not find the tree
behind which he had left the axe. He knew what was wrong.
It was as though with the cessation of that interminable voice
he had become aware not of silence but of elapsed time, that
on the instant it had ceased he had retraced and resumed at
the moment it began in the store at six oclock in the afternoon, and now he was six hours late. You're trying too hard,
he told himself. You got to slow up. So he held himself
still for the space of a hundred, trying to orient himself by
looking back up the slope, to establish whether he was above
or below the tree, to the right or left of it. Then he went back
halfway through the corn and looked back at the bottom
from there, trying to recognise by its shape and position the
tree where he had left the axe, standing in the roar not of
silence now but of time's friction. He thought of starting
from some point which he knew was below the tree he
sought and searching each tree as he came to it. But the
sound of time was too loud, so when he began to move, to
run, it was toward neither the bottom nor the cabin but
across the slope, quartering, out of the corn and on into the
road a half mile beyond his house.

He ran for another mile and came to another cabin, smaller
and shabbier than his. It belonged to the negro who had
found the gun. There was a dog here, a mongrel terrier, a
feice, not much larger than a cat and noisy as a calliope; at

once it came boiling out from beneath the house and rushed toward him in shrill hysteria. He knew it and it should know him; he spoke to it to quiet it but it continued to yap, the sound seeming to come from a dozen different points out of the darkness before him until he ran suddenly at it, whereupon the shrill uproar faded rapidly back toward the house. He continued to run, on toward the woodpile which he knew too; the axe was there. As he caught it up a voice said from the dark cabin: "Who there?" He didn't answer. He ran on, the terrier still yapping behind him though from beneath the house now. Now he was in corn again, better than his. He ran on through it, descending, toward the bottom.

Before entering the bottom, he stopped and took his bearings on a star. He did not expect to find the tree from this point, it was the old sunken road he aimed for; once in that, he could orient himself again. His surest course, even though it would be longer, would be to skirt the bottom until he reached country he knew in the dark and strike in for the tree from there, but when he examined the sky to fix his bearing, he thought, It's after one oclock.

Yet, thirty minutes later, he had not found the road. He had been able to see the sky only intermittently, and not always the star he guided by then. But he believed he had not deviated much. Also, he had cautioned himself: You will expect to come onto it before you do; you will have to watch for that. But in this time he had travelled twice the distance in which he should have found it. When he realised, admitted at last that he was lost, it was with neither alarm nor despair, but rage. It was as though, like the cousin and his dishonesty two or three hours ago, ruthlessness likewise had repudiated the disciple who had flagged for a moment in ruthlessness; that it was that humanity which had caused him to waste three hours in hope that the cousin would tire and go away instead of striking the other over the head when he ran past the tree where he had lost the axe, which had brought him to this.

His first impulse was to run, not in panic but to keep ahead of that avalanche of accumulating seconds which was now his enemy. But he quelled it, holding himself motionless, his spent body shaking faintly and steadily with exhaustion, until he was satisfied his muscles would not be able to take him by surprise and run with him. Then he turned deliberately and carefully until he believed he was facing his back trail and the direction from which he had come, and walked forward. After a while he came to an opening in which he could see the sky. The star on which he had fixed his course when he entered the bottom was directly in front of him. And now it's after two oclock, he thought.

Now he began to run, or as fast as he dared, that is. He could not help himself. I got to find the road now, he thought. If I try to go back and start over, it will be daylight before I get out of the bottom. So he hurried on, stumbling and thrashing among the briers and undergrowth, one arm extended to fend himself from the trees, voiceless, panting, blind, the muscles about his eyelids strained and aching against the flat impenetrable face of the darkness, until suddenly there was no earth under his feet; he made another stride, running upon nothing, then he was falling and then he was on his back, panting. He was in the road. But he did not know where. But I aint crossed it, he thought. I am still on the west side of it. And now it's past two oclock.

Now he was oriented again. By turning his back on the road and holding a straight course, he would reach the edge of the bottom. Then he would be able to ascertain where he was. When he found himself falling, he had flung the axe away. He hunted for it on his hands and knees and found it and climbed out of the road and went on. He did not run now. Now he knew that he dared not lose himself again. When, an hour later, he emerged from the bottom, it was at the corner of a corn-patch. It was his own; the bizarre erst-fluid earth became fixed and stable in the old solid dimensions and juxtapositions. He saw the squat roof-line of his own house, and running again, stumbling a little among the rows of whispering stalks, panting through his dry lips and his dry clenched teeth, he saw and recognised the tree behind which he had left the axe, and again it was as if he had retraced and resumed at some dead point in time and only time was lost. He turned and approached it, he was about to pass it when a thicker shadow detached itself from the other shadow, rising without haste, and the cousin's voice said, weakly and harshly: "Forgot your durned axe, hah? Here it is. Take it."

He had stopped with no sound, no ejaculation, no catch of breath. Except I better not use the axe, he thought, still, immobile, while the other breathed harshly above him and the harsh, weak, outraged voice went on: "You durn little fratricidal murderer, if I hadn't just about stood all one man can stand, for twenty-five dollars or twenty-five thousand either, I'd be a good mind to knock you in the head with it and tote you out and throw you into Hampton's surrey myself. And by God it aint your fault it wasn't Hampton instead of me sitting here waiting for you. Hell fire, you hadn't hardly got started good chuckling over them other twenty-five dollars you thought you had just got before Hampton and the whole durn mess of them was in that crib, untying me and throwing water in my face. And I lied for you again. I told them you had knocked me in the head and tied me up and robbed me and lit out for the railroad. Now just how much longer do you figure I aim to keep telling lies just to save your neck? Hah?—Well? What are we waiting for? For Hampton?"

"Yes," he said. "All right." But not the axe, he thought. He turned and went on, into the trees. The other followed him, right at his heels now, the fierce adenoidal breath, the weak, outraged voice almost over his head, so that when he stooped and groped with his hand about the ground at his feet, the other walked into him.

"What the hell you doing now? Have you lost the durn axe again? Find it and give it to me and then get on and show me where it's at before not only sunup but ever durn vote-sucking——" His hand touched and found a stick large enough. I cant see this time, so I got to be ready to hit twice, he thought, rising. He struck toward the harsh, enraged voice, recovering and striking again though one blow had been enough.

He knew where he was now. He needed no guide, though presently he knew that he had one and he went quite fast now, nosing into the thin taint of air, needing to go fast now. Because it's more than three oclock now, he thought, thinking: I had forgot that. It's like just about everything was in cahoots against one man killing another. Then he knew that

he smelled it, because now there was no focal point, no guiding point, it was everywhere; he saw the opening, the topless
shell of the blasted oak rising against the leaf-frayed patch of
rainless sky. He squared himself away for proper distance by
touching his hand against the shell and swung the axe. The
entire head sank helve-deep into the rotten pith. He wrenched
at it, twisting it free, and raised it again. Then—there was no
sound, the darkness itself merely sighed and flowed behind
him, and he tried to turn but it was too late—something
struck him between the shoulders. He knew at once what it
was. He was not surprised even, feeling the breath and hearing the teeth as he fell, turning, trying to raise the axe,
hearing the teeth again at his throat and feeling the hot
breath-reek as he hurled the hound temporarily back with
his forearm and got onto his knees and got both hands on the
axe. He could see its eyes now as it leaped the second time.
They seemed to float toward him interminably. He struck at
them, striking nothing; the axe-head went into the ground,
almost snatching him after it onto his face. This time when he
saw the eyes, he was on his feet. He rushed at them, the axe
lifted. He went charging on even after the eyes vanished,
crashing and plunging in the undergrowth, stopping at last,
the axe raised and poised, panting, listening, seeing and hearing nothing. He returned to the tree.

At the first stroke of the axe, the dog sprang again. He was
expecting it. He did not bury the head this time and he had
the axe raised and ready as he whirled. He struck at the eyes
and felt the axe strike and leap spinning from his hands, and
he sprang toward where the animal thrashed and groaned in
the underbrush, leaping toward the sound, stamping furiously
about him, pausing crouched, to listen, leaping toward another sound and stamping again, but again in vain. Then he
got down on his hands and knees and crawled in widening
circles about the tree, hunting the axe. When he found it at
last he could see, above the jagged top of the shell, the morning star.

He chopped again at the base of the shell, stopping after
each blow to listen, the axe already poised, his feet and knees
braced to whirl. But he heard nothing. Then he began to
chop steadily, the axe sinking helve-deep at each stroke as

though into sand or sawdust. Then the axe sank, helve and all, into the rotten wood, he knew now it was not imagination he had smelled and he dropped the axe and began to tear at the shell with his hands, his head averted, his teeth bared and clenched, his breath hissing through them, freeing one arm momentarily to fling the hound back though it surged against him again, whimpering, and then thrust its head into the growing orifice out of which the foul air seemed to burst with an audible sound. "Get back, God damn you!" he panted as though he were speaking to a man, trying again to hurl the hound away; "give me room!" He dragged at the body, feeling it slough upon its bones as though it were too large for itself. Now the hound had its entire head and shoulders in the opening, howling.

When the body came suddenly free, he went over backward, lying on his back in the mud, the body across his legs, while the hound stood over it, howling. He got up and kicked at it. It moved back, but when he stooped and took hold of the legs and began to walk backward, the hound was beside him again. But it was intent on the body and as long as they were in motion, it did not howl. But when he stopped to get his breath, it began to howl again and again he braced himself and kicked at it and this time as he did so he discovered that he was actually seeing the animal and that dawn had come, the animal visible now, gaunt, thin, with a fresh bloody gash across its face, howling. Watching it, he stooped and groped until his hand found a stick. It was foul with slime but still fairly sound. When the hound raised its head to howl again, he struck. The dog whirled; he saw the long scar of the gunshot running from its shoulder to its flank as it sprang at him. This time the stick took it fairly between the eyes. He picked up the ankles, facing forward now, and tried to run.

When he came out of the undergrowth and onto the river bank, the east was turning red. The stream itself was still invisible—a long bank of mist like cotton batting, beneath which the water ran. He stooped; once more he raised the body which was half again his size, and hurled it outward into the mist and, even as he released it, springing after it, catching himself back just before he followed it, seeing at the instant of its vanishing the sluggish sprawl of three limbs where there should have been four, and recovering balance to turn, already running as the pattering rush of the hound whispered behind him and the animal struck him in the back. It did not pause. On his hands and knees he saw it in midair like a tremendous wingless bird soar out and vanish into the mist. He got to his feet and ran. He stumbled and fell once and got up, running. Then he heard the swift soft feet behind him and he fell again and on his hands and knees again he watched it soar over him and turn in midair so that it landed facing him, its eyes like two cigar-coals as it sprang at him before he could rise. He struck at its face with his hands and got up and ran. They reached the stump together. The hound leaped at him again, slashing at his shoulder as he ducked into the opening he had made and groped furiously for the missing arm, the hound still slashing at his back and legs. Then the dog was gone. A voice said: "All right, Mink. We've got him. You can come out now."

The surrey was waiting among the trees behind his house, where he had found the marks of it two days ago. He sat with a deputy in the back seat, their inside wrists manacled together. The sheriff rode beside the other deputy, who drove. The driver swung the team around to return to Varner's store and the Jefferson highroad, but the sheriff stopped him. "Wait," the sheriff said and turned in the front seat—a tremendous man, neckless, in an unbuttoned waistcoat and a collarless starched shirt. In his broad heavy face his small, cold, shrewd eyes resembled two bits of black glass pressed into uncooked dough. He addressed both of them. "Where does this road come out at the other end?"

"Into the old Whiteleaf Bridge road," the deputy said. "That's fourteen miles. And you are still nine miles from Whiteleaf store then. And when you reach Whiteleaf store, you are still eight miles from Jefferson. It's just twenty-five miles by Varner's."

"I reckon we'll skip Varner's this time," the sheriff said. "Drive on, Jim."

"Sure," the deputy said. "Drive on, Jim. It wouldn't be our money we saved, it would just be the county's." The sheriff, turning to face forward again, paused and looked at the deputy. They looked at one another. "I said all right, didn't I?" the deputy said. "Drive on."

Through the rest of that morning and into noon they wound among the pine hills. The sheriff had a shoe box of cold food and even a stone jug of buttermilk wrapped in wet gunnysacks. They ate without stopping save to let the team drink at a branch which crossed the road. Then the road came down out of the hills and in the early afternoon they passed Whiteleaf store in the long broad rich flatlands lush with the fine harvest, the fired and heavy corn and the cotton-pickers still moving through the spilling rows, and he saw the men squatting and sitting on the gallery beneath the patent medicine and tobacco posters stand suddenly up. "Well, well," the deputy said. "There are folks here too that act willing to believe their name is Houston for maybe ten or fifteen minutes anyway."

"Drive on," the sheriff said. They went on, pacing in the thick, soft dust the long, parched summer afternoon, though actually they could not keep pace with it and presently the fierce sun slanted into the side of the surrey where he sat. The sheriff spoke now without turning his head or removing his cob pipe: "George, swap sides with him. Let him ride in the shade."

"I'm all right," he said. "It dont bother me." After a while it did not bother him, or it was no worse for him than for the others, because the road approached the hills again, rising and winding again as the long shadows of the pines wheeled slowly over the slow surrey in the now slanting sun; soon Jefferson itself would appear beyond the final valley, with the poised fierce ball of the sun dropping down beyond it, shining from directly ahead and almost level into the surrey, upon all their faces. There was a board on a tree, bearing a merchant's name above the legend *Jefferson 4 mi*, drawing up and then past, yet with no semblance of motion, and he moved his feet slightly and braced his inside elbow for the coming jerk and gathered and hurled himself feet foremost out of the moving surrey, snapping his arm and shoulder forward against the expected jerk but too late, so that even as his body swung out and free of the wheel his head slipped down into the V of the stanchion which supported the top and the weight and momentum of his whole body came down on his vised neck. In a moment now he would hear the bone, the vertebrae, and he wrenched his body again, kicking backward now toward where he believed the moving wheel would be, thinking, If I can just hook my foot in them spokes, something will have to give; lashing with his foot toward the wheel, feeling each movement of his body travel back to his neck as though he were attempting, in a cold fury of complete detachment, to see which would go first: the living bone or the dead metal. Then something struck him a terrific blow at the base of his neck and ceased to be a blow and became instead a pressure, rational and furious with deadly intent. He believed he heard the bone and he knew he heard the deputy's voice: "Break! God damn it, break! Break!" and he felt the surge of the surrey and he even seemed to see the sheriff leaning over the seat-back and grappling with the raging deputy; choking, gasping, trying to close his mouth and he could not, trying to roll his head from beneath the cold hard blow of the water and there was a bough over his head against the sunny sky, with a faint wind in the leaves, and the three faces. But after a while he could breathe again all right, and the faint wind of motion had dried the water from his face and only his shirt was a little damp, not a cool wind yet but just a wind free at last of the unendurable sun, blowing out of the beginning of dusk, the surrey moving now beneath an ordered overarch of sunshot trees, between the clipped and tended lawns where children shrieked and played in bright small garments in the sunset and the ladies sat rocking in the fresh dresses of afternoon and the men coming home from work turned into the neat painted gates, toward plates of food and cups of coffee in the long beginning of twilight.

They approached the jail from the rear and drove into the enclosed yard. "Jump," the sheriff said. "Lift him out."

"I'm all right," he said. But he had to speak twice before he made any sound, and even then it was not his voice. "I can walk."

After the doctor had gone, he lay on his cot. There was a small, high, barred window in the wall, but there was nothing beyond the window save twilight. Then he smelled supper cooking somewhere—ham and hot bread and coffee—and suddenly a hot, thin, salty liquid began to run in his mouth, though when he tried to swallow, it was so painful that he sat up, swallowing the hot salt, moving his neck and head rigidly and gingerly to ease the swallowing. Then a loud trampling of feet began beyond the barred door, coming rapidly nearer, and he rose and went to it and looked through the bars into the common room where the negro victims of a thousand petty white man's misdemeanors ate and slept together. He could see the head of the stairs; the trampling came from it and he watched a disorderly clump of heads in battered hats and caps and bodies in battered overalls and broken shoes erupt and fill the foul barren room with a subdued uproar of scuffling feet and mellow witless singsong voices—the chain gang which worked on the streets, seven or eight of them, in jail for vagrancy or razor fights or shooting dice for ten or fifteen cents, freed of their shovels and rock hammers for ten hours at least. He held to the bars and looked at them. "It—" he said. His voice made no sound at all. He put his hand to his throat and spoke again, making a dry, croaking sound. The negroes fell completely still, looking at him, their eyeballs white and still in the already fading faces. "I was all right," he said, "until it started coming to pieces. I could have handled that dog." He held his throat, his voice harsh and dry and croaking. "But the son of a bitch started coming to pieces on me."

"Who him?" one of the negroes said. They whispered among themselves, murmuring. The white eyeballs rolled at him.

"I was all right," he said. "But the son of a bitch—"

"Hush, white man," the negro said. "Hush. Dont be telling us no truck like that."

"I would have been all right," he said, harsh, whispering. Then his voice failed altogether again and he held to the bars with one hand, holding his throat with the other, while the negroes watched him, huddled, their eyeballs white and still in the failing light. Then with one accord they turned and rushed toward the stairs and he heard the slow steps too and then he smelled the food, and he clung to the bars, trying to see the stairhead. Are they going to feed them niggers before they do a white man? he thought, smelling the coffee and the ham.

3.

That was the fall before the winter from which the people as they became older were to establish time and date events. The summer's rainless heat—the blazing days beneath which even the oak leaves turned brown and died, the nights during which the ordered stars seemed to glare down in cold and lidless amazement at an earth being drowned in dust—broke at last, and for the three weeks of Indian summer the ardor-wearied earth, ancient Lilith, reigned, throned and crowned amid the old invincible courtesan's formal defunction. Through these blue and drowsy and empty days filled with silence and the smell of burning leaves and woodsmoke, Ratliff, passing to and fro between his home and the Square, would see the two small grimed hands, immobile and clasping loosely the bars of the jail window at a height not a great deal above that at which a child would have held them. And in the afternoons he would watch his three guests, the wife and the two children, entering or leaving the jail on their daily visit. On the first day, the day he had brought her home with him, she had insisted on doing some of the housework, all of it which his sister would permit, sweeping and washing dishes and chopping wood for fires which his nieces and nephews had heretofore done (and incidentally, in doing so, gaining their juvenile contempt too), apparently oblivious of the sister's mute and outraged righteousness, big yet not fat, actually slender as Ratliff realised at last in a sort of shocked and sober . . . not pity: rather, concern; usually barefoot, with the untidy mass of bleached hair long since turning back to dark at the roots, and the cold face in which there was something of a hard not-quite-lost beauty, though it may have been only an ingrained and ineradicable self-confidence or perhaps just toughness. Because the prisoner had refused not only bond (if he could have made one) but counsel. He had stood between two officers—small, his face like a mask of intractability carved in wood, wasted and almost skeleton-thin—before the committing magistrate, and he might not even have been present, hearing or perhaps not hearing himself being arraigned, then at a touch from one of the officers turning back toward the jail, the cell. So the case was pretermitted from sheer desuetude of physical material for formal suttee, like a half-cast play, through the October term of court, to the spring term next May; and perhaps three afternoons a week Ratliff would watch his guests as, the children dressed in cast-off garments of his nephews and nieces, the three of them entered the jail, thinking of the four of them sitting in the close cell rank with creosote and old wraiths of human excreta—the sweat, the urine, the vomit discharged of all the old agonies: terror, impotence, hope. Waiting for Flem Snopes, he thought. For Flem Snopes.

Then the winter, the cold, came. By that time she had a job. He had known as well as she that the other arrangement could not last, since in a way it was his sister's house, even if only by a majority of voting strength. So he was not only not surprised, he was relieved when she came and told him she was going to move. Then, as soon as she told him she was going to leave, something happened to him. He told himself that it was the two children. "That's all right about the job," he said. "That's fine. But you dont need to move. You'll have to pay board and lodging if you move. And you will need to save. You will need money."

"Yes," she said harshly. "I'll need money."

"Does he still think—" He stopped himself. He said, "You aint heard yet when Flem will be back, have you?" She didn't answer. He didn't expect her to. "You will need to save all you can," he said. "So you stay here. Pay her a dollar a week board for the children if that would make you feel better about it. I dont reckon a kid would eat more than four bits' worth in seven days. But you stay here."

So she stayed. He had given up his room to them and he slept with his oldest nephew. Her job was in a rambling shabby side-street boarding-house with an equivocal reputation, named the Savoy Hotel. Her work began at daybreak and ended sometime after dark, sometimes well after dark. She swept and made the beds and did some of the cooking, since there was a negro porter who washed the dishes and kept up the fires. She had her meals there and received three dollars a week. "Only she's going to keep her heels blistered running barefooted in and out of them horse-traders' and petty jurys' and agents for nigger insurances' rooms all night long," a town wit said. But that was her affair. Ratliff knew nothing about that and cared less and, to his credit, believed even still less than that. So now he would not see her at all save on Sunday afternoons as, the children in the new over-coats which he had bought for them and the woman in his old one which she had insisted on paying him fifty cents for, they would enter the gate to the jail or perhaps emerge from it. That was when it occurred to him how not once had any of his kin—old Ab or the schoolmaster or the blacksmith or the new clerk—come in to see him. And if all the facts about that business was knowed, he thought, There's one of them that ought to be there in that cell too. Or in another one just like it, since you cant hang a man twice—granted of course that a Snopes carries the death penalty even for another Snopes.

There was snow on Thanksgiving and though it did not remain two days, it was followed early in December by an iron cold which locked the earth in a frozen rigidity, so that after a week or so actual dust blew from it. Smoke turned white before it left the chimney, unable to rise, becoming the same color as the misty sky itself in which all day long the sun stood pale as an uncooked biscuit and as heatless. Now they dont even need to have to not come in to see him, Ratliff told himself. For a man to drive them twenty miles in from Frenchman's Bend just on a errand of mercy, even a Snopes dont have to excuse himself from it. There was a window-pane now between the bars and the hands; they were not visible now, even if anyone had paused along before the jail to look for them. Instead he would be walking fast when he passed, hunched in his overcoat, holding his ears in turn with his yarn-mitted hands, his breath wisping about the crimson tip of his nose and his watering eyes and into the empty Square across which perhaps one country wagon moved, its occupants wrapped in quilts with a lighted lantern on the seat between them while the frosted windows of the stores seemed to stare at it without comprehension or regret like the faces of cataracted old men.

Christmas passed beneath that same salt-colored sky, without even any surface softening of the iron ground, but in January a wind set up out of the north-west and blew the sky clear. The sun drew shadows on the frozen ground and for three days patches of it thawed a little at noon, for an inch or so, like a spreading of butter or axle-grease; and toward noon people would emerge, like rats or roaches, Ratliff told himself, amazed and tentative at the sun or at the patches of earth soft again out of an old, almost forgotten time, capable again of taking a footprint. "It wont freeze again tonight," they told one another. "It's clouding up from the south-west. It will rain and wash the frost out of the ground and we will be all right again." It did rain. The wind moved counter-clockwise into the east. "It will go through to the north-west again and freeze again. Even that would be better than snow," they told one another, even though the rain had already begun to solidify and by nightfall had become snow, falling for two days and dissolving into the mud as it fell until the mud itself froze at last and still the snow fell and stopped too finally and the windless iron cold came down upon it without even a heatless wafer of sun to preside above a dead earth cased in ice; January and then February, no movement anywhere save the low constant smoke and the infrequent people unable to stand up on the sidewalks creeping townward or homeward in the middle of the streets where no horse could have kept its feet, and no sound save the chopping of axes and the lonely whistles of the daily trains and Ratliff would seem to see them, black, without dimension and unpeopled and plumed with fading vapor, rushing without purpose through the white and rigid solitude. At home now, sitting over his own fire on those Sunday afternoons, he would hear the woman arrive for the children after dinner and put the new overcoats on them above the outgrown garments in which regardless of temperature they had gone to Sunday school (his sister saw to that) with the nephew and nieces who had discarded them; and he would think of the four of them sitting, huddled still in the coats, about the small ineffective sheet-iron stove which did not warm the cell but merely drew from the walls like tears the old sweat of the old agonies and despairs which had harbored there. Later they would return. She would never stay for supper, but once a month she would bring to him the eight dollars she had saved out of her twelve-dollar salary, and the other coins and bills (once she had nine dollars more) which he never asked how she had come by. He was her banker. His sister may or may not have known this, though she probably did. The sum mounted up. "But it will take a lot of weeks," he said. She didn't answer. "Maybe he might answer a letter," he said. "After all, blood is blood."

The freeze could not last forever. On the ninth of March it even snowed again and this snow even went away without turning to ice. So people could move about again, and one Saturday he entered the restaurant of which he was half owner and saw Bookwright sitting again before a plate containing a mass of jumbled food a good deal of which was eggs. They had not seen one another in almost six months. No greeting passed between them. "She's back home again," Bookwright said. "Got in last week."

"She gets around fast," Ratliff said. "I just saw her toting a scuttle of ashes out the back door of the Savoy Hotel five minutes ago."

"I mean the other one," Bookwright said, eating. "Flem's wife. Will drove over to Mottstown and picked them up last week."

"Them?"

"Not Flem. Her and the baby."

So he has already heard, Ratliff thought. Somebody has done already wrote him. He said: "The baby. Well well. February, January, December, November, October, September, August. And some of March. It aint hardly big enough to be chewing tobacco yet, I reckon."

"It wouldn't chew," Bookwright said. "It's a girl."

So for a while he didn't know what to do, though it did not take him long to decide. Better now, he told himself. Even if she was ever hoping without knowing she was. He waited at home the next afternoon until she came for the children. "His wife's back," he said. For just an instant she did not move at all. "You never really expected nothing else, did you?" he said.

"No," she said.

Then even that winter was over at last. It ended as it had begun, in rain, not cold rain but loud fierce gusts of warm water washing out of the earth the iron enduring frost, the belated spring hard on its bright heels and all coming at once, pell mell and disordered, fruit and bloom and leaf, pied meadow and blossoming wood and the long fields shearing dark out of winter's slumber, to the shearing plow. The school was already closed for the planting year when he passed it and drove up to the store and hitched his team to the old familiar post and mounted among the seven or eight men squatting and lounging about the gallery as if they had not moved since he had looked back last at them almost six months ago. "Well, men," he said. "School's already closed I see. Chillen can go to the field now and give you folks a chance to rest."

"It's been closed since last October," Quick said. "Teacher quit."

"I.O.? Quit?"

"His wife come in one day. He looked up and saw her and lit out."

"His what?" Ratliff said.

"His wife," Tull said. "Or so she claimed. A kind of big gray-colored woman with a—"

"Ah shucks," Ratliff said. "He aint married. Aint he been here three years? You mean his mother."

"No, no," Tull said. "She was young all right. She just had a kind of gray color all over. In a buggy. With a baby about six months old."

"A baby?" Ratliff said. He looked from face to face among them, blinking. "Look here," he said. "What's all this anyway? How'd he get a wife, let alone a baby six months old? Aint he been right here three years? Hell a mile, he aint been out of hearing long enough to done that."

"Wallstreet says they are his," Tull said.

"Wallstreet?" Ratliff said. "Who's Wallstreet?"

"That boy of Eck's."

"That boy about ten years old?" Ratliff blinked at Tull now. "They never had that panic until a year or two back. How'd a boy ten years old get to be named Wall street?"

"I dont know," Tull said.

"I reckon it's his all right," Quick said. "Leastways he taken one look at that buggy and he aint been seen since."

"Sho now," Ratliff said. "A baby is one thing in pants that will make any man run, provided he's still got room enough to start in. Which it seems I.O. had."

"He needed room," Bookwright said in his harsh, abrupt voice. "This one could have held him, provided somebody just throwed I.O. down first and give it time to get a hold. It was bigger than he was already."

"It might hold him yet," Quick said.

"Yes," Tull said. "She just stopped long enough to buy a can of sardines and crackers. Then she druv on down the road in the same direction somebody told her I.O. had been going. He was walking. Her and the baby both et the sardines."

"Well, well," Ratliff said. "Them Snopes. Well, well—" He ceased. They watched quietly as the Varner surrey came up the road, going home. The negro was driving; in the back seat with her mother, Mrs Flem Snopes sat. The beautiful face did not even turn as the surrey drew abreast of the store. It passed in profile, calm, oblivious, incurious. It was not a tragic face: it was just damned. The surrey went on.

"Is he really waiting in that jail yonder for Flem Snopes to come back and get him out?" the fourth man said.

"He's still in jail," Ratliff said.

"But is he waiting for Flem?" Quick said.

"No," Ratliff said. "Because Flem aint coming back here until that trial is over and finished." Then Mrs Littlejohn stood on her veranda, ringing the dinner bell, and they rose and began to disperse. Ratliff and Bookwright descended the steps together.

"Shucks," Bookwright said. "Even Flem Snopes aint going to let his own blood cousin be hung just to save money."

"I reckon Flem knows it aint going to go that far. Jack Houston was shot from in front, and everybody knows he never went anywhere without that pistol, and they found it laying there in the road where they found the marks where the horse had whirled and run, whether it had dropped out of his hand or fell out of his pocket when he fell or not. I reckon Flem had done inquired into all that. And so he aint coming back until it's all finished. He aint coming back here where Mink's wife can worry him or folks can talk about him for leaving his cousin in jail. There's some things even a Snopes wont do. I dont know just exactly what they are, but they's some somewhere."

Then Bookwright went on, and he untied the team and drove the buckboard on into Mrs Littlejohn's lot and unharnessed and carried the harness into the barn. He had not seen it since that afternoon in September either, and something, he did not know what, impelled and moved him; he hung the gear up and went on through the dim high ammoniac tunnel, between the empty stalls, to the last one and looked into it and saw the thick, female, sitting buttocks, the shapeless figure quiet in the gloom, the blasted face turning and looking up at him, and for a fading instant there was something almost like recognition even if there could have been no remembering, in the devastated eyes, and the drooling mouth slacking and emitting a sound, hoarse, abject, not loud. Upon the overalled knees Ratliff saw the battered wooden effigy of a cow such as children receive on Christmas.

He heard the hammer before he reached the shop. The hammer stopped, poised; the dull, open, healthy face looked up at him without either surprise or interrogation, almost without recognition. "Howdy, Eck," Ratliff said. "Can you pull the old shoes off my team right after dinner and shoe them again? I got a trip to make tonight."

"All right," the other said. "Anytime you bring them in."

"All right," Ratliff said. "That boy of yours. You changed his name lately, aint you?" The other looked at him, the hammer poised. On the anvil the ruby tip of the iron he was shaping faded slowly. "Wall street."

"Oh," the other said. "No, sir. It wasn't changed. He never had no name to speak of until last year. I left him with his grandma after my first wife died, while I was getting settled down; I was just sixteen then. She called him after his grandpa, but he never had no actual name. Then last year after I got settled down and sent for him, I thought maybe he better have a name. I.O. read about that one in the paper. He figured if we named him Wallstreet Panic it might make him get rich like the folks that run that Wallstreet panic."

"Oh," Ratliff said. "Sixteen. And one kid wasn't enough to settle you down. How many did it take?"

"I got three."

"Two more beside Wallstreet. What—"

"Three more besides Wall," the other said.

"Oh," Ratliff said. The other waited a moment. Then he raised the hammer again. But he stopped it and stood looking at the cold iron on the anvil and laid the hammer down and turned back to the forge. "So you had to pay all that twenty dollars," Ratliff said. The other looked back at him. "For that cow last summer."

"Yes. And another two bits for that ere toy one."

"You bought him that too?"

"Yes. I felt sorry for him. I thought maybe anytime he would happen to start thinking, that ere toy one would give him something to think about."

BOOK FOUR

THE PEASANTS
Chapter One

I.

A LITTLE WHILE before sundown the men lounging about the gallery of the store saw, coming up the road from the south, a covered wagon drawn by mules and followed by a considerable string of obviously alive objects which in the levelling sun resembled vari-sized and -colored tatters torn at random from large billboards—circus posters, say—attached to the rear of the wagon and inherent with its own separate and collective motion, like the tail of a kite.

"What in the hell is that?" one said.

"It's a circus," Quick said. They began to rise, watching the wagon. Now they could see that the animals behind the wagon were horses. Two men rode in the wagon.

"Hell fire," the first man—his name was Freeman—said. "It's Flem Snopes." They were all standing when the wagon came up and stopped and Snopes got down and approached the steps. He might have departed only this morning. He wore the same cloth cap, the minute bow tie against the white shirt, the same gray trousers. He mounted the steps.

"Howdy, Flem," Quick said. The other looked briefly at all of them and none of them, mounting the steps. "Starting you a circus?"

"Gentlemen," he said. He crossed the gallery; they made way for him. Then they descended the steps and approached the wagon, at the tail of which the horses stood in a restive clump, larger than rabbits and gaudy as parrots and shackled to one another and to the wagon itself with sections of barbed wire. Calico-coated, small-bodied, with delicate legs and pink faces in which their mismatched eyes rolled wild and subdued, they huddled, gaudy motionless and alert, wild as deer, deadly as rattlesnakes, quiet as doves. The men stood at a respectful distance, looking at them. At that moment Jody Varner came through the group, shouldering himself to the front of it.

"Watch yourself, doc," a voice said from the rear. But it was already too late. The nearest animal rose on its hind legs with lightning rapidity and struck twice with its fore feet at Varner's face, faster than a boxer, the movement of its surge against the wire which held it travelling backward among the rest of the band in a wave of thuds and lunges. "Hup, you broom-tailed hay-burning sidewinders," the same voice said. This was the second man who had arrived in the wagon. He was a stranger. He wore a heavy densely black moustache, a wide pale hat. When he thrust himself through and turned to herd them back from the horses they saw, thrust into the hip pockets of his tight jeans pants, the butt of a heavy pearl-handled pistol and a florid carton such as small cakes come in. "Keep away from them, boys," he said. "They've got kind of skittish, they aint been rode in so long."

"Since when have they been rode?" Quick said. The stranger looked at Quick. He had a broad, quite cold, wind-gnawed face and bleak cold eyes. His belly fitted neat and smooth as a peg into the tight trousers.

"I reckon that was when they were rode on the ferry to get across the Mississippi River," Varner said. The stranger looked at him. "My name's Varner," Jody said.

"Hipps," the other said. "Call me Buck." Across the left side of his head, obliterating the tip of that ear, was a savage and recent gash gummed over with a blackish substance like axle-grease. They looked at the scar. Then they watched him remove the carton from his pocket and tilt a gingersnap into his hand and put the gingersnap into his mouth, beneath the moustache.

"You and Flem have some trouble back yonder?" Quick said. The stranger ceased chewing. When he looked directly at anyone, his eyes became like two pieces of flint turned suddenly up in dug earth.

"Back where?" he said.

"Your nigh ear," Quick said.

"Oh," the other said. "That." He touched his ear. "That was my mistake. I was absent-minded one night when I was staking them out. Studying about something else and forgot how long the wire was." He chewed. They looked at his ear. "Happen to any man careless around a horse. Put a little axle-dope on it and you wont notice it tomorrow though. They're pretty lively now, lazing along all day doing nothing. It'll work out of them in a couple of days." He put another gingersnap into his mouth, chewing. "Dont you believe they'll gentle?" No one answered. They looked at the ponies, grave and noncommittal. Jody turned and went back into the store. "Them's good, gentle ponies," the stranger said. "Watch now." He put the carton back into his pocket and approached the horses, his hand extended. The nearest one was standing on three legs now. It appeared to be asleep. Its eyelid drooped over the cerulean eye; its head was shaped like an ironing-board. Without even raising the eyelid it flicked its head, the yellow teeth cropped. For an instant it and the man appeared to be inextricable in one violence. Then they became motionless, the stranger's high heels dug into the earth, one hand gripping the animal's nostrils, holding the horse's head wrenched half around while it breathed in hoarse, smothered groans. "See?" the stranger said in a panting voice, the veins standing white and rigid in his neck and along his jaw. "See? All you got to do is handle them a little and work hell out of them for a couple of days. Now look out. Give me room back there." They gave back a little. The stranger gathered himself then sprang away. As he did so, a second horse slashed at his back, severing his vest from collar to hem down the back exactly as the trick swordsman severs a floating veil with one stroke.

"Sho now," Quick said. "But suppose a man dont happen to own a vest."

At that moment Jody Varner, followed by the blacksmith, thrust through them again. "All right, Buck," he said. "Better get them on into the lot. Eck here will help you." The stranger, the severed halves of the vest swinging from either shoulder, mounted to the wagon seat, the blacksmith following.

"Get up, you transmogrified hallucinations of Job and Jezebel," the stranger said. The wagon moved on, the tethered ponies coming gaudily into motion behind it, behind which in turn the men followed at a respectful distance, on up the road and into the lane and so to the lot gate behind Mrs Littlejohn's. Eck got down and opened the gate. The wagon passed through but when the ponies saw the fence the herd surged backward against the wire which attached it to the wagon, standing on its collective hind legs and then trying to turn within itself, so that the wagon moved backward for a few feet until the Texan, cursing, managed to saw the mules about and so lock the wheels. The men following had already fallen rapidly back. "Here, Eck," the Texan said. "Get up here and take the reins." The blacksmith got back in the wagon and took the reins. Then they watched the Texan descend, carrying a looped-up blacksnake whip, and go around to the rear of the herd and drive it through the gate, the whip snaking about the harlequin rumps in methodical and pistol-like reports. Then the watchers hurried across Mrs Littlejohn's yard and mounted to the veranda, one end of which overlooked the lot.

"How you reckon he ever got them tied together?" Freeman said.

"I'd a heap rather watch how he aims to turn them loose," Quick said. The Texan had climbed back into the halted wagon. Presently he and Eck both appeared at the rear end of the open hood. The Texan grasped the wire and began to draw the first horse up to the wagon, the animal plunging and surging back against the wire as though trying to hang itself, the contagion passing back through the herd from animal to animal until they were rearing and plunging again against the wire.

"Come on, grab a holt," the Texan said. Eck grasped the wire also. The horses laid back against it, the pink faces tossing above the back-surging mass. "Pull him up, pull him up," the Texan said sharply. "They couldn't get up here in the wagon even if they wanted to." The wagon moved gradually backward until the head of the first horse was snubbed up to the tail-gate. The Texan took a turn of the wire quickly about one of the wagon stakes. "Keep the slack out of it," he said. He vanished and reappeared, almost in the same second, with a pair of heavy wire-cutters. "Hold them like that," he said, and leaped. He vanished, broad hat, flapping vest, wire-cutters and all, into a kaleidoscopic maelstrom of long teeth and wild eyes and slashing feet, from which presently the horses began to burst one by one like partridges flushing, each wearing a necklace of barbed wire. The first one crossed the lot at top speed, on a straight line. It galloped into the fence without any diminution whatever. The wire gave, recovered, and slammed the horse to earth where it lay for a moment, glaring, its legs still galloping in air. It scrambled up without having ceased to gallop and crossed the lot and galloped into the opposite fence and was slammed again to earth. The others were now freed. They whipped and whirled about the lot like dizzy fish in a bowl. It had seemed like a big lot until now, but now the very idea that all that fury and motion should be transpiring inside any one fence was something to be repudiated with contempt, like a mirror trick. From the ultimate dust the stranger, carrying the wire-cutters and his vest completely gone now, emerged. He was not running, he merely moved with a light-poised and watchful celerity, weaving among the calico rushes of the animals, feinting and dodging like a boxer until he reached the gate and crossed the yard and mounted to the veranda. One sleeve of his shirt hung only at one point from his shoulder. He ripped it off and wiped his face with it and threw it away and took out the paper carton and shook a gingersnap into his hand. He was breathing only a little heavily. "Pretty lively now," he said. "But it'll work out of them in a couple of days." The ponies still streaked back and forth through the growing dusk like hysterical fish, but not so violently now.

"What'll you give a man to reduce them odds a little for you?" Quick said. The Texan looked at him, the eyes bleak, pleasant and hard above the chewing jaw, the heavy moustache. "To take one of them off your hands?" Quick said.

At that moment the little periwinkle-eyed boy came along the veranda, saying, "Papa, papa; where's papa?"

"Who you looking for, sonny?" one said.

"It's Eck's boy," Quick said. "He's still out yonder in the wagon. Helping Mr Buck here." The boy went on to the end of the veranda, in diminutive overalls—a miniature replica of the men themselves.

"Papa," he said. "Papa." The blacksmith was still leaning from the rear of the wagon, still holding the end of the severed wire. The ponies, bunched for the moment, now slid past the wagon, flowing, stringing out again so that they appeared to have doubled in number, rushing on; the hard rapid light patter of unshod hooves came out of the dust. "Mamma says to come on to supper," the boy said.

The moon was almost full then. When supper was over and they had gathered again along the veranda, the alteration was hardly one of visibility even. It was merely a translation from the lapidary-dimensional of day to the treacherous and silver receptivity in which the horses huddled in mazy camouflage, or singly or in pairs rushed, fluid, phantom, and unceasing, to huddle again in mirage-like clumps from which came high abrupt squeals and the vicious thudding of hooves.

Ratliff was among them now. He had returned just before supper. He had not dared take his team into the lot at all. They were now in Bookwright's stable a half mile from the store. "So Flem has come home again," he said. "Well, well, well. Will Varner paid to get him to Texas, so I reckon it aint no more than fair for you fellows to pay the freight on him back." From the lot there came a high thin squeal. One of the animals emerged. It seemed not to gallop but to flow, bodiless, without dimension. Yet there was the rapid light beat of hard hooves on the packed earth.

"He aint said they was his yet," Quick said.

"He aint said they aint neither," Freeman said.

"I see," Ratliff said. "That's what you are holding back on. Until he tells you whether they are his or not. Or maybe you can wait until the auction's over and split up and some can follow Flem and some can follow that Texas fellow and watch to see which one spends the money. But then, when a man's done got trimmed, I dont reckon he cares who's got the money."

"Maybe if Ratliff would leave here tonight, they wouldn't make him buy one of them ponies tomorrow," a third said.

"That's a fact," Ratliff said. "A fellow can dodge a Snopes if he just starts lively enough. In fact, I dont believe he would have to pass more than two folks before he would have another victim intervened betwixt them. You folks aint going to buy them things sho enough, are you?" Nobody answered. They sat on the steps, their backs against the veranda posts, or on the railing itself. Only Ratliff and Quick sat in chairs, so that to them the others were black silhouettes against the dreaming lambence of the moonlight beyond the veranda. The pear tree across the road opposite was now in full and frosty bloom, the twigs and branches springing not outward from the limbs but standing motionless and perpendicular above the horizontal boughs like the separate and upstreaming hair of a drowned woman sleeping upon the uttermost floor of the windless and tideless sea.

"Anse McCallum brought two of them horses back from Texas once," one of the men on the steps said. He did not move to speak. He was not speaking to anyone. "It was a good team. A little light. He worked it for ten years. Light work, it was."

"I mind it," another said. "Anse claimed he traded fourteen rifle cartridges for both of them, didn't he?"

"It was the rifle too, I heard," a third said.

"No, it was just the shells," the first said. "The fellow wanted to swap him four more for the rifle too, but Anse said he never needed them. Cost too much to get six of them back to Mississippi."

"Sho," the second said. "When a man dont have to invest so much into a horse or a team, he dont need to expect so much from it." The three of them were not talking any louder, they were merely talking among themselves, to one another, as if they sat there alone. Ratliff, invisible in the shadow against the wall, made a sound, harsh, sardonic, not loud.

"Ratliff's laughing," a fourth said.

"Dont mind me," Ratliff said. The three speakers had not moved. They did not move now, yet there seemed to gather about the three silhouettes something stubborn, convinced, and passive, like children who have been chidden. A bird, a shadow, fleet and dark and swift, curved across the moonlight, upward into the pear tree and began to sing; a mockingbird.

"First one I've noticed this year," Freeman said.

"You can hear them along Whiteleaf every night," the first man said. "I heard one in February. In that snow. Singing in a gum."

"Gum is the first tree to put out," the third said. "That was why. It made it feel like singing, fixing to put out that way. That was why it taken a gum."

"Gum first to put out?" Quick said. "What about willow?"

"Willow aint a tree," Freeman said. "It's a weed."

"Well, I dont know what it is," the fourth said. "But it aint no weed. Because you can grub up a weed and you are done with it. I been grubbing up a clump of willows outen my spring pasture for fifteen years. They are the same size every year. Only difference is, it's just two or three more trees every time."

"And if I was you," Ratliff said, "that's just exactly where I would be come sunup tomorrow. Which of course you aint going to do. I reckon there aint nothing under the sun or in Frenchman's Bend neither that can keep you folks from giving Flem Snopes and that Texas man your money. But I'd sholy like to know just exactly who I was giving my money to. Seems like Eck here would tell you. Seems like he'd do that for his neighbors, dont it? Besides being Flem's cousin, him and that boy of his, Wallstreet, helped that Texas man tote water for them tonight and Eck's going to help him feed them in the morning too. Why, maybe Eck will be the one that will catch them and lead them up one at a time for you folks to bid on them. Aint that right, Eck?"

The other man sitting on the steps with his back against the post was the blacksmith. "I dont know," he said.

"Boys," Ratliff said, "Eck knows all about them horses. Flem's told him, how much they cost and how much him and that Texas man aim to get for them, make off of them. Come on, Eck. Tell us." The other did not move, sitting on the top step, not quite facing them, sitting there beneath the successive layers of their quiet and intent concentrated listening and waiting.

"I dont know," he said. Ratliff began to laugh. He sat in the chair, laughing while the others sat or lounged upon the steps and the railing, sitting beneath his laughing as Eck had sat beneath their listening and waiting. Ratliff ceased laughing. He rose. He yawned, quite loud.

"All right. You folks can buy them critters if you want to. But me, I'd just as soon buy a tiger or a rattlesnake. And if Flem Snopes offered me either one of them, I would be afraid to touch it for fear it would turn out to be a painted dog or a piece of garden hose when I went up to take possession of it. I bid you one and all goodnight." He entered the house. They did not look after him, though after a while they all shifted a little and looked down into the lot, upon the splotchy, sporadic surge and flow of the horses, from among which from time to time came an abrupt squeal, a thudding blow. In the pear tree the mockingbird's idiot reiteration pulsed and purled.

"Anse McCallum made a good team outen them two of hisn," the first man said. "They was a little light. That was all."

When the sun rose the next morning a wagon and three saddled mules stood in Mrs Littlejohn's lane and six men and Eck Snopes' son were already leaning on the fence, looking at the horses which huddled in a quiet clump before the barn door, watching the men in their turn. A second wagon came up the road and into the lane and stopped, and then there were eight men beside the boy standing at the fence, beyond which the horses stood, their blue-and-brown eyeballs rolling alertly in their gaudy faces. "So this here is the Snopes circus, is it?" one of the newcomers said. He glanced at the faces, then he went to the end of the row and stood beside the blacksmith and the little boy. "Are them Flem's horses?" he said to the blacksmith.

"Eck dont know who them horses belong to anymore than we do," one of the others said. "He knows that Flem come here on the same wagon with them, because he saw him. But that's all."

"And all he will know," a second said. "His own kin will be the last man in the world to find out anything about Flem Snopes' business."

"No," the first said. "He wouldn't even be that. The first man Flem would tell his business to would be the man that was left after the last man died. Flem Snopes dont even tell himself what he is up to. Not if he was laying in bed with himself in an empty house in the dark of the moon."

"That's a fact," a third said. "Flem would trim Eck or any other of his kin quick as he would us. Aint that right, Eck?"

"I dont know," Eck said. They were watching the horses,

which at that moment broke into a high-eared, stiff-kneed swirl and flowed in a patchwork wave across the lot and brought up again, facing the men along the fence, so they did not hear the Texan until he was among them. He wore a new shirt and another vest a little too small for him and he was just putting the paper carton back into his hip pocket.

"Morning, morning," he said. "Come to get an early pick, have you? Want to make me an offer for one or two before the bidding starts and runs the prices up?" They had not looked at the stranger long. They were not looking at him now, but at the horses in the lot, which had lowered their heads, snuffing into the dust.

"I reckon we'll look a while first," one said.

"You are in time to look at them eating breakfast, anyhow," the Texan said. "Which is more than they done without they staid up all night." He opened the gate and entered it. At once the horses jerked their heads up, watching him. "Here, Eck," the Texan said over his shoulder, "two or three of you boys help me drive them into the barn." After a moment Eck and two others approached the gate, the little boy at his father's heels, though the other did not see him until he turned to shut the gate.

"You stay out of here," Eck said. "One of them things will snap your head off same as a acorn before you even know it." He shut the gate and went on after the others, whom the Texan had now waved fanwise outward as he approached the horses which now drew into a restive huddle, beginning to mill slightly, watching the men. Mrs Littlejohn came out of the kitchen and crossed the yard to the woodpile, watching the lot. She picked up two or three sticks of wood and paused, watching the lot again. Now there were two more men standing at the fence.

"Come on, come on," the Texan said. "They wont hurt you. They just aint never been in under a roof before."

"I just as lief let them stay out here, if that's what they want to do," Eck said.

"Get yourself a stick—there's a bunch of wagon-stakes against the fence yonder—and when one of them tries to rush you, bust him over the head so he will understand what you mean." One of the men went to the fence and got three

of the stakes and returned and distributed them. Mrs Littlejohn, her armful of wood complete now, paused again halfway back to the house, looking into the lot. The little boy was
directly behind his father again, though this time the father
had not discovered him yet. The men advanced toward the
horses, the huddle of which began to break into gaudy units
turning inward upon themselves. The Texan was cursing them
in a loud steady cheerful voice. "Get in there, you banjo-faced
jackrabbits. Dont hurry them, now. Let them take their time.
Hi! Get in there. What do you think that barn is—a law-
court maybe? Or maybe a church and somebody is going to
take up a collection on you?" The animals fell slowly back.
Now and then one feinted to break from the huddle, the
Texan driving it back each time with skillfully-thrown bits of
dirt. Then one at the rear saw the barn door just behind it but
before the herd could break the Texan snatched the wagon-
stake from Eck and, followed by one of the other men, rushed
at the horses and began to lay about the heads and shoulders,
choosing by unerring instinct the point animal and striking it
first square in the face then on the withers as it turned and
then on the rump as it turned further, so that when the break
came it was reversed and the entire herd rushed into the long
open hallway and brought up against the further wall with a
hollow, thunderous sound like that of a collapsing mine-shaft.
"Seems to have held all right," the Texan said. He and the
other man slammed the half-length doors and looked over
them into the tunnel of the barn, at the far end of which the
ponies were now a splotchy phantom moiling punctuated by
crackings of wooden partitions and the dry reports of hooves
which gradually died away. "Yep, it held all right," the Texan
said. The other two came to the doors and looked over them.
The little boy came up beside his father now, trying to see
through a crack, and Eck saw him.

"Didn't I tell you to stay out of here?" Eck said. "Dont you
know them things will kill you quicker than you can say scat?
You go and get outside of that fence and stay there."

"Why dont you get your paw to buy you one of them,
Wall?" one of the men said.

"Me buy one of them things?" Eck said. "When I can go
to the river anytime and catch me a snapping turtle or a moc-

casin for nothing? You go on, now. Get out of here and stay out." The Texan had entered the barn. One of the men closed the doors after him and put the bar up again and over the top of the doors they watched the Texan go on down the hallway, toward the ponies which now huddled like gaudy phantoms in the gloom, quiet now and already beginning to snuff experimentally into the long lipworn trough fastened against the rear wall. The little boy had merely gone around behind his father, to the other side, where he stood peering now through a knot-hole in a plank. The Texan opened a smaller door in the wall and entered it, though almost immediately he reappeared.

"I dont see nothing but shelled corn in here," he said. "Snopes said he would send some hay up here last night."

"Wont they eat corn either?" one of the men said.

"I dont know," the Texan said. "They aint never seen any that I know of. We'll find out in a minute though." He disappeared, though they could still hear him in the crib. Then he emerged once more, carrying a big double-ended feed-basket, and retreated into the gloom where the parti-colored rumps of the horses were now ranged quietly along the feeding-trough. Mrs Littlejohn appeared once more, on the veranda this time, carrying a big brass dinner bell. She raised it to make the first stroke. A small commotion set up among the ponies as the Texan approached but he began to speak to them at once, in a brisk loud unemphatic mixture of cursing and cajolery, disappearing among them. The men at the door heard the dry rattling of the corn-pellets into the trough, a sound broken by a single snort of amazed horror. A plank cracked with a loud report; before their eyes the depths of the hallway dissolved in loud fury, and while they stared over the doors, unable yet to begin to move, the entire interior exploded into mad tossing shapes like a downrush of flames.

"Hell fire," one of them said. "Jump!" he shouted. The three turned and ran frantically for the wagon, Eck last. Several voices from the fence were now shouting something but Eck did not even hear them until, in the act of scrambling madly at the tail-gate, he looked behind him and saw the little boy still leaning to the knot-hole in the door which in the next instant vanished into matchwood, the knot-hole itself exploding from his eye and leaving him, motionless in the diminutive overalls and still leaning forward a little until he vanished utterly beneath the towering parti-colored wave full of feet and glaring eyes and wild teeth which, overtopping, burst into scattering units, revealing at last the gaping orifice and the little boy still standing in it, unscathed, his eye still leaned to the vanished knot-hole.

"Wall!" Eck roared. The little boy turned and ran for the wagon. The horses were whipping back and forth across the lot, as if while in the barn they had once more doubled their number; two of them rushed up quartering and galloped all over the boy again without touching him as he ran, earnest and diminutive and seemingly without progress, though he reached the wagon at last, from which Eck, his sunburned skin now a sickly white, reached down and snatched the boy into the wagon by the straps of his overalls and slammed him face down across his knees and caught up a coiled hitching-rope from the bed of the wagon.

"Didn't I tell you to get out of here?" Eck said in a shaking voice. "Didn't I tell you?"

"If you're going to whip him, you better whip the rest of us too and then one of us can frail hell out of you," one of the others said.

"Or better still, take the rope and hang that durn fellow yonder," the second said. The Texan was now standing in the wrecked door of the barn, taking the gingersnap carton from his hip pocket. "Before he kills the rest of Frenchman's Bend too."

"You mean Flem Snopes," the first said. The Texan tilted the carton above his other open palm. The horses still rushed and swirled back and forth but they were beginning to slow now, trotting on high, stiff legs, although their eyes were still rolling whitely and various.

"I misdoubted that damn shell corn all along," the Texan said. "But at least they have seen what it looks like. They cant claim they aint got nothing out of this trip." He shook the carton over his open hand. Nothing came out of it. Mrs Littlejohn on the veranda made the first stroke with the dinner bell; at the sound the horses rushed again, the earth of the lot becoming vibrant with the light dry clatter of hooves. The

Texan crumpled the carton and threw it aside. "Chuck wagon," he said. There were three more wagons in the lane now and there were twenty or more men at the fence when the Texan, followed by his three assistants and the little boy, passed through the gate. The bright cloudless early sun gleamed upon the pearl butt of the pistol in his hip pocket and upon the bell which Mrs Littlejohn still rang, peremptory, strong, and loud.

When the Texan, picking his teeth with a splintered kitchen match, emerged from the house twenty minutes later, the tethered wagons and riding horses and mules extended from the lot gate to Varner's store, and there were more than fifty men now standing along the fence beside the gate, watching him quietly, a little covertly, as he approached, rolling a little, slightly bowlegged, the high heels of his carved boots printing neatly into the dust. "Morning, gents," he said. "Here, Bud," he said to the little boy, who stood slightly behind him, looking at the protruding butt of the pistol. He took a coin from his pocket and gave it to the boy. "Run to the store and get me a box of gingersnaps." He looked about at the quiet faces, protuberant, sucking his teeth. He rolled the match from one side of his mouth to the other without touching it. "You boys done made your picks, have you? Ready to start her off, hah?" They did not answer. They were not looking at him now. That is, he began to have the feeling that each face had stopped looking at him the second before his gaze reached it. After a moment Freeman said:

"Aint you going to wait for Flem?"

"Why?" the Texan said. Then Freeman stopped looking at him too. There was nothing in Freeman's face either. There was nothing, no alteration, in the Texan's voice. "Eck, you done already picked out yours. So we can start her off when you are ready."

"I reckon not," Eck said. "I wouldn't buy nothing I was afraid to walk up and touch."

"Them little ponies?" the Texan said. "You helped water and feed them. I bet that boy of yours could walk up to any one of them."

"He better not let me catch him," Eck said. The Texan looked about at the quiet faces, his gaze at once abstract and alert, with an impenetrable surface quality like flint, as though the surface were impervious or perhaps there was nothing behind it.

"Them ponies is gentle as a dove, boys. The man that buys them will get the best piece of horseflesh he ever forked or druv for the money. Naturally they got spirit; I aint selling crowbait. Besides, who'd want Texas crowbait anyway, with Mississippi full of it?" His stare was still absent and unwinking; there was no mirth or humor in his voice and there was neither mirth nor humor in the single guffaw which came from the rear of the group. Two wagons were now drawing out of the road at the same time, up to the fence. The men got down from them and tied them to the fence and approached. "Come up, boys," the Texan said. "You're just in time to buy a good gentle horse cheap."

"How about that one that cut your vest off last night?" a voice said. This time three or four guffawed. The Texan looked toward the sound, bleak and unwinking.

"What about it?" he said. The laughter, if it had been laughter, ceased. The Texan turned to the nearest gatepost and climbed to the top of it, his alternate thighs deliberate and bulging in the tight trousers, the butt of the pistol catching and losing the sun in pearly gleams. Sitting on the post, he looked down at the faces along the fence which were attentive, grave, reserved and not looking at him. "All right," he said. "Who's going to start her off with a bid? Step right up; take your pick and make your bid, and when the last one is sold, walk in that lot and put your rope on the best piece of horseflesh you ever forked or druv for the money. There aint a pony there that aint worth fifteen dollars. Young, sound, good for saddle or work stock, guaranteed to outlast four ordinary horses; you couldn't kill one of them with a axletree——" There was a small violent commotion at the rear of the group. The little boy appeared, burrowing among the motionless overalls. He approached the post, the new and unbroken paper carton lifted. The Texan leaned down and took it and tore the end from it and shook three or four of the cakes into the boy's hand, a hand as small and almost as black as that of a coon. He held the carton in his hand while he talked, pointing out the horses with it as he indicated them.

"Look at that one with the three stocking feet and the frost-bit ear; watch him now when they pass again. Look at that shoulder-action; that horse is worth twenty dollars of any man's money. Who'll make me a bid on him to start her off?" His voice was harsh, ready, forensic. Along the fence below him the men stood with, buttoned close in their overalls, the tobacco-sacks and worn purses the sparse silver and frayed bills hoarded a coin at a time in the cracks of chimneys or chinked into the logs of walls. From time to time the horses broke and rushed with purposeless violence and huddled again, watching the faces along the fence with wild mis-matched eyes. The lane was full of wagons now. As the others arrived they would have to stop in the road beyond it and the occupants came up the lane on foot. Mrs Littlejohn came out of her kitchen. She crossed the yard, looking toward the lot gate. There was a blackened washpot set on four bricks in the corner of the yard. She built a fire beneath the pot and came to the fence and stood there for a time, her hands on her hips and the smoke from the fire drifting blue and slow behind her. Then she turned and went back into the house. "Come on, boys," the Texan said. "Who'll make me a bid?"

"Four bits," a voice said. The Texan did not even glance toward it.

"Or, if he dont suit you, how about that fiddle-head horse without no mane to speak of? For a saddle pony, I'd rather have him than that stocking-foot. I heard somebody say fifty cents just now. I reckon he meant five dollars, didn't he? Do I hear five dollars?"

"Four bits for the lot," the same voice said. This time there were no guffaws. It was the Texan who laughed, harshly, with only his lower face, as if he were reciting a multiplication table.

"Fifty cents for the dried mud offen them, he means," he said. "Who'll give a dollar more for the genuine Texas cockle-burrs?" Mrs Littlejohn came out of the kitchen, carrying the sawn half of a wooden hogshead which she set on a stump beside the smoking pot, and stood with her hands on her hips, looking into the lot for a while without coming to the fence this time. Then she went back into the house. "What's the matter with you boys?" the Texan said. "Here, Eck, you been helping me and you know them horses. How about making me a bid on that wall-eyed one you picked out last night? Here. Wait a minute." He thrust the paper carton into his other hip pocket and swung his feet inward and dropped, cat-light, into the lot. The ponies, huddled, watched him. Then they broke before him and slid stiffly along the fence. He turned them and they whirled and rushed back across the lot; whereupon, as though he had been waiting his chance when they should have turned their backs on him, the Texan began to run too, so that when they reached the opposite side of the lot and turned, slowing to huddle again, he was almost upon them. The earth became thunderous; dust arose, out of which the animals began to burst like flushed quail and into which, with that apparently unflagging faith in his own invulnerability, the Texan rushed. For an instant the watchers could see them in the dust—the pony backed into the angle of the fence and the stable, the man facing it, reaching toward his hip. Then the beast rushed at him in a sort of fatal and hopeless desperation and he struck it between the eyes with the pistol-butt and felled it and leaped onto its prone head. The pony recovered almost at once and pawed itself to its knees and heaved at its prisoned head and fought itself up, dragging the man with it; for an instant in the dust the watchers saw the man free of the earth and in violent lateral motion like a rag attached to the horse's head. Then the Texan's feet came back to earth and the dust blew aside and revealed them, motionless, the Texan's sharp heels braced into the ground, one hand gripping the pony's forelock and the other its nostrils, the long evil muzzle wrung backward over its scarred shoulder while it breathed in labored and hollow groans. Mrs Littlejohn was in the yard again. No one had seen her emerge this time. She carried an armful of clothing and a metal-ridged wash-board and she was standing motionless at the kitchen steps, looking into the lot. Then she moved across the yard, still looking into the lot, and dumped the garments into the tub, still looking into the lot. "Look him over, boys," the Texan panted, turning his own suffused face and the protuberant glare of his eyes toward the fence. "Look him over quick. Them shoulders and——" He had relaxed for an instant apparently. The animal exploded again; again for an instant the Texan was free of the earth, though he was still talking: "—and legs you whoa I'll tear your face right look him over quick boys worth fifteen dollars of let me get a holt of who'll make me a bid whoa you blare-eyed jack rabbit, whoa!" They were moving now—a kaleidoscope of inextricable and incredible violence on the periphery of which the metal clasps of the Texan's suspenders sun-glinted in ceaseless orbit, with terrific slowness across the lot. Then the broad clay-colored hat soared deliberately outward; an instant later the Texan followed it, though still on his feet, and the pony shot free in mad, staglike bounds. The Texan picked up the hat and struck the dust from it against his leg, and returned to the fence and mounted the post again. He was breathing heavily. Still the faces did not look at him as he took the carton from his hip and shook a cake from it and put the cake into his mouth, chewing, breathing harshly. Mrs Littlejohn turned away and began to bail water from the pot into the tub, though after each bucketful she turned her head and looked into the lot again. "Now, boys," the Texan said. "Who says that pony aint worth fifteen dollars? You couldn't buy that much dynamite for just fifteen dollars. There aint one of them cant do a mile in three minutes; turn them into pasture and they will board themselves; work them like hell all day and every time you think about it, lay them over the head with a single-tree and after a couple of days every jackrabbit one of them will be so tame you will have to put them out of the house at night like a cat." He shook another cake from the carton and ate it. "Come on, Eck," he said. "Start her off. How about ten dollars for that horse, Eck?"

"What need I got for a horse I would need a bear-trap to catch?" Eck said.

"Didn't you just see me catch him?"

"I seen you," Eck said. "And I dont want nothing as big as a horse if I got to wrastle with it every time it finds me on the same side of a fence it's on."

"All right," the Texan said. He was still breathing harshly, but now there was nothing of fatigue or breathlessness in it. He shook another cake into his palm and inserted it beneath his moustache. "All right. I want to get this auction started. I aint come here to live, no matter how good a country you folks claim you got. I'm going to give you that horse." For a moment there was no sound, not even that of breathing except the Texan's.

"You going to give it to me?" Eck said.

"Yes. Provided you will start the bidding on the next one." Again there was no sound save the Texan's breathing, and then the clash of Mrs Littlejohn's pail against the rim of the pot.

"I just start the bidding," Eck said. "I dont have to buy it lessen I aint over-topped." Another wagon had come up the lane. It was battered and paintless. One wheel had been repaired by crossed planks bound to the spokes with baling wire and the two underfed mules wore a battered harness patched with bits of cotton rope; the reins were ordinary cotton plow-lines, not new. It contained a woman in a shapeless gray garment and a faded sunbonnet, and a man in faded and patched though clean overalls. There was not room for the wagon to draw out of the lane so the man left it standing where it was and got down and came forward—a thin man, not large, with something about his eyes, something strained and washed-out, at once vague and intense, who shoved into the crowd at the rear, saying,

"What? What's that? Did he give him that horse?"

"All right," the Texan said. "That wall-eyed horse with the scarred neck belongs to you. Now. That one that looks like he's had his head in a flour barrel. What do you say? Ten dollars?"

"Did he give him that horse?" the newcomer said.

"A dollar," Eck said. The Texan's mouth was still open for speech; for an instant his face died so behind the hard eyes.

"A dollar?" he said. "One dollar? Did I actually hear that?"

"Durn it," Eck said. "Two dollars then. But I aint—"

"Wait," the newcomer said. "You, up there on the post." The Texan looked at him. When the others turned, they saw that the woman had left the wagon too, though they had not known she was there since they had not seen the wagon drive up. She came among them behind the man, gaunt in the gray shapeless garment and the sunbonnet, wearing stained canvas gymnasium shoes. She overtook the man but she did not touch him, standing just behind him, her hands rolled before her into the gray dress.

"Henry," she said in a flat voice. The man looked over his shoulder.

"Get back to that wagon," he said.

"Here, missus," the Texan said. "Henry's going to get the bargain of his life in about a minute. Here, boys, let the missus come up close where she can see. Henry's going to pick out that saddle-horse the missus has been wanting. Who says ten——"

"Henry," the woman said. She did not raise her voice. She had not once looked at the Texan. She touched the man's arm. He turned and struck her hand down.

"Get back to that wagon like I told you." The woman stood behind him, her hands rolled again into her dress. She was not looking at anything, speaking to anyone.

"He aint no more despair than to buy one of them things," she said. "And us not but five dollars away from the poor-house, he aint no more despair." The man turned upon her with that curious air of leashed, of dreamlike fury. The others lounged along the fence in attitudes gravely inattentive, almost oblivious. Mrs Littlejohn had been washing for some time now, pumping rhythmically up and down above the wash-board in the sud-foamed tub. She now stood erect again, her soap-raw hands on her hips, looking into the lot.

"Shut your mouth and get back in that wagon," the man said. "Do you want me to take a wagon stake to you?" He turned and looked up at the Texan. "Did you give him that horse?" he said. The Texan was looking at the woman. Then he looked at the man; still watching him, he tilted the paper carton over his open palm. A single cake came out of it.

"Yes," he said.

"Is the fellow that bids in this next horse going to get that first one too?"

"No," the Texan said.

"All right," the other said. "Are you going to give a horse to the man that makes the first bid on the next one?"

"No," the Texan said.

"Then if you were just starting the auction off by giving

away a horse, why didn't you wait till we were all here?" The Texan stopped looking at the other. He raised the empty carton and squinted carefully into it, as if it might contain a precious jewel or perhaps a deadly insect. Then he crumpled it and dropped it carefully beside the post on which he sat.

"Eck bids two dollars," he said. "I believe he still thinks he's bidding on them scraps of bob-wire they come here in instead of on one of the horses. But I got to accept it. But are you boys—"

"So Eck's going to get two horses at a dollar a head," the newcomer said. "Three dollars." The woman touched him again. He flung her hand off without turning and she stood again, her hands rolled into her dress across her flat stomach, not looking at anything.

"Misters," she said, "we got chaps in the house that never had shoes last winter. We aint got corn to feed the stock. We got five dollars I earned weaving by firelight after dark. And he aint no more despair."

"Henry bids three dollars," the Texan said. "Raise him a dollar, Eck, and the horse is yours." Beyond the fence the horses rushed suddenly and for no reason and as suddenly stopped, staring at the faces along the fence.

"Henry," the woman said. The man was watching Eck. His stained and broken teeth showed a little beneath his lip. His wrists dangled into fists below the faded sleeves of his shirt too short from many washings.

"Four dollars," Eck said.

"Five dollars!" the husband said, raising one clenched hand. He shouldered himself forward toward the gate-post. The woman did not follow him. She now looked at the Texan for the first time. Her eyes were a washed gray also, as though they had faded too like the dress and the sunbonnet.

"Mister," she said, "if you take that five dollars I earned my chaps a-weaving for one of them things, it'll be a curse on you and yours during all the time of man."

"Five dollars!" the husband shouted. He thrust himself up to the post, his clenched hand on a level with the Texan's knees. He opened it upon a wad of frayed banknotes and silver. "Five dollars! And the man that raises it will have to beat my head off or I'll beat hisn."

"All right," the Texan said. "Five dollars is bid. But dont you shake your hand at me."

At five oclock that afternoon the Texan crumpled the third paper carton and dropped it to the earth beneath him. In the copper slant of the leveling sun which fell also upon the line of limp garments in Mrs Littlejohn's backyard and which cast his shadow and that of the post on which he sat long across the lot where now and then the ponies still rushed in purposeless and tireless surges, the Texan straightened his leg and thrust his hand into his pocket and took out a coin and leaned down to the little boy. His voice was now hoarse, spent. "Here, bud," he said. "Run to the store and get me a box of gingersnaps." The men still stood along the fence, tireless, in their overalls and faded shirts. Flem Snopes was there now, appeared suddenly from nowhere, standing beside the fence with a space the width of three or four men on either side of him, standing there in his small yet definite isolation, chewing tobacco, in the same gray trousers and minute bow tie in which he had departed last summer but in a new cap, gray too like the other, but new, and overlaid with a bright golfer's plaid, looking also at the horses in the lot. All of them save two had been sold for sums ranging from three dollars and a half to eleven and twelve dollars. The purchasers, as they had bid them in, had gathered as though by instinct into a separate group on the other side of the gate, where they stood with their hands lying upon the top strand of the fence, watching with a still more sober intensity the animals which some of them had owned for seven and eight hours now but had not yet laid hands upon. The husband, Henry, stood beside the post on which the Texan sat. The wife had gone back to the wagon, where she sat gray in the gray garment, motionless, looking at nothing still; she might have been something inanimate which he had loaded into the wagon to move it somewhere, waiting now in the wagon until he should be ready to go on again, patient, insensate, timeless.

"I bought a horse and I paid cash for it," he said. His voice was harsh and spent too, the mad look in his eyes had a quality glazed now and even sightless. "And yet you expect me to stand around here till they are all sold before I can get my horse. Well, you can do all the expecting you want. I'm going to take my horse out of there and go home." The Texan looked down at him. The Texan's shirt was blotched with sweat. His big face was cold and still, his voice level.

"Take your horse then." After a moment Henry looked away. He stood with his head bent a little, swallowing from time to time.

"Aint you going to catch him for me?"

"It aint my horse," the Texan said in that flat still voice. After a while Henry raised his head. He did not look at the Texan.

"Who'll help me catch my horse?" he said. Nobody answered. They stood along the fence, looking quietly into the lot where the ponies huddled, already beginning to fade a little where the long shadow of the house lay upon them, deepening. From Mrs Littlejohn's kitchen the smell of frying ham came. A noisy cloud of sparrows swept across the lot and into a chinaberry tree beside the house, and in the high soft vague blue swallows stooped and whirled in erratic indecision, their cries like strings plucked at random. Without looking back, Henry raised his voice: "Bring that ere plow-line." After a time the wife moved. She got down from the wagon and took a coil of new cotton rope from it and approached. The husband took the rope from her and moved toward the gate. The Texan began to descend from the post, stiffly, as Henry put his hand on the latch. "Come on here," he said. The wife had stopped when he took the rope from her. She moved again, obediently, her hands rolled into the dress across her stomach, passing the Texan without looking at him.

"Dont you go in there, missus," he said. She stopped, not looking at him, not looking at anything. The husband opened the gate and entered the lot and turned, holding the gate open but without raising his eyes.

"Come on here," he said.

"Dont you go in there, missus," the Texan said. The wife stood motionless between them, her face almost concealed by the sunbonnet, her hands folded across her stomach.

"I reckon I better," she said. The other men did not look at her at all, at her or Henry either. They stood along the fence, grave and quiet and inattentive, almost bemused. Then the wife passed through the gate; the husband shut it behind

them and turned and began to move toward the huddled
ponies, the wife following in the gray and shapeless garment
within which she moved without inference of locomotion,
like something on a moving platform, a float. The horses
were watching them. They clotted and blended and shifted
among themselves, on the point of breaking though not
breaking yet. The husband shouted at them. He began to
curse them, advancing, the wife following. Then the huddle
broke, the animals moving with high, stiff knees, circling the
two people who turned and followed again as the herd flowed
and huddled again at the opposite side of the lot.

"There he is," the husband said. "Get him into that corner." The herd divided; the horse which the husband had
bought jolted on stiff legs. The wife shouted at it; it spun and
poised, plunging, then the husband struck it across the face
with the coiled rope and it whirled and slammed into the
corner of the fence. "Keep him there now," the husband said.
He shook out the rope, advancing. The horse watched him
with wild, glaring eyes; it rushed again, straight toward the
wife. She shouted at it and waved her arms but it soared past
her in a long bound and rushed again into the huddle of its
fellows. They followed and hemmed it again into another corner; again the wife failed to stop its rush for freedom and the
husband turned and struck her with the coiled rope. "Why
didn't you head him?" he said. "Why didn't you?" He struck
her again; she did not move, not even to fend the rope with a
raised arm. The men along the fence stood quietly, their faces
lowered as though brooding upon the earth at their feet.
Only Flem Snopes was still watching—if he ever had been
looking into the lot at all, standing in his little island of isolation, chewing with his characteristic faint sidewise thrust
beneath the new plaid cap.

The Texan said something, not loud, harsh and short. He
entered the lot and went to the husband and jerked the uplifted rope from his hand. The husband whirled as though he
were about to spring at the Texan, crouched slightly, his knees
bent and his arms held slightly away from his sides, though
his gaze never mounted higher than the Texan's carved and
dusty boots. Then the Texan took the husband by the arm
and led him back toward the gate, the wife following, and

through the gate which he held open for the woman and then closed. He took a wad of banknotes from his trousers and removed a bill from it and put it into the woman's hand. "Get him into the wagon and get him on home," he said.

"What's that for?" Flem Snopes said. He had approached. He now stood beside the post on which the Texan had been sitting. The Texan did not look at him.

"Thinks he bought one of them ponies," the Texan said. He spoke in a flat still voice, like that of a man after a sharp run. "Get him on away, missus."

"Give him back that money," the husband said, in his lifeless, spent tone. "I bought that horse and I aim to have him if I got to shoot him before I can put a rope on him." The Texan did not even look at him.

"Get him on away from here, missus," he said.

"You take your money and I take my horse," the husband said. He was shaking slowly and steadily now, as though he were cold. His hands open and shut below the frayed cuffs of his shirt. "Give it back to him," he said.

"You dont own no horse of mine," the Texan said. "Get him on home, missus." The husband raised his spent face, his mad glazed eyes. He reached out his hand. The woman held the banknote in her folded hands across her stomach. For a while the husband's shaking hand merely fumbled at it. Then he drew the banknote free.

"It's my horse," he said. "I bought it. These fellows saw me. I paid for it. It's my horse. Here." He turned and extended the banknote toward Snopes. "You got something to do with these horses. I bought one. Here's the money for it. I bought one. Ask him." Snopes took the banknote. The others stood, gravely inattentive, in relaxed attitudes along the fence. The sun had gone now; there was nothing save violet shadow upon them and upon the lot where once more and for no reason the ponies rushed and flowed. At that moment the little boy came up, tireless and indefatiguable still, with the new paper carton. The Texan took it, though he did not open it at once. He had dropped the rope and now the husband stooped for it, fumbling at it for sometime before he lifted it from the ground. Then he stood with his head bent, his knuckles whitening on the rope. The woman had not moved.

Twilight was coming fast now; there was a last mazy swirl of swallows against the high and changing azure. Then the Texan tore the end from the carton and tilted one of the cakes into his hand; he seemed to be watching the hand as it shut slowly upon the cake until a fine powder of snuff-colored dust began to rain from his fingers. He rubbed the hand carefully on his thigh and raised his head and glanced about until he saw the little boy and handed the carton back to him.

"Here, bud," he said. Then he looked at the woman, his voice flat, quiet again. "Mr Snopes will have your money for you tomorrow. Better get him in the wagon and get him on home. He dont own no horse. You can get your money to-morrow from Mr Snopes." The wife turned and went back to the wagon and got into it. No one watched her, nor the hus-band who still stood, his head bent, passing the rope from one hand to the other. They leaned along the fence, grave and quiet, as though the fence were in another land, another time.

"How many you got left?" Snopes said. The Texan roused; they all seemed to rouse then, returning, listening again.

"Got three now," the Texan said. "Swap all three of them for a buggy or a———"

"It's out in the road," Snopes said, a little shortly, a little quickly, turning away. "Get your mules." He went on up the lane. They watched the Texan enter the lot and cross it, the horses flowing before him but without the old irrational vio-lence, as if they too were spent, vitiated with the long day, and enter the barn and then emerge, leading the two har-nessed mules. The wagon had been backed under the shed beside the barn. The Texan entered this and came out a mo-ment later, carrying a bedding-roll and his coat, and led the mules back toward the gate, the ponies huddled again and watching him with their various unmatching eyes, quietly now, as if they too realised there was not only an armistice between them at last but that they would never look upon each other again in both their lives. Someone opened the gate. The Texan led the mules through it and they followed in a body, leaving the husband standing beside the closed gate, his head still bent and the coiled rope in his hand. They passed the wagon in which the wife sat, her gray gar-ment fading into the dusk, almost the same color and as still, looking at nothing; they passed the clothesline with its limp and unwinded drying garments, walking through the hot vivid smell of ham from Mrs Littlejohn's kitchen. When they reached the end of the lane they could see the moon, almost full, tremendous and pale and still lightless in the sky from which day had not quite gone. Snopes was standing at the end of the lane beside an empty buggy. It was the one with the glittering wheels and the fringed parasol top in which he and Will Varner had used to drive. The Texan was motionless too, looking at it.

"Well well well," he said. "So this is it."

"If it dont suit you, you can ride one of the mules back to Texas," Snopes said.

"You bet," the Texan said. "Only I ought to have a powder puff or at least a mandolin to ride it with." He backed the mules onto the tongue and lifted the breast-yoke. Two of them came forward and fastened the traces for him. Then they watched him get into the buggy and raise the reins.

"Where you heading for?" one said. "Back to Texas?"

"In this?" the Texan said. "I wouldn't get past the first Texas saloon without starting the vigilance committee. Besides, I aint going to waste all this here lace-trimmed top and these spindle wheels just on Texas. Long as I am this far, I reckon I'll go on a day or two and look-see them northern towns. Washington and New York and Baltimore. What's the short way to New York from here?" They didn't know. But they told him how to reach Jefferson.

"You're already headed right," Freeman said. "Just keep right on up the road past the schoolhouse."

"All right," the Texan said. "Well, remember about busting them ponies over the head now and then until they get used to you. You wont have any trouble with them then." He lifted the reins again. As he did so Snopes stepped forward and got into the buggy.

"I'll ride as far as Varner's with you," he said.

"I didn't know I was going past Varner's," the Texan said.

"You can go to town that way," Snopes said. "Drive on." The Texan shook the reins. Then he said,

"Whoa." He straightened his leg and put his hand into his pocket. "Here, bud," he said to the little boy, "run to the store and— Never mind. I'll stop and get it myself, long as I am going back that way. Well, boys," he said. "Take care of yourselves." He swung the team around. The buggy went on. They looked after it.

"I reckon he aims to kind of come up on Jefferson from behind," Quick said.

"He'll be lighter when he gets there," Freeman said. "He can come up to it easy from any side he wants."

"Yes," Bookwright said. "His pockets wont rattle." They went back to the lot; they passed on through the narrow way between the two lines of patient and motionless wagons, which at the end was completely closed by the one in which the woman sat. The husband was still standing beside the gate with his coiled rope, and now night had completely come. The light itself had not changed so much; if anything, it was brighter but with that other-worldly quality of moonlight, so that when they stood once more looking into the lot, the splotchy bodies of the ponies had a distinctness, almost a brilliance, but without individual shape and without depth—no longer horses, no longer flesh and bone directed by a principle capable of calculated violence, no longer inherent with the capacity to hurt and harm.

"Well, what are we waiting for?" Freeman said. "For them to go to roost?"

"We better all get our ropes first," Quick said. "Get your ropes everybody." Some of them did not have ropes. When they left home that morning, they had not heard about the horses, the auction. They had merely happened through the village by chance and learned of it and stopped.

"Go to the store and get some then," Freeman said.

"The store will be closed now," Quick said.

"No it wont," Freeman said. "If it was closed, Lump Snopes would a been up here." So while the ones who had come prepared got their ropes from the wagons, the others went down to the store. The clerk was just closing it.

"You all aint started catching them yet, have you?" he said. "Good; I was afraid I wouldn't get there in time." He opened the door again and amid the old strong sunless smells of cheese and leather and molasses he measured and cut off sections of plow-line for them and in a body and the clerk in the center and still talking, voluble and unlistened to, they returned up the road. The pear tree before Mrs Littlejohn's was like drowned silver now in the moon. The mockingbird of last night, or another one, was already singing in it, and they now saw, tied to the fence, Ratliff's buckboard and team.

"I thought something was wrong all day," one said. "Ratliff wasn't there to give nobody advice." When they passed down the lane, Mrs Littlejohn was in her backyard, gathering the garments from the clothesline; they could still smell the ham. The others were waiting at the gate, beyond which the ponies, huddled again, were like phantom fish, suspended apparently without legs now in the brilliant treachery of the moon.

"I reckon the best way will be for us all to take and catch them one at a time," Freeman said.

"One at a time," the husband, Henry, said. Apparently he had not moved since the Texan had led his mules through the gate, save to lift his hands to the top of the gate, one of them still clutching the coiled rope. "One at a time," he said. He began to curse in a harsh, spent monotone. "After I've stood around here all day, waiting for that——" He cursed. He began to jerk at the gate, shaking it with spent violence until one of the others slid the latch back and it swung open and Henry entered it, the others following, the little boy pressing close behind his father until Eck became aware of him and turned.

"Here," he said. "Give me that rope. You stay out of here."

"Aw, paw," the boy said.

"No sir. Them things will kill you. They almost done it this morning. You stay out of here."

"But we got two to catch." For a moment Eck stood looking down at the boy.

"That's right," he said. "We got two. But you stay close to me now. And when I holler run, you run. You hear me?"

"Spread out, boys," Freeman said. "Keep them in front of us." They began to advance across the lot in a ragged crescent-shaped line, each one with his rope. The ponies were now at the far side of the lot. One of them snorted; the mass shifted within itself but without breaking. Freeman, glancing back, saw the little boy. "Get that boy out of here," he said.

"I reckon you better," Eck said to the boy. "You go and get in the wagon yonder. You can see us catch them from there." The little boy turned and trotted toward the shed beneath which the wagon stood. The line of men advanced, Henry a little in front.

"Watch them close now," Freeman said. "Maybe we better try to get them into the barn first——" At that moment the huddle broke. It parted and flowed in both directions along the fence. The men at the ends of the line began to run, waving their arms and shouting. "Head them," Freeman said tensely. "Turn them back." They turned them, driving them back upon themselves again; the animals merged and spun in short, huddling rushes, phantom and inextricable. "Hold them now," Freeman said. "Dont let them get by us." The line advanced again. Eck turned; he did not know why—whether a sound, what. The little boy was just behind him again.

"Didn't I tell you to get in that wagon and stay there?" Eck said.

"Watch out, paw!" the boy said. "There he is! There's ourn!" It was the one the Texan had given Eck. "Catch him, paw!"

"Get out of my way," Eck said. "Get back to that wagon." The line was still advancing. The ponies milled, clotting, forced gradually backward toward the open door of the barn. Henry was still slightly in front, crouched slightly, his thin figure, even in the mazy moonlight, emanating something of that spent fury. The splotchy huddle of animals seemed to be moving before the advancing line of men like a snowball which they might have been pushing before them by some invisible means, gradually nearer and nearer to the black yawn of the barn door. Later it was obvious that the ponies were so intent upon the men that they did not realise the barn was even behind them until they backed into the shadow of it. Then an indescribable sound, a movement desperate and despairing, arose among them; for an instant of static horror men and animals faced one another, then the men whirled and ran before a gaudy vomit of long wild faces and splotched chests which overtook and scattered them and flung them sprawling aside and completely obliterated from sight Henry and the little boy, neither of whom had moved though Henry had flung up both arms, still holding his coiled rope, the herd sweeping on across the lot, to crash through the gate which the last man through it had neglected to close, leaving it slightly ajar, carrying all of the gate save the upright to which the hinges were nailed with them, and so among the teams and wagons which choked the lane, the teams springing and lunging too, snapping hitch-reins and tongues. Then the whole inextricable mass crashed among the wagons and eddied and divided about the one in which the woman sat, and rushed on down the lane and into the road, dividing, one half going one way and one half the other.

The men in the lot, except Henry, got to their feet and ran toward the gate. The little boy once more had not been touched, not even thrown off his feet; for a while his father held him clear of the ground in one hand, shaking him like a rag doll. "Didn't I tell you to stay in that wagon?" Eck cried. "Didn't I tell you?"

"Look out, paw!" the boy chattered out of the violent shaking, "there's ourn! There he goes!" It was the horse the Texan had given them again. It was as if they owned no other, the other one did not exist; as if by some absolute and instantaneous rapport of blood they had relegated to oblivion the one for which they had paid money. They ran to the gate and down the lane where the other men had disappeared. They saw the horse the Texan had given them whirl and dash back and rush through the gate into Mrs Littlejohn's yard and run up the front steps and crash once on the wooden veranda and vanish through the front door. Eck and the boy ran up onto the veranda. A lamp sat on a table just inside the door. In its mellow light they saw the horse fill the long hallway like a pinwheel, gaudy, furious and thunderous. A little further down the hall there was a varnished yellow melodeon. The horse crashed into it; it produced a single note, almost a chord, in bass, resonant and grave, of deep and sober astonishment; the horse with its monstrous and antic shadow whirled again and vanished through another door. It was a bedroom; Ratliff, in his underclothes and one sock and with the other sock in his hand and his back to the door, was leaning out the open window facing the lane, the lot. He looked back over his shoulder. For an instant he and the horse glared at one another. Then he sprang through the window as the horse backed out of the room and into the hall again and whirled and saw Eck and the little boy just entering the front door, Eck still carrying his rope. It whirled again and rushed on down the hall and onto the back porch just as Mrs Little-john, carrying an armful of clothes from the line and the wash-board, mounted the steps.

"Get out of here, you son of a bitch," she said. She struck with the wash-board; it divided neatly on the long mad face and the horse whirled and rushed back up the hall, where Eck and the boy now stood.

"Get to hell out of here, Wall!" Eck roared. He dropped to the floor, covering his head with his arms. The boy did not move, and for the third time the horse soared above the un-winking eyes and the unbowed and untouched head and onto the front veranda again just as Ratliff, still carrying the sock, ran around the corner of the house and up the steps. The horse whirled without breaking or pausing. It galloped to the end of the veranda and took the railing and soared outward, hobgoblin and floating, in the moon. It landed in the lot still running and crossed the lot and galloped through the wrecked gate and among the overturned wagons and the still intact one in which Henry's wife still sat, and on down the lane and into the road.

A quarter of a mile further on, the road gashed pallid and moony between the moony shadows of the bordering trees, the horse still galloping, galloping its shadow into the dust, the road descending now toward the creek and the bridge. It was of wood, just wide enough for a single vehicle. When the horse reached it, it was occupied by a wagon coming from the opposite direction and drawn by two mules already asleep in the harness and the soporific motion. On the seat were Tull and his wife, in splint chairs in the wagon behind them sat their four daughters, all returning belated from an all-day visit with some of Mrs Tull's kin. The horse neither checked nor swerved. It crashed once on the wooden bridge and rushed between the two mules which waked lunging in opposite di-rections in the traces, the horse now apparently scrambling along the wagon-tongue itself like a mad squirrel and scrab-bling at the end-gate of the wagon with its fore feet as if it intended to climb into the wagon while Tull shouted at it and struck at its face with his whip. The mules were now trying to turn the wagon around in the middle of the bridge. It slewed and tilted, the bridge-rail cracked with a sharp report above the shrieks of the women; the horse scrambled at last across the back of one of the mules and Tull stood up in the wagon and kicked at its face. Then the front end of the wagon rose, flinging Tull, the reins now wrapped several times about his wrist, backward into the wagon bed among the overturned chairs and the exposed stockings and undergarments of his women. The pony scrambled free and crashed again on the wooden planking, galloping again. The wagon lurched again; the mules had finally turned it on the bridge where there was not room for it to turn and were now kicking themselves free of the traces. When they came free, they snatched Tull bodily out of the wagon. He struck the bridge on his face and was dragged for several feet before the wrist-wrapped reins broke. Far up the road now, distancing the frantic mules, the pony faded on. While the five women still shrieked above Tull's unconscious body, Eck and the little boy came up, trotting, Eck still carrying his rope. He was panting. "Which way'd he go?" he said.

In the now empty and moon-drenched lot, his wife and Mrs Littlejohn and Ratliff and Lump Snopes, the clerk, and three other men raised Henry out of the trampled dust and carried him into Mrs Littlejohn's back yard. His face was blanched and stony, his eyes were closed, the weight of his head tautened his throat across the protruding larynx; his teeth glinted dully beneath his lifted lip. They carried him on toward the house, through the dappled shade of the chinaberry trees. Across the dreaming and silver night a faint sound like remote thunder came and ceased. "There's one of them on the creek bridge," one of the men said.

"It's that one of Eck Snopes," another said. "The one that was in the house." Mrs Littlejohn had preceded them into the hall. When they entered with Henry, she had already taken the lamp from the table and she stood beside an open door, holding the lamp high.

"Bring him in here," she said. She entered the room first and set the lamp on the dresser. They followed with clumsy

scufflings and pantings and laid Henry on the bed and Mrs
Littlejohn came to the bed and stood looking down at
Henry's peaceful and bloodless face. "I'll declare," she said. "You
men." They had drawn back a little, clumped, shifting from
one foot to another, not looking at her nor at his wife either,
who stood at the foot of the bed, motionless, her hands
folded into her dress. "You all get out of here, V.K.," she said
to Ratliff. "Go outside. See if you cant find something else to
play with that will kill some more of you."

"All right," Ratliff said. "Come on boys. Aint no more
horses to catch in here." They followed him toward the door,
on tiptoe, their shoes scuffing, their shadows monstrous on
the wall.

"Go get Will Varner," Mrs Littlejohn said. "I reckon you
can tell him it's still a mule." They went out; they didn't look
back. They tiptoed up the hall and crossed the veranda and
descended into the moonlight. Now that they could pay attention to it, the silver air seemed to be filled with faint and
sourceless sounds—shouts, thin and distant, again a brief
thunder of hooves on a wooden bridge, more shouts faint and
thin and earnest and clear as bells; once they even distinguished the words: "Whooey. Head him."

"He went through that house quick," Ratliff said. "He
must have found another woman at home." Then Henry
screamed in the house behind them. They looked back into
the dark hall where a square of light fell through the bedroom
door, listening while the scream sank into a harsh respiration:
"Ah. Ah. Ah" on a rising note about to become screaming
again. "Come on," Ratliff said. "We better get Varner." They
went up the road in a body, treading the moon-blanched dust
in the tremulous April night murmurous with the moving of
sap and the wet bursting of burgeoning leaf and bud and constant with the thin and urgent cries and the brief and fading
bursts of galloping hooves. Varner's house was dark, blank
and without depth in the moonlight. They stood, clumped
darkly in the silver yard and called up at the blank windows
until suddenly someone was standing in one of them. It was
Flem Snopes' wife. She was in a white garment; the heavy
braided club of her hair looked almost black against it. She
did not lean out, she merely stood there, full in the moon,

apparently blank-eyed or certainly not looking downward at them—the heavy gold hair, the mask not tragic and perhaps not even doomed: just damned, the strong faint lift of breasts beneath the marblelike fall of the garment; to those below what Brunhilde, what Rhinemaiden on what spurious river-rock of papier-mache, what Helen returned to what topless and shoddy Argos, waiting for no one. "Evening, Mrs Snopes," Ratliff said. "We want Uncle Will. Henry Armstid is hurt at Mrs Littlejohn's." She vanished from the window. They waited in the moonlight, listening to the faint remote shouts and cries, until Varner emerged, sooner than they had actually expected, hunching into his coat and buttoning his trousers over the tail of his nightshirt, his suspenders still dangling in twin loops below the coat. He was carrying the battered bag which contained the plumber-like tools with which he drenched and wormed and blistered and floated or drew the teeth of horses and mules; he came down the steps, lean and loosejointed, his shrewd ruthless head cocked a little as he listened also to the faint bell-like cries and shouts with which the silver air was full.

"Are they still trying to catch them rabbits?" he said.

"All of them except Henry Armstid," Ratliff said. "He caught his."

"Hah," Varner said. "That you, V.K.? How many did you buy?"

"I was too late," Ratliff said. "I never got back in time."

"Hah," Varner said. They moved on to the gate and into the road again. "Well, it's a good bright cool night for running them." The moon was now high overhead, a pearled and mazy yawn in the soft sky, the ultimate ends of which rolled onward, whorl on whorl, beyond the pale stars and by pale stars surrounded. They walked in a close clump, tramping their shadows into the road's mild dust, blotting the shadows of the burgeoning trees which soared, trunk branch and twig against the pale sky, delicate and finely thinned. They passed the dark store. Then the pear tree came in sight. It rose in mazed and silver immobility like exploding snow; the mockingbird still sang in it. "Look at that tree," Varner said. "It ought to make this year, sho."

"Corn'll make this year too," one said.

"A moon like this is good for every growing thing outen earth," Varner said. "I mind when me and Mrs Varner was expecting Eula. Already had a mess of children and maybe we ought to quit then. But I wanted some more gals. Others had done married and moved away, and a passel of boys, soon as they get big enough to be worth anything, they aint got time to work. Got to set around store and talk. But a gal will stay home and work until she does get married. So there was a old woman told my mammy once that if a woman showed her belly to the full moon after she had done caught, it would be a gal. So Mrs Varner taken and laid every night with the moon on her nekid belly, until it fulled and after. I could lay my ear to her belly and hear Eula kicking and scrouging like all get-out, feeling the moon."

"You mean it actually worked sho enough, Uncle Will?" the other said.

"Hah," Varner said. "You might try it. You get enough women showing their nekid bellies to the moon or the sun either or even just to your hand fumbling around often enough and more than likely after a while there will be something in it you can lay your ear and listen to, provided something come up and you aint got away by that time. Hah, V.K.?" Someone guffawed.

"Dont ask me," Ratliff said. "I cant even get nowhere in time to buy a cheap horse." Two or three guffawed this time. Then they began to hear Henry's respirations from the house: "Ah. Ah. Ah" and they ceased abruptly, as if they had not been aware of their closeness to it. Varner walked on in front, lean, shambling, yet moving quite rapidly, though his head was still slanted with listening as the faint, urgent, indomitable cries murmured in the silver lambence, sourceless, at times almost musical, like fading bell-notes; again there was a brief rapid thunder of hooves on wooden planking.

"There's another one on the creek bridge," one said.

"They are going to come out even on them things, after all," Varner said. "They'll get the money back in exercise and relaxation. You take a man that aint got no other relaxation all year long except dodging mule-dung up and down a field furrow. And a night like this one, when a man aint old enough yet to lay still and sleep, and yet he aint young enough anymore to be tomcatting in and out of other folks' back windows, something like this is good for him. It'll make him sleep tomorrow night anyhow, provided he gets back home by then. If we had just knowed about this in time, we could have trained up a pack of horse-dogs. Then we could have held one of these field trials."

"That's one way to look at it, I reckon," Ratliff said. "In fact, it might be a considerable comfort to Bookwright and Quick and Freeman and Eck Snopes and them other new horse-owners if that side of it could be brought to their attention, because the chances are aint none of them thought to look at it in that light yet. Probably there aint a one of them that believes now there's any cure a-tall for that Texas disease Flem Snopes and that Dead-eye Dick brought here."

"Hah," Varner said. He opened Mrs Littlejohn's gate. The dim light still fell outward across the hall from the bedroom door; beyond it, Armstid was saying "Ah. Ah. Ah" steadily. "There's a pill for every ill but the last one."

"Even if there was always time to take it," Ratliff said.

"Hah," Varner said again. He glanced back at Ratliff for an instant, pausing. But the little hard bright eyes were invisible now; it was only the bushy overhang of the brows which seemed to concentrate downward toward him in writhen immobility, not frowning but with a sort of fierce risibility. "Even if there was time to take it. Breathing is a sight-draft dated yesterday."

At nine oclock on the second morning after that, five men were sitting or squatting along the gallery of the store. The sixth was Ratliff. He was standing up, and talking: "Maybe there wasn't but one of them things in Mrs Littlejohn's house that night, like Eck says. But it was the biggest drove of just one horse I ever seen. It was in my room and it was on the front porch and I could hear Mrs Littlejohn hitting it over the head with that wash-board in the back yard all at the same time. And still it was missing everybody everytime. I reckon that's what that Texas man meant by calling them bargains: that a man would need to be powerful unlucky to ever get close enough to one of them to get hurt." They laughed, all except Eck himself. He and the little boy were eating. When they mounted the steps, Eck had gone on into the store and emerged with a paper sack, from which he took a segment of cheese and with his pocket knife divided it carefully into two exact halves and gave one to the boy and took a handful of crackers from the sack and gave them to the boy, and now they squatted against the wall, side by side and, save for the difference in size, identical, eating.

"I wonder what that horse thought Ratliff was," one said. He held a spray of peach bloom between his teeth. It bore four blossoms like miniature ballet skirts of pink tulle. "Jumping out windows and running in doors in his shirt-tail? I wonder how many Ratliffs that horse thought he saw."

"I dont know," Ratliff said. "But if he saw just half as many of me as I saw of him, he was sholy surrounded. Everytime I turned my head, that thing was just running over me or just swirling to run back over that boy again. And that boy there, he stayed right under it one time to my certain knowledge for a full one-and-one-half minutes without ducking his head or even batting his eyes. Yes sir, when I looked around and seen that varmint in the door behind me blaring its eyes at me, I'd a made sho Flem Snopes had brought a tiger back from Texas except I knowed that couldn't no just one tiger completely fill a entire room." They laughed again, quietly. Lump Snopes, the clerk, sitting in the only chair tilted back against the door-facing and partly blocking the entrance, cackled suddenly.

"If Flem had knowed how quick you fellows was going to snap them horses up, he'd a probably brought some tigers," he said. "Monkeys too."

"So they was Flem's horses," Ratliff said. The laughter stopped. The other three had open knives in their hands, with which they had been trimming idly at chips and slivers of wood. Now they sat apparently absorbed in the delicate and almost tedious movements of the knife-blades. The clerk had looked quickly up and found Ratliff watching him. His constant expression of incorrigible and mirthful disbelief had left him now; only the empty wrinkles of it remained about his mouth and eyes.

"Has Flem ever said they was?" he said. "But you town fellows are smarter than us country folks. Likely you done already read Flem's mind." But Ratliff was not looking at him now.

"And I reckon we'd a bought them," he said. He stood above them again, easy, intelligent, perhaps a little sombre but still perfectly impenetrable. "Eck here, for instance. With a wife and family to support. He owns two of them, though to be sho he never had to pay money for but one. I heard folks chasing them things up until midnight last night, but Eck and that boy aint been home a-tall in two days." They laughed again, except Eck. He pared off a bite of cheese and speared it on the knife-point and put it into his mouth.

"Eck caught one of hisn," the second man said.

"That so?" Ratliff said. "Which one was it, Eck? The one he give you or the one you bought?"

"The one he give me," Eck said, chewing.

"Well, well," Ratliff said. "I hadn't heard about that. But Eck's still one horse short. And the one he had to pay money for. Which is pure proof enough that them horses wasn't Flem's because wouldn't no man ever give his own blood kin something he couldn't even catch." They laughed again, but they stopped when the clerk spoke. There was no mirth in his voice at all.

"Listen," he said. "All right. We done all admitted you are too smart for anybody to get ahead of. You never bought no horse from Flem or nobody else, so maybe it aint none of your business and maybe you better just leave it at that."

"Sholy," Ratliff said. "It's done already been left at that two nights ago. The fellow that forgot to shut that lot gate done that. With the exception of Eck's horse. And we know that wasn't Flem's, because that horse was give to Eck for nothing."

"There's others besides Eck that aint got back home yet," the man with the peach spray said. "Bookwright and Quick are still chasing theirs. They was reported three miles west of Burtsboro Old Town at eight oclock last night. They aint got close enough to it yet to tell which one it belongs to."

"Sholy," Ratliff said. "The only new horse-owner in this country that could a been found without bloodhounds since whoever it was left that gate open two nights ago, is Henry Armstid. He's laying right there in Mrs Littlejohn's bedroom where he can watch the lot so that any time the one he bought happens to run back into it, all he's got to do is to

holler at his wife to run out with the rope and catch it——"
He ceased, though he said, "Morning, Flem," so immediately
afterward and with no change whatever in tone, that the
pause was not even discernible. With the exception of the
clerk, who sprang up, vacated the chair with a sort of servile
alacrity, and Eck and the little boy who continued to eat, they
watched above their stilled hands as Snopes in the gray trousers and the minute tie and the new cap with its bright over-
plaid mounted the steps. He was chewing; he already carried
a piece of white pine board; he jerked his head at them, looking at nobody, and took the vacated chair and opened his
knife and began to whittle. The clerk now leaned in the opposite side of the door, rubbing his back against the facing. The
expression of merry and invincible disbelief had returned to
his face, with a quality watchful and secret.

"You're just in time," he said. "Ratliff here seems to be in a
considerable sweat about who actually owned them horses."
Snopes drew his knife-blade neatly along the board, the neat,
surgeon-like sliver curling before it. The others were whittling
again, looking carefully at nothing, except Eck and the boy,
who were still eating, and the clerk rubbing his back against
the door-facing and watching Snopes with that secret and
alert intensity. "Maybe you could put his mind at rest."
Snopes turned his head slightly and spat, across the gallery
and the steps and into the dust beyond them. He drew the
knife back and began another curling sliver.

"He was there too," Snopes said. "He knows as much as
anybody else." This time the clerk guffawed, chortling, his
features gathering toward the center of his face as though
plucked there by a hand. He slapped his leg, cackling.

"You might as well to quit," he said. "You cant beat him."

"I reckon not," Ratliff said. He stood above them, not
looking at any of them, his gaze fixed apparently on the
empty road beyond Mrs Littlejohn's house, impenetrable,
brooding even. A hulking, half-grown boy in overalls too
small for him, appeared suddenly from nowhere in particular.
He stood for a while in the road, just beyond spitting-range
of the gallery, with that air of having come from nowhere in
particular and of not knowing where he would go next when
he should move again and of not being troubled by that fact.

He was looking at nothing, certainly not toward the gallery, and no one on the gallery so much as looked at him except the little boy, who now watched the boy in the road, his periwinkle eyes grave and steady above the bitten cracker in his halted hand. The boy in the road moved on, thickly undulant in the tight overalls, and vanished beyond the corner of the store, the round head and the unwinking eyes of the little boy on the gallery turning steadily to watch him out of sight. Then the little boy bit the cracker again, chewing. "Of course there's Mrs Tull," Ratliff said. "But that's Eck she's going to sue for damaging Tull against that bridge. And as for Henry Armstid——"

"If a man aint got gumption enough to protect himself, it's his own look-out," the clerk said.

"Sholy," Ratliff said, still in that dreamy, abstracted tone, actually speaking over his shoulder even. "And Henry Armstid, that's all right because from what I hear of the conversation that taken place, Henry had already stopped owning that horse he thought was his before that Texas man left. And as for that broke leg, that wont put him out none because his wife can make his crop." The clerk had ceased to rub his back against the door. He watched the back of Ratliff's head, unwinking too, sober and intent; he glanced at Snopes who, chewing, was watching another sliver curl away from the advancing knife-blade, then he watched the back of Ratliff's head again.

"It wont be the first time she has made their crop," the man with the peach spray said. Ratliff glanced at him.

"You ought to know. This wont be the first time I ever saw you in their field, doing plowing Henry never got around to. How many days have you already given them this year?" The man with the peach spray removed it and spat carefully and put the spray back between his teeth.

"She can run a furrow straight as I can," the second said.

"They're unlucky," the third said. "When you are unlucky, it dont matter much what you do."

"Sholy," Ratliff said. "I've heard laziness called bad luck so much that maybe it is."

"He aint lazy," the third said. "When their mule died three or four years ago, him and her broke their land working time about in the traces with the other mule. They aint lazy."

"So that's all right," Ratliff said, gazing up the empty road again. "Likely she will begin right away to finish the plowing; that oldest gal is pretty near big enough to work with a mule, aint she? or at least to hold the plow steady while Mrs Armstid helps the mule?" He glanced again toward the man with the peach spray as though for an answer, but he was not looking at the other and he went on talking without any pause. The clerk stood with his rump and back pressed against the door-facing as if he had paused in the act of scratching, watching Ratliff quite hard now, unwinking. If Ratliff had looked at Flem Snopes, he would have seen nothing below the down-slanted peak of the cap save the steady motion of his jaws. Another sliver was curling with neat deliberation before the moving knife. "Plenty of time now because all she's got to do after she finishes washing Mrs Littlejohn's dishes and sweeping out the house to pay hers and Henry's board, is to go out home and milk and cook up enough vittles to last the children until tomorrow and feed them and get the littlest ones to sleep and wait outside the door until that biggest gal gets the bar up and gets into bed herself with the axe—"

"The axe?" the man with the peach spray said.

"She takes it to bed with her. She's just twelve, and what with this country still more or less full of them uncaught horses that never belonged to Flem Snopes, likely she feels maybe she cant swing a mere wash-board like Mrs Littlejohn can.—and then come back and wash up the supper dishes. And after that, not nothing to do until morning except to stay close enough where Henry can call her until it's light enough to chop the wood to cook breakfast and then help Mrs Little-john wash the dishes and make the beds and sweep while watching the road. Because likely any time now Flem Snopes will get back from wherever he has been since the auction, which of course is to town naturally to see about his cousin that's got into a little legal trouble, and so get that five dollars. 'Only maybe he wont give it back to me,' she says, and maybe that's what Mrs Littlejohn thought too, because she never said nothing. I could hear her—"

"And where did you happen to be during all this?" the clerk said.

"Listening," Ratliff said. He glanced back at the clerk, then he was looking away again, almost standing with his back to them. "—could hear her dumping the dishes into the pan like she was throwing them at it. 'Do you reckon he will give it back to me?' Mrs Armstid says. 'That Texas man give it to him and said he would. All the folks there saw him give Mr Snopes the money and heard him say I could get it from Mr Snopes tomorrow.' Mrs Littlejohn was washing the dishes now, washing them like a man would, like they was made out of iron. 'No,' she says. 'But asking him wont do no hurt.'—'If he wouldn't give it back, it aint no use to ask,' Mrs Armstid says.—'Suit yourself,' Mrs Littlejohn says. 'It's your money.' Then I couldn't hear nothing but the dishes for a while. 'Do you reckon he might give it back to me?' Mrs Armstid says. 'That Texas man said he would. They all heard him say it.'—'Then go and ask him for it,' Mrs Littlejohn says. Then I couldn't hear nothing but the dishes again. 'He wont give it back to me,' Mrs Armstid says.—'All right,' Mrs Littlejohn says. 'Dont ask him, then.' Then I just heard the dishes. They would have two pans, both washing. 'You dont reckon he would, do you?' Mrs Armstid says. Mrs Littlejohn never said nothing. It sounded like she was throwing the dishes at one another. 'Maybe I better go and talk to Henry,' Mrs Armstid says.—'I would,' Mrs Littlejohn says. And I be dog if it didn't sound exactly like she had two plates in her hands, beating them together like these here brass bucket-lids in a band. 'Then Henry can buy another five-dollar horse with it. Maybe he'll buy one next time that will out and out kill him. If I just thought he would, I'd give him back that money, myself.'—'I reckon I better talk to him first,' Mrs Armstid says. And then it sounded just like Mrs Littlejohn taken up the dishes and pans and all and throwed the whole business at the cook-stove—" Ratliff ceased. Behind him the clerk was hissing "Psst! Psst! Flem. Flem!" Then he stopped, and all of them watched Mrs Armstid approach and mount the steps, gaunt in the shapeless gray garment, the stained tennis shoes hissing faintly on the boards. She came among them and stood, facing Snopes but not looking at anyone, her hands rolled into her apron.

"He said that day he wouldn't sell Henry that horse," she said in a flat toneless voice. "He said you had the money and I could get it from you." Snopes raised his head and turned it slightly again and spat neatly past the woman, across the gallery and into the road.

"He took all the money with him when he left," he said. Motionless, the gray garment hanging in rigid, almost formal folds like drapery in bronze, Mrs Armstid appeared to be watching something near Snopes' feet, as though she had not heard him, or as if she had quitted her body as soon as she finished speaking and although her body, hearing, had received the words, they would have no life nor meaning until she returned. The clerk was rubbing his back steadily against the door-facing again, watching her. The little boy was watching her too with his unwinking ineffable gaze, but nobody else was. The man with the peach spray removed it and spat and put the twig back into his mouth.

"He said Henry hadn't bought no horse," she said. "He said I could get the money from you."

"I reckon he forgot it," Snopes said. "He took all the money away with him when he left." He watched her a moment longer, then he trimmed again at the stick. The clerk rubbed his back gently against the door, watching her. After a time Mrs Armstid raised her head and looked up the road where it went on, mild with spring dust, past Mrs Littlejohn's, beginning to rise, on past the not-yet-bloomed (that would be in June) locust grove across the way, on past the schoolhouse, the weathered roof of which, rising beyond an orchard of peach and pear trees, resembled a hive swarmed about by a cloud of pink-and-white bees, ascending, mounting toward the crest of the hill where the church stood among its sparse gleam of marble headstones in the sombre cedar grove where during the long afternoons of summer the constant mourning doves called back and forth. She moved; once more the rubber soles hissed on the gnawed boards.

"I reckon it's about time to get dinner started," she said.

"How's Henry this morning, Mrs Armstid?" Ratliff said.

She looked at him, pausing, the blank eyes waking for an instant.

"He's resting, I thank you kindly," she said. Then the eyes died again and she moved again. Snopes rose from the chair, closing his knife with his thumb and brushing a litter of minute shavings from his lap.

"Wait a minute," he said. Mrs Armstid paused again, half-turning, though still not looking at Snopes nor at any of them. Because she cant possibly actually believe it, Ratliff told himself. Anymore than I do. Snopes entered the store, the clerk, motionless again, his back and rump pressed against the door-facing as though waiting to start rubbing again, watched him enter, his head turning as the other passed him like the head of an owl, the little eyes blinking rapidly now. Jody Varner came up the road on his horse. He did not pass but instead turned in beside the store, toward the mulberry tree behind it where he was in the habit of hitching his horse. A wagon came up the road, creaking past. The man driving it lifted his hand; one or two of the men on the gallery lifted theirs in response. The wagon went on. Mrs Armstid looked after it. Snopes came out of the door, carrying a small striped paper bag and approached Mrs Armstid. "Here," he said. Her hand turned just enough to receive it. "A little sweetening for the chaps," he said. His other hand was already in his pocket, and as he turned back to the chair, he drew something from his pocket and handed it to the clerk, who took it. It was a five-cent piece. He sat down in the chair and tilted it back against the door again. He now had the knife in his hand again, already open. He turned his head slightly and spat again, neatly past the gray garment, into the road. The little boy was watching the sack in Mrs Armstid's hand. Then she seemed to discover it also, rousing.

"You're right kind," she said. She rolled the sack into the apron, the little boy's unwinking gaze fixed upon the lump her hands made beneath the cloth. She moved again. "I reckon I better get on and help with dinner," she said. She descended the steps, though as soon as she reached the level earth and began to retreat, the gray folds of the garment once more lost all inference and intimation of locomotion, so that she seemed to progress without motion like a figure on a retreating and diminishing float; a gray and blasted tree-trunk moving, somehow intact and upright, upon an unhurried flood. The clerk in the doorway cackled suddenly, explosively, chortling. He slapped his thigh.

"By God," he said, "you cant beat him."

Jody Varner, entering the store from the rear, paused in midstride like a pointing bird-dog. Then, on tiptoe, in complete silence and with astonishing speed, he darted behind the counter and sped up the gloomy tunnel, at the end of which a hulking, bear-shaped figure stooped, its entire head and shoulders wedged into the glass case which contained the needles and thread and snuff and tobacco and the stale gaudy candy. He snatched the boy savagely and viciously out; the boy gave a choked cry and struggled flabbily, cramming a final handful of something into his mouth, chewing. But he ceased to struggle almost at once and became slack and inert save for his jaws. Varner dragged him around the counter as the clerk entered, seemed to bounce suddenly into the store with a sort of alert concern. "You, Saint Elmo!" he said.

"Aint I told you and told you to keep him out of here?" Varner demanded, shaking the boy. "He's damn near eaten that candy-case clean. Stand up!" The boy hung like a half-filled sack from Varner's hand, chewing with a kind of fatalistic desperation, the eyes shut tight in the vast flaccid colorless face, the ears moving steadily and faintly to the chewing. Save for the jaw and the ears, he appeared to have gone to sleep chewing.

"You, Saint Elmo!" the clerk said. "Stand up!" The boy assumed his own weight, though he did not open his eyes yet nor cease to chew. Varner released him. "Git on home," the clerk said. The boy turned obediently to re-enter the store. Varner jerked him about again.

"Not that way," he said. The boy crossed the gallery and descended the steps, the tight overalls undulant and reluctant across his flabby thighs. Before he reached the ground, his hand rose from his pocket to his mouth; again his ears moved faintly to the motion of chewing.

"He's worse than a rat, aint he?" the clerk said.

"Rat, hell," Varner said, breathing harshly. "He's worse than a goat. First thing I know, he'll graze on back and work through that lace leather and them hame-strings and lap-links and ring-bolts and eat me and you and him all three clean out the back door. And then be damned if I wouldn't be afraid to turn my back for fear he would cross the road and start in on the gin and the blacksmith shop. Now you mind what I say. If I catch him hanging around here one more time, I'm going to set a bear-trap for him." He went out onto the gallery, the clerk following. "Morning, gentlemen," he said.

"Who's that one, Jody?" Ratliff said. Save for the clerk in the background, they were the only two standing, and now, in juxtaposition, you could see the resemblance between them—a resemblance intangible, indefinite, not in figure, speech, dress, intelligence; certainly not in morals. Yet it was there, but with this bridgeless difference, this hallmark of his fate upon him: he would become an old man; Ratliff, too: but an old man who at about sixty-five would be caught and married by a creature not yet seventeen probably, who would for the rest of his life continue to take revenge upon him for her whole sex; Ratliff, never. The boy was moving without haste up the road. His hand rose again from his pocket to his mouth.

"That boy of I.O.'s," Varner said. "By God, I've done everything but put out poison for him."

"What?" Ratliff said. He glanced quickly about at the faces; for an instant there was in his own not only bewilderment but something almost like terror. "I thought—the other day you fellows told me—You said it was a woman, a young woman with a baby—Here now," he said. "Wait."

"This here's another one," Varner said. "I wish to hell he couldn't walk. Well, Eck, I hear you caught one of your horses."

"That's right," Eck said. He and the little boy had finished the crackers and cheese and he had sat for some time now, holding the empty bag.

"It was the one he give you, wasn't it?" Varner said.

"That's right," Eck said.

"Give the other one to me, paw," the little boy said.

"What happened?" Varner said.

"He broke his neck," Eck said.

"I know," Varner said. "But how?" Eck did not move.

Watching him, they could almost see him visibly gathering and arranging words, speech. Varner, looking down at him, began to laugh steadily and harshly, sucking his teeth. "I'll tell you what happened. Eck and that boy finally run it into that blind lane of Freeman's, after a chase of about twenty-four hours. They figured it couldn't possibly climb them eight-foot fences of Freeman's so him and the boy tied their rope across the end of the lane, about three feet off the ground. And sho enough, soon as the horse come to the end of the lane and seen Freeman's barn, it whirled just like Eck figured it would and come helling back up that lane like a scared hen-hawk. It probably never even seen the rope at all. Mrs Freeman was watching from where she had run up onto the porch. She said that when it hit that rope, it looked just like one of these here great big Christmas pinwheels. But the one you bought got clean away, didn't it?"

"That's right," Eck said. "I never had time to see which way the other one went."

"Give him to me, paw," the little boy said.

"You wait till we catch him," Eck said. "We'll see about it then."

That afternoon Ratliff sat in the halted buckboard in front of Bookwright's gate. Bookwright stood in the road beside it. "You were wrong," Bookwright said. "He come back."

"He come back," Ratliff said. "I misjudged his . . . nerve aint the word I want, and sholy lack of it aint. But I wasn't wrong."

"Nonsense," Bookwright said. "He was gone all day yesterday. Nobody saw him going to town or coming back, but that's bound to be where he was at. Aint no man, I dont care if his name is Snopes, going to let his own blood kin rot in jail."

"He wont be in jail long. Court is next month, and after they send him to Parchman, he can stay out doors again. He will even go back to farming, plowing. Of course it wont be his cotton, but then he never did make enough out of his own cotton to quite pay him for staying alive."

"Nonsense," Bookwright said. "I dont believe it. Flem aint going to let him go to the penitentiary."

"Yes," Ratliff said. "Because Flem Snopes has got to cancel

all them loose-flying notes that turns up here and there every now and then. He's going to discharge at least some of them notes for good and all." They looked at one another—Ratliff grave and easy in the blue shirt, Bookwright sober too, black-browed, intent.

"I thought you said you and him burned them notes."

"I said we burned two notes that Mink Snopes gave me. Do you think that any Snopes is going to put all of anything on one piece of paper that can be destroyed by one match? Do you think there is any Snopes that dont know that?"

"Oh," Bookwright said. "Hah," he said, with no mirth. "I reckon you gave Henry Armstid back his five dollars too." Then Ratliff looked away. His face changed—something fleeting, quizzical, but not smiling, his eyes did not smile; it was gone.

"I could have," he said. "But I didn't. I might have if I could just been sho he would buy something this time that would sho enough kill him, like Mrs Littlejohn said. Besides, I wasn't protecting a Snopes from Snopeses; I wasn't even protecting a people from a Snopes. I was protecting something that wasn't even a people, that wasn't nothing but something that dont want nothing but to walk and feel the sun and wouldn't know how to hurt no man even if it would and wouldn't want to even if it could, just like I wouldn't stand by and see you steal a meat-bone from a dog. I never made them Snopeses and I never made the folks that cant wait to bare their backsides to them. I could do more, but I wont. I wont, I tell you!"

"All right," Bookwright said. "Hook your drag up; it aint nothing but a hill. I said it's all right."

2.

The two actions of Armstid pl. vs. Snopes, and Tull pl. vs. Eckrum Snopes (and anyone else named Snopes or Varner either which Tull's irate wife could contrive to involve, as the village well knew) were accorded a change of venue by mutual agreement and arrangement among the litigants. Three of the parties did, that is, because Flem Snopes flatly refused to recognise the existence of the suit against himself, stating once and without heat and first turning his head slightly aside to spit, "They wasn't none of my horses," then fell to whittling again while the baffled and helpless bailiff stood before the tilted chair with the papers he was trying to serve.

"What a opportunity for that Snopes family lawyer this would a been," Ratliff said when told about it. "What's his name? that quick-fatherer, the Moses with his mouth full of mottoes and his coat-tail full of them already halfgrown retro-active sons? I dont understand yet how a man that has to spend as much time as I do being constantly reminded of them folks, still cant keep the names straight. I.O. That he never had time to wait. This here would be probably the one tried case in his whole legal existence where he wouldn't be bothered with no narrow-ideaed client trying to make him stop talking, and the squire presiding himself would be the only man in company with authority to tell him to shut up."

So neither did the Varner surrey nor Ratliff's buckboard make one among the wagons, the buggies, and the saddled horses and mules which moved out of the village on that May Saturday morning, to converge upon Whiteleaf store eight miles away, coming not only from Frenchman's Bend but from other directions too since by that time, what Ratliff had called 'that Texas sickness', that spotted corruption of frantic and uncatchable horses, had spread as far as twenty and thirty miles. So by the time the Frenchman's Bend people began to arrive, there were two dozen wagons, the teams reversed and eased of harness and tied to the rear wheels in order to pass the day, and twice that many saddled animals already standing about the locust grove beside the store and the site of the hearing had already been transferred from the store to an ad-jacent shed where in the fall cotton would be stored. But by nine oclock it was seen that even the shed would not hold them all, so the palladium was moved again, from the shed to the grove itself. The horses and mules and wagons were cleared from it; the single chair, the gnawed table bearing a thick bible which had the appearance of loving and constant use of a piece of old and perfectly-kept machinery and an al-manac and a copy of Mississippi Reports dated 1881 and bear-ing along its opening edge a single thread-thin line of soilure as if during all the time of his possession its owner (or user)

had opened it at only one page though that quite often, were
fetched from the shed to the grove; a wagon and four
men were dispatched and returned presently from the church
a mile away with four wooden pews for the litigants and
their clansmen and witnesses; behind these in turn the spectators stood—the men, the women, the children, sober, attentive, and neat, not in their Sunday clothes to be sure, but in
the clean working garments donned that morning for the
Saturday's diversion of sitting about the country stores or
trips into the county seat, and in which they would return to
the field on Monday morning and would wear all that week
until Friday night came round again. The Justice of the Peace
was a neat, small, plump old man resembling a tender carica-
ture of all grandfathers who ever breathed, in a beautifully
laundered though collarless white shirt with immaculate
starch-gleaming cuffs and bosom, and steel-framed spectacles
and neat, faintly curling white hair. He sat behind the table
and looked at them—at the gray woman in the gray sunbonnet and dress, her clasped and motionless hands on her lap
resembling a gnarl of pallid and drowned roots from a
drained swamp; at Tull in his faded but absolutely clean shirt
and the overalls which his womenfolks not only kept immac-
ulately washed but starched and ironed also, and not creased
through the legs but flat across them from seam to seam, so
that on each Saturday morning they resembled the short
pants of a small boy, and the sedate and innocent blue of his
eyes above the month-old cornsilk beard which concealed
most of his abraded face and which gave him an air of incredible and paradoxical dissoluteness, not as though at last and
without warning he had appeared in the sight of his fellow-
men in his true character, but as if an old Italian portrait of a
child saint had been defaced by a vicious and idle boy; at Mrs
Tull, a strong, full-bosomed though slightly dumpy woman
with an expression of grim and seething outrage which the
elapsed four weeks had apparently neither increased nor diminished but had merely set, an outrage which curiously and
almost at once began to give the impression of being directed
not at any Snopes or at any other man in particular but at all
men, all males, and of which Tull himself was not at all the
victim but the subject, who sat on one side of her husband

while the biggest of the four daughters sat on the other as
if they (or Mrs Tull at least) were not so much convinced that
Tull might leap up and flee, as determined that he would not;
and at Eck and the little boy, identical save for size, and
Lump the clerk in a gray cap which someone actually recognised as being the one which Flem Snopes had worn when
he went to Texas last year, who between spells of rapid blinking would sit staring at the Justice with the lidless intensity
of a rat—and into the lens-distorted and irisless old-man's
eyes of the Justice there grew an expression not only of
amazement and bewilderment but, as in Ratliff's eyes while
he stood on the store gallery four weeks ago, something very
like terror.

"This—" he said. "I didn't expect—I didn't look to see——.
I'm going to pray," he said. "I aint going to pray aloud. But I
hope—" He looked at them. "I wish. . . . Maybe some of
you all anyway had better do the same." He bowed his head.
They watched him, quiet and grave, while he sat motionless
behind the table, the light morning wind moving faintly in
his thin hair and the shadow-stipple of windy leaves gliding
and flowing across the starched bulge of bosom and the
gleaming bone-buttoned cuffs, as rigid and almost as large as
sections of six-inch stovepipe, at his joined hands. He raised
his head. "Armstid against Snopes," he said. Mrs Armstid
spoke. She did not move, she looked at nothing, her hands
clasped in her lap, speaking in that flat, toneless and hopeless
voice:

"That Texas man said——"

"Wait," the Justice said. He looked about at the faces, the
blurred eyes fleeing behind the thick lenses. "Where is the
defendant? I dont see him."

"He wouldn't come," the bailiff said.

"Wouldn't come?" the Justice said. "Didn't you serve the
papers on him?"

"He wouldn't take them," the bailiff said. "He said—"

"Then he is in contempt!" the Justice cried.

"What for?" Lump Snopes said. "Aint nobody proved yet
they was his horses." The Justice looked at him.

"Are you representing the defendant?" he said. Snopes
blinked at him for a moment.

"What's that mean?" he said. "That you aim for me to pay whatever fine you think you can clap onto him?"

"So he refuses to defend himself," the Justice said. "Dont he know that I can find against him for that reason, even if pure justice and decency aint enough?"

"It'll be pure something," Snopes said. "It dont take no mind-reader to see how your mind is——"

"Shut up, Snopes," the bailiff said. "If you aint in this case, you keep out of it." He turned back to the Justice. "What you want me to do: go over to the Bend and fetch Snopes here anyway? I reckon I can do it."

"No," the Justice said. "Wait." He looked about at the sober faces again with that bafflement, that dread. "Does anybody here know for sho who them horses belonged to? Anybody?" They looked back at him, sober, attentive—at the neat immaculate old man sitting with his hands locked together on the table before him to still the trembling. "All right, Mrs Armstid," he said. "Tell the court what happened." She told it, unmoving, in the flat, inflectionless voice, looking at nothing, while they listened quietly, coming to the end and ceasing without even any fall of voice, as though the tale mattered nothing and came to nothing. The Justice was looking down at his hands. When she ceased, he looked up at her. "But you haven't showed yet that Snopes owned the horses. The one you want to sue is that Texas man. And he's gone. If you got a judgment against him, you couldn't collect the money. Dont you see?"

"Mr Snopes brought him here," Mrs Armstid said. "Likely that Texas man wouldn't have knowed where Frenchman's Bend was if Mr Snopes hadn't showed him."

"But it was the Texas man that sold the horses and collected the money for them." The Justice looked about again at the faces. "Is that right? You, Bookwright, is that what happened?"

"Yes," Bookwright said. The Justice looked at Mrs Armstid again, with that pity and grief. As the morning increased the wind had risen, so that from time to time gusts of it ran through the branches overhead, bringing a faint snow of petals, prematurely bloomed as the spring itself had condensed with spendthrift speed after the hard winter, and the heavy and drowsing scent of them, about the motionless heads.

"He give Mr Snopes Henry's money. He said Henry hadn't bought no horse. He said I could get the money from Mr Snopes tomorrow."

"And you have witnesses that saw and heard him?"

"Yes, sir. The other men that was there saw him give Mr Snopes the money and say that I could get it——"

"And you asked Snopes for the money?"

"Yes, sir. He said that Texas man taken it away with him when he left. But I would. . . ." She ceased again, perhaps looking down at her hands also. Certainly she was not looking at anyone.

"Yes?" the Justice said. "You would what?"

"I would know them five dollars. I earned them myself, weaving at night after Henry and the chaps was asleep. Some of the ladies in Jefferson would save up string and such and give it to me and I would weave things and sell them. I earned that money a little at a time and I would know it when I saw it because I would take the can outen the chimney and count it now and then while it was making up to enough to buy my chaps some shoes for next winter. I would know it if I was to see it again. If Mr Snopes would just let——"

"Suppose there was somebody seen Flem give that money back to that Texas fellow," Lump Snopes said suddenly.

"Did anybody here see that?" the Justice said.

"Yes," Snopes said, harshly and violently. "Eck here did." He looked at Eck. "Go on. Tell him." The Justice looked at Eck; the four Tull girls turned their heads as one head and looked at him, and Mrs Tull leaned forward to look past her husband, her face cold, furious, and contemptuous, and those standing shifted to look past one another's heads at Eck sitting motionless on the bench.

"Did you see Snopes give Armstid's money back to the Texas man, Eck?" the Justice said. Still Eck did not answer nor move. Lump Snopes made a gross violent sound through the side of his mouth.

"By God, I aint afraid to say it if Eck is. I seen him do it."

"Will you swear that as testimony?" Snopes looked at the Justice. He did not blink now.

"So you wont take my word," he said.

"I want the truth," the Justice said. "If I cant find that, I got to have sworn evidence of what I will have to accept as truth." He lifted the bible from the two other books.

"All right," the bailiff said. "Step up here." Snopes rose from the bench and approached. They watched him, though now there was no shifting nor craning, no movement at all among the faces, the still eyes. Snopes at the table looked back at them once, his gaze traversing swiftly the crescent-shaped rank; he looked at the Justice again. The bailiff grasped the bible, though the Justice did not release it yet.

"You are ready to swear you saw Snopes give that Texas man back the money he took from Henry Armstid for that horse?" he said.

"I said I was, didn't I?" Snopes said. The Justice released the bible.

"Swear him," he said.

"Put your left hand on the Book raise your right hand you solemnly swear and affirm—" the bailiff said rapidly. But Snopes had already done so, his left hand clapped onto the extended bible and the other hand raised and his head turned away as once more his gaze went rapidly along the circle of expressionless and intent faces, saying in that harsh and snarling voice:

"Yes. I saw Flem Snopes give back to that Texas man whatever money Henry Armstid or anybody else thinks Henry Armstid or anybody else paid Flem for any of them horses. Does that suit you?"

"Yes," the Justice said. Then there was no movement, no sound anywhere among them. The bailiff placed the bible quietly on the table beside the Justice's locked hands, and there was no movement save the flow and recover of the windy shadows and the drift of the locust petals. Then Mrs Armstid rose; she stood once more (or still) looking at nothing, her hands clasped across her middle.

"I reckon I can go now, cant I?" she said.

"Yes," the Justice said, rousing. "Unless you would like—"

"I better get started," she said. "It's a right far piece." She had not come in the wagon, but on one of the gaunt and underfed mules. One of the men followed her across the grove and untied the mule for her and led it up to a wagon, from one hub of which she mounted. Then they looked at the Justice again. He sat behind the table, his hands still joined before him, though his head was not bowed now. Yet he did not move until the bailiff leaned and spoke to him, when he roused, came suddenly awake without starting, as an old man wakes from an old man's light sleep. He removed his hands from the table and, looking down, he spoke exactly as if he were reading from a paper:

"Tull against Snopes. Assault and—"

"Yes!" Mrs Tull said. "I'm going to say a word before you start." She leaned, looking past Tull at Lump Snopes again. "If you think you are going to lie and perjure Flem and Eck Snopes out of—"

"Now, mamma," Tull said. Now she spoke to Tull, without changing her position or her tone or even any break or pause in her speech:

"Dont you say hush to me! You'll let Eck Snopes or Flem Snopes or that whole Varner tribe snatch you out of the wagon and beat you half to death against a wooden bridge. But when it comes to suing them for your just rights and a punishment, oh no. Because that wouldn't be neighborly. What's neighborly got to do with you lying flat on your back in the middle of planting time while we pick splinters out of your face?" By this time the bailiff was shouting,

"Order! Order! This here's a law court!" Mrs Tull ceased. She sat back, breathing hard, staring at the Justice, who sat and spoke again as if he were reading aloud:

"—assault and battery on the person of Vernon Tull, through the agency and instrument of one horse, unnamed, belonging to Eckrum Snopes. Evidence of physical detriment and suffering, defendant himself. Witnesses, Mrs Tull and daughters—"

"Eck Snopes saw it too," Mrs Tull said, though with less violence now. "He was there. He got there in plenty of time to see it. Let him deny it. Let him look me in the face and deny it if he—"

"If you please, ma'am," the Justice said. He said it so quietly that Mrs Tull hushed and became quite calm, almost a rational and composed being. "The injury to your husband aint disputed. And the agency of the horse aint disputed. The law says that when a man owns a creature which he knows to be dangerous and if that creature is restrained and restricted from the public commons by a pen or enclosure capable of restraining and restricting it, if a man enter that pen or enclosure, whether he knows the creature in it is dangerous or not dangerous, then that man has committed trespass and the owner of that creature is not liable. But if that creature known to him to be dangerous ceases to be restrained by that suitable pen or enclosure, either by accident or design and either with or without the owner's knowledge, then that owner is liable. That's the law. All necessary now is to establish first, the ownership of the horse, and second, that the horse was a dangerous creature within the definition of the law as provided."

"Hah," Mrs Tull said. She said it exactly as Bookwright would have. "Dangerous. Ask Vernon Tull. Ask Henry Armstid if them things was pets."

"If you please, ma'am," the Justice said. He was looking at Eck. "What is the defendant's position? Denial of ownership?"

"What?" Eck said.

"Was that your horse that ran over Mr Tull?"

"Yes," Eck said. "It was mine. How much do I have to p——"

"Hah," Mrs Tull said again. "Denial of ownership. When there were at least forty men—fools too, or they wouldn't have been there. But even a fool's word is good about what he saw and heard.—at least forty men heard that Texas murderer give that horse to Eck Snopes. Not sell it to him, mind; give it to him."

"What?" the Justice said. "Gave it to him?"

"Yes," Eck said. "He give it to me. I'm sorry Tull happened to be using that bridge too at the same time. How much do I——"

"Wait," the Justice said. "What did you give him? a note? a swap of some kind?"

"No," Eck said. "He just pointed to it in the lot and told me it belonged to me."

"And he didn't give you a bill of sale or a deed or anything in writing?"

"I reckon he never had time," Eck said. "And after Lon Quick forgot and left that gate open, never nobody had time to do no writing even if we had a thought of it."

"What's all this?" Mrs Tull said. "Eck Snopes has just told you he owned that horse. And if you wont take his word, there were forty men standing at that gate all day long doing nothing, that heard that murdering card-playing whiskey-drinking antichrist—" This time the Justice raised one hand, in its enormous pristine cuff, toward her. He did not look at her.

"Wait," he said. "Then what did he do?" he said to Eck. "Just lead the horse up and put the rope in your hand?"

"No," Eck said. "Him nor nobody else never got no ropes on none of them. He just pointed to the horse in the lot and said it was mine and auctioned off the rest of them and got into the buggy and said goodbye and druv off. And we got our ropes and went into the lot, only Lon Quick forgot to shut the gate. I'm sorry it made Tull's mules snatch him outen the wagon. How much do I owe him?" Then he stopped, because the Justice was no longer looking at him and, as he realised a moment later, no longer listening either. Instead, he was sitting back in the chair, actually leaning back in it for the first time, his head bent slightly and his hands resting on the table before him, the fingers lightly overlapped. They watched him quietly for almost a half-minute before anyone realised that he was looking quietly and steadily at Mrs Tull.

"Well, Mrs Tull," he said, "by your own testimony, Eck never owned that horse."

"What?" Mrs Tull said. It was not loud at all. "What did you say?"

"In the law, ownership cant be conferred or invested by word-of-mouth. It must be established either by recorded or authentic document, or by possession or occupation. By your testimony and his both, he never gave that Texas man any-thing in exchange for that horse, and by his testimony the Texas man never gave him any paper to prove he owned it, and by his testimony and by what I know myself from these last four weeks, nobody yet has ever laid hand or rope either on any one of them. So that horse never came into Eck's pos-session at all. That Texas man could have given that same horse to a dozen other men standing around that gate that day, without even needing to tell Eck he had done it; and Eck himself could have transferred all his title and equity in it to Mr Tull right there while Mr Tull was lying unconscious on that bridge just by thinking it to himself, and Mr Tull's title would be just as legal as Eck's."

"So I get nothing," Mrs Tull said. Her voice was still calm, quiet, though probably no one but Tull realised that it was too calm and quiet. "My team is made to run away by a wild spotted mad-dog, my wagon is wrecked; my husband is jerked out of it and knocked unconscious and unable to work for a whole week with less than half of our seed in the ground, and I get nothing."

"Wait," the Justice said. "The law—"

"The law," Mrs Tull said. She stood suddenly up—a short, broad, strong woman, balanced on the balls of her planted feet.

"Now, mamma," Tull said.

"Yes, ma'am," the Justice said. "Your damages are fixed by statute. The law says that when a suit for damages is brought against the owner of an animal which has committed damage or injury, if the owner of the animal either cant or wont assume liability, the injured or damaged party shall find recompense in the body of the animal. And since Eck Snopes never owned that horse at all, and since you just heard a case here this morning that failed to prove that Flem Snopes had any equity in any of them, that horse still belongs to that Texas man. Or did belong. Because now that horse that made your team run away and snatch your husband out of the wagon, belongs to you and Mr Tull."

"Now, mamma!" Tull said. He rose quickly. But Mrs Tull was still quiet, only quite rigid and breathing hard, until Tull spoke. Then she turned on him, not screaming: shouting; presently the bailiff was banging the table-top with his hand-polished hickory cane and roaring "Order! Order!" while the neat old man, thrust backward in his chair as though about to dodge and trembling with an old man's palsy, looked on with amazed unbelief.

"The horse!" Mrs Tull shouted. "We see it for five seconds, while it is climbing into the wagon with us and then out

again. Then it's gone, God dont know where and thank the
Lord He dont! And the mules gone with it and the wagon
wrecked and you laying there on the bridge with your face
full of kindling-wood and bleeding like a hog and dead for all
we knew. And he gives us the horse! Dont you hush me! Get
on to that wagon, fool that would sit there behind a pair of
young mules with the reins tied around his wrist! Get on to
that wagon, all of you!"

"I cant stand no more!" the old Justice cried. "I wont! This
court's adjourned! Adjourned!"

There was another trial then. It began on the following
Monday and most of those same faces watched it too, in the
county court house in Jefferson when the prisoner entered between two officers and looking hardly larger than a child, in a
suit of brand-new overalls, thin, almost frail-looking, the sombre violent face thin in repose and pallid from the eight
months in jail, and was arraigned and then plead by the counsel appointed him by the Court—a young man graduated
only last June from the State University's law school and admitted to the Bar, who did what he could and overdid what
he could not, zealous and, for all practical purposes and results, ignored, having exhausted all his challenges before the
State had made one and in despite of which seeing himself
faced by an authenticated jury in almost record time as if the
State, the public, all rational mankind, possessed an inexhaustible pool of interchangeable faces and names all cradling
one identical conviction and intention, so that his very challenges could have been discharged for him by the janitor who
opened the court-room, by merely counting off the first members of the panel corresponding to that number. And, if the
defendant's counsel had had any detachment and objectivity
left at all by then, he probably realised soon that it was not his
client but himself who was embattled with that jury. Because
his client was paying no attention whatever to what was
going on. He did not seem to be interested in watching and
listening to it as someone else's trial. He sat where they had
placed him, manacled to one of the officers, small, in the new
iron-hard board-stiff overalls, the back of his head toward the
Bar and what was going on there and his upper body shifting
constantly until they realised that he was trying to watch the

rear of the room, the doors and who entered them. He had to be spoken to twice before he stood up and plead and continued to stand, his back completely turned to the Court now, his face sombre, thin, curiously urgent and quite calm and with something else in it which was not even just hope but was actual faith, looking not at his wife who sat on the bench just behind him but out into the crowded room, among the ranked and intent faces some of which, most of which, he knew, until the officer he was handcuffed to pulled him down again. And he sat that way through the rest of the brief and record day-and-a-quarter of his trial, the small, neatly-combed, vicious and ironlike incorrigible head turning and craning constantly to see backward past the bulk of the two officers, watching the entrance while his attorney did what he could, talked himself frantic and at last voiceless before the grave impassivity of the jury which resembled a conclave of grown men self-delegated with the necessity (though for a definitely specified and limited time) of listening to prattle of a licensed child. And still the client listened to none of it, watching constantly the rear of the room while toward the end of the first day the faith went out of his face, leaving only the hope, and at the beginning of the second day the hope was gone too and there was only the urgency, the grim and intractable sombreness, while still he watched the door. The State finished in mid-morning of the second day. The jury was out twenty minutes and returned with a ballot of murder in the second degree; the prisoner stood again and was sentenced by the Court to be transported to the State Penal Farm and there remain until he died. But he was not listening to that either; he had not only turned his back to the Court to look out into the crowded room, he was speaking himself even before the Judge had ceased, continuing to speak even while the Judge hammered the desk with his gavel and the two officers and three bailiffs converged upon the prisoner as he struggled, flinging them back and for a short time actually successful, staring out into the room. "Flem Snopes!" he said. "Flem Snopes! Is Flem Snopes in this room? Tell that son of a bitch——"

Chapter Two

I.

RATLIFF STOPPED the buckboard at Bookwright's gate. The house was dark, but at once three or four of Bookwright's dogs came yelling out from beneath it or behind it. Armstid swung his leg stiffly out and prepared to get down. "Wait," Ratliff said. "I'll go get him."

"I can walk," Armstid said harshly.

"Sholy," Ratliff said. "Besides, them dogs knows me."

"They'll know me, after the first one runs at me once," Armstid said.

"Sholy," Ratliff said. He was already out of the buckboard. "You wait here and hold the team." Armstid swung his leg back into the buckboard, not invisible even in the moonless August darkness, but on the contrary, because of his faded overalls, quite distinct against the buckboard's dark upholstery; it was only his features beneath his hatbrim which could not be distinguished. Ratliff handed him the reins and turned past the metal mailbox on its post in the starlight, toward the gate beyond it and the mellow uproar of the dogs. When he was through the gate he could see them—a yelling clump of blackness against the slightly paler earth which broke and spread fanwise before him, braced, yelling, holding him bayed—three black-and-tan hounds whose tan the starlight had transposed to black too so that, not quite invisible but almost and without detail, they might have been the three intact carbons of burned newspaper-sheets standing upright from the earth, yelling at him. He shouted at them. They should have recognised him already by smell. When he shouted, he knew that they already had, because for perhaps a second they hushed, then as he moved forward they retreated before him, keeping the same distance, baying. Then he saw Bookwright, pale too in overalls against the black house. When Bookwright shouted at the hounds, they did hush.

"Git," he said. "Shut up and git." He approached, becoming black in his turn against the paler earth, to where Ratliff waited. "Where's Henry?" he said.

1044

"In the buggy," Ratliff said. He turned back toward the gate.

"Wait," Bookwright said. Ratliff stopped. The other came up beside him. They looked at one another, each face invisible to the other. "You aint let him persuade you into this, have you?" Bookwright said. "Between having to remember them five dollars every time he looks at his wife maybe, and that broke leg, and that horse he bought from Flem Snopes with it he aint even seen again, he's plumb crazy now. Not that he had far to go. You aint just let him persuade you?"

"I dont think so," Ratliff said. "I know I aint," he said. "There's something there. I've always knowed it. Just like Will Varner knows there is something there. If there wasn't, he wouldn't never bought it. And he wouldn't a kept it, selling the balance of it off and still keeping that old house, paying taxes on it when he could a got something for it, setting there in that flour-barrel chair to watch it and claiming he did it because it rested him to set there where somebody had gone to all that work and expense just to build something to sleep and eat and lay with his wife in. And I knowed it for sho when Flem Snopes took it. When he had Will Varner just where he wanted him, and then he sold out to Will by taking that old house and them ten acres that wouldn't hardly raise goats. And I went with Henry last night. I saw it too. You dont have to come in, if you feel uncertain. I'd rather you wouldn't."

"All right," Bookwright said. He moved on. "That's all I wanted to know." They returned to the buckboard. Henry moved to the middle of the seat and they got in. "Dont let me crowd your leg," Bookwright said.

"There aint anything wrong with my leg," Armstid said in that harsh voice. "I can walk as far as you or any man any day."

"Sholy," Ratliff said quickly, taking the reins. "Henry's leg is all right now. You cant even notice it."

"Let's get on," Bookwright said. "Wont nobody have to walk for a while, if that team can."

"It's shorter through the Bend," Ratliff said. "But we better not go that way."

"Let them see," Armstid said. "If anybody here is afraid, I dont need no help. I can—"

"Sholy," Ratliff said. "If folks sees us, we might have too much help. That's what we want to dodge." Armstid hushed. He said no more from then on, sitting between them in an immobility which was almost like a temperature, thinner, as though it had not been the sickness (after being in bed about a month, he had got up one day and broken the leg again; nobody ever knew how, what he had been doing, trying to do, because he never talked about it) but impotence and fury which had wasted him.

Ratliff asked neither advice nor directions; there was little anybody could have told him about the back roads and lanes of that or any of the other country he travelled. They passed nobody; the dark and sleeping land was empty, the scattered and remote homesteads indicated only by the occasional baying of dogs. The lanes he followed ran pale between the broad spread of fields felt rather than seen, where the corn was beginning to fire and the cotton to bloom, then into tunnels of trees rising and feathered lushly with summer's full leaf against the sky of August heavy and thick with stars. Then they were in the old lane which for years now had been marked by nothing save the prints of Varner's old white horse and, for a brief time, by the wheels of the parasol-topped runabout—the old scar almost healed now, where thirty years ago a courier (perhaps a neighbor's slave flogging a mule taken out of the plow) had galloped with the news of Sumter, where perhaps the barouche had moved, the women swaying and pliant in hooped crinoline beneath parasols, the men in broadcloth riding the good horses at the wheels, talking about it, where the son and perhaps the master himself had ridden into Jefferson with his pistols and his portmanteau and a body-servant on the spare horse behind, talking of regiments and victory; where the Federal patrols had ridden the land peopled by women and negro slaves about the time of the battle of Jefferson.

There was nothing to show of that now. There was hardly a road; where the sand darkened into the branch and then rose again, there was no trace left of the bridge. Now the scar ran straight as a plumb-line along a shaggy hedgerow of spaced cedars decreed there by the same nameless architect who had planned and built the house for its nameless master, now two and three feet thick, the boughs interlocked and massed now. Ratliff turned in among them. He seemed to know exactly where he was going. But then Bookwright remembered that he had been here last night.

Armstid didn't wait for them. Ratliff tied the team hurriedly and they overtook him—a shadow, still faintly visible because of his overalls faded pale with washing, hurrying stiffly on through the undergrowth. The earth yawned black before them, a long gash: a ravine, a ditch. Bookwright remembered that Armstid had been here for more than one night, nevertheless the limping shadow seemed about to hurl itself into the black abyss. "You better help him," Bookwright said. "He's going to break—"

"Hush!" Ratliff hissed. "The garden is just up the hill yonder."

"—break that leg again," Bookwright said, quieter now. "Then we'll be into it."

"He'll be all right," Ratliff whispered. "It's been this way every night. Just dont push him too close. But dont let him get too far ahead. Once last night while we were laying there I had to hold him." They went on, just behind the figure which moved now in absolute silence and with surprising speed. They were in a ravine massed with honeysuckle and floored with dry sand in which they could hear the terrific laboring of the lame leg. Yet still they could hardly keep up with him. After about two hundred yards Armstid turned to climb up out of the ravine. Ratliff followed him. "Careful now," he whispered back to Bookwright. "We're right at it." But Bookwright was watching Armstid. He wont never make it, he thought. He wont never climb that bank. But the other did it, dragging the stiffened and once-fragile and hence maybe twice-fragile leg at the almost sheer slope, silent and unaided and emanating that trigger-like readiness to repudiate assistance and to deny that he might possibly need it. Then on hands and knees Bookwright was crawling after the others in a path through a mass of man-tall briers and weeds and persimmon shoots, overtaking them where they lay flat at the edge of a vague slope which rose to the shaggy crest on which, among oaks, the shell of the tremendous house stood where it had been decreed too by the imported and nameless architect and its master whose anonymous dust lay with that of his blood and of the progenitors of saxophone players in Harlem honkytonks beneath the weathered and illegible headstones on another knoll four hundred yards away, with its broken roof and topless chimneys and one high rectangle of window through which he could see the stars in the opposite sky. The slope had probably been a rose-garden. None of them knew or cared, just as they, who had seen it, walked past and looked at it perhaps a hundred times, did not know that the fallen pediment in the middle of the slope had once been a sundial. Ratliff reached across Armstid's body and gripped his arm, then, above the sound of their panting breath, Bookwright heard the steady and unhurried sigh of a shovel and the measured thud of spaded earth somewhere on the slope above them. "There!" Ratliff whispered.

"I hear somebody digging," Bookwright whispered. "How do I know it's Flem Snopes?"

"Hasn't Henry been laying here every night since ten days ago, listening to him? Wasn't I right here last night with Henry myself, listening to him? Didn't we lay right here until he quit and left and then we crawled up there and found every place where he had dug and then filled the hole back up and smoothed the dirt to hide it?"

"All right," Bookwright whispered. "You and Armstid have been watching somebody digging. But how do I know it is Flem Snopes?"

"All right," Armstid said, with a cold restrained violence, almost aloud; both of them could feel him trembling where he lay between them, jerking and shaking through his gaunt and wasted body like a leashed dog. "It aint Flem Snopes then. Go on back home."

"Hush!" Ratliff hissed. Armstid had turned, looking toward Bookwright. His face was not a foot from Bookwright's, the features more indistinguishable than ever now.

"Go on," he said. "Go on back home."

"Hush, Henry!" Ratliff whispered. "He's going to hear you!" But Armstid had already turned his head, glaring up the dark slope again, shaking and trembling between them, cursing in a dry whisper. "If you knowed it was Flem, would you believe then?" Ratliff whispered across Armstid's body. Bookwright didn't answer. He lay there too, with the others, while Armstid's thin body shook and jerked beside him, listening to the steady and unhurried whisper of the shovel and to Armstid's dry and furious cursing. Then the sound of the shovel ceased. For a moment nobody moved. Then Armstid said,

"He's done found it!" He surged suddenly and violently between them. Bookwright heard or felt Ratliff grasp him.

"Stop!" Ratliff whispered. "Stop! Help hold him, Odum!" Bookwright grasped Armstid's other arm. Between them they held the furious body until Armstid ceased and lay again between them, rigid, glaring, cursing in that dry whisper. His arms felt no larger than sticks; the strength in them was unbelievable. "He aint found it yet!" Ratliff whispered at him. "He just knows it's there somewhere; maybe he found a paper somewhere in the house telling where it is. But he's got to hunt to find it same as we will. He knows it's somewhere in that garden, but he's got to hunt to find it same as us. Aint we been watching him hunting for it?" Bookwright could hear both the voices now speaking in hissing whispers, the one cursing, the other cajoling and reasoning while the owners of them glared as one up the starlit slope. Now Ratliff was speaking to him. "You dont believe it's Flem," he said. "All right. Just watch." They lay in the weeds; they were all holding their breaths now, Bookwright too. Then he saw the digger—a shadow, a thicker darkness, moving against the slope, mounting it. "Watch," Ratliff whispered. Bookwright could hear him and Armstid where they lay glaring up the slope, breathing in hissing exhalations, in passionate and dying sighs. Then Bookwright saw the white shirt; an instant later the figure came into complete relief against the sky as if it had paused for a moment on the crest of the slope. Then it was gone. "There!" Ratliff whispered. "Wasn't that Flem Snopes? Do you believe now?" Bookwright drew a long breath and let it out again. He was still holding Armstid's arm. He had forgotten about it. Now he felt it again under his hand like a taut steel cable vibrating.

"It's Flem," he said.

"Certainly it's Flem," Ratliff said. "Now all we got to do is find out tomorrow night where it's at and—"

"Tomorrow night, hell!" Armstid said. He surged forward again, attempting to rise. "Let's get up there now and find it. That's what we got to do. Before he—" They both held him again while Ratliff argued with him, sibilant and expostulant. They held him flat on the ground again at last, cursing.

"We got to find where it is first," Ratliff panted. "We got to find exactly where it is the first time. We aint got time just to hunt. We got to find it the first night because we cant afford to leave no marks for him to find when he comes back. Cant you see that? that we aint going to have but one chance to find it because we dont dare be caught looking?"

"What we going to do?" Bookwright said.

"Ha," Armstid said. "Ha." It was harsh, furious, restrained. There was no mirth in it. "What *we* going to do. I thought you had gone back home."

"Shut up, Henry," Ratliff said. He rose to his knees, though he still held Armstid's arm. "We agreed to take Odum in with us. At least let's wait till we find that money before we start squabbling over it."

"Suppose it aint nothing but Confederate money," Bookwright said.

"All right," Ratliff said. "What do you reckon that old Frenchman did with all the money he had before there was any such thing as Confederate money? Besides, a good deal of it was probably silver spoons and jewelry."

"You all can have the silver spoons and jewelry," Bookwright said. "I'll take my share in money."

"So you believe now, do you?" Ratliff said. Bookwright didn't answer.

"What we going to do now?" he said.

"I'm going up the bottom tomorrow and get Uncle Dick Bolivar," Ratliff said. "I ought to get back here a little after dark. But then we cant do anything here until after midnight, after Flem has done got through hunting it."

"And finding it tomorrow night," Armstid said. "By God, I aint—" They were all standing now. Armstid began to struggle, sudden and furious, to free his arm. But Ratliff held him.

He flung both arms around Armstid and held him until he stopped struggling.

"Listen," Ratliff said. "Flem Snopes aint going to find it. If he knowed where to look, do you think he'd a been here digging for it every night for two weeks? Dont you know folks have been looking for that money for thirty years? That every foot of this whole place has been turned over at least ten times? That there aint a piece of land in this whole country that's been worked as much and as often as this here little shirt-tail of garden? Will Varner could have raised cotton or corn either in it so tall he would have to gather it on horseback just by putting the seed in the ground. The reason aint nobody found it yet is it's buried so deep aint nobody had time to dig that far in just one night and then get the hole filled back up where Will Varner wouldn't find it when he got out here at daylight to sit in that flour-barrel chair and watch. No sir. There aint but one thing in this world can keep us from finding it." Armstid had ceased. He and Bookwright both looked toward Ratliff's indistinguishable face. After a while Armstid said harshly:

"And what's that?"

"That's for Flem Snopes to find out somebody else is hunting for it," Ratliff said.

It was about midnight the next night when Ratliff turned his buckboard into the cedars again. Bookwright now rode his horse, because there were already three people in the buckboard, and again Armstid did not wait for Ratliff to tie the team. He was out as soon as the buckboard stopped; he dragged a shovel clashing and clanging out of the dog-kennel box, making no effort whatever to be quiet, and was gone limping terrifically into the darkness before Ratliff and Bookwright were on the ground. "We might as well go back home," Bookwright said.

"No, no," Ratliff said. "He aint never there this late. But we better catch up with Henry anyway." The third man in the buckboard had not moved yet. Even in the obscurity his long white beard had a faintly luminous quality, as if it had absorbed something of the starlight through which Ratliff had fetched him and were now giving it back to the dark. Ratliff and Bookwright helped him, groping and fumbling, out of

the buckboard, and carrying the other shovel and the pick and
half-carrying the old man, they hurried down into the ravine
and then ran, trying to overtake the sound of Armstid's limping progress. They never overtook him. They climbed up out
of the ditch, carrying the old man bodily now, and even before they reached the foot of the garden they could hear the
sound of Armstid's rapid shovel up the slope. They released
the old man, who sank to the ground between them, breathing in reedy gasps, and as one Ratliff and Bookwright glared
up the dark slope toward the hushed furious sound of the
shovel. "We got to make him stop until Uncle Dick can find
it," Ratliff said. They ran toward the sound, shoulder to
shoulder in the stumbling dark, among the rank weeds.
"Here, Henry!" Ratliff whispered. "Wait for Uncle Dick."
Armstid didn't pause, digging furiously, flinging the dirt and
thrusting the shovel again all in one motion. Ratliff grasped
at the shovel. Armstid jerked it free and whirled, the shovel
raised like an axe, their faces invisible to one another,
strained, spent. Ratliff had not had his clothes off in three
nights, but Armstid had probably been in his for the whole
two weeks.

"Touch it!" Armstid whispered. "Touch it!"

"Wait now," Ratliff said. "Give Uncle Dick a chance to find
where it's at."

"Get away," Armstid said. "I warn you. Get outen my
hole." He resumed his furious digging. Ratliff watched him
for a second.

"Come on," he said. He turned, running, Bookwright behind him. The old man was sitting up when they reached
him. Ratliff plunged down beside him and began to scrabble
among the weeds for the other shovel. It was the pick he
found first. He flung it away and plunged down again; he and
Bookwright found the shovel at the same time. Then they
were standing, struggling for the shovel, snatching and jerking at it, their breathing harsh and repressed, hearing even
above their own breathing the rapid sound of Armstid's
shovel up the slope. "Leave go!" Ratliff whispered. "Leave
go!" The old man, unaided now, was struggling to get up.

"Wait," he said. "Wait." Then Ratliff seemed to realise

what he was doing. He released the shovel; he almost hurled it at Bookwright.

"Take it," he said. He drew a long shuddering breath. "God," he whispered. "Just look at what even the money a man aint got yet will do to him." He stooped and jerked the old man to his feet, not with intentional roughness but merely out of his urgency. He had to hold him up for a moment.

"Wait," the old man said in a reedy, quavering voice. He was known through all that country. He had no kin, no ties, and he antedated everyone; nobody knew how old he was—a tall thin man in a filthy frock coat and no shirt beneath it and a long, perfectly white beard reaching below his waist, who lived in a mud-daubed hut in the river bottom five or six miles from any road. He made and sold nostrums and charms, and it was said of him that he ate not only frogs and snakes but bugs as well—anything that he could catch. There was nothing in his hut but his pallet bed, a few cooking vessels, a tremendous bible and a faded daguerreotype of a young man in a Confederate uniform which was believed by those who had seen it to be his son. "Wait," he said. "There air anger in the yearth. Ye must make that ere un quit a-bruisin hit."

"That's so," Ratliff said. "It wont work unless the ground is quiet. We got to make him stop." Again when they stood over him, Henry continued to dig; again when Ratliff touched him he whirled, the shovel raised, and stood cursing them in a spent whisper until the old man himself walked up and touched his shoulder.

"Ye kin dig and ye kin dig, young man," the reedy voice said. "For what's rendered to the yearth, the yearth will keep until hit's ready to reveal hit."

"That's right, Henry," Ratliff said. "We got to give Uncle Dick room to find where it is. Come on, now." Armstid lowered the shovel and came out of his pit (it was already nearly a foot deep). But he would not relinquish the shovel; he still held to it until the old man drove them back to the edge of the garden and produced from the tail-pocket of his frock coat a forked peach branch, from the butt-end of which something dangled on a length of string; Ratliff, who had seen it before at least, knew what it was—an empty cloth tobacco-sack containing a gold-filled human tooth. He held them there for ten minutes, stooping now and then to lay his hand flat on the earth. Then, with the three of them clumped and silent at his heels, he went to the weed-choked corner of the old garden and grasped the two prongs of the branch in his hands, the string and the tobacco-sack hanging plumblike and motionless before him, and stood for a time, muttering to himself.

"How do I—" Bookwright said.

"Hush," Ratliff said. The old man began to walk, the three of them following. They moved like a procession, with something at once outrageously pagan and orthodoxly funereal about them, slowly back and forth across the garden, mounting the slope gradually in overlapping traverses. Suddenly the old man stopped; Armstid, limping just behind him, bumped into him.

"There's somebody agin it," he said. He didn't look back. "It aint you," he said, and they all knew he was talking to Ratliff. "And it aint that cripple. It's that other one. That black one. Let him get offen this ground and quieten hit, or you can take me on back home."

"Go back to the edge," Ratliff said quietly over his shoulder to Bookwright. "It'll be all right then."

"But I—" Bookwright said.

"Get off the garden," Ratliff said. "It's after midnight. It'll be daylight in four hours." Bookwright returned to the foot of the slope. That is, he faded into the darkness, because they did not watch him; they were moving again now, Armstid and Ratliff close at the old man's heels. Again they began to mount the slope in traverses, passing the place where Henry had begun to dig, passing the place where Ratliff had found signs of the other man's excavation on the first night Armstid had brought him here; now Ratliff could feel Armstid beginning to tremble again. The old man stopped. They did not bump into him this time, and Ratliff did not know that Bookwright was behind him again until the old man spoke:

"Tech my elbers," he said. "Not you," he said. "You that didn't believe." When Bookwright touched them, inside the sleeves the arms—arms thin and frail and dead as rotten sticks—were jerking faintly and steadily; when the old man stopped suddenly again and Bookwright blundered into him, he felt the whole thin body straining backward. Armstid was cursing steadily in his dry whisper. "Tech the peach fork," the old man panted. "You that didn't believe." When Bookwright touched it, it was arched into a rigid down-pointing curve, the string taut as wire. Armstid made a choked sound; Bookwright felt his hand on the branch too. The branch sprang free; the old man staggered, the fork lying dead on the ground at his feet until Armstid, digging furiously with his bare hands, flung it away.

They turned as one and plunged back down the slope to where they had left the tools. They could hardly keep up with Armstid. "Dont let him get the pick," Bookwright panted. "He will kill somebody with it." But Armstid was not after the pick. He went straight to where he had left his shovel when the old man produced the forked branch and refused to start until he put the shovel down, and snatched it up and ran back up the slope. He was already digging when Ratliff and Bookwright reached him. They all dug then, frantically, hurling the dirt aside, in each other's way, the tools clashing and ringing together, while the old man stood above them behind the faint gleam of his beard in the starlight and his white brows above the two caverns from which, even if they had paused to look, they could not have told whether his eyes even watched them or not, musing, detached, without interest in their panting frenzy. Suddenly the three of them became frozen in the attitudes of digging for perhaps a second. Then they leaped into the hole together; the six hands at the same instant touched the object—a heavy solid sack of heavy cloth through which they all felt the round milled edges of coins. They struggled for it, jerking it back and forth among them, clutching it, gripping it, panting.

"Stop it!" Ratliff panted. "Stop it! Aint we all three partners alike?" But Armstid clung to it, trying to jerk it away from the others, cursing. "Let go, Odum," Ratliff said. "Let him have it." They turned it loose. Armstid clutched it to himself, stooping, glaring at them as they climbed out of the hole. "Let him keep it," Ratliff said. "Dont you know that aint all?" He turned quickly away. "Come on, Uncle Dick," he said. "Get your—" He ceased. The old man was standing motionless behind them, his head turned as if he were listening toward the ditch from which they had come. "What?" Ratliff whispered. They were all three motionless now, rigid, still stooped a little as when they had stepped away from Armstid. "Do you hear something?" Ratliff whispered. "Is somebody down there?"

"I feel four bloods lust-running," the old man said. "Hit's four sets of blood here lusting for trash." They crouched, rigid. But there was no sound.

"Well, aint it four of us here?" Bookwright whispered.

"Uncle Dick dont care nothing about money," Ratliff whispered. "If somebody's hiding there—" They were running. Armstid was the first to start, still carrying his shovel. Again they could hardly keep up with him as they went plunging down the slope.

"Kill him," Armstid said. "Watch every bush and kill him."

"No," Ratliff said. "Catch him first." When he and Bookwright reached the ditch, they could hear Armstid beating along the edge of it, making no effort whatever to be quiet, slashing at the dark undergrowth with the axe-like shovel-edge with the same fury he had dug with. But they found nothing, nobody.

"Maybe Uncle Dick never heard nothing," Bookwright said.

"Well, whatever it was is gone, anyway," Ratliff said. "Maybe it—" He ceased. He and Bookwright stared at one another; above their held breaths they heard the horse. It was in the old road beyond the cedars; it was as if it had been dropped there from the sky in full gallop. They heard it until it ceased into the sand at the branch. After a moment they heard it again on the hard ground beyond, fainter now. Then it ceased altogether. They stared at one another in the darkness, across their held breaths. Then Ratliff exhaled. "That means we got till daylight," he said. "Come on."

Twice more the old man's peach branch sprang and bent; twice more they found small bulging canvas bags solid and unmistakable even in the dark. "Now," Ratliff said, "we got a hole a piece and till daylight to do it in. Dig, boys."

When the east began to turn gray, they had found nothing

else. But digging three holes at once, as they had been doing, none of them had been able to go very deep. And the bulk of the treasure would be deep; as Ratliff had said, if it were not it would have been found ten times over during the last thirty years since there probably were not many square feet of the ten acres which comprised the old mansion-site which had not been dug into between some sunset and dawn by someone without a light, trying to dig fast and dig quiet at the same time. So at last he and Bookwright prevailed on Armstid to see a little of reason, and they desisted and filled up the holes and removed the traces of digging. Then they opened the bags in the gray light. Ratliff's and Bookwright's contained twenty-five silver dollars each. Armstid refused to tell what his contained or to let anyone see it. He crouched over it, his back toward them, cursing them when they tried to look. "All right," Ratliff said. Then a thought struck him. He looked down at Armstid. "Of course aint nobody fool enough to try to spend any of it now."

"Mine's mine," Armstid said. "I found it. I worked for it. I'm going to do any God damn thing I want to with it."

"All right," Ratliff said. "How are you going to explain it?"

"How am I—" Armstid said. Squatting, he looked up at Ratliff. They could see one another's faces now. All three of them were strained, spent with sleeplessness and fatigue.

"Yes," Ratliff said. "How are you going to explain to folks where you got it? Got twenty-five dollars all coined before 1861?" He quit looking at Armstid. He and Bookwright looked at one another quietly in the growing light. "There was somebody in the ditch, watching us," he said. "We got to buy it."

"We got to buy it quick," Bookwright said. "Tomorrow."

"You mean today," Ratliff said. Bookwright looked about him. It was as though he were waking from an anaesthetic, as if he saw the dawn, the earth, for the first time.

"That's right," he said. "It's already tomorrow now."

The old man lay under a tree beside the ditch, asleep, flat on his back, his mouth open, his beard dingy and stained in the increasing dawn; they hadn't even missed him since they really began to dig. They waked him and helped him back to the buckboard. The dog-kennel box in which Ratliff carried the sewing-machines had a padlocked door. He took a few ears of corn from the box, then he stowed his and Bookwright's bags of coins beneath the odds and ends of small and still-frozen traded objects at the back of it and locked it again.

"You put yours in here too, Henry," he said. "What we want to do now is to forget we even got them until we find the rest of it and get it out of the ground." But Armstid would not. He climbed stiffly onto the horse behind Bookwright, unaided, repudiating the aid which had not even been offered yet, clutching his bag inside the bib of his patched and faded overalls, and they departed. Ratliff fed his team and watered them at the branch; he too was on the road before the sun rose. Just before nine oclock he paid the old man his dollar fee and put him down where the five-mile path to his hut entered the river bottom, and turned the wiry and indefatiguable little horses back toward Frenchman's Bend. There was somebody hid in that ditch, he thought. We got to buy it damn quick.

Later it seemed to him that, until he reached the store, he had not actually realised himself how quick they would have to buy it. Almost as soon as he came in sight of the store, he saw the new face among the familiar ones along the gallery and recognised it—Eustace Grimm, a young tenant-farmer living ten or twelve miles away in the next county with his wife of a year, to whom Ratliff intended to sell a sewing-machine as soon as they had finished paying for the baby born two months ago; as he tied his team to one of the gallery posts and mounted the heel-gnawed steps, he thought, Maybe sleeping rests a man, but it takes staying up all night for two or three nights and being worried and scared half to death during them, to sharpen him. Because as soon as he recognised Grimm, something in him had clicked, though it would be three days before he would know what it was. He had not had his clothes off in more than sixty hours; he had had no breakfast today and what eating he had done in the last two days had been more than spotty—all of which showed in his face. But it didn't show in his voice or anywhere else, and nothing else but that showed anywhere at all. "Morning, gentlemen," he said.

"Be durn if you dont look like you aint been to bed in a

week, V.K.," Freeman said. "What you up to now? Lon Quick said his boy seen your team and buckboard hid out in the bottom below Armstid's two mornings ago, but I told him I didn't reckon them horses had done nothing to have to hide from. So it must be you."

"I reckon not," Ratliff said. "Or I'd a been caught too, same as the team. I used to think I was too smart to be caught by anybody around here. But I dont know now." He looked at Grimm, his face, except for the sleeplessness and fatigue, as bland and quizzical and impenetrable as ever. "Eustace," he said, "you're strayed."

"It looks like it," Grimm said. "I come to see—"

"He's paid his road-tax," Lump Snopes, the clerk, sitting as usual in the single chair tilted in the doorway, said. "Do you object to him using Yoknapatawpha roads too?"

"Sholy not," Ratliff said. "And if he'd a just paid his poll-tax in the right place, he could drive his wagon through the store and through Will Varner's house too." They guffawed, all except Lump.

"Maybe I will yet," Grimm said. "I come up here to see—" He ceased, looking up at Ratliff. He was perfectly motionless, squatting, a sliver of wood in one hand and his open and arrested knife in the other. Ratliff watched him.

"Couldn't you see him last night either?" he said.

"Couldn't I see who last night?" Grimm said.

"How could he have seen anybody in Frenchman's Bend last night when he wasn't in Frenchman's Bend last night?" Lump Snopes said. "Go on to the house, Eustace," he said. "Dinner's about ready. I'll be along in a few minutes."

"I got—" Grimm said.

"You got twelve miles to drive to get home tonight," Snopes said. "Go on, now." Grimm looked at him a moment longer. Then he rose and descended the steps and went on up the road. Ratliff was no longer watching him. He was looking at Snopes.

"Eustace eating with you during his visit?" he said.

"He happens to be eating at Winterbottom's where I happen to be boarding," Snopes said harshly. "Where a few other folks happens to be eating and paying board too."

"Sho now," Ratliff said. "You hadn't ought to druv him

away like that. Likely Eustace dont get to town very often to spend a day or two examining the country and setting around store."

"He'll have his feet under his own table tonight," Snopes said. "You can go down there and look at him. Then you can be in his back yard even before he opens his mouth."

"Sho now," Ratliff said, pleasant, bland, inscrutable, with his spent and sleepless face. "When you expecting Flem back?"

"Back from where?" Snopes said, in that harsh voice. "From laying up yonder in that barrel-slat hammock, taking time about with Will Varner, sleeping? Likely never."

"Him and Will and the womenfolks was in Jefferson yesterday," Freeman said. "Will said they was coming home this morning."

"Sho now," Ratliff said. "Sometimes it takes a man even longer than a year to get his new wife out of the idea that money was just made to shop with." He stood above them, leaning against a gallery post, indolent and easy, as if he had not ever even heard of haste. So Flem Snopes has been in Jefferson since yesterday, he thought. And Lump Snopes didn't want it mentioned. And Eustace Grimm—again his mind clicked; still it would be three days before he would know what had clicked, because now he believed he did know, that he saw the pattern complete—and Eustace Grimm has been here since last night, since we heard that galloping horse anyway. Maybe they was both on the horse. Maybe that's why it sounded so loud. He could see that too—Lump Snopes and Grimm on the single horse, fleeing, galloping in the dark back to Frenchman's Bend where Flem Snopes would still be absent until sometime in the early afternoon. And Lump Snopes didn't want that mentioned either, he thought, and Eustace Grimm had to be sent home to keep folks from talking to him. And Lump Snopes aint just worried and mad: he's scared. They might even have found the hidden buckboard. They probably had, and so knew at least one of those who were digging in the garden; now Snopes would not only have to get hold of his cousin first through his agent, Grimm, he might even then become involved in a bidding contest for the place against someone who (Ratliff added this without vanity) had more to outbid him with; he thought, musing, amazed as always though still impenetrable, how even a Snopes was not safe from another Snopes. Damn quick, he thought. He stood away from the post and turned back toward the steps. "I reckon I'll get along," he said. "See you boys tomorrow."

"Come home with me and take dinner," Freeman said.

"Much obliged," Ratliff said. "I ate breakfast late at Bookwright's. I want to collect a machine note from Ike McCaslin this afternoon and be back here by dark." He got into the buckboard and turned the team back down the road. Presently they had fallen into their road gait, trotting rapidly on their short legs in the traces though their forward motion was not actually fast, on until they had passed Varner's house, beyond which the road turned off to McCaslin's farm and so out of sight from the store. They entered this road galloping, the dust bursting from their shaggy backs in long spurts where the whip slashed them. He had three miles to go. After the first half-mile it would be all winding and little-used lane, but he could do it in twenty minutes. And it was only a little after noon, and it had probably been at least nine oclock before Will Varner got his wife away from the Jefferson church-ladies' auxiliary with which she was affiliated. He made it in nineteen minutes, hurtling and bouncing among the ruts ahead of his spinning dust, and slowed the now-lathered team and swung them into the Jefferson highroad a mile from the village, letting them trot for another half-mile, slowing, to cool them out gradually. But there was no sign of the surrey yet, so he went on at a walk until he reached a crest from which he could see the road for some distance ahead, and pulled out of the road into the shade of a tree and stopped. Now he had had no dinner either. But he was not quite hungry, and although after he had put the old man out and turned back toward the village this morning he had had an almost irresistible desire to sleep, that was gone too now. So he sat in the buckboard, lax now, blinking painfully against the glare of noon, while the team (he never used check-reins) nudged the lines slack and grazed over the breast-yoke. People would probably pass and see him there; some might even be going toward the village, where they might tell of seeing him. But he would take care of that when it arose. It was as though he said to himself, Now I got a little while at least when I can let down.

Then he saw the surrey. He was already in the road, going at that road-gait which the whole countryside knew, full of rapid little hooves which still did not advance a great deal faster than two big horses could have walked, before anyone in the surrey could have seen him. And he knew that they had already seen and recognised him when, still two hundred yards from it, he pulled up and sat in the buckboard, affable, bland and serene except for his worn face, until Varner stopped the surrey beside him. "Howdy, V.K.," Varner said.

"Morning," Ratliff said. He raised his hat to the two women in the back seat. "Mrs Varner. Mrs Snopes."

"Where you headed?" Varner said. "Town?" Ratliff told no lie; he attempted none, smiling a little, courteous, perhaps even a little deferential.

"I come out to meet you. I want to speak to Flem a minute." He looked at Snopes for the first time. "I'll drive you on home," he said.

"Hah," Varner said. "You had to come two miles to meet him and then turn around and go two miles back, to talk to him."

"That's right," Ratliff said. He was still looking at Snopes.

"You got better sense than to try to sell Flem Snopes anything," Varner said. "And you sholy aint fool enough by God to buy anything from him, are you?"

"I dont know," Ratliff said in that same pleasant and unchanged and impenetrable voice out of his spent and sleepless face, still looking at Snopes. "I used to think I was smart, but now I dont know. I'll bring you on home," he said. "You wont be late for dinner."

"Go on and get out," Varner said to his son-in-law. "He aint going to tell you till you do." But Snopes was already moving. He spat outward over the wheel and turned and climbed down over it, backward, broad and deliberate in the soiled light-gray trousers, the white shirt, the plaid cap; the surrey went on. Ratliff cramped the wheel and Snopes got into the buckboard beside him and he turned the buckboard and again the team fell into their tireless and familiar road-gait. But this time Ratliff reined them back until they were walking and held them so while Snopes chewed steadily beside him. They didn't look at one another again.

"That Old Frenchman place," Ratliff said. The surrey went on a hundred yards ahead, pacing its own dust, as they themselves were now doing. "What are you going to ask Eustace Grimm for it?" Snopes spat tobacco juice over the moving wheel. He did not chew fast nor did he seem to find it necessary to stop chewing in order to spit or speak either.

"He's at the store, is he?" he said.

"Aint this the day you told him to come?" Ratliff said. "How much are you going to ask him for it?" Snopes told him. Ratliff made a short sound, something like Varner's habitual ejaculation. "Do you reckon Eustace Grimm can get his hands on that much money?"

"I dont know," Snopes said. He spat over the moving wheel again. Ratliff might have said, Then you dont want to sell it; Snopes would have answered, I'll sell anything. But they did not. They didn't need to.

"All right," Ratliff said. "What are you going to ask me for it?" Snopes told him. It was the same amount. This time Ratliff used Varner's ejaculation. "I'm just talking about them ten acres where that old house is. I aint trying to buy all Yoknapatawpha County from you." They crossed the last hill; the surrey began to move faster, drawing away from them. The village was not far now. "We'll let this one count," Ratliff said. "How much do you want for that Old Frenchman place?" His team was trying to trot too, ahead of the buckboard's light weight. Ratliff held them in, the road beginning to curve to pass the schoolhouse and enter the village. The surrey had already vanished beyond the curve.

"What do you want with it?" Snopes said.

"To start a goat-ranch," Ratliff said. "How much?" Snopes spat over the moving wheel. He named the sum for the third time. Ratliff slacked off the reins and the little strong tireless team began to trot, sweeping around the last curve and past the empty schoolhouse, the village now in sight, the surrey in sight too, already beyond the store, going on. "That fellow, that teacher you had three-four years ago. Labove. Did anybody ever hear what become of him?"

A little after six that evening, in the empty and locked store,

Ratliff and Bookwright and Armstid bought the Old French-man place from Snopes. Ratliff gave a quit-claim deed to his half of the side-street lunch-room in Jefferson. Armstid gave a mortgage on his farm, including the buildings and tools and live-stock and about two miles of three-strand wire fence; Bookwright paid his third in cash. Then Snopes let them out the front door and locked it again and they stood on the empty gallery in the fading August afterglow and watched him depart up the road toward Varner's house—two of them did, that is, because Armstid had already gone ahead and got into the buckboard, where he sat motionless and waiting and emanating that patient and seething fury. "It's ours now," Ratliff said. "And now we better get on out there and watch it before somebody fetches in Uncle Dick Bolivar some night and starts hunting buried money."

They went first to Bookwright's house (he was a bachelor) and got the mattress from his bed and two quilts and his coffee-pot and skillet and another pick and shovel, then they went to Armstid's home. He had but one mattress too, but then he had a wife and five small children; besides, Ratliff, who had seen the mattress, knew that it would not even bear being lifted from the bed. So Armstid got a quilt and they helped him fill an empty feed sack with shucks for a pillow and returned to the buckboard, passing the house in the door of which his wife still stood, with four of the children huddled about her now. But she still said nothing, and when Ratliff looked back from the moving buckboard, the door was empty.

When they turned from the old road and drove up through the shaggy park to the shell of the ruined house, there was still light enough for them to see the wagon and mules stand-ing before it, and at that moment a man came out of the house itself and stopped, looking at them. It was Eustace Grimm, but Ratliff never knew if Armstid recognised him or even bothered to try to, because once more before the buck-board had even stopped Armstid was out of it and snatched the other shovel from beneath Bookwright's and Ratliff's feet and rushed with his limping and painful fury toward Grimm, who moved swiftly too and put the wagon between Armstid and himself, standing there and watching Armstid across the wagon as Armstid slashed across the wagon at him with the shovel. "Catch him!" Ratliff said. "He'll kill him!"

"Or break that damn leg again," Bookwright said. When they overtook him, he was trying to double the wagon, the shovel raised and poised like an axe. But Grimm had already darted around to the other side, where he now saw Ratliff and Bookwright running up, and he sprang away from them too, watching them, poised and alert. Bookwright caught Armstid from behind in both arms and held him.

"Get away quick, if you dont want anything," Ratliff told Grimm.

"No, I dont want anything," Grimm said.

"Then go on while Bookwright's got him." Grimm moved toward the wagon, watching Armstid with something curious and veiled in his look.

"He's going to get in trouble with that sort of foolishness," he said.

"He'll be all right," Ratliff said. "You just get on away from here." Grimm got into the wagon and went on. "You can let him go now," Ratliff said. Armstid flung free of Bookwright and turned toward the garden. "Wait, Henry," Ratliff said. "Let's eat supper first. Let's get our beds into the house." But Armstid hurried on, limping in the fading light toward the garden. "We ought to eat first," Ratliff said. Then he let out a long breath like a sigh; he and Bookwright ran side by side to the rear of the sewing-machine box, which Ratliff unlocked, and they snatched out the other shovels and picks and ran down the slope and into the old garden where Armstid was already digging. Just before they reached him he stood up and began to run toward the road, the shovel raised, whereupon they too saw that Grimm had not departed but was sitting in the wagon in the road, watching them across the ruined fence of iron pickets until Armstid had almost reached it. Then he drove on.

They dug all that night, Armstid in one hole, Ratliff and Bookwright working together in another. From time to time they would stop to rest while the summer constellations marched overhead. Ratliff and Bookwright would move about to flex their cramped muscles, then they would squat (They did not smoke; they could not risk showing any light.

Armstid had probably never had the extra nickel or dime to buy tobacco with.) and talk quietly while they listened to the steady sound of Armstid's shovel below them. He would be digging when they stopped; he would still be digging, unflagging and tireless, when they started again, though now and then one of them would remember him and pause to see him sitting on the side of his pit, immobile as the lumps of earth he had thrown out of it. Then he would be digging again before he had actually had time to rest; this until dawn began and Ratliff and Bookwright stood over him in the wan light, arguing with him. "We got to quit," Ratliff said. "It's already light enough for folks to see us." Armstid didn't pause.

"Let them," he said. "It's mine now. I can dig all day if I want."

"All right," Ratliff said. "You'll have plenty of help then." Now Armstid paused, looking up at him out of his pit. "How can we dig all night and then set up all day to keep other folks out of it?" Ratliff said. "Come on now," he said. "We got to eat and then sleep some." They got the mattress and the quilts from the buckboard and carried them into the house, the hall in whose gaping door-frames no doors any longer hung and from whose ceiling depended the skeleton of what had been once a crystal chandelier, with its sweep of stairs whose treads had long since been prized off and carried away to patch barns and chicken-houses and privies, whose spindles and walnut railings and newel-posts had long ago been chopped up and burned as firewood. The room they chose had a fourteen-foot ceiling. There were the remains of a once-gilt filigree of cornice above the gutted windows and the ribbed and serrated grin of lathing from which the plaster had fallen, and the skeleton of another prismed chandelier. They spread the mattress and the quilts upon the dust of plaster, and Ratliff and Bookwright returned to the buckboard and got the food they had brought, and the two sacks of coins. They hid the two sacks in the chimney, foul now with bird-droppings, behind the mantel in which there were still wedged a few shards of the original marble. Armstid didn't produce his bag. They didn't know what he had done with it. They didn't ask.

They built no fire. Ratliff would probably have objected, but nobody suggested it; they ate cold the tasteless food, too tired to taste it; removing only their shoes stained with the dampening earth from the deepening pits, they lay among the quilts and slept fitfully, too tired to sleep completely also, dreaming of gold. Toward noon jagged scraps and flecks of sun came through the broken roof and the two rotted floors overhead and crept eastward across the floor and the tumbled quilts and then the prone bodies and the slack-mouthed up-flung faces, whereupon they turned and shifted or covered their heads and faces with their arms, as though, still sleeping, they fled the weightless shadow of that for which, awake, they had betrayed themselves. They were awake at sunset without having rested. They moved stiffly about, not talking, while the coffee-pot boiled on the broken hearth; they ate again, wolfing the cold and tasteless food while the crimson glow from the dying west faded in the high ruined room. Armstid was the first one to finish. He put his cup down and rose, turning first onto his hands and knees as an infant gets up, dragging his stiff twice-broken leg painfully beneath him, and limped toward the door. "We ought to wait till full dark," Ratliff said, to no one; certainly no one answered him. It was as if he spoke to himself and had answered himself. He rose too. Bookwright was already standing. When they reached the garden, Armstid was already in his pit, digging.

They dug through that brief summer night as through the previous one while the familiar stars wheeled overhead, stop-ping now and then to rest and ease their muscles and listen to the steady sigh and recover of Armstid's shovel below them; they prevailed upon him to stop at dawn and returned to the house and ate—the canned salmon, the sidemeat cold in its own congealed grease, the cold cooked bread—and slept again among the tumbled quilts while noon came and the creeping and probing golden sun at whose touch they turned and shifted as though in impotent nightmare flight from that impalpable and weightless burden. They had finished the bread that morning. When the others waked at the second sunset, Ratliff had the coffee-pot on the fire and was cooking another batch of cornbread in the skillet. Armstid would not wait for it. He ate his portion of meat alone and drank his coffee and got to his feet again as small children do, and went out. Bookwright was standing also. Ratliff, squatting beside the skillet, looked up at him. "Go on then," he said. "You dont need to wait either."

"We're down six foot," Bookwright said. "Four foot wide and near ten foot long. I'll start where we found the third sack."

"All right," Ratliff said. "Go on and start." Because something had clicked in his mind again. It might have been while he was asleep, he didn't know. But he knew that this time it was right. Only I dont want to look at it, hear it, he thought, squatting, holding the skillet steady over the fire, squinting his watering eyes against the smoke which the broken chimney no longer drew out of the house, I dont dare to. Anyway, I dont have to yet. I can dig again tonight. We even got a new place to dig. So he waited until the bread was done. Then he took it out of the skillet and set it near the ashes and sliced some of the bacon into the skillet and cooked it; he had his first hot meal in three days, and he ate it without haste, squatting, sipping his coffee while the last of the sunset's crimson gathered along the ruined ceiling and died from there too, and the room had only the glow of the dying fire.

Bookwright and Armstid were already digging. When he came close enough to see, Armstid unaided was three feet down and his pit was very nearly as long as the one Ratliff and Bookwright had dug together. He went on to where Bookwright had started the new pit and took up his shovel (Bookwright had fetched it for him) and began to dig. They dug on through that night too, beneath the marching and familiar stars, stopping now and then to rest although Armstid did not stop when they did, squatting on the lip of the new excavation while Ratliff talked, murmurous, not about gold, money, but anecdotal, humorous, his invisible face quizzical, bemused, impenetrable. They dug again. Daylight will be time enough to look at it, he thought. Because I done already looked at it, he thought. I looked at it three days ago. Then it began to be dawn. In the wan beginning of that light he put his shovel down and straightened up. Bookwright's pick rose and fell steadily in front of him; twenty feet beyond, he could now see Armstid waist-deep in the ground as if he had been cut in two at the hips, the dead torso, not even knowing it was dead, laboring on in measured stoop and recover like a metronome as Armstid dug himself back into that earth which had produced him to be its born and fated thrall forever until he died. Ratliff climbed out of the pit and stood in the dark fresh loam which they had thrown out of it, his muscles flinching and jerking with fatigue, and stood looking quietly at Bookwright until Bookwright became aware of him and paused, the pick raised for the next stroke, and looked up at him. They looked at each other—the two gaunt, unshaven, weary faces. "Odum," Ratliff said, "who was Eustace Grimm's wife?"

"I dont know," Bookwright said.

"I do," Ratliff said. "She was one of them Calhoun County Dosheys. And that aint right. And his ma was a Fite. And that aint right either." Bookwright quit looking at him. He laid the pick down carefully, almost gently, as if it were a spoon level-full of soup or of that much nitro-glycerin, and climbed out of the pit, wiping his hands on his trousers.

"I thought you knew," he said. "I thought you knew everything about folks in this country."

"I reckon I know now," Ratliff said. "But I reckon you'll still have to tell me."

"Fite was his second wife's name. She wasn't Eustace's ma. Pa told me about it when Ab Snopes first rented that place from the Varners five years ago."

"All right," Ratliff said. "Tell me."

"Eustace's ma was Ab Snopes' youngest sister." They looked at one another, blinking a little. Soon the light would begin to increase fast.

"Sholy now," Ratliff said. "You finished?"

"Yes," Bookwright said. "I'm finished."

"Bet you one of them I beat you," Ratliff said. They mounted the slope and entered the house, the room where they slept. It was still dark in the room, so while Ratliff fumbled the two bags out of the chimney, Bookwright lit the lantern and set it on the floor and they squatted facing each other across the lantern, opening the bags.

"I reckon we ought to knowed wouldn't no cloth sack—" Bookwright said. "After thirty years—" They emptied the bags onto the floor. Each of them took up a coin, examined it briefly, then set them one upon the other like a crowned king

in checkers, close to the lantern. Then one by one they examined the other coins by the light of the dingy lantern. "But
how did he know it would be us?" Bookwright said.

"He didn't," Ratliff said. "He didn't care. He just come out
here every night and dug for a while. He knowed he couldn't
possibly dig over two weeks before somebody saw him." He
laid his last coin down and sat back on his heels until Bookwright had finished. "1871," he said.

"1879," Bookwright said. "I even got one that was made last
year. You beat me."

"I beat you," Ratliff said. He took up the two coins and
they put the money back into the bags. They didn't hide
them. They left each bag on its owner's quilt and blew out the
lantern. It was lighter now and they could see Armstid quite
well where he stooped and rose and stooped in his thigh-deep
pit. The sun would rise soon; already there were three buzzards soaring against the high yellow-blue. Armstid did not
even look up when they approached; he continued to dig
even while they stood beside the pit, looking down at him.
"Henry," Ratliff said. Then Ratliff leaned down and touched
his shoulder. He whirled, the shovel raised and turned edge-
wise and glinting a thin line of steel-colored dawn as the edge
of an axe would.

"Get out of my hole," he said. "Get outen it."

2.

The wagons containing the men, the women and the children approaching the village from that direction, stopped,
and the men who had walked up from the store to stand
along Varner's fence, watched, while Lump and Eck Snopes
and Varner's negro, Sam, loaded the furniture and the trunks
and the boxes into the wagon backed up to the edge of the
veranda. It was the same wagon drawn by the same mules
which had brought Flem Snopes back from Texas in April,
and the three men came and went between it and the house,
Eck or the negro backing clumsily through the door with the
burden between them and Lump Snopes scuttling along beside it in a constant patter of his own exhortations and commands, holding to it, to be sure, but carrying no weight, to

load that into the wagon and return, pausing at the door and stepping aside as Mrs Varner bustled out with another armful of small crocks and hermetic jars of fruit and vegetables. The watchers along the fence checked the objects off—the dismantled bed, the dresser, the washstand with its flowered matching bowl and ewer and slop-jar and chamber-pot, the trunk which doubtless contained the wife's and the child's clothing, the wooden box which the women at least knew doubtless contained dishes and cutlery and cooking vessels, and lastly a tightly-roped mass of brown canvas. "What's that?" Freeman said. "It looks like a tent."

"It is a tent," Tull said. "Eck brought it out from the express office in town last week."

"They aint going to move to Jefferson and live in a tent, are they?" Freeman said.

"I dont know," Tull said. At last the wagon was loaded; Eck and the negro bumped through the door for the last time, Mrs Varner bustled out with the final hermetic jar; Lump Snopes re-entered the house and emerged with the straw suitcase which they all knew, then Flem Snopes and then his wife came out. She was carrying the baby which was too large to have been born at only seven months but which had certainly not waited until May, and stood there for a moment, Olympus-tall, a head above her mother or husband either, in a tailored suit despite the rich heat of summer's full maturing, whose complexion alone showed that she was not yet eighteen since the unseeing and expressionless mask-face had no age, while the women in the wagons looked at her and thought how that was the first tailored suit ever seen in Frenchman's Bend and how she had got some clothes out of Flem Snopes anyway because it would not be Will Varner that bought them now, and the men along the fence looked at her and thought of Hoake McCarron and how any one of them would have bought the suit or anything else for her if she had wanted it.

Mrs Varner took the child from her and they watched her sweep the skirts inward into one hand with the gesture immemorial and female and troubling, and climb the wheel to the seat where Snopes already sat with the reins, and lean down and take the child from Mrs Varner. The wagon moved,

lurched into motion, the team swinging to cross the yard toward the open gate into the lane, and that was all. If farewell
was said, that was it, the halted wagons along the road creaking into motion again though Freeman and Tull and the other
four men merely turned, relaxed again, their backs against the
picket fence now, their faces identically grave, a little veiled
and perhaps even sober, not quite watching the laden wagon
as it turned out of the lane and approached and then was
passing them—the plaid cap, the steady and deliberate jaw,
the minute bow and the white shirt; the other face calm and
beautiful and by its expression carven or even corpse-like,
looking not at them certainly and maybe not at anything they
knew. "So long, Flem," Freeman said. "Save me a steak when
you get your hand in at cooking." He didn't answer. He
might not have heard even. The wagon went on. Watching it,
not moving yet, they saw it turn into the old road which until
two weeks ago had been marked only by the hooves of
Varner's fat white horse for more than twenty years.

"He'll have to drive three extra miles to get back into the
road to town that way," Tull said in an anxious voice.

"Maybe he aims to take them three miles on into town with
him and swap them to Aaron Rideout for the other half of
that restaurant," Freeman said.

"Maybe he'll swap them to Ratliff and Bookwright and
Henry Armstid for something else," a third man—his name
was Rideout also, a brother of the other one, both of whom
were Ratliff's cousins—said. "He'll find Ratliff in town too."

"He'll find Henry Armstid without having to go that far,"
Freeman said.

That road was no longer a fading and almost healed scar. It
was rutted now, because there had been rain a week ago, and
now the untroubled grass and weeds of almost thirty years
bore four distinct paths: the two outer ones where iron
wheel-rims had run, the two inner ones where the harnessed
teams had walked daily since that first afternoon when the
first ones had turned into it—the weathered and creaking
wagons, the plow-galled horses and mules, the men and
women and children entering another world, traversing
another land, moving in another time, another afternoon
without time or name.

Where the sand darkened into the shallow water of the branch and then lightened and rose again, the countless over-lapping prints of rims and iron shoes were like shouts in a deserted church. Then the wagons would begin to come into sight, drawn up in line at the roadside, the smaller children squatting in the wagons, the women still sitting in the splint chairs in the wagon beds, holding the infants and nursing them when need arose, the men and the larger children stand-ing quietly along the ruined and honeysuckle-choked iron fence, watching Armstid as he spaded the earth steadily down the slope of the old garden. They had been watching him for two weeks. After the first day, after the first ones had seen him and gone home with the news of it, they began to come in by wagon and on horse- and mule-back from as far away as ten and fifteen miles, men, women, and children, octogenar-ian and suckling, four generations in one battered and weath-ered wagon-bed still littered with dried manure or hay and grain chaff, to sit in the wagons and stand along the fence with the decorum of a formal reception, the rapt interest of a crowd watching a magician at a fair. On the first day, when the first one descended and approached the fence, Armstid climbed out of his pit and ran at him, dragging the stiffened leg, the shovel raised, cursing in a harsh, light, gasping whis-per, and drove the man away. But soon he quit that; he ap-peared to be not even aware of them where they stood along the fence, watching him spading himself steadily back and forth across the slope with that spent and unflagging fury. But none of them attempted to enter the garden again, and now it was only the half-grown boys who ever bothered him.

Toward the middle of the afternoon the ones who had come the long distances would begin to depart. But there were always some who would remain, even though it meant unharnessing and feeding and perhaps even milking in the dark. Then, just before sunset, the last wagon would arrive— the two gaunt, rabbit-like mules, the braced and dishing and ungreased wheels—and they would turn along the fence and watch quietly while the woman in the gray and shapeless gar-ment and the faded sunbonnet got down and lifted from beneath the seat a tin pail and approached the fence beyond which the man still had not looked up nor faltered in his metronome-like labor. She would set the pail in the corner of the fence and stand for a time, motionless, the gray garment falling in rigid carven folds to her stained tennis shoes, her hands clasped and rolled into her apron, against her stomach. If she were looking at the man, they could not tell it; if she were looking at anything, they did not know it. Then she would turn and go back to the wagon (she had feeding and milking to do too, as well as the children's supper to get) and mount to the seat and take up the rope reins and turn the wagon and drive away. Then the last of the watchers would depart, leaving Armstid in the middle of his fading slope, spading himself into the waxing twilight with the regularity of a mechanical toy and with something monstrous in his unflagging effort, as if the toy were too light for what it had been set to do, or too tightly wound. In the hot summer mornings, squatting with slow tobacco or snuff-sticks on the gallery of Varner's store, or at quiet cross-roads about the land in the long slant of afternoon, they talked about it, wagon to wagon, wagon to rider, rider to rider or from wagon or rider to one waiting beside a mail-box or a gate: "Is he still at it?"

"He's still at it."

"He's going to kill himself. Well, I dont know as it will be any loss."

"Not to his wife, anyway."

"That's a fact. It will save her that trip every day toting food to him. That Flem Snopes."

"That's a fact. Wouldn't no other man have done it."

"Couldn't no other man have done it. Anybody might have fooled Henry Armstid. But couldn't nobody but Flem Snopes have fooled Ratliff."

Now though it was only a little after ten, so not only had the day's quota all arrived, they were still there, including even the ones who, like Snopes, were going all the way in to Jefferson, when he drove up. He did not pull out of the road into line. Instead, he drove on past the halted wagons while the heads of the women holding the nursing children turned to look at him and the heads of the men along the fence turned to watch him pass, the faces grave, veiled too, still looking at him when he stopped the wagon and sat, chewing with that steady and measured thrust and looking over their heads into the garden. Then the heads along the ruined fence turned as though to follow his look, and they watched two half-grown boys emerge from the undergrowth on the far side of the garden and steal across it, approaching Armstid from behind. He had not looked up nor even ceased to dig, yet the boys were not within twenty feet of him when he whirled and dragged himself out of the trench and ran at them, the shovel lifted. He said nothing; he did not even curse now. He just ran at them, dragging his leg, stumbling among the clods he had dug while the boys fled before him, distancing him. Even after they had vanished in the undergrowth from which they had come, Armstid continued to run until he stumbled and fell headlong and lay there for a time while beyond the fence the people watched him in a silence so complete that they could hear the dry whisper of his panting breath. Then he got up, onto his hands and knees first as small children do, and picked up the shovel and returned to the trench. He did not glance up at the sun, as a man pausing in work does to gauge the time. He came straight back to the trench, hurrying back to it with that painful and laboring slowness, the gaunt unshaven face which was now completely that of a madman. He got back into the trench and began to dig.

Snopes turned his head and spat over the wagon wheel. He jerked the reins slightly. "Come up," he said.

END VOLUME ONE.

Chronology

recognize different birds. The Falkner brothers become
close to cousin Sallie Murry Wilkins (b. 1899), daughter of
aunt Mary Holland Falkner Wilkins.

1903   Meets and occasionally plays with Lida Estelle Oldham (b.
1896), daughter of Republican attorney Lemuel Oldham,
when her family moves to Oxford in fall.

1905   Enters first grade. Enjoys drawing and painting with
watercolors.

1906   Skips to third grade. Grandmother Sallie Murry Falkner
dies December 21.

1907   Grandmother Lelia Butler dies June 1. Third brother,
Dean Swift Falkner, born August 15.

1909–13   Begins working in father's livery stable in June. Athletic
activities are curtailed in late 1910 when he is put in a tight
canvas brace to correct shoulder stoop. Draws, writes
stories and poems, and starts to play hooky. Becomes increasingly attracted to Estelle Oldham and shows her his
poems. Reads comic magazine *The Arkansas Traveller*, *Pilgrim's Progress*, *Moby-Dick* (telling his brother Murry, "It's
one of the best books ever written"), Mark Twain, Joel
Chandler Harris, Shakespeare, Fielding, Conrad, Balzac,
and Hugo, among others. Shoots his dog accidentally
while hunting rabbits in the fall of 1911 and does not hunt
again for several years. Becomes active Boy Scout and begins to play high school football in fall 1913.

1914–15   Shows his poetry to law student Phil Stone, four years his
senior. Stone becomes close friend, gives him books to
read ("Swinburne, Keats and a number of the then
moderns, such as Conrad Aiken and the Imagists in verse
and Sherwood Anderson and the others in prose," Stone
recalls), and introduces him to writer and fellow towns-
man Stark Young. Helps plan yearbook and does sketches
for it. Pitches and plays shortstop on baseball team. Returns to school briefly in fall 1915 to play football, then
drops out. Hunts deer and bear at camp of "General"
James Stone, Phil's father, near Batesville, in the Mississippi Delta thirty miles west of Oxford.

1916–17   Begins working early in 1916 as clerk at grandfather's bank, the First National, and hates it. Drinks his grandfather's liquor. ("Grandfather thought it was the janitor.") By end of 1916 spends most of his time on campus of University of Mississippi, where he becomes friends with freshman Ben Wasson. Contributes drawings to "Social Activities" section of university yearbook, *Ole Miss*. Continues to write verse influenced by Swinburne and A. E. Housman, among others.

1918   Estelle Oldham tells Falkner she is "ready to elope" with him, despite her engagement to Cornell Franklin, a University of Mississippi graduate now successfully practicing law in Hawaii who is preferred by her family. Falkner insists on getting the Oldhams' consent, but both families oppose marriage, and Estelle's wedding to Franklin is set for April 18. Joins Phil Stone, then studying law at Yale, in New Haven early in April. Meets poets Stephen Vincent Benét and Robert Hillyer. Reads Yeats. Works as ledger clerk at Winchester Repeating Arms Co., where his name is recorded "Faulkner." Determined to join British forces, he and Stone practice English accents and mannerisms. Accepted by Royal Air Force in mid-June. Visits Oxford before reporting to Toronto Recruits' Depot on July 9, where he lists birthplace as Finchley, Middlesex, England, birthdate as May 25, 1898, and spells his name "Faulkner." Brother Murry, serving in the Marines, is wounded in the Argonne on November 1. Faulkner's service is limited to attending ground school. ("The war quit on us before we could do anything about it.") Discharged in December, returns to Oxford wearing newly-purchased officer's uniform and Royal Flying Corps wings and suffering, he claims, from effects of crashing a plane.

1919   Continues to work on poetry. Drinks with friends in gambling houses and brothels in Clarksdale and Charleston, Mississippi, Memphis, and New Orleans. Composes long cycle of poems influenced by classic pastoral tradition and modern poetry, especially T. S. Eliot. Sees Estelle frequently during her four-month visit home from Hawaii with her daughter, Victoria. "L'Apres-Midi d'un Faune," 40-line poem, appears in *The New Republic* August 6. Other poems are not accepted. Registers in September as a special student at University of Mississippi, where father is now assistant secretary of university. Studies French, Spanish, and Shakespeare; publishes poems in campus paper, *The Mississippian*, and Oxford *Eagle*. First published story, "Landing in Luck," appears in *The Mississippian* in November. In December, agrees to be initiated into Sigma Alpha Epsilon fraternity because of family tradition. Given nicknames "Count" and "Count No 'Count" by fellow students, who consider him aloof and affected.

1920   Inscribes *The Lilacs*, 36-page hand-lettered giftbook of poems, to Phil Stone on New Year's Day. Translates four poems by Paul Verlaine that are published in *The Mississippian* in February and March. Contributes drawings to the yearbook. Awarded $10 poetry prize by Professor Calvin S. Brown in June. Does odd jobs and assists with Boy Scout troop. Helps build clay tennis court beside Falkners' university-owned home; becomes a good player. Joins The Marionettes, a new university drama group; finishes one-act play (not produced) and works on stage props and set design. Withdraws from university in November during crackdown on fraternities. Receives commission as honorary second lieutenant in RAF; wears uniform with pips on various occasions. Writes *Marionettes*, an experimental verse play; hand-letters several copies of its 55 pages, adding illustrations influenced by Aubrey Beardsley. Wasson sells five at $5 apiece. The Marionettes decline to produce it.

1921   Favorably reviews *Turns and Movies*, volume of verse by Conrad Aiken, in *The Mississippian*. Paints buildings on campus. Presents Estelle Franklin with 88-page bound typescript volume of poems entitled *Vision in Spring* during her visit home in the summer. Accepts invitation of Stark Young to visit him in New York City in the fall. Revisits New Haven, October–November, then rents rooms in New York City and works as clerk in Lord & Taylor bookstore managed by Stark Young's friend Elizabeth Prall. Returns home in December after Phil Stone and Lemuel Oldham secure him position as postmaster at university post office at salary of $1,500 a year.

1922   Writes while on duty at the post office, neglects customers, is reluctant to sort mail, does not always forward it, and keeps patrons' magazines and periodicals in the office until he and his friends have read them. Praises Edna St. Vincent Millay and Eugene O'Neill in articles published in *The Mississippian*. Grandfather John Wesley Thompson Falkner dies March 13. Faulkner does last drawing for yearbook *Ole Miss*. Plays golf. Writes poems, stories, and criticism. *The Double Dealer*, a New Orleans magazine, publishes his short poem "Portrait." Continues to read widely, including works by Conrad Aiken, Eugene O'Neill, and Elinor Wylie.

1923   Begins driving his own car. Becomes scoutmaster during summer. Submits collection *Orpheus, and Other Poems* to The Four Seas Company of Boston in June. They agree to publish it if Faulkner will pay manufacturing costs; Faulkner declines in November, saying "on re-reading some of the things, I see that they aren't particularly significant."

1924   Receives gift of James Joyce's *Ulysses* from Phil Stone. Reads Voltaire and stories by Thomas Beer, a popular magazine writer of the time. (Faulkner later said that Beer "influenced me a lot.") In May, Four Seas agrees to publish cycle of pastoral poems, *The Marble Faun*, and Faulkner sends $400 to cover publication costs. Phil Stone writes preface and takes active role in negotiations. Continues to write stories and verse, compiling gift volumes for friends. Removed as scoutmaster after local minister denounces his drinking. Faulkner resigns as postmaster October 31. ("I reckon I'll be at the beck and call of folks with money all my life, but thank God I won't ever again have to be at the beck and call of every son of a bitch who's got two cents to buy a stamp.") Visits Elizabeth Prall in New Orleans and meets her husband, Sherwood Anderson, whose work he admires. *The Marble Faun* published in December.

1925   Leaves for New Orleans in January, intending to earn his passage to Europe. Accepts Elizabeth Prall Anderson's invitation to stay in spare room while Sherwood Anderson is away on a lecture tour, then moves into quarters rented from artist William Spratling. Contributes essays, poems, stories, and sketches to the New Orleans *Times-Picayune* and *The Double Dealer*. Meets Anita Loos. Begins work on novel *Mayday*, which Sherwood Anderson, now a close friend, praises. ("We would meet in the afternoons, we'd walk and he'd talk and I'd listen, we'd meet in the evenings and we'd go to a drinking place and we'd sit around till one or two o'clock drinking . . .") Anderson recommends Faulkner's novel to publisher Boni & Liveright. Visits Stone's brother and his family at Pascagoula on Gulf Coast in June; falls in love with Helen Baird (b. 1904), a sculptor he had met in New Orleans. Sails as passenger on a freighter from New Orleans to Genoa with William Spratling July 7; throws mass of manuscript overboard en route. Travels through Italy and Switzerland to Paris, settling on Left Bank. Grows beard. Goes to Louvre and various galleries; writes to mother in August: "went to a very very modernist exhibition the other day—futurist and vorticist. I was talking to a painter, a real one. He wont go to the exhibitions at all. He says its all right to paint the damn things, but as far as looking at them, he'd rather go to the Luxembourg gardens and watch the children sail their boats. And I agree with him." In September writes, "I have spent afternoon after afternoon in the Louvre . . . I have seen Rodin's museum, and 2 private collections of Matisse and Picasso (who are yet alive and painting) as well as numberless young and struggling moderns. And Cezanne! That man dipped his brush in light . . ." Years later, says of James Joyce in Paris: "I would go to some effort to go to the café that he inhabited to look at him. But that was the only literary man that I remember seeing in Europe in those days." Works on articles, poems, and fiction, including two novels, *Mosquito* and *Elmer* (about a young American painter, never finished). Tours France on foot and by train; visits World War I battlefields which still show scars of fighting. Visits England briefly in October, writes of Kent countryside: "Quietest most restful country under the sun. No wonder that Joseph Conrad could write such fine books here." Finds England too expensive and returns to France. Writes his mother, "I am expecting to hear from Liveright when I reach Paris. I waked up yesterday with such a grand feeling that something out of the ordinary has happened to me that I am firmly expecting news of some sort—either very good or very bad." Learns in Paris that

novel *Mayday* has been accepted for publication by Boni
& Liveright and retitled *Soldiers' Pay*; Faulkner likes new
title. Sails to the United States in December. Visits his
publishers in New York before returning to Oxford.

1926   Inscribes a hand-lettered, illustrated allegorical tale *May-
          day* (the same title originally given novel) to Helen Baird
          in January. Moves in with Spratling at 632 St. Peter Street,
          New Orleans, in February, going back to Oxford for brief
          visits. *Soldiers' Pay* published by Boni & Liveright Feb-
          ruary 25 in printing of 2,500 copies (sells 2,084 by May).
          Mother, shocked by sexual material in the novel, says that
          the best thing he could do is leave the country; father re-
          fuses to read it. Reviews are generally favorable—one re-
          viewer notes its "hard intelligence as well as consummate
          pity." Hand-letters a sequence of poems called *Helen: A
          Courtship* for Helen Baird in June. Vacations in Pascagoula,
          where he finishes typescript of novel *Mosquitoes* in early
          September. Returns to New Orleans in fall. Begins novels
          Father Abraham, about an avaricious Mississippi family
          named Snopes, and *Flags in the Dust*, depicting four
          generations of Sartoris family, based on Southern and
          family lore. Parodies Anderson's style in foreword to *Sher-
          wood Anderson & Other Famous Creoles*, a collection of
          Spratling's sketches, which they publish themselves in an
          edition of 400 copies that sells out in a week at $1.50 a
          copy. Book offends Anderson and causes breach between
          him and Faulkner. Returns to Oxford at Christmas.

1927   Sees Estelle, who has returned to Oxford after beginning
          divorce proceedings against Cornell Franklin. Gives her
          daughter, Victoria, a 47-page tale, *The Wishing Tree*, typed
          and bound in varicolored paper, in February as a present
          for her eighth birthday. Helen Baird marries Guy C. Ly-
          man in March. *Mosquitoes* published April 30. Puts *Father
          Abraham* aside to concentrate on *Flags in the Dust*. Works
          on it at Pascagoula during summer, and finishes revised
          typescript in late September. Horace Liveright rejects
          Flags in the Dust in late November and advises Faulkner
          not to offer it elsewhere.

1928   Begins "Twilight," story about the Compson family, early
          in the year. ("One day I seemed to shut a door, between

me and all publishers' addresses and book lists. I said to
myself, Now I can write.") Centered on Caddie Compson,
it becomes *The Sound and the Fury*. ("I loved her so much
I couldn't decide to give her life just for the duration of a
short story. She deserved more than that. So my novel was
created, almost in spite of myself.") Sends *Flags in the
Dust*, extensively revised, and group of short stories to
Ben Wasson, now New York literary agent. Wasson submits *Flags in the Dust* to eleven publishers, all of whom
reject it. Faulkner continues to work on new novel. In
September, Wasson shows *Flags in the Dust* to Harrison
(Hal) Smith, editor at Harcourt, Brace and Company,
who writes favorable report. Alfred Harcourt agrees to
publish book on condition that it be cut. Faulkner uses
$300 advance to go to New York. Dismayed at the cuts
Wasson says are necessary, allows him to do most of the
cutting. (" 'The trouble is,' he said, 'is that you had about
6 books in here. You were trying to write them all at
once.' He showed me what he meant, what he had done,
and I realized for the first time that I had done better than
I knew . . .") Tries unsuccessfully to sell short stories.
Rents a small furnished flat in Greenwich Village and revises and types manuscript of *The Sound and the Fury*. Finishes in October, drinks heavily, and is found unconscious
by friends Eric J. (Jim) Devine and Leon Scales, who take
care of him in their apartment. Moves in with painter
Owen Crump after recovering. Returns to Oxford in
December.

1929   *Sartoris* (the cut and retitled *Flags in the Dust*) published
by Harcourt, Brace and Company January 31 in first printing of 1,998. Starts writing *Sanctuary*. *The Sound and the
Fury* accepted by new firm of Jonathan Cape and Harrison
Smith in February; Faulkner receives $200 advance. Es-
telle's divorce becomes final on April 29. Faulkner receives
$200 advance for new novel from Cape & Smith in early
May. Completes *Sanctuary* in late May; Smith writes him
that it is too shocking to publish. Asks Smith for an additional $500 advance so that he can get married. Marries
Estelle in Presbyterian Church in nearby College Hill,
June 20. Borrows money from cousin Sallie Murry
(Wilkins) Williams and her husband to go to Pascagoula,
where he and Estelle have troubled honeymoon. Reads
proofs of *The Sound and the Fury*, restoring italicized

passages changed by Wasson. Returns to Oxford and takes job on night shift at the university power plant. Visits mother daily. *The Sound and the Fury* published October 7 in printing of 1,789. Reviews are enthusiastic, sales disappointing. Writes *As I Lay Dying* while at work, beginning October 25 and finishing December 11. ("I am going to write a book by which, at a pinch, I can stand or fall if I never touch ink again.")

1930   Finishes typescript of *As I Lay Dying* on January 12. Begins publishing stories in national magazines when *Forum* accepts "A Rose for Emily" for its April issue. Achieves mass-market success when *The Saturday Evening Post* accepts "Thrift" (appears September) and *Scribner's* accepts "Dry September" (published January 1931). April, purchases rundown antebellum house (lacks electricity and plumbing) and four acres of land in Oxford for $6,000 at 6% interest, with no money down. Names it Rowanoak (or Rowan Oak), and begins renovation, doing much of the work himself. Moves into it in June with Estelle and her children, Victoria (born 1919) and Malcolm (born 1923). Household staff includes Caroline Barr and Ned ("Uncle Ned") Barnett, former slave who had been servant of great-grandfather William Clark Falkner. Chatto & Windus publishes *Soldiers' Pay*, with introduction by Richard Hughes, June 20, first of Faulkner's works to appear in England. Sells "Red Leaves" and "Lizards in Jamshyd's Courtyard" to *The Saturday Evening Post* for $750 each (more than he had received for any novel). *As I Lay Dying*, where for the first time in print the Mississippi locale is identified as Yoknapatawpha County, published October 6 by Cape & Smith in printing of 2,522 copies. Harrison Smith now thinks *Sanctuary* may make money for ailing publishing firm, and sends galley proofs in November. Though the resetting costs Faulkner $270, he revises extensively "to make out of it something which would not shame *The Sound and the Fury* and *As I Lay Dying*." Finishes revision in December.

1931   Daughter Alabama, named for Faulkner's great-aunt Alabama, is born prematurely on January 11 and dies after nine days. *Sanctuary*, published February 9 by Cape & Smith, sells 3,519 copies by March 4—more than combined sales of *The Sound and the Fury* and *As I Lay Dying*; elicits high praise and increasing attention for Faulkner abroad. Gallimard acquires the rights to publish *As I Lay Dying* and *Sanctuary* in French. Many in Oxford are shocked by *Sanctuary*; Faulkner's father tells a coed carrying the book that it isn't fit for a nice girl to read, but his mother defends him. Chatto & Windus publishes *The Sound and the Fury* in April. "Spotted Horses" appears in *Scribner's* in June. Begins work on novel tentatively titled *Dark House* in August, developing theme used in rejected short story "Rose of Lebanon." *These 13*, a collection of stories, published by Cape & Smith September 21; sells better than any of his works except *Sanctuary*. Attends Southern Writers' Conference at University of Virginia in Charlottesville on his way to New York in October. Drinks heavily. Wooed by publishers Bennett Cerf and Donald Klopfer of Random House, Harold Guinzberg and George Oppenheimer of Viking, and Alfred A. Knopf. To keep him away from other publishers, Harrison Smith has Milton Abernethy take Faulkner on ship cruise to Jacksonville, Florida, and back to New York. Firm of Cape & Smith is dissolved by Jonathan Cape; Faulkner signs with new firm, Harrison Smith, Inc. Meets his French translator, Princeton professor Maurice Coindreau, banker and future secretary of defense Robert Lovett, Dorothy Parker, H. L. Mencken, Robert Benchley, John O'Hara, John Dos Passos, Frank Sullivan, and Corey Ford (will continue to see some of them on later trips). Spends hours talking and drinking with Dashiell Hammett and Lillian Hellman. Meets Nathanael West. Works on new novel (now called *Light in August*) and stories, one of them—"Turn About"—inspired by war stories told by Lovett (finished in Oxford, and published in *The Saturday Evening Post*, March 1932). Finishes self-deprecatory introduction ("This book . . . is a cheap idea, because it was deliberately conceived to make money") to Random House's Modern Library edition of *Sanctuary* (published 1932). Makes contacts with film studios and writes film treatments. Earns enough money during stay in New York to pay bills at home. Drinks heavily; friends contact Estelle. She arrives early in December, and they return to Oxford before the middle of the month.

Random House publishes story "Idyll in the Desert" in limited edition of 400 copies.

1932   Finishes manuscript of *Light in August* in February and revised typescript in March. Cape's new partnership, Cape & Ballou, goes into receivership in March, owing Faulkner $4,000 in royalties. Goes to work May 7 at Metro-Goldwyn-Mayer studio in Culver City, California, on six-week, $500-per-week contract. Leaves the studio almost immediately, not returning for a week. ("When they took me into a projection room and kept assuring me that it was all going to be very, very easy, I got flustered.") Takes a $30-a-month cottage on Jackson Street near studio and works unsuccessfully on series of treatments and scripts. At the end of contract makes plans to return home, but director-producer Howard Hawks hires him as scriptwriter for film *Today We Live*, based on "Turn About," beginning his longest Hollywood association. Father dies of heart attack August 7, and Faulkner returns home as head of family. "Dad left mother solvent for only about 1 year," he writes Ben Wasson. "Then it is me." Agreement with Hawks allows him to work in Oxford. Takes stepson Malcolm on walks through woods and bottoms, teaching him to distinguish dangerous from harmless snakes. Returns to Hollywood in October for three weeks, taking mother and brother Dean with him. *Light in August* published October 6 by new firm of Harrison Smith and Robert Haas. Paramount buys film rights to *Sanctuary* (released as *The Story of Temple Drake*, May 12, 1933). Faulkner receives $6,000 from sale. Continues working for MGM in Oxford. Spends part of Hollywood earnings on renovation of Rowan Oak.

1933   Begins flying lessons with Captain Vernon Omlie in February, and makes first solo flight April 20 after seventeen hours of dual instruction. *Today We Live* premieres in Oxford, April 12. *A Green Bough*, poems, published April 20 by Smith & Haas. Travels to New Orleans in May to work on film *Louisiana Lou* with director Tod Browning, but refuses to return to Hollywood for revisions; studio terminates contract May 13. Buys more land adjoining Rowan Oak. Works on stories and novel, *The Peasants*, which uses

Snopes characters. Daughter Jill born June 24. Prepares a marked copy (apparently now lost) for a projected Random House limited edition of *The Sound and the Fury* (never published) that would print the Benjy section in three colors, and writes an introduction. ("I wrote this book and learned to read. . . . I discovered that there is actually something to which the shabby term Art not only can, but must, be applied.") Receives $500 for his work on it. Plans novel *Requiem for a Nun*. Buys Omlie's Waco C cabin biplane in fall. Concerned about brother Dean's future, arranges to have Omlie train Dean as a pilot. Flies with Omlie and Dean to New York to meet with publishers early in November, returning in time to go hunting. Earns pilot's license December 14.

1934   Begins new novel *A Dark House* in February, using material from stories "Evangeline" (written 1931) and "Wash" (written 1933). Flies with Omlie to New Orleans for dedication of Shushan Airport February 15. Participates in Mississippi air shows with Omlie, Dean, and others in spring, billed as "William Faulkner's (Famous Author) Air Circus" on one occasion; Faulkner avoids flying aerobatics. *Doctor Martino and Other Stories* published April 16 by Smith & Haas. Pressed for money, writes "Ambuscade," "Retreat," and "Raid," series of Civil War stories centering on Bayard Sartoris and black companion Ringo, hoping to sell them to *The Saturday Evening Post* (they appear in fall). Goes back to work with Hawks in Hollywood for $1,000 a week, from the end of June to late July. Finishes script *Sutter's Gold* in Oxford. Brother Murry is member of FBI team that kills John Dillinger in Chicago, July 22. Writes Smith in August that new novel "is not quite ripe yet," but "I have a title for it which I like, by the way: ABSALOM, ABSALOM; the story is of a man who wanted a son through pride, and got too many of them and they destroyed him." Puts it aside and converts unpublished story "This Kind of Courage" into novel, *Pylon*. Sends first chapter to Harrison Smith in November and finishes it by end of December.

1935   Forms Okatoba Fishing and Hunting Club with R. L. Sullivan and Whitson Cook, receiving hunting and fishing rights to several thousand acres of General Stone's land

near Batesville, Mississippi, at eastern edge of the Mississippi Delta. *Pylon* published by Smith & Haas, March 25.
Pressed for money, works intensively at writing stories
meant to sell. Writes his agent Morton Goldman in April:
"What I really need is $10,000.00. With that I could pay
my debts, and insurance for two years and really write. I
mean, write." Returns to *Absalom, Absalom!* Resumes occasional flying, though the Waco now belongs to Dean.
Goes to New York September 23 to negotiate a better contract with Smith & Haas and to sell stories to magazines.
Returns home October 15, without gaining much from the
trip. Brother Dean and his three passengers are killed
when the Waco crashes November 10. Faulkner assists un-
dertaker in futile attempt to prepare Dean's body for
open-casket funeral. Distraught and guilt-ridden, assumes
responsibility for Dean's pregnant wife, Louise, and stays
for several weeks with her and his grieving mother, who
feels suicidal. On December 10, goes to Hollywood for
five-week, $1,000-per-week assignment with Hawks for
Twentieth Century–Fox, taking *Absalom, Absalom!* with
him. Works on novel early in the morning before going to
the studio. Begins intermittent and sometimes intense
fifteen-year affair with Hawks's 28-year-old secretary (later
his script supervisor), Mississippi divorcée Meta Doherty
Carpenter.

1936   After successful completion of draft of script (*The Road to
Glory*), begins to drink heavily. Returns to Oxford on sick
leave January 13. Finishes manuscript of *Absalom, Absalom!*
January 31. Drinks heavily and is hospitalized in Wright's
Sanitarium, small private hospital in Byhalia, Mississippi,
fifty miles north of Oxford. Reluctant to delay revision of
novel by writing stories to make money, signs new contract with Twentieth Century–Fox (again for $1,000 a
week until "employment shall be terminated by either
party"). Returns to Hollywood February 26, moving into
the Beverly Hills Hotel. Works on several scripts, sees old
friends. Dean, daughter of brother Dean Faulkner, born
March 22; Faulkner assumes role of surrogate father. Goes
boar hunting on Santa Cruz Island with Nathanael West
in April. Returns to Oxford early in June and writes to
agent when his stories don't sell: "Since last summer I
seem to have got out of the habit of writing trash . . ."
Draws map of Yoknapatawpha County for *Absalom, Ab-*

salom! Goes back to Hollywood in mid-July (for six-month, $750-per-week contract), taking Estelle, Jill, and two servants with him, and moves into a large house just north of Santa Monica. Captain Omlie dies in crash as passenger on commercial flight August 6. Sees Meta Carpenter, who has decided to marry pianist Wolfgang Rebner. Estelle and Faulkner both drink heavily. *Absalom, Absalom!*, published October 26 by Random House (which has absorbed the firm of Smith & Haas), receives some critical praise, though sales are not enough to allow freedom from script-writing, and Faulkner is unable to sell film rights (had hoped to receive $50,000 for them). Becomes increasingly unproductive at Twentieth Century–Fox and is laid off in December after earning almost $20,000 for the year. Proposes to convert Bayard Sartoris–Ringo stories (now six in number) into novel and is encouraged by Bennett Cerf and Robert Haas. Harrison Smith leaves Random House. Makes final payment on Rowan Oak.

1937   Returns to studio from layoff February 26 at salary of $1,000 a week. Family moves closer to studio. Unhappiness at work and home exacerbates Faulkner's drinking. March to June, works on film script for *Drums Along the Mohawk*, directed by John Ford. Estelle and Jill return to Oxford in late May. Maurice Coindreau stays with Faulkner for week in June to discuss French translation of *The Sound and the Fury*. Writes "An Odor of Verbena," concluding episode in Bayard-Ringo series. Returns to Rowan Oak in late August, having earned over $21,000 for the year working for Twentieth Century–Fox. Begins story "The Wild Palms," then starts to expand it into a novel. Goes to New York in mid-October to prepare the Bayard-Ringo stories for publication with new Random House editor, Saxe Commins. Stays at Algonquin Hotel; sees old friends, including Harrison Smith, Joel Sayre, Eric J. Devine, and Meta Rebner. Renews friendship with Sherwood Anderson ("a giant in an earth populated . . . by pigmies"). Drinks heavily, collapses against steam pipe in hotel room, and suffers palm-sized third-degree burn on his back. Treated by doctor, then cared for by Eric J. Devine. Sherwood Anderson visits him. Returns to Oxford accompanied by Devine. Resumes work on novel, *If I Forget Thee, Jerusalem* (to be published as *The Wild Palms* at publisher's insistence); says the theme of the book is:

"Between grief and nothing I will take grief." Reads Keats and Housman aloud and does crossword puzzles with stepdaughter Victoria after breakup of her first marriage ("He kept me alive," she later says). Intense pain from burn makes sleeping difficult.

1938 *The Unvanquished*, Bayard-Ringo stories reworked with new material into novel, published February 15 by Random House. MGM buys screen rights for $25,000, of which Faulkner receives $19,000 after payment of commissions. Buys 320-acre farm seventeen miles northeast of Oxford and names it Greenfield Farm; insists on raising mules despite brother John's (who is tenant manager) preference for more profitable cattle (later acquires cattle for farm). Despite infection from skin graft performed at the end of February, continues work on *If I Forget Thee, Jerusalem*. Writes to Haas in July: "To me, it was written just as if I had sat on the one side of a wall and the paper was on the other and my hand with the pen thrust through the wall and writing not only on invisible paper but in pitch darkness too . . ." Goes to New York to read proofs of novel, now titled *The Wild Palms*, in late September. Returns to work on Snopes book *The Peasants* and plots out two more volumes, *Rus in Urbe* and *Ilium Falling*, to form trilogy. Takes Harold Ober as new literary agent.

1939 Elected to National Institute of Arts and Letters in January. *The Wild Palms*, published January 19, reviewed in *Time* cover story, sells more than 1,000 copies a week and tops sales of *Sanctuary* by late March. Raises $6,000 (by cashing in life insurance policy and obtaining advance from Random House) to save Phil Stone from financial disaster. Writes stories, hoping to earn money, and works on Snopes trilogy, retitling volumes *The Hamlet*, *The Town*, and *The Mansion*. Helps brother John at Greenfield Farm, sometimes serving tenants in commissary. Influential favorable essays on Faulkner published by George Marion O'Donnell (*Kenyon Review*, summer) and Conrad Aiken (*The Atlantic Monthly*, November). Takes short holidays in New York City in October and December after testifying in Washington, D.C., in plagiarism suit brought against Twentieth Century–Fox by writer who claims (wrongly) to have written *The Road to Glory*. Donates manuscript of *Absalom, Absalom!* to relief fund for Spanish Loyalists. "Barn Burning" wins first O. Henry Memorial Award ($300 prize) for best short story published in an American magazine.

1940   Works on proofs of *The Hamlet*. Caroline Barr, in her mid-nineties, suffers stroke and dies January 31. Faulkner gives eulogy in parlor of Rowan Oak. ("She was born in bondage and with a dark skin and most of her early maturity was passed in a dark and tragic time for the land of her birth. She went through vicissitudes which she had not caused; she assumed cares and griefs which were not even her cares and griefs. She was paid wages for this, but pay is still just money. And she never received very much of that . . .") Writes stories about black families. *The Hamlet*, published by Random House April 1, is reviewed favorably, but sales fall below those of *The Wild Palms*. Faces mounting financial pressure from debts, family obligations, and back taxes, but is reluctant to raise funds by selling property. (Writes Haas in June: "It's probably vanity as much as anything else which makes me want to hold onto it. I own a larger parcel of it than anybody else in town and nobody gave me any of it or loaned me a nickel to buy any of it with and all my relations and fellow townsmen, including the borrowers and frank spongers, all prophesied I'd never be more than a bum.") Appeals to Random House for higher advances against royalties, and proposes to make a novel out of series of stories about related black and white families. Tries to get a job in Hollywood. After unsatisfactory negotiations with Random House, goes to New York late in June to negotiate with Harold Guinzburg of The Viking Press, but Viking cannot substantially improve on the Random House offer. Resumes writing stories (five published in the year).

1941   Wires literary agent Harold Ober on January 16 asking for $100; uses part of it to pay electric bill. Organizes Lafayette County aircraft warning system in late June. Wishing to do more in anticipation of U.S. entry into World War II, thinks about securing military commission and hopes to teach air navigation. "The Bear" accepted by

The Saturday Evening Post for $1,000 in November. Finishes work on series of stories forming novel *Go Down, Moses* in December.

1942   Goes to Washington, D.C., in unsuccessful attempt to secure military or naval commission. *Go Down, Moses and Other Stories*, dedicated to Caroline Barr, published by Random House May 11. (Faulkner considers it a novel; "and Other Stories" added by publisher.) Deeply in debt and unable to sell enough stories to remain solvent, seeks Hollywood work through publishers, agents, and friends. Reports for five-month segment of low-paying ($300 a week), long-term Warner Bros. contract on July 27. Moves into Highland Hotel. Works with producer Robert Buckner on film about Charles de Gaulle until project is dropped. Resumes affair with Meta Carpenter (now divorced from Rebner). Sees other old friends, including Ruth Ford (University of Mississippi alumna who had once dated brother Dean), and Clark Gable and Howard Hawks, with whom he goes fishing and hunting. Becomes friends with writers A. I. ("Buzz") Bezzerides and Jo Pagano. Eats often at favorite restaurant in Hollywood, Musso & Frank Grill. Writes two scenes for *Air Force*, directed by Hawks. Gets month's leave to return to Oxford for Christmas while remaining on payroll.

1943   Returns to Warner Bros. January 16 on a 26-week, $350-per-week contract. Begins working with Hawks in March on *Battle Cry*, film depicting various Allied nations' roles in the war. Sends one of his RAF pips to nephew James Faulkner, who is training to become Marine Corps fighter pilot (pip is lost when nephew is forced to ditch his Corsair off Okinawa in 1945). Warner Bros. picks up 52-week option at $400 a week in late June; Faulkner drinks and collapses. Writes and revises lengthy and complex script for *Battle Cry*. When the film is canceled in August due to its high cost, takes leave of absence without pay to return to Oxford. Receives $1,000 advance from producer William Bacher to work at home on film treatment about the Unknown Soldier of World War I. Describes it in letter to Ober as "a fable, an indictment of war perhaps" and writes 51-page synopsis in fall.

1944   Reports back to Warner Bros. February 14, and moves in
        with Bezzerides family on Saltair Street, just north of
        Santa Monica. Begins work for Hawks on film version of
        Ernest Hemingway's *To Have and Have Not*. Estelle and
        Jill join him in June, and they move to an apartment in
        East Hollywood. Works with Hawks and screenwriter
        Leigh Brackett on film of Raymond Chandler's *The Big
        Sleep*. Depression, drinking, and periods of hospitalization
        follow departure of Jill and Estelle in September. Critic
        Malcolm Cowley writes the first of several essays on
        Faulkner to "redress the balance between his worth and
        his reputation," comparing him to Balzac and noting that
        all his works except for *Sanctuary* are out of print. Works
        on filmscript for *Mildred Pierce*, directed by Michael
        Curtiz. Requests leave without pay and returns home De-
        cember 15, taking with him the script for *The Big Sleep*,
        which he finishes in Oxford. Offered $5,000 advance to
        write a nonfiction book on the Mississippi River by Dou-
        bleday. Provisionally turns it down, saying: "I am 47. I
        have 3 more books of my own I want to write. I am like
        an aging mare, who has three more gestations in her be-
        fore her time is over, and doesn't want to spend one of
        them breeding what she considers . . . a mule."

1945   Works on the "fable" about the Unknown Soldier ("writ-
        ing and rewriting, weighing every word"), hoping to
        make it into a novel. Returns to Hollywood and Warner
        Bros. in June, now at $500 a week. Cowley obtains pub-
        lishers' approval in August to edit a collection of
        Faulkner's works for the Viking Portable Library series;
        Faulkner advises him on selections. Works on scripts for
        Stallion Road and briefly with Jean Renoir on *The South-
        erner*. Continues work on the "fable," rising at 4:00 A.M.
        and working until 8:00 A.M. before going to the studio.
        Hollywood agent William Herndon refuses to release him
        from agent-client agreement and Warner Bros. refuses to
        release him from exclusive contract. Writes: "I dont like
        this damn place any better than I ever did. That is one
        comfort: at least I cant be any sicker tomorrow for Missis-
        sippi than I was yesterday." Refusing to assign Warner
        Bros. film rights to his own writings (including the
        "fable"), leaves studio without permission September 18.
        Returns to Rowan Oak, bringing Lady Go-lightly, the
        mare Jill rode during her stay in California. Redraws map

of Yoknapatawpha County and writes "1699–1945 The Compsons" to go with excerpt from *The Sound and the Fury* in Cowley's *Portable Faulkner*; says, "I should have done this when I wrote the book. Then the whole thing would have fallen into pattern like a jigsaw puzzle when the magician's wand touched it." Takes part in annual hunt in November. Short story, "An Error in Chemistry," wins second prize ($250) in *Ellery Queen's Mystery Magazine* contest in December (had received $300 for story itself).

1946   Feels trapped and depressed, drinks heavily. Cerf, Haas, and Ober persuade Jack Warner to give Faulkner leave of absence and release from rights assignment so he can finish his novel. Random House pays immediate advance of $1,000 and $500 a month after that. Faulkner worries that novel will take longer to complete than advances can cover. *The Portable Faulkner* published by Viking April 29. Tells class at University of Mississippi in May that the four greatest influences on his work were the Old Testament, Melville, Dostoevski, and Conrad. European reputation, especially in France, grows as works are translated. Jean-Paul Sartre writes of Faulkner's significance in "American Novelists in French Eyes," in September *Atlantic Monthly*. Sells film rights for stories "Death Drag" and "Honor" to RKO for combined net of $6,600, and "Two Soldiers" to Cagney Productions for $3,750. Random House issues *The Sound and the Fury* (with "1699–1945 The Compsons" retitled "Appendix/Compson: 1699–1945" added as first part) and *As I Lay Dying* together in Modern Library edition in October. Nearly hits trees while landing airplane and does not fly as pilot again. Continues work on "fable" ("I dont write as fast as I used to"). Works secretly, because of exclusive Warner Bros. contract, on film script (unidentified) at home.

1947   Meets in April with six literature classes at University of Mississippi on condition no notes be taken. Ranks Hemingway among top contemporaries, along with Thomas Wolfe, John Dos Passos, and John Steinbeck, but is quoted in wire-service account as saying that Hemingway "has no courage, has never gone out on a limb. He has never used a word where the reader might check his usage in a dictionary." Hemingway is deeply offended, and Faulkner writes apology. ("I have believed for years that the human voice has caused all human ills and I thought I had broken myself of talking. Maybe this will be my valedictory lesson.") Long-time family servant Ned Barnett dies. In November *Partisan Review* refuses excerpt about a horse race from the "fable."

1948   Begins mystery novel in January, based on idea mentioned to Haas in 1940; calls it *Intruder in the Dust*, and finishes it in April. MGM buys film rights for $50,000 before publication. Published by Random House September 27, it is his most commercially successful book, selling over 15,000 copies. Feels free of financial pressure for the first time. Turns down Hamilton Basso's proposal of *New Yorker* profile: "I am working tooth and nail at my lifetime ambition to be the last private individual on earth . . ." Works on short-story collection proposed earlier in the year by Random House. Eager to visit friends, goes to New York for holiday in October and meets Malcolm Cowley for the first time. Collapses after few days and recuperates at Cowley's home in Sherman, Connecticut. Decides to arrange stories in collection by cycles, an idea suggested by Cowley three years earlier. Elected to the American Academy of Arts and Letters November 23.

1949   Director Clarence Brown brings MGM company to Oxford to film *Intruder in the Dust*. Faulkner revises screenplay and helps scout locations, but is not given credit because of legal complications with Warner Bros. Rewrites unpublished 1942 mystery story "Knight's Gambit," expanding it into novella. Buys sloop, which he names *The Ring Dove*, and sails it on Sardis Reservoir, 25 miles northwest of Oxford, during spring and summer. Eudora Welty visits and Faulkner takes her sailing. In August is sought out by 20-year-old Joan Williams, Bard College student and aspiring writer from Memphis, who admires his work. Reluctantly attends world premiere of *Intruder in the Dust* on October 9 at refurbished Lyric Theatre, owned by cousin Sallie Murry Williams and her husband. Event is considered to have caused the most excitement since Union General A. J. Smith burned Oxford in Civil War. "A Courtship" wins O. Henry Award for 1949. Random House publishes *Knight's Gambit*, volume of mystery stories, November 27.

1950   Writes to Joan Williams in January, offering help as a mentor. Goes to New York for ten days in February, staying at Algonquin; sees publishers, old friends (actress Ruth Ford, Joel Sayre, and others), and Joan Williams. Begins sending her notes for a play he hopes they will write together. Writes letter to Memphis *Commercial Appeal* in March protesting failure of Mississippi jury to give death penalty to a white man convicted of murdering three black children. Receives American Academy's William Dean Howells Medal for Fiction in May; does not attend ceremony. Personal involvement with Joan Williams deepens when she returns to Memphis for summer. Gives her manuscript of *The Sound and the Fury*. She is reluctant to rewrite his material for play *Requiem for a Nun*, and their collaboration becomes increasingly difficult. *Collected Stories of William Faulkner* published August 2 by Random House and adopted by Book-of-the-Month Club as alternate fiction selection, receiving generally good reviews. Informed November 10 he will receive 1949 (delayed until 1950) Nobel Prize for Literature. Reluctant to attend, drinks heavily at annual hunt, contracts bad cold, but finally agrees to go to Stockholm with Jill to receive award on December 10. Meets Else Jonsson, widow of Thorsten Jonsson, one of Faulkner's earliest Swedish translators. Gives widely quoted address ("I believe that man will not merely endure: he will prevail"). Afterwards, writes to friend, "I fear that some of my fellow Mississippians will never forgive that 30,000$ that durn foreign country gave me for just sitting on my ass writing stuff that makes my own state ashamed to own me." *The New York Times* reports that 100,000 copies of his books have been sold in Modern Library editions, and that 2.5 million paperback copies are in print.

1951   Takes $5,000 of Nobel Prize money for his own use, establishes "Faulkner Memorial" trust fund with remainder for scholarships and other educational purposes. Goes to Hollywood in February for five weeks scriptwriting on *The Left Hand of God* for Hawks. Earns $14,000, including bonus, for finishing script ahead of schedule (Hawks does not direct film, and Faulkner does not receive writing credit when it is released in 1955). Sees Meta Carpenter for last time. The Levee Press of Greenville, Mississippi, publishes horse-race piece as *Notes on a Horsethief* February 10.

Collected Stories receives National Book Award for Fiction
March 6. Releases statement to Memphis *Commercial Appeal* doubting guilt and opposing execution of Willie McGee, a black man convicted of raping a white woman
(McGee later executed). Takes three-week trip in April to
New York, England, and France, visiting Verdun battlefield, which figures in his "fable." Gives short commencement address at Jill's high school graduation in Oxford
May 28. Finishes manuscript of *Requiem for a Nun* in early
June. (Writes in letter to Else Jonsson: "I am really tired of
writing, the agony and sweat of it. I'll probably never quit
though, until I die. But now I feel like nothing would be
as peaceful as to break the pencil, throw it away, admit I
dont know why, the answers either.") Hears from Ruth
Ford that Lemuel Ayers would like to produce *Requiem
for a Nun* on stage, and goes to New York for week in July
to work on it. Drives Jill to school at Pine Manor Junior
College in Wellesley, Massachusetts, with Estelle. *Requiem
for a Nun*, with long prose introductions to its three acts,
published by Random House October 2. Works on stage
version in Cambridge, Massachusetts, in October and November. Becomes officer in the Legion of Honor of the
Republic of France at ceremony at French Consulate in
New Orleans October 26.

1952   Works on "fable" and trains horse; has two falls in February and March, injuring his back. Attends ceremony commemorating ninetieth anniversary of battle of Shiloh with
novelist Shelby Foote, and walks over battlefield with him.
Although work now widely taught in colleges, turns
down honorary degree of Doctor of Letters from Tulane
University, writing: "I feel that for one who did not even
graduate from grammar school, to accept an honorary degree representative not only of higher learning but of
post-graduate labor in it, would debase and nullify the
whole aim of learning." (Later declines all other attempts
to award him honorary degrees, often using this same reply.) Attacks "welfare and other bureaus of economic or
industrial regimentation" in address delivered May 15 to
Delta Council in Cleveland, Mississippi. Takes one-month
trip to Europe, though plans to produce his play during
Paris cultural festival had fallen through. Collapses in
severe pain in Paris; doctors discover two old spinal
compression fractures, possibly riding injuries, and advise

surgical fusion. Faulkner refuses and visits Harold Raymond of Chatto & Windus in England, still suffering severe pain. Treated near Oslo, Norway, by masseur on advice of Else Jonsson. Returns home feeling better than he has in years, but is not allowed to ride. Helps Joan Williams with her writing, but relationship is increasingly troubled. Injures back in boating accident in August. Hospitalized in Memphis in September for convulsive seizure brought on by drinking and back pain, and again in October, after fall down stairs. X-rays reveal three additional old spinal compression fractures. Wears back brace. Helps Ford Foundation prepare *Omnibus* production of "The Faulkner Story" for television in November. Accepts editor and friend Saxe Commins' invitation to write at his Princeton home. Depression and drinking precipitate collapse and is admitted to private hospital in New York. After discharge stays in New York, working on "fable"; sees Joan Williams. Returns home for Christmas.

1953   Stays in Oxford until Estelle recovers from cataract operation. Returns to New York January 31 for indefinite stay, hoping to finish the "fable." Medical problems continue; has extensive physiological and neurological examinations to determine cause of memory lapses, but nothing new is discovered. Writes semi-autobiographical essay "Mississippi" for *Holiday* (appears April 1954). Returns to Oxford with Jill in late April when Estelle is hospitalized for severe hemorrhage. Goes back to New York May 9, when danger is over. Estelle accompanies him when he gives commencement address at Jill's graduation from Pine Manor. Jill attends University of Mexico in fall, and Estelle goes with her when she leaves in late August. Faulkner stays at Rowan Oak, working on "fable." Hospitalized in September in Memphis and in Wright's Sanitarium in Byhalia. Angered when *Life* magazine publishes two-part article on him, September 28–October 5. Drives to New York with Joan Williams in October; they see Dylan Thomas (whose earlier poetry reading Faulkner had found moving) shortly before Thomas's death in November, and attend subsequent memorial service. Finishes *A Fable* at Commins' house in early November. Leaves for Paris to work with Hawks and screenwriter Harry Kurnitz on film, *Land of the Pharaohs*. Meets 19-year-old admirer, Jean

Stein, in St. Moritz on Christmas Eve. Spends Christmas holidays in Stockholm and sees Else Jonsson.

1954   Stays with Harold Raymond in Biddenden, Kent, England, in early January, and then goes to Switzerland, Paris, and Rome, visiting friends, seeing Jean Stein, and working on film. Arrives in Cairo in mid-February suffering from alcoholic collapse and is taken to Anglo-American Hospital. Continues working on film, but Hawks and Kurnitz do not use most of what he writes. Joan Williams marries Ezra Bowen on March 6. Leaves Egypt March 29. Stays three weeks in Paris, spending one night in hospital. Returns home in late April, after short stay in New York. Writes preface for *A Fable*, but decides not to use it. Works on farm most of May; sells livestock and then rents it out for a year. *A Fable* published by Random House, August 2. At request of U.S. State Department, attends International Writers' Conference in São Paulo, Brazil, stopping off on the way at Lima, Peru. Enjoys trip and offers his services again on return home. Jill marries Paul D. Summers, Jr., August 21, and moves to Charlottesville, Virginia, where Paul attends law school. Faulkner checks into Algonquin Hotel, New York, September 10; divides time between New York and Oxford for next six months. Makes spoken record for Caedmon Records, works on stories and magazine pieces, and feels reassured of ability to earn money. Sees Jean Stein often.

1955   Writes article on hockey game at Madison Square Garden, "An Innocent at Rinkside," for *Sports Illustrated* (appears January 24). Accepts National Book Award for Fiction for *A Fable*, January 25. Works on script for *The Era of Fear*, ABC television program about McCarthyism, but in March angrily rejects contract which includes morals clause and requires membership in unions ABC deals with. Becomes increasingly involved in civil rights issues; writes letters to editors advocating school integration; receives abusive letters and phone calls, and his position angers his brothers. Gives lecture "On Privacy. The American Dream: What Happened to It" at the University of Oregon and University of Montana in April (published in *Harper's*, May). *A Fable* wins Pulitzer Prize in May. Writes article on eighty-first running of Kentucky

Derby for *Sports Illustrated*. Helps publicize *Land of the Pharaohs*. Leaves on State Department trip July 29. Spends three weeks in Japan, visiting Tokyo, Nagano, and Kyoto, and delighting Japanese hosts (remarks from colloquia published as *Faulkner at Nagano*, 1956). Returns to New York by way of Philippines (to visit stepdaughter and family), Italy, France, England, and Iceland, combining State Department appearances and vacation. *Big Woods*, collection of hunting stories with new linking material, illustrated by Edward Shenton, published by Random House, October 14. Rushes to Oxford October 23 when mother, almost eighty-five, suffers cerebral hemorrhage; remains while she recuperates. Speaks against discrimination to integrated audience at Memphis meeting of Southern Historical Association, November 10; receives more threatening letters and phone calls. When Jean Stein visits the South, shows her New Orleans and Gulf Coast; they encounter Helen Baird Lyman on a Pascagoula beach. Begins second Snopes volume (*The Town*) in early December.

1956   Columbia Pictures takes option on *The Sound and the Fury* for $3,500 (film is released by Twentieth Century–Fox in 1959), and Universal buys *Pylon* for $50,000 (released in 1958 as *The Tarnished Angels*, directed by Douglas Sirk). Goes to New York February 8 to discuss finances with Ober: "what to do with money I have, where my kin and friends cant borrow it, against my old age." Worried about imminent violence, writes two articles urging voluntary integration in South to prevent Northern intervention: "On Fear: The South in Labor" (*Harper's*, June), and "A Letter to the North" (*Life*, March). Increasingly alarmed by rising tensions over court-ordered integration of University of Alabama, agrees to interview with *The Reporter* magazine; desperate and drinking, says if South were pushed too hard there would be civil war. Interviewer quotes him as saying that "if it came to fighting I'd fight for Mississippi against the United States even if it meant . . . shooting Negroes." (Later repudiates the interview: "They are statements which no sober man would make, nor it seems to me, any sane man believe.") Does extensive interview with Jean Stein for *The Paris Review*. On return to Oxford, injures back again when he is thrown by horse. Begins vomiting blood March 18; hospitalized in

Memphis. By early April feels well enough to go with Estelle to Charlottesville, Virginia, where first grandson,
Paul D. Summers III, is born April 15. Works on *The Town*
in Oxford during summer. With P. D. East, starts semi-
annual satirical paper for Southern moderates, entitled *The
Southern Reposure*. First and only issue appears in mid-
summer. Writes essay for *Ebony*, appealing for moderation
and urging blacks to "learn . . . the responsibility of
equality." Albert Camus' adaptation of *Requiem for a Nun*
successfully staged in Paris. Goes to Washington, D.C., for
four days in September as chairman of writers' group in
Eisenhower Administration's People-to-People Program.
Chooses Harvey Breit of *The New York Times* as co-
chairman; attends meeting at Breit's home November 29.

1957   Continues chairman's work into early February. Refuses
Estelle's offer of a divorce. Depressed by changing re-
lationship with Jean Stein, suffers collapse. Goes to
Charlottesville as University of Virginia's first writer-
in-residence February 9; moves into house on Rugby
Road. Meets professors Frederick L. Gwynn and Joseph
Blotner, who assist him in setting schedules. Arrives in
Athens March 17 for two-week visit at invitation of State
Department; sees Greek adaptation of *Requiem for a Nun*.
Cruises four days on private yacht in the Aegean. Accepts
Silver Medal from Greek Academy. *The Town*, published
May 1 by Random House, receives mixed reviews. Extensive exhibition of Faulkner materials, including many
manuscripts and typescripts, opens at Princeton University
on May 10. Presents National Institute of Arts and Letters'
Gold Medal for Fiction to John Dos Passos May 22. Con-
cludes successful university semester of classroom and
public appearances. Rides with friends and in the Farmington Hunt, and tours Civil War battlefields near Richmond. Returns to Rowan Oak for summer, tends to farm
and boat, visits mother. Ignores telegrams from producer
Jerry Wald reporting on production of film *The Long Hot
Summer*, based on *The Hamlet* (released 1958). Goes to
Charlottesville in November, intending to ride and fox-
hunt, but falls ill with strep throat. Hunts quail near
Oxford in December.

1958   Begins to type first draft of *The Mansion*, third and last
of the Snopes trilogy, at Rowan Oak in early January.

Returns to Charlottesville for second term as writer-in-residence, January 30, meeting classes and public groups. (Remarks are published in *Faulkner in the University: Class Conferences at the University of Virginia, 1957–58* in 1959.) At one session presents "A Word to Virginians," an appeal to state to take the lead in teaching blacks "the responsibilities of equality." Goes to Princeton for two weeks, March 1, meeting with students individually and in groups. Returns to Oxford in May. Declines, for political reasons, invitation to visit Soviet Union with group of writers. Saxe Commins dies July 17. Gives away niece Dean Faulkner, daughter of brother Dean, at her wedding November 9, and hosts large reception for her at Rowan Oak. Goes to Princeton for another week of student sessions, and then to New York to work on *The Mansion* with Random House editor Albert Erskine. Returns to Charlottesville and rides in the Keswick and Farmington hunts; is described by a fellow rider as "all nerve." Second grandchild, William Cuthbert Faulkner Summers, born December 2.

1959   Works on *The Mansion* and hunts quail in Oxford. *Requiem for a Nun*, version adapted for the stage by Ruth Ford, opens on Broadway January 30 after successful London run; closes after forty-three performances. Though not reappointed as writer-in-residence for the year, takes position as consultant on contemporary literature to Alderman Library at University of Virginia, and is assigned library study and typewriter. Accepted as outside member in Farmington Hunt and continues riding with Keswick Hunt. Fractures collarbone when horse falls at Farmington hunter trials March 14. Rides again in May at Rowan Oak despite slow and painful recovery; another horse fall causes additional injuries, necessitating use of crutches for two weeks. Works with Albert Erskine in New York on *The Mansion*, eliminating some of the discrepancies between it and *The Hamlet*. Writes preface to *The Mansion* explaining others. Completes purchase of Charlottesville home on Rugby Road, August 21. Attends four-day UNESCO conference in Denver late September. Harold Ober, long-time agent and friend, dies October 31. *The Mansion* published by Random House, November 13. Continues riding and hunting, suffering occasional falls.

1960   Divides time between Oxford and Charlottesville. Hospitalized briefly at Byhalia for collapse brought on by bourbon administered for self-diagnosed pleurisy. Accepts appointment as Balch Lecturer in American Literature at University of Virginia with minimal duties (salary $250 a year) in August. Mother suffers cerebral hemorrhage, dies October 16. Sees Charlottesville friends often, including Joseph and Yvonne Blotner. Becomes full member of Farmington Hunt; writes to Albert Erskine, "I have been awarded a pink coat, a splendor worthy of being photographed in." Establishes William Faulkner Foundation December 28, providing scholarships for black Mississippians and prize for first novels; bequeaths to it the manuscripts he has deposited in the Alderman Library.

1961   Hunts quail in Oxford in January. Reluctantly leaves on two-week State Department trip to Venezuela April 1. Receives the Order of Andrés Bello, Venezuela's highest civilian award; gives speech expressing gratitude in Spanish. Third grandson, A. Burks Summers, born May 30. Shocked by news of Hemingway's suicide, July 2. Returns to Rowan Oak. Begins writing *The Horse Stealers: A Reminiscence*, conceived years earlier as novel about "a sort of Huck Finn"; enjoys work and finishes first draft August 21. Returns to Charlottesville in mid-October. Novel, re-titled *The Reivers*, taken by Book-of-the-Month Club eight months before publication. Checks into Algonquin Hotel to work on book with editor Albert Erskine, November 27. Hospitalized in Charlottesville, December 18, suffering from acute respiratory infection, back trouble, and drinking. Leaves after several days, but soon has relapse and is treated at Tucker Neurological and Psychiatric Hospital in Richmond until December 29.

1962   Injured in fall from horse, January 3. Readmitted to Tucker suffering from chest pain, fever, and drinking, January 8. Goes to Rowan Oak to recuperate in mid-January and hunts with nephew James Faulkner. Returns to Charlottesville in early April; intends to make move permanent. Travels to West Point with Estelle, Jill, and Paul, April 19, and reads from *The Reivers*. Turns down President John F. Kennedy's invitation to attend dinner for American Nobel Prize winners. Accepts Gold Medal for

Fiction of National Institute of Arts and Letters, presented by Eudora Welty, May 24. Returns to Oxford. *The Reivers* published by Random House, June 4. Thrown by horse near Rowan Oak, June 17. Endures much pain, but continues to go for walks, and negotiates purchase of Red Acres, 250-acre estate outside Charlottesville, for $200,000. Pain and drinking increase; taken by Estelle and James Faulkner to Wright's Sanitarium at Byhalia, July 5. Dies of heart attack, 1:30 A.M. on July 6. After service at Rowan Oak is buried on July 7 in St. Peter's Cemetery, Oxford, Mississippi.

Note on the Texts

This volume reproduces the texts of *Absalom, Absalom!*, *The Unvanquished*, *If I Forget Thee, Jerusalem* [*The Wild Palms*], and *The Hamlet* that have been established by Noel Polk for publication by Faulkner's publisher. (The first of these was published by Random House in 1986 as *Absalom, Absalom! The Corrected Text*.) All texts are based upon Faulkner's own typescripts, the texts of which have been emended to account for his revisions in proofs, his indisputable typing errors, and certain other errors and inconsistencies that clearly demand correction. The underlying holograph manuscript for each work has been consulted regularly throughout the editorial process and has supplied the editor with numerous corrections of Faulkner's own typing; indeed, comparison has been made of all relevant extant forms of these works, published and unpublished, to determine the nature and causes of the variants among the texts. The goal of these labors—to discover the forms of these works that Faulkner wanted in print at the time of their original publication—is sometimes elusive. Although thousands of pages of typescript and manuscript and proof are available to the editor, it is not always clear what Faulkner's final intentions were, or even whether Faulkner had any "final" intentions regarding the individual components of his novels.

Copy-texts for *Absalom, Absalom!*, *If I Forget Thee, Jerusalem*, and *The Hamlet* are his own ribbon typescript copies, which were used by the typesetters of the first editions; for *The Unvanquished*, copy-text is a combination of his extant ribbon typescript and the carbon typescripts underlying the magazine tearsheets that were used by the printer as part of the setting copy of the first edition. Except for a few pages of *Absalom, Absalom!* and several of *The Unvanquished*, Faulkner typed (or assembled) and proofread these documents himself, with varying degrees of care; they bear his own holograph corrections and revisions, as well as editorial alterations of varying extent. Faulkner was in some ways an extremely consistent writer. He never included apostrophes in the words "dont", "wont", "aint", "cant", or "oclock", and very seldom used an apostrophe to indicate a dropped letter in a spoken dialect word, such as "bout" or "runnin". He never used a period after the titles "Mr", "Mrs", or "Dr". The original editors generally, but inconsistently, accepted these practices, but compositors often made mistakes and many periods and apostrophes slipped in. More serious problems also frequently occurred. The publisher of *If I Forget Thee, Jerusalem*, for example, forced him to accept the title of one of its sections, "The Wild Palms," as the title for the entire work. The editors of *Absalom, Absalom!* made drastic revisions of its prose that worked toward normalizing the radical stylistic experimentation for which the novel is well known. They shortened some long sentences, clarified and smoothed perceived syntactical difficulties, removed parentheses, placed syntactical elements of some sentences closer together, frequently replaced deliberately ambiguous or vague pronominal references with proper names, and, in more than one instance, simply deleted material they deemed repetitious or otherwise unnecessary, sometimes ten lines at a time.

Faulkner's attitude toward such intervention is neither consistent nor entirely clear. Almost from the beginning of his career, he was a supremely confident craftsman; he was at the same time aware of the complexity of the demands his work would make, not merely on the reader, but also on publisher and editor and proofreader. His response to Ben Wasson's tampering with the Benjy section of *The Sound and the Fury*—that he would rewrite it if publishing were not grown up enough to publish it as he wanted it—reflects both his flexibility toward the realities of publication and his impatience with those mechanical processes of publication beyond his control that might thwart the accomplishment of his artistic goals. This response also specifically displays an irritation with editors who failed to understand what he was trying to do. He seems to have been indifferent to some types of editorial changes, and he acquiesced to them; he seems not to have cared whether certain words were spelled consistently or not, whether certain of his archaisms were modernized or not; and he seems to have expected his editor to divine from his typescript whether each sentence was punctuated exactly as he wanted it—that is, whether or not a variation from an apparent pattern was in fact a deliberate variation or merely an inadvertency he assumed an editor would correct. Thus while some of his marks on galley and page proofs were genuine revisions of his own, many others were clearly attempts to repair damage of one sort or another made by someone else on the typescript setting copy.

With the benefit of decades of intense scholarship, we are now perhaps in a better position to understand Faulkner's intentions, although clearly many of the original editorial problems remain. The Polk texts attempt to reproduce Faulkner's typescripts as he presented them to his publishers, before editorial intervention. Only those revisions on typescript or in proof that Faulkner seems to have initiated himself in response to his own text are accepted, not those he made in response to a revision or a correction suggested or inserted by an editor; this is a very conservative policy that rejects some of Faulkner's proof revisions in favor of his original typescript.

Polk's interventions, then, strive to be minimal, and every effort has been made to preserve Faulkner's idiosyncrasies in spelling and punctuation. Nevertheless, certain corrections of the typescripts have been necessary. Unmistakable typing errors and other demonstrable errors have been corrected. Faulkner's punctuation has been regularized in two cases: although he used three hyphens (---) to indicate a one-em dash, Faulkner was inconsistent throughout his career in the number of hyphens he typed to indicate a dash longer than one em, and in the number of dots he typed to indicate ellipses; he frequently typed as many as twelve or thirteen hyphens or dots. In the Polk texts, generally, three or four hyphens become a one-em dash, five or more become a two-em dash; up to six dots of ellipses are regularized to three or four according to traditional usage, seven or more become seven.

The text of *Absalom, Absalom!* reproduced here is that of *Absalom, Absalom! The Corrected Text*, prepared by Polk and published by Random House in 1986. Copy-text for this edition was the typescript setting copy at the Alderman Library of the University of Virginia; other relevant documents used in preparing the text were the complete holograph manuscript, at the Harry Ransom Humanities Research Center of the University of Texas, and the corrected galley proofs made available to the editor by Professor Carvel Collins.

Absalom, Absalom! was a particularly difficult novel for Faulkner to write. He began writing it in early 1934 — manuscripts of material entitled "Dark House" and "A Dark House" are dated February 11, 1934 — though its central narrative concerning Thomas Sutpen derives from a short story, "Evangeline," which was submitted unsuccessfully to *The Saturday Evening Post* in July 1931, and its narrative method of dialogue between two young male talkers can be traced to several earlier stories, such as "Mistral" and "The Big Shot" in the late 1920s. By August of 1934 Faulkner had decided on *Absalom, Absalom!* as the title of the novel, and described it as the story "of a man who wanted a son through pride, and got too many of them and they destroyed him." At the same time, he wrote his editor that the novel was "not quite ripe" and that only one chapter of his materials suited him — years later he told a group at the University of Virginia that the material had become "inchoate" — and so he put it aside and wrote *Pylon* very quickly in the late fall of 1934. Almost immediately after *Pylon* was published, he again took up work on *Absalom, Absalom!* — the date on the first page of the holograph manuscript is March 30, 1935 — and proceeded to completion steadily over the next thirteen months, despite three extended stints in Hollywood, the death of his brother Dean, and increasing marital difficulties. It was edited and proofread during the summer of 1936, and published on October 26 in a text marred by hundreds of instances of outright editorial revision.

Absalom, Absalom! The Corrected Text of 1986 made the novel available for the first time in a text that was as faithful to Faulkner's usage as surviving evidence permitted, and that text is printed here with the following exceptions, keyed to the page and line numbers of the present volume: "between papa and" replaces "between" at 16.17; "handful" replaces "handfull" at 67.34; "perish. . . . . . ." replaces "perish . . ." at 105.36; "spoke——";" replaces "spoke——;" " at 106.35; "*up from*" replaces "*up*" at 131.15; "*up* thinking" replaces "*up*, thinking," at 174.37–38; "faces" replaces "faces," at 246.38; "*mothers' and fathers' hell*" replaces "*mother's and father's hell*" at 286.24; "semestrial" replaces "semesterial" at 296.14; "now'." replaces "now'" at 305.1; and "wife" replaces "wife," at 312.10. Accent marks have been removed from "fiance" at 8.34, 103.38, 112.15, 149.1, 149.40, and 270.7. They have also been removed from "*elan*" at 107.32, "*embusque*" at 140.27, and "communique" at 251.15. (These corrections will be made in future printings of the Random House and Vintage texts.)

The Unvanquished had its beginning as a short story about a white boy, Bayard Sartoris, and his Negro slave and friend, Ringo, during the Civil War. It was written in the spring of 1934, while Faulkner was taking a break from his work on *Absalom, Absalom!* He needed to "boil the pot," he claimed, and make some money from magazine sales. "Ambuscade," published in *The Saturday Evening Post* on September 29, 1934, then, became the first of a series of seven stories about these boys, covering a period of about a decade and a half in their lives. Other stories in the series followed quickly: "Retreat," (*Saturday Evening Post*, October 13, 1934); "Raid" (*Saturday Evening Post*, November 3, 1934); and "Drusilla" (*Scribner's*, April 1935; retitled "Skirmish at Sartoris" in the book). At this point Faulkner broke off the series in order to complete *Absalom, Absalom!*, but took up the series again almost immediately after that novel was published in October 1936. "The Unvanquished" (retitled "Riposte in Tertio" in the book) was published in *The Saturday Evening Post* on November 14, 1936, and "Vendée" in *The Saturday Evening Post* on December 5 of the same year. In late December of 1936, Faulkner wrote to Random House proposing a book of these Civil War stories, but it was not until the end of the following July that he wrote the final story, "An Odor of Verbena," to complete the series. He was not able to sell this story to a magazine.

His preparation of the stories for book publication, in the fall of 1937, reflects the same sort of commercial haste that had gone into their writing. Although he revised and rewrote a good bit of the text, expanding and elaborating and doing much to weld the separate stories into a single narrative, for the most part he gave to the printer magazine tearsheets only slightly revised in ink. The setting copy is thus a combination of the magazine tearsheets and many revised and newly typed pages; it is a setting copy that complicates editorial work on the current edition. The *Post* and *Scribner's* editors had, of course, heavily edited Faulkner's text in fairly predictable ways for family magazines; they not only normalized his punctuation—supplying apostrophes in "wont", "dont", and "cant", and periods for "Mr" and "Mrs", for example—but also bowdlerized many of the mild epithets and prettied up some of the more colorful dialect language. Since Faulkner did not emend the magazine texts back toward his normal usage in such matters, the changes made by the magazine editors were retained in the portions of the book version set from the magazine tearsheets. To complicate matters further, though it is clear that Faulkner typed most of the new pages himself, some of the pages were definitely typed by someone else, and others may have been.

Thus copy-text for the Polk edition of *The Unvanquished* consists of the new ribbon typescript Faulkner prepared as he revised, the carbon typescripts underlying those portions of the text represented by tearsheets (since the ribbon typescripts of the magazine versions are not known to exist), and certain smaller passages that appeared for the first time in the magazine text. (All of the extant materials relevant to the editing of *The Unvanquished*—Faulkner's typescript/tearsheet setting copy, the carbon typescripts of the magazine versions of the individual stories, and the holograph manuscripts—are in the Rowan Oak Papers at the University of Mississippi; one typescript of "The Unvanquished" is in the Alderman Library of the University of Virginia.) The copy-text has been emended to account for changes, either on the magazine or book galleys (none of the galleys is known to exist) or on the original ribbon typescript pages from which the magazine texts were set, that might reasonably be attributed to Faulkner. Significant inconsistencies, such as those in chronology, have not been altered.

If I Forget Thee, Jerusalem is published here for the first time under Faulkner's title. The novel was originally published on January 19, 1939, under the title of one of its parts, "The Wild Palms," a change made over his objections, and in a text that, while not so drastically changed by editors as that of *Absalom, Absalom!*, was also edited in ways that altered the texture and meaning of the prose in numerous minor ways, including one instance of bowdlerization: in the typescript, the tall convict's final words to the Warden, and the novel's closing line, is "Women, shit"; in the first printing of the published novel, this line is editorially rendered "Women——!" The editing, however, shows some inconsistency; though the word "shit" was marked out here, where it was easy to see, two other words, "prick" and "cunt", imbedded in the middle of the book, were not altered—and perhaps were not even noticed.

Faulkner began work on this novel in 1937 in order, he said, to "stave off" a broken heart, probably referring to the breakup of his romance with Meta Carpenter. He first began it as a short story, entitled "Wild Palms" and set on the Mississippi Gulf Coast, about a middle-aged doctor and his wife who encounter a couple named Harry and Charlotte. Perceiving that there was material here for a longer work, he did not try to sell the story, but began work on the novel on September 15, 1937, (his holograph date on the first page of the manuscript) and he completed it in June of 1938. All the evidence of the typescripts and the manuscripts in the Alderman Library of the University of Virginia (no galleys are known to exist), indicates that Faulkner did not take two separate stories and interleave them, but rather wrote, in alternating stints, first a "Wild Palms" section, then an "Old Man" section. He invented the story of the "tall convict," he later said, as a counterpoint to the story of Harry and Charlotte, in an effort to maintain the intensity of the latter story without allowing it to become shrill. Copy-text for the Polk edition printed here is the ribbon typescript setting copy at the University of Virginia.

The novel that eventually became *The Hamlet* began as a group of sketches and fragments about the Snopes clan written very early in Faulkner's career (probably in the mid-1920s) and elaborated in a series of short stories over the next decade or so. In late 1926 or early 1927, he began a novel, entitled *Father Abraham*, which he abandoned after writing about 18,000 words. He then wrote several versions of what would become "Spotted Horses" (versions entitled, variously, "As I Lay Dying," "Aria con Amore," and "The Peasants"), though he was unable to interest any magazine in the stories.

During the next four years, he went on to write *Flags in the Dust*, *The Sound and the Fury*, *As I Lay Dying*, and *Sanctuary*, but he never completely let go of the Snopes clan. Snopes characters appear regularly in these books, and Faulkner continued to develop the material in such stories as "Lizards in Jamshyd's Courtyard" (*Saturday Evening Post*, February 27, 1932), "The Hound" (not a Snopes story, but incorporated into *The Hamlet* as one; *Harper's*, August 1931), "Afternoon of a Cow" (1937; unpublished in English until 1947), and two others, "Centaur in Brass" (*American Mercury*, February 1932) and "Mule in the Yard" (*Scribner's*, August 1934), which were incorporated into *The Town*, the second novel of the Snopes trilogy, published in 1957.

Faulkner turned his full attention to what he called "the Snopes book" in the early fall of 1938, writing to his editor at Random House about his plans to make a trilogy out of the material; the first novel would be called "The Peasants," the second "Rus in Urbe," the third "Ilium Falling." This plan, the execution of which would stretch over two decades, resulted in the Snopes trilogy: *The Hamlet* (1940), *The Town* (1957), and *The Mansion* (1959). He first began *The Hamlet* with another short story, "Barn Burning" (*Harper's*, June 1939), intending it to be a kind of prologue, but changed his mind and instead incorporated elements from the story into other parts of the novel. He worked steadily on *The Hamlet* until its completion in early December 1939 and returned galleys to Random House on February 5, 1940. The book was published by Random House on April 1, 1940. Although the editors did not make the kind of revisions they had made in other works by Faulkner, the text was marred by many typographical and compositorial errors. Copy-text for the Polk edition printed here is the ribbon typescript setting copy at the Alderman Library of the University of Virginia (other relevant documents consulted were the holograph manuscript, also at the University of Virginia, and two sets of uncorrected galleys, one privately owned and the other at the Mississippi Department of Archives and History in Jackson).

American English continues to fluctuate; for example, a word may be spelled in more than one way, even in the same work. Commas are sometimes used expressively to suggest the movements of voice, and capitals are sometimes meant to give significance to a word beyond those it might have in its uncapitalized form. Since standardization would remove such effects, this volume preserves the spelling, punctuation, and wording of the texts established by Noel Polk, which strive to be as faithful to Faulkner's usage as surviving evidence permits. In this volume the reader has the results of the most detailed scholarly efforts thus far made to establish the texts of *Absalom, Absalom!*, *The Unvanquished*, *If I Forget Thee, Jerusalem*, and *The Hamlet*.

Errors corrected second printing (cited by page and line number): 330.1, sissippi (*LOA*).

Notes

In the notes that follow, the reference numbers denote page and line of this volume (the line count includes chapter headings). No note is made for material included in a standard desk-reference book. For more detailed notes, references to other studies, and further biographical background than is contained in the Chronology, see: Joseph Blotner, *Faulkner, A Biography*, two volumes (New York: Random House, 1974); Joseph Blotner, *Faulkner, A Biography, One-Volume Edition* (New York: Random House, 1984); Calvin S. Brown, *A Glossary of Faulkner's South* (New Haven: Yale University Press, 1976); *Selected Letters of William Faulkner* (New York: Random House, 1977), edited by Joseph Blotner; James Hinkle, *Reading Faulkner's The Unvanquished* (Jackson: University Press of Mississippi, forthcoming).

ABSALOM, ABSALOM!

1.1   ABSALOM, ABSALOM!]   Cf. 2 Samuel 13–19.

6.22–23   *Be Light.*]   Genesis 1:3.

64.20–21   Lincoln's . . . Sumpter]   Lincoln was elected president on November 6, 1860. Confederate forces began firing on Fort Sumter in Charleston, S.C., April 12, 1861, and it was surrendered by Major Robert Anderson on April 14.

66.6   Mississippi seceded]   On January 9, 1861, Mississippi became the second state to secede.

101.35   strap oil]   Oil for harness straps.

140.27   *embusque*]   French; literally, one who waits in ambush; in military usage, a shirker, a soldier not at the front.

183.1–4   And there . . . until—"]   Having failed to overturn Virginia's ordinance of secession passed on April 17, 1861, inhabitants of the poorer, largely non-slaveholding northwestern counties voted to form a separate state. West Virginia was admitted to the Union on June 20, 1863.

184.5–6   Tidewater]   Coastal Virginia, as far inland as the rivers are affected by the ebb and flow of the ocean tides.

223.11–12   Pittsburg Landing]   On the Tennessee River. An alternate name for the battle of Shiloh, April 6–7, 1862.

285.32   *Old Joe*]   Confederate General Joseph E. Johnston (1807–91) commanded the Army of Tennessee from December 27, 1863, to July 17, 1864, and again from February 23, 1865, until its surrender on April 26, 1865.

296.12   Bayard] Pierre Terrail, Seigneur de Bayard, was a heroic French soldier of the Middle Ages whose name came to suggest a man of courage and honor. In the medieval French romance *Renaud de Montauban* or *Four Sons of Aymon*, Bayard is a bright-colored magic steed that can elongate to accommodate more than one rider. The Oxford English Dictionary defines "bayard" as a kind of blindness, or blind recklessness; a person blind to the light of knowledge, having the self-confidence of ignorance.

303.10–11   saw chunk] A large section of tree trunk sawed flat at both ends to make a seat or table.

THE UNVANQUISHED

326.37   chinkapin] The dwarf chestnut, a shrubby tree 6 to 20 feet high that produces a small nut in a chestnut-like husk.

329.12   Barksdale] Confederate General William Barksdale (1821–63) commanded a brigade of Mississippi troops at Antietam, Fredericksburg, Chancellorsville, and Gettysburg, where he was mortally wounded.

329.34–35   Patroller] A member of a county patrol responsible for returning slaves absent without written permission.

330.5   F.R.S.S.] Fellow of the Royal Statistical Society.

353.6   Second Manassas] In the South, the battles of Bull Run were referred to as First and Second Manassas (July 21, 1861, and August 29–30, 1862).

363.14   boring] Lowering his head to drive against the pressure of the bit being pulled to restrain him.

379.20–21   croker sack] A sack of heavy, loosely-woven cloth used for the harvesting of crops such as cotton, barley, and corn.

400.1   RIPOSTE IN TERTIO] Fencing terms. A riposte is an attack by the defender after a successful parry, delivered after the opponent's recovery; a tertio, or tierce, is an outside thrust. A riposte in tertio suggests here an attack out of turn that violates the spirit and rules of the sport.

401.9   Smith] Union General Andrew Jackson Smith (1815–97), whose troops in 1864 burned much of Oxford and Ripley, including the home of Col. William C. Falkner.

404.15   saw chunk] See note to 303.10–11.

424.1   VENDÉE] La Vendée, a region in western France, was a scene of several counterrevolutionary peasant uprisings from 1793–1832. According to his French translator, Maurice Coindreau, Faulkner used the title "Vendée" because, after reading Balzac's novel *Les Chouans*, he felt that Southerners had much in common with Vendeans. Both were conquered, and their regions occupied, by people who spoke their own language.

431.24   short coupled]   Short-bodied.

IF I FORGET THEE, JERUSALEM [THE WILD PALMS]

493.1–2   IF . . . JERUSALEM]   Psalms 137:5.

512.39   sandboils]   Places where water mixed with sand comes up through the landward side of a levee, forced up by the pressure of the water contained in the levee.

513.15   Ahenobarbus']   The paternal name of Nero (A.D. 37–68), first called Lucius Domitius Ahenobarbus, later Nero Claudius Caesar.

514.14   Mound's Landing]   Two miles west of Scott, Mississippi, and 14 miles north of Greenville.

518.23   Vieux Carre]   The old French Quarter, in the heart of New Orleans.

521.4   Rat]   A slang term for student, especially a freshman.

534.20   'If . . . whole'.]   Cf. Matthew 5:29, Mark 9:47.

551.32   urped]   Vomited.

554.14–15   Mrs . . . cow]   According to popular legend, the great Chicago fire of October 8–9, 1871, started when Mrs. O'Leary's cow knocked over a lantern.

588.4–5   French post-cards]   Pornographic photographs.

589.31   choriated]   From "choric," i.e., a heavenly choir.

656.32   Carnarvon]   Caernarvon, on the eastern bank of the Mississippi, 14 miles south of New Orleans, where the levee was dynamited on April 29, 1927, to ease the strain on the levee at New Orleans.

THE HAMLET

753.11   cramped]   Steered the horses sharply to one side to turn the front of the wheel against the buckboard.

776.2   bead]   Bubbles in a shaken bottle of moonshine whiskey that indicate the strength and quality of the liquor.

877.7   feice]   A feist or fice, a small mongrel dog.

995.22   frail]   Variant of flail.

1073.35   dishing]   Concave on the outside and likely to fall apart.

CATALOGING INFORMATION

Faulkner, William, 1897–1962.
Novels, 1936–1940.
Edited by Joseph Blotner and Noel Polk.

(The Library of America ; 48)
Contents: Absalom, Absalom! — The unvanquished —
If I forget thee, Jerusalem [The wild palms] — The hamlet.
I. Title: Absalom, Absalom!. II. Title: The unvanquished.
III. Title: If I forget thee, Jerusalem [The wild palms].
IV. The hamlet. V. Series.
PS3511.A86A6   1990   813′54   89-62931
ISBN 0-940450-55-0 (alk. paper)

THE LIBRARY OF AMERICA SERIES

This book is set in 10 point Linotron Galliard,
a face designed for photocomposition by Matthew Carter
and based on the sixteenth-century face Granjon. The paper
is acid-free Ecusta Nyalite and meets the requirements for perma-
nence of the American National Standards Institute. The binding
material is Brillianta, a 100% woven rayon cloth made by
Van Heek-Scholco Textielfabrieken, Holland. The com-
position is by Haddon Craftsmen, Inc., and The
Clarinda Company. Printing and binding
by R. R. Donnelley & Sons Company.
Designed by Bruce Campbell.